The Complete Works of Rudyard Kipling

Rudyard Kipling

GRAPEVINE INDIA

Published by

GRAPEVINE INDIA PUBLISHERS PVT LTD

www.grapevineindia.com
Delhi | Mumbai
email: grapevineindiapublishers@gmail.com

Ordering Information:
Quantity sales: Special discounts are available on quantity
purchases by corporations, associations, and others.
For details, reach out to the publisher.

First published by Grapevine India 2023
Copyright © Grapevine 2023

"CAPTAINS COURAGEOUS"
A STORY OF THE GRAND BANKS
by
Rudyard Kipling

TO
JAMES CONLAND, M.D.,
Brattleboro, Vermont

I ploughed the land with horses,
But my heart was ill at ease,
For the old sea-faring men
Came to me now and then,
With their sagas of the seas.

Longfellow.

CHAPTER I

The weather door of the smoking-room had been left open to the North Atlantic fog, as the big liner rolled and lifted, whistling to warn the fishing-fleet.

"That Cheyne boy's the biggest nuisance aboard," said a man in a frieze overcoat, shutting the door with a bang. "He isn't wanted here. He's too fresh."

A white-haired German reached for a sandwich, and grunted between bites: "I know der breed. Ameriga is full of dot kind. I dell you you should imbort ropes' ends free under your dariff."

"Pshaw! There isn't any real harm to him. He's more to be pitied than anything," a man from New York drawled, as he lay at full length along the cushions under the wet skylight. "They've dragged him around from hotel to hotel ever since he was a kid. I was talking to his mother this morning. She's a lovely lady, but she don't pretend to manage him. He's going to Europe to finish his education."

"Education isn't begun yet." This was a Philadelphian, curled up in a corner. "That boy gets two hundred a month pocket-money, he told me. He isn't sixteen either."

"Railroads, his father, aind't it?" said the German.

"Yep. That and mines and lumber and shipping. Built one place at San Diego, the old man has; another at Los Angeles; owns half a dozen railroads, half the lumber on the Pacific slope, and lets his wife spend the money," the Philadelphian went on lazily. "The West don't suit her, she says. She just tracks around with the boy and her nerves, trying to find out what'll amuse him, I guess. Florida, Adirondacks, Lakewood, Hot Springs, New York, and round again. He isn't much more than a second-hand hotel clerk now. When he's finished in Europe he'll be a holy terror."

"What's the matter with the old man attending to him personally?" said a voice from the frieze ulster.

"Old man's piling up the rocks. 'Don't want to be disturbed, I guess. He'll find out his error a few years from now. 'Pity, because there's a heap of good in the boy if you could get at it."

"Mit a rope's end; mit a rope's end!" growled the German.

Once more the door banged, and a slight, slim-built boy perhaps fifteen years old, a half-smoked cigarette hanging from one corner of his mouth, leaned in over the high footway. His pasty yellow complexion did not show well on a person of his years, and his look was a mixture of irresolution, bravado, and very cheap smartness. He was dressed in a cherry-coloured blazer, knickerbockers, red stockings, and bicycle shoes, with a red flannel cap at the back of the head. After whistling between his teeth, as he eyed the company, he said in a loud, high voice: "Say, it's thick outside. You can hear the fish-boats squawking all around us. Say, wouldn't it be great if we ran down one?"

"Shut the door, Harvey," said the New Yorker. "Shut the door and stay outside. You're not wanted here."

"Who'll stop me?" he answered, deliberately. "Did you pay for my passage, Mister Martin? 'Guess I've as good right here as the next man."

He picked up some dice from a checkerboard and began throwing, right hand against left.

"Say, gen'elmen, this is deader'n mud. Can't we make a game of poker between us?"

There was no answer, and he puffed his cigarette, swung his legs, and drummed on the table with rather dirty fingers. Then he pulled out a roll of bills as if to count them.

"How's your mamma this afternoon?" a man said. "I didn't see her at lunch."

"In her state-room, I guess. She's 'most always sick on the ocean. I'm going to give the stewardess fifteen dollars for looking after her. I don't go down more 'n I can avoid. It makes me feel mysterious to pass that butler's-pantry place. Say, this is the first time I've been on the ocean."

"Oh, don't apologize, Harvey."

"Who's apologizing? This is the first time I've crossed the ocean, gen'elmen, and, except the first day, I haven't been sick one little bit. No, sir!" He brought down his fist with a triumphant bang, wetted his finger, and went on counting the bills.

"Oh, you're a high-grade machine, with the writing in plain sight," the Philadelphian yawned. "You'll blossom into a credit to your country if you don't take care."

"I know it. I'm an American—first, last, and all the time. I'll show 'em that when I strike Europe. Piff! My cig's out. I can't smoke the truck the steward sells. Any gen'elman got a real Turkish cig on him?"

The chief engineer entered for a moment, red, smiling, and wet. "Say, Mac," cried Harvey cheerfully, "how are we hitting it?"

"Vara much in the ordinary way," was the grave reply. "The young are as polite as ever to their elders, an' their elders are e'en tryin' to appreciate it."

A low chuckle came from a corner. The German opened his cigar-case and handed a skinny black cigar to Harvey.

"Dot is der broper apparatus to smoke, my young friendt," he said. "You vill dry it? Yes? Den you vill be efer so happy."

Harvey lit the unlovely thing with a flourish: he felt that he was getting on in grownup society.

"It would take more 'n this to keel me over," he said, ignorant that he was lighting that terrible article, a Wheeling "stogie".

"Dot we shall bresently see," said the German. "Where are we now, Mr. Mactonal'?"

"Just there or thereabouts, Mr. Schaefer," said the engineer. "We'll be on the Grand Bank to-night; but in a general way o' speakin', we're all among the fishing-fleet now. We've shaved three dories an' near scalped the boom off a Frenchman since noon, an' that's close sailing', ye may say."

"You like my cigar, eh?" the German asked, for Harvey's eyes were full of tears.

"Fine, full flavor," he answered through shut teeth. "Guess we've slowed down a little, haven't we? I'll skip out and see what the log says."

"I might if I vhas you," said the German.

Harvey staggered over the wet decks to the nearest rail. He was very unhappy; but he saw the deck-steward lashing chairs together, and, since he had boasted before the man that he was never seasick, his pride made him go aft to the second-saloon deck at the stern, which was finished in a turtle-back. The deck was deserted, and he crawled to the extreme end of it, near the flag-pole. There he doubled up in limp agony, for the Wheeling "stogie" joined with the surge and jar of the screw to sieve out his soul. His head swelled; sparks of fire danced before his eyes; his body seemed to lose weight, while his heels wavered in the breeze. He was fainting from seasickness, and a roll of the ship tilted him over the rail on to the smooth lip of the turtle-back. Then a low, gray mother-wave swung out of the fog, tucked Harvey under one arm, so to speak, and pulled him off and away to leeward; the great green closed over him, and he went quietly to sleep.

He was roused by the sound of a dinner-horn such as they used to blow at a summer-school he had once attended in the Adirondacks. Slowly he remembered that he was Harvey Cheyne, drowned and dead in mid-ocean, but was too weak to fit things together. A new smell filled his nostrils; wet and clammy chills ran down his back, and he was helplessly full of salt water. When he opened his eyes, he perceived that he was still on the top of the sea, for it was running round him in silver-coloured hills, and he was lying on a pile of half-dead fish, looking at a broad human back clothed in a blue jersey.

"It's no good," thought the boy. "I'm dead, sure enough, and this thing is in charge."

He groaned, and the figure turned its head, showing a pair of little gold rings half hidden in curly black hair.

"Aha! You feel some pretty well now?" it said. "Lie still so: we trim better."

With a swift jerk he sculled the flickering boat-head on to a foamless sea that lifted her twenty full feet, only to slide her into a glassy pit beyond. But this mountain-climbing did not interrupt blue-jersey's talk. "Fine good job, I say, that I catch you. Eh, wha-at? Better good job, I say, your boat not catch me. How you come to fall out?"

"I was sick," said Harvey; "sick, and couldn't help it."

"Just in time I blow my horn, and your boat she yaw a little. Then I see you come all down. Eh, wha-at? I think you are cut into baits by the screw, but you dreeft—dreeft to me, and I make a big fish of you. So you shall not die this time."

"Where am I?" said Harvey, who could not see that life was particularly safe where he lay.

"You are with me in the dory—Manuel my name, and I come from schooner We're Here of Gloucester. I live to Gloucester. By-and-by we get supper. Eh, wha-at?"

He seemed to have two pairs of hands and a head of cast-iron, for, not content with blowing through a big conch-shell, he must needs stand up to it, swaying with the sway of the flat-bottomed dory, and send a grinding, thuttering shriek through the fog. How long this entertainment lasted, Harvey could not remember, for he lay back terrified at the sight of the smoking swells. He fancied he heard a gun and a horn and shouting. Something bigger than the dory, but quite as lively, loomed alongside. Several voices talked at once; he was dropped into a dark, heaving hole, where men in oilskins gave him a hot drink and took off his clothes, and he fell asleep.

When he waked he listened for the first breakfast-bell on the steamer, wondering why his state-

room had grown so small. Turning, he looked into a narrow, triangular cave, lit by a lamp hung against a huge square beam. A three-cornered table within arm's reach ran from the angle of the bows to the foremast. At the after end, behind a well-used Plymouth stove, sat a boy about his own age, with a flat red face and a pair of twinkling gray eyes. He was dressed in a blue jersey and high rubber boots. Several pairs of the same sort of foot-wear, an old cap, and some worn-out woollen socks lay on the floor, and black and yellow oilskins swayed to and fro beside the bunks. The place was packed as full of smells as a bale is of cotton. The oilskins had a peculiarly thick flavor of their own which made a sort of background to the smells of fried fish, burnt grease, paint, pepper, and stale tobacco; but these, again, were all hooped together by one encircling smell of ship and salt water. Harvey saw with disgust that there were no sheets on his bed-place. He was lying on a piece of dingy ticking full of lumps and nubbles. Then, too, the boat's motion was not that of a steamer. She was neither sliding nor rolling, but rather wriggling herself about in a silly, aimless way, like a colt at the end of a halter. Water-noises ran by close to his ear, and beams creaked and whined about him. All these things made him grunt despairingly and think of his mother.

"Feelin' better?" said the boy, with a grin. "Hev some coffee?" He brought a tin cup full and sweetened it with molasses.

"Isn't there milk?" said Harvey, looking round the dark double tier of bunks as if he expected to find a cow there.

"Well, no," said the boy. "Ner there ain't likely to be till 'baout mid-September. 'Tain't bad coffee. I made it."

Harvey drank in silence, and the boy handed him a plate full of pieces of crisp fried pork, which he ate ravenously.

"I've dried your clothes. Guess they've shrunk some," said the boy. "They ain't our style much—none of 'em. Twist round an' see if you're hurt any."

Harvey stretched himself in every direction, but could not report any injuries.

"That's good," the boy said heartily. "Fix yerself an' go on deck. Dad wants to see you. I'm his son,—Dan, they call me,—an' I'm cook's helper an' everything else aboard that's too dirty for the men. There ain't no boy here 'cep' me sence Otto went overboard—an' he was only a Dutchy, an' twenty year old at that. How'd you come to fall off in a dead flat ca'am?"

"'Twasn't a calm," said Harvey, sulkily. "It was a gale, and I was seasick. Guess I must have rolled over the rail."

"There was a little common swell yes'day an' last night," said the boy. "But ef thet's your notion of a gale——" He whistled. "You'll know more 'fore you're through. Hurry! Dad's waitin'."

Like many other unfortunate young people, Harvey had never in all his life received a direct order—never, at least, without long, and sometimes tearful, explanations of the advantages of obedience and the reasons for the request. Mrs. Cheyne lived in fear of breaking his spirit, which, perhaps, was the reason that she herself walked on the edge of nervous prostration. He could not see why he should be expected to hurry for any man's pleasure, and said so. "Your dad can come down here if he's so anxious to talk to me. I want him to take me to New York right away. It'll pay him."

Dan opened his eyes as the size and beauty of this joke dawned on him. "Say, Dad!" he shouted up the foc'sle hatch, "he says you kin slip down an' see him ef you're anxious that way. 'Hear,

Dad?"

The answer came back in the deepest voice Harvey had ever heard from a human chest: "Quit foolin', Dan, and send him to me."

Dan sniggered, and threw Harvey his warped bicycle shoes. There was something in the tones on the deck that made the boy dissemble his extreme rage and console himself with the thought of gradually unfolding the tale of his own and his father's wealth on the voyage home. This rescue would certainly make him a hero among his friends for life. He hoisted himself on deck up a perpendicular ladder, and stumbled aft, over a score of obstructions, to where a small, thick-set, clean-shaven man with gray eyebrows sat on a step that led up to the quarter-deck. The swell had passed in the night, leaving a long, oily sea, dotted round the horizon with the sails of a dozen fishing-boats. Between them lay little black specks, showing where the dories were out fishing. The schooner, with a triangular riding-sail on the mainmast, played easily at anchor, and except for the man by the cabin-roof—"house" they call it—she was deserted.

"Mornin'—Good afternoon, I should say. You've nigh slep' the clock round, young feller," was the greeting.

"Mornin'," said Harvey. He did not like being called "young feller"; and, as one rescued from drowning, expected sympathy. His mother suffered agonies whenever he got his feet wet; but this mariner did not seem excited.

"Naow let's hear all abaout it. It's quite providential, first an' last, fer all concerned. What might be your name? Where from (we mistrust it's Noo York), an' where baound (we mistrust it's Europe)?"

Harvey gave his name, the name of the steamer, and a short history of the accident, winding up with a demand to be taken back immediately to New York, where his father would pay anything any one chose to name.

"H'm," said the shaven man, quite unmoved by the end of Harvey's speech. "I can't say we think special of any man, or boy even, that falls overboard from that kind o' packet in a flat ca'am. Least of all when his excuse is that he's seasick."

"Excuse!" cried Harvey. "D'you suppose I'd fall overboard into your dirty little boat for fun?"

"Not knowin' what your notions o' fun may be, I can't rightly say, young feller. But if I was you, I wouldn't call the boat which, under Providence, was the means o' savin' ye, names. In the first place, it's blame irreligious. In the second, it's annoyin' to my feelin's—an' I'm Disko Troop o' the We're Here o' Gloucester, which you don't seem rightly to know."

"I don't know and I don't care," said Harvey. "I'm grateful enough for being saved and all that, of course! but I want you to understand that the sooner you take me back to New York the better it'll pay you."

"Meanin'—haow?" Troop raised one shaggy eyebrow over a suspiciously mild blue eye.

"Dollars and cents," said Harvey, delighted to think that he was making an impression. "Cold dollars and cents." He thrust a hand into a pocket, and threw out his stomach a little, which was his way of being grand. "You've done the best day's work you ever did in your life when you pulled me in. I'm all the son Harvey Cheyne has."

"He's bin favoured," said Disko, dryly.

"And if you don't know who Harvey Cheyne is, you don't know much—that's all. Now turn her around and let's hurry."

Harvey had a notion that the greater part of America was filled with people discussing and envying his father's dollars.

"Mebbe I do, an' mebbe I don't. Take a reef in your stummick, young feller. It's full o' my vittles."

Harvey heard a chuckle from Dan, who was pretending to be busy by the stump-foremast, and blood rushed to his face. "We'll pay for that too," he said. "When do you suppose we shall get to New York?"

"I don't use Noo York any. Ner Boston. We may see Eastern Point about September; an' your pa—I'm real sorry I hain't heerd tell of him—may give me ten dollars efter all your talk. Then o' course he mayn't."

"Ten dollars! Why, see here, I—" Harvey dived into his pocket for the wad of bills. All he brought up was a soggy packet of cigarettes.

"Not lawful currency; an' bad for the lungs. Heave 'em overboard, young feller, and try agin."

"It's been stolen!" cried Harvey, hotly.

"You'll hev to wait till you see your pa to reward me, then?"

"A hundred and thirty-four dollars—all stolen," said Harvey, hunting wildly through his pockets. "Give them back."

A curious change flitted across old Troop's hard face. "What might you have been doin' at your time o' life with one hundred an' thirty-four dollars, young feller?"

"It was part of my pocket-money—for a month." This Harvey thought would be a knock-down blow, and it was—indirectly.

"Oh! One hundred and thirty-four dollars is only part of his pocket-money—for one month only! You don't remember hittin' anything when you fell over, do you? Crack agin a stanchion, le's say. Old man Hasken o' the East Wind"—Troop seemed to be talking to himself—"he tripped on a hatch an' butted the mainmast with his head—hardish. 'Baout three weeks afterwards, old man Hasken he would hev it that the "East Wind" was a commerce-destroyin' man-o'-war, an' so he declared war on Sable Island because it was Bridish, an' the shoals run aout too far. They sewed him up in a bed-bag, his head an' feet appearin', fer the rest o' the trip, an' now he's to home in Essex playin' with little rag dolls."

Harvey choked with rage, but Troop went on consolingly: "We're sorry fer you. We're very sorry fer you—an' so young. We won't say no more abaout the money, I guess."

"'Course you won't. You stole it."

"Suit yourself. We stole it ef it's any comfort to you. Naow, abaout goin' back. Allowin' we could do it, which we can't, you ain't in no fit state to go back to your home, an' we've jest come on to the Banks, workin' fer our bread. We don't see the ha'af of a hundred dollars a month, let alone pocket-money; an' with good luck we'll be ashore again somewheres abaout the first weeks o' September."

"But—but it's May now, and I can't stay here doin' nothing just because you want to fish. I can't, I tell you!"

"Right an' jest; jest an' right. No one asks you to do nothin'. There's a heap as you can do, for Otto he went overboard on Le Have. I mistrust he lost his grip in a gale we f'und there. Anyways, he never come back to deny it. You've turned up, plain, plumb providential for all concerned. I mistrust, though, there's ruther few things you kin do. Ain't thet so?"

"I can make it lively for you and your crowd when we get ashore," said Harvey, with a vicious nod, murmuring vague threats about "piracy," at which Troop almost—not quite—smiled.

"Excep' talk. I'd forgot that. You ain't asked to talk more'n you've a mind to aboard the We're Here. Keep your eyes open, an' help Dan to do ez he's bid, an' sechlike, an' I'll give you—you ain't wuth it, but I'll give—ten an' a ha'af a month; say thirty-five at the end o' the trip. A little work will ease up your head, and you kin tell us all abaout your dad an' your ma an' your money afterwards."

"She's on the steamer," said Harvey, his eyes filling with tears. "Take me to New York at once."

"Poor woman—poor woman! When she has you back she'll forgit it all, though. There's eight of us on the We're Here, an' ef we went back naow—it's more'n a thousand mile—we'd lose the season. The men they wouldn't hev it, allowin' I was agreeable."

"But my father would make it all right."

"He'd try. I don't doubt he'd try," said Troop; "but a whole season's catch is eight men's bread; an' you'll be better in your health when you see him in the fall. Go forward an' help Dan. It's ten an' a ha'af a month, e I said, an' o' course, all f'und, same e the rest o' us."

"Do you mean I'm to clean pots and pans and things?" said Harvey.

"An' other things. You've no call to shout, young feller."

"I won't! My father will give you enough to buy this dirty little fish-kettle"—Harvey stamped on the deck—"ten times over, if you take me to New York safe; and—and—you're in a hundred and thirty by me, anyhow."

"Haow?" said Troop, the iron face darkening.

"How? You know how, well enough. On top of all that, you want me to do menial work"—Harvey was very proud of that adjective—"till the Fall. I tell you I will not. You hear?"

Troop regarded the top of the mainmast with deep interest for a while, as Harvey harangued fiercely all around him.

"Hsh!" he said at last. "I'm figurin' out my responsibilities in my own mind. It's a matter o' jedgment."

Dan stole up and plucked Harvey by the elbow. "Don't go to tamperin' with Dad any more," he pleaded. "You've called him a thief two or three times over, an' he don't take that from any livin' bein'."

"I won't!" Harvey almost shrieked, disregarding the advice, and still Troop meditated.

"Seems kinder unneighbourly," he said at last, his eye travelling down to Harvey. "I—don't

lame you, not a mite, young feeler, nor you won't blame me when the bile's out o' your systim. 3e sure you sense what I say? Ten an' a ha'af fer second boy on the schooner—an' all found— er to teach you an' fer the sake o' your health. Yes or no?"

'No!" said Harvey. "Take me back to New York or I'll see you—"

Ie did not exactly remember what followed. He was lying in the scuppers, holding on to a nose hat bled while Troop looked down on him serenely.

"Dan," he said to his son, "I was sot agin this young feeler when I first saw him on account o' asty jedgments. Never you be led astray by hasty jedgments, Dan. Naow I'm sorry for him, ecause he's clear distracted in his upper works. He ain't responsible fer the names he's give me, or fer his other statements—nor fer jumpin' overboard, which I'm abaout ha'af convinced he lid. You be gentle with him, Dan, 'r I'll give you twice what I've give him. Them hemmeridges lears the head. Let him sluice it off!"

Troop went down solemnly into the cabin, where he and the older men bunked, leaving Dan to comfort the luckless heir to thirty millions.

CHAPTER II

"I warned ye," said Dan, as the drops fell thick and fast on the dark, oiled planking. "Dad ain't noways hasty, but you fair earned it. Pshaw! there's no sense takin' on so." Harvey's shoulders were rising and falling in spasms of dry sobbing. "I know the feelin'. First time Dad laid me out was the last—and that was my first trip. Makes ye feel sickish an' lonesome. I know."

"It does," moaned Harvey. "That man's either crazy or drunk, and—and I can't do anything."

"Don't say that to Dad," whispered Dan. "He's set agin all liquor, an'—well, he told me you was the madman. What in creation made you call him a thief? He's my dad."

Harvey sat up, mopped his nose, and told the story of the missing wad of bills. "I'm not crazy," he wound up. "Only—your father has never seen more than a five-dollar bill at a time, and my father could buy up this boat once a week and never miss it."

"You don't know what the We're Here's worth. Your dad must hev a pile o' money. How did he git it? Dad sez loonies can't shake out a straight yarn. Go ahead."

"In gold mines and things, West."

"I've read o' that kind o' business. Out West, too? Does he go around with a pistol on a trick-pony, same ez the circus? They call that the Wild West, and I've heard that their spurs an' bridles was solid silver."

"You are a chump!" said Harvey, amused in spite of himself. "My father hasn't any use for ponies. When he wants to ride he takes his car."

"Haow? Lobster-car?"

"No. His own private car, of course. You've seen a private car some time in your life?"

"Slatin Beeman he hez one," said Dan, cautiously. "I saw her at the Union Depot in Boston, with three niggers hoggin' her run." (Dan meant cleaning the windows.) "But Slatin Beeman he owns 'baout every railroad on Long Island, they say, an' they say he's bought 'baout ha'af Noo Hampshire an' run a line fence around her, an' filled her up with lions an' tigers an' bears an' buffalo an' crocodiles an' such all. Slatin Beeman he's a millionaire. I've seen his car. Yes?"

"Well, my father's what they call a multi-millionaire, and he has two private cars. One's named for me, the 'Harvey', and one for my mother, the 'Constance'."

"Hold on," said Dan. "Dad don't ever let me swear, but I guess you can. 'Fore we go ahead, I want you to say hope you may die if you're lyin'."

"Of course," said Harvey.

"The ain't 'niff. Say, 'Hope I may die if I ain't speaking' truth.'"

"Hope I may die right here," said Harvey, "if every word I've spoken isn't the cold truth."

"Hundred an' thirty-four dollars an' all?" said Dan. "I heard ye talkin' to Dad, an' I ha'af looked you'd be swallered up, same's Jonah."

Harvey protested himself red in the face. Dan was a shrewd young person along his own lines,

and ten minutes' questioning convinced him that Harvey was not lying—much. Besides, he had bound himself by the most terrible oath known to boyhood, and yet he sat, alive, with a red-ended nose, in the scuppers, recounting marvels upon marvels.

"Gosh!" said Dan at last from the very bottom of his soul when Harvey had completed an inventory of the car named in his honour. Then a grin of mischievous delight overspread his broad face. "I believe you, Harvey. Dad's made a mistake fer once in his life."

"He has, sure," said Harvey, who was meditating an early revenge.

"He'll be mad clear through. Dad jest hates to be mistook in his jedgments." Dan lay back and slapped his thigh. "Oh, Harvey, don't you spile the catch by lettin' on."

"I don't want to be knocked down again. I'll get even with him, though."

"Never heard any man ever got even with dad. But he'd knock ye down again sure. The more he was mistook the more he'd do it. But gold-mines and pistols—"

"I never said a word about pistols," Harvey cut in, for he was on his oath.

"Thet's so; no more you did. Two private cars, then, one named fer you an' one fer her; an' two hundred dollars a month pocket-money, all knocked into the scuppers fer not workin' fer ten an' a ha'af a month! It's the top haul o' the season." He exploded with noiseless chuckles.

"Then I was right?" said Harvey, who thought he had found a sympathiser.

"You was wrong; the wrongest kind o' wrong! You take right hold an' pitch in 'longside o' me, or you'll catch it, an' I'll catch it fer backin' you up. Dad always gives me double helps 'cause I'm his son, an' he hates favourin' folk. 'Guess you're kinder mad at dad. I've been that way time an' again. But dad's a mighty jest man; all the fleet says so."

"Looks like justice, this, don't it?" Harvey pointed to his outraged nose.

"Thet's nothin'. Lets the shore blood outer you. Dad did it for yer health. Say, though, I can't have dealin's with a man that thinks me or dad or any one on the We're Here's a thief. We ain't any common wharf-end crowd by any manner o' means. We're fishermen, an' we've shipped together for six years an' more. Don't you make any mistake on that! I told ye dad don't let me swear. He calls 'em vain oaths, and pounds me; but ef I could say what you said 'baout your pap an' his fixin's, I'd say that 'baout your dollars. I dunno what was in your pockets when I dried your kit, fer I didn't look to see; but I'd say, using the very same words ez you used jest now, neither me nor dad—an' we was the only two that teched you after you was brought aboard—knows anythin' 'baout the money. Thet's my say. Naow?"

The bloodletting had certainly cleared Harvey's brain, and maybe the loneliness of the sea had something to do with it. "That's all right," he said. Then he looked down confusedly. "'Seems to me that for a fellow just saved from drowning I haven't been over and above grateful, Dan."

"Well, you was shook up and silly," said Dan. "Anyway, there was only dad an' me aboard to see it. The cook he don't count."

"I might have thought about losing the bills that way," Harvey said, half to himself, "instead of calling everybody in sight a thief. Where's your father?"

"In the cabin. What d' you want o' him again?"

"You'll see," said Harvey, and he stepped, rather groggily, for his head was still singing, to the cabin steps where the little ship's clock hung in plain sight of the wheel. Troop, in the chocolate-and-yellow painted cabin, was busy with a note-book and an enormous black pencil which he sucked hard from time to time.

"I haven't acted quite right," said Harvey, surprised at his own meekness.

"What's wrong naow?" said the skipper. "Walked into Dan, hev ye?"

"No; it's about you."

"I'm here to listen."

"Well, I—I'm here to take things back," said Harvey very quickly. "When a man's saved from drowning—" he gulped.

"Ey? You'll make a man yet ef you go on this way."

"He oughtn't begin by calling people names."

"Jest an' right—right an' jest," said Troop, with the ghost of a dry smile.

"So I'm here to say I'm sorry." Another big gulp.

Troop heaved himself slowly off the locker he was sitting on and held out an eleven-inch hand. "I mistrusted 'twould do you sights o' good; an' this shows I weren't mistook in my jedgments." A smothered chuckle on deck caught his ear. "I am very seldom mistook in my jedgments." The eleven-inch hand closed on Harvey's, numbing it to the elbow. "We'll put a little more gristle to that 'fore we've done with you, young feller; an' I don't think any worse of ye fer anythin' the's gone by. You wasn't fairly responsible. Go right abaout your business an' you won't take no hurt."

"You're white," said Dan, as Harvey regained the deck, flushed to the tips of his ears.

"I don't feel it," said he.

"I didn't mean that way. I heard what Dad said. When Dad allows he don't think the worse of any man, Dad's give himself away. He hates to be mistook in his jedgments too. Ho! ho! Onct Dad has a jedgment, he'd sooner dip his colours to the British than change it. I'm glad it's settled right eend up. Dad's right when he says he can't take you back. It's all the livin' we make here—fishin'. The men'll be back like sharks after a dead whale in ha'af an hour."

"What for?" said Harvey.

"Supper, o' course. Don't your stummick tell you? You've a heap to learn."

"Guess I have," said Harvey, dolefully, looking at the tangle of ropes and blocks overhead.

"She's a daisy," said Dan, enthusiastically, misunderstanding the look. "Wait till our mainsail's bent, an' she walks home with all her salt wet. There's some work first, though." He pointed down into the darkness of the open main-hatch between the two masts.

"What's that for? It's all empty," said Harvey.

"You an' me an' a few more hev got to fill it," said Dan. "That's where the fish goes."

"Alive?" said Harvey.

"Well, no. They're so's to be ruther dead—an' flat—an' salt. There's a hundred hogshead o' salt in the bins, an' we hain't more'n covered our dunnage to now."

"Where are the fish, though?"

"'In the sea they say, in the boats we pray,'" said Dan, quoting a fisherman's proverb. "You come in last night with 'baout forty of 'em."

He pointed to a sort of wooden pen just in front of the quarter-deck.

"You an' me we'll sluice that out when they're through. 'Send we'll hev full pens to-night! I've seen her down ha'af a foot with fish waitin' to clean, an' we stood to the tables till we was splittin' ourselves instid o' them, we was so sleepy. Yes, they're comm' in naow." Dan looked over the low bulwarks at half a dozen dories rowing towards them over the shining, silky sea.

"I've never seen the sea from so low down," said Harvey. "It's fine."

The low sun made the water all purple and pinkish, with golden lights on the barrels of the long swells, and blue and green mackerel shades in the hollows. Each schooner in sight seemed to be pulling her dories towards her by invisible strings, and the little black figures in the tiny boats pulled like clockwork toys.

"They've struck on good," said Dan, between his half-shut eyes. "Manuel hain't room fer another fish. Low ez a lily-pad in still water, Aeneid he?"

"Which is Manuel? I don't see how you can tell 'em 'way off, as you do."

"Last boat to the south'ard. He fund you last night," said Dan, pointing. "Manuel rows Portugoosey; ye can't mistake him. East o' him—he's a heap better'n he rows—is Pennsylvania. Loaded with saleratus, by the looks of him. East o' him—see how pretty they string out all along—with the humpy shoulders, is Long Jack. He's a Galway man inhabitin' South Boston, where they all live mostly, an' mostly them Galway men are good in a boat. North, away yonder—you'll hear him tune up in a minute is Tom Platt. Man-o'-war's man he was on the old Ohio first of our navy, he says, to go araound the Horn. He never talks of much else, 'cept when he sings, but he has fair fishin' luck. There! What did I tell you?"

A melodious bellow stole across the water from the northern dory. Harvey heard something about somebody's hands and feet being cold, and then:

"Bring forth the chart, the doleful chart,
See where them mountings meet!
The clouds are thick around their heads,
The mists around their feet."

"Full boat," said Dan, with a chuckle. "If he give us 'O Captain' it's topping' too!"

The bellow continued:

"And naow to thee, O Capting,
Most earnestly I pray,
That they shall never bury me
In church or cloister gray."

"Double game for Tom Platt. He'll tell you all about the old Ohio tomorrow. 'See that blue dory behind him? He's my uncle,—Dad's own brother,—an' ef there's any bad luck loose on the Banks she'll fetch up agin Uncle Salters, sure. Look how tender he's rowin'. I'll lay my wage and share he's the only man stung up to-day—an' he's stung up good."

"What'll sting him?" said Harvey, getting interested.

"Strawberries, mostly. Pumpkins, sometimes, an' sometimes lemons an' cucumbers. Yes, he's stung up from his elbows down. That man's luck's perfectly paralyzin'. Naow we'll take a-holt o' the tackles an' hist 'em in. Is it true what you told me jest now, that you never done a hand's turn o' work in all your born life? Must feel kinder awful, don't it?"

"I'm going to try to work, anyway," Harvey replied stoutly. "Only it's all dead new."

"Lay a-holt o' that tackle, then. Behind ye!"

Harvey grabbed at a rope and long iron hook dangling from one of the stays of the mainmast, while Dan pulled down another that ran from something he called a "topping-lift," as Manuel drew alongside in his loaded dory. The Portuguese smiled a brilliant smile that Harvey learned to know well later, and with a short-handled fork began to throw fish into the pen on deck. "Two hundred and thirty-one," he shouted.

"Give him the hook," said Dan, and Harvey ran it into Manuel's hands. He slipped it through a loop of rope at the dory's bow, caught Dan's tackle, hooked it to the stern-becket, and clambered into the schooner.

"Pull!" shouted Dan, and Harvey pulled, astonished to find how easily the dory rose.

"Hold on, she don't nest in the crosstrees!" Dan laughed; and Harvey held on, for the boat lay in the air above his head.

"Lower away," Dan shouted, and as Harvey lowered, Dan swayed the light boat with one hand till it landed softly just behind the mainmast. "They don't weigh nothin' empty. Thet was right smart fer a passenger. There's more trick to it in a sea-way."

"Ah ha!" said Manuel, holding out a brown hand. "You are some pretty well now? This time last night the fish they fish for you. Now you fish for fish. Eh, wha-at?"

"I'm—I'm ever so grateful," Harvey stammered, and his unfortunate hand stole to his pocket once more, but he remembered that he had no money to offer. When he knew Manuel better the mere thought of the mistake he might have made would cover him with hot, uneasy blushes in his bunk.

"There is no to be thankful for to me!" said Manuel. "How shall I leave you dreeft, dreeft all around the Banks? Now you are a fisherman eh, wha-at? Ouh! Auh!" He bent backward and forward stiffly from the hips to get the kinks out of himself.

"I have not cleaned boat to-day. Too busy. They struck on queek. Danny, my son, clean for me."

Harvey moved forward at once. Here was something he could do for the man who had saved his life.

Dan threw him a swab, and he leaned over the dory, mopping up the slime clumsily, but with great good-will. "Hike out the foot-boards; they slide in them grooves," said Dan. "Swab 'em an' lay 'em down. Never let a foot-board jam. Ye may want her bad some day. Here's Long

ack."

A stream of glittering fish flew into the pen from a dory alongside.

"Manuel, you take the tackle. I'll fix the tables. Harvey, clear Manuel's boat. Long Jack's restin' on the top of her."

Harvey looked up from his swabbing at the bottom of another dory just above his head.

"Jest like the Injian puzzle-boxes, ain't they?" said Dan, as the one boat dropped into the other.

"Takes to ut like a duck to water," said Long Jack, a grizzly-chinned, long-lipped Galway man, bending to and fro exactly as Manuel had done. Disko in the cabin growled up the hatchway, and they could hear him suck his pencil.

"Wan hunder an' forty-nine an' a half-bad luck to ye, Discobolus!" said Long Jack. "I'm murderin' meself to fill your pockuts. Slate ut for a bad catch. The Portugee has bate me."

Whack came another dory alongside, and more fish shot into the pen.

"Two hundred and three. Let's look at the passenger!" The speaker was even larger than the Galway man, and his face was made curious by a purple cut running slant-ways from his left eye to the right corner of his mouth.

Not knowing what else to do, Harvey swabbed each dory as it came down, pulled out the foot-boards, and laid them in the bottom of the boat.

"He's caught on good," said the scarred man, who was Tom Platt, watching him critically. "There are two ways o' doin' everything. One's fisher-fashion—any end first an' a slippery hitch over all—an' the other's—"

"What we did on the old Ohio!" Dan interrupted, brushing into the knot of men with a long board on legs. "Get out o' here, Tom Platt, an' leave me fix the tables."

He jammed one end of the board into two nicks in the bulwarks, kicked out the leg, and ducked just in time to avoid a swinging blow from the man-o'-war's man.

"An' they did that on the Ohio, too, Danny. See?" said Tom Platt, laughing.

"Guess they was swivel-eyed, then, fer it didn't git home, and I know who'll find his boots on the main-truck ef he don't leave us alone. Haul ahead! I'm busy, can't ye see?"

"Danny, ye lie on the cable an' sleep all day," said Long Jack. "You're the hoight av impidence, an' I'm persuaded ye'll corrupt our supercargo in a week."

"His name's Harvey," said Dan, waving two strangely shaped knives, "an' he'll be worth five of any Sou' Boston clam-digger 'fore long." He laid the knives tastefully on the table, cocked his head on one side, and admired the effect.

"I think it's forty-two," said a small voice overside, and there was a roar of laughter as another voice answered, "Then my luck's turned fer onct, 'caze I'm forty-five, though I be stung outer all shape."

"Forty-two or forty-five. I've lost count," the small voice said.

"It's Penn an' Uncle Salters caountin' catch. This beats the circus any day," said Dan. "Jest

look at 'em!"

"Come in—come in!" roared Long Jack. "It's wet out yondher, children."

"Forty-two, ye said." This was Uncle Salters.

"I'll count again, then," the voice replied meekly. The two dories swung together and bunted into the schooner's side.

"Patience o' Jerusalem!" snapped Uncle Salters, backing water with a splash. "What possest a farmer like you to set foot in a boat beats me. You've nigh stove me all up."

"I am sorry, Mr. Salters. I came to sea on account of nervous dyspepsia. You advised me, I think."

"You an' your nervis dyspepsy be drowned in the Whale-hole," roared Uncle Salters, a fat and tubby little man. "You're comin' down on me again. Did ye say forty-two or forty-five?"

"I've forgotten, Mr. Salters. Let's count."

"Don't see as it could be forty-five. I'm forty-five," said Uncle Salters. "You count keerful, Penn."

Disko Troop came out of the cabin. "Salters, you pitch your fish in naow at once," he said in the tone of authority.

"Don't spile the catch, Dad," Dan murmured. "Them two are on'y jest beginnin'."

"Mother av delight! He's forkin' them wan by wan," howled Long Jack, as Uncle Salters got to work laboriously; the little man in the other dory counting a line of notches on the gunwale.

"That was last week's catch," he said, looking up plaintively, his forefinger where he had left off.

Manuel nudged Dan, who darted to the after-tackle, and, leaning far overside, slipped the hook into the stern-rope as Manuel made her fast forward. The others pulled gallantly and swung the boat in—man, fish, and all.

"One, two, four-nine," said Tom Platt, counting with a practised eye. "Forty-seven. Penn, you're it!" Dan let the after-tackle run, and slid him out of the stern on to the deck amid a torrent of his own fish.

"Hold on!" roared Uncle Salters, bobbing by the waist. "Hold on, I'm a bit mixed in my caount."

He had no time to protest, but was hove inboard and treated like "Pennsylvania."

"Forty-one," said Tom Platt. "Beat by a farmer, Salters. An' you sech a sailor, too!"

"'Tween't fair caount," said he, stumbling out of the pen; "an' I'm stung up all to pieces."

His thick hands were puffy and mottled purply white.

"Some folks will find strawberry-bottom," said Dan, addressing the newly risen moon, "ef they hev to dive fer it, seems to me."

"An' others," said Uncle Salters, "eats the fat o' the land in sloth, an' mocks their own blood-kin."

"Seat ye! Seat ye!" a voice Harvey had not heard called from the foc'sle. Disko Troop, Tom Platt, Long Jack, and Salters went forward on the word. Little Penn bent above his square deep-sea reel and the tangled cod-lines; Manuel lay down full length on the deck, and Dan dropped into the hold, where Harvey heard him banging casks with a hammer.

"Salt," he said, returning. "Soon as we're through supper we git to dressing-down. You'll pitch to Dad. Tom Platt an' Dad they stow together, an' you'll hear 'em arguin'. We're second ha'af, you an' me an' Manuel an' Penn—the youth an' beauty o' the boat."

"What's the good of that?" said Harvey. "I'm hungry."

"They'll be through in a minute. Suff! She smells good to-night. Dad ships a good cook ef he do suffer with his brother. It's a full catch today, Aeneid it?" He pointed at the pens piled high with cod. "What water did ye hev, Manuel?"

"Twenty-fife father," said the Portuguese, sleepily. "They strike on good an' queek. Some day I show you, Harvey."

The moon was beginning to walk on the still sea before the elder men came aft. The cook had no need to cry "second half." Dan and Manuel were down the hatch and at table ere Tom Platt, last and most deliberate of the elders, had finished wiping his mouth with the back of his hand. Harvey followed Penn, and sat down before a tin pan of cod's tongues and sounds, mixed with scraps of pork and fried potato, a loaf of hot bread, and some black and powerful coffee. Hungry as they were, they waited while "Pennsylvania" solemnly asked a blessing. Then they stoked in silence till Dan drew a breath over his tin cup and demanded of Harvey how he felt.

"'Most full, but there's just room for another piece."

The cook was a huge, jet-black negro, and, unlike all the negroes Harvey had met, did not talk, contenting himself with smiles and dumb-show invitations to eat more.

"See, Harvey," said Dan, rapping with his fork on the table, "it's jest as I said. The young an' handsome men—like me an' Pennsy an' you an' Manuel—we're second ha'af, an' we eats when the first ha'af are through. They're the old fish; an' they're mean an' humpy, an' their stummicks has to be humoured; so they come first, which they don't deserve. Aeneid that so, doctor?"

The cook nodded.

"Can't he talk?" said Harvey in a whisper.

"'Nough to get along. Not much o' anything we know. His natural tongue's kinder curious. Comes from the innards of Cape Breton, he does, where the farmers speak homemade Scotch. Cape Breton's full o' niggers whose folk run in there durin' aour war, an' they talk like farmers—all huffy-chuffy."

"That is not Scotch," said "Pennsylvania." "That is Gaelic. So I read in a book."

"Penn reads a heap. Most of what he says is so—'cep' when it comes to a caount o' fish—eh?"

"Does your father just let them say how many they've caught without checking them?" said Harvey.

"Why, yes. Where's the sense of a man lyin' fer a few old cod?"

"Was a man once lied for his catch," Manuel put in. "Lied every day. Fife, ten, twenty-fife more fish than come he say there was."

"Where was that?" said Dan. "None o' aour folk."

"Frenchman of Anguille."

"Ah! Them West Shore Frenchmen don't caount anyway. Stands to reason they can't caount. Ef you run acrost any of their soft hooks, Harvey, you'll know why," said Dan, with an awful contempt.

"Always more and never less,
Every time we come to dress,"

Long Jack roared down the hatch, and the "second ha'af" scrambled up at once.

The shadow of the masts and rigging, with the never-furled riding-sail, rolled to and fro on the heaving deck in the moonlight; and the pile of fish by the stern shone like a dump of fluid silver. In the hold there were tramplings and rumblings where Disko Troop and Tom Platt moved among the salt-bins. Dan passed Harvey a pitchfork, and led him to the inboard end of the rough table, where Uncle Salters was drumming impatiently with a knife-haft. A tub of salt water lay at his feet.

"You pitch to dad an' Tom Platt down the hatch, an' take keer Uncle Salters don't cut yer eye out," said Dan, swinging himself into the hold. "I'll pass salt below."

Penn and Manuel stood knee deep among cod in the pen, flourishing drawn knives. Long Jack, a basket at his feet and mittens on his hands, faced Uncle Salters at the table, and Harvey stared at the pitchfork and the tub.

"Hi!" shouted Manuel, stooping to the fish, and bringing one up with a finger under its gill and a finger in its eyes. He laid it on the edge of the pen; the knife-blade glimmered with a sound of tearing, and the fish, slit from throat to vent, with a nick on either side of the neck, dropped at Long Jack's feet.

"Hi!" said Long Jack, with a scoop of his mittened hand. The cod's liver dropped in the basket. Another wrench and scoop sent the head and offal flying, and the empty fish slid across to Uncle Salters, who snorted fiercely. There was another sound of tearing, the backbone flew over the bulwarks, and the fish, headless, gutted, and open, splashed in the tub, sending the salt water into Harvey's astonished mouth. After the first yell, the men were silent. The cod moved along as though they were alive, and long ere Harvey had ceased wondering at the miraculous dexterity of it all, his tub was full.

"Pitch!" grunted Uncle Salters, without turning his head, and Harvey pitched the fish by twos and threes down the hatch.

"Hi! Pitch 'em bunchy," shouted Dan. "Don't scatter! Uncle Salters is the best splitter in the fleet. Watch him mind his book!"

Indeed, it looked a little as though the round uncle were cutting magazine pages against time. Manuel's body, cramped over from the hips, stayed like a statue; but his long arms grabbed the fish without ceasing. Little Penn toiled valiantly, but it was easy to see he was weak. Once or twice Manuel found time to help him without breaking the chain of supplies, and once Manuel howled because he had caught his finger in a Frenchman's hook. These hooks are made of soft metal, to be rebent after use; but the cod very often get away with them and are hooked again

elsewhere; and that is one of the many reasons why the Gloucester boats despise the Frenchmen.

Down below, the rasping sound of rough salt rubbed on rough flesh sounded like the whirring of a grindstone—steady undertune to the "click-nick" of knives in the pen; the wrench and shloop of torn heads, dropped liver, and flying offal; the "caraaah" of Uncle Salters's knife scooping away backbones; and the flap of wet, open bodies falling into the tub.

At the end of an hour Harvey would have given the world to rest; for fresh, wet cod weigh more than you would think, and his back ached with the steady pitching. But he felt for the first time in his life that he was one of the working gang of men, took pride in the thought, and held on sullenly.

"Knife oh!" shouted Uncle Salters at last. Penn doubled up, gasping among the fish, Manuel bowed back and forth to supple himself, and Long Jack leaned over the bulwarks. The cook appeared, noiseless as a black shadow, collected a mass of backbones and heads, and retreated.

"Blood-ends for breakfast an' head-chowder," said Long Jack, smacking his lips.

"Knife oh!" repeated Uncle Salters, waving the flat, curved splitter's weapon.

"Look by your foot, Harve," cried Dan below.

Harvey saw half a dozen knives stuck in a cleat in the hatch combing. He dealt these around, taking over the dulled ones.

"Water!" said Disko Troop.

"Scuttle-butt's for'ard an' the dipper's alongside. Hurry, Harve," said Dan.

He was back in a minute with a big dipperful of stale brown water which tasted like nectar, and loosed the jaws of Disko and Tom Platt.

"These are cod," said Disko. "They ain't Damarskus figs, Tom Platt, nor yet silver bars. I've told you that ever single time since we've sailed together."

"A matter o' seven seasons," returned Tom Platt coolly. "Good stowin's good stowin' all the same, an' there's a right an' a wrong way o' stowin' ballast even. If you'd ever seen four hundred ton o' iron set into the—"

"Hi!" With a yell from Manuel the work began again, and never stopped till the pen was empty. The instant the last fish was down, Disko Troop rolled aft to the cabin with his brother; Manuel and Long Jack went forward; Tom Platt only waited long enough to slide home the hatch ere he too disappeared. In half a minute Harvey heard deep snores in the cabin, and he was staring blankly at Dan and Penn.

"I did a little better that time, Danny," said Penn, whose eyelids were heavy with sleep. "But I think it is my duty to help clean."

"'Wouldn't hev your conscience fer a thousand quintal," said Dan. "Turn in, Penn. You've no call to do boy's work. Draw a bucket, Harvey. Oh, Penn, dump these in the gurry-butt 'fore you sleep. Kin you keep awake that long?"

Penn took up the heavy basket of fish-livers, emptied them into a cask with a hinged top lashed by the foc's'le; then he too dropped out of sight in the cabin.

"Boys clean up after dressin' down an' first watch in ca'am weather is boy's watch on the We're Here." Dan sluiced the pen energetically, unshipped the table, set it up to dry in the moonlight, ran the red knife-blades through a wad of oakum, and began to sharpen them on a tiny grindstone, as Harvey threw offal and backbones overboard under his direction.

At the first splash a silvery-white ghost rose bolt upright from the oily water and sighed a weird whistling sigh. Harvey started back with a shout, but Dan only laughed.

"Grampus," said he. "Beggin' fer fish-heads. They up-eend the way when they're hungry. Breath on him like the doleful tombs, hain't he?" A horrible stench of decayed fish filled the air as the pillar of white sank, and the water bubbled oilily. "Hain't ye never seen a grampus up-eend before? You'll see 'em by hundreds 'fore ye're through. Say, it's good to hev a boy aboard again. Otto was too old, an' a Dutchy at that. Him an' me we fought consid'ble. 'Wouldn't ha' keered fer that ef he'd hed a Christian tongue in his head. Sleepy?"

"Dead sleepy," said Harvey, nodding forward.

"Mustn't sleep on watch. Rouse up an' see ef our anchor-light's bright an' shinin'. You're on watch now, Harve."

"Pshaw! What's to hurt us? Bright's day. Sn-orrr!"

"Jest when things happen, Dad says. Fine weather's good sleepin', an' 'fore you know, mebbe, you're cut in two by a liner, an' seventeen brass-bound officers, all gen'elmen, lift their hand to it that your lights was aout an' there was a thick fog. Harve, I've kinder took to you, but ef you nod onct more I'll lay into you with a rope's end."

The moon, who sees many strange things on the Banks, looked down on a slim youth in knickerbockers and a red jersey, staggering around the cluttered decks of a seventy-ton schooner, while behind him, waving a knotted rope, walked, after the manner of an executioner, a boy who yawned and nodded between the blows he dealt.

The lashed wheel groaned and kicked softly, the riding-sail slatted a little in the shifts of the light wind, the windlass creaked, and the miserable procession continued. Harvey expostulated, threatened, whimpered, and at last wept outright, while Dan, the words clotting on his tongue, spoke of the beauty of watchfulness and slashed away with the rope's end, punishing the dories as often as he hit Harvey. At last the clock in the cabin struck ten, and upon the tenth stroke little Penn crept on deck. He found two boys in two tumbled heaps side by side on the main hatch, so deeply asleep that he actually rolled them to their berths.

CHAPTER III

t was the forty-fathom slumber that clears the soul and eye and heart, and sends you to breakfast ravening. They emptied a big tin dish of juicy fragments of fish—the blood-ends the cook had collected overnight. They cleaned up the plates and pans of the elder mess, who were out fishing, sliced pork for the midday meal, swabbed down the foc'sle, filled the lamps, drew coal and water for the cook, and investigated the fore-hold, where the boat's stores were stacked. It was another perfect day—soft, mild, and clear; and Harvey breathed to the very bottom of his lungs.

More schooners had crept up in the night, and the long blue seas were full of sails and dories. Far away on the horizon, the smoke of some liner, her hull invisible, smudged the blue, and to eastward a big ship's top-gallant sails, just lifting, made a square nick in it. Disko Troop was smoking by the roof of the cabin—one eye on the craft around, and the other on the little fly at the main-mast-head.

"When Dad kerflummoxes that way," said Dan in a whisper, "he's doin' some high-line thinkin' fer all hands. I'll lay my wage an' share we'll make berth soon. Dad he knows the cod, an' the Fleet they know Dad knows. 'See 'em comm' up one by one, lookin' fer nothin' in particular, o' course, but scrowgin' on us all the time? There's the Prince Leboo; she's a Chat-ham boat. She's crep' up sence last night. An' see that big one with a patch in her foresail an' a new jib? She's the Carrie Pitman from West Chat-ham. She won't keep her canvas long onless her luck's changed since last season. She don't do much 'cep' drift. There ain't an anchor made 'll hold her. . . . When the smoke puffs up in little rings like that, Dad's studyin' the fish. Ef we speak to him now, he'll git mad. Las' time I did, he jest took an' hove a boot at me."

Disko Troop stared forward, the pipe between his teeth, with eyes that saw nothing. As his son said, he was studying the fish—pitting his knowledge and experience on the Banks against the roving cod in his own sea. He accepted the presence of the inquisitive schooners on the horizon as a compliment to his powers. But now that it was paid, he wished to draw away and make his berth alone, till it was time to go up to the Virgin and fish in the streets of that roaring town upon the waters. So Disko Troop thought of recent weather, and gales, currents, food-supplies, and other domestic arrangements, from the point of view of a twenty-pound cod; was, in fact, for an hour a cod himself, and looked remarkably like one. Then he removed the pipe from his teeth.

"Dad," said Dan, "we've done our chores. Can't we go overside a piece? It's good catchin' weather."

"Not in that cherry-coloured rig ner them ha'af baked brown shoes. Give him suthin' fit to wear."

"Dad's pleased—that settles it," said Dan, delightedly, dragging Harvey into the cabin, while Troop pitched a key down the steps. "Dad keeps my spare rig where he kin overhaul it, 'cause Ma sez I'm keerless." He rummaged through a locker, and in less than three minutes Harvey was adorned with fisherman's rubber boots that came half up his thigh, a heavy blue jersey well darned at the elbows, a pair of nippers, and a sou'wester.

"Naow ye look somethin' like," said Dan. "Hurry!"

"Keep nigh an' handy," said Troop "an' don't go visitin' raound the Fleet. If any one asks you what I'm cal'latin' to do, speak the truth—fer ye don't know."

A little red dory, labelled Hattie S., lay astern of the schooner. Dan hauled in the painter, and dropped lightly on to the bottom boards, while Harvey tumbled clumsily after.

"That's no way o' gettin' into a boat," said Dan. "Ef there was any sea you'd go to the bottom, sure. You got to learn to meet her."

Dan fitted the thole-pins, took the forward thwart and watched Harvey's work. The boy had rowed, in a lady-like fashion, on the Adirondack ponds; but there is a difference between squeaking pins and well-balanced ruflocks—light sculls and stubby, eight-foot sea-oars. They stuck in the gentle swell, and Harvey grunted.

"Short! Row short!" said Dan. "Ef you cramp your oar in any kind o' sea you're liable to turn her over. Ain't she a daisy? Mine, too."

The little dory was specklessly clean. In her bows lay a tiny anchor, two jugs of water, and some seventy fathoms of thin, brown dory-roding. A tin dinner-horn rested in cleats just under Harvey's right hand, beside an ugly-looking maul, a short gaff, and a shorter wooden stick. A couple of lines, with very heavy leads and double cod-hooks, all neatly coiled on square reels, were stuck in their place by the gunwale.

"Where's the sail and mast?" said Harvey, for his hands were beginning to blister.

Dan chuckled. "Ye don't sail fishin'-dories much. Ye pull; but ye needn't pull so hard. Don't you wish you owned her?"

"Well, I guess my father might give me one or two if I asked 'em," Harvey replied. He had been too busy to think much of his family till then.

"That's so. I forgot your dad's a millionaire. You don't act milliony any, naow. But a dory an' craft an' gear"—Dan spoke as though she were a whaleboat—"costs a heap. Think your dad 'u'd give you one fer—fer a pet like?"

"Shouldn't wonder. It would be 'most the only thing I haven't stuck him for yet."

"Must be an expensive kinder kid to home. Don't slitheroo thet way, Harve. Short's the trick, because no sea's ever dead still, an' the swells 'll—"

Crack! The loom of the oar kicked Harvey under the chin and knocked him backwards.

"That was what I was goin' to say. I hed to learn too, but I wasn't more than eight years old when I got my schoolin'."

Harvey regained his seat with aching jaws and a frown.

"No good gettin' mad at things, Dad says. It's our own fault ef we can't handle 'em, he says. Le's try here. Manuel 'll give us the water."

The "Portugee" was rocking fully a mile away, but when Dan up-ended an oar he waved his left arm three times.

"Thirty fathom," said Dan, stringing a salt clam on to the hook. "Over with the doughboys. Bait same's I do, Harvey, an' don't snarl your reel."

Dan's line was out long before Harvey had mastered the mystery of baiting and heaving out the leads. The dory drifted along easily. It was not worth while to anchor till they were sure of good ground.

"Here we come!" Dan shouted, and a shower of spray rattled on Harvey's shoulders as a big cod flapped and kicked alongside. "Muckle, Harvey, muckle! Under your hand! Quick!"

Evidently "muckle" could not be the dinner-horn, so Harvey passed over the maul, and Dan scientifically stunned the fish before he pulled it inboard, and wrenched out the hook with the short wooden stick he called a "gob-stick." Then Harvey felt a tug, and pulled up zealously.

"Why, these are strawberries!" he shouted. "Look!"

The hook had fouled among a bunch of strawberries, red on one side and white on the other—perfect reproductions of the land fruit, except that there were no leaves, and the stem was all pipy and slimy.

"Don't tech 'em. Slat 'em off. Don't—"

The warning came too late. Harvey had picked them from the hook, and was admiring them.

"Ouch!" he cried, for his fingers throbbed as though he had grasped many nettles.

"Now ye know what strawberry-bottom means. Nothin' 'cep' fish should be teched with the naked fingers, Dad says. Slat 'em off agin the gunnel, an' bait up, Harve. Lookin' won't help any. It's all in the wages."

Harvey smiled at the thought of his ten and a half dollars a month, and wondered what his mother would say if she could see him hanging over the edge of a fishing-dory in mid-ocean. She suffered agonies whenever he went out on Saranac Lake; and, by the way, Harvey remembered distinctly that he used to laugh at her anxieties. Suddenly the line flashed through his hand, stinging even through the "nippers," the woolen circlets supposed to protect it.

"He's a logy. Give him room accordin' to his strength," cried Dan. "I'll help ye."

"No, you won't," Harvey snapped, as he hung on to the line. "It's my first fish. Is—is it a whale?"

"Halibut, mebbe." Dan peered down into the water alongside, and flourished the big "muckle," ready for all chances. Something white and oval flickered and fluttered through the green. "I'll lay my wage an' share he's over a hundred. Are you so everlastin' anxious to land him alone?"

Harvey's knuckles were raw and bleeding where they had been banged against the gunwale; his face was purple-blue between excitement and exertion; he dripped with sweat, and was half-blinded from staring at the circling sunlit ripples about the swiftly moving line. The boys were tired long ere the halibut, who took charge of them and the dory for the next twenty minutes. But the big flat fish was gaffed and hauled in at last.

"Beginner's luck," said Dan, wiping his forehead. "He's all of a hundred."

Harvey looked at the huge gray-and-mottled creature with unspeakable pride. He had seen halibut many times on marble slabs ashore, but it had never occurred to him to ask how they came inland. Now he knew; and every inch of his body ached with fatigue.

"Ef Dad was along," said Dan, hauling up, "he'd read the signs plain's print. The fish are runnin' smaller an' smaller, an' you've took 'baout as logy a halibut's we're apt to find this trip. Yesterday's catch—did ye notice it?—was all big fish an' no halibut. Dad he'd read them signs right off. Dad says everythin' on the Banks is signs, an' can be read wrong er right. Dad's deeper'n the Whale-hole."

Even as he spoke some one fired a pistol on the We're Here, and a potato-basket was run up in the fore-rigging.

"What did I say, naow? That's the call fer the whole crowd. Dad's onter something, er he'd never break fishin' this time o' day. Reel up, Harve, an' we'll pull back."

They were to windward of the schooner, just ready to flirt the dory over the still sea, when sounds of woe half a mile off led them to Penn, who was careering around a fixed point for all the world like a gigantic water-bug. The little man backed away and came down again with enormous energy, but at the end of each maneuver his dory swung round and snubbed herself on her rope.

"We'll hev to help him, else he'll root an' seed here," said Dan.

"What's the matter?" said Harvey. This was a new world, where he could not lay down the law to his elders, but had to ask questions humbly. And the sea was horribly big and unexcited.

"Anchor's fouled. Penn's always losing 'em. Lost two this trip a'ready—on sandy bottom too— an' Dad says next one he loses, sure's fishin', he'll give him the kelleg. That 'u'd break Penn's heart."

"What's a 'kelleg'?" said Harvey, who had a vague idea it might be some kind of marine torture, like keel-hauling in the storybooks.

"Big stone instid of an anchor. You kin see a kelleg ridin' in the bows fur's you can see a dory, an' all the fleet knows what it means. They'd guy him dreadful. Penn couldn't stand that no more'n a dog with a dipper to his tail. He's so everlastin' sensitive. Hello, Penn! Stuck again? Don't try any more o' your patents. Come up on her, and keep your rodin' straight up an' down."

"It doesn't move," said the little man, panting. "It doesn't move at all, and instead I tried everything."

"What's all this hurrah's-nest for'ard?" said Dan, pointing to a wild tangle of spare oars and dory-roding, all matted together by the hand of inexperience.

"Oh, that," said Penn proudly, "is a Spanish windlass. Mr. Salters showed me how to make it; but even that doesn't move her."

Dan bent low over the gunwale to hide a smile, twitched once or twice on the roding, and, behold, the anchor drew at once.

"Haul up, Penn," he said laughing, "er she'll git stuck again."

They left him regarding the weed-hung flukes of the little anchor with big, pathetic blue eyes, and thanking them profusely.

"Oh, say, while I think of it, Harve," said Dan when they were out of ear-shot, "Penn ain't quite all caulked. He ain't nowise dangerous, but his mind's give out. See?"

"Is that so, or is it one of your father's judgments?"

Harvey asked as he bent to his oars. He felt he was learning to handle them more easily.

"Dad ain't mistook this time. Penn's a sure 'nuff loony."

"No, he ain't thet exactly, so much ez a harmless ijut. It was this way (you're rowin' quite so, Harve), an' I tell you 'cause it's right you orter know. He was a Moravian preacher once. Jacob Boiler wuz his name, Dad told me, an' he lived with his wife an' four children somewheres out Pennsylvania way. Well, Penn he took his folks along to a Moravian meetin'—camp-meetin' most like—an' they stayed over jest one night in Johns-town. You've heered talk o' Johnstown?"

Harvey considered. "Yes, I have. But I don't know why. It sticks in my head same as Ashtabula."

"Both was big accidents—thet's why, Harve. Well, that one single night Penn and his folks was to the hotel Johnstown was wiped out. 'Dam bust an' flooded her, an' the houses struck adrift an' bumped into each other an' sunk. I've seen the pictures, an' they're dretful. Penn he saw his folk drowned all'n a heap 'fore he rightly knew what was comin'. His mind give out from that on. He mistrusted somethin' hed happened up to Johnstown, but for the poor life of him he couldn't remember what, an' he jest drifted araound smilin' an' wonderin'. He didn't know what he was, nor yit what he hed bin, an' thet way he run agin Uncle Salters, who was visitin' 'n Allegheny City. Ha'af my mother's folks they live scattered inside o' Pennsylvania, an' Uncle Salters he visits araound winters. Uncle Salters he kinder adopted Penn, well knowin' what his trouble wuz; an' he brought him East, an' he give him work on his farm."

"Why, I heard him calling Penn a farmer last night when the boats bumped. Is your Uncle Salters a farmer?"

"Farmer!" shouted Dan. "There ain't water enough 'tween here an' Hatt'rus to wash the furrer-mold off'n his boots. He's jest everlastin' farmer. Why, Harve, I've seen thet man hitch up a bucket, long towards sundown, an' set twiddlin' the spigot to the scuttle-butt same's ef 'twas a cow's bag. He's thet much farmer. Well, Penn an' he they ran the farm—up Exeter way 'twur. Uncle Salters he sold it this spring to a jay from Boston as wanted to build a summer-haouse, an' he got a heap for it. Well, them two loonies scratched along till, one day, Penn's church—he'd belonged to the Moravians—found out where he wuz drifted an' layin', an' wrote to Uncle Salters. 'Never heerd what they said exactly; but Uncle Salters was mad. He's a 'piscopolian mostly—but he jest let 'em hev it both sides o' the bow, 's if he was a Baptist; an' sez he warn't goin' to give up Penn to any blame Moravian connection in Pennsylvania or anywheres else. Then he come to Dad, towin' Penn,—thet was two trips back,—an' sez he an' Penn must fish a trip fer their health. 'Guess he thought the Moravians wouldn't hunt the Banks fer Jacob Boiler. Dad was agreeable, fer Uncle Salters he'd been fishin' off an' on fer thirty years, when he warn't inventin' patent manures, an' he took quarter-share in the We're Here; an' the trip done Penn so much good, Dad made a habit o' takin' him. Some day, Dad sez, he'll remember his wife an' kids an' Johnstown, an' then, like as not, he'll die, Dad sez. Don't ye talk abaout Johnstown ner such things to Penn, 'r Uncle Salters he'll heave ye overboard."

"Poor Penn!" murmured Harvey. "I shouldn't ever have thought Uncle Salters cared for him by the look of 'em together."

"I like Penn, though; we all do," said Dan. "We ought to ha' give him a tow, but I wanted to tell ye first."

They were close to the schooner now, the other boats a little behind them.

"You needn't heave in the dories till after dinner," said Troop from the deck. "We'll dress daown right off. Fix table, boys!"

"Deeper'n the Whale-deep," said Dan, with a wink, as he set the gear for dressing down. "Look at them boats that hev edged up since mornin'. They're all waitin' on Dad. See 'em, Harve?"

"They are all alike to me." And indeed to a landsman, the nodding schooners around seemed run from the same mold.

"They ain't, though. That yaller, dirty packet with her bowsprit steeved that way, she's the Hope of Prague. Nick Brady's her skipper, the meanest man on the Banks. We'll tell him so when we strike the Main Ledge. 'Way off yonder's the Day's Eye. The two Jeraulds own her. She's from Harwich; fastish, too, an' hez good luck; but Dad he'd find fish in a graveyard. Them other three, side along, they're the Margie Smith, Rose, and Edith S. Walen, all from home. 'Guess we'll see the Abbie M. Deering to-morrer, Dad, won't we? They're all slippin' over from the shaol o' 'Oueereau.'"

"You won't see many boats to-morrow, Danny." When Troop called his son Danny, it was a sign that the old man was pleased. "Boys, we're too crowded," he went on, addressing the crew as they clambered inboard. "We'll leave 'em to bait big an' catch small." He looked at the catch in the pen, and it was curious to see how little and level the fish ran. Save for Harvey's halibut, there was nothing over fifteen pounds on deck.

"I'm waitin' on the weather," he added.

"Ye'll have to make it yourself, Disko, for there's no sign I can see," said Long Jack, sweeping the clear horizon.

And yet, half an hour later, as they were dressing down, the Bank fog dropped on them, "between fish and fish," as they say. It drove steadily and in wreaths, curling and smoking along the colourless water. The men stopped dressing-down without a word. Long Jack and Uncle Salters slipped the windlass brakes into their sockets, and began to heave up the anchor; the windlass jarring as the wet hempen cable strained on the barrel. Manuel and Tom Platt gave a hand at the last. The anchor came up with a sob, and the riding-sail bellied as Troop steadied her at the wheel. "Up jib and foresail," said he.

"Slip 'em in the smother," shouted Long Jack, making fast the jib-sheet, while the others raised the clacking, rattling rings of the foresail; and the foreboom creaked as the We're Here looked up into the wind and dived off into blank, whirling white.

"There's wind behind this fog," said Troop.

It was wonderful beyond words to Harvey; and the most wonderful part was that he heard no orders except an occasional grunt from Troop, ending with, "That's good, my son!"

"Never seen anchor weighed before?" said Tom Platt, to Harvey gaping at the damp canvas of the foresail.

"No. Where are we going?"

"Fish and make berth, as you'll find out 'fore you've been a week aboard. It's all new to you, but we never know what may come to us. Now, take me—Tom Platt—I'd never ha' thought—"

"It's better than fourteen dollars a month an' a bullet in your belly," said Troop, from the wheel. "Ease your jumbo a grind."

"Dollars an' cents better," returned the man-o'-war's man, doing something to a big jib with a wooden spar tied to it. "But we didn't think o' that when we manned the windlass-brakes on the Miss Jim Buck, I outside Beau-fort Harbor, with Fort Macon heavin' hot shot at our stern, an' a livin' gale atop of all. Where was you then, Disko?"

"Jest here, or hereabouts," Disko replied, "earnin' my bread on the deep waters, an' dodgin' Reb privateers. Sorry I can't accommodate you with red-hot shot, Tom Platt; but I guess we'll come aout all right on wind 'fore we see Eastern Point."

There was an incessant slapping and chatter at the bows now, varied by a solid thud and a little spout of spray that clattered down on the foc'sle. The rigging dripped clammy drops, and the men lounged along the lee of the house—all save Uncle Salters, who sat stiffly on the main-hatch nursing his stung hands.

"Guess she'd carry stays'l," said Disko, rolling one eye at his brother.

"Guess she wouldn't to any sorter profit. What's the sense o' wastin' canvas?" the farmer-sailor replied.

The wheel twitched almost imperceptibly in Disko's hands. A few seconds later a hissing wave-top slashed diagonally across the boat, smote Uncle Salters between the shoulders, and drenched him from head to foot. He rose sputtering, and went forward only to catch another.

"See Dad chase him all around the deck," said Dan. "Uncle Salters he thinks his quarter share's our canvas. Dad's put this duckin' act up on him two trips runnin'. Hi! That found him where he feeds." Uncle Salters had taken refuge by the foremast, but a wave slapped him over the knees. Disko's face was as blank as the circle of the wheel.

"Guess she'd lie easier under stays'l, Salters," said Disko, as though he had seen nothing.

"Set your old kite, then," roared the victim through a cloud of spray; "only don't lay it to me if anything happens. Penn, you go below right off an' git your coffee. You ought to hev more sense than to bum araound on deck this weather."

"Now they'll swill coffee an' play checkers till the cows come home," said Dan, as Uncle Salters hustled Penn into the fore-cabin. "'Looks to me like's if we'd all be doin' so fer a spell. There's nothin' in creation deader-limpsey-idler'n a Banker when she ain't on fish."

"I'm glad ye spoke, Danny," cried Long Jack, who had been casting round in search of amusement. "I'd clean forgot we'd a passenger under that T-wharf hat. There's no idleness for thim that don't know their ropes. Pass him along, Tom Platt, an' we'll larn him."

"'Tain't my trick this time," grinned Dan. "You've got to go it alone. Dad learned me with a rope's end."

For an hour Long Jack walked his prey up and down, teaching, as he said, "things at the sea that ivry man must know, blind, dhrunk, or asleep." There is not much gear to a seventy-ton schooner with a stump-foremast, but Long Jack had a gift of expression. When he wished to draw Harvey's attention to the peak-halyards, he dug his knuckles into the back of the boy's neck and kept him at gaze for half a minute. He emphasized the difference between fore and aft generally by rubbing Harvey's nose along a few feet of the boom, and the lead of each rope was fixed in Harvey's mind by the end of the rope itself.

The lesson would have been easier had the deck been at all free; but there appeared to be a place on it for everything and anything except a man. Forward lay the windlass and its tackle, with the chain and hemp cables, all very unpleasant to trip over; the foc'sle stovepipe, and the gurry-butts by the foc'sle hatch to hold the fish-livers. Aft of these the foreboom and booby of the main-hatch took all the space that was not needed for the pumps and dressing-pens. Then came the nests of dories lashed to ring-bolts by the quarter-deck; the house, with tubs and oddments

lashed all around it; and, last, the sixty-foot main-boom in its crutch, splitting things length-wise, to duck and dodge under every time.

Tom Platt, of course, could not keep his oar out of the business, but ranged alongside with enormous and unnecessary descriptions of sails and spars on the old Ohio.

"Niver mind fwhat he says; attind to me, Innocince. Tom Platt, this bally-hoo's not the Ohio, an' you're mixing the bhoy bad."

"He'll be ruined for life, beginnin' on a fore-an'-after this way," Tom Platt pleaded. "Give him a chance to know a few leadin' principles. Sailin's an art, Harvey, as I'd show you if I had ye in the fore-top o' the—"

"I know ut. Ye'd talk him dead an' cowld. Silince, Tom Platt! Now, after all I've said, how'd you reef the foresail, Harve? Take your time answerin'."

"Haul that in," said Harvey, pointing to leeward.

"Fwhat? The North Atlantuc?"

"No, the boom. Then run that rope you showed me back there—"

"That's no way," Tom Platt burst in.

"Quiet! He's larnin', an' has not the names good yet. Go on, Harve."

"Oh, it's the reef-pennant. I'd hook the tackle on to the reef-pennant, and then let down—"

"Lower the sail, child! Lower!" said Tom Platt, in a professional agony.

"Lower the throat and peak halyards," Harvey went on. Those names stuck in his head.

"Lay your hand on thim," said Long Jack.

Harvey obeyed. "Lower till that rope-loop—on the after-leach-kris—no, it's cringle—till the cringle was down on the boom. Then I'd tie her up the way you said, and then I'd hoist up the peak and throat halyards again."

"You've forgot to pass the tack-earing, but wid time and help ye'll larn. There's good and just reason for ivry rope aboard, or else 'twould be overboard. D'ye follow me? 'Tis dollars an' cents I'm puttin' into your pocket, ye skinny little supercargo, so that fwhin ye've filled out ye can ship from Boston to Cuba an' tell thim Long Jack larned you. Now I'll chase ye around a piece, callin' the ropes, an' you'll lay your hand on thim as I call."

He began, and Harvey, who was feeling rather tired, walked slowly to the rope named. A rope's end licked round his ribs, and nearly knocked the breath out of him.

"When you own a boat," said Tom Platt, with severe eyes, "you can walk. Till then, take all orders at the run. Once more—to make sure!"

Harvey was in a glow with the exercise, and this last cut warmed him thoroughly. Now he was a singularly smart boy, the son of a very clever man and a very sensitive woman, with a fine resolute temper that systematic spoiling had nearly turned to mulish obstinacy. He looked at the other men, and saw that even Dan did not smile. It was evidently all in the day's work, though it hurt abominably; so he swallowed the hint with a gulp and a gasp and a grin. The same smartness that led him to take such advantage of his mother made him very sure that no one on

the boat, except, maybe, Penn, would stand the least nonsense. One learns a great deal from a mere tone. Long Jack called over half a dozen ropes, and Harvey danced over the deck like an eel at ebb-tide, one eye on Tom Platt.

"Ver' good. Ver' good don," said Manuel. "After supper I show you a little schooner I make, with all her ropes. So we shall learn."

"Fust-class fer—a passenger," said Dan. "Dad he's jest allowed you'll be wuth your salt maybe 'fore you're draownded. Thet's a heap fer Dad. I'll learn you more our next watch together."

"Taller!" grunted Disko, peering through the fog as it smoked over the bows. There was nothing to be seen ten feet beyond the surging jib-boom, while alongside rolled the endless procession of solemn, pale waves whispering and lipping one to the other.

"Now I'll learn you something Long Jack can't," shouted Tom Platt, as from a locker by the stern he produced a battered deep-sea lead hollowed at one end, smeared the hollow from a saucer full of mutton tallow, and went forward. "I'll learn you how to fly the Blue Pigeon. Shooo!"

Disko did something to the wheel that checked the schooner's way, while Manuel, with Harvey to help (and a proud boy was Harvey), let down the jib in a lump on the boom. The lead sung a deep droning song as Tom Platt whirled it round and round.

"Go ahead, man," said Long Jack, impatiently. "We're not drawin' twenty-five fut off Fire Island in a fog. There's no trick to ut."

"Don't be jealous, Galway." The released lead plopped into the sea far ahead as the schooner surged slowly forward.

"Soundin' is a trick, though," said Dan, "when your dipsey lead's all the eye you're like to hev for a week. What d'you make it, Dad?"

Disko's face relaxed. His skill and honour were involved in the march he had stolen on the rest of the Fleet, and he had his reputation as a master artist who knew the Banks blindfold. "Sixty, mebbe—ef I'm any judge," he replied, with a glance at the tiny compass in the window of the house.

"Sixty," sung out Tom Platt, hauling in great wet coils.

The schooner gathered way once more. "Heave!" said Disko, after a quarter of an hour.

"What d'you make it?" Dan whispered, and he looked at Harvey proudly. But Harvey was too proud of his own performances to be impressed just then.

"Fifty," said the father. "I mistrust we're right over the nick o' Green Bank on old Sixty-Fifty."

"Fifty!" roared Tom Platt. They could scarcely see him through the fog. "She's bust within a yard—like the shells at Fort Macon."

"Bait up, Harve," said Dan, diving for a line on the reel.

The schooner seemed to be straying promiscuously through the smother, her headsail banging wildly. The men waited and looked at the boys who began fishing.

"Heugh!" Dan's lines twitched on the scored and scarred rail. "Now haow in thunder did Dad

know? Help us here, Harve. It's a big un. Poke-hooked, too." They hauled together, and landed a goggle-eyed twenty-pound cod. He had taken the bait right into his stomach.

"Why, he's all covered with little crabs," cried Harvey, turning him over.

"By the great hook-block, they're lousy already," said Long Jack. "Disko, ye kape your spare eyes under the keel."

Splash went the anchor, and they all heaved over the lines, each man taking his own place at the bulwarks.

"Are they good to eat?" Harvey panted, as he lugged in another crab-covered cod.

"Sure. When they're lousy it's a sign they've all been herdin' together by the thousand, and when they take the bait that way they're hungry. Never mind how the bait sets. They'll bite on the bare hook."

"Say, this is great!" Harvey cried, as the fish came in gasping and splashing—nearly all poke-hooked, as Dan had said. "Why can't we always fish from the boat instead of from the dories?"

"Allus can, till we begin to dress daown. Efter thet, the heads and offals 'u'd scare the fish to Fundy. Boatfishin' ain't reckoned progressive, though, unless ye know as much as dad knows. Guess we'll run aout aour trawl to-night. Harder on the back, this, than frum the dory, ain't it?"

It was rather back-breaking work, for in a dory the weight of a cod is water-borne till the last minute, and you are, so to speak, abreast of him; but the few feet of a schooner's freeboard make so much extra dead-hauling, and stooping over the bulwarks cramps the stomach. But it was wild and furious sport so long as it lasted; and a big pile lay aboard when the fish ceased biting.

"Where's Penn and Uncle Salters?" Harvey asked, slapping the slime off his oilskins, and reeling up the line in careful imitation of the others.

"Git 's coffee and see."

Under the yellow glare of the lamp on the pawl-post, the foc'sle table down and opened, utterly unconscious of fish or weather, sat the two men, a checker-board between them, Uncle Salters snarling at Penn's every move.

"What's the matter naow?" said the former, as Harvey, one hand in the leather loop at the head of the ladder, hung shouting to the cook.

"Big fish and lousy—heaps and heaps," Harvey replied, quoting Long Jack. "How's the game?"

Little Penn's jaw dropped. "'Tweren't none o' his fault," snapped Uncle Salters. "Penn's deef."

"Checkers, weren't it?" said Dan, as Harvey staggered aft with the steaming coffee in a tin pail. "That lets us out o' cleanin' up to-night. Dad's a jest man. They'll have to do it."

"An' two young fellers I know'll bait up a tub or so o' trawl, while they're cleanin'," said Disko, lashing the wheel to his taste.

"Um! Guess I'd ruther clean up, Dad."

"Don't doubt it. Ye wun't, though. Dress daown! Dress daown! Penn'll pitch while you two bait up."

"Why in thunder didn't them blame boys tell us you'd struck on?" said Uncle Salters, shuffling to his place at the table. "This knife's gum-blunt, Dan."

"Ef stickin' out cable don't wake ye, guess you'd better hire a boy o' your own," said Dan, muddling about in the dusk over the tubs full of trawl-line lashed to windward of the house. "Oh, Harve, don't ye want to slip down an' git 's bait?"

"Bait ez we are," said Disko. "I mistrust shag-fishin' will pay better, ez things go."

That meant the boys would bait with selected offal of the cod as the fish were cleaned—an improvement on paddling bare-handed in the little bait-barrels below. The tubs were full of neatly coiled line carrying a big hook each few feet; and the testing and baiting of every single hook, with the stowage of the baited line so that it should run clear when shot from the dory, was a scientific business. Dan managed it in the dark, without looking, while Harvey caught his fingers on the barbs and bewailed his fate. But the hooks flew through Dan's fingers like tatting on an old maid's lap. "I helped bait up trawl ashore 'fore I could well walk," he said. "But it's a putterin' job all the same. Oh, Dad!" This shouted towards the hatch, where Disko and Tom Platt were salting. "How many skates you reckon we'll need?"

"'Baout three. Hurry!"

"There's three hundred fathom to each tub," Dan explained; "more'n enough to lay out to-night. Ouch! 'Slipped up there, I did." He stuck his finger in his mouth. "I tell you, Harve, there ain't money in Gloucester 'u'd hire me to ship on a reg'lar trawler. It may be progressive, but, barrin' that, it's the putterin'est, slimjammest business top of earth."

"I don't know what this is, if 'tisn't regular trawling," said Harvey sulkily. "My fingers are all cut to frazzles."

"Pshaw! This is just one o' Dad's blame experiments. He don't trawl 'less there's mighty good reason fer it. Dad knows. Thet's why he's baitin' ez he is. We'll hev her saggin' full when we take her up er we won't see a fin."

Penn and Uncle Salters cleaned up as Disko had ordained, but the boys profited little. No sooner were the tubs furnished than Tom Platt and Long Jack, who had been exploring the inside of a dory with a lantern, snatched them away, loaded up the tubs and some small, painted trawl-buoys, and hove the boat overboard into what Harvey regarded as an exceedingly rough sea. "They'll be drowned. Why, the dory's loaded like a freight-car," he cried.

"We'll be back," said Long Jack, "an' in case you'll not be lookin' for us, we'll lay into you both if the trawl's snarled."

The dory surged up on the crest of a wave, and just when it seemed impossible that she could avoid smashing against the schooner's side, slid over the ridge, and was swallowed up in the damp dusk.

"Take ahold here, an' keep ringin' steady," said Dan, passing Harvey the lanyard of a bell that hung just behind the windlass.

Harvey rang lustily, for he felt two lives depended on him. But Disko in the cabin, scrawling in the log-book, did not look like a murderer, and when he went to supper he even smiled dryly at the anxious Harvey.

"This ain't no weather," said Dan. "Why, you an' me could set thet trawl! They've only gone out jest far 'nough so's not to foul our cable. They don't need no bell reelly."

"Clang! clang! clang!" Harvey kept it up, varied with occasional rub-a-dubs, for another half-hour. There was a bellow and a bump alongside. Manuel and Dan raced to the hooks of the dory-tackle; Long Jack and Tom Platt arrived on deck together, it seemed, one half the North Atlantic at their backs, and the dory followed them in the air, landing with a clatter.

"Nary snarl," said Tom Platt as he dripped. "Danny, you'll do yet."

"The pleasure av your comp'ny to the banquit," said Long Jack, squelching the water from his boots as he capered like an elephant and stuck an oil-skinned arm into Harvey's face. "We do be condescending to honour the second half wid our presence." And off they all four rolled to supper, where Harvey stuffed himself to the brim on fish-chowder and fried pies, and fell fast asleep just as Manuel produced from a locker a lovely two-foot model of the Lucy Holmes, his first boat, and was going to show Harvey the ropes. Harvey never even twiddled his fingers as Penn pushed him into his bunk.

"It must be a sad thing—a very sad thing," said Penn, watching the boy's face, "for his mother and his father, who think he is dead. To lose a child—to lose a man-child!"

"Git out o' this, Penn," said Dan. "Go aft and finish your game with Uncle Salters. Tell Dad I'll stand Harve's watch ef he don't keer. He's played aout."

"Ver' good boy," said Manuel, slipping out of his boots and disappearing into the black shadows of the lower bunk. "Expec' he make good man, Danny. I no see he is any so mad as your parpa he says. Eh, wha-at?"

Dan chuckled, but the chuckle ended in a snore.

It was thick weather outside, with a rising wind, and the elder men stretched their watches. The hour struck clear in the cabin; the nosing bows slapped and scuffed with the seas; the foc'sle stove-pipe hissed and sputtered as the spray caught it; and the boys slept on, while Disko, Long Jack, Tom Platt, and Uncle Salters, each in turn, stumped aft to look at the wheel, forward to see that the anchor held, or to veer out a little more cable against chafing, with a glance at the dim anchor-light between each round.

CHAPTER IV

Harvey waked to find the "first half" at breakfast, the foc'sle door drawn to a crack, and every square inch of the schooner singing its own tune. The black bulk of the cook balanced behind the tiny galley over the glare of the stove, and the pots and pans in the pierced wooden board before it jarred and racketed to each plunge. Up and up the foc'sle climbed, yearning and urging and quivering, and then, with a clear, sickle-like swoop, came down into the seas. He could hear the flaring bows cut and squelch, and there was a pause ere the divided waters came down on the deck above, like a volley of buckshot. Followed the woolly sound of the cable in the hawse-hole; and a grunt and squeal of the windlass; a yaw, a punt, and a kick, and the We're Here gathered herself together to repeat the motions.

"Now, ashore," he heard Long Jack saying, "ye've chores, an' ye must do thim in any weather. Here we're well clear of the fleet, an' we've no chores—an' that's a blessin'. Good night, all." He passed like a big snake from the table to his bunk, and began to smoke. Tom Platt followed his example; Uncle Salters, with Penn, fought his way up the ladder to stand his watch, and the cook set for the "second half."

It came out of its bunks as the others had entered theirs, with a shake and a yawn. It ate till it could eat no more; and then Manuel filled his pipe with some terrible tobacco, crotched himself between the pawl-post and a forward bunk, cocked his feet up on the table, and smiled tender and indolent smiles at the smoke. Dan lay at length in his bunk, wrestling with a gaudy, gilt-stopped accordion, whose tunes went up and down with the pitching of the We're Here. The cook, his shoulders against the locker where he kept the fried pies (Dan was fond of fried pies), peeled potatoes, with one eye on the stove in event of too much water finding its way down the pipe; and the general smell and smother were past all description.

Harvey considered affairs, wondered that he was not deathly sick, and crawled into his bunk again, as the softest and safest place, while Dan struck up, "I don't want to play in your yard," as accurately as the wild jerks allowed.

"How long is this for?" Harvey asked of Manuel.

"Till she get a little quiet, and we can row to trawl. Perhaps to-night. Perhaps two days more. You do not like? Eh, wha-at?"

"I should have been crazy sick a week ago, but it doesn't seem to upset me now—much."

"That is because we make you fisherman, these days. If I was you, when I come to Gloucester I would give two, three big candles for my good luck."

"Give who?"

"To be sure—the Virgin of our Church on the Hill. She is very good to fishermen all the time. That is why so few of us Portugee men ever are drowned."

"You're a Roman Catholic, then?"

"I am a Madeira man. I am not a Porto Pico boy. Shall I be Baptist, then? Eh, wha-at? I always give candles—two, three more when I come to Gloucester. The good Virgin she never forgets me, Manuel."

"I don't sense it that way," Tom Platt put in from his bunk, his scarred face lit up by the glare of

a match as he sucked at his pipe. "It stands to reason the sea's the sea; and you'll get jest abou what's goin', candles or kerosene, fer that matter."

"'Tis a mighty good thing," said Long Jack, "to have a frind at coort, though. I'm o' Manuel's way o' thinkin'. About tin years back I was crew to a Sou' Boston market-boat. We was of Minot's Ledge wid a northeaster, butt first, atop of us, thicker'n burgoo. The ould man was dhrunk, his chin waggin' on the tiller, an' I sez to myself, 'If iver I stick my boat-huk into T-wharf again, I'll show the saints fwhat manner o' craft they saved me out av.' Now, I'm here, as ye can well see, an' the model of the dhirty ould Kathleen, that took me a month to make, I gave ut to the priest, an' he hung ut up forninst the altar. There's more sense in givin' a model that's by way o' bein' a work av art than any candle. Ye can buy candles at store, but a model shows the good saints ye've tuk trouble an' are grateful."

"D'you believe that, Irish?" said Tom Platt, turning on his elbow.

"Would I do ut if I did not, Ohio?"

"Wa-al, Enoch Fuller he made a model o' the old Ohio, and she's to Calem museum now. Mighty pretty model, too, but I guess Enoch he never done it fer no sacrifice; an' the way I take it is—"

There were the makings of an hour-long discussion of the kind that fishermen love, where the talk runs in shouting circles and no one proves anything at the end, had not Dan struck up this cheerful rhyme:

"Up jumped the mackerel with his stripe'd back.
Reef in the mainsail, and haul on the tack;
For it's windy weather—"

Here Long Jack joined in:

"And it's blowy weather;
When the winds begin to blow, pipe all hands together!"

Dan went on, with a cautious look at Tom Platt, holding the accordion low in the bunk:

"Up jumped the cod with his chuckle-head,
Went to the main-chains to heave at the lead;
For it's windy weather," etc.

Tom Platt seemed to be hunting for something. Dan crouched lower, but sang louder:

"Up jumped the flounder that swims to the ground.
Chuckle-head! Chuckle-head! Mind where ye sound!"

Tom Platt's huge rubber boot whirled across the foc's'le and caught Dan's uplifted arm. There was war between the man and the boy ever since Dan had discovered that the mere whistling of that tune would make him angry as he heaved the lead.

"Thought I'd fetch yer," said Dan, returning the gift with precision. "Ef you don't like my music, git out your fiddle. I ain't goin' to lie here all day an' listen to you an' Long Jack arguin' 'baout candles. Fiddle, Tom Platt; or I'll learn Harve here the tune!"

Tom Platt leaned down to a locker and brought up an old white fiddle. Manuel's eye glistened, and from somewhere behind the pawl-post he drew out a tiny, guitar-like thing with wire strings,

which he called a machette.

"'Tis a concert," said Long Jack, beaming through the smoke. "A reg'lar Boston concert."

There was a burst of spray as the hatch opened, and Disko, in yellow oilskins, descended.

"Ye're just in time, Disko. Fwhat's she doin' outside?"

"Jest this!" He dropped on to the lockers with the push and heave of the We're Here.

"We're singin' to kape our breakfasts down. Ye'll lead, av course, Disko," said Long Jack.

"Guess there ain't more'n 'baout two old songs I know, an' ye've heerd them both."

His excuses were cut short by Tom Platt launching into a most dolorous tune, like unto the moaning of winds and the creaking of masts. With his eyes fixed on the beams above, Disko began this ancient, ancient ditty, Tom Platt flourishing all round him to make the tune and words fit a little:

"There is a crack packet—crack packet o' fame,
She hails from Noo York, an' the Dreadnought's her name.
You may talk o' your fliers—Swallowtail and Black Ball—
But the Dreadnought's the packet that can beat them all.
"Now the Dreadnought she lies in the River Mersey,
Because of the tug-boat to take her to sea;
But when she's off soundings you shortly will know

(Chorus.)

She's the Liverpool packet—O Lord, let her go!

"Now the Dreadnought she's howlin' crost the Banks o' Newfoundland,
Where the water's all shallow and the bottom's all sand.
Sez all the little fishes that swim to and fro:

(Chorus.)

'She's the Liverpool packet—O Lord, let her go!'",

There were scores of verses, for he worked the Dreadnought every mile of the way between Liverpool and New York as conscientiously as though he were on her deck, and the accordion pumped and the fiddle squeaked beside him. Tom Platt followed with something about "the rough and tough McGinn, who would pilot the vessel in." Then they called on Harvey, who felt very flattered, to contribute to the entertainment; but all that he could remember were some pieces of "Skipper Ireson's Ride" that he had been taught at the camp-school in the Adirondacks. It seemed that they might be appropriate to the time and place, but he had no more than mentioned the title when Disko brought down one foot with a bang, and cried, "Don't go on, young feller. That's a mistaken jedgment—one o' the worst kind, too, becaze it's catchin' to the ear."

"I orter ha' warned you," said Dan. "Thet allus fetches Dad."

"What's wrong?" said Harvey, surprised and a little angry.

"All you're goin' to say," said Disko. "All dead wrong from start to finish, an' Whittier he's to blame. I have no special call to right any Marblehead man, but 'tweren't no fault o' Ireson's.

My father he told me the tale time an' again, an' this is the way 'twuz."

"For the wan hundredth time," put in Long Jack under his breath

"Ben Ireson he was skipper o' the Betty, young feller, comin' home frum the Banks—that was before the war of 1812, but jestice is jestice at all times. They fund the Active o' Portland, an' Gibbons o' that town he was her skipper; they fund her leakin' off Cape Cod Light. There was a terr'ble gale on, an' they was gettin' the Betty home 's fast as they could craowd her. Well, Ireson he said there warn't any sense to reskin' a boat in that sea; the men they wouldn't hev it; and he laid it before them to stay by the Active till the sea run daown a piece. They wouldn't hev that either, hangin' araound the Cape in any sech weather, leak or no leak. They jest up stays'l an' quit, nat'rally takin' Ireson with 'em. Folks to Marblehead was mad at him not runnin' the risk, and becaze nex' day, when the sea was ca'am (they never stopped to think o' that), some of the Active's folks was took off by a Truro man. They come into Marblehead with their own tale to tell, sayin' how Ireson had shamed his town, an' so forth an' so on, an' Ireson's men they was scared, seein' public feelin' agin' 'em, an' they went back on Ireson, an' swore he was respons'ble for the hull act. 'Tweren't the women neither that tarred and feathered him— Marblehead women don't act that way—'twas a passel o' men an' boys, an' they carted him araound town in an old dory till the bottom fell aout, and Ireson he told 'em they'd be sorry for it some day. Well, the facts come aout later, same's they usually do, too late to be any ways useful to an honest man; an' Whittier he come along an' picked up the slack eend of a lyin' tale, an' tarred and feathered Ben Ireson all over onct more after he was dead. 'Twas the only tune Whittier ever slipped up, an' 'tweren't fair. I whaled Dan good when he brought that piece back from school. You don't know no better, o' course; but I've give you the facts, hereafter an' evermore to be remembered. Ben Ireson weren't no sech kind o' man as Whittier makes aout; my father he knew him well, before an' after that business, an' you beware o' hasty jedgments, young feller. Next!"

Harvey had never heard Disko talk so long, and collapsed with burning cheeks; but, as Dan said promptly, a boy could only learn what he was taught at school, and life was too short to keep track of every lie along the coast.

Then Manuel touched the jangling, jarring little machette to a queer tune, and sang something in Portuguese about "Nina, innocente!" ending with a full-handed sweep that brought the song up with a jerk. Then Disko obliged with his second song, to an old-fashioned creaky tune, and all joined in the chorus. This is one stanza:

"Now Aprile is over and melted the snow,
And outer Noo Bedford we shortly must tow;
Yes, out o' Noo Bedford we shortly must clear,
We're the whalers that never see wheat in the ear."

Here the fiddle went very softly for a while by itself, and then:

"Wheat-in-the-ear, my true-love's posy blowin,
Wheat-in-the-ear, we're goin' off to sea;
Wheat-in-the-ear, I left you fit for sowin,
When I come back a loaf o' bread you'll be!"

That made Harvey almost weep, though he could not tell why. But it was much worse when the cook dropped the potatoes and held out his hands for the fiddle. Still leaning against the locker door, he struck into a tune that was like something very bad but sure to happen whatever you did. After a little he sang, in an unknown tongue, his big chin down on the fiddle-tail, his white eyeballs glaring in the lamplight. Harvey swung out of his bunk to hear better; and amid the

straining of the timbers and the wash of the waters the tune crooned and moaned on, like lee surf in a blind fog, till it ended with a wail.

"Jimmy Christmas! Thet gives me the blue creevles," said Dan. "What in thunder is it?"

"The song of Fin McCoul," said the cook, "when he wass going to Norway." His English was not thick, but all clear-cut, as though it came from a phonograph.

"Faith, I've been to Norway, but I didn't make that unwholesim noise. 'Tis like some of the old songs, though," said Long Jack, sighing.

"Don't let's hev another 'thout somethin' between," said Dan; and the accordion struck up a rattling, catchy tune that ended:

"It's six an' twenty Sundays sence las' we saw the land,
With fifteen hunder quintal,
An' fifteen hunder quintal,
'Teen hunder toppin' quintal,
'Twix' old 'Queereau an' Grand!"

"Hold on!" roared Tom Platt. "D'ye want to nail the trip, Dan? That's Jonah sure, 'less you sing it after all our salt's wet."

"No, 'tain't, is it, Dad? Not unless you sing the very las' verse. You can't learn me anything on Jonahs!"

"What's that?" said Harvey. "What's a Jonah?"

"A Jonah's anything that spoils the luck. Sometimes it's a man—sometimes it's a boy—or a bucket. I've known a splittin'-knife Jonah two trips till we was on to her," said Tom Platt. "There's all sorts o' Jonahs. Jim Bourke was one till he was drowned on Georges. I'd never ship with Jim Bourke, not if I was starvin'. There wuz a green dory on the Ezra Flood. Thet was a Jonah, too, the worst sort o' Jonah. Drowned four men, she did, an' used to shine fiery O, nights in the nest."

"And you believe that?" said Harvey, remembering what Tom Platt had said about candles and models. "Haven't we all got to take what's served?"

A mutter of dissent ran round the bunks. "Outboard, yes; inboard, things can happen," said Disko. "Don't you go makin' a mock of Jonahs, young feller."

"Well, Harve ain't no Jonah. Day after we catched him," Dan cut in, "we had a toppin' good catch."

The cook threw up his head and laughed suddenly—a queer, thin laugh. He was a most disconcerting nigger.

"Murder!" said Long Jack. "Don't do that again, doctor. We ain't used to ut."

"What's wrong?" said Dan. "Ain't he our mascot, and didn't they strike on good after we'd struck him?"

"Oh! yess," said the cook. "I know that, but the catch iss not finish yet."

"He ain't goin' to do us any harm," said Dan, hotly. "Where are ye hintin' an' edgin' to? He's all right."

"No harm. No. But one day he will be your master, Danny."

"That all?" said Dan, placidly. "He wun't—not by a jugful."

"Master!" said the cook, pointing to Harvey. "Man!" and he pointed to Dan.

"That's news. Haow soon?" said Dan, with a laugh.

"In some years, and I shall see it. Master and man—man and master."

"How in thunder d'ye work that out?" said Tom Platt.

"In my head, where I can see."

"Haow?" This from all the others at once.

"I do not know, but so it will be." He dropped his head, and went on peeling the potatoes, and not another word could they get out of him.

"Well," said Dan, "a heap o' things'll hev to come abaout 'fore Harve's any master o' mine; but I'm glad the doctor ain't choosen to mark him for a Jonah. Now, I mistrust Uncle Salters fer the Jonerest Jonah in the Fleet regardin' his own special luck. Dunno ef it's spreadin' same's smallpox. He ought to be on the Carrie Pitman. That boat's her own Jonah, sure—crews an' gear made no differ to her driftin'. Jiminy Christmas! She'll etch loose in a flat ca'am."

"We're well clear o' the Fleet, anyway," said Disko. "Carrie Pitman an' all." There was a rapping on the deck.

"Uncle Salters has catched his luck," said Dan as his father departed.

"It's blown clear," Disko cried, and all the foc'sle tumbled up for a bit of fresh air. The fog had gone, but a sullen sea ran in great rollers behind it. The We're Here slid, as it were, into long, sunk avenues and ditches which felt quite sheltered and homelike if they would only stay still; but they changed without rest or mercy, and flung up the schooner to crown one peak of a thousand gray hills, while the wind hooted through her rigging as she zigzagged down the slopes. Far away a sea would burst into a sheet of foam, and the others would follow suit as at a signal, till Harvey's eyes swam with the vision of interlacing whites and grays. Four or five Mother Carey's chickens stormed round in circles, shrieking as they swept past the bows. A rain-squall or two strayed aimlessly over the hopeless waste, ran down 'wind and back again, and melted away.

"Seems to me I saw somethin' flicker jest naow over yonder," said Uncle Salters, pointing to the northeast.

"Can't be any of the fleet," said Disko, peering under his eyebrows, a hand on the foc'sle gangway as the solid bows hatcheted into the troughs. "Sea's oilin' over dretful fast. Danny, don't you want to skip up a piece an' see how aour trawl-buoy lays?"

Danny, in his big boots, trotted rather than climbed up the main rigging (this consumed Harvey with envy), hitched himself around the reeling cross-trees, and let his eye rove till it caught the tiny black buoy-flag on the shoulder of a mile-away swell.

"She's all right," he hailed. "Sail O! Dead to the no'th'ard, comin' down like smoke! Schooner she be, too."

They waited yet another half-hour, the sky clearing in patches, with a flicker of sickly sun from time to time that made patches of olive-green water. Then a stump-foremast lifted, ducked, and disappeared, to be followed on the next wave by a high stern with old-fashioned wooden snail's-horn davits. The snails were red-tanned.

"Frenchmen!" shouted Dan. "No, 'tain't, neither. Da-ad!"

"That's no French," said Disko. "Salters, your blame luck holds tighter'n a screw in a keg-head."

"I've eyes. It's Uncle Abishai."

"You can't nowise tell fer sure."

"The head-king of all Jonahs," groaned Tom Platt. "Oh, Salters, Salters, why wasn't you abed an' asleep?"

"How could I tell?" said poor Salters, as the schooner swung up.

She might have been the very Flying Dutchman, so foul, draggled, and unkempt was every rope and stick aboard. Her old-style quarterdeck was some or five feet high, and her rigging flew knotted and tangled like weed at a wharf-end. She was running before the wind—yawing frightfully—her staysail let down to act as a sort of extra foresail,—"scandalized," they call it,—and her foreboom guyed out over the side. Her bowsprit cocked up like an old-fashioned frigate's; her jib-boom had been fished and spliced and nailed and clamped beyond further repair; and as she hove herself forward, and sat down on her broad tail, she looked for all the world like a blouzy, frouzy, bad old woman sneering at a decent girl.

"That's Abishai," said Salters. "Full o' gin an' Judique men, an' the judgments o' Providence layin' fer him an' never takin' good holt He's run in to bait, Miquelon way."

"He'll run her under," said Long Jack. "That's no rig fer this weather."

"Not he, 'r he'd 'a done it long ago," Disko replied. "Looks 's if he cal'lated to run us under. Ain't she daown by the head more 'n natural, Tom Platt?"

"Ef it's his style o' loadin' her she ain't safe," said the sailor slowly. "Ef she's spewed her oakum he'd better git to his pumps mighty quick."

The creature threshed up, wore round with a clatter and raffle, and lay head to wind within ear-shot.

A gray-beard wagged over the bulwark, and a thick voice yelled something Harvey could not understand. But Disko's face darkened. "He'd resk every stick he hez to carry bad news. Says we're in fer a shift o' wind. He's in fer worse. Abishai! Abi-shai!" He waved his arm up and down with the gesture of a man at the pumps, and pointed forward. The crew mocked him and laughed.

"Jounce ye, an' strip ye an' trip ye!" yelled Uncle Abishai. "A livin' gale—a livin' gale. Yab! Cast up fer your last trip, all you Gloucester haddocks. You won't see Gloucester no more, no more!"

"Crazy full—as usual," said Tom Platt. "Wish he hadn't spied us, though."

She drifted out of hearing while the gray-head yelled something about a dance at the Bay of

Bulls and a dead man in the foc'sle. Harvey shuddered. He had seen the sloven tilled decks and the savage-eyed crew.

"An' that's a fine little floatin' hell fer her draught," said Long Jack. "I wondher what mischief he's been at ashore."

"He's a trawler," Dan explained to Harvey, "an' he runs in fer bait all along the coast. Oh, no, not home, he don't go. He deals along the south an' east shore up yonder." He nodded in the direction of the pitiless Newfoundland beaches. "Dad won't never take me ashore there. They're a mighty tough crowd—an' Abishai's the toughest. You saw his boat? Well, she's nigh seventy year old, they say; the last o' the old Marblehead heel-tappers. They don't make them quarterdecks any more. Abishai don't use Marblehead, though. He ain't wanted there. He jes' drif's araound, in debt, trawlin' an' cussin' like you've heard. Bin a Jonah fer years an' years, he hez. 'Gits liquor frum the Feecamp boats fer makin' spells an' selling winds an' such truck. Crazy, I guess."

"'Twon't be any use underrunnin' the trawl to-night," said Tom Platt, with quiet despair. "He come alongside special to cuss us. I'd give my wage an' share to see him at the gangway o' the old Ohio 'fore we quit floggin'. Jest abaout six dozen, an' Sam Mocatta layin' 'em on criss-cross!"

The disheveled "heel-tapper" danced drunkenly down wind, and all eyes followed her. Suddenly the cook cried in his phonograph voice: "It wass his own death made him speak so! He iss fey—fey, I tell you! Look!" She sailed into a patch of watery sunshine three or four miles distant. The patch dulled and faded out, and even as the light passed so did the schooner. She dropped into a hollow and—was not.

"Run under, by the Great Hook-Block!" shouted Disko, jumping aft. "Drunk or sober, we've got to help 'em. Heave short and break her out! Smart!"

Harvey was thrown on the deck by the shock that followed the setting of the jib and foresail, for they hove short on the cable, and to save time, jerked the anchor bodily from the bottom, heaving in as they moved away. This is a bit of brute force seldom resorted to except in matters of life and death, and the little We're Here complained like a human. They ran down to where Abishai's craft had vanished; found two or three trawl-tubs, a gin-bottle, and a stove-in dory, but nothing more. "Let 'em go," said Disko, though no one had hinted at picking them up. "I wouldn't hev a match that belonged to Abishai aboard. Guess she run clear under. Must ha' been spewin' her oakum fer a week, an' they never thought to pump her. That's one more boat gone along o' leavin' port all hands drunk."

"Glory be!" said Long Jack. "We'd ha' been obliged to help 'em if they was top o' water."

"'Thinkin' o' that myself," said Tom Platt.

"Fey! Fey!" said the cook, rolling his eyes. "He haas taken his own luck with him."

"Ver' good thing, I think, to tell the Fleet when we see. Eh, wha-at?" said Manuel. "If you runna that way before the 'wind, and she work open her seams—" He threw out his hands with an indescribable gesture, while Penn sat down on the house and sobbed at the sheer horror and pity of it all. Harvey could not realize that he had seen death on the open waters, but he felt very sick. Then Dan went up the cross-trees, and Disko steered them back to within sight of their own trawl-buoys just before the fog blanketed the sea once again.

"We go mighty quick hereabouts when we do go," was all he said to Harvey. "You think on that

fer a spell, young feller. That was liquor."

"After dinner it was calm enough to fish from the decks,—Penn and Uncle Salters were very zealous this time,—and the catch was large and large fish.

"Abishai has shorely took his luck with him," said Salters. "The wind hain't backed ner riz ner nothin'. How abaout the trawl? I despise superstition, anyway."

Tom Platt insisted that they had much better haul the thing and make a new berth. But the cook said: "The luck iss in two pieces. You will find it so when you look. I know." This so tickled Long Jack that he overbore Tom Platt and the two went out together.

Underrunning a trawl means pulling it in on one side of the dory, picking off the fish, rebaiting the hooks, and passing them back to the sea again—something like pinning and unpinning linen on a wash-line. It is a lengthy business and rather dangerous, for the long, sagging line may twitch a boat under in a flash. But when they heard, "And naow to thee, O Capting," booming out of the fog, the crew of the We're Here took heart. The dory swirled alongside well loaded, Tom Platt yelling for Manuel to act as relief-boat.

"The luck's cut square in two pieces," said Long Jack, forking in the fish, while Harvey stood open-mouthed at the skill with which the plunging dory was saved from destruction. "One half was jest punkins. Tom Platt wanted to haul her an' ha' done wid ut; but I said, "I'll back the doctor that has the second sight, an' the other half come up sagging full o' big uns. Hurry, Man'nle, an' bring's a tub o' bait. There's luck afloat to-night."

The fish bit at the newly baited hooks from which their brethren had just been taken, and Tom Platt and Long Jack moved methodically up and down the length of the trawl, the boat's nose surging under the wet line of hooks, stripping the sea-cucumbers that they called pumpkins, slatting off the fresh-caught cod against the gunwale, rebaiting, and loading Manuel's dory till dusk.

"I'll take no risks," said Disko then—"not with him floatin' around so near. Abishai won't sink fer a week. Heave in the dories an' we'll dress daown after supper."

That was a mighty dressing-down, attended by three or four blowing grampuses. It lasted till nine o'clock, and Disko was thrice heard to chuckle as Harvey pitched the split fish into the hold.

"Say, you're haulin' ahead dretful fast," said Dan, when they ground the knives after the men had turned in. "There's somethin' of a sea to-night, an' I hain't heard you make no remarks on it."

"Too busy," Harvey replied, testing a blade's edge. "Come to think of it, she is a high-kicker."

The little schooner was gambolling all around her anchor among the silver-tipped waves. Backing with a start of affected surprise at the sight of the strained cable, she pounced on it like a kitten, while the spray of her descent burst through the hawse-holes with the report of a gun. Shaking her head, she would say: "Well, I'm sorry I can't stay any longer with you. I'm going North," and would sidle off, halting suddenly with a dramatic rattle of her rigging. "As I was just going to observe," she would begin, as gravely as a drunken man addressing a lamp-post. The rest of the sentence (she acted her words in dumb-show, of course) was lost in a fit of the fidgets, when she behaved like a puppy chewing a string, a clumsy woman in a side-saddle, a hen with her head cut off, or a cow stung by a hornet, exactly as the whims of the sea took her.

"See her sayin' her piece. She's Patrick Henry naow," said Dan.

She swung sideways on a roller, and gesticulated with her jib-boom from port to starboard.

"But-ez-fer me, give me liberty-er give me-death!"

Wop! She sat down in the moon-path on the water, courtesying with a flourish of pride impressive enough had not the wheel-gear sniggered mockingly in its box.

Harvey laughed aloud. "Why, it's just as if she was alive," he said.

"She's as stiddy as a haouse an' as dry as a herrin'," said Dan enthusiastically, as he was slung across the deck in a batter of spray. "Fends 'em off an' fends 'em off, an' 'Don't ye come anigh me,' she sez. Look at her—jest look at her! Sakes! You should see one o' them toothpicks histin' up her anchor on her spike outer fifteen-fathom water."

"What's a toothpick, Dan?"

"Them new haddockers an' herrin'-boats. Fine's a yacht forward, with yacht sterns to 'em, an' spike bowsprits, an' a haouse that 'u'd take our hold. I've heard that Burgess himself he made the models fer three or four of 'em. Dad's sot agin 'em on account o' their pitchin' an' joltin', but there's heaps o' money in 'em. Dad can find fish, but he ain't no ways progressive—he don't go with the march o' the times. They're chock-full o' labour-savin' jigs an' sech all. 'Ever seed the Elector o' Gloucester? She's a daisy, ef she is a toothpick."

"What do they cost, Dan?"

"Hills o' dollars. Fifteen thousand, p'haps; more, mebbe. There's gold-leaf an' everything you kin think of." Then to himself, half under his breath, "Guess I'd call her Hattie S., too."

CHAPTER V

That was the first of many talks with Dan, who told Harvey why he would transfer his dory's name to the imaginary Burgess-modelled haddocker. Harvey heard a good deal about the real Hattie at Gloucester; saw a lock of her hair—which Dan, finding fair words of no avail, had "hooked" as she sat in front of him at school that winter—and a photograph. Hattie was about fourteen years old, with an awful contempt for boys, and had been trampling on Dan's heart through the winter. All this was revealed under oath of solemn secrecy on moonlit decks, in the dead dark, or in choking fog; the whining wheel behind them, the climbing deck before, and without, the unresting, clamorous sea. Once, of course, as the boys came to know each other, there was a fight, which raged from bow to stern till Penn came up and separated them, but promised not to tell Disko, who thought fighting on watch rather worse than sleeping. Harvey was no match for Dan physically, but it says a great deal for his new training that he took his defeat and did not try to get even with his conqueror by underhand methods.

That was after he had been cured of a string of boils between his elbows and wrists, where the wet jersey and oilskins cut into the flesh. The salt water stung them unpleasantly, but when they were ripe Dan treated them with Disko's razor, and assured Harvey that now he was a "blooded Banker"; the affliction of gurry-sores being the mark of the caste that claimed him.

Since he was a boy and very busy, he did not bother his head with too much thinking. He was exceedingly sorry for his mother, and often longed to see her and above all to tell her of this wonderful new life, and how brilliantly he was acquitting himself in it. Otherwise he preferred not to wonder too much how she was bearing the shock of his supposed death. But one day, as he stood on the foc's'le ladder, guying the cook, who had accused him and Dan of hooking fried pies, it occurred to him that this was a vast improvement on being snubbed by strangers in the smoking-room of a hired liner.

He was a recognized part of the scheme of things on the We're Here; had his place at the table and among the bunks; and could hold his own in the long talks on stormy days, when the others were always ready to listen to what they called his "fairy-tales" of his life ashore. It did not take him more than two days and a quarter to feel that if he spoke of his own life—it seemed very far away—no one except Dan (and even Dan's belief was sorely tried) credited him. So he invented a friend, a boy he had heard of, who drove a miniature four-pony drag in Toledo, Ohio, and ordered five suits of clothes at a time and led things called "germans" at parties where the oldest girl was not quite fifteen, but all the presents were solid silver. Salters protested that this kind of yarn was desperately wicked, if not indeed positively blasphemous, but he listened as greedily as the others; and their criticisms at the end gave Harvey entirely new notions on "germans," clothes, cigarettes with gold-leaf tips, rings, watches, scent, small dinner-parties, champagne, card-playing, and hotel accommodation. Little by little he changed his tone when speaking of his "friend," whom Long Jack had christened "the Crazy Kid," "the Gilt-edged Baby," "the Suckin' Vanderpoop," and other pet names; and with his sea-booted feet cocked up on the table would even invent histories about silk pajamas and specially imported neckwear, to the "friend's" discredit. Harvey was a very adaptable person, with a keen eye and ear for every face and tone about him.

Before long he knew where Disko kept the old greencrusted quadrant that they called the "hog-yoke"—under the bed-bag in his bunk. When he took the sun, and with the help of "The Old Farmer's" almanac found the latitude, Harvey would jump down into the cabin and scratch the reckoning and date with a nail on the rust of the stove-pipe. Now, the chief engineer of the liner could have done no more, and no engineer of thirty years' service could have assumed one half of the ancient-mariner air with which Harvey, first careful to spit over the side, made public the

schooner's position for that day, and then and not till then relieved Disko of the quadrant. There is an etiquette in all these things.

The said "hog-yoke," an Eldridge chart, the farming almanac, Blunt's "Coast Pilot," and Bowditch's "Navigator" were all the weapons Disko needed to guide him, except the deep-sea lead that was his spare eye. Harvey nearly slew Penn with it when Tom Platt taught him first how to "fly the blue pigeon"; and, though his strength was not equal to continuous sounding in any sort of a sea, for calm weather with a seven-pound lead on shoal water Disko used him freely. As Dan said:

"'Tain't soundin's dad wants. It's samples. Grease her up good, Harve." Harvey would tallow the cup at the end, and carefully bring the sand, shell, sludge, or whatever it might be, to Disko, who fingered and smelt it and gave judgment As has been said, when Disko thought of cod he thought as a cod; and by some long-tested mixture of instinct and experience, moved the We're Here from berth to berth, always with the fish, as a blindfolded chess-player moves on the unseen board.

But Disko's board was the Grand Bank—a triangle two hundred and fifty miles on each side—a waste of wallowing sea, cloaked with dank fog, vexed with gales, harried with drifting ice, scored by the tracks of the reckless liners, and dotted with the sails of the fishing-fleet.

For days they worked in fog—Harvey at the bell—till, grown familiar with the thick airs, he went out with Tom Platt, his heart rather in his mouth. But the fog would not lift, and the fish were biting, and no one can stay helplessly afraid for six hours at a time. Harvey devoted himself to his lines and the gaff or gob-stick as Tom Platt called for them; and they rowed back to the schooner guided by the bell and Tom's instinct; Manuel's conch sounding thin and faint beside them. But it was an unearthly experience, and, for the first time in a month, Harvey dreamed of the shifting, smoking floors of water round the dory, the lines that strayed away into nothing, and the air above that melted on the sea below ten feet from his straining eyes. A few days later he was out with Manuel on what should have been forty-fathom bottom, but the whole length of the roding ran out, and still the anchor found nothing, and Harvey grew mortally afraid, for that his last touch with earth was lost. "Whale-hole," said Manuel, hauling in. "That is good joke on Disko. Come!" and he rowed to the schooner to find Tom Platt and the others jeering at the skipper because, for once, he had led them to the edge of the barren Whale-deep, the blank hole of the Grand Bank. They made another berth through the fog, and that time the hair of Harvey's head stood up when he went out in Manuel's dory. A whiteness moved in the whiteness of the fog with a breath like the breath of the grave, and there was a roaring, a plunging, and spouting. It was his first introduction to the dread summer berg of the Banks, and he cowered in the bottom of the boat while Manuel laughed. There were days, though, clear and soft and warm, when it seemed a sin to do anything but loaf over the hand-lines and spank the drifting "sun-scalds" with an oar; and there were days of light airs, when Harvey was taught how to steer the schooner from one berth to another.

It thrilled through him when he first felt the keel answer to his band on the spokes and slide over the long hollows as the foresail scythed back and forth against the blue sky. That was magnificent, in spite of Disko saying that it would break a snake's back to follow his wake. But, as usual, pride ran before a fall. They were sailing on the wind with the staysail—an old one, luckily—set, and Harvey jammed her right into it to show Dan how completely he had mastered the art. The foresail went over with a bang, and the foregaff stabbed and ripped through the staysail, which was, of course, prevented from going over by the mainstay. They lowered the wreck in awful silence, and Harvey spent his leisure hours for the next few days under Tom Platt's lee, learning to use a needle and palm. Dan hooted with joy, for, as he said, he had made the very same blunder himself in his early days.

Boylike, Harvey imitated all the men by turns, till he had combined Disko's peculiar stoop at the wheel, Long Jack's swinging overhand when the lines were hauled, Manuel's round-shouldered but effective stroke in a dory, and Tom Platt's generous Ohio stride along the deck.

"'Tis beautiful to see how he takes to ut," said Long Jack, when Harvey was looking out by the windlass one thick noon. "I'll lay my wage an' share 'tis more'n half play-actin' to him, an' he consates himself he's a bowld mariner. Watch his little bit av a back now!"

"That's the way we all begin," said Tom Platt. "The boys they make believe all the time till they've cheated 'emselves into bein' men, an' so till they die—pretendin' an' pretendin'. I done it on the old Ohio, I know. Stood my first watch—harbor-watch—feelin' finer'n Farragut. Dan's full o' the same kind o' notions. See 'em now, actin' to be genewine moss-backs—very hair a rope-yarn an' blood Stockholm tar." He spoke down the cabin stairs. "Guess you're mistook in your judgments fer once, Disko. What in Rome made ye tell us all here the kid was crazy?"

"He wuz," Disko replied. "Crazy ez a loon when he come aboard; but I'll say he's sobered up consid'ble sence. I cured him."

"He yarns good," said Tom Platt. "T'other night he told us abaout a kid of his own size steerin' a cunnin' little rig an' four ponies up an' down Toledo, Ohio, I think 'twas, an' givin' suppers to a crowd o' sim'lar kids. Cur'us kind o' fairy-tale, but blame interestin'. He knows scores of 'em."

"Guess he strikes 'em outen his own head," Disko called from the cabin, where he was busy with the logbook. "Stands to reason that sort is all made up. It don't take in no one but Dan, an' he laughs at it. I've heard him, behind my back."

"Yever hear what Sim'on Peter Ca'houn said when they whacked up a match 'twix' his sister Hitty an' Lorin' Jerauld, an' the boys put up that joke on him daown to Georges?" drawled Uncle Salters, who was dripping peaceably under the lee of the starboard dory-nest.

Tom Platt puffed at his pipe in scornful silence: he was a Cape Cod man, and had not known that tale more than twenty years. Uncle Salters went on with a rasping chuckie:

"Sim'on Peter Ca'houn he said, an' he was jest right, abaout Lorin', 'Ha'af on the taown,' he said, 'an' t'other ha'af blame fool; an' they told me she's married a 'ich man.' Sim'on Peter Ca'houn he hedn't no roof to his mouth, an' talked that way."

"He didn't talk any Pennsylvania Dutch," Tom Platt replied. "You'd better leave a Cape man to tell that tale. The Ca'houns was gypsies frum 'way back."

"Wal, I don't profess to be any elocutionist," Salters said. "I'm comin' to the moral o' things. That's jest abaout what aour Harve be! Ha'af on the taown, an' t'other ha'af blame fool; an' there's some'll believe he's a rich man. Yah!"

"Did ye ever think how sweet 'twould be to sail wid a full crew o' Salterses?" said Long Jack. "Ha'af in the furrer an' other ha'af in the muck-heap, as Ca'houn did not say, an' makes out he's a fisherman!"

A little laugh went round at Salters's expense.

Disko held his tongue, and wrought over the log-book that he kept in a hatchet-faced, square hand; this was the kind of thing that ran on, page after soiled page:

"July 17. This day thick fog and few fish. Made berth to northward. So ends this day.

"July 18. This day comes in with thick fog. Caught a few fish.

"July 19. This day comes in with light breeze from N.E. and fine weather. Made a berth to eastward. Caught plenty fish.

"July 20. This, the Sabbath, comes in with fog and light winds. So ends this day. Total fish caught this week, 3,478."

They never worked on Sundays, but shaved, and washed themselves if it were fine, and Pennsylvania sang hymns. Once or twice he suggested that, if it was not an impertinence, he thought he could preach a little. Uncle Salters nearly jumped down his throat at the mere notion, reminding him that he was not a preacher and mustn't think of such things. "We'd hev him rememberin' Johns-town next," Salters explained, "an' what would happen then?" so they compromised on his reading aloud from a book called "Josephus." It was an old leather-bound volume, smelling of a hundred voyages, very solid and very like the Bible, but enlivened with accounts of battles and sieges; and they read it nearly from cover to cover. Otherwise Penn was a silent little body. He would not utter a word for three days on end sometimes, though he played checkers, listened to the songs, and laughed at the stories. When they tried to stir him up, he would answer: "I don't wish to seem unneighbourly, but it is because I have nothing to say. My head feels quite empty. I've almost forgotten my name." He would turn to Uncle Salters with an expectant smile.

"Why, Pennsylvania Pratt," Salters would shout "You'll fergit me next!"

"No—never," Penn would say, shutting his lips firmly. "Pennsylvania Pratt, of course," he would repeat over and over. Sometimes it was Uncle Salters who forgot, and told him he was Haskins or Rich or McVitty; but Penn was equally content—till next time.

He was always very tender with Harvey, whom he pitied both as a lost child and as a lunatic; and when Salters saw that Penn liked the boy, he relaxed, too. Salters was not an amiable person (He esteemed it his business to keep the boys in order); and the first time Harvey, in fear and trembling, on a still day, managed to shin up to the main-truck (Dan was behind him ready to help), he esteemed it his duty to hang Salters's big sea-boots up there—a sight of shame and derision to the nearest schooner. With Disko, Harvey took no liberties; not even when the old man dropped direct orders, and treated him, like the rest of the crew, to "Don't you want to do so and so?" and "Guess you'd better," and so forth. There was something about the clean-shaven lips and the puckered corners of the eyes that was mightily sobering to young blood.

Disko showed him the meaning of the thumbed and pricked chart, which, he said, laid over any government publication whatsoever; led him, pencil in hand, from berth to berth over the whole string of banks—Le Have, Western, Banquereau, St. Pierre, Green, and Grand—talking "cod" meantime. Taught him, too, the principle on which the "hog-yoke" was worked.

In this Harvey excelled Dan, for he had inherited a head for figures, and the notion of stealing information from one glimpse of the sullen Bank sun appealed to all his keen wits. For other sea-matters his age handicapped him. As Disko said, he should have begun when he was ten. Dan could bait up trawl or lay his hand on any rope in the dark; and at a pinch, when Uncle Salters had a gurry-score on his palm, could dress down by sense of touch. He could steer in anything short of half a gale from the feel of the wind on his face, humouring the We're Here just when she needed it. These things he did as automatically as he skipped about the rigging, or made his dory a part of his own will and body. But he could not communicate his knowledge to Harvey.

Still there was a good deal of general information flying about the schooner on stormy days, when they lay up in the foc'sle or sat on the cabin lockers, while spare eye-bolts, leads, and

rings rolled and rattled in the pauses of the talk. Disko spoke of whaling voyages in the Fifties; of great she-whales slain beside their young; of death agonies on the black tossing seas, and blood that spurted forty feet in the air; of boats smashed to splinters; of patent rockets that went off wrong-end-first and bombarded the trembling crews; of cutting-in and boiling-down, and that terrible "nip" of '71, when twelve hundred men were made homeless on the ice in three days—wonderful tales, all true. But more wonderful still were his stories of the cod, and how they argued and reasoned on their private businesses deep down below the keel.

Long Jack's tastes ran more to the supernatural. He held them silent with ghastly stories of the "Yo-hoes" on Monomoy Beach, that mock and terrify lonely clam-diggers; of sand-walkers and dune-haunters who were never properly buried; of hidden treasure on Fire Island guarded by the spirits of Kidd's men; of ships that sailed in the fog straight over Truro township; of that harbor in Maine where no one but a stranger will lie at anchor twice in a certain place because of a dead crew who row alongside at midnight with the anchor in the bow of their old-fashioned boat, whistling—not calling, but whistling—for the soul of the man who broke their rest.

Harvey had a notion that the east coast of his native land, from Mount Desert south, was populated chiefly by people who took their horses there in the summer and entertained in country-houses with hardwood floors and Vantine portires. He laughed at the ghost-tales,—not as much as he would have done a month before,—but ended by sitting still and shuddering.

Tom Platt dealt with his interminable trip round the Horn on the old Ohio in flogging days, with a navy more extinct than the dodo—the navy that passed away in the great war. He told them how red-hot shot are dropped into a cannon, a wad of wet clay between them and the cartridge; how they sizzle and reek when they strike wood, and how the little ship-boys of the Miss Jim Buck hove water over them and shouted to the fort to try again. And he told tales of blockade— long weeks of swaying at anchor, varied only by the departure and return of steamers that had used up their coal (there was no chance for the sailing-ships); of gales and cold that kept two hundred men, night and day, pounding and chopping at the ice on cable, blocks, and rigging, when the galley was as red-hot as the fort's shot, and men drank cocoa by the bucket. Tom Platt had no use for steam. His service closed when that thing was comparatively new. He admitted that it was a specious invention in time of peace, but looked hopefully for the day when sails should come back again on ten-thousand-ton frigates with hundred-and-ninety-foot booms.

Manuel's talk was slow and gentle—all about pretty girls in Madeira washing clothes in the dry beds of streams, by moonlight, under waving bananas; legends of saints, and tales of queer dances or fights away in the cold Newfoundland baiting-ports. Salters was mainly agricultural; for, though he read "Josephus" and expounded it, his mission in life was to prove the value of green manures, and specially of clover, against every form of phosphate whatsoever. He grew libellous about phosphates; he dragged greasy "Orange Judd" books from his bunk and intoned them, wagging his finger at Harvey, to whom it was all Greek. Little Penn was so genuinely pained when Harvey made fun of Salters's lectures that the boy gave it up, and suffered in polite silence. That was very good for Harvey.

The cook naturally did not join in these conversations. As a rule, he spoke only when it was absolutely necessary; but at times a queer gift of speech descended on him, and he held forth, half in Gaelic, half in broken English, an hour at a time. He was especially communicative with the boys, and he never withdrew his prophecy that one day Harvey would be Dan's master, and that he would see it. He told them of mail-carrying in the winter up Cape Breton way, of the dog-train that goes to Coudray, and of the ram-steamer Arctic, that breaks the ice between the mainland and Prince Edward Island. Then he told them stories that his mother had told him, of life far to the southward, where water never froze; and he said that when he died his soul would go to lie down on a warm white beach of sand with palm-trees waving above. That seemed to

the boys a very odd idea for a man who had never seen a palm in his life. Then, too, regularly at each meal, he would ask Harvey, and Harvey alone, whether the cooking was to his taste; and this always made the "second half" laugh. Yet they had a great respect for the cook's judgment, and in their hearts considered Harvey something of a mascot by consequence.

And while Harvey was taking in knowledge of new things at each pore and hard health with every gulp of the good air, the We're Here went her ways and did her business on the Bank, and the silvery-gray kenches of well-pressed fish mounted higher and higher in the hold. No one day's work was out of common, but the average days were many and close together.

Naturally, a man of Disko's reputation was closely watched—"scrowged upon," Dan called it—by his neighbours, but he had a very pretty knack of giving them the slip through the curdling, glidy fog-banks. Disko avoided company for two reasons. He wished to make his own experiments, in the first place; and in the second, he objected to the mixed gatherings of a fleet of all nations. The bulk of them were mainly Gloucester boats, with a scattering from Provincetown, Harwich, Chatham, and some of the Maine ports, but the crews drew from goodness knows where. Risk breeds recklessness, and when greed is added there are fine chances for every kind of accident in the crowded fleet, which, like a mob of sheep, is huddled round some unrecognized leader. "Let the two Jeraulds lead 'em," said Disko. "We're baound to lay among 'em for a spell on the Eastern Shoals; though ef luck holds, we won't hev to lay long. Where we are naow, Harve, ain't considered noways good graound."

"Ain't it?" said Harvey, who was drawing water (he had learned just how to wiggle the bucket), after an unusually long dressing-down. "Shouldn't mind striking some poor ground for a change, then."

"All the graound I want to see—don't want to strike her—is Eastern Point," said Dan. "Say, Dad, it looks's if we wouldn't hev to lay more'n two weeks on the Shoals. You'll meet all the comp'ny you want then, Harve. That's the time we begin to work. No reg'lar meals fer no one then. 'Mug-up when ye're hungry, an' sleep when ye can't keep awake. Good job you wasn't picked up a month later than you was, or we'd never ha' had you dressed in shape fer the Old Virgin."

Harvey understood from the Eldridge chart that the Old Virgin and a nest of curiously named shoals were the turning-point of the cruise, and that with good luck they would wet the balance of their salt there. But seeing the size of the Virgin (it was one tiny dot), he wondered how even Disko with the hog-yoke and the lead could find her. He learned later that Disko was entirely equal to that and any other business and could even help others. A big four-by-five blackboard hung in the cabin, and Harvey never understood the need of it till, after some blinding thick days, they heard the unmelodious tooting of a foot-power fog-horn—a machine whose note is as that of a consumptive elephant.

They were making a short berth, towing the anchor under their foot to save trouble. "Square-rigger bellowin' fer his latitude," said Long Jack. The dripping red head-sails of a bark glided out of the fog, and the We're Here rang her bell thrice, using sea shorthand.

The larger boat backed her topsail with shrieks and shoutings.

"Frenchman," said Uncle Salters, scornfully. "Miquelon boat from St. Malo." The farmer had a weatherly sea-eye. "I'm 'most outer 'baccy, too, Disko."

"Same here," said Tom Platt. "Hi! Backez vous—backez vous! Standez awayez, you butt-ended mucho-bono! Where you from—St. Malo, eh?"

"Ah, ha! Mucho bono! Oui! oui! Clos Poulet—St. Malo! St. Pierre et Miquelon," cried the other crowd, waving woollen caps and laughing. Then all together, "Bord! Bord!"

"Bring up the board, Danny. Beats me how them Frenchmen fetch anywheres, exceptin' America's fairish broadly. Forty-six forty-nine's good enough fer them; an' I guess it's abaout right, too."

Dan chalked the figures on the board, and they hung it in the main-rigging to a chorus of mercis from the bark.

"Seems kinder uneighbourly to let 'em swedge off like this," Salters suggested, feeling in his pockets.

"Hev ye learned French then sence last trip?" said Disko. "I don't want no more stone-ballast hove at us 'long o' your callin' Miquelon boats 'footy cochins,' same's you did off Le Have."

"Harmon Rush he said that was the way to rise 'em. Plain United States is good enough fer me. We're all dretful short on terbakker. Young feller, don't you speak French?"

"Oh, yes," said Harvey valiantly; and he bawled: "Hi! Say! Arretez vous! Attendez! Nous sommes venant pour tabac."

"Ah, tabac, tabac!" they cried, and laughed again.

"That hit 'em. Let's heave a dory over, anyway," said Tom Platt. "I don't exactly hold no certificates on French, but I know another lingo that goes, I guess. Come on, Harve, an' interpret."

The raffle and confusion when he and Harvey were hauled up the bark's black side was indescribable. Her cabin was all stuck round with glaring coloured prints of the Virgin—the Virgin of Newfoundland, they called her. Harvey found his French of no recognized Bank brand, and his conversation was limited to nods and grins. But Tom Platt waved his arms and got along swimmingly. The captain gave him a drink of unspeakable gin, and the opera-comique crew, with their hairy throats, red caps, and long knives, greeted him as a brother. Then the trade began. They had tobacco, plenty of it—American, that had never paid duty to France. They wanted chocolate and crackers. Harvey rowed back to arrange with the cook and Disko, who owned the stores, and on his return the cocoa-tins and cracker-bags were counted out by the Frenchman's wheel. It looked like a piratical division of loot; but Tom Platt came out of it roped with black pigtail and stuffed with cakes of chewing and smoking tobacco. Then those jovial mariners swung off into the mist, and the last Harvey heard was a gay chorus:

"Par derriere chez ma tante,
Il'y a un bois joli,
Et le rossignol y chante
Et le jour et la nuit....

Que donneriez vous, belle,
Qui l'amenerait ici?
Je donnerai Quebec,
Sorel et Saint Denis."

"How was it my French didn't go, and your sign-talk did?" Harvey demanded when the barter had been distributed among the We're Heres.

"Sign-talk!" Platt guffawed. "Well, yes, 'twas sign-talk, but a heap older'n your French, Harve.

Them French boats are chockfull o' Freemasons, an' that's why."

"Are you a Freemason, then?"

"Looks that way, don't it?" said the man-o'-war's man, stuffing his pipe; and Harvey had another mystery of the deep sea to brood upon.

CHAPTER VI

The thing that struck him most was the exceedingly casual way in which some craft loafed about the broad Atlantic. Fishing-boats, as Dan said, were naturally dependent on the courtesy and wisdom of their neighbours; but one expected better things of steamers. That was after another interesting interview, when they had been chased for three miles by a big lumbering old cattle-boat, all boarded over on the upper deck, that smelt like a thousand cattle-pens. A very excited officer yelled at them through a speaking-trumpet, and she lay and lollopped helplessly on the water while Disko ran the We're Here under her lee and gave the skipper a piece of his mind. "Where might ye be—eh? Ye don't deserve to be anywhere. You barn-yard tramps go hoggin' the road on the high seas with no blame consideration fer your neighbours, an' your eyes in your coffee-cups instid o' in your silly heads."

At this the skipper danced on the bridge and said something about Disko's own eyes. "We haven't had an observation for three days. D'you suppose we can run her blind?" he shouted.

"Wa-al, I can," Disko retorted. "What's come to your lead? Et it? Can't ye smell bottom, or are them cattle too rank?"

"What d' ye feed 'em?" said Uncle Salters with intense seriousness, for the smell of the pens woke all the farmer in him. "They say they fall off dretful on a v'yage. Dunno as it's any o' my business, but I've a kind o' notion that oil-cake broke small an' sprinkled—"

"Thunder!" said a cattle-man in a red jersey as he looked over the side. "What asylum did they let His Whiskers out of?"

"Young feller," Salters began, standing up in the fore-rigging, "let me tell yeou 'fore we go any further that I've—"

The officer on the bridge took off his cap with immense politeness. "Excuse me," he said, "but I've asked for my reckoning. If the agricultural person with the hair will kindly shut his head, the sea-green barnacle with the wall-eye may per-haps condescend to enlighten us."

"Naow you've made a show o' me, Salters," said Disko, angrily. He could not stand up to that particular sort of talk, and snapped out the latitude and longitude without more lectures.

"Well, that's a boat-load of lunatics, sure," said the skipper, as he rang up the engine-room and tossed a bundle of newspapers into the schooner.

"Of all the blamed fools, next to you, Salters, him an' his crowd are abaout the likeliest I've ever seen," said Disko as the We're Here slid away. "I was jest givin' him my jedgment on lullsikin' round these waters like a lost child, an' you must cut in with your fool farmin'. Can't ye never keep things sep'rate?"

Harvey, Dan, and the others stood back, winking one to the other and full of joy; but Disko and Salters wrangled seriously till evening, Salters arguing that a cattle-boat was practically a barn on blue water, and Disko insisting that, even if this were the case, decency and fisher-pride demanded that he should have kept "things sep'rate." Long Jack stood it in silence for a time,—an angry skipper makes an unhappy crew,—and then he spoke across the table after supper:

"Fwhat's the good o' bodderin' fwhat they'll say?" said he.

"They'll tell that tale agin us fer years—that's all," said Disko. "Oil-cake sprinkled!"

"With salt, o' course," said Salters, impenitent, reading the farming reports from a week-old New York paper.

"It's plumb mortifyin' to all my feelin's," the skipper went on.

"Can't see ut that way," said Long Jack, the peacemaker "Look at here, Disko! Is there another packet afloat this day in this weather cud ha' met a tramp an' over an' above givin' her her reckonin',—over an' above that, I say,—cud ha' discoorsed wid her quite intelligent on the management av steers an' such at sea? Forgit ut! Av coorse they will not. 'Twas the most compenjus conversation that iver accrued. Double game an' twice runnin'—all to us." Dan kicked Harvey under the table, and Harvey choked in his cup.

"Well," said Salters, who felt that his honour had been somewhat plastered, "I said I didn't know as 'twuz any business o' mine, 'fore I spoke."

"An' right there," said Tom Platt, experienced in discipline and etiquette—"right there, I take it, Disko, you should ha' asked him to stop ef the conversation wuz likely, in your jedgment, to be anyways—what it shouldn't."

"Dunno but that's so," said Disko, who saw his way to an honourable retreat from a fit of the dignities.

"Why, o' course it was so," said Salters, "you bein' skipper here; an' I'd cheerful hev stopped on a hint—not from any leadin' or conviction, but fer the sake o' bearin' an example to these two blame boys of aours."

"Didn't I tell you, Harve, 'twould come araound to us 'fore we'd done? Always those blame boys. But I wouldn't have missed the show fer a half-share in a halibutter," Dan whispered.

"Still, things should ha' been kep' sep'rate," said Disko, and the light of new argument lit in Salters's eye as he crumbled cut plug into his pipe.

"There's a power av vartue in keepin' things sep'rate," said Long Jack, intent on stilling the storm. "That's fwhat Steyning of Steyning and Hare's f'und when he sent Counahan fer skipper on the Marilla D. Kuhn, instid o' Cap. Newton that was took with inflam'try rheumatism an' couldn't go. Counahan the Navigator we called him."

"Nick Counahan he never went aboard fer a night 'thout a pond o' rum somewheres in the manifest," said Tom Platt, playing up to the lead. "He used to bum araound the c'mission houses to Boston lookin' fer the Lord to make him captain of a tow-boat on his merits. Sam Coy, up to Atlantic Avenoo, give him his board free fer a year or more on account of his stories."

"Counahan the Navigator! Tck! Tck! Dead these fifteen year, ain't he?"

"Seventeen, I guess. He died the year the Caspar McVeagh was built; but he could niver keep things sep'rate. Steyning tuk him fer the reason the thief tuk the hot stove—bekaze there was nothin' else that season. The men was all to the Banks, and Counahan he whacked up an iverlastin' hard crowd fer crew. Rum! Ye cud ha' floated the Marilla, insurance an' all, in fwhat they stowed aboard her. They lef' Boston Harbour for the great Grand Bank wid a roarin' nor'wester behind 'em an' all hands full to the bung. An' the hivens looked after thim, for divil a watch did they set, an' divil a rope did they lay hand to, till they'd seen the bottom av a fifteen-gallon cask o' bug-juice. That was about wan week, so far as Counahan remembered. (If I cud only tell the tale as he told ut!) All that whoile the wind blew like ould glory, an' the Marilla—'twas summer, and they'd give her a foretopmast—struck her gait and kept ut.

Then Counahan tuk the hog-yoke an' thrembled over it for a whoile, an' made out, betwix' that an' the chart an' the singin' in his head, that they was to the south'ard o' Sable Island, gettin' along glorious, but speakin' nothin'. Then they broached another keg, an' quit speculatin' about anythin' fer another spell. The Marilla she lay down whin she dropped Boston Light, and she never lufted her lee-rail up to that time—hustlin' on one an' the same slant. But they saw no weed, nor gulls, nor schooners; an' prisintly they obsarved they'd bin out a matter o' fourteen days and they mis-trusted the Bank has suspinded payment. So they sounded, an' got sixty fathom. 'That's me,' sez Counahan. 'That's me iv'ry time! I've run her slat on the Bank fer you, an' when we get thirty fathom we'll turn in like little men. Counahan is the b'y,' sez he. 'Counahan the Navigator!'

"Nex' cast they got ninety. Sez Counahan: 'Either the lead-line's tuk to stretchin' or else the Bank's sunk.'

"They hauled ut up, bein' just about in that state when ut seemed right an' reasonable, and sat down on the deck countin' the knots, an' gettin' her snarled up hijjus. The Marilla she'd struck her gait, an' she hild ut, an' prisintly along came a tramp, an' Counahan spoke her.

"'Hev ye seen any fishin'-boats now?' sez he, quite casual.

"'There's lashin's av them off the Irish coast,' sez the tramp.

"'Aah! go shake yerself,' sez Counahan. 'Fwhat have I to do wid the Irish coast?'

"'Then fwhat are ye doin' here?' sez the tramp.

"'Sufferin' Christianity!' sez Counahan (he always said that whin his pumps sucked an' he was not feelin' good)—'Sufferin' Christianity!' he sez, 'where am I at?'

"'Thirty-five mile west-sou'west o' Cape Clear,' sez the tramp, 'if that's any consolation to you.'

"Counahan fetched wan jump, four feet sivin inches, measured by the cook.

"'Consolation!' sez he, bould as brass. 'D'ye take me fer a dialect? Thirty-five mile from Cape Clear, an' fourteen days from Boston Light. Sufferin' Christianity, 'tis a record, an' by the same token I've a mother to Skibbereen!' Think av ut! The gall av um! But ye see he could niver keep things sep'rate.

"The crew was mostly Cork an' Kerry men, barrin' one Marylander that wanted to go back, but they called him a mutineer, an' they ran the ould Marilla into Skibbereen, an' they had an illigant time visitin' around with frinds on the ould sod fer a week. Thin they wint back, an' it cost 'em two an' thirty days to beat to the Banks again. 'Twas gettin' on towards fall, and grub was low, so Counahan ran her back to Boston, wid no more bones to ut."

"And what did the firm say?" Harvey demanded.

"Fwhat could they? The fish was on the Banks, an' Counahan was at T-wharf talkin' av his record trip east! They tuk their satisfaction out av that, an' ut all came av not keepin' the crew and the rum sep'rate in the first place; an' confusin' Skibbereen wid 'Queereau, in the second. Counahan the Navigator, rest his sowl! He was an imprompju citizen!"

"Once I was in the Lucy Holmes," said Manuel, in his gentle voice. "They not want any of her feesh in Gloucester. Eh, wha-at? Give us no price. So we go across the water, and think to sell to some Fayal man. Then it blow fresh, and we cannot see well. Eh, wha-at? Then it blow some

more fresh, and we go down below and drive very fast—no one know where. By and by we see a land, and it get some hot. Then come two, three nigger in a brick. Eh, wha-at? We ask where we are, and they say—now, what you all think?"

"Grand Canary," said Disko, after a moment. Manuel shook his head, smiling.

"Blanco," said Tom Platt.

"No. Worse than that. We was below Bezagos, and the brick she was from Liberia! So we sell our feesh there! Not bad, so? Eh, wha-at?"

"Can a schooner like this go right across to Africa?" said Harvey.

"Go araound the Horn ef there's anythin' worth goin' fer, and the grub holds aout," said Disko. "My father he run his packet, an' she was a kind o' pinkey, abaout fifty ton, I guess,—the Rupert,—he run her over to Greenland's icy mountains the year ha'af our fleet was tryin' after cod there. An' what's more, he took my mother along with him,—to show her haow the money was earned, I presoom,—an' they was all iced up, an' I was born at Disko. Don't remember nothin' abaout it, o' course. We come back when the ice eased in the spring, but they named me fer the place. Kinder mean trick to put up on a baby, but we're all baound to make mistakes in aour lives."

"Sure! Sure!" said Salters, wagging his head. "All baound to make mistakes, an' I tell you two boys here thet after you've made a mistake—ye don't make fewer'n a hundred a day—the next best thing's to own up to it like men."

Long Jack winked one tremendous wink that embraced all hands except Disko and Salters, and the incident was closed.

Then they made berth after berth to the northward, the dories out almost every day, running along the east edge of the Grand Bank in thirty- to forty-fathom water, and fishing steadily.

It was here Harvey first met the squid, who is one of the best cod-baits, but uncertain in his moods. They were waked out of their bunks one black night by yells of "Squid O!" from Salters, and for an hour and a half every soul aboard hung over his squid-jig—a piece of lead painted red and armed at the lower end with a circle of pins bent backward like half-opened umbrella ribs. The squid—for some unknown reason—likes, and wraps himself round, this thing, and is hauled up ere he can escape from the pins. But as he leaves his home he squirts first water and next ink into his captor's face; and it was curious to see the men weaving their heads from side to side to dodge the shot. They were as black as sweeps when the flurry ended; but a pile of fresh squid lay on the deck, and the large cod thinks very well of a little shiny piece of squid tentacle at the tip of a clam-baited hook. Next day they caught many fish, and met the Carrie Pitman, to whom they shouted their luck, and she wanted to trade—seven cod for one fair-sized squid; but Disko would not agree at the price, and the Carrie dropped sullenly to leeward and anchored half a mile away, in the hope of striking on to some for herself.

Disko said nothing till after supper, when he sent Dan and Manuel out to buoy the We're Here's cable and announced his intention of turning in with the broad-axe. Dan naturally repeated these remarks to the dory from the Carrie, who wanted to know why they were buoying their cable, since they were not on rocky bottom.

"Dad sez he wouldn't trust a ferryboat within five mile o' you," Dan howled cheerfully.

"Why don't he git out, then? Who's hinderin'?" said the other.

"'Cause you've jest the same ez lee-bowed him, an' he don't take that from any boat, not to speak o' sech a driftin' gurry-butt as you be."

"She ain't driftin' any this trip," said the man angrily, for the Carrie Pitman had an unsavory reputation for breaking her ground-tackle.

"Then haow d'you make berths?" said Dan. "It's her best p'int o' sailin'. An' ef she's quit driftin', what in thunder are you doin' with a new jib-boom?" That shot went home.

"Hey, you Portugoosy organ-grinder, take your monkey back to Gloucester. Go back to school, Dan Troop," was the answer.

"O-ver-alls! O-ver-alls!" yelled Dan, who knew that one of the Carrie's crew had worked in an overall factory the winter before.

"Shrimp! Gloucester shrimp! Git aout, you Novy!"

To call a Gloucester man a Nova Scotian is not well received. Dan answered in kind.

"Novy yourself, ye Scrabble-towners! ye Chatham wreckers! Git aout with your brick in your stockin'!" And the forces separated, but Chatham had the worst of it.

"I knew haow 'twould be," said Disko. "She's drawed the wind raound already. Some one oughter put a deesist on thet packet. She'll snore till midnight, an' jest when we're gettin' our sleep she'll strike adrift. Good job we ain't crowded with craft hereaways. But I ain't goin' to up anchor fer Chatham. She may hold."

The wind, which had hauled round, rose at sundown and blew steadily. There was not enough sea, though, to disturb even a dory's tackle, but the Carrie Pitman was a law unto herself. At the end of the boys' watch they heard the crack-crack-crack of a huge muzzle-loading revolver aboard her.

"Glory, glory, hallelujah!" sung Dan. "Here she comes, Dad; butt-end first, walkin' in her sleep same's she done on 'Queereau.'"

Had she been any other boat Disko would have taken his chances, but now he cut the cable as the Carrie Pitman, with all the North Atlantic to play in, lurched down directly upon them. The We're Here, under jib and riding-sail, gave her no more room than was absolutely necessary,—Disko did not wish to spend a week hunting for his cable,—but scuttled up into the wind as the Carrie passed within easy hail, a silent and angry boat, at the mercy of a raking broadside of Bank chaff.

"Good evenin'," said Disko, raising his head-gear, "an' haow does your garden grow?"

"Go to Ohio an' hire a mule," said Uncle Salters. "We don't want no farmers here."

"Will I lend YOU my dory-anchor?" cried Long Jack.

"Unship your rudder an' stick it in the mud," bawled Tom Platt.

"Say!" Dan's voice rose shrill and high, as he stood on the wheel-box. "Sa-ay! Is there a strike in the o-ver-all factory; or hev they hired girls, ye Shackamaxons?"

"Veer out the tiller-lines," cried Harvey, "and nail 'em to the bottom!" That was a salt-flavoured jest he had been put up to by Tom Platt. Manuel leaned over the stern and yelled: "Johanna

Morgan play the organ! Ahaaaa!" He flourished his broad thumb with a gesture of unspeakable contempt and derision, while little Penn covered himself with glory by piping up: "Gee a little! Hssh! Come here. Haw!"

They rode on their chain for the rest of the night, a short, snappy, uneasy motion, as Harvey found, and wasted half the forenoon recovering the cable. But the boys agreed the trouble was cheap at the price of triumph and glory, and they thought with grief over all the beautiful things that they might have said to the discomfited Carrie.

CHAPTER VII

Next day they fell in with more sails, all circling slowly from the east northerly towards the west. But just when they expected to make the shoals by the Virgin the fog shut down, and they anchored, surrounded by the tinklings of invisible bells. There was not much fishing, but occasionally dory met dory in the fog and exchanged news.

That night, a little before dawn, Dan and Harvey, who had been sleeping most of the day, tumbled out to "hook" fried pies. There was no reason why they should not have taken them openly; but they tasted better so, and it made the cook angry. The heat and smell below drove them on deck with their plunder, and they found Disko at the bell, which he handed over to Harvey.

"Keep her goin'," said he. "I mistrust I hear somethin'. Ef it's anything, I'm best where I am so's to get at things."

It was a forlorn little jingle; the thick air seemed to pinch it off, and in the pauses Harvey heard the muffled shriek of a liner's siren, and he knew enough of the Banks to know what that meant. It came to him, with horrible distinctness, how a boy in a cherry-coloured jersey—he despised fancy blazers now with all a fisher-man's contempt—how an ignorant, rowdy boy had once said it would be "great" if a steamer ran down a fishing-boat. That boy had a stateroom with a hot and cold bath, and spent ten minutes each morning picking over a gilt-edged bill of fare. And that same boy—no, his very much older brother—was up at four of the dim dawn in streaming, crackling oilskins, hammering, literally for the dear life, on a bell smaller than the steward's breakfast-bell, while somewhere close at hand a thirty-foot steel stem was storming along at twenty miles an hour! The bitterest thought of all was that there were folks asleep in dry, upholstered cabins who would never learn that they had massacred a boat before breakfast. So Harvey rang the bell.

"Yes, they slow daown one turn o' their blame propeller," said Dan, applying himself to Manuel's conch, "fer to keep inside the law, an' that's consolin' when we're all at the bottom. Hark to her! She's a humper!"

"Aooo-whoo-whupp!" went the siren. "Wingle-tingle-tink," went the bell. "Graaa-ouch!" went the conch, while sea and sky were all mired up in milky fog. Then Harvey felt that he was near a moving body, and found himself looking up and up at the wet edge of a cliff-like bow, leaping, it seemed, directly over the schooner. A jaunty little feather of water curled in front of it, and as it lifted it showed a long ladder of Roman numerals-XV., XVI., XVII., XVIII., and so forth—on a salmon-coloured gleaming side. It tilted forward and downward with a heart-stilling "Sssssooo"; the ladder disappeared; a line of brass-rimmed port-holes flashed past; a jet of steam puffed in Harvey's helplessly uplifted hands; a spout of hot water roared along the rail of the We're Here, and the little schooner staggered and shook in a rush of screw-torn water, as a liner's stern vanished in the fog. Harvey got ready to faint or be sick, or both, when he heard a crack like a trunk thrown on a sidewalk, and, all small in his ear, a far-away telephone voice drawling: "Heave to! You've sunk us!"

"Is it us?" he gasped.

"No! Boat out yonder. Ring! We're goin' to look," said Dan, running out a dory.

In half a minute all except Harvey, Penn, and the cook were overside and away. Presently a schooner's stump-foremast, snapped clean across, drifted past the bows. Then an empty green

dory came by, knocking on the We're Here's side, as though she wished to be taken in. Then followed something, face down, in a blue jersey, but—it was not the whole of a man. Penn changed colour and caught his breath with a click. Harvey pounded despairingly at the bell, for he feared they might be sunk at any minute, and he jumped at Dan's hail as the crew came back.

"The Jennie Cushman," said Dan, hysterically, "cut clean in half—graound up an' trompled on at that! Not a quarter of a mile away. Dad's got the old man. There ain't any one else, and—there was his son, too. Oh, Harve, Harve, I can't stand it! I've seen—" He dropped his head on his arms and sobbed while the others dragged a gray-headed man aboard.

"What did you pick me up for?" the stranger groaned. "Disko, what did you pick me up for?"

Disko dropped a heavy hand on his shoulder, for the man's eyes were wild and his lips trembled as he stared at the silent crew. Then up and spoke Pennsylvania Pratt, who was also Haskins or Rich or McVitty when Uncle Salters forgot; and his face was changed on him from the face of a fool to the countenance of an old, wise man, and he said in a strong voice: "The Lord gave, and the Lord hath taken away; blessed be the name of the Lord! I was—I am a minister of the Gospel. Leave him to me."

"Oh, you be, be you?" said the man. "Then pray my son back to me! Pray back a nine-thousand-dollar boat an' a thousand quintal of fish. If you'd left me alone my widow could ha' gone on to the Provident an' worked fer her board, an' never known—an' never known. Now I'll hev to tell her."

"There ain't nothin' to say," said Disko. "Better lie down a piece, Jason Olley."

When a man has lost his only son, his summer's work, and his means of livelihood, in thirty counted seconds, it is hard to give consolation.

"All Gloucester men, wasn't they?" said Tom Platt, fiddling helplessly with a dory-becket.

"Oh, that don't make no odds," said Jason, wringing the wet from his beard. "I'll be rowin' summer boarders araound East Gloucester this fall." He rolled heavily to the rail, singing:

"Happy birds that sing and fly
Round thine altars, O Most High!"

"Come with me. Come below!" said Penn, as though he had a right to give orders. Their eyes met and fought for a quarter of a minute.

"I dunno who you be, but I'll come," said Jason submissively. "Mebbe I'll get back some o' the—some o' the-nine thousand dollars." Penn led him into the cabin and slid the door behind.

"That ain't Penn," cried Uncle Salters. "It's Jacob Boiler, an'—he's remembered Johnstown! I never seed such eyes in any livin' man's head. What's to do naow? What'll I do naow?"

They could hear Penn's voice and Jason's together. Then Penn's went on alone, and Salters slipped off his hat, for Penn was praying. Presently the little man came up the steps, huge drops of sweat on his face, and looked at the crew. Dan was still sobbing by the wheel.

"He don't know us," Salters groaned. "It's all to do over again, checkers and everything—an' what'll he say to me?"

Penn spoke; they could hear that it was to strangers. "I have prayed," said he. "Our people believe in prayer. I have prayed for the life of this man's son. Mine were drowned before my

eyes—she and my eldest and—the others. Shall a man be more wise than his Maker? I prayed never for their lives, but I have prayed for this man's son, and he will surely be sent him."

Salters looked pleadingly at Penn to see if he remembered.

"How long have I been mad?" Penn asked suddenly. His mouth was twitching.

"Pshaw, Penn! You weren't never mad," Salters began "Only a little distracted like."

"I saw the houses strike the bridge before the fires broke out. I do not remember any more. How long ago is that?"

"I can't stand it! I can't stand it!" cried Dan, and Harvey whimpered in sympathy.

"Abaout five year," said Disko, in a shaking voice.

"Then I have been a charge on some one for every day of that time. Who was the man?"

Disko pointed to Salters.

"Ye hain't—ye hain't!" cried the sea-farmer, twisting his hands together. "Ye've more'n earned your keep twice-told; an' there's money owin' you, Penn, besides ha'af o' my quarter-share in the boat, which is yours fer value received."

"You are good men. I can see that in your faces. But—"

"Mother av Mercy," whispered Long Jack, "an' he's been wid us all these trips! He's clean bewitched."

A schooner's bell struck up alongside, and a voice hailed through the fog: "O Disko! 'Heard abaout the Jennie Cushman?"

"They have found his son," cried Penn. "Stand you still and see the salvation of the Lord!"

"Got Jason aboard here," Disko answered, but his voice quavered. "There—warn't any one else?"

"We've fund one, though. 'Run acrost him snarled up in a mess o' lumber thet might ha' bin a foc'sle. His head's cut some."

"Who is he?"

The We're Here's heart-beats answered one another.

"Guess it's young Olley," the voice drawled.

Penn raised his hands and said something in German. Harvey could have sworn that a bright sun was shining upon his lifted face; but the drawl went on: "Sa-ay! You fellers guyed us consid'rable t'other night."

"We don't feel like guyin' any now," said Disko.

"I know it; but to tell the honest truth we was kinder—kinder driftin' when we run agin young Olley."

It was the irrepressible Carrie Pitman, and a roar of unsteady laughter went up from the deck

of the We're Here.

"Hedn't you 'baout's well send the old man aboard? We're runnin' in fer more bait an' graound-tackle. Guess you won't want him, anyway, an' this blame windlass work makes us short-handed. We'll take care of him. He married my woman's aunt."

"I'll give you anything in the boat," said Troop.

"Don't want nothin', 'less, mebbe, an anchor that'll hold. Say! Young Olley's gittin' kinder baulky an' excited. Send the old man along."

Penn waked him from his stupor of despair, and Tom Platt rowed him over. He went away without a word of thanks, not knowing what was to come; and the fog closed over all.

"And now," said Penn, drawing a deep breath as though about to preach. "And now"—the erect body sank like a sword driven home into the scabbard; the light faded from the overbright eyes; the voice returned to its usual pitiful little titter—"and now," said Pennsylvania Pratt, "do you think it's too early for a little game of checkers, Mr. Salters?"

"The very thing—the very thing I was goin' to say myself," cried Salters promptly. "It beats all, Penn, how ye git on to what's in a man's mind."

The little fellow blushed and meekly followed Salters forward.

"Up anchor! Hurry! Let's quit these crazy waters," shouted Disko, and never was he more swiftly obeyed.

"Now what in creation d'ye suppose is the meanin' o' that all?" said Long Jack, when they were working through the fog once more, damp, dripping, and bewildered.

"The way I sense it," said Disko, at the wheel, "is this: The Jennie Cushman business comin' on an empty stummick—"

"H-he saw one of them go by," sobbed Harvey.

"An' that, o' course, kinder hove him outer water, julluk runnin' a craft ashore; hove him right aout, I take it, to rememberin' Johnstown an' Jacob Boiler an' such-like reminiscences. Well, consolin' Jason there held him up a piece, same's shorin' up a boat. Then, bein' weak, them props slipped an' slipped, an' he slided down the ways, an' naow he's water-borne agin. That's haow I sense it."

They decided that Disko was entirely correct.

"'Twould ha' bruk Salters all up," said Long Jack, "if Penn had stayed Jacob Boilerin'. Did ye see his face when Penn asked who he'd been charged on all these years? How is ut, Salters?"

"Asleep—dead asleep. Turned in like a child," Salters replied, tiptoeing aft. "There won't be no grub till he wakes, natural. Did ye ever see sech a gift in prayer? He everlastin'ly hiked young Olley outer the ocean. Thet's my belief. Jason was tur'ble praoud of his boy, an' I mistrusted all along 'twas a jedgment on worshippin' vain idols."

"There's others jes as sot," said Disko.

"That's difrunt," Salters retorted quickly. "Penn's not all caulked, an' I ain't only but doin' my duty by him."

They waited, those hungry men, three hours, till Penn reappeared with a smooth face and a blank mind. He said he believed that he had been dreaming. Then he wanted to know why they were so silent, and they could not tell him.

Disko worked all hands mercilessly for the next three or four days; and when they could not go out, turned them into the hold to stack the ship's stores into smaller compass, to make more room for the fish. The packed mass ran from the cabin partition to the sliding door behind the foc'sle stove; and Disko showed how there is great art in stowing cargo so as to bring a schooner to her best draft. The crew were thus kept lively till they recovered their spirits; and Harvey was tickled with a rope's end by Long Jack for being, as the Galway man said, "sorrowful as a sick cat over fwhat couldn't be helped." He did a great deal of thinking in those weary days, and told Dan what he thought, and Dan agreed with him—even to the extent of asking for fried pies instead of hooking them.

But a week later the two nearly upset the Hattie S. in a wild attempt to stab a shark with an old bayonet tied to a stick. The grim brute rubbed alongside the dory begging for small fish, and between the three of them it was a mercy they all got off alive.

At last, after playing blindman's-buff in the fog, there came a morning when Disko shouted down the foc'sle: "Hurry, boys! We're in taown!"

CHAPTER VIII

To the end of his days, Harvey will never forget that sight. The sun was just clear of the horizon they had not seen for nearly a week, and his low red light struck into the riding-sails of three fleets of anchored schooners—one to the north, one to the westward, and one to the south. There must have been nearly a hundred of them, of every possible make and build, with, far away, a square-rigged Frenchman, all bowing and courtesying one to the other. From every boat dories were dropping away like bees from a crowded hive, and the clamour of voices, the rattling of ropes and blocks, and the splash of the oars carried for miles across the heaving water. The sails turned all colours, black, pearly-gray, and white, as the sun mounted; and more boats swung up through the mists to the southward.

The dories gathered in clusters, separated, reformed, and broke again, all heading one way; while men hailed and whistled and cat-called and sang, and the water was speckled with rubbish thrown overboard.

"It's a town," said Harvey. "Disko was right. It IS a town!"

"I've seen smaller," said Disko. "There's about a thousand men here; an' yonder's the Virgin." He pointed to a vacant space of greenish sea, where there were no dories.

The We're Here skirted round the northern squadron, Disko waving his hand to friend after friend, and anchored as nearly as a racing yacht at the end of the season. The Bank fleet pass good seamanship in silence; but a bungler is jeered all along the line.

"Jest in time fer the caplin," cried the Mary Chilton.

"'Salt 'most wet?" asked the King Philip.

"Hey, Tom Platt! Come t' supper to-night?" said the Henry Clay; and so questions and answers flew back and forth. Men had met one another before, dory-fishing in the fog, and there is no place for gossip like the Bank fleet. They all seemed to know about Harvey's rescue, and asked if he were worth his salt yet. The young bloods jested with Dan, who had a lively tongue of his own, and inquired after their health by the town-nicknames they least liked. Manuel's countrymen jabbered at him in their own language; and even the silent cook was seen riding the jib-boom and shouting Gaelic to a friend as black as himself. After they had buoyed the cable— all around the Virgin is rocky bottom, and carelessness means chafed ground-tackle and danger from drifting—after they had buoyed the cable, their dories went forth to join the mob of boats anchored about a mile away. The schooners rocked and dipped at a safe distance, like mother ducks watching their brood, while the dories behaved like mannerless ducklings.

As they drove into the confusion, boat banging boat, Harvey's ears tingled at the comments on his rowing. Every dialect from Labrador to Long Island, with Portuguese, Neapolitan, Lingua Franca, French, and Gaelic, with songs and shoutings and new oaths, rattled round him, and he seemed to be the butt of it all. For the first time in his life he felt shy—perhaps that came from living so long with only the We're Heres—among the scores of wild faces that rose and fell with the reeling small craft. A gentle, breathing swell, three furlongs from trough to barrel, would quietly shoulder up a string of variously painted dories. They hung for an instant, a wonderful frieze against the sky-line, and their men pointed and hailed. Next moment the open mouths, waving arms, and bare chests disappeared, while on another swell came up an entirely new line of characters like paper figures in a toy theatre. So Harvey stared. "Watch out!" said Dan, flourishing a dip-net "When I tell you dip, you dip. The caplin'll school any time from naow on.

Where'll we lay, Tom Platt?"

Pushing, shoving, and hauling, greeting old friends here and warning old enemies there, Commodore Tom Platt led his little fleet well to leeward of the general crowd, and immediately three or four men began to haul on their anchors with intent to lee-bow the We're Heres. But a yell of laughter went up as a dory shot from her station with exceeding speed, its occupant pulling madly on the roding.

"Give her slack!" roared twenty voices. "Let him shake it out."

"What's the matter?" said Harvey, as the boat flashed away to the southward. "He's anchored, isn't he?"

"Anchored, sure enough, but his graound-tackle's kinder shifty," said Dan, laughing. "Whale's fouled it. . . . Dip Harve! Here they come!"

The sea round them clouded and darkened, and then frizzed up in showers of tiny silver fish, and over a space of five or six acres the cod began to leap like trout in May; while behind the cod three or four broad gray-backs broke the water into boils.

Then everybody shouted and tried to haul up his anchor to get among the school, and fouled his neighbour's line and said what was in his heart, and dipped furiously with his dip-net, and shrieked cautions and advice to his companions, while the deep fizzed like freshly opened soda-water, and cod, men, and whales together flung in upon the luckless bait. Harvey was nearly knocked overboard by the handle of Dan's net. But in all the wild tumult he noticed, and never forgot, the wicked, set little eye—something like a circus elephant's eye—of a whale that drove along almost level with the water, and, so he said, winked at him. Three boats found their rodings fouled by these reckless mid-sea hunters, and were towed half a mile ere their horses shook the line free.

Then the caplin moved off, and five minutes later there was no sound except the splash of the sinkers overside, the flapping of the cod, and the whack of the muckles as the men stunned them. It was wonderful fishing. Harvey could see the glimmering cod below, swimming slowly in droves, biting as steadily as they swam. Bank law strictly forbids more than one hook on one line when the dories are on the Virgin or the Eastern Shoals; but so close lay the boats that even single hooks snarled, and Harvey found himself in hot argument with a gentle, hairy Newfoundlander on one side and a howling Portuguese on the other.

Worse than any tangle of fishing-lines was the confusion of the dory-rodings below water. Each man had anchored where it seemed good to him, drifting and rowing round his fixed point. As the fish struck on less quickly, each man wanted to haul up and get to better ground; but every third man found himself intimately connected with some four or five neighbours. To cut another's roding is crime unspeakable on the Banks; yet it was done, and done without detection, three or four times that day. Tom Platt caught a Maine man in the black act and knocked him over the gunwale with an oar, and Manuel served a fellow-countryman in the same way. But Harvey's anchor-line was cut, and so was Penn's, and they were turned into relief-boats to carry fish to the We're Here as the dories filled. The caplin schooled once more at twilight, when the mad clamour was repeated; and at dusk they rowed back to dress down by the light of kerosene-lamps on the edge of the pen.

It was a huge pile, and they went to sleep while they were dressing. Next day several boats fished right above the cap of the Virgin; and Harvey, with them, looked down on the very weed of that lonely rock, which rises to within twenty feet of the surface. The cod were there in legions, marching solemnly over the leathery kelp. When they bit, they bit all together; and so when they

stopped. There was a slack time at noon, and the dories began to search for amusement. It was Dan who sighted the Hope Of Prague just coming up, and as her boats joined the company they were greeted with the question: "Who's the meanest man in the Fleet?"

Three hundred voices answered cheerily: "Nick Bra-ady." It sounded like an organ chant.

"Who stole the lampwicks?" That was Dan's contribution.

"Nick Bra-ady," sang the boats.

"Who biled the salt bait fer soup?" This was an unknown backbiter a quarter of a mile away.

Again the joyful chorus. Now, Brady was not especially mean, but he had that reputation, and the Fleet made the most of it. Then they discovered a man from a Truro boat who, six years before, had been convicted of using a tackle with five or six hooks—a "scrowger," they call it—in the Shoals. Naturally, he had been christened "Scrowger Jim"; and though he had hidden himself on the Georges ever since, he found his honours waiting for him full blown. They took it up in a sort of firecracker chorus: "Jim! O Jim! Jim! O Jim! Ssssrowger Jim!" That pleased everybody. And when a poetical Beverly man—he had been making it up all day, and talked about it for weeks—sang, "The Carrie Pitman's anchor doesn't hold her for a cent" the dories felt that they were indeed fortunate. Then they had to ask that Beverly man how he was off for beans, because even poets must not have things all their own way. Every schooner and nearly every man got it in turn. Was there a careless or dirty cook anywhere? The dories sang about him and his food. Was a schooner badly found? The Fleet was told at full length. Had a man hooked tobacco from a mess-mate? He was named in meeting; the name tossed from roller to roller. Disko's infallible judgments, Long Jack's market-boat that he had sold years ago, Dan's sweetheart (oh, but Dan was an angry boy!), Penn's bad luck with dory-anchors, Salter's views on manure, Manuel's little slips from virtue ashore, and Harvey's ladylike handling of the oar—all were laid before the public; and as the fog fell around them in silvery sheets beneath the sun, the voices sounded like a bench of invisible judges pronouncing sentence.

The dories roved and fished and squabbled till a swell underran the sea. Then they drew more apart to save their sides, and some one called that if the swell continued the Virgin would break. A reckless Galway man with his nephew denied this, hauled up anchor, and rowed over the very rock itself. Many voices called them to come away, while others dared them to hold on. As the smooth-backed rollers passed to the southward, they hove the dory high and high into the mist, and dropped her in ugly, sucking, dimpled water, where she spun round her anchor, within a foot or two of the hidden rock. It was playing with death for mere bravado; and the boats looked on in uneasy silence till Long Jack rowed up behind his countrymen and quietly cut their roding.

"Can't ye hear ut knockin'?" he cried. "Pull for you miserable lives! Pull!"

The men swore and tried to argue as the boat drifted; but the next swell checked a little, like a man tripping on a carpet. There was a deep sob and a gathering roar, and the Virgin flung up a couple of acres of foaming water, white, furious, and ghastly over the shoal sea. Then all the boats greatly applauded Long Jack, and the Galway men held their tongue.

"Ain't it elegant?" said Dan, bobbing like a young seal at home. "She'll break about once every ha'af hour now, 'les the swell piles up good. What's her reg'lar time when she's at work, Tom Platt?"

"Once ivry fifteen minutes, to the tick. Harve, you've seen the greatest thing on the Banks; an' but for Long Jack you'd seen some dead men too."

There came a sound of merriment where the fog lay thicker and the schooners were ringing their bells. A big bark nosed cautiously out of the mist, and was received with shouts and cries of, "Come along, darlin'," from the Irishry.

"Another Frenchman?" said Harvey.

"Hain't you eyes? She's a Baltimore boat; goin' in fear an' tremblin'," said Dan. "We'll guy the very sticks out of her. Guess it's the fust time her skipper ever met up with the Fleet this way."

She was a black, buxom, eight-hundred-ton craft. Her mainsail was looped up, and her topsail flapped undecidedly in what little wind was moving. Now a bark is feminine beyond all other daughters of the sea, and this tall, hesitating creature, with her white and gilt figurehead, looked just like a bewildered woman half lifting her skirts to cross a muddy street under the jeers of bad little boys. That was very much her situation. She knew she was somewhere in the neighbourhood of the Virgin, had caught the roar of it, and was, therefore, asking her way. This is a small part of what she heard from the dancing dories:

"The Virgin? Fwhat are you talkin' of? 'This is Le Have on a Sunday mornin'. Go home an' sober up."

"Go home, ye tarrapin! Go home an' tell 'em we're comin'."

Half a dozen voices together, in a most tuneful chorus, as her stern went down with a roll and a bubble into the troughs: "Thay-aah-she-strikes!"

"Hard up! Hard up fer your life! You're on top of her now."

"Daown! Hard daown! Let go everything!"

"All hands to the pumps!"

"Daown jib an' pole her!"

Here the skipper lost his temper and said things. Instantly fishing was suspended to answer him, and he heard many curious facts about his boat and her next port of call. They asked him if he were insured; and whence he had stolen his anchor, because, they said, it belonged to the Carrie Pitman; they called his boat a mud-scow, and accused him of dumping garbage to frighten the fish; they offered to tow him and charge it to his wife; and one audacious youth slipped up almost under the counter, smacked it with his open palm, and yelled: "Gid up, Buck!"

The cook emptied a pan of ashes on him, and he replied with cod-heads. The bark's crew fired small coal from the galley, and the dories threatened to come aboard and "razee" her. They would have warned her at once had she been in real peril; but, seeing her well clear of the Virgin, they made the most of their chances. The fun was spoilt when the rock spoke again, a half-mile to windward, and the tormented bark set everything that would draw and went her ways; but the dories felt that the honours lay with them.

All that night the Virgin roared hoarsely; and next morning, over an angry, white-headed sea, Harvey saw the Fleet with flickering masts waiting for a lead. Not a dory was hove out till ten o'clock, when the two Jeraulds of the Day's Eye, imagining a lull which did not exist, set the example. In a minute half the boats were out and bobbing in the cockly swells, but Troop kept the We're Heres at work dressing down. He saw no sense in "dares"; and as the storm grew that evening they had the pleasure of receiving wet strangers only too glad to make any refuge in the gale. The boys stood by the dory-tackles with lanterns, the men ready to haul, one eye cocked for the sweeping wave that would make them drop everything and hold on for dear life. Out of

the dark would come a yell of "Dory, dory!" They would hook up and haul in a drenched man and a half-sunk boat, till their decks were littered down with nests of dories and the bunks were full. Five times in their watch did Harvey, with Dan, jump at the foregaff where it lay lashed on the boom, and cling with arms, legs, and teeth to rope and spar and sodden canvas as a big wave filled the decks. One dory was smashed to pieces, and the sea pitched the man head first on to the decks, cutting his forehead open; and about dawn, when the racing seas glimmered white all along their cold edges, another man, blue and ghastly, crawled in with a broken hand, asking news of his brother. Seven extra mouths sat down to breakfast: A Swede; a Chatham skipper; a boy from Hancock, Maine; one Duxbury, and three Provincetown men.

There was a general sorting out among the Fleet next day; and though no one said anything, all ate with better appetites when boat after boat reported full crews aboard. Only a couple of Portuguese and an old man from Gloucester were drowned, but many were cut or bruised; and two schooners had parted their tackle and been blown to the southward, three days' sail. A man died on a Frenchman—it was the same bark that had traded tobacco with the We're Heres. She slipped away quite quietly one wet, white morning, moved to a patch of deep water, her sails all hanging anyhow, and Harvey saw the funeral through Disko's spy-glass. It was only an oblong bundle slid overside. They did not seem to have any form of service, but in the night, at anchor, Harvey heard them across the star-powdered black water, singing something that sounded like a hymn. It went to a very slow tune.

"La brigantine
Qui va tourner,
Roule et s'incline
Pour m'entrainer.
Oh, Vierge Marie,
Pour moi priez Dieu!
Adieu, patrie;
Quebec, adieu!"

Tom Platt visited her, because, he said, the dead man was his brother as a Freemason. It came out that a wave had doubled the poor fellow over the heel of the bowsprit and broken his back. The news spread like a flash, for, contrary to general custom, the Frenchman held an auction of the dead man's kit,—he had no friends at St Malo or Miquelon,—and everything was spread out on the top of the house, from his red knitted cap to the leather belt with the sheath-knife at the back. Dan and Harvey were out on twenty-fathom water in the Hattie S., and naturally rowed over to join the crowd. It was a long pull, and they stayed some little time while Dan bought the knife, which had a curious brass handle. When they dropped overside and pushed off into a drizzle of rain and a lop of sea, it occurred to them that they might get into trouble for neglecting the lines.

"Guess 'twon't hurt us any to be warmed up," said Dan, shivering under his oilskins, and they rowed on into the heart of a white fog, which, as usual, dropped on them without warning.

"There's too much blame tide hereabouts to trust to your instinks," he said. "Heave over the anchor, Harve, and we'll fish a piece till the thing lifts. Bend on your biggest lead. Three pound ain't any too much in this water. See how she's tightened on her rodin' already."

There was quite a little bubble at the bows, where some irresponsible Bank current held the dory full stretch on her rope; but they could not see a boat's length in any direction. Harvey turned up his collar and bunched himself over his reel with the air of a wearied navigator. Fog had no special terrors for him now. They fished a while in silence, and found the cod struck on well. Then Dan drew the sheath-knife and tested the edge of it on the gunwale.

"That's a daisy," said Harvey. "How did you get it so cheap?"

"On account o' their blame Cath'lic superstitions," said Dan, jabbing with the bright blade. "They don't fancy takin' iron from off a dead man, so to speak. 'See them Arichat Frenchmen step back when I bid?"

"But an auction ain't taking anythink off a dead man. It's business."

"We know it ain't, but there's no goin' in the teeth o' superstition. That's one o' the advantages o' livin' in a progressive country." And Dan began whistling:

"Oh, Double Thatcher, how are you?
Now Eastern Point comes inter view.
The girls an' boys we soon shall see,
At anchor off Cape Ann!"

"Why didn't that Eastport man bid, then? He bought his boots. Ain't Maine progressive?"

"Maine? Pshaw! They don't know enough, or they hain't got money enough, to paint their haouses in Maine. I've seen 'em. The Eastport man he told me that the knife had been used—so the French captain told him—used up on the French coast last year."

"Cut a man? Heave 's the muckle." Harvey hauled in his fish, rebaited, and threw over.

"Killed him! Course, when I heard that I was keener'n ever to get it."

"Christmas! I didn't know it," said Harvey, turning round. "I'll give you a dollar for it when I—get my wages. Say, I'll give you two dollars."

"Honest? D'you like it as much as all that?" said Dan, flushing. "Well, to tell the truth, I kinder got it for you—to give; but I didn't let on till I saw how you'd take it. It's yours and welcome, Harve, because we're dory-mates, and so on and so forth, an' so followin'. Catch a-holt!"

He held it out, belt and all.

"But look at here. Dan, I don't see—"

"Take it. 'Tain't no use to me. I wish you to hev it." The temptation was irresistible. "Dan, you're a white man," said Harvey. "I'll keep it as long as I live."

"That's good hearin'," said Dan, with a pleasant laugh; and then, anxious to change the subject: "'Look's if your line was fast to somethin'."

"Fouled, I guess," said Harve, tugging. Before he pulled up he fastened the belt round him, and with deep delight heard the tip of the sheath click on the thwart. "Concern the thing!" he cried. "She acts as though she were on strawberry-bottom. It's all sand here, ain't it?"

Dan reached over and gave a judgmatic tweak. "Hollbut'll act that way 'f he's sulky. Thet's no strawberry-bottom. Yank her once or twice. She gives, sure. Guess we'd better haul up an' make certain."

They pulled together, making fast at each turn on the cleats, and the hidden weight rose sluggishly.

"Prize, oh! Haul!" shouted Dan, but the shout ended in a shrill, double shriek of horror, for out of the sea came the body of the dead Frenchman buried two days before! The hook had caught

him under the right armpit, and he swayed, erect and horrible, head and shoulders above water. His arms were tied to his side, and—he had no face. The boys fell over each other in a heap at the bottom of the dory, and there they lay while the thing bobbed alongside, held on the shortened line.

"The tide—the tide brought him!" said Harvey with quivering lips, as he fumbled at the clasp of the belt.

"Oh, Lord! Oh, Harve!" groaned Dan, "be quick. He's come for it. Let him have it. Take it off."

"I don't want it! I don't want it!" cried Harvey. "I can't find the bu-buckle."

"Quick, Harve! He's on your line!"

Harvey sat up to unfasten the belt, facing the head that had no face under its streaming hair. "He's fast still," he whispered to Dan, who slipped out his knife and cut the line, as Harvey flung the belt far overside. The body shot down with a plop, and Dan cautiously rose to his knees, whiter than the fog.

"He come for it. He come for it. I've seen a stale one hauled up on a trawl and I didn't much care, but he come to us special."

"I wish—I wish I hadn't taken the knife. Then he'd have come on your line."

"Dunno as thet would ha' made any differ. We're both scared out o' ten years' growth. Oh, Harve, did ye see his head?"

"Did I? I'll never forget it. But look at here, Dan; it couldn't have been meant. It was only the tide."

"Tide! He come for it, Harve. Why, they sunk him six miles to south'ard o' the Fleet, an' we're two miles from where she's lyin' now. They told me he was weighted with a fathom an' a half o' chain-cable."

"Wonder what he did with the knife—up on the French coast?"

"Something bad. 'Guess he's bound to take it with him to the Judgment, an' so— What are you doin' with the fish?"

"Heaving 'em overboard," said Harvey.

"What for? We sha'n't eat 'em."

"I don't care. I had to look at his face while I was takin' the belt off. You can keep your catch if you like. I've no use for mine."

Dan said nothing, but threw his fish over again.

"Guess it's best to be on the safe side," he murmured at last. "I'd give a month's pay if this fog 'u'd lift. Things go abaout in a fog that ye don't see in clear weather—yo-hoes an' hollerers and such like. I'm sorter relieved he come the way he did instid o' walkin'. He might ha' walked."

"Don't, Dan! We're right on top of him now. 'Wish I was safe aboard, hem' pounded by Uncle Salters."

"They'll be lookin' fer us in a little. Gimme the tooter." Dan took the tin dinner-horn, but paused before he blew.

Go on," said Harvey. "I don't want to stay here all night"

"Question is, haow he'd take it. There was a man frum down the coast told me once he was in a schooner where they darsen't ever blow a horn to the dories, becaze the skipper—not the man he was with, but a captain that had run her five years before—he'd drowned a boy alongside in a drunk fit; an' ever after, that boy he'd row along-side too and shout, 'Dory! dory!' with the rest."

"Dory! dory!" a muffled voice cried through the fog. They cowered again, and the horn dropped from Dan's hand.

"Hold on!" cried Harvey; "it's the cook."

"Dunno what made me think o' thet fool tale, either," said Dan. "It's the doctor, sure enough."

"Dan! Danny! Oooh, Dan! Harve! Harvey! Oooh, Haarveee!"

"We're here," sung both boys together. They heard oars, but could see nothing till the cook, shining and dripping, rowed into them.

"What iss happened?" said he. "You will be beaten at home."

"Thet's what we want. Thet's what we're sufferin' for" said Dan. "Anything homey's good enough fer us. We've had kinder depressin' company." As the cook passed them a line, Dan told him the tale.

"Yess! He come for hiss knife," was all he said at the end.

Never had the little rocking We're Here looked so deliciously home-like as when the cook, born and bred in fogs, rowed them back to her. There was a warm glow of light from the cabin and a satisfying smell of food forward, and it was heavenly to hear Disko and the others, all quite alive and solid, leaning over the rail and promising them a first-class pounding. But the cook was a black; master of strategy. He did not get the dories aboard till he had given the more striking points of the tale, explaining as he backed and bumped round the counter how Harvey was the mascot to destroy any possible bad luck. So the boys came override as rather uncanny heroes, and every one asked them questions instead of pounding them for making trouble. Little Penn delivered quite a speech on the folly of superstitions; but public opinion was against him and in favour of Long Jack, who told the most excruciating ghost-stories, till nearly midnight. Under that influence no one except Salters and Penn said anything about "idolatry," when the cook put a lighted candle, a cake of flour and water, and a pinch of salt on a shingle, and floated them out astern to keep the Frenchman quiet in case he was still restless. Dan lit the candle because he had bought the belt, and the cook grunted and muttered charms as long as he could see the ducking point of flame.

Said Harvey to Dan, as they turned in after watch:

"How about progress and Catholic superstitions?"

"Huh! I guess I'm as enlightened and progressive as the next man, but when it comes to a dead St. Malo deck-hand scarin' a couple o' pore boys stiff fer the sake of a thirty-cent knife, why, then, the cook can take hold fer all o' me. I mistrust furriners, livin' or dead."

Next morning all, except the cook, were rather ashamed of the ceremonies, and went to work double tides, speaking gruffly to one another.

The We're Here was racing neck and neck for her last few loads against the Parry Norman; and so close was the struggle that the Fleet took side and betted tobacco. All hands worked at the lines or dressing-down till they fell asleep where they stood—beginning before dawn and ending when it was too dark to see. They even used the cook as pitcher, and turned Harvey into the hold to pass salt, while Dan helped to dress down. Luckily a Parry Norman man sprained his ankle falling down the foc'sle, and the We're Heres gained. Harvey could not see how one more fish could be crammed into her, but Disko and Tom Platt stowed and stowed, and planked the mass down with big stones from the ballast, and there was always "jest another day's work." Disko did not tell them when all the salt was wetted. He rolled to the lazarette aft the cabin and began hauling out the big mainsail. This was at ten in the morning. The riding-sail was down and the main- and topsail were up by noon, and dories came alongside with letters for home, envying their good fortune. At last she cleared decks, hoisted her flag,—as is the right of the first boat off the Banks,—up-anchored, and began to move. Disko pretended that he wished to accomodate folk who had not sent in their mail, and so worked her gracefully in and out among the schooners. In reality, that was his little triumphant procession, and for the fifth year running it showed what kind of mariner he was. Dan's accordion and Tom Platt's fiddle supplied the music of the magic verse you must not sing till all the salt is wet:

"Hih! Yih! Yoho! Send your letters raound!
All our salt is wetted, an' the anchor's off the graound!
Bend, oh, bend your mains'l, we're back to Yankeeland—
 With fifteen hunder' quintal,
 An' fifteen hunder' quintal,
 'Teen hunder' toppin' quintal,
'Twix' old 'Queereau an' Grand."

The last letters pitched on deck wrapped round pieces of coal, and the Gloucester men shouted messages to their wives and womenfolks and owners, while the We're Here finished the musical ride through the Fleet, her headsails quivering like a man's hand when he raises it to say good-by.

Harvey very soon discovered that the We're Here, with her riding-sail, strolling from berth to berth, and the We're Here headed west by south under home canvas, were two very different boats. There was a bite and kick to the wheel even in "boy's" weather; he could feel the dead weight in the hold flung forward mightily across the surges, and the streaming line of bubbles overside made his eyes dizzy.

Disko kept them busy fiddling with the sails; and when those were flattened like a racing yacht's, Dan had to wait on the big topsail, which was put over by hand every time she went about. In spare moments they pumped, for the packed fish dripped brine, which does not improve a cargo. But since there was no fishing, Harvey had time to look at the sea from another point of view. The low-sided schooner was naturally on most intimate terms with her surroundings. They saw little of the horizon save when she topped a swell; and usually she was elbowing, fidgeting, and coasting her steadfast way through gray, gray-blue, or black hollows laced across and across with streaks of shivering foam; or rubbing herself caressingly along the flank of some bigger water-hill. It was as if she said: "You wouldn't hurt me, surely? I'm only the little We're Here." Then she would slide away chuckling softly to herself till she was brought up by some fresh obstacle. The dullest of folk cannot see this kind of thing hour after hour through long days without noticing it; and Harvey, being anything but dull, began to comprehend and enjoy the dry chorus of wave-tops turning over with a sound of incessant tearing; the hurry of the winds working across open spaces and herding the purple-blue cloud-shadows; the splendid upheaval of the red sunrise; the folding and packing away of the morning mists, wall after wall withdrawn across the white floors; the salty glare and blaze of noon; the kiss of rain falling over thousands of dead, flat square miles; the chilly blackening of everything at the day's end; and the million

wrinkles of the sea under the moonlight, when the jib-boom solemnly poked at the low stars, and Harvey went down to get a doughnut from the cook.

But the best fun was when the boys were put on the wheel together, Tom Platt within hail, and she cuddled her lee-rail down to the crashing blue, and kept a little home-made rainbow arching unbroken over her windlass. Then the jaws of the booms whined against the masts, and the sheets creaked, and the sails filled with roaring; and when she slid into a hollow she trampled like a woman tripped in her own silk dress, and came out, her jib wet half-way up, yearning and peering for the tall twin-lights of Thatcher's Island.

They left the cold gray of the Bank sea, saw the lumber-ships making for Quebec by the Straits of St. Lawrence, with the Jersey salt-brigs from Spain and Sicily; found a friendly northeaster off Artimon Bank that drove them within view of the East light of Sable Island,—a sight Disko did not linger over,—and stayed with them past Western and Le Have, to the northern fringe of George's. From there they picked up the deeper water, and let her go merrily.

"Hattie's pulling on the string," Dan confided to Harvey. "Hattie an' Ma. Next Sunday you'll be hirin' a boy to throw water on the windows to make ye go to sleep. 'Guess you'll keep with us till your folks come. Do you know the best of gettin' ashore again?"

"Hot bath?" said Harvey. His eyebrows were all white with dried spray.

"That's good, but a night-shirt's better. I've been dreamin' o' night-shirts ever since we bent our mainsail. Ye can wiggle your toes then. Ma'll hev a new one fer me, all washed soft. It's home, Harve. It's home! Ye can sense it in the air. We're runnin' into the aidge of a hot wave naow, an' I can smell the bayberries. Wonder if we'll get in fer supper. Port a trifle."

The hesitating sails flapped and lurched in the close air as the deep smoothed out, blue and oily, round them. When they whistled for a wind only the rain came in spiky rods, bubbling and drumming, and behind the rain the thunder and the lightning of mid-August. They lay on the deck with bare feet and arms, telling one another what they would order at their first meal ashore; for now the land was in plain sight. A Gloucester swordfish-boat drifted alongside, a man in the little pulpit on the bowsprit flourished his harpoon, his bare head plastered down with the wet. "And all's well!" he sang cheerily, as though he were watch on a big liner. "Wouverman's waiting fer you, Disko. What's the news o' the Fleet?"

Disko shouted it and passed on, while the wild summer storm pounded overhead and the lightning flickered along the capes from four different quarters at once. It gave the low circle of hills round Gloucester Harbor, Ten Pound Island, the fish-sheds, with the broken line of house-roofs, and each spar and buoy on the water, in blinding photographs that came and went a dozen times to the minute as the We're Here crawled in on half-flood, and the whistling-buoy moaned and mourned behind her. Then the storm died out in long, separated, vicious dags of blue-white flame, followed by a single roar like the roar of a mortar-battery, and the shaken air tingled under the stars as it got back to silence.

"The flag, the flag!" said Disko, suddenly, pointing upward.

"What is ut?" said Long Jack.

"Otto! Ha'af mast. They can see us frum shore now."

"I'd clean forgot. He's no folk to Gloucester, has he?"

"Girl he was goin' to be married to this fall."

"Mary pity her!" said Long Jack, and lowered the little flag half-mast for the sake of Otto, swept

overboard in a gale off Le Have three months before.

Disko wiped the wet from his eyes and led the We're Here to Wouverman's wharf, giving his orders in whispers, while she swung round moored tugs and night-watchmen hailed her from the ends of inky-black piers. Over and above the darkness and the mystery of the procession, Harvey could feel the land close round him once more, with all its thousands of people asleep, and the smell of earth after rain, and the familiar noise of a switching-engine coughing to herself in a freight-yard; and all those things made his heart beat and his throat dry up as he stood by the foresheet. They heard the anchor-watch snoring on a lighthouse-tug, nosed into a pocket of darkness where a lantern glimmered on either side; somebody waked with a grunt, threw them a rope, and they made fast to a silent wharf flanked with great iron-roofed sheds fall of warm emptiness, and lay there without a sound.

Then Harvey sat down by the wheel, and sobbed and sobbed as though his heart would break, and a tall woman who had been sitting on a weigh-scale dropped down into the schooner and kissed Dan once on the cheek; for she was his mother, and she had seen the We're Here by the lightning flashes. She took no notice of Harvey till he had recovered himself a little and Disko had told her his story. Then they went to Disko's house together as the dawn was breaking; and until the telegraph office was open and he could wire his folk, Harvey Cheyne was perhaps the loneliest boy in all America. But the curious thing was that Disko and Dan seemed to think none the worse of him for crying.

Wouverman was not ready for Disko's prices till Disko, sure that the We're Here was at least a week ahead of any other Gloucester boat, had given him a few days to swallow them; so all hands played about the streets, and Long Jack stopped the Rocky Neck trolley, on principle, as he said, till the conductor let him ride free. But Dan went about with his freckled nose in the air, bung-full of mystery and most haughty to his family.

"Dan, I'll hev to lay inter you ef you act this way," said Troop, pensively. "Sence we've come ashore this time you've bin a heap too fresh."

"I'd lay into him naow ef he was mine," said Uncle Salters, sourly. He and Penn boarded with the Troops.

"Oho!" said Dan, shuffling with the accordion round the backyard, ready to leap the fence if the enemy advanced. "Dad, you're welcome to your own judgment, but remember I've warned ye. Your own flesh an' blood ha' warned ye! 'Tain't any o' my fault ef you're mistook, but I'll be on deck to watch ye. An' ez fer yeou, Uncle Salters, Pharaoh's chief butler ain't in it 'longside o' you! You watch aout an' wait. You'll be plowed under like your own blamed clover; but me—Dan Troop—I'll flourish like a green bay-tree because I warn't stuck on my own opinion."

Disko was smoking in all his shore dignity and a pair of beautiful carpet-slippers. "You're gettin' ez crazy as poor Harve. You two go araound gigglin' an' squinchin' an' kickin' each other under the table till there's no peace in the haouse," said he.

"There's goin' to be a heap less—fer some folks," Dan replied. "You wait an' see."

He and Harvey went out on the trolley to East Gloucester, where they tramped through the bayberry bushes to the lighthouse, and lay down on the big red boulders and laughed themselves hungry. Harvey had shown Dan a telegram, and the two swore to keep silence till the shell burst.

"Harve's folk?" said Dan, with an unruffled face after supper. "Well, I guess they don't amount to much of anything, or we'd ha' heard from 'em by naow. His pop keeps a kind o' store out West. Maybe he'll give you 's much as five dollars, Dad."

"What did I tell ye?" said Salters. "Don't sputter over your vittles, Dan."

CHAPTER IX

Whatever his private sorrows may be, a multimillionaire, like any other workingman, should keep abreast of his business. Harvey Cheyne, senior, had gone East late in June to meet a woman broken down, half mad, who dreamed day and night of her son drowning in the gray seas. He had surrounded her with doctors, trained nurses, massage-women, and even faith-cure companions, but they were useless. Mrs. Cheyne lay still and moaned, or talked of her boy by the hour together to any one who would listen. Hope she had none, and who could offer it? All she needed was assurance that drowning did not hurt; and her husband watched to guard lest she should make the experiment. Of his own sorrow he spoke little—hardly realized the depth of it till he caught himself asking the calendar on his writing-desk, "What's the use of going on?"

There had always lain a pleasant notion at the back of his head that, some day, when he had rounded off everything and the boy had left college, he would take his son to his heart and lead him into his possessions. Then that boy, he argued, as busy fathers do, would instantly become his companion, partner, and ally, and there would follow splendid years of great works carried out together—the old head backing the young fire. Now his boy was dead—lost at sea, as it might have been a Swede sailor from one of Cheyne's big teaships; the wife dying, or worse; he himself was trodden down by platoons of women and doctors and maids and attendants; worried almost beyond endurance by the shift and change of her poor restless whims; hopeless, with no heart to meet his many enemies.

He had taken the wife to his raw new palace in San Diego, where she and her people occupied a wing of great price, and Cheyne, in a veranda-room, between a secretary and a typewriter, who was also a telegraphist, toiled along wearily from day to day. There was a war of rates among four Western railroads in which he was supposed to be interested; a devastating strike had developed in his lumber camps in Oregon, and the legislature of the State of California, which has no love for its makers, was preparing open war against him.

Ordinarily he would have accepted battle ere it was offered, and have waged a pleasant and unscrupulous campaign. But now he sat limply, his soft black hat pushed forward on to his nose, his big body shrunk inside his loose clothes, staring at his boots or the Chinese junks in the bay, and assenting absently to the secretary's questions as he opened the Saturday mail.

Cheyne was wondering how much it would cost to drop everything and pull out. He carried huge insurances, could buy himself royal annuities, and between one of his places in Colorado and a little society (that would do the wife good), say in Washington and the South Carolina islands, a man might forget plans that had come to nothing. On the other hand—

The click of the typewriter stopped; the girl was looking at the secretary, who had turned white.

He passed Cheyne a telegram repeated from San Francisco:

Picked up by fishing schooner We're Here having fallen off boat great times on Banks fishing all well waiting Gloucester Mass care Disko Troop for money or orders wire what shall do and how is Mama Harvey N. Cheyne.

The father let it fall, laid his head down on the roller-top of the shut desk, and breathed heavily. The secretary ran for Mrs. Cheyne's doctor who found Cheyne pacing to and fro.

"What—what d' you think of it? Is it possible? Is there any meaning to it? I can't quite make it out," he cried.

"I can," said the doctor. "I lose seven thousand a year—that's all." He thought of the struggling New York practice he had dropped at Cheyne's imperious bidding, and returned the telegram with a sigh.

"You mean you'd tell her? 'May be a fraud?'"

"What's the motive?" said the doctor, coolly. "Detection's too certain. It's the boy sure enough."

Enter a French maid, impudently, as an indispensable one who is kept on only by large wages.

"Mrs. Cheyne she say you must come at once. She think you are seek."

The master of thirty millions bowed his head meekly and followed Suzanne; and a thin, high voice on the upper landing of the great white-wood square staircase cried: "What is it? What has happened?"

No doors could keep out the shriek that rang through the echoing house a moment later, when her husband blurted out the news.

"And that's all right," said the doctor, serenely, to the typewriter. "About the only medical statement in novels with any truth to it is that joy don't kill, Miss Kinzey."

"I know it; but we've a heap to do first." Miss Kinzey was from Milwaukee, somewhat direct of speech; and as her fancy leaned towards the secretary, she divined there was work in hand. He was looking earnestly at the vast roller-map of America on the wall.

"Milsom, we're going right across. Private car—straight through—Boston. Fix the connections," shouted Cheyne down the staircase.

"I thought so."

The secretary turned to the typewriter, and their eyes met (out of that was born a story—nothing to do with this story). She looked inquiringly, doubtful of his resources. He signed to her to move to the Morse as a general brings brigades into action. Then he swept his hand musician-wise through his hair, regarded the ceiling, and set to work, while Miss Kinzey's white fingers called up the Continent of America.

"K. H. Wade, Los Angeles— The 'Constance' is at Los Angeles, isn't she, Miss Kinzey?"

"Yep." Miss Kinzey nodded between clicks as the secretary looked at his watch.

"Ready? Send 'Constance,' private car, here, and arrange for special to leave here Sunday in time to connect with New York Limited at Sixteenth Street, Chicago, Tuesday next."

Click-click-click! "Couldn't you better that?"

"Not on those grades. That gives 'em sixty hours from here to Chicago. They won't gain anything by taking a special east of that. Ready? Also arrange with Lake Shore and Michigan Southern to take 'Constance' on New York Central and Hudson River Buffalo to Albany, and B. and A. the same Albany to Boston. Indispensable I should reach Boston Wednesday evening. Be sure nothing prevents. Have also wired Canniff, Toucey, and Barnes.—Sign, Cheyne."

Miss Kinzey nodded, and the secretary went on.

"Now then. Canniff, Toucey, and Barnes, of course. Ready? Canniff, Chicago. Please take my private car 'Constance' from Santa Fe at Sixteenth Street next Tuesday p. m. on N. Y. Limited

hrough to Buffalo and deliver N. Y. C. for Albany.—Ever bin to N' York, Miss Kinzey? We'll go some day.—Ready? Take car Buffalo to Albany on Limited Tuesday p. m. That's for Toucey."

"Haven't bin to Noo York, but I know that!" with a toss of the head.

"Beg pardon. Now, Boston and Albany, Barnes, same instructions from Albany through to Boston. Leave three-five P. M. (you needn't wire that); arrive nine-five P. M. Wednesday. That covers everything Wade will do, but it pays to shake up the managers."

"It's great," said Miss Kinzey, with a look of admiration. This was the kind of man she understood and appreciated.

"'Tisn't bad," said Milsom, modestly. "Now, any one but me would have lost thirty hours and spent a week working out the run, instead of handing him over to the Santa Fe straight through to Chicago."

"But see here, about that Noo York Limited. Chauncey Depew himself couldn't hitch his car to her," Miss Kinzey suggested, recovering herself.

"Yes, but this isn't Chauncey. It's Cheyne—lightning. It goes."

"Even so. Guess we'd better wire the boy. You've forgotten that, anyhow."

"I'll ask."

When he returned with the father's message bidding Harvey meet them in Boston at an appointed hour, he found Miss Kinzey laughing over the keys. Then Milsom laughed too, for the frantic clicks from Los Angeles ran: "We want to know why-why-why? General uneasiness developed and spreading."

Ten minutes later Chicago appealed to Miss Kinzey in these words: "If crime of century is maturing please warn friends in time. We are all getting to cover here."

This was capped by a message from Topeka (and wherein Topeka was concerned even Milsom could not guess): "Don't shoot, Colonel. We'll come down."

Cheyne smiled grimly at the consternation of his enemies when the telegrams were laid before him. "They think we're on the warpath. Tell 'em we don't feel like fighting just now, Milsom. Tell 'em what we're going for. I guess you and Miss Kinsey had better come along, though it isn't likely I shall do any business on the road. Tell 'em the truth—for once."

So the truth was told. Miss Kinzey clicked in the sentiment while the secretary added the memorable quotation, "Let us have peace," and in board rooms two thousand miles away the representatives of sixty-three million dollars' worth of variously manipulated railroad interests breathed more freely. Cheyne was flying to meet the only son, so miraculously restored to him. The bear was seeking his cub, not the bulls. Hard men who had their knives drawn to fight for their financial lives put away the weapons and wished him God-speed, while half a dozen panic-smitten tin-pot toads perked up their heads and spoke of the wonderful things they would have done had not Cheyne buried the hatchet.

It was a busy week-end among the wires; for now that their anxiety was removed, men and cities hastened to accommodate. Los Angeles called to San Diego and Barstow that the Southern California engineers might know and be ready in their lonely roundhouses; Barstow passed the word to the Atlantic and Pacific; and Albuquerque flung it the whole length of the

Atchinson, Topeka, and Santa Fe management, even into Chicago. An engine, combination-car with crew, and the great and gilded "Constance" private car were to be "expedited" over those two thousand three hundred and fifty miles. The train would take precedence of one hundred and seventy-seven others meeting and passing; despatchers and crews of every one of those said trains must be notified. Sixteen locomotives, sixteen engineers, and sixteen firemen would be needed—each and every one the best available. Two and one half minutes would be allowed for changing engines, three for watering, and two for coaling. "Warn the men, and arrange tanks and chutes accordingly; for Harvey Cheyne is in a hurry, a hurry, a hurry," sang the wires. "Forty miles an hour will be expected, and division superintendents will accompany this special over their respective divisions. From San Diego to Sixteenth Street, Chicago, let the magic carpet be laid down. Hurry! Oh, hurry!"

"It will be hot," said Cheyne, as they rolled out of San Diego in the dawn of Sunday. "We're going to hurry, Mama, just as fast as ever we can; but I really don't think there's any good of your putting on your bonnet and gloves yet. You'd much better lie down and take your medicine. I'd play you a game of dominoes, but it's Sunday."

"I'll be good. Oh, I will be good. Only—taking off my bonnet makes me feel as if we'd never get there."

"Try to sleep a little, Mama, and we'll be in Chicago before you know."

"But it's Boston, Father. Tell them to hurry."

The six-foot drivers were hammering their way to San Bernardino and the Mohave wastes, but this was no grade for speed. That would come later. The heat of the desert followed the heat of the hills as they turned east to the Needles and the Colorado River. The car cracked in the utter drouth and glare, and they put crushed ice to Mrs. Cheyne's neck, and toiled up the long, long grades, past Ash Fork, towards Flagstaff, where the forests and quarries are, under the dry, remote skies. The needle of the speed-indicator flicked and wagged to and fro; the cinders rattled on the roof, and a whirl of dust sucked after the whirling wheels. The crew of the combination sat on their bunks, panting in their shirtsleeves, and Cheyne found himself among them shouting old, old stories of the railroad that every trainman knows, above the roar of the car. He told them about his son, and how the sea had given up its dead, and they nodded and spat and rejoiced with him; asked after "her, back there," and whether she could stand it if the engineer "let her out a piece," and Cheyne thought she could. Accordingly, the great fire-horse was "let 'ut" from Flagstaff to Winslow, till a division superintendent protested.

But Mrs. Cheyne, in the boudoir stateroom, where the French maid, sallow-white with fear, clung to the silver door-handle, only moaned a little and begged her husband to bid them "hurry." And so they dropped the dry sands and moon-struck rocks of Arizona behind them, and grilled on till the crash of the couplings and the wheeze of the brake-hose told them they were at Coolidge by the Continental Divide.

Three bold and experienced men—cool, confident, and dry when they began; white, quivering, and wet when they finished their trick at those terrible wheels—swung her over the great lift from Albuquerque to Glorietta and beyond Springer, up and up to the Raton Tunnel on the State line, whence they dropped rocking into La Junta, had sight of the Arkansaw, and tore down the long slope to Dodge City, where Cheyne took comfort once again from setting his watch an hour ahead.

There was very little talk in the car. The secretary and typewriter sat together on the stamped Spanish-leather cushions by the plate-glass observation-window at the rear end, watching the surge and ripple of the ties crowded back behind them, and, it is believed, making notes of the

scenery. Cheyne moved nervously between his own extravagant gorgeousness and the naked necessity of the combination, an unlit cigar in his teeth, till the pitying crews forgot that he was their tribal enemy, and did their best to entertain him.

At night the bunched electrics lit up that distressful palace of all the luxuries, and they fared sumptuously, swinging on through the emptiness of abject desolation.

Now they heard the swish of a water-tank, and the guttural voice of a Chinaman, the click-clink of hammers that tested the Krupp steel wheels, and the oath of a tramp chased off the rear-platform; now the solid crash of coal shot into the tender; and now a beating back of noises as they flew past a waiting train. Now they looked out into great abysses, a trestle purring beneath their tread, or up to rocks that barred out half the stars. Now scour and ravine changed and rolled back to jagged mountains on the horizon's edge, and now broke into hills lower and lower, till at last came the true plains.

At Dodge City an unknown hand threw in a copy of a Kansas paper containing some sort of an interview with Harvey, who had evidently fallen in with an enterprising reporter, telegraphed on from Boston. The joyful journalese revealed that it was beyond question their boy, and it soothed Mrs. Cheyne for a while. Her one word "hurry" was conveyed by the crews to the engineers at Nickerson, Topeka, and Marceline, where the grades are easy, and they brushed the Continent behind them. Towns and villages were close together now, and a man could feel here that he moved among people.

"I can't see the dial, and my eyes ache so. What are we doing?"

"The very best we can, Mama. There's no sense in getting in before the Limited. We'd only have to wait."

"I don't care. I want to feel we're moving. Sit down and tell me the miles."

Cheyne sat down and read the dial for her (there were some miles which stand for records to this day), but the seventy-foot car never changed its long steamer-like roll, moving through the heat with the hum of a giant bee. Yet the speed was not enough for Mrs. Cheyne; and the heat, the remorseless August heat, was making her giddy; the clock-hands would not move, and when, oh, when would they be in Chicago?

It is not true that, as they changed engines at Fort Madison, Cheyne passed over to the Amalgamated Brotherhood of Locomotive Engineers an endowment sufficient to enable them to fight him and his fellows on equal terms for evermore. He paid his obligations to engineers and firemen as he believed they deserved, and only his bank knows what he gave the crews who had sympathized with him. It is on record that the last crew took entire charge of switching operations at Sixteenth Street, because "she" was in a doze at last, and Heaven was to help any one who bumped her.

Now the highly paid specialist who conveys the Lake Shore and Michigan Southern Limited from Chicago to Elkhart is something of an autocrat, and he does not approve of being told how to back up to a car. None the less he handled the "Constance" as if she might have been a load of dynamite, and when the crew rebuked him, they did it in whispers and dumb show.

"Pshaw!" said the Atchinson, Topeka, and Santa Fe men, discussing life later, "we weren't runnin' for a record. Harvey Cheyne's wife, she were sick back, an' we didn't want to jounce her. 'Come to think of it, our runnin' time from San Diego to Chicago was 57.54. You can tell that to them Eastern way-trains. When we're tryin' for a record, we'll let you know."

To the Western man (though this would not please either city) Chicago and Boston are cheek by jowl, and some railroads encourage the delusion. The Limited whirled the "Constance" into Buffalo and the arms of the New York Central and Hudson River (illustrious magnates with white whiskers and gold charms on their watch-chains boarded her here to talk a little business to Cheyne), who slid her gracefully into Albany, where the Boston and Albany completed the run from tide-water to tide-water—total time, eighty-seven hours and thirty-five minutes, or three days, fifteen hours and one half. Harvey was waiting for them.

After violent emotion most people and all boys demand food. They feasted the returned prodigal behind drawn curtains, cut off in their great happiness, while the trains roared in and out around them. Harvey ate, drank, and enlarged on his adventures all in one breath, and when he had a hand free his mother fondled it. His voice was thickened with living in the open, salt air; his palms were rough and hard, his wrists dotted with marks of gurrysores; and a fine full flavour of codfish hung round rubber boots and blue jersey.

The father, well used to judging men, looked at him keenly. He did not know what enduring harm the boy might have taken. Indeed, he caught himself thinking that he knew very little whatever of his son; but he distinctly remembered an unsatisfied, dough-faced youth who took delight in "calling down the old man," and reducing his mother to tears—such a person as adds to the gaiety of public rooms and hotel piazzas, where the ingenuous young of the wealthy play with or revile the bell-boys. But this well set-up fisher-youth did not wriggle, looked at him with eyes steady, clear, and unflinching, and spoke in a tone distinctly, even startlingly, respectful. There was that in his voice, too, which seemed to promise that the change might be permanent, and that the new Harvey had come to stay.

"Some one's been coercing him," thought Cheyne. "Now Constance would never have allowed that. Don't see as Europe could have done it any better."

"But why didn't you tell this man, Troop, who you were?" the mother repeated, when Harvey had expanded his story at least twice.

"Disko Troop, dear. The best man that ever walked a deck. I don't care who the next is."

"Why didn't you tell him to put you ashore? You know Papa would have made it up to him ten times over."

"I know it; but he thought I was crazy. I'm afraid I called him a thief because I couldn't find the bills in my pocket."

"A sailor found them by the flagstaff that—that night," sobbed Mrs. Cheyne.

"That explains it, then. I don't blame Troop any. I just said I wouldn't work—on a Banker, too—and of course he hit me on the nose, and oh! I bled like a stuck hog."

"My poor darling! They must have abused you horribly."

"Dunno quite. Well, after that, I saw a light."

Cheyne slapped his leg and chuckled. This was going to be a boy after his own hungry heart. He had never seen precisely that twinkle in Harvey's eye before.

"And the old man gave me ten and a half a month; he's paid me half now; and I took hold with Dan and pitched right in. I can't do a man's work yet. But I can handle a dory 'most as well as Dan, and I don't get rattled in a fog—much; and I can take my trick in light winds—that's steering, dear—and I can 'most bait up a trawl, and I know my ropes, of course; and I can pitch

fish till the cows come home, and I'm great on old Josephus, and I'll show you how I can clear coffee with a piece of fish-skin, and—I think I'll have another cup, please. Say, you've no notion what a heap of work there is in ten and a half a month!"

"I began with eight and a half, my son," said Cheyne.

"That so? You never told me, sir."

"You never asked, Harve. I'll tell you about it some day, if you care to listen. Try a stuffed olive."

"Troop says the most interesting thing in the world is to find out how the next man gets his vittles. It's great to have a trimmed-up meal again. We were well fed, though. But mug on the Banks. Disko fed us first-class. He's a great man. And Dan—that's his son—Dan's my partner. And there's Uncle Salters and his manures, an' he reads Josephus. He's sure I'm crazy yet. And there's poor little Penn, and he is crazy. You mustn't talk to him about Johnstown, because—

"And, oh, you must know Tom Platt and Long Jack and Manuel. Manuel saved my life. I'm sorry he's a Portuguee. He can't talk much, but he's an everlasting musician. He found me struck adrift and drifting, and hauled me in."

"I wonder your nervous system isn't completely wrecked," said Mrs. Cheyne.

"What for, Mama? I worked like a horse and I ate like a hog and I slept like a dead man."

That was too much for Mrs. Cheyne, who began to think of her visions of a corpse rocking on the salty seas. She went to her stateroom, and Harvey curled up beside his father, explaining his indebtedness.

"You can depend upon me to do everything I can for the crowd, Harve. They seem to be good men on your showing."

"Best in the Fleet, sir. Ask at Gloucester," said Harvey. "But Disko believes still he's cured me of being crazy. Dan's the only one I've let on to about you, and our private cars and all the rest of it, and I'm not quite sure Dan believes. I want to paralyze 'em to-morrow. Say, can't they run the 'Constance' over to Gloucester? Mama don't look fit to be moved, anyway, and we're bound to finish cleaning out by tomorrow. Wouverman takes our fish. You see, we're the first off the Banks this season, and it's four twenty-five a quintal. We held out till he paid it. They want it quick."

"You mean you'll have to work to-morrow, then?"

"I told Troop I would. I'm on the scales. I've brought the tallies with me." He looked at the greasy notebook with an air of importance that made his father choke. "There isn't but three—no—two ninety-four or five quintal more by my reckoning."

"Hire a substitute," suggested Cheyne, to see what Harvey would say.

"Can't, sir. I'm tally-man for the schooner. Troop says I've a better head for figures than Dan. Troop's a mighty just man."

"Well, suppose I don't move the 'Constance' to-night, how'll you fix it?"

Harvey looked at the clock, which marked twenty past eleven.

"Then I'll sleep here till three and catch the four o'clock freight. They let us men from the Fleet ride free as a rule."

"That's a notion. But I think we can get the 'Constance' around about as soon as your men's freight. Better go to bed now."

Harvey spread himself on the sofa, kicked off his boots, and was asleep before his father could shade the electrics. Cheyne sat watching the young face under the shadow of the arm thrown over the forehead, and among many things that occurred to him was the notion that he might perhaps have been neglectful as a father.

"One never knows when one's taking one's biggest risks," he said. "It might have been worse than drowning; but I don't think it has—I don't think it has. If it hasn't, I haven't enough to pay Troop, that's all; and I don't think it has."

Morning brought a fresh sea breeze through the windows, the "Constance" was side-tracked among freight-cars at Gloucester, and Harvey had gone to his business.

"Then he'll fall overboard again and be drowned," the mother said bitterly.

"We'll go and look, ready to throw him a rope in case. You've never seen him working for his bread," said the father.

"What nonsense! As if any one expected—"

"Well, the man that hired him did. He's about right, too."

They went down between the stores full of fishermen's oilskins to Wouverman's wharf where the We're Here rode high, her Bank flag still flying, all hands busy as beavers in the glorious morning light. Disko stood by the main hatch superintending Manuel, Penn, and Uncle Salters at the tackle. Dan was swinging the loaded baskets inboard as Long Jack and Tom Platt filled them, and Harvey, with a notebook, represented the skipper's interests before the clerk of the scales on the salt-sprinkled wharf-edge.

"Ready!" cried the voices below. "Haul!" cried Disko. "Hi!" said Manuel. "Here!" said Dan, swinging the basket. Then they heard Harvey's voice, clear and fresh, checking the weights.

The last of the fish had been whipped out, and Harvey leaped from the string-piece six feet to a ratline, as the shortest way to hand Disko the tally, shouting, "Two ninety-seven, and an empty hold!"

"What's the total, Harve?" said Disko.

"Eight sixty-five. Three thousand six hundred and seventy-six dollars and a quarter. 'Wish I'd share as well as wage."

"Well, I won't go so far as to say you hevn't deserved it, Harve. Don't you want to slip up to Wouverman's office and take him our tallies?"

"Who's that boy?" said Cheyne to Dan, well used to all manner of questions from those idle imbeciles called summer boarders.

"Well, he's kind o' supercargo," was the answer. "We picked him up struck adrift on the Banks. Fell overboard from a liner, he sez. He was a passenger. He's by way o' hem' a fisherman now."

"Is he worth his keep?"

"Ye-ep. Dad, this man wants to know ef Harve's worth his keep. Say, would you like to go aboard? We'll fix up a ladder for her."

"I should very much, indeed. 'Twon't hurt you, Mama, and you'll be able to see for yourself."

The woman who could not lift her head a week ago scrambled down the ladder, and stood aghast amid the mess and tangle aft.

"Be you anyways interested in Harve?" said Disko.

"Well, ye-es."

"He's a good boy, an' ketches right hold jest as he's bid. You've heard haow we found him? He was sufferin' from nervous prostration, I guess, 'r else his head had hit somethin', when we hauled him aboard. He's all over that naow. Yes, this is the cabin. 'Tain't in order, but you're quite welcome to look araound. Those are his figures on the stove-pipe, where we keep the reckonin' mostly."

"Did he sleep here?" said Mrs. Cheyne, sitting on a yellow locker and surveying the disorderly bunks.

"No. He berthed forward, madam, an' only fer him an' my boy hookin' fried pies an muggin' up when they ought to ha' been asleep, I dunno as I've any special fault to find with him."

"There weren't nothin' wrong with Harve," said Uncle Salters, descending the steps. "He hung my boots on the main-truck, and he ain't over an' above respectful to such as knows more'n he do, specially about farmin'; but he were mostly misled by Dan."

Dan in the meantime, profiting by dark hints from Harvey early that morning, was executing a war-dance on deck. "Tom, Tom!" he whispered down the hatch. "His folks has come, an' Dad hain't caught on yet, an' they're pow-wowin' in the cabin. She's a daisy, an' he's all Harve claimed he was, by the looks of him."

"Howly Smoke!" said Long Jack, climbing out covered with salt and fish-skin. "D'ye belave his tale av the kid an' the little four-horse rig was thrue?"

"I knew it all along," said Dan. "Come an' see Dad mistook in his judgments."

They came delightedly, just in time to hear Cheyne say: "I'm glad he has a good character, because—he's my son."

Disko's jaw fell,—Long Jack always vowed that he heard the click of it,—and he stared alternately at the man and the woman.

"I got his telegram in San Diego four days ago, and we came over."

"In a private car?" said Dan. "He said ye might."

"In a private car, of course."

Dan looked at his father with a hurricane of irreverent winks.

"There was a tale he told us av drivin' four little ponies in a rig av his own," said Long Jack. "Was that thrue now?"

"Very likely," said Cheyne. "Was it, Mama?"

"He had a little drag when we were in Toledo, I think," said the mother.

Long Jack whistled. "Oh, Disko!" said he, and that was all.

"I wuz—I am mistook in my jedgments—worse'n the men o' Marblehead," said Disko, as though the words were being windlassed out of him. "I don't mind ownin' to you, Mr. Cheyne, as I mistrusted the boy to be crazy. He talked kinder odd about money."

"So he told me."

"Did he tell ye anything else? 'Cause I pounded him once." This with a somewhat anxious glance at Mrs. Cheyne.

"Oh, yes," Cheyne replied. "I should say it probably did him more good than anything else in the world."

"I jedged 'twuz necessary, er I wouldn't ha' done it. I don't want you to think we abuse our boys any on this packet."

"I don't think you do, Mr. Troop."

Mrs. Cheyne had been looking at the faces—Disko's ivory-yellow, hairless, iron countenance; Uncle Salters's, with its rim of agricultural hair; Penn's bewildered simplicity; Manuel's quiet smile; Long Jack's grin of delight, and Tom Platt's scar. Rough, by her standards, they certainly were; but she had a mother's wits in her eyes, and she rose with out-stretched hands.

"Oh, tell me, which is who?" said she, half sobbing. "I want to thank you and bless you—all of you."

"Faith, that pays me a hunder time," said Long Jack.

Disko introduced them all in due form. The captain of an old-time Chinaman could have done no better, and Mrs. Cheyne babbled incoherently. She nearly threw herself into Manuel's arms when she understood that he had first found Harvey.

"But how shall I leave him dreeft?" said poor Manuel. "What do you yourself if you find him so? Eh, wha-at? We are in one good boy, and I am ever so pleased he come to be your son."

"And he told me Dan was his partner!" she cried. Dan was already sufficiently pink, but he turned a rich crimson when Mrs. Cheyne kissed him on both cheeks before the assembly. Then they led her forward to show her the foc'sle, at which she wept again, and must needs go down to see Harvey's identical bunk, and there she found the nigger cook cleaning up the stove, and he nodded as though she were some one he had expected to meet for years. They tried, two at a time, to explain the boat's daily life to her, and she sat by the pawl-post, her gloved hands on the greasy table, laughing with trembling lips and crying with dancing eyes.

"And who's ever to use the We're Here after this?" said Long Jack to Tom Platt. "I feel as if she'd made a cathedral av ut all."

"Cathedral!" sneered Tom Platt. "Oh, if it had bin even the Fish C'mmission boat instid of this bally-hoo o' blazes. If we only hed some decency an' order an' side-boys when she goes over! She'll have to climb that ladder like a hen, an' we—we ought to be mannin' the yards!"

"Then Harvey was not mad," said Penn, slowly, to Cheyne.

"No, indeed—thank God," the big millionaire replied, stooping down tenderly.

"It must be terrible to be mad. Except to lose your child, I do not know anything more terrible. But your child has come back? Let us thank God for that."

"Hello!" cried Harvey, looking down upon them benignly from the wharf.

"I wuz mistook, Harve. I wuz mistook," said Disko, swiftly, holding up a hand. "I wuz mistook in my jedgments. Ye needn't rub in any more."

"Guess I'll take care o' that," said Dan, under his breath.

"You'll be goin' off naow, won't ye?"

"Well, not without the balance of my wages, 'less you want to have the We're Here attached."

"Thet's so; I'd clean forgot"; and he counted out the remaining dollars. "You done all you contracted to do, Harve; and you done it 'baout's well as if you'd been brought up—" Here Disko brought himself up. He did not quite see where the sentence was going to end.

"Outside of a private car?" suggested Dan, wickedly.

"Come on, and I'll show her to you," said Harvey.

Cheyne stayed to talk with Disko, but the others made a procession to the depot, with Mrs. Cheyne at the head. The French maid shrieked at the invasion; and Harvey laid the glories of the "Constance" before them without a word. They took them in in equal silence—stamped leather, silver door-handles and rails, cut velvet, plate-glass, nickel, bronze, hammered iron, and the rare woods of the continent inlaid.

"I told you," said Harvey; "I told you." This was his crowning revenge, and a most ample one.

Mrs. Cheyne decreed a meal, and that nothing might be lacking to the tale Long Jack told afterwards in his boarding-house, she waited on them herself. Men who are accustomed to eat at tiny tables in howling gales have curiously neat and finished manners; but Mrs. Cheyne, who did not know this, was surprised. She longed to have Manuel for a butler; so silently and easily did he comport himself among the frail glassware and dainty silver. Tom Platt remembered the great days on the Ohio and the manners of foreign potentates who dined with the officers; and Long Jack, being Irish, supplied the small talk till all were at their ease.

In the We're Here's cabin the fathers took stock of each other behind their cigars. Cheyne knew well enough when he dealt with a man to whom he could not offer money; equally well he knew that no money could pay for what Disko had done. He kept his own counsel and waited for an opening.

"I hevn't done anything to your boy or fer your boy excep' make him work a piece an' learn him how to handle the hog-yoke," said Disko. "He has twice my boy's head for figgers."

"By the way," Cheyne answered casually, "what d'you calculate to make of your boy?"

Disko removed his cigar and waved it comprehensively round the cabin. "Dan's jest plain boy, an' he don't allow me to do any of his thinkin'. He'll hev this able little packet when I'm laid by. He ain't noways anxious to quit the business. I know that."

"Mmm! 'Ever been West, Mr. Troop?"

"'Bin's fer ez Noo York once in a boat. I've no use for railroads. No more hez Dan. Salt water's good enough fer the Troops. I've been 'most everywhere—in the nat'ral way, o' course."

"I can give him all the salt water he's likely to need—till he's a skipper."

"Haow's that? I thought you wuz a kinder railroad king. Harve told me so when—I was mistook in my jedgments."

"We're all apt to be mistaken. I fancied perhaps you might know I own a line of tea-clippers—San Francisco to Yokohama—six of 'em—iron-built, about seventeen hundred and eighty tons apiece.

"Blame that boy! He never told. I'd ha' listened to that, instid o' his truck abaout railroads an' pony-carriages."

"He didn't know."

"'Little thing like that slipped his mind, I guess."

"No, I only capt—took hold of the 'Blue M.' freighters—Morgan and McQuade's old line—this summer." Disko collapsed where he sat, beside the stove.

"Great Caesar Almighty! I mistrust I've been fooled from one end to the other. Why, Phil Airheart he went from this very town six year back—no, seven—an' he's mate on the San Jose—now—twenty-six days was her time out. His sister she's livin' here yet, an' she reads his letters to my woman. An' you own the 'Blue M.' freighters?"

Cheyne nodded.

"If I'd known that I'd ha' jerked the We're Here back to port all standin', on the word."

"Perhaps that wouldn't have been so good for Harvey."

"If I'd only known! If he'd only said about the cussed Line, I'd ha' understood! I'll never stand on my own jedgments again—never. They're well-found packets. Phil Airheart he says so."

"I'm glad to have a recommend from that quarter. Airheart's skipper of the San Jose now. What I was getting at is to know whether you'd lend me Dan for a year or two, and we'll see if we can't make a mate of him. Would you trust him to Airheart?"

"It's a resk taking a raw boy—"

"I know a man who did more for me."

"That's diff'runt. Look at here naow, I ain't recommendin' Dan special because he's my own flesh an' blood. I know Bank ways ain't clipper ways, but he hain't much to learn. Steer he can—no boy better, if I say it—an' the rest's in our blood an' get; but I could wish he warn't so cussed weak on navigation."

"Airheart will attend to that. He'll ship as boy for a voyage or two, and then we can put him in the way of doing better. Suppose you take him in hand this winter, and I'll send for him early in the spring. I know the Pacific's a long ways off—"

"Pshaw! We Troops, livin' an' dead, are all around the earth an' the seas thereof."

"But I want you to understand—and I mean this—any time you think you'd like to see him, tell me, and I'll attend to the transportation. 'Twon't cost you a cent."

"If you'll walk a piece with me, we'll go to my house an' talk this to my woman. I've bin so crazy mistook in all my jedgments, it don't seem to me this was like to be real."

They went blue-trimmed of nasturtiums over to Troop's eighteen-hundred-dollar, white house, with a retired dory full in the front yard and a shuttered parlour which was a museum of oversea plunder. There sat a large woman, silent and grave, with the dim eyes of those who look long to sea for the return of their beloved. Cheyne addressed himself to her, and she gave consent wearily.

"We lose one hundred a year from Gloucester only, Mr. Cheyne," she said—"one hundred boys an' men; and I've come so's to hate the sea as if 'twuz alive an' listenin'. God never made it fer humans to anchor on. These packets o' yours they go straight out, I take it' and straight home again?"

"As straight as the winds let 'em, and I give a bonus for record passages. Tea don't improve by being at sea."

"When he wuz little he used to play at keeping store, an' I had hopes he might follow that up. But soon's he could paddle a dory I knew that were goin' to be denied me."

"They're square-riggers, Mother; iron-built an' well found. Remember what Phil's sister reads you when she gits his letters."

"I've never known as Phil told lies, but he's too venturesome (like most of 'em that use the sea). If Dan sees fit, Mr. Cheyne, he can go—fer all o' me."

"She jest despises the ocean," Disko explained, "an' I—I dunno haow to act polite, I guess, er I'd thank you better."

"My father—my own eldest brother—two nephews—an' my second sister's man," she said, dropping her head on her hand. "Would you care fer any one that took all those?"

Cheyne was relieved when Dan turned up and accepted with more delight than he was able to put into words. Indeed, the offer meant a plain and sure road to all desirable things; but Dan thought most of commanding watch on broad decks, and looking into far-away harbours.

Mrs. Cheyne had spoken privately to the unaccountable Manuel in the matter of Harvey's rescue. He seemed to have no desire for money. Pressed hard, he said that he would take five dollars, because he wanted to buy something for a girl. Otherwise—"How shall I take money when I make so easy my eats and smokes? You will giva some if I like or no? Eh, wha-at? Then you shall giva me money, but not that way. You shall giva all you can think." He introduced her to a snuffy Portuguese priest with a list of semi-destitute widows as long as his cassock. As a strict Unitarian, Mrs. Cheyne could not sympathize with the creed, but she ended by respecting the brown, voluble little man.

Manuel, faithful son of the Church, appropriated all the blessings showered on her for her charity. "That letta me out," said he. "I have now ver' good absolutions for six months"; and he strolled forth to get a handkerchief for the girl of the hour and to break the hearts of all the others.

Salters went West for a season with Penn, and left no address behind. He had a dread that these millinary people, with wasteful private cars, might take undue interest in his companion. It was

better to visit inland relatives till the coast was clear. "Never you be adopted by rich folk, Penn," he said in the cars, "or I'll take 'n' break this checker-board over your head. Ef you forgit your name agin—which is Pratt—you remember you belong with Salters Troop, an' set down right where you are till I come fer you. Don't go taggin' araound after them whose eyes bung out with fatness, accordin' to Scripcher."

CHAPTER X

But it was otherwise with the We're Here's silent cook, for he came up, his kit in a handkerchief, and boarded the "Constance." Pay was no particular object, and he did not in the least care where he slept. His business, as revealed to him in dreams, was to follow Harvey for the rest of his days. They tried argument and, at last, persuasion; but there is a difference between one Cape Breton and two Alabama negroes, and the matter was referred to Cheyne by the cook and porter. The millionaire only laughed. He presumed Harvey might need a body-servant some day or other, and was sure that one volunteer was worth five hirelings. Let the man stay, therefore; even though he called himself MacDonald and swore in Gaelic. The car could go back to Boston, where, if he were still of the same mind, they would take him West.

With the "Constance," which in his heart of hearts he loathed, departed the last remnant of Cheyne's millionairedom, and he gave himself up to an energetic idleness. This Gloucester was a new town in a new land, and he purposed to "take it in," as of old he had taken in all the cities from Snohomish to San Diego of that world whence he hailed. They made money along the crooked street which was half wharf and half ship's store: as a leading professional he wished to learn how the noble game was played. Men said that four out of every five fish-balls served at New England's Sunday breakfast came from Gloucester, and overwhelmed him with figures in proof—statistics of boats, gear, wharf-frontage, capital invested, salting, packing, factories, insurance, wages, repairs, and profits. He talked with the owners of the large fleets whose skippers were little more than hired men, and whose crews were almost all Swedes or Portuguese. Then he conferred with Disko, one of the few who owned their craft, and compared notes in his vast head. He coiled himself away on chain-cables in marine junk-shops, asking questions with cheerful, unslaked Western curiosity, till all the water-front wanted to know "what in thunder that man was after, anyhow." He prowled into the Mutual Insurance rooms, and demanded explanations of the mysterious remarks chalked up on the blackboard day by day; and that brought down upon him secretaries of every Fisherman's Widow and Orphan Aid Society within the city limits. They begged shamelessly, each man anxious to beat the other institution's record, and Cheyne tugged at his beard and handed them all over to Mrs. Cheyne.

She was resting in a boarding-house near Eastern Point—a strange establishment, managed, apparently, by the boarders, where the table-cloths were red-and-white-checkered and the population, who seemed to have known one another intimately for years, rose up at midnight to make Welsh rarebits if it felt hungry. On the second morning of her stay Mrs. Cheyne put away her diamond solitaires before she came down to breakfast.

"They're most delightful people," she confided to her husband; "so friendly and simple, too, though they are all Boston, nearly."

"That isn't simpleness, Mama," he said, looking across the boulders behind the apple-trees where the hammocks were slung. "It's the other thing, that what I haven't got."

"It can't be," said Mrs. Cheyne quietly. "There isn't a woman here owns a dress that cost a hundred dollars. Why, we—"

"I know it, dear. We have—of course we have. I guess it's only the style they wear East. Are you having a good time?"

"I don't see very much of Harvey; he's always with you; but I ain't near as nervous as I was."

"I haven't had such a good time since Willie died. I never rightly understood that I had a son

before this. Harve's got to be a great boy. 'Anything I can fetch you, dear? 'Cushion under your head? Well, we'll go down to the wharf again and look around."

Harvey was his father's shadow in those days, and the two strolled along side by side, Cheyne using the grades as an excuse for laying his hand on the boy's square shoulder. It was then that Harvey noticed and admired what had never struck him before—his father's curious power of getting at the heart of new matters as learned from men in the street.

"How d'you make 'em tell you everything without opening your head?" demanded the son, as they came out of a rigger's loft.

"I've dealt with quite a few men in my time, Harve, and one sizes 'em up somehow, I guess. I know something about myself, too." Then, after a pause, as they sat down on a wharf-edge: "Men can 'most always tell when a man has handled things for himself, and then they treat him as one of themselves."

"Same as they treat me down at Wouverman's wharf. I'm one of the crowd now. Disko has told every one I've earned my pay." Harvey spread out his hands and rubbed the palms together. "They're all soft again," he said dolefully.

"Keep 'em that way for the next few years, while you're getting your education. You can harden 'em up after."

"Ye-es, I suppose so," was the reply, in no delighted voice.

"It rests with you, Harve. You can take cover behind your mama, of course, and put her on to fussing about your nerves and your high-strungness and all that kind of poppycock."

"Have I ever done that?" said Harvey, uneasily.

His father turned where he sat and thrust out a long hand. "You know as well as I do that I can't make anything of you if you don't act straight by me. I can handle you alone if you'll stay alone, but I don't pretend to manage both you and Mama. Life's too short, anyway."

"Don't make me out much of a fellow, does it?"

"I guess it was my fault a good deal; but if you want the truth, you haven't been much of anything up to date. Now, have you?"

"Umm! Disko thinks . . . Say, what d'you reckon it's cost you to raise me from the start—first, last and all over?"

Cheyne smiled. "I've never kept track, but I should estimate, in dollars and cents, nearer fifty than forty thousand; maybe sixty. The young generation comes high. It has to have things, and it tires of 'em, and—the old man foots the bill."

Harvey whistled, but at heart he was rather pleased to think that his upbringing had cost so much. "And all that's sunk capital, isn't it?"

"Invested, Harve. Invested, I hope."

"Making it only thirty thousand, the thirty I've earned is about ten cents on the hundred. That's a mighty poor catch." Harvey wagged his head solemnly.

Cheyne laughed till he nearly fell off the pile into the water.

"Disko has got a heap more than that out of Dan since he was ten; and Dan's at school half the year, too."

"Oh, that's what you're after, is it?"

"No. I'm not after anything. I'm not stuck on myself any just now—that's all. . . . I ought to be kicked."

"I can't do it, old man; or I would, I presume, if I'd been made that way."

"Then I'd have remembered it to the last day I lived—and never forgiven you," said Harvey, his chin on his doubled fists.

"Exactly. That's about what I'd do. You see?"

"I see. The fault's with me and no one else. All the same, something's got to be done about it."

Cheyne drew a cigar from his vest-pocket, bit off the end, and fell to smoking. Father and son were very much alike; for the beard hid Cheyne's mouth, and Harvey had his father's slightly aquiline nose, close-set black eyes, and narrow, high cheek-bones. With a touch of brown paint he would have made up very picturesquely as a Red Indian of the story-books.

"Now you can go on from here," said Cheyne, slowly, "costing me between six or eight thousand a year till you're a voter. Well, we'll call you a man then. You can go right on from that, living on me to the tune of forty or fifty thousand, besides what your mother will give you, with a valet and a yacht or a fancy-ranch where you can pretend to raise trotting-stock and play cards with your own crowd."

"Like Lorry Tuck?" Harvey put in.

"Yep; or the two De Vitre boys or old man McQuade's son. California's full of 'em, and here's an Eastern sample while we're talking."

A shiny black steam-yacht, with mahogany deck-house, nickel-plated binnacles, and pink-and-white-striped awnings puffed up the harbour, flying the burgee of some New York club. Two young men in what they conceived to be sea costumes were playing cards by the saloon skylight; and a couple of women with red and blue parasols looked on and laughed noisily.

"Shouldn't care to be caught out in her in any sort of a breeze. No beam," said Harvey, critically, as the yacht slowed to pick up her mooring-buoy.

"They're having what stands them for a good time. I can give you that, and twice as much as that, Harve. How'd you like it?"

"Caesar! That's no way to get a dinghy overside," said Harvey, still intent on the yacht. "If I couldn't slip a tackle better than that I'd stay ashore. . . . What if I don't?"

"Stay ashore—or what?"

"Yacht and ranch and live on 'the old man,' and—get behind Mama where there's trouble," said Harvey, with a twinkle in his eye.

"Why, in that case, you come right in with me, my son."

"Ten dollars a month?" Another twinkle.

"Not a cent more until you're worth it, and you won't begin to touch that for a few years."

"I'd sooner begin sweeping out the office—isn't that how the big bugs start?—and touch something now than—"

"I know it; we all feel that way. But I guess we can hire any sweeping we need. I made the same mistake myself of starting in too soon."

"Thirty million dollars' worth o' mistake, wasn't it? I'd risk it for that."

"I lost some; and I gained some. I'll tell you."

Cheyne pulled his beard and smiled as he looked over the still water, and spoke away from Harvey, who presently began to be aware that his father was telling the story of his life. He talked in a low, even voice, without gesture and without expression; and it was a history for which a dozen leading journals would cheerfully have paid many dollars—the story of forty years that was at the same time the story of the New West, whose story is yet to be written.

It began with a kinless boy turned loose in Texas, and went on fantastically through a hundred changes and chops of life, the scenes shifting from State after Western State, from cities that sprang up in a month and—in a season utterly withered away, to wild ventures in wilder camps that are now laborious, paved municipalities. It covered the building of three railroads and the deliberate wreck of a fourth. It told of steamers, townships, forests, and mines, and the men of every nation under heaven, manning, creating, hewing, and digging these. It touched on chances of gigantic wealth flung before eyes that could not see, or missed by the merest accident of time and travel; and through the mad shift of things, sometimes on horseback, more often afoot, now rich, now poor, in and out, and back and forth, deck-hand, train-hand, contractor, boarding-house keeper, journalist, engineer, drummer, real-estate agent, politician, dead-beat, rum-seller, mine-owner, speculator, cattle-man, or tramp, moved Harvey Cheyne, alert and quiet, seeking his own ends, and, so he said, the glory and advancement of his country.

He told of the faith that never deserted him even when he hung on the ragged edge of despair— the faith that comes of knowing men and things. He enlarged, as though he were talking to himself, on his very great courage and resource at all times. The thing was so evident in the man's mind that he never even changed his tone. He described how he had bested his enemies, or forgiven them, exactly as they had bested or forgiven him in those careless days; how he had entreated, cajoled, and bullied towns, companies, and syndicates, all for their enduring good; crawled round, through, or under mountains and ravines, dragging a string and hoop-iron railroad after him, and in the end, how he had sat still while promiscuous communities tore the last fragments of his character to shreds.

The tale held Harvey almost breathless, his head a little cocked to one side, his eyes fixed on his father's face, as the twilight deepened and the red cigar-end lit up the furrowed cheeks and heavy eyebrows. It seemed to him like watching a locomotive storming across country in the dark—a mile between each glare of the open fire-door: but this locomotive could talk, and the words shook and stirred the boy to the core of his soul. At last Cheyne pitched away the cigar-butt, and the two sat in the dark over the lapping water.

"I've never told that to any one before," said the father.

Harvey gasped. "It's just the greatest thing that ever was!" said he.

"That's what I got. Now I'm coming to what I didn't get. It won't sound much of anything to you, but I don't wish you to be as old as I am before you find out. I can handle men, of course,

and I'm no fool along my own lines, but—but—I can't compete with the man who has been taught! I've picked up as I went along, and I guess it sticks out all over me."

"I've never seen it," said the son, indignantly.

"You will, though, Harve. You will—just as soon as you're through college. Don't I know it? Don't I know the look on men's faces when they think me a—a 'mucker,' as they call it out here? I can break them to little pieces—yes—but I can't get back at 'em to hurt 'em where they live. I don't say they're 'way 'way up, but I feel I'm 'way, 'way, 'way off, somehow. Now you've got your chance. You've got to soak up all the learning that's around, and you'll live with a crowd that are doing the same thing. They'll be doing it for a few thousand dollars a year at most; but remember you'll be doing it for millions. You'll learn law enough to look after your own property when I'm out o' the light, and you'll have to be solid with the best men in the market (they are useful later); and above all, you'll have to stow away the plain, common, sit-down-with-your chin-on your-elbows book-learning. Nothing pays like that, Harve, and it's bound to pay more and more each year in our country—in business and in politics. You'll see."

"There's no sugar in my end of the deal," said Harvey. "Four years at college! 'Wish I'd chosen the valet and the yacht!"

"Never mind, my son," Cheyne insisted. "You're investing your capital where it'll bring in the best returns; and I guess you won't find our property shrunk any when you're ready to take hold. Think it over, and let me know in the morning. Hurry! We'll be late for supper!"

As this was a business talk, there was no need for Harvey to tell his mother about it; and Cheyne naturally took the same point of view. But Mrs. Cheyne saw and feared, and was a little jealous. Her boy, who rode rough-shod over her, was gone, and in his stead reigned a keen-faced youth, abnormally silent, who addressed most of his conversation to his father. She understood it was business, and therefore a matter beyond her premises. If she had any doubts, they were resolved when Cheyne went to Boston and brought back a new diamond marquise ring.

"What have you two been doing now?" she said, with a weak little smile, as she turned it in the light.

"Talking—just talking, Mama; there's nothing mean about Harvey."

There was not. The boy had made a treaty on his own account. Railroads, he explained gravely, interested him as little as lumber, real estate, or mining. What his soul yearned after was control of his father's newly purchased sailing-ship. If that could be promised him within what he conceived to be a reasonable time, he, for his part, guaranteed diligence and sobriety at college for four or five years. In vacation he was to be allowed full access to all details connected with the line—he had not asked more than two thousand questions about it,—from his father's most private papers in the safe to the tug in San Francisco harbour.

"It's a deal," said Cheyne at the last. "You'll alter your mind twenty times before you leave college, o' course; but if you take hold of it in proper shape, and if you don't tie it up before you're twenty-three, I'll make the thing over to you. How's that, Harve?"

"Nope; never pays to split up a going concern. There's too much competition in the world anyway, and Disko says 'blood-kin hev to stick together.' His crowd never go back on him. That's one reason, he says, why they make such big fares. Say, the We're Here goes off to the Georges on Monday. They don't stay long ashore, do they?"

"Well, we ought to be going, too, I guess. I've left my business hung up at loose ends between

two oceans, and it's time to connect again. I just hate to do it, though; haven't had a holiday like this for twenty years."

"We can't go without seeing Disko off," said Harvey; "and Monday's Memorial Day. Let's stay over that, anyway."

"What is this memorial business? They were talking about it at the boarding-house," said Cheyne weakly. He, too, was not anxious to spoil the golden days.

"Well, as far as I can make out, this business is a sort of song-and-dance act, whacked up for the summer boarders. Disko don't think much of it, he says, because they take up a collection for the widows and orphans. Disko's independent. Haven't you noticed that?"

"Well—yes. A little. In spots. Is it a town show, then?"

"The summer convention is. They read out the names of the fellows drowned or gone astray since last time, and they make speeches, and recite, and all. Then, Disko says, the secretaries of the Aid Societies go into the back yard and fight over the catch. The real show, he says, is in the spring. The ministers all take a hand then, and there aren't any summer boarders around."

"I see," said Cheyne, with the brilliant and perfect comprehension of one born into and bred up to city pride. "We'll stay over for Memorial Day, and get off in the afternoon."

"Guess I'll go down to Disko's and make him bring his crowd up before they sail. I'll have to stand with them, of course."

"Oh, that's it, is it," said Cheyne. "I'm only a poor summer boarder, and you're—"

"A Banker—full-blooded Banker," Harvey called back as he boarded a trolley, and Cheyne went on with his blissful dreams for the future.

Disko had no use for public functions where appeals were made for charity, but Harvey pleaded that the glory of the day would be lost, so far as he was concerned, if the We're Heres absented themselves. Then Disko made conditions. He had heard—it was astonishing how all the world knew all the world's business along the water-front—he had heard that a "Philadelphia actress-woman" was going to take part in the exercises; and he mistrusted that she would deliver "Skipper Ireson's Ride." Personally, he had as little use for actresses as for summer boarders; but justice was justice, and though he himself (here Dan giggled) had once slipped up on a matter of judgment, this thing must not be. So Harvey came back to East Gloucester, and spent half a day explaining to an amused actress with a royal reputation on two seaboards the inwardness of the mistake she contemplated; and she admitted that it was justice, even as Disko had said.

Cheyne knew by old experience what would happen; but anything of the nature of a public palaver was meat and drink to the man's soul. He saw the trolleys hurrying west, in the hot, hazy morning, full of women in light summer dresses, and white-faced straw-hatted men fresh from Boston desks; the stack of bicycles outside the post office; the come-and-go of busy officials, greeting one another; the slow flick and swash of bunting in the heavy air; and the important man with a hose sluicing the brick sidewalk.

"Mother," he said suddenly, "don't you remember—after Seattle was burned out—and they got her going again?"

Mrs. Cheyne nodded, and looked critically down the crooked street. Like her husband, she understood these gatherings, all the West over, and compared them one against another. The fishermen began to mingle with the crowd about the town-hall doors—blue-jowled Portuguese,

their women bare-headed or shawled for the most part; clear-eyed Nova Scotians, and men of the Maritime Provinces; French, Italians, Swedes, and Danes, with outside crews of coasting schooners; and everywhere women in black, who saluted one another with gloomy pride, for this was their day of great days. And there were ministers of many creeds,—pastors of great, gilt-edged congregations, at the seaside for a rest, with shepherds of the regular work,—from the priests of the Church on the Hill to bush-bearded ex-sailor Lutherans, hail-fellow with the men of a score of boats. There were owners of lines of schooners, large contributors to the societies, and small men, their few craft pawned to the mastheads, with bankers and marine-insurance agents, captains of tugs and water-boats, riggers, fitters, lumpers, salters, boat-builders, and coopers, and all the mixed population of the water-front.

They drifted along the line of seats made gay with the dresses of the summer boarders, and one of the town officials patrolled and perspired till he shone all over with pure civic pride. Cheyne had met him for five minutes a few days before, and between the two there was entire understanding.

"Well, Mr. Cheyne, and what d'you think of our city?—Yes, madam, you can sit anywhere you please.—You have this kind of thing out West, I presume?"

"Yes, but we aren't as old as you."

"That's so, of course. You ought to have been at the exercises when we celebrated our two hundred and fiftieth birthday. I tell you, Mr. Cheyne, the old city did herself credit."

"So I heard. It pays, too. What's the matter with the town that it don't have a first-class hotel, though?"

"—Right over there to the left, Pedro. Heaps o' room for you and your crowd.—Why, that's what I tell 'em all the time, Mr. Cheyne. There's big money in it, but I presume that don't affect you any. What we want is—"

A heavy hand fell on his broadcloth shoulder, and the flushed skipper of a Portland coal-and-ice coaster spun him half round. "What in thunder do you fellows mean by clappin' the law on the town when all decent men are at sea this way? Heh? Town's dry as a bone, an' smells a sight worse sence I quit. 'Might ha' left us one saloon for soft drinks, anyway."

"Don't seem to have hindered your nourishment this morning, Carsen. I'll go into the politics of it later. Sit down by the door and think over your arguments till I come back."

"What good is arguments to me? In Miquelon champagne's eighteen dollars a case and—" The skipper lurched into his seat as an organ-prelude silenced him.

"Our new organ," said the official proudly to Cheyne. "Cost us four thousand dollars, too. We'll have to get back to high-license next year to pay for it. I wasn't going to let the ministers have all the religion at their convention. Those are some of our orphans standing up to sing. My wife taught 'em. See you again later, Mr. Cheyne. I'm wanted on the platform."

High, clear, and true, children's voices bore down the last noise of those settling into their places.

"O all ye Works of the Lord, bless ye the Lord: praise him and magnify him for ever!"

The women throughout the hall leaned forward to look as the reiterated cadences filled the air. Mrs. Cheyne, with some others, began to breathe short; she had hardly imagined there were so many widows in the world; and instinctively searched for Harvey. He had found the We're

Heres at the back of the audience, and was standing, as by right, between Dan and Disko. Uncle Salters, returned the night before with Penn, from Pamlico Sound, received him suspiciously.

"Hain't your folk gone yet?" he grunted. "What are you doin' here, young feller?"

"O ye Seas and Floods, bless ye the Lord: praise him, and magnify him for ever!"

"Hain't he good right?" said Dan. "He's bin there, same as the rest of us."

"Not in them clothes," Salters snarled.

"Shut your head, Salters," said Disko. "Your bile's gone back on you. Stay right where ye are, Harve."

Then up and spoke the orator of the occasion, another pillar of the municipality, bidding the world welcome to Gloucester, and incidentally pointing out wherein Gloucester excelled the rest of the world. Then he turned to the sea-wealth of the city, and spoke of the price that must be paid for the yearly harvest. They would hear later the names of their lost dead one hundred and seventeen of them. (The widows stared a little, and looked at one another here.) Gloucester could not boast any overwhelming mills or factories. Her sons worked for such wage as the sea gave; and they all knew that neither Georges nor the Banks were cow-pastures. The utmost that folk ashore could accomplish was to help the widows and the orphans, and after a few general remarks he took this opportunity of thanking, in the name of the city, those who had so public-spiritedly consented to participate in the exercises of the occasion.

"I jest despise the beggin' pieces in it," growled Disko. "It don't give folk a fair notion of us."

"Ef folk won't be fore-handed an' put by when they've the chance," returned Salters, "it stands in the nature o' things they hev to be 'shamed. You take warnin' by that, young feller. Riches endureth but for a season, ef you scatter them araound on lugsuries—"

"But to lose everything, everything," said Penn. "What can you do then? Once I"—the watery blue eyes stared up and down as if looking for something to steady them—"once I read—in a book, I think—of a boat where every one was run down—except some one—and he said to me—"

"Shucks!" said Salters, cutting in. "You read a little less an' take more int'rust in your vittles, and you'll come nearer earnin' your keep, Penn."

Harvey, jammed among the fishermen, felt a creepy, crawly, tingling thrill that began in the back of his neck and ended at his boots. He was cold, too, though it was a stifling day.

"That the actress from Philadelphia?" said Disko Troop, scowling at the platform. "You've fixed it about old man Ireson, hain't ye, Harve? Ye know why naow."

It was not "Ireson's Ride" that the woman delivered, but some sort of poem about a fishing-port called Brixham and a fleet of trawlers beating in against storm by night, while the women made a guiding fire at the head of the quay with everything they could lay hands on.

"They took the grandma's blanket,
Who shivered and bade them go;
They took the baby's cradle,
Who could not say them no."

"Whew!" said Dan, peering over Long Jack's shoulder. "That's great! Must ha' bin expensive, though."

"Ground-hog case," said the Galway man. "Badly lighted port, Danny."

* * * * * *

"And knew not all the while
If they were lighting a bonfire
Or only a funeral pile."

The wonderful voice took hold of people by their heartstrings; and when she told how the drenched crews were flung ashore, living and dead, and they carried the bodies to the glare of the fires, asking: "Child, is this your father?" or "Wife, is this your man?" you could hear hard breathing all over the benches.

"And when the boats of Brixham
Go out to face the gales,
Think of the love that travels
Like light upon their sails!"

There was very little applause when she finished. The women were looking for their handkerchiefs, and many of the men stared at the ceiling with shiny eyes.

"H'm," said Salters; "that 'u'd cost ye a dollar to hear at any theatre—maybe two. Some folk, I presoom, can afford it. 'Seems downright waste to me. . . . Naow, how in Jerusalem did Cap. Bart Edwardes strike adrift here?"

"No keepin' him under," said an Eastport man behind. "He's a poet, an' he's baound to say his piece. 'Comes from daown aour way, too."

He did not say that Captain B. Edwardes had striven for five consecutive years to be allowed to recite a piece of his own composition on Gloucester Memorial Day. An amused and exhausted committee had at last given him his desire. The simplicity and utter happiness of the old man, as he stood up in his very best Sunday clothes, won the audience ere he opened his mouth. They sat unmurmuring through seven-and-thirty hatchet-made verses describing at fullest length the loss of the schooner Joan Hasken off the Georges in the gale of 1867, and when he came to an end they shouted with one kindly throat.

A far-sighted Boston reporter slid away for a full copy of the epic and an interview with the author; so that earth had nothing more to offer Captain Bart Edwardes, ex-whaler, shipwright, master-fisherman, and poet, in the seventy-third year of his age.

"Naow, I call that sensible," said the Eastport man. "I've bin over that graound with his writin', jest as he read it, in my two hands, and I can testify that he's got it all in."

"If Dan here couldn't do better'n that with one hand before breakfast, he ought to be switched," said Salters, upholding the honor of Massachusetts on general principles. "Not but what I'm free to own he's considerable litt'ery—fer Maine. Still—"

"Guess Uncle Salters's goin' to die this trip. Fust compliment he's ever paid me," Dan sniggered. "What's wrong with you, Harve? You act all quiet and you look greenish. Feelin' sick?"

"Don't know what's the matter with me," Harvey implied. "Seems if my insides were too big for my outsides. I'm all crowded up and shivery."

"Dispepsy? Pshaw—too bad. We'll wait for the readin', an' then we'll quit, an' catch the tide."

The widows—they were nearly all of that season's making—braced themselves rigidly like

people going to be shot in cold blood, for they knew what was coming. The summer-boarder girls in pink and blue shirt-waists stopped tittering over Captain Edwardes's wonderful poem, and looked back to see why all was silent. The fishermen pressed forward as that town official who had talked to Cheyne bobbed up on the platform and began to read the year's list of losses, dividing them into months. Last September's casualties were mostly single men and strangers, but his voice rang very loud in the stillness of the hall.

"September 9th. Schooner Florrie Anderson lost, with all aboard, off the Georges.

"Reuben Pitman, master, 50, single, Main Street, City.

"Emil Olsen, 19, single, 329 Hammond Street, City. Denmark.

"Oscar Standberg, single, 25. Sweden.

"Carl Stanberg, single, 28, Main Street. City.

"Pedro, supposed Madeira, single, Keene's boardinghouse. City.

"Joseph Welsh, alias Joseph Wright, 30, St. John's, Newfoundland."

"No—Augusty, Maine," a voice cried from the body of the hall.

"He shipped from St. John's," said the reader, looking to see.

"I know it. He belongs in Augusty. My nevvy."

The reader made a pencilled correction on the margin of the list, and resumed.

"Same schooner, Charlie Ritchie, Liverpool, Nova Scotia, 33, single.

"Albert May, 267 Rogers Street, City, 27, single.

"September 27th.—Orvin Dollard, 30, married, drowned in dory off Eastern Point."

That shot went home, for one of the widows flinched where she sat, clasping and unclasping her hands. Mrs. Cheyne, who had been listening with wide-opened eyes, threw up her head and choked. Dan's mother, a few seats to the right, saw and heard and quickly moved to her side. The reading went on. By the time they reached the January and February wrecks the shots were falling thick and fast, and the widows drew breath between their teeth.

"February 14th.—Schooner Harry Randolph dismasted on the way home from Newfoundland; Asa Musie, married, 32, Main Street, City, lost overboard.

"February 23d.—Schooner Gilbert Hope; went astray in dory, Robert Beavon, 29, married, native of Pubnico, Nova Scotia."

But his wife was in the hall. They heard a low cry, as though a little animal had been hit. It was stifled at once, and a girl staggered out of the hall. She had been hoping against hope for months, because some who have gone adrift in dories have been miraculously picked up by deep-sea sailing-ships. Now she had her certainty, and Harvey could see the policeman on the sidewalk hailing a hack for her. "It's fifty cents to the depot"—the driver began, but the policeman held up his hand—"but I'm goin' there anyway. Jump right in. Look at here, Al; you don't pull me next time my lamps ain't lit. See?"

The side-door closed on the patch of bright sunshine, and Harvey's eyes turned again to the

reader and his endless list.

"April 19th.—Schooner Mamie Douglas lost on the Banks with all hands.

"Edward Canton, 43, master, married, City.

"D. Hawkins, alias Williams, 34, married, Shelbourne, Nova Scotia.

"G. W. Clay, coloured, 28, married, City."

And so on, and so on. Great lumps were rising in Harvey's throat, and his stomach reminded him of the day when he fell from the liner.

"May 10th.—Schooner We're Here [the blood tingled all over him] Otto Svendson, 20, single, City, lost overboard."

Once more a low, tearing cry from somewhere at the back of the hall.

"She shouldn't ha' come. She shouldn't ha' come," said Long Jack, with a cluck of pity.

"Don't scrowge, Harve," grunted Dan. Harvey heard that much, but the rest was all darkness spotted with fiery wheels. Disko leaned forward and spoke to his wife, where she sat with one arm round Mrs. Cheyne, and the other holding down the snatching, catching, ringed hands.

"Lean your head daown—right daown!" he whispered. "It'll go off in a minute."

"I ca-an't! I do-don't! Oh, let me—" Mrs. Cheyne did not at all know what she said.

"You must," Mrs. Troop repeated. "Your boy's jest fainted dead away. They do that some when they're gettin' their growth. 'Wish to tend to him? We can git aout this side. Quite quiet. You come right along with me. Psha', my dear, we're both women, I guess. We must tend to aour men-folk. Come!"

The We're Heres promptly went through the crowd as a body-guard, and it was a very white and shaken Harvey that they propped up on a bench in an anteroom.

"Favours his ma," was Mrs. Troop's only comment, as the mother bent over her boy.

"How d'you suppose he could ever stand it?" she cried indignantly to Cheyne, who had said nothing at all. "It was horrible—horrible! We shouldn't have come. It's wrong and wicked! It—it isn't right! Why—why couldn't they put these things in the papers, where they belong? Are you better, darling?"

That made Harvey very properly ashamed. "Oh, I'm all right, I guess," he said, struggling to his feet, with a broken giggle. "Must ha' been something I ate for breakfast."

"Coffee, perhaps," said Cheyne, whose face was all in hard lines, as though it had been cut out of bronze. "We won't go back again."

"Guess 'twould be 'baout's well to git daown to the wharf," said Disko. "It's close in along with them Dagoes, an' the fresh air will fresh Mrs. Cheyne up."

Harvey announced that he never felt better in his life; but it was not till he saw the We're Here, fresh from the lumper's hands, at Wouverman's wharf, that he lost his all-overish feelings in a queer mixture of pride and sorrowfulness. Other people—summer boarders and such-like— played about in cat-boats or looked at the sea from pier-heads; but he understood things from

the inside—more things than he could begin to think about. None the less, he could have sat down and howled because the little schooner was going off. Mrs. Cheyne simply cried and cried every step of the way and said most extraordinary things to Mrs. Troop, who "babied" her till Dan, who had not been "babied" since he was six, whistled aloud.

And so the old crowd—Harvey felt like the most ancient of mariners dropped into the old schooner among the battered dories, while Harvey slipped the stern-fast from the pier-head, and they slid her along the wharf-side with their hands. Every one wanted to say so much that no one said anything in particular. Harvey bade Dan take care of Uncle Salters's sea-boots and Penn's dory-anchor, and Long Jack entreated Harvey to remember his lessons in seamanship; but the jokes fell flat in the presence of the two women, and it is hard to be funny with green harbour-water widening between good friends.

"Up jib and fores'l!" shouted Disko, getting to the wheel, as the wind took her. "See you later, Harve. Dunno but I come near thinkin' a heap o' you an' your folks."

Then she glided beyond ear-shot, and they sat down to watch her up the harbour, And still Mrs. Cheyne wept.

"Pshaw, my dear," said Mrs. Troop: "we're both women, I guess. Like's not it'll ease your heart to hev your cry aout. God He knows it never done me a mite o' good, but then He knows I've had something to cry fer!"

Now it was a few years later, and upon the other edge of America, that a young man came through the clammy sea fog up a windy street which is flanked with most expensive houses built of wood to imitate stone. To him, as he was standing by a hammered iron gate, entered on horseback—and the horse would have been cheap at a thousand dollars—another young man. And this is what they said:

"Hello, Dan!"

"Hello, Harve!"

"What's the best with you?"

"Well, I'm so's to be that kind o' animal called second mate this trip. Ain't you most through with that triple invoiced college of yours?"

"Getting that way. I tell you, the Leland Stanford Junior, isn't a circumstance to the old We're Here; but I'm coming into the business for keeps next fall."

"Meanin' aour packets?"

"Nothing else. You just wait till I get my knife into you, Dan. I'm going to make the old line lie down and cry when I take hold."

"I'll resk it," said Dan, with a brotherly grin, as Harvey dismounted and asked whether he were coming in.

"That's what I took the cable fer; but, say, is the doctor anywheres araound? I'll draown that crazy nigger some day, his one cussed joke an' all."

There was a low, triumphant chuckle, as the ex-cook of the We're Here came out of the fog to take the horse's bridle. He allowed no one but himself to attend to any of Harvey's wants.

"Thick as the Banks, ain't it, doctor?" said Dan, propitiatingly.

But the coal-black Celt with the second-sight did not see fit to reply till he had tapped Dan on the shoulder, and for the twentieth time croaked the old, old prophecy in his ear.

"Master—man. Man—master," said he. "You remember, Dan Troop, what I said? On the We're Here?"

"Well, I won't go so far as to deny that it do look like it as things stand at present," said Dan. "She was a noble packet, and one way an' another I owe her a heap—her and Dad."

'Me too," quoth Harvey Cheyne.

KIM

CHAPTER I

O ye who tread the Narrow Way
By Tophet-flare to Judgment Day,
Be gentle when "the heathen" pray
To Buddha at Kamakura!

He sat, in defiance of municipal orders, astride the gun Zam Zammah on her brick platform opposite the old Ajaib-Gher—the Wonder House, as the natives call the Lahore Museum. Who hold Zam-Zammah, that "fire-breathing dragon", hold the Punjab, for the great green-bronze piece is always first of the conqueror's loot.

There was some justification for Kim—he had kicked Lala Dinanath's boy off the trunnions—since the English held the Punjab and Kim was English. Though he was burned black as any native; though he spoke the vernacular by preference, and his mother-tongue in a clipped uncertain sing-song; though he consorted on terms of perfect equality with the small boys of the bazar; Kim was white—a poor white of the very poorest. The half-caste woman who looked after him (she smoked opium, and pretended to keep a second-hand furniture shop by the square where the cheap cabs wait) told the missionaries that she was Kim's mother's sister; but his mother had been nursemaid in a Colonel's family and had married Kimball O'Hara, a young colour-sergeant of the Mavericks, an Irish regiment. He afterwards took a post on the Sind, Punjab, and Delhi Railway, and his Regiment went home without him. The wife died of cholera in Ferozepore, and O'Hara fell to drink and loafing up and down the line with the keen-eyed three-year-old baby. Societies and chaplains, anxious for the child, tried to catch him, but O'Hara drifted away, till he came across the woman who took opium and learned the taste from her, and died as poor whites die in India. His estate at death consisted of three papers—one he called his "ne varietur" because those words were written below his signature thereon, and another his "clearance-certificate". The third was Kim's birth-certificate. Those things, he was used to say, in his glorious opium-hours, would yet make little Kimball a man. On no account was Kim to part with them, for they belonged to a great piece of magic—such magic as men practised over yonder behind the Museum, in the big blue-and-white Jadoo-Gher—the Magic House, as we name the Masonic Lodge. It would, he said, all come right some day, and Kim's horn would be exalted between pillars—monstrous pillars—of beauty and strength. The Colonel himself, riding on a horse, at the head of the finest Regiment in the world, would attend to Kim—little Kim that should have been better off than his father. Nine hundred first-class devils, whose God was a Red Bull on a green field, would attend to Kim, if they had not forgotten O'Hara—poor O'Hara that was gang-foreman on the Ferozepore line. Then he would weep bitterly in the broken rush chair on the veranda. So it came about after his death that the woman sewed parchment, paper, and birth-certificate into a leather amulet-case which she strung round Kim's neck.

"And some day," she said, confusedly remembering O'Hara's prophecies, "there will come for you a great Red Bull on a green field, and the Colonel riding on his tall horse, yes, and" dropping into English—"nine hundred devils."

"Ah," said Kim, "I shall remember. A Red Bull and a Colonel on a horse will come, but first, my father said, will come the two men making ready the ground for these matters. That is how my father said they always did; and it is always so when men work magic."

If the woman had sent Kim up to the local Jadoo-Gher with those papers, he would, of course, have been taken over by the Provincial Lodge, and sent to the Masonic Orphanage in the Hills; but what she had heard of magic she distrusted. Kim, too, held views of his own. As he reached the years of indiscretion, he learned to avoid missionaries and white men of serious aspect who asked who he was, and what he did. For Kim did nothing with an immense success. True, he knew the wonderful walled city of Lahore from the Delhi Gate to the outer Fort Ditch; was hand in glove with men who led lives stranger than anything Haroun al Raschid dreamed of; and he lived in a life wild as that of the Arabian Nights, but missionaries and secretaries of charitable societies could not see the beauty of it. His nickname through the wards was "Little Friend of all the World"; and very often, being lithe and inconspicuous, he executed commissions by night on the crowded housetops for sleek and shiny young men of fashion. It was intrigue,—of course he knew that much, as he had known all evil since he could speak,—but what he loved was the game for its own sake—the stealthy prowl through the dark gullies and lanes, the crawl up a waterpipe, the sights and sounds of the women's world on the flat roofs, and the headlong flight from housetop to housetop under cover of the hot dark. Then there were holy men, ash-smeared faquirs by their brick shrines under the trees at the riverside, with whom he was quite familiar—greeting them as they returned from begging-tours, and, when no one was by, eating from the same dish. The woman who looked after him insisted with tears that he should wear European clothes—trousers, a shirt and a battered hat. Kim found it easier to slip into Hindu or Mohammedan garb when engaged on certain businesses. One of the young men of fashion—he who was found dead at the bottom of a well on the night of the earthquake—had once given him a complete suit of Hindu kit, the costume of a lowcaste street boy, and Kim stored it in a secret place under some baulks in Nila Ram's timber-yard, beyond the Punjab High Court, where the fragrant deodar logs lie seasoning after they have driven down the Ravi. When there was business or frolic afoot, Kim would use his properties, returning at dawn to the veranda, all tired out from shouting at the heels of a marriage procession, or yelling at a Hindu festival. Sometimes there was food in the house, more often there was not, and then Kim went out again to eat with his native friends.

As he drummed his heels against Zam-Zammah he turned now and again from his king-of-the-castle game with little Chota Lal and Abdullah the sweetmeat-seller's son, to make a rude remark to the native policeman on guard over rows of shoes at the Museum door. The big Punjabi grinned tolerantly: he knew Kim of old. So did the water-carrier, sluicing water on the dry road from his goat-skin bag. So did Jawahir Singh, the Museum carpenter, bent over new packing-cases. So did everybody in sight except the peasants from the country, hurrying up to the Wonder House to view the things that men made in their own province and elsewhere. The Museum was given up to Indian arts and manufactures, and anybody who sought wisdom could ask the Curator to explain.

"Off! Off! Let me up!" cried Abdullah, climbing up Zam-Zammah's wheel.

"Thy father was a pastry-cook, Thy mother stole the ghi," sang Kim. "All Mussalmans fell off Zam-Zammah long ago!"

"Let me up!" shrilled little Chota Lal in his gilt-embroidered cap. His father was worth perhaps half a million sterling, but India is the only democratic land in the world.

"The Hindus fell off Zam-Zammah too. The Mussalmans pushed them off. Thy father was a pastry-cook—"

He stopped; for there shuffled round the corner, from the roaring Motee Bazar, such a man as Kim, who thought he knew all castes, had never seen. He was nearly six feet high, dressed in fold upon fold of dingy stuff like horse-blanketing, and not one fold of it could Kim refer to any

known trade or profession. At his belt hung a long open-work iron pencase and a wooden rosary such as holy men wear. On his head was a gigantic sort of tam-o'-shanter. His face was yellow and wrinkled, like that of Fook Shing, the Chinese bootmaker in the bazar. His eyes turned up at the corners and looked like little slits of onyx.

"Who is that?" said Kim to his companions.

"Perhaps it is a man," said Abdullah, finger in mouth, staring.

"Without doubt," returned Kim; "but he is no man of India that I have ever seen."

"A priest, perhaps," said Chota Lal, spying the rosary. "See! He goes into the Wonder House!"

"Nay, nay," said the policeman, shaking his head. "I do not understand your talk." The constable spoke Punjabi. "O Friend of all the World, what does he say?"

"Send him hither," said Kim, dropping from Zam-Zammah, flourishing his bare heels. "He is a foreigner, and thou art a buffalo."

The man turned helplessly and drifted towards the boys. He was old, and his woollen gaberdine still reeked of the stinking artemisia of the mountain passes.

"O Children, what is that big house?" he said in very fair Urdu.

"The Ajaib-Gher, the Wonder House!" Kim gave him no title—such as Lala or Mian. He could not divine the man's creed.

"Ah! The Wonder House! Can any enter?"

"It is written above the door—all can enter."

"Without payment?"

"I go in and out. I am no banker," laughed Kim.

"Alas! I am an old man. I did not know." Then, fingering his rosary, he half turned to the Museum.

"What is your caste? Where is your house? Have you come far?" Kim asked.

"I came by Kulu—from beyond the Kailas—but what know you? From the Hills where"—he sighed—"the air and water are fresh and cool."

"Aha! Khitai [a Chinaman]," said Abdullah proudly. Fook Shing had once chased him out of his shop for spitting at the joss above the boots.

"Pahari [a hillman]," said little Chota Lal.

"Aye, child—a hillman from hills thou'lt never see. Didst hear of Bhotiyal [Tibet]? I am no Khitai, but a Bhotiya [Tibetan], since you must know—a lama—or, say, a guru in your tongue."

"A guru from Tibet," said Kim. "I have not seen such a man. They be Hindus in Tibet, then?"

"We be followers of the Middle Way, living in peace in our lamasseries, and I go to see the Four Holy Places before I die. Now do you, who are children, know as much as I do who am old." He smiled benignantly on the boys.

"Hast thou eaten?"

He fumbled in his bosom and drew forth a worn, wooden begging-bowl. The boys nodded. All priests of their acquaintance begged.

"I do not wish to eat yet." He turned his head like an old tortoise in the sunlight. "Is it true that there are many images in the Wonder House of Lahore?" He repeated the last words as one making sure of an address.

"That is true," said Abdullah. "It is full of heathen būts. Thou also art an idolater."

"Never mind him," said. Kim. "That is the Government's house and there is no idolatry in it, but only a Sahib with a white beard. Come with me and I will show."

"Strange priests eat boys," whispered Chota Lal.

"And he is a stranger and a būt-parast (idolater)," said Abdullah, the Mohammedan.

Kim laughed. "He is new. Run to your mothers' laps, and be safe. Come!"

Kim clicked round the self-registering turnstile; the old man followed and halted amazed. In the entrance-hall stood the larger figures of the Greco-Buddhist sculptures done, savants know how long since, by forgotten workmen whose hands were feeling, and not unskilfully, for the mysteriously transmitted Grecian touch. There were hundreds of pieces, friezes of figures in relief, fragments of statues and slabs crowded with figures that had encrusted the brick walls of the Buddhist stupas and viharas of the North Country and now, dug up and labelled, made the pride of the Museum. In open-mouthed wonder the lama turned to this and that, and finally checked in rapt attention before a large alto-relief representing a coronation or apotheosis of the Lord Buddha. The Master was represented seated on a lotus the petals of which were so deeply undercut as to show almost detached. Round Him was an adoring hierarchy of kings, elders, and old-time Buddhas. Below were lotus-covered waters with fishes and water-birds. Two butterfly-winged devas held a wreath over His head; above them another pair supported an umbrella surmounted by the jewelled headdress of the Bodhisat.

"The Lord! The Lord! It is Sakya Muni himself," the lama half sobbed; and under his breath began the wonderful Buddhist invocation:

"To Him the Way,—the Law,—Apart—
Whom Maya held beneath her heart,
Ananda's Lord—the Bodhisat."

"And He is here! The Most Excellent Law is here also. My pilgrimage is well begun. And what work! What work!"

"Yonder is the Sahib." said Kim, and dodged sideways among the cases of the arts and manufacturers wing. A white-bearded Englishman was looking at the lama, who gravely turned and saluted him and after some fumbling drew forth a note-book and a scrap of paper.

"Yes, that is my name," smiling at the clumsy, childish print.

"One of us who had made pilgrimage to the Holy Places—he is now Abbot of the Lung-Cho Monastery—gave it me," stammered the lama. "He spoke of these." His lean hand moved tremulously round.

"Welcome, then, O lama from Tibet. Here be the images, and I am here"—he glanced at the

lama's face—"to gather knowledge. Come to my office awhile." The old man was trembling with excitement.

The office was but a little wooden cubicle partitioned off from the sculpture-lined gallery. Kim laid himself down, his ear against a crack in the heat-split cedar door, and, following his instinct, stretched out to listen and watch.

Most of the talk was altogether above his head. The lama, haltingly at first, spoke to the Curator of his own lamassery, the Such-zen, opposite the Painted Rocks, four months' march away. The Curator brought out a huge book of photos and showed him that very place, perched on its crag, overlooking the gigantic valley of many-hued strata.

"Ay, ay!" The lama mounted a pair of horn-rimmed spectacles of Chinese work. "Here is the little door through which we bring wood before winter. And thou—the English know of these things? He who is now Abbot of Lung-Cho told me, but I did not believe. The Lord—the Excellent One—He has honour here too? And His life is known?"

"It is all carven upon the stones. Come and see, if thou art rested."

Out shuffled the lama to the main hall, and, the Curator beside him, went through the collection with the reverence of a devotee and the appreciative instinct of a craftsman.

Incident by incident in the beautiful story he identified on the blurred stone, puzzled here and there by the unfamiliar Greek convention, but delighted as a child at each new trove. Where the sequence failed, as in the Annunciation, the Curator supplied it from his mound of books— French and German, with photographs and reproductions.

Here was the devout Asita, the pendant of Simeon in the Christian story, holding the Holy Child on his knee while mother and father listened; and here were incidents in the legend of the cousin Devadatta. Here was the wicked woman who accused the Master of impurity, all confounded; here was the teaching in the Deer-park; the miracle that stunned the fire-worshippers; here was the Bodhisat in royal state as a prince; the miraculous birth; the death at Kusinagara, where the weak disciple fainted; while there were almost countless repetitions of the meditation under the Bodhi tree; and the adoration of the alms-bowl was everywhere. In a few minutes the Curator saw that his guest was no mere bead-telling mendicant, but a scholar of parts. And they went at it all over again, the lama taking snuff, wiping his spectacles, and talking at railway speed in a bewildering mixture of Urdu and Tibetan. He had heard of the travels of the Chinese pilgrims, Fu-Hiouen and Hwen-Tsiang, and was anxious to know if there was any translation of their record. He drew in his breath as he turned helplessly over the pages of Beal and Stanislas Julien. "'Tis all here. A treasure locked." Then he composed himself reverently to listen to fragments hastily rendered into Urdu. For the first time he heard of the labours of European scholars, who by the help of these and a hundred other documents have identified the Holy Places of Buddhism. Then he was shown a mighty map, spotted and traced with yellow. The brown finger followed the Curator's pencil from point to point. Here was Kapilavastu, here the Middle Kingdom, and here Mahabodhi, the Mecca of Buddhism; and here was Kusinagara, sad place of the Holy One's death. The old man bowed his head over the sheets in silence for a while, and the Curator lit another pipe. Kim had fallen asleep. When he waked, the talk, still in spate, was more within his comprehension.

"And thus it was, O Fountain of Wisdom, that I decided to go to the Holy Places which His foot had trod—to the Birthplace, even to Kapila; then to Mahabodhi, which is Buddh Gaya—to the Monastery—to the Deer-park—to the place of His death."

The lama lowered his voice. "And I come here alone. For five—seven—eighteen—forty years it

was in my mind that the Old Law was not well followed; being overlaid, as thou knowest, with devildom, charms, and idolatry. Even as the child outside said but now. Ay, even as the child said, with būt-parasti."

"So it comes with all faiths."

"Thinkest thou? The books of my lamassery I read, and they were dried pith; and the later ritual with which we of the Reformed Law have cumbered ourselves—that, too, had no worth to these old eyes. Even the followers of the Excellent One are at feud on feud with one another. It is all illusion. Ay, maya, illusion. But I have another desire"—the seamed yellow face drew within three inches of the Curator, and the long forefinger-nail tapped on the table. "Your scholars, by these books, have followed the Blessed Feet in all their wanderings; but there are things which they have not sought out. I know nothing—nothing do I know—but I go to free myself from the Wheel of Things by a broad and open road." He smiled with most simple triumph. "As a pilgrim to the Holy Places I acquire merit. But there is more. Listen to a true thing. When our gracious Lord, being as yet a youth, sought a mate, men said, in His father's Court, that He was too tender for marriage. Thou knowest?"

The Curator nodded, wondering what would come next.

"So they made the triple trial of strength against all comers. And at the test of the Bow, our Lord first breaking that which they gave Him, called for such a bow as none might bend. Thou knowest?"

"It is written. I have read."

"And, overshooting all other marks, the arrow passed far and far beyond sight. At the last it fell; and, where it touched earth, there broke out a stream which presently became a River, whose nature, by our Lord's beneficence, and that merit He acquired ere He freed himself, is that whoso bathes in it washes away all taint and speckle of sin."

"So it is written," said the Curator sadly.

The lama drew a long breath. "Where is that River? Fountain of Wisdom, where fell the arrow?"

"Alas, my brother, I do not know," said the Curator.

"Nay, if it please thee to forget—the one thing only that thou hast not told me. Surely thou must know? See, I am an old man! I ask with my head between thy feet, O Fountain of Wisdom. We know He drew the bow! We know the arrow fell! We know the stream gushed! Where, then, is the River? My dream told me to find it. So I came. I am here. But where is the River?"

"If I knew, think you I would not cry it aloud?"

"By it one attains freedom from the Wheel of Things," the lama went on, unheeding. "The River of the Arrow! Think again! Some little stream, maybe—dried in the heats? But the Holy One would never so cheat an old man."

"I do not know. I do not know."

The lama brought his thousand-wrinkled face once more a handsbreadth from the Englishman's. "I see thou dost not know. Not being of the Law, the matter is hid from thee."

"Ay—hidden—hidden."

"We are both bound, thou and I, my brother. But I"—he rose with a sweep of the soft thick drapery—"I go to cut myself free. Come also!"

"I am bound," said the Curator. "But whither goest thou?"

"First to Kashi [Benares]: where else? There I shall meet one of the pure faith in a Jain temple of that city. He also is a Seeker in secret, and from him haply I may learn. Maybe he will go with me to Buddh Gaya. Thence north and west to Kapilavastu, and there will I seek for the River. Nay, I will seek everywhere as I go—for the place is not known where the arrow fell."

"And how wilt thou go? It is a far cry to Delhi, and farther to Benares."

"By road and the trains. From Pathânkot, having left the Hills, I came hither in a te-rain. It goes swiftly. At first I was amazed to see those tall poles by the side of the road snatching up and snatching up their threads,"—he illustrated the stoop and whirl of a telegraph-pole flashing past the train. "But later, I was cramped and desired to walk, as I am used."

"And thou art sure of thy road?" said the Curator.

"Oh, for that one but asks a question and pays money, and the appointed persons despatch all to the appointed place. That much I knew in my lamassery from sure report," said the lama proudly.

"And when dost thou go?" The Curator smiled at the mixture of old-world piety and modern progress that is the note of India today.

"As soon as may be. I follow the places of His life till I come to the River of the Arrow. There is, moreover, a written paper of the hours of the trains that go south."

"And for food?" Lamas, as a rule, have good store of money somewhere about them, but the Curator wished to make sure.

"For the journey, I take up the Master's begging-bowl. Yes. Even as He went so go I, forsaking the ease of my monastery. There was with me when I left the hills a chela (disciple) who begged for me as the Rule demands, but halting in Kulu awhile a fever took him and he died. I have now no chela, but I will take the alms-bowl and thus enable the charitable to acquire merit." He nodded his head valiantly. Learned doctors of a lamassery do not beg, but the lama was an enthusiast in this quest.

"Be it so," said the Curator, smiling. "Suffer me now to acquire merit. We be craftsmen together, thou and I. Here is a new book of white English paper: here be sharpened pencils two and three—thick and thin, all good for a scribe. Now lend me thy spectacles."

The Curator looked through them. They were heavily scratched, but the power was almost exactly that of his own pair, which he slid into the lama's hand, saying: "Try these."

"A feather! A very feather upon the face." The old man turned his head delightedly and wrinkled up his nose. "How scarcely do I feel them! How clearly do I see!"

"They be bilaur—crystal—and will never scratch. May they help thee to thy River, for they are thine."

"I will take them and the pencils and the white note-book," said the lama, "as a sign of friendship between priest and priest—and now—" He fumbled at his belt, detached the open-work iron pincers, and laid it on the Curator's table. "That is for a memory between thee and me—my

pencase. It is something old—even as I am."

It was a piece of ancient design, Chinese, of an iron that is not smelted these days; and the collector's heart in the Curator's bosom had gone out to it from the first. For no persuasion would the lama resume his gift.

"When I return, having found the River, I will bring thee a written picture of the Padma Samthora such as I used to make on silk at the lamassery. Yes—and of the Wheel of Life," he chuckled, "for we be craftsmen together, thou and I."

The Curator would have detained him: they are few in the world who still have the secret of the conventional brush-pen Buddhist pictures which are, as it were, half written and half drawn. But the lama strode out, head high in air, and pausing an instant before the great statue of a Bodhisat in meditation, brushed through the turnstiles.

Kim followed like a shadow. What he had overheard excited him wildly. This man was entirely new to all his experience, and he meant to investigate further, precisely as he would have investigated a new building or a strange festival in Lahore city. The lama was his trove, and he purposed to take possession. Kim's mother had been Irish, too.

The old man halted by Zam-Zammah and looked round till his eye fell on Kim. The inspiration of his pilgrimage had left him for awhile, and he felt old, forlorn, and very empty.

"Do not sit under that gun," said the policeman loftily.

"Huh! Owl!" was Kim's retort on the lama's behalf. "Sit under that gun if it please thee. When didst thou steal the milkwoman's slippers, Dunnoo?"

That was an utterly unfounded charge sprung on the spur of the moment, but it silenced Dunnoo, who knew that Kim's clear yell could call up legions of bad bazaar boys if need arose.

"And whom didst thou worship within?" said Kim affably, squatting in the shade beside the lama.

"I worshipped none, child. I bowed before the Excellent Law."

Kim accepted this new God without emotion. He knew already a few score.

"And what dost thou do?"

"I beg. I remember now it is long since I have eaten or drunk. What is the custom of charity in this town? In silence, as we do of Tibet, or speaking aloud?"

"Those who beg in silence starve in silence," said Kim, quoting a native proverb. The lama tried to rise, but sank back again, sighing for his disciple, dead in far-away Kulu. Kim watched head to one side, considering and interested.

"Give me the bowl. I know the people of this city—all who are charitable. Give, and I will bring it back filled."

Simply as a child the old man handed him the bowl.

"Rest, thou. I know the people."

He trotted off to the open shop of a kunjri, a low-caste vegetable-seller, which lay opposite the belt-tramway line down the Motee Bazar. She knew Kim of old.

"Oho, hast thou turned yogi with thy begging-bowl?" she cried.

"Nay." said Kim proudly. "There is a new priest in the city—a man such as I have never seen."

"Old priest—young tiger," said the woman angrily. "I am tired of new priests! They settle on our wares like flies. Is the father of my son a well of charity to give to all who ask?"

"No," said Kim. "Thy man is rather yagi (bad-tempered) than yogi (a holy man). But this priest is new. The Sahib in the Wonder House has talked to him like a brother. O my mother, fill me this bowl. He waits."

"That bowl indeed! That cow-bellied basket! Thou hast as much grace as the holy bull of Shiv. He has taken the best of a basket of onions already, this morn; and forsooth, I must fill thy bowl. He comes here again."

The huge, mouse-coloured Brahmini bull of the ward was shouldering his way through the many-coloured crowd, a stolen plantain hanging out of his mouth. He headed straight for the shop, well knowing his privileges as a sacred beast, lowered his head, and puffed heavily along the line of baskets ere making his choice. Up flew Kim's hard little heel and caught him on his moist blue nose. He snorted indignantly, and walked away across the tram-rails, his hump quivering with rage.

"See! I have saved more than the bowl will cost thrice over. Now, mother, a little rice and some dried fish atop—yes, and some vegetable curry."

A growl came out of the back of the shop, where a man lay.

"He drove away the bull," said the woman in an undertone. "It is good to give to the poor." She took the bowl and returned it full of hot rice.

"But my yogi is not a cow," said Kim gravely, making a hole with his fingers in the top of the mound. "A little curry is good, and a fried cake, and a morsel of conserve would please him, I think."

"It is a hole as big as thy head," said the woman fretfully. But she filled it, none the less, with good, steaming vegetable curry, clapped a fried cake atop, and a morsel of clarified butter on the cake, dabbed a lump of sour tamarind conserve at the side; and Kim looked at the load lovingly.

"That is good. When I am in the bazar the bull shall not come to this house. He is a bold beggar-man."

"And thou?" laughed the woman. "But speak well of bulls. Hast thou not told me that some day a Red Bull will come out of a field to help thee? Now hold all straight and ask for the holy man's blessing upon me. Perhaps, too, he knows a cure for my daughter's sore eyes. Ask. him that also, O thou Little Friend of all the World."

But Kim had danced off ere the end of the sentence, dodging pariah dogs and hungry acquaintances.

"Thus do we beg who know the way of it," said he proudly to the lama, who opened his eyes at the contents of the bowl. "Eat now and—I will eat with thee. Ohé bhistie!" he called to the water-carrier, sluicing the crotons by the Museum. "Give water here. We men are thirsty."

"We men!" said the bhistie, laughing. "Is one skinful enough for such a pair? Drink, then, in the name of the Compassionate."

He loosed a thin stream into Kim's hands, who drank native fashion; but the lama must needs pull out a cup from his inexhaustible upper draperies and drink ceremonially.

"Pardesi (a foreigner)," Kim explained, as the old man delivered in an unknown tongue what was evidently a blessing.

They ate together in great content, clearing the beggingbowl. Then the lama took snuff from a portentous wooden snuff-gourd, fingered his rosary awhile, and so dropped into the easy sleep of age, as the shadow of Zam-Zammah grew long.

Kim loafed over to the nearest tobacco-seller, a rather lively young Mohammedan woman, and begged a rank cigar of the brand that they sell to students of the Punjab University who copy English customs. Then he smoked and thought, knees to chin, under the belly of the gun, and the outcome of his thoughts was a sudden and stealthy departure in the direction of Nila Ram's timber-yard.

The lama did not wake till the evening life of the city had begun with lamp-lighting and the return of white-robed clerks and subordinates from the Government offices. He stared dizzily in all directions, but none looked at him save a Hindu urchin in a dirty turban and Isabella-coloured clothes. Suddenly he bowed his head on his knees and wailed.

"What is this?" said the boy, standing before him. "Hast thou been robbed?"

"It is my new chela (disciple) that is gone away from me, and I know not where he is."

"And what like of man was thy disciple?"

"It was a boy who came to me in place of him who died, on account of the merit which I had gained when I bowed before the Law within there." He pointed towards the Museum. "He came upon me to show me a road which I had lost. He led me into the Wonder House, and by his talk emboldened me to speak to the Keeper of the Images, so that I was cheered and made strong. And when I was faint with hunger he begged for me, as would a chela for his teacher. Suddenly was he sent. Suddenly has he gone away. It was in my mind to have taught him the Law upon the road to Benares."

Kim stood amazed at this, because he had overheard the talk in the Museum, and knew that the old man was speaking the truth, which is a thing a native on the road seldom presents to a stranger.

"But I see now that he was but sent for a purpose. By this I know that I shall find a certain River for which I seek."

"The River of the Arrow?" said Kim, with a superior smile.

"Is this yet another Sending?" cried the lama. "To none have I spoken of my search, save to the Priest of the Images. Who art thou?"

"Thy chela," said Kim simply, sitting on his heels. "I have never seen anyone like to thee in all this my life. I go with thee to Benares. And, too, I think that so old a man as thou, speaking the truth to chance-met people at dusk, is in great need of a disciple."

"But the River—the River of the Arrow?"

"Oh, that I heard when thou wast speaking to the Englishman. I lay against the door."

The lama sighed. "I thought thou hadst been a guide permitted. Such things fall sometimes—but I am not worthy. Thou dost not, then, know the River?"

"Not I," Kim laughed uneasily. "I go to look for—for a bull—a Red. Bull on a green field who shall help me." Boylike, if an acquaintance had a scheme, Kim was quite ready with one of his own; and, boylike, he had really thought for as much as twenty minutes at a time of his father's prophecy.

"To what, child?" said the lama.

"God knows, but so my father told me". I heard thy talk in the Wonder House of all those new strange places in the Hills, and if one so old and so little—so used to truth-telling—may go out for the small matter of a river, it seemed to me that I too must go a-travelling. If it is our fate to find those things we shall find them—thou, thy River; and I, my Bull, and the Strong Pillars and some other matters that I forget."

"It is not pillars but a Wheel from which I would be free," said the lama.

"That is all one. Perhaps they will make me a king," said Kim, serenely prepared for anything.

"I will teach thee other and better desires upon the road," the lama replied in the voice of authority. "Let us go to Benares."

"Not by night. Thieves are abroad. Wait till the day."

"But there is no place to sleep." The old man was used to the order of his monastery, and though he slept on the ground, as the Rule decrees, preferred a decency in these things.

"We shall get good lodging at the Kashmir Serai," said Kim, laughing at his perplexity. "I have a friend there. Come!"

The hot and crowded bazars blazed with light as they made their way through the press of all the races in Upper India, and the lama mooned through it like a man in a dream. It was his first experience of a large manufacturing city, and the crowded tram-car with its continually squealing brakes frightened him. Half pushed, half towed, he arrived at the high gate of the Kashmir Serai: that huge open square over against the railway station, surrounded with arched cloisters, where the camel and horse caravans put up on their return from Central Asia. Here were all manner of Northern folk, tending tethered ponies and kneeling camels; loading and unloading bales and bundles; drawing water for the evening meal at the creaking well-windlasses; piling grass before the shrieking, wild-eyed stallions; cuffing the surly caravan dogs; paying off camel-drivers; taking on new grooms; swearing, shouting, arguing, and chaffering in the packed square. The cloisters, reached by three or four masonry steps, made a haven of refuge around this turbulent sea. Most of them were rented to traders, as we rent the arches of a viaduct; the space between pillar and pillar being bricked or boarded off into rooms, which were guarded by heavy wooden doors and cumbrous native padlocks. Locked doors showed that the owner was away, and a few rude—sometimes very rude—chalk or paint scratches told where he had gone. Thus: "Lutuf Ullah is gone to Kurdistan." Below, in coarse verse: "O Allah, who sufferest lice to live on the coat of a Kabuli, why hast thou allowed this louse Lutuf to live so long?"

Kim, fending the lama between excited men and excited beasts, sidled along the cloisters to the far end, nearest the railway station, where Mahbub Ali, the horse-trader, lived when he came in from that mysterious land beyond the Passes of the North.

Kim had had many dealings with Mahbub in his little life, especially between his tenth and his

thirteenth year—and the big burly Afghan, his beard dyed scarlet with lime (for he was elderly and did not wish his grey hairs to show), knew the boy's value as a gossip. Sometimes he would tell Kim to watch a man who had nothing whatever to do with horses: to follow him for one whole day and report every soul with whom he talked. Kim would deliver himself of his tale at evening, and Mahbub would listen without a word or gesture. It was intrigue of some kind, Kim knew; but its worth lay in saying nothing whatever to anyone except Mahbub, who gave him beautiful meals all hot from the cookshop at the head of the serai, and once as much as eight annas in money.

"He is here," said Kim, hitting a bad-tempered camel on the nose. "Ohé, Mahbub Ali!" He halted at a dark arch and slipped behind the bewildered lama.

The horse-trader, his deep, embroidered Bokhariot belt unloosed, was lying on a pair of silk carpet saddle-bags, pulling lazily at an immense silver hookah. He turned his head very slightly at the cry; and seeing only the tall silent figure, chuckled in his deep chest.

"Allah! A lama! A Red Lama! It is far from Lahore to the Passes. What dost thou do here?"

The lama held out the begging-bowl mechanically.

"God's curse on all unbelievers!" said Mahbub. "I do not give to a lousy Tibetan; but ask my Baltis over yonder behind the camels. They may value your blessings. Oh, horseboys, here is a countryman of yours. See if he be hungry."

A shaven, crouching Balti, who had come down with the horses, and who was nominally some sort of degraded Buddhist, fawned upon the priest, and in thick gutturals besought the Holy One to sit at the horseboys' fire.

"Go!" said Kim, pushing him lightly, and the lama strode away, leaving Kim at the edge of the cloister.

"Go!" said Mahbub Ali, returning to his hookah. "Little Hindu, run away. God's curse on all unbelievers! Beg from those of my tail who are of thy faith."

"Maharaj," whined Kim, using the Hindu form of address, and thoroughly enjoying the situation; "my father is dead—my mother is dead—my stomach is empty."

"Beg from my men among the horses, I say. There must be some Hindus in my tail."

"Oh, Mahbub Ali, but am I a Hindu?" said Kim in English.

The trader gave no sign of astonishment, but looked under shaggy eyebrows.

"Little Friend of all the World," said he, "what is this?"

"Nothing. I am now that holy man's disciple; and we go a pilgrimage together—to Benares, he says. He is quite mad, and I am tired of Lahore city. I wish new air and water."

"But for whom dost thou work? Why come to me?" The voice was harsh with suspicion.

"To whom else should I come? I have no money. It is not good to go about without money. Thou wilt sell many horses to the officers. They are very fine horses, these new ones: I have seen them. Give me a rupee, Mahbub Ali, and when I come to my wealth I will give thee a bond and pay."

"Um!" said Mahbub Ali, thinking swiftly. "Thou hast never before lied to me. Call that lama—stand back in the dark."

"Oh, our tales will agree," said Kim, laughing.

"We go to Benares," said the lama, as soon as he understood the drift of Mahbub Ali's questions. "The boy and I, I go to seek for a certain River."

"Maybe—but the boy?"

"He is my disciple. He was sent, I think, to guide me to that River. Sitting under a gun was I when he came suddenly. Such things have befallen the fortunate to whom guidance was allowed. But I remember now, he said he was of this world—a Hindu."

"And his name?"

"That I did not ask. Is he not my disciple?"

"His country—his race—his village? Mussalman—Sikh Hindu—Jain—low caste or high?"

"Why should I ask? There is neither high nor low in the Middle Way. If he is my chela—does—will—can anyone take him from me? for, look you, without him I shall not find my River." He wagged his head solemnly.

"None shall take him from thee. Go, sit among my Baltis," said Mahbub Ali, and the lama drifted off, soothed by the promise.

"Is he not quite mad?" said Kim, coming forward to the light again. "Why should I lie to thee, Hajji?"

Mahbub puffed his hookah in silence. Then he began, almost whispering: "Umballa is on the road to Benares—if indeed ye two go there."

"Tck! Tck! I tell thee he does not know how to lie—as we two know."

"And if thou wilt carry a message for me as far as Umballa, I will give thee money. It concerns a horse—a white stallion which I have sold to an officer upon the last time I returned from the Passes. But then—stand nearer and hold up hands as begging—the pedigree of the white stallion was not fully established, and that officer, who is now at Umballa, bade me make it clear." (Mahbub here described the horse and the appearance of the officer.) "So the message to that officer will be: 'The pedigree of the white stallion is fully established.' By this will he know that thou comest from me. He will then say 'What proof hast thou?' and thou wilt answer: 'Mahbub Ali has given me the proof.'"

"And all for the sake of a white stallion," said Kim, with a giggle, his eyes aflame.

"That pedigree I will give thee now—in my own fashion and some hard words as well." A shadow passed behind Kim, and a feeding camel. Mahbub Ali raised his voice.

"Allah! Art thou the only beggar in the city? Thy mother is dead. Thy father is dead. So is it with all of them. Well, well—"

He turned as feeling on the floor beside him and tossed a flap of soft, greasy Mussalman bread to the boy. "Go and lie down among my horseboys for tonight—thou and the lama. Tomorrow I may give thee service."

Kim slunk away, his teeth in the bread, and, as he expected, he found a small wad of folded tissue-paper wrapped in oilskin, with three silver rupees—enormous largesse. He smiled and thrust money and paper into his leather amulet-case. The lama, sumptuously fed by Mahbub's Baltis, was already asleep in a corner of one of the stalls. Kim lay down beside him and laughed. He knew he had rendered a service to Mahbub Ali, and not for one little minute did he believe the tale of the stallion's pedigree.

But Kim did not suspect that Mahbub Ali, known as one of the best horse-dealers in the Punjab, a wealthy and enterprising trader, whose caravans penetrated far and far into the Back of Beyond, was registered in one of the locked books of the Indian Survey Department as C25 IB. Twice or thrice yearly C25 would send in a little story, baldly told but most interesting, and generally—it was checked by the statements of R17 and M4—quite true. It concerned all manner of out-of-the-way mountain principalities, explorers of nationalities other than English, and the guntrade—was, in brief, a small portion of that vast mass of "information received" on which the Indian Government acts. But, recently, five confederated Kings, who had no business to confederate, had been informed by a kindly Northern Power that there was a leakage of news from their territories into British India. So those Kings' Prime Ministers were seriously annoyed and took steps, after the Oriental fashion. They suspected, among many others, the bullying, red-bearded horsedealer whose caravans ploughed through their fastnesses belly-deep in snow. At least, his caravan that season had been ambushed and shot at twice on the way down, when Mahbub's men accounted for three strange ruffians who might, or might not, have been hired for the job. Therefore Mahbub had avoided halting at the insalubrious city of Peshawur, and had come through without stop to Lahore, where, knowing his country-people, he anticipated curious developments.

And there was that on Mahbub Ali which he did not wish to keep an hour longer than was necessary—a wad of closely folded tissue-paper, wrapped in oilskin—an impersonal, unaddressed statement, with five microscopic pin-holes in one corner, that most scandalously betrayed the five confederated Kings, the sympathetic Northern Power, a Hindu banker in Peshawur, a firm of gun-makers in Belgium, and an important, semi-independent Mohammedan ruler to the south. This last was R17's work, which Mahbub had picked up beyond the Dora Pass and was carrying in for R17, who, owing to circumstances over which he had no control, could not leave his post of observation. Dynamite was milky and innocuous beside that report of C25; and even an Oriental, with an Oriental's views of the value of time, could see that the sooner it was in the proper hands the better. Mahbub had no particular desire to die by violence, because two or three family blood-feuds across the Border hung unfinished on his hands, and when these scores were cleared he intended to settle down as a more or less virtuous citizen. He had never passed the serai gate since his arrival two days ago, but had been ostentatious in sending telegrams to Bombay, where he banked some of his money; to Delhi, where a sub-partner of his own clan was selling horses to the agent of a Rajputana state; and to Umballa, where an Englishman was excitedly demanding the pedigree of a white stallion. The public letter-writer, who knew English, composed excellent telegrams, such as: "Creighton, Laurel Bank, Umballa. Horse is Arabian as already advised. Sorrowful delayed pedigree which am translating." And later to the same address: "Much sorrowful delay. Will forward pedigree." To his sub-partner at Delhi he wired: "Lutuf Ullah. Have wired two thousand rupees your credit Luchman Narain's bank.—" This was entirely in the way of trade, but every one of those telegrams was discussed and rediscussed, by parties who conceived themselves to be interested, before they went over to the railway station in charge of a foolish Balti, who allowed all sorts of people to read them on the road.

When, in Mahbub's own picturesque language, he had muddied the wells of inquiry with the stick of precaution, Kim had dropped on him, sent from Heaven; and, being as prompt as he was unscrupulous, Mahbub Ali used to taking all sorts of gusty chances, pressed him into service on the spot.

A wandering lama with a low-caste boy-servant might attract a moment's interest as they wandered about India, the land of pilgrims; but no one would suspect them or, what was more to the point, rob.

He called for a new light-ball to his hookah, and considered the case. If the worst came to the worst, and the boy came to harm, the paper would incriminate nobody. And he would go up to Umballa leisurely and—at a certain risk of exciting fresh suspicion—repeat his tale by word of mouth to the people concerned.

But R17's report was the kernel of the whole affair, and it would be distinctly inconvenient if that failed to come to hand. However, God was great, and Mahbub Ali felt he had done all he could for the time being. Kim was the one soul in the world who had never told him a lie. That would have been a fatal blot on Kim's character if Mahbub had not known that to others, for his own ends or Mahbub's business, Kim could lie like an Oriental.

Then Mahbub Ali rolled across the serai to the Gate of the Harpies who paint their eyes and trap the stranger, and was at some pains to call on the one girl who, he had reason to believe, was a particular friend of a smooth-faced Kashmiri pundit who had waylaid his simple Balti in the matter of the telegrams. It was an utterly foolish thing to do; because they fell to drinking perfumed brandy against the Law of the Prophet, and Mahbub grew wonderfully drunk, and the gates of his mouth were loosened, and he pursued the Flower of Delight with the feet of intoxication till he fell flat among the cushions, where the Flower of Delight, aided by a smooth-faced Kashmiri pundit, searched him from head to foot most thoroughly.

About the same hour Kim heard soft feet in Mahbub's deserted stall. The horse-trader, curiously enough, had left his door unlocked, and his men were busy celebrating their return to India with a whole sheep of Mahbub's bounty. A sleek young gentleman from Delhi, armed with a bunch of keys which the Flower had unshackled from the senseless one's belt, went through every single box, bundle, mat, and saddle-bag in Mahbub's possession even more systematically than the Flower and the pundit were searching the owner.

"And I think." said the Flower scornfully an hour later, one rounded elbow on the snoring carcass, "that he is no more than a pig of an Afghan horse-dealer, with no thought except women and horses. Moreover, he may have sent it away by now—if ever there were such a thing."

"Nay—in a matter touching Five Kings it would be next his black heart," said the pundit. "Was there nothing?"

The Delhi man laughed and resettled his turban as he entered. "I searched between the soles of his slippers as the Flower searched his clothes. This is not the man but another. I leave little unseen."

"They did not say he was the very man," said the pundit thoughtfully. "They said, 'Look if he be the man, since our counsels are troubled.'"

"That North country is full of horse-dealers as an old coat of lice. There is Sikandar Khan, Nur Ali Beg, and Farrukh Shah all heads of kafilas [caravans]—who deal there," said the Flower.

"They have not yet come in," said the pundit. "Thou must ensnare them later."

Phew!" said the Flower with deep disgust, rolling Mahbub's head from her lap. "I earn my money. Farrukh Shah is a bear, Ali Beg a swashbuckler, and old Sikandar Khan—yaie! Go! I sleep now. This swine will not stir till dawn."

When Mahbub woke, the Flower talked to him severely on the sin of drunkenness. Asiatics do not wink when they have outmanoeuvred an enemy, but as Mahbub Ali cleared his throat, tightened his belt, and staggered forth under the early morning stars, he came very near to it.

"What a colt's trick!" said he to himself. "As if every girl in Peshawur did not use it! But 'twas prettily done. Now God He knows how many more there be upon the Road who have orders to test me—perhaps with the knife. So it stands that the boy must go to Umballa—and by rail—for the writing is something urgent. I abide here, following the Flower and drinking wine as an Afghan coper should."

He halted at the stall next but one to his own. His men lay there heavy with sleep. There was no sign of Kim or the lama.

"Up!" He stirred a sleeper. "Whither went those who lay here last even—the lama and the boy? Is aught missing?"

"Nay," grunted the man, "the old madman rose at second cockcrow saying he would go to Benares, and the young one led him away."

"The curse of Allah on all unbelievers!" said Mahbub heartily, and climbed into his own stall, growling in his beard.

But it was Kim who had wakened the lama—Kim with one eye laid against a knot-hole in the planking, who had seen the Delhi man's search through the boxes. This was no common thief that turned over letters, bills, and saddles—no mere burglar who ran a little knife sideways into the soles of Mahbub's slippers, or picked the seams of the saddle-bags so deftly. At first Kim had been minded to give the alarm—the long-drawn cho-or—choor! (thief! thief!) that sets the serai ablaze of nights; but he looked more carefully, and, hand on amulet, drew his own conclusions.

"It must be the pedigree of that made-up horse-lie," said he, "the thing that I carry to Umballa. Better that we go now. Those who search bags with knives may presently search bellies with knives. Surely there is a woman behind this. Hai! Hai! in a whisper to the light-sleeping old man. "Come. It is time—time to go to Benares."

The lama rose obediently, and they passed out of the serai like shadows.

CHAPTER II

And whoso will, from Pride released;
Contemning neither creed nor priest,
May feel the Soul of all the East.
About him at Kamakura.

They entered the fort-like railway station, black in the end of night; the electrics sizzling over the goods-yard where they handle the heavy Northern grain-traffic.

"This is the work of devils!" said the lama, recoiling from the hollow echoing darkness, the glimmer of rails between the masonry platforms, and the maze of girders above. He stood in a gigantic stone hall paved, it seemed, with the sheeted dead third-class passengers who had taken their tickets overnight and were sleeping in the waiting-rooms. All hours of the twenty-four are alike to Orientals, and their passenger traffic is regulated accordingly.

"This is where the fire-carriages come. One stands behind that hole"—Kim pointed to the ticket-office—"who will give thee a paper to take thee to Umballa."

"But we go to Benares," he replied petulantly.

"All one. Benares then. Quick: she comes!"

"Take thou the purse."

The lama, not so well used to trains as he had pretended, started as the 3.25 a.m. south-bound roared in. The sleepers sprang to life, and the station filled with clamour and shoutings, cries of water and sweetmeat vendors, shouts of native policemen, and shrill yells of women gathering up their baskets, their families, and their husbands.

"It is the train—only the te-rain. It will not come here. Wait!" Amazed at the lama's immense simplicity (he had handed him a small bag full of rupees), Kim asked and paid for a ticket to Umballa. A sleepy clerk grunted and flung out a ticket to the next station, just six miles distant.

"Nay," said Kim, scanning it with a grin. "This may serve for farmers, but I live in the city of Lahore. It was cleverly done, Babu. Now give the ticket to Umballa."

The Babu scowled and dealt the proper ticket.

"Now another to Amritzar," said Kim, who had no notion of spending Mahbub Ali's money on anything so crude as a paid ride to Umballa. "The price is so much. The small money in return is just so much. I know the ways of the te-rain ... Never did yogi need chela as thou dost," he went on merrily to the bewildered lama. "They would have flung thee out at Mian Mir but for me. This way! Come!" He returned the money, keeping only one anna in each rupee of the price of the Umballa ticket as his commission—the immemorial commission of Asia.

The lama jibbed at the open door of a crowded third-class carriage. "Were it not better to walk?" said he weakly.

A burly Sikh artisan thrust forth his bearded head. "Is he afraid? Do not be afraid. I remember the time when I was afraid of the train. Enter! This thing is the work of the Government."

"I do not fear," said the lama. "Have ye room within for two?"

"There is no room even for a mouse," shrilled the wife of a well-to-do cultivator—a Hindu Jat from the rich Jullundur, district. Our night trains are not as well looked after as the day ones, where the sexes are very strictly kept to separate carriages.

"Oh, mother of my son, we can make space," said the blueturbaned husband. "Pick up the child. It is a holy man, see'st thou?"

"And my lap full of seventy times seven bundles! Why not bid him sit on my knee, Shameless? But men are ever thus!" She looked round for approval. An Amritzar courtesan near the window sniffed behind her head drapery.

"Enter! Enter!" cried a fat Hindu money-lender, his folded account-book in a cloth under his arm. With an oily smirk: "It is well to be kind to the poor."

"Ay, at seven per cent a month with a mortgage on the unborn calf," said a young Dogra soldier going south on leave; and they all laughed.

"Will it travel to Benares?" said the lama.

"Assuredly. Else why should we come? Enter, or we are left," cried Kim.

"See!" shrilled the Amritzar girl. "He has never entered a train. Oh, see!"

"Nay, help," said the cultivator, putting out a large brown hand and hauling him in. "Thus is it done, father."

"But—but—I sit on the floor. It is against the Rule to sit on a bench," said the lama. "Moreover, it cramps me."

"I say," began the money-lender, pursing his lips, "that there is not one rule of right living which these te-rains do not cause us to break. We sit, for example, side by side with all castes and peoples."

"Yea, and with most outrageously shameless ones," said the wife, scowling at the Amritzar girl making eyes at the young sepoy.

"I said we might have gone by cart along the road," said the husband, "and thus have saved some money."

"Yes—and spent twice over what we saved on food by the way. That was talked out ten thousand times."

"Ay, by ten thousand tongues," grunted he.

"The Gods help us poor women if we may not speak. Oho! He is of that sort which may not look at or reply to a woman." For the lama, constrained by his Rule, took not the faintest notice of her. "And his disciple is like him?"

"Nay, mother," said Kim most promptly. "Not when the woman is well-looking and above all charitable to the hungry."

"A beggar's answer," said the Sikh, laughing. "Thou hast brought it on thyself, sister!" Kim's hands were crooked in supplication.

"And whither goest thou?" said the woman, handing him the half of a cake from a greasy package.

"Even to Benares."

"Jugglers belike?" the young soldier suggested. "Have ye any tricks to pass the time? Why does not that yellow man answer?"

"Because," said Kim stoutly, "he is holy, and thinks upon matters hidden from thee."

"That may be well. We of the Ludhiana Sikhs"—he rolled it out sonorously—"do not trouble our heads with doctrine. We fight."

"My sister's brother's son is naik (corporal) in that regiment," said the Sikh craftsman quietly. "There are also some Dogra companies there." The soldier glared, for a Dogra is of other caste than a Sikh, and the banker tittered.

"They are all one to me," said the Amritzar girl.

"That we believe," snorted the cultivator's wife malignantly.

"Nay, but all who serve the Sirkar with weapons in their hands are, as it were, one brotherhood. There is one brotherhood of the caste, but beyond that again"—she looked round timidly—"the bond of the Pulton—the Regiment—eh?"

"My brother is in a Jat regiment," said the cultivator. "Dogras be good men."

"Thy Sikhs at least were of that opinion," said the soldier, with a scowl at the placid old man in the corner. "Thy Sikhs thought so when our two companies came to help them at the Pirzai Kotal in the face of eight Afridi standards on the ridge not three months gone."

He told the story of a Border action in which the Dogra companies of the Ludhiana Sikhs had acquitted themselves well. The Amritzar girl smiled; for she knew the talk was to win her approval.

"Alas!" said the cultivator's wife at the end. "So their villages were burnt and their little children made homeless?"

"They had marked our dead. They paid a great payment after we of the Sikhs had schooled them. So it was. Is this Amritzar?"

"Ay, and here they cut our tickets," said the banker, fumbling at his belt.

The lamps were paling in the dawn when the half-caste guard came round. Ticket-collecting is a slow business in the East, where people secrete their tickets in all sorts of curious places. Kim produced his and was told to get out.

"But I go to Umballa," he protested. "I go with this holy man."

"Thou canst go to Jehannum for aught I care. This ticket is only—"

Kim burst into a flood of tears, protesting that the lama was his father and his mother, that he was the prop of the lama's declining years, and that the lama would die without his care. All the carriage bade the guard be merciful—the banker was specially eloquent here—but the guard hauled Kim on to the platform. The lama blinked—he could not overtake the situation and Kim lifted up his voice and wept outside the carriage window.

"I am very poor. My father is dead—my mother is dead. O charitable ones, if I am left here, who shall tend that old man?"

"What—what is this?" the lama repeated. "He must go to Benares. He must come with me. He is my chela. If there is money to be paid—"

"Oh, be silent," whispered Kim; "are we Rajahs to throw away good silver when the world is so charitable?"

The Amritzar girl stepped out with her bundles, and it was on her that Kim kept his watchful eye. Ladies of that persuasion, he knew, were generous.

"A ticket—a little tikkut to Umballa—O Breaker of Hearts!" She laughed. "Hast thou no charity?"

"Does the holy man come from the North?"

"From far and far in the North he comes," cried Kim. "From among the hills."

"There is snow among the pine-trees in the North—in the hills there is snow. My mother was from Kulu. Get thee a ticket. Ask him for a blessing."

"Ten thousand blessings," shrilled Kim. "O Holy One, a woman has given us in charity so that I can come with thee—a woman with a golden heart. I run for the tikkut."

The girl looked up at the lama, who had mechanically followed Kim to the platform. He bowed his head that he might not see her, and muttered in Tibetan as she passed on with the crowd.

"Light come—light go," said the cultivator's wife viciously.

"She has acquired merit," returned the lama. "Beyond doubt it was a nun."

"There be ten thousand such nuns in Amritzar alone. Return, old man, or the te-rain may depart without thee," cried the banker.

"Not only was it sufficient for the ticket, but for a little food also," said Kim, leaping to his place. "Now eat, Holy One. Look. Day comes!"

Golden, rose, saffron, and pink, the morning mists smoked away across the flat green levels. All the rich Punjab lay out in the splendour of the keen sun. The lama flinched a little as the telegraph-posts swung by.

"Great is the speed of the te-rain," said the banker, with a patronizing grin. "We have gone farther since Lahore than thou couldst walk in two days: at even, we shall enter Umballa."

"And that is still far from Benares," said the lama wearily, mumbling over the cakes that Kim offered. They all unloosed their bundles and made their morning meal. Then the banker, the cultivator, and the soldier prepared their pipes and wrapped the compartment in choking, acrid smoke, spitting and coughing and enjoying themselves. The Sikh and the cultivator's wife chewed pan; the lama took snuff and told his beads, while Kim, cross-legged, smiled over the comfort of a full stomach.

"What rivers have ye by Benares?" said the lama of a sudden to the carriage at large.

"We have Gunga," returned the banker, when the little titter had subsided.

"What others?"

"What other than Gunga?"

"Nay, but in my mind was the thought of a certain River of healing."

"That is Gunga. Who bathes in her is made clean and goes to the Gods. Thrice have I made pilgrimage to Gunga." He looked round proudly.

"There was need," said the young sepoy drily, and the travellers' laugh turned against the banker.

"Clean—to return again to the Gods," the lama muttered. "And to go forth on the round of lives anew—still tied to the Wheel." He shook his head testily. "But maybe there is a mistake. Who, then, made Gunga in the beginning?"

"The Gods. Of what known faith art thou?" the banker said, appalled.

"I follow the Law—the Most Excellent Law. So it was the Gods that made Gunga. What like of Gods were they?"

The carriage looked at him in amazement. It was inconceivable that anyone should be ignorant of Gunga.

"What—what is thy God?" said the money-lender at last.

"Hear!" said the lama, shifting the rosary to his hand. "Hear: for I speak of Him now! O people of Hind, listen!"

He began in Urdu the tale of the Lord Buddha, but, borne by his own thoughts, slid into Tibetan and long-droned texts from a Chinese book of the Buddha's life. The gentle, tolerant folk looked on reverently. All India is full of holy men stammering gospels in strange tongues; shaken and consumed in the fires of their own zeal; dreamers, babblers, and visionaries: as it has been from the beginning and will continue to the end.

"Um!" said the soldier of the Ludhiana Sikhs. "There was a Mohammedan regiment lay next to us at the Pirzai Kotal, and a priest of theirs—he was, as I remember, a naik—when the fit was on him, spake prophecies. But the mad all are in God's keeping. His officers overlooked much in that man."

The lama fell back on Urdu, remembering that he was in a strange land. "Hear the tale of the Arrow which our Lord loosed from the bow," he said.

This was much more to their taste, and they listened curiously while he told it. "Now, O people of Hind, I go to seek that River. Know ye aught that may guide me, for we be all men and women in evil case."

"There is Gunga—and Gunga alone—who washes away sin." ran the murmur round the carriage.

"Though past question we have good Gods Jullundur-way," said the cultivator's wife, looking out of the window. "See how they have blessed the crops."

"To search every river in the Punjab is no small matter," said her husband. "For me, a stream that leaves good silt on my land suffices, and I thank Bhumia, the God of the Home-stead." He shrugged one knotted, bronzed shoulder.

"Think you our Lord came so far North?" said the lama, turning to Kim.

"It may be," Kim replied soothingly, as he spat red pan-juice on the floor.

"The last of the Great Ones," said the Sikh with authority, "was Sikander Julkarn [Alexander the Great]. He paved the streets of Jullundur and built a great tank near Umballa. That pavement holds to this day; and the tank is there also. I never heard of thy God."

"Let thy hair grow long and talk Punjabi," said the young soldier jestingly to Kim, quoting a Northern proverb. "That is all that makes a Sikh." But he did not say this very loud.

The lama sighed and shrank into himself, a dingy, shapeless mass. In the pauses of their talk they could hear the low droning "Om mane pudme hum! Om mane pudme hum!"—and the thick click of the wooden rosary beads.

"It irks me," he said at last. "The speed and the clatter irk me. Moreover, my chela, I think that maybe we have over-passed that River."

"Peace, peace," said Kim. "Was not the River near Benares? We are yet far from the place."

"But—if our Lord came North, it may be any one of these little ones that we have run across."

"I do not know."

"But thou wast sent to me—wast thou sent to me?—for the merit I had acquired over yonder at Such-zen. From beside the cannon didst thou come—bearing two faces—and two garbs."

"Peace. One must not speak of these things here," whispered Kim. "There was but one of me. Think again and thou wilt remember. A boy—a Hindu boy—by the great green cannon."

"But was there not also an Englishman with a white beard holy among images—who himself made more sure my assurance of the River of the Arrow?"

"He—we—went to the Ajaib-Gher in Lahore to pray before the Gods there," Kim explained to the openly listening company. "And the Sahib of the Wonder House talked to him—yes, this is truth as a brother. He is a very holy man, from far beyond the Hills. Rest, thou. In time we come to Umballa."

"But my River—the River of my healing?"

"And then, if it please thee, we will go hunting for that River on foot. So that we miss nothing—not even a little rivulet in a field-side."

"But thou hast a Search of thine own?" The lama—very pleased that he remembered so well—sat bolt upright.

"Ay," said Kim, humouring him. The boy was entirely happy to be out chewing pan and seeing new people in the great good-tempered world.

"It was a bull—a Red Bull that shall come and help thee and carry thee—whither? I have forgotten. A Red Bull on a green field, was it not?"

"Nay, it will carry me nowhere," said Kim. "It is but a tale I told thee."

"What is this?" The cultivator's wife leaned forward, her bracelets clinking on her arm. "Do ye both dream dreams? A Red Bull on a green field, that shall carry thee to the heavens or what? Was it a vision? Did one make a prophecy? We have a Red Bull in our village behind Jullundur city, and he grazes by choice in the very greenest of our fields!"

"Give a woman an old wife's tale and a weaver-bird a leaf and a thread", they will weave wonderful things," said the Sikh. "All holy men dream dreams, and by following holy men their disciples attain that power."

"A Red Bull on a green field, was it?" the lama repeated. "In a former life it may be thou hast acquired merit, and the Bull will come to reward thee."

"Nay—nay—it was but a tale one told to me—for a jest belike. But I will seek the Bull about Umballa, and thou canst look for thy River and rest from the clatter of the train."

"It may be that the Bull knows—that he is sent to guide us both." said the lama, hopefully as a child. Then to the company, indicating Kim: "This one was sent to me but yesterday. He is not, I think, of this world."

"Beggars aplenty have I met, and holy men to boot, but never such a yogi nor such a disciple," said the woman.

Her husband touched his forehead lightly with one finger and smiled. But the next time the lama would eat they took care to give him of their best.

And at last—tired, sleepy, and dusty—they reached Umballa City Station.

"We abide here upon a law-suit," said the cultivator's wife to Kim. "We lodge with my man's cousin's younger brother. There is room also in the courtyard for thy yogi and for thee. Will—will he give me a blessing?"

"O holy man! A woman with a heart of gold gives us lodging for the night. It is a kindly land, this land of the South. See how we have been helped since the dawn!"

The lama bowed his head in benediction.

"To fill my cousin's younger brother's house with wastrels—" the husband began, as he shouldered his heavy bamboo staff.

"Thy cousin's younger brother owes my father's cousin something yet on his daughter's marriage-feast," said the woman crisply. "Let him put their food to that account. The yogi will beg, I doubt not."

"Ay, I beg for him," said Kim, anxious only to get the lama under shelter for the night, that he might seek Mahbub Ali's Englishman and deliver himself of the white stallion's pedigree.

"Now," said he, when the lama had come to an anchor in the inner courtyard of a decent Hindu house behind the cantonments, "I go away for a while—to—to buy us victual in the bazar. Do not stray abroad till I return."

"Thou wilt return? Thou wilt surely return?" The old man caught at his wrist. "And thou wilt return in this very same shape? Is it too late to look tonight for the River?"

"Too late and too dark. Be comforted. Think how far thou art on the road—an hundred kos from Lahore already."

"Yea—and farther from my monastery. Alas! It is a great and terrible world."

Kim stole out and away, as unremarkable a figure as ever carried his own and a few score thousand other folk's fate slung round his neck. Mahbub Ali's directions left him little doubt of

he house in which his Englishman lived; and a groom, bringing a dog-cart home from the Club, made him quite sure. It remained only to identify his man, and Kim slipped through the garden hedge and hid in a clump of plumed grass close to the veranda. The house blazed with lights, and servants moved about tables dressed with flowers, glass, and silver. Presently forth came an Englishman, dressed in black and white, humming a tune. It was too dark to see his face, so Kim, beggar-wise, tried an old experiment.

"Protector of the Poor!"

The man backed towards the voice.

"Mahbub Ali says—"

'Hah! What says Mahbub Ali?" He made no attempt to look for the speaker, and that showed Kim that he knew.

"The pedigree of the white stallion is fully established."

"What proof is there?" The Englishman switched at the rose-hedge in the side of the drive.

"Mahbub Ali has given me this proof." Kim flipped the wad of folded paper into the air, and it fell in the path beside the man, who put his foot on it as a gardener came round the corner. When the servant passed he picked it up, dropped a rupee—Kim could hear the clink—and strode into the house, never turning round. Swiftly Kim took up the money; but for all his training, he was Irish enough by birth to reckon silver the least part of any game. What he desired was the visible effect of action; so, instead of slinking away, he lay close in the grass and wormed nearer to the house.

He saw—Indian bungalows are open through and through—the Englishman return to a small dressing-room, in a corner of the veranda, that was half office, littered with papers and despatch-boxes, and sit down to study Mahbub Ali's message. His face, by the full ray of the kerosene lamp, changed and darkened, and Kim, used as every beggar must be to watching countenances, took good note.

"Will! Will, dear!" called a woman's voice. "You ought to be in the drawing-room. They'll be here in a minute."

The man still read intently.

"Will!" said the voice, five minutes later. "He's come. I can hear the troopers in the drive."

The man dashed out bareheaded as a big landau with four native troopers behind it halted at the veranda, and a tall, black haired man, erect as an arrow, swung out, preceded by a young officer who laughed pleasantly.

Flat on his belly lay Kim, almost touching the high wheels. His man and the black stranger exchanged two sentences.

"Certainly, sir," said the young officer promptly. "Everything waits while a horse is concerned."

"We shan't be more than twenty minutes," said Kim's man. "You can do the honours—keep 'em amused, and all that."

"Tell one of the troopers to wait," said the tall man, and they both passed into the dressing-room together as the landau rolled away. Kim saw their heads bent over Mahbub Ali's message, and

heard the voices—one low and deferential, the other sharp and decisive.

"It isn't a question of weeks. It is a question of days—hours almost," said the elder. "I'd been expecting it for some time, but this"—he tapped Mahbub Ali's paper—"clinches it. Grogan's dining here to-night, isn't he?"

"Yes, sir, and Macklin too."

"Very good. I'll speak to them myself. The matter will be referred to the Council, of course, but this is a case where one is justified in assuming that we take action at once. Warn the Pined and Peshawar brigades. It will disorganize all the summer reliefs, but we can't help that. This comes of not smashing them thoroughly the first time. Eight thousand should be enough."

"What about artillery, sir?"

"I must consult Macklin."

"Then it means war?"

"No. Punishment. When a man is bound by the action of his predecessor—"

"But C25 may have lied."

"He bears out the other's information. Practically, they showed their hand six months back. But Devenish would have it there was a chance of peace. Of course they used it to make themselves stronger. Send off those telegrams at once—the new code, not the old—mine and Wharton's. I don't think we need keep the ladies waiting any longer. We can settle the rest over the cigars. I thought it was coming. It's punishment—not war."

As the trooper cantered off, Kim crawled round to the back of the house, where, going on his Lahore experiences, he judged there would be food—and information. The kitchen was crowded with excited scullions, one of whom kicked him.

"Aie," said Kim, feigning tears. "I came only to wash dishes in return for a bellyful."

"All Umballa is on the same errand. Get hence. They go in now with the soup. Think you that we who serve Creighton Sahib need strange scullions to help us through a big dinner?"

"It is a very big dinner," said Kim, looking at the plates.

"Small wonder. The guest of honour is none other than the Jang-i-Lat Sahib [the Commander-in-Chief]."

"Ho!" said Kim, with the correct guttural note of wonder. He had learned what he wanted, and when the scullion turned he was gone.

"And all that trouble," said he to himself, thinking as usual in Hindustani, "for a horse's pedigree! Mahbub Ali should have come to me to learn a little lying. Every time before that I have borne a message it concerned a woman. Now it is men. Better. The tall man said that they will loose a great army to punish someone—somewhere—the news goes to Pindi and Peshawur. There are also guns. Would I had crept nearer. It is big news!"

He returned to find the cultivator's cousin's younger brother discussing the family law-suit in all its bearings with the cultivator and his wife and a few friends, while the lama dozed. After the evening meal some one passed him a water-pipe; and Kim felt very much of a man as he

pulled at the smooth coconut-shell, his legs spread abroad in the moonlight, his tongue clicking in remarks from time to time. His hosts were most polite; for the cultivator's wife had told them of his vision of the Red Bull, and of his probable descent from another world. Moreover, the lama was a great and venerable curiosity.

The family priest, an old, tolerant Sarsut Brahmin, dropped in later, and naturally started a theological argument to impress the family. By creed, of course, they were all on their priest's side, but the lama was the guest and the novelty. His gentle kindliness, and his impressive Chinese quotations, that sounded like spells, delighted them hugely; and in this sympathetic, simple air, he expanded like the Bodhisat's own lotus, speaking of his life in the great hills of Such-zen, before, as he said, "I rose up to seek enlightenment."

Then it came out that in those worldly days he had been a master-hand at casting horoscopes and nativities; and the family priest led him on to describe his methods; each giving the planets names that the other could not understand, and pointing upwards as the big stars sailed across the dark. The children of the house tugged unrebuked at his rosary; and he clean forgot the Rule which forbids looking at women as he talked of enduring snows, landslips, blocked passes, the remote cliffs where men find sapphires and turquoise, and that wonderful upland road that leads at last into Great China itself.

"How thinkest thou of this one?" said the cultivator aside to the priest.

"A holy man—a holy man indeed. His Gods are not the Gods, but his feet are upon the Way," was the answer. "And his methods of nativities, though that is beyond thee, are wise and sure."

"Tell me," said Kim lazily, "whether I find my Red Bull on a green field, as was promised me."

"What knowledge hast thou of thy birth-hour?" the priest asked, swelling with importance.

"Between first and second cockcrow of the first night in May."

"Of what year?"

"I do not know; but upon the hour that I cried first fell the great earthquake in Srinagar which is in Kashmir." This Kim had from the woman who took care of him, and she again from Kimball O'Hara. The earthquake had been felt in India, and for long stood a leading date in the Punjab.

"Ai!" said a woman excitedly. This seemed to make Kim's supernatural origin more certain. "Was not such an one's daughter born then—"

"And her mother bore her husband four sons in four years all likely boys," cried the cultivator's wife, sitting outside the circle in the shadow.

"None reared in the knowledge," said the family priest, "forget how the planets stood in their Houses upon that night." He began to draw in the dust of the courtyard. "At least thou hast good claim to a half of the House of the Bull. How runs thy prophecy?"

"Upon a day," said Kim, delighted at the sensation he was creating, "I shall be made great by means of a Red Bull on a green field, but first there will enter two men making all things ready."

"Yes: thus ever at the opening of a vision. A thick darkness that clears slowly; anon one enters with a broom making ready the place. Then begins the Sight. Two men—thou sayest? Ay, ay. The Sun, leaving the House of the Bull, enters that of the Twins. Hence the two men of the prophecy. Let us now consider. Fetch me a twig, little one."

He knitted his brows, scratched, smoothed out, and scratched again in the dust mysterious signs—to the wonder of all save the lama, who, with fine instinct, forbore to interfere.

At the end of half an hour, he tossed the twig from him with a grunt.

"Hm! Thus say the stars. Within three days come the two men to make all things ready. After them follows the Bull; but the sign over against him is the sign of War and armed men."

"There was indeed a man of the Ludhiana Sikhs in the carriage from Lahore," said the cultivator's wife hopefully.

"Tck! Armed men—many hundreds. What concern hast thou with war?" said the priest to Kim. "Thine is a red and an angry sign of War to be loosed very soon."

"None—none." said the lama earnestly. "We seek only peace and our River."

Kim smiled, remembering what he had overheard in the dressing-room. Decidedly he was a favourite of the stars.

The priest brushed his foot over the rude horoscope. "More than this I cannot see. In three days comes the Bull to thee, boy."

"And my River, my River," pleaded the lama. "I had hoped his Bull would lead us both to the River."

"Alas, for that wondrous River, my brother," the priest replied. "Such things are not common."

Next morning, though they were pressed to stay, the lama insisted on departure. They gave Kim a large bundle of good food and nearly three annas in copper money for the needs of the road, and with many blessings watched the two go southward in the dawn.

"Pity it is that these and such as these could not be freed from—"

"Nay, then would only evil people be left on the earth, and who would give us meat and shelter?" quoth Kim, stepping merrily under his burden.

"Yonder is a small stream. Let us look," said the lama, and he led from the white road across the fields; walking into a very hornets' nest of pariah dogs.

CHAPTER III

Yea, voice of every Soul that clung
To life that strove from rung to rung
When Devadatta's rule was young,
The warm wind brings Kamakura.

Behind them an angry farmer brandished a bamboo pole. He was a market-gardener, Arain by caste, growing vegetables and flowers for Umballa city, and well Kim knew the breed.

"Such an one," said the lama, disregarding the dogs, "is impolite to strangers, intemperate of speech and uncharitable. Be warned by his demeanour, my disciple."

"Ho, shameless beggars!" shouted the farmer. "Begone! Get hence!"

"We go," the lama returned, with quiet dignity. "We go from these unblessed fields."

"Ah," said Kim, sucking in his breath. "If the next crops fail, thou canst only blame thine own tongue."

The man shuffled uneasily in his slippers. "The land is full of beggars," he began, half apologetically.

"And by what sign didst thou know that we would beg from thee, O Mali?" said Kim tartly, using the name that a market-gardener least likes. "All we sought was to look at that river beyond the field there."

"River, forsooth!" the man snorted. "What city do ye hail from not to know a canal-cut? It runs as straight as an arrow, and I pay for the water as though it were molten silver. There is a branch of a river beyond. But if ye need water I can give that—and milk."

"Nay, we will go to the river," said the lama, striding out.

"Milk and a meal." the man stammered, as he looked at the strange tall figure. "I—I would not draw evil upon myself—or my crops. But beggars are so many in these hard days."

"Take notice." The lama turned to Kim. "He was led to speak harshly by the Red Mist of anger. That clearing from his eyes, he becomes courteous and of an affable heart. May his fields be blessed! Beware not to judge men too hastily, O farmer."

"I have met holy ones who would have cursed thee from hearthstone to byre," said Kim to the abashed man. "Is he not wise and holy? I am his disciple."

He cocked his nose in the air loftily and stepped across the narrow field-borders with great dignity.

"There is no pride," said the lama, after a pause, "there is no pride among such as follow the Middle Way."

"But thou hast said he was low-caste and discourteous."

"Low-caste I did not say, for how can that be which is not? Afterwards he amended his discourtesy, and I forgot the offence. Moreover, he is as we are, bound upon the Wheel of Things; but he does not tread the way of deliverance." He halted at a little runlet among the fields, and considered the hoof-pitted bank.

"Now, how wilt thou know thy River?" said Kim, squatting in the shade of some tall sugar-cane.

"When I find it, an enlightenment will surely be given. This, I feel, is not the place. O littlest among the waters, if only thou couldst tell me where runs my River! But be thou blessed to make the fields bear!"

"Look! Look!" Kim sprang to his side and dragged him back. A yellow-and-brown streak glided from the purple rustling stems to the bank, stretched its neck to the water, drank, and lay still—a big cobra with fixed, lidless eyes.

"I have no stick—I have no stick," said Kim. "I will get me one and break his back."

"Why? He is upon the Wheel as we are—a life ascending or descending—very far from deliverance. Great evil must the soul have done that is cast into this shape."

"I hate all snakes," said Kim. No native training can quench the white man's horror of the Serpent.

"Let him live out his life." The coiled thing hissed and half opened its hood. "May thy release come soon, brother!" the lama continued placidly. "Hast thou knowledge, by chance, of my River?"

"Never have I seen such a man as thou art," Kim whispered, overwhelmed. "Do the very snakes understand thy talk?"

"Who knows?" He passed within a foot of the cobra's poised head. It flattened itself among the dusty coils.

"Come, thou!" he called over his shoulder.

"Not I," said Kim". "I go round."

"Come. He does no hurt."

Kim hesitated for a moment. The lama backed his order by some droned Chinese quotation which Kim took for a charm. He obeyed and bounded across the rivulet, and the snake, indeed, made no sign.

"Never have I seen such a man." Kim wiped the sweat from his forehead. "And now, whither go we?"

"That is for thee to say. I am old, and a stranger—far from my own place. But that the rêl-carriage fills my head with noises of devil-drums I would go in it to Benares now ... Yet by so going we may miss the River. Let us find another river."

Where the hard-worked soil gives three and even four crops a year through patches of sugar-cane, tobacco, long white radishes, and nol-kol, all that day they strolled on, turning aside to every glimpse of water; rousing village dogs and sleeping villages at noonday; the lama replying to the volleyed questions with an unswerving simplicity. They sought a River: a River of miraculous healing. Had any one knowledge of such a stream?

Sometimes men laughed, but more often heard the story out to the end and offered them a place in the shade, a drink of milk, and a meal. The women were always kind, and the little children as children are the world over, alternately shy and venturesome.

Evening found them at rest under the village tree of a mud-walled, mud-roofed hamlet, talking to the headman as the cattle came in from the grazing-grounds and the women prepared the day's last meal. They had passed beyond the belt of market-gardens round hungry Umballa, and were among the mile-wide green of the staple crops.

He was a white-bearded and affable elder, used to entertaining strangers. He dragged out a string bedstead for the lama, set warm cooked food before him, prepared him a pipe, and, the evening ceremonies being finished in the village temple, sent for the village priest.

Kim told the older children tales of the size and beauty of Lahore, of railway travel, and such-like city things, while the men talked, slowly as their cattle chew the cud.

"I cannot fathom it," said the headman at last to the priest. "How readest thou this talk?" The lama, his tale told, was silently telling his beads.

"He is a Seeker." the priest answered. "The land is full of such. Remember him who came only last, month—the faquir with the tortoise?"

"Ay, but that man had right and reason, for Krishna Himself appeared in a vision promising him Paradise without the burning-pyre if he journeyed to Prayag. This man seeks no God who is within my knowledge."

"Peace, he is old: he comes from far off, and he is mad," the smooth-shaven priest replied. "Hear me." He turned to the lama. "Three kos (six miles) to the westward runs the great road to Calcutta."

"But I would go to Benares—to Benares."

"And to Benares also. It crosses all streams on this side of Hind. Now my word to thee, Holy One, is rest here till tomorrow. Then take the road" (it was the Grand Trunk Road he meant) "and test each stream that it overpasses; for, as I understand, the virtue of thy River lies neither in one pool nor place, but throughout its length. Then, if thy Gods will, be assured that thou wilt come upon thy freedom."

"That is well said." The lama was much impressed by the plan. "We will begin tomorrow, and a blessing on thee for showing old feet such a near road." A deep, sing-song Chinese half-chant closed the sentence. Even the priest was impressed, and the headman feared an evil spell: but none could look at the lama's simple, eager face and doubt him long.

"Seest thou my chela?" he said, diving into his snuff-gourd with an important sniff. It was his duty to repay courtesy with courtesy.

"I see—and hear." The headman rolled his eye where Kim was chatting to a girl in blue as she laid crackling thorns on a fire.

"He also has a Search of his own. No river, but a Bull. Yea, a Red Bull on a green field will some day raise him to honour. He is, I think, not altogether of this world. He was sent of a sudden to aid me in this search, and his name is Friend of all the World."

The priest smiled. "Ho, there, Friend of all the World," he cried across the sharp-smelling smoke, "what art thou?"

"This Holy One's disciple," said Kim.

"He says thou are a būt (a spirit)."

"Can būts eat?" said Kim, with a twinkle. "For I am hungry."

"It is no jest," cried the lama. "A certain astrologer of that city whose name I have forgotten—"

"That is no more than the city of Umballa where we slept last night," Kim whispered to the priest.

"Ay, Umballa was it? He cast a horoscope and declared that my chela should find his desire within two days. But what said he of the meaning of the stars, Friend of all the World?"

Kim cleared his throat and looked around at the village greybeards.

"The meaning of my Star is War," he replied pompously.

Somebody laughed at the little tattered figure strutting on the brickwork plinth under the great tree. Where a native would have lain down, Kim's white blood set him upon his feet.

"Ay, War," he answered.

"That is a sure prophecy," rumbled a deep voice. "For there is always war along the Border—as I know."

It was an old, withered man, who had served the Government in the days of the Mutiny as a native officer in a newly raised cavalry regiment. The Government had given him a good holding in the village, and though the demands of his sons, now grey-bearded officers on their own account, had impoverished him, he was still a person of consequence. English officials—Deputy Commissioners even—turned aside from the main road to visit him, and on those occasions he dressed himself in the uniform of ancient days, and stood up like a ramrod.

"But this shall be a great war—a war of eight thousand." Kim's voice shrilled across the quick-gathering crowd, astonishing himself.

"Redcoats or our own regiments?" the old man snapped, as though he were asking an equal. His tone made men respect Kim.

"Redcoats," said Kim at a venture. "Redcoats and guns."

"But—but the astrologer said no word of this," cried the lama, snuffing prodigiously in his excitement.

"But I know. The word has come to me, who am this Holy One's disciple. There will rise a war—a war of eight thousand redcoats. From Pindi and Peshawur they will be drawn. This is sure."

"The boy has heard bazar-talk," said the priest.

"But he was always by my side," said the lama. "How should he know? I did not know."

"He will make a clever juggler when the old man is dead," muttered the priest to the headman. "What new trick is this?"

"A sign. Give me a sign," thundered the old soldier suddenly. "If there were war my sons would have told me."

"When all is ready, thy sons, doubt not, will be told. But it is a long road from thy sons to the man in whose hands these things lie." Kim warmed to the game, for it reminded him of

experiences in the letter-carrying line, when, for the sake of a few pice, he pretended to know more than he knew. But now he was playing for larger things—the sheer excitement and the sense of power. He drew a new breath and went on.

"Old man, give me a sign. Do underlings order the goings of eight thousand redcoats—with guns?"

"No." Still the old man answered as though Kim were an equal.

"Dost thou know who He is, then, that gives the order?"

"I have seen Him."

"To know again?"

"I have known Him since he was a lieutenant in the top-khana (the Artillery)."

"A tall man. A tall man with black hair, walking thus?" Kim took a few paces in a stiff, wooden style.

"Ay. But that anyone may have seen." The crowd were breathless—still through all this talk.

"That is true," said Kim. "But I will say more. Look now. First the great man walks thus. Then He thinks thus." (Kim drew a forefinger over his forehead and downwards till it came to rest by the angle of the jaw.) "Anon He twitches his fingers thus. Anon He thrusts his hat under his left armpit." Kim illustrated the motion and stood like a stork.

The old man groaned, inarticulate with amazement; and the crowd shivered.

"So—so—so. But what does He when He is about to give an order?"

"He rubs the skin at the back of his neck—thus. Then falls one finger on the table and He makes a small sniffing noise through his nose. Then He speaks, saying: 'Loose such and such a regiment. Call out such guns.'"

The old man rose stiffly and saluted.

"'For'"—Kim translated into the vernacular the clinching sentences he had heard in the dressing-room at Umballa—"'For,' says He, 'we should have done this long ago. It is not war—it is a chastisement. Snff!'"

"Enough. I believe. I have seen Him thus in the smoke of battles. Seen and heard. It is He!"

"I saw no smoke"—Kim's voice shifted to the rapt sing-song of the wayside fortune-teller. "I saw this in darkness. First came a man to make things clear. Then came horsemen. Then came He standing in a ring of light. The rest followed as I have said. Old man, have I spoken truth?"

"It is He. Past all doubt it is He."

The crowd drew a long, quavering breath, staring alternately at the old man, still at attention, and ragged Kim against the purple twilight.

"Said I not—said I not he was from the other world?" cried the lama proudly. "He is the Friend of all the World. He is the Friend of the Stars!"

"At least it does not concern us," a man cried. "O thou young soothsayer, if the gift abides with

thee at all seasons, I have a red-spotted cow. She may be sister to thy Bull for aught I know—"

"Or I care," said Kim. "My Stars do not concern themselves with thy cattle."

"Nay, but she is very sick," a woman struck in. "My man is a buffalo, or he would have chosen his words better. Tell me if she recover?"

Had Kim been at all an ordinary boy, he would have carried on the play; but one does not know Lahore city, and least of all the faquirs by the Taksali Gate, for thirteen years without also knowing human nature.

The priest looked at him sideways, something bitterly—a dry and blighting smile.

"Is there no priest, then, in the village? I thought I had seen a great one even now," cried Kim.

"Ay—but—" the woman began.

"But thou and thy husband hoped to get the cow cured for a handful of thanks." The shot told: they were notoriously the closest-fisted couple in the village. "It is not well to cheat the temples. Give a young calf to thine own priest, and, unless thy Gods are angry past recall, she will give milk within a month."

"A master-beggar art thou," purred the priest approvingly. "Not the cunning of forty years could have done better. Surely thou hast made the old man rich?"

"A little flour, a little butter and a mouthful of cardamoms," Kim retorted, flushed with the praise, but still cautious—"Does one grow rich on that? And, as thou canst see, he is mad. But it serves me while I learn the road at least."

He knew what the faquirs of the Taksali Gate were like when they talked among themselves, and copied the very inflection of their lewd disciples.

"Is his Search, then, truth or a cloak to other ends? It may be treasure."

"He is mad—many times mad. There is nothing else."

Here the old soldier bobbled up and asked if Kim would accept his hospitality for the night. The priest recommended him to do so, but insisted that the honour of entertaining the lama belonged to the temple—at which the lama smiled guilelessly. Kim glanced from one face to the other, and drew his own conclusions.

"Where is the money?" he whispered, beckoning the old man off into the darkness.

"In my bosom. Where else?"

"Give it me. Quietly and swiftly give it me."

"But why? Here is no ticket to buy."

"Am I thy chela, or am I not? Do I not safeguard thy old feet about the ways? Give me the money and at dawn I will return it." He slipped his hand above the lama's girdle and brought away the purse.

"Be it so—be it so." The old man nodded his head. "This is a great and terrible world. I never knew there were so many men alive in it."

Next morning the priest was in a very bad temper, but the lama was quite happy; and Kim had enjoyed a most interesting evening with the old man, who brought out his cavalry sabre and, balancing it on his dry knees, told tales of the Mutiny and young captains thirty years in their graves, till Kim dropped off to sleep.

"Certainly the air of this country is good," said the lama. "I sleep lightly, as do all old men; but last night I slept unwaking till broad day. Even now I am heavy."

"Drink a draught of hot milk," said Kim, who had carried not a few such remedies to opium-smokers of his acquaintance. "It is time to take the Road again."

"The long Road that overpasses all the rivers of Hind," said the lama gaily. "Let us go. But how thinkest thou, chela, to recompense these people, and especially the priest, for their great kindness? Truly they are būt-parast, but in other lives, maybe, they will receive enlightenment. A rupee to the temple? The thing within is no more than stone and red paint, but the heart of man we must acknowledge when and where it is good."

"Holy One, hast thou ever taken the Road alone?" Kim looked up sharply, like the Indian crows so busy about the fields.

"Surely, child: from Kulu to Pathânkot—from Kulu, where my first chela died. When men were kind to us we made offerings, and all men were well-disposed throughout all the Hills."

"It is otherwise in Hind," said Kim drily. "Their Gods are many-armed and malignant. Let them alone."

"I would set thee on thy road for a little, Friend of all the World, thou and thy yellow man." The old soldier ambled up the village street, all shadowy in the dawn, on a punt, scissor-hocked pony. "Last night broke up the fountains of remembrance in my so-dried heart, and it was as a blessing to me. Truly there is war abroad in the air. I smell it. See! I have brought my sword."

He sat long-legged on the little beast, with the big sword at his side—hand dropped on the pommel—staring fiercely over the flat lands towards the North. "Tell me again how He showed in thy vision. Come up and sit behind me. The beast will carry two."

"I am this Holy One's disciple," said Kim, as they cleared the village-gate. The villagers seemed almost sorry to be rid of them, but the priest's farewell was cold and distant. He had wasted some opium on a man who carried no money.

"That is well spoken. I am not much used to holy men, but respect is always good. There is no respect in these days—not even when a Commissioner Sahib comes to see me. But why should one whose Star leads him to war follow a holy man?"

"But he is a holy man," said Kim earnestly. "In truth, and in talk and in act, holy. He is not like the others. I have never seen such an one. We be not fortune-tellers, or jugglers, or beggars."

"Thou art not. That I can see. But I do not know that other. He marches well, though."

The first freshness of the day carried the lama forward with long, easy, camel-like strides. He was deep in meditation, mechanically clicking his rosary.

They followed the rutted and worn country road that wound across the flat between the great dark-green mango-groves, the line of the snowcapped Himalayas faint to the eastward. All India was at work in the fields, to the creaking of well-wheels, the shouting of ploughmen behind their cattle, and the clamour of the crows. Even the pony felt the good influence and almost broke into

a trot as Kim laid a hand on the stirrup-leather.

"It repents me that I did not give a rupee to the shrine," said the lama on the last bead of his eighty-one.

The old soldier growled in his beard, so that the lama for the first time was aware of him.

"Seekest thou the River also?" said he, turning.

"The day is new," was the reply. "What need of a river save to water at before sundown? I come to show thee a short lane to the Big Road."

"That is a courtesy to be remembered, O man of good will. But why the sword?"

The old soldier looked as abashed as a child interrupted in his game of make-believe.

"The sword," he said, fumbling it. "Oh, that was a fancy of mine an old man's fancy. Truly the police orders are that no man must bear weapons throughout Hind, but"—he cheered up and slapped the hilt—"all the constabeels hereabout know me."

"It is not a good fancy," said the lama. "What profit to kill men?"

"Very little—as I know; but if evil men were not now and then slain it would not be a good world for weaponless dreamers. I do not speak without knowledge who have seen the land from Delhi south awash with blood."

"What madness was that, then?"

"The Gods, who sent it for a plague, alone know. A madness ate into all the Army, and they turned against their officers. That was the first evil, but not past remedy if they had then held their hands. But they chose to kill the Sahibs' wives and children. Then came the Sahibs from over the sea and called them to most strict account."

"Some such rumour, I believe, reached me once long ago. They called it the Black Year, as I remember."

"What manner of life hast thou led, not to know The Year? A rumour indeed! All earth knew, and trembled!"

"Our earth never shook but once—upon the day that the Excellent One received Enlightenment."

"Umph! I saw Delhi shake at least—and Delhi is the navel of the world."

"So they turned against women and children? That was a bad deed, for which the punishment cannot be avoided."

"Many strove to do so, but with very small profit. I was then in a regiment of cavalry. It broke. Of six hundred and eighty sabres stood fast to their salt—how many, think you? Three. Of whom I was one."

"The greater merit."

"Merit! We did not consider it merit in those days. My people, my friends, my brothers fell from me. They said: 'The time of the English is accomplished. Let each strike out a little holding for himself.' But I had talked with the men of Sobraon, of Chilianwallah, of Moodkee and Ferozeshah. I said: 'Abide a little and the wind turns. There is no blessing in this work.' In those

days I rode seventy miles with an English Memsahib and her babe on my saddle-bow. (Wow! That was a horse fit for a man!) I placed them in safety, and back came I to my officer—the one that was not killed of our five. 'Give me work,' said I, 'for I am an outcast among my own kind, and my cousin's blood is wet on my sabre.' 'Be content,' said he. 'There is great work forward. When this madness is over there is a recompense.'"

"Ay, there is a recompense when the madness is over, surely?" the lama muttered half to himself.

"They did not hang medals in those days on all who by accident had heard a gun fired. No! In nineteen pitched battles was I; in six-and-forty skirmishes of horse; and in small affairs without number. Nine wounds I bear; a medal and four clasps and the medal of an Order, for my captains, who are now generals, remembered me when the Kaisar-i-Hind had accomplished fifty years of her reign, and all the land rejoiced. They said: 'Give him the Order of Berittish India.' I carry it upon my neck now. I have also my jaghir (holding) from the hands of the State—a free gift to me and mine. The men of the old days—they are now Commissioners— come riding to me through the crops—high upon horses so that all the village sees—and we talk out the old skirmishes, one dead man's name leading to another."

"And after?" said the lama.

"Oh, afterwards they go away, but not before my village has seen."

"And at the last what wilt thou do?"

"At the last I shall die."

"And after?"

"Let the Gods order it. I have never pestered Them with prayers. I do not think They will pester me. Look you, I have noticed in my long life that those who eternally break in upon Those Above with complaints and reports and bellowings and weepings are presently sent for in haste, as our Colonel used to send for slack-jawed down-country men who talked too much. No, I have never wearied the Gods. They will remember this, and give me a quiet place where I can drive my lance in the shade, and wait to welcome my sons: I have no less than three Rissaldar— majors all—in the regiments."

"And they likewise, bound upon the Wheel, go forth from life to life—from despair to despair," said the lama below his breath, "hot, uneasy, snatching."

"Ay," the old soldier chuckled. "Three Rissaldar—majors in three regiments. Gamblers a little, but so am I. They must be well mounted; and one cannot take the horses as in the old days one took women. Well, well, my holding can pay for all. How thinkest thou? It is a well-watered strip, but my men cheat me. I do not know how to ask save at the lance's point. Ugh! I grow angry and I curse them, and they feign penitence, but behind my back I know they call me a toothless old ape."

"Hast thou never desired any other thing?"

"Yes—yes—a thousand times! A straight back and a close-clinging knee once more; a quick wrist and a keen eye; and the marrow that makes a man. Oh, the old days—the good days of my strength!"

"That strength is weakness."

"It has turned so; but fifty years since I could have proved it otherwise," the old soldier retorted,

driving his stirrup-edge into the pony's lean flank.

"But I know a River of great healing."

"I have drank Gunga-water to the edge of dropsy. All she gave me was a flux, and no sort of strength."

"It is not Gunga. The River that I know washes from all taint of sin. Ascending the far bank one is assured of Freedom. I do not know thy life, but thy face is the face of the honourable and courteous. Thou hast clung to thy Way, rendering fidelity when it was hard to give, in that Black Year of which I now remember other tales. Enter now upon the Middle Way which is the path to Freedom. Hear the Most Excellent Law, and do not follow dreams."

"Speak, then, old man," the soldier smiled, half saluting. "We be all babblers at our age."

The lama squatted under the shade of a mango, whose shadow played checkerwise over his face; the soldier sat stiffly on the pony; and Kim, making sure that there were no snakes, lay down in the crotch of the twisted roots.

There was a drowsy buzz of small life in hot sunshine, a cooing of doves, and a sleepy drone of well-wheels across the fields. Slowly and impressively the lama began. At the end of ten minutes the old soldier slid from his pony, to hear better as he said, and sat with the reins round his wrist. The lama's voice faltered, the periods lengthened. Kim was busy watching a grey squirrel. When the little scolding bunch of fur, close pressed to the branch, disappeared, preacher and audience were fast asleep, the old officer's strong-cut head pillowed on his arm, the lama's thrown back against the tree-bole, where it showed like yellow ivory. A naked child toddled up, stared, and, moved by some quick impulse of reverence, made a solemn little obeisance before the lama—only the child was so short and fat that it toppled over sideways, and Kim laughed at the sprawling, chubby legs. The child, scared and indignant, yelled aloud.

"Hai! Hai!" said the soldier, leaping to his feet. "What is it? What orders? ... It is ... a child! I dreamed it was an alarm. Little one—little one—do not cry. Have I slept? That was discourteous indeed!"

"I fear! I am afraid!" roared the child.

"What is it to fear? Two old men and a boy? How wilt thou ever make a soldier, Princeling?"

The lama had waked too, but, taking no direct notice of the child, clicked his rosary.

"What is that?" said the child, stopping a yell midway. "I have never seen such things. Give them me."

"Aha." said the lama, smiling, and trailing a loop of it on the grass:

This is a handful of cardamoms,
 This is a lump of ghi:
This is millet and chillies and rice,
 A supper for thee and me!

The child shrieked with joy, and snatched at the dark, glancing beads.

"Oho!" said the old soldier. "Whence hadst thou that song, despiser of this world?"

"I learned it in Pathânkot—sitting on a doorstep," said the lama shyly. "It is good to be kind to

babes."

"As I remember, before the sleep came on us, thou hadst told me that marriage and bearing were darkeners of the true light, stumbling-blocks upon the Way. Do children drop from Heaven in thy country? Is it the Way to sing them songs?"

"No man is all perfect," said the lama gravely, recoiling the rosary. "Run now to thy mother, little one."

"Hear him!" said the soldier to Kim. "He is ashamed for that he has made a child happy. There was a very good householder lost in thee, my brother. Hai, child!" He threw it a pice. "Sweetmeats are always sweet." And as the little figure capered away into the sunshine: "They grow up and become men. Holy One, I grieve that I slept in the midst of thy preaching. Forgive me."

"We be two old men," said the lama. "The fault is mine. I listened to thy talk of the world and its madness, and one fault led to the next."

"Hear him! What harm do thy Gods suffer from play with a babe? And that song was very well sung. Let us go on and I will sing thee the song of Nikal Seyn before Delhi—the old song."

And they fared out from the gloom of the mango-tope, the old man's high, shrill voice ringing across the field, as wail by long-drawn wail he unfolded the story of Nikal Seyn [Nicholson]— the song that men sing in the Punjab to this day. Kim was delighted, and the lama listened with deep interest.

"Ahi! Nikal Seyn is dead—he died before Delhi! Lances of the North, take vengeance for Nikal Seyn." He quavered it out to the end, marking the trills with the flat of his sword on the pony's rump.

"And now we come to the Big Road," said he, after receiving the compliments of Kim; for the lama was markedly silent. "It is long since I have ridden this way, but thy boy's talk stirred me. See, Holy One—the Great Road which is the backbone of all Hind. For the most part it is shaded, as here, with four lines of trees; the middle road—all hard—takes the quick traffic. In the days before rail-carriages the Sahibs travelled up and down here in hundreds. Now there are only country-carts and such like. Left and right is the rougher road for the heavy carts—grain and cotton and timber, fodder, lime and hides. A man goes in safety here for at every few kos is a police-station. The police are thieves and extortioners (I myself would patrol it with cavalry— young recruits under a strong captain), but at least they do not suffer any rivals. All castes and kinds of men move here.

"Look! Brahmins and chumars, bankers and tinkers, barbers and bunnias, pilgrims and potters— all the world going and coming. It is to me as a river from which I am withdrawn like a log after a flood."

And truly the Grand Trunk Road is a wonderful spectacle. It runs straight, bearing without crowding India's traffic for fifteen hundred miles—such a river of life as nowhere else exists in the world. They looked at the green-arched, shade-flecked length of it, the white breadth speckled with slow-pacing folk; and the two-roomed police-station opposite.

"Who bears arms against the law?" a constable called out laughingly, as he caught sight of the soldier's sword. "Are not the police enough to destroy evil-doers?"

"It was because of the police I bought it," was the answer. "Does all go well in Hind?"

"Rissaldar Sahib, all goes well."

"I am like an old tortoise, look you, who puts his head out from the bank and draws it in again. Ay, this is the Road of Hindustan. All men come by this way..."

"Son of a swine, is the soft part of the road meant for thee to scratch thy back upon? Father of all the daughters of shame and husband of ten thousand virtueless ones, thy mother was devoted to a devil, being led thereto by her mother. Thy aunts have never had a nose for seven generations! Thy sister—What Owl's folly told thee to draw thy carts across the road? A broken wheel? Then take a broken head and put the two together at leisure!"

The voice and a venomous whip-cracking came out of a pillar of dust fifty yards away, where a cart had broken down. A thin, high Kathiawar mare, with eyes and nostrils aflame, rocketed out of the jam, snorting and wincing as her rider bent her across the road in chase of a shouting man. He was tall and grey-bearded, sitting the almost mad beast as a piece of her, and scientifically lashing his victim between plunges.

The old man's face lit with pride. "My child!" said he briefly, and strove to rein the pony's neck to a fitting arch.

"Am I to be beaten before the police?" cried the carter. "Justice! I will have Justice—"

"Am I to be blocked by a shouting ape who upsets ten thousand sacks under a young horse's nose? That is the way to ruin a mare."

"He speaks truth. He speaks truth. But she follows her man close," said the old man. The carter ran under the wheels of his cart and thence threatened all sorts of vengeance.

"They are strong men, thy sons," said the policeman serenely, picking his teeth.

The horseman delivered one last vicious cut with his whip and came on at a canter.

"My father!" He reigned back ten yards and dismounted.

The old man was off his pony in an instant, and they embraced as do father and son in the East.

CHAPTER IV

Good Luck, she is never a lady,
But the cursedest quean alive,
Tricksy, wincing, and jady—
Kittle to lead or drive.
Greet her—she's hailing a stranger!
Meet her—she's busking to leave!
Let her alone for a shrew to the bone
And the hussy comes plucking your sleeve!
Largesse! Largesse, O Fortune!
Give or hold at your will.
If I've no care for Fortune,
Fortune must follow me still!

The Wishing-Caps.

Then, lowering their voices, they spoke together. Kim came to rest under a tree, but the lama tugged impatiently at his elbow.

"Let us go on. The River is not here."

"Hai mai! Have we not walked enough for a little? Our River will not run away. Patience, and he will give us a dole."

"This." said the old soldier suddenly, "is the Friend of the Stars. He brought me the news yesterday. Having seen the very man Himself, in a vision, giving orders for the war."

"Hm!" said his son, all deep in his broad chest. "He came by a bazar-rumour and made profit of it."

His father laughed. "At least he did not ride to me begging for a new charger, and the Gods know how many rupees. Are thy brothers' regiments also under orders?"

"I do not know. I took leave and came swiftly to thee in case—"

"In case they ran before thee to beg. O gamblers and spendthrifts all! But thou hast never yet ridden in a charge. A good horse is needed there, truly. A good follower and a good pony also for the marching. Let us see—let us see." He thrummed on the pommel.

"This is no place to cast accounts in, my father. Let us go to thy house."

"At least pay the boy, then: I have no pice with me, and he brought auspicious news. Ho! Friend of all the World, a war is toward as thou hast said."

"Nay, as I know, the war," returned Kim composedly.

"Eh?" said the lama, fingering his beads, all eager for the road.

"My master does not trouble the Stars for hire. We brought the news bear witness, we brought the news, and now we go." Kim half-crooked his hand at his side.

The son tossed a silver coin through the sunlight, grumbling something about beggars and

jugglers. It was a four-anna piece, and would feed them well for days. The lama, seeing the flash of the metal, droned a blessing.

"Go thy way, Friend of all the World," piped the old soldier, wheeling his scrawny mount. "For once in all my days I have met a true prophet—who was not in the Army."

Father and son swung round together: the old man sitting as erect as the younger.

A Punjabi constable in yellow linen trousers slouched across the road. He had seen the money pass.

"Halt!" he cried in impressive English. "Know ye not that there is a takkus of two annas a head, which is four annas, on those who enter the Road from this side-road? It is the order of the Sirkar, and the money is spent for the planting of trees and the beautification of the ways."

"And the bellies of the police," said Kim, slipping out of arm's reach. "Consider for a while, man with a mud head. Think you we came from the nearest pond like the frog, thy father-in-law? Hast thou ever heard the name of thy brother?"

"And who was he? Leave the boy alone," cried a senior constable, immensely delighted, as he squatted down to smoke his pipe in the veranda.

"He took a label from a bottle of belaitee-pani (soda-water), and, affixing it to a bridge, collected taxes for a month from those who passed, saying that it was the Sirkar's order. Then came an Englishman and broke his head. Ah, brother, I am a town-crow, not a village-crow!"

The policeman drew back abashed, and Kim hooted at him all down the road.

"Was there ever such a disciple as I?" he cried merrily to the lama. "All earth would have picked thy bones within ten mile of Lahore city if I had not guarded thee."

"I consider in my own mind whether thou art a spirit, sometimes, or sometimes an evil imp," said the lama, smiling slowly.

"I am thy chela." Kim dropped into step at his side—that indescribable gait of the long-distance tramp all the world over.

"Now let us walk," muttered the lama, and to the click of his rosary they walked in silence mile upon mile. The lama as usual, was deep in meditation, but Kim's bright eyes were open wide. This broad, smiling river of life, he considered, was a vast improvement on the cramped and crowded Lahore streets. There were new people and new sights at every stride—castes he knew and castes that were altogether out of his experience.

They met a troop of long-haired, strong-scented Sansis with baskets of lizards and other unclean food on their backs, their lean dogs sniffing at their heels. These people kept their own side of the road, moving at a quick, furtive jog-trot, and all other castes gave them ample room; for the Sansi is deep pollution. Behind them, walking wide and stiffly across the strong shadows, the memory of his leg-irons still on him, strode one newly released from the jail; his full stomach and shiny skin to prove that the Government fed its prisoners better than most honest men could feed themselves. Kim knew that walk well, and made broad jest of it as they passed. Then an Akali, a wild-eyed, wild-haired Sikh devotee in the blue-checked clothes of his faith, with polished-steel quoits glistening on the cone of his tall blue turban, stalked past, returning from a visit to one of the independent Sikh States, where he had been singing the ancient glories of the Khalsa to College-trained princelings in top-boots and white-cord breeches. Kim was careful not to irritate that man; for the Akali's temper is short and his arm quick. Here and

here they met or were overtaken by the gaily dressed crowds of whole villages turning out to some local fair; the women, with their babes on their hips, walking behind the men, the older boys prancing on sticks of sugar-cane, dragging rude brass models of locomotives such as they sell for a halfpenny, or flashing the sun into the eyes of their betters from cheap toy mirrors. One could see at a glance what each had bought; and if there were any doubt it needed only to watch the wives comparing, brown arm against brown arm, the newly purchased dull glass bracelets that come from the North-West. These merry-makers stepped slowly, calling one to the other and stopping to haggle with sweetmeat-sellers, or to make a prayer before one of the wayside shrines—sometimes Hindu, sometimes Mussalman—which the low-caste of both creeds share with beautiful impartiality. A solid line of blue, rising and falling like the back of a caterpillar in haste, would swing up through the quivering dust and trot past to a chorus of quick cackling. That was a gang of changars—the women who have taken all the embankments of all the Northern railways under their charge—a flat-footed, big-bosomed, strong-limbed, blue-petticoated clan of earth-carriers, hurrying north on news of a job, and wasting no time by the road. They belong to the caste whose men do not count, and they walked with squared elbows, swinging hips, and heads on high, as suits women who carry heavy weights. A little later a marriage procession would strike into the Grand Trunk with music and shoutings, and a smell of marigold and jasmine stronger even than the reek of the dust. One could see the bride's litter, a blur of red and tinsel, staggering through the haze, while the bridegroom's bewreathed pony turned aside to snatch a mouthful from a passing fodder-cart. Then Kim would join the Kentish-fire of good wishes and bad jokes, wishing the couple a hundred sons and no daughters, as the saying is. Still more interesting and more to be shouted over it was when a strolling juggler with some half-trained monkeys, or a panting, feeble bear, or a woman who tied goats' horns to her feet, and with these danced on a slack-rope, set the horses to shying and the women to shrill, long-drawn quavers of amazement.

The lama never raised his eyes. He did not note the money-lender on his goose-rumped pony, hastening along to collect the cruel interest; or the long-shouting, deep-voiced little mob—still in military formation—of native soldiers on leave, rejoicing to be rid of their breeches and puttees, and saying the most outrageous things to the most respectable women in sight. Even the seller of Ganges-water he did not see, and Kim expected that he would at least buy a bottle of that precious stuff. He looked steadily at the ground, and strode as steadily hour after hour, his soul busied elsewhere. But Kim was in the seventh heaven of joy. The Grand Trunk at this point was built on an embankment to guard against winter floods from the foothills, so that one walked, as it were, a little above the country, along a stately corridor, seeing all India spread out to left and right. It was beautiful to behold the many-yoked grain and cotton wagons crawling over the country roads: one could hear their axles, complaining a mile away, coming nearer, till with shouts and yells and bad words they climbed up the steep incline and plunged on to the hard main road, carter reviling carter. It was equally beautiful to watch the people, little clumps of red and blue and pink and white and saffron, turning aside to go to their own villages, dispersing and growing small by twos and threes across the level plain. Kim felt these things, though he could not give tongue to his feelings, and so contented himself with buying peeled sugar-cane and spitting the pith generously about his path. From time to time the lama took snuff, and at last Kim could endure the silence no longer.

"This is a good land—the land of the South!" said he. "The air is good; the water is good. Eh?"

"And they are all bound upon the Wheel," said the lama. "Bound from life after life. To none of these has the Way been shown." He shook himself back to this world.

"And now we have walked a weary way," said Kim. "Surely we shall soon come to a parao (a resting-place). Shall we stay there? Look, the sun is sloping."

"Who will receive us this evening?"

"That is all one. This country is full of good folk. Besides" he sunk his voice beneath a whisper—"we have money."

The crowd thickened as they neared the resting-place which marked the end of their day's journey. A line of stalls selling very simple food and tobacco, a stack of firewood, a police-station, a well, a horse-trough, a few trees, and, under them, some trampled ground dotted with the black ashes of old fires, are all that mark a parao on the Grand Trunk; if you except the beggars and the crows—both hungry.

By this time the sun was driving broad golden spokes through the lower branches of the mango-trees; the parakeets and doves were coming home in their hundreds; the chattering, grey-backed Seven Sisters, talking over the day's adventures, walked back and forth in twos and threes almost under the feet of the travellers; and shufflings and scufflings in the branches showed that the bats were ready to go out on the night-picket. Swiftly the light gathered itself together, painted for an instant the faces and the cartwheels and the bullocks' horns as red as blood. Then the night fell, changing the touch of the air, drawing a low, even haze, like a gossamer veil of blue, across the face of the country, and bringing out, keen and distinct, the smell of wood-smoke and cattle and the good scent of wheaten cakes cooked on ashes. The evening patrol hurried out of the police-station with important coughings and reiterated orders; and a live charcoal ball in the cup of a wayside carter's hookah glowed red while Kim's eye mechanically watched the last flicker of the sun on the brass tweezers.

The life of the parao was very like that of the Kashmir Serai on a small scale. Kim dived into the happy Asiatic disorder which, if you only allow time, will bring you everything that a simple man needs.

His wants were few, because, since the lama had no caste scruples, cooked food from the nearest stall would serve; but, for luxury's sake, Kim bought a handful of dung-cakes to build a fire. All about, coming and going round the little flames, men cried for oil, or grain, or sweetmeats, or tobacco, jostling one another while they waited their turn at the well; and under the men's voices you heard from halted, shuttered carts the high squeals and giggles of women whose faces should not be seen in public.

Nowadays, well-educated natives are of opinion that when their womenfolk travel—and they visit a good deal—it is better to take them quickly by rail in a properly screened compartment; and that custom is spreading. But there are always those of the old rock who hold by the use of their forefathers; and, above all, there are always the old women—more conservative than the men—who toward the end of their days go on a pilgrimage. They, being withered and undesirable, do not, under certain circumstances, object to unveiling. After their long seclusion, during which they have always been in business touch with a thousand outside interests, they love the bustle and stir of the open road, the gatherings at the shrines, and the infinite possibilities of gossip with like-minded dowagers. Very often it suits a longsuffering family that a strong-tongued, iron-willed old lady should disport herself about India in this fashion; for certainly pilgrimage is grateful to the Gods. So all about India, in the most remote places, as in the most public, you find some knot of grizzled servitors in nominal charge of an old lady who is more or less curtained and hid away in a bullock-cart. Such men are staid and discreet, and when a European or a high-caste native is near will net their charge with most elaborate precautions; but in the ordinary haphazard chances of pilgrimage the precautions are not taken. The old lady is, after all, intensely human, and lives to look upon life.

Kim marked down a gaily ornamented ruth or family bullock-cart, with a broidered canopy of two domes, like a double-humped camel, which had just been drawn into the parao. Eight

men made its retinue, and two of the eight were armed with rusty sabres—sure signs that they followed a person of distinction, for the common folk do not bear arms. An increasing cackle of complaints, orders, and jests, and what to a European would have been bad language, came from behind the curtains. Here was evidently a woman used to command.

Kim looked over the retinue critically. Half of them were thin-legged, grey-bearded Ooryas from down country. The other half were duffle-clad, felt-hatted hillmen of the North; and that mixture told its own tale, even if he had not overheard the incessant sparring between the two divisions. The old lady was going south on a visit—probably to a rich relative, most probably to a son-in-law, who had sent up an escort as a mark of respect. The hillmen would be of her own people—Kulu or Kangra folk. It was quite clear that she was not taking her daughter down to be wedded, or the curtains would have been laced home and the guard would have allowed no one near the car. A merry and a high-spirited dame, thought Kim, balancing the dung-cake in one hand, the cooked food in the other, and piloting the lama with a nudging shoulder. Something might be made out of the meeting. The lama would give him no help, but, as a conscientious chela, Kim was delighted to beg for two.

He built his fire as close to the cart as he dared, waiting for one of the escort to order him away. The lama dropped wearily to the ground, much as a heavy fruit-eating bat cowers, and returned to his rosary.

"Stand farther off, beggar!" The order was shouted in broken Hindustani by one of the hillmen.

"Huh! It is only a pahari (a hillman)", said Kim over his shoulder. "Since when have the hill-asses owned all Hindustan?"

The retort was a swift and brilliant sketch of Kim's pedigree for three generations.

"Ah!" Kim's voice was sweeter than ever, as he broke the dung-cake into fit pieces. "In my country we call that the beginning of love-talk."

A harsh, thin cackle behind the curtains put the hillman on his mettle for a second shot.

"Not so bad—not so bad," said Kim with calm. "But have a care, my brother, lest we—we, I say—be minded to give a curse or so in return. And our curses have the knack of biting home."

The Ooryas laughed; the hillman sprang forward threateningly. The lama suddenly raised his head, bringing his huge tam-o'-shanter hat into the full light of Kim's new-started fire.

"What is it?" said he.

The man halted as though struck to stone. "I—I—am saved from a great sin," he stammered.

"The foreigner has found him a priest at last," whispered one of the Ooryas.

"Hai! Why is that beggar-brat not well beaten?" the old woman cried.

The hillman drew back to the cart and whispered something to the curtain. There was dead silence, then a muttering.

"This goes well," thought Kim, pretending neither to see nor hear.

"When—when—he has eaten"—the hillman fawned on Kim—"it—it is requested that the Holy One will do the honour to talk to one who would speak to him."

"After he has eaten he will sleep," Kim returned loftily. He could not quite see what new turn the game had taken, but stood resolute to profit by it. "Now I will get him his food." The last sentence, spoken loudly, ended with a sigh as of faintness.

"I—I myself and the others of my people will look to that—if it is permitted."

"It is permitted," said Kim, more loftily than ever. "Holy One, these people will bring us food."

"The land is good. All the country of the South is good—a great and a terrible world," mumbled the lama drowsily.

"Let him sleep," said Kim, "but look to it that we are well fed when he wakes. He is a very holy man."

Again one of the Ooryas said something contemptuously.

"He is not a faquir. He is not a down-country beggar," Kim went on severely, addressing the stars. "He is the most holy of holy men. He is above all castes. I am his chela."

"Come here!" said the flat thin voice behind the curtain; and Kim came, conscious that eyes he could not see were staring at him. One skinny brown finger heavy with rings lay on the edge of the cart, and the talk went this way:

"Who is that one?"

"An exceedingly holy one. He comes from far off. He comes from Tibet."

"Where in Tibet?"

"From behind the snows—from a very far place. He knows the stars; he makes horoscopes; he reads nativities. But he does not do this for money. He does it for kindness and great charity. I am his disciple. I am called also the Friend of the Stars."

"Thou art no hillman."

"Ask him. He will tell thee I was sent to him from the Stars to show him an end to his pilgrimage."

"Humph! Consider, brat, that I am an old woman and not altogether a fool. Lamas I know, and to these I give reverence, but thou art no more a lawful chela than this my finger is the pole of this wagon. Thou art a casteless Hindu—a bold and unblushing beggar, attached, belike, to the Holy One for the sake of gain."

"Do we not all work for gain?" Kim changed his tone promptly to match that altered voice. "I have heard"—this was a bow drawn at a venture—"I have heard—"

"What hast thou heard?" she snapped, rapping with the finger.

"Nothing that I well remember, but some talk in the bazars, which is doubtless a lie, that even Rajahs—small Hill Rajahs—"

"But none the less of good Rajput blood."

"Assuredly of good blood. That these even sell the more comely of their womenfolk for gain. Down south they sell them—to zemindars and such—all of Oudh."

If there be one thing in the world that the small Hill Rajahs deny it is just this charge; but it

happens to be one thing that the bazars believe, when they discuss the mysterious slave-traffics of India. The old lady explained to Kim, in a tense, indignant whisper, precisely what manner and fashion of malignant liar he was. Had Kim hinted this when she was a girl, he would have been pommelled to death that same evening by an elephant. This was perfectly true.

"Ahai! I am only a beggar's brat, as the Eye of Beauty has said," he wailed in extravagant terror.

"Eye of Beauty, forsooth! Who am I that thou shouldst fling beggar-endearments at me?" And yet she laughed at the long-forgotten word. "Forty years ago that might have been said, and not without truth. Ay. thirty years ago. But it is the fault of this gadding up and down Hind that a king's widow must jostle all the scum of the land, and be made a mock by beggars."

"Great Queen," said Kim promptly, for he heard her shaking with indignation, "I am even what the Great Queen says I am; but none the less is my master holy. He has not yet heard the Great Queen's order that—"

"Order? I order a Holy One—a Teacher of the Law—to come and speak to a woman? Never!"

"Pity my stupidity. I thought it was given as an order—"

"It was not. It was a petition. Does this make all clear?"

A silver coin clicked on the edge of the cart. Kim took it and salaamed profoundly. The old lady recognized that, as the eyes and the ears of the lama, he was to be propitiated.

"I am but the Holy One's disciple. When he has eaten perhaps he will come."

"Oh, villain and shameless rogue!" The jewelled forefinger shook itself at him reprovingly; but he could hear the old lady's chuckle.

"Nay, what is it?" he said, dropping into his most caressing and confidential tone—the one, he well knew, that few could resist. "Is—is there any need of a son in thy family? Speak freely, for we priests—" That last was a direct plagiarism from a faquir by the Taksali Gate.

"We priests! Thou art not yet old enough to—" She checked the joke with another laugh. "Believe me, now and again, we women, O priest, think of other matters than sons. Moreover, my daughter has borne her man-child."

"Two arrows in the quiver are better than one; and three are better still." Kim quoted the proverb with a meditative cough, looking discreetly earthward.

"True—oh, true. But perhaps that will come. Certainly those down-country Brahmins are utterly useless. I sent gifts and monies and gifts again to them, and they prophesied."

"Ah," drawled Kim, with infinite contempt, "they prophesied!" A professional could have done no better.

"And it was not till I remembered my own Gods that my prayers were heard. I chose an auspicious hour, and—perhaps thy Holy One has heard of the Abbot of the Lung-Cho lamassery. It was to him I put the matter, and behold in the due time all came about as I desired. The Brahmin in the house of the father of my daughter's son has since said that it was through his prayers—which is a little error that I will explain to him when we reach our journey's end. And so afterwards I go to Buddh Gaya, to make shraddha for the father of my children."

"Thither go we."

"Doubly auspicious," chirruped the old lady. "A second son at least!"

"O Friend of all the World!" The lama had waked, and, simply as a child bewildered in a strange bed, called for Kim.

"I come! I come, Holy One!" He dashed to the fire, where he found the lama already surrounded by dishes of food, the hillmen visibly adoring him and the Southerners looking sourly.

"Go back! Withdraw!" Kim cried. "Do we eat publicly like dogs?" They finished the meal in silence, each turned a little from the other, and Kim topped it with a native-made cigarette.

"Have I not said an hundred times that the South is a good land? Here is a virtuous and high-born widow of a Hill Rajah on pilgrimage, she says, to Buddha Gay. She it is sends us those dishes; and when thou art well rested she would speak to thee."

"Is this also thy work?" The lama dipped deep into his snuff-gourd.

"Who else watched over thee since our wonderful journey began?" Kim's eyes danced in his head as he blew the rank smoke through his nostrils and stretched him on the dusty ground. "Have I failed to oversee thy comforts, Holy One?"

"A blessing on thee." The lama inclined his solemn head. "I have known many men in my so long life, and disciples not a few. But to none among men, if so be thou art woman-born, has my heart gone out as it has to thee—thoughtful, wise, and courteous; but something of a small imp."

"And I have never seen such a priest as thou." Kim considered the benevolent yellow face wrinkle by wrinkle. "It is less than three days since we took the road together, and it is as though it were a hundred years."

"Perhaps in a former life it was permitted that I should have rendered thee some service. Maybe"—he smiled—"I freed thee from a trap; or, having caught thee on a hook in the days when I was not enlightened, cast thee back into the river."

"Maybe," said Kim quietly. He had heard this sort of speculation again and again, from the mouths of many whom the English would not consider imaginative. "Now, as regards that woman in the bullock-cart. I think she needs a second son for her daughter."

"That is no part of the Way," sighed the lama. "But at least she is from the Hills. Ah, the Hills, and the snow of the Hills!"

He rose and stalked to the cart. Kim would have given his ears to come too, but the lama did not invite him; and the few words he caught were in an unknown tongue, for they spoke some common speech of the mountains. The woman seemed to ask questions which the lama turned over in his mind before answering. Now and again he heard the singsong cadence of a Chinese quotation. It was a strange picture that Kim watched between drooped eyelids. The lama, very straight and erect, the deep folds of his yellow clothing slashed with black in the light of the parao fires precisely as a knotted tree-trunk is slashed with the shadows of the low sun, addressed a tinsel and lacquered ruth which burned like a many-coloured jewel in the same uncertain light. The patterns on the gold-worked curtains ran up and down, melting and reforming as the folds shook and quivered to the night wind; and when the talk grew more earnest the jewelled forefinger snapped out little sparks of light between the embroideries. Behind the cart was a wall of uncertain darkness speckled with little flames and alive with half-caught forms and faces and shadows. The voices of early evening had settled down to one soothing hum whose deepest note was the steady chumping of the bullocks above their chopped

straw, and whose highest was the tinkle of a Bengali dancing-girl's sitar. Most men had eaten and pulled deep at their gurgling, grunting hookahs, which in full blast sound like bull-frogs.

At last the lama returned. A hillman walked behind him with a wadded cotton-quilt and spread it carefully by the fire.

"She deserves ten thousand grandchildren," thought Kim. "None the less, but for me, those gifts would not have come."

"A virtuous woman—and a wise one." The lama slackened off, joint by joint, like a slow camel. "The world is full of charity to those who follow the Way." He flung a fair half of the quilt over Kim.

"And what said she?" Kim rolled up in his share of it.

"She asked me many questions and propounded many problems—the most of which were idle tales which she had heard from devil-serving priests who pretend to follow the Way. Some I answered, and some I said were foolish. Many wear the Robe, but few keep the Way."

"True. That is true." Kim used the thoughtful, conciliatory tone of those who wish to draw confidences.

"But by her lights she is most right-minded. She desires greatly that we should go with her to Buddh Gaya; her road being ours, as I understand, for many days' journey to the southward."

"And?"

"Patience a little. To this I said that my Search came before all things. She had heard many foolish legends, but this great truth of my River she had never heard. Such are the priests of the lower hills! She knew the Abbot of Lung-Cho, but she did not know of my River—nor the tale of the Arrow."

"And?"

"I spoke therefore of the Search, and of the Way, and of matters that were profitable; she desiring only that I should accompany her and make prayer for a second son."

"Aha! 'We women' do not think of anything save children," said Kim sleepily.

"Now, since our roads run together for a while, I do not see that we in any way depart from our Search if so be we accompany her—at least as far as—I have forgotten the name of the city."

"Ohé!" said Kim, turning and speaking in a sharp whisper to one of the Ooryas a few yards away. "Where is your master's house?"

"A little behind Saharunpore, among the fruit gardens." He named the village.

"That was the place," said the lama. "So far, at least, we can go with her."

"Flies go to carrion," said the Oorya, in an abstracted voice.

"For the sick cow a crow; for the sick man a Brahmin." Kim breathed the proverb impersonally to the shadow-tops of the trees overhead.

The Oorya grunted and held his peace.

"So then we go with her, Holy One?"

"Is there any reason against? I can still step aside and try all the rivers that the road overpasses. She desires that I should come. She very greatly desires it."

Kim stifled a laugh in the quilt. When once that imperious old lady had recovered from her natural awe of a lama he thought it probable that she would be worth listening to.

He was nearly asleep when the lama suddenly quoted a proverb: "The husbands of the talkative have a great reward hereafter." Then Kim heard him snuff thrice, and dozed off, still laughing.

The diamond-bright dawn woke men and crows and bullocks together. Kim sat up and yawned, shook himself, and thrilled with delight. This was seeing the world in real truth; this was life as he would have it—bustling and shouting, the buckling of belts, and beating of bullocks and creaking of wheels, lighting of fires and cooking of food, and new sights at every turn of the approving eye. The morning mist swept off in a whorl of silver, the parrots shot away to some distant river in shrieking green hosts: all the well-wheels within ear-shot went to work. India was awake, and Kim was in the middle of it, more awake and more excited than anyone, chewing on a twig that he would presently use as a toothbrush; for he borrowed right- and left-handedly from all the customs of the country he knew and loved. There was no need to worry about food—no need to spend a cowrie at the crowded stalls. He was the disciple of a holy man annexed by a strong-willed old lady. All things would be prepared for them, and when they were respectfully invited so to do they would sit and eat. For the rest—Kim giggled here as he cleaned his teeth—his hostess would rather heighten the enjoyment of the road. He inspected her bullocks critically, as they came up grunting and blowing under the yokes. If they went too fast—it was not likely—there would be a pleasant seat for himself along the pole; the lama would sit beside the driver. The escort, of course, would walk. The old lady, equally of course, would talk a great deal, and by what he had heard that conversation would not lack salt. She was already ordering, haranguing, rebuking, and, it must be said, cursing her servants for delays.

"Get her her pipe. In the name of the Gods, get her her pipe and stop her ill-omened mouth," cried an Oorya, tying up his shapeless bundles of bedding. "She and the parrots are alike. They screech in the dawn."

"The lead-bullocks! Hai! Look to the lead-bullocks!" They were backing and wheeling as a grain-cart's axle caught them by the horns. "Son of an owl, where dost thou go?" This to the grinning carter.

"Ai! Yai! Yai! That within there is the Queen of Delhi going to pray for a son," the man called back over his high load. "Room for the Queen of Delhi and her Prime Minister the grey monkey climbing up his own sword!" Another cart loaded with bark for a down-country tannery followed close behind, and its driver added a few compliments as the ruth-bullocks backed and backed again.

From behind the shaking curtains came one volley of invective. It did not last long, but in kind and quality, in blistering, biting appropriateness, it was beyond anything that even Kim had heard. He could see the carter's bare chest collapse with amazement, as the man salaamed reverently to the voice, leaped from the pole, and helped the escort haul their volcano on to the main road. Here the voice told him truthfully what sort of wife he had wedded, and what she was doing in his absence.

"Oh, shabash!" murmured Kim, unable to contain himself, as the man slunk away.

"Well done, indeed? It is a shame and a scandal that a poor woman may not go to make prayer

to her Gods except she be jostled and insulted by all the refuse of Hindustan—that she must eat gâli (abuse) as men eat ghi. But I have yet a wag left to my tongue—a word or two well spoken that serves the occasion. And still am I without my tobacco! Who is the one-eyed and luckless son of shame that has not yet prepared my pipe?"

It was hastily thrust in by a hillman, and a trickle of thick smoke from each corner of the curtains showed that peace was restored.

If Kim had walked proudly the day before, disciple of a holy man, today he paced with tenfold pride in the train of a semi-royal procession, with a recognized place under the patronage of an old lady of charming manners and infinite resource. The escort, their heads tied up native-fashion, fell in on either side the cart, shuffling enormous clouds of dust.

The lama and Kim walked a little to one side; Kim chewing his stick of sugarcane, and making way for no one under the status of a priest. They could hear the old lady's tongue clack as steadily as a rice-husker. She bade the escort tell her what was going on on the road; and so soon as they were clear of the parao she flung back the curtains and peered out, her veil a third across her face. Her men did not eye her directly when she addressed them, and thus the proprieties were more or less observed.

A dark, sallowish District Superintendent of Police, faultlessly uniformed, an Englishman, trotted by on a tired horse, and, seeing from her retinue what manner of person she was, chaffed her.

"O mother," he cried, "do they do this in the zenanas? Suppose an Englishman came by and saw that thou hast no nose?"

"What?" she shrilled back. "Thine own mother has no nose? Why say so, then, on the open road?"

It was a fair counter. The Englishman threw up his hand with the gesture of a man hit at sword-play. She laughed and nodded.

"Is this a face to tempt virtue aside?" She withdrew all her veil and stared at him.

It was by no means lovely, but as the man gathered up his reins he called it a Moon of Paradise, a Disturber of Integrity, and a few other fantastic epithets which doubled her up with mirth.

"That is a nut-cut (rogue)," she said. "All police-constables are nut-cuts; but the police-wallahs are the worst. Hai, my son, thou hast never learned all that since thou camest from Belait (Europe). Who suckled thee?"

"A pahareen—a hillwoman of Dalhousie, my mother. Keep thy beauty under a shade—O Dispenser of Delights," and he was gone.

"These be the sort"—she took a fine judicial tone, and stuffed her mouth with pan—"These be the sort to oversee justice. They know the land and the customs of the land. The others, all new from Europe, suckled by white women and learning our tongues from books, are worse than the pestilence. They do harm to Kings." Then she told a long, long tale to the world at large, of an ignorant young policeman who had disturbed some small Hill Rajah, a ninth cousin of her own, in the matter of a trivial land-case, winding up with a quotation from a work by no means devotional.

Then her mood changed, and she bade one of the escort ask whether the lama would walk alongside and discuss matters of religion. So Kim dropped back into the dust and returned to

his sugar-cane. For an hour or more the lama's tam-o'shanter showed like a moon through the haze; and, from all he heard, Kim gathered that the old woman wept. One of the Ooryas half apologized for his rudeness overnight, saying that he had never known his mistress of so bland a temper, and he ascribed it to the presence of the strange priest. Personally, he believed in Brahmins, though, like all natives, he was acutely aware of their cunning and their greed. Still, when Brahmins but irritated with begging demands the mother of his master's wife, and when she sent them away so angry that they cursed the whole retinue (which was the real reason of the second off-side bullock going lame, and of the pole breaking the night before), he was prepared to accept any priest of any other denomination in or out of India. To this Kim assented with wise nods, and bade the Oorya observe that the lama took no money, and that the cost of his and Kim's food would be repaid a hundred times in the good luck that would attend the caravan henceforward. He also told stories of Lahore city, and sang a song or two which made the escort laugh. As a town-mouse well acquainted with the latest songs by the most fashionable composers—they are women for the most part—Kim had a distinct advantage over men from a little fruit-village behind Saharunpore, but he let that advantage be inferred.

At noon they turned aside to eat, and the meal was good, plentiful, and well-served on plates of clean leaves, in decency, out of drift of the dust. They gave the scraps to certain beggars, that all requirements might be fulfilled, and sat down to a long, luxurious smoke. The old lady had retreated behind her curtains, but mixed most freely in the talk, her servants arguing with and contradicting her as servants do throughout the East. She compared the cool and the pines of the Kangra and Kulu hills with the dust and the mangoes of the South; she told a tale of some old local Gods at the edge of her husband's territory; she roundly abused the tobacco which she was then smoking, reviled all Brahmins, and speculated without reserve on the coming of many grandsons.

CHAPTER V

Here come I to my own again
Fed, forgiven, and known again
Claimed by bone of my bone again,
And sib to flesh of my flesh!
The fatted calf is dressed for me,
But the husks have greater zest for me ...
I think my pigs will be best for me,
So I'm off to the styes afresh.

The Prodigal Son.

Once more the lazy, string-tied, shuffling procession got under way, and she slept till they reached the next halting-stage. It was a very short march, and time lacked an hour to sundown, so Kim cast about for means of amusement.

"But why not sit and rest?" said one of the escort. "Only the devils and the English walk to and fro without reason."

"Never make friends with the Devil, a Monkey, or a Boy. No man knows what they will do next," said his fellow.

Kim turned a scornful back—he did not want to hear the old story how the Devil played with the boys and repented of it and walked idly across country.

The lama strode after him. All that day, whenever they passed a stream, he had turned aside to look at it, but in no case had he received any warning that he had found his River. Insensibly, too, the comfort of speaking to someone in a reasonable tongue, and of being properly considered and respected as her spiritual adviser by a well-born woman, had weaned his thoughts a little from the Search. And further, he was prepared to spend serene years in his quest; having nothing of the white man's impatience, but a great faith.

"Where goest thou?" he called after Kim.

"Nowhither—it was a small march, and all this"—Kim waved his hands abroad—"is new to me."

"She is beyond question a wise and a discerning woman. But it is hard to meditate when—"

"All women are thus." Kim spoke as might have Solomon.

"Before the lamassery was a broad platform," the lama muttered, looping up the well-worn rosary, "of stone. On that I have left the marks of my feet—pacing to and fro with these."

He clicked the beads, and began the "Om mane pudme hum" of his devotion; grateful for the cool, the quiet, and the absence of dust.

One thing after another drew Kim's idle eye across the plain. There was no purpose in his wanderings, except that the build of the huts near by seemed new, and he wished to investigate.

They came out on a broad tract of grazing-ground, brown and purple in the afternoon light, with a heavy clump of mangoes in the centre. It struck Kim as curious that no shrine stood in so

eligible a spot: the boy was observing as any priest for these things. Far across the plain walked side by side four men, made small by the distance. He looked intently under his curved palms and caught the sheen of brass.

"Soldiers. White soldiers!" said he. "Let us see."

"It is always soldiers when thou and I go out alone together. But I have never seen the white soldiers."

"They do no harm except when they are drunk. Keep behind this tree."

They stepped behind the thick trunks in the cool dark of the mango-tope. Two little figures halted; the other two came forward uncertainly. They were the advance-party of a regiment on the march, sent out, as usual, to mark the camp. They bore five-foot sticks with fluttering flags, and called to each other as they spread over the flat earth.

At last they entered the mango-grove, walking heavily.

"It's here or hereabouts—officers' tents under the trees, I take it, an' the rest of us can stay outside. Have they marked out for the baggage-wagons behind?"

They cried again to their comrades in the distance, and the rough answer came back faint and mellowed.

"Shove the flag in here, then," said one.

"What do they prepare?" said the lama, wonderstruck. "This is a great and terrible world. What is the device on the flag?"

A soldier thrust a stave within a few feet of them, grunted discontentedly, pulled it up again, conferred with his companion, who looked up and down the shaded cave of greenery, and returned it.

Kim stared with all his eyes, his breath coming short and sharp between his teeth. The soldiers stamped off into the sunshine.

"O Holy One!" he gasped. "My horoscope! The drawing in the dust by the priest at Umballa! Remember what he said. First come two—ferashes—to make all things ready—in a dark place, as it is always at the beginning of a vision."

"But this is not vision," said the lama. "It is the world's Illusion, and no more."

"And after them comes the Bull—the Red Bull on the green field. Look! It is he!"

He pointed to the flag that was snap snapping in the evening breeze not ten feet away. It was no more than an ordinary camp marking-flag; but the regiment, always punctilious in matters of millinery, had charged it with the regimental device, the Red Bull, which is the crest of the Mavericks—the great Red Bull on a background of Irish green.

"I see, and now I remember." said the lama. "Certainly it is thy Bull. Certainly, also, the two men came to make all ready."

"They are soldiers—white soldiers. What said the priest? 'The sign over against the Bull is the sign of War and armed men.' Holy One, this thing touches my Search."

"True. It is true." The lama stared fixedly at the device that flamed like a ruby in the dusk. "The

priest at Umballa said that thine was the sign of War."

"What is to do now?"

"Wait. Let us wait."

"Even now the darkness clears," said Kim. It was only natural that the descending sun should at last strike through the tree-trunks, across the grove, filling it with mealy gold light for a few minutes; but to Kim it was the crown of the Umballa Brahmin's prophecy.

"Hark!" said the lama. "One beats a drum—far off!"

At first the sound, carrying diluted through the still air, resembled the beating of an artery in the head. Soon a sharpness was added.

"Ah! The music," Kim explained. He knew the sound of a regimental band, but it amazed the lama.

At the far end of the plain a heavy, dusty column crawled in sight. Then the wind brought the tune:

We crave your condescension
To tell you what we know
Of marching in the Mulligan Guards
To Sligo Port below!

Here broke in the shrill-tongued fifes:

We shouldered arms,
We marched—we marched away.
From Phœnix Park
We marched to Dublin Bay.
The drums and the fifes,
Oh, sweetly they did play,
As we marched—marched—marched—with the
Mulligan Guards!

It was the band of the Mavericks playing the regiment to camp; for the men were route-marching with their baggage. The rippling column swung into the level—carts behind it divided left and right, ran about like an ant-hill, and ...

"But this is sorcery!" said the lama.

The plain dotted itself with tents that seemed to rise, all spread, from the carts. Another rush of men invaded the grove, pitched a huge tent in silence, ran up yet eight or nine more by the side of it, unearthed cooking-pots, pans, and bundles, which were taken possession of by a crowd of native servants; and behold the mango-tope turned into an orderly town as they watched!

"Let us go," said the lama, sinking back afraid, as the fires twinkled and white officers with jingling swords stalked into the Mess-tent.

"Stand back in the shadow. No one can see beyond the light of a fire," said Kim, his eyes still on the flag. He had never before watched the routine of a seasoned regiment pitching camp in thirty minutes.

"Look! look! look!" clucked the lama. "Yonder comes a priest." It was Bennett, the Church of England Chaplain of the regiment, limping in dusty black. One of his flock had made some rude remarks about the Chaplain's mettle; and to abash him Bennett had marched step by step with the men that day. The black dress, gold cross on the watch-chain, the hairless face, and the soft, black wideawake hat would have marked him as a holy man anywhere in all India. He dropped into a camp-chair by the door of the Mess-tent and slid off his boots. Three or four officers gathered round him, laughing and joking over his exploit.

"The talk of white men is wholly lacking in dignity," said the lama, who judged only by tone. "But I considered the countenance of that priest and I think he is learned. Is it likely that he will understand our talk? I would talk to him of my Search."

"Never speak to a white man till he is fed," said Kim, quoting a well-known proverb. "They will eat now, and—and I do not think they are good to beg from. Let us go back to the resting-place. After we have eaten we will come again. It certainly was a Red Bull—my Red Bull."

They were both noticeably absent-minded when the old lady's retinue set their meal before them; so none broke their reserve, for it is not lucky to annoy guests.

"Now," said Kim, picking his teeth, "we will return to that place; but thou, O Holy One, must wait a little way off, because thy feet are heavier than mine and I am anxious to see more of that Red Bull."

"But how canst thou understand the talk? Walk slowly. The road is dark," the lama replied uneasily.

Kim put the question aside. "I marked a place near to the trees," said he, "where thou canst sit till I call. Nay," as the lama made some sort of protest, "remember this is my Search—the Search for my Red Bull. The sign in the Stars was not for thee. I know a little of the customs of white soldiers, and I always desire to see some new things."

"What dost thou not know of this world?" The lama squatted obediently in a little hollow of the ground not a hundred yards from the hump of the mango-trees dark against the star-powdered sky.

"Stay till I call." Kim flitted into the dusk. He knew that in all probability there would be sentries round the camp, and smiled to himself as he heard the thick boots of one. A boy who can dodge over the roofs of Lahore city on a moonlight night, using every little patch and corner of darkness to discomfit his pursuer, is not likely to be checked by a line of well-trained soldiers. He paid them the compliment of crawling between a couple, and, running and halting, crouching and dropping flat, worked his way toward the lighted Mess-tent where, close pressed behind the mango-tree, he waited till some chance word should give him a returnable lead.

The one thing now in his mind was further information as to the Red Bull. For aught he knew, and Kim's limitations were as curious and sudden as his expansions, the men, the nine hundred thorough devils of his father's prophecy, might pray to the beast after dark, as Hindus pray to the Holy Cow. That at least would be entirely right and logical, and the padre with the gold cross would be therefore the man to consult in the matter. On the other hand, remembering sober-faced padres whom he had avoided in Lahore city, the priest might be an inquisitive nuisance who would bid him learn. But had it not been proven at Umballa that his sign in the high heavens portended War and armed men? Was he not the Friend of the Stars as well as of all the World, crammed to the teeth with dreadful secrets? Lastly—and firstly as the undercurrent of all his quick thoughts—this adventure, though he did not know the English word, was a stupendous lark—a delightful continuation of his old flights across the housetops, as well as the fulfilment

of sublime prophecy. He lay belly-flat and wriggled towards the Mess-tent door, a hand on the amulet round his neck.

It was as he suspected. The Sahibs prayed to their God; for in the centre of the Mess-table—its sole ornament when they were on the line of march—stood a golden bull fashioned from old-time loot of the Summer Palace at Pekin—a red-gold bull with lowered head, ramping upon a field of Irish green. To him the Sahibs held out their glasses and cried aloud confusedly.

Now the Reverend Arthur Bennett always left Mess after that toast, and being rather tired by his march his movements were more abrupt than usual. Kim, with slightly raised head, was still staring at his totem on the table, when the Chaplain stepped on his right shoulder-blade. Kim flinched under the leather, and, rolling sideways, brought down the Chaplain, who, ever a man of action, caught him by the throat and nearly choked the life out of him. Kim then kicked him desperately in the stomach. Mr Bennett gasped and doubled up, but without relaxing his grip, rolled over again, and silently hauled Kim to his own tent. The Mavericks were incurable practical jokers; and it occurred to the Englishman that silence was best till he had made complete inquiry.

"Why, it's a boy!" he said, as he drew his prize under the light of the tent-pole lantern, then shaking him severely cried: "What were you doing? You're a thief. Choor? Mallum?" His Hindustanee was very limited, and the ruffled and disgusted Kim intended to keep to the character laid down for him. As he recovered his breath he was inventing a beautifully plausible tale of his relations to some scullion, and at the same time keeping a keen eye on and a little under the Chaplain's left arm-pit. The chance came; he ducked for the doorway, but a long arm shot out and clutched at his neck, snapping the amulet-string and closing on the amulet.

"Give it me. O, give it me. Is it lost? Give me the papers."

The words were in English—the tinny, saw-cut English of the native-bred, and the Chaplain jumped.

"A scapular," said he, opening his hand. "No, some sort of heathen charm. Why—why, do you speak English? Little boys who steal are beaten. You know that?"

"I do not—I did not steal." Kim danced in agony like a terrier at a lifted stick. "Oh, give it me. It is my charm. Do not thieve it from me."

The Chaplain took no heed, but, going to the tent door, called aloud. A fattish, clean-shaven man appeared.

"I want your advice, Father Victor," said Bennett. "I found this boy in the dark outside the Mess-tent. Ordinarily, I should have chastised him and let him go, because I believe him to be a thief. But it seems he talks English, and he attaches some sort of value to a charm round his neck. I thought perhaps you might help me."

Between himself and the Roman Catholic Chaplain of the Irish contingent lay, as Bennett believed, an unbridgeable gulf, but it was noticeable that whenever the Church of England dealt with a human problem she was very likely to call in the Church of Rome. Bennett's official abhorrence of the Scarlet Woman and all her ways was only equalled by his private respect for Father Victor.

"A thief talking English, is it? Let's look at his charm. No, it's not a scapular, Bennett." He held out his hand.

"But have we any right to open it? A sound whipping—"

"I did not thieve," protested Kim. "You have hit me kicks all over my body. Now give me my charm and I will go away."

"Not quite so fast. We'll look first," said Father Victor, leisurely rolling out poor Kimball O'Hara's "ne varietur" parchment, his clearance-certificate, and Kim's baptismal certificate. On this last O'Hara—with some confused idea that he was doing wonders for his son—had scrawled scores of times: "Look after the boy. Please look after the boy"—signing his name and regimental number in full.

"Powers of Darkness below!" said Father Victor, passing all over to Mr Bennett. "Do you know what these things are?"

"Yes." said Kim. "They are mine, and I want to go away."

"I do not quite understand," said Mr Bennett. "He probably brought them on purpose. It may be a begging trick of some kind."

"I never saw a beggar less anxious to stay with his company, then. There's the makings of a gay mystery here. Ye believe in Providence, Bennett?"

"I hope so."

"Well, I believe in miracles, so it comes to the same thing. Powers of Darkness! Kimball O'Hara! And his son! But then he's a native, and I saw Kimball married myself to Annie Shott. How long have you had these things, boy?"

"Ever since I was a little baby."

Father Victor stepped forward quickly and opened the front of Kim's upper garment. "You see, Bennett, he's not very black. What's your name?"

"Kim."

"Or Kimball?"

"Perhaps. Will you let me go away?"

"What else?"

"They call me Kim Rishti ke. That is Kim of the Rishti."

"What is that—'Rishti'?"

"Eye-rishti—that was the Regiment—my father's."

"Irish—oh, I see."

"Yess. That was how my father told me. My father, he has lived."

"Has lived where?"

"Has lived. Of course he is dead—gone-out."

"Oh! That's your abrupt way of putting it, is it?"

Bennett interrupted. "It is possible I have done the boy an injustice. He is certainly white, though evidently neglected. I am sure I must have bruised him. I do not think spirits—"

"Get him a glass of sherry, then, and let him squat on the cot. Now, Kim," continued Father Victor, "no one is going to hurt you. Drink that down and tell us about yourself. The truth, if you've no objection."

Kim coughed a little as he put down the empty glass, and considered. This seemed a time for caution and fancy. Small boys who prowl about camps are generally turned out after a whipping. But he had received no stripes; the amulet was evidently working in his favour, and it looked as though the Umballa horoscope and the few words that he could remember of his father's maunderings fitted in most miraculously. Else why did the fat padre seem so impressed, and why the glass of hot yellow drink from the lean one?

"My father, he is dead in Lahore city since I was very little. The woman, she kept kabarri shop near where the hire-carriages are." Kim began with a plunge, not quite sure how far the truth would serve him.

"Your mother?"

"No!"—with a gesture of disgust. "She went out when I was born. My father, he got these papers from the Jadoo-Gher what do you call that?" (Bennett nodded) "because he was in good-standing. What do you call that?" (again Bennett nodded). "My father told me that. He said, too, and also the Brahmin who made the drawing in the dust at Umballa two days ago, he said, that I shall find a Red Bull on a green field and that the Bull shall help me."

"A phenomenal little liar," muttered Bennett.

"Powers of Darkness below, what a country!" murmured Father Victor. "Go on, Kim."

"I did not thieve. Besides, I am just now disciple of a very holy man. He is sitting outside. We saw two men come with flags, making the place ready. That is always so in a dream, or on account of a—a—prophecy. So I knew it was come true. I saw the Red Bull on the green field, and my father he said: 'Nine hundred pukka devils and the Colonel riding on a horse will look after you when you find the Red Bull!' I did not know what to do when I saw the Bull, but I went away and I came again when it was dark. I wanted to see the Bull again, and I saw the Bull again with the—the Sahibs praying to it. I think the Bull shall help me. The holy man said so too. He is sitting outside. Will you hurt him, if I call him a shout now? He is very holy. He can witness to all the things I say, and he knows I am not a thief."

"'Sahibs praying to a bull!' What in the world do you make of that?" said Bennett. "'Disciple of a holy man!' Is the boy mad?"

"It's O'Hara's boy, sure enough. O'Hara's boy leagued with all the Powers of Darkness. It's very much what his father would have done if he was drunk. We'd better invite the holy man. He may know something."

"He does not know anything," said Kim. "I will show you him if you come. He is my master. Then afterwards we can go."

"Powers of Darkness!" was all that Father Victor could say, as Bennett marched off, with a firm hand on Kim's shoulder.

They found the lama where he had dropped.

"The Search is at an end for me," shouted Kim in the vernacular. "I have found the Bull, but God knows what comes next. They will not hurt you. Come to the fat priest's tent with this thin man and see the end. It is all new, and they cannot talk Hindi. They are only uncurried donkeys."

"Then it is not well to make a jest of their ignorance," the lama returned. "I am glad if thou art rejoiced, chela."

Dignified and unsuspicious, he strode into the little tent, saluted the Churches as a Churchman, and sat down by the open charcoal brazier. The yellow lining of the tent reflected in the lamplight made his face red-gold.

Bennett looked at him with the triple-ringed uninterest of the creed that lumps nine-tenths of the world under the title of "heathen".

"And what was the end of the Search? What gift has the Red Bull brought?" The lama addressed himself to Kim.

"He says, 'What are you going to do?'" Bennett was staring uneasily at Father Victor, and Kim, for his own ends, took upon himself the office of interpreter.

"I do not see what concern this faquir has with the boy, who is probably his dupe or his confederate," Bennett began. "We cannot allow an English boy—Assuming that he is the son of a Mason, the sooner he goes to the Masonic Orphanage the better."

"Ah! That's your opinion as Secretary to the Regimental Lodge," said Father Victor; "but we might as well tell the old man what we are going to do. He doesn't look like a villain."

"My experience is that one can never fathom the Oriental mind. Now, Kimball, I wish you to tell this man what I say word for word."

Kim gathered the import of the next few sentences and began thus:

"Holy One, the thin fool who looks like a camel says that I am the son of a Sahib."

"But how?"

"Oh, it is true. I knew it since my birth, but he could only find it out by rending the amulet from my neck and reading all the papers. He thinks that once a Sahib is always a Sahib, and between the two of them they purpose to keep me in this Regiment or to send me to a madrissah (a school). It has happened before. I have always avoided it. The fat fool is of one mind and the camel-like one of another. But that is no odds. I may spend one night here and perhaps the next. It has happened before. Then I will run away and return to thee."

"But tell them that thou art my chela. Tell them how thou didst come to me when I was faint and bewildered. Tell them of our Search, and they will surely let thee go now."

"I have already told them. They laugh, and they talk of the police."

"What are you saying?" asked Mr Bennett.

"Oah. He only says that if you do not let me go it will stop him in his business—his ur-gent private af-fairs." This last was a reminiscence of some talk with a Eurasian clerk in the Canal Department, but it only drew a smile, which nettled him. "And if you did know what his business was you would not be in such a beastly hurry to interfere."

"What is it then?" said Father Victor, not without feeling, as he watched the lama's face.

"There is a River in this country which he wishes to find so verree much. It was put out by an Arrow which—" Kim tapped his foot impatiently as he translated in his own mind from the vernacular to his clumsy English. "Oah, it was made by our Lord God Buddha, you know, and if you wash there you are washed away from all your sins and made as white as cotton-wool." (Kim had heard mission-talk in his time.) "I am his disciple, and we must find that River. It is so verree valuable to us."

"Say that again," said Bennett. Kim obeyed, with amplifications.

"But this is gross blasphemy!" cried the Church of England.

"Tck! Tck!" said Father Victor sympathetically. "I'd give a good deal to be able to talk the vernacular. A river that washes away sin! And how long have you two been looking for it?"

"Oh, many days. Now we wish to go away and look for it again. It is not here, you see."

"I see," said Father Victor gravely. "But he can't go on in that old man's company. It would be different, Kim, if you were not a soldier's son. Tell him that the Regiment will take care of you and make you as good a man as your—as good a man as can be. Tell him that if he believes in miracles he must believe that—"

"There is no need to play on his credulity," Bennett interrupted.

"I'm doing no such thing. He must believe that the boy's coming here—to his own Regiment— in search of his Red Bull is in the nature of a miracle. Consider the chances against it, Bennett. This one boy in all India, and our Regiment of all others on the line o' march for him to meet with! It's predestined on the face of it. Yes, tell him it's Kismet. Kismet, mallum? (Do you understand?)"

He turned towards the lama, to whom he might as well have talked of Mesopotamia.

"They say,"—the old man's eye lighted at Kim's speech "they say that the meaning of my horoscope is now accomplished, and that being led back—though as thou knowest I went out of curiosity—to these people and their Red Bull I must needs go to a madrissah and be turned into a Sahib. Now I make pretence of agreement, for at the worst it will be but a few meals eaten away from thee. Then I will slip away and follow down the road to Saharunpore. Therefore, Holy One, keep with that Kulu woman—on no account stray far from her cart till I come again. Past question, my sign is of War and of armed men. See how they have given me wine to drink and set me upon a bed of honour! My father must have been some great person. So if they raise me to honour among them, good. If not, good again. However it goes, I will run back to thee when I am tired. But stay with the Rajputni, or I shall miss thy feet ... Oah yess," said the boy, "I have told him everything you tell me to say."

"And I cannot see any need why he should wait," said Bennett, feeling in his trouser-pocket. "We can investigate the details later—and I will give him a ru—"

"Give him time. Maybe he's fond of the lad," said Father Victor, half arresting the clergyman's motion.

The lama dragged forth his rosary and pulled his huge hat-brim over his eyes.

"What can he want now?"

"He says"—Kim put up one hand. "He says: 'Be quiet.' He wants to speak to me by himself. You see, you do not know one little word of what he says, and I think if you talk he will perhaps give you very bad curses. When he takes those beads like that, you see, he always wants to be quiet."

The two Englishmen sat overwhelmed, but there was a look in Bennett's eye that promised ill for Kim when he should be relaxed to the religious arm.

"A Sahib and the son of a Sahib—" The lama's voice was harsh with pain. "But no white man knows the land and the customs of the land as thou knowest. How comes it this is true?"

"What matter, Holy One?—but remember it is only for a night or two. Remember, I can change swiftly. It will all be as it was when I first spoke to thee under Zam-Zammah the great gun—"

"As a boy in the dress of white men—when I first went to the Wonder House. And a second time thou wast a Hindu. What shall the third incarnation be?" He chuckled drearily. "Ah, chela, thou has done a wrong to an old man because my heart went out to thee."

"And mine to thee. But how could I know that the Red Bull would bring me to this business?"

The lama covered his face afresh, and nervously rattled the rosary. Kim squatted beside him and laid hold upon a fold of his clothing.

"Now it is understood that the boy is a Sahib?" he went on in a muffled tone. "Such a Sahib as was he who kept the images in the Wonder House." The lama's experience of white men was limited. He seemed to be repeating a lesson. "So then it is not seemly that he should do other than as the Sahibs do. He must go back to his own people."

"For a day and a night and a day," Kim pleaded.

"No, ye don't!" Father Victor saw Kim edging towards the door, and interposed a strong leg.

"I do not understand the customs of white men. The Priest of the Images in the Wonder House in Lahore was more courteous than the thin one here. This boy will be taken from me. They will make a Sahib of my disciple? Woe to me! How shall I find my River? Have they no disciples? Ask."

"He says he is very sorree that he cannot find the River now any more. He says, Why have you no disciples, and stop bothering him? He wants to be washed of his sins."

Neither Bennett nor Father Victor found any answer ready.

Said Kim in English, distressed for the lama's agony: "I think if you will let me go now we will walk away quietly and not steal. We will look for that River like before I was caught. I wish I did not come here to find the Red Bull and all that sort of thing. I do not want it."

"It's the very best day's work you ever did for yourself, young man," said Bennett.

"Good heavens, I don't know how to console him," said Father Victor, watching the lama intently. "He can't take the boy away with him, and yet he's a good man—I'm sure he's a good man. Bennett, if you give him that rupee he'll curse you root and branch!"

They listened to each other's breathing—three—five full minutes. Then the lama raised his head, and looked forth across them into space and emptiness.

"And I am a Follower of the Way," he said bitterly. "The sin is mine and the punishment is mine. I made believe to myself for now I see it was but make-belief—that thou wast sent to me to aid in the Search. So my heart went out to thee for thy charity and thy courtesy and the wisdom of thy little years. But those who follow the Way must permit not the fire of any desire or attachment, for that is all Illusion. As says ..." He quoted an old, old Chinese text, backed it with another, and reinforced these with a third. "I stepped aside from the Way, my chela. It was no fault of thine. I delighted in the sight of life, the new people upon the roads, and in thy joy at seeing these things. I was pleased with thee who should have considered my Search and my Search alone. Now I am sorrowful because thou art taken away and my River is far from me. It is the Law which I have broken!"

"Powers of Darkness below!" said Father Victor, who, wise in the confessional, heard the pain in every sentence.

"I see now that the sign of the Red Bull was a sign for me as well as for thee. All Desire is red—and evil. I will do penance and find my River alone."

"At least go back to the Kulu woman," said Kim, "otherwise thou wilt be lost upon the roads. She will feed thee till I run back to thee."

The lama waved a hand to show that the matter was finally settled in his mind.

"Now,"—his tone altered as he turned to Kim,—"what will they do with thee? At least I may, acquiring merit, wipe out past ill."

"Make me a Sahib—so they think. The day after tomorrow I return. Do not grieve."

"Of what sort? Such an one as this or that man?" He pointed to Father Victor. "Such an one as those I saw this evening, men wearing swords and stamping heavily?"

"Maybe."

"That is not well. These men follow desire and come to emptiness. Thou must not be of their sort."

"The Umballa priest said that my Star was War," Kim interjected. "I will ask these fools—but there is truly no need. I will run away this night, for all I wanted to see the new things."

Kim put two or three questions in English to Father Victor, translating the replies to the lama.

Then: "He says, 'You take him from me and you cannot say what you will make him.' He says, 'Tell me before I go, for it is not a small thing to make a child.'"

"You will be sent to a school. Later on, we shall see. Kimball, I suppose you'd like to be a soldier?"

"Gorah-log (white-folk). No-ah! No-ah!" Kim shook his head violently. There was nothing in his composition to which drill and routine appealed. "I will not be a soldier."

"You will be what you're told to be," said Bennett; "and you should be grateful that we're going to help you."

Kim smiled compassionately. If these men lay under the delusion that he would do anything that he did not fancy, so much the better.

Another long silence followed. Bennett fidgeted with impatience, and suggested calling a sentry to evict the faquir.

"Do they give or sell learning among the Sahibs? Ask them," said the lama, and Kim interpreted.

"They say that money is paid to the teacher—but that money the Regiment will give ... What need? It is only for a night."

"And—the more money is paid the better learning is given?" The lama disregarded Kim's plans for an early flight. "It is no wrong to pay for learning. To help the ignorant to wisdom is always a merit." The rosary clicked furiously as an abacus. Then he faced his oppressors.

"Ask them for how much money do they give a wise and suitable teaching? And in what city is that teaching given?"

"Well," said Father Victor in English, when Kim had translated, "that depends. The Regiment would pay for you all the time you are at the Military Orphanage; or you might go on the Punjab Masonic Orphanage's list (not that he or you 'ud understand what that means); but the best schooling a boy can get in India is, of course, at St Xavier's in Partibus at Lucknow." This took some time to interpret, for Bennett wished to cut it short.

"He wants to know how much?" said Kim placidly.

"Two or three hundred rupees a year." Father Victor was long past any sense of amazement. Bennett, impatient, did not understand.

"He says: 'Write that name and the money upon a paper and give it him.' And he says you must write your name below, because he is going to write a letter in some days to you. He says you are a good man. He says the other man is a fool. He is going away."

The lama rose suddenly. "I follow my Search," he cried, and was gone.

"He'll run slap into the sentries," cried Father Victor, jumping up as the lama stalked out; "but I can't leave the boy." Kim made swift motion to follow, but checked himself. There was no sound of challenge outside. The lama had disappeared.

Kim settled himself composedly on the Chaplain's cot. At least the lama had promised that he would stay with the Raiput woman from Kulu, and the rest was of the smallest importance. It pleased him that the two padres were so evidently excited. They talked long in undertones, Father Victor urging some scheme on Mr Bennett, who seemed incredulous. All this was very new and fascinating, but Kim felt sleepy. They called men into the tent—one of them certainly was the Colonel, as his father had prophesied—and they asked him an infinity of questions, chiefly about the woman who looked after him, all of which Kim answered truthfully. They did not seem to think the woman a good guardian.

After all, this was the newest of his experiences. Sooner or later, if he chose, he could escape into great, grey, formless India, beyond tents and padres and colonels. Meantime, if the Sahibs were to be impressed, he would do his best to impress them. He too was a white man.

After much talk that he could not comprehend, they handed him over to a sergeant, who had strict instructions not to let him escape. The Regiment would go on to Umballa, and Kim would be sent up, partly at the expense of the Lodge and in part by subscription, to a place called Sanawar.

"It's miraculous past all whooping, Colonel," said Father Victor, when he had talked without

a break for ten minutes. "His Buddhist friend has levanted after taking my name and address. I can't quite make out whether he'll pay for the boy's education or whether he is preparing some sort of witchcraft on his own account." Then to Kim: "You'll live to be grateful to your friend the Red Bull yet. We'll make a man of you at Sanawar—even at the price o' making you a Protestant."

"Certainly—most certainly," said Bennett.

"But you will not go to Sanawar," said Kim.

"But we will go to Sanawar, little man. That's the order of the Commander-in-Chief, who's a trifle more important than O'Hara's son."

"You will not go to Sanawar. You will go to thee War."

There was a shout of laughter from the full tent.

"When you know your own Regiment a trifle better you won't confuse the line of march with line of battle, Kim. We hope to go to 'thee War' sometime."

"Oah, I know all thatt." Kim drew his bow again at a venture. If they were not going to the war, at least they did not know what he knew of the talk in the veranda at Umballa.

"I know you are not at thee war now; but I tell you that as soon as you get to Umballa you will be sent to the war—the new war. It is a war of eight thousand men, besides the guns."

"That's explicit. D'you add prophecy to your other gifts? Take him along, sergeant. Take up a suit for him from the Drums, an' take care he doesn't slip through your fingers. Who says the age of miracles is gone by? I think I'll go to bed. My poor mind's weakening."

At the far end of the camp, silent as a wild animal, an hour later sat Kim, newly washed all over, in a horrible stiff suit that rasped his arms and legs.

"A most amazin' young bird," said the sergeant. "He turns up in charge of a yellow-headed buck-Brahmin priest, with his father's Lodge certificates round his neck, talkin' God knows what all of a red bull. The buck-Brahmin evaporates without explanations, an' the bhoy sets cross-legged on the Chaplain's bed prophesyin' bloody war to the men at large. Injia's a wild land for a God-fearin' man. I'll just tie his leg to the tent-pole in case he'll go through the roof. What did ye say about the war?"

"Eight thousand men, besides guns," said Kim. "Very soon you will see."

"You're a consolin' little imp. Lie down between the Drums an' go to bye-bye. Those two boys will watch your slumbers."

CHAPTER VI

Now I remember comrades—
Old playmates on new seas—
Whenas we traded orpiment
Among the savages.
Ten thousand leagues to southward,
And thirty years removed—
They knew not noble Valdez,
But me they knew and loved.

Song of Diego Valdez.

Very early in the morning the white tents came down and disappeared as the Mavericks took a side-road to Umballa. It did not skirt the resting-place, and Kim, trudging beside a baggage-cart under fire of comments from soldiers' wives, was not so confident as overnight. He discovered that he was closely watched—Father Victor on the one side, and Mr Bennett on the other.

In the forenoon the column checked. A camel-orderly handed the Colonel a letter. He read it, and spoke to a Major. Half a mile in the rear, Kim heard a hoarse and joyful clamour rolling down on him through the thick dust. Then someone beat him on the back, crying: "Tell us how ye knew, ye little limb of Satan? Father dear, see if ye can make him tell."

A pony ranged alongside, and he was hauled on to the priest's saddlebow.

"Now, my son, your prophecy of last night has come true. Our orders are to entrain at Umballa for the Front tomorrow."

"What is thatt?" said Kim, for "front" and "entrain" were newish words to him.

"We are going to 'thee War,' as you called it."

"Of course you are going to thee War. I said last night."

"Ye did; but, Powers o' Darkness, how did ye know?"

Kim's eyes sparkled. He shut his lips, nodded his head, and looked unspeakable things. The Chaplain moved on through the dust, and privates, sergeants, and subalterns called one another's attention to the boy. The Colonel, at the head of the column, stared at him curiously. "It was probably some bazar rumour." he said; "but even then—" He referred to the paper in his hand. "Hang it all, the thing was only decided within the last forty-eight hours."

"Are there many more like you in India?" said Father Victor, "or are you by way o' being a lusus naturæ?"

"Now I have told you," said the boy, "will you let me go back to my old man? If he has not stayed with that woman from Kulu, I am afraid he will die."

"By what I saw of him he's as well able to take care of himself as you. No. Ye've brought us luck, an' we're goin' to make a man of you. I'll take ye back to your baggage-cart and ye'll come to me this evening."

For the rest of the day Kim found himself an object of distinguished consideration among a few

hundred white men. The story of his appearance in camp, the discovery of his parentage, and his prophecy, had lost nothing in the telling. A big, shapeless white woman on a pile of bedding asked him mysteriously whether he thought her husband would come back from the war. Kim reflected gravely, and said that he would, and the woman gave him food. In many respects, this big procession that played music at intervals—this crowd that talked and laughed so easily— resembled a festival in Lahore city. So far, there was no sign of hard work, and he resolved to lend the spectacle his patronage. At evening there came out to meet them bands of music, and played the Mavericks into camp near Umballa railway station. That was an interesting night. Men of other regiments came to visit the Mavericks. The Mavericks went visiting on their own account. Their pickets hurried forth to bring them back, met pickets of strange regiments on the same duty; and, after a while, the bugles blew madly for more pickets with officers to control the tumult. The Mavericks had a reputation for liveliness to live up to. But they fell in on the platform next morning in perfect shape and condition; and Kim, left behind with the sick, women, and boys, found himself shouting farewells excitedly as the trains drew away. Life as a Sahib was amusing so far; but he touched it with a cautious hand. Then they marched him back in charge of a drummer-boy to empty, lime-washed barracks, whose floors were covered with rubbish and string and paper, and whose ceilings gave back his lonely footfall. Native-fashion, he curled himself up on a stripped cot and went to sleep. An angry man stumped down the veranda, woke him up, and said he was a schoolmaster. This was enough for Kim, and he retired into his shell. He could just puzzle out the various English Police notices in Lahore city, because they affected his comfort; and among the many guests of the woman who looked after him had been a queer German who painted scenery for the Parsee travelling theatre. He told Kim that he had been "on the barricades in "Forty-eight," and therefore—at least that was how it struck Kim—he would teach the boy to write in return for food. Kim had been kicked as far as single letters, but did not think well of them.

"I do not know anything. Go away!" said Kim, scenting evil. Hereupon the man caught him by the ear, dragged him to a room in a far-off wing where a dozen drummer-boys were sitting on forms, and told him to be still if he could do nothing else. This he managed very successfully. The man explained something or other with white lines on a black board for at least half an hour, and Kim continued his interrupted nap. He much disapproved of the present aspect of affairs, for this was the very school and discipline he had spent two-thirds of his young life in avoiding. Suddenly a beautiful idea occurred to him, and he wondered that he had not thought of it before.

The man dismissed them, and first to spring through the veranda into the open sunshine was Kim.

"'Ere, you! 'Alt! Stop!" said a high voice at his heels. "I've got to look after you. My orders are not to let you out of my sight. Where are you goin'?"

It was the drummer-boy who had been hanging round him all the forenoon—a fat and freckled person of about fourteen, and Kim loathed him from the soles of his boots to his cap-ribbons.

"To the bazar—to get sweets—for you," said Kim, after thought.

"Well, the bazar's out o' bounds. If we go there we'll get a dressing-down. You come back."

"How near can we go?" Kim did not know what bounds meant, but he wished to be polite—for the present.

"'Ow near? 'Ow far, you mean! We can go as far as that tree down the road."

"Then I will go there."

"All right. I ain't goin'. It's too 'ot. I can watch you from 'ere. It's no good your runninv away. If you did, they'd spot you by your clothes. That's regimental stuff you're wearin'. There ain't a picket in Umballa wouldn't 'ead you back quicker than you started out."

This did not impress Kim as much as the knowledge that his raiment would tire him out if he tried to run. He slouched to the tree at the corner of a bare road leading towards the bazar, and eyed the natives passing. Most of them were barrack-servants of the lowest caste. Kim hailed a sweeper, who promptly retorted with a piece of unnecessary insolence, in the natural belief that the European boy could not follow it. The low, quick answer undeceived him. Kim put his fettered soul into it, thankful for the late chance to abuse somebody in the tongue he knew best. "And now, go to the nearest letter-writer in the bazar and tell him to come here. I would write a letter."

"But—but what manner of white man's son art thou to need a bazar letter-writer? Is there not a schoolmaster in the barracks?"

"Ay; and Hell is full of the same sort. Do my order, you—you Od! Thy mother was married under a basket! Servant of Lal Beg" (Kim knew the God of the sweepers), "run on my business or we will talk again."

The sweeper shuffled off in haste. "There is a white boy by the barracks waiting under a tree who is not a white boy," he stammered to the first bazar letter-writer he came across. "He needs thee."

"Will he pay?" said the spruce scribe, gathering up his desk and pens and sealing-wax all in order.

"I do not know. He is not like other boys. Go and see. It is well worth."

Kim danced with impatience when the slim young Kayeth hove in sight. As soon as his voice could carry he cursed him volubly.

"First I will take my pay," the letter-writer said. "Bad words have made the price higher. But who art thou, dressed in that fashion, to speak in this fashion?"

"Aha! That is in the letter which thou shalt write. Never was such a tale. But I am in no haste. Another writer will serve me. Umballa city is as full of them as is Lahore."

"Four annas," said the writer, sitting down and spreading his cloth in the shade of a deserted barrack-wing.

Mechanically Kim squatted beside him—squatted as only the natives can—in spite of the abominable clinging trousers.

The writer regarded him sideways.

"That is the price to ask of Sahibs," said Kim. "Now fix me a true one."

"An anna and a half. How do I know, having written the letter, that thou wilt not run away?"

I must not go beyond this tree, and there is also the stamp to be considered."

"I get no commission on the price of the stamp. Once more, what manner of white boy art thou?"

"That shall be said in the letter, which is to Mahbub Ali, the horse-dealer in the Kashmir Serai, at Lahore. He is my friend."

"Wonder on wonder!" murmured the letter-writer, dipping a reed in the inkstand. "To be written in Hindi?"

"Assuredly. To Mahbub Ali then. Begin! I have come down with the old man as far as Umballa in the train. At Umballa I carried the news of the bay mare's pedigree." After what he had seen in the garden, he was not going to write of white stallions.

"Slower a little. What has a bay mare to do ... Is it Mahbub Ali, the great dealer?"

"Who else? I have been in his service. Take more ink. Again. As the order was, so I did it. We then went on foot towards Benares, but on the third day we found a certain regiment. Is that down?"

"Ay, pulton," murmured the writer, all ears.

"I went into their camp and was caught, and by means of the charm about my neck, which thou knowest, it was established that I was the son of some man in the regiment: according to the prophecy of the Red Bull, which thou knowest was common talk of our bazar." Kim waited for this shaft to sink into the letter-writer's heart, cleared his throat, and continued: "A priest clothed me and gave me a new name ... One priest, however, was a fool. The clothes are very heavy, but I am a Sahib and my heart is heavy too. They send me to a school and beat me. I do not like the air and water here. Come then and help me, Mahbub Ali, or send me some money, for I have not sufficient to pay the writer who writes this."

"'Who writes this.' It is my own fault that I was tricked. Thou art as clever as Husain Bux that forged the Treasury stamps at Nucklao. But what a tale! What a tale! Is it true by any chance?"

"It does not profit to tell lies to Mahbub Ali. It is better to help his friends by lending them a stamp. When the money comes I will repay."

The writer grunted doubtfully, but took a stamp out of his desk, sealed the letter, handed it over to Kim, and departed. Mahbub Ali's was a name of power in Umballa.

"That is the way to win a good account with the Gods," Kim shouted after him.

"Pay me twice over when the money comes," the man cried over his shoulder.

"What was you bukkin' to that nigger about?" said the drummer-boy when Kim returned to the veranda. "I was watch-in' you."

"I was only talkin' to him."

"You talk the same as a nigger, don't you?"

"No-ah! No-ah! I onlee speak a little. What shall we do now?"

"The bugles'll go for dinner in arf a minute. My Gawd! I wish I'd gone up to the Front with the Regiment. It's awful doin' nothin' but school down 'ere. Don't you 'ate it?"

"Oah yess!"

I'd run away if I knew where to go to, but, as the men say, in this bloomin' Injia you're only a prisoner at large. You can't desert without bein' took back at once. I'm fair sick of it."

"You have been in Be—England?"

"W'y, I only come out last troopin' season with my mother. I should think I 'ave been in England. What a ignorant little beggar you are! You was brought up in the gutter, wasn't you?"

"Oah yess. Tell me something about England. My father he came from there."

Though he would not say so, Kim of course disbelieved every word the drummer-boy spoke about the Liverpool suburb which was his England. It passed the heavy time till dinner—a most unappetizing meal served to the boys and a few invalids in a corner of a barrack-room. But that he had written to Mahbub Ali, Kim would have been almost depressed. The indifference of native crowds he was used to; but this strong loneliness among white men preyed on him. He was grateful when, in the course of the afternoon, a big soldier took him over to Father Victor, who lived in another wing across another dusty parade-ground. The priest was reading an English letter written in purple ink. He looked at Kim more curiously than ever.

"An' how do you like it, my son, as far as you've gone? Not much, eh? It must be hard—very hard on a wild animal. Listen now. I've an amazin' epistle from your friend."

"Where is he? Is he well? Oah! If he knows to write me letters, it is all right."

"You're fond of him then?"

"Of course I am fond of him. He was fond of me."

"It seems so by the look of this. He can't write English, can he?"

"Oah no. Not that I know, but of course he found a letter-writer who can write English verree well, and so he wrote. I do hope you understand."

"That accounts for it. D'you know anything about his money affairs?" Kim's face showed that he did not.

"How can I tell?"

"That's what I'm askin'. Now listen if you can make head or tail o' this. We'll skip the first part ... It's written from Jagadhir Road ... 'Sitting on wayside in grave meditation, trusting to be favoured with your Honour's applause of present step, which recommend your Honour to execute for Almighty God's sake. Education is greatest blessing if of best sorts. Otherwise no earthly use.' Faith, the old man's hit the bull's-eye that time! 'If your Honour condescending giving my boy best educations Xavier' (I suppose that's St Xavier's in Partibus) 'in terms of our conversation dated in your tent 15th instant' (a business-like touch there!) 'then Almighty God blessing your Honour's succeedings to third an' fourth generation and'—now listen!—'confide in your Honour's humble servant for adequate remuneration per hoondi per annum three hundred rupees a year to one expensive education St Xavier, Lucknow, and allow small time to forward same per hoondi sent to any part of India as your Honour shall address yourself. This servant of your Honour has presently no place to lay crown of his head, but going to Benares by train on account of persecution of old woman talking so much and unanxious residing Saharunpore in any domestic capacity.' Now what in the world does that mean?"

"She has asked him to be her puro—her clergyman—at Saharunpore, I think. He would not do that on account of his River. She did talk."

"It's clear to you, is it? It beats me altogether. 'So going to Benares, where will find address and forward rupees for boy who is apple of eye, and for Almighty God's sake execute this education,

and your petitioner as in duty bound shall ever awfully pray. Written by Sobrao Satai, Failed Entrance Allahabad University, for Venerable Teshoo Lama the priest of Such-zen looking for a River, address care of Tirthankars' Temple, Benares. P. M.—Please note boy is apple of eye, and rupees shall be sent per hoondi three hundred per annum. For God Almighty's sake.' Now, is that ravin' lunacy or a business proposition? I ask you, because I'm fairly at my wits' end."

"He says he will give me three hundred rupees a year? So he will give me them."

"Oh, that's the way you look at it, is it?"

"Of course. If he says so!"

The priest whistled; then he addressed Kim as an equal. "I don't believe it; but we'll see. You were goin' off today to the Military Orphanage at Sanawar, where the Regiment would keep you till you were old enough to enlist. Ye'd be brought up to the Church of England. Bennett arranged for that. On the other hand, if ye go to St Xavier's ye'll get a better education an—an can have the religion. D'ye see my dilemma?" Kim saw nothing save a vision of the lama going south in a train with none to beg for him.

"Like most people, I'm going to temporize. If your friend sends the money from Benares— Powers of Darkness below, where's a street-beggar to raise three hundred rupees?—ye'll go down to Lucknow and I'll pay your fare, because I can't touch the subscription-money if I intend, as I do, to make ye a Catholic. If he doesn't, ye'll go to the Military Orphanage at the Regiment's expense. I'll allow him three days' grace, though I don't believe it at all. Even then, if he fails in his payments later on ... but it's beyond me. We can only walk one step at a time in this world, praise God! An' they sent Bennett to the Front an' left me behind. Bennett can't expect everything."

"Oah yess," said Kim vaguely.

The priest leaned forward. "I'd give a month's pay to find what's goin' on inside that little round head of yours."

"There is nothing," said Kim, and scratched it. He was wondering whether Mahbub Ali would send him as much as a whole rupee. Then he could pay the letter-writer and write letters to the lama at Benares. Perhaps Mahbub Ali would visit him next time he came south with horses. Surely he must know that Kim's delivery of the letter to the officer at Umballa had caused the great war which the men and boys had discussed so loudly over the barrack dinner-tables. But if Mahbub Ali did not know this, it would be very unsafe to tell him so. Mahbub Ali was hard upon boys who knew, or thought they knew, too much.

"Well, till I get further news"—Father Victor's voice interrupted the reverie. "Ye can run along now and play with the other boys. They'll teach ye something—but I don't think ye'll like it."

The day dragged to its weary end. When he wished to sleep he was instructed how to fold up his clothes and set out his boots; the other boys deriding. Bugles waked him in the dawn; the schoolmaster caught him after breakfast, thrust a page of meaningless characters under his nose, gave them senseless names and whacked him without reason. Kim meditated poisoning him with opium borrowed from a barrack-sweeper, but reflected that, as they all ate at one table in public (this was peculiarly revolting to Kim, who preferred to turn his back on the world at meals), the stroke might be dangerous. Then he attempted running off to the village where the priest had tried to drug the lama—the village where the old soldier lived. But far-seeing sentries at every exit headed back the little scarlet figure. Trousers and jacket crippled body and mind alike so he abandoned the project and fell back, Oriental-fashion, on time and chance. Three

days of torment passed in the big, echoing white rooms. He walked out of afternoons under escort of the drummer-boy, and all he heard from his companions were the few useless words which seemed to make two-thirds of the white man's abuse. Kim knew and despised them all long ago. The boy resented his silence and lack of interest by beating him, as was only natural. He did not care for any of the bazars which were in bounds. He styled all natives "niggers"; yet servants and sweepers called him abominable names to his face, and, misled by their deferential attitude, he never understood. This somewhat consoled Kim for the beatings.

On the morning of the fourth day a judgement overtook that drummer. They had gone out together towards Umballa racecourse. He returned alone, weeping, with news that young O'Hara, to whom he had been doing nothing in particular, had hailed a scarlet-bearded nigger on horseback; that the nigger had then and there laid into him with a peculiarly adhesive quirt, picked up young O'Hara, and borne him off at full gallop. These tidings came to Father Victor, and he drew down his long upper lip. He was already sufficiently startled by a letter from the Temple of the Tirthankars at Benares, enclosing a native banker's note of hand for three hundred rupees, and an amazing prayer to "Almighty God". The lama would have been more annoyed than the priest had he known how the bazar letter-writer had translated his phrase "to acquire merit."

"Powers of Darkness below!" Father Victor fumbled with the note. "An' now he's off with another of his peep-o'-day friends. I don't know whether it will be a greater relief to me to get him back or to have him lost. He's beyond my comprehension. How the Divil—yes, he's the man I mean—can a street-beggar raise money to educate white boys?"

Three miles off, on Umballa racecourse, Mahbub Ali, reining a grey Kabuli stallion with Kim in front of him, was saying:

"But, Little Friend of all the World, there is my honour and reputation to be considered. All the officer-Sahibs in all the regiments, and all Umballa, know Mahbub Ali. Men saw me pick thee up and chastise that boy. We are seen now from far across this plain. How can I take thee away, or account for thy disappearing if I set thee down and let thee run off into the crops? They would put me in jail. Be patient. Once a Sahib, always a Sahib. When thou art a man—who knows?—thou wilt be grateful to Mahbub Ali."

"Take me beyond their sentries where I can change this red. Give me money and I will go to Benares and be with my lama again. I do not want to be a Sahib, and remember I did deliver that message."

The stallion bounded wildly. Mahbub Ali had incautiously driven home the sharp-edged stirrup. (He was not the new sort of fluent horse-dealer who wears English boots and spurs.) Kim drew his own conclusions from that betrayal.

"That was a small matter. It lay on the straight road to Benares. I and the Sahib have by this time forgotten it. I send so many letters and messages to men who ask questions about horses, I cannot well remember one from the other. Was it some matter of a bay mare that Peters Sahib wished the pedigree of?"

Kim saw the trap at once. If he had said "bay mare" Mahbub would have known by his very readiness to fall in with the amendment that the boy suspected something. Kim replied therefore:

"Bay mare. No. I do not forget my messages thus. It was a white stallion."

"Ay, so it was. A white Arab stallion. But thou didst write 'bay mare' to me."

"Who cares to tell truth to a letter-writer?" Kim answered, feeling Mahbub's palm on his heart.

"Hi! Mahbub, you old villain, pull up!" cried a voice, and an Englishman raced alongside on a little polo-pony. "I've been chasing you half over the country. That Kabuli of yours can go. For sale, I suppose?"

"I have some young stuff coming on made by Heaven for the delicate and difficult polo-game. He has no equal. He—"

"Plays polo and waits at table. Yes. We know all that. What the deuce have you got there?"

"A. boy," said Mahbub gravely. "He was being beaten by another boy. His father was once a white soldier in the big war. The boy was a child in Lahore city. He played with my horses when he was a babe. Now I think they will make him a soldier. He has been newly caught by his father's Regiment that went up to the war last week. But I do not think he wants to be a soldier. I take him for a ride. Tell me where thy barracks are and I will set thee there."

"Let me go. I can find the barracks alone."

"And if thou runnest away who will say it is not my fault?"

"He'll run back to his dinner. Where has he to run to?" the Englishman asked.

"He was born in the land. He has friends. He goes where he chooses. He is a chabuk sawai (a sharp chap). It needs only to change his clothing, and in a twinkling he would be a low-caste Hindu boy."

"The deuce he would!" The Englishman looked critically at the boy as Mahbub headed towards the barracks. Kim ground his teeth. Mahbub was mocking him, as faithless Afghans will; for he went on:

"They will send him to a school and put heavy boots on his feet and swaddle him in these clothes. Then he will forget all he knows. Now, which of the barracks is thine?"

Kim pointed—he could not speak—to Father Victor's wing, all staring white near by.

"Perhaps he will make a good soldier," said Mahbub reflectively.

"He will make a good orderly at least. I sent him to deliver a message once from Lahore. A message concerning the pedigree of a white stallion."

Here was deadly insult on deadlier injury—and the Sahib to whom he had so craftily given that war-waking letter heard it all. Kim beheld Mahbub Ali frying in flame for his treachery, but for himself he saw one long grey vista of barracks, schools, and barracks again. He gazed imploringly at the clear-cut face in which there was no glimmer of recognition; but even at this extremity it never occurred to him to throw himself on the white man's mercy or to denounce the Afghan. And Mahbub stared deliberately at the Englishman, who stared as deliberately at Kim, quivering and tongue-tied.

"My horse is well trained," said the dealer. "Others would have kicked, Sahib."

"Ah," said the Englishman at last, rubbing his pony's damp withers with his whip-butt. "Who makes the boy a soldier?"

"He says the Regiment that found him, and especially the Padre-sahib of that regiment.

"There is the Padre!" Kim choked as bare-headed Father Victor sailed down upon them from the veranda.

"Powers O' Darkness below, O'Hara! How many more mixed friends do you keep in Asia?" he cried, as Kim slid down and stood helplessly before him.

"Good morning, Padre," the Englishman said cheerily. "I know you by reputation well enough. Meant to have come over and called before this. I'm Creighton."

"Of the Ethnological Survey?" said Father Victor. The Englishman nodded. "Faith, I'm glad to meet ye then; an' I owe you some thanks for bringing back the boy."

"No thanks to me, Padre. Besides, the boy wasn't going away. You don't know old Mahbub Ali." The horse-dealer sat impassive in the sunlight. "You will when you have been in the station a month. He sells us all our crocks. That boy is rather a curiosity. Can you tell me anything about him?"

"Can I tell you?" puffed Father Victor. "You'll be the one man that could help me in my quandaries. Tell you! Powers o' Darkness, I'm bursting to tell someone who knows something o' the native!"

A groom came round the corner. Colonel Creighton raised his voice, speaking in Urdu. "Very good, Mahbub Ali, but what is the use of telling me all those stories about the pony? Not one pice more than three hundred and fifty rupees will I give."

"The Sahib is a little hot and angry after riding," the horse-dealer returned, with the leer of a privileged jester. "Presently, he will see my horse's points more clearly. I will wait till he has finished his talk with the Padre. I will wait under that tree."

"Confound you!" The Colonel laughed. "That comes of looking at one of Mahbub's horses. He's a regular old leech, Padre. Wait, then, if thou hast so much time to spare, Mahbub. Now I'm at your service, Padre. Where is the boy? Oh, he's gone off to collogue with Mahbub. Queer sort of boy. Might I ask you to send my mare round under cover?"

He dropped into a chair which commanded a clear view of Kim and Mahbub Ali in conference beneath the tree. The Padre went indoors for cheroots.

Creighton heard Kim say bitterly: "Trust a Brahmin before a snake, and a snake before an harlot, and an harlot before a Pathan, Mahbub Ali."

"That is all one." The great red beard wagged solemnly. "Children should not see a carpet on the loom till the pattern is made plain. Believe me, Friend of all the World, I do thee great service. They will not make a soldier of thee."

"You crafty old sinner!" thought Creighton. "But you're not far wrong. That boy mustn't be wasted if he is as advertised."

"Excuse me half a minute," cried the Padre from within, "but I'm gettin' the documents in the case."

"If through me the favour of this bold and wise Colonel Sahib comes to thee, and thou art raised to honour, what thanks wilt thou give Mahbub Ali when thou art a man?"

"Nay, nay! I begged thee to let me take the Road again, where I should have been safe; and thou hast sold me back to the English. What will they give thee for blood-money?"

"A cheerful young demon!" The Colonel bit his cigar, and turned politely to Father Victor.

"What are the letters that the fat priest is waving before the Colonel? Stand behind the stallion as though looking at my bridle!" said Mahbub Ali.

"A letter from my lama which he wrote from Jagadhir Road, saying that he will pay three hundred rupees by the year for my schooling."

"Oho! Is old Red Hat of that sort? At which school?"

"God knows. I think in Nucklao."

"Yes. There is a big school there for the sons of Sahibs—and half-Sahibs. I have seen it when I sell horses there. So the lama also loved the Friend of all the World?"

"Ay; and he did not tell lies, or return me to captivity."

"Small wonder the Padre does not know how to unravel the thread. How fast he talks to the Colonel Sahib!" Mahbub Ali chuckled. "By Allah!" the keen eyes swept the veranda for an instant—"thy lama has sent what to me looks like a note of hand. I have had some few dealings in hoondies. The Colonel Sahib is looking at it."

"What good is all this to me?" said Kim wearily. "Thou wilt go away, and they will return me to those empty rooms where there is no good place to sleep and where the boys beat me."

"I do not think that. Have patience, child. All Pathans are not faithless—except in horseflesh."

Five—ten—fifteen minutes passed, Father Victor talking energetically or asking questions which the Colonel answered.

"Now I've told you everything that I know about the boy from beginnin to end; and it's a blessed relief to me. Did ye ever hear the like?"

"At any rate, the old man has sent the money. Gobind Sahai's notes of hand are good from here to China," said the Colonel. "The more one knows about natives the less can one say what they will or won't do."

"That's consolin'—from the head of the Ethnological Survey. It's this mixture of Red Bulls and Rivers of Healing (poor heathen, God help him!) an' notes of hand and Masonic certificates. Are you a Mason, by any chance?"

"By Jove, I am, now I come to think of it. That's an additional reason," said the Colonel absently.

"I'm glad ye see a reason in it. But as I said, it's the mixture o' things that's beyond me. An' his prophesyin' to our Colonel, sitting on my bed with his little shimmy torn open showing his white skin; an' the prophecy comin' true! They'll cure all that nonsense at St Xavier's, eh?"

"Sprinkle him with holy water," the Colonel laughed.

"On my word, I fancy I ought to sometimes. But I'm hoping he'll be brought up as a good Catholic. All that troubles me is what'll happen if the old beggar-man—"

"Lama, lama, my dear sir; and some of them are gentlemen in their own country."

"The lama, then, fails to pay next year. He's a fine business head to plan on the spur of the moment, but he's bound to die some day. An' takin' a heathen's money to give a child a Christian education—"

"But he said explicitly what he wanted. As soon as he knew the boy was white he seems to have made his arrangements accordingly. I'd give a month's pay to hear how he explained it all at the Tirthankars' Temple at Benares. Look here, Padre, I don't pretend to know much about natives, but if he says he'll pay, he'll pay—dead or alive. I mean, his heirs will assume the debt. My advice to you is, send the boy down to Lucknow. If your Anglican Chaplain thinks you've stolen a march on him—"

"Bad luck to Bennett! He was sent to the Front instead o' me. Doughty certified me medically unfit. I'll excommunicate Doughty if he comes back alive! Surely Bennett ought to be content with—"

"Glory, leaving you the religion. Quite so! As a matter of fact I don't think Bennett will mind. Put the blame on me. I—er—strongly recommend sending the boy to St Xavier's. He can go down on pass as a soldier's orphan, so the railway fare will be saved. You can buy him an outfit from the Regimental subscription. The Lodge will be saved the expense of his education, and that will put the Lodge in a good temper. It's perfectly easy. I've got to go down to Lucknow next week. I'll look after the boy on the way—give him in charge of my servants, and so on."

"You're a good man."

"Not in the least. Don't make that mistake. The lama has sent us money for a definite end. We can't very well return it. We shall have to do as he says. Well, that's settled, isn't it? Shall we say that, Tuesday next, you'll hand him over to me at the night train south? That's only three days. He can't do much harm in three days."

"It's a weight off my mind, but—this thing here?"—he waved the note of hand—"I don't know Gobind Sahai: or his bank, which may be a hole in a wall."

"You've never been a subaltern in debt. I'll cash it if you like, and send you the vouchers in proper order."

"But with all your own work too! It's askin'—"

"It's not the least trouble indeed. You see, as an ethnologist, the thing's very interesting to me. I'd like to make a note of it for some Government work that I'm doing. The transformation of a regimental badge like your Red Bull into a sort of fetish that the boy follows is very interesting."

"But I can't thank you enough."

"There's one thing you can do. All we Ethnological men are as jealous as jackdaws of one another's discoveries. They're of no interest to anyone but ourselves, of course, but you know what book-collectors are like. Well, don't say a word, directly or indirectly, about the Asiatic side of the boy's character—his adventures and his prophecy, and so on. I'll worm them out of the boy later on and—you see?"

"I do. Ye'll make a wonderful account of it. Never a word will I say to anyone till I see it in print."

"Thank you. That goes straight to an ethnologist's heart. Well, I must be getting back to my breakfast. Good Heavens! Old Mahbub here still?" He raised his voice, and the horse-dealer came out from under the shadow of the tree, "Well, what is it?"

"As regards that young horse," said Mahbub, "I say that when a colt is born to be a polo-pony, closely following the ball without teaching—when such a colt knows the game by divination—then I say it is a great wrong to break that colt to a heavy cart, Sahib!"

"So say I also, Mahbub. The colt will be entered for polo only. (These fellows think of nothing in the world but horses, Padre.) I'll see you tomorrow, Mahbub, if you've anything likely for sale."

The dealer saluted, horseman-fashion, with a sweep of the off hand. "Be patient a little, Friend of all the World," he whispered to the agonized Kim. "Thy fortune is made. In a little while thou goest to Nucklao, and—here is something to pay the letter-writer. I shall see thee again, I think, many times," and he cantered off down the road.

"Listen to me," said the Colonel from the veranda, speaking in the vernacular. "In three days thou wilt go with me to Lucknow, seeing and hearing new things all the while. Therefore sit still for three days and do not run away. Thou wilt go to school at Lucknow."

"Shall I meet my Holy One there?" Kim whimpered.

"At least Lucknow is nearer to Benares than Umballa. It may be thou wilt go under my protection. Mahbub Ali knows this, and he will be angry if thou returnest to the Road now. Remember—much has been told me which I do not forget."

"I will wait," said Kim, "but the boys will beat me."

Then the bugles blew for dinner.

CHAPTER VII

Unto whose use the pregnant suns are poised
With idiot moons and stars retracing stars?
Creep thou betweene—thy coming's all unnoised.
Heaven hath her high, as Earth her baser, wars.
Heir to these tumults, this affright, that fraye
(By Adam's, fathers', own, sin bound alway);
Peer up, draw out thy horoscope and say
Which planet mends thy threadbare fate or mars!

Sir John Christie.

In the afternoon the red-faced schoolmaster told Kim that he had been "struck off the strength", which conveyed no meaning to him till he was ordered to go away and play. Then he ran to the bazar, and found the young letter-writer to whom he owed a stamp.

"Now I pay," said Kim royally, "and now I need another letter to be written."

"Mahbub Ali is in Umballa," said the writer jauntily. He was, by virtue of his office, a bureau of general misinformation.

"This is not to Mahbub, but to a priest. Take thy pen and write quickly. To Teshoo Lama, the Holy One from Bhotiyal seeking for a River, who is now in the Temple of the Tirthankars at Benares. Take more ink! In three days I am to go down to Nucklao to the school at Nucklao. The name of the school is Xavier. I do not know where that school is, but it is at Nucklao."

"But I know Nucklao," the writer interrupted. "I know the school."

"Tell him where it is, and I give half an anna."

The reed pen scratched busily. "He cannot mistake." The man lifted his head. "Who watches us across the street?"

Kim looked up hurriedly and saw Colonel Creighton in tennis-flannels.

"Oh, that is some Sahib who knows the fat priest in the barracks. He is beckoning me."

"What dost thou?" said the Colonel, when Kim trotted up.

"I—I am not running away. I send a letter to my Holy One at Benares."

"I had not thought of that. Hast thou said that I take thee to Lucknow?"

"Nay, I have not. Read the letter, if there be a doubt."

"Then why hast thou left out my name in writing to that Holy One?" The Colonel smiled a queer smile. Kim took his courage in both hands.

"It was said once to me that it is inexpedient to write the names of strangers concerned in any matter, because by the naming of names many good plans are brought to confusion."

"Thou hast been well taught," the Colonel replied, and Kim flushed. "I have left my cheroot-case in the Padre's veranda. Bring it to my house this even."

"Where is the house?" said Kim. His quick wit told him that he was being tested in some fashion or another, and he stood on guard.

"Ask anyone in the big bazar." The Colonel walked on.

"He has forgotten his cheroot-case," said Kim, returning. "I must bring it to him this evening. That is all my letter except, thrice over, Come to me! Come to me! Come to me! Now I will pay for a stamp and put it in the post. He rose to go, and as an afterthought asked: "Who is that angry-faced Sahib who lost the cheroot-case?"

"Oh, he is only Creighton Sahib—a very foolish Sahib, who is a Colonel Sahib without a regiment."

"What is his business?"

"God knows. He is always buying horses which he cannot ride, and asking riddles about the works of God—such as plants and stones and the customs of people. The dealers call him the father of fools, because he is so easily cheated about a horse. Mahbub Ali says he is madder than most other Sahibs."

"Oh!" said Kim, and departed. His training had given him some small knowledge of character, and he argued that fools are not given information which leads to calling out eight thousand men besides guns. The Commander-in-Chief of all India does not talk, as Kim had heard him talk, to fools. Nor would Mahbub Ali's tone have changed, as it did every time he mentioned the Colonel's name, if the Colonel had been a fool. Consequently—and this set Kim to skipping—there was a mystery somewhere, and Mahbub Ali probably spied for the Colonel much as Kim had spied for Mahbub. And, like the horse-dealer, the Colonel evidently respected people who did not show themselves to be too clever.

He rejoiced that he had not betrayed his knowledge of the Colonel's house; and when, on his return to barracks, he discovered that no cheroot-case had been left behind, he beamed with delight. Here was a man after his own heart—a tortuous and indirect person playing a hidden game. Well, if he could be a fool, so could Kim.

He showed nothing of his mind when Father Victor, for three long mornings, discoursed to him of an entirely new set of Gods and Godlings—notably of a Goddess called Mary, who, he gathered, was one with Bibi Miriam of Mahbub Ali's theology. He betrayed no emotion when, after the lecture, Father Victor dragged him from shop to shop buying articles of outfit, nor when envious drummer-boys kicked him because he was going to a superior school did he complain, but awaited the play of circumstances with an interested soul. Father Victor, good man, took him to the station, put him into an empty second-class next to Colonel Creighton's first, and bade him farewell with genuine feeling.

"They'll make a man o' you, O'Hara, at St Xavier's—a white man, an', I hope, a good man. They know all about your comin', an' the Colonel will see that ye're not lost or mislaid anywhere on the road. I've given you a notion of religious matters,—at least I hope so,—and you'll remember, when they ask you your religion, that you're a Cath'lic. Better say Roman Cath'lic, tho' I'm not fond of the word."

Kim lit a rank cigarette—he had been careful to buy a stock in the bazar—and lay down to think. This solitary passage was very different from that joyful down-journey in the third-class with the lama. "Sahibs get little pleasure of travel," he reflected. "Hai mai! I go from one place to another as it might be a kickball. It is my Kismet. No man can escape his Kismet. But I am to pray to Bibi Miriam, and I am a Sahib." He looked at his boots ruefully. "No; I am Kim. This

is the great world, and I am only Kim. Who is Kim?" He considered his own identity, a thing he had never done before, till his head swam. He was one insignificant person in all this roaring whirl of India, going southward to he knew not what fate.

Presently the Colonel sent for him, and talked for a long time. So far as Kim could gather, he was to be diligent and enter the Survey of India as a chain-man. If he were very good, and passed the proper examinations, he would be earning thirty rupees a month at seventeen years old, and Colonel Creighton would see that he found suitable employment.

Kim pretended at first to understand perhaps one word in three of this talk. Then the Colonel, seeing his mistake, turned to fluent and picturesque Urdu and Kim was contented. No man could be a fool who knew the language so intimately, who moved so gently and silently, and whose eyes were so different from the dull fat eyes of other Sahibs.

"Yes, and thou must learn how to make pictures of roads and mountains and rivers, to carry these pictures in thine eye till a suitable time comes to set them upon paper. Perhaps some day, when thou art a chain-man, I may say to thee when we are working together: 'Go across those hills and see what lies beyond.' Then one will say: 'There are bad people living in those hills who will slay the chain-man if he be seen to look like a Sahib.' What then?"

Kim thought. Would it be safe to return the Colonel's lead?

"I would tell what that other man had said."

"But if I answered: 'I will give thee a hundred rupees for knowledge of what is behind those hills—for a picture of a river and a little news of what the people say in the villages there'?"

"How can I tell? I am only a boy. Wait till I am a man." Then, seeing the Colonel's brow clouded, he went on: "But I think I should in a few days earn the hundred rupees."

"By what road?"

Kim shook his head resolutely. "If I said how I would earn them, another man might hear and forestall me. It is not good to sell knowledge for nothing."

"Tell now." The Colonel held up a rupee. Kim's hand half reached towards it, and dropped.

"Nay, Sahib; nay. I know the price that will be paid for the answer, but I do not know why the question is asked."

"Take it for a gift, then," said Creighton, tossing it over. "There is a good spirit in thee. Do not let it be blunted at St Xavier's. There are many boys there who despise the black men."

"Their mothers were bazar-women," said Kim. He knew well there is no hatred like that of the half-caste for his brother-in-law.

"True; but thou art a Sahib and the son of a Sahib. Therefore, do not at any time be led to contemn the black men. I have known boys newly entered into the service of the Government who feigned not to understand the talk or the customs of black men. Their pay was cut for ignorance. There is no sin so great as ignorance. Remember this."

Several times in the course of the long twenty-four hours' run south did the Colonel send for Kim, always developing this latter text.

"We be all on one lead-rope, then," said Kim at last, "the Colonel, Mahbub Ali, and I—when

I become a chain-man. He will use me as Mahbub Ali employed me, I think. That is good, if it allows me to return to the Road again. This clothing grows no easier by wear."

When they came to the crowded Lucknow station there was no sign of the lama. He swallowed his disappointment, while the Colonel bundled him into a ticca-gharri with his neat belongings and despatched him alone to St Xavier's.

"I do not say farewell, because we shall meet again," he cried. "Again, and many times, if thou art one of good spirit. But thou art not yet tried."

"Not when I brought thee"—Kim actually dared to use the tum of equals—"a white stallion's pedigree that night?"

"Much is gained by forgetting, little brother," said the Colonel, with a look that pierced through Kim's shoulder-blades as he scuttled into the carriage.

It took him nearly five minutes to recover. Then he sniffed the new air appreciatively. "A rich city," he said. "Richer than Lahore. How good the bazars must be! Coachman, drive me a little through the bazars here."

"My order is to take thee to the school." The driver used the "thou", which is rudeness when applied to a white man. In the clearest and most fluent vernacular Kim pointed out his error, climbed on to the box-seat, and, perfect understanding established, drove for a couple of hours up and down, estimating, comparing, and enjoying. There is no city—except Bombay, the queen of all—more beautiful in her garish style than Lucknow, whether you see her from the bridge over the river, or from the top of the Imambara looking down on the gilt umbrellas of the Chutter Munzil, and the trees in which the town is bedded. Kings have adorned her with fantastic buildings, endowed her with charities, crammed her with pensioners, and drenched her with blood. She is the centre of all idleness, intrigue, and luxury, and shares with Delhi the claim to talk the only pure Urdu.

"A fair city—a beautiful city." The driver, as a Lucknow man, was pleased with the compliment, and told Kim many astounding things where an English guide would have talked of the Mutiny.

"Now we will go to the school," said Kim at last. The great old school of St Xavier's in Partibus, block on block of low white buildings, stands in vast grounds over against the Gumti River, at some distance from the city.

"What like of folk are they within?" said Kim.

"Young Sahibs—all devils. But to speak truth, and I drive many of them to and fro from the railway station, I have never seen one that had in him the making of a more perfect devil than thou—this young Sahib whom I am now driving."

Naturally, for he was never trained to consider them in any way improper, Kim had passed the time of day with one or two frivolous ladies at upper windows in a certain street, and naturally, in the exchange of compliments, had acquitted himself well. He was about to acknowledge the driver's last insolence, when his eye—it was growing dusk—caught a figure sitting by one of the white plaster gate-pillars in the long sweep of wall.

"Stop!" he cried. "Stay here. I do not go to the school at once."

"But what is to pay me for this coming and re-coming?" said the driver petulantly. "Is the boy mad? Last time it was a dancing-girl. This time it is a priest."

Kim was in the road headlong, patting the dusty feet beneath the dirty yellow robe.

"I have waited here a day and a half," the lama's level voice began. "Nay, I had a disciple with me. He that was my friend at the Temple of the Tirthankars gave me a guide for this journey. I came from Benares in the te-rain, when thy letter was given me. Yes, I am well fed. I need nothing."

"But why didst thou not stay with the Kulu woman, O Holy One? In what way didst thou get to Benares? My heart has been heavy since we parted."

"The woman wearied me by constant flux of talk and requiring charms for children. I separated myself from that company, permitting her to acquire merit by gifts. She is at least a woman of open hands, and I made a promise to return to her house if need arose. Then, perceiving myself alone in this great and terrible world, I bethought me of the te-rain to Benares, where I knew one abode in the Tirthankars' Temple who was a Seeker, even as I."

"Ah! Thy River," said Kim. "I had forgotten the River."

"So soon, my chela? I have never forgotten it. But when I had left thee it seemed better that I should go to the Temple and take counsel, for, look you, India is very large, and it may be that wise men before us, some two or three, have left a record of the place of our River. There is debate in the Temple of the Tirthankars on this matter; some saying one thing, and some another. They are courteous folk."

"So be it; but what dost thou do now?"

"I acquire merit in that I help thee, my chela, to wisdom. The priest of that body of men who serve the Red Bull wrote me that all should be as I desired for thee. I sent the money to suffice for one year, and then I came, as thou seest me, to watch for thee going up into the Gates of Learning. A day and a half have I waited, not because I was led by any affection towards thee— that is no part of the Way—but, as they said at the Tirthankars' Temple, because, money having been paid for learning, it was right that I should oversee the end of the matter. They resolved my doubts most clearly. I had a fear that, perhaps, I came because I wished to see thee—misguided by the Red Mist of affection. It is not so ... Moreover, I am troubled by a dream."

"But surely, Holy One, thou hast not forgotten the Road and all that befell on it. Surely it was a little to see me that thou didst come?"

"The horses are cold, and it is past their feeding-time," whined the driver.

"Go to Jehannum and abide there with thy reputationless aunt!" Kim snarled over his shoulder. "I am all alone in this land; I know not where I go nor what shall befall me. My heart was in that letter I sent thee. Except for Mahbub Ali, and he is a Pathan, I have no friend save thee, Holy One. Do not altogether go away."

"I have considered that also," the lama replied, in a shaking voice. "It is manifest that from time to time I shall acquire merit if before that I have not found my River—by assuring myself that thy feet are set on wisdom. What they will teach thee I do not know, but the priest wrote me that no son of a Sahib in all India will be better taught than thou. So from time to time, therefore, I will come again. Maybe thou wilt be such a Sahib as he who gave me these spectacles"—the lama wiped them elaborately—"in the Wonder House at Lahore. That is my hope, for he was a Fountain of Wisdom—wiser than many abbots Again, maybe thou wilt forget me and our meetings."

"If I eat thy bread," cried Kim passionately, "how shall I ever forget thee?"

"No—no." He put the boy aside. "I must go back to Benares. From time to time, now that I know the customs of letter-writers in this land, I will send thee a letter, and from time to time I will come and see thee."

"But whither shall I send my letters?" wailed Kim, clutching at the robe, all forgetful that he was a Sahib.

"To the Temple of the Tirthankars at Benares. That is the place I have chosen till I find my River. Do not weep; for, look you, all Desire is Illusion and a new binding upon the Wheel. Go up to the Gates of Learning. Let me see thee go ... Dost thou love me? Then go, or my heart cracks ... I will come again. Surely I will come again."

The lama watched the ticca-gharri rumble into the compound, and strode off, snuffing between each long stride.

"The Gates of Learning" shut with a clang.

The country born and bred boy has his own manners and customs, which do not resemble those of any other land; and his teachers approach him by roads which an English master would not understand. Therefore, you would scarcely be interested in Kim's experiences as a St Xavier's boy among two or three hundred precocious youths, most of whom had never seen the sea. He suffered the usual penalties for breaking out of bounds when there was cholera in the city. This was before he had learned to write fair English, and so was obliged to find a bazar letter-writer. He was, of course, indicted for smoking and for the use of abuse more full-flavoured than even St Xavier's had ever heard. He learned to wash himself with the Levitical scrupulosity of the native-born, who in his heart considers the Englishman rather dirty. He played the usual tricks on the patient coolies pulling the punkahs in the sleeping-rooms where the boys threshed through the hot nights telling tales till the dawn; and quietly he measured himself against his self-reliant mates.

They were sons of subordinate officials in the Railway, Telegraph, and Canal Services; of warrant-officers, sometimes retired and sometimes acting as commanders-in-chief to a feudatory Rajah's army; of captains of the Indian Marine Government pensioners, planters, Presidency shopkeepers, and missionaries. A few were cadets of the old Eurasian houses that have taken strong root in Dhurrumtollah—Pereiras, De Souzas, and D'Silvas. Their parents could well have educated them in England, but they loved the school that had served their own youth, and generation followed sallow-hued generation at St Xavier's. Their homes ranged from Howrah of the railway people to abandoned cantonments like Monghyr and Chunar; lost tea-gardens Shillong-way; villages where their fathers were large landholders in Oudh or the Deccan; Mission-stations a week from the nearest railway line; seaports a thousand miles south, facing the brazen Indian surf; and cinchona-plantations south of all. The mere story of their adventures, which to them were no adventures, on their road to and from school would have crisped a Western boy's hair. They were used to jogging off alone through a hundred miles of jungle, where there was always the delightful chance of being delayed by tigers; but they would no more have bathed in the English Channel in an English August than their brothers across the world would have lain still while a leopard snuffed at their palanquin. There were boys of fifteen who had spent a day and a half on an islet in the middle of a flooded river, taking charge, as by right, of a camp of frantic pilgrims returning from a shrine. There were seniors who had requisitioned a chance-met Rajah's elephant, in the name of St Francis Xavier, when the Rains once blotted out the cart-track that led to their father's estate, and had all but lost the huge beast in a quicksand. There was a boy who, he said, and none doubted, had helped his father to beat off with rifles from the veranda a rush of Akas in the days when those head-hunters were bold against lonely plantations.

And every tale was told in the even, passionless voice of the native-born, mixed with quaint reflections, borrowed unconsciously from native foster-mothers, and turns of speech that showed they had been that instant translated from the vernacular. Kim watched, listened, and approved. This was not insipid, single-word talk of drummer-boys. It dealt with a life he knew and in part understood. The atmosphere suited him, and he throve by inches. They gave him a white drill suit as the weather warmed, and he rejoiced in the new-found bodily comforts as he rejoiced to use his sharpened mind over the tasks they set him. His quickness would have delighted an English master; but at St Xavier's they know the first rush of minds developed by sun and surroundings, as they know the half-collapse that sets in at twenty-two or twenty-three.

None the less he remembered to hold himself lowly. When tales were told of hot nights, Kim did not sweep the board with his reminiscences; for St Xavier's looks down on boys who "go native all-together." One must never forget that one is a Sahib, and that some day, when examinations are passed, one will command natives. Kim made a note of this, for he began to understand where examinations led.

Then came the holidays from August to October—the long holidays imposed by the heat and the Rains. Kim was informed that he would go north to some station in the hills behind Umballa, where Father Victor would arrange for him.

"A barrack-school?" said Kim, who had asked many questions and thought more.

"Yes, I suppose so," said the master. "It will not do you any harm to keep you out of mischief. You can go up with young De Castro as far as Delhi."

Kim considered it in every possible light. He had been diligent, even as the Colonel advised. A boy's holiday was his own property—of so much the talk of his companions had advised him,—and a barrack-school would be torment after St Xavier's. Moreover—this was magic worth anything else—he could write. In three months he had discovered how men can speak to each other without a third party, at the cost of half an anna and a little knowledge. No word had come from the lama, but there remained the Road. Kim yearned for the caress of soft mud squishing up between the toes, as his mouth watered for mutton stewed with butter and cabbages, for rice speckled with strong scented cardamoms, for the saffron-tinted rice, garlic and onions, and the forbidden greasy sweetmeats of the bazars. They would feed him raw beef on a platter at the barrack-school, and he must smoke by stealth. But again, he was a Sahib and was at St Xavier's, and that pig Mahbub Ali ... No, he would not test Mahbub's hospitality—and yet ... He thought it out alone in the dormitory, and came to the conclusion he had been unjust to Mahbub.

The school was empty; nearly all the masters had gone away; Colonel Creighton's railway pass lay in his hand, and Kim puffed himself that he had not spent Colonel Creighton's or Mahbub's money in riotous living. He was still lord of two rupees seven annas. His new bullock-trunk, marked "K. O'H.", and bedding-roll lay in the empty sleeping-room.

"Sahibs are always tied to their baggage," said Kim, nodding at them. "You will stay here" He went out into the warm rain, smiling sinfully, and sought a certain house whose outside he had noted down some time before...

"Arre"! Dost thou know what manner of women we be in this quarter? Oh, shame!"

"Was I born yesterday?" Kim squatted native-fashion on the cushions of that upper room. "A little dyestuff and three yards of cloth to help out a jest. Is it much to ask?"

"Who is she? Thou art full young, as Sahibs go, for this devilry."

'Oh, she? She is the daughter of a certain schoolmaster of a regiment in the cantonments. He has beaten me twice because I went over their wall in these clothes. Now I would go as a gardener's boy. Old men are very jealous."

"That is true. Hold thy face still while I dab on the juice."

"Not too black, Naikan. I would not appear to her as a hubshi (nigger)."

"Oh, love makes nought of these things. And how old is she?"

"Twelve years, I think," said the shameless Kim. "Spread it also on the breast. It may be her father will tear my clothes off me, and if I am piebald—" he laughed.

The girl worked busily, dabbing a twist of cloth into a little saucer of brown dye that holds longer than any walnut-juice.

"Now send out and get me a cloth for the turban. Woe is me, my head is all unshaved! And he will surely knock off my turban."

"I am not a barber, but I will make shift. Thou wast born to be a breaker of hearts! All this disguise for one evening? Remember, the stuff does not wash away." She shook with laughter till her bracelets and anklets jingled. "But who is to pay me for this? Huneefa herself could not have given thee better stuff."

"Trust in the Gods, my sister," said Kim gravely, screwing his face round as the stain dried. "Besides, hast thou ever helped to paint a Sahib thus before?"

"Never indeed. But a jest is not money."

"It is worth much more."

"Child, thou art beyond all dispute the most shameless son of Shaitan that I have ever known to take up a poor girl's time with this play, and then to say: 'Is not the jest enough?' Thou wilt go very far in this world." She gave the dancing-girls' salutation in mockery.

"All one. Make haste and rough-cut my head." Kim shifted from foot to foot, his eyes ablaze with mirth as he thought of the fat days before him. He gave the girl four annas, and ran down the stairs in the likeness of a low-caste Hindu boy—perfect in every detail. A cookshop was his next point of call, where he feasted in extravagance and greasy luxury.

On Lucknow station platform he watched young De Castro, all covered with prickly-heat, get into a second-class compartment. Kim patronized a third, and was the life and soul of it. He explained to the company that he was assistant to a juggler who had left him behind sick with fever, and that he would pick up his master at Umballa. As the occupants of the carriage changed, he varied this tale, or adorned it with all the shoots of a budding fancy, the more rampant for being held off native speech so long. In all India that night was no human being so joyful as Kim. At Umballa he got out and headed eastward, plashing over the sodden fields to the village where the old soldier lived.

About this time Colonel Creighton at Simla was advised from Lucknow by wire that young O'Hara had disappeared. Mahbub Ali was in town selling horses, and to him the Colonel confided the affair one morning cantering round Annandale racecourse.

"Oh, that is nothing," said the horse-dealer. "Men are like horses. At certain times they need salt, and if that salt is not in the mangers they will lick it up from the earth. He has gone back to

the Road again for a while. The madrissah wearied him. I knew it would. Another time, I will take him upon the Road myself. Do not be troubled, Creighton Sahib. It is as though a polo-pony, breaking loose, ran out to learn the game alone."

"Then he is not dead, think you?"

"Fever might kill him. I do not fear for the boy otherwise. A monkey does not fall among trees."

Next morning, on the same course, Mahbub's stallion ranged alongside the Colonel.

"It is as I had thought," said the horse-dealer. "He has come through Umballa at least, and there he has written a letter to me, having learned in the bazar that I was here."

"Read," said the Colonel, with a sigh of relief. It was absurd that a man of his position should take an interest in a little country-bred vagabond; but the Colonel remembered the conversation in the train, and often in the past few months had caught himself thinking of the queer, silent, self-possessed boy. His evasion, of course, was the height of insolence, but it argued some resource and nerve.

Mahbub's eyes twinkled as he reined out into the centre of the cramped little plain, where none could come near unseen.

"'The Friend of the Stars, who is the Friend of all the World—'"

"What is this?"

"A name we give him in Lahore city. 'The Friend of all the World takes leave to go to his own places. He will come back upon the appointed day. Let the box and the bedding-roll be sent for; and if there has been a fault, let the Hand of Friendship turn aside the Whip of Calamity.' There is yet a little more, but—"

"No matter, read."

"'Certain things are not known to those who eat with forks. It is better to eat with both hands for a while. Speak soft words to those who do not understand this that the return may be propitious.' Now the manner in which that was cast is, of course, the work of the letter-writer, but see how wisely the boy has devised the matter of it so that no hint is given except to those who know!"

"Is this the Hand of Friendship to avert the Whip of Calamity?" laughed the Colonel.

"See how wise is the boy. He would go back to the Road again, as I said. Not knowing yet thy trade—"

"I am not at all sure of that," the Colonel muttered.

"He turns to me to make a peace between you. Is he not wise? He says he will return. He is but perfecting his knowledge. Think, Sahib! He has been three months at the school. And he is not mouthed to that bit. For my part, I rejoice. The pony learns the game."

"Ay, but another time he must not go alone."

"Why? He went alone before he came under the Colonel Sahib's protection. When he comes to the Great Game he must go alone—alone, and at peril of his head. Then, if he spits, or sneezes, or sits down other than as the people do whom he watches, he may be slain. Why hinder him now? Remember how the Persians say: The jackal that lives in the wilds of Mazanderan can

only be caught by the hounds of Mazanderan."

"True. It is true, Mahbub Ali. And if he comes to no harm, I do not desire anything better. But it is great insolence on his part."

"He does not tell me, even, whither he goes," said Mahbub. "He is no fool. When his time is accomplished he will come to me. It is time the healer of pearls took him in hand. He ripens too quickly—as Sahibs reckon."

This prophecy was fulfilled to the letter a month later. Mahbub had gone down to Umballa to bring up a fresh consignment of horses, and Kim met him on the Kalka road at dusk riding alone, begged an alms of him, was sworn at, and replied in English. There was nobody within earshot to hear Mahbub's gasp of amazement.

"Oho! And where hast thou been?"

"Up and down—down and up."

"Come under a tree, out of the wet, and tell."

"I stayed for a while with an old man near Umballa; anon with a household of my acquaintance in Umballa. With one of these I went as far as Delhi to the southward. That is a wondrous city. Then I drove a bullock for a teli (an oilman) coming north; but I heard of a great feast forward in Patiala, and thither went I in the company of a firework-maker. It was a great feast" (Kim rubbed his stomach). "I saw Rajahs, and elephants with gold and silver trappings; and they lit all the fireworks at once, whereby eleven men were killed, my fire-work-maker among them, and I was blown across a tent but took no harm. Then I came back to the rêl with a Sikh horseman, to whom I was groom for my bread; and so here."

"Shabash!" said Mahbub Ali.

"But what does the Colonel Sahib say? I do not wish to be beaten."

"The Hand of Friendship has averted the Whip of Calamity; but another time, when thou takest the Road it will be with me. This is too early."

"Late enough for me. I have learned to read and to write English a little at the madrissah. I shall soon be altogether a Sahib."

"Hear him!" laughed Mahbub, looking at the little drenched figure dancing in the wet. "Salaam—Sahib," and he saluted ironically.

"Well, art tired of the Road, or wilt thou come on to Umballa with me and work back with the horses?"

"I come with thee, Mahbub Ali."

CHAPTER VIII

> Something I owe to the soil that grew—
> More to the life that fed—
> But most to Allah Who gave me two
> Separate sides to my head.
>
> I would go without shirts or shoes,
> Friends, tobacco or bread
> Sooner than for an instant lose
> Either side of my head."

"Then in God's name take blue for red," said Mahbub, alluding to the Hindu colour of Kim's disreputable turban.

Kim countered with the old proverb, "I will change my faith and my bedding, but thou must pay for it."

The dealer laughed till he nearly fell from his horse. At a shop on the outskirts of the city the change was made, and Kim stood up, externally at least, a Mohammedan.

Mahbub hired a room over against the railway station, sent for a cooked meal of the finest with the almond-curd sweet-meats (balushai we call it) and fine-chopped Lucknow tobacco.

"This is better than some other meat that I ate with the Sikh," said Kim, grinning as he squatted, "and assuredly they give no such victuals at my madrissah."

"I have a desire to hear of that same madrissah." Mahbub stuffed himself with great boluses of spiced mutton fried in fat with cabbage and golden-brown onions. "But tell me first, altogether and truthfully, the manner of thy escape. For, O Friend of all the World,"—he loosed his cracking belt—"I do not think it is often that a Sahib and the son of a Sahib runs away from there."

"How should they? They do not know the land. It was nothing," said Kim, and began his tale. When he came to the disguisement and the interview with the girl in the bazar, Mahbub Ali's gravity went from him. He laughed aloud and beat his hand on his thigh.

"Shabash! Shabash! Oh, well done, little one! What will the healer of turquoises say to this? Now, slowly, let us hear what befell afterwards—step by step, omitting nothing."

Step by step then, Kim told his adventures between coughs as the full-flavoured tobacco caught his lungs.

"I said," growled Mahbub Ali to himself, "I said it was the pony breaking out to play polo. The fruit is ripe already—except that he must learn his distances and his pacings, and his rods and his compasses. Listen now. I have turned aside the Colonel's whip from thy skin, and that is no small service."

"True." Kim pulled serenely. "That is true."

"But it is not to be thought that this running out and in is any way good."

"It was my holiday, Hajji. I was a slave for many weeks. Why should I not run away when the

school was shut? Look, too, how I, living upon my friends or working for my bread, as I did with the Sikh, have saved the Colonel Sahib a great expense."

Mahbub's lips twitched under his well-pruned Mohammedan moustache.

"What are a few rupees"—the Pathan threw out his open hand carelessly—"to the Colonel Sahib? He spends them for a purpose, not in any way for love of thee."

"That," said Kim slowly, "I knew a very long time ago."

"Who told?"

"The Colonel Sahib himself. Not in those many words, but plainly enough for one who is not altogether a mud-head. Yea, he told me in the te-rain when we went down to Lucknow."

"Be it so. Then I will tell thee more, Friend of all the World, though in the telling I lend thee my head."

"It was forfeit to me," said Kim, with deep relish, "in Umballa, when thou didst pick me up on the horse after the drummer-boy beat me."

"Speak a little plainer. All the world may tell lies save thou and I. For equally is thy life forfeit to me if I chose to raise my finger here."

"And this is known to me also," said Kim, readjusting the live charcoal-ball on the weed. "It is a very sure tie between us. Indeed, thy hold is surer even than mine; for who would miss a boy beaten to death, or, it may be, thrown into a well by the roadside? Most people here and in Simla and across the passes behind the Hills would, on the other hand, say: 'What has come to Mahbub Ali?' if he were found dead among his horses. Surely, too, the Colonel Sahib would make inquiries. But again,"—Kim's face puckered with cunning,—"he would not make overlong inquiry, lest people should ask: 'What has this Colonel Sahib to do with that horse-dealer?' But I—if I lived—"

"As thou wouldst surely die—"

"It may be; but I say, if I lived, I, and I alone, would know that one had come by night, as a common thief perhaps, to Mahbub Ali's bulkhead in the serai, and there had slain him, either before or after that thief had made a full search into his saddlebags and between the soles of his slippers. Is that news to tell to the Colonel, or would he say to me—(I have not forgotten when he sent me back for a cigar-case that he had not left behind him)—'What is Mahbub Ali to me?'?"

Up went a gout of heavy smoke. There was a long pause: then Mahbub Ali spoke in admiration: "And with these things on thy mind, dost thou lie down and rise again among all the Sahibs' little sons at the madrissah and meekly take instruction from thy teachers?"

"It is an order," said Kim blandly. "Who am I to dispute an order?"

"A most finished Son of Eblis," said Mahbub Ali. "But what is this tale of the thief and the search?"

"That which I saw," said Kim, "the night that my lama and I lay next thy place in the Kashmir Serai. The door was left unlocked, which I think is not thy custom, Mahbub. He came in as one assured that thou wouldst not soon return. My eye was against a knot-hole in the plank. He searched as it were for something—not a rug, not stirrups, nor a bridle, nor brass pots—

something little and most carefully hid. Else why did he prick with an iron between the soles of thy slippers?"

"Ha!" Mahbub Ali smiled gently. "And seeing these things, what tale didst thou fashion to thyself, Well of the Truth?"

"None. I put my hand upon my amulet, which lies always next to my skin, and, remembering the pedigree of a white stallion that I had bitten out of a piece of Mussalmani bread, I went away to Umballa perceiving that a heavy trust was laid upon me. At that hour, had I chosen, thy head was forfeit. It needed only to say to that man, 'I have here a paper concerning a horse which I cannot read.' And then?" Kim peered at Mahbub under his eyebrows.

"Then thou wouldst have drunk water twice—perhaps thrice, afterwards. I do not think more than thrice," said Mahbub simply.

"It is true. I thought of that a little, but most I thought that I loved thee, Mahbub. Therefore I went to Umballa, as thou knowest, but (and this thou dost not know) I lay hid in the garden-grass to see what Colonel Creighton Sahib might do upon reading the white stallion's pedigree."

"And what did he?" for Kim had bitten off the conversation.

"Dost thou give news for love, or dost thou sell it?" Kim asked.

"I sell and—I buy." Mahbub took a four-anna piece out of his belt and held it up.

"Eight!" said Kim, mechanically following the huckster instinct of the East.

Mahbub laughed, and put away the coin. "It is too easy to deal in that market, Friend of all the World. Tell me for love. Our lives lie in each other's hand."

"Very good. I saw the Jang-i-Lat Sahib [the Commander-in-Chief] come to a big dinner. I saw him in Creighton Sahib's office. I saw the two read the white stallion's pedigree. I heard the very orders given for the opening of a great war."

"Hah!" Mahbub nodded with deepest eyes afire. "The game is well played. That war is done now, and the evil, we hope, nipped before the flower—thanks to me—and thee. What didst thou later?"

"I made the news as it were a hook to catch me victual and honour among the villagers in a village whose priest drugged my lama. But I bore away the old man's purse, and the Brahmin found nothing. So next morning he was angry. Ho! Ho! And I also used the news when I fell into the hands of that white Regiment with their Bull!"

"That was foolishness." Mahbub scowled. "News is not meant to be thrown about like dung-cakes, but used sparingly—like bhang."

"So I think now, and moreover, it did me no sort of good. But that was very long ago," he made as to brush it all away with a thin brown hand—"and since then, and especially in the nights under the punkah at the madrissah, I have thought very greatly."

"Is it permitted to ask whither the Heaven-born's thought might have led?" said Mahbub, with an elaborate sarcasm, smoothing his scarlet beard.

"It is permitted," said Kim, and threw back the very tone. "They say at Nucklao that no Sahib must tell a black man that he has made a fault."

Mahbub's hand shot into his bosom, for to call a Pathan a "black man" (kala admi) is a blood-insult. Then he remembered and laughed. "Speak, Sahib. Thy black man hears."

"But," said Kim, "I am not a Sahib, and I say I made a fault to curse thee, Mahbub Ali, on that day at Umballa when I thought I was betrayed by a Pathan. I was senseless; for I was but newly caught, and I wished to kill that low-caste drummer-boy. I say now, Hajji, that it was well done; and I see my road all clear before me to a good service. I will stay in the madrissah till I am ripe."

"Well said. Especially are distances and numbers and the manner of using compasses to be learned in that game. One waits in the Hills above to show thee."

"I will learn their teaching upon a condition—that my time is given to me without question when the madrissah is shut. Ask that for me of the Colonel."

"But why not ask the Colonel in the Sahibs' tongue?"

"The Colonel is the servant of the Government. He is sent hither and yon at a word, and must consider his own advancement. (See how much I have already learned at Nucklao!) Moreover, the Colonel I know since three months only. I have known one Mahbub Ali for six years. So! To the madrissah I will go. At the madrissah I will learn. In the madrissah I will be a Sahib. But when the madrissah is shut, then must I be free and go among my people. Otherwise I die!"

"And who are thy people, Friend of all the World?"

"This great and beautiful land," said Kim, waving his paw round the little clay-walled room where the oil-lamp in its niche burned heavily through the tobacco-smoke. "And, further, I would see my lama again. And, further, I need money."

"That is the need of everyone," said Mahbub ruefully. "I will give thee eight annas, for much money is not picked out of horses' hooves, and it must suffice for many days. As to all the rest, I am well pleased, and no further talk is needed. Make haste to learn, and in three years, or it may be less, thou wilt be an aid—even to me."

"Have I been such a hindrance till now?" said Kim, with a boy's giggle.

"Do not give answers," Mahbub grunted. "Thou art my new horse-boy. Go and bed among my men. They are near the north end of the station, with the horses."

"They will beat me to the south end of the station if I come without authority."

Mahbub felt in his belt, wetted his thumb on a cake of Chinese ink, and dabbed the impression on a piece of soft native paper. From Balkh to Bombay men know that rough-ridged print with the old scar running diagonally across it.

"That is enough to show my headman. I come in the morning."

"By which road?" said Kim.

"By the road from the city. There is but one, and then we return to Creighton Sahib. I have saved thee a beating."

"Allah! What is a beating when the very head is loose on the shoulders?"

Kim slid out quietly into the night, walked half round the house, keeping close to the walls, and

headed away from the station for a mile or so. Then, fetching a wide compass, he worked back at leisure, for he needed time to invent a story if any of Mahbub's retainers asked questions.

They were camped on a piece of waste ground beside the railway, and, being natives, had not, of course, unloaded the two trucks in which Mahbub's animals stood among a consignment of country-breds bought by the Bombay tram-company. The headman, a broken-down, consumptive-looking Mohammedan, promptly challenged Kim, but was pacified at sight of Mahbub's sign-manual.

"The Hajji has of his favour given me service," said Kim testily. "If this be doubted, wait till he comes in the morning. Meantime, a place by the fire."

Followed the usual aimless babble that every low-caste native must raise on every occasion. It died down, and Kim lay out behind the little knot of Mahbub's followers, almost under the wheels of a horse-truck, a borrowed blanket for covering. Now a bed among brickbats and ballast-refuse on a damp night, between overcrowded horses and unwashed Baltis, would not appeal to many white boys; but Kim was utterly happy. Change of scene, service, and surroundings were the breath of his little nostrils, and thinking of the neat white cots of St Xavier's all arow under the punkah gave him joy as keen as the repetition of the multiplication-table in English.

"I am very old," he thought sleepily. "Every month I become a year more old. I was very young, and a fool to boot, when I took Mahbub's message to Umballa. Even when I was with that white Regiment I was very young and small and had no wisdom. But now I learn every day, and in three years the Colonel will take me out of the madrissah and let me go upon the Road with Mahbub hunting for horses' pedigrees, or maybe I shall go by myself; or maybe I shall find the lama and go with him. Yes; that is best. To walk again as a chela with my lama when he comes back to Benares."

The thoughts came more slowly and disconnectedly. He was plunging into a beautiful dreamland when his ears caught a whisper, thin and sharp, above the monotonous babble round the fire. It came from behind the iron-skinned horse-truck.

"He is not here, then?"

"Where should he be but roystering in the city. Who looks for a rat in a frog-pond? Come away. He is not our man."

"He must not go back beyond the Passes a second time. It is the order."

"Hire some woman to drug him. It is a few rupees only, and there is no evidence."

"Except the woman. It must be more certain; and remember the price upon his head."

"Ay, but the police have a long arm, and we are far from the Border. If it were in Peshawur, now!"

"Yes—in Peshawur," the second voice sneered. "Peshawur, full of his blood-kin—full of bolt-holes and women behind whose clothes he will hide. Yes, Peshawur or Jehannum would suit us equally well."

"Then what is the plan?"

"O fool, have I not told it a hundred times? Wait till he comes to lie down, and then one sure shot. The trucks are between us and pursuit. We have but to run back over the lines and go our

way. They will not see whence the shot came. Wait here at least till the dawn. What manner of faquir art thou, to shiver at a little watching?"

"Oho!" thought Kim, behind close-shut eyes. "Once again it is Mahbub. Indeed a white stallion's pedigree is not a good thing to peddle to Sahibs! Or maybe Mahbub has been selling other news. Now what is to do, Kim? I know not where Mahbub houses, and if he comes here before the dawn they will shoot him. That would be no profit for thee, Kim. And this is not a matter for the police. That would be no profit for Mahbub; and"—he giggled almost aloud—"I do not remember any lesson at Nucklao which will help me. Allah! Here is Kim and yonder are they. First, then, Kim must wake and go away, so that they shall not suspect. A bad dream wakes a man—thus—"

He threw the blanket off his face, and raised himself suddenly with the terrible, bubbling, meaningless yell of the Asiatic roused by nightmare.

"Urr-urr-urr-urr! Ya-la-la-la-la! Narain! The churel! The churel!"

A churel is the peculiarly malignant ghost of a woman who has died in child-bed. She haunts lonely roads, her feet are turned backwards on the ankles, and she leads men to torment.

Louder rose Kim's quavering howl, till at last he leaped to his feet and staggered off sleepily, while the camp cursed him for waking them. Some twenty yards farther up the line he lay down again, taking care that the whisperers should hear his grunts and groans as he recomposed himself. After a few minutes he rolled towards the road and stole away into the thick darkness.

He paddled along swiftly till he came to a culvert, and dropped behind it, his chin on a level with the coping-stone. Here he could command all the night-traffic, himself unseen.

Two or three carts passed, jingling out to the suburbs; a coughing policeman and a hurrying foot-passenger or two who sang to keep off evil spirits. Then rapped the shod feet of a horse.

"Ah! This is more like Mahbub," thought Kim, as the beast shied at the little head above the culvert.

"Ohé", Mahbub Ali," he whispered, "have a care!"

The horse was reined back almost on its haunches, and forced towards the culvert.

"Never again," said Mahbub, "will I take a shod horse for night-work. They pick up all the bones and nails in the city." He stooped to lift its forefoot, and that brought his head within a foot of Kim's.

"Down—keep down," he muttered. "The night is full of eyes."

"Two men wait thy coming behind the horse-trucks. They will shoot thee at thy lying down, because there is a price on thy head. I heard, sleeping near the horses."

"Didst thou see them? ... Hold still, Sire of Devils!" This furiously to the horse.

"No."

"Was one dressed belike as a faquir?"

"One said to the other, 'What manner of faquir art thou, to shiver at a little watching?'"

"Good. Go back to the camp and lie down. I do not die tonight."

Mahbub wheeled his horse and vanished. Kim tore back down the ditch till he reached a point opposite his second resting-place, slipped across the road like a weasel, and re-coiled himself in the blanket.

"At least Mahbub knows," he thought contentedly. "And certainly he spoke as one expecting it. I do not think those two men will profit by tonight's watch."

An hour passed, and, with the best will in the world to keep awake all night, he slept deeply. Now and again a night train roared along the metals within twenty feet of him; but he had all the Oriental's indifference to mere noise, and it did not even weave a dream through his slumber.

Mahbub was anything but asleep. It annoyed him vehemently that people outside his tribe and unaffected by his casual amours should pursue him for the life. His first and natural impulse was to cross the line lower down, work up again, and, catching his well-wishers from behind, summarily slay them. Here, he reflected with sorrow, another branch of the Government, totally unconnected with Colonel Creighton, might demand explanations which would be hard to supply; and he knew that south of the Border a perfectly ridiculous fuss is made about a corpse or so. He had not been troubled in this way since he sent Kim to Umballa with the message, and hoped that suspicion had been finally diverted.

Then a most brilliant notion struck him.

"The English do eternally tell the truth," he said, "therefore we of this country are eternally made foolish. By Allah, I will tell the truth to an Englishman! Of what use is the Government police if a poor Kabuli be robbed of his horses in their very trucks. This is as bad as Peshawur! I should lay a complaint at the station. Better still, some young Sahib on the Railway! They are zealous, and if they catch thieves it is remembered to their honour."

He tied up his horse outside the station, and strode on to the platform.

"Hullo, Mahbub Ali" said a young Assistant District Traffic Superintendent who was waiting to go down the line—a tall, tow-haired, horsey youth in dingy white linen. "What are you doing here? Selling weeds—eh?"

"No; I am not troubled for my horses. I come to look for Lutuf Ullah. I have a truck-load up the line. Could anyone take them out without the Railway's knowledge?"

"Shouldn't think so, Mahbub. You can claim against us if they do."

"I have seen two men crouching under the wheels of one of the trucks nearly all night. Faquirs do not steal horses, so I gave them no more thought. I would find Lutuf Ullah, my partner."

"The deuce you did? And you didn't bother your head about it? 'Pon my word, it's just almost as well that I met you. What were they like, eh?"

"They were only faquirs. They will no more than take a little grain, perhaps, from one of the trucks. There are many up the line. The State will never miss the dole. I came here seeking for my partner, Lutuf Ullah."

"Never mind your partner. Where are your horse-trucks?"

"A little to this side of the farthest place where they make lamps for the trains."—

"The signal-box! Yes."

"And upon the rail nearest to the road upon the right-hand side—looking up the line thus. But as regards Lutuf Ullah—a tall man with a broken nose, and a Persian greyhound Aie!"

The boy had hurried off to wake up a young and enthusiastic policeman; for, as he said, the Railway had suffered much from depredations in the goods-yard. Mahbub Ali chuckled in his dyed beard.

"They will walk in their boots, making a noise, and then they will wonder why there are no faquirs. They are very clever boys—Barton Sahib and Young Sahib."

He waited idly for a few minutes, expecting to see them hurry up the line girt for action. A light engine slid through the station, and he caught a glimpse of young Barton in the cab.

"I did that child an injustice. He is not altogether a fool," said Mahbub Ali. "To take a fire-carriage for a thief is a new game!"

When Mahbub Ali came to his camp in the dawn, no one thought it worth while to tell him any news of the night. No one, at least, but one small horseboy, newly advanced to the great man's service, whom Mahbub called to his tiny tent to assist in some packing.

"It is all known to me," whispered Kim, bending above saddlebags. 'Two Sahibs came up on a te-train. I was running to and fro in the dark on this side of the trucks as the te-train moved up and down slowly. They fell upon two men sitting under this truck—Hajji, what shall I do with this lump of tobacco? Wrap it in paper and put it under the salt-bag? Yes—and struck them down. But one man struck at a Sahib with a faquir's buck's horn" (Kim meant the conjoined black-buck horns, which are a faquir's sole temporal weapon)—"the blood came. So the other Sahib, first smiting his own man senseless, smote the stabber with a short gun which had rolled from the first man's hand. They all raged as though mad together."

Mahbub smiled with heavenly resignation. "No! That is not so much dewanee (madness, or a case for the civil court—the word can be punned upon both ways) as nizamut (a criminal case). A gun, sayest thou? Ten good years in jail."

"Then they both lay still, but I think they were nearly dead when they were put on the te-train. Their heads moved thus. And there is much blood on the line. Come and see?"

"I have seen blood before. Jail is the sure place—and assuredly they will give false names, and assuredly no man will find them for a long time. They were unfriends of mine. Thy fate and mine seem on one string. What a tale for the healer of pearls! Now swiftly with the saddle-bags and the cooking-platter. We will take out the horses and away to Simla."

Swiftly—as Orientals understand speed—with long explanations, with abuse and windy talk, carelessly, amid a hundred checks for little things forgotten, the untidy camp broke up and led the half-dozen stiff and fretful horses along the Kalka road in the fresh of the rain-swept dawn. Kim, regarded as Mahbub Ali's favourite by all who wished to stand well with the Pathan, was not called upon to work. They strolled on by the easiest of stages, halting every few hours at a wayside shelter. Very many Sahibs travel along the Kalka road; and, as Mahbub Ali says, every young Sahib must needs esteem himself a judge of a horse, and, though he be over head in debt to the money-lender, must make as if to buy. That was the reason that Sahib after Sahib, rolling along in a stage-carriage, would stop and open talk. Some would even descend from their vehicles and feel the horses' legs; asking inane questions, or, through sheer ignorance of the vernacular, grossly insulting the imperturbable trader.

"When first I dealt with Sahibs, and that was when Colonel Soady Sahib was Governor of Fort

Abazai and flooded the Commissioner's camping-ground for spite," Mahbub confided to Kim as the boy filled his pipe under a tree, "I did not know how greatly they were fools, and this made me wroth. As thus—," and he told Kim a tale of an expression, misused in all innocence, that doubled Kim up with mirth. "Now I see, however,"—he exhaled smoke slowly—"that it is with them as with all men—in certain matters they are wise, and in others most foolish. Very foolish it is to use the wrong word to a stranger; for though the heart may be clean of offence, how is the stranger to know that? He is more like to search truth with a dagger."

"True. True talk," said Kim solemnly. "Fools speak of a cat when a woman is brought to bed, for instance. I have heard them."

"Therefore, in one situate as thou art, it particularly behoves thee to remember this with both kinds of faces. Among Sahibs, never forgetting thou art a Sahib; among the folk of Hind, always remembering thou art—" He paused, with a puzzled smile.

"What am I? Mussalman, Hindu, Jain, or Buddhist? That is a hard knot."

"Thou art beyond question an unbeliever, and therefore thou wilt be damned. So says my Law—or I think it does. But thou art also my Little Friend of all the World, and I love thee. So says my heart. This matter of creeds is like horseflesh. The wise man knows horses are good— that there is a profit to be made from all; and for myself—but that I am a good Sunni and hate the men of Tirah—I could believe the same of all the Faiths. Now manifestly a Kathiawar mare taken from the sands of her birthplace and removed to the west of Bengal founders—nor is even a Balkh stallion (and there are no better horses than those of Balkh, were they not so heavy in the shoulder) of any account in the great Northern deserts beside the snow-camels I have seen. Therefore I say in my heart the Faiths are like the horses. Each has merit in its own country."

"But my lama said altogether a different thing."

"Oh, he is an old dreamer of dreams from Bhotiyal. My heart is a little angry, Friend of all the World, that thou shouldst see such worth in a man so little known."

"It is true, Hajji; but that worth do I see, and to him my heart is drawn."

"And his to thine, I hear. Hearts are like horses. They come and they go against bit or spur. Shout Gul Sher Khan yonder to drive in that bay stallion's pickets more firmly. We do not want a horse-fight at every resting-stage, and the dun and the black will be locked in a little ... Now hear me. Is it necessary to the comfort of thy heart to see that lama?"

"It is one part of my bond," said Kim. "If I do not see him, and if he is taken from me, I will go out of that madrissah in Nucklao and, and—once gone, who is to find me again?"

"It is true. Never was colt held on a lighter heel-rope than thou." Mahbub nodded his head.

"Do not be afraid." Kim spoke as though he could have vanished on the moment. "My lama has said that he will come to see me at the madrissah—"

"A beggar and his bowl in the presence of those young Sa—"

"Not all!" Kim cut in with a snort. "Their eyes are blued and their nails are blackened with low-caste blood, many of them. Sons of mehteeranees—brothers-in-law to the bhungi (sweeper)."

We need not follow the rest of the pedigree; but Kim made his little point clearly and without heat, chewing a piece of sugar-cane the while.

"Friend of all the World," said Mahbub, pushing over the pipe for the boy to clean, "I have met many men, women, and boys, and not a few Sahibs. I have never in all my days met such an imp as thou art."

"And why? When I always tell thee the truth."

"Perhaps the very reason, for this is a world of danger to honest men." Mahbub Ali hauled himself off the ground, girt in his belt, and went over to the horses.

"Or sell it?"

There was that in the tone that made Mahbub halt and turn. "What new devilry?"

"Eight annas, and I will tell," said Kim, grinning. "It touches thy peace."

"O Shaitan!" Mahbub gave the money.

"Rememberest thou the little business of the thieves in the dark, down yonder at Umballa?"

"Seeing they sought my life, I have not altogether forgotten. Why?"

"Rememberest thou the Kashmir Serai?"

"I will twist thy ears in a moment—Sahib."

"No need—Pathan. Only, the second faquir, whom the Sahibs beat senseless, was the man who came to search thy bulkhead at Lahore. I saw his face as they helped him on the engine. The very same man."

"Why didst thou not tell before?"

"Oh, he will go to jail, and be safe for some years. There is no need to tell more than is necessary at any one time. Besides, I did not then need money for sweetmeats."

"Allah kerim!" said Mahbub Ah. "Wilt thou some day sell my head for a few sweetmeats if the fit takes thee?"

Kim will remember till he dies that long, lazy journey from Umballa, through Kalka and the Pinjore Gardens near by, up to Simla. A sudden spate in the Gugger River swept down one horse (the most valuable, be sure), and nearly drowned Kim among the dancing boulders. Farther up the road the horses were stampeded by a Government elephant, and being in high condition of grass food, it cost a day and a half to get them together again. Then they met Sikandar Khan coming down with a few unsaleable screws—remnants of his string—and Mahbub, who has more of horse-coping in his little fingernail than Sikandar Khan in all his tents, must needs buy two of the worst, and that meant eight hours' laborious diplomacy and untold tobacco. But it was all pure delight—the wandering road, climbing, dipping, and sweeping about the growing spurs; the flush of the morning laid along the distant snows; the branched cacti, tier upon tier on the stony hillsides; the voices of a thousand water-channels; the chatter of the monkeys; the solemn deodars, climbing one after another with down-drooped branches; the vista of the Plains rolled out far beneath them; the incessant twanging of the tonga-horns and the wild rush of the led horses when a tonga swung round a curve; the halts for prayers (Mahbub was very religious in dry-washings and bellowings when time did not press); the evening conferences by the halting-places, when camels and bullocks chewed solemnly together and the stolid drivers told the news of the Road—all these things lifted Kim's heart to song within him.

"But, when the singing and dancing is done," said Mahbub Ali, "comes the Colonel Sahib's, and that is not so sweet."

"A fair land—a most beautiful land is this of Hind—and the land of the Five Rivers is fairer than all," Kim half chanted. "Into it I will go again if Mahbub Ali or the Colonel lift hand or foot against me. Once gone, who shall find me? Look, Hajji, is yonder the city of Simla? Allah, what a city!"

"My father's brother, and he was an old man when Mackerson Sahib's well was new at Peshawur, could recall when there were but two houses in it."

He led the horses below the main road into the lower Simla bazar—the crowded rabbit-warren that climbs up from the valley to the Town Hall at an angle of forty-five. A man who knows his way there can defy all the police of India's summer capital, so cunningly does veranda communicate with veranda, alley-way with alley-way, and bolt-hole with bolt-hole. Here live those who minister to the wants of the glad city—jhampanis who pull the pretty ladies' 'rickshaws by night and gamble till the dawn; grocers, oil-sellers, curio-vendors, firewood-dealers, priests, pickpockets, and native employees of the Government. Here are discussed by courtesans the things which are supposed to be profoundest secrets of the India Council; and here gather all the sub-sub-agents of half the Native States. Here, too, Mahbub Ali rented a room, much more securely locked than his bulkhead at Lahore, in the house of a Mohammedan cattle-dealer. It was a place of miracles, too, for there went in at twilight a Mohammedan horseboy, and there came out an hour later a Eurasian lad—the Lucknow girl's dye was of the best—in badly-fitting shop-clothes.

"I have spoken with Creighton Sahib," quoth Mahbub Ali, "and a second time has the Hand of Friendship averted the Whip of Calamity. He says that thou hast altogether wasted sixty days upon the Road, and it is too late, therefore, to send thee to any Hill-school."

"I have said that my holidays are my own. I do not go to school twice over. That is one part of my bond."

"The Colonel Sahib is not yet aware of that contract. Thou art to lodge in Lurgan Sahib's house till it is time to go again to Nucklao."

"I had sooner lodge with thee, Mahbub."

"Thou dost not know the honour. Lurgan Sahib himself asked for thee. Thou wilt go up the hill and along the road atop, and there thou must forget for a while that thou hast ever seen or spoken to me, Mahbub Ali, who sells horses to Creighton Sahib, whom thou dost not know. Remember this order."

Kim nodded. "Good," said he, "and who is Lurgan Sahib? Nay"—he caught Mahbub's sword-keen glance—"indeed I have never heard his name. Is he by chance—he lowered his voice—"one of us?"

"What talk is this of us, Sahib?" Mahbub Ali returned, in the tone he used towards Europeans. "I am a Pathan; thou art a Sahib and the son of a Sahib. Lurgan Sahib has a shop among the European shops. All Simla knows it. Ask there ... and, Friend of all the World, he is one to be obeyed to the last wink of his eyelashes. Men say he does magic, but that should not touch thee. Go up the hill and ask. Here begins the Great Game."

CHAPTER IX

S' doaks was son of Yelth the wise—
Chief of the Raven clan.
Itswoot the Bear had him in care
To make him a medicine-man.

He was quick and quicker to learn—
Bold and bolder to dare:
He danced the dread Kloo-Kwallie Dance
To tickle Itswoot the Bear!

Oregon Legend.

Kim flung himself whole-heartedly upon the next turn of the wheel. He would be a Sahib again for a while. In that idea, so soon as he had reached the broad road under Simla Town Hall, he cast about for one to impress. A Hindu child, some ten years old, squatted under a lamp-post.

"Where is Mr Lurgan's house?" demanded Kim.

"I do not understand English," was the answer, and Kim shifted his speech accordingly.

"I will show."

Together they set off through the mysterious dusk, full of the noises of a city below the hillside, and the breath of a cool wind in deodar-crowned Jakko, shouldering the stars. The house-lights, scattered on every level, made, as it were, a double firmament. Some were fixed, others belonged to the "rickshaws of the careless, open-spoken English folk, going out to dinner.

"It is here," said Kim's guide, and halted in a veranda flush with the main road. No door stayed them, but a curtain of beaded reeds that split up the lamplight beyond.

"He is come," said the boy, in a voice little louder than a sigh, and vanished. Kim felt sure that the boy had been posted to guide him from the first, but, putting a bold face on it, parted the curtain. A black-bearded man, with a green shade over his eyes, sat at a table, and, one by one, with short, white hands, picked up globules of light from a tray before him, threaded them on a glancing silken string, and hummed to himself the while. Kim was conscious that beyond the circle of light the room was full of things that smelt like all the temples of all the East. A whiff of musk, a puff of sandal-wood, and a breath of sickly jessamine-oil caught his opened nostrils.

"I am here," said Kim at last, speaking in the vernacular: the smells made him forget that he was to be a Sahib.

"Seventy-nine, eighty, eighty-one," the man counted to himself, stringing pearl after pearl so quickly that Kim could scarcely follow his fingers. He slid off the green shade and looked fixedly at Kim for a full half-minute. The pupils of the eye dilated and closed to pin-pricks, as if at will. There was a faquir by the Taksali Gate who had just this gift and made money by it, especially when cursing silly women. Kim stared with interest. His disreputable friend could further twitch his ears, almost like a goat, and Kim was disappointed that this new man could not imitate him.

"Do not be afraid," said Lurgan Sahib suddenly.

"Why should I fear?"

"Thou wilt sleep here tonight, and stay with me till it is time to go again to Nucklao. It is an order."

"It is an order," Kim repeated. "But where shall I sleep?"

"Here, in this room." Lurgan Sahib waved his hand towards the darkness behind him.

"So be it," said Kim composedly. "Now?"

He nodded and held the lamp above his head. As the light swept them, there leaped out from the walls a collection of Tibetan devil-dance masks, hanging above the fiend-embroidered draperies of those ghastly functions—horned masks, scowling masks, and masks of idiotic terror. In a corner, a Japanese warrior, mailed and plumed, menaced him with a halberd, and a score of lances and khandas and kuttars gave back the unsteady gleam. But what interested Kim more than all these things—he had seen devil-dance masks at the Lahore Museum—was a glimpse of the soft-eyed Hindu child who had left him in the doorway, sitting cross-legged under the table of pearls with a little smile on his scarlet lips.

"I think that Lurgan Sahib wishes to make me afraid. And I am sure that that devil's brat below the table wishes to see me afraid.

"This place," he said aloud, "is like a Wonder House. Where is my bed?"

Lurgan Sahib pointed to a native quilt in a corner by the loathsome masks, picked up the lamp, and left the room black.

"Was that Lurgan Sahib?" Kim asked as he cuddled down. No answer. He could hear the Hindu boy breathing, however, and, guided by the sound, crawled across the floor, and cuffed into the darkness, crying: "Give answer, devil! Is this the way to lie to a Sahib?"

From the darkness he fancied he could hear the echo of a chuckle. It could not be his soft-fleshed companion, because he was weeping. So Kim lifted up his voice and called aloud:

"Lurgan Sahib! O Lurgan Sahib! Is it an order that thy servant does not speak to me?"

"It is an order." The voice came from behind him and he started.

"Very good. But remember," he muttered, as he resought the quilt, "I will beat thee in the morning. I do not love Hindus."

That was no cheerful night; the room being overfull of voices and music. Kim was waked twice by someone calling his name. The second time he set out in search, and ended by bruising his nose against a box that certainly spoke with a human tongue, but in no sort of human accent. It seemed to end in a tin trumpet and to be joined by wires to a smaller box on the floor—so far, at least, as he could judge by touch. And the voice, very hard and whirring, came out of the trumpet. Kim rubbed his nose and grew furious, thinking, as usual, in Hindi.

"This with a beggar from the bazar might be good, but—I am a Sahib and the son of a Sahib and, which is twice as much more beside, a student of Nucklao. Yess" (here he turned to English), "a boy of St Xavier's. Damn Mr Lurgan's eyes!—It is some sort of machinery like a sewing-machine. Oh, it is a great cheek of him—we are not frightened that way at Lucknow—No!" Then in Hindi: "But what does he gain? He is only a trader—I am in his shop. But Creighton Sahib is a Colonel—and I think Creighton Sahib gave orders that it should be done. How I will

beat that Hindu in the morning! What is this?"

The trumpet-box was pouring out a string of the most elaborate abuse that even Kim had ever heard, in a high uninterested voice, that for a moment lifted the short hairs of his neck. When the vile thing drew breath, Kim was reassured by the soft, sewing-machine-like whirr.

"Chûp! (Be still)" he cried, and again he heard a chuckle that decided him. "Chûp—or I break your head."

The box took no heed. Kim wrenched at the tin trumpet and something lifted with a click. He had evidently raised a lid. If there were a devil inside, now was its time, for—he sniffed—thus did the sewing-machines of the bazar smell. He would clean that shaitan. He slipped off his jacket, and plunged it into the box's mouth. Something long and round bent under the pressure, there was a whirr and the voice stopped—as voices must if you ram a thrice-doubled coat on to the wax cylinder and into the works of an expensive phonograph. Kim finished his slumbers with a serene mind.

In the morning he was aware of Lurgan Sahib looking down on him.

"Oah!" said Kim, firmly resolved to cling to his Sahib-dom. "There was a box in the night that gave me bad talk. So I stopped it. Was it your box?"

The man held out his hand.

"Shake hands, O'Hara," he said. "Yes, it was my box. I keep such things because my friends the Rajahs like them. That one is broken, but it was cheap at the price. Yes, my friends, the Kings, are very fond of toys—and so am I sometimes."

Kim looked him over out of the corners of his eyes. He was a Sahib in that he wore Sahib's clothes; the accent of his Urdu, the intonation of his English, showed that he was anything but a Sahib. He seemed to understand what moved in Kim's mind ere the boy opened his mouth, and he took no pains to explain himself as did Father Victor or the Lucknow masters. Sweetest of all—he treated Kim as an equal on the Asiatic side.

"I am sorry you cannot beat my boy this morning. He says he will kill you with a knife or poison. He is jealous, so I have put him in the corner and I shall not speak to him today. He has just tried to kill me. You must help me with the breakfast. He is almost too jealous to trust, just now."

Now a genuine imported Sahib from England would have made a great to-do over this tale. Lurgan Sahib stated it as simply as Mahbub Ali was used to record his little affairs in the North.

The back veranda of the shop was built out over the sheer hillside, and they looked down into their neighbours' chimney-pots, as is the custom of Simla. But even more than the purely Persian meal cooked by Lurgan Sahib with his own hands, the shop fascinated Kim. The Lahore Museum was larger, but here were more wonders—ghost-daggers and prayer-wheels from Tibet; turquoise and raw amber necklaces; green jade bangles; curiously packed incense-sticks in jars crusted over with raw garnets; the devil-masks of overnight and a wall full of peacock-blue draperies; gilt figures of Buddha, and little portable lacquer altars; Russian samovars with turquoises on the lid; egg-shell china sets in quaint octagonal cane boxes; yellow ivory crucifixes—from Japan of all places in the world, so Lurgan Sahib said; carpets in dusty bales, smelling atrociously, pushed back behind torn and rotten screens of geometrical work; Persian water-jugs for the hands after meals; dull copper incense-burners neither Chinese nor Persian, with friezes of fantastic devils running round them; tarnished silver belts that knotted like raw

hide; hairpins of jade, ivory, and plasma; arms of all sorts and kinds, and a thousand other oddments were cased, or piled, or merely thrown into the room, leaving a clear space only round the rickety deal table, where Lurgan Sahib worked.

"Those things are nothing," said his host, following Kim's glance. "I buy them because they are pretty, and sometimes I sell—if I like the buyer's look. My work is on the table—some of it."

It blazed in the morning light—all red and blue and green flashes, picked out with the vicious blue-white spurt of a diamond here and there. Kim opened his eyes.

"Oh, they are quite well, those stones. It will not hurt them to take the sun. Besides, they are cheap. But with sick stones it is very different." He piled Kim's plate anew. "There is no one but me can doctor a sick pearl and re-blue turquoises. I grant you opals—any fool can cure an opal—but for a sick pearl there is only me. Suppose I were to die! Then there would be no one ... Oh no! You cannot do anything with jewels. It will be quite enough if you understand a little about the Turquoise—some day."

He moved to the end of the veranda to refill the heavy, porous clay water-jug from the filter.

"Do you want drink?"

Kim nodded. Lurgan Sahib, fifteen feet off, laid one hand on the jar. Next instant, it stood at Kim's elbow, full to within half an inch of the brim—the white cloth only showing, by a small wrinkle, where it had slid into place.

"Wah!" said Kim in most utter amazement. "That is magic." Lurgan Sahib's smile showed that the compliment had gone home.

"Throw it back."

"It will break."

"I say, throw it back."

Kim pitched it at random. It fell short and crashed into fifty pieces, while the water dripped through the rough veranda boarding.

"I said it would break."

"All one. Look at it. Look at the largest piece."

That lay with a sparkle of water in its curve, as it were a star on the floor. Kim looked intently. Lurgan Sahib laid one hand gently on the nape of his neck, stroked it twice or thrice, and whispered: "Look! It shall come to life again, piece by piece. First the big piece shall join itself to two others on the right and the left—on the right and the left. Look!"

To save his life, Kim could not have turned his head. The light touch held him as in a vice, and his blood tingled pleasantly through him. There was one large piece of the jar where there had been three, and above them the shadowy outline of the entire vessel. He could see the veranda through it, but it was thickening and darkening with each beat of his pulse. Yet the jar—how slowly the thoughts came!—the jar had been smashed before his eyes. Another wave of prickling fire raced down his neck, as Lurgan Sahib moved his hand.

"Look! It is coming into shape," said Lurgan Sahib.

So far Kim had been thinking in Hindi, but a tremor came on him, and with an effort like that of a swimmer before sharks, who hurls himself half out of the water, his mind leaped up from a darkness that was swallowing it and took refuge in—the multiplication-table in English!

"Look! It is coming into shape," whispered Lurgan Sahib.

The jar had been smashed—yess, smashed—not the native word, he would not think of that—but smashed—into fifty pieces, and twice three was six, and thrice three was nine, and four times three was twelve. He clung desperately to the repetition. The shadow-outline of the jar cleared like a mist after rubbing eyes. There were the broken shards; there was the spilt water drying in the sun, and through the cracks of the veranda showed, all ribbed, the white house-wall below—and thrice twelve was thirty-six!

"Look! Is it coming into shape?" asked Lurgan Sahib.

"But it is smashed—smashed," he gasped—Lurgan Sahib had been muttering softly for the last half-minute. Kim wrenched his head aside. "Look! Dekho! It is there as it was there."

"It is there as it was there," said Lurgan, watching Kim closely while the boy rubbed his neck. "But you are the first of many who has ever seen it so." He wiped his broad forehead.

"Was that more magic?" Kim asked suspiciously. The tingle had gone from his veins; he felt unusually wide awake.

"No, that was not magic. It was only to see if there was—a flaw in a jewel. Sometimes very fine jewels will fly all to pieces if a man holds them in his hand, and knows the proper way. That is why one must be careful before one sets them. Tell me, did you see the shape of the pot?"

"For a little time. It began to grow like a flower from the ground."

"And then what did you do? I mean, how did you think?"

"Oah! I knew it was broken, and so, I think, that was what I thought—and it was broken."

"Hm! Has anyone ever done that same sort of magic to you before?"

"If it was," said Kim "do you think I should let it again? I should run away."

"And now you are not afraid—eh?"

"Not now."

Lurgan Sahib looked at him more closely than ever. "I shall ask Mahbub Ali—not now, but some day later," he muttered. "I am pleased with you—yes; and I am pleased with you—no. You are the first that ever saved himself. I wish I knew what it was that ... But you are right. You should not tell that—not even to me."

He turned into the dusky gloom of the shop, and sat down at the table, rubbing his hands softly. A small, husky sob came from behind a pile of carpets. It was the Hindu child obediently facing towards the wall. His thin shoulders worked with grief.

"Ah! He is jealous, so jealous. I wonder if he will try to poison me again in my breakfast, and make me cook it twice.

"Kubbee—kubbee nahin," came the broken answer.

"And whether he will kill this other boy?"

"Kubbee—kubbee nahin." (Never—never. No!)

"What do you think he will do?" He turned suddenly on Kim.

"Oah! I do not know. Let him go, perhaps. Why did he want to poison you?"

"Because he is so fond of me. Suppose you were fond of someone, and you saw someone come, and the man you were fond of was more pleased with him than he was with you, what would you do?"

Kim thought. Lurgan repeated the sentence slowly in the vernacular.

"I should not poison that man," said Kim reflectively, "but I should beat that boy—if that boy was fond of my man. But first, I would ask that boy if it were true."

"Ah! He thinks everyone must be fond of me."

"Then I think he is a fool."

"Hearest thou?" said Lurgan Sahib to the shaking shoulders. "The Sahib's son thinks thou art a little fool. Come out, and next time thy heart is troubled, do not try white arsenic quite so openly. Surely the Devil Dasim was lord of our table-cloth that day! It might have made me ill, child, and then a stranger would have guarded the jewels. Come!"

The child, heavy-eyed with much weeping, crept out from behind the bale and flung himself passionately at Lurgan Sahib's feet, with an extravagance of remorse that impressed even Kim.

"I will look into the ink-pools—I will faithfully guard the jewels! Oh, my Father and my Mother, send him away!" He indicated Kim with a backward jerk of his bare heel.

"Not yet—not yet. In a little while he will go away again. But now he is at school—at a new madrissah—and thou shalt be his teacher. Play the Play of the Jewels against him. I will keep tally."

The child dried his tears at once, and dashed to the back of the shop, whence he returned with a copper tray.

"Give me!" he said to Lurgan Sahib. "Let them come from thy hand, for he may say that I knew them before."

"Gently—gently," the man replied, and from a drawer under the table dealt a half-handful of clattering trifles into the tray.

"Now," said the child, waving an old newspaper. "Look on them as long as thou wilt, stranger. Count and, if need be, handle. One look is enough for me." He turned his back proudly.

"But what is the game?"

"When thou hast counted and handled and art sure that thou canst remember them all, I cover them with this paper, and thou must tell over the tally to Lurgan Sahib. I will write mine."

"Oah!" The instinct of competition waked in his breast. He bent over the tray. There were but fifteen stones on it. "That is easy," he said after a minute. The child slipped the paper over the winking jewels and scribbled in a native account-book.

"There are under that paper five blue stones—one big, one smaller, and three small," said Kim, all in haste. "There are four green stones, and one with a hole in it; there is one yellow stone that I can see through, and one like a pipe-stem. There are two red stones, and—and—I made the count fifteen, but two I have forgotten. No! Give me time. One was of ivory, little and brownish; and—and—give me time..."

"One—two"—Lurgan Sahib counted him out up to ten. Kim shook his head.

"Hear my count!" the child burst in, trilling with laughter. "First, are two flawed sapphires—one of two ruttees and one of four as I should judge. The four-ruttee sapphire is chipped at the edge. There is one Turkestan turquoise, plain with black veins, and there are two inscribed—one with a Name of God in gilt, and the other being cracked across, for it came out of an old ring, I cannot read. We have now all five blue stones. Four flawed emeralds there are, but one is drilled in two places, and one is a little carven—"

"Their weights?" said Lurgan Sahib impassively.

"Three—five—five—and four ruttees as I judge it. There is one piece of old greenish pipe amber, and a cut topaz from Europe. There is one ruby of Burma, of two ruttees, without a flaw, and there is a balas-ruby, flawed, of two ruttees. There is a carved ivory from China representing a rat sucking an egg; and there is last—ah ha!—a ball of crystal as big as a bean set on a gold leaf."

He clapped his hands at the close.

"He is thy master," said Lurgan Sahib, smiling.

"Huh! He knew the names of the stones," said Kim, flushing. "Try again! With common things such as he and I both know."

They heaped the tray again with odds and ends gathered from the shop, and even the kitchen, and every time the child won, till Kim marvelled.

"Bind my eyes—let me feel once with my fingers, and even then I will leave thee opened-eyed behind," he challenged.

Kim stamped with vexation when the lad made his boast good.

"If it were men—or horses," he said, "I could do better. This playing with tweezers and knives and scissors is too little."

"Learn first—teach later," said Lurgan Sahib. "Is he thy master?"

"Truly. But how is it done?"

"By doing it many times over till it is done perfectly—for it is worth doing."

The Hindu boy, in highest feather, actually patted Kim on the back.

"Do not despair," he said. "I myself will teach thee."

"And I will see that thou art well taught," said Lurgan Sahib, still speaking in the vernacular, "for except my boy here—it was foolish of him to buy so much white arsenic when, if he had asked, I could have given it—except my boy here I have not in a long time met with one better worth teaching. And there are ten days more ere thou canst return to Lucknao where they teach

nothing—at the long price. We shall, I think, be friends."

They were a most mad ten days, but Kim enjoyed himself too much to reflect on their craziness. In the morning they played the Jewel Game—sometimes with veritable stones, sometimes with piles of swords and daggers, sometimes with photo-graphs of natives. Through the afternoons he and the Hindu boy would mount guard in the shop, sitting dumb behind a carpet-bale or a screen and watching Mr Lurgan's many and very curious visitors. There were small Rajahs, escorts coughing in the veranda, who came to buy curiosities—such as phonographs and mechanical toys. There were ladies in search of necklaces, and men, it seemed to Kim—but his mind may have been vitiated by early training—in search of the ladies; natives from independent and feudatory Courts whose ostensible business was the repair of broken necklaces—rivers of light poured out upon the table—but whose true end seemed to be to raise money for angry Maharanees or young Rajahs. There were Babus to whom Lurgan Sahib talked with austerity and authority, but at the end of each interview he gave them money in coined silver and currency notes. There were occasional gatherings of long-coated theatrical natives who discussed metaphysics in English and Bengali, to Mr Lurgan's great edification. He was always interested in religions. At the end of the day, Kim and the Hindu boy—whose name varied at Lurgan's pleasure—were expected to give a detailed account of all that they had seen and heard—their view of each man's character, as shown in his face, talk, and manner, and their notions of his real errand. After dinner, Lurgan Sahib's fancy turned more to what might be called dressing-up, in which game he took a most informing interest. He could paint faces to a marvel; with a brush-dab here and a line there changing them past recognition. The shop was full of all manner of dresses and turbans, and Kim was apparelled variously as a young Mohammedan of good family, an oilman, and once—which was a joyous evening—as the son of an Oudh landholder in the fullest of full dress. Lurgan Sahib had a hawk's eye to detect the least flaw in the make-up; and lying on a worn teak-wood couch, would explain by the half-hour together how such and such a caste talked, or walked, or coughed, or spat, or sneezed, and, since "hows" matter little in this world, the "why" of everything. The Hindu child played this game clumsily. That little mind, keen as an icicle where tally of jewels was concerned, could not temper itself to enter another's soul; but a demon in Kim woke up and sang with joy as he put on the changing dresses, and changed speech and gesture therewith.

Carried away by enthusiasm, he volunteered to show Lurgan Sahib one evening how the disciples of a certain caste of faquir, old Lahore acquaintances, begged doles by the roadside; and what sort of language he would use to an Englishman, to a Punjabi farmer going to a fair, and to a woman without a veil. Lurgan Sahib laughed immensely, and begged Kim to stay as he was, immobile for half an hour—cross-legged, ash-smeared, and wild-eyed, in the back room. At the end of that time entered a hulking, obese Babu whose stockinged legs shook with fat, and Kim opened on him with a shower of wayside chaff. Lurgan Sahib—this annoyed Kim—watched the Babu and not the play.

"I think," said the Babu heavily, lighting a cigarette, "I am of opeenion that it is most extraordinary and effeecient performance. Except that you had told me I should have opined that—that—that you were pulling my legs. How soon can he become approximately effeecient chain-man? Because then I shall indent for him."

"That is what he must learn at Lucknow."

"Then order him to be jolly-dam'-quick. Good-night, Lurgan." The Babu swung out with the gait of a bogged cow.

When they were telling over the day's list of visitors, Lurgan Sahib asked Kim who he thought the man might be.

"God knows!" said Kim cheerily. The tone might almost have deceived Mahbub Ali, but it failed entirely with the healer of sick pearls.

"That is true. God, He knows; but I wish to know what you think."

Kim glanced sideways at his companion, whose eye had a way of compelling truth.

"I—I think he will want me when I come from the school, but"—confidentially, as Lurgan Sahib nodded approval—"I do not understand how he can wear many dresses and talk many tongues."

"Thou wilt understand many things later. He is a writer of tales for a certain Colonel. His honour is great only in Simla, and it is noticeable that he has no name, but only a number and a letter—that is a custom among us."

"And is there a price upon his head too—as upon Mah—all the others?"

"Not yet; but if a boy rose up who is now sitting here and went—look, the door is open!—as far as a certain house with a red-painted veranda, behind that which was the old theatre in the Lower Bazar, and whispered through the shutters: 'Hurree Chunder Mookerjee bore the bad news of last month', that boy might take away a belt full of rupees."

"How many?" said Kim promptly.

"Five hundred—a thousand—as many as he might ask for."

"Good. And for how long might such a boy live after the news was told?" He smiled merrily at Lurgan's Sahib's very beard.

"Ah! That is to be well thought of. Perhaps if he were very clever, he might live out the day—but not the night. By no means the night."

"Then what is the Babu's pay if so much is put upon his head?"

"Eighty—perhaps a hundred—perhaps a hundred and fifty rupees; but the pay is the least part of the work. From time to time, God causes men to be born—and thou art one of them—who have a lust to go abroad at the risk of their lives and discover news—today it may be of far-off things, tomorrow of some hidden mountain, and the next day of some near-by men who have done a foolishness against the State. These souls are very few; and of these few, not more than ten are of the best. Among these ten I count the Babu, and that is curious. How great, therefore, and desirable must be a business that brazens the heart of a Bengali!"

"True. But the days go slowly for me. I am yet a boy, and it is only within two months I learned to write Angrezi. Even now I cannot read it well. And there are yet years and years and long years before I can be even a chain-man."

"Have patience, Friend of all the World"—Kim started at the title. "Would I had a few of the years that so irk thee. I have proved thee in several small ways. This will not be forgotten when I make my report to the Colonel Sahib." Then, changing suddenly into English with a deep laugh:

"By Jove! O'Hara, I think there is a great deal in you; but you must not become proud and you must not talk. You must go back to Lucknow and be a good little boy and mind your book, as the English say, and perhaps, next holidays if you care, you can come back to me!" Kim's face fell. "Oh, I mean if you like. I know where you want to go."

Four days later a seat was booked for Kim and his small trunk at the rear of a Kalka tonga. His companion was the whale-like Babu, who, with a fringed shawl wrapped round his head, and his fat openwork-stockinged left leg tucked under him, shivered and grunted in the morning chill.

"How comes it that this man is one of us?" thought Kim considering the jelly back as they jolted down the road; and the reflection threw him into most pleasant day-dreams. Lurgan Sahib had given him five rupees—a splendid sum—as well as the assurance of his protection if he worked. Unlike Mahbub, Lurgan Sahib had spoken most explicitly of the reward that would follow obedience, and Kim was content. If only, like the Babu, he could enjoy the dignity of a letter and a number—and a price upon his head! Some day he would be all that and more. Some day he might be almost as great as Mahbub Ali! The housetops of his search should be half India; he would follow Kings and Ministers, as in the old days he had followed vakils and lawyers' touts across Lahore city for Mahbub Ali's sake. Meantime, there was the present, and not at all unpleasant, fact of St Xavier's immediately before him. There would be new boys to condescend to, and there would be tales of holiday adventures to hear. Young Martin, son of the tea-planter at Manipur, had boasted that he would go to war, with a rifle, against the head-hunters.

That might be, but it was certain young Martin had not been blown half across the forecourt of a Patiala palace by an explosion of fireworks; nor had he... Kim fell to telling himself the story of his own adventures through the last three months. He could paralyse St Xavier's—even the biggest boys who shaved—with the recital, were that permitted. But it was, of course, out of the question. There would be a price upon his head in good time, as Lurgan Sahib had assured him; and if he talked foolishly now, not only would that price never be set, but Colonel Creighton would cast him off—and he would be left to the wrath of Lurgan Sahib and Mahbub Ali—for the short space of life that would remain to him.

"So I should lose Delhi for the sake of a fish," was his proverbial philosophy. It behoved him to forget his holidays (there would always remain the fun of inventing imaginary adventures) and, as Lurgan Sahib had said, to work. Of all the boys hurrying back to St Xavier's, from Sukkur in the sands to Galle beneath the palms, none was so filled with virtue as Kimball O'Hara, jiggeting down to Umballa behind Hurree Chunder Mookerjee, whose name on the books of one section of the Ethnological Survey was R.17.

And if additional spur were needed, the Babu supplied it. After a huge meal at Kalka, he spoke uninterruptedly. Was Kim going to school? Then he, an M A of Calcutta University, would explain the advantages of education. There were marks to be gained by due attention to Latin and Wordsworth's Excursion (all this was Greek to Kim). French, too was vital, and the best was to be picked up in Chandernagore a few miles from Calcutta. Also a man might go far, as he himself had done, by strict attention to plays called Lear and Julius Cæsar, both much in demand by examiners. Lear was not so full of historical allusions as Julius Cæsar; the book cost four annas, but could be bought second-hand in Bow Bazar for two. Still more important than Wordsworth, or the eminent authors, Burke and Hare, was the art and science of mensuration. A boy who had passed his examination in these branches—for which, by the way, there were no cram-books—could, by merely marching over a country with a compass and a level and a straight eye, carry away a picture of that country which might be sold for large sums in coined silver. But as it was occasionally inexpedient to carry about measuring-chains a boy would do well to know the precise length of his own foot-pace, so that when he was deprived of what Hurree Chunder called adventitious aids he might still tread his distances. To keep count of thousands of paces, Hurree Chunder's experience had shown him nothing more valuable than a rosary of eighty-one or a hundred and eight beads, for "it was divisible and sub-divisible into many multiples and sub-multiples". Through the volleying drifts of English, Kim caught the

general trend of the talk, and it interested him very much. Here was a new craft that a man could tuck away in his head and by the look of the large wide world unfolding itself before him, it seemed that the more a man knew the better for him.

Said the Babu when he had talked for an hour and a half "I hope some day to enjoy your offeecial acquaintance. Ad interim, if I may be pardoned that expression, I shall give you this betel-box, which is highly valuable article and cost me two rupees only four years ago." It was a cheap, heart-shaped brass thing with three compartments for carrying the eternal betel-nut, lime and pan-leaf; but it was filled with little tabloid-bottles.

"That is reward of merit for your performance in character of that holy man. You see, you are so young you think you will last for ever and not take care of your body. It is great nuisance to go sick in the middle of business. I am fond of drugs myself, and they are handy to cure poor people too. These are good Departmental drugs—quinine and so on. I give it you for souvenir. Now good-bye. I have urgent private business here by the roadside."

He slipped out noiselessly as a cat, on the Umballa road, hailed a passing cart and jingled away, while Kim, tongue-tied, twiddled the brass betel-box in his hands.

The record of a boy's education interests few save his parents, and, as you know, Kim was an orphan. It is written in the books of St Xavier's in Partibus that a report of Kim's progress was forwarded at the end of each term to Colonel Creighton and to Father Victor, from whose hands duly came the money for his schooling. It is further recorded in the same books that he showed a great aptitude for mathematical studies as well as map-making, and carried away a prize (The Life of Lord Lawrence, tree-calf, two vols., nine rupees, eight annas) for proficiency therein; and the same term played in St Xavier's eleven against the Alighur Mohammedan College, his age being fourteen years and ten months. He was also re-vaccinated (from which we may assume that there had been another epidemic of smallpox at Lucknow) about the same time. Pencil notes on the edge of an old muster-roll record that he was punished several times for "conversing with improper persons", and it seems that he was once sentenced to heavy pains for "absenting himself for a day in the company of a street beggar". That was when he got over the gate and pleaded with the lama through a whole day down the banks of the Gumti to accompany him on the Road next holidays—for one month—for a little week; and the lama set his face as a flint against it, averring that the time had not yet come. Kim's business, said the old man as they ate cakes together, was to get all the wisdom of the Sahibs and then he would see. The Hand of Friendship must in some way have averted the Whip of Calamity, for six weeks later Kim seems to have passed an examination in elementary surveying "with great credit", his age being fifteen years and eight months. From this date the record is silent. His name does not appear in the year's batch of those who entered for the subordinate Survey of India, but against it stand the words "removed on appointment."

Several times in those three years, cast up at the Temple of the Tirthankars in Benares the lama, a little thinner and a shade yellower, if that were possible, but gentle and untainted as ever. Sometimes it was from the South that he came—from south of Tuticorin, whence the wonderful fire-boats go to Ceylon where are priests who know Pali; sometimes it was from the wet green West and the thousand cotton-factory chimneys that ring Bombay; and once from the North, where he had doubled back eight hundred miles to talk for a day with the Keeper of the Images in the Wonder House. He would stride to his cell in the cool, cut marble—the priests of the Temple were good to the old man,—wash off the dust of travel, make prayer, and depart for Lucknow, well accustomed now to the way of the rail, in a third-class carriage. Returning, it was noticeable, as his friend the Seeker pointed out to the head-priest, that he ceased for a while to mourn the loss of his River, or to draw wondrous pictures of the Wheel of Life, but preferred to talk of the beauty and wisdom of a certain mysterious chela whom no man of the Temple had

ever seen. Yes, he had followed the traces of the Blessed Feet throughout all India. (The Curator has still in his possession a most marvellous account of his wanderings and meditations.) There remained nothing more in life but to find the River of the Arrow. Yet it was shown to him in dreams that it was a matter not to be undertaken with any hope of success unless that seeker had with him the one chela appointed to bring the event to a happy issue, and versed in great wisdom—such wisdom as white-haired Keepers of Images possess. For example (here came out the snuff-gourd, and the kindly Jain priests made haste to be silent):

"Long and long ago, when Devadatta was King of Benares—let all listen to the Jâtaka!—an elephant was captured for a time by the king's hunters and ere he broke free, beringed with a grievous legiron. This he strove to remove with hate and frenzy in his heart, and hurrying up and down the forests, besought his brother-elephants to wrench it asunder. One by one, with their strong trunks, they tried and failed. At the last they gave it as their opinion that the ring was not to be broken by any bestial power. And in a thicket, new-born, wet with moisture of birth, lay a day-old calf of the herd whose mother had died. The fettered elephant, forgetting his own agony, said: 'If I do not help this suckling it will perish under our feet.' So he stood above the young thing, making his legs buttresses against the uneasily moving herd; and he begged milk of a virtuous cow, and the calf throve, and the ringed elephant was the calf's guide and defence. Now the days of an elephant—let all listen to the Jâtaka!—are thirty-five years to his full strength, and through thirty-five Rains the ringed elephant befriended the younger, and all the while the fetter ate into the flesh.

"Then one day the young elephant saw the half-buried iron, and turning to the elder said: 'What is this?' 'It is even my sorrow,' said he who had befriended him. Then that other put out his trunk and in the twinkling of an eyelash abolished the ring, saying: 'The appointed time has come.' So the virtuous elephant who had waited temperately and done kind acts was relieved, at the appointed time, by the very calf whom he had turned aside to cherish—let all listen to the Jâtaka! for the Elephant was Ananda, and the Calf that broke the ring was none other than The Lord Himself..."

Then he would shake his head benignly, and over the ever-clicking rosary point out how free that elephant-calf was from the sin of pride. He was as humble as a chela who, seeing his master sitting in the dust outside the Gates of Learning, over-leapt the gates (though they were locked) and took his master to his heart in the presence of the proud-stomached city. Rich would be the reward of such a master and such a chela when the time came for them to seek freedom together!

So did the lama speak, coming and going across India as softly as a bat. A sharp-tongued old woman in a house among the fruit-trees behind Saharunpore honoured him as the woman honoured the prophet, but his chamber was by no means upon the wall. In an apartment of the forecourt overlooked by cooing doves he would sit, while she laid aside her useless veil and chattered of spirits and fiends of Kulu, of grandchildren unborn, and of the free-tongued brat who had talked to her in the resting-place. Once, too, he strayed alone from the Grand Trunk Road below Umballa to the very village whose priest had tried to drug him; but the kind Heaven that guards lamas sent him at twilight through the crops, absorbed and unsuspicious, to the Rissaldar's door. Here was like to have been a grave misunderstanding, for the old soldier asked him why the Friend of the Stars had gone that way only six days before.

"That may not be," said the lama. "He has gone back to his own people."

"He sat in that corner telling a hundred merry tales five nights ago," his host insisted. "True, he vanished somewhat suddenly in the dawn after foolish talk with my granddaughter. He grows apace, but he is the same Friend of the Stars as brought me true word of the war. Have ye parted?"

"Yes—and no," the lama replied. "We—we have not altogether parted, but the time is not ripe that we should take the Road together. He acquires wisdom in another place. We must wait."

"All one—but if it were not the boy how did he come to speak so continually of thee?"

"And what said he?" asked the lama eagerly.

"Sweet words—an hundred thousand—that thou art his father and mother and such all. Pity that he does not take the Qpeen's service. He is fearless."

This news amazed the lama, who did not then know how religiously Kim kept to the contract made with Mahbub Ali, and perforce ratified by Colonel Creighton...

"There is no holding the young pony from the game," said the horse-dealer when the Colonel pointed out that vagabonding over India in holiday time was absurd. "If permission be refused to go and come as he chooses, he will make light of the refusal. Then who is to catch him? Colonel Sahib, only once in a thousand years is a horse born so well fitted for the game as this our colt. And we need men."

CHAPTER X

Your tiercel's too long at hack, Sire. He's no eyass
But a passage-hawk that footed ere we caught him,
Dangerously free o' the air. Faith! were he mine
(As mine's the glove he binds to for his tirings)
I'd fly him with a make-hawk. He's in yarak
Plumed to the very point—so manned, so weathered...
Give him the firmament God made him for,
And what shall take the air of him?—Old Play.

Lurgan Sahib did not use as direct speech, but his advice tallied with Mahbub's; and the upshot was good for Kim. He knew better now than to leave Lucknow city in native garb, and if Mahbub were anywhere within reach of a letter, it was to Mahbub's camp he headed, and made his change under the Pathan's wary eye. Could the little Survey paint-box that he used for map-tinting in term-time have found a tongue to tell of holiday doings, he might have been expelled. Once Mahbub and he went together as far as the beautiful city of Bombay, with three truckloads of tram-horses, and Mahbub nearly melted when Kim proposed a sail in a dhow across the Indian Ocean to buy Gulf Arabs, which, he understood from a hanger-on of the dealer Abdul Rahman, fetched better prices than mere Kabulis.

He dipped his hand into the dish with that great trader when Mahbub and a few co-religionists were invited to a big Haj dinner. They came back by way of Karachi by sea, when Kim took his first experience of sea-sickness sitting on the fore-hatch of a coasting-steamer, well persuaded he had been poisoned. The Babu's famous drug-box proved useless, though Kim had restocked it at Bombay. Mahbub had business at Quetta, and there Kim, as Mahbub admitted, earned his keep, and perhaps a little over, by spending four curious days as scullion in the house of a fat Commissariat sergeant, from whose office-box, in an auspicious moment, he removed a little vellum ledger which he copied out—it seemed to deal entirely with cattle and camel sales—by moonlight, lying behind an outhouse, all through one hot night. Then he returned the ledger to its place, and, at Mahbub's word, left that service unpaid, rejoining him six miles down the road, the clean copy in his bosom.

"That soldier is a small fish," Mahbub Ali explained, "but in time we shall catch the larger one. He only sells oxen at two prices—one for himself and one for the Government—which I do not think is a sin."

"Why could not I take away the little book and be done with it?"

"Then he would have been frightened, and he would have told his master. Then we should miss, perhaps, a great number of new rifles which seek their way up from Quetta to the North. The Game is so large that one sees but a little at a time."

"Oho!" said Kim, and held his tongue. That was in the monsoon holidays, after he had taken the prize for mathematics. The Christmas holidays he spent—deducting ten days for private amusements—with Lurgan Sahib, where he sat for the most part in front of a roaring wood-fire—Jakko road was four feet deep in snow that year—and—the small Hindu had gone away to be married—helped Lurgan to thread pearls. He made Kim learn whole chapters of the Koran by heart, till he could deliver them with the very roll and cadence of a mullah. Moreover, he told Kim the names and properties of many native drugs, as well as the runes proper to recite when you administer them. And in the evenings he wrote charms on parchment—elaborate pentagrams crowned with the names of devils—Murra, and Awan the Companion of Kings—

all fantastically written in the corners. More to the point, he advised Kim as to the care of his own body, the cure of fever-fits, and simple remedies of the Road. A week before it was time to go down, Colonel Creighton Sahib—this was unfair—sent Kim a written examination paper that concerned itself solely with rods and chains and links and angles.

Next holidays he was out with Mahbub, and here, by the way, he nearly died of thirst, plodding through the sand on a camel to the mysterious city of Bikanir, where the wells are four hundred feet deep, and lined throughout with camel-bone. It was not an amusing trip from Kim's point of view, because—in defiance of the contract—the Colonel ordered him to make a map of that wild, walled city; and since Mohammedan horse-boys and pipe-tenders are not expected to drag Survey-chains round the capital of an independent Native State, Kim was forced to pace all his distances by means of a bead rosary. He used the compass for bearings as occasion served—after dark chiefly, when the camels had been fed—and by the help of his little Survey paint-box of six colour-cakes and three brushes, he achieved something not remotely unlike the city of Jeysulmir. Mahbub laughed a great deal, and advised him to make up a written report as well; and in the back of the big account-book that lay under the flap of Mahbub's pet saddle Kim fell to work..

"It must hold everything that thou hast seen or touched or considered. Write as though the Jung-i-Lat Sahib himself had come by stealth with a vast army outsetting to war."

"How great an army?"

"Oh, half a lakh of men."

"Folly! Remember how few and bad were the wells in the sand. Not a thousand thirsty men could come near by here."

"Then write that down—also all the old breaches in the walls and whence the firewood is cut—and what is the temper and disposition of the King. I stay here till all my horses are sold. I will hire a room by the gateway, and thou shalt be my accountant. There is a good lock to the door."

The report in its unmistakable St Xavier's running script, and the brown, yellow, and lake-daubed map, was on hand a few years ago (a careless clerk filed it with the rough notes of E's second Seistan survey), but by now the pencil characters must be almost illegible. Kim translated it, sweating under the light of an oil-lamp, to Mahbub, the second day of their return-journey.

The Pathan rose and stooped over his dappled saddle-bags.

"I knew it would be worthy a dress of honour, and so I made one ready," he said, smiling. "Were I Amir of Afghanistan (and some day we may see him), I would fill thy mouth with gold." He laid the garments formally at Kim's feet. There was a gold-embroidered Peshawur turban-cap, rising to a cone, and a big turban-cloth ending in a broad fringe of gold. There was a Delhi embroidered waistcoat to slip over a milky white shirt, fastening to the right, ample and flowing; green pyjamas with twisted silk waist-string; and that nothing might be lacking, russia-leather slippers, smelling divinely, with arrogantly curled tips.

"Upon a Wednesday, and in the morning, to put on new clothes is auspicious," said Mahbub solemnly. "But we must not forget the wicked folk in the world. So!"

He capped all the splendour, that was taking Kim's delighted breath away, with a mother-of-pearl, nickel-plated, self-extracting .450 revolver.

"I had thought of a smaller bore, but reflected that this takes Government bullets. A man can always come by those—especially across the Border. Stand up and let me look." He clapped Kim on the shoulder. "May you never be tired, Pathan! Oh, the hearts to be broken! Oh, the eyes under the eyelashes, looking sideways!"

Kim turned about, pointed his toes, stretched, and felt mechanically for the moustache that was just beginning. Then he stooped towards Mahbub's feet to make proper acknowledgment with fluttering, quick-patting hands; his heart too full for words. Mahbub forestalled and embraced him.

"My son, said he, "what need of words between us? But is not the little gun a delight? All six cartridges come out at one twist. It is borne in the bosom next the skin, which, as it were, keeps it oiled. Never put it elsewhere, and please God, thou shalt some day kill a man with it."

"Hai mai!" said Kim ruefully. "If a Sahib kills a man he is hanged in the jail."

"True: but one pace beyond the Border, men are wiser. Put it away; but fill it first. Of what use is a gun unfed?"

"When I go back to the madrissah I must return it. They do not allow little guns. Thou wilt keep it for me?"

"Son, I am wearied of that madrissah, where they take the best years of a man to teach him what he can only learn upon the Road. The folly of the Sahibs has neither top nor bottom. No matter. Maybe thy written report shall save thee further bondage; and God He knows we need men more and more in the Game."

They marched, jaw-bound against blowing sand, across the salt desert to Jodhpur, where Mahbub and his handsome nephew Habib Ullah did much trading; and then sorrowfully, in European clothes, which he was fast outgrowing, Kim went second-class to St Xavier's. Three weeks later, Colonel Creighton, pricing Tibetan ghost-daggers at Lurgan's shop, faced Mahbub Ali openly mutinous. Lurgan Sahib operated as support in reserve.

"The pony is made—finished—mouthed and paced, Sahib! From now on, day by day, he will lose his manners if he is kept at tricks. Drop the rein on his back and let go," said the horse-dealer. "We need him."

"But he is so young, Mahbub—not more than sixteen—is he?"

"When I was fifteen, I had shot my man and begot my man, Sahib."

"You impenitent old heathen!" Creighton turned to Lurgan. The black beard nodded assent to the wisdom of the Afghan's dyed scarlet.

"I should have used him long ago," said Lurgan. "The younger the better. That is why I always have my really valuable jewels watched by a child. You sent him to me to try. I tried him in every way: he is the only boy I could not make to see things."

"In the crystal—in the ink-pool?" demanded Mahbub.

"No. Under my hand, as I told you. That has never happened before. It means that he is strong enough—but you think it skittles, Colonel Creighton—to make anyone do anything he wants. And that is three years ago. I have taught him a good deal since, Colonel Creighton. I think you waste him now."

"Hmm! Maybe you're right. But, as you know, there is no Survey work for him at present."

"Let him out let him go," Mahbub interrupted. "Who expects any colt to carry heavy weight at first? Let him run with the caravans—like our white camel-colts—for luck. I would take him myself, but—"

"There is a little business where he would be most useful—in the South," said Lurgan, with peculiar suavity, dropping his heavy blued eyelids.

"E.23 has that in hand," said Creighton quickly. "He must not go down there. Besides, he knows no Turki."

"Only tell him the shape and the smell of the letters we want and he will bring them back," Lurgan insisted.

"No. That is a man's job," said Creighton.

It was a wry-necked matter of unauthorized and incendiary correspondence between a person who claimed to be the ultimate authority in all matters of the Mohammedan religion throughout the world, and a younger member of a royal house who had been brought to book for kidnapping women within British territory. The Moslem Archbishop had been emphatic and over-arrogant; the young prince was merely sulky at the curtailment of his privileges, but there was no need he should continue a correspondence which might some day compromise him. One letter indeed had been procured, but the finder was later found dead by the roadside in the habit of an Arab trader, as E.23, taking up the work, duly reported.

These facts, and a few others not to be published, made both Mahbub and Creighton shake their heads.

"Let him go out with his Red Lama," said the horse-dealer with visible effort. "He is fond of the old man. He can learn his paces by the rosary at least."

"I have had some dealings with the old man—by letter," said Colonel Creighton, smiling to himself. "Whither goes he?"

"Up and down the land, as he has these three years. He seeks a River of Healing. God's curse upon all—" Mahbub checked himself. "He beds down at the Temple of the Tirthankars or at Buddh Gaya when he is in from the Road. Then he goes to see the boy at the madrissah, as we know for the boy was punished for it twice or thrice. He is quite mad, but a peaceful man. I have met him. The Babu also has had dealings with him. We have watched him for three years. Red Lamas are not so common in Hind that one loses track."

"Babus are very curious," said Lurgan meditatively. "Do you know what Hurree Babu really wants? He wants to be made a member of the Royal Society by taking ethnological notes. I tell you, I tell him about the lama everything which Mahbub and the boy have told me. Hurree Babu goes down to Benares—at his own expense, I think."

"I don't," said Creighton briefly. He had paid Hurree's travelling expenses, out of a most lively curiosity to learn what the lama might be.

"And he applies to the lama for information on lamaism, and devil-dances, and spells and charms, several times in these few years. Holy Virgin! I could have told him all that yeears ago. I think Hurree Babu is getting too old for the Road. He likes better to collect manners and customs information. Yes, he wants to be an FRS."

"Hurree thinks well of the boy, doesn't he?"

"Oh, very indeed—we have had some pleasant evenings at my little place—but I think it would be waste to throw him away with Hurree on the Ethnological side."

"Not for a first experience. How does that strike you, Mahbub? Let the boy run with the lama for six months. After that we can see. He will get experience."

"He has it already, Sahib—as a fish controls the water he swims in. But for every reason it will be well to loose him from the school."

"Very good, then," said Creighton, half to himself. "He can go with the lama, and if Hurree Babu cares to keep an eye on them so much the better. He won't lead the boy into any danger as Mahbub would. Curious—his wish to be an F R S. Very human, too. He is best on the Ethnological side—Hurree."

No money and no preferment would have drawn Creighton from his work on the Indian Survey, but deep in his heart also lay the ambition to write "F R S" after his name. Honours of a sort he knew could be obtained by ingenuity and the help of friends, but, to the best of his belief, nothing save work—papers representing a life of it—took a man into the Society which he had bombarded for years with monographs on strange Asiatic cults and unknown customs. Nine men out of ten would flee from a Royal Society soiree in extremity of boredom; but Creighton was the tenth, and at times his soul yearned for the crowded rooms in easy London where silver-haired, bald-headed gentlemen who know nothing of the Army move among spectroscopic experiments, the lesser plants of the frozen tundras, electric flight-measuring machines, and apparatus for slicing into fractional millimetres the left eye of the female mosquito. By all right and reason, it was the Royal Geographical that should have appealed to him, but men are as chancy as children in their choice of playthings. So Creighton smiled, and thought the better of Hurree Babu, moved by like desire.

He dropped the ghost-dagger and looked up at Mahbub.

"How soon can we get the colt from the stable?" said the horse-dealer, reading his eyes.

"Hmm! If I withdraw him by order now—what will he do, think you? I have never before assisted at the teaching of such an one."

"He will come to me," said Mahbub promptly. "Lurgan Sahib and I will prepare him for the Road."

"So be it, then. For six months he shall run at his choice. But who will be his sponsor?"

Lurgan slightly inclined his head. "He will not tell anything, if that is what you are afraid of, Colonel Creighton."

"It's only a boy, after all."

"Ye-es; but first, he has nothing to tell; and secondly, he knows what would happen. Also, he is very fond of Mahbub, and of me a little."

"Will he draw pay?" demanded the practical horse-dealer.

"Food and water allowance only. Twenty rupees a month."

One advantage of the Secret Service is that it has no worrying audit. That Service is ludicrously

starved, of course, but the funds are administered by a few men who do not call for vouchers or present itemized accounts. Mahbub's eyes lighted with almost a Sikh's love of money. Even Lurgan's impassive face changed. He considered the years to come when Kim would have been entered and made to the Great Game that never ceases day and night, throughout India. He foresaw honour and credit in the mouths of a chosen few, coming to him from his pupil. Lurgan Sahib had made E.23 what E.23 was, out of a bewildered, impertinent, lying, little North-West Province man.

But the joy of these masters was pale and smoky beside the joy of Kim when St Xavier's Head called him aside, with word that Colonel Creighton had sent for him.

"I understand, O'Hara, that he has found you a place as an assistant chain-man in the Canal Department: that comes of taking up mathematics. It is great luck for you, for you are only sixteen; but of course you understand that you do not become pukka (permanent) till you have passed the autumn examination. So you must not think you are going out into the world to enjoy yourself, or that your fortune is made. There is a great deal of hard work before you. Only, if you succeed in becoming pukka, you can rise, you know, to four hundred and fifty a month." Whereat the Principal gave him much good advice as to his conduct, and his manners, and his morals; and others, his elders, who had not been wafted into billets, talked as only Anglo-Indian lads can, of favouritism and corruption. Indeed, young Cazalet, whose father was a pensioner at Chunar, hinted very broadly that Colonel Creighton's interest in Kim was directly paternal; and Kim, instead of retaliating, did not even use language. He was thinking of the immense fun to come, of Mahbub's letter of the day before, all neatly written in English, making appointment for that afternoon in a house the very name of which would have crisped the Principal's hair with horror...

Said Kim to Mahbub in Lucknow railway station that evening, above the luggage-scales: "I feared lest at the last, the roof would fall upon me and cheat me. It is indeed all finished, O my father?"

Mahbub snapped his fingers to show the utterness of that end, and his eyes blazed like red coals.

"Then where is the pistol that I may wear it?"

"Softly! A half-year, to run without heel-ropes. I begged that much from Colonel Creighton Sahib. At twenty rupees a month. Old Red Hat knows that thou art coming."

"I will pay thee dustoorie (commission) on my pay for three months," said Kim gravely. "Yea, two rupees a month. But first we must get rid of these." He plucked his thin linen trousers and dragged at his collar. "I have brought with me all that I need on the Road. My trunk has gone up to Lurgan Sahib's."

"Who sends his salaams to thee—Sahib."

"Lurgan Sahib is a very clever man. But what dost thou do?"

"I go North again, upon the Great Game. What else? Is thy mind still set on following old Red Hat?"

"Do not forget he made me that I am—though he did not know it. Year by year, he sent the money that taught me."

"I would have done as much—had it struck my thick head," Mahbub growled. "Come away. The lamps are lit now, and none will mark thee in the bazar. We go to Huneefa's house."

On the way thither, Mahbub gave him much the same sort of advice as his mother gave to Lemuel, and curiously enough, Mahbub was exact to point out how Huneefa and her likes destroyed kings.

"And I remember," he quoted maliciously, "one who said, 'Trust a snake before an harlot, and an harlot before a Pathan, Mahbub Ali.' Now, excepting as to Pathans, of whom I am one, all that is true. Most true is it in the Great Game, for it is by means of women that all plans come to ruin and we lie out in the dawning with our throats cut. So it happened to such a one." He gave the reddest particulars.

"Then why—?" Kim paused before a filthy staircase that climbed to the warm darkness of an upper chamber, in the ward that is behind Azim Ullah's tobacco-shop. Those who know it call it The Birdcage—it is so full of whisperings and whistlings and chirrupings.

The room, with its dirty cushions and half-smoked hookahs, smelt abominably of stale tobacco. In one corner lay a huge and shapeless woman clad in greenish gauzes, and decked, brow, nose, ear, neck, wrist, arm, waist, and ankle with heavy native jewellery. When she turned it was like the clashing of copper pots. A lean cat in the balcony outside the window mewed hungrily. Kim checked, bewildered, at the door-curtain.

"Is that the new stuff, Mahbub?" said Huneefa lazily, scarce troubling to remove the mouthpiece from her lips. "O Buktanoos!"—like most of her kind, she swore by the Djinns—"O Buktanoos! He is very good to look upon."

"That is part of the selling of the horse," Mahbub explained to Kim, who laughed.

"I have heard that talk since my Sixth Day," he replied, squatting by the light. "Whither does it lead?"

"To protection. Tonight we change thy colour. This sleeping under roofs has blanched thee like an almond. But Huneefa has the secret of a colour that catches. No painting of a day or two. Also, we fortify thee against the chances of the Road. That is my gift to thee, my son. Take out all metals on thee and lay them here. Make ready, Huneefa."

Kim dragged forth his compass, Survey paint-box, and the new-filled medicine-box. They had all accompanied his travels, and boylike he valued them immensely.

The woman rose slowly and moved with her hands a little spread before her. Then Kim saw that she was blind. "No, no," she muttered, "the Pathan speaks truth—my colour does not go in a week or a month, and those whom I protect are under strong guard."

"When one is far off and alone, it would not be well to grow blotched and leprous of a sudden," said Mahbub. "When thou wast with me I could oversee the matter. Besides, a Pathan is a fair-skin. Strip to the waist now and look how thou art whitened." Huneefa felt her way back from an inner room. "It is no matter, she cannot see." He took a pewter bowl from her ringed hand.

The dye-stuff showed blue and gummy. Kim experimented on the back of his wrist, with a dab of cotton-wool; but Huneefa heard him.

"No, no," she cried, "the thing is not done thus, but with the proper ceremonies. The colouring is the least part. I give thee the full protection of the Road."

"Jadoo? (magic)," said Kim, with a half start. He did not like the white, sightless eyes. Mahbub's hand on his neck bowed him to the floor, nose within an inch of the boards.

"Be still. No harm comes to thee, my son. I am thy sacrifice!"

He could not see what the woman was about, but heard the dish-clash of her jewellery for many minutes. A match lit up the darkness; he caught the well-known purr and fizzle of grains of incense. Then the room filled with smoke—heavy aromatic, and stupefying. Through growing drowse he heard the names of devils—of Zulbazan, Son of Eblis, who lives in bazars and paraos, making all the sudden lewd wickedness of wayside halts; of Dulhan, invisible about mosques, the dweller among the slippers of the faithful, who hinders folk from their prayers; and Musboot, Lord of lies and panic. Huneefa, now whispering in his ear, now talking as from an immense distance, touched him with horrible soft fingers, but Mahbub's grip never shifted from his neck till, relaxing with a sigh, the boy lost his senses.

"Allah! How he fought! We should never have done it but for the drugs. That was his white blood, I take it," said Mahbub testily. "Go on with the dawut (invocation). Give him full Protection."

"O Hearer! Thou that hearest with ears, be present. Listen, O Hearer!" Huneefa moaned, her dead eyes turned to the west. The dark room filled with moanings and snortings.

From the outer balcony, a ponderous figure raised a round bullet head and coughed nervously.

"Do not interrupt this ventriloquial necromanciss, my friend," it said in English. "I opine that it is very disturbing to you, but no enlightened observer is jolly-well upset."

"...I will lay a plot for their ruin! O Prophet, bear with the unbelievers. Let them alone awhile!" Huneefa's face, turned to the northward, worked horribly, and it was as though voices from the ceiling answered her.

Hurree Babu returned to his note-book, balanced on the window-sill, but his hand shook. Huneefa, in some sort of drugged ecstasy, wrenched herself to and fro as she sat cross-legged by Kim's still head, and called upon devil after devil, in the ancient order of the ritual, binding them to avoid the boy's every action.

"With Him are the keys of the Secret Things! None knoweth them besides Himself He knoweth that which is in the dry land and in the sea!" Again broke out the unearthly whistling responses.

"I—I apprehend it is not at all malignant in its operation?" said the Babu, watching the throat-muscles quiver and jerk as Huneefa spoke with tongues. "It—it is not likely that she has killed the boy? If so, I decline to be witness at the trial What was the last hypothetical devil mentioned?"

"Babuji," said Mahbub in the vernacular. "I have no regard for the devils of Hind, but the Sons of Eblis are far otherwise, and whether they be jumalee (well-affected) or jullalee (terrible) they love not Kafirs."

"Then you think I had better go?" said Hurree Babu, half rising. "They are, of course, dematerialized phenomena. Spencer says."

Huneefa's crisis passed, as these things must, in a paroxysm of howling, with a touch of froth at the lips. She lay spent and motionless beside Kim, and the crazy voices ceased.

"Wah! That work is done. May the boy be better for it; and Huneefa is surely a mistress of dawut. Help haul her aside, Babu. Do not be afraid."

"How am I to fear the absolutely non-existent?" said Hurree Babu, talking English to reassure

himself. It is an awful thing still to dread the magic that you contemptuously investigate—to collect folk-lore for the Royal Society with a lively belief in all Powers of Darkness.

Mahbub chuckled. He had been out with Hurree on the Road ere now. "Let us finish the colouring," said he. "The boy is well protected if—if the Lords of the Air have ears to hear. I am a sufi (free-thinker), but when one can get blind-sides of a woman, a stallion, or a devil, why go round to invite a kick? Set him upon the way, Babu, and see that old Red Hat does not lead him beyond our reach. I must get back to my horses."

"All raight," said Hurree Babu. "He is at present curious spectacle."

About third cockcrow, Kim woke after a sleep of thousands of years. Huneefa, in her corner, snored heavily, but Mahbub was gone.

"I hope you were not frightened," said an oily voice at his elbow. "I superintended entire operation, which was most interesting from ethnological point of view. It was high-class dawut."

"Huh!" said Kim, recognizing Hurree Babu, who smiled ingratiatingly.

"And also I had honour to bring down from Lurgan your present costume. I am not in the habit offeecially of carrying such gauds to subordinates, but"—he giggled—"your case is noted as exceptional on the books. I hope Mr Lurgan will note my action."

Kim yawned and stretched himself. It was good to turn and twist within loose clothes once again.

"What is this?" He looked curiously at the heavy duffle-stuff loaded with the scents of the far North.

"Oho! That is inconspicuous dress of chela attached to service of lamaistic lama. Complete in every particular," said Hurree Babu, rolling into the balcony to clean his teeth at a goglet. "I am of opeenion it is not your old gentleman's precise releegion, but rather sub-variant of same. I have contributed rejected notes To Whom It May Concern: Asiatic Quarterly Review on these subjects. Now it is curious that the old gentleman himself is totally devoid of releegiosity. He is not a dam' particular."

"Do you know him?"

Hurree Babu held up his hand to show he was engaged in the prescribed rites that accompany tooth-cleaning and such things among decently bred Bengalis. Then he recited in English an Arya-Somaj prayer of a theistical nature, and stuffed his mouth with pan and betel.

"Oah yes. I have met him several times at Benares, and also at Buddh Gaya, to interrogate him on releegious points and devil-worship. He is pure agnostic—same as me."

Huneefa stirred in her sleep, and Hurree Babu jumped nervously to the copper incense-burner, all black and discoloured in morning-light, rubbed a finger in the accumulated lamp-black, and drew it diagonally across his face.

"Who has died in thy house?" asked Kim in the vernacular.

"None. But she may have the Evil Eye—that sorceress," the Babu replied.

"What dost thou do now, then?"

"I will set thee on thy way to Benares, if thou goest thither, and tell thee what must be known by Us."

"I go. At what hour runs the te-rain?" He rose to his feet, looked round the desolate chamber and at the yellow-wax face of Huneefa as the low sun stole across the floor. "Is there money to be paid that witch?"

"No. She has charmed thee against all devils and all dangers in the name of her devils. It was Mahbub's desire." In English: "He is highly obsolete, I think, to indulge in such supersteetion. Why, it is all ventriloquy. Belly-speak—eh?"

Kim snapped his fingers mechanically to avert whatever evil—Mahbub, he knew, meditated none—might have crept in through Huneefa's ministrations; and Hurree giggled once more. But as he crossed the room he was careful not to step in Huneefa's blotched, squat shadow on the boards. Witches—when their time is on them—can lay hold of the heels of a man's soul if he does that.

"Now you must well listen," said the Babu when they were in the fresh air. "Part of these ceremonies which we witnessed they include supply of effeecient amulet to those of our Department. If you feel in your neck you will find one small silver amulet, verree cheap. That is ours. Do you understand?"

"Oah yes, hawa-dilli (a heart-lifter)," said Kim, feeling at his neck.

"Huneefa she makes them for two rupees twelve annas with—oh, all sorts of exorcisms. They are quite common, except they are partially black enamel, and there is a paper inside each one full of names of local saints and such things. Thatt is Huneefa's look-out, you see? Huneefa makes them onlee for us, but in case she does not, when we get them we put in, before issue, one small piece of turquoise. Mr Lurgan he gives them. There is no other source of supply; but it was me invented all this. It is strictly unoffeecial of course, but convenient for subordinates. Colonel Creighton he does not know. He is European. The turquoise is wrapped in the paper ... Yes, that is road to railway station ... Now suppose you go with the lama, or with me, I hope, some day, or with Mahbub. Suppose we get into a dam'-tight place. I am a fearful man—most fearful—but I tell you I have been in dam'-tight places more than hairs on my head. You say: 'I am Son of the Charm.' Verree good."

"I do not understand quite. We must not be heard talking English here."

"That is all raight. I am only Babu showing off my English to you. All we Babus talk English to show off;" said Hurree, flinging his shoulder-cloth jauntily. "As I was about to say, 'Son of the Charm' means that you may be member of the Sat Bhai—the Seven Brothers, which is Hindi and Tantric. It is popularly supposed to be extinct Society, but I have written notes to show it is still extant. You see, it is all my invention. Verree good. Sat Bhai has many members, and perhaps before they jolly-well-cut-your-throat they may give you just a chance of life. That is useful, anyhow. And moreover, these foolish natives—if they are not too excited—they always stop to think before they kill a man who says he belongs to any speecific organization. You see? You say then when you are in tight place, 'I am Son of the Charm', and you get—perhaps—ah—your second wind. That is only in extreme instances, or to open negotiations with a stranger. Can you quite see? Verree good. But suppose now, I, or any one of the Department, come to you dressed quite different. You would not know me at all unless I choose, I bet you. Some day I will prove it. I come as Ladakhi trader—oh, anything—and I say to you: 'You want to buy precious stones?' You say: 'Do I look like a man who buys precious stones?' Then I say:

'Even verree poor man can buy a turquoise or tarkeean.'"

"That is kichree—vegetable curry," said Kim.

"Of course it is. You say: 'Let me see the tarkeean.' Then I say: 'It was cooked by a woman, and perhaps it is bad for your caste.' Then you say: 'There is no caste when men go to—look for tarkeean.' You stop a little between those words, 'to—look'. That is thee whole secret. The little stop before the words."

Kim repeated the test-sentence.

"That is all right. Then I will show you my turquoise if there is time, and then you know who I am, and then we exchange views and documents and those-all things. And so it is with any other man of us. We talk sometimes about turquoises and sometimes about tarkeean, but always with that little stop in the words. It is verree easy. First, 'Son of the Charm', if you are in a tight place. Perhaps that may help you—perhaps not. Then what I have told you about the tarkeean, if you want to transact offeecial business with a strange man. Of course, at present, you have no offeecial business. You are—ah ha!—supernumerary on probation. Quite unique specimen. If you were Asiatic of birth you might be employed right off; but this half-year of leave is to make you de-Englishized, you see? The lama he expects you, because I have demi-offeecially informed him you have passed all your examinations, and will soon obtain Government appointment. Oh ho! You are on acting-allowance, you see: so if you are called upon to help Sons of the Charm mind you jolly-well try. Now I shall say good-bye, my dear fellow, and I hope you—ah—will come out top-side all raight."

Hurree Babu stepped back a pace or two into the crowd at the entrance of Lucknow station and— was gone. Kim drew a deep breath and hugged himself all over. The nickel-plated revolver he could feel in the bosom of his sad-coloured robe, the amulet was on his neck; begging-gourd, rosary, and ghost-dagger (Mr Lurgan had forgotten nothing) were all to hand, with medicine, paint-box, and compass, and in a worn old purse-belt embroidered with porcupine-quill patterns lay a month's pay. Kings could be no richer. He bought sweetmeats in a leaf-cup from a Hindu trader, and ate them with glad rapture till a policeman ordered him off the steps.

CHAPTER XI

Give the man who is not made
To his trade
Swords to fling and catch again,
Coins to ring and snatch again,
Men to harm and cure again,
Snakes to charm and lure again—
He'll be hurt by his own blade,
By his serpents disobeyed,
By his clumsiness bewrayed,"
By the people mocked to scorn—
So 'tis not with juggler born!
Pinch of dust or withered flower,
Chance-flung fruit or borrowed staff,
Serve his need and shore his power,
Bind the spell, or loose the laugh!

But a man who, etc., Op. 15

Followed a sudden natural reaction.

"Now am I alone—all alone," he thought. "In all India is no one so alone as I! If I die today, who shall bring the news—and to whom? If I live and God is good, there will be a price upon my head, for I am a Son of the Charm—I, Kim."

A very few white people, but many Asiatics, can throw themselves into a mazement as it were by repeating their own names over and over again to themselves, letting the mind go free upon speculation as to what is called personal identity. When one grows older, the power, usually, departs, but while it lasts it may descend upon a man at any moment.

"Who is Kim—Kim—Kim?"

He squatted in a corner of the clanging waiting-room, rapt from all other thoughts; hands folded in lap, and pupils contracted to pin-points. In a minute—in another half-second—he felt he would arrive at the solution of the tremendous puzzle; but here, as always happens, his mind dropped away from those heights with a rush of a wounded bird, and passing his hand before his eyes, he shook his head.

A long-haired Hindu bairagi (holy man), who had just bought a ticket, halted before him at that moment and stared intently.

"I also have lost it," he said sadly. "It is one of the Gates to the Way, but for me it has been shut many years."

"What is the talk?" said Kim, abashed.

"Thou wast wondering there in thy spirit what manner of thing thy soul might be. The seizure came of a sudden. I know. Who should know but I? Whither goest thou?"

"Toward Kashi [Benares]."

"There are no Gods there. I have proved them. I go to Prayag [Allahabad] for the fifth time—

seeking the Road to Enlightenment. Of what faith art thou?"

"I too am a Seeker," said Kim, using one of the lama's pet words. "Though"—he forgot his Northern dress for the moment—"though Allah alone knoweth what I seek."

The old fellow slipped the bairagi's crutch under his armpit and sat down on a patch of ruddy leopard's skin as Kim rose at the call for the Benares train.

"Go in hope, little brother," he said. "It is a long road to the feet of the One; but thither do we all travel."

Kim did not feel so lonely after this, and ere he had sat out twenty miles in the crowded compartment, was cheering his neighbours with a string of most wonderful yarns about his own and his master's magical gifts.

Benares struck him as a peculiarly filthy city, though it was pleasant to find how his cloth was respected. At least one-third of the population prays eternally to some group or other of the many million deities, and so reveres every sort of holy man. Kim was guided to the Temple of the Tirthankars, about a mile outside the city, near Sarnath, by a chance-met Punjabi farmer—a Kamboh from Jullundur-way who had appealed in vain to every God of his homestead to cure his small son, and was trying Benares as a last resort.

"Thou art from the North?" he asked, shouldering through the press of the narrow, stinking streets much like his own pet bull at home.

"Ay, I know the Punjab. My mother was a pahareen, but my father came from Amritzar—by Jandiala," said Kim, oiling his ready tongue for the needs of the Road.

"Jandiala—Jullundur? Oho! Then we be neighbours in some sort, as it were." He nodded tenderly to the wailing child in his arms. "Whom dost thou serve?"

"A most holy man at the Temple of the Tirthankers."

"They are all most holy and—most greedy," said the Jat with bitterness. "I have walked the pillars and trodden the temples till my feet are flayed, and the child is no whit better. And the mother being sick too ... Hush, then, little one ... We changed his name when the fever came. We put him into girl's clothes. There was nothing we did not do, except—I said to his mother when she bundled me off to Benares—she should have come with me—I said Sakhi Sarwar Sultan would serve us best. We know His generosity, but these down-country Gods are strangers."

The child turned on the cushion of the huge corded arms and looked at Kim through heavy eyelids.

"And was it all worthless?" Kim asked, with easy interest.

"All worthless—all worthless," said the child, lips cracking with fever.

"The Gods have given him a good mind, at least" said the father proudly. "To think he should have listened so cleverly. Yonder is thy Temple. Now I am a poor man—many priests have dealt with me—but my son is my son, and if a gift to thy master can cure him—I am at my very wits' end."

Kim considered for a while, tingling with pride. Three years ago he would have made prompt profit on the situation and gone his way without a thought; but now, the very respect the Jat paid him proved that he was a man. Moreover, he had tasted fever once or twice already, and knew

enough to recognize starvation when he saw it.

"Call him forth and I will give him a bond on my best yoke, so that the child is cured."

Kim halted at the carved outer door of the temple. A white-clad Oswal banker from Ajmir, his sins of usury new wiped out, asked him what he did.

"I am chela to Teshoo Lama, an Holy One from Bhotiyal—within there. He bade me come. I wait. Tell him."

"Do not forget the child," cried the importunate Jat over his shoulder, and then bellowed in Punjabi; "O Holy One—O disciple of the Holy One—O Gods above all the Worlds—behold affliction sitting at the gate!" That cry is so common in Benares that the passers never turned their heads.

The Oswal, at peace with mankind, carried the message into the darkness behind him, and the easy, uncounted Eastern minutes slid by; for the lama was asleep in his cell, and no priest would wake him. When the click of his rosary again broke the hush of the inner court where the calm images of the Arhats stand, a novice whispered, "Thy chela is here," and the old man strode forth, forgetting the end of that prayer.

Hardly had the tall figure shown in the doorway than the Jat ran before him, and, lifting up the child, cried: "Look upon this, Holy One; and if the Gods will, he lives—he lives!"

He fumbled in his waist-belt and drew out a small silver coin.

"What is now?" The lama's eyes turned to Kim. It was noticeable he spoke far clearer Urdu than long ago, under ZamZammah; but father would allow no private talk.

"It is no more than a fever," said Kim. "The child is not well fed."

"He sickens at everything, and his mother is not here."

"If it be permitted, I may cure, Holy One."

"What! Have they made thee a healer? Wait here," said the lama, and he sat down by the Jat upon the lowest step of the temple, while Kim, looking out of the corner of his eyes, slowly opened the little betel-box. He had dreamed dreams at school of returning to the lama as a Sahib—of chaffing the old man before he revealed himself—boy's dreams all. There was more drama in this abstracted, brow-puckered search through the tabloid-bottles, with a pause here and there for thought and a muttered invocation between whiles. Quinine he had in tablets, and dark brown meat-lozenges—beef most probably, but that was not his business. The little thing would not eat, but it sucked at a lozenge greedily, and said it liked the salt taste.

"Take then these six." Kim handed them to the man. "Praise the Gods, and boil three in milk; other three in water. After he has drunk the milk give him this" (it was the half of a quinine pill), "and wrap him warm. Give him the water of the other three, and the other half of this white pill when he wakes. Meantime, here is another brown medicine that he may suck at on the way home."

"Gods, what wisdom!" said the Kamboh, snatching.

It was as much as Kim could remember of his own treatment in a bout of autumn malaria—if you except the patter that he added to impress the lama.

"Now go! Come again in the morning."

"But the price—the price," said the Jat, and threw back his sturdy shoulders. "My son is my son. Now that he will be whole again, how shall I go back to his mother and say I took help by the wayside and did not even give a bowl of curds in return?"

"They are alike, these Jats," said Kim softly. "The Jat stood on his dunghill and the King's elephants went by. 'O driver,' said he, 'what will you sell those little donkeys for?'"

The Jat burst into a roar of laughter, stifled with apologies to the lama. "It is the saying of my own country the very talk of it. So are we Jats all. I will come tomorrow with the child; and the blessing of the Gods of the Homesteads—who are good little Gods—be on you both ... Now, son, we grow strong again. Do not spit it out, little Princeling! King of my Heart, do not spit it out, and we shall be strong men, wrestlers and club-wielders, by morning."

He moved away, crooning and mumbling. The lama turned to Kim, and all the loving old soul of him looked out through his narrow eyes.

"To heal the sick is to acquire merit; but first one gets knowledge. That was wisely done, O Friend of all the World."

"I was made wise by thee, Holy One," said Kim, forgetting the little play just ended; forgetting St Xavier's; forgetting his white blood; forgetting even the Great Game as he stooped, Mohammedan-fashion, to touch his master's feet in the dust of the Jain temple. "My teaching I owe to thee. I have eaten thy bread three years. My time is finished. I am loosed from the schools. I come to thee."

"Herein is my reward. Enter! Enter! And is all well?" They passed to the inner court, where the afternoon sun sloped golden across. "Stand that I may see. So!" He peered critically. "It is no longer a child, but a man, ripened in wisdom, walking as a physician. I did well—I did well when I gave thee up to the armed men on that black night. Dost thou remember our first day under Zam-Zammah?"

"Ay," said Kim. "Dost thou remember when I leapt off the carriage the first day I went to—"

"The Gates of Learning? Truly. And the day that we ate the cakes together at the back of the river by Nucklao. Aha! Many times hast thou begged for me, but that day I begged for thee."

"Good reason," quoth Kim. "I was then a scholar in the Gates of Learning, and attired as a Sahib. Do not forget, Holy One," he went on playfully. "I am still a Sahib—by thy favour."

"True. And a Sahib in most high esteem. Come to my cell, chela."

"How is that known to thee?"

The lama smiled. "First by means of letters from the kindly priest whom we met in the camp of armed men; but he is now gone to his own country, and I sent the money to his brother." Colonel Creighton, who had succeeded to the trusteeship when Father Victor went to England with the Mavericks, was hardly the Chaplain's brother. "But I do not well understand Sahibs' letters. They must be interpreted to me. I chose a surer way. Many times when I returned from my Search to this Temple, which has always been a nest to me, there came one seeking Enlightenment—a man from Leh—that had been, he said, a Hindu, but wearied of all those Gods." The lama pointed to the Arhats.

"A fat man?" said Kim, a twinkle in his eye.

"Very fat; but I perceived in a little his mind was wholly given up to useless things—such as devils and charms and the form and fashion of our tea-drinkings in the monasteries, and by what road we initiated the novices. A man abounding in questions; but he was a friend of thine, chela. He told me that thou wast on the road to much honour as a scribe. And I see thou art a physician."

"Yes, that am I—a scribe, when I am a Sahib, but it is set aside when I come as thy disciple. I have accomplished the years appointed for a Sahib."

"As it were a novice?" said the lama, nodding his head. "Art thou freed from the schools? I would not have thee unripe."

"I am all free. In due time I take service under the Government as a scribe—"

"Not as a warrior. That is well."

"But first I come to wander with thee. Therefore I am here. Who begs for thee, these days?" he went on quickly. The ice was thin.

"Very often I beg myself; but, as thou knowest, I am seldom here, except when I come to look again at my disciple. From one end to another of Hind have I travelled afoot and in the te-rain. A great and a wonderful land! But here, when I put in, is as though I were in my own Bhotiyal."

He looked round the little clean cell complacently. A low cushion gave him a seat, on which he had disposed himself in the cross-legged attitude of the Bodhisat emerging from meditation; a black teak-wood table, not twenty inches high, set with copper tea-cups, was before him. In one corner stood a tiny altar, also of heavily carved teak, bearing a copper-gilt image of the seated Buddha and fronted by a lamp, an incense-holder, and a pair of copper flower-pots.

"The Keeper of the Images in the Wonder House acquired merit by giving me these a year since," he said, following Kim's eye. "When one is far from one's own land such things carry remembrance; and we must reverence the Lord for that He showed the Way. See!" He pointed to a curiously-built mound of coloured rice crowned with a fantastic metal ornament. "When I was Abbot in my own place—before I came to better knowledge I made that offering daily. It is the Sacrifice of the Universe to the Lord. Thus do we of Bhotiyal offer all the world daily to the Excellent Law. And I do it even now, though I know that the Excellent One is beyond all pinchings and pattings." He snuffed from his gourd.

"It is well done, Holy One," Kim murmured, sinking at ease on the cushions, very happy and rather tired.

"And also," the old man chuckled, "I write pictures of the Wheel of Life. Three days to a picture. I was busied on it—or it may be I shut my eyes a little—when they brought word of thee. It is good to have thee here: I will show thee my art—not for pride's sake, but because thou must learn. The Sahibs have not all this world's wisdom."

He drew from under the table a sheet of strangely scented yellow Chinese paper, the brushes, and slab of Indian ink. In cleanest, severest outline he had traced the Great Wheel with its six spokes, whose centre is the conjoined Hog, Snake, and Dove (Ignorance, Anger, and Lust), and whose compartments are all the Heavens and Hells, and all the chances of human life. Men say that the Bodhisat Himself first drew it with grains of rice upon dust, to teach His disciples the cause of things. Many ages have crystallized it into a most wonderful convention crowded with hundreds of little figures whose every line carries a meaning. Few can translate the picture-parable; there are not twenty in all the world who can draw it surely without a copy: of those

who can both draw and expound are but three.

"I have a little learned to draw," said Kim. "But this is a marvel beyond marvels."

"I have written it for many years," said the lama. "Time was when I could write it all between one lamp-lighting and the next. I will teach thee the art—after due preparation; and I will show thee the meaning of the Wheel."

"We take the Road, then?"

"The Road and our Search. I was but waiting for thee. It was made plain to me in a hundred dreams—notably one that came upon the night of the day that the Gates of Learning first shut that without thee I should never find my River. Again and again, as thou knowest, I put this from me, fearing an illusion. Therefore I would not take thee with me that day at Lucknow, when we ate the cakes. I would not take thee till the time was ripe and auspicious. From the Hills to the Sea, from the Sea to the Hills have I gone, but it was vain. Then I remembered the Jâtaka."

He told Kim the story of the elephant with the leg-iron, as he had told it so often to the Jain priests.

"Further testimony is not needed," he ended serenely. "Thou wast sent for an aid. That aid removed, my Search came to naught. Therefore we will go out again together, and our Search sure."

"Whither go we?"

"What matters, Friend of all the World? The Search, I say, is sure. If need be, the River will break from the ground before us. I acquired merit when I sent thee to the Gates of Learning, and gave thee the jewel that is Wisdom. Thou didst return, I saw even now, a follower of Sakyamuni, the Physician, whose altars are many in Bhotiyal. It is sufficient. We are together, and all things are as they were—Friend of all the World—Friend of the Stars—my chela!"

Then they talked of matters secular; but it was noticeable that the lama never demanded any details of life at St Xavier's, nor showed the faintest curiosity as to the manners and customs of Sahibs. His mind moved all in the past, and he revived every step of their wonderful first journey together, rubbing his hands and chuckling, till it pleased him to curl himself up into the sudden sleep of old age.

Kim watched the last dusty sunshine fade out of the court, and played with his ghost-dagger and rosary. The clamour of Benares, oldest of all earth's cities awake before the Gods, day and night, beat round the walls as the sea's roar round a breakwater. Now and again, a Jain priest crossed the court, with some small offering to the images, and swept the path about him lest by chance he should take the life of a living thing. A lamp twinkled, and there followed the sound of a prayer. Kim watched the stars as they rose one after another in the still, sticky dark, till he fell asleep at the foot of the altar. That night he dreamed in Hindustani, with never an English word...

"Holy One, there is the child to whom we gave the medicine," he said, about three o'clock in the morning, when the lama, also waking from dreams, would have fared forth on pilgrimage. "The Jat will be here at the light."

"I am well answered. In my haste I would have done a wrong." He sat down on the cushions and returned to his rosary. "Surely old folk are as children," he said pathetically. "They desire a matter—behold, it must be done at once, or they fret and weep! Many times when I was upon

the Road I have been ready to stamp with my feet at the hindrance of an ox-cart in the way, or a mere cloud of dust. It was not so when I was a man—a long time ago. None the less it is wrongful—"

"But thou art indeed old, Holy One."

"The thing was done. A Cause was put out into the world, and, old or young, sick or sound, knowing or unknowing, who can rein in the effect of that Cause? Does the Wheel hang still if a child spin it—or a drunkard? Chela, this is a great and a terrible world."

"I think it good," Kim yawned. "What is there to eat? I have not eaten since yesterday even."

"I had forgotten thy need. Yonder is good Bhotiyal tea and cold rice."

"We cannot walk far on such stuff." Kim felt all the European's lust for flesh-meat, which is not accessible in a Jain temple. Yet, instead of going out at once with the begging-bowl, he stayed his stomach on slabs of cold rice till the full dawn. It brought the farmer, voluble, stuttering with gratitude.

"In the night the fever broke and the sweat came," he cried. "Feel here—his skin is fresh and new! He esteemed the salt lozenges, and took milk with greed." He drew the cloth from the child's face, and it smiled sleepily at Kim. A little knot of Jain priests, silent but all-observant, gathered by the temple door. They knew, and Kim knew that they knew, how the old lama had met his disciple. Being courteous folk, they had not obtruded themselves overnight by presence, word, or gesture. Wherefore Kim repaid them as the sun rose.

"Thank the Gods of the Jains, brother," he said, not knowing how those Gods were named. "The fever is indeed broken."

"Look! See!" The lama beamed in the background upon his hosts of three years. "Was there ever such a chela? He follows our Lord the Healer."

Now the Jains officially recognize all the Gods of the Hindu creed, as well as the Lingam and the Snake. They wear the Brahminical thread; they adhere to every claim of Hindu caste-law. But, because they knew and loved the lama, because he was an old man, because he sought the Way, because he was their guest, and because he collogued long of nights with the head-priest—as free-thinking a metaphysician as ever split one hair into seventy—they murmured assent.

"Remember,"—Kim bent over the child—. "this trouble may come again."

"Not if thou hast the proper spell," said the father.

"But in a little while we go away."

"True," said the lama to all the Jains. "We go now together upon the Search whereof I have often spoken. I waited till my chela was ripe. Behold him! We go North. Never again shall I look upon this place of my rest, O people of good will."

"But I am not a beggar." The cultivator rose to his feet, clutching the child.

"Be still. Do not trouble the Holy One," a priest cried.

"Go," Kim whispered. "Meet us again under the big railway bridge, and for the sake of all the Gods of our Punjab, bring food—curry, pulse, cakes fried in fat, and sweetmeats. Specially sweetmeats. Be swift!"

The pallor of hunger suited Kim very well as he stood, tall and slim, in his sand-coloured, sweeping robes, one hand on his rosary and the other in the attitude of benediction, faithfully copied from the lama. An English observer might have said that he looked rather like the young saint of a stained-glass window, whereas he was but a growing lad faint with emptiness.

Long and formal were the farewells, thrice ended and thrice renewed. The Seeker—he who had invited the lama to that haven from far-away Tibet, a silver-faced, hairless ascetic—took no part in it, but meditated, as always, alone among the images. The others were very human; pressing small comforts upon the old man—a betel-box, a fine new iron pencase, a food-bag, and such-like—warning him against the dangers of the world without, and prophesying a happy end to the Search. Meantime Kim, lonelier than ever, squatted on the steps, and swore to himself in the language of St Xavier's.

"But it is my own fault," he concluded. "With Mahbub, I ate Mahbub's bread, or Lurgan Sahib's. At St Xavier's, three meals a day. Here I must jolly-well look out for myself. Besides, I am not in good training. How I could eat a plate of beef now! ... Is it finished, Holy One?"

The lama, both hands raised, intoned a final blessing in ornate Chinese. "I must lean on thy shoulder," said he, as the temple gates closed. "We grow stiff, I think."

The weight of a six-foot man is not light to steady through miles of crowded streets, and Kim, loaded down with bundles and packages for the way, was glad to reach the shadow of the railway bridge.

"Here we eat," he said resolutely, as the Kamboh, blue-robed and smiling, hove in sight, a basket in one hand and the child in the other.

"Fall to, Holy Ones!" he cried from fifty yards. (They were by the shoal under the first bridge-span, out of sight of hungry priests.) "Rice and good curry, cakes all warm and well scented with hing (asafœtida), curds and sugar. King of my fields,"—this to the small son—"let us show these holy men that we Jats of Jullundur can pay a service ... I had heard the Jains would eat nothing that they had not cooked, but truly"—he looked away politely over the broad river—"where there is no eye there is no caste."

"And we," said Kim, turning his back and heaping a leafplatter for the lama, "are beyond all castes."

They gorged themselves on the good food in silence. Nor till he had licked the last of the sticky sweetstuff from his little finger did Kim note that the Kamboh too was girt for travel.

"If our roads lie together," he said roughly, "I go with thee. One does not often find a worker of miracles, and the child is still weak. But I am not altogether a reed." He picked up his lathi—a five-foot male-bamboo ringed with bands of polished iron—and flourished it in the air. "The Jats are called quarrel-some, but that is not true. Except when we are crossed, we are like our own buffaloes."

"So be it," said Kim. "A good stick is a good reason."

The lama gazed placidly up-stream, where in long, smudged perspective the ceaseless columns of smoke go up from the burning-ghats by the river. Now and again, despite all municipal regulations, the fragment of a half-burned body bobbed by on the full current.

"But for thee," said the Kamboh to Kim, drawing the child into his hairy breast, "I might today have gone thither—with this one. The priests tell us that Benares is holy—which none doubt—

and desirable to die in. But I do not know their Gods, and they ask for money; and when one has done one worship a shaved-head vows it is of none effect except one do another. Wash here! Wash there! Pour, drink, lave, and scatter flowers—but always pay the priests. No, the Punjab for me, and the soil of the Jullundur-doab for the best soil in it."

"I have said many times—in the Temple, I think—that if need be, the River will open at our feet. We will therefore go North," said the lama, rising. "I remember a pleasant place, set about with fruit-trees, where one can walk in meditation—and the air is cooler there. It comes from the Hills and the snow of the Hills."

"What is the name?" said Kim.

"How should I know? Didst thou not—no, that was after the Army rose out of the earth and took thee away. I abode there in meditation in a room against the dovecot—except when she talked eternally."

"Oho! the woman from Kulu. That is by Saharunpore." Kim laughed.

"How does the spirit move thy master? Does he go afoot, for the sake of past sins?" the Jat demanded cautiously. "It is a far cry to Delhi."

"No," said Kim. "I will beg a tikkut for the te-rain." One does not own to the possession of money in India.

"Then, in the name of the Gods, let us take the fire-carriage. My son is best in his mother's arms. The Government has brought on us many taxes, but it gives us one good thing—the te-rain that joins friends and unites the anxious. A wonderful matter is the te-rain."

They all piled into it a couple of hours later, and slept through the heat of the day. The Kamboh plied Kim with ten thousand questions as to the lama's walk and work in life, and received some curious answers. Kim was content to be where he was, to look out upon the flat North-Western landscape, and to talk to the changing mob of fellow-passengers. Even today, tickets and ticket-clipping are dark oppression to Indian rustics. They do not understand why, when they have paid for a magic piece of paper, strangers should punch great pieces out of the charm. So, long and furious are the debates between travellers and Eurasian ticket-collectors. Kim assisted at two or three with grave advice, meant to darken counsel and to show off his wisdom before the lama and the admiring Kamboh. But at Somna Road the Fates sent him a matter to think upon. There tumbled into the compartment, as the train was moving off, a mean, lean little person—a Mahratta, so far as Kim could judge by the cock of the tight turban. His face was cut, his muslin upper-garment was badly torn, and one leg was bandaged. He told them that a country-cart had upset and nearly slain him: he was going to Delhi, where his son lived. Kim watched him closely. If, as he asserted, he had been rolled over and over on the earth, there should have been signs of gravel-rash on the skin. But all his injuries seemed clean cuts, and a mere fall from a cart could not cast a man into such extremity of terror. As, with shaking fingers, he knotted up the torn cloth about his neck he laid bare an amulet of the kind called a keeper-up of the heart. Now, amulets are common enough, but they are not generally strung on square-plaited copper wire, and still fewer amulets bear black enamel on silver. There were none except the Kamboh and the lama in the compartment, which, luckily, was of an old type with solid ends. Kim made as to scratch in his bosom, and thereby lifted his own amulet. The Mahratta's face changed altogether at the sight, and he disposed the amulet fairly on his breast.

"Yes," he went on to the Kamboh, "I was in haste, and the cart, driven by a bastard, bound its wheel in a water-cut, and besides the harm done to me there was lost a full dish of tarkeean. I was not a Son of the Charm [a lucky man] that day."

"That was a great loss," said the Kamboh, withdrawing interest. His experience of Benares had made him suspicious.

"Who cooked it?" said Kim.

"A woman." The Mahratta raised his eyes.

"But all women can cook tarkeean," said the Kamboh. "It is a good curry, as I know."

"Oh yes, it is a good curry," said the Mahratta.

"And cheap," said Kim. "But what about caste?"

"Oh, there is no caste where men go to—look for tarkeean," the Mahratta replied, in the prescribed cadence. "Of whose service art thou?"

"Of the service of this Holy One." Kim pointed to the happy, drowsy lama, who woke with a jerk at the well-loved word.

"Ah, he was sent from Heaven to aid me. He is called the Friend of all the World. He is also called the Friend of the Stars. He walks as a physician—his time being ripe. Great is his wisdom."

"And a Son of the Charm," said Kim under his breath, as the Kamboh made haste to prepare a pipe lest the Mahratta should beg.

"And who is that?" the Mahratta asked, glancing sideways nervously.

"One whose child I—we have cured, who lies under great debt to us. Sit by the window, man from Jullundur. Here is a sick one."

"Humph! I have no desire to mix with chance-met wastrels. My ears are not long. I am not a woman wishing to overhear secrets." The Jat slid himself heavily into a far corner.

"Art thou anything of a healer? I am ten leagues deep in calamity," cried the Mahratta, picking up the cue.

"This man is cut and bruised all over. I go about to cure him," Kim retorted. "None interfered between thy babe and me."

"I am rebuked," said the Kamboh meekly. "I am thy debtor for the life of my son. Thou art a miracle-worker—I know it."

"Show me the cuts." Kim bent over the Mahratta's neck, his heart nearly choking him; for this was the Great Game with a vengeance. "Now, tell thy tale swiftly, brother, while I say a charm."

"I come from the South, where my work lay. One of us they slew by the roadside. Hast thou heard?" Kim shook his head. He, of course, knew nothing of E's predecessor, slain down South in the habit of an Arab trader. "Having found a certain letter which I was sent to seek, I came away. I escaped from the city and ran to Mhow. So sure was I that none knew, I did not change my face. At Mhow a woman brought charge against me of theft of jewellery in that city which I had left. Then I saw the cry was out against me. I ran from Mhow by night, bribing the police, who had been bribed to hand me over without question to my enemies in the South. Then I lay in old Chitor city a week, a penitent in a temple, but I could not get rid of the letter which was my charge. I buried it under the Queen's Stone, at Chitor, in the place known to us all."

Kim did not know, but not for worlds would he have broken the thread.

"At Chitor, look you, I was all in Kings' country; for Kotah to the east is beyond the Queen's law, and east again lie Jaipur and Gwalior. Neither love spies, and there is no justice. I was hunted like a wet jackal; but I broke through at Bandakui, where I heard there was a charge against me of murder in the city I had left—of the murder of a boy. They have both the corpse and the witnesses waiting."

"But cannot the Government protect?"

"We of the Game are beyond protection. If we die, we die. Our names are blotted from the book. That is all. At Bandakui, where lives one of Us, I thought to slip the scent by changing my face, and so made me a Mahratta. Then I came to Agra, and would have turned back to Chitor to recover the letter. So sure I was I had slipped them. Therefore I did not send a tar [telegram] to any one saying where the letter lay. I wished the credit of it all."

Kim nodded. He understood that feeling well.

"But at Agra, walking in the streets, a man cried a debt against me, and approaching with many witnesses, would hale me to the courts then and there. Oh, they are clever in the South! He recognized me as his agent for cotton. May he burn in Hell for it!"

"And wast thou?"

"O fool! I was the man they sought for the matter of the letter! I ran into the Fleshers' Ward and came out by the House of the Jew, who feared a riot and pushed me forth. I came afoot to Somna Road—I had only money for my tikkut to Delhi—and there, while I lay in a ditch with a fever, one sprang out of the bushes and beat me and cut me and searched me from head to foot. Within earshot of the te-rain it was!"

"Why did he not slay thee out of hand?"

"They are not so foolish. If I am taken in Delhi at the instance of lawyers, upon a proven charge of murder, my body is handed over to the State that desires it. I go back guarded, and then—I die slowly for an example to the rest of Us. The South is not my country. I run in circles—like a goat with one eye. I have not eaten for two days. I am marked"—he touched the filthy bandage on his leg—"so that they will know me at Delhi."

"Thou art safe in the te-rain, at least."

"Live a year at the Great Game and tell me that again! The wires will be out against me at Delhi, describing every tear and rag upon me. Twenty—a hundred, if need be—will have seen me slay that boy. And thou art useless!"

Kim knew enough of native methods of attack not to doubt that the case would be deadly complete—even to the corpse. The Mahratta twitched his fingers with pain from time to time. The Kamboh in his corner glared sullenly; the lama was busy over his beads; and Kim, fumbling doctor-fashion at the man's neck, thought out his plan between invocations.

"Hast thou a charm to change my shape? Else I am dead. Five—ten minutes alone, if I had not been so pressed, and I might—"

"Is he cured yet, miracle-worker?" said the Kamboh jealously. "Thou hast chanted long enough."

"Nay. There is no cure for his hurts, as I see, except he sit for three days in the habit of a bairagi." This is a common penance, often imposed on a fat trader by his spiritual teacher.

"One priest always goes about to make another priest," was the retort. Like most grossly superstitious folk, the Kamboh could not keep his tongue from deriding his Church.

"Will thy son be a priest, then? It is time he took more of my quinine."

"We Jats are all buffaloes," said the Kamboh, softening anew.

Kim rubbed a finger-tip of bitterness on the child's trusting little lips. "I have asked for nothing," he said sternly to the father, "except food. Dost thou grudge me that? I go to heal another man. Have I thy leave—Prince?"

Up flew the man's huge paws in supplication. "Nay—nay. Do not mock me thus."

"It pleases me to cure this sick one. Thou shalt acquire merit by aiding. What colour ash is there in thy pipe-bowl? White. That is auspicious. Was there raw turmeric among thy foodstuffs?"

"I—I—"

"Open thy bundle!"

It was the usual collection of small oddments: bits of cloth, quack medicines, cheap fairings, a clothful of atta—greyish, rough-ground native flour—twists of down-country tobacco, tawdry pipe-stems, and a packet of curry-stuff, all wrapped in a quilt. Kim turned it over with the air of a wise warlock, muttering a Mohammedan invocation.

"This is wisdom I learned from the Sahibs," he whispered to the lama; and here, when one thinks of his training at Lurgan's, he spoke no more than the truth. "There is a great evil in this man's fortune, as shown by the Stars, which—which troubles him. Shall I take it away?"

"Friend of the Stars, thou hast done well in all things. Let it be at thy pleasure. Is it another healing?"

"Quick! Be quick!" gasped the Mahratta. "The train may stop."

"A healing against the shadow of death," said Kim, mixing the Kamboh's flour with the mingled charcoal and tobacco ash in the red-earth bowl of the pipe. E, without a word, slipped off his turban and shook down his long black hair.

"That is my food—priest," the jat growled.

"A buffalo in the temple! Hast thou dared to look even thus far?" said Kim. "I must do mysteries before fools; but have a care for thine eyes. Is there a film before them already? I save the babe, and for return thou—oh, shameless!" The man flinched at the direct gaze, for Kim was wholly in earnest.

"Shall I curse thee, or shall I—" He picked up the outer cloth of the bundle and threw it over the bowed head. "Dare so much as to think a wish to see, and—and—even I cannot save thee. Sit! Be dumb!"

"I am blind—dumb. Forbear to curse! Co—come, child; we will play a game of hiding. Do not, for my sake, look from under the cloth."

"I see hope," said E23. "What is thy scheme?"

"This comes next," said Kim, plucking the thin body-shirt. E23 hesitated, with all a North-West man's dislike of baring his body.

"What is caste to a cut throat?" said Kim, rending it to the waist. "We must make thee a yellow Saddhu all over. Strip—strip swiftly, and shake thy hair over thine eyes while I scatter the ash. Now, a caste-mark on thy forehead." He drew from his bosom the little Survey paint-box and a cake of crimson lake.

"Art thou only a beginner?" said E23, labouring literally for the dear life, as he slid out of his body-wrappings and stood clear in the loin-cloth while Kim splashed in a noble caste-mark on the ash-smeared brow.

"But two days entered to the Game, brother," Kim replied. "Smear more ash on the bosom."

"Hast thou met—a physician of sick pearls?" He switched out his long, tight-rolled turban-cloth and, with swiftest hands, rolled it over and under about his loins into the intricate devices of a Saddhu's cincture.

"Hah! Dost thou know his touch, then? He was my teacher for a while. We must bar thy legs. Ash cures wounds. Smear it again."

"I was his pride once, but thou art almost better. The Gods are kind to us! Give me that."

It was a tin box of opium pills among the rubbish of the Jat's bundle. E23 gulped down a half handful. "They are good against hunger, fear, and chill. And they make the eyes red too," he explained. "Now I shall have heart to play the Game. We lack only a Saddhu's tongs. What of the old clothes?"

Kim rolled them small, and stuffed them into the slack folds of his tunic. With a yellow-ochre paint cake he smeared the legs and the breast, great streaks against the background of flour, ash, and turmeric.

"The blood on them is enough to hang thee, brother."

"Maybe; but no need to throw them out of the window ... It is finished." His voice thrilled with a boy's pure delight in the Game. "Turn and look, O Jat!"

"The Gods protect us," said the hooded Kamboh, emerging like a buffalo from the reeds. "But—whither went the Mahratta? What hast thou done?"

Kim had been trained by Lurgan Sahib; E23, by virtue of his business, was no bad actor. In place of the tremulous, shrinking trader there lolled against the corner an all but naked, ash-smeared, ochre-barred, dusty-haired Saddhu, his swollen eyes—opium takes quick effect on an empty stomach—luminous with insolence and bestial lust, his legs crossed under him, Kim's brown rosary round his neck, and a scant yard of worn, flowered chintz on his shoulders. The child buried his face in his amazed father's arms.

"Look up, Princeling! We travel with warlocks, but they will not hurt thee. Oh, do not cry ... What is the sense of curing a child one day and killing him with fright the next?"

"The child will be fortunate all his life. He has seen a great healing. When I was a child I made clay men and horses."

"I have made them too. Sír Banás, he comes in the night and makes them all alive at the back of our kitchen-midden," piped the child.

"And so thou art not frightened at anything. Eh, Prince?"

"I was frightened because my father was frightened. I felt his arms shake."

"Oh, chicken-man!" said Kim, and even the abashed Jat laughed. "I have done a healing on this poor trader. He must forsake his gains and his account-books, and sit by the wayside three nights to overcome the malignity of his enemies. The Stars are against him."

"The fewer money-lenders the better, say I; but, Saddhu or no Saddhu, he should pay for my stuff on his shoulders."

"So? But that is thy child on thy shoulder—given over to the burning-ghat not two days ago. There remains one thing more. I did this charm in thy presence because need was great. I changed his shape and his soul. None the less, if, by any chance, O man from Jullundur, thou rememberest what thou hast seen, either among the elders sitting under the village tree, or in thine own house, or in company of thy priest when he blesses thy cattle, a murrain will come among the buffaloes, and a fire in thy thatch, and rats in the corn-bins, and the curse of our Gods upon thy fields that they may be barren before thy feet and after thy ploughshare." This was part of an old curse picked up from a faquir by the Taksali Gate in the days of Kim's innocence. It lost nothing by repetition.

"Cease, Holy One! In mercy, cease!" cried the Jat. "Do not curse the household. I saw nothing! I heard nothing! I am thy cow!" and he made to grab at Kim's bare foot beating rhythmically on the carriage floor. "But since thou hast been permitted to aid me in the matter of a pinch of flour and a little opium and such trifles as I have honoured by using in my art, so will the Gods return a blessing," and he gave it at length, to the man's immense relief. It was one that he had learned from Lurgan Sahib.

The lama stared through his spectacles as he had not stared at the business of disguisement. "Friend of the Stars," he said at last, "thou hast acquired great wisdom. Beware that it do not give birth to pride. No man having the Law before his eyes speaks hastily of any matter which he has seen or encountered."

"No—no—no, indeed," cried the farmer, fearful lest the master should be minded to improve on the pupil. E23, with relaxed mouth, gave himself up to the opium that is meat, tobacco, and medicine to the spent Asiatic.

So, in a silence of awe and great miscomprehension, they slid into Delhi about lamp-lighting time.

CHAPTER XII

Who hath desired the Sea—the sight of salt-water unbounded?
The heave and the halt and the hurl and the crash of the comber wind-hounded?
The sleek-barrelled swell before storm—grey, foamless, enormous, and growing?
Stark calm on the lap of the Line—or the crazy-eyed hurricane blowing?
His Sea in no showing the same—his Sea and the same 'neath all showing—
His Sea that his being fulfils?
So and no otherwise—so and no otherwise Hill-men desire their Hills!

The Sea and the Hills.

"I have found my heart again," said E23, under cover of the platform's tumult. "Hunger and fear make men dazed, or I might have thought of this escape before. I was right. They come to hunt for me. Thou hast saved my head."

A group of yellow-trousered Punjab policemen, headed by a hot and perspiring young Englishman, parted the crowd about the carriages. Behind them, inconspicuous as a cat, ambled a small fat person who looked like a lawyer's tout.

"See the young Sahib reading from a paper. My description is in his hand," said E23. "They go carriage by carriage, like fisher-folk netting a pool."

When the procession reached their compartment, E23 was counting his beads with a steady jerk of the wrist; while Kim jeered at him for being so drugged as to have lost the ringed fire-tongs which are the Saddhu's distinguishing mark. The lama, deep in meditation, stared straight before him; and the farmer, glancing furtively, gathered up his belongings.

"Nothing here but a parcel of holy-bolies," said the Englishman aloud, and passed on amid a ripple of uneasiness; for native police mean extortion to the native all India over.

"The trouble now," whispered E23, "lies in sending a wire as to the place where I hid that letter I was sent to find. I cannot go to the tar-office in this guise."

"Is it not enough I have saved thy neck?"

"Not if the work be left unfinished. Did never the healer of sick pearls tell thee so? Comes another Sahib! Ah!"

This was a tallish, sallowish District Superintendent of Police—belt, helmet, polished spurs and all—strutting and twirling his dark moustache.

"What fools are these Police Sahibs!" said Kim genially.

E23 glanced up under his eyelids. "It is well said," he muttered in a changed voice. "I go to drink water. Keep my place."

He blundered out almost into the Englishman's arms, and was bad-worded in clumsy Urdu.

"Tum mut? You drunk? You mustn't bang about as though Delhi station belonged to you, my friend."

E23, not moving a muscle of his countenance, answered with a stream of the filthiest abuse, at

which Kim naturally rejoiced. It reminded him of the drummer-boys and the barrack-sweepers at Umballa in the terrible time of his first schooling.

"My good fool," the Englishman drawled. "Nickle-jao! Go back to your carriage."

Step by step, withdrawing deferentially and dropping his voice, the yellow Saddhu clomb back to the carriage, cursing the D.S.P. to remotest posterity, by—here Kim almost jumped—by the curse of the Queen's Stone, by the writing under the Queen's Stone, and by an assortment of Gods with wholly, new names.

"I don't know what you're saying,"—the Englishman flushed angrily—"but it's some piece of blasted impertinence. Come out of that!"

E23, affecting to misunderstand, gravely produced his ticket, which the Englishman wrenched angrily from his hand.

"Oh, zoolum! What oppression!" growled the Jat from his corner. "All for the sake of a jest too." He had been grinning at the freedom of the Saddhu's tongue. "Thy charms do not work well today, Holy One!"

The Saddhu followed the policeman, fawning and supplicating. The ruck of passengers, busy, with their babies and their bundles, had not noticed the affair. Kim slipped out behind him; for it flashed through his head that he had heard this angry, stupid Sahib discoursing loud personalities to an old lady near Umballa three years ago.

"It is well", the Saddhu whispered, jammed in the calling, shouting, bewildered press—a Persian greyhound between his feet and a cageful of yelling hawks under charge of a Rajput falconer in the small of his back. "He has gone now to send word of the letter which I hid. They told me he was in Peshawur. I might have known that he is like the crocodile—always at the other ford. He has saved me from present calamity, but I owe my life to thee."

"Is he also one of Us?" Kim ducked under a Mewar camel-driver's greasy armpit and cannoned off a covey of jabbering Sikh matrons.

"Not less than the greatest. We are both fortunate! I will make report to him of what thou hast done. I am safe under his protection."

He bored through the edge of the crowd besieging the carriages, and squatted by the bench near the telegraph-office.

"Return, or they take thy place! Have no fear for the work, brother—or my life. Thou hast given me breathing-space, and Strickland Sahib has pulled me to land. We may work together at the Game yet. Farewell!"

Kim hurried to his carriage: elated, bewildered, but a little nettled in that he had no key to the secrets about him.

"I am only a beginner at the Game, that is sure. I could not have leaped into safety as did the Saddhu. He knew it was darkest under the lamp. I could not have thought to tell news under pretence of cursing ... and how clever was the Sahib! No matter, I saved the life of one ... Where is the Kamboh gone, Holy One?" he whispered, as he took his seat in the now crowded compartment.

"A fear gripped him," the lama replied, with a touch of tender malice. "He saw thee change the Mahratta to a Saddhu in the twinkling of an eye, as a protection against evil. That shook him.

Then he saw the Saddhu fall sheer into the hands of the polis—all the effect of thy art. Then he gathered up his son and fled; for he said that thou didst change a quiet trader into an impudent bandier of words with the Sahibs, and he feared a like fate. Where is the Saddhu?"

"With the polis," said Kim ... "Yet I saved the Kamboh's child."

The lama snuffed blandly.

"Ah, chela, see how thou art overtaken! Thou didst cure the Kamboh's child solely to acquire merit. But thou didst put a spell on the Mahratta with prideful workings—I watched thee—and with sidelong glances to bewilder an old old man and a foolish farmer: whence calamity and suspicion."

Kim controlled himself with an effort beyond his years. Not more than any other youngster did he like to eat dirt or to be misjudged, but he saw himself in a cleft stick. The train rolled out of Delhi into the night.

"It is true," he murmured. "Where I have offended thee I have done wrong."

"It is more, chela. Thou hast loosed an Act upon the world, and as a stone thrown into a pool so spread the consequences thou canst not tell how far."

This ignorance was well both for Kim's vanity and for the lama's peace of mind, when we think that there was then being handed in at Simla a code-wire reporting the arrival of E23 at Delhi, and, more important, the whereabouts of a letter he had been commissioned to—abstract. Incidentally, an over-zealous policeman had arrested, on charge of murder done in a far southern State, a horribly indignant Ajmir cotton-broker, who was explaining himself to a Mr Strickland on Delhi platform, while E23 was paddling through byways into the locked heart of Delhi city. In two hours several telegrams had reached the angry minister of a southern State reporting that all trace of a somewhat bruised Mahratta had been lost; and by the time the leisurely train halted at Saharunpore the last ripple of the stone Kim had helped to heave was lapping against the steps of a mosque in far-away Roum—where it disturbed a pious man at prayers.

The lama made his in ample form near the dewy bougainvillea-trellis near the platform, cheered by the clear sunshine and the presence of his disciple. "We will put these things behind us," he said, indicating the brazen engine and the gleaming track. "The jolting of the te-rain—though a wonderful thing—has turned my bones to water. We will use clean air henceforward."

"Let us go to the Kulu woman's house" said Kim, and stepped forth cheerily under the bundles. Early morning Saharunpore-way is clean and well scented. He thought of the other mornings at St Xavier's, and it topped his already thrice-heaped contentment.

"Where is this new haste born from? Wise men do not run about like chickens in the sun. We have come hundreds upon hundreds of kos already, and, till now, I have scarcely been alone with thee an instant. How canst thou receive instruction all jostled of crowds? How can I, whelmed by a flux of talk, meditate upon the Way?"

"Her tongue grows no shorter with the years, then?" the disciple smiled.

"Nor her desire for charms. I remember once when I spoke of the Wheel of Life"—the lama fumbled in his bosom for his latest copy—"she was only curious about the devils that besiege children. She shall acquire merit by entertaining us—in a little while—at an after-occasion—softly, softly. Now we will wander loose-foot, waiting upon the Chain of Things. The Search is sure."

So they travelled very easily across and among the broad bloomful fruit-gardens—by way of Aminabad, Sahaigunge, Akrola of the Ford, and little Phulesa—the line of the Siwaliks always to the north, and behind them again the snows. After long, sweet sleep under the dry stars came the lordly, leisurely passage through a waking village—begging-bowl held forth in silence, but eyes roving in defiance of the Law from sky's edge to sky's edge. Then would Kim return soft-footed through the soft dust to his master under the shadow of a mango-tree or the thinner shade of a white Doon siris, to eat and drink at ease. At mid-day, after talk and a little wayfaring, they slept; meeting the world refreshed when the air was cooler. Night found them adventuring into new territory—some chosen village spied three hours before across the fat land, and much discussed upon the road.

There they told their tale—a new one each evening so far as Kim was concerned—and there were they made welcome, either by priest or headman, after the custom of the kindly East.

When the shadows shortened and the lama leaned more heavily upon Kim, there was always the Wheel of Life to draw forth, to hold flat under wiped stones, and with a long straw to expound cycle by cycle. Here sat the Gods on high—and they were dreams of dreams. Here was our Heaven and the world of the demi-Gods—horsemen fighting among the hills. Here were the agonies done upon the beasts, souls ascending or descending the ladder and therefore not to be interfered with. Here were the Hells, hot and cold, and the abodes of tormented ghosts. Let the chela study the troubles that come from over-eating—bloated stomach and burning bowels. Obediently, then, with bowed head and brown finger alert to follow the pointer, did the chela study; but when they came to the Human World, busy and profitless, that is just above the Hells, his mind was distracted; for by the roadside trundled the very Wheel itself, eating, drinking, trading, marrying, and quarrelling—all warmly alive. Often the lama made the living pictures the matter of his text, bidding Kim—too ready—note how the flesh takes a thousand shapes, desirable or detestable as men reckon, but in truth of no account either way; and how the stupid spirit, bond-slave to the Hog, the Dove, and the Serpent—lusting after betel-nut, a new yoke of oxen, women, or the favour of kings—is bound to follow the body through all the Heavens and all the Hells, and strictly round again. Sometimes a woman or a poor man, watching the ritual—it was nothing less—when the great yellow chart was unfolded, would throw a few flowers or a handful of cowries upon its edge. It sufficed these humble ones that they had met a Holy One who might be moved to remember them in his prayers.

"Cure them if they are sick," said the lama, when Kim's sporting instincts woke. "Cure them if they have fever, but by no means work charms. Remember what befell the Mahratta."

"Then all Doing is evil?" Kim replied, lying out under a big tree at the fork of the Doon road, watching the little ants run over his hand.

"To abstain from action is well—except to acquire merit."

"At the Gates of Learning we were taught that to abstain from action was unbefitting a Sahib. And I am a Sahib."

"Friend of all the World,"—the lama looked directly at Kim—"I am an old man—pleased with shows as are children. To those who follow the Way there is neither black nor white, Hind nor Bhotiyal. We be all souls seeking escape. No matter what thy wisdom learned among Sahibs, when we come to my River thou wilt be freed from all illusion—at my side. Hai! My bones ache for that River, as they ached in the te-rain; but my spirit sits above my bones, waiting. The Search is sure!"

"I am answered. Is it permitted to ask a question?"

The lama inclined his stately head.

"I ate thy bread for three years—as thou knowest. Holy One, whence came—?"

"There is much wealth, as men count it, in Bhotiyal," the lama returned with composure. "In my own place I have the illusion of honour. I ask for that I need. I am not concerned with the account. That is for my monastery. Ai! The black high seats in the monastery, and novices all in order!"

And he told stories, tracing with a finger in the dust, of the immense and sumptuous ritual of avalanche-guarded cathedrals; of processions and devil-dances; of the changing of monks and nuns into swine; of holy cities fifteen thousand feet in the air; of intrigue between monastery and monastery; of voices among the hills, and of that mysterious mirage that dances on dry snow. He spoke even of Lhassa and of the Dalai Lama, whom he had seen and adored.

Each long, perfect day rose behind Kim for a barrier to cut him off from his race and his mother-tongue. He slipped back to thinking and dreaming in the vernacular, and mechanically followed the lama's ceremonial observances at eating, drinking, and the like. The old man's mind turned more and more to his monastery as his eyes turned to the steadfast snows. His River troubled him nothing. Now and again, indeed, he would gaze long and long at a tuft or a twig, expecting, he said, the earth to cleave and deliver its blessing; but he was content to be with his disciple, at ease in the temperate wind that comes down from the Doon. This was not Ceylon, nor Buddh Gaya, nor Bombay, nor some grass-tangled ruins that he seemed to have stumbled upon two years ago. He spoke of those places as a scholar removed from vanity, as a Seeker walking in humility, as an old man, wise and temperate, illumining knowledge with brilliant insight. Bit by bit, disconnectedly, each tale called up by some wayside thing, he spoke of all his wanderings up and down Hind; till Kim, who had loved him without reason, now loved him for fifty good reasons. So they enjoyed themselves in high felicity, abstaining, as the Rule demands, from evil words, covetous desires; not over-eating, not lying on high beds, nor wearing rich clothes. Their stomachs told them the time, and the people brought them their food, as the saying is. They were lords of the villages of Aminabad, Sahaigunge, Akrola of the Ford, and little Phulesa, where Kim gave the soulless woman a blessing.

But news travels fast in India, and too soon shuffled across the crop-land, bearing a basket of fruits with a box of Kabul grapes and gilt oranges, a white-whiskered servitor—a lean, dry Oorya—begging them to bring the honour of their presence to his mistress, distressed in her mind that the lama had neglected her so long.

"Now do I remember"—the lama spoke as though it were a wholly new proposition. "She is virtuous, but an inordinate talker."

Kim was sitting on the edge of a cow's manger, telling stories to a village smith's children.

"She will only ask for another son for her daughter. I have not forgotten her," he said. "Let her acquire merit. Send word that we will come."

They covered eleven miles through the fields in two days, and were overwhelmed with attentions at the end; for the old lady held a fine tradition of hospitality, to which she forced her son-in-law, who was under the thumb of his women-folk and bought peace by borrowing of the money-lender. Age had not weakened her tongue or her memory, and from a discreetly barred upper window, in the hearing of not less than a dozen servants, she paid Kim compliments that would have flung European audiences into unclean dismay.

"But thou art still the shameless beggar-brat of the parao," she shrilled. "I have not forgotten

thee. Wash ye and eat. The father of my daughter's son is gone away awhile. So we poor women are dumb and useless."

For proof, she harangued the entire household unsparingly till food and drink were brought; and in the evening—the smoke-scented evening, copper-dun and turquoise across the fields—it pleased her to order her palanquin to be set down in the untidy forecourt by smoky torchlight; and there, behind not too closely drawn curtains, she gossiped.

"Had the Holy One come alone, I should have received him otherwise; but with this rogue, who can be too careful?"

"Maharanee," said Kim, choosing as always the amplest title, "is it my fault that none other than a Sahib—a polis-sahib—called the Maharanee whose face he—" "Chutt! That was on the pilgrimage. When we travel—thou knowest the proverb."

"Called the Maharanee a Breaker of Hearts and a Dispenser of Delights?"

"To remember that! It was true. So he did. That was in the time of the bloom of my beauty." She chuckled like a contented parrot above the sugar lump. "Now tell me of thy goings and comings—as much as may be without shame. How many maids, and whose wives, hang upon thine eyelashes? Ye hail from Benares? I would have gone there again this year, but my daughter—we have only two sons. Phaii! Such is the effect of these low plains. Now in Kulu men are elephants. But I would ask thy Holy One—stand aside, rogue—a charm against most lamentable windy colics that in mango-time overtake my daughter's eldest. Two years back he gave me a powerful spell."

"Oh, Holy One!" said Kim, bubbling with mirth at the lama's rueful face.

"It is true. I gave her one against wind."

"Teeth—teeth—teeth," snapped the old woman.

"'Cure them if they are sick,'" Kim quoted relishingly, "'but by no means work charms. Remember what befell the Mahratta.'"

"That was two Rains ago; she wearied me with her continual importunity." The lama groaned as the Unjust Judge had groaned before him. "Thus it comes—take note, my chela—that even those who would follow the Way are thrust aside by idle women. Three days through, when the child was sick, she talked to me."

"Arre! and to whom else should I talk? The boy's mother knew nothing, and the father—in the nights of the cold weather it was—'Pray to the Gods,' said he, forsooth, and turning over, snored!"

"I gave her the charm. What is an old man to do?"

"'To abstain from action is well—except to acquire merit.'"

"Ah chela, if thou desertest me, I am all alone."

"He found his milk-teeth easily at any rate," said the old lady. "But all priests are alike."

Kim coughed severely. Being young, he did not approve of her flippancy. "To importune the wise out of season is to invite calamity."

"There is a talking mynah"—the thrust came back with the well-remembered snap of the jewelled fore-finger—"over the stables which has picked up the very tone of the family priest. Maybe I forget honour to my guests, but if ye had seen him double his fists into his belly, which was like a half-grown gourd, and cry: 'Here is the pain!' ye would forgive. I am half minded to take the hakim's medicine. He sells it cheap, and certainly it makes him fat as Shiv's own bull. He does not deny remedies, but I doubted for the child because of the in-auspicious colour of the bottles."

The lama, under cover of the monologue, had faded out into the darkness towards the room prepared.

"Thou hast angered him, belike," said Kim.

"Not he. He is wearied, and I forgot, being a grandmother. (None but a grandmother should ever oversee a child. Mothers are only fit for bearing.) Tomorrow, when he sees how my daughter's son is grown, he will write the charm. Then, too, he can judge of the new hakim's drugs."

"Who is the hakim, Maharanee?"

"A wanderer, as thou art, but a most sober Bengali from Dacca—a master of medicine. He relieved me of an oppression after meat by means of a small pill that wrought like a devil unchained. He travels about now, vending preparations of great value. He has even papers, printed in Angrezi, telling what things he has done for weak-backed men and slack women. He has been here four days; but hearing ye were coming (hakims and priests are snake and tiger the world over) he has, as I take it, gone to cover."

While she drew breath after this volley, the ancient servant, sitting unrebuked on the edge of the torchlight, muttered: "This house is a cattle-pound, as it were, for all charlatans and—priests. Let the boy stop eating mangoes ... but who can argue with a grandmother?" He raised his voice respectfully: "Sahiba, the hakim sleeps after his meat. He is in the quarters behind the dovecote."

Kim bristled like an expectant terrier. To outface and down-talk a Calcutta-taught Bengali, a voluble Dacca drug-vendor, would be a good game. It was not seemly that the lama, and incidentally himself, should be thrown aside for such an one. He knew those curious bastard English advertisements at the backs of native newspapers. St Xavier's boys sometimes brought them in by stealth to snigger over among their mates; for the language of the grateful patient recounting his symptoms is most simple and revealing. The Oorya, not unanxious to play off one parasite against the other, slunk away towards the dovecote.

"Yes," said Kim, with measured scorn. "Their stock-in-trade is a little coloured water and a very great shamelessness. Their prey are broken-down kings and overfed Bengalis. Their profit is in children—who are not born."

The old lady chuckled. "Do not be envious. Charms are better, eh? I never gainsaid it. See that thy Holy One writes me a good amulet by the morning."

"None but the ignorant deny"—a thick, heavy voice boomed through the darkness, as a figure came to rest squatting—"None but the ignorant deny the value of charms. None but the ignorant deny the value of medicines."

"A rat found a piece of turmeric. Said he: 'I will open a grocer's shop,'" Kim retorted.

Battle was fairly joined now, and they heard the old lady stiffen to attention.

"The priest's son knows the names of his nurse and three Gods. Says he: 'Hear me, or I will curse you by the three million Great Ones.'" Decidedly this invisible had an arrow or two in his quiver. He went on: "I am but a teacher of the alphabet. I have learned all the wisdom of the Sahibs."

"The Sahibs never grow old. They dance and they play like children when they are grandfathers. A strong-backed breed," piped the voice inside the palanquin.

"I have, too, our drugs which loosen humours of the head in hot and angry men. Siná well compounded when the moon stands in the proper House; yellow earths I have—arplan from China that makes a man renew his youth and astonish his household; saffron from Kashmir, and the best salep of Kabul. Many people have died before—"

"That I surely believe," said Kim.

"They knew the value of my drugs. I do not give my sick the mere ink in which a charm is written, but hot and rending drugs which descend and wrestle with the evil."

"Very mightily they do so," sighed the old lady.

The voice launched into an immense tale of misfortune and bankruptcy, studded with plentiful petitions to the Government. "But for my fate, which overrules all, I had been now in Government employ. I bear a degree from the great school at Calcutta—whither, maybe, the son of this House shall go."

"He shall indeed. If our neighbour's brat can in a few years be made an F A" (First Arts—she used the English word, of which she had heard so often), "how much more shall children clever as some that I know bear away prizes at rich Calcutta."

"Never," said the voice, "have I seen such a child! Born in an auspicious hour, and—but for that colic which, alas! turning into black cholers, may carry him off like a pigeon—destined to many years, he is enviable."

"Hai mai!" said the old lady. "To praise children is inauspicious, or I could listen to this talk. But the back of the house is unguarded, and even in this soft air men think themselves to be men, and women we know ... The child's father is away too, and I must be chowkedar (watchman) in my old age. Up! Up! Take up the palanquin. Let the hakim and the young priest settle between them whether charms or medicine most avail. Ho! worthless people, fetch tobacco for the guests, and—round the homestead go I!"

The palanquin reeled off, followed by straggling torches and a horde of dogs. Twenty villages knew the Sahiba—her failings, her tongue, and her large charity. Twenty villages cheated her after immemorial custom, but no man would have stolen or robbed within her jurisdiction for any gift under heaven. None the less, she made great parade of her formal inspections, the riot of which could be heard half-way to Mussoorie.

Kim relaxed, as one augur must when he meets another. The hakim, still squatting, slid over his hookah with a friendly foot, and Kim pulled at the good weed. The hangers-on expected grave professional debate, and perhaps a little free doctoring.

"To discuss medicine before the ignorant is of one piece with teaching the peacock to sing," said the hakim.

"True courtesy," Kim echoed, "is very often inattention."

These, be it understood, were company-manners, designed to impress.

"Hi! I have an ulcer on my leg," cried a scullion. "Look at it!"

"Get hence! Remove!" said the hakim. "Is it the habit of the place to pester honoured guests? Ye crowd in like buffaloes."

"If the Sahiba knew—" Kim began.

"Ai! Ai! Come away. They are meat for our mistress. When her young Shaitan's colics are cured perhaps we poor people may be suffered to—"

"The mistress fed thy wife when thou wast in jail for breaking the money-lender's head. Who speaks against her?" The old servitor curled his white moustaches savagely in the young moonlight. "I am responsible for the honour of this house. Go!" and he drove the underlings before him.

Said the hakim, hardly more than shaping the words with his lips: "How do you do, Mister O'Hara? I am jolly glad to see you again."

Kim's hand clenched about the pipe-stem. Anywhere on the open road, perhaps, he would not have been astonished; but here, in this quiet backwater of life, he was not prepared for Hurree Babu. It annoyed him, too, that he had been hoodwinked.

"Ah ha! I told you at Lucknow—resurgam—I shall rise again and you shall not know me. How much did you bet—eh?"

He chewed leisurely upon a few cardamom seeds, but he breathed uneasily.

"But why come here, Babuji?"

"Ah! Thatt is the question, as Shakespeare hath it. I come to congratulate you on your extraordinary effeecient performance at Delhi. Oah! I tell you we are all proud of you. It was verree neat and handy. Our mutual friend, he is old friend of mine. He has been in some dam'-tight places. Now he will be in some more. He told me; I tell Mr Lurgan; and he is pleased you graduate so nicely. All the Department is pleased."

For the first time in his life, Kim thrilled to the clean pride (it can be a deadly pitfall, none the less) of Departmental praise—ensnaring praise from an equal of work appreciated by fellow-workers. Earth has nothing on the same plane to compare with it. But, cried the Oriental in him, Babus do not travel far to retail compliments.

"Tell thy tale, Babu," he said authoritatively.

"Oah, it is nothing. Onlee I was at Simla when the wire came in about what our mutual friend said he had hidden, and old Creighton—" He looked to see how Kim would take this piece of audacity.

"The Colonel Sahib," the boy from St Xavier's corrected.

"Of course. He found me at a loose string, and I had to go down to Chitor to find that beastly letter. I do not like the South—too much railway travel; but I drew good travelling allowance. Ha! Ha! I meet our mutual at Delhi on the way back. He lies quiett just now, and says Saddhu-disguise suits him to the ground. Well, there I hear what you have done so well, so quickly, upon the instantaneous spur of the moment. I tell our mutual you take the bally bun, by Jove! It was

splendid. I come to tell you so."

"Umm!"

The frogs were busy in the ditches, and the moon slid to her setting. Some happy servant had gone out to commune with the night and to beat upon a drum. Kim's next sentence was in the vernacular.

"How didst thou follow us?"

"Oah. Thatt was nothing. I know from our mutual friend you go to Saharunpore. So I come on. Red Lamas are not inconspicuous persons. I buy myself my drug-box, and I am very good doctor really. I go to Akrola of the Ford, and hear all about you, and I talk here and talk there. All the common people know what you do. I knew when the hospitable old lady sent the dooli. They have great recollections of the old lama's visits here. I know old ladies cannot keep their hands from medicines. So I am a doctor, and—you hear my talk? I think it is verree good. My word, Mister O'Hara, they know about you and the lama for fifty miles—the common people. So I come. Do you mind?"

"Babuji," said Kim, looking up at the broad, grinning face, "I am a Sahib."

"My dear Mister O'Hara—"

"And I hope to play the Great Game."

"You are subordinate to me departmentally at present."

"Then why talk like an ape in a tree? Men do not come after one from Simla and change their dress, for the sake of a few sweet words. I am not a child. Talk Hindi and let us get to the yolk of the egg. Thou art here—speaking not one word of truth in ten. Why art thou here? Give a straight answer."

"That is so verree disconcerting of the Europeans, Mister O'Hara. You should know a heap better at your time of life."

"But I want to know," said Kim, laughing. "If it is the Game, I may help. How can I do anything if you bukh (babble) all round the shop?"

Hurree Babu reached for the pipe, and sucked it till it gurgled again.

"Now I will speak vernacular. You sit tight, Mister O'Hara ... It concerns the pedigree of a white stallion."

"Still? That was finished long ago."

"When everyone is dead the Great Game is finished. Not before. Listen to me till the end. There were Five Kings who prepared a sudden war three years ago, when thou wast given the stallion's pedigree by Mahbub Ali. Upon them, because of that news, and ere they were ready, fell our Army."

"Ay—eight thousand men with guns. I remember that night."

"But the war was not pushed. That is the Government custom. The troops were recalled because the Government believed the Five Kings were cowed; and it is not cheap to feed men among the high Passes. Hilás and Bunár—Rajahs with guns—undertook for a price to guard the Passes

against all coming from the North. They protested both fear and friendship." He broke off with a giggle into English: "Of course, I tell you this unoffeecially to elucidate political situation, Mister O'Hara. Offeecially, I am debarred from criticizing any action of superiors. Now I go on.—This pleased the Government, anxious to avoid expense, and a bond was made for so many rupees a month that Hilás and Bunár should guard the Passes as soon as the State's troops were withdrawn. At that time—it was after we two met—I, who had been selling tea in Leh, became a clerk of accounts in the Army. When the troops were withdrawn, I was left behind to pay the coolies who made new roads in the Hills. This road-making was part of the bond between Bunár, Hilás, and the Government."

"So? And then?"

"I tell you, it was jolly-beastly cold up there too, after summer," said Hurree Babu confidentially. "I was afraid these Bunár men would cut my throat every night for thee pay-chest. My native sepoy-guard, they laughed at me! By Jove! I was such a fearful man. Nevar mind thatt. I go on colloquially ... I send word many times that these two Kings were sold to the North; and Mahbub Ali, who was yet farther North, amply confirmed it. Nothing was done. Only my feet were frozen, and a toe dropped off. I sent word that the roads for which I was paying money to the diggers were being made for the feet of strangers and enemies."

"For?"

"For the Russians. The thing was an open jest among the coolies. Then I was called down to tell what I knew by speech of tongue. Mahbub came South too. See the end! Over the Passes this year after snow-melting"—he shivered afresh—"come two strangers under cover of shooting wild goats. They bear guns, but they bear also chains and levels and compasses."

"Oho! The thing gets clearer."

"They are well received by Hilás and Bunár. They make great promises; they speak as the mouthpiece of a Kaisar with gifts. Up the valleys, down the valleys go they, saying, 'Here is a place to build a breastwork; here can ye pitch a fort. Here can ye hold the road against an army'—the very roads for which I paid out the rupees monthly. The Government knows, but does nothing. The three other Kings, who were not paid for guarding the Passes, tell them by runner of the bad faith of Bunár and Hilás. When all the evil is done, look you—when these two strangers with the levels and the compasses make the Five Kings to believe that a great army will sweep the Passes tomorrow or the next day—Hill-people are all fools—comes the order to me, Hurree Babu, 'Go North and see what those strangers do.' I say to Creighton Sahib, 'This is not a lawsuit, that we go about to collect evidence.'" Hurree returned to his English with a jerk: "'By Jove,' I said, 'why the dooce do you not issue demi-offeecial orders to some brave man to poison them, for an example? It is, if you permit the observation, most reprehensible laxity on your part.' And Colonel Creighton, he laughed at me! It is all your beastly English pride. You think no one dare conspire! That is all tommy-rott."

Kim smoked slowly, revolving the business, so far as he understood it, in his quick mind.

"Then thou goest forth to follow the strangers?"

"No. To meet them. They are coming in to Simla to send down their horns and heads to be dressed at Calcutta. They are exclusively sporting gentlemen, and they are allowed special faceelities by the Government. Of course, we always do that. It is our British pride."

"Then what is to fear from them?"

"By Jove, they are not black people. I can do all sorts of things with black people, of course. They are Russians, and highly unscrupulous people. I—I do not want to consort with them without a witness."

"Will they kill thee?"

"Oah, thatt is nothing. I am good enough Herbert Spencerian, I trust, to meet little thing like death, which is all in my fate, you know. But—but they may beat me."

"Why?"

Hurree Babu snapped his fingers with irritation. "Of course I shall affeeliate myself to their camp in supernumerary capacity as perhaps interpreter, or person mentally impotent and hungree, or some such thing. And then I must pick up what I can, I suppose. That is as easy for me as playing Mister Doctor to the old lady. Onlee—onlee—you see, Mister O'Hara, I am unfortunately Asiatic, which is serious detriment in some respects. And allso I am Bengali—a fearful man."

"God made the Hare and the Bengali. What shame?" said Kim, quoting the proverb.

"It was process of Evolution, I think, from Primal Necessity, but the fact remains in all the cui bono. I am, oh, awfully fearful!—I remember once they wanted to cut off my head on the road to Lhassa. (No, I have never reached to Lhassa.) I sat down and cried, Mister O'Hara, anticipating Chinese tortures. I do not suppose these two gentlemen will torture me, but I like to provide for possible contingency with European assistance in emergency." He coughed and spat out the cardamoms. "It is purely unoffeecial indent, to which you can say 'No, Babu'. If you have no pressing engagement with your old man—perhaps you might divert him; perhaps I can seduce his fancies—I should like you to keep in Departmental touch with me till I find those sporting coves. I have great opeenion of you since I met my friend at Delhi. And also I will embody your name in my offeecial report when matter is finally adjudicated. It will be a great feather in your cap. That is why I come really."

"Humph! The end of the tale, I think, is true; but what of the fore-part?"

"About the Five Kings? Oah! there is ever so much truth in it. A lots more than you would suppose," said Hurree earnestly. "You come—eh? I go from here straight into the Doon. It is verree verdant and painted meads. I shall go to Mussoorie to good old Munsoorie Pahar, as the gentlemen and ladies say. Then by Rampur into Chini. That is the only way they can come. I do not like waiting in the cold, but we must wait for them. I want to walk with them to Simla. You see, one Russian is a Frenchman, and I know my French pretty well. I have friends in Chandernagore."

"He would certainly rejoice to see the Hills again," said Kim meditatively. "All his speech these ten days past has been of little else. If we go together—"

"Oah! We can be quite strangers on the road, if your lama prefers. I shall just be four or five miles ahead. There is no hurry for Hurree—that is an Europe pun, ha! ha!—and you come after. There is plenty of time; they will plot and survey and map, of course. I shall go tomorrow, and you the next day, if you choose. Eh? You go think on it till morning. By Jove, it is near morning now." He yawned ponderously, and with never a civil word lumbered off to his sleeping-place. But Kim slept little, and his thoughts ran in Hindustani:

"Well is the Game called great! I was four days a scullion at Quetta, waiting on the wife of the man whose book I stole. And that was part of the Great Game! From the South—God knows

how far—came up the Mahratta, playing the Great Game in fear of his life. Now I shall go far and far into the North playing the Great Game. Truly, it runs like a shuttle throughout all Hind. And my share and my joy"—he smiled to the darkness—"I owe to the lama here. Also to Mahbub Ali—also to Creighton Sahib, but chiefly to the Holy One. He is right—a great and a wonderful world—and I am Kim—Kim—Kim—alone—one person—in the middle of it all. But I will see these strangers with their levels and chains..."

"What was the upshot of last night's babble?" said the lama, after his orisons.

"There came a strolling seller of drugs—a hanger-on of the Sahiba's. Him I abolished by arguments and prayers, proving that our charms are worthier than his coloured waters."

"Alas, my charms! Is the virtuous woman still bent upon a new one?"

"Very strictly."

"Then it must be written, or she will deafen me with her clamour." He fumbled at his pencase.

"In the Plains," said Kim, "are always too many people. In the Hills, as I understand, there are fewer."

"Oh! the Hills, and the snows upon the Hills." The lami tore off a tiny square of paper fit to go in an amulet. "But what dost thou know of the Hills?"

"They are very close." Kim thrust open the door and looked at the long, peaceful line of the Himalayas flushed in morning-gold. "Except in the dress of a Sahib, I have never set foot among them."

The lama snuffed the wind wistfully.

"If we go North,"—Kim put the question to the waking sunrise—"would not much mid-day heat be avoided by walking among the lower hills at least? ... Is the charm made, Holy One?"

"I have written the names of seven silly devils—not one of whom is worth a grain of dust in the eye. Thus do foolish women drag us from the Way!"

Hurree Babu came out from behind the dovecote washing his teeth with ostentatious ritual. Full-fleshed, heavy-haunched, bull-necked, and deep-voiced, he did not look like "a fearful man". Kim signed almost imperceptibly that matters were in good train, and when the morning toilet was over, Hurree Babu, in flowery speech, came to do honour to the lama. They ate, of course, apart, and afterwards the old lady, more or less veiled behind a window, returned to the vital business of green-mango colics in the young. The lama's knowledge of medicine was, of course, sympathetic only. He believed that the dung of a black horse, mixed with sulphur, and carried in a snake-skin, was a sound remedy for cholera; but the symbolism interested him far more than the science. Hurree Babu deferred to these views with enchanting politeness, so that the lama called him a courteous physician. Hurree Babu replied that he was no more than an inexpert dabbler in the mysteries; but at least—he thanked the Gods therefore—he knew when he sat in the presence of a master. He himself had been taught by the Sahibs, who do not consider expense, in the lordly halls of Calcutta; but, as he was ever first to acknowledge, there lay a wisdom behind earthly wisdom—the high and lonely lore of meditation. Kim looked on with envy. The Hurree Babu of his knowledge—oily, effusive, and nervous—was gone; gone, too, was the brazen drug-vendor of overnight. There remained—polished, polite, attentive—a sober, learned son of experience and adversity, gathering wisdom from the lama's lips. The old lady confided to Kim that these rare levels were beyond her. She liked charms with plenty of

ink that one could wash off in water, swallow, and be done with. Else what was the use of the Gods? She liked men and women, and she spoke of them—of kinglets she had known in the past; of her own youth and beauty; of the depredations of leopards and the eccentricities of love Asiatic; of the incidence of taxation, rack-renting, funeral ceremonies, her son-in-law (this by allusion, easy to be followed), the care of the young, and the age's lack of decency. And Kim, as interested in the life of this world as she soon to leave it, squatted with his feet under the hem of his robe, drinking all in, while the lama demolished one after another every theory of body-curing put forward by Hurree Babu.

At noon the Babu strapped up his brass-bound drug-box, took his patent-leather shoes of ceremony in one hand, a gay blue-and-white umbrella in the other, and set off northwards to the Doon, where, he said, he was in demand among the lesser kings of those parts.

"We will go in the cool of the evening, chela," said the lama. "That doctor, learned in physic and courtesy, affirms that the people among these lower hills are devout, generous, and much in need of a teacher. In a very short time—so says the hakim—we come to cool air and the smell of pines."

"Ye go to the Hills? And by Kulu road? Oh, thrice happy!" shrilled the old lady. "But that I am a little pressed with the care of the homestead I would take palanquin ... but that would be shameless, and my reputation would be cracked. Ho! Ho! I know the road—every march of the road I know. Ye will find charity throughout—it is not denied to the well-looking. I will give orders for provision. A servant to set you forth upon your journey? No ... Then I will at least cook ye good food."

"What a woman is the Sahiba!" said the white-bearded Oorya, when a tumult rose by the kitchen quarters. "She has never forgotten a friend: she has never forgotten an enemy in all her years. And her cookery—wah!" He rubbed his slim stomach.

There were cakes, there were sweetmeats, there was cold fowl stewed to rags with rice and prunes—enough to burden Kim like a mule.

"I am old and useless," she said. "None now love me—and none respect—but there are few to compare with me when I call on the Gods and squat to my cooking-pots. Come again, O people of good will. Holy One and disciple, come again. The room is always prepared; the welcome is always ready ... See the women do not follow thy chela too openly. I know the women of Kulu. Take heed, chela, lest he run away when he smells his Hills again ... Hai! Do not tilt the rice-bag upside down ... Bless the household, Holy One, and forgive thy servant her stupidities."

She wiped her red old eyes on a corner of her veil, and clucked throatily.

"Women talk," said the lama at last, "but that is a woman's infirmity. I gave her a charm. She is upon the Wheel and wholly given over to the shows of this life, but none the less, chela, she is virtuous, kindly, hospitable—of a whole and zealous heart. Who shall say she does not acquire merit?"

"Not I, Holy One," said Kim, reslinging the bountiful provision on his shoulders. "In my mind—behind my eyes—I have tried to picture such an one altogether freed from the Wheel—desiring nothing, causing nothing—a nun, as it were."

"And, O imp?" The lama almost laughed aloud.

"I cannot make the picture."

"Nor I. But there are many, many millions of lives before her. She will get wisdom a little, it may be, in each one."

"And will she forget how to make stews with saffron upon that road?"

"Thy mind is set on things unworthy. But she has skill. I am refreshed all over. When we reach the lower hills I shall be yet stronger. The hakim spoke truly to me this morn when he said a breath from the snows blows away twenty years from the life of a man. We will go up into the Hills—the high hills—up to the sound of snow-waters and the sound of the trees—for a little while. The hakim said that at any time we may return to the Plains, for we do no more than skirt the pleasant places. The hakim is full of learning; but he is in no way proud. I spoke to him—when thou wast talking to the Sahiba—of a certain dizziness that lays hold upon the back of my neck in the night, and he said it rose from excessive heat—to be cured by cool air. Upon consideration, I marvelled that I had not thought of such a simple remedy."

"Didst thou tell him of thy Search?" said Kim, a little jealously. He preferred to sway the lama by his own speech—not through the wiles of Hurree Babu.

"Assuredly. I told him of my dream, and of the manner by which I had acquired merit by causing thee to be taught wisdom."

"Thou didst not say I was a Sahib?"

"What need? I have told thee many times we be but two souls seeking escape. He said—and he is just herein—that the River of Healing will break forth even as I dreamed—at my feet, if need be. Having found the Way, seest thou, that shall free me from the Wheel, need I trouble to find a way about the mere fields of earth—which are illusion? That were senseless. I have my dreams, night upon night repeated; I have Jâtaka; and I have thee, Friend of all the World. It was written in thy horoscope that a Red Bull on a green field—I have not forgotten—should bring thee to honour. Who but I saw that prophecy accomplished? Indeed, I was the instrument. Thou shalt find me my River, being in return the instrument. The Search is sure!"

He set his ivory-yellow face, serene and untroubled, towards the beckoning Hills; his shadow shouldering far before him in the dust.

CHAPTER XIII

Who hath desired the Sea—the immense and contemptuous surges?
The shudder, the stumble, the swerve ere the star-stabbing bowsprit merges—
The orderly clouds of the Trades and the ridged roaring sapphire thereunder—
Unheralded cliff-lurking flaws and the head-sails' low-volleying thunder?
His Sea in no wonder the same—his Sea and the same in each wonder—
His Sea that his being fulfils?
So and no otherwise—so and no otherwise hill-men desire their hills!

The Sea and the Hills.

"Who goes to the hills goes to his mother."

They had crossed the Siwaliks and the half-tropical Doon, left Mussoorie behind them, and headed north along the narrow hill-roads. Day after day they struck deeper into the huddled mountains, and day after day Kim watched the lama return to a man's strength. Among the terraces of the Doon he had leaned on the boy's shoulder, ready to profit by wayside halts. Under the great ramp to Mussoorie he drew himself together as an old hunter faces a well-remembered bank, and where he should have sunk exhausted swung his long draperies about him, drew a deep double-lungful of the diamond air, and walked as only a hillman can. Kim, plains-bred and plains-fed, sweated and panted astonished. "This is my country," said the lama. "Beside Such-zen, this is flatter than a rice-field"; and with steady, driving strokes from the loins he strode upwards. But it was on the steep downhill marches, three thousand feet in three hours, that he went utterly away from Kim, whose back ached with holding back, and whose big toe was nigh cut off by his grass sandal-string. Through the speckled shadow of the great deodar-forests; through oak feathered and plumed with ferns; birch, ilex, rhododendron, and pine, out on to the bare hillsides' slippery sunburnt grass, and back into the woodlands' coolth again, till oak gave way to bamboo and palm of the valley, the lama swung untiring.

Glancing back in the twilight at the huge ridges behind him and the faint, thin line of the road whereby they had come, he would lay out, with a hillman's generous breadth of vision, fresh marches for the morrow; or, halting in the neck of some uplifted pass that gave on Spiti and Kulu, would stretch out his hands yearningly towards the high snows of the horizon. In the dawns they flared windy-red above stark blue, as Kedarnath and Badrinath—kings of that wilderness—took the first sunlight. All day long they lay like molten silver under the sun, and at evening put on their jewels again. At first they breathed temperately upon the travellers, winds good to meet when one crawled over some gigantic hog's-back; but in a few days, at a height of nine or ten thousand feet, those breezes bit; and Kim kindly allowed a village of hillmen to acquire merit by giving him a rough blanket-coat. The lama was mildly surprised that anyone should object to the knife-edged breezes which had cut the years off his shoulders.

"These are but the lower hills, chela. There is no cold till we come to the true Hills."

"Air and water are good, and the people are devout enough, but the food is very bad," Kim growled; "and we walk as though we were mad—or English. It freezes at night, too."

"A little, maybe; but only enough to make old bones rejoice in the sun. We must not always delight in soft beds and rich food."

"We might at least keep to the road."

Kim had all a plainsman's affection for the well-trodden track, not six feet wide, that snaked among the mountains; but the lama, being Tibetan, could not refrain from short cuts over spurs and the rims of gravel-strewn slopes. As he explained to his limping disciple, a man bred among mountains can prophesy the course of a mountain-road, and though low-lying clouds might be a hindrance to a short-cutting stranger, they made no earthly difference to a thoughtful man. Thus, after long hours of what would be reckoned very fair mountaineering in civilized countries, they would pant over a saddle-back, sidle past a few landslips, and drop through forest at an angle of forty-five onto the road again. Along their track lay the villages of the hillfolk—mud and earth huts, timbers now and then rudely carved with an axe—clinging like swallows' nests against the steeps, huddled on tiny flats half-way down a three-thousand-foot glissade; jammed into a corner between cliffs that funnelled and focused every wandering blast; or, for the sake of summer pasture, cowering down on a neck that in winter would be ten feet deep in snow. And the people—the sallow, greasy, duffle-clad people, with short bare legs and faces almost Esquimaux—would flock out and adore. The Plains—kindly and gentle—had treated the lama as a holy man among holy men. But the Hills worshipped him as one in the confidence of all their devils. Theirs was an almost obliterated Buddhism, overlaid with a nature-worship fantastic as their own landscapes, elaborate as the terracing of their tiny fields; but they recognized the big hat, the clicking rosary, and the rare Chinese texts for great authority; and they respected the man beneath the hat.

"We saw thee come down over the black Breasts of Eua," said a Betah who gave them cheese, sour milk, and stone-hard bread one evening. "We do not use that often—except when calving cows stray in summer. There is a sudden wind among those stones that casts men down on the stillest day. But what should such folk care for the Devil of Eua!"

Then did Kim, aching in every fibre, dizzy with looking down, footsore with cramping desperate toes into inadequate crannies, take joy in the day's march—such joy as a boy of St Xavier's who had won the quarter-mile on the flat might take in the praises of his friends. The hills sweated the ghi and sugar suet off his bones; the dry air, taken sobbingly at the head of cruel passes, firmed and built out his upper ribs; and the tilted levels put new hard muscles into calf and thigh.

They meditated often on the Wheel of Life—the more so since, as the lama said, they were freed from its visible temptations. Except the grey eagle and an occasional far-seen bear grubbing and rooting on the hillside; a vision of a furious painted leopard met at dawn in a still valley devouring a goat; and now and again a bright-coloured bird, they were alone with the winds and the grass singing under the wind. The women of the smoky huts over whose roofs the two walked as they descended the mountains, were unlovely and unclean, wives of many husbands, and afflicted with goitre. The men were woodcutters when they were not farmers—meek, and of an incredible simplicity. But that suitable discourse might not fail, Fate sent them, overtaking and overtaken upon the road, the courteous Dacca physician, who paid for his food in ointments good for goitre and counsels that restore peace between men and women. He seemed to know these hills as well as he knew the hill dialects, and gave the lama the lie of the land towards Ladakh and Tibet. He said they could return to the Plains at any moment. Meantime, for such as loved mountains, yonder road might amuse. This was not all revealed in a breath, but at evening encounters on the stone threshing-floors, when, patients disposed of, the doctor would smoke and the lama snuff, while Kim watched the wee cows grazing on the housetops, or threw his soul after his eyes across the deep blue gulfs between range and range. And there were talks apart in the dark woods, when the doctor would seek herbs, and Kim, as budding physician, must accompany him.

"You see, Mister O'Hara, I do not know what the deuce-an' all I shall do when I find our sporting friends; but if you will kindly keep within sight of my umbrella, which is fine fixed point for cadastral survey, I shall feel much better."

Kim looked out across the jungle of peaks. "This is not my country, hakim. Easier, I think, to find one louse in a bear-skin."

"Oah, thatt is my strong points. There is no hurry for Hurree. They were at Leh not so long ago. They said they had come down from the Karakorum with their heads and horns and all. I am onlee afraid they will have sent back all their letters and compromising things from Leh into Russian territoree. Of course they will walk away as far to the East as possible—just to show that they were never among the Western States. You do not know the Hills?" He scratched with a twig on the earth. "Look! They should have come in by Srinagar or Abbottabad. Thatt is their short road—down the river by Bunji and Astor. But they have made mischief in the West. So"—he drew a furrow from left to right—"they march and they march away East to Leh (ah! it is cold there), and down the Indus to Hanlé (I know that road), and then down, you see, to Bushahr and Chini valley. That is ascertained by process of elimination, and also by asking questions from people that I cure so well. Our friends have been a long time playing about and producing impressions. So they are well known from far off. You will see me catch them somewhere in Chini valley. Please keep your eye on the umbrella."

It nodded like a wind-blown harebell down the valleys and round the mountain sides, and in due time the lama and Kim, who steered by compass, would overhaul it, vending ointments and powders at eventide. "We came by such and such a way!" The lama would throw a careless finger backward at the ridges, and the umbrella would expend itself in compliments.

They crossed a snowy pass in cold moonlight, when the lama, mildly chaffing Kim, went through up to his knees, like a Bactrian camel—the snow-bred, shag-haired sort that came into the Kashmir Serai. They dipped across beds of light snow and snow-powdered shale, where they took refuge from a gale in a camp of Tibetans hurrying down tiny sheep, each laden with a bag of borax. They came out upon grassy shoulders still snow-speckled, and through forest, to grass anew. For all their marchings, Kedarnath and Badrinath were not impressed; and it was only after days of travel that Kim, uplifted upon some insignificant ten-thousand-foot hummock, could see that a shoulder-knot or horn of the two great lords had—ever so slightly—changed outline.

At last they entered a world within a world—a valley of leagues where the high hills were fashioned of a mere rubble and refuse from off the knees of the mountains. Here one day's march carried them no farther, it seemed, than a dreamer's clogged pace bears him in a nightmare. They skirted a shoulder painfully for hours, and, behold, it was but an outlying boss in an outlying buttress of the main pile! A rounded meadow revealed itself, when they had reached it, for a vast tableland running far into the valley. Three days later, it was a dim fold in the earth to southward.

"Surely the Gods live here!" said Kim, beaten down by the silence and the appalling sweep and dispersal of the cloud-shadows after rain. "This is no place for men!"

"Long and long ago," said the lama, as to himself, "it was asked of the Lord whether the world were everlasting. On this the Excellent One returned no answer ... When I was in Ceylon, a wise Seeker confirmed that from the gospel which is written in Pali. Certainly, since we know the way to Freedom, the question were unprofitable, but—look, and know illusion, chela! These—are the true Hills! They are like my hills by Suchzen. Never were such hills!"

Above them, still enormously above them, earth towered away towards the snow-line, where from east to west across hundreds of miles, ruled as with a ruler, the last of the bold birches stopped. Above that, in scarps and blocks upheaved, the rocks strove to fight their heads above the white smother. Above these again, changeless since the world's beginning, but changing to every mood of sun and cloud, lay out the eternal snow. They could see blots and blurs on

its face where storm and wandering wullie-wa got up to dance. Below them, as they stood, the forest slid away in a sheet of blue-green for mile upon mile; below the forest was a village in its sprinkle of terraced fields and steep grazing-grounds. Below the village they knew, though a thunderstorm worried and growled there for the moment, a pitch of twelve or fifteen hundred feet gave to the moist valley where the streams gather that are the mothers of young Sutluj.

As usual, the lama had led Kim by cow-track and by-road, far from the main route along which Hurree Babu, that "fearful man", had bucketed three days before through a storm to which nine Englishmen out of ten would have given full right of way. Hurree was no game-shot—the snick of a trigger made him change colour—but, as he himself would have said, he was "fairly effeecient stalker", and he had raked the huge valley with a pair of cheap binoculars to some purpose. Moreover, the white of worn canvas tents against green carries far. Hurree Babu had seen all he wanted to see when he sat on the threshing-floor of Ziglaur, twenty miles away as the eagle flies, and forty by road—that is to say, two small dots which one day were just below the snow-line, and the next had moved downward perhaps six inches on the hillside. Once cleaned out and set to the work, his fat bare legs could cover a surprising amount of ground, and this was the reason why, while Kim and the lama lay in a leaky hut at Ziglaur till the storm should be over-past, an oily, wet, but always smiling Bengali, talking the best of English with the vilest of phrases, was ingratiating himself with two sodden and rather rheumatic foreigners. He had arrived, revolving many wild schemes, on the heels of a thunderstorm which had split a pine over against their camp, and so convinced a dozen or two forcibly impressed baggage-coolies the day was inauspicious for farther travel that with one accord they had thrown down their loads and jibbed. They were subjects of a Hill Rajah who farmed out their services, as is the custom, for his private gain; and, to add to their personal distresses, the strange Sahibs had already threatened them with rifles. The most of them knew rifles and Sahibs of old: they were trackers and shikarris of the Northern valleys, keen after bear and wild goat; but they had never been thus treated in their lives. So the forest took them to her bosom, and, for all oaths and clamour, refused to restore. There was no need to feign madness or—the Babu had thought of another means of securing a welcome. He wrung out his wet clothes, slipped on his patent-leather shoes, opened the blue-and-white umbrella, and with mincing gait and a heart beating against his tonsils appeared as "agent for His Royal Highness, the Rajah of Rampur, gentlemen. What can I do for you, please?"

The gentlemen were delighted. One was visibly French, the other Russian, but they spoke English not much inferior to the Babu's. They begged his kind offices. Their native servants had gone sick at Leh. They had hurried on because they were anxious to bring the spoils of the chase to Simla ere the skins grew moth-eaten. They bore a general letter of introduction (the Babu salaamed to it orientally) to all Government officials. No, they had not met any other shooting-parties en route. They did for themselves. They had plenty of supplies. They only wished to push on as soon as might be. At this he waylaid a cowering hillman among the trees, and after three minutes' talk and a little silver (one cannot be economical upon State service, though Hurree's heart bled at the waste) the eleven coolies and the three hangers-on reappeared. At least the Babu would be a witness to their oppression.

"My royal master, he will be much annoyed, but these people are onlee common people and grossly ignorant. If your honours will kindly overlook unfortunate affair, I shall be much pleased. In a little while rain will stop and we can then proceed. You have been shooting, eh? That is fine performance!"

He skipped nimbly from one kilta to the next, making pretence to adjust each conical basket. The Englishman is not, as a rule, familiar with the Asiatic, but he would not strike across the wrist a kindly Babu who had accidentally upset a kilta with a red oilskin top. On the other hand, he would not press drink upon a Babu were he never so friendly, nor would he invite him to

meat. The strangers did all these things, and asked many questions—about women mostly—to which Hurree returned gay and unstudied answers. They gave him a glass of whitish fluid like to gin, and then more; and in a little time his gravity departed from him. He became thickly treasonous, and spoke in terms of sweeping indecency of a Government which had forced upon him a white man's education and neglected to supply him with a white man's salary. He babbled tales of oppression and wrong till the tears ran down his cheeks for the miseries of his land. Then he staggered off, singing love-songs of Lower Bengal, and collapsed upon a wet tree-trunk. Never was so unfortunate a product of English rule in India more unhappily thrust upon aliens.

"They are all just of that pattern," said one sportsman to the other in French. "When we get into India proper thou wilt see. I should like to visit his Rajah. One might speak the good word there. It is possible that he has heard of us and wishes to signify his good-will."

"We have not time. We must get into Simla as soon as may be," his companion replied. "For my own part, I wish our reports had been sent back from Hilás, or even Leh."

"The English post is better and safer. Remember we are given all facilities—and Name of God!—they give them to us too! Is it unbelievable stupidity?"

"It is pride—pride that deserves and will receive punishment."

"Yes! To fight a fellow-Continental in our game is something. There is a risk attached, but these people—bah! It is too easy."

"Pride—all pride, my friend."

"Now what the deuce is good of Chandernagore being so close to Calcutta and all," said Hurree, snoring open-mouthed on the sodden moss, "if I cannot understand their French? They talk so particularly fast! It would have been much better to cut their beastly throats."

When he presented himself again he was racked with a headache—penitent, and volubly afraid that in his drunkenness he might have been indiscreet. He loved the British Government—it was the source of all prosperity and honour, and his master at Rampur held the very same opinion. Upon this the men began to deride him and to quote past words, till step by step, with deprecating smirks, oily grins, and leers of infinite cunning, the poor Babu was beaten out of his defences and forced to speak—truth. When Lurgan was told the tale later, he mourned aloud that he could not have been in the place of the stubborn, inattentive coolies, who with grass mats over their heads and the raindrops puddling in their footprints, waited on the weather. All the Sahibs of their acquaintance—rough-clad men joyously returning year after year to their chosen gullies—had servants and cooks and orderlies, very often hillmen. These Sahibs travelled without any retinue. Therefore they were poor Sahibs, and ignorant; for no Sahib in his senses would follow a Bengali's advice. But the Bengali, appearing from somewhere, had given them money, and could make shift with their dialect. Used to comprehensive ill-treatment from their own colour, they suspected a trap somewhere, and stood by to run if occasion offered.

Then through the new-washed air, steaming with delicious earth-smells, the Babu led the way down the slopes—walking ahead of the coolies in pride; walking behind the foreigners in humility. His thoughts were many and various. The least of them would have interested his companions beyond words. But he was an agreeable guide, ever keen to point out the beauties of his royal master's domain. He peopled the hills with anything they had a mind to slay—thar, ibex, or markhor, and bear by Elisha's allowance. He discoursed of botany and ethnology with unimpeachable inaccuracy, and his store of local legends—he had been a trusted agent of the State for fifteen years, remember—was inexhaustible.

"Decidedly this fellow is an original," said the taller of the two foreigners. "He is like the nightmare of a Viennese courier."

"He represents in petto India in transition—the monstrous hybridism of East and West," the Russian replied. "It is we who can deal with Orientals."

"He has lost his own country and has not acquired any other. But he has a most complete hatred of his conquerors. Listen. He confided to me last night," said the other.

Under the striped umbrella Hurree Babu was straining ear and brain to follow the quick-poured French, and keeping both eyes on a kilta full of maps and documents—an extra-large one with a double red oil-skin cover. He did not wish to steal anything. He only desired to know what to steal, and, incidentally, how to get away when he had stolen it. He thanked all the Gods of Hindustan, and Herbert Spencer, that there remained some valuables to steal.

On the second day the road rose steeply to a grass spur above the forest; and it was here, about sunset, that they came across an aged lama—but they called him a bonze—sitting cross-legged above a mysterious chart held down by stones, which he was explaining to a young man, evidently a neophyte, of singular, though unwashen, beauty. The striped umbrella had been sighted half a march away, and Kim had suggested a halt till it came up to them.

"Ha!" said Hurree Babu, resourceful as Puss-in-Boots. "That is eminent local holy man. Probably subject of my royal master."

"What is he doing? It is very curious."

"He is expounding holy picture—all hand-worked."

The two men stood bareheaded in the wash of the afternoon sunlight low across the gold-coloured grass. The sullen coolies, glad of the check, halted and slid down their loads.

"Look!" said the Frenchman. "It is like a picture for the birth of a religion—the first teacher and the first disciple. Is he a Buddhist?"

"Of some debased kind," the other answered. "There are no true Buddhists among the Hills. But look at the folds of the drapery. Look at his eyes—how insolent! Why does this make one feel that we are so young a people?" The speaker struck passionately at a tall weed. "We have nowhere left our mark yet. Nowhere! That, do you understand, is what disquiets me." He scowled at the placid face, and the monumental calm of the pose.

"Have patience. We shall make your mark together—we and you young people. Meantime, draw his picture."

The Babu advanced loftily; his back out of all keeping with his deferential speech, or his wink towards Kim.

"Holy One, these be Sahibs. My medicines cured one of a flux, and I go into Simla to oversee his recovery. They wish to see thy picture—"

"To heal the sick is always good. This is the Wheel of Life," said the lama, "the same I showed thee in the hut at Ziglaur when the rain fell."

"And to hear thee expound it."

The lama's eyes lighted at the prospect of new listeners. "To expound the Most Excellent Way

is good. Have they any knowledge of Hindi, such as had the Keeper of Images?"

"A little, maybe."

Hereat, simply as a child engrossed with a new game, the lama threw back his head and began the full-throated invocation of the Doctor of Divinity ere he opens the full doctrine. The strangers leaned on their alpenstocks and listened. Kim, squatting humbly, watched the red sunlight on their faces, and the blend and parting of their long shadows. They wore un-English leggings and curious girt-in belts that reminded him hazily of the pictures in a book in St Xavier's library 'The Adventures of a Young Naturalist in Mexico' was its name. Yes, they looked very like the wonderful M. Sumichrast of that tale, and very unlike the "highly unscrupulous folk" of Hurree Babu's imagining. The coolies, earth-coloured and mute, crouched reverently some twenty or thirty yards away, and the Babu, the slack of his thin gear snapping like a marking-flag in the chill breeze, stood by with an air of happy proprietorship.

"These are the men," Hurree whispered, as the ritual went on and the two whites followed the grass-blade sweeping from Hell to Heaven and back again. "All their books are in the large kilta with the reddish top—books and reports and maps—and I have seen a King's letter that either Hilás or Bunár has written. They guard it most carefully. They have sent nothing back from Hilás or Leh. That is sure."

"Who is with them?"

"Only the beegar-coolies. They have no servants. They are so close they cook their own food."

"But what am I to do?"

"Wait and see. Only if any chance comes to me thou wilt know where to seek for the papers."

"This were better in Mahbub Ali's hands than a Bengali's," said Kim scornfully.

"There are more ways of getting to a sweetheart than butting down a wall."

"See here the Hell appointed for avarice and greed. Flanked upon the one side by Desire and on the other by Weariness." The lama warmed to his work, and one of the strangers sketched him in the quick-fading light.

"That is enough," the man said at last brusquely. "I cannot understand him, but I want that picture. He is a better artist than I. Ask him if he will sell it."

"He says 'No, sar,'" the Babu replied. The lama, of course, would no more have parted with his chart to a casual wayfarer than an archbishop would pawn the holy vessels of his cathedral. All Tibet is full of cheap reproductions of the Wheel; but the lama was an artist, as well as a wealthy Abbot in his own place.

"Perhaps in three days, or four, or ten, if I perceive that the Sahib is a Seeker and of good understanding, I may myself draw him another. But this was used for the initiation of a novice. Tell him so, hakim."

"He wishes it now—for money."

The lama shook his head slowly and began to fold up the Wheel. The Russian, on his side, saw no more than an unclean old man haggling over a dirty piece of paper. He drew out a handful of rupees, and snatched half-jestingly at the chart, which tore in the lama's grip. A low murmur of horror went up from the coolies—some of whom were Spiti men and, by their lights, good

Buddhists. The lama rose at the insult; his hand went to the heavy iron pencase that is the priest's weapon, and the Babu danced in agony.

"Now you see—you see why I wanted witnesses. They are highly unscrupulous people. Oh, sar! sar! You must not hit holyman!"

"Chela! He has defiled the Written Word!"

It was too late. Before Kim could ward him off, the Russian struck the old man full on the face. Next instant he was rolling over and over downhill with Kim at his throat. The blow had waked every unknown Irish devil in the boy's blood, and the sudden fall of his enemy did the rest. The lama dropped to his knees, half-stunned; the coolies under their loads fled up the hill as fast as plainsmen run aross the level. They had seen sacrilege unspeakable, and it behoved them to get away before the Gods and devils of the hills took vengeance. The Frenchman ran towards the lama, fumbling at his revolver with some notion of making him a hostage for his companion. A shower of cutting stones—hillmen are very straight shots—drove him away, and a coolie from Ao-chung snatched the lama into the stampede. All came about as swiftly as the sudden mountain-darkness.

"They have taken the baggage and all the guns," yelled the Frenchman, firing blindly into the twilight.

"All right, sar! All right! Don't shoot. I go to rescue," and Hurree, pounding down the slope, cast himself bodily upon the delighted and astonished Kim, who was banging his breathless foe's head against a boulder.

"Go back to the coolies," whispered the Babu in his ear. "They have the baggage. The papers are in the kilta with the red top, but look through all. Take their papers, and specially the murasla (King's letter). Go! The other man comes!"

Kim tore uphill. A revolver-bullet rang on a rock by his side, and he cowered partridge-wise.

"If you shoot," shouted Hurree, "they will descend and annihilate us. I have rescued the gentleman, sar. This is particularly dangerous."

"By Jove!" Kim was thinking hard in English. "This is dam'-tight place, but I think it is self-defence." He felt in his bosom for Mahbub's gift, and uncertainly—save for a few practice shots in the Bikanir desert, he had never used the little gun—pulled the trigger.

"What did I say, sar!" The Babu seemed to be in tears. "Come down here and assist to resuscitate. We are all up a tree, I tell you."

The shots ceased. There was a sound of stumbling feet, and Kim hurried upward through the gloom, swearing like a cat—or a country-bred.

"Did they wound thee, chela?" called the lama above him.

"No. And thou?" He dived into a clump of stunted firs.

"Unhurt. Come away. We go with these folk to Shamlegh-under-the-Snow."

"But not before we have done justice," a voice cried. "I have got the Sahibs' guns—all four. Let us go down."

"He struck the Holy One—we saw it! Our cattle will be barren—our wives will cease to bear!

The snows will slide upon us as we go home... Atop of all other oppression too!"

The little fir-clump filled with clamouring coolies—panic-stricken, and in their terror capable of anything. The man from Ao-chung clicked the breech-bolt of his gun impatiently, and made as to go downhill.

"Wait a little, Holy One; they cannot go far. Wait till I return," said he.

"It is this person who has suffered wrong," said the lama, his hand over his brow.

"For that very reason," was the reply.

"If this person overlooks it, your hands are clean. Moreover, ye acquire merit by obedience."

"Wait, and we will all go to Shamlegh together," the man insisted.

For a moment, for just so long as it needs to stuff a cartridge into a breech-loader, the lama hesitated. Then he rose to his feet, and laid a finger on the man's shoulder.

"Hast thou heard? I say there shall be no killing—I who was Abbot of Such-zen. Is it any lust of thine to be re-born as a rat, or a snake under the eaves—a worm in the belly of the most mean beast? Is it thy wish to—"

The man from Ao-chung fell to his knees, for the voice boomed like a Tibetan devil-gong.

"Ai! ai!" cried the Spiti men. "Do not curse us—do not curse him. It was but his zeal, Holy One! ... Put down the rifle, fool!"

"Anger on anger! Evil on evil! There will be no killing. Let the priest-beaters go in bondage to their own acts. Just and sure is the Wheel, swerving not a hair! They will be born many times—in torment." His head drooped, and he leaned heavily on Kim's shoulder.

"I have come near to great evil, chela," he whispered in that dead hush under the pines. "I was tempted to loose the bullet; and truly, in Tibet there would have been a heavy and a slow death for them ... He struck me across the face ... upon the flesh ..." He slid to the ground, breathing heavily, and Kim could hear the over-driven heart bump and check.

"Have they hurt him to the death?" said the Ao-chung man, while the others stood mute.

Kim knelt over the body in deadly fear. "Nay," he cried passionately, "this is only a weakness." Then he remembered that he was a white man, with a white man's camp-fittings at his service. "Open the kiltas! The Sahibs may have a medicine."

"Oho! Then I know it," said the Ao-chung man with a laugh. "Not for five years was I Yankling Sahib's shikarri without knowing that medicine. I too have tasted it. Behold!"

He drew from his breast a bottle of cheap whisky—such as is sold to explorers at Leh—and cleverly forced a little between the lama's teeth.

"So I did when Yankling Sahib twisted his foot beyond Astor. Aha! I have already looked into their baskets—but we will make fair division at Shamlegh. Give him a little more. It is good medicine. Feel! His heart goes better now. Lay his head down and rub a little on the chest. If he had waited quietly while I accounted for the Sahibs this would never have come. But perhaps the Sahibs may chase us here. Then it would not be wrong to shoot them with their own guns, heh?"

"One is paid, I think, already," said Kim between his teeth. "I kicked him in the groin as we went downhill. Would I had killed him!"

"It is well to be brave when one does not live in Rampur," said one whose hut lay within a few miles of the Rajah's rickety palace. "If we get a bad name among the Sahibs, none will employ us as shikarris any more."

"Oh, but these are not Angrezi Sahibs—not merry-minded men like Fostum Sahib or Yankling Sahib. They are foreigners—they cannot speak Angrezi as do Sahibs."

Here the lama coughed and sat up, groping for the rosary.

"There shall be no killing," he murmured. "Just is the Wheel! Evil on evil—"

"Nay, Holy One. We are all here." The Ao-chung man timidly patted his feet. "Except by thy order, no one shall be slain. Rest awhile. We will make a little camp here, and later, as the moon rises, we go to Shamlegh-under-the-Snow."

"After a blow," said a Spiti man sententiously, "it is best to sleep."

"There is, as it were, a dizziness at the back of my neck, and a pinching in it. Let me lay my head on thy lap, chela. I am an old man, but not free from passion ... We must think of the Cause of Things."

"Give him a blanket. We dare not light a fire lest the Sahibs see."

"Better get away to Shamlegh. None will follow us to Shamlegh."

This was the nervous Rampur man.

"I have been Fostum Sahib's shikarri, and I am Yankling Sahib's shikarri. I should have been with Yankling Sahib now but for this cursed beegar (the corvée). Let two men watch below with the guns lest the Sahibs do more foolishness. I shall not leave this Holy One."

They sat down a little apart from the lama, and, after listening awhile, passed round a water-pipe whose receiver was an old Day and Martin blacking-bottle. The glow of the red charcoal as it went from hand to hand lit up the narrow, blinking eyes, the high Chinese cheek-bones, and the bull-throats that melted away into the dark duffle folds round the shoulders. They looked like kobolds from some magic mine—gnomes of the hills in conclave. And while they talked, the voices of the snow-waters round them diminished one by one as the night-frost choked and clogged the runnels.

"How he stood up against us!" said a Spiti man admiring. "I remember an old ibex, out Ladakh-way, that Dupont Sahib missed on a shoulder-shot, seven seasons back, standing up just like him. Dupont Sahib was a good shikarri."

"Not as good as Yankling Sahib." The Ao-chung man took a pull at the whisky-bottle and passed it over. "Now hear me—unless any other man thinks he knows more."

The challenge was not taken up.

"We go to Shamlegh when the moon rises. There we will fairly divide the baggage between us. I am content with this new little rifle and all its cartridges."

"Are the bears only bad on thy holding? said a mate, sucking at the pipe.

"No; but musk-pods are worth six rupees apiece now, and thy women can have the canvas of the tents and some of the cooking-gear. We will do all that at Shamlegh before dawn. Then we all go our ways, remembering that we have never seen or taken service with these Sahibs, who may, indeed, say that we have stolen their baggage."

"That is well for thee, but what will our Rajah say?"

"Who is to tell him? Those Sahibs, who cannot speak our talk, or the Babu, who for his own ends gave us money? Will he lead an army against us? What evidence will remain? That we do not need we shall throw on Shamlegh-midden, where no man has yet set foot."

"Who is at Shamlegh this summer?" The place was only a grazing centre of three or four huts."

"The Woman of Shamlegh. She has no love for Sahibs, as we know. The others can be pleased with little presents; and here is enough for us all." He patted the fat sides of the nearest basket.

"But—but—"

"I have said they are not true Sahibs. All their skins and heads were bought in the bazar at Leh. I know the marks. I showed them to ye last march."

"True. They were all bought skins and heads. Some had even the moth in them."

That was a shrewd argument, and the Ao-chung man knew his fellows.

"If the worst comes to the worst, I shall tell Yankling Sahib, who is a man of a merry mind, and he will laugh. We are not doing any wrong to any Sahibs whom we know. They are priest-beaters. They frightened us. We fled! Who knows where we dropped the baggage? Do ye think Yankling Sahib will permit down-country police to wander all over the hills, disturbing his game? It is a far cry from Simla to Chini, and farther from Shamlegh to Shamlegh-midden."

"So be it, but I carry the big kilta. The basket with the red top that the Sahibs pack themselves every morning."

"Thus it is proved," said the Shamlegh man adroitly, "that they are Sahibs of no account. Who ever heard of Fostum Sahib, or Yankling Sahib, or even the little Peel Sahib that sits up of nights to shoot serow—I say, who, ever heard of these Sahibs coming into the hills without a down-country cook, and a bearer, and—and all manner of well-paid, high-handed and oppressive folk in their tail? How can they make trouble? What of the kilta?"

"Nothing, but that it is full of the Written Word—books and papers in which they wrote, and strange instruments, as of worship."

"Shamlegh-midden will take them all."

"True! But how if we insult the Sahibs' Gods thereby! I do not like to handle the Written Word in that fashion. And their brass idols are beyond my comprehension. It is no plunder for simple hill-folk."

"The old man still sleeps. Hst! We will ask his chela." The Ao-chung man refreshed himself, and swelled with pride of leadership.

"We have here," he whispered, "a kilta whose nature we do not know."

"But I do," said Kim cautiously. The lama drew breath in natural, easy sleep, and Kim had been

thinking of Hurree's last words. As a player of the Great Game, he was disposed just then to reverence the Babu. "It is a kilta with a red top full of very wonderful things, not to be handled by fools."

"I said it; I said it," cried the bearer of that burden. "Thinkest thou it will betray us?"

"Not if it be given to me. I can draw out its magic. Otherwise it will do great harm."

"A priest always takes his share." Whisky was demoralizing the Ao-chung man.

"It is no matter to me." Kim answered, with the craft of his mother-country. "Share it among you, and see what comes!"

"Not I. I was only jesting. Give the order. There is more than enough for us all. We go our way from Shamlegh in the dawn."

They arranged and re-arranged their artless little plans for another hour, while Kim shivered with cold and pride. The humour of the situation tickled the Irish and the Oriental in his soul. Here were the emissaries of the dread Power of the North, very possibly as great in their own land as Mahbub or Colonel Creighton, suddenly smitten helpless. One of them, he privately knew, would be lame for a time. They had made promises to Kings. Tonight they lay out somewhere below him, chartless, foodless, tentless, gunless—except for Hurree Babu, guideless. And this collapse of their Great Game (Kim wondered to whom they would report it), this panicky bolt into the night, had come about through no craft of Hurree's or contrivance of Kim's, but simply, beautifully, and inevitably as the capture of Mahbub's faquir-friends by the zealous young policeman at Umballa.

"They are there—with nothing; and, by Jove, it is cold! I am here with all their things. Oh, they will be angry! I am sorry for Hurree Babu."

Kim might have saved his pity, for though at that moment the Bengali suffered acutely in the flesh, his soul was puffed and lofty. A mile down the hill, on the edge of the pine-forest, two half-frozen men—one powerfully sick at intervals—were varying mutual recriminations with the most poignant abuse of the Babu, who seemed distraught with terror. They demanded a plan of action. He explained that they were very lucky to be alive; that their coolies, if not then stalking them, had passed beyond recall; that the Rajah, his master, was ninety miles away, and, so far from lending them money and a retinue for the Simla journey, would surely cast them into prison if he heard that they had hit a priest. He enlarged on this sin and its consequences till they bade him change the subject. Their one hope, said he, was unostentatious flight from village to village till they reached civilization; and, for the hundredth time dissolved in tears, he demanded of the high stars why the Sahibs "had beaten holy man".

Ten steps would have taken Hurree into the creaking gloom utterly beyond their reach—to the shelter and food of the nearest village, where glib-tongued doctors were scarce. But he preferred to endure cold, belly-pinch, bad words, and occasional blows in the company of his honoured employers. Crouched against a tree-trunk, he sniffed dolefully.

"And have you thought," said the uninjured man hotly, "what sort of spectacle we shall present wandering through these hills among these aborigines?"

Hurree Babu had thought of little else for some hours, but the remark was not to his address.

"We cannot wander! I can hardly walk," groaned Kim's victim.

"Perhaps the holy man will be merciful in loving-kindness, sar, otherwise—"

"I promise myself a peculiar pleasure in emptying my revolver into that young bonze when next we meet," was the unchristian answer.

"Revolvers! Vengeance! Bonzes!" Hurree crouched lower. The war was breaking out afresh. "Have you no consideration for our loss? The baggage! The baggage!" He could hear the speaker literally dancing on the grass. "Everything we bore! Everything we have secured! Our gains! Eight months' work! Do you know what that means? 'Decidedly it is we who can deal with Orientals!' Oh, you have done well."

They fell to it in several tongues, and Hurree smiled. Kim was with the kiltas, and in the kiltas lay eight months of good diplomacy. There was no means of communicating with the boy, but he could be trusted. For the rest, Hurree could so stage-manage the journey through the hills that Hilás, Bunár, and four hundred miles of hill-roads should tell the tale for a generation. Men who cannot control their own coolies are little respected in the Hills, and the hillman has a very keen sense of humour.

"If I had done it myself," thought Hurree, "it would not have been better; and, by Jove, now I think of it, of course I arranged it myself. How quick I have been! Just when I ran downhill I thought it! Thee outrage was accidental, but onlee me could have worked it—ah—for all it was dam'-well worth. Consider the moral effect upon these ignorant peoples! No treaties— no papers—no written documents at all—and me to interpret for them. How I shall laugh with the Colonel! I wish I had their papers also: but you cannot occupy two places in space simultaneously. Thatt is axiomatic."

CHAPTER XIV

My brother kneels (so saith Kabir)
To stone and brass in heathen wise,
But in my brother's voice I hear
My own unanswered agonies.
His God is as his Fates assign—
His prayer is all the world's—and mine.

KABIR.

At moonrise the cautious coolies got under way. The lama, refreshed by his sleep and the spirit, needed no more than Kim's shoulder to bear him along—a silent, swift-striding man. They held the shale-sprinkled grass for an hour, swept round the shoulder of an immortal cliff, and climbed into a new country entirely blocked off from all sight of Chini valley. A huge pasture-ground ran up fan-shaped to the living snow. At its base was perhaps half an acre of flat land, on which stood a few soil and timber huts. Behind them—for, hill-fashion, they were perched on the edge of all things—the ground fell sheer two thousand feet to Shamlegh-midden, where never yet man has set foot.

The men made no motion to divide the plunder till they had seen the lama bedded down in the best room of the place, with Kim shampooing his feet, Mohammedan-fashion.

"We will send food," said the Ao-chung man, "and the red-topped kilta. By dawn there will be none to give evidence, one way or the other. If anything is not needed in the kilta—see here!"

He pointed through the window—opening into space that was filled with moonlight reflected from the snow—and threw out an empty whisky-bottle.

"No need to listen for the fall. This is the world's end," he said, and went out. The lama looked forth, a hand on either sill, with eyes that shone like yellow opals. From the enormous pit before him white peaks lifted themselves yearning to the moonlight. The rest was as the darkness of interstellar space.

"These," he said slowly, "are indeed my Hills. Thus should a man abide, perched above the world, separated from delights, considering vast matters."

"Yes; if he has a chela to prepare tea for him, and to fold a blanket for his head, and to chase out calving cows."

A smoky lamp burned in a niche, but the full moonlight beat it down; and by the mixed light, stooping above the food-bag and cups, Kim moved like a tall ghost.

"Ai! But now I have let the blood cool, my head still beats and drums, and there is a cord round the back of my neck."

"No wonder. It was a strong blow. May he who dealt it—"

"But for my own passions there would have been no evil."

"What evil? Thou hast saved the Sahibs from the death they deserved a hundred times."

"The lesson is not well learnt, chela." The lama came to rest on a folded blanket, as Kim went

forward with his evening routine. "The blow was but a shadow upon a shadow. Evil in itself—my legs weary apace these latter days!—it met evil in me: anger, rage, and a lust to return evil. These wrought in my blood, woke tumult in my stomach, and dazzled my ears." Here he drank scalding black-tea ceremonially, taking the hot cup from Kim's hand. "Had I been passionless, the evil blow would have done only bodily evil—a scar, or a bruise—which is illusion. But my mind was not abstracted, for rushed in straightway a lust to let the Spiti men kill. In fighting that lust, my soul was torn and wrenched beyond a thousand blows. Not till I had repeated the Blessings" (he meant the Buddhist Beatitudes) "did I achieve calm. But the evil planted in me by that moment's carelessness works out to its end. Just is the Wheel, swerving not a hair! Learn the lesson, chela."

"It is too high for me," Kim muttered. "I am still all shaken. I am glad I hurt the man."

"I felt that, sleeping upon thy knees, in the wood below. It disquieted me in my dreams—the evil in thy soul working through to mine. Yet on the other hand"—he loosed his rosary—"I have acquired merit by saving two lives—the lives of those that wronged me. Now I must see into the Cause of Things. The boat of my soul staggers."

"Sleep, and be strong. That is wisest."

"I meditate. There is a need greater than thou knowest."

Till the dawn, hour after hour, as the moonlight paled on the high peaks, and that which had been belted blackness on the sides of the far hills showed as tender green forest, the lama stared fixedly at the wall. From time to time he groaned. Outside the barred door, where discomfited kine came to ask for their old stable, Shamlegh and the coolies gave itself up to plunder and riotous living. The Ao-chung man was their leader, and once they had opened the Sahibs' tinned foods and found that they were very good they dared not turn back. Shamlegh kitchen-midden took the dunnage.

When Kim, after a night of bad dreams, stole forth to brush his teeth in the morning chill, a fair-coloured woman with turquoise-studded headgear drew him aside.

"The others have gone. They left thee this kilta as the promise was. I do not love Sahibs, but thou wilt make us a charm in return for it. We do not wish little Shamlegh to get a bad name on account of the—accident. I am the Woman of Shamlegh." She looked him over with bold, bright eyes, unlike the usual furtive glance of hillwomen.

"Assuredly. But it must be done in secret."

She raised the heavy kilta like a toy and slung it into her own hut.

"Out and bar the door! Let none come near till it is finished," said Kim.

"But afterwards—we may talk?"

Kim tilted the kilta on the floor—a cascade of Survey-instruments, books, diaries, letters, maps, and queerly scented native correspondence. At the very bottom was an embroidered bag covering a sealed, gilded, and illuminated document such as one King sends to another. Kim caught his breath with delight, and reviewed the situation from a Sahib's point of view.

"The books I do not want. Besides, they are logarithms—Survey, I suppose." He laid them aside. "The letters I do not understand, but Colonel Creighton will. They must all be kept. The maps—they draw better maps than me—of course. All the native letters—oho!—and particularly the murasla." He sniffed the embroidered bag. "That must be from Hilás or Bunár,

and Hurree Babu spoke truth. By Jove! It is a fine haul. I wish Hurree could know ... The rest must go out of the window." He fingered a superb prismatic compass and the shiny top of a theodolite. But after all, a Sahib cannot very well steal, and the things might be inconvenient evidence later. He sorted out every scrap of manuscript, every map, and the native letters. They made one softish slab. The three locked ferril-backed books, with five worn pocket-books, he put aside.

"The letters and the murasla I must carry inside my coat and under my belt, and the hand-written books I must put into the food-bag. It will be very heavy. No. I do not think there is anything more. If there is, the coolies have thrown it down the khud, so thatt is all right. Now you go too." He repacked the kilta with all he meant to lose, and hove it up on to the windowsill. A thousand feet below lay a long, lazy, round-shouldered bank of mist, as yet untouched by the morning sun. A thousand feet below that was a hundred-year-old pine-forest. He could see the green tops looking like a bed of moss when a wind-eddy thinned the cloud.

"No! I don't think any one will go after you!"

The wheeling basket vomited its contents as it dropped. The theodolite hit a jutting cliff-ledge and exploded like a shell; the books, inkstands, paint-boxes, compasses, and rulers showed for a few seconds like a swarm of bees. Then they vanished; and, though Kim, hanging half out of the window, strained his young ears, never a sound came up from the gulf.

"Five hundred—a thousand rupees could not buy them," he thought sorrowfully. "It was verree wasteful, but I have all their other stuff—everything they did—I hope. Now how the deuce am I to tell Hurree Babu, and whatt the deuce am I to do? And my old man is sick. I must tie up the letters in oilskin. That is something to do first—else they will get all sweated ... And I am all alone!" He bound them into a neat packet, swedging down the stiff, sticky oilskin at the comers, for his roving life had made him as methodical as an old hunter in matters of the road. Then with double care he packed away the books at the bottom of the food-bag.

The woman rapped at the door.

"But thou hast made no charm," she said, looking about.

"There is no need." Kim had completely overlooked the necessity for a little patter-talk. The woman laughed at his confusion irreverently.

"None—for thee. Thou canst cast a spell by the mere winking of an eye. But think of us poor people when thou art gone. They were all too drunk last night to hear a woman. Thou art not drunk?"

"I am a priest." Kim had recovered himself, and, the woman being aught but unlovely, thought best to stand on his office.

"I warned them that the Sahibs will be angry and will make an inquisition and a report to the Rajah. There is also the Babu with them. Clerks have long tongues."

"Is that all thy trouble?" The plan rose fully formed in Kim's mind, and he smiled ravishingly.

"Not all," quoth the woman, putting out a hard brown hand all covered with turquoises set in silver.

"I can finish that in a breath," he went on quickly. "The Babu is the very hakim (thou hast heard of him?) who was wandering among the hills by Ziglaur. I know him."

"He will tell for the sake of a reward. Sahibs cannot distinguish one hillman from another, but Babus have eyes for men—and women."

"Carry a word to him from me."

"There is nothing I would not do for thee."

He accepted the compliment calmly, as men must in lands where women make the love, tore a leaf from a note-book, and with a patent indelible pencil wrote in gross Shikast—the script that bad little boys use when they write dirt on walls: "I have everything that they have written: their pictures of the country, and many letters. Especially the murasla. Tell me what to do. I am at Shamlegh-under-the-Snow. The old man is sick."

"Take this to him. It will altogether shut his mouth. He cannot have gone far."

"Indeed no. They are still in the forest across the spur. Our children went to watch them when the light came, and have cried the news as they moved."

Kim looked his astonishment; but from the edge of the sheep-pasture floated a shrill, kite-like trill. A child tending cattle had picked it up from a brother or sister on the far side of the slope that commanded Chini valley.

"My husbands are also out there gathering wood." She drew a handful of walnuts from her bosom, split one neatly, and began to eat. Kim affected blank ignorance.

"Dost thou not know the meaning of the walnut—priest?" she said coyly, and handed him the half-shells.

"Well thought of." He slipped the piece of paper between them quickly. "Hast thou a little wax to close them on this letter?"

The woman sighed aloud, and Kim relented.

"There is no payment till service has been rendered. Carry this to the Babu, and say it was sent by the Son of the Charm."

"Ai! Truly! Truly! By a magician—who is like a Sahib."

"Nay, a Son of the Charm: and ask if there be any answer."

"But if he offer a rudeness? I—I am afraid."

Kim laughed. "He is, I have no doubt, very tired and very hungry. The Hills make cold bedfellows. Hai, my"—it was on the tip of his tongue to say Mother, but he turned it to Sister— "thou art a wise and witty woman. By this time all the villages know what has befallen the Sahibs—eh?"

"True. News was at Ziglaur by midnight, and by tomorrow should be at Kotgarh. The villages are both afraid and angry."

"No need. Tell the villages to feed the Sahibs and pass them on, in peace. We must get them quietly away from our valleys. To steal is one thing—to kill another. The Babu will understand, and there will be no after-complaints. Be swift. I must tend my master when he wakes."

"So be it. After service—thou hast said?—comes the reward. I am the Woman of Shamlegh, and I hold from the Rajah. I am no common bearer of babes. Shamlegh is thine: hoof and horn

[270] RUDYARD KIPLING

and hide, milk and butter. Take or leave."

She turned resolutely uphill, her silver necklaces clicking on her broad breast, to meet the morning sun fifteen hundred feet above them. This time Kim thought in the vernacular as he waxed down the oilskin edges of the packets.

"How can a man follow the Way or the Great Game when he is so—always pestered by women? There was that girl at Akrola of the Ford; and there was the scullion's wife behind the dovecot—not counting the others—and now comes this one! When I was a child it was well enough, but now I am a man and they will not regard me as a man. Walnuts, indeed! Ho! ho! It is almonds in the Plains!"

He went out to levy on the village—not with a begging-bowl, which might do for down-country, but in the manner of a prince. Shamlegh's summer population is only three families—four women and eight or nine men. They were all full of tinned meats and mixed drinks, from ammoniated quinine to white vodka, for they had taken their full share in the overnight loot. The neat Continental tents had been cut up and shared long ago, and there were patent aluminium saucepans abroad.

But they considered the lama's presence a perfect safeguard against all consequences, and impenitently brought Kim of their best—even to a drink of chang—the barley-beer that comes from Ladakh-way. Then they thawed out in the sun, and sat with their legs hanging over infinite abysses, chattering, laughing, and smoking. They judged India and its Government solely from their experience of wandering Sahibs who had employed them or their friends as shikarris. Kim heard tales of shots missed upon ibex, serow, or markhor, by Sahibs twenty years in their graves—every detail lighted from behind like twigs on tree-tops seen against lightning. They told him of their little diseases, and, more important, the diseases of their tiny, sure-footed cattle; of trips as far as Kotgarh, where the strange missionaries live, and beyond even to marvellous Simla, where the streets are paved with silver, and anyone, look you, can get service with the Sahibs, who ride about in two-wheeled carts and spend money with a spade. Presently, grave and aloof, walking very heavily, the lama joined himself to the chatter under the eaves, and they gave him great room. The thin air refreshed him, and he sat on the edge of precipices with the best of them, and, when talk languished, flung pebbles into the void. Thirty miles away, as the eagle flies, lay the next range, seamed and channelled and pitted with little patches of brush—forests, each a day's dark march. Behind the village, Shamlegh hill itself cut off all view to southward. It was like sitting in a swallow's nest under the eaves of the roof of the world.

From time to time the lama stretched out his hand, and with a little low-voiced prompting would point out the road to Spiti and north across the Parungla.

"Beyond, where the hills lie thickest, lies De-ch'en" (he meant Han-lé'), "the great Monastery. s'Tag-stan-ras-ch'en built it, and of him there runs this tale." Whereupon he told it: a fantastic piled narrative of bewitchment and miracles that set Shamlegh a-gasping. Turning west a little, he steered for the green hills of Kulu, and sought Kailung under the glaciers. "For thither came I in the old, old days. From Leh I came, over the Baralachi."

"Yes, yes; we know it," said the far-faring people of Shamlegh.

"And I slept two nights with the priests of Kailung. These are the Hills of my delight! Shadows blessed above all other shadows! There my eyes opened on this world; there my eyes were opened to this world; there I found Enlightenment; and there I girt my loins for my Search. Out of the Hills I came—the high Hills and the strong winds. Oh, just is the Wheel!" He blessed them in detail—the great glaciers, the naked rocks, the piled moraines and tumbled shale; dry upland, hidden salt-lake, age-old timber and fruitful water-shot valley one after the other, as a

dying man blesses his folk; and Kim marvelled at his passion.

"Yes—yes. There is no place like our Hills," said the people of Shamlegh. And they fell to wondering how a man could live in the hot terrible Plains where the cattle run as big as elephants, unfit to plough on a hillside; where village touches village, they had heard, for a hundred miles; where folk went about stealing in gangs, and what the robbers spared the Police carried utterly away.

So the still forenoon wore through, and at the end of it Kim's messenger dropped from the steep pasture as unbreathed as when she had set out.

"I sent a word to the hakim," Kim explained, while she made reverence.

"He joined himself to the idolaters? Nay, I remember he did a healing upon one of them. He has acquired merit, though the healed employed his strength for evil. Just is the Wheel! What of the hakim?"

"I feared that thou hadst been bruised and—and I knew he was wise." Kim took the waxed walnut-shell and read in English on the back of his note: Your favour received. Cannot get away from present company at present, but shall take them into Simla. After which, hope to rejoin you. Inexpedient to follow angry gentlemen. Return by same road you came, and will overtake. Highly gratified about correspondence due to my forethought. "He says, Holy One, that he will escape from the idolaters, and will return to us. Shall we wait awhile at Shamlegh, then?"

The lama looked long and lovingly upon the hills and shook his head.

"That may not be, chela. From my bones outward I do desire it, but it is forbidden. I have seen the Cause of Things."

"Why? When the Hills give thee back thy strength day by day? Remember we were weak and fainting down below there in the Doon."

"I became strong to do evil and to forget. A brawler and a swashbuckler upon the hillsides was I." Kim bit back a smile. "Just and perfect is the Wheel, swerving not a hair. When I was a man—a long time ago—I did pilgrimage to Guru Ch'wan among the poplars" (he pointed Bhotanwards), "where they keep the Sacred Horse."

"Quiet, be quiet!" said Shamlegh, all arow. "He speaks of Jam-lin-nin-k'or, the Horse That Can Go Round The World In a Day."

"I speak to my chela only," said the lama, in gentle reproof, and they scattered like frost on south eaves of a morning. "I did not seek truth in those days, but the talk of doctrine. All illusion! I drank the beer and ate the bread of Guru Ch'wan. Next day one said: 'We go out to fight Sangor Gutok down the valley to discover' (mark again how Lust is tied to Anger!) 'which Abbot shall bear rule in the valley and take the profit of the prayers they print at Sangor Gutok.' I went, and we fought a day."

"But how, Holy One?"

"With our long pencases as I could have shown ... I say, we fought under the poplars, both Abbots and all the monks, and one laid open my forehead to the bone. See!" He tilted back his cap and showed a puckered silvery scar. "Just and perfect is the Wheel! Yesterday the scar itched, and after fifty years I recalled how it was dealt and the face of him who dealt it; dwelling a little in illusion. Followed that which thou didst see—strife and stupidity. Just is the Wheel! The idolater's blow fell upon the scar. Then I was shaken in my soul: my soul was darkened,

and the boat of my soul rocked upon the waters of illusion. Not till I came to Shamlegh could I meditate upon the Cause of Things, or trace the running grass-roots of Evil. I strove all the long night."

"But, Holy One, thou art innocent of all evil. May I be thy sacrifice!"

Kim was genuinely distressed at the old man's sorrow, and Mahbub Ali's phrase slipped out unawares.

"In the dawn," the lama went on more gravely, ready rosary clicking between the slow sentences, "came enlightenment. It is here ... I am an old man ... hill-bred, hill-fed, never to sit down among my Hills. Three years I travelled through Hind, but—can earth be stronger than Mother Earth? My stupid body yearned to the Hills and the snows of the Hills, from below there. I said, and it is true, my Search is sure. So, at the Kulu woman's house I turned hillward, over-persuaded by myself. There is no blame to the hakim. He—following Desire—foretold that the Hills would make me strong. They strengthened me to do evil, to forget my Search. I delighted in life and the lust of life. I desired strong slopes to climb. I cast about to find them. I measured the strength of my body, which is evil, against the high Hills, I made a mock of thee when thy breath came short under Jamnotri. I jested when thou wouldst not face the snow of the pass."

"But what harm? I was afraid. It was just. I am not a hillman; and I loved thee for thy new strength."

"More than once I remember"—he rested his cheek dolefully on his hand—"I sought thy praise and the hakim's for the mere strength of my legs. Thus evil followed evil till the cup was full. Just is the Wheel! All Hind for three years did me all honour. From the Fountain of Wisdom in the Wonder House to"—he smiled—"a little child playing by a big gun—the world prepared my road. And why?"

"Because we loved thee. It is only the fever of the blow. I myself am still sick and shaken."

"No! It was because I was upon the Way—tuned as are si-nen (cymbals) to the purpose of the Law. I departed from that ordinance. The tune was broken: followed the punishment. In my own Hills, on the edge of my own country, in the very place of my evil desire, comes the buffet—here!" (He touched his brow.) "As a novice is beaten when he misplaces the cups, so am I beaten, who was Abbot of Such-zen. No word, look you, but a blow, chela."

"But the Sahibs did not know thee, Holy One?"

"We were well matched. Ignorance and Lust met Ignorance and Lust upon the road, and they begat Anger. The blow was a sign to me, who am no better than a strayed yak, that my place is not here. Who can read the Cause of an act is halfway to Freedom! 'Back to the path,' says the Blow. 'The Hills are not for thee. Thou canst not choose Freedom and go in bondage to the delight of life.'"

"Would we had never met that cursed Russian!"

"Our Lord Himself cannot make the Wheel swing backward. And for my merit that I had acquired I gain yet another sign." He put his hand in his bosom, and drew forth the Wheel of Life. "Look! I considered this after I had meditated. There remains untorn by the idolater no more than the breadth of my fingernail."

"I see."

"So much, then, is the span of my life in this body. I have served the Wheel all my days. Now

the Wheel serves me. But for the merit I have acquired in guiding thee upon the Way, there would have been added to me yet another life ere I had found my River. Is it plain, chela?"

Kim stared at the brutally disfigured chart. From left to right diagonally the rent ran—from the Eleventh House where Desire gives birth to the Child (as it is drawn by Tibetans)—across the human and animal worlds, to the Fifth House—the empty House of the Senses. The logic was unanswerable.

"Before our Lord won Enlightenment"—the lama folded all away with reverence—"He was tempted. I too have been tempted, but it is finished. The Arrow fell in the Plains—not in the Hills. Therefore, what make we here?"

"Shall we at least wait for the hakim?"

"I know how long I shall live in this body. What can a hakim do?"

"But thou art all sick and shaken. Thou canst not walk."

"How can I be sick if I see Freedom?" He rose unsteadily to his feet.

"Then I must get food from the village. Oh, the weary Road!" Kim felt that he too needed rest.

"That is lawful. Let us eat and go. The Arrow fell in the Plains ... but I yielded to Desire. Make ready, chela."

Kim turned to the woman with the turquoise headgear who had been idly pitching pebbles over the cliff. She smiled very kindly.

"I found him like a strayed buffalo in a cornfield—the Babu; snorting and sneezing with cold. He was so hungry that he forgot his dignity and gave me sweet words. The Sahibs have nothing." She flung out an empty palm. "One is very sick about the stomach. Thy work?"

Kim nodded, with a bright eye.

"I spoke to the Bengali first—and to the people of a near-by village after. The Sahibs will be given food as they need it—nor will the people ask money. The plunder is already distributed. The Babu makes lying speeches to the Sahibs. Why does he not leave them?"

"Out of the greatness of his heart."

"Was never a Bengali yet had one bigger than a dried walnut. But it is no matter ... Now as to walnuts. After service comes reward. I have said the village is thine."

"It is my loss," Kim began. "Even now I had planned desirable things in my heart which"—there is no need to go through the compliments proper to these occasions. He sighed deeply ... "But my master, led by a vision—"

"Huh! What can old eyes see except a full begging-bowl?"

"—turns from this village to the Plains again."

"Bid him stay."

Kim shook his head. "I know my Holy One, and his rage if he be crossed," he replied impressively. "His curses shake the Hills."

"Pity they did not save him from a broken head! I heard that thou wast the tiger-hearted one who smote the Sahib. Let him dream a little longer. Stay!"

"Hillwoman," said Kim, with austerity that could not harden the outlines of his young oval face, "these matters are too high for thee."

"The Gods be good to us! Since when have men and women been other than men and women?"

"A priest is a priest. He says he will go upon this hour. I am his chela, and I go with him. We need food for the Road. He is an honoured guest in all the villages, but"—he broke into a pure boy's grin—"the food here is good. Give me some."

"What if I do not give it thee? I am the woman of this village."

"Then I curse thee—a little—not greatly, but enough to remember." He could not help smiling.

"Thou hast cursed me already by the down-dropped eyelash and the uplifted chin. Curses? What should I care for mere words?" She clenched her hands upon her bosom ... "But I would not have thee to go in anger, thinking hardly of me—a gatherer of cow-dung and grass at Shamlegh, but still a woman of substance."

"I think nothing," said Kim, "but that I am grieved to go, for I am very weary; and that we need food. Here is the bag."

The woman snatched it angrily. "I was foolish," said she. "Who is thy woman in the Plains? Fair or black? I was fair once. Laughest thou? Once, long ago, if thou canst believe, a Sahib looked on me with favour. Once, long ago, I wore European clothes at the Mission-house yonder." She pointed towards Kotgarh. "Once, long ago. I was Ker-lis-ti-an and spoke English—as the Sahibs speak it. Yes. My Sahib said he would return and wed me—yes, wed me. He went away—I had nursed him when he was sick—but he never returned. Then I saw that the Gods of the Kerlistians lied, and I went back to my own people ... I have never set eyes on a Sahib since. (Do not laugh at me. The fit is past, little priestling.) Thy face and thy walk and thy fashion of speech put me in mind of my Sahib, though thou art only a wandering mendicant to whom I give a dole. Curse me? Thou canst neither curse nor bless!" She set her hands on her hips and laughed bitterly. "Thy Gods are lies; thy works are lies; thy words are lies. There are no Gods under all the Heavens. I know it ... But for awhile I thought it was my Sahib come back, and he was my God. Yes, once I made music on a pianno in the Mission-house at Kotgarh. Now I give alms to priests who are heatthen." She wound up with the English word, and tied the mouth of the brimming bag.

"I wait for thee, chela," said the lama, leaning against the door-post.

The woman swept the tall figure with her eyes. "He walk! He cannot cover half a mile. Whither would old bones go?"

At this Kim, already perplexed by the lama's collapse and foreseeing the weight of the bag, fairly lost his temper.

"What is it to thee, woman of ill-omen, where he goes?"

"Nothing—but something to thee, priest with a Sahib's face. Wilt thou carry him on thy shoulders?"

"I go to the Plains. None must hinder my return. I have wrestled with my soul till I am strengthless. The stupid body is spent, and we are far from the Plains."

"Behold!" she said simply, and drew aside to let Kim see his own utter helplessness. "Curse me. Maybe it will give him strength. Make a charm! Call on thy great God. Thou art a priest." She turned away.

The lama had squatted limply, still holding by the door-post. One cannot strike down an old man that he recovers again like a boy in the night. Weakness bowed him to the earth, but his eyes that hung on Kim were alive and imploring.

"It is all well," said Kim. "It is the thin air that weakens thee. In a little while we go! It is the mountain-sickness. I too am a little sick at stomach,"—and he knelt and comforted with such poor words as came first to his lips. Then the woman returned, more erect than ever.

"Thy Gods useless, heh? Try mine. I am the Woman of Shamlegh." She hailed hoarsely, and there came out of a cow-pen her two husbands and three others with a dooli, the rude native litter of the Hills, that they use for carrying the sick and for visits of state. "These cattle"—she did not condescend to look at them—"are thine for so long as thou shalt need."

"But we will not go Simla-way. We will not go near the Sahibs," cried the first husband.

"They will not run away as the others did, nor will they steal baggage. Two I know for weaklings. Stand to the rear-pole, Sonoo and Taree." They obeyed swiftly. "Lower now, and lift in that holy man. I will see to the village and your virtuous wives till ye return."

"When will that be?"

"Ask the priests. Do not pester me. Lay the food-bag at the foot, it balances better so."

"Oh, Holy One, thy Hills are kinder than our Plains!" cried Kim, relieved, as the lama tottered to the litter. "It is a very king's bed—a place of honour and ease. And we owe it to—"

"A woman of ill-omen. I need thy blessings as much as I do thy curses. It is my order and none of thine. Lift and away! Here! Hast thou money for the road?"

She beckoned Kim to her hut, and stooped above a battered English cash-box under her cot.

"I do not need anything," said Kim, angered where he should have been grateful. "I am already rudely loaded with favours."

She looked up with a curious smile and laid a hand on his shoulder. "At least, thank me. I am foul-faced and a hillwoman, but, as thy talk goes, I have acquired merit. Shall I show thee how the Sahibs render thanks?" and her hard eyes softened.

"I am but a wandering priest," said Kim, his eyes lighting in answer. "Thou needest neither my blessings nor my curses."

"Nay. But for one little moment—thou canst overtake the dooli in ten strides—if thou wast a Sahib, shall I show thee what thou wouldst do?"

"How if I guess, though?" said Kim, and putting his arm round her waist, he kissed her on the cheek, adding in English: "Thank you verree much, my dear."

Kissing is practically unknown among Asiatics, which may have been the reason that she leaned back with wide-open eyes and a face of panic.

"Next time," Kim went on, "you must not be so sure of your heatthen priests. Now I say good-

bye." He held out his hand English-fashion. She took it mechanically. "Good-bye, my dear."

"Good-bye, and—and"—she was remembering her English words one by one—"you will come back again? Good-bye, and—thee God bless you."

Half an hour later, as the creaking litter jolted up the hill path that leads south-easterly from Shamlegh, Kim saw a tiny figure at the hut door waving a white rag.

"She has acquired merit beyond all others," said the lama. "For to set a man upon the way to Freedom is half as great as though she had herself found it."

"Umm," said Kim thoughtfully, considering the past. "It may be that I have acquired merit also ... At least she did not treat me like a child." He hitched the front of his robe, where lay the slab of documents and maps, re-stowed the precious food-bag at the lama's feet, laid his hand on the litter's edge, and buckled down to the slow pace of the grunting husbands.

"These also acquire merit," said the lama after three miles.

"More than that, they shall be paid in silver," quoth Kim. The Woman of Shamlegh had given it to him; and it was only fair, he argued, that her men should earn it back again.

CHAPTER XV

I'd not give room for an Emperor—
I'd hold my road for a King.
To the Triple Crown I'd not bow down—
But this is a different thing!
I'll not fight with the Powers of Air—
Sentries pass him through!
Drawbridge let fall—He's the Lord of us all—
The Dreamer whose dream came true!

The Siege of the Fairies.

Two hundred miles north of Chini, on the blue shale of Ladakh, lies Yankling Sahib, the merry-minded man, spy-glassing wrathfully across the ridges for some sign of his pet tracker—a man from Ao-chung. But that renegade, with a new Mannlicher rifle and two hundred cartridges, is elsewhere, shooting musk-deer for the market, and Yankling Sahib will learn next season how very ill he has been.

Up the valleys of Bushahr—the far-beholding eagles of the Himalayas swerve at his new blue-and-white gored umbrella—hurries a Bengali, once fat and well-looking, now lean and weather-worn. He has received the thanks of two foreigners of distinction, piloted not unskilfully to Mashobra tunnel, which leads to the great and gay capital of India. It was not his fault that, blanketed by wet mists, he conveyed them past the telegraph-station and European colony of Kotgarh. It was not his fault, but that of the Gods, of whom he discoursed so engagingly, that he led them into the borders of Nahan, where the Rajah of that state mistook them for deserting British soldiery. Hurree Babu explained the greatness and glory, in their own country, of his companions, till the drowsy kinglet smiled. He explained it to everyone who asked—many times—aloud—variously. He begged food, arranged accommodation, proved a skilful leech for an injury of the groin—such a blow as one may receive rolling down a rock-covered hillside in the dark—and in all things indispensable. The reason of his friendliness did him credit. With millions of fellow-serfs, he had learned to look upon Russia as the great deliverer from the North. He was a fearful man. He had been afraid that he could not save his illustrious employers from the anger of an excited peasantry. He himself would just as lief hit a holy man as not, but ... He was deeply grateful and sincerely rejoiced that he had done his "little possible" towards bringing their venture to—barring the lost baggage—a successful issue, he had forgotten the blows; denied that any blows had been dealt that unseemly first night under the pines. He asked neither pension nor retaining fee, but, if they deemed him worthy, would they write him a testimonial? It might be useful to him later, if others, their friends, came over the Passes. He begged them to remember him in their future greatnesses, for he "opined subtly" that he, even he, Mohendro Lal Dutt, MA of Calcutta, had "done the State some service".

They gave him a certificate praising his courtesy, helpfulness, and unerring skill as a guide. He put it in his waist-belt and sobbed with emotion; they had endured so many dangers together. He led them at high noon along crowded Simla Mall to the Alliance Bank of Simla, where they wished to establish their identity. Thence he vanished like a dawn-cloud on Jakko.

Behold him, too fine-drawn to sweat, too pressed to vaunt the drugs in his little brass-bound box, ascending Shamlegh slope, a just man made perfect. Watch him, all Babudom laid aside, smoking at noon on a cot, while a woman with turquoise-studded headgear points south-easterly across the bare grass. Litters, she says, do not travel as fast as single men, but his birds should now be in the Plains. The holy man would not stay though Lispeth pressed him. The Babu

groans heavily, girds up his huge loins, and is off again. He does not care to travel after dusk; but his days' marches—there is none to enter them in a book—would astonish folk who mock at his race. Kindly villagers, remembering the Dacca drug-vendor of two months ago, give him shelter against evil spirits of the wood. He dreams of Bengali Gods, University text-books of education, and the Royal Society, London, England. Next dawn the bobbing blue-and-white umbrella goes forward.

On the edge of the Doon, Mussoorie well behind them and the Plains spread out in golden dust before, rests a worn litter in which—all the Hills know it—lies a sick lama who seeks a River for his healing. Villages have almost come to blows over the honour of bearing it, for not only has the lama given them blessings, but his disciple good money—full one-third Sahibs' prices. Twelve miles a day has the dooli travelled, as the greasy, rubbed pole-ends show, and by roads that few Sahibs use. Over the Nilang Pass in storm when the driven snow-dust filled every fold of the impassive lama's drapery; between the black horns of Raieng where they heard the whistle of the wild goats through the clouds; pitching and strained on the shale below; hard-held between shoulder and clenched jaw when they rounded the hideous curves of the Cut Road under Bhagirati; swinging and creaking to the steady jog-trot of the descent into the Valley of the Waters; pressed along the steamy levels of that locked valley; up, up and out again, to meet the roaring gusts off Kedarnath; set down of mid-days in the dun gloom of kindly oak-forests; passed from village to village in dawn-chill, when even devotees may be forgiven for swearing at impatient holy men; or by torchlight, when the least fearful think of ghosts—the dooli has reached her last stage. The little hill-folk sweat in the modified heat of the lower Siwaliks, and gather round the priests for their blessing and their wage.

"Ye have acquired merit," says the lama. "Merit greater than your knowing. And ye will return to the Hills," he sighs.

"Surely. The high Hills as soon as may be." The bearer rubs his shoulder, drinks water, spits it out again, and readjusts his grass sandal. Kim—his face is drawn and tired—pays very small silver from his belt, heaves out the food-bag, crams an oilskin packet—they are holy writings—into his bosom, and helps the lama to his feet. The peace has come again into the old man's eyes, and he does not look for the hills to fall down and crush him as he did that terrible night when they were delayed by the flooded river.

The men pick up the dooli and swing out of sight between the scrub clumps.

The lama raises a hand toward the rampart of the Himalayas. "Not with you, O blessed among all hills, fell the Arrow of Our Lord! And never shall I breathe your airs again!"

"But thou art ten times the stronger man in this good air," says Kim, for to his wearied soul appeal the well-cropped, kindly Plains. "Here, or hereabouts, fell the Arrow, yes. We will go very softly, perhaps, a kos a day, for the Search is sure. But the bag weighs heavy."

"Ay, our Search is sure. I have come out of great temptation."

It was never more than a couple of miles a day now, and Kim's shoulders bore all the weight of it—the burden of an old man, the burden of the heavy food-bag with the locked books, the load of the writings on his heart, and the details of the daily routine. He begged in the dawn, set blankets for the lama's meditation, held the weary head on his lap through the noonday heats, fanning away the flies till his wrists ached, begged again in the evenings, and rubbed the lama's feet, who rewarded him with promise of Freedom—today, tomorrow, or, at furthest, the next day.

"Never was such a chela. I doubt at times whether Ananda more faithfully nursed Our Lord.

And thou art a Sahib? When I was a man—a long time ago—I forgot that. Now I look upon thee often, and every time I remember that thou art a Sahib. It is strange."

"Thou hast said there is neither black nor white. Why plague me with this talk, Holy One? Let me rub the other foot. It vexes me. I am not a Sahib. I am thy chela, and my head is heavy on my shoulders."

"Patience a little! We reach Freedom together. Then thou and I, upon the far bank of the River, will look back upon our lives as in the Hills we saw our days' marches laid out behind us. Perhaps I was once a Sahib."

"Was never a Sahib like thee, I swear it."

"I am certain the Keeper of the Images in the Wonder House was in past life a very wise Abbot. But even his spectacles do not make my eyes see. There fall shadows when I would look steadily. No matter—we know the tricks of the poor stupid carcass—shadow changing to another shadow. I am bound by the illusion of Time and Space. How far came we today in the flesh?"

"Perhaps half a koss." (Three quarters of a mile, and it was a weary march.)

"Half a koss. Ha! I went ten thousand thousand in the spirit. How, we are all lapped and swathed and swaddled in these senseless things." He looked at his thin blue-veined hand that found the beads so heavy. "Chela, hast thou never a wish to leave me?"

Kim thought of the oilskin packet and the books in the food-bag. If someone duly authorized would only take delivery of them the Great Game might play itself for aught he then cared. He was tired and hot in his head, and a cough that came from the stomach worried him.

"No." he said almost sternly. "I am not a dog or a snake to bite when I have learned to love."

"Thou art too tender towards me."

"Not that either. I have moved in one matter without consulting thee. I have sent a message to the Kulu woman by that woman who gave us the goat's milk this morn, saying that thou wast a little feeble and wouldst need a litter. I beat myself in my mind that I did not do it when we entered the Doon. We stay in this place till the litter returns."

"I am content. She is a woman with a heart of gold, as thou sayest, but a talker—something of a talker."

"She will not weary thee. I have looked to that also. Holy One, my heart is very heavy for my many carelessnesses towards thee." An hysterical catch rose in his throat. "I have walked thee too far: I have not picked good food always for thee; I have not considered the heat; I have talked to people on the road and left thee alone ... I have—I have ... Hai mai! But I love thee ... and it is all too late ... I was a child ... Oh, why was I not a man? ..." Overborne by strain, fatigue, and the weight beyond his years, Kim broke down and sobbed at the lama's feet.

"What a to-do is here!" said the old man gently. "Thou hast never stepped a hair's breadth from the Way of Obedience. Neglect me? Child, I have lived on thy strength as an old tree lives on the lime of a new wall. Day by day, since Shamlegh down, I have stolen strength from thee. Therefore, not through any sin of thine, art thou weakened. It is the Body—the silly, stupid Body—that speaks now. Not the assured Soul. Be comforted! Know at least the devils that thou fightest. They are earth-born—children of illusion. We will go to the woman from Kulu. She shall acquire merit in housing us, and specially in tending me. Thou shalt run free till strength

returns. I had forgotten the stupid Body. If there be any blame, I bear it. But we are too close to the Gates of Deliverance to weigh blame. I could praise thee, but what need? In a little—in a very little—we shall sit beyond all needs."

And so he petted and comforted Kim with wise saws and grave texts on that little-understood beast, our Body, who, being but a delusion, insists on posing as the Soul, to the darkening of the Way, and the immense multiplication of unnecessary devils.

"Hai! hai! Let us talk of the woman from Kulu. Think you she will ask another charm for her grandsons? When I was a young man, a very long time ago, I was plagued with these vapours—and some others—and I went to an Abbot—a very holy man and a seeker after truth, though then I knew it not. Sit up and listen, child of my soul! My tale was told. Said he to me, 'Chela, know this. There are many lies in the world, and not a few liars, but there are no liars like our bodies, except it be the sensations of our bodies.' Considering this I was comforted, and of his great favour he suffered me to drink tea In his presence. Suffer me now to drink tea, for I am thirsty."

With a laugh across his tears, Kim kissed the lama's feet, and set about the tea-making.

"Thou leanest on me in the body, Holy One, but I lean on thee for some other things. Dost know it?"

"I have guessed maybe," and the lama's eyes twinkled. "We must change that."

So, when with scufflings and scrapings and a hot air of importance, paddled up nothing less than the Sahiba's pet palanquin sent twenty miles, with that same grizzled old Oorya servant in charge, and when they reached the disorderly order of the long white rambling house behind Saharunpore, the lama took his own measures.

Said the Sahiba cheerily from an upper window, after compliments: "What is the good of an old woman's advice to an old man? I told thee—I told thee, Holy One, to keep an eye upon the chela. How didst thou do it? Never answer me! I know. He has been running among the women. Look at his eyes—hollow and sunk—and the Betraying Line from the nose down! He has been sifted out! Fie! Fie! And a priest, too!"

Kim looked up, over-weary to smile, shaking his head in denial.

"Do not jest," said the lama. "That time is done. We are here upon great matters. A sickness of soul took me in the Hills, and him a sickness of the body. Since then I have lived upon his strength—eating him."

"Children together—young and old," she sniffed, but forbore to make any new jokes. "May this present hospitality restore ye! Hold awhile and I will come to gossip of the high good Hills."

At evening time—her son-in-law was returned, so she did not need to go on inspection round the farm—she won to the meat of the matter, explained low-voicedly by the lama. The two old heads nodded wisely together. Kim had reeled to a room with a cot in it, and was dozing soddenly. The lama had forbidden him to set blankets or get food.

"I know—I know. Who but I?" she cackled. "We who go down to the burning-ghats clutch at the hands of those coming up from the River of Life with full water-jars—yes, brimming water-jars. I did the boy wrong. He lent thee his strength? It is true that the old eat the young daily. Stands now we must restore him."

"Thou hast many times acquired merit—"

"My merit. What is it? Old bag of bones making curries for men who do not ask 'Who cooked this?' Now if it were stored up for my grandson—"

"He that had the belly-pain?"

"To think the Holy One remembers that! I must tell his mother. It is most singular honour! 'He that had the belly-pain'—straightway the Holy One remembered. She will be proud."

"My chela is to me as is a son to the unenlightened."

"Say grandson, rather. Mothers have not the wisdom of our years. If a child cries they say the heavens are falling. Now a grandmother is far enough separated from the pain of bearing and the pleasure of giving the breast to consider whether a cry is wickedness pure or the wind. And since thou speakest once again of wind, when last the Holy One was here, maybe I offended in pressing for charms."

"Sister," said the lama, using that form of address a Buddhist monk may sometimes employ towards a nun, "if charms comfort thee—"

"They are better than ten thousand doctors."

"I say, if they comfort thee, I who was Abbot of Such-zen, will make as many as thou mayest desire. I have never seen thy face—"

"That even the monkeys who steal our loquats count for again. Hee! hee!"

"But as he who sleeps there said,"—he nodded at the shut door of the guest-chamber across the forecourt—"thou hast a heart of gold... And he is in the spirit my very 'grandson' to me."

"Good! I am the Holy One's cow." This was pure Hinduism, but the lama never heeded. "I am old. I have borne sons in the body. Oh, once I could please men! Now I can cure them." He heard her armlets tinkle as though she bared arms for action. "I will take over the boy and dose him, and stuff him, and make him all whole. Hai! hai! We old people know something yet."

Wherefore when Kim, aching in every bone, opened his eyes, and would go to the cook-house to get his master's food, he found strong coercion about him, and a veiled old figure at the door, flanked by the grizzled manservant, who told him very precisely the things that he was on no account to do.

"Thou must have? Thou shalt have nothing. What? A locked box in which to keep holy books? Oh, that is another matter. Heavens forbid I should come between a priest and his prayers! It shall be brought, and thou shalt keep the key."

They pushed the coffer under his cot, and Kim shut away Mahbub's pistol, the oilskin packet of letters, and the locked books and diaries, with a groan of relief. For some absurd reason their weight on his shoulders was nothing to their weight on his poor mind. His neck ached under it of nights.

"Thine is a sickness uncommon in youth these days: since young folk have given up tending their betters. The remedy is sleep, and certain drugs," said the Sahiba; and he was glad to give himself up to the blankness that half menaced and half soothed him.

She brewed drinks, in some mysterious Asiatic equivalent to the still-room—drenches that smelt pestilently and tasted worse. She stood over Kim till they went down, and inquired exhaustively after they had come up. She laid a taboo upon the forecourt, and enforced it by

means of an armed man. It is true he was seventy odd, that his scabbarded sword ceased at the hilt; but he represented the authority of the Sahiba, and loaded wains, chattering servants, calves, dogs, hens, and the like, fetched a wide compass by those parts. Best of all, when the body was cleared, she cut out from the mass of poor relations that crowded the back of the buildings—house-hold dogs, we name them—a cousin's widow, skilled in what Europeans, who know nothing about it, call massage. And the two of them, laying him east and west, that the mysterious earth-currents which thrill the clay of our bodies might help and not hinder, took him to pieces all one long afternoon—bone by bone, muscle by muscle, ligament by ligament, and lastly, nerve by nerve. Kneaded to irresponsible pulp, half hypnotized by the perpetual flick and readjustment of the uneasy chudders that veiled their eyes, Kim slid ten thousand miles into slumber—thirty-six hours of it—sleep that soaked like rain after drought.

Then she fed him, and the house spun to her clamour. She caused fowls to be slain; she sent for vegetables, and the sober, slow-thinking gardener, nigh as old as she, sweated for it; she took spices, and milk, and onion, with little fish from the brooks—anon limes for sherbets, fat quails from the pits, then chicken-livers upon a skewer, with sliced ginger between.

"I have seen something of this world," she said over the crowded trays, "and there are but two sorts of women in it—those who take the strength out of a man and those who put it back. Once I was that one, and now I am this. Nay—do not play the priestling with me. Mine was but a jest. If it does not hold good now, it will when thou takest the road again. Cousin,"—this to the poor relation, never wearied of extolling her patroness's charity—"he is getting a bloom on the skin of a new-curried horse. Our work is like polishing jewels to be thrown to a dance-girl—eh?"

Kim sat up and smiled. The terrible weakness had dropped from him like an old shoe. His tongue itched for free speech again, and but a week back the lightest word clogged it like ashes. The pain in his neck (he must have caught it from the lama) had gone with the heavy dengue-aches and the evil taste in the mouth. The two old women, a little, but not much, more careful about their veils now, clucked as merrily as the hens that had entered pecking through the open door.

"Where is my Holy One?" he demanded.

"Hear him! Thy Holy One is well," she snapped viciously. "Though that is none of his merit. Knew I a charm to make him wise, I'd sell my jewels and buy it. To refuse good food that I cooked myself—and go roving into the fields for two nights on an empty belly—and to tumble into a brook at the end of it—call you that holiness? Then, when he has nearly broken what thou hast left of my heart with anxiety, he tells me that he has acquired merit. Oh, how like are all men! No, that was not it—he tells me that he is freed from all sin. I could have told him that before he wetted himself all over. He is well now—this happened a week ago—but burn me such holiness! A babe of three would do better. Do not fret thyself for the Holy One. He keeps both eyes on thee when he is not wading our brooks."

"I do not remember to have seen him. I remember that the days and nights passed like bars of white and black, opening and shutting. I was not sick: I was but tired."

"A lethargy that comes by right some few score years later. But it is done now."

"Maharanee," Kim began, but led by the look in her eye, changed it to the title of plain love—"Mother, I owe my life to thee. How shall I make thanks? Ten thousand blessings upon thy house and—"

"The house be unblessed!" (It is impossible to give exactly the old lady's word.) "Thank the Gods as a priest if thou wilt, but thank me, if thou carest, as a son. Heavens above! Have I

shifted thee and lifted thee and slapped and twisted thy ten toes to find texts flung at my head? Somewhere a mother must have borne thee to break her heart. What used thou to her—son?"

"I had no mother, my mother," said Kim. "She died, they tell me, when I was young."

"Hai mai! Then none can say I have robbed her of any right if—when thou takest the road again and this house is but one of a thousand used for shelter and forgotten, after an easy-flung blessing. No matter. I need no blessings, but—but—" She stamped her foot at the poor relation. "Take up the trays to the house. What is the good of stale food in the room, O woman of ill-omen?"

"I ha—have borne a son in my time too, but he died," whimpered the bowed sister-figure behind the chudder. "Thou knowest he died! I only waited for the order to take away the tray."

"It is I that am the woman of ill-omen," cried the old lady penitently. "We that go down to the chattris (the big umbrellas above the burning-ghats where the priests take their last dues) clutch hard at the bearers of the chattis (water-jars—young folk full of the pride of life, she meant; but the pun is clumsy). When one cannot dance in the festival one must e'en look out of the window, and grandmothering takes all a woman's time. Thy master gives me all the charms I now desire for my daughter's eldest, by reason—is it?—that he is wholly free from sin. The hakim is brought very low these days. He goes about poisoning my servants for lack of their betters."

"What hakim, mother?"

"That very Dacca man who gave me the pill which rent me in three pieces. He cast up like a strayed camel a week ago, vowing that he and thou had been blood-brothers together up Kulu-way, and feigning great anxiety for thy health. He was very thin and hungry, so I gave orders to have him stuffed too—him and his anxiety!"

"I would see him if he is here."

"He eats five times a day, and lances boils for my hinds to save himself from an apoplexy. He is so full of anxiety for thy health that he sticks to the cook-house door and stays himself with scraps. He will keep. We shall never get rid of him."

"Send him here, mother"—the twinkle returned to Kim's eye for a flash—"and I will try."

"I'll send him, but to chase him off is an ill turn. At least he had the sense to fish the Holy One out of the brook; thus, as the Holy One did not say, acquiring merit."

"He is a very wise hakim. Send him, mother."

"Priest praising priest? A miracle! If he is any friend of thine (ye squabbled at your last meeting) I'll hale him here with horse-ropes and—and give him a caste-dinner afterwards, my son ... Get up and see the world! This lying abed is the mother of seventy devils ... my son! my son!"

She trotted forth to raise a typhoon off the cook-house, and almost on her shadow rolled in the Babu, robed as to the shoulders like a Roman emperor, jowled like Titus, bare-headed, with new patent-leather shoes, in highest condition of fat, exuding joy and salutations.

"By Jove, Mister O'Hara, but I am jolly glad to see you. I will kindly shut the door. It is a pity you are sick. Are you very sick?"

"The papers—the papers from the kilta. The maps and the murasla!" He held out the key

impatiently; for the present need on his soul was to get rid of the loot.

"You are quite right. That is correct Departmental view to take. You have got everything?"

"All that was handwritten in the kilta I took. The rest I threw down the hill." He could hear the key's grate in the lock, the sticky pull of the slow-rending oilskin, and a quick shuffling of papers. He had been annoyed out of all reason by the knowledge that they lay below him through the sick idle days—a burden incommunicable. For that reason the blood tingled through his body, when Hurree, skipping elephantinely, shook hands again.

"This is fine! This is finest! Mister O'Hara! you have—ha! ha! swiped the whole bag of tricks—locks, stocks, and barrels. They told me it was eight months' work gone up the spouts! By Jove, how they beat me! ... Look, here is the letter from Hilás!" He intoned a line or two of Court Persian, which is the language of authorized and unauthorized diplomacy. "Mister Rajah Sahib has just about put his foot in the holes. He will have to explain offeecially how the deuce-an'-all he is writing love-letters to the Czar. And they are very clever maps ... and there is three or four Prime Ministers of these parts implicated by the correspondence. By Gad, sar! The British Government will change the succession in Hilás and Bunár, and nominate new heirs to the throne. 'Trea-son most base' ... but you do not understand? Eh?"

"Are they in thy hands?" said Kim. It was all he cared for.

"Just you jolly-well bet yourself they are." He stowed the entire trove about his body, as only Orientals can. "They are going up to the office, too. The old lady thinks I am permanent fixture here, but I shall go away with these straight off—immediately. Mr Lurgan will be proud man. You are offeecially subordinate to me, but I shall embody your name in my verbal report. It is a pity we are not allowed written reports. We Bengalis excel in thee exact science." He tossed back the key and showed the box empty.

"Good. That is good. I was very tired. My Holy One was sick, too. And did he fall into—"

"Oah yess. I am his good friend, I tell you. He was behaving very strange when I came down after you, and I thought perhaps he might have the papers. I followed him on his meditations, and to discuss ethnological points also. You see, I am verree small person here nowadays, in comparison with all his charms. By Jove, O'Hara, do you know, he is afflicted with infirmity of fits. Yess, I tell you. Cataleptic, too, if not also epileptic. I found him in such a state under a tree in articulo mortem, and he jumped up and walked into a brook and he was nearly drowned but for me. I pulled him out."

"Because I was not there!" said Kim. "He might have died."

"Yes, he might have died, but he is dry now, and asserts he has undergone transfiguration." The Babu tapped his forehead knowingly. "I took notes of his statements for Royal Society—in posse. You must make haste and be quite well and come back to Simla, and I will tell you all my tale at Lurgan's. It was splendid. The bottoms of their trousers were quite torn, and old Nahan Rajah, he thought they were European soldiers deserting."

"Oh, the Russians? How long were they with thee?"

"One was a Frenchman. Oh, days and days and days! Now all the hill-people believe all Russians are all beggars. By Jove! they had not one dam'-thing that I did not get them. And I told the common people—oah, such tales and anecdotes!—I will tell you at old Lurgan's when you come up. We will have—ah—a night out! It is feather in both our caps! Yess, and they gave me a certificate. That is creaming joke. You should have seen them at the Alliance Bank identifying

themselves! And thank Almighty God you got their papers so well! You do not laugh verree much, but you shall laugh when you are well. Now I will go straight to the railway and get out. You shall have all sorts of credits for your game. When do you come along? We are very proud of you though you gave us great frights. And especially Mahbub."

"Ay, Mahbub. And where is he?"

"Selling horses in this vi-cinity, of course."

"Here! Why? Speak slowly. There is a thickness in my head still."

The Babu looked shyly down his nose. "Well, you see, I am fearful man, and I do not like responsibility. You were sick, you see, and I did not know where deuce-an'-all the papers were, and if so, how many. So when I had come down here I slipped in private wire to Mahbub—he was at Meerut for races—and I tell him how case stands. He comes up with his men and he consorts with the lama, and then he calls me a fool, and is very rude—"

"But wherefore—wherefore?"

"That is what I ask. I only suggest that if anyone steals the papers I should like some good strong, brave men to rob them back again. You see, they are vitally important, and Mahbub Ali he did not know where you were."

"Mahbub Ali to rob the Sahiba's house? Thou art mad, Babu," said Kim with indignation.

"I wanted the papers. Suppose she had stole them? It was only practical suggestion, I think. You are not pleased, eh?"

A native proverb—unquotable—showed the blackness of Kim's disapproval.

"Well,"—Hurree shrugged his shoulders—"there is no accounting for thee taste. Mahbub was angry too. He has sold horses all about here, and he says old lady is pukka (thorough) old lady and would not condescend to such ungentlemanly things. I do not care. I have got the papers, and I was very glad of moral support from Mahbub. I tell you, I am fearful man, but, somehow or other, the more fearful I am the more dam'-tight places I get into. So I was glad you came with me to Chini, and I am glad Mahbub was close by. The old lady she is sometimes very rude to me and my beautiful pills."

"Allah be merciful!" said Kim on his elbow, rejoicing. "What a beast of wonder is a Babu! And that man walked alone—if he did walk—with robbed and angry foreigners!"

"Oah, thatt was nothing, after they had done beating me; but if I lost the papers it was pretty-jolly serious. Mahbub he nearly beat me too, and he went and consorted with the lama no end. I shall stick to ethnological investigations henceforwards. Now good-bye, Mister O'Hara. I can catch 4.25 p.m. to Umballa if I am quick. It will be good times when we all tell thee tale up at Mr Lurgan's. I shall report you offeecially better. Good-bye, my dear fallow, and when next you are under thee emotions please do not use the Mohammedan terms with the Tibetan dress."

He shook hands twice—a Babu to his boot-heels—and opened the door. With the fall of the sunlight upon his still triumphant face he returned to the humble Dacca quack.

"He robbed them," thought Kim, forgetting his own share in the game. "He tricked them. He lied to them like a Bengali. They give him a chit (a testimonial). He makes them a mock at the risk of his life—I never would have gone down to them after the pistol-shots—and then he says he is a fearful man ... And he is a fearful man. I must get into the world again."

At first his legs bent like bad pipe-stems, and the flood and rush of the sunlit air dazzled him. He squatted by the white wall, the mind rummaging among the incidents of the long dooli journey, the lama's weaknesses, and, now that the stimulus of talk was removed, his own self-pity, of which, like the sick, he had great store. The unnerved brain edged away from all the outside, as a raw horse, once rowelled, sidles from the spur. It was enough, amply enough, that the spoil of the kilta was away—off his hands—out of his possession. He tried to think of the lama—to wonder why he had tumbled into a brook—but the bigness of the world, seen between the forecourt gates, swept linked thought aside. Then he looked upon the trees and the broad fields, with the thatched huts hidden among crops—looked with strange eyes unable to take up the size and proportion and use of things—stared for a still half-hour. All that while he felt, though he could not put it into words, that his soul was out of gear with its surroundings—a cog-wheel unconnected with any machinery, just like the idle cog-wheel of a cheap Beheea sugar-crusher laid by in a corner. The breezes fanned over him, the parrots shrieked at him, the noises of the populated house behind—squabbles, orders, and reproofs—hit on dead ears.

"I am Kim. I am Kim. And what is Kim?" His soul repeated it again and again.

He did not want to cry—had never felt less like crying in his life—but of a sudden easy, stupid tears trickled down his nose, and with an almost audible click he felt the wheels of his being lock up anew on the world without. Things that rode meaningless on the eyeball an instant before slid into proper proportion. Roads were meant to be walked upon, houses to be lived in, cattle to be driven, fields to be tilled, and men and women to be talked to. They were all real and true—solidly planted upon the feet—perfectly comprehensible—clay of his clay, neither more nor less. He shook himself like a dog with a flea in his ear, and rambled out of the gate. Said the Sahiba, to whom watchful eyes reported this move: "Let him go. I have done my share. Mother Earth must do the rest. When the Holy One comes back from meditation, tell him."

There stood an empty bullock-cart on a little knoll half a mile away, with a young banyan tree behind—a look-out, as it were, above some new-ploughed levels; and his eyelids, bathed in soft air, grew heavy as he neared it. The ground was good clean dust—no new herbage that, living, is half-way to death already, but the hopeful dust that holds the seeds of all life. He felt it between his toes, patted it with his palms, and joint by joint, sighing luxuriously, laid him down full length along in the shadow of the wooden-pinned cart. And Mother Earth was as faithful as the Sahiba. She breathed through him to restore the poise he had lost lying so long on a cot cut off from her good currents. His head lay powerless upon her breast, and his opened hands surrendered to her strength. The many-rooted tree above him, and even the dead manhandled wood beside, knew what he sought, as he himself did not know. Hour upon hour he lay deeper than sleep.

Towards evening, when the dust of returning kine made all the horizons smoke, came the lama and Mahbub Ali, both afoot, walking cautiously, for the house had told them where he had gone.

"Allah! What a fool's trick to play in open country!" muttered the horse-dealer. "He could be shot a hundred times—but this is not the Border."

"And," said the lama, repeating a many-times-told tale, "never was such a chela. Temperate, kindly, wise, of ungrudging disposition, a merry heart upon the road, never forgetting, learned, truthful, courteous. Great is his reward!"

"I know the boy—as I have said."

"And he was all those things?"

"Some of them—but I have not yet found a Red Hat's charm for making him overly truthful.

He has certainly been well nursed."

"The Sahiba is a heart of gold," said the lama earnestly. "She looks upon him as her son."

"Hmph! Half Hind seems that way disposed. I only wished to see that the boy had come to no harm and was a free agent. As thou knowest, he and I were old friends in the first days of your pilgrimage together."

"That is a bond between us." The lama sat down. "We are at the end of the pilgrimage."

"No thanks to thee thine was not cut off for good and all a week back. I heard what the Sahiba said to thee when we bore thee up on the cot." Mahbub laughed, and tugged his newly dyed beard.

"I was meditating upon other matters that tide. It was the hakim from Dacca broke my meditations."

"Otherwise"—this was in Pushtu for decency's sake—"thou wouldst have ended thy meditations upon the sultry side of Hell—being an unbeliever and an idolater for all thy child's simplicity. But now, Red Hat, what is to be done?"

"This very night,"—the words came slowly, vibrating with triumph—"this very night he will be as free as I am from all taint of sin—assured as I am, when he quits this body, of Freedom from the Wheel of Things. I have a sign"—he laid his hand above the torn chart in his bosom—"that my time is short; but I shall have safeguarded him throughout the years. Remember, I have reached Knowledge, as I told thee only three nights back."

"It must be true, as the Tirah priest said when I stole his cousin's wife, that I am a sufi (a free-thinker); for here I sit," said Mahbub to himself, "drinking in blasphemy unthinkable ... I remember the tale. On that, then, he goes to Jannatu l'Adn (the Gardens of Eden). But how? Wilt thou slay him or drown him in that wonderful river from which the Babu dragged thee?"

"I was dragged from no river," said the lama simply. "Thou hast forgotten what befell. I found it by Knowledge."

"Oh, ay. True," stammered Mahbub, divided between high indignation and enormous mirth. "I had forgotten the exact run of what happened. Thou didst find it knowingly."

"And to say that I would take life is—not a sin, but a madness simple. My chela aided me to the River. It is his right to be cleansed from sin—with me."

"Ay, he needs cleansing. But afterwards, old man—afterwards?"

"What matter under all the Heavens? He is sure of Nibban—enlightened—as I am."

"Well said. I had a fear he might mount Mohammed's Horse and fly away."

"Nay—he must go forth as a teacher."

"Aha! Now I see! That is the right gait for the colt. Certainly he must go forth as a teacher. He is somewhat urgently needed as a scribe by the State, for instance."

"To that end he was prepared. I acquired merit in that I gave alms for his sake. A good deed does not die. He aided me in my Search. I aided him in his. Just is the Wheel, O horse-seller from the North. Let him be a teacher; let him be a scribe—what matter? He will have attained Freedom

at the end. The rest is illusion."

"What matter? When I must have him with me beyond Balkh in six months! I come up with ten lame horses and three strong-backed men—thanks to that chicken of a Babu—to break a sick boy by force out of an old trot's house. It seems that I stand by while a young Sahib is hoisted into Allah knows what of an idolater's Heaven by means of old Red Hat. And I am reckoned something of a player of the Game myself! But the madman is fond of the boy; and I must be very reasonably mad too."

"What is the prayer?" said the lama, as the rough Pushtu rumbled into the red beard.

"No matter at all; but now I understand that the boy, sure of Paradise, can yet enter Government service, my mind is easier. I must get to my horses. It grows dark. Do not wake him. I have no wish to hear him call thee master."

"But he is my disciple. What else?"

"He has told me." Mahbub choked down his touch of spleen and rose laughing. "I am not altogether of thy faith, Red Hat—if so small a matter concern thee."

"It is nothing," said the lama.

"I thought not. Therefore it will not move thee, sinless, new-washed and three parts drowned to boot, when I call thee a good man—a very good man. We have talked together some four or five evenings now, and for all I am a horse-coper I can still, as the saying is, see holiness beyond the legs of a horse. Yea, can see, too, how our Friend of all the World put his hand in thine at the first. Use him well, and suffer him to return to the world as a teacher, when thou hast—bathed his legs, if that be the proper medicine for the colt."

"Why not follow the Way thyself, and so accompany the boy?"

Mahbub stared stupefied at the magnificent insolence of the demand, which across the Border he would have paid with more than a blow. Then the humour of it touched his worldly soul.

"Softly—softly—one foot at a time, as the lame gelding went over the Umballa jumps. I may come to Paradise later—I have workings that way—great motions—and I owe them to thy simplicity. Thou hast never lied?"

"What need?"

"O Allah, hear him! 'What need' in this Thy world! Nor ever harmed a man?"

"Once—with a pencase—before I was wise."

"So? I think the better of thee. Thy teachings are good. Thou hast turned one man that I know from the path of strife." He laughed immensely. "He came here open-minded to commit a dacoity (a house-robbery with violence). Yes, to cut, rob, kill, and carry off what he desired."

"A great foolishness!"

"Oh! black shame too. So he thought after he had seen thee—and a few others, male and female. So he abandoned it; and now he goes to beat a big fat Babu man."

"I do not understand."

"Allah forbid it! Some men are strong in knowledge, Red Hat. Thy strength is stronger still.

Keep it—I think thou wilt. If the boy be not a good servant, pull his ears off."

With a hitch of his broad Bokhariot belt the Pathan swaggered off into the gloaming, and the lama came down from his clouds so far as to look at the broad back.

"That person lacks courtesy, and is deceived by the shadow of appearances. But he spoke well of my chela, who now enters upon his reward. Let me make the prayer! ... Wake, O fortunate above all born of women. Wake! It is found!"

Kim came up from those deep wells, and the lama attended his yawning pleasure; duly snapping fingers to head off evil spirits.

"I have slept a hundred years. Where—? Holy One, hast thou been here long? I went out to look for thee, but"—he laughed drowsily—"I slept by the way. I am all well now. Hast thou eaten? Let us go to the house. It is many days since I tended thee. And the Sahiba fed thee well? Who shampooed thy legs? What of the weaknesses—the belly and the neck, and the beating in the ears?"

"Gone—all gone. Dost thou not know?"

"I know nothing, but that I have not seen thee in a monkey's age. Know what?"

"Strange the knowledge did not reach out to thee, when all my thoughts were theeward."

"I cannot see the face, but the voice is like a gong. Has the Sahiba made a young man of thee by her cookery?"

He peered at the cross-legged figure, outlined jet-black against the lemon-coloured drift of light. So does the stone Bodhisat sit who looks down upon the patent self-registering turnstiles of the Lahore Museum.

The lama held his peace. Except for the click of the rosary and a faint clop-clop of Mahbub's retreating feet, the soft, smoky silence of evening in India wrapped them close.

"Hear me! I bring news."

"But let us—"

Out shot the long yellow hand compelling silence. Kim tucked his feet under his robe-edge obediently.

"Hear me! I bring news! The Search is finished. Comes now the Reward... Thus. When we were among the Hills, I lived on thy strength till the young branch bowed and nigh broke. When we came out of the Hills, I was troubled for thee and for other matters which I held in my heart. The boat of my soul lacked direction; I could not see into the Cause of Things. So I gave thee over to the virtuous woman altogether. I took no food. I drank no water. Still I saw not the Way. They pressed food upon me and cried at my shut door. So I removed myself to a hollow under a tree. I took no food. I took no water. I sat in meditation two days and two nights, abstracting my mind; inbreathing and outbreathing in the required manner ... Upon the second night—so great was my reward—the wise Soul loosed itself from the silly Body and went free. This I have never before attained, though I have stood on the threshold of it. Consider, for it is a marvel!"

"A marvel indeed. Two days and two nights without food! Where was the Sahiba?" said Kim under his breath.

"Yea, my Soul went free, and, wheeling like an eagle, saw indeed that there was no Teshoo Lama nor any other soul. As a drop draws to water, so my Soul drew near to the Great Soul which is beyond all things. At that point, exalted in contemplation, I saw all Hind, from Ceylon in the sea to the Hills, and my own Painted Rocks at Such-zen; I saw every camp and village, to the least, where we have ever rested. I saw them at one time and in one place; for they were within the Soul. By this I knew the Soul had passed beyond the illusion of Time and Space and of Things. By this I knew that I was free. I saw thee lying in thy cot, and I saw thee falling downhill under the idolater—at one time, in one place, in my Soul, which, as I say, had touched the Great Soul. Also I saw the stupid body of Teshoo Lama lying down, and the hakim from Dacca kneeled beside, shouting in its ear. Then my Soul was all alone, and I saw nothing, for I was all things, having reached the Great Soul. And I meditated a thousand thousand years, passionless, well aware of the Causes of all Things. Then a voice cried: 'What shall come to the boy if thou art dead?' and I was shaken back and forth in myself with pity for thee; and I said: 'I will return to my chela, lest he miss the Way.' Upon this my Soul, which is the Soul of Teshoo Lama, withdrew itself from the Great Soul with strivings and yearnings and retchings and agonies not to be told. As the egg from the fish, as the fish from the water, as the water from the cloud, as the cloud from the thick air, so put forth, so leaped out, so drew away, so fumed up the Soul of Teshoo Lama from the Great Soul. Then a voice cried: 'The River! Take heed to the River!' and I looked down upon all the world, which was as I had seen it before—one in time, one in place—and I saw plainly the River of the Arrow at my feet. At that hour my Soul was hampered by some evil or other whereof I was not wholly cleansed, and it lay upon my arms and coiled round my waist; but I put it aside, and I cast forth as an eagle in my flight for the very place of the River. I pushed aside world upon world for thy sake. I saw the River below me—the River of the Arrow—and, descending, the waters of it closed over me; and behold I was again in the body of Teshoo Lama, but free from sin, and the hakim from Decca bore up my head in the waters of the River. It is here! It is behind the mango-tope here—even here!"

"Allah kerim! Oh, well that the Babu was by! Wast thou very wet?"

"Why should I regard? I remember the hakim was concerned for the body of Teshoo Lama. He haled it out of the holy water in his hands, and there came afterwards thy horse-seller from the North with a cot and men, and they put the body on the cot and bore it up to the Sahiba's house."

"What said the Sahiba?"

"I was meditating in that body, and did not hear. So thus the Search is ended. For the merit that I have acquired, the River of the Arrow is here. It broke forth at our feet, as I have said. I have found it. Son of my Soul, I have wrenched my Soul back from the Threshold of Freedom to free thee from all sin—as I am free, and sinless! Just is the Wheel! Certain is our deliverance! Come!"

He crossed his hands on his lap and smiled, as a man may who has won salvation for himself and his beloved.

VOLUME I
DEPARTMENTAL DITTIES AND OTHER VERSES

I have eaten your bread and salt,
 I have drunk your water and wine,
The deaths ye died I have watched beside,
 And the lives that ye led were mine.

Was there aught that I did not share
 In vigil or toil or ease,
One joy or woe that I did not know,
 Dear hearts across the seas?

I have written the tale of our life
 For a sheltered people's mirth,
In jesting guise—but ye are wise,
And ye know what the jest is worth.

GENERAL SUMMARY

We are very slightly changed

From the semi-apes who ranged

 India's prehistoric clay;

Whoso drew the longest bow,

Ran his brother down, you know,

 As we run men down today.

"Dowb," the first of all his race,

Met the Mammoth face to face

 On the lake or in the cave,

Stole the steadiest canoe,

Ate the quarry others slew,

 Died—and took the finest grave.

When they scratched the reindeer-bone

Someone made the sketch his own,

 Filched it from the artist—then,

Even in those early days,

Won a simple Viceroy's praise

 Through the toil of other men.

Ere they hewed the Sphinx's visage

Favoritism governed kissage,

Even as it does in this age.

Who shall doubt the secret hid

Under Cheops' pyramid

Was that the contractor did

 Cheops out of several millions?

Or that Joseph's sudden rise

To Comptroller of Supplies

Was a fraud of monstrous size

 On King Pharoah's swart Civilians?

Thus, the artless songs I sing

Do not deal with anything

 New or never said before.

As it was in the beginning,

Is today official sinning,

 And shall be forevermore.

ARMY HEADQUARTERS

Old is the song that I sing—

 Old as my unpaid bills—

Old as the chicken that kitmutgars bring

Men at dak-bungalows—old as the Hills.

Ahasuerus Jenkins of the "Operatic Own"

 Was dowered with a tenor voice of super-Santley tone.

His views on equitation were, perhaps, a trifle queer;

He had no seat worth mentioning, but oh! he had an ear.

He clubbed his wretched company a dozen times a day,

He used to quit his charger in a parabolic way,

His method of saluting was the joy of all beholders,

But Ahasuerus Jenkins had a head upon his shoulders.

He took two months to Simla when the year was at the spring,

And underneath the deodars eternally did sing.

He warbled like a bulbul, but particularly at

Cornelia Agrippina who was musical and fat.

She controlled a humble husband, who, in turn, controlled a Dept.,

Where Cornelia Agrippina's human singing-birds were kept

From April to October on a plump retaining fee,

Supplied, of course, per mensem, by the Indian Treasury.

Cornelia used to sing with him, and Jenkins used to play;

He praised unblushingly her notes, for he was false as they:

So when the winds of April turned the budding roses brown,

Cornelia told her husband: "Tom, you mustn't send him down."

They haled him from his regiment which didn't much regret him;

They found for him an office-stool, and on that stool they set him,

To play with maps and catalogues three idle hours a day,

And draw his plump retaining fee—which means his double pay.

Now, ever after dinner, when the coffeecups are brought,

Ahasuerus waileth o'er the grand pianoforte;

And, thanks to fair Cornelia, his fame hath waxen great,

And Ahasuerus Jenkins is a power in the State.

STUDY OF AN ELEVATION, IN INDIAN INK

This ditty is a string of lies.

But—how the deuce did Gubbins rise?

POTIPHAR GUBBINS, C. E.,

Stands at the top of the tree;

And I muse in my bed on the reasons that led

To the hoisting of Potiphar G.

Potiphar Gubbins, C. E.,

Is seven years junior to Me;

Each bridge that he makes he either buckles or breaks,

And his work is as rough as he.

Potiphar Gubbins, C. E.,

Is coarse as a chimpanzee;

And I can't understand why you gave him your hand,

Lovely Mehitabel Lee.

Potiphar Gubbins, C. E.,

Is dear to the Powers that Be;

For They bow and They smile in an affable style

Which is seldom accorded to Me.

Potiphar Gubbins, C. E.,

Is certain as certain can be

Of a highly-paid post which is claimed by a host

Of seniors—including Me.

Careless and lazy is he,

Greatly inferior to Me.

What is the spell that you manage so well,

Commonplace Potiphar G.?

Lovely Mehitabel Lee,

Let me inquire of thee,

Should I have riz to what Potiphar is,

Hadst thou been mated to me?

A LEGEND

This is the reason why Rustum Beg,

Rajah of Kolazai,

Drinketh the "simpkin" and brandy peg,

Maketh the money to fly,

Vexeth a Government, tender and kind,

Also—but this is a detail—blind.

RUSTUM BEG of Kolazai—slightly backward native state

Lusted for a C. S. I.,—so began to sanitate.

Built a Jail and Hospital—nearly built a City drain—

Till his faithful subjects all thought their Ruler was insane.

Strange departures made he then—yea, Departments stranger still,

Half a dozen Englishmen helped the Rajah with a will,

Talked of noble aims and high, hinted of a future fine

For the state of Kolazai, on a strictly Western line.

Rajah Rustum held his peace; lowered octroi dues a half;

Organized a State Police; purified the Civil Staff;

Settled cess and tax afresh in a very liberal way;

Cut temptations of the flesh—also cut the Bukhshi's pay;

Roused his Secretariat to a fine Mahratta fury,

By a Hookum hinting at supervision of dasturi;

Turned the State of Kolazai very nearly upside-down;

When the end of May was nigh, waited his achievement crown.

When the Birthday Honors came,

Sad to state and sad to see,

Stood against the Rajah's name nothing more than C. I. E.!

Things were lively for a week in the State of Kolazai.

Even now the people speak of that time regretfully.

How he disendowed the Jail—stopped at once the City drain;

Turned to beauty fair and frail—got his senses back again;

Doubled taxes, cesses, all; cleared away each new-built thana;

Turned the two-lakh Hospital into a superb Zenana;

Heaped upon the Bukhshi Sahib wealth and honors manifold;

Clad himself in Eastern garb—squeezed his people as of old.

Happy, happy Kolazai! Never more will Rustum Beg

Play to catch the Viceroy's eye. He prefers the "simpkin" peg.

THE STORY OF URIAH

"Now there were two men in one city;

the one rich and the other poor."

Jack Barrett went to Quetta

 Because they told him to.

He left his wife at Simla

 On three-fourths his monthly screw:

Jack Barrett died at Quetta

 Ere the next month's pay he drew.

Jack Barrett went to Quetta.

 He didn't understand

The reason of his transfer

 From the pleasant mountain-land:

The season was September,

 And it killed him out of hand.

Jack Barrett went to Quetta,

 And there gave up the ghost,

Attempting two men's duty

 In that very healthy post;

And Mrs. Barrett mourned for him

 Five lively months at most.

Jack Barrett's bones at Quetta

 Enjoy profound repose;

But I shouldn't be astonished

If now his spirit knows

The reason of his transfer

From the Himalayan snows.

And, when the Last Great Bugle Call

Adown the Hurnal throbs,

When the last grim joke is entered

In the big black Book of Jobs,

And Quetta graveyards give again

Their victims to the air,

I shouldn't like to be the man

Who sent Jack Barrett there.

THE POST THAT FITTED

Though tangled and twisted the course of true love

 This ditty explains,

No tangle's so tangled it cannot improve

 If the Lover has brains.

Ere the steamer bore him Eastward, Sleary was engaged to marry

An attractive girl at Tunbridge, whom he called "my little Carrie."

Sleary's pay was very modest; Sleary was the other way.

Who can cook a two-plate dinner on eight poor rupees a day?

Long he pondered o'er the question in his scantly furnished quarters—

Then proposed to Minnie Boffkin, eldest of Judge Boffkin's daughters.

Certainly an impecunious Subaltern was not a catch,

But the Boffkins knew that Minnie mightn't make another match.

So they recognised the business and, to feed and clothe the bride,

Got him made a Something Something somewhere on the Bombay side.

Anyhow, the billet carried pay enough for him to marry—

As the artless Sleary put it:—"Just the thing for me and Carrie."

Did he, therefore, jilt Miss Boffkin—impulse of a baser mind?

No! He started epileptic fits of an appalling kind.

[Of his modus operandi only this much I could gather:—

"Pears's shaving sticks will give you little taste and lots of lather."]

Frequently in public places his affliction used to smite

Sleary with distressing vigour—always in the Boffkins' sight.

Ere a week was over Minnie weepingly returned his ring,

Told him his "unhappy weakness" stopped all thought of marrying.

Sleary bore the information with a chastened holy joy,—

Epileptic fits don't matter in Political employ,—

Wired three short words to Carrie—took his ticket, packed his kit—

Bade farewell to Minnie Boffkin in one last, long, lingering fit.

Four weeks later, Carrie Sleary read—and laughed until she wept—

Mrs. Boffkin's warning letter on the "wretched epilept."...

Year by year, in pious patience, vengeful Mrs. Boffkin sits

Waiting for the Sleary babies to develop Sleary's fits.

PUBLIC WASTE

Walpole talks of "a man and his price."

 List to a ditty queer—

The sale of a Deputy-Acting-Vice-

 Resident-Engineer,

Bought like a bullock, hoof and hide,

By the Little Tin Gods on the Mountain Side.

By the Laws of the Family Circle 'tis written in letters of brass

That only a Colonel from Chatham can manage the Railways of State,

Because of the gold on his breeks, and the subjects wherein he must pass;

Because in all matters that deal not with Railways his knowledge is great.

Now Exeter Battleby Tring had laboured from boyhood to eld

On the Lines of the East and the West, and eke of the North and South;

Many Lines had he built and surveyed—important the posts which he held;

And the Lords of the Iron Horse were dumb when he opened his mouth.

Black as the raven his garb, and his heresies jettier still—

Hinting that Railways required lifetimes of study and knowledge—

Never clanked sword by his side—Vauban he knew not nor drill—

Nor was his name on the list of the men who had passed through the "College."

Wherefore the Little Tin Gods harried their little tin souls,

Seeing he came not from Chatham, jingled no spurs at his heels,

Knowing that, nevertheless, was he first on the Government rolls

For the billet of "Railway Instructor to Little Tin Gods on Wheels."

Letters not seldom they wrote him, "having the honour to state,"

It would be better for all men if he were laid on the shelf.

Much would accrue to his bank-book, an he consented to wait

Until the Little Tin Gods built him a berth for himself,

"Special, well paid, and exempt from the Law of the Fifty and Five,

Even to Ninety and Nine"—these were the terms of the pact:

Thus did the Little Tin Gods (long may Their Highnesses thrive!)

Silence his mouth with rupees, keeping their Circle intact;

Appointing a Colonel from Chatham who managed the Bhamo State Line

(The which was one mile and one furlong—a guaranteed twenty-inch gauge),

So Exeter Battleby Tring consented his claims to resign,

And died, on four thousand a month, in the ninetieth year of his age!

DELILAH

We have another viceroy now,—those days are dead and done
Of Delilah Aberyswith and depraved Ulysses Gunne.

Delilah Aberyswith was a lady—not too young—
With a perfect taste in dresses and a badly-bitted tongue,
With a thirst for information, and a greater thirst for praise,
And a little house in Simla in the Prehistoric Days.

By reason of her marriage to a gentleman in power,
Delilah was acquainted with the gossip of the hour;
And many little secrets, of the half-official kind,
Were whispered to Delilah, and she bore them all in mind.

She patronized extensively a man, Ulysses Gunne,
Whose mode of earning money was a low and shameful one.
He wrote for certain papers, which, as everybody knows,
Is worse than serving in a shop or scaring off the crows.

He praised her "queenly beauty" first; and, later on, he hinted
At the "vastness of her intellect" with compliment unstinted.
He went with her a-riding, and his love for her was such
That he lent her all his horses and—she galled them very much.

One day, THEY brewed a secret of a fine financial sort;
It related to Appointments, to a Man and a Report.
'Twas almost worth the keeping,—only seven people knew it—
And Gunne rose up to seek the truth and patiently pursue it.

It was a Viceroy's Secret, but—perhaps the wine was red—

Perhaps an Aged Councillor had lost his aged head—

Perhaps Delilah's eyes were bright—Delilah's whispers sweet—

The Aged Member told her what 'twere treason to repeat.

Ulysses went a-riding, and they talked of love and flowers;

Ulysses went a-calling, and he called for several hours;

Ulysses went a-waltzing, and Delilah helped him dance—

Ulysses let the waltzes go, and waited for his chance.

The summer sun was setting, and the summer air was still,

The couple went a-walking in the shade of Summer Hill.

The wasteful sunset faded out in Turkish-green and gold,

Ulysses pleaded softly, and— that bad Delilah told!

Next morn, a startled Empire learnt the all-important news;

Next week, the Aged Councillor was shaking in his shoes.

Next month, I met Delilah and she did not show the least

Hesitation in affirming that Ulysses was a "beast."

We have another Viceroy now, those days are dead and done—

Of Delilah Aberyswith and most mean Ulysses Gunne!

WHAT HAPPENED

Hurree Chunder Mookerjee, pride of Bow Bazaar,

Owner of a native press, "Barrishter-at-Lar,"

Waited on the Government with a claim to wear

Sabres by the bucketful, rifles by the pair.

Then the Indian Government winked a wicked wink,

Said to Chunder Mookerjee: "Stick to pen and ink.

They are safer implements, but, if you insist,

We will let you carry arms wheresoe'er you list."

Hurree Chunder Mookerjee sought the gunsmith and

Bought the tubes of Lancaster, Ballard, Dean, and Bland,

Bought a shiny bowie-knife, bought a town-made sword,

Jingled like a carriage-horse when he went abroad.

But the Indian Government, always keen to please,

Also gave permission to horrid men like these—

Yar Mahommed Yusufzai, down to kill or steal,

Chimbu Singh from Bikaneer, Tantia the Bhil;

Killar Khan the Marri chief, Jowar Singh the Sikh,

Nubbee Baksh Punjabi Jat, Abdul Huq Rafiq—

He was a Wahabi; last, little Boh Hla-oo

Took advantage of the Act—took a Snider too.

They were unenlightened men, Ballard knew them not.

They procured their swords and guns chiefly on the spot;

And the lore of centuries, plus a hundred fights,

Made them slow to disregard one another's rights.

With a unanimity dear to patriot hearts

All those hairy gentlemen out of foreign parts

Said: "The good old days are back—let us go to war!"

 Swaggered down the Grand Trunk Road into Bow Bazaar,

Nubbee Baksh Punjabi Jat found a hide-bound flail;

Chimbu Singh from Bikaneer oiled his Tonk jezail;

Yar Mahommed Yusufzai spat and grinned with glee

As he ground the butcher-knife of the Khyberee.

Jowar Singh the Sikh procured sabre, quoit, and mace,

Abdul Huq, Wahabi, jerked his dagger from its place,

While amid the jungle-grass danced and grinned and jabbered

Little Boh Hla-oo and cleared his dah-blade from the scabbard.

What became of Mookerjee? Soothly, who can say?

Yar Mahommed only grins in a nasty way,

Jowar Singh is reticent, Chimbu Singh is mute.

But the belts of all of them simply bulge with loot.

What became of Ballard's guns? Afghans black and grubby

Sell them for their silver weight to the men of Pubbi;

And the shiny bowie-knife and the town-made sword are

Hanging in a Marri camp just across the Border.

What became of Mookerjee? Ask Mahommed Yar

Prodding Siva's sacred bull down the Bow Bazaar.

Speak to placid Nubbee Baksh—question land and sea—

Ask the Indian Congressmen—only don't ask me!

PINK DOMINOES

They are fools who kiss and tell"—

 Wisely has the poet sung.

Man may hold all sorts of posts

 If he'll only hold his tongue.

Jenny and Me were engaged, you see,

 On the eve of the Fancy Ball;

So a kiss or two was nothing to you

 Or any one else at all.

Jenny would go in a domino—

 Pretty and pink but warm;

While I attended, clad in a splendid

 Austrian uniform.

Now we had arranged, through notes exchanged

 Early that afternoon,

At Number Four to waltz no more,

 But to sit in the dusk and spoon.

I wish you to see that Jenny and Me

 Had barely exchanged our troth;

So a kiss or two was strictly due

 By, from, and between us both.

When Three was over, an eager lover,

 I fled to the gloom outside;

And a Domino came out also

 Whom I took for my future bride.

That is to say, in a casual way,

 I slipped my arm around her;

With a kiss or two (which is nothing to you),

 And ready to kiss I found her.

She turned her head and the name she said

 Was certainly not my own;

But ere I could speak, with a smothered shriek

 She fled and left me alone.

Then Jenny came, and I saw with shame

 She'd doffed her domino;

And I had embraced an alien waist—

 But I did not tell her so.

Next morn I knew that there were two

 Dominoes pink, and one

Had cloaked the spouse of Sir Julian House,

 Our big Political gun.

Sir J. was old, and her hair was gold,

 And her eye was a blue cerulean;

And the name she said when she turned her head

 Was not in the least like "Julian."

THE MAN WHO COULD WRITE

Shun—shun the Bowl! That fatal, facile drink
 Has ruined many geese who dipped their quills in 't;
Bribe, murder, marry, but steer clear of Ink
 Save when you write receipts for paid-up bills in 't.

There may be silver in the "blue-black"—all
I know of is the iron and the gall.

Boanerges Blitzen, servant of the Queen,
Is a dismal failure—is a Might-have-been.
In a luckless moment he discovered men
Rise to high position through a ready pen.
Boanerges Blitzen argued therefore—"I,
With the selfsame weapon, can attain as high."
 Only he did not possess when he made the trial,
Wicked wit of C-lv-n, irony of L—l.

[Men who spar with Government need, to back their blows,
Something more than ordinary journalistic prose.]

Never young Civilian's prospects were so bright,
Till an Indian paper found that he could write:
Never young Civilian's prospects were so dark,
When the wretched Blitzen wrote to make his mark.
Certainly he scored it, bold, and black, and firm,
In that Indian paper—made his seniors squirm,
Quoted office scandals, wrote the tactless truth—

Was there ever known a more misguided youth?

When the Rag he wrote for praised his plucky game,

Boanerges Blitzen felt that this was Fame;

When the men he wrote of shook their heads and swore,

Boanerges Blitzen only wrote the more:

Posed as Young Ithuriel, resolute and grim,

Till he found promotion didn't come to him;

Till he found that reprimands weekly were his lot,

And his many Districts curiously hot.

Till he found his furlough strangely hard to win,

Boanerges Blitzen didn't care to pin:

Then it seemed to dawn on him something wasn't right—

Boanerges Blitzen put it down to "spite";

Languished in a District desolate and dry;

Watched the Local Government yearly pass him by;

Wondered where the hitch was; called it most unfair.

* * * * * * * * *

That was seven years ago—and he still is there!

MUNICIPAL

"Why is my District death-rate low?"

 Said Binks of Hezabad.

"Well, drains, and sewage-outfalls are

 "My own peculiar fad.

"I learnt a lesson once, It ran

"Thus," quoth that most veracious man:—

It was an August evening and, in snowy garments clad,

I paid a round of visits in the lines of Hezabad;

When, presently, my Waler saw, and did not like at all,

A Commissariat elephant careering down the Mall.

I couldn't see the driver, and across my mind it rushed

That that Commissariat elephant had suddenly gone musth.

I didn't care to meet him, and I couldn't well get down,

So I let the Waler have it, and we headed for the town.

The buggy was a new one and, praise Dykes, it stood the strain,

Till the Waler jumped a bullock just above the City Drain;

And the next that I remember was a hurricane of squeals,

And the creature making toothpicks of my five-foot patent wheels.

He seemed to want the owner, so I fled, distraught with fear,

To the Main Drain sewage-outfall while he snorted in my ear—

Reached the four-foot drain-head safely and, in darkness and despair,

Felt the brute's proboscis fingering my terror-stiffened hair.

Heard it trumpet on my shoulder—tried to crawl a little higher—

Found the Main Drain sewage outfall blocked, some eight feet up, with mire;

And, for twenty reeking minutes, Sir, my very marrow froze,

While the trunk was feeling blindly for a purchase on my toes!

It missed me by a fraction, but my hair was turning grey

Before they called the drivers up and dragged the brute away.

Then I sought the City Elders, and my words were very plain.

They flushed that four-foot drain-head and—it never choked again!

You may hold with surface-drainage, and the sun-for-garbage cure,

Till you've been a periwinkle shrinking coyly up a sewer.

I believe in well-flushed culverts....

This is why the death-rate's small;

And, if you don't believe me, get shikarred yourself. That's all.

A CODE OF MORALS

Lest you should think this story true

I merely mention I

Evolved it lately. 'Tis a most

Unmitigated misstatement.

Now Jones had left his new-wed bride to keep his house in order,

And hied away to the Hurrum Hills above the Afghan border,

To sit on a rock with a heliograph; but ere he left he taught

His wife the working of the Code that sets the miles at naught.

And Love had made him very sage, as Nature made her fair;

So Cupid and Apollo linked, per heliograph, the pair.

At dawn, across the Hurrum Hills, he flashed her counsel wise—

At e'en, the dying sunset bore her husband's homilies.

He warned her 'gainst seductive youths in scarlet clad and gold,

As much as 'gainst the blandishments paternal of the old;

But kept his gravest warnings for (hereby the ditty hangs)

That snowy-haired Lothario, Lieutenant-General Bangs.

'Twas General Bangs, with Aide and Staff, who tittupped on the way,

When they beheld a heliograph tempestuously at play.

They thought of Border risings, and of stations sacked and burnt—

So stopped to take the message down—and this is what they learnt—

"Dash dot dot, dot, dot dash, dot dash dot" twice. The General swore.

"Was ever General Officer addressed as 'dear' before?

"'My Love,' i' faith! 'My Duck,' Gadzooks! 'My darling popsy-wop!'

"Spirit of great Lord Wolseley, who is on that mountaintop?"

The artless Aide-de-camp was mute; the gilded Staff were still,

As, dumb with pent-up mirth, they booked that message from the hill;

For clear as summer lightning-flare, the husband's warning ran:—

"Don't dance or ride with General Bangs—a most immoral man."

[At dawn, across the Hurrum Hills, he flashed her counsel wise—

But, howsoever Love be blind, the world at large hath eyes.]

With damnatory dot and dash he heliographed his wife

Some interesting details of the General's private life.

The artless Aide-de-camp was mute, the shining Staff were still,

And red and ever redder grew the General's shaven gill.

And this is what he said at last (his feelings matter not):—

"I think we've tapped a private line. Hi! Threes about there! Trot!"

All honour unto Bangs, for ne'er did Jones thereafter know

By word or act official who read off that helio.

But the tale is on the Frontier, and from Michni to Mooltan

They know the worthy General as "that most immoral man."

THE LAST DEPARTMENT

Twelve hundred million men are spread

About this Earth, and I and You

Wonder, when You and I are dead,

"What will those luckless millions do?"

None whole or clean, we cry, "or free from stain

Of favour." Wait awhile, till we attain

The Last Department where nor fraud nor fools,

Nor grade nor greed, shall trouble us again.

Fear, Favour, or Affection—what are these

To the grim Head who claims our services?

I never knew a wife or interest yet

Delay that pukka step, miscalled "decease";

When leave, long overdue, none can deny;

When idleness of all Eternity

Becomes our furlough, and the marigold

Our thriftless, bullion-minting Treasury

Transferred to the Eternal Settlement,

Each in his strait, wood-scantled office pent,

No longer Brown reverses Smith's appeals,

Or Jones records his Minute of Dissent.

And One, long since a pillar of the Court,

As mud between the beams thereof is wrought;

And One who wrote on phosphates for the crops

Is subject-matter of his own Report.

These be the glorious ends whereto we pass—

Let Him who Is, go call on Him who Was;

 And He shall see the mallie steals the slab

For currie-grinder, and for goats the grass.

A breath of wind, a Border bullet's flight,

A draught of water, or a horse's fright—

 The droning of the fat Sheristadar

Ceases, the punkah stops, and falls the night

For you or Me. Do those who live decline

The step that offers, or their work resign?

 Trust me, Today's Most Indispensables,

Five hundred men can take your place or mine.

OTHER VERSES
RECESSIONAL

(A Victorian Ode)

God of our fathers, known of old—
 Lord of our far-flung battle line—
Beneath whose awful hand we hold
 Dominion over palm and pine—

Lord God of Hosts, be with us yet,
Lest we forget—lest we forget!

The tumult and the shouting dies—
 The Captains and the Kings depart—
Still stands Thine ancient sacrifice,
 An humble and a contrite heart.

Lord God of Hosts, be with us yet,
Lest we forget—lest we forget!

Far-called our navies melt away—
 On dune and headland sinks the fire—
Lo, all our pomp of yesterday
 Is one with Nineveh and Tyre!

Judge of the Nations, spare us yet,
Lest we forget—lest we forget!

If, drunk with sight of power, we loose

Wild tongues that have not Thee in awe—

Such boastings as the Gentiles use,

Or lesser breeds without the Law—

Lord God of Hosts, be with us yet,

Lest we forget—lest we forget!

For heathen heart that puts her trust

In reeking tube and iron shard—

All valiant dust that builds on dust,

And guarding calls not Thee to guard.

For frantic boast and foolish word,

Thy Mercy on Thy People, Lord!

Amen.

THE VAMPIRE

The verses—as suggested by the painting by Philip Burne Jones, first
exhibited at the new gallery in London in 1897.

A fool there was and he made his prayer

 (Even as you and I!)

To a rag and a bone and a hank of hair

(We called her the woman who did not care),

But the fool he called her his lady fair

 (Even as you and I!)

Oh the years we waste and the tears we waste

 And the work of our head and hand,

Belong to the woman who did not know

(And now we know that she never could know)

 And did not understand.

A fool there was and his goods he spent

 (Even as you and I!)

Honor and faith and a sure intent

But a fool must follow his natural bent

(And it wasn't the least what the lady meant),

 (Even as you and I!)

Oh the toil we lost and the spoil we lost

 And the excellent things we planned,

Belong to the woman who didn't know why

(And now we know she never knew why)

And did not understand.

The fool we stripped to his foolish hide

(Even as you and I!)

Which she might have seen when she threw him aside—

(But it isn't on record the lady tried)

So some of him lived but the most of him died—

(Even as you and I!)

And it isn't the shame and it isn't the blame

That stings like a white hot brand.

It's coming to know that she never knew why

(Seeing at last she could never know why)

And never could understand.

TO THE UNKNOWN GODDESS

Will you conquer my heart with your beauty; my soul going out from afar?

Shall I fall to your hand as a victim of crafty and cautious shikar?

Have I met you and passed you already, unknowing, unthinking and blind?

Shall I meet you next session at Simla, O sweetest and best of your kind?

Does the P. and O. bear you to meward, or, clad in short frocks in the West,

Are you growing the charms that shall capture and torture the heart in my

breast?

Will you stay in the Plains till September—my passion as warm as the day?

Will you bring me to book on the Mountains, or where the thermantidotes play?

When the light of your eyes shall make pallid the mean lesser lights I pursue,

And the charm of your presence shall lure me from love of the gay "thirteen-

two";

When the peg and the pig-skin shall please not; when I buy me Calcutta-build

clothes;

When I quit the Delight of Wild Asses; forswearing the swearing of oaths;

As a deer to the hand of the hunter when I turn 'mid the gibes of my friends;

When the days of my freedom are numbered, and the life of the bachelor ends.

Ah, Goddess! child, spinster, or widow—as of old on Mars Hill whey they

raised

To the God that they knew not an altar—so I, a young Pagan, have praised

The Goddess I know not nor worship; yet, if half that men tell me be true,

You will come in the future, and therefore these verses are written to you.

[326] RUDYARD KIPLING

THE RUPAIYAT OF OMAR KAL'VIN

[Allowing for the difference 'twixt prose and rhymed exaggeration, this ought
to reproduce the sense of what Sir A— told the nation sometime ago, when the
Government struck from our incomes two per cent.]

Now the New Year, reviving last Year's Debt,

The Thoughtful Fisher casteth wide his Net;

 So I with begging Dish and ready Tongue

Assail all Men for all that I can get.

Imports indeed are gone with all their Dues—

Lo! Salt a Lever that I dare not use,

 Nor may I ask the Tillers in Bengal—

Surely my Kith and Kin will not refuse!

Pay—and I promise by the Dust of Spring,

Retrenchment. If my promises can bring

 Comfort, Ye have Them now a thousandfold—

By Allah! I will promise Anything!

Indeed, indeed, Retrenchment oft before

I swore—but did I mean it when I swore?

 And then, and then, We wandered to the Hills,

And so the Little Less became Much More.

Whether a Boileaugunge or Babylon,

I know not how the wretched Thing is done,

 The Items of Receipt grow surely small;

The Items of Expense mount one by one.

I cannot help it. What have I to do

With One and Five, or Four, or Three, or Two?

 Let Scribes spit Blood and Sulphur as they please,

Or Statesmen call me foolish—Heed not you.

Behold, I promise—Anything You will.

Behold, I greet you with an empty Till—

 Ah! Fellow-Sinners, of your Charity

Seek not the Reason of the Dearth, but fill.

For if I sinned and fell, where lies the Gain

Of Knowledge? Would it ease you of your Pain

 To know the tangled Threads of Revenue,

I ravel deeper in a hopeless Skein?

"Who hath not Prudence"—what was it I said,

Of Her who paints her Eyes and tires Her Head,

 And gibes and mocks the People in the Street,

And fawns upon them for Her thriftless Bread?

Accursed is She of Eve's daughters—She

Hath cast off Prudence, and Her End shall be

 Destruction... Brethren, of your Bounty

Some portion of your daily Bread to Me.

LA NUIT BLANCHE

A much-discerning Public hold
 The Singer generally sings
And prints and sells his past for gold.

Whatever I may here disclaim,
 The very clever folk I sing to
 Will most indubitably cling to
Their pet delusion, just the same.

I had seen, as the dawn was breaking
 And I staggered to my rest,
Tari Devi softly shaking
 From the Cart Road to the crest.

I had seen the spurs of Jakko
 Heave and quiver, swell and sink.
Was it Earthquake or tobacco,
 Day of Doom, or Night of Drink?

In the full, fresh fragrant morning
 I observed a camel crawl,
Laws of gravitation scorning,
 On the ceiling and the wall;
Then I watched a fender walking,
 And I heard grey leeches sing,
And a red-hot monkey talking
 Did not seem the proper thing.

Then a Creature, skinned and crimson,
 Ran about the floor and cried,
And they said that I had the "jims" on,
 And they dosed me with bromide,
And they locked me in my bedroom—
 Me and one wee Blood Red Mouse—
Though I said: "To give my head room
 You had best unroof the house."

But my words were all unheeded,
 Though I told the grave M.D.
That the treatment really needed
 Was a dip in open sea
That was lapping just below me,
 Smooth as silver, white as snow,
And it took three men to throw me
 When I found I could not go.

Half the night I watched the Heavens
 Fizz like '81 champagne—
Fly to sixes and to sevens,
 Wheel and thunder back again;
And when all was peace and order
 Save one planet nailed askew,
Much I wept because my warder
 Would not let me set it true.

After frenzied hours of waiting,

When the Earth and Skies were dumb,

Pealed an awful voice dictating

 An interminable sum,

Changing to a tangle story—

 "What she said you said I said"—

Till the Moon arose in glory,

 And I found her... in my head;

Then a Face came, blind and weeping,

 And It couldn't wipe its eyes,

And It muttered I was keeping

 Back the moonlight from the skies;

So I patted it for pity,

 But it whistled shrill with wrath,

And a huge black Devil City

 Poured its peoples on my path.

So I fled with steps uncertain

 On a thousand-year long race,

But the bellying of the curtain

 Kept me always in one place;

While the tumult rose and maddened

 To the roar of Earth on fire,

Ere it ebbed and sank and saddened

 To a whisper tense as wire.

In tolerable stillness

 Rose one little, little star,

And it chuckled at my illness,

And it mocked me from afar;

And its brethren came and eyed me,

 Called the Universe to aid,

Till I lay, with naught to hide me,

 'Neath the Scorn of All Things Made.

Dun and saffron, robed and splendid,

 Broke the solemn, pitying Day,

And I knew my pains were ended,

 And I turned and tried to pray;

But my speech was shattered wholly,

 And I wept as children weep.

Till the dawn-wind, softly, slowly,

 Brought to burning eyelids sleep.

MY RIVAL

I go to concert, party, ball—
 What profit is in these?
I sit alone against the wall
 And strive to look at ease.

The incense that is mine by right
 They burn before her shrine;
And that's because I'm seventeen
 And She is forty-nine.

I cannot check my girlish blush,
 My color comes and goes;
I redden to my finger-tips,
 And sometimes to my nose.

But She is white where white should be,
 And red where red should shine.
The blush that flies at seventeen
 Is fixed at forty-nine.

I wish I had Her constant cheek;
 I wish that I could sing
All sorts of funny little songs,
 Not quite the proper thing.

I'm very gauche and very shy,
 Her jokes aren't in my line;

And, worst of all, I'm seventeen
 While She is forty-nine.

The young men come, the young men go
 Each pink and white and neat,
She's older than their mothers, but
 They grovel at Her feet.

They walk beside Her 'rickshaw wheels—
 None ever walk by mine;
And that's because I'm seventeen
 And She is forty-nine.

She rides with half a dozen men,
 (She calls them "boys" and "mashers")
I trot along the Mall alone;
 My prettiest frocks and sashes
Don't help to fill my programme-card,
 And vainly I repine
From ten to two A.M. Ah me!
 Would I were forty-nine!

She calls me "darling," "pet," and "dear,"
 And "sweet retiring maid."
I'm always at the back, I know,
 She puts me in the shade.

She introduces me to men,
 "Cast" lovers, I opine,

For sixty takes to seventeen,

 Nineteen to forty-nine.

But even She must older grow

 And end Her dancing days,

She can't go on forever so

 At concerts, balls and plays.

One ray of priceless hope I see

 Before my footsteps shine;

Just think, that She'll be eighty-one

 When I am forty-nine.

THE LOVERS' LITANY

Eyes of grey—a sodden quay,

Driving rain and falling tears,

As the steamer wears to sea

In a parting storm of cheers.

Sing, for Faith and Hope are high—

None so true as you and I—

Sing the Lovers' Litany:

"Love like ours can never die!"

Eyes of black—a throbbing keel,

Milky foam to left and right;

Whispered converse near the wheel

In the brilliant tropic night.

Cross that rules the Southern Sky!

Stars that sweep and wheel and fly,

Hear the Lovers' Litany:

Love like ours can never die!"

Eyes of brown—a dusty plain

Split and parched with heat of June,

Flying hoof and tightened rein,

Hearts that beat the old, old tune.

Side by side the horses fly,

Frame we now the old reply

Of the Lovers' Litany:

"Love like ours can never die!"

Eyes of blue—the Simla Hills

Silvered with the moonlight hoar;

Pleading of the waltz that thrills,

Dies and echoes round Benmore.

"Mabel," "Officers," "Goodbye,"

Glamour, wine, and witchery—

On my soul's sincerity,

"Love like ours can never die!"

Maidens of your charity,

Pity my most luckless state.

Four times Cupid's debtor I—

Bankrupt in quadruplicate.

Yet, despite this evil case,

And a maiden showed me grace,

Four-and-forty times would I

Sing the Lovers' Litany:

"Love like ours can never die!"

A BALLAD OF BURIAL

("Saint @Proxed's ever was the Church for peace")

If down here I chance to die,
 Solemnly I beg you take
All that is left of "I"
 To the Hills for old sake's sake,
Pack me very thoroughly
 In the ice that used to slake
Pegs I drank when I was dry—
 This observe for old sake's sake.

To the railway station hie,
 There a single ticket take
For Umballa—goods-train—I
 Shall not mind delay or shake.

I shall rest contentedly
 Spite of clamor coolies make;
Thus in state and dignity
 Send me up for old sake's sake.

Next the sleepy Babu wake,
 Book a Kalka van "for four."
Few, I think, will care to make
 Journeys with me any more
As they used to do of yore.

I shall need a "special" break—

Thing I never took before—

 Get me one for old sake's sake.

After that—arrangements make.

 No hotel will take me in,

And a bullock's back would break

 'Neath the teak and leaden skin

Tonga ropes are frail and thin,

 Or, did I a back-seat take,

In a tonga I might spin,—

 Do your best for old sake's sake.

After that—your work is done.

 Recollect a Padre must

Mourn the dear departed one—

 Throw the ashes and the dust.

Don't go down at once. I trust

 You will find excuse to "snake

Three days' casual on the bust."

 Get your fun for old sake's sake.

I could never stand the Plains.

 Think of blazing June and May

Think of those September rains

 Yearly till the Judgment Day!

I should never rest in peace,

 I should sweat and lie awake.

Rail me then, on my decease,

 To the Hills for old sake's sake.

DIVIDED DESTINIES

It was an artless Bandar, and he danced upon a pine,

And much I wondered how he lived, and where the beast might dine,

And many, many other things, till, o'er my morning smoke,

I slept the sleep of idleness and dreamt that Bandar spoke.

He said: "O man of many clothes! Sad crawler on the Hills!

Observe, I know not Ranken's shop, nor Ranken's monthly bills;

I take no heed to trousers or the coats that you call dress;

Nor am I plagued with little cards for little drinks at Mess.

"I steal the bunnia's grain at morn, at noon and eventide,

(For he is fat and I am spare), I roam the mountain side,

I follow no man's carriage, and no, never in my life

Have I flirted at Peliti's with another Bandar's wife.

"O man of futile fopperies—unnecessary wraps;

I own no ponies in the hills, I drive no tall-wheeled traps;

I buy me not twelve-button gloves, 'short-sixes' eke, or rings,

Nor do I waste at Hamilton's my wealth on 'pretty things.'

"I quarrel with my wife at home, we never fight abroad;

But Mrs. B. has grasped the fact I am her only lord.

I never heard of fever—dumps nor debts depress my soul;

And I pity and despise you!" Here he poached my breakfast-roll.

His hide was very mangy, and his face was very red,

And ever and anon he scratched with energy his head.

His manners were not always nice, but how my spirit cried

To be an artless Bandar loose upon the mountain side!

So I answered: "Gentle Bandar, an inscrutable Decree

Makes thee a gleesome fleasome Thou, and me a wretched Me.

Go! Depart in peace, my brother, to thy home amid the pine;

Yet forget not once a mortal wished to change his lot for thine."

THE MASQUE OF PLENTY

Argument.—The Indian Government being minded to discover the economic condition of their lands, sent a Committee to inquire into it; and saw that it was good.

Scene.—The wooded heights of Simla. The Incarnation of the Government of India in the raiment of the Angel of Plenty sings, to pianoforte accompaniment:—

"How sweet is the shepherd's sweet life!
　From the dawn to the even he strays—
And his tongue shall be filled with praise.

　(adagio dim.) Filled with praise!"

(largendo con sp.) Now this is the position,
　　　　Go make an inquisition
　　　　Into their real condition
　　　　As swiftly as ye may.

　　　(p) Ay, paint our swarthy billions
　　　　The richest of vermillions
　　　　Ere two well-led cotillions
　　　　Have danced themselves away.

Turkish Patrol, as able and intelligent Investigators wind
　　　down the Himalayas:—

What is the state of the Nation? What is its occupation?

Hi! get along, get along, get along—lend us the information!

(dim.) Census the byle and the yabu—capture a first-class Babu,

 Set him to file Gazetteers—Gazetteers...

 (ff) What is the state of the Nation, etc., etc.

Interlude, from Nowhere in Particular, to stringed and Oriental
instruments.

Our cattle reel beneath the yoke they bear—

 The earth is iron and the skies are brass—

And faint with fervour of the flaming air

 The languid hours pass.

The well is dry beneath the village tree—

 The young wheat withers ere it reach a span,

And belts of blinding sand show cruelly

 Where once the river ran.

Pray, brothers, pray, but to no earthly King—

 Lift up your hands above the blighted grain,

Look westward—if they please, the Gods shall bring

 Their mercy with the rain.

Look westward—bears the blue no brown cloud-bank?

 Nay, it is written—wherefore should we fly?

On our own field and by our cattle's flank

 Lie down, lie down to die!

Semi-Chorus

By the plumed heads of Kings

Waving high,

Where the tall corn springs

O'er the dead.

If they rust or rot we die,

If they ripen we are fed.

Very mighty is the power of our Kings!

Triumphal return to Simla of the Investigators, attired after

the manner of Dionysus, leading a pet tiger-cub in wreaths

of rhubarb-leaves, symbolical of India under medical treatment.

They sing:—

We have seen, we have written—behold it, the proof of our manifold toil!

In their hosts they assembled and told it—the tale of the Sons of the Soil.

We have said of the Sickness—"Where is it?"—and of Death—"It is far from

our ken,"—

We have paid a particular visit to the affluent children of men.

We have trodden the mart and the well-curb—we have stooped to the field and

the byre;

And the King may the forces of Hell curb for the People have all they desire!

Castanets and step-dance:—

Oh, the dom and the mag and the thakur and the thag,

 And the nat and the brinjaree,

And the bunnia and the ryot are as happy and as quiet

And as plump as they can be!

Yes, the jain and the jat in his stucco-fronted hut,

 And the bounding bazugar,

By the favour of the King, are as fat as anything,

 They are—they are—they are!

Recitative, Government of India, with white satin wings and electro-plated

 harp:—

How beautiful upon the Mountains—in peace reclining,

Thus to be assured that our people are unanimously dining.

And though there are places not so blessed as others in natural advantages,

which, after all, was only to be expected,

Proud and glad are we to congratulate you upon the work you have thus ably

effected.

(Cres.) How be-ewtiful upon the Mountains!

Hired Band, brasses only, full chorus:—

 God bless the Squire

And all his rich relations

Who teach us poor people

We eat our proper rations—

 We eat our proper rations,

 In spite of inundations,

 Malarial exhalations,

 And casual starvations,

We have, we have, they say we have—

We have our proper rations!

Chorus of the Crystallised Facts

 Before the beginning of years

 There came to the rule of the State

 Men with a pair of shears,

 Men with an Estimate—

 Strachey with Muir for leaven,

 Lytton with locks that fell,

 Ripon fooling with Heaven,

 And Temple riding like H—ll!

 And the bigots took in hand

 Cess and the falling of rain,

 And the measure of sifted sand

 The dealer puts in the grain—

 Imports by land and sea,

 To uttermost decimal worth,

 And registration—free—

 In the houses of death and of birth.

And fashioned with pens and paper,

And fashioned in black and white,

With Life for a flickering taper

And Death for a blazing light—

With the Armed and the Civil Power,

That his strength might endure for a span—

From Adam's Bridge to Peshawur,

The Much Administered Man.

In the towns of the North and the East,

They gathered as unto rule,

They bade him starve his priest

And send his children to school.

Railways and roads they wrought,

For the needs of the soil within;

A time to squabble in court,

A time to bear and to grin.

And gave him peace in his ways,

Jails—and Police to fight,

Justice—at length of days,

And Right—and Might in the Right.

His speech is of mortgaged bedding,

On his kine he borrows yet,

At his heart is his daughter's wedding,

In his eye foreknowledge of debt.

He eats and hath indigestion,

He toils and he may not stop;

His life is a long-drawn question

Between a crop and a crop.

THE MARE'S NEST

Jane Austen Beecher Stowe de Rouse
 Was good beyond all earthly need;
But, on the other hand, her spouse
 Was very, very bad indeed.

He smoked cigars, called churches slow,
And raced—but this she did not know.

For Belial Machiavelli kept
 The little fact a secret, and,
Though o'er his minor sins she wept,
 Jane Austen did not understand
That Lilly—thirteen-two and bay
Absorbed one-half her husband's pay.

She was so good, she made him worse;
 (Some women are like this, I think;)
He taught her parrot how to curse,
 Her Assam monkey how to drink.

He vexed her righteous soul until
She went up, and he went down hill.

Then came the crisis, strange to say,
 Which turned a good wife to a better.

A telegraphic peon, one day,

Brought her—now, had it been a letter

For Belial Machiavelli, I

Know Jane would just have let it lie.

But 'twas a telegram instead,

　Marked "urgent," and her duty plain

To open it. Jane Austen read:

　"Your Lilly's got a cough again.

Can't understand why she is kept

At your expense." Jane Austen wept.

It was a misdirected wire.

　Her husband was at Shaitanpore.

She spread her anger, hot as fire,

　Through six thin foreign sheets or more.

Sent off that letter, wrote another

To her solicitor—and mother.

Then Belial Machiavelli saw

　Her error and, I trust, his own,

Wired to the minion of the Law,

　And traveled wifeward—not alone.

For Lilly—thirteen-two and bay—

Came in a horse-box all the way.

There was a scene—a weep or two—

　With many kisses. Austen Jane

Rode Lilly all the season through,

 And never opened wires again.

She races now with Belial. This

Is very sad, but so it is.

POSSIBILITIES

Ay, lay him 'neath the Simla pine—

 A fortnight fully to be missed,

 Behold, we lose our fourth at whist,

A chair is vacant where we dine.

His place forgets him; other men

 Have bought his ponies, guns, and traps.

 His fortune is the Great Perhaps

And that cool rest-house down the glen,

Whence he shall hear, as spirits may,

 Our mundane revel on the height,

 Shall watch each flashing 'rickshaw-light

Sweep on to dinner, dance, and play.

Benmore shall woo him to the ball

 With lighted rooms and braying band;

 And he shall hear and understand

"Dream Faces" better than us all.

For, think you, as the vapours flee

 Across Sanjaolie after rain,

 His soul may climb the hill again

To each field of victory.

Unseen, who women held so dear,

 The strong man's yearning to his kind

Shall shake at most the window-blind,
Or dull awhile the card-room's cheer.

@In his own place of power unknown,
 His Light o' Love another's flame,
And he an alien and alone!

Yet may he meet with many a friend—
 Shrewd shadows, lingering long unseen
 Among us when "God save the Queen"
Shows even "extras" have an end.

And, when we leave the heated room,
 And, when at four the lights expire,
 The crew shall gather round the fire
And mock our laughter in the gloom;

Talk as we talked, and they ere death—
 Flirt wanly, dance in ghostly-wise,
 With ghosts of tunes for melodies,
And vanish at the morning's breath.

CHRISTMAS IN INDIA

Dim dawn behind the tamarisks—the sky is saffron-yellow—

 As the women in the village grind the corn,

And the parrots seek the riverside, each calling to his fellow

 That the Day, the staring Easter Day is born.

 Oh the white dust on the highway! Oh the stenches in the byway!

 Oh the clammy fog that hovers o'er the earth;

 And at Home they're making merry 'neath the white and scarlet berry—

 What part have India's exiles in their mirth?

Full day behind the tamarisks—the sky is blue and staring—

 As the cattle crawl afield beneath the yoke,

And they bear One o'er the field-path, who is past all hope or caring,

 To the ghat below the curling wreaths of smoke.

 Call on Rama, going slowly, as ye bear a brother lowly—

 Call on Rama—he may hear, perhaps, your voice!

 With our hymn-books and our psalters we appeal to other altars,

 And today we bid "good Christian men rejoice!"

High noon behind the tamarisks—the sun is hot above us—

 As at Home the Christmas Day is breaking wan.

They will drink our healths at dinner—those who tell us how they love us,

 And forget us till another year be gone!

 Oh the toil that knows no breaking! Oh the Heimweh, ceaseless, aching!

 Oh the black dividing Sea and alien Plain!

Youth was cheap—wherefore we sold it.

Gold was good—we hoped to hold it,

And today we know the fulness of our gain.

Grey dusk behind the tamarisks—the parrots fly together—

As the sun is sinking slowly over Home;

And his last ray seems to mock us shackled in a lifelong tether.

That drags us back howe'er so far we roam.

Hard her service, poor her payment—she is ancient, tattered raiment—

India, she the grim Stepmother of our kind.

If a year of life be lent her, if her temple's shrine we enter,

The door is shut—we may not look behind.

Black night behind the tamarisks—the owls begin their chorus—

As the conches from the temple scream and bray.

With the fruitless years behind us, and the hopeless years before us,

Let us honor, O my brother, Christmas Day!

Call a truce, then, to our labors—let us feast with friends and
neighbors,

And be merry as the custom of our caste;

For if "faint and forced the laughter," and if sadness follow after,

We are richer by one mocking Christmas past.

PAGETT, M.P.

The toad beneath the harrow knows

Exactly where each tooth-point goes.

The butterfly upon the road

Preaches contentment to that toad.

Pagett, M.P., was a liar, and a fluent liar therewith—

He spoke of the heat of India as the "Asian Solar Myth";

Came on a four months' visit, to "study the East," in November,

And I got him to sign an agreement vowing to stay till September.

March came in with the koil. Pagett was cool and gay,

Called me a "bloated Brahmin," talked of my "princely pay."

March went out with the roses. "Where is your heat?" said he.

"Coming," said I to Pagett, "Skittles!" said Pagett, M.P.

April began with the punkah, coolies, and prickly-heat,—

Pagett was dear to mosquitoes, sandflies found him a treat.

He grew speckled and mumpy—hammered, I grieve to say,

Aryan brothers who fanned him, in an illiberal way.

May set in with a dust-storm,—Pagett went down with the sun.

All the delights of the season tickled him one by one.

Imprimis—ten day's "liver"—due to his drinking beer;

Later, a dose of fever—slight, but he called it severe.

Dysent'ry touched him in June, after the Chota Bursat—

Lowered his portly person—made him yearn to depart.

He didn't call me a "Brahmin," or "bloated," or "overpaid,"

 But seemed to think it a wonder that any one stayed.

July was a trifle unhealthy,—Pagett was ill with fear.

'Called it the "Cholera Morbus," hinted that life was dear.

He babbled of "Eastern Exile," and mentioned his home with tears;

But I haven't seen my children for close upon seven years.

We reached a hundred and twenty once in the Court at noon,

(I've mentioned Pagett was portly) Pagett, went off in a swoon.

That was an end to the business; Pagett, the perjured, fled

With a practical, working knowledge of "Solar Myths" in his head.

And I laughed as I drove from the station, but the mirth died out on my lips

As I thought of the fools like Pagett who write of their "Eastern trips,"

 And the sneers of the traveled idiots who duly misgovern the land,

And I prayed to the Lord to deliver another one into my hand.

THE SONG OF THE WOMEN

How shall she know the worship we would do her?

 The walls are high, and she is very far.

How shall the woman's message reach unto her

 Above the tumult of the packed bazaar?

 Free wind of March, against the lattice blowing,

 Bear thou our thanks, lest she depart unknowing.

Go forth across the fields we may not roam in,

 Go forth beyond the trees that rim the city,

To whatsoe'er fair place she hath her home in,

 Who dowered us with wealth of love and pity.

 Out of our shadow pass, and seek her singing—

 "I have no gifts but Love alone for bringing."

Say that we be a feeble folk who greet her,

 But old in grief, and very wise in tears;

Say that we, being desolate, entreat her

 That she forget us not in after years;

 For we have seen the light, and it were grievous

 To dim that dawning if our lady leave us.

By life that ebbed with none to stanch the failing

 By Love's sad harvest garnered in the spring,

When Love in ignorance wept unavailing

 O'er young buds dead before their blossoming;

 By all the grey owl watched, the pale moon viewed,

 In past grim years, declare our gratitude!

By hands uplifted to the Gods that heard not,

 By fits that found no favor in their sight,

By faces bent above the babe that stirred not,

 By nameless horrors of the stifling night;

 By ills foredone, by peace her toils discover,

 Bid Earth be good beneath and Heaven above her!

If she have sent her servants in our pain

 If she have fought with Death and dulled his sword;

If she have given back our sick again.

 And to the breast the waking lips restored,

 Is it a little thing that she has wrought?

 Then Life and Death and Motherhood be nought.

Go forth, O wind, our message on thy wings,

 And they shall hear thee pass and bid thee speed,

In reed-roofed hut, or white-walled home of kings,

 Who have been helpen by her in their need.

 All spring shall give thee fragrance, and the wheat

 Shall be a tasselled floorcloth to thy feet.

Haste, for our hearts are with thee, take no rest!

 Loud-voiced ambassador, from sea to sea

Proclaim the blessing, manifold, confessed.

 Of those in darkness by her hand set free.

 Then very softly to her presence move,

 And whisper: "Lady, lo, they know and love!"

A BALLAD OF JAKKO HILL

One moment bid the horses wait,
　Since tiffin is not laid till three,
Below the upward path and straight
　You climbed a year ago with me.

Love came upon us suddenly
　And loosed—an idle hour to kill—
A headless, armless armory
　That smote us both on Jakko Hill.

Ah Heaven! we would wait and wait
　Through Time and to Eternity!
Ah Heaven! we could conquer Fate
　With more than Godlike constancy
I cut the date upon a tree—
　Here stand the clumsy figures still:
"10-7-85, A.D."
　Damp with the mist of Jakko Hill.

What came of high resolve and great,
　And until Death fidelity!
Whose horse is waiting at your gate?
　Whose 'rickshaw-wheels ride over me?
No Saint's, I swear; and—let me see
　Tonight what names your programme fill—
We drift asunder merrily,
　As drifts the mist on Jakko Hill.

L'ENVOI.

Princess, behold our ancient state

 Has clean departed; and we see

'Twas Idleness we took for Fate

 That bound light bonds on you and me.

Amen! Here ends the comedy

 Where it began in all good will;

Since Love and Leave together flee

 As driven mist on Jakko Hill!

THE PLEA OF THE SIMLA DANCERS

Too late, alas! the song

To remedy the wrong;—

The rooms are taken from us, swept and

 garnished for their fate.

 But these tear-besprinkled pages

 Shall attest to future ages

That we cried against the crime of it—

 too late, alas! too late!

"What have we ever done to bear this grudge?"

 Was there no room save only in Benmore

For docket, duftar, and for office drudge,

 That you usurp our smoothest dancing floor?

Must babus do their work on polished teak?

 Are ball-rooms fittest for the ink you spill?

Was there no other cheaper house to seek?

 You might have left them all at Strawberry Hill.

We never harmed you! Innocent our guise,

 Dainty our shining feet, our voices low;

And we revolved to divers melodies,

 And we were happy but a year ago.

Tonight, the moon that watched our lightsome wiles—

 That beamed upon us through the deodars—

Is wan with gazing on official files,

 And desecrating desks disgust the stars.

Nay! by the memory of tuneful nights—

 Nay! by the witchery of flying feet—

Nay! by the glamour of foredone delights—

 By all things merry, musical, and meet—

By wine that sparkled, and by sparkling eyes—

 By wailing waltz—by reckless galop's strain—

By dim verandas and by soft replies,

 Give us our ravished ball-room back again!

Or—hearken to the curse we lay on you!

 The ghosts of waltzes shall perplex your brain,

And murmurs of past merriment pursue

 Your 'wildered clerks that they indite in vain;

And when you count your poor Provincial millions,

 The only figures that your pen shall frame

Shall be the figures of dear, dear cotillions

 Danced out in tumult long before you came.

Yea! "See Saw" shall upset your estimates,

 "Dream Faces" shall your heavy heads bemuse,

Because your hand, unheeding, desecrates

 Our temple; fit for higher, worthier use.

And all the long verandas, eloquent

 With echoes of a score of Simla years,

Shall plague you with unbidden sentiment—

 Babbling of kisses, laughter, love, and tears.

So shall you mazed amid old memories stand,

So shall you toil, and shall accomplish nought,

And ever in your ears a phantom Band

Shall blare away the staid official thought.

Wherefore—and ere this awful curse he spoken,

Cast out your swarthy sacrilegious train,

And give—ere dancing cease and hearts be broken—

Give us our ravished ball-room back again!

THE BALLAD OF FISHER'S BOARDING-HOUSE

That night, when through the mooring-chains
 The wide-eyed corpse rolled free,
 To blunder down by Garden Reach
 And rot at Kedgeree,
 The tale the Hughli told the shoal
 The lean shoal told to me.

'T was Fultah Fisher's boarding-house,
 Where sailor-men reside,
And there were men of all the ports
 From Mississip to Clyde,
And regally they spat and smoked,
 And fearsomely they lied.

They lied about the purple Sea
 That gave them scanty bread,
They lied about the Earth beneath,
 The Heavens overhead,
For they had looked too often on
 Black rum when that was red.

They told their tales of wreck and wrong,
 Of shame and lust and fraud,
They backed their toughest statements with
 The Brimstone of the Lord,
And crackling oaths went to and fro
 Across the fist-banged board.

And there was Hans the blue-eyed Dane,

 Bull-throated, bare of arm,

Who carried on his hairy chest

 The maid Ultruda's charm—

The little silver crucifix

 That keeps a man from harm.

And there was Jake Without-the-Ears,

 And Pamba the Malay,

And Carboy Gin the Guinea cook,

 And Luz from Vigo Bay,

And Honest Jack who sold them slops

 And harvested their pay.

And there was Salem Hardieker,

 A lean Bostonian he—

Russ, German, English, Halfbreed, Finn,

 Yank, Dane, and Portuguee,

At Fultah Fisher's boarding-house

 They rested from the sea.

Now Anne of Austria shared their drinks,

 Collinga knew her fame,

From Tarnau in Galicia

 To Juan Bazaar she came,

To eat the bread of infamy

 And take the wage of shame.

She held a dozen men to heel—

Rich spoil of war was hers,

In hose and gown and ring and chain,

From twenty mariners,

And, by Port Law, that week, men called

her Salem Hardieker's.

But seamen learnt—what landsmen know—

That neither gifts nor gain

Can hold a winking Light o' Love

Or Fancy's flight restrain,

When Anne of Austria rolled her eyes

On Hans the blue-eyed Dane.

Since Life is strife, and strife means knife,

From Howrah to the Bay,

And he may die before the dawn

Who liquored out the day,

In Fultah Fisher's boarding-house

We woo while yet we may.

But cold was Hans the blue-eyed Dane,

Bull-throated, bare of arm,

And laughter shook the chest beneath

The maid Ultruda's charm—

The little silver crucifix

That keeps a man from harm.

"You speak to Salem Hardieker;

"You was his girl, I know.

"I ship mineselfs tomorrow, see,

 "Und round the Skaw we go,

"South, down the Cattegat, by Hjelm,

 "To Besser in Saro."

When love rejected turns to hate,

 All ill betide the man.

"You speak to Salem Hardieker"—

 She spoke as woman can.

A scream—a sob—"He called me—names!"

 And then the fray began.

An oath from Salem Hardieker,

 A shriek upon the stairs,

A dance of shadows on the wall,

 A knife-thrust unawares—

And Hans came down, as cattle drop,

 Across the broken chairs.

* * * * * *

In Anne of Austria's trembling hands

 The weary head fell low:—

"I ship mineselfs tomorrow, straight

 "For Besser in Saro;

"Und there Ultruda comes to me

 "At Easter, und I go—

"South, down the Cattegat—What's here?

"There—are—no—lights—to guide!"

The mutter ceased, the spirit passed,

And Anne of Austria cried

In Fultah Fisher's boarding-house

When Hans the mighty died.

Thus slew they Hans the blue-eyed Dane,

Bull-throated, bare of arm,

But Anne of Austria looted first

The maid Ultruda's charm—

The little silver crucifix

That keeps a man from harm.

AS THE BELL CLINKS

As I left the Halls at Lumley, rose the vision of a comely

Maid last season worshipped dumbly, watched with fervor from afar;

And I wondered idly, blindly, if the maid would greet me kindly.

That was all—the rest was settled by the clinking tonga-bar.

Yea, my life and hers were coupled by the tonga coupling-bar.

For my misty meditation, at the second changin'-station,

Suffered sudden dislocation, fled before the tuneless jar

Of a Wagner obbligato, scherzo, doublehand staccato,

Played on either pony's saddle by the clacking tonga-bar—

Played with human speech, I fancied, by the jigging, jolting bar.

"She was sweet," thought I, "last season, but 'twere surely wild unreason

Such tiny hope to freeze on as was offered by my Star,

When she whispered, something sadly: 'I—we feel your going badly!'"

"And you let the chance escape you?" rapped the rattling tonga-bar.

"What a chance and what an idiot!" clicked the vicious tonga-bar.

Heart of man—oh, heart of putty! Had I gone by Kakahutti,

On the old Hill-road and rutty, I had 'scaped that fatal car.

But his fortune each must bide by, so I watched the milestones slide by,

To "You call on Her tomorrow!"—fugue with cymbals by the bar—

"You must call on Her tomorrow!"—post-horn gallop by the bar.

Yet a further stage my goal on—we were whirling down to Solon,

With a double lurch and roll on, best foot foremost, ganz und gar—

"She was very sweet," I hinted. "If a kiss had been imprinted?"—

"'Would ha' saved a world of trouble!" clashed the busy tonga-bar.

"'Been accepted or rejected!" banged and clanged the tonga-bar.

Then a notion wild and daring, 'spite the income tax's paring,

And a hasty thought of sharing—less than many incomes are,

Made me put a question private, you can guess what I would drive at.

"You must work the sum to prove it," clanked the careless tonga-bar.

"Simple Rule of Two will prove it," lilted back the tonga-bar.

It was under Khyraghaut I mused. "Suppose the maid be haughty—

(There are lovers rich—and rotty)—wait some wealthy Avatar?

Answer monitor untiring, 'twixt the ponies twain perspiring!"

 "Faint heart never won fair lady," creaked the straining tonga-bar.

"Can I tell you ere you ask Her?" pounded slow the tonga-bar.

Last, the Tara Devi turning showed the lights of Simla burning,

Lit my little lazy yearning to a fiercer flame by far.

As below the Mall we jingled, through my very heart it tingled—

Did the iterated order of the threshing tonga-bar—

"Try your luck—you can't do better!" twanged the loosened tonga-bar.

[372] RUDYARD KIPLING

AN OLD SONG

So long as 'neath the Kalka hills

 The tonga-horn shall ring,

So long as down the Solon dip

 The hard-held ponies swing,

So long as Tara Devi sees

 The lights of Simla town,

So long as Pleasure calls us up,

 Or Duty drives us down,

 If you love me as I love you

 What pair so happy as we two?

So long as Aces take the King,

 Or backers take the bet,

So long as debt leads men to wed,

 Or marriage leads to debt,

So long as little luncheons, Love,

 And scandal hold their vogue,

While there is sport at Annandale

 Or whisky at Jutogh,

 If you love me as I love you

 What knife can cut our love in two?

So long as down the rocking floor

 The raving polka spins,

So long as Kitchen Lancers spur

 The maddened violins,

So long as through the whirling smoke

We hear the oft-told tale—

"Twelve hundred in the Lotteries,"

And Whatshername for sale?

If you love me as I love you

We'll play the game and win it too.

So long as Lust or Lucre tempt

Straight riders from the course,

So long as with each drink we pour

Black brewage of Remorse,

So long as those unloaded guns

We keep beside the bed,

Blow off, by obvious accident,

The lucky owner's head,

If you love me as I love you

What can Life kill or Death undo?

So long as Death 'twixt dance and dance

Chills best and bravest blood,

And drops the reckless rider down

The rotten, rain-soaked khud,

So long as rumours from the North

Make loving wives afraid,

So long as Burma takes the boy

Or typhoid kills the maid,

If you love me as I love you

What knife can cut our love in two?

By all that lights our daily life

Or works our lifelong woe,

From Boileaugunge to Simla Downs

And those grim glades below,

Where, heedless of the flying hoof

And clamour overhead,

Sleep, with the grey langur for guard

Our very scornful Dead,

If you love me as I love you

All Earth is servant to us two!

By Docket, Billetdoux, and File,

By Mountain, Cliff, and Fir,

By Fan and Sword and Office-box,

By Corset, Plume, and Spur

By Riot, Revel, Waltz, and War,

By Women, Work, and Bills,

By all the life that fizzes in

The everlasting Hills,

If you love me as I love you

What pair so happy as we two?

CERTAIN MAXIMS OF HAFIZ

I.

If It be pleasant to look on, stalled in the packed serai,

Does not the Young Man try Its temper and pace ere he buy?

If She be pleasant to look on, what does the Young Man say?

"Lo! She is pleasant to look on, give Her to me today!"

II.

Yea, though a Kafir die, to him is remitted Jehannum

If he borrowed in life from a native at sixty per cent. per annum.

III.

Blister we not for bursati? So when the heart is vexed,

The pain of one maiden's refusal is drowned in the pain of the next.

IV.

The temper of chums, the love of your wife, and a new piano's tune—

Which of the three will you trust at the end of an Indian June?

V.

Who are the rulers of Ind—to whom shall we bow the knee?

Make your peace with the women, and men will make you L. G.

VI.

Does the woodpecker flit round the young ferash?

Does grass clothe a new-built wall?

Is she under thirty, the woman who holds a boy in her thrall?

VII.

If She grow suddenly gracious—reflect. Is it all for thee?

The black-buck is stalked through the bullock, and Man through jealousy.

VIII.

Seek not for favor of women. So shall you find it indeed.

Does not the boar break cover just when you're lighting a weed?

IX.

If He play, being young and unskilful, for shekels of silver and gold,

Take his money, my son, praising Allah. The kid was ordained to be sold.

X.

With a "weed" among men or horses verily this is the best,

That you work him in office or dog-cart lightly—but give him no rest.

XI.

Pleasant the snaffle of Courtship, improving the manners and carriage;

But the colt who is wise will abstain from the terrible thorn-bit of Marriage.

XII.

As the thriftless gold of the babul, so is the gold that we spend

On a derby Sweep, or our neighbor's wife, or the horse that we buy from a

friend.

XIII.

The ways of man with a maid be strange, yet simple and tame

To the ways of a man with a horse, when selling or racing that same.

XIV.

In public Her face turneth to thee, and pleasant Her smile when ye meet.

It is ill. The cold rocks of El-Gidar smile thus on the waves at their feet.

In public Her face is averted, with anger. She nameth thy name.

It is well. Was there ever a loser content with the loss of the game?

XV.

If She have spoken a word, remember thy lips are sealed,

And the Brand of the Dog is upon him by whom is the secret revealed.

If She have written a letter, delay not an instant, but burn it.

Tear it to pieces, O Fool, and the wind to her mate shall return it!

If there be trouble to Herward, and a lie of the blackest can clear,

Lie, while thy lips can move or a man is alive to hear.

XVI.

My Son, if a maiden deny thee and scufflingly bid thee give o'er,

Yet lip meets with lip at the last word—get out!

 She has been there before.

They are pecked on the ear and the chin and the nose who are lacking in lore.

XVII.

If we fall in the race, though we win, the hoof-slide is scarred on the

course.

Though Allah and Earth pardon Sin, remaineth forever Remorse.

XVIII.

"By all I am misunderstood!" if the Matron shall say, or the Maid:

"Alas! I do not understand," my son, be thou nowise afraid.

In vain in the sight of the Bird is the net of the Fowler displayed.

XIX.

My son, if I, Hafiz, the father, take hold of thy knees in my pain,

Demanding thy name on stamped paper, one day or one hour—refrain.

Are the links of thy fetters so light that thou cravest another man's chain?

THE GRAVE OF THE HUNDRED HEAD

There's a widow in sleepy Chester
 Who weeps for her only son;
There's a grave on the Pabeng River,
 A grave that the Burmans shun,
And there's Subadar Prag Tewarri
 Who tells how the work was done.

A Snider squibbed in the jungle,
 Somebody laughed and fled,
And the men of the First Shikaris
 Picked up their Subaltern dead,
With a big blue mark in his forehead
 And the back blown out of his head.

Subadar Prag Tewarri,
 Jemadar Hira Lal,
Took command of the party,
 Twenty rifles in all,
Marched them down to the river
 As the day was beginning to fall.

They buried the boy by the river,
 A blanket over his face—
They wept for their dead Lieutenant,
 The men of an alien race—
They made a samadh in his honor,
 A mark for his resting-place.

For they swore by the Holy Water,

 They swore by the salt they ate,

That the soul of Lieutenant Eshmitt Sahib

 Should go to his God in state;

With fifty file of Burman

 To open him Heaven's gate.

The men of the First Shikaris

 Marched till the break of day,

Till they came to the rebel village,

 The village of Pabengmay—

A jingal covered the clearing,

 Calthrops hampered the way.

Subadar Prag Tewarri,

 Bidding them load with ball,

Halted a dozen rifles

 Under the village wall;

Sent out a flanking-party

 With Jemadar Hira Lal.

The men of the First Shikaris

 Shouted and smote and slew,

Turning the grinning jingal

 On to the howling crew.

The Jemadar's flanking-party

 Butchered the folk who flew.

Long was the morn of slaughter,

Long was the list of slain,

Five score heads were taken,

 Five score heads and twain;

And the men of the First Shikaris

 Went back to their grave again,

Each man bearing a basket

 Red as his palms that day,

Red as the blazing village—

 The village of Pabengmay,

And the "drip-drip-drip" from the baskets

 Reddened the grass by the way.

They made a pile of their trophies

 High as a tall man's chin,

Head upon head distorted,

 Set in a sightless grin,

Anger and pain and terror

 Stamped on the smoke-scorched skin.

Subadar Prag Tewarri

 Put the head of the Boh

On the top of the mound of triumph,

 The head of his son below,

With the sword and the peacock-banner

 That the world might behold and know.

Thus the samadh was perfect,

 Thus was the lesson plain

Of the wrath of the First Shikaris—

 The price of a white man slain;

And the men of the First Shikaris

 Went back into camp again.

Then a silence came to the river,

 A hush fell over the shore,

And Bohs that were brave departed,

 And Sniders squibbed no more;

 For the Burmans said

 That a kullah's head

Must be paid for with heads five score.

There's a widow in sleepy Chester

 Who weeps for her only son;

There's a grave on the Pabeng River,

 A grave that the Burmans shun,

And there's Subadar Prag Tewarri

 Who tells how the work was done.

THE MOON OF OTHER DAYS

Beneath the deep veranda's shade,
 When bats begin to fly,
I sit me down and watch—alas!—
 Another evening die.

Blood-red behind the sere ferash
 She rises through the haze.
Sainted Diana! can that be
 The Moon of Other Days?

Ah! shade of little Kitty Smith,
 Sweet Saint of Kensington!
Say, was it ever thus at Home
 The Moon of August shone,
When arm in arm we wandered long
 Through Putney's evening haze,
And Hammersmith was Heaven beneath
 The Moon of Other Days?

But Wandle's stream is Sutlej now,
 And Putney's evening haze
The dust that half a hundred kine
 Before my window raise.
Unkempt, unclean, athwart the mist
 The seething city looms,
In place of Putney's golden gorse
 The sickly babul blooms.

Glare down, old Hecate, through the dust,

 And bid the pie-dog yell,

Draw from the drain its typhoid-germ,

 From each bazaar its smell;

Yea, suck the fever from the tank

 And sap my strength therewith:

Thank Heaven, you show a smiling face

 To little Kitty Smith!

THE OVERLAND MAIL

(Foot-Service to the Hills)

In the name of the Empress of India, make way,

 O Lords of the Jungle, wherever you roam.

The woods are astir at the close of the day—

 We exiles are waiting for letters from Home.

Let the robber retreat—let the tiger turn tail—

In the Name of the Empress, the Overland Mail!

With a jingle of bells as the dusk gathers in,

 He turns to the foot-path that heads up the hill—

The bags on his back and a cloth round his chin,

 And, tucked in his waist-belt, the Post Office bill:

"Despatched on this date, as received by the rail,

Per runner, two bags of the Overland Mail."

Is the torrent in spate? He must ford it or swim.

 Has the rain wrecked the road? He must climb by the cliff.

Does the tempest cry "Halt"? What are tempests to him?

 The Service admits not a "but" or and "if."

While the breath's in his mouth, he must bear without fail,

In the Name of the Empress, the Overland Mail.

From aloe to rose-oak, from rose-oak to fir,

 From level to upland, from upland to crest,

From rice-field to rock-ridge, from rock-ridge to spur,

 Fly the soft sandalled feet, strains the brawny brown chest.

From rail to ravine—to the peak from the vale—

Up, up through the night goes the Overland Mail.

There's a speck on the hillside, a dot on the road—

 A jingle of bells on the foot-path below—

There's a scuffle above in the monkey's abode—

 The world is awake, and the clouds are aglow.

For the great Sun himself must attend to the hail:

"In the name of the Empress the Overland Mail!"

WHAT THE PEOPLE SAID

June 21st, 1887

By the well, where the bullocks go

Silent and blind and slow—

By the field where the young corn dies

In the face of the sultry skies,

They have heard, as the dull Earth hears

The voice of the wind of an hour,

The sound of the Great Queen's voice:

"My God hath given me years,

Hath granted dominion and power:

And I bid you, O Land, rejoice."

And the ploughman settles the share

More deep in the grudging clod;

For he saith: "The wheat is my care,

And the rest is the will of God.

He sent the Mahratta spear

As He sendeth the rain,

And the Mlech, in the fated year,

Broke the spear in twain.

And was broken in turn. Who knows

How our Lords make strife?

It is good that the young wheat grows,

For the bread is Life."

Then, far and near, as the twilight drew,

Hissed up to the scornful dark

Great serpents, blazing, of red and blue,

That rose and faded, and rose anew.

That the Land might wonder and mark

"Today is a day of days," they said,

"Make merry, O People, all!"

And the Ploughman listened and bowed his head:

"Today and tomorrow God's will," he said,

As he trimmed the lamps on the wall.

"He sendeth us years that are good,

As He sendeth the dearth,

He giveth to each man his food,

Or Her food to the Earth.

Our Kings and our Queens are afar—

On their peoples be peace—

God bringeth the rain to the Bar,

That our cattle increase."

And the Ploughman settled the share

More deep in the sun-dried clod:

"Mogul Mahratta, and Mlech from the North,

And White Queen over the Seas—

God raiseth them up and driveth them forth

As the dust of the ploughshare flies in the breeze;

But the wheat and the cattle are all my care,

And the rest is the will of God."

[388] RUDYARD KIPLING

THE UNDERTAKER'S HORSE

"To-tschin-shu is condemned to death.

How can he drink tea with the Executioner?"

Japanese Proverb.

The eldest son bestrides him,

And the pretty daughter rides him,

And I meet him oft o' mornings on the Course;

And there kindles in my bosom

An emotion chill and gruesome

As I canter past the Undertaker's Horse.

Neither shies he nor is restive,

But a hideously suggestive

Trot, professional and placid, he affects;

And the cadence of his hoof-beats

To my mind this grim reproof beats:—

"Mend your pace, my friend, I'm coming. Who's the next?"

Ah! stud-bred of ill-omen,

I have watched the strongest go—men

Of pith and might and muscle—at your heels,

Down the plantain-bordered highway,

(Heaven send it ne'er be my way!)

In a lacquered box and jetty upon wheels.

Answer, sombre beast and dreary,

Where is Brown, the young, the cheery,

Smith, the pride of all his friends and half the Force?

You were at that last dread dak

We must cover at a walk,

Bring them back to me, O Undertaker's Horse!

With your mane unhogged and flowing,

And your curious way of going,

And that businesslike black crimping of your tail,

E'en with Beauty on your back, Sir,

Pacing as a lady's hack, Sir,

What wonder when I meet you I turn pale?

It may be you wait your time, Beast,

Till I write my last bad rhyme, Beast—

Quit the sunlight, cut the rhyming, drop the glass—

Follow after with the others,

Where some dusky heathen smothers

Us with marigolds in lieu of English grass.

Or, perchance, in years to follow,

I shall watch your plump sides hollow,

See Carnifex (gone lame) become a corse—

See old age at last o'erpower you,

And the Station Pack devour you,

I shall chuckle then, O Undertaker's Horse!

But to insult, jibe, and quest, I've

Still the hideously suggestive

Trot that hammers out the unrelenting text,

And I hear it hard behind me

In what place soe'er I find me:—

"'Sure to catch you sooner or later. Who's the next?"

THE FALL OF JOCK GILLESPIE

This fell when dinner-time was done—
 'Twixt the first an' the second rub—
That oor mon Jock cam' hame again
 To his rooms ahist the Club.

An' syne he laughed, an' syne he sang,
 An' syne we thocht him fou,
An' syne he trumped his partner's trick,
 An' garred his partner rue.

Then up and spake an elder mon,
 That held the Spade its Ace—
"God save the lad! Whence comes the licht
 "That wimples on his face?"

An' Jock he sniggered, an' Jock he smiled,
 An' ower the card-brim wunk:—
"I'm a' too fresh fra' the stirrup-peg,
 "May be that I am drunk."

"There's whusky brewed in Galashils
 "An' L. L. L. forbye;
"But never liquor lit the lowe
 "That keeks fra' oot your eye.

"There's a third o' hair on your dress-coat breast,
 "Aboon the heart a wee?"

"Oh! that is fra' the lang-haired Skye

 "That slobbers ower me."

"Oh! lang-haired Skyes are lovin' beasts,

 "An' terrier dogs are fair,

"But never yet was terrier born,

 "Wi' ell-lang gowden hair!

"There's a smirch o' pouther on your breast,

 "Below the left lappel?"

"Oh! that is fra' my auld cigar,

 "Whenas the stump-end fell."

"Mon Jock, ye smoke the Trichi coarse,

 "For ye are short o' cash,

"An' best Havanas couldna leave

 "Sae white an' pure an ash.

"This nicht ye stopped a story braid,

 "An' stopped it wi' a curse.

"Last nicht ye told that tale yoursel'—

 "An' capped it wi' a worse!

"Oh! we're no fou! Oh! we're no fou!

 "But plainly we can ken

"Ye're fallin', fallin' fra the band

 "O' cantie single men!"

An' it fell when sirris-shaws were sere,

An' the nichts were lang and mirk,

In braw new breeks, wi' a gowden ring,

Oor Jock gaed to the Kirk!

ARITHMETIC ON THE FRONTIER

A great and glorious thing it is
 To learn, for seven years or so,
The Lord knows what of that and this,
 Ere reckoned fit to face the foe—
The flying bullet down the Pass,
That whistles clear: "All flesh is grass."

Three hundred pounds per annum spent
 On making brain and body meeter
For all the murderous intent
 Comprised in "villainous saltpetre!"
And after—ask the Yusufzaies
What comes of all our 'ologies.

A scrimmage in a Border Station—
 A canter down some dark defile—
Two thousand pounds of education
 Drops to a ten-rupee jezail—
The Crammer's boast, the Squadron's pride,
Shot like a rabbit in a ride!

No proposition Euclid wrote,
 No formulae the text-books know,
Will turn the bullet from your coat,
 Or ward the tulwar's downward blow
Strike hard who cares—shoot straight who can—
The odds are on the cheaper man.

One sword-knot stolen from the camp

 Will pay for all the school expenses

Of any Kurrum Valley scamp

 Who knows no word of moods and tenses,

But, being blessed with perfect sight,

Picks off our messmates left and right.

With home-bred hordes the hillsides teem,

 The troop-ships bring us one by one,

At vast expense of time and steam,

 To slay Afridis where they run.

The "captives of our bow and spear"

 Are cheap—alas! as we are dear.

THE BETROTHED

"You must choose between me and your cigar."

—BREACH OF PROMISE CASE, CIRCA 1885.

Open the old cigar-box, get me a Cuba stout,

For things are running crossways, and Maggie and I are out.

We quarrelled about Havanas—we fought o'er a good cheroot,

And I knew she is exacting, and she says I am a brute.

Open the old cigar-box—let me consider a space;

In the soft blue veil of the vapour musing on Maggie's face.

Maggie is pretty to look at—Maggie's a loving lass,

But the prettiest cheeks must wrinkle, the truest of loves must pass.

There's peace in a Larranaga, there's calm in a Henry Clay;

But the best cigar in an hour is finished and thrown away—

Thrown away for another as perfect and ripe and brown—

But I could not throw away Maggie for fear o' the talk o' the town!

Maggie, my wife at fifty—grey and dour and old—

With never another Maggie to purchase for love or gold!

And the light of Days that have Been the dark of the Days that Are,

And Love's torch stinking and stale, like the butt of a dead cigar—

The butt of a dead cigar you are bound to keep in your pocket—

With never a new one to light tho' it's charred and black to the socket!

Open the old cigar-box—let me consider a while.

Here is a mild Manila—there is a wifely smile.

Which is the better portion—bondage bought with a ring,

Or a harem of dusky beauties, fifty tied in a string?

Counsellors cunning and silent—comforters true and tried,

And never a one of the fifty to sneer at a rival bride?

Thought in the early morning, solace in time of woes,

Peace in the hush of the twilight, balm ere my eyelids close,

This will the fifty give me, asking nought in return,

With only a Suttee's passion—to do their duty and burn.

This will the fifty give me. When they are spent and dead,

Five times other fifties shall be my servants instead.

The furrows of far-off Java, the isles of the Spanish Main,

When they hear my harem is empty will send me my brides again.

I will take no heed to their raiment, nor food for their mouths withal,

So long as the gulls are nesting, so long as the showers fall.

I will scent 'em with best vanilla, with tea will I temper their hides,

And the Moor and the Mormon shall envy who read of the tale of my brides.

For Maggie has written a letter to give me my choice between

The wee little whimpering Love and the great god Nick o' Teen.

And I have been servant of Love for barely a twelvemonth clear,

But I have been Priest of Cabanas a matter of seven year;

And the gloom of my bachelor days is flecked with the cheery light

Of stumps that I burned to Friendship and Pleasure and Work and Fight.

And I turn my eyes to the future that Maggie and I must prove,

But the only light on the marshes is the Will-o'-the-Wisp of Love.

Will it see me safe through my journey or leave me bogged in the mire?

Since a puff of tobacco can cloud it, shall I follow the fitful fire?

Open the old cigar-box—let me consider anew—

Old friends, and who is Maggie that I should abandon you?

A million surplus Maggies are willing to bear the yoke;

And a woman is only a woman, but a good Cigar is a Smoke.

Light me another Cuba—I hold to my first-sworn vows.

If Maggie will have no rival, I'll have no Maggie for Spouse!

A TALE OF TWO CITIES

Where the sober-colored cultivator smiles

 On his byles;

Where the cholera, the cyclone, and the crow

 Come and go;

Where the merchant deals in indigo and tea,

 Hides and ghi;

Where the Babu drops inflammatory hints

 In his prints;

Stands a City—Charnock chose it—packed away

 Near a Bay—

By the Sewage rendered fetid, by the sewer

 Made impure,

By the Sunderbunds unwholesome, by the swamp

 Moist and damp;

And the City and the Viceroy, as we see,

 Don't agree.

Once, two hundred years ago, the trader came

 Meek and tame.

Where his timid foot first halted, there he stayed,

 Till mere trade

Grew to Empire, and he sent his armies forth

 South and North

Till the country from Peshawur to Ceylon

 Was his own.

Thus the midday halt of Charnock—more's the pity!

Grew a City.

As the fungus sprouts chaotic from its bed,
 So it spread—
Chance-directed, chance-erected, laid and built
 On the silt—
Palace, byre, hovel—poverty and pride—
 Side by side;
And, above the packed and pestilential town,
 Death looked down.

But the Rulers in that City by the Sea
 Turned to flee—
Fled, with each returning spring-tide from its ills
 To the Hills.

From the clammy fogs of morning, from the blaze
 Of old days,
From the sickness of the noontide, from the heat,
 Beat retreat;
For the country from Peshawur to Ceylon
 Was their own.

But the Merchant risked the perils of the Plain
 For his gain.

Now the resting-place of Charnock, 'neath the palms,
 Asks an alms,
And the burden of its lamentation is,

Briefly, this:

"Because for certain months, we boil and stew,

So should you.

Cast the Viceroy and his Council, to perspire

In our fire!"

And for answer to the argument, in vain

We explain

That an amateur Saint Lawrence cannot fry:

"All must fry!"

That the Merchant risks the perils of the Plain

For gain.

Nor can Rulers rule a house that men grow rich in,

From its kitchen.

Let the Babu drop inflammatory hints

In his prints;

And mature—consistent soul—his plan for stealing

To Darjeeling:

Let the Merchant seek, who makes his silver pile,

England's isle;

Let the City Charnock pitched on—evil day!

Go Her way.

Though the argosies of Asia at Her doors

Heap their stores,

Though Her enterprise and energy secure

Income sure,

Though "out-station orders punctually obeyed"

　　Swell Her trade—

Still, for rule, administration, and the rest,

　　Simla's best.

The End

*　*　*　*　*　*　*　*

VOLUME II BALLADS AND BARRACK-ROOM BALLADS

BALLADS

THE BALLAD OF EAST AND WEST

Oh, East is East, and West is West, and never the twain shall
meet,

Till Earth and Sky stand presently at God's great Judgment
Seat;

But there is neither East nor West, Border, nor Breed, nor Birth,

When two strong men stand face to face,

tho' they come from the ends of the earth!

Kamal is out with twenty men to raise the Border-side,

And he has lifted the Colonel's mare that is the Colonel's pride:

He has lifted her out of the stable-door between the dawn and the day,

And turned the calkins upon her feet, and ridden her far away.

Then up and spoke the Colonel's son that led a troop of the Guides:

"Is there never a man of all my men can say where Kamal hides?"

Then up and spoke Mahommed Khan, the son of the Ressaldar:

"If ye know the track of the morning-mist, ye know where his pickets are.

"At dusk he harries the Abazai—at dawn he is into Bonair,

But he must go by Fort Bukloh to his own place to fare,

So if ye gallop to Fort Bukloh as fast as a bird can fly,

By the favour of God ye may cut him off ere he win to the Tongue of Jagai.

"But if he be past the Tongue of Jagai, right swiftly turn ye then,

For the length and the breadth of that grisly plain is sown with Kamal's men.

There is rock to the left, and rock to the right, and low lean thorn between,

And ye may hear a breech-bolt snick where never a man is seen.”

The Colonel's son has taken a horse, and a raw rough dun was he,

With the mouth of a bell and the heart of Hell and the head of the gallows-

tree.

The Colonel's son to the Fort has won, they bid him stay to eat—

Who rides at the tail of a Border thief, he sits not long at his meat.

He's up and away from Fort Bukloh as fast as he can fly,

Till he was aware of his father's mare in the gut of the Tongue of Jagai,

Till he was aware of his father's mare with Kamal upon her back,

And when he could spy the white of her eye, he made the pistol crack.

He has fired once, he has fired twice, but the whistling ball went wide.

“Ye shoot like a soldier,” Kamal said. “Show now if ye can ride.”

It's up and over the Tongue of Jagai, as blown dustdevils go,

The dun he fled like a stag of ten, but the mare like a barren doe.

The dun he leaned against the bit and slugged his head above,

But the red mare played with the snaffle-bars, as a maiden plays with a glove.

There was rock to the left and rock to the right, and low lean thorn between,

And thrice he heard a breech-bolt snick tho’ never a man was seen.

They have ridden the low moon out of the sky, their hoofs drum up the dawn,

The dun he went like a wounded bull, but the mare like a new-roused fawn.

The dun he fell at a water-course—in a woful heap fell he,

And Kamal has turned the red mare back, and pulled the rider free.

He has knocked the pistol out of his hand—small room was there to strive,

"'Twas only by favour of mine," quoth he, "ye rode so long alive:

There was not a rock for twenty mile, there was not a clump of tree,

But covered a man of my own men with his rifle cocked on his knee.

"If I had raised my bridle-hand, as I have held it low,

The little jackals that flee so fast were feasting all in a row:

If I had bowed my head on my breast, as I have held it high,

The kite that whistles above us now were gorged till she could not fly."

Lightly answered the Colonel's son: "Do good to bird and beast,

But count who come for the broken meats before thou makest a feast.

"If there should follow a thousand swords to carry my bones away,

Belike the price of a jackal's meal were more than a thief could pay.

"They will feed their horse on the standing crop, their men on the garnered

grain,

The thatch of the byres will serve their fires when all the cattle are slain.

"But if thou thinkest the price be fair,—thy brethren wait to sup,

The hound is kin to the jackal-spawn,—howl, dog, and call them up!

And if thou thinkest the price be high, in steer and gear and stack,

Give me my father's mare again, and I'll fight my own way back!"

Kamal has gripped him by the hand and set him upon his feet.

"No talk shall be of dogs," said he, "when wolf and gray wolf meet.

"May I eat dirt if thou hast hurt of me in deed or breath;

What dam of lances brought thee forth to jest at the dawn with Death?"

Lightly answered the Colonel's son: "I hold by the blood of my clan:

Take up the mare for my father's gift—by God, she has carried a man!"

The red mare ran to the Colonel's son, and nuzzled against his breast;

"We be two strong men," said Kamal then, "but she loveth the younger best.

So she shall go with a lifter's dower, my turquoise-studded rein,

My broidered saddle and saddle-cloth, and silver stirrups twain."

The Colonel's son a pistol drew and held it muzzle-end,

"Ye have taken the one from a foe," said he;

 "will ye take the mate from a friend?"

 "A gift for a gift," said Kamal straight; "a limb for the risk of a limb.

"Thy father has sent his son to me, I'll send my son to him!"

With that he whistled his only son, that dropped from a mountain-crest—

He trod the ling like a buck in spring, and he looked like a lance in rest.

"Now here is thy master," Kamal said, "who leads a troop of the Guides,

And thou must ride at his left side as shield on shoulder rides.

Till Death or I cut loose the tie, at camp and board and bed,

Thy life is his—thy fate it is to guard him with thy head.

"So, thou must eat the White Queen's meat, and all her foes are thine,

And thou must harry thy father's hold for the peace of the Border-line,

And thou must make a trooper tough and hack thy way to power—

Belike they will raise thee to Ressaldar when I am hanged in Peshawur."

They have looked each other between the eyes, and there they found no fault,

They have taken the Oath of the Brother-in-Blood on leavened bread and salt:

They have taken the Oath of the Brother-in-Blood on fire and fresh-cut sod,

On the hilt and the haft of the Khyber knife, and the Wondrous Names of God.

The Colonel's son he rides the mare and Kamal's boy the dun,

And two have come back to Fort Bukloh where there went forth but one.

And when they drew to the Quarter-Guard, full twenty swords flew clear—

There was not a man but carried his feud with the blood of the mountaineer.

"Ha' done! ha' done!" said the Colonel's son.

 "Put up the steel at your sides!

Last night ye had struck at a Border thief—

 tonight 'tis a man of the Guides!"

Oh, East is East, and West is West, and never the twain shall meet,

Till Earth and Sky stand presently at God's great Judgment Seat;

But there is neither East nor West, Border, nor Breed, nor Birth,

When two strong men stand face to face,

 tho' they come from the ends of the earth!

THE LAST SUTTEE

Not many years ago a King died in one of the Rajpoot States. His wives,

disregarding the orders of the English against Suttee, would have broken out

of the palace had not the gates been barred.

But one of them, disguised as the King's favourite dancing-girl, passed

through the line of guards and reached the pyre. There, her courage failing,

she prayed her cousin, a baron of the court, to kill her. This he did, not

knowing who she was.

Udai Chand lay sick to death

 In his hold by Gungra hill.

All night we heard the death-gongs ring

For the soul of the dying Rajpoot King,

All night beat up from the women's wing

 A cry that we could not still.

All night the barons came and went,

 The lords of the outer guard:

All night the cressets glimmered pale

On Ulwar sabre and Tonk jezail,

Mewar headstall and Marwar mail,

 That clinked in the palace yard.

In the Golden room on the palace roof

 All night he fought for air:

And there was sobbing behind the screen,

Rustle and whisper of women unseen,

And the hungry eyes of the Boondi Queen

On the death she might not share.

He passed at dawn—the death-fire leaped

 From ridge to river-head,

From the Malwa plains to the Abu scars:

And wail upon wail went up to the stars

Behind the grim zenana-bars,

 When they knew that the King was dead.

The dumb priest knelt to tie his mouth

 And robe him for the pyre.

The Boondi Queen beneath us cried:

"See, now, that we die as our mothers died

In the bridal-bed by our master's side!

 Out, women!—to the fire!"

We drove the great gates home apace:

 White hands were on the sill:

But ere the rush of the unseen feet

Had reached the turn to the open street,

The bars shot down, the guard-drum beat—

 We held the dovecot still.

A face looked down in the gathering day,

 And laughing spoke from the wall:

"Ohe', they mourn here: let me by—

Azizun, the Lucknow nautch-girl, I!

When the house is rotten, the rats must fly,

 And I seek another thrall.

"For I ruled the King as ne'er did Queen,—

 Tonight the Queens rule me!

Guard them safely, but let me go,

Or ever they pay the debt they owe

In scourge and torture!" She leaped below,

 And the grim guard watched her flee.

They knew that the King had spent his soul

 On a North-bred dancing-girl:

That he prayed to a flat-nosed Lucknow god,

And kissed the ground where her feet had trod,

And doomed to death at her drunken nod,

 And swore by her lightest curl.

We bore the King to his fathers' place,

 Where the tombs of the Sun-born stand:

Where the gray apes swing, and the peacocks preen

On fretted pillar and jewelled screen,

And the wild boar couch in the house of the Queen

 On the drift of the desert sand.

The herald read his titles forth,

 We set the logs aglow:

"Friend of the English, free from fear,

Baron of Luni to Jeysulmeer,

Lord of the Desert of Bikaneer,

 King of the Jungle,—go!"

All night the red flame stabbed the sky

 With wavering wind-tossed spears:

And out of a shattered temple crept

A woman who veiled her head and wept,

And called on the King—but the great King slept,

 And turned not for her tears.

Small thought had he to mark the strife—

 Cold fear with hot desire—

When thrice she leaped from the leaping flame,

And thrice she beat her breast for shame,

And thrice like a wounded dove she came

 And moaned about the fire.

One watched, a bow-shot from the blaze,

 The silent streets between,

Who had stood by the King in sport and fray,

To blade in ambush or boar at bay,

And he was a baron old and gray,

 And kin to the Boondi Queen.

He said: "O shameless, put aside

 The veil upon thy brow!

Who held the King and all his land

To the wanton will of a harlot's hand!

Will the white ash rise from the blistered brand?

 Stoop down, and call him now!"

Then she: "By the faith of my tarnished soul,

All things I did not well,

I had hoped to clear ere the fire died,

And lay me down by my master's side

To rule in Heaven his only bride,

 While the others howl in Hell.

"But I have felt the fire's breath,

 And hard it is to die!

Yet if I may pray a Rajpoot lord

To sully the steel of a Thakur's sword

With base-born blood of a trade abhorred,"—

 And the Thakur answered, "Ay."

He drew and struck: the straight blade drank

 The life beneath the breast.

"I had looked for the Queen to face the flame,

But the harlot dies for the Rajpoot dame—

Sister of mine, pass, free from shame,

 Pass with thy King to rest!"

The black log crashed above the white:

 The little flames and lean,

Red as slaughter and blue as steel,

That whistled and fluttered from head to heel,

Leaped up anew, for they found their meal

 On the heart of—the Boondi Queen!

THE BALLAD OF THE KING'S MERCY

Abdhur Rahman, the Durani Chief,

 of him is the story told.

His mercy fills the Khyber hills—

 his grace is manifold;

He has taken toll of the North and the South—

 his glory reacheth far,

And they tell the tale of his charity

 from Balkh to Kandahar.

Before the old Peshawur Gate, where Kurd and Kaffir meet,

 The Governor of Kabul dealt the Justice of the Street,

 And that was strait as running noose and swift as plunging knife,

 Tho' he who held the longer purse might hold the longer life.

There was a hound of Hindustan had struck a Euzufzai,

 Wherefore they spat upon his face and led him out to die.

It chanced the King went forth that hour when throat was bared to knife;

 The Kaffir grovelled under-hoof and clamoured for his life.

Then said the King: "Have hope, O friend! Yea, Death disgraced is hard;

 Much honour shall be thine"; and called the Captain of the Guard,

 Yar Khan, a bastard of the Blood, so city-babble saith,

 And he was honoured of the King—the which is salt to Death;

 And he was son of Daoud Shah, the Reiver of the Plains,

 And blood of old Durani Lords ran fire in his veins;

 And 'twas to tame an Afghan pride nor Hell nor Heaven could bind,

 The King would make him butcher to a yelping cur of Hind.

"Strike!" said the King. "King's blood art thou—his death shall be his

 pride!"

Then louder, that the crowd might catch: "Fear not—his arms are tied!"

Yar Khan drew clear the Khyber knife, and struck, and sheathed again.

"O man, thy will is done," quoth he; "a King this dog hath slain."

Abdhur Rahman, the Durani Chief,

 to the North and the South is sold.

The North and the South shall open their mouth

 to a Ghilzai flag unrolled,

When the big guns speak to the Khyber peak,

 and his dog-Heratis fly:

Ye have heard the song—How long? How long?

 Wolves of the Abazai!

That night before the watch was set, when all the streets were clear,

The Governor of Kabul spoke: "My King, hast thou no fear?

Thou knowest—thou hast heard,"—his speech died at his master's face.

And grimly said the Afghan King: "I rule the Afghan race.

My path is mine—see thou to thine—tonight upon thy bed

Think who there be in Kabul now that clamour for thy head."

That night when all the gates were shut to City and to throne,

Within a little garden-house the King lay down alone.

Before the sinking of the moon, which is the Night of Night,

Yar Khan came softly to the King to make his honour white.

The children of the town had mocked beneath his horse's hoofs,

The harlots of the town had hailed him "butcher!" from their roofs.

But as he groped against the wall, two hands upon him fell,

The King behind his shoulder spake: "Dead man, thou dost not well!

'Tis ill to jest with Kings by day and seek a boon by night;

And that thou bearest in thy hand is all too sharp to write.

"But three days hence, if God be good, and if thy strength remain,

Thou shalt demand one boon of me and bless me in thy pain.

For I am merciful to all, and most of all to thee.

"My butcher of the shambles, rest—no knife hast thou for me!"

 Abdhur Rahman, the Durani Chief,

 holds hard by the South and the North;

 But the Ghilzai knows, ere the melting snows,

 when the swollen banks break forth,

 When the red-coats crawl to the sungar wall,

 and his Usbeg lances fail:

 Ye have heard the song—How long? How long?

 Wolves of the Zuka Kheyl!

They stoned him in the rubbish-field when dawn was in the sky,

According to the written word, "See that he do not die."

They stoned him till the stones were piled above him on the plain,

And those the labouring limbs displaced they tumbled back again.

One watched beside the dreary mound that veiled the battered

thing,

And him the King with laughter called the Herald of the King.

It was upon the second night, the night of Ramazan,

The watcher leaning earthward heard the message of Yar Khan.

From shattered breast through shrivelled lips broke forth the rattling breath,
"Creature of God, deliver me from agony of Death."

They sought the King among his girls, and risked their lives thereby:
"Protector of the Pitiful, give orders that he die!"

"Bid him endure until the day," a lagging answer came;
"The night is short, and he can pray and learn to bless my name."

Before the dawn three times he spoke, and on the day once more:
"Creature of God, deliver me, and bless the King therefor!"

They shot him at the morning prayer, to ease him of his pain,
And when he heard the matchlocks clink, he blessed the King again.

Which thing the singers made a song for all the world to sing,
So that the Outer Seas may know the mercy of the King.

Abdhur Rahman, the Durani Chief,
 of him is the story told,
He has opened his mouth to the North and the South,
 they have stuffed his mouth with gold.

Ye know the truth of his tender ruth—
 and sweet his favours are:
Ye have heard the song—How long? How long?
 from Balkh to Kandahar.

THE BALLAD OF THE KING'S JEST

When spring-time flushes the desert grass,

Our kafilas wind through the Khyber Pass.

Lean are the camels but fat the frails,

Light are the purses but heavy the bales,

As the snowbound trade of the North comes down

To the market-square of Peshawur town.

In a turquoise twilight, crisp and chill,

A kafila camped at the foot of the hill.

Then blue smoke-haze of the cooking rose,

And tent-peg answered to hammer-nose;

And the picketed ponies, shag and wild,

Strained at their ropes as the feed was piled;

And the bubbling camels beside the load

Sprawled for a furlong adown the road;

And the Persian pussy-cats, brought for sale,

Spat at the dogs from the camel-bale;

And the tribesmen bellowed to hasten the food;

And the camp-fires twinkled by Fort Jumrood;

And there fled on the wings of the gathering dusk

A savour of camels and carpets and musk,

A murmur of voices, a reek of smoke,

To tell us the trade of the Khyber woke.

The lid of the flesh-pot chattered high,

The knives were whetted and—then came I

To Mahbub Ali the muleteer,

Patching his bridles and counting his gear,

Crammed with the gossip of half a year.

But Mahbub Ali the kindly said,

"Better is speech when the belly is fed."

So we plunged the hand to the mid-wrist deep

In a cinnamon stew of the fat-tailed sheep,

And he who never hath tasted the food,

By Allah! he knoweth not bad from good.

We cleansed our beards of the mutton-grease,

We lay on the mats and were filled with peace,

And the talk slid north, and the talk slid south,

With the sliding puffs from the hookah-mouth.

Four things greater than all things are,—

Women and Horses and Power and War.

We spake of them all, but the last the most,

For I sought a word of a Russian post,

Of a shifty promise, an unsheathed sword

And a gray-coat guard on the Helmund ford.

Then Mahbub Ali lowered his eyes

In the fashion of one who is weaving lies.

Quoth he: "Of the Russians who can say?

When the night is gathering all is gray.

But we look that the gloom of the night shall die

In the morning flush of a blood-red sky.

"Friend of my heart, is it meet or wise

To warn a King of his enemies?

We know what Heaven or Hell may bring,

But no man knoweth the mind of the King.

"That unsought counsel is cursed of God

Attesteth the story of Wali Dad.

"His sire was leaky of tongue and pen,

His dam was a clucking Khuttuck hen;

And the colt bred close to the vice of each,

For he carried the curse of an unstanched speech.

"Therewith madness—so that he sought

The favour of kings at the Kabul court;

And travelled, in hope of honour, far

To the line where the gray-coat squadrons are.

"There have I journeyed too—but I

Saw naught, said naught, and—did not die!

He harked to rumour, and snatched at a breath

Of 'this one knoweth' and 'that one saith',—

Legends that ran from mouth to mouth

Of a gray-coat coming, and sack of the South.

"These have I also heard—they pass

With each new spring and the winter grass.

"Hot-foot southward, forgotten of God,

Back to the city ran Wali Dad,

Even to Kabul—in full durbar

The King held talk with his Chief in War.

"Into the press of the crowd he broke,

And what he had heard of the coming spoke.

"Then Gholam Hyder, the Red Chief, smiled,

As a mother might on a babbling child;

But those who would laugh restrained their breath,

When the face of the King showed dark as death.

"Evil it is in full durbar

To cry to a ruler of gathering war!

Slowly he led to a peach-tree small,

That grew by a cleft of the city wall.

"And he said to the boy: 'They shall praise thy zeal

So long as the red spurt follows the steel.

"And the Russ is upon us even now?

Great is thy prudence—await them, thou.

Watch from the tree. Thou art young and strong,

Surely thy vigil is not for long.

"The Russ is upon us, thy clamour ran?

Surely an hour shall bring their van.

Wait and watch. When the host is near,

Shout aloud that my men may hear.'

"Friend of my heart, is it meet or wise

To warn a King of his enemies?

A guard was set that he might not flee—

A score of bayonets ringed the tree.

"The peach-bloom fell in showers of snow,

When he shook at his death as he looked below.

By the power of God, who alone is great,

Till the seventh day he fought with his fate.

"Then madness took him, and men declare

He mowed in the branches as ape and bear,

And last as a sloth, ere his body failed,

And he hung as a bat in the forks, and wailed,

And sleep the cord of his hands untied,

And he fell, and was caught on the points and died.

"Heart of my heart, is it meet or wise

To warn a King of his enemies?

We know what Heaven or Hell may bring,

But no man knoweth the mind of the King.

"Of the gray-coat coming who can say?

When the night is gathering all is gray.

"To things greater than all things are,

The first is Love, and the second War.

"And since we know not how War may prove,

Heart of my heart, let us talk of Love!"

THE BALLAD OF BOH DA THONE

This is the ballad of Boh Da Thone,

Erst a Pretender to Theebaw's throne,

Who harried the district of Alalone:

How he met with his fate and the V.P.P.

At the hand of Harendra Mukerji,

Senior Gomashta, G.B.T.

Boh Da Thone was a warrior bold:

His sword and his Snider were bossed with gold,

And the Peacock Banner his henchmen bore

Was stiff with bullion, but stiffer with gore.

He shot at the strong and he slashed at the weak

From the Salween scrub to the Chindwin teak:

He crucified noble, he sacrificed mean,

He filled old ladies with kerosene:

While over the water the papers cried,

"The patriot fights for his countryside!"

But little they cared for the Native Press,

The worn white soldiers in Khaki dress,

Who tramped through the jungle and camped in the byre,

Who died in the swamp and were tombed in the mire,

Who gave up their lives, at the Queen's Command,

For the Pride of their Race and the Peace of the Land.

Now, first of the foemen of Boh Da Thone

Was Captain O'Neil of the "Black Tyrone",

And his was a Company, seventy strong,

Who hustled that dissolute Chief along.

There were lads from Galway and Louth and Meath

Who went to their death with a joke in their teeth,

And worshipped with fluency, fervour, and zeal

The mud on the boot-heels of "Crook" O'Neil.

But ever a blight on their labours lay,

And ever their quarry would vanish away,

Till the sun-dried boys of the Black Tyrone

Took a brotherly interest in Boh Da Thone:

And, sooth, if pursuit in possession ends,

The Boh and his trackers were best of friends.

The word of a scout—a march by night—

A rush through the mist—a scattering fight—

A volley from cover—a corpse in the clearing—

The glimpse of a loin-cloth and heavy jade earring—

The flare of a village—the tally of slain—

And...the Boh was abroad "on the raid" again!

They cursed their luck, as the Irish will,

They gave him credit for cunning and skill,

They buried their dead, they bolted their beef,

And started anew on the track of the thief

Till, in place of the "Kalends of Greece", men said,

"When Crook and his darlings come back with the head."

They had hunted the Boh from the hills to the plain—

He doubled and broke for the hills again:

They had crippled his power for rapine and raid,

They had routed him out of his pet stockade,

And at last, they came, when the Day Star tired,

To a camp deserted—a village fired.

A black cross blistered the Morning-gold,

And the body upon it was stark and cold.

The wind of the dawn went merrily past,

The high grass bowed her plumes to the blast.

And out of the grass, on a sudden, broke

A spirtle of fire, a whorl of smoke—

And Captain O'Neil of the Black Tyrone

Was blessed with a slug in the ulnar-bone—

The gift of his enemy Boh Da Thone.

(Now a slug that is hammered from telegraph-wire

Is a thorn in the flesh and a rankling fire.)

The shot-wound festered—as shot-wounds may
In a steaming barrack at Mandalay.

The left arm throbbed, and the Captain swore,
"I'd like to be after the Boh once more!"
The fever held him—the Captain said,
"I'd give a hundred to look at his head!"

The Hospital punkahs creaked and whirred,
But Babu Harendra (Gomashta) heard.

He thought of the cane-brake, green and dank,
That girdled his home by the Dacca tank.
He thought of his wife and his High School son,
He thought—but abandoned the thought—of a gun.
His sleep was broken by visions dread
Of a shining Boh with a silver head.

He kept his counsel and went his way,
And swindled the cartmen of half their pay.

And the months went on, as the worst must do,
And the Boh returned to the raid anew.

But the Captain had quitted the long-drawn strife,
And in far Simoorie had taken a wife.
And she was a damsel of delicate mould,
With hair like the sunshine and heart of gold,

And little she knew the arms that embraced

Had cloven a man from the brow to the waist:

And little she knew that the loving lips

Had ordered a quivering life's eclipse,

And the eye that lit at her lightest breath

Had glared unawed in the Gates of Death.

(For these be matters a man would hide,

As a general rule, from an innocent Bride.)

And little the Captain thought of the past,

And, of all men, Babu Harendra last.

But slow, in the sludge of the Kathun road,

The Government Bullock Train toted its load.

Speckless and spotless and shining with ghee,

In the rearmost cart sat the Babu-jee.

And ever a phantom before him fled

Of a scowling Boh with a silver head.

Then the lead-cart stuck, though the coolies slaved,

And the cartmen flogged and the escort raved;

And out of the jungle, with yells and squeals,

Pranced Boh Da Thone, and his gang at his heels!

Then belching blunderbuss answered back

The Snider's snarl and the carbine's crack,

And the blithe revolver began to sing

To the blade that twanged on the locking-ring,

And the brown flesh blued where the bay'net kissed,

As the steel shot back with a wrench and a twist,

And the great white bullocks with onyx eyes

Watched the souls of the dead arise,

And over the smoke of the fusillade

The Peacock Banner staggered and swayed.

Oh, gayest of scrimmages man may see

Is a well-worked rush on the G.B.T.!

The Babu shook at the horrible sight,

And girded his ponderous loins for flight,

But Fate had ordained that the Boh should start

On a lone-hand raid of the rearmost cart,

And out of that cart, with a bellow of woe,

The Babu fell—flat on the top of the Boh!

For years had Harendra served the State,

To the growth of his purse and the girth of his pet.

There were twenty stone, as the tally-man knows,

On the broad of the chest of this best of Bohs.

And twenty stone from a height discharged

Are bad for a Boh with a spleen enlarged.

Oh, short was the struggle—severe was the shock—

He dropped like a bullock—he lay like a block;

And the Babu above him, convulsed with fear,

Heard the labouring life-breath hissed out in his ear.

And thus in a fashion undignified

The princely pest of the Chindwin died.

Turn now to Simoorie where, lapped in his ease,

The Captain is petting the Bride on his knees,

Where the whit of the bullet, the wounded man's scream

Are mixed as the mist of some devilish dream—

Forgotten, forgotten the sweat of the shambles

Where the hill-daisy blooms and the gray monkey gambols,

From the sword-belt set free and released from the steel,

The Peace of the Lord is with Captain O'Neil.

Up the hill to Simoorie—most patient of drudges—

The bags on his shoulder, the mail-runner trudges.

"For Captain O'Neil, Sahib. One hundred and ten

Rupees to collect on delivery."

 Then

(Their breakfast was stopped while the screw-jack and hammer

Tore waxcloth, split teak-wood, and chipped out the dammer;)

Open-eyed, open-mouthed, on the napery's snow,

With a crash and a thud, rolled—the Head of the Boh!

And gummed to the scalp was a letter which ran:—

"IN FIELDING FORCE SERVICE.

Encampment,
—th Jan.

"Dear Sir,—I have honour to send, as you said,
For final approval (see under) Boh's Head;

"Was took by myself in most bloody affair.

By High Education brought pressure to bear.

"Now violate Liberty, time being bad,
To mail V.P.P. (rupees hundred) Please add

"Whatever Your Honour can pass. Price of Blood
Much cheap at one hundred, and children want food;

"So trusting Your Honour will somewhat retain
True love and affection for Govt. Bullock Train,

"And show awful kindness to satisfy me,
I am,
Graceful Master,
Your
H. MUKERJI."

As the rabbit is drawn to the rattlesnake's power,
As the smoker's eye fills at the opium hour,

As a horse reaches up to the manger above,

As the waiting ear yearns for the whisper of love,

From the arms of the Bride, iron-visaged and slow,

The Captain bent down to the Head of the Boh.

And e'en as he looked on the Thing where It lay

'Twixt the winking new spoons and the napkins' array,

The freed mind fled back to the long-ago days—

The hand-to-hand scuffle—the smoke and the blaze—

The forced march at night and the quick rush at dawn—

The banjo at twilight, the burial ere morn—

The stench of the marshes—the raw, piercing smell

When the overhand stabbing-cut silenced the yell—

The oaths of his Irish that surged when they stood

Where the black crosses hung o'er the Kuttamow flood.

As a derelict ship drifts away with the tide

The Captain went out on the Past from his Bride,

Back, back, through the springs to the chill of the year,

When he hunted the Boh from Maloon to Tsaleer.

As the shape of a corpse dimmers up through deep water,

In his eye lit the passionless passion of slaughter,

And men who had fought with O'Neil for the life

Had gazed on his face with less dread than his wife.

For she who had held him so long could not hold him—

Though a four-month Eternity should have controlled him—

But watched the twin Terror—the head turned to head—
The scowling, scarred Black, and the flushed savage Red—
The spirit that changed from her knowing and flew to
Some grim hidden Past she had never a clue to.

But It knew as It grinned, for he touched it unfearing,
And muttered aloud, "So you kept that jade earring!"

Then nodded, and kindly, as friend nods to friend,
"Old man, you fought well, but you lost in the end."

The visions departed, and Shame followed Passion:—
"He took what I said in this horrible fashion,

"I'll write to Harendra!" With language unsainted
The Captain came back to the Bride... who had fainted.

And this is a fiction? No. Go to Simoorie
And look at their baby, a twelve-month old Houri,
A pert little, Irish-eyed Kathleen Mavournin—
She's always about on the Mall of a mornin'—

And you'll see, if her right shoulder-strap is displaced,
This: Gules upon argent, a Boh's Head, erased!

THE LAMENT OF THE BORDER CATTLE THIEF

O woe is me for the merry life
 I led beyond the Bar,
And a treble woe for my winsome wife
 That weeps at Shalimar.

They have taken away my long jezail,
 My shield and sabre fine,
And heaved me into the Central jail
 For lifting of the kine.

The steer may low within the byre,
 The Jat may tend his grain,
But there'll be neither loot nor fire
 Till I come back again.

And God have mercy on the Jat
 When once my fetters fall,
And Heaven defend the farmer's hut
 When I am loosed from thrall.

It's woe to bend the stubborn back
 Above the grinching quern,
It's woe to hear the leg-bar clack
 And jingle when I turn!
But for the sorrow and the shame,
 The brand on me and mine,
I'll pay you back in leaping flame
 And loss of the butchered kine.

For every cow I spared before
 In charity set free,
If I may reach my hold once more
 I'll reive an honest three.

For every time I raised the low
 That scared the dusty plain,
By sword and cord, by torch and tow
 I'll light the land with twain!

Ride hard, ride hard to Abazai,
 Young Sahib with the yellow hair—
Lie close, lie close as khuttucks lie,
 Fat herds below Bonair!

The one I'll shoot at twilight-tide,
 At dawn I'll drive the other;
The black shall mourn for hoof and hide,
 The white man for his brother.

'Tis war, red war, I'll give you then,
 War till my sinews fail;
For the wrong you have done to a chief of men,
 And a thief of the Zukka Kheyl.

And if I fall to your hand afresh
 I give you leave for the sin,
That you cram my throat with the foul pig's flesh,
 And swing me in the skin!

THE RHYME OF THE THREE CAPTAINS

This ballad appears to refer to one of the exploits of the notorious Paul
Jones, the American pirate. It is founded on fact.

... At the close of a winter day,

Their anchors down, by London town, the Three Great Captains lay;

And one was Admiral of the North from Solway Firth to Skye,

And one was Lord of the Wessex coast and all the lands thereby,

And one was Master of the Thames from Limehouse to Blackwall,

And he was Captain of the Fleet—the bravest of them all.

Their good guns guarded their great gray sides that were thirty foot in the
sheer,

When there came a certain trading-brig with news of a privateer.

Her rigging was rough with the clotted drift that drives in a Northern breeze,

Her sides were clogged with the lazy weed that spawns in the Eastern seas.

Light she rode in the rude tide-rip, to left and right she rolled,

And the skipper sat on the scuttle-butt and stared at an empty hold.

"I ha' paid Port dues for your Law," quoth he, "and where is the Law ye boast

If I sail unscathed from a heathen port to be robbed on a Christian coast?

Ye have smoked the hives of the Laccadives as we burn the lice in a bunk,

We tack not now to a Gallang prow or a plunging Pei-ho junk;

I had no fear but the seas were clear as far as a sail might fare

Till I met with a lime-washed Yankee brig that rode off Finisterre.

"There were canvas blinds to his bow-gun ports to screen the weight he bore,

And the signals ran for a merchantman from Sandy Hook to the Nore.

"He would not fly the Rovers' flag—the bloody or the black,

But now he floated the Gridiron and now he flaunted the Jack.

He spoke of the Law as he crimped my crew—he swore it was only a loan;

But when I would ask for my own again, he swore it was none of my own.

"He has taken my little parrakeets that nest beneath the Line,

He has stripped my rails of the shaddock-frails and the green unripened pine;

He has taken my bale of dammer and spice I won beyond the seas,

He has taken my grinning heathen gods—and what should he want o' these?

My foremast would not mend his boom, my deckhouse patch his boats;

He has whittled the two, this Yank Yahoo, to peddle for shoe-peg oats.

"I could not fight for the failing light and a rough beam-sea beside,

But I hulled him once for a clumsy crimp and twice because he lied.

"Had I had guns (as I had goods) to work my Christian harm,

I had run him up from his quarter-deck to trade with his own yard-arm;

I had nailed his ears to my capstan-head, and ripped them off with a saw,

And soused them in the bilgewater, and served them to him raw;

I had flung him blind in a rudderless boat to rot in the rocking dark,

I had towed him aft of his own craft, a bait for his brother shark;

I had lapped him round with cocoa husk, and drenched him with the oil,

And lashed him fast to his own mast to blaze above my spoil;

I had stripped his hide for my hammock-side, and tasselled his beard i' the mesh,

And spitted his crew on the live bamboo that grows through the gangrened flesh;

I had hove him down by the mangroves brown, where the mud-reef sucks and draws,

Moored by the heel to his own keel to wait for the land-crab's claws!

He is lazar within and lime without, ye can nose him far enow,

For he carries the taint of a musky ship—the reek of the slaver's dhow!"

The skipper looked at the tiering guns and the bulwarks tall and cold,

And the Captains Three full courteously peered down at the gutted hold,

And the Captains Three called courteously from deck to scuttle-butt:—

"Good Sir, we ha' dealt with that merchantman or ever your teeth were cut.

"Your words be words of a lawless race, and the Law it standeth thus:

He comes of a race that have never a Law, and he never has boarded us.

"We ha' sold him canvas and rope and spar—we know that his price is fair,

And we know that he weeps for the lack of a Law as he rides off Finisterre.

"And since he is damned for a gallows-thief by you and better than you,

We hold it meet that the English fleet should know that we hold him true."

The skipper called to the tall taffrail:—"And what is that to me?

Did ever you hear of a Yankee brig that rifled a Seventy-three?

Do I loom so large from your quarter-deck that I lift like a ship o' the Line?

He has learned to run from a shotted gun and harry such craft as mine.

"There is never a Law on the Cocos Keys to hold a white man in,

But we do not steal the niggers' meal, for that is a nigger's sin.

"Must he have his Law as a quid to chaw, or laid in brass on his wheel?

Does he steal with tears when he buccaneers? 'Fore Gad, then, why does he steal?"

The skipper bit on a deep-sea word, and the word it was not sweet,

For he could see the Captains Three had signalled to the Fleet.

But three and two, in white and blue, the whimpering flags began:—

"We have heard a tale of a—foreign sail, but he is a merchantman."

The skipper peered beneath his palm and swore by the Great Horn Spoon:—

"'Fore Gad, the Chaplain of the Fleet would bless my picaroon!"

By two and three the flags blew free to lash the laughing air:—

"We have sold our spars to the merchantman—we know that his price is fair."

The skipper winked his Western eye, and swore by a China storm:—

"They ha' rigged him a Joseph's jury-coat to keep his honour warm."

The halliards twanged against the tops, the bunting bellied broad,

The skipper spat in the empty hold and mourned for a wasted cord.

Masthead—masthead, the signal sped by the line o' the British craft;

The skipper called to his Lascar crew, and put her about and laughed:—

"It's mainsail haul, my bully boys all—we'll out to the seas again—

Ere they set us to paint their pirate saint, or scrub at his grapnel-chain.

"It's fore-sheet free, with her head to the sea, and the swing of the unbought brine—

We'll make no sport in an English court till we come as a ship o' the Line:

Till we come as a ship o' the Line, my lads, of thirty foot in the sheer,

Lifting again from the outer main with news of a privateer;

Flying his pluck at our mizzen-truck for weft of Admiralty,

Heaving his head for our dipsey-lead in sign that we keep the sea.

"Then fore-sheet home as she lifts to the foam—we stand on the outward tack,

We are paid in the coin of the white man's trade—the bezant is hard, ay, and

black.

"The frigate-bird shall carry my word to the Kling and the Orang-Laut

How a man may sail from a heathen coast to be robbed in a Christian port;

How a man may be robbed in Christian port while Three Great Captains there

Shall dip their flag to a slaver's rag—to show that his trade is fair!"

THE BALLAD OF THE CLAMPHERDOWN

It was our war-ship Clampherdown

 Would sweep the Channel clean,

Wherefore she kept her hatches close

When the merry Channel chops arose,

 To save the bleached marine.

She had one bow-gun of a hundred ton,

 And a great stern-gun beside;

They dipped their noses deep in the sea,

They racked their stays and stanchions free

 In the wash of the wind-whipped tide.

It was our war-ship Clampherdown,

 Fell in with a cruiser light

That carried the dainty Hotchkiss gun

And a pair o' heels wherewith to run

 From the grip of a close-fought fight.

She opened fire at seven miles—

 As ye shoot at a bobbing cork—

And once she fired and twice she fired,

Till the bow-gun drooped like a lily tired

 That lolls upon the stalk.

"Captain, the bow-gun melts apace,

 The deck-beams break below,

'Twere well to rest for an hour or twain,

And patch the shattered plates again."

 And he answered, "Make it so."

She opened fire within the mile—

 As ye shoot at the flying duck—

And the great stern-gun shot fair and true,

With the heave of the ship, to the stainless blue,

 And the great stern-turret stuck.

"Captain, the turret fills with steam,

 The feed-pipes burst below—

You can hear the hiss of the helpless ram,

You can hear the twisted runners jam."

 And he answered, "Turn and go!"

It was our war-ship Clampherdown,

 And grimly did she roll;

Swung round to take the cruiser's fire

As the White Whale faces the Thresher's ire

 When they war by the frozen Pole.

"Captain, the shells are falling fast,

 And faster still fall we;

And it is not meet for English stock

To bide in the heart of an eight-day clock

 The death they cannot see."

"Lie down, lie down, my bold A.B.,

 We drift upon her beam;

We dare not ram, for she can run;

And dare ye fire another gun,

And die in the peeling steam?"

It was our war-ship Clampherdown

That carried an armour-belt;

But fifty feet at stern and bow

Lay bare as the paunch of the purser's sow,

To the hail of the Nordenfeldt.

"Captain, they hack us through and through;

The chilled steel bolts are swift!

We have emptied the bunkers in open sea,

Their shrapnel bursts where our coal should be."

And he answered, "Let her drift."

It was our war-ship Clampherdown,

Swung round upon the tide,

Her two dumb guns glared south and north,

And the blood and the bubbling steam ran forth,

And she ground the cruiser's side.

"Captain, they cry, the fight is done,

They bid you send your sword."

And he answered, "Grapple her stern and bow.

They have asked for the steel. They shall have it now;

Out cutlasses and board!"

It was our war-ship Clampherdown

Spewed up four hundred men;

And the scalded stokers yelped delight,

As they rolled in the waist and heard the fight

Stamp o'er their steel-walled pen.

They cleared the cruiser end to end,

From conning-tower to hold.

They fought as they fought in Nelson's fleet;

They were stripped to the waist, they were bare to the feet,

As it was in the days of old.

It was the sinking Clampherdown

Heaved up her battered side—

And carried a million pounds in steel,

To the cod and the corpse-fed conger-eel,

And the scour of the Channel tide.

It was the crew of the Clampherdown

Stood out to sweep the sea,

On a cruiser won from an ancient foe,

As it was in the days of long ago,

And as it still shall be.

THE BALLAD OF THE "BOLIVAR"

Seven men from all the world, back to Docks again,

Rolling down the Ratcliffe Road drunk and raising Cain:

Give the girls another drink 'fore we sign away—

We that took the Bolivar out across the Bay!

We put out from Sunderland loaded down with rails;

We put back to Sunderland 'cause our cargo shifted;

We put out from Sunderland—met the winter gales—

Seven days and seven nights to the Start we drifted.

Racketing her rivets loose, smoke-stack white as snow,

All the coals adrift adeck, half the rails below,

Leaking like a lobster-pot, steering like a dray—

Out we took the Bolivar, out across the Bay!

One by one the Lights came up, winked and let us by;

Mile by mile we waddled on, coal and fo'c'sle short;

Met a blow that laid us down, heard a bulkhead fly;

Left the Wolf behind us with a two-foot list to port.

Trailing like a wounded duck, working out her soul;

Clanging like a smithy-shop after every roll;

Just a funnel and a mast lurching through the spray—

So we threshed the Bolivar out across the Bay!

'Felt her hog and felt her sag, betted when she'd break;

Wondered every time she raced if she'd stand the shock;

Heard the seas like drunken men pounding at her strake;

Hoped the Lord 'ud keep his thumb on the plummer-block.

 Banged against the iron decks, bilges choked with coal;

 Flayed and frozen foot and hand, sick of heart and soul;

 Last we prayed she'd buck herself into judgment Day—

 Hi! we cursed the Bolivar—knocking round the Bay!

O her nose flung up to sky, groaning to be still—

Up and down and back we went, never time for breath;

Then the money paid at Lloyd's caught her by the heel,

And the stars ran round and round dancin' at our death.

 Aching for an hour's sleep, dozing off between;

 'Heard the rotten rivets draw when she took it green;

 'Watched the compass chase its tail like a cat at play—

 That was on the Bolivar, south across the Bay.

Once we saw between the squalls, lyin' head to swell—

Mad with work and weariness, wishin' they was we—

Some damned Liner's lights go by like a long hotel;

Cheered her from the Bolivar—swampin' in the sea.

 Then a grayback cleared us out, then the skipper laughed;

 "Boys, the wheel has gone to Hell—rig the winches aft!

 Yoke the kicking rudder-head—get her under way!"

 So we steered her, pulley-haul, out across the Bay!

Just a pack o' rotten plates puttied up with tar,

In we came, an' time enough, 'cross Bilbao Bar.

Overloaded, undermanned, meant to founder, we

Euchred God Almighty's storm, bluffed the Eternal Sea!

Seven men from all the world, back to town again,

Rollin' down the Ratcliffe Road drunk and raising Cain:

Seven men from out of Hell. Ain't the owners gay,

'Cause we took the "Bolivar" safe across the Bay?

THE ENGLISH FLAG

Above the portico a flag-staff, bearing the Union Jack,

remained fluttering in the flames for some time, but ultimately

when it fell the crowds rent the air with shouts,

and seemed to see significance in the incident.—DAILY PAPERS.

Winds of the World, give answer! They are whimpering to and fro—

And what should they know of England who only England know?—

The poor little street-bred people that vapour and fume and brag,

They are lifting their heads in the stillness to yelp at the English Flag!

Must we borrow a clout from the Boer—to plaster anew with dirt?

An Irish liar's bandage, or an English coward's shirt?

We may not speak of England; her Flag's to sell or share.

What is the Flag of England? Winds of the World, declare!

The North Wind blew:—"From Bergen my steel-shod vanguards go;

I chase your lazy whalers home from the Disko floe;

By the great North Lights above me I work the will of God,

And the liner splits on the ice-field or the Dogger fills with cod.

"I barred my gates with iron, I shuttered my doors with flame,

Because to force my ramparts your nutshell navies came;

I took the sun from their presence, I cut them down with my blast,

And they died, but the Flag of England blew free ere the spirit passed.

"The lean white bear hath seen it in the long, long Arctic night,

The musk-ox knows the standard that flouts the Northern Light:

What is the Flag of England? Ye have but my bergs to dare,

Ye have but my drifts to conquer. Go forth, for it is there!"

The South Wind sighed:—"From the Virgins my mid-sea course was ta'en

Over a thousand islands lost in an idle main,

Where the sea-egg flames on the coral and the long-backed breakers croon

Their endless ocean legends to the lazy, locked lagoon.

"Strayed amid lonely islets, mazed amid outer keys,

I waked the palms to laughter—I tossed the scud in the breeze—

Never was isle so little, never was sea so lone,

But over the scud and the palm-trees an English flag was flown.

"I have wrenched it free from the halliard to hang for a wisp on the Horn;

I have chased it north to the Lizard—ribboned and rolled and torn;

I have spread its fold o'er the dying, adrift in a hopeless sea;

I have hurled it swift on the slaver, and seen the slave set free.

"My basking sunfish know it, and wheeling albatross,

Where the lone wave fills with fire beneath the Southern Cross.

What is the Flag of England? Ye have but my reefs to dare,

Ye have but my seas to furrow. Go forth, for it is there!"

The East Wind roared:—"From the Kuriles, the Bitter Seas, I come,

And me men call the Home-Wind, for I bring the English home.

Look—look well to your shipping! By the breath of my mad typhoon

I swept your close-packed Praya and beached your best at Kowloon!

"The reeling junks behind me and the racing seas before,

I raped your richest roadstead—I plundered Singapore!

I set my hand on the Hoogli; as a hooded snake she rose,

And I flung your stoutest steamers to roost with the startled crows.

"Never the lotus closes, never the wild-fowl wake,

But a soul goes out on the East Wind that died for England's sake—

Man or woman or suckling, mother or bride or maid—

Because on the bones of the English the English Flag is stayed.

"The desert-dust hath dimmed it, the flying wild-ass knows,

The scared white leopard winds it across the taintless snows.

What is the Flag of England? Ye have but my sun to dare,

Ye have but my sands to travel. Go forth, for it is there!"

The West Wind called:—"In squadrons the thoughtless galleons fly

That bear the wheat and cattle lest street-bred people die.

They make my might their porter, they make my house their path,

Till I loose my neck from their rudder and whelm them all in my wrath.

"I draw the gliding fog-bank as a snake is drawn from the hole,

They bellow one to the other, the frighted ship-bells toll,

For day is a drifting terror till I raise the shroud with my breath,

And they see strange bows above them and the two go locked to death.

"But whether in calm or wrack-wreath, whether by dark or day,

I heave them whole to the conger or rip their plates away,

First of the scattered legions, under a shrieking sky,

Dipping between the rollers, the English Flag goes by.

"The dead dumb fog hath wrapped it—the frozen dews have kissed—

The naked stars have seen it, a fellow-star in the mist.

What is the Flag of England? Ye have but my breath to dare,

Ye have but my waves to conquer. Go forth, for it is there!"

"CLEARED"

(In Memory of a Commission)

Help for a patriot distressed, a spotless spirit hurt,

Help for an honorable clan sore trampled in the dirt!

From Queenstown Bay to Donegal, O listen to my song,

The honorable gentlemen have suffered grievous wrong.

Their noble names were mentioned—O the burning black disgrace!—

By a brutal Saxon paper in an Irish shooting-case;

They sat upon it for a year, then steeled their heart to brave it,

And "coruscating innocence" the learned Judges gave it.

Bear witness, Heaven, of that grim crime beneath the surgeon's knife,

The honorable gentlemen deplored the loss of life;

Bear witness of those chanting choirs that burk and shirk and snigger,

No man laid hand upon the knife or finger to the trigger!

Cleared in the face of all mankind beneath the winking skies,

Like phoenixes from Phoenix Park (and what lay there) they rise!

Go shout it to the emerald seas-give word to Erin now,

Her honorable gentlemen are cleared—and this is how:

They only paid the Moonlighter his cattle-hocking price,

They only helped the murderer with council's best advice,

But—sure it keeps their honor white—the learned Court believes

They never gave a piece of plate to murderers and thieves.

They ever told the ramping crowd to card a woman's hide,

They never marked a man for death—what fault of theirs he died?—

They only said "intimidate," and talked and went away—

By God, the boys that did the work were braver men than they!

Their sin it was that fed the fire—small blame to them that heard

The "bhoys" get drunk on rhetoric, and madden at the word—

They knew whom they were talking at, if they were Irish too,

The gentlemen that lied in Court, they knew and well they knew.

They only took the Judas-gold from Fenians out of jail,

They only fawned for dollars on the blood-dyed Clan-na-Gael.

If black is black or white is white, ill black and white it's down,

They're only traitors to the Queen and rebels to the Crown.

"Cleared," honorable gentlemen. Be thankful it's no more:

The widow's curse is on your house, the dead are at your door.

On you the shame of open shame, on you from North to South

The band of every honest man flat-heeled across your mouth.

"Less black than we were painted"?—Faith, no word of black was said;

The lightest touch was human blood, and that, ye know, runs red.

It's sticking to your fist today for all your sneer and scoff,

And by the Judge's well-weighed word you cannot wipe it off.

Hold up those hands of innocence—go, scare your sheep, together,

The blundering, tripping tups that bleat behind the old bell-wether;

And if they snuff the taint and break to find another pen,

Tell them it's tar that glistens so, and daub them yours again!

[452] RUDYARD KIPLING

"The charge is old"?—As old as Cain—as fresh as yesterday;

Old as the Ten Commandments, have ye talked those laws away?

If words are words, or death is death, or powder sends the ball,

You spoke the words that sped the shot—the curse be on you all.

"Our friends believe"? Of course they do—as sheltered women may;

But have they seen the shrieking soul ripped from the quivering clay?

They—If their own front door is shut, they'll swear the whole world's warm;

What do they know of dread of death or hanging fear of harm?

The secret half a country keeps, the whisper in the lane,

The shriek that tells the shot went home behind the broken pane,

The dry blood crisping in the sun that scares the honest bees,

And shows the "bhoys" have heard your talk—what do they know of these?

But you—you know—ay, ten times more; the secrets of the dead,

Black terror on the country-side by word and whisper bred,

The mangled stallion's scream at night, the tail-cropped heifer's low.

Who set the whisper going first? You know, and well you know!

My soul! I'd sooner lie in jail for murder plain and straight,

Pure crime I'd done with my own hand for money, lust, or hate,

Than take a seat in Parliament by fellow-felons cheered,

While one of those "not provens" proved me cleared as you are cleared.

Cleared—you that "lost" the League accounts—go, guard our honor still,

Go, help to make our country's laws that broke God's laws at will—

One hand stuck out behind the back, to signal "strike again";

The other on your dress-shirt front to show your heart is @dane,

If black is black or white is white, in black and white it's down,

You're only traitors to the Queen and but rebels to the Crown

If print is print or words are words, the learned Court perpends:

We are not ruled by murderers, only—by their friends.

AN IMPERIAL RESCRIPT

Now this is the tale of the Council the German Kaiser decreed,

To ease the strong of their burden, to help the weak in their need,

He sent a word to the peoples, who struggle, and pant, and sweat,

That the straw might be counted fairly and the tally of bricks be set.

The Lords of Their Hands assembled; from the East and the West they drew—

Baltimore, Lille, and Essen, Brummagem, Clyde, and Crewe.

And some were black from the furnace, and some were brown from the soil,

And some were blue from the dye-vat; but all were wearied of toil.

And the young King said:—"I have found it, the road to the rest ye seek:

The strong shall wait for the weary, the hale shall halt for the weak;

With the even tramp of an army where no man breaks from the line,

Ye shall march to peace and plenty in the bond of brotherhood—sign!"

The paper lay on the table, the strong heads bowed thereby,

And a wail went up from the peoples:—"Ay, sign—give rest, for we die!"

A hand was stretched to the goose-quill, a fist was cramped to scrawl,

When—the laugh of a blue-eyed maiden ran clear through the council-hall.

And each one heard Her laughing as each one saw Her plain—

Saidie, Mimi, or Olga, Gretchen, or Mary Jane.

And the Spirit of Man that is in Him to the light of the vision woke;

And the men drew back from the paper, as a Yankee delegate spoke:—

"There's a girl in Jersey City who works on the telephone;

We're going to hitch our horses and dig for a house of our own,

With gas and water connections, and steam-heat through to the top;

And, W. Hohenzollern, I guess I shall work till I drop."

And an English delegate thundered:—"The weak an' the lame be blowed!

I've a berth in the Sou'-West workshops, a home in the Wandsworth Road;

And till the 'sociation has footed my buryin' bill,

I work for the kids an' the missus. Pull up? I be damned if I will!"

And over the German benches the bearded whisper ran:—

"Lager, der girls und der dollars, dey makes or dey breaks a man.

If Schmitt haf collared der dollars, he collars der girl deremit;

But if Schmitt bust in der pizness, we collars der girl from Schmitt."

They passed one resolution:—"Your sub-committee believe

You can lighten the curse of Adam when you've lightened the curse of Eve.

But till we are built like angels, with hammer and chisel and pen,

We will work for ourself and a woman, for ever and ever, amen."

Now this is the tale of the Council the German Kaiser held—

The day that they razored the Grindstone, the day that the Cat was belled,

The day of the Figs from Thistles, the day of the Twisted Sands,

The day that the laugh of a maiden made light of the Lords of Their Hands.

TOMLINSON

Now Tomlinson gave up the ghost in his house in Berkeley Square,

And a Spirit came to his bedside and gripped him by the hair—

A Spirit gripped him by the hair and carried him far away,

Till he heard as the roar of a rain-fed ford the roar of the Milky Way:

Till he heard the roar of the Milky Way die down and drone and cease,

And they came to the Gate within the Wall where Peter holds the keys.

"Stand up, stand up now, Tomlinson, and answer loud and high

The good that ye did for the sake of men or ever ye came to die—

The good that ye did for the sake of men in little earth so lone!"

And the naked soul of Tomlinson grew white as a rain-washed bone.

"O I have a friend on earth," he said, "that was my priest and guide,

And well would he answer all for me if he were by my side."

—"For that ye strove in neighbour-love it shall be written fair,

But now ye wait at Heaven's Gate and not in Berkeley Square:

Though we called your friend from his bed this night, he could not speak for

you,

For the race is run by one and one and never by two and two."

Then Tomlinson looked up and down, and little gain was there,

For the naked stars grinned overhead, and he saw that his soul was bare:

The Wind that blows between the worlds, it cut him like a knife,

And Tomlinson took up his tale and spoke of his good in life.

"This I have read in a book," he said, "and that was told to me,

And this I have thought that another man thought of a Prince in Muscovy."

The good souls flocked like homing doves and bade him clear the path,

And Peter twirled the jangling keys in weariness and wrath.

"Ye have read, ye have heard, ye have thought," he said, "and the tale is yet
to run:

By the worth of the body that once ye had, give answer—what ha'ye done?"

Then Tomlinson looked back and forth, and little good it bore,

For the Darkness stayed at his shoulder-blade and Heaven's Gate before:—

"O this I have felt, and this I have guessed, and this I have heard men say,

And this they wrote that another man wrote of a carl in Norroway."

—"Ye have read, ye have felt, ye have guessed, good lack! Ye have hampered
Heaven's Gate;

There's little room between the stars in idleness to prate!

O none may reach by hired speech of neighbour, priest, and kin

Through borrowed deed to God's good meed that lies so fair within;

Get hence, get hence to the Lord of Wrong, for doom has yet to run,

And... the faith that ye share with Berkeley Square uphold you, Tomlinson!"

The Spirit gripped him by the hair, and sun by sun they fell

Till they came to the belt of Naughty Stars that rim the mouth of Hell:

The first are red with pride and wrath, the next are white with pain,

But the third are black with clinkered sin that cannot burn again:

They may hold their path, they may leave their path, with never a soul to
mark,

They may burn or freeze, but they must not cease in the Scorn of the Outer
Dark.

The Wind that blows between the worlds, it nipped him to the bone,

And he yearned to the flare of Hell-Gate there as the light of his own hearth-
stone.

The Devil he sat behind the bars, where the desperate legions drew,

But he caught the hasting Tomlinson and would not let him through.

"Wot ye the price of good pit-coal that I must pay?" said he,

"That ye rank yoursel' so fit for Hell and ask no leave of me?

I am all o'er-sib to Adam's breed that ye should give me scorn,

For I strove with God for your First Father the day that he was born.

"Sit down, sit down upon the slag, and answer loud and high

The harm that ye did to the Sons of Men or ever you came to die."

And Tomlinson looked up and up, and saw against the night

The belly of a tortured star blood-red in Hell-Mouth light;

And Tomlinson looked down and down, and saw beneath his feet

The frontlet of a tortured star milk-white in Hell-Mouth heat.

"O I had a love on earth," said he, "that kissed me to my fall,

And if ye would call my love to me I know she would answer all."

—"All that ye did in love forbid it shall be written fair,

But now ye wait at Hell-Mouth Gate and not in Berkeley Square:

Though we whistled your love from her bed tonight, I trow she would not run,

For the sin ye do by two and two ye must pay for one by one!"

The Wind that blows between the worlds, it cut him like a knife,

And Tomlinson took up the tale and spoke of his sin in life:—

"Once I ha' laughed at the power of Love and twice at the grip of the Grave,

And thrice I ha' patted my God on the head that men might call me brave."

The Devil he blew on a brandered soul and set it aside to cool:—

"Do ye think I would waste my good pit-coal on the hide of a brain-sick fool?

I see no worth in the hobnailed mirth or the jolthead jest ye did

That I should waken my gentlemen that are sleeping three on a grid."

Then Tomlinson looked back and forth, and there was little grace,

For Hell-Gate filled the houseless Soul with the Fear of Naked Space.

"Nay, this I ha' heard," quo' Tomlinson, "and this was noised abroad,

And this I ha' got from a Belgian book on the word of a dead French lord."

—"Ye ha' heard, ye ha' read, ye ha' got, good lack! and the tale begins

afresh—

Have ye sinned one sin for the pride o' the eye or the sinful lust of the

flesh?"

Then Tomlinson he gripped the bars and yammered, "Let me in—

For I mind that I borrowed my neighbour's wife to sin the deadly sin."

The Devil he grinned behind the bars, and banked the fires high:

"Did ye read of that sin in a book?" said he; and Tomlinson said, "Ay!"

The Devil he blew upon his nails, and the little devils ran,

And he said: "Go husk this whimpering thief that comes in the guise of a man:

Winnow him out 'twixt star and star, and sieve his proper worth:

There's sore decline in Adam's line if this be spawn of earth."

Empusa's crew, so naked-new they may not face the fire,

But weep that they bin too small to sin to the height of their desire,

Over the coal they chased the Soul, and racked it all abroad,

As children rifle a caddis-case or the raven's foolish hoard.

And back they came with the tattered Thing, as children after play,

And they said: "The soul that he got from God he has bartered clean away.

"We have threshed a stook of print and book, and winnowed a chattering wind

And many a soul wherefrom he stole, but his we cannot find:

We have handled him, we have dandled him, we have seared him to the bone,

And sure if tooth and nail show truth he has no soul of his own."

The Devil he bowed his head on his breast and rumbled deep and low:—

"I'm all o'er-sib to Adam's breed that I should bid him go.

"Yet close we lie, and deep we lie, and if I gave him place,

My gentlemen that are so proud would flout me to my face;

They'd call my house a common stews and me a careless host,

And—I would not anger my gentlemen for the sake of a shiftless ghost."

The Devil he looked at the mangled Soul that prayed to feel the flame,

And he thought of Holy Charity, but he thought of his own good name:—

"Now ye could haste my coal to waste, and sit ye down to fry:

Did ye think of that theft for yourself?" said he; and Tomlinson said, "Ay!"

The Devil he blew an outward breath, for his heart was free from care:—

"Ye have scarce the soul of a louse," he said, "but the roots of sin are

there,

And for that sin should ye come in were I the lord alone.

But sinful pride has rule inside—and mightier than my own.

"Honour and Wit, fore-damned they sit, to each his priest and whore:

Nay, scarce I dare myself go there, and you they'd torture sore.

"Ye are neither spirit nor spirk," he said; "ye are neither book nor brute—

Go, get ye back to the flesh again for the sake of Man's repute.

"I'm all o'er-sib to Adam's breed that I should mock your pain,

But look that ye win to worthier sin ere ye come back again.

Get hence, the hearse is at your door—the grim black stallions wait—

They bear your clay to place today. Speed, lest ye come too late!

Go back to Earth with a lip unsealed—go back with an open eye,

And carry my word to the Sons of Men or ever ye come to die:

That the sin they do by two and two they must pay for one by one—

And... the God that you took from a printed book be with you, Tomlinson!"

* * * * * * *

BARRACK-ROOM BALLADS

Dedication

To T. A.

I have made for you a song,

And it may be right or wrong,

But only you can tell me if it's true;

I have tried for to explain

Both your pleasure and your pain,

And, Thomas, here's my best respects to you!

O there'll surely come a day

When they'll give you all your pay,

And treat you as a Christian ought to do;

So, until that day comes round,

Heaven keep you safe and sound,

And, Thomas, here's my best respects to you!

—R. K.

DANNY DEEVER

"What are the bugles blowin' for?" said Files-on-Parade.

"To turn you out, to turn you out", the Colour-Sergeant said.

"What makes you look so white, so white?" said Files-on-Parade.

"I'm dreadin' what I've got to watch", the Colour-Sergeant said.

For they're hangin' Danny Deever, you can hear the Dead March play,

The regiment's in 'ollow square—they're hangin' him today;

They've taken of his buttons off an' cut his stripes away,

An' they're hangin' Danny Deever in the mornin'.

"What makes the rear-rank breathe so 'ard?" said Files-on-Parade.

"It's bitter cold, it's bitter cold", the Colour-Sergeant said.

"What makes that front-rank man fall down?" said Files-on-Parade.

"A touch o' sun, a touch o' sun", the Colour-Sergeant said.

They are hangin' Danny Deever, they are marchin' of 'im round,

They 'ave 'alted Danny Deever by 'is coffin on the ground;

An' 'e'll swing in 'arf a minute for a sneakin' shootin' hound—

O they're hangin' Danny Deever in the mornin'!

"'Is cot was right-'and cot to mine", said Files-on-Parade.

"'E's sleepin' out an' far tonight", the Colour-Sergeant said.

"I've drunk 'is beer a score o' times", said Files-on-Parade.

"'E's drinkin' bitter beer alone", the Colour-Sergeant said.

They are hangin' Danny Deever, you must mark 'im to 'is place,

For 'e shot a comrade sleepin'—you must look 'im in the face;

Nine 'undred of 'is county an' the regiment's disgrace,

While they're hangin' Danny Deever in the mornin'.

"What's that so black agin' the sun?" said Files-on-Parade.

"It's Danny fightin' 'ard for life", the Colour-Sergeant said.

"What's that that whimpers over'ead?" said Files-on-Parade.

"It's Danny's soul that's passin' now", the Colour-Sergeant said.

For they're done with Danny Deever, you can 'ear the quickstep play,

The regiment's in column, an' they're marchin' us away;

Ho! the young recruits are shakin', an' they'll want their beer today,

After hangin' Danny Deever in the mornin'.

TOMMY

I went into a public-'ouse to get a pint o' beer,

The publican 'e up an' sez, "We serve no red-coats here."

The girls be'ind the bar they laughed an' giggled fit to die,

I outs into the street again an' to myself sez I:

 O it's Tommy this, an' Tommy that, an' "Tommy, go away";

 But it's "Thank you, Mister Atkins", when the band begins to play,

 The band begins to play, my boys, the band begins to play,

 O it's "Thank you, Mister Atkins", when the band begins to play.

I went into a theatre as sober as could be,

They gave a drunk civilian room, but 'adn't none for me;

They sent me to the gallery or round the music-'alls,

But when it comes to fightin', Lord! they'll shove me in the stalls!

 For it's Tommy this, an' Tommy that, an' "Tommy, wait outside";

 But it's "Special train for Atkins" when the trooper's on the tide,

 The troopship's on the tide, my boys, the troopship's on the tide,

 O it's "Special train for Atkins" when the trooper's on the tide.

Yes, makin' mock o' uniforms that guard you while you sleep

Is cheaper than them uniforms, an' they're starvation cheap;

An' hustlin' drunken soldiers when they're goin' large a bit

Is five times better business than paradin' in full kit.

 Then it's Tommy this, an' Tommy that, an' "Tommy, 'ow's yer soul?"

 But it's "Thin red line of 'eroes" when the drums begin to roll,

 The drums begin to roll, my boys, the drums begin to roll,

 O it's "Thin red line of 'eroes" when the drums begin to roll.

We aren't no thin red 'eroes, nor we aren't no blackguards too,

But single men in barricks, most remarkable like you;

An' if sometimes our conduck isn't all your fancy paints,

Why, single men in barricks don't grow into plaster saints;

 While it's Tommy this, an' Tommy that, an' "Tommy, fall be'ind",

 But it's "Please to walk in front, sir", when there's trouble in the wind,

 There's trouble in the wind, my boys, there's trouble in the wind,

 O it's "Please to walk in front, sir", when there's trouble in the wind.

You talk o' better food for us, an' schools, an' fires, an' all:

We'll wait for extry rations if you treat us rational.

Don't mess about the cook-room slops, but prove it to our face

The Widow's Uniform is not the soldier-man's disgrace.

 For it's Tommy this, an' Tommy that, an' "Chuck him out, the brute!"

 But it's "Saviour of 'is country" when the guns begin to shoot;

 An' it's Tommy this, an' Tommy that, an' anything you please;

 An' Tommy ain't a bloomin' fool—you bet that Tommy sees!

FUZZY-WUZZY

(Soudan Expeditionary Force)

We've fought with many men acrost the seas,

 An' some of 'em was brave an' some was not:

The Paythan an' the Zulu an' Burmese;

 But the Fuzzy was the finest o' the lot.

We never got a ha'porth's change of 'im:

 'E squatted in the scrub an' 'ocked our 'orses,

'E cut our sentries up at Suakim,

An' 'e played the cat an' banjo with our forces.

So 'ere's to you, Fuzzy-Wuzzy, at your 'ome in the Soudan;

You're a pore benighted 'eathen but a first-class fightin' man;

We gives you your certificate, an' if you want it signed

We'll come an' 'ave a romp with you whenever you're inclined.

We took our chanst among the Khyber 'ills,

 The Boers knocked us silly at a mile,

The Burman give us Irriwaddy chills,

 An' a Zulu impi dished us up in style:

But all we ever got from such as they

 Was pop to what the Fuzzy made us swaller;

We 'eld our bloomin' own, the papers say,

 But man for man the Fuzzy knocked us 'oller.

Then 'ere's to you, Fuzzy-Wuzzy, an' the missis and the kid;

 Our orders was to break you, an' of course we went an' did.

We sloshed you with Martinis, an' it wasn't 'ardly fair;

 But for all the odds agin' you, Fuzzy-Wuz, you broke the square.

'E 'asn't got no papers of 'is own,

 'E 'asn't got no medals nor rewards,

So we must certify the skill 'e's shown

 In usin' of 'is long two-'anded swords:

When 'e's 'oppin' in an' out among the bush

 With 'is coffin-'eaded shield an' shovel-spear,

An 'appy day with Fuzzy on the rush

 Will last an 'ealthy Tommy for a year.

So 'ere's to you, Fuzzy-Wuzzy, an' your friends which are no more,

If we 'adn't lost some messmates we would 'elp you to deplore;

But give an' take's the gospel, an' we'll call the bargain fair,

For if you 'ave lost more than us, you crumpled up the square!

'E rushes at the smoke when we let drive,

 An', before we know, 'e's 'ackin' at our 'ead;

'E's all 'ot sand an' ginger when alive,

 An' 'e's generally shammin' when 'e's dead.

'E's a daisy, 'e's a ducky, 'e's a lamb!

 'E's a injia-rubber idiot on the spree,

'E's the on'y thing that doesn't give a damn

 For a Regiment o' British Infantree!

 So 'ere's to you, Fuzzy-Wuzzy, at your 'ome in the Soudan;

 You're a pore benighted 'eathen but a first-class fightin' man;

 An' 'ere's to you, Fuzzy-Wuzzy, with your 'ayrick 'ead of 'air—

 You big black boundin' beggar—for you broke a British square!

SOLDIER, SOLDIER

"Soldier, soldier come from the wars,

Why don't you march with my true love?"

"We're fresh from off the ship an' 'e's maybe give the slip,

An' you'd best go look for a new love."

New love! True love!

Best go look for a new love,

The dead they cannot rise, an' you'd better dry your eyes,

An' you'd best go look for a new love.

"Soldier, soldier come from the wars,

What did you see o' my true love?"

"I seed 'im serve the Queen in a suit o' rifle-green,

An' you'd best go look for a new love."

"Soldier, soldier come from the wars,

Did ye see no more o' my true love?"

"I seed 'im runnin' by when the shots begun to fly—

But you'd best go look for a new love."

"Soldier, soldier come from the wars,

Did aught take 'arm to my true love?"

"I couldn't see the fight, for the smoke it lay so white—

An' you'd best go look for a new love."

"Soldier, soldier come from the wars,

I'll up an' tend to my true love!"

"'E's lying on the dead with a bullet through 'is 'ead,

An' you'd best go look for a new love."

"Soldier, soldier come from the wars,

I'll down an' die with my true love!"

"The pit we dug'll 'ide 'im an' the twenty men beside 'im—

An' you'd best go look for a new love."

"Soldier, soldier come from the wars,

Do you bring no sign from my true love?"

"I bring a lock of 'air that 'e allus used to wear,

An' you'd best go look for a new love."

"Soldier, soldier come from the wars,

O then I know it's true I've lost my true love!"

"An' I tell you truth again—when you've lost the feel o' pain

You'd best take me for your true love."

True love! New love!

Best take 'im for a new love,

The dead they cannot rise, an' you'd better dry your eyes,

An' you'd best take 'im for your true love.

SCREW-GUNS

Smokin' my pipe on the mountings,

 sniffin' the mornin' cool,

I walks in my old brown gaiters

 along o' my old brown mule,

With seventy gunners be'ind me,

 an' never a beggar forgets

It's only the pick of the Army

 that handles the dear little pets—'Tss! 'Tss!

 For you all love the screw-guns—the screw-guns they all love you!

So when we call round with a few guns,

 o' course you will know what to do—hoo! hoo!

Jest send in your Chief an' surrender—

 it's worse if you fights or you runs:

You can go where you please, you can skid up the trees,

 but you don't get away from the guns!

They sends us along where the roads are, but mostly we goes where they ain't:

We'd climb up the side of a sign-board an' trust to the stick o' the paint:

We've chivied the Naga an' Looshai,

 we've give the Afreedeeman fits,

For we fancies ourselves at two thousand,

 we guns that are built in two bits—'Tss! 'Tss!

 For you all love the screw-guns...

If a man doesn't work, why, we drills 'im

 an' teaches 'im 'ow to behave;

If a beggar can't march, why, we kills 'im

an' rattles 'im into 'is grave.

You've got to stand up to our business

an' spring without snatchin' or fuss.

D'you say that you sweat with the field-guns?

By God, you must lather with us—'Tss! 'Tss!

For you all love the screw-guns...

The eagles is screamin' around us,

the river's a-moanin' below,

We're clear o' the pine an' the oak-scrub,

we're out on the rocks an' the snow,

An' the wind is as thin as a whip-lash

what carries away to the plains

The rattle an' stamp o' the lead-mules—

the jinglety-jink o' the chains—'Tss! 'Tss!

For you all love the screw-guns...

There's a wheel on the Horns o' the Mornin',

an' a wheel on the edge o' the Pit,

An' a drop into nothin' beneath you as straight as a beggar can spit:

With the sweat runnin' out o' your shirt-sleeves,

an' the sun off the snow in your face,

An' 'arf o' the men on the drag-ropes

to hold the old gun in 'er place—'Tss! 'Tss!

For you all love the screw-guns...

Smokin' my pipe on the mountings,

sniffin' the mornin' cool,

I climbs in my old brown gaiters

along o' my old brown mule.

The monkey can say what our road was—

 the wild-goat 'e knows where we passed.

Stand easy, you long-eared old darlin's!

 Out drag-ropes! With shrapnel! Hold fast—'Tss! 'Tss!

For you all love the screw-guns—the screw-guns they all love
you!

So when we take tea with a few guns,

 o' course you will know what to do—hoo! hoo!

Jest send in your Chief an' surrender—

 it's worse if you fights or you runs:

You may hide in the caves, they'll be only your graves,

 but you can't get away from the guns!

GUNGA DIN

You may talk o' gin and beer

When you're quartered safe out 'ere,

An' you're sent to penny-fights an' Aldershot it;

But when it comes to slaughter

You will do your work on water,

An' you'll lick the bloomin' boots of 'im that's got it.

Now in Injia's sunny clime,

Where I used to spend my time

A-servin' of 'Er Majesty the Queen,

Of all them blackfaced crew

The finest man I knew

Was our regimental bhisti, Gunga Din.

He was "Din! Din! Din!

You limpin' lump o' brick-dust, Gunga Din!

Hi! slippy hitherao!

Water, get it! Panee lao!1

You squidgy-nosed old idol, Gunga Din."

The uniform 'e wore

Was nothin' much before,

An' rather less than 'arf o' that be'ind,

For a piece o' twisty rag

An' a goatskin water-bag

Was all the field-equipment 'e could find.

When the sweatin' troop-train lay

In a sidin' through the day,

Where the 'eat would make your bloomin' eyebrows crawl,

We shouted "Harry By!" 2

Till our throats were bricky-dry,

Then we wopped 'im 'cause 'e couldn't serve us all.

It was "Din! Din! Din!

You 'eathen, where the mischief 'ave you been?

You put some juldee 3 in it

Or I'll marrow 4 you this minute

If you don't fill up my helmet, Gunga Din!"

'E would dot an' carry one

Till the longest day was done;

An' 'e didn't seem to know the use o' fear.

If we charged or broke or cut,

You could bet your bloomin' nut,

'E'd be waitin' fifty paces right flank rear.

With 'is mussick 5 on 'is back,

'E would skip with our attack,

An' watch us till the bugles made "Retire",

An' for all 'is dirty 'ide

'E was white, clear white, inside

When 'e went to tend the wounded under fire!

It was "Din! Din! Din!"

With the bullets kickin' dust-spots on the green.

When the cartridges ran out,

You could hear the front-files shout,

"Hi! ammunition-mules an' Gunga Din!"

I shan't forgit the night

When I dropped be'ind the fight

With a bullet where my belt-plate should 'a' been.

I was chokin' mad with thirst,

An' the man that spied me first

Was our good old grinnin', gruntin' Gunga Din.

'E lifted up my 'ead,

An' he plugged me where I bled,

An' 'e guv me 'arf-a-pint o' water-green:

It was crawlin' and it stunk,

But of all the drinks I've drunk,

I'm gratefullest to one from Gunga Din.

It was "Din! Din! Din!

'Ere's a beggar with a bullet through 'is spleen;

'E's chawin' up the ground,

An' 'e's kickin' all around:

For Gawd's sake git the water, Gunga Din!"

'E carried me away

To where a dooli lay,

An' a bullet come an' drilled the beggar clean.

'E put me safe inside,

An' just before 'e died,

"I 'ope you liked your drink", sez Gunga Din.

So I'll meet 'im later on

At the place where 'e is gone—

Where it's always double drill and no canteen;

'E'll be squattin' on the coals

Givin' drink to poor damned souls,

An' I'll get a swig in hell from Gunga Din!

 Yes, Din! Din! Din!

 You Lazarushian-leather Gunga Din!

 Though I've belted you and flayed you,

 By the livin' Gawd that made you,

 You're a better man than I am, Gunga Din!

1 Bring water swiftly.

2 Mr Atkins' equivalent for "O Brother."

3 Hit you.

4 Be quick.

5 Water skin.

OONTS

(Northern India Transport Train)

Wot makes the soldier's 'eart to @penk, wot makes 'im to perspire?

It isn't standin' up to charge nor lyin' down to fire;

But it's everlastin' waitin' on a everlastin' road

For the commissariat camel an' 'is commissariat load.

 O the oont, 1 O the oont, O the commissariat oont!

 With 'is silly neck a-bobbin' like a basket full o' snakes;

 We packs 'im like an idol, an' you ought to 'ear 'im grunt,

 An' when we gets 'im loaded up 'is blessed girth-rope breaks.

Wot makes the rear-guard swear so 'ard when night is drorin' in,

An' every native follower is shiverin' for 'is skin?

It ain't the chanst o' being rushed by Paythans from the 'ills,

It's the commissariat camel puttin' on 'is bloomin' frills!

 O the oont, O the oont, O the hairy scary oont!

 A-trippin' over tent-ropes when we've got the night alarm!

 We socks 'im with a stretcher-pole an' 'eads 'im off in front,

 An' when we've saved 'is bloomin' life 'e chaws our bloomin' arm.

The 'orse 'e knows above a bit, the bullock's but a fool,

The elephant's a gentleman, the battery-mule's a mule;

But the commissariat cam-u-el, when all is said an' done,

'E's a devil an' a ostrich an' a orphan-child in one.

 O the oont, O the oont, O the Gawd-forsaken oont!

 The lumpy-'umpy 'ummin'-bird a-singin' where 'e lies,

 'E's blocked the whole division from the rear-guard to the front,

 An' when we get him up again—the beggar goes an' dies!

'E'll gall an' chafe an' lame an' fight—'e smells most awful vile;

'E'll lose 'isself for ever if you let 'im stray a mile;

'E's game to graze the 'ole day long an' 'owl the 'ole night through,

An' when 'e comes to greasy ground 'e splits 'isself in two.

 O the oont, O the oont, O the floppin', droppin' oont!

 When 'is long legs give from under an' 'is meltin' eye is dim,

 The tribes is up be'ind us, and the tribes is out in front—

 It ain't no jam for Tommy, but it's kites an' crows for 'im.

So when the cruel march is done, an' when the roads is blind,

An' when we sees the camp in front an' 'ears the shots be'ind,

Ho! then we strips 'is saddle off, and all 'is woes is past:

'E thinks on us that used 'im so, and gets revenge at last.

 O the oont, O the oont, O the floatin', bloatin' oont!

 The late lamented camel in the water-cut 'e lies;

 We keeps a mile be'ind 'im an' we keeps a mile in front,

 But 'e gets into the drinkin'-casks, and then o' course we dies.

1 Camel—oo is pronounced like u in "bull," but by Mr. Atkins to rhyme with "front."

LOOT

If you've ever stole a pheasant-egg be'ind the keeper's back,

If you've ever snigged the washin' from the line,

If you've ever crammed a gander in your bloomin' 'aversack,

You will understand this little song o' mine.

But the service rules are 'ard, an' from such we are debarred,

For the same with English morals does not suit.

 (Cornet: Toot! toot!)

W'y, they call a man a robber if 'e stuffs 'is marchin' clobber

With the—

(Chorus) Loo! loo! Lulu! lulu! Loo! loo! Loot! loot! loot!

 Ow the loot!

 Bloomin' loot!

 That's the thing to make the boys git up an' shoot!

 It's the same with dogs an' men,

 If you'd make 'em come again

 Clap 'em forward with a Loo! loo! Lulu! Loot!

 (ff) Whoopee! Tear 'im, puppy! Loo! loo! Lulu! Loot! loot! loot!

If you've knocked a nigger edgeways when 'e's thrustin' for your life,

You must leave 'im very careful where 'e fell;

An' may thank your stars an' gaiters if you didn't feel 'is knife

That you ain't told off to bury 'im as well.

Then the sweatin' Tommies wonder as they spade the beggars under

Why lootin' should be entered as a crime;

So if my song you'll 'ear, I will learn you plain an' clear

 'Ow to pay yourself for fightin' overtime.

(Chorus) With the loot,...

Now remember when you're 'acking round a gilded Burma god

 That 'is eyes is very often precious stones;

An' if you treat a nigger to a dose o' cleanin'-rod

 'E's like to show you everything 'e owns.

When 'e won't prodooce no more, pour some water on the floor

 Where you 'ear it answer 'ollow to the boot

 (Cornet: Toot! toot!)—

When the ground begins to sink, shove your baynick down the chink,

 An' you're sure to touch the—

(Chorus) Loo! loo! Lulu! Loot! loot! loot!

 Ow the loot!...

When from 'ouse to 'ouse you're 'unting, you must always work in pairs—

 It 'alves the gain, but safer you will find—

For a single man gets bottled on them twisty-wisty stairs,

 An' a woman comes and clobs 'im from be'ind.

When you've turned 'em inside out, an' it seems beyond a doubt

 As if there weren't enough to dust a flute

 (Cornet: Toot! toot!)—

Before you sling your 'ook, at the 'ousetops take a look,

 For it's underneath the tiles they 'ide the loot.

(Chorus) Ow the loot!...

You can mostly square a Sergint an' a Quartermaster too,

If you only take the proper way to go;

I could never keep my pickin's, but I've learned you all I knew—

An' don't you never say I told you so.

An' now I'll bid good-bye, for I'm gettin' rather dry,

 An' I see another tunin' up to toot

 (Cornet: Toot! toot!)—

So 'ere's good-luck to those that wears the Widow's clo'es,

 An' the Devil send 'em all they want o' loot!

(Chorus) Yes, the loot,

 Bloomin' loot!

 In the tunic an' the mess-tin an' the boot!

 It's the same with dogs an' men,

 If you'd make 'em come again

 (fff) Whoop 'em forward with a Loo! loo! Lulu! Loot! loot! loot!

 Heeya! Sick 'im, puppy! Loo! loo! Lulu! Loot! loot! loot!

'SNARLEYOW'

This 'appened in a battle to a batt'ry of the corps

Which is first among the women an' amazin' first in war;

An' what the bloomin' battle was I don't remember now,

But Two's off-lead 'e answered to the name o' Snarleyow.

 Down in the Infantry, nobody cares;

 Down in the Cavalry, Colonel 'e swears;

 But down in the lead with the wheel at the flog

 Turns the bold Bombardier to a little whipped dog!

They was movin' into action, they was needed very sore,

To learn a little schoolin' to a native army corps,

They 'ad nipped against an uphill, they was tuckin' down the brow,

When a tricky, trundlin' roundshot give the knock to Snarleyow.

They cut 'im loose an' left 'im—'e was almost tore in two—

But he tried to follow after as a well-trained 'orse should do;

'E went an' fouled the limber, an' the Driver's Brother squeals:

"Pull up, pull up for Snarleyow—'is head's between 'is 'eels!"

The Driver 'umped 'is shoulder, for the wheels was goin' round,

An' there ain't no "Stop, conductor!" when a batt'ry's changin' ground;

Sez 'e: "I broke the beggar in, an' very sad I feels,

But I couldn't pull up, not for you—your 'ead between your 'eels!"

'E 'adn't 'ardly spoke the word, before a droppin' shell

A little right the batt'ry an' between the sections fell;

An' when the smoke 'ad cleared away, before the limber wheels,
There lay the Driver's Brother with 'is 'ead between 'is 'eels.

Then sez the Driver's Brother, an' 'is words was very plain,
"For Gawd's own sake get over me, an' put me out o' pain."
They saw 'is wounds was mortial, an' they judged that it was best,
So they took an' drove the limber straight across 'is back an' chest.

The Driver 'e give nothin' 'cept a little coughin' grunt,
But 'e swung 'is 'orses 'andsome when it came to "Action Front!"
An' if one wheel was juicy, you may lay your Monday head
'Twas juicier for the niggers when the case begun to spread.

The moril of this story, it is plainly to be seen:
You 'avn't got no families when servin' of the Queen—
You 'avn't got no brothers, fathers, sisters, wives, or sons—
If you want to win your battles take an' work your bloomin' guns!

Down in the Infantry, nobody cares;
Down in the Cavalry, Colonel 'e swears;
But down in the lead with the wheel at the flog
Turns the bold Bombardier to a little whipped dog!

THE WIDOW AT WINDSOR

'Ave you 'eard o' the Widow at Windsor

With a hairy gold crown on 'er 'ead?

She 'as ships on the foam—she 'as millions at 'ome,

An' she pays us poor beggars in red.

 (Ow, poor beggars in red!)

There's 'er nick on the cavalry 'orses,

There's 'er mark on the medical stores—

An' 'er troopers you'll find with a fair wind be'ind

That takes us to various wars.

 (Poor beggars!—barbarious wars!)

 Then 'ere's to the Widow at Windsor,

 An' 'ere's to the stores an' the guns,

 The men an' the 'orses what makes up the forces

 O' Missis Victorier's sons.

 (Poor beggars! Victorier's sons!)

Walk wide o' the Widow at Windsor,

For 'alf o' Creation she owns:

We 'ave bought 'er the same with the sword an' the flame,

An' we've salted it down with our bones.

 (Poor beggars!—it's blue with our bones!)

Hands off o' the sons o' the Widow,

Hands off o' the goods in 'er shop,

For the Kings must come down an' the Emperors frown

When the Widow at Windsor says "Stop"!

 (Poor beggars!—we're sent to say "Stop"!)

Then 'ere's to the Lodge o' the Widow,

From the Pole to the Tropics it runs—

To the Lodge that we tile with the rank an' the file,

An' open in form with the guns.

(Poor beggars!—it's always they guns!)

We 'ave 'eard o' the Widow at Windsor,

It's safest to let 'er alone:

For 'er sentries we stand by the sea an' the land

Wherever the bugles are blown.

(Poor beggars!—an' don't we get blown!)

Take 'old o' the Wings o' the Mornin',

An' flop round the earth till you're dead;

But you won't get away from the tune that they play

To the bloomin' old rag over'ead.

(Poor beggars!—it's 'ot over'ead!)

Then 'ere's to the sons o' the Widow,

Wherever, 'owever they roam.

'Ere's all they desire, an' if they require

A speedy return to their 'ome.

(Poor beggars!—they'll never see 'ome!)

BELTS

There was a row in Silver Street that's near to Dublin Quay,

Between an Irish regiment an' English cavalree;

It started at Revelly an' it lasted on till dark:

The first man dropped at Harrison's, the last forninst the Park.

 For it was:—"Belts, belts, belts, an' that's one for you!"

 An' it was "Belts, belts, belts, an' that's done for you!"

 O buckle an' tongue

 Was the song that we sung

 From Harrison's down to the Park!

There was a row in Silver Street—the regiments was out,

They called us "Delhi Rebels", an' we answered "Threes about!"

 That drew them like a hornet's nest—we met them good an' large,

The English at the double an' the Irish at the charge.

 Then it was:—"Belts...

There was a row in Silver Street—an' I was in it too;

We passed the time o' day, an' then the belts went whirraru!

I misremember what occurred, but subsequint the storm

A Freeman's Journal Supplemint was all my uniform.

 O it was:—"Belts...

There was a row in Silver Street—they sent the Polis there,

 The English were too drunk to know, the Irish didn't care;

 But when they grew impertinint we simultaneous rose,

Till half o' them was Liffey mud an' half was tatthered clo'es.

For it was:—"Belts...

There was a row in Silver Street—it might ha' raged till now,
But some one drew his side-arm clear, an' nobody knew how;
'Twas Hogan took the point an' dropped; we saw the red blood run:
An' so we all was murderers that started out in fun.

While it was:—"Belts...

There was a row in Silver Street—but that put down the shine,
Wid each man whisperin' to his next: "'Twas never work o' mine!"
We went away like beaten dogs, an' down the street we bore him,
The poor dumb corpse that couldn't tell the bhoys were sorry for him.

When it was:—"Belts...

There was a row in Silver Street—it isn't over yet,
For half of us are under guard wid punishments to get;
'Tis all a merricle to me as in the Clink I lie:
There was a row in Silver Street—begod, I wonder why!

But it was:—"Belts, belts, belts, an' that's one for you!"
An' it was "Belts, belts, belts, an' that's done for you!"
O buckle an' tongue
Was the song that we sung
From Harrison's down to the Park!

THE YOUNG BRITISH SOLDIER

When the 'arf-made recruity goes out to the East

'E acts like a babe an' 'e drinks like a beast,

An' 'e wonders because 'e is frequent deceased

 Ere 'e's fit for to serve as a soldier.

 Serve, serve, serve as a soldier,

 Serve, serve, serve as a soldier,

 Serve, serve, serve as a soldier,

 So-oldier of the Queen!

Now all you recruities what's drafted today,

You shut up your rag-box an' 'ark to my lay,

An' I'll sing you a soldier as far as I may:

 A soldier what's fit for a soldier.

 Fit, fit, fit for a soldier...

First mind you steer clear o' the grog-sellers' huts,

For they sell you Fixed Bay'nets that rots out your guts—

Ay, drink that 'ud eat the live steel from your butts—

 An' it's bad for the young British soldier.

 Bad, bad, bad for the soldier...

When the cholera comes—as it will past a doubt—

Keep out of the wet and don't go on the shout,

For the sickness gets in as the liquor dies out,

An' it crumples the young British soldier.

 Crum-, crum-, crumples the soldier...

But the worst o' your foes is the sun over'ead:
You must wear your 'elmet for all that is said:
If 'e finds you uncovered 'e'll knock you down dead,
 An' you'll die like a fool of a soldier.

 Fool, fool, fool of a soldier...

If you're cast for fatigue by a sergeant unkind,
Don't grouse like a woman nor crack on nor blind;
Be handy and civil, and then you will find
 That it's beer for the young British soldier.

 Beer, beer, beer for the soldier...

Now, if you must marry, take care she is old—
A troop-sergeant's widow's the nicest I'm told,
For beauty won't help if your rations is cold,
 Nor love ain't enough for a soldier.

 'Nough, 'nough, 'nough for a soldier...

If the wife should go wrong with a comrade, be loath
To shoot when you catch 'em—you'll swing, on my oath!—
Make 'im take 'er and keep 'er: that's Hell for them both,
 An' you're shut o' the curse of a soldier.

Curse, curse, curse of a soldier...

When first under fire an' you're wishful to duck,

Don't look nor take 'eed at the man that is struck,

Be thankful you're livin', and trust to your luck

 And march to your front like a soldier.

 Front, front, front like a soldier...

When 'arf of your bullets fly wide in the ditch,

Don't call your Martini a cross-eyed old bitch;

She's human as you are—you treat her as sich,

 An' she'll fight for the young British soldier.

 Fight, fight, fight for the soldier...

When shakin' their bustles like ladies so fine,

The guns o' the enemy wheel into line,

Shoot low at the limbers an' don't mind the shine,

 For noise never startles the soldier.

 Start-, start-, startles the soldier...

If your officer's dead and the sergeants look white,

Remember it's ruin to run from a fight:

So take open order, lie down, and sit tight,

 And wait for supports like a soldier.

 Wait, wait, wait like a soldier...

When you're wounded and left on Afghanistan's plains,

And the women come out to cut up what remains,

Jest roll to your rifle and blow out your brains

 An' go to your Gawd like a soldier.

 Go, go, go like a soldier,

 Go, go, go like a soldier,

 Go, go, go like a soldier,

 So-oldier of the Queen!

MANDALAY

By the old Moulmein Pagoda, lookin' lazy at the sea,

There's a Burma girl a-settin', and I know she thinks o' me;

For the wind is in the palm-trees, and the temple-bells they say:

"Come you back, you British soldier; come you back to Mandalay!"

 Come you back to Mandalay,

 Where the old Flotilla lay:

 Can't you 'ear their paddles chunkin' from Rangoon to Mandalay?

 On the road to Mandalay,

 Where the flyin'-fishes play,

 An' the dawn comes up like thunder outer China 'crost the Bay!

'Er petticoat was yaller an' 'er little cap was green,

An' 'er name was Supi-yaw-lat—jes' the same as Theebaw's Queen,

An' I seed her first a-smokin' of a whackin' white cheroot,

An' a-wastin' Christian kisses on an 'eathen idol's foot:

 Bloomin' idol made o'mud—

 Wot they called the Great Gawd Budd—

 Plucky lot she cared for idols when I kissed 'er where she stud!

 On the road to Mandalay...

When the mist was on the rice-fields an' the sun was droppin' slow,

She'd git 'er little banjo an' she'd sing "Kulla-lo-lo!"

With 'er arm upon my shoulder an' 'er cheek agin' my cheek

We useter watch the steamers an' the hathis pilin' teak.

 Elephints a-pilin' teak

 In the sludgy, squdgy creek,

 Where the silence 'ung that 'eavy you was 'arf afraid to speak!

On the road to Mandalay...

But that's all shove be'ind me—long ago an' fur away,

An' there ain't no 'busses runnin' from the Bank to Mandalay;

An' I'm learnin' 'ere in London what the ten-year soldier tells:

"If you've 'eard the East a-callin', you won't never 'eed naught else."

No! you won't 'eed nothin' else

But them spicy garlic smells,

An' the sunshine an' the palm-trees an' the tinkly temple-bells;

On the road to Mandalay...

I am sick o' wastin' leather on these gritty pavin'-stones,

An' the blasted Henglish drizzle wakes the fever in my bones;

Tho' I walks with fifty 'ousemaids outer Chelsea to the Strand,

An' they talks a lot o' lovin', but wot do they understand?

Beefy face an' grubby 'and—

Law! wot do they understand?

I've a neater, sweeter maiden in a cleaner, greener land!

On the road to Mandalay...

Ship me somewheres east of Suez, where the best is like the worst,

Where there aren't no Ten Commandments an' a man can raise a thirst;

For the temple-bells are callin', an' it's there that I would be—

By the old Moulmein Pagoda, looking lazy at the sea;

On the road to Mandalay,

Where the old Flotilla lay,

With our sick beneath the awnings when we went to Mandalay!

On the road to Mandalay,

Where the flyin'-fishes play,

An' the dawn comes up like thunder outer China 'crost the Bay!

TROOPIN'

(Our Army in the East)

Troopin', troopin', troopin' to the sea:

'Ere's September come again—the six-year men are free.

O leave the dead be'ind us, for they cannot come away

To where the ship's a-coalin' up that takes us 'ome today.

 We're goin' 'ome, we're goin' 'ome,

 Our ship is at the shore,

 An' you must pack your 'aversack,

 For we won't come back no more.

 Ho, don't you grieve for me,

 My lovely Mary-Ann,

 For I'll marry you yit on a fourp'ny bit

 As a time-expired man.

The Malabar's in 'arbour with the Jumner at 'er tail,

An' the time-expired's waitin' of 'is orders for to sail.

Ho! the weary waitin' when on Khyber 'ills we lay,

But the time-expired's waitin' of 'is orders 'ome today.

They'll turn us out at Portsmouth wharf in cold an' wet an' rain,

All wearin' Injian cotton kit, but we will not complain;

They'll kill us of pneumonia—for that's their little way—

But damn the chills and fever, men, we're goin' 'ome today!

Troopin', troopin', winter's round again!

See the new draf's pourin' in for the old campaign;

Ho, you poor recruities, but you've got to earn your pay—

What's the last from Lunnon, lads? We're goin' there today.

Troopin', troopin', give another cheer—

'Ere's to English women an' a quart of English beer.

The Colonel an' the regiment an' all who've got to stay,

Gawd's mercy strike 'em gentle—Whoop! we're goin' 'ome today.

 We're goin' 'ome, we're goin' 'ome,

 Our ship is at the shore,

 An' you must pack your 'aversack,

 For we won't come back no more.

 Ho, don't you grieve for me,

 My lovely Mary-Ann,

 For I'll marry you yit on a fourp'ny bit

 As a time-expired man.

FORD O' KABUL RIVER

Kabul town's by Kabul river—

Blow the bugle, draw the sword—

There I lef' my mate for ever,

Wet an' drippin' by the ford.

 Ford, ford, ford o' Kabul river,

 Ford o' Kabul river in the dark!

 There's the river up and brimmin', an' there's 'arf a squadron swimmin'

 'Cross the ford o' Kabul river in the dark.

Kabul town's a blasted place—

Blow the bugle, draw the sword—

'Strewth I sha'n't forget 'is face

Wet an' drippin' by the ford!

 Ford, ford, ford o' Kabul river,

 Ford o' Kabul river in the dark!

 Keep the crossing-stakes beside you, an' they will surely guide you

 'Cross the ford o' Kabul river in the dark.

Kabul town is sun and dust—

Blow the bugle, draw the sword—

I'd ha' sooner drownded fust

'Stead of 'im beside the ford.

 Ford, ford, ford o' Kabul river,

 Ford o' Kabul river in the dark!

 You can 'ear the 'orses threshin', you can 'ear the men a-splashin',

 'Cross the ford o' Kabul river in the dark.

Kabul town was ours to take—

Blow the bugle, draw the sword—

I'd ha' left it for 'is sake—

'Im that left me by the ford.

 Ford, ford, ford o' Kabul river,

 Ford o' Kabul river in the dark!

 It's none so bloomin' dry there; ain't you never comin' nigh there,

 'Cross the ford o' Kabul river in the dark?

Kabul town'll go to hell—

Blow the bugle, draw the sword—

'Fore I see him 'live an' well—

'Im the best beside the ford.

 Ford, ford, ford o' Kabul river,

 Ford o' Kabul river in the dark!

 Gawd 'elp 'em if they blunder, for their boots'll pull 'em under,

 By the ford o' Kabul river in the dark.

Turn your 'orse from Kabul town—

Blow the bugle, draw the sword—

'Im an' 'arf my troop is down,

Down an' drownded by the ford.

 Ford, ford, ford o' Kabul river,

 Ford o' Kabul river in the dark!

 There's the river low an' fallin', but it ain't no use o' callin'

 'Cross the ford o' Kabul river in the dark.

ROUTE MARCHIN'

We're marchin' on relief over Injia's sunny plains,

A little front o' Christmas-time an' just be'ind the Rains;

Ho! get away you bullock-man, you've 'eard the bugle blowed,

There's a regiment a-comin' down the Grand Trunk Road;

 With its best foot first

 And the road a-sliding past,

 An' every bloomin' campin'-ground exactly like the last;

 While the Big Drum says,

 With 'is "rowdy-dowdy-dow!"—

 "Kiko kissywarsti don't you hamsher argy jow?" 2

Oh, there's them Injian temples to admire when you see,

There's the peacock round the corner an' the monkey up the tree,

An' there's that rummy silver grass a-wavin' in the wind,

An' the old Grand Trunk a-trailin' like a rifle-sling be'ind.

 While it's best foot first,...

At half-past five's Revelly, an' our tents they down must come,

Like a lot of button mushrooms when you pick 'em up at 'ome.

But it's over in a minute, an' at six the column starts,

While the women and the kiddies sit an' shiver in the carts.

 An' it's best foot first,...

Oh, then it's open order, an' we lights our pipes an' sings,

An' we talks about our rations an' a lot of other things,

An' we thinks o' friends in England, an' we wonders what they're at,

An' 'ow they would admire for to hear us sling the bat.1

 An' it's best foot first,...

It's none so bad o' Sunday, when you're lyin' at your ease,

To watch the kites a-wheelin' round them feather-'eaded trees,

For although there ain't no women, yet there ain't no barrick-yards,

So the orficers goes shootin' an' the men they plays at cards.

 Till it's best foot first,...

So 'ark an' 'eed, you rookies, which is always grumblin' sore,

There's worser things than marchin' from Umballa to Cawnpore;

An' if your 'eels are blistered an' they feels to 'urt like 'ell,

You drop some tallow in your socks an' that will make 'em well.

 For it's best foot first,...

We're marchin' on relief over Injia's coral strand,

Eight 'undred fightin' Englishmen, the Colonel, and the Band;

Ho! get away you bullock-man, you've 'eard the bugle blowed,

There's a regiment a-comin' down the Grand Trunk Road;

 With its best foot first

 And the road a-sliding past,

 An' every bloomin' campin'-ground exactly like the last;

 While the Big Drum says,

 With 'is "rowdy-dowdy-dow!"—

 "Kiko kissywarsti don't you hamsher argy jow?" 2

1 Thomas's first and firmest conviction is that he is a profound Orientalist and a fluent speaker of Hindustani. As a matter of fact, he depends largely on the sign-language.

2 Why don't you get on

The end

* * * * * *

VOLUME III. THE PHANTOM 'RICKSHAW AND OTHER GHOST STORIES

THE PHANTOM 'RICKSHAW

May no ill dreams disturb my rest,

Nor Powers of Darkness me molest.

—Evening Hymn.

ONE of the few advantages that India has over England is a great Knowability. After five years' service a man is directly or indirectly acquainted with the two or three hundred Civilians in his Province, all the Messes of ten or twelve Regiments and Batteries, and some fifteen hundred other people of the non-official caste. In ten years his knowledge should be doubled, and at the end of twenty he knows, or knows something about, every Englishman in the Empire, and may travel anywhere and everywhere without paying hotel-bills.

Globe-trotters who expect entertainment as a right, have, even within my memory, blunted this open-heartedness, but none the less today, if you belong to the Inner Circle and are neither a Bear nor a Black Sheep, all houses are open to you, and our small world is very, very kind and helpful.

Rickett of Kamartha stayed with Polder of Kumaon some fifteen years ago. He meant to stay two nights, but was knocked down by rheumatic fever, and for six weeks disorganized Polder's establishment, stopped Polder's work, and nearly died in Polder's bedroom. Polder behaves as though he had been placed under eternal obligation by Rickett, and yearly sends the little Ricketts a box of presents and toys. It is the same everywhere. The men who do not take the trouble to conceal from you their opinion that you are an incompetent ass, and the women who blacken your character and misunderstand your wife's amusements, will work themselves to the bone in your behalf if you fall sick or into serious trouble.

Heatherlegh, the Doctor, kept, in addition to his regular practice, a hospital on his private account—an arrangement of loose boxes for Incurables, his friend called it—but it was really a sort of fitting-up shed for craft that had been damaged by stress of weather. The weather in India is often sultry, and since the tale of bricks is always a fixed quantity, and the only liberty allowed is permission to work overtime and get no thanks, men occasionally break down and become as mixed as the metaphors in this sentence.

Heatherlegh is the dearest doctor that ever was, and his invariable prescription to all his patients is, "lie low, go slow, and keep cool." He says that more men are killed by overwork than the importance of this world justifies. He maintains that overwork slew Pansay, who died under his hands about three years ago. He has, of course, the right to speak authoritatively, and he laughs at my theory that there was a crack in Pansay's head and a little bit of the Dark World came through and pressed him to death. "Pansay went off the handle," says Heatherlegh, "after the stimulus of long leave at Home. He may or he may not have behaved like a blackguard to Mrs. Keith-Wessington. My notion is that the work of the Katabundi Settlement ran him off his legs, and that he took to brooding and making much of an ordinary P. & 0. flirtation. He certainly was engaged to Miss Mannering, and she certainly broke off the engagement. Then he took a feverish chill and all that nonsense about ghosts developed. Overwork started his illness, kept it alight, and killed him poor devil. Write him off to the System—one man to take the work of two and a half men."

I do not believe this. I used to sit up with Pansay sometimes when Heatherlegh was called out to patients, and I happened to be within claim. The man would make me most unhappy by describing in a low, even voice, the procession that was always passing at the bottom of his bed. He had a sick man's command of language.

When he recovered I suggested that he should write out the whole affair from beginning to end, knowing that ink might assist him to ease his mind. When little boys have learned a new bad word they are never happy till they have chalked it up on a door. And this also is Literature.

He was in a high fever while he was writing, and the blood-and-thunder Magazine diction he adopted did not calm him. Two months afterward he was reported fit for duty, but, in spite of the fact that he was urgently needed to help an undermanned Commission stagger through a deficit, he preferred to die; vowing at the last that he was hag-ridden. I got his manuscript before he died, and this is his version of the affair, dated 1885:

My doctor tells me that I need rest and change of air. It is not improbable that I shall get both ere long—rest that neither the red-coated messenger nor the midday gun can break, and change of air far beyond that which any homeward-bound steamer can give me. In the meantime I am resolved to stay where I am; and, in flat defiance of my doctor's orders, to take all the world into my confidence. You shall learn for yourselves the precise nature of my malady; and shall, too, judge for yourselves whether any man born of woman on this weary earth was ever so tormented as I.

Speaking now as a condemned criminal might speak ere the drop-bolts are drawn, my story, wild and hideously improbable as it may appear, demands at least attention. That it will ever receive credence I utterly disbelieve. Two months ago I should have scouted as mad or drunk the man who had dared tell me the like. Two months ago I was the happiest man in India. Today, from Peshawur to the sea, there is no one more wretched. My doctor and I are the only two who know this. His explanation is, that my brain, digestion, and eyesight are all slightly affected; giving rise to my frequent and persistent "delusions." Delusions, indeed! I call him a fool; but he attends me still with the same unwearied smile, the same bland professional manner, the same neatly trimmed red whiskers, till I begin to suspect that I am an ungrateful, evil-tempered invalid. But you shall judge for yourselves.

Three years ago it was my fortune—my great misfortune—to sail from Gravesend to Bombay, on return from long leave, with one Agnes Keith-Wessington, wife of an officer on the Bombay side. It does not in the least concern you to know what manner of woman she was. Be content with the knowledge that, ere the voyage had ended, both she and I were desperately and unreasoningly in love with one another. Heaven knows that I can make the admission now without one particle of vanity. In matters of this sort there is always one who gives and another who accepts. From the first day of our ill-omened attachment, I was conscious that Agnes's passion was a stronger, a more dominant, and—if I may use the expression—a purer sentiment than mine. Whether she recognized the fact then, I do not know. Afterward it was bitterly plain to both of us.

Arrived at Bombay in the spring of the year, we went our respective ways, to meet no more for the next three or four months, when my leave and her love took us both to Simla. There we spent the season together; and there my fire of straw burned itself out to a pitiful end with the closing year. I attempt no excuse. I make no apology. Mrs. Wessington had given up much for my sake, and was prepared to give up all. From my own lips, in August, 1882, she learned that I was sick of her presence, tired of her company, and weary of the sound of her voice. Ninety-nine women out of a hundred would have wearied of me as I wearied of them; seventy-five of that number would have promptly avenged themselves by active and obtrusive flirtation with other

men. Mrs. Wessington was the hundredth. On her neither my openly expressed aversion nor the cutting brutalities with which I garnished our interviews had the least effect. "Jack, darling!" was her one eternal cuckoo cry: "I'm sure it's all a mistake—a hideous mistake; and we'll be good friends again some day. Please forgive me, Jack, dear."

I was the offender, and I knew it. That knowledge transformed my pity into passive endurance, and, eventually, into blind hate—the same instinct, I suppose, which prompts a man to savagely stamp on the spider he has but half killed. And with this hate in my bosom the season of 1882 came to an end.

Next year we met again at Simla—she with her monotonous face and timid attempts at reconciliation, and I with loathing of her in every fibre of my frame. Several times I could not avoid meeting her alone; and on each occasion her words were identically the same. Still the unreasoning wail that it was all a "mistake"; and still the hope of eventually "making friends." I might have seen had I cared to look, that that hope only was keeping her alive. She grew more wan and thin month by month. You will agree with me, at least, that such conduct would have driven any one to despair. It was uncalled for; childish; unwomanly. I maintain that she was much to blame. And again, sometimes, in the black, fever-stricken night-watches, I have begun to think that I might have been a little kinder to her. But that really is a "delusion." I could not have continued pretending to love her when I didn't; could I? It would have been unfair to us both.

Last year we met again—on the same terms as before. The same weary appeal, and the same curt answers from my lips. At least I would make her see how wholly wrong and hopeless were her attempts at resuming the old relationship. As the season wore on, we fell apart—that is to say, she found it difficult to meet me, for I had other and more absorbing interests to attend to. When I think it over quietly in my sick-room, the season of 1884 seems a confused nightmare wherein light and shade were fantastically intermingled—my courtship of little Kitty Mannering; my hopes, doubts, and fears; our long rides together; my trembling avowal of attachment; her reply; and now and again a vision of a white face flitting by in the 'rickshaw with the black and white liveries I once watched for so earnestly; the wave of Mrs. Wessington's gloved hand; and, when she met me alone, which was but seldom, the irksome monotony of her appeal. I loved Kitty Mannering; honestly, heartily loved her, and with my love for her grew my hatred for Agnes. In August Kitty and I were engaged. The next day I met those accursed "magpie" jhampanies at the back of Jakko, and, moved by some passing sentiment of pity, stopped to tell Mrs. Wessington everything. She knew it already.

"So I hear you're engaged, Jack dear." Then, without a moment's pause—"I'm sure it's all a mistake—a hideous mistake. We shall be as good friends some day, Jack, as we ever were."

My answer might have made even a man wince. It cut the dying woman before me like the blow of a whip. "Please forgive me, Jack; I didn't mean to make you angry; but it's true, it's true!"

And Mrs. Wessington broke down completely. I turned away and left her to finish her journey in peace, feeling, but only for a moment or two, that I had been an unutterably mean hound. I looked back, and saw that she had turned her 'rickshaw with the idea, I suppose, of overtaking me.

The scene and its surroundings were photographed on my memory.

The rain-swept sky (we were at the end of the wet weather), the sodden, dingy pines, the muddy road, and the black powder-riven cliffs formed a gloomy background against which the black and white liveries of the jhampanies, the yellow-paneled 'rickshaw and Mrs. Wessington's down-bowed golden head stood out clearly. She was holding her handkerchief in her left hand

and was leaning back exhausted against the 'rickshaw cushions. I turned my horse up a bypath near the Sanjowlie Reservoir and literally ran away. Once I fancied I heard a faint call of "Jack!" This may have been imagination. I never stopped to verify it. Ten minutes later I came across Kitty on horseback; and, in the delight of a long ride with her, forgot all about the interview.

A week later Mrs. Wessington died, and the inexpressible burden of her existence was removed from my life. I went Plainsward perfectly happy. Before three months were over I had forgotten all about her, except that at times the discovery of some of her old letters reminded me unpleasantly of our bygone relationship. By January I had disinterred what was left of our correspondence from among my scattered belongings and had burned it. At the beginning of April of this year, 1885, I was at Simla—semi-deserted Simla—once more, and was deep in lover's talks and walks with Kitty. It was decided that we should be married at the end of June. You will understand, therefore, that, loving Kitty as I did, I am not saying too much when I pronounce myself to have been, at that time, the happiest man in India.

Fourteen delightful days passed almost before I noticed their flight.

Then, aroused to the sense of what was proper among mortals circumstanced as we were, I pointed out to Kitty that an engagement ring was the outward and visible sign of her dignity as an engaged girl; and that she must forthwith come to Hamilton's to be measured for one. Up to that moment, I give you my word, we had completely forgotten so trivial a matter. To Hamilton's we accordingly went on the 15th of April, 1885. Remember that—whatever my doctor may say to the contrary—I was then in perfect health, enjoying a well-balanced mind and an absolute tranquil spirit. Kitty and I entered Hamilton's shop together, and there, regardless of the order of affairs, I measured Kitty for the ring in the presence of the amused assistant. The ring was a sapphire with two diamonds. We then rode out down the slope that leads to the Combermere Bridge and Peliti's shop.

While my Waler was cautiously feeling his way over the loose shale, and Kitty was laughing and chattering at my side—while all Simla, that is to say as much of it as had then come from the Plains, was grouped round the Reading-room and Peliti's veranda,—I was aware that some one, apparently at a vast distance, was calling me by my Christian name. It struck me that I had heard the voice before, but when and where I could not at once determine. In the short space it took to cover the road between the path from Hamilton's shop and the first plank of the Combermere Bridge I had thought over half a dozen people who might have committed such a solecism, and had eventually decided that it must have been singing in my ears. Immediately opposite Peliti's shop my eye was arrested by the sight of four jhampanies in "magpie" livery, pulling a yellow-paneled, cheap, bazar 'rickshaw. In a moment my mind flew back to the previous season and Mrs. Wessington with a sense of irritation and disgust. Was it not enough that the woman was dead and done with, without her black and white servitors reappearing to spoil the day's happiness? Whoever employed them now I thought I would call upon, and ask as a personal favor to change her jhampanies' livery. I would hire the men myself, and, if necessary, buy their coats from off their backs. It is impossible to say here what a flood of undesirable memories their presence evoked.

"Kitty," I cried, "there are poor Mrs. Wessington's jhampanies turned up again! I wonder who has them now?"

Kitty had known Mrs. Wessington slightly last season, and had always been interested in the sickly woman. "What? Where?" she asked. "I can't see them anywhere."

Even as she spoke her horse, swerving from a laden mule, threw himself directly in front of the advancing 'rickshaw. I had scarcely time to utter a word of warning when, to my unutterable horror, horse and rider passed through men and carriage as if they had been thin air.

"What's the matter?" cried Kitty; "what made you call out so foolishly, Jack? If I am engaged I don't want all creation to know about it. There was lots of space between the mule and the veranda; and, if you think I can't ride—

"—There!"

Whereupon wilful Kitty set off, her dainty little head in the air, at a hand-gallop in the direction of the Bandstand; fully expecting, as she herself afterward told me, that I should follow her. What was the matter? Nothing indeed. Either that I was mad or drunk, or that Simla was haunted with devils. I reined in my impatient cob, and turned round. The 'rickshaw had turned too, and now stood immediately facing me, near the left railing of the Combermere Bridge.

"Jack! Jack, darling!" (There was no mistake about the words this time: they rang through my brain as if they had been shouted in my ear.) "It's some hideous mistake, I'm sure. Please forgive me, jack, and let's be friends again."

The 'rickshaw-hood had fallen back, and inside, as I hope and pray daily for the death I dread by night, sat Mrs. Keith-Wessington, handkerchief in hand, and golden head bowed on her breast.

How long I stared motionless I do not know. Finally, I was aroused by my syce taking the Waler's bridle and asking whether I was ill. From the horrible to the commonplace is but a step. I tumbled off my horse and dashed, half fainting, into Peliti's for a glass of cherry-brandy. There two or three couples were gathered round the coffee-tables discussing the gossip of the day. Their trivialities were more comforting to me just then than the consolations of religion could have been. I plunged into the midst of the conversation at once; chatted, laughed, and jested with a face (when I caught a glimpse of it in a mirror) as white and drawn as that of a corpse. Three or four men noticed my condition; and, evidently setting it down to the results of over-many pegs, charitably endeavoured to draw me apart from the rest of the loungers. But I refused to be led away. I wanted the company of my kind—as a child rushes into the midst of the dinner-party after a fright in the dark. I must have talked for about ten minutes or so, though it seemed an eternity to me, when I heard Kitty's clear voice outside inquiring for me. In another minute she had entered the shop, prepared to roundly upbraid me for failing so signally in my duties. Something in my face stopped her.

"Why, Jack," she cried, "what have you been doing? What has happened? Are you ill?" Thus driven into a direct lie, I said that the sun had been a little too much for me. It was close upon five o'clock of a cloudy April afternoon, and the sun had been hidden all day. I saw my mistake as soon as the words were out of my mouth: attempted to recover it; blundered hopelessly and followed Kitty in a regal rage, out of doors, amid the smiles of my acquaintances. I made some excuse (I have forgotten what) on the score of my feeling faint; and cantered away to my hotel, leaving Kitty to finish the ride by herself.

In my room I sat down and tried calmly to reason out the matter.

Here was I, Theobald Jack Pansay, a well-educated Bengal Civilian in the year of grace, 1885, presumably sane, certainly healthy, driven in terror from my sweetheart's side by the apparition of a woman who had been dead and buried eight months ago. These were facts that I could not blink. Nothing was further from my thought than any memory of Mrs. Wessington when Kitty and I left Hamilton's shop. Nothing was more utterly commonplace than the stretch of wall opposite Peliti's. It was broad daylight. The road was full of people; and yet here, look you, in defiance of every law of probability, in direct outrage of Nature's ordinance, there had appeared to me a face from the grave.

Kitty's Arab had gone through the 'rickshaw: so that my first hope that some woman marvelously

like Mrs. Wessington had hired the carriage and the coolies with their old livery was lost. Again and again I went round this treadmill of thought; and again and again gave up baffled and in despair. The voice was as inexplicable as the apparition. I had originally some wild notion of confiding it all to Kitty; of begging her to marry me at once; and in her arms defying the ghostly occupant of the 'rickshaw. "After all," I argued, "the presence of the 'rickshaw is in itself enough to prove the existence of a spectral illusion. One may see ghosts of men and women, but surely never of coolies and carriages. The whole thing is absurd. Fancy the ghost of a hill-man!"

Next morning I sent a penitent note to Kitty, imploring her to overlook my strange conduct of the previous afternoon. My Divinity was still very wroth, and a personal apology was necessary. I explained, with a fluency born of night-long pondering over a falsehood, that I had been attacked with sudden palpitation of the heart—the result of indigestion. This eminently practical solution had its effect; and Kitty and I rode out that afternoon with the shadow of my first lie dividing us.

Nothing would please her save a canter round Jakko. With my nerves still unstrung from the previous night I feebly protested against the notion, suggesting Observatory Hill, Jutogh, the Boileaugunge road—anything rather than the Jakko round. Kitty was angry and a little hurt: so I yielded from fear of provoking further misunderstanding, and we set out together toward Chota Simla. We walked a greater part of the way, and, according to our custom, cantered from a mile or so below the Convent to the stretch of level road by the Sanjowlie Reservoir. The wretched horses appeared to fly, and my heart beat quicker and quicker as we neared the crest of the ascent. My mind had been full of Mrs. Wessington all the afternoon; and every inch of the Jakko road bore witness to our oldtime walks and talks. The bowlders were full of it; the pines sang it aloud overhead; the rain-fed torrents giggled and chuckled unseen over the shameful story; and the wind in my ears chanted the iniquity aloud.

As a fitting climax, in the middle of the level men call the Ladies' Mile the Horror was awaiting me. No other 'rickshaw was in sight—only the four black and white jhampanies, the yellow-paneled carriage, and the golden head of the woman within—all apparently just as I had left them eight months and one fortnight ago! For an instant I fancied that Kitty must see what I saw—we were so marvelously sympathetic in all things. Her next words undeceived me—"Not a soul in sight! Come along, Jack, and I'll race you to the Reservoir buildings!" Her wiry little Arab was off like a bird, my Waler following close behind, and in this order we dashed under the cliffs. Half a minute brought us within fifty yards of the 'rickshaw. I pulled my Waler and fell back a little. The 'rickshaw was directly in the middle of the road; and once more the Arab passed through it, my horse following. "Jack! Jack dear! Please forgive me," rang with a wail in my ears, and, after an interval:—"It's a mistake, a hideous mistake!"

I spurred my horse like a man possessed. When I turned my head at the Reservoir works, the black and white liveries were still waiting—patiently waiting—under the grey hillside, and the wind brought me a mocking echo of the words I had just heard. Kitty bantered me a good deal on my silence throughout the remainder of the ride. I had been talking up till then wildly and at random.

To save my life I could not speak afterward naturally, and from Sanjowlie to the Church wisely held my tongue.

I was to dine with the Mannerings that night, and had barely time to canter home to dress. On the road to Elysium Hill I overheard two men talking together in the dusk.—"It's a curious thing," said one, "how completely all trace of it disappeared. You know my wife was insanely fond of the woman ('never could see anything in her myself), and wanted me to pick up her old 'rickshaw and coolies if they were to be got for love or money. Morbid sort of fancy I call it; but

I've got to do what the Memsahib tells me.

"Would you believe that the man she hired it from tells me that all four of the men—they were brothers—died of cholera on the way to Hardwar, poor devils, and the 'rickshaw has been broken up by the man himself. 'Told me he never used a dead Memsahib's 'rickshaw. 'Spoiled his luck.' Queer notion, wasn't it? Fancy poor little Mrs. Wessington spoiling any one's luck except her own!" I laughed aloud at this point; and my laugh jarred on me as I uttered it. So there were ghosts of 'rickshaws after all, and ghostly employments in the other world! How much did Mrs. Wessington give her men? What were their hours? Where did they go?

And for visible answer to my last question I saw the infernal Thing blocking my path in the twilight. The dead travel fast, and by short cuts unknown to ordinary coolies. I laughed aloud a second time and checked my laughter suddenly, for I was afraid I was going mad. Mad to a certain extent I must have been, for I recollect that I reined in my horse at the head of the 'rickshaw, and politely wished Mrs. Wessington "Good evening." Her answer was one I knew only too well. I listened to the end; and replied that I had heard it all before, but should be delighted if she had anything further to say. Some malignant devil stronger than I must have entered into me that evening, for I have a dim recollection of talking the commonplaces of the day for five minutes to the Thing in front of me.

"Mad as a hatter, poor devil—or drunk. Max, try and get him to come home."

Surely that was not Mrs. Wessington's voice! The two men had overheard me speaking to the empty air, and had returned to look after me. They were very kind and considerate, and from their words evidently gathered that I was extremely drunk. I thanked them confusedly and cantered away to my hotel, there changed, and arrived at the Mannerings' ten minutes late. I pleaded the darkness of the night as an excuse; was rebuked by Kitty for my unlover-like tardiness; and sat down.

The conversation had already become general; and under cover of it, I was addressing some tender small talk to my sweetheart when I was aware that at the further end of the table a short red-whiskered man was describing, with much broidery, his encounter with a mad unknown that evening.

A few sentences convinced me that he was repeating the incident of half an hour ago. In the middle of the story he looked round for applause, as professional story-tellers do, caught my eye, and straightway collapsed. There was a moment's awkward silence, and the red-whiskered man muttered something to the effect that he had "forgotten the rest," thereby sacrificing a reputation as a good story-teller which he had built up for six seasons past. I blessed him from the bottom of my heart, and—went on with my fish.

In the fulness of time that dinner came to an end; and with genuine regret I tore myself away from Kitty—as certain as I was of my own existence that It would be waiting for me outside the door. The red-whiskered man, who had been introduced to me as Doctor Heatherlegh, of Simla, volunteered to bear me company as far as our roads lay together. I accepted his offer with gratitude.

My instinct had not deceived me. It lay in readiness in the Mall, and, in what seemed devilish mockery of our ways, with a lighted head-lamp. The red-whiskered man went to the point at once, in a manner that showed he bad been thinking over it all dinner time.

"I say, Pansay, what the deuce was the matter with you this evening on the Elysium road?" The suddenness of the question wrenched an answer from me before I was aware.

"That!" said I, pointing to It.

"That may be either D. T. or Eyes for aught I know. Now you don't liquor. I saw as much at dinner, so it can't be D. T. There's nothing whatever where you're pointing, though you're sweating and trembling with fright like a scared pony. Therefore, I conclude that it's Eyes. And I ought to understand all about them. Come along home with me. I'm on the Blessington lower road."

To my intense delight the 'rickshaw instead of waiting for us kept about twenty yards ahead—and this, too whether we walked, trotted, or cantered. In the course of that long night ride I had told my companion almost as much as I have told you here.

"Well, you've spoiled one of the best tales I've ever laid tongue to," said he, "but I'll forgive you for the sake of what you've gone through. Now come home and do what I tell you; and when I've cured you, young man, let this be a lesson to you to steer clear of women and indigestible food till the day of your death."

The 'rickshaw kept steady in front; and my red-whiskered friend seemed to derive great pleasure from my account of its exact whereabouts.

"Eyes, Pansay—all Eyes, Brain, and Stomach. And the greatest of these three is Stomach. You've too much conceited Brain, too little Stomach, and thoroughly unhealthy Eyes. Get your Stomach straight and the rest follows. And all that's French for a liver pill.

"I'll take sole medical charge of you from this hour! for you're too interesting a phenomenon to be passed over."

By this time we were deep in the shadow of the Blessington lower road and the 'rickshaw came to a dead stop under a pine-clad, over-hanging shale cliff. Instinctively I halted too, giving my reason. Heatherlegh rapped out an oath.

"Now, if you think I'm going to spend a cold night on the hillside for the sake of a stomach-cum-Brain-cum-Eye illusion—Lord, ha' mercy! What's that?"

There was a muffled report, a blinding smother of dust just in front of us, a crack, the noise of rent boughs, and about ten yards of the cliff-side—pines, undergrowth, and all—slid down into the road below, completely blocking it up. The uprooted trees swayed and tottered for a moment like drunken giants in the gloom, and then fell prone among their fellows with a thunderous crash. Our two horses stood motionless and sweating with fear. As soon as the rattle of falling earth and stone had subsided, my companion muttered:—"Man, if we'd gone forward we should have been ten feet deep in our graves by now. 'There are more things in heaven and earth...' Come home, Pansay, and thank God. I want a peg badly."

We retraced our way over the Church Ridge, and I arrived at Dr. Heatherlegh's house shortly after midnight.

His attempts toward my cure commenced almost immediately, and for a week I never left his sight. Many a time in the course of that week did I bless the good fortune which had thrown me in contact with Simla's best and kindest doctor. Day by day my spirits grew lighter and more equable. Day by day, too, I became more and more inclined to fall in with Heatherlegh's "spectral illusion" theory, implicating eyes, brain, and stomach. I wrote to Kitty, telling her that a slight sprain caused by a fall from my horse kept me indoors for a few days; and that I should be recovered before she had time to regret my absence.

Heatherlegh's treatment was simple to a degree. It consisted of liver pills, cold-water baths, and strong exercise, taken in the dusk or at early dawn—for, as he sagely observed:—"A man with a sprained ankle doesn't walk a dozen miles a day, and your young woman might be wondering if she saw you."

At the end of the week, after much examination of pupil and pulse, and strict injunction' as to diet and pedestrianism, Heatherlegh dismissed me as brusquely as he had taken charge of me. Here is his parting benediction:—"Man, I can certify to your mental cure, and that's as much as to say I've cured most of your bodily ailments. Now, get your traps out of this as soon as you can; and be off to make love to Miss Kitty."

I was endeavoring to express my thanks for his kindness. He cut me short.

"Don't think I did this because I like you. I gather that you've behaved like a blackguard all through. But, all the same, you re a phenomenon, and as queer a phenomenon as you are a blackguard. No!"—checking me a second time—"not a rupee please. Go out and see if you can find the eyes-brain-and-stomach business again. I'll give you a lakh for each time you see it."

Half an hour later I was in the Mannerings' drawing-room with Kitty—drunk with the intoxication of present happiness and the fore-knowledge that I should never more be troubled with Its hideous presence. Strong in the sense of my new-found security, I proposed a ride at once; and, by preference, a canter round Jakko.

Never had I felt so well, so overladen with vitality and mere animal spirits, as I did on the afternoon of the 30th of April. Kitty was delighted at the change in my appearance, and complimented me on it in her delightfully frank and outspoken manner. We left the Mannerings' house together, laughing and talking, and cantered along the Chota Simla road as of old.

I was in haste to reach the Sanjowlie Reservoir and there make my assurance doubly sure. The horses did their best, but seemed all too slow to my impatient mind. Kitty was astonished at my boisterousness. "Why, Jack!" she cried at last, "you are behaving like a child. What are you doing?"

We were just below the Convent, and from sheer wantonness I was making my Waler plunge and curvet across the road as I tickled it with the loop of my riding-whip.

"Doing?" I answered; "nothing, dear. That's just it. If you'd been doing nothing for a week except lie up, you'd be as riotous as I."

"'Singing and murmuring in your feastful mirth, Joying to feel yourself alive; Lord over Nature, Lord of the visible Earth, Lord of the senses five.'"

My quotation was hardly out of my lips before we had rounded the corner above the Convent; and a few yards further on could see across to Sanjowlie. In the centre of the level road stood the black and white liveries, the yellow-paneled 'rickshaw, and Mrs. Keith-Wessington. I pulled up, looked, rubbed my eyes, and, I believe must have said something. The next thing I knew was that I was lying face downward on the road with Kitty kneeling above me in tears.

"Has it gone, child?" I gasped. Kitty only wept more bitterly.

"Has what gone, Jack dear? what does it all mean? There must be a mistake somewhere, Jack. A hideous mistake." Her last words brought me to my feet—mad—raving for the time being.

"Yes, there is a mistake somewhere," I repeated, "a hideous mistake. Come and look at It."

I have an indistinct idea that I dragged Kitty by the wrist along the road up to where It stood, and implored her for pity's sake to speak to It; to tell It that we were betrothed; that neither Death nor Hell could break the tie between us; and Kitty only knows how much more to the same effect. Now and again I appealed passionately to the Terror in the 'rickshaw to bear witness to all I had said, and to release me from a torture that was killing me. As I talked I suppose I must have told Kitty of my old relations with Mrs. Wessington, for I saw her listen intently with white face and blazing eyes.

"Thank you, Mr. Pansay," she said, "that's quite enough. Syce ghora lao."

The syces, impassive as Orientals always are, had come up with the recaptured horses; and as Kitty sprang into her saddle I caught hold of the bridle, entreating her to hear me out and forgive. My answer was the cut of her riding-whip across my face from mouth to eye, and a word or two of farewell that even now I cannot write down. So I judged, and judged rightly, that Kitty knew all; and I staggered back to the side of the 'rickshaw. My face was cut and bleeding, and the blow of the riding-whip had raised a livid blue wheal on it. I had no self-respect. Just then, Heatherlegh, who must have been following Kitty and me at a distance, cantered up.

"Doctor," I said, pointing to my face, "here's Miss Mannering's signature to my order of dismissal and—I'll thank you for that lakh as soon as convenient."

Heatherlegh's face, even in my abject misery, moved me to laughter.

"I'll stake my professional reputation"—he began.

"Don't be a fool," I whispered. "I've lost my life's happiness and you'd better take me home."

As I spoke the 'rickshaw was gone. Then I lost all knowledge of what was passing. The crest of Jakko seemed to heave and roll like the crest of a cloud and fall in upon me.

Seven days later (on the 7th of May, that is to say) I was aware that I was lying in Heatherlegh's room as weak as a little child. Heatherlegh was watching me intently from behind the papers on his writing-table. His first words were not encouraging; but I was too far spent to be much moved by them.

"Here's Miss Kitty has sent back your letters. You corresponded a good deal, you young people. Here's a packet that looks like a ring, and a cheerful sort of a note from Mannering Papa, which I've taken the liberty of reading and burning. The old gentleman's not pleased with you."

"And Kitty?" I asked, dully.

"Rather more drawn than her father from what she says. By the same token you must have been letting out any number of queer reminiscences just before I met you. 'Says that a man who would have behaved to a woman as you did to Mrs. Wessington ought to kill himself out of sheer pity for his kind. She's a hot-headed little virago, your mash. 'Will have it too that you were suffering from D. T. when that row on the Jakko road turned up. 'Says she'll die before she ever speaks to you again."

I groaned and turned over to the other side.

"Now you've got your choice, my friend. This engagement has to be broken off; and the Mannerings don't want to be too hard on you. Was it broken through D. T. or epileptic fits? Sorry I can't offer you a better exchange unless you'd prefer hereditary insanity. Say the word and I'll tell 'em it's fits. All Simla knows about that scene on the Ladies' Mile. Come! I'll give you five minutes to think over it."

During those five minutes I believe that I explored thoroughly the lowest circles of the Inferno which it is permitted man to tread on earth. And at the same time I myself was watching myself faltering through the dark labyrinths of doubt, misery, and utter despair. I wondered, as Heatherlegh in his chair might have wondered, which dreadful alternative I should adopt. Presently I heard myself answering in a voice that I hardly recognized, "—They're confoundedly particular about morality in these parts. Give 'em fits, Heatherlegh, and my love. Now let me sleep a bit longer."

Then my two selves joined, and it was only I (half crazed, devil-driven) that tossed in my bed, tracing step by step the history of the past month.

"But I am in Simla," I kept repeating to myself. "I, Jack Pansay, am in Simla and there are no ghosts here. It's unreasonable of that woman to pretend there are. Why couldn't Agnes have left me alone? I never did her any harm. It might just as well have been me as Agnes. Only I'd never have come back on purpose to kill her. Why can't I be left alone—left alone and happy?"

It was high noon when I first awoke, and the sun was low in the sky before I slept—slept as the tortured criminal sleeps on his rack, too worn to feel further pain.

Next day I could not leave my bed. Heatherlegh told me in the morning that he had received an answer from Mr. Mannering, and that, thanks to his (Heatherlegh's) friendly offices, the story of my affliction had traveled through the length and breadth of Simla, where I was on all sides much pitied.

"And that's rather more than you deserve," he concluded, pleasantly, "though the Lord knows you've been going through a pretty severe mill. Never mind; we'll cure you yet, you perverse phenomenon."

I declined firmly to be cured. "You've been much too good to me already, old man," said I; "but I don't think I need trouble you further."

In my heart I knew that nothing Heatherlegh could do would lighten the burden that had been laid upon me.

With that knowledge came also a sense of hopeless, impotent rebellion against the unreasonableness of it all. There were scores of men no better than I whose punishments had at least been reserved for another world; and I felt that it was bitterly, cruelly unfair that I alone should have been singled out for so hideous a fate. This mood would in time give place to another where it seemed that the 'rickshaw and I were the only realities in a world of shadows; that Kitty was a ghost; that Mannering, Heatherlegh, and all the other men and women I knew were all ghosts; and the great, grey hills themselves but vain shadows devised to torture me. From mood to mood I tossed backward and forward for seven weary days; my body growing daily stronger and stronger, until the bedroom looking-glass told me that I had returned to everyday life, and was as other men once more. Curiously enough my face showed no signs of the struggle I had gone through. It was pale indeed, but as expressionless and commonplace as ever. I had expected some permanent alteration—visible evidence of the disease that was eating me away. I found nothing.

On the 15th of May, I left Heatherlegh's house at eleven o'clock in the morning; and the instinct of the bachelor drove me to the Club. There I found that every man knew my story as told by Heatherlegh, and was, in clumsy fashion, abnormally kind and attentive. Nevertheless I recognized that for the rest of my natural life I should be among but not of my fellows; and I envied very bitterly indeed the laughing coolies on the Mall below. I lunched at the Club, and at four o'clock wandered aimlessly down the Mall in the vague hope of meeting Kitty. Close to the

Band-stand the black and white liveries joined me; and I heard Mrs. Wessington's old appeal at my side. I had been expecting this ever since I came out; and was only surprised at her delay. The phantom 'rickshaw and I went side by side along the Chota Simla road in silence. Close to the bazar, Kitty and a man on horseback overtook and passed us. For any sign she gave I might have been a dog in the road. She did not even pay me the compliment of quickening her pace; though the rainy afternoon had served for an excuse.

So Kitty and her companion, and I and my ghostly Light-o'-Love, crept round Jakko in couples. The road was streaming with water; the pines dripped like roof-pipes on the rocks below, and the air was full of fine, driving rain. Two or three times I found myself saying to myself almost aloud: "I'm Jack Pansay on leave at Simla—at Simla! Everyday, ordinary Simla. I mustn't forget that—I mustn't forget that." Then I would try to recollect some of the gossip I had heard at the Club: the prices of So-and-So's horses—anything, in fact, that related to the workaday Anglo-Indian world I knew so well. I even repeated the multiplication-table rapidly to myself, to make quite sure that I was not taking leave of my senses. It gave me much comfort; and must have prevented my hearing Mrs. Wessington for a time.

Once more I wearily climbed the Convent slope and entered the level road. Here Kitty and the man started off at a canter, and I was left alone with Mrs. Wessington. "Agnes," said I, "will you put back your hood and tell me what it all means?" The hood dropped noiselessly, and I was face to face with my dead and buried mistress. She was wearing the dress in which I had last seen her alive; carried the same tiny handkerchief in her right hand; and the same cardcase in her left. (A woman eight months dead with a cardcase!) I had to pin myself down to the multiplication-table, and to set both hands on the stone parapet of the road, to assure myself that that at least was real.

"Agnes," I repeated, "for pity's sake tell me what it all means." Mrs. Wessington leaned forward, with that odd, quick turn of the head I used to know so well, and spoke.

If my story had not already so madly overleaped the hounds of all human belief I should apologize to you now. As I know that no one—no, not even Kitty, for whom it is written as some sort of justification of my conduct—will believe me, I will go on. Mrs. Wessington spoke and I walked with her from the Sanjowlie road to the turning below the Commander-in-Chief's house as I might walk by the side of any living woman's 'rickshaw, deep in conversation. The second and most tormenting of my moods of sickness had suddenly laid hold upon me, and like the Prince in Tennyson's poem, "I seemed to move amid a world of ghosts." There had been a garden-party at the Commander-in-Chief's, and we two joined the crowd of homeward-bound folk. As I saw them then it seemed that they were the shadows—impalpable, fantastic shadows—that divided for Mrs. Wessington's 'rickshaw to pass through. What we said during the course of that weird interview I cannot—indeed, I dare not—tell. Heatherlegh's comment would have been a short laugh and a remark that I had been "mashing a brain-eye-and-stomach chimera." It was a ghastly and yet in some indefinable way a marvelously dear experience. Could it be possible, I wondered, that I was in this life to woo a second time the woman I had killed by my own neglect and cruelty?

I met Kitty on the homeward road—a shadow among shadows.

If I were to describe all the incidents of the next fortnight in their order, my story would never come to an end; and your patience would Be exhausted. Morning after morning and evening after evening the ghostly 'rickshaw and I used to wander through Simla together. Wherever I went there the four black and white liveries followed me and bore me company to and from my hotel. At the Theatre I found them amid the crowd of yelling jhampanies; outside the Club veranda, after a long evening of whist; at the Birthday Ball, waiting patiently for my reappearance; and

in broad daylight when I went calling. Save that it cast no shadow, the 'rickshaw was in every respect as real to look upon as one of wood and iron. More than once, indeed, I have had to check myself from warning some hard-riding friend against cantering over it. More than once I have walked down the Mall deep in conversation with Mrs. Wessington to the unspeakable amazement of the passers-by.

Before I had been out and about a week I learned that the "fit" theory had been discarded in favor of insanity. However, I made no change in my mode of life. I called, rode, and dined out as freely as ever. I had a passion for the society of my kind which I had never felt before; I hungered to be among the realities of life; and at the same time I felt vaguely unhappy when I had been separated too long from my ghostly companion. It would be almost impossible to describe my varying moods from the 15th of May up to today.

The presence of the 'rickshaw filled me by turns with horror, blind fear, a dim sort of pleasure, and utter despair. I dared not leave Simla; and I knew that my stay there was killing me. I knew, moreover, that it was my destiny to die slowly and a little every day. My only anxiety was to get the penance over as quietly as might be. Alternately I hungered for a sight of Kitty and watched her outrageous flirtations with my successor—to speak more accurately, my successors—with amused interest. She was as much out of my life as I was out of hers. By day I wandered with Mrs. Wessington almost content. By night I implored Heaven to let me return to the world as I used to know it. Above all these varying moods lay the sensation of dull, numbing wonder that the Seen and the Unseen should mingle so strangely on this earth to hound one poor soul to its grave.

August 27.—Heatherlegh has been indefatigable in his attendance on me; and only yesterday told me that I ought to send in an application for sick leave. An application to escape the company of a phantom! A request that the Government would graciously permit me to get rid of five ghosts and an airy 'rickshaw by going to England. Heatherlegh's proposition moved me to almost hysterical laughter. I told him that I should await the end quietly at Simla; and I am sure that the end is not far off. Believe me that I dread its advent more than any word can say; and I torture myself nightly with a thousand speculations as to the manner of my death.

Shall I die in my bed decently and as an English gentleman should die; or, in one last walk on the Mall, will my soul be wrenched from me to take its place forever and ever by the side of that ghastly phantasm? Shall I return to my old lost allegiance in the next world, or shall I meet Agnes loathing her and bound to her side through all eternity? Shall we two hover over the scene of our lives till the end of Time? As the day of my death draws nearer, the intense horror that all living flesh feels toward escaped spirits from beyond the grave grows more and more powerful. It is an awful thing to go down quick among the dead with scarcely one-half of your life completed. It is a thousand times more awful to wait as I do in your midst, for I know not what unimaginable terror. Pity me, at least on the score of my "delusion," for I know you will never believe what I have written here Yet as surely as ever a man was done to death by the Powers of Darkness I am that man.

In justice, too, pity her. For as surely as ever woman was killed by man, I killed Mrs. Wessington. And the last portion of my punishment is ever now upon me.

MY OWN TRUE GHOST STORY

As I came through the Desert thus it was—

As I came through the Desert.

 —The City of Dreadful Night.

Somewhere in the Other World, where there are books and pictures and plays and shop windows to look at, and thousands of men who spend their lives in building up all four, lives a gentleman who writes real stories about the real insides of people; and his name is Mr. Walter Besant. But he will insist upon treating his ghosts—he has published half a workshopful of them—with levity. He makes his ghost-seers talk familiarly, and, in some cases, flirt outrageously, with the phantoms. You may treat anything, from a Viceroy to a Vernacular Paper, with levity; but you must behave reverently toward a ghost, and particularly an Indian one.

There are, in this land, ghosts who take the form of fat, cold, pobby corpses, and hide in trees near the roadside till a traveler passes. Then they drop upon his neck and remain. There are also terrible ghosts of women who have died in child-bed. These wander along the pathways at dusk, or hide in the crops near a village, and call seductively. But to answer their call is death in this world and the next. Their feet are turned backward that all sober men may recognize them. There are ghosts of little children who have been thrown into wells. These haunt well curbs and the fringes of jungles, and wail under the stars, or catch women by the wrist and beg to be taken up and carried. These and the corpse ghosts, however, are only vernacular articles and do not attack Sahibs. No native ghost has yet been authentically reported to have frightened an Englishman; but many English ghosts have scared the life out of both white and black.

Nearly every other Station owns a ghost. There are said to be two at Simla, not counting the woman who blows the bellows at Syree dak-bungalow on the Old Road; Mussoorie has a house haunted of a very lively Thing; a White Lady is supposed to do night-watchman round a house in Lahore; Dalhousie says that one of her houses "repeats" on autumn evenings all the incidents of a horrible horse-and-precipice accident; Murree has a merry ghost, and, now that she has been swept by cholera, will have room for a sorrowful one; there are Officers' Quarters in Mian Mir whose doors open without reason, and whose furniture is guaranteed to creak, not with the heat of June but with the weight of Invisibles who come to lounge in the chairs; Peshawur possesses houses that none will willingly rent; and there is something—not fever—wrong with a big bungalow in Allahabad. The older Provinces simply bristle with haunted houses, and march phantom armies along their main thoroughfares.

Some of the dak-bungalows on the Grand Trunk Road have handy little cemeteries in their compound—witnesses to the "changes and chances of this mortal life" in the days when men drove from Calcutta to the Northwest. These bungalows are objectionable places to put up in. They are generally very old, always dirty, while the khansamah is as ancient as the bungalow. He either chatters senilely, or falls into the long trances of age. In both moods he is useless. If you get angry with him, he refers to some Sahib dead and buried these thirty years, and says that when he was in that Sahib's service not a khansamah in the Province could touch him. Then he jabbers and mows and trembles and fidgets among the dishes, and you repent of your irritation.

In these dak-bungalows, ghosts are most likely to be found, and when found, they should be made a note of. Not long ago it was my business to live in dak-bungalows. I never inhabited the same house for three nights running, and grew to be learned in the breed. I lived in Government-built ones with red brick walls and rail ceilings, an inventory of the furniture posted in every

room, and an excited snake at the threshold to give welcome. I lived in "converted" ones—old houses officiating as dak-bungalows—where nothing was in its proper place and there wasn't even a fowl for dinner. I lived in second-hand palaces where the wind blew through open-work marble tracery just as uncomfortably as through a broken pane. I lived in dak-bungalows where the last entry in the visitors' book was fifteen months old, and where they slashed off the curry-kid's head with a sword. It was my good luck to meet all sorts of men, from sober traveling missionaries and deserters flying from British Regiments, to drunken loafers who threw whisky bottles at all who passed; and my still greater good fortune just to escape a maternity case. Seeing that a fair proportion of the tragedy of our lives out here acted itself in dak-bungalows, I wondered that I had met no ghosts. A ghost that would voluntarily hang about a dak-bungalow would be mad of course; but so many men have died mad in dak-bungalows that there must be a fair percentage of lunatic ghosts.

In due time I found my ghost, or ghosts rather, for there were two of them. Up till that hour I had sympathized with Mr. Besant's method of handling them, as shown in "The Strange Case of Mr. Lucraft and Other Stories." I am now in the Opposition.

We will call the bungalow Katmal dak-bungalow. But THAT was the smallest part of the horror. A man with a sensitive hide has no right to sleep in dak-bungalows. He should marry. Katmal dak-bungalow was old and rotten and unrepaired. The floor was of worn brick, the walls were filthy, and the windows were nearly black with grime. It stood on a bypath largely used by native Sub-Deputy Assistants of all kinds, from Finance to Forests; but real Sahibs were rare. The khansamah, who was nearly bent double with old age, said so.

When I arrived, there was a fitful, undecided rain on the face of the land, accompanied by a restless wind, and every gust made a noise like the rattling of dry bones in the stiff toddy palms outside. The khansamah completely lost his head on my arrival. He had served a Sahib once. Did I know that Sahib? He gave me the name of a well-known man who has been buried for more than a quarter of a century, and showed me an ancient daguerreotype of that man in his prehistoric youth. I had seen a steel engraving of him at the head of a double volume of Memoirs a month before, and I felt ancient beyond telling.

The day shut in and the khansamah went to get me food. He did not go through the pretense of calling it "khana"—man's victuals. He said "ratub," and that means, among other things, "grub"—dog's rations. There was no insult in his choice of the term. He had forgotten the other word, I suppose.

While he was cutting up the dead bodies of animals, I settled myself down, after exploring the dak-bungalow. There were three rooms, beside my own, which was a corner kennel, each giving into the other through dingy white doors fastened with long iron bars. The bungalow was a very solid one, but the partition walls of the rooms were almost jerry-built in their flimsiness. Every step or bang of a trunk echoed from my room down the other three, and every footfall came back tremulously from the far walls. For this reason I shut the door. There were no lamps—only candles in long glass shades. An oil wick was set in the bathroom.

For bleak, unadulterated misery that dak-bungalow was the worst of the many that I had ever set foot in. There was no fireplace, and the windows would not open; so a brazier of charcoal would have been useless. The rain and the wind splashed and gurgled and moaned round the house, and the toddy palms rattled and roared.

Half a dozen jackals went through the compound singing, and a hyena stood afar off and mocked them. A hyena would convince a Sadducee of the Resurrection of the Dead—the worst sort of Dead. Then came the ratub—a curious meal, half native and half English in composition—with the old khansamah babbling behind my chair about dead and gone English people, and the

wind-blown candles playing shadow-bo-peep with the bed and the mosquito-curtains. It was just the sort of dinner and evening to make a man think of every single one of his past sins, and of all the others that he intended to commit if he lived.

Sleep, for several hundred reasons, was not easy. The lamp in the bath-room threw the most absurd shadows into the room, and the wind was beginning to talk nonsense.

Just when the reasons were drowsy with blood-sucking I heard the regular—"Let—us—take—and—heave—him—over" grunt of doolie-bearers in the compound. First one doolie came in, then a second, and then a third. I heard the doolies dumped on the ground, and the shutter in front of my door shook. "That's some one trying to come in," I said. But no one spoke, and I persuaded myself that it was the gusty wind. The shutter of the room next to mine was attacked, flung back, and the inner door opened. "That's some Sub-Deputy Assistant," I said, "and he has brought his friends with him. Now they'll talk and spit and smoke for an hour."

But there were no voices and no footsteps. No one was putting his luggage into the next room. The door shut, and I thanked Providence that I was to be left in peace. But I was curious to know where the doolies had gone. I got out of bed and looked into the darkness. There was never a sign of a doolie. Just as I was getting into bed again, I heard, in the next room, the sound that no man in his senses can possibly mistake—the whir of a billiard ball down the length of the slates when the striker is stringing for break. No other sound is like it. A minute afterwards there was another whir, and I got into bed. I was not frightened—indeed I was not. I was very curious to know what had become of the doolies. I jumped into bed for that reason.

Next minute I heard the double click of a cannon and my hair sat up. It is a mistake to say that hair stands up. The skin of the head tightens and you can feel a faint, prickly, bristling all over the scalp. That is the hair sitting up.

There was a whir and a click, and both sounds could only have been made by one thing—a billiard ball. I argued the matter out at great length with myself; and the more I argued the less probable it seemed that one bed, one table, and two chairs—all the furniture of the room next to mine—could so exactly duplicate the sounds of a game of billiards. After another cannon, a three—cushion one to judge by the whir, I argued no more. I had found my ghost and would have given worlds to have escaped from that dak-bungalow. I listened, and with each listen the game grew clearer.

There was whir on whir and click on click. Sometimes there was a double click and a whir and another click. Beyond any sort of doubt, people were playing billiards in the next room. And the next room was not big enough to hold a billiard table!

Between the pauses of the wind I heard the game go forward—stroke after stroke. I tried to believe that I could not hear voices; but that attempt was a failure.

Do you know what fear is? Not ordinary fear of insult, injury or death, but abject, quivering dread of something that you cannot see—fear that dries the inside of the mouth and half of the throat—fear that makes you sweat on the palms of the hands, and gulp in order to keep the uvula at work? This is a fine Fear—a great cowardice, and must be felt to be appreciated. The very improbability of billiards in a dak-bungalow proved the reality of the thing. No man—drunk or sober—could imagine a game at billiards, or invent the spitting crack of a "screw-cannon."

A severe course of dak-bungalows has this disadvantage—it breeds infinite credulity. If a man said to a confirmed dak-bungalow-haunter:—"There is a corpse in the next room, and there's a mad girl in the next but one, and the woman and man on that camel have just eloped from a place sixty miles away," the hearer would not disbelieve because he would know that nothing

is too wild, grotesque, or horrible to happen in a dak-bungalow.

This credulity, unfortunately, extends to ghosts. A rational person fresh from his own house would have turned on his side and slept. I did not. So surely as I was given up as a bad carcass by the scores of things in the bed because the bulk of my blood was in my heart, so surely did I hear every stroke of a long game at billiards played in the echoing room behind the iron-barred door. My dominant fear was that the players might want a marker. It was an absurd fear; because creatures who could play in the dark would be above such superfluities. I only know that that was my terror; and it was real.

After a long, long while the game stopped, and the door banged. I slept because I was dead tired. Otherwise I should have preferred to have kept awake. Not for everything in Asia would I have dropped the door-bar and peered into the dark of the next room.

When the morning came, I considered that I had done well and wisely, and inquired for the means of departure.

"By the way, khansamah," I said, "what were those three doolies doing in my compound in the night?"

"There were no doolies," said the khansamah.

I went into the next room and the daylight streamed through the open door. I was immensely brave. I would, at that hour, have played Black Pool with the owner of the big Black Pool down below.

"Has this place always been a dak-bungalow?" I asked.

"No," said the khansamah. "Ten or twenty years ago, I have forgotten how long, it was a billiard room."

"A how much?"

"A billiard room for the Sahibs who built the Railway. I was khansamah then in the big house where all the Railway-Sahibs lived, and I used to come across with brandy-shrab. These three rooms were all one, and they held a big table on which the Sahibs played every evening. But the Sahibs are all dead now, and the Railway runs, you say, nearly to Kabul."

"Do you remember anything about the Sahibs?"

"It is long ago, but I remember that one Sahib, a fat man and always angry, was playing here one night, and he said to me:—'Mangal Khan, brandy-pani do,' and I filled the glass, and he bent over the table to strike, and his head fell lower and lower till it hit the table, and his spectacles came off, and when we—the Sahibs and I myself—ran to lift him he was dead. I helped to carry him out. Aha, he was a strong Sahib! But he is dead and I, old Mangal Khan, am still living, by your favor."

That was more than enough! I had my ghost—a firsthand, authenticated article. I would write to the Society for Psychical Research—I would paralyze the Empire with the news! But I would, first of all, put eighty miles of assessed crop land between myself and that dak-bungalow before nightfall. The Society might send their regular agent to investigate later on.

I went into my own room and prepared to pack after noting down the facts of the case. As I smoked I heard the game begin again,—with a miss in balk this time, for the whir was a short one.

The door was open and I could see into the room. Click—click! That was a cannon. I entered the room without fear, for there was sunlight within and a fresh breeze without. The unseen game was going on at a tremendous rate. And well it might, when a restless little rat was running to and fro inside the dingy ceiling-cloth, and a piece of loose window-sash was making fifty breaks off the window-bolt as it shook in the breeze!

Impossible to mistake the sound of billiard balls! Impossible to mistake the whir of a ball over the slate! But I was to be excused. Even when I shut my enlightened eyes the sound was marvelously like that of a fast game.

Entered angrily the faithful partner of my sorrows, Kadir Baksh.

"This bungalow is very bad and low-caste! No wonder the Presence was disturbed and is speckled. Three sets of doolie-bearers came to the bungalow late last night when I was sleeping outside, and said that it was their custom to rest in the rooms set apart for the English people! What honor has the khansamah? They tried to enter, but I told them to go. No wonder, if these Oorias have been here, that the Presence is sorely spotted. It is shame, and the work of a dirty man!"

Kadir Baksh did not say that he had taken from each gang two annas for rent in advance, and then, beyond my earshot, had beaten them with the big green umbrella whose use I could never before divine. But Kadir Baksh has no notions of morality.

There was an interview with the khansamah, but as he promptly lost his head, wrath gave place to pity, and pity led to a long conversation, in the course of which he put the fat Engineer-Sahib's tragic death in three separate stations—two of them fifty miles away. The third shift was to Calcutta, and there the Sahib died while driving a dogcart.

If I had encouraged him the khansamah would have wandered all through Bengal with his corpse.

I did not go away as soon as I intended. I stayed for the night, while the wind and the rat and the sash and the window-bolt played a ding-dong "hundred and fifty up." Then the wind ran out and the billiards stopped, and I felt that I had ruined my one genuine, hall-marked ghost story.

Had I only stopped at the proper time, I could have made anything out of it.

That was the bitterest thought of all!

THE STRANGE RIDE OF MORROWBIE JUKES

Alive or dead-there is no other way.

—Native Proverb.

THERE is, as the conjurers say, no deception about this tale. Jukes by accident stumbled upon a village that is well known to exist, though he is the only Englishman who has been there. A somewhat similar institution used to flourish on the outskirts of Calcutta, and there is a story that if you go into the heart of Bikanir, which is in the heart of the Great Indian Desert, you shall come across not a village but a town where the Dead who did not die but may not live have established their headquarters. And, since it is perfectly true that in the same Desert is a wonderful city where all the rich money lenders retreat after they have made their fortunes (fortunes so vast that the owners cannot trust even the strong hand of the Government to protect them, but take refuge in the waterless sands), and drive sumptuous C-spring barouches, and buy beautiful girls and decorate their palaces with gold and ivory and Minton tiles and mother-of-pearl, I do not see why Jukes's tale should not be true. He is a Civil Engineer, with a head for plans and distances and things of that kind, and he certainly would not take the trouble to invent imaginary traps. He could earn more by doing his legitimate work. He never varies the tale in the telling, and grows very hot and indignant when he thinks of the disrespectful treatment he received. He wrote this quite straightforwardly at first, but he has since touched it up in places and introduced Moral Reflections, thus:

In the beginning it all arose from a slight attack of fever. My work necessitated my being in camp for some months between Pakpattan and Muharakpur—a desolate sandy stretch of country as every one who has had the misfortune to go there may know. My coolies were neither more nor less exasperating than other gangs, and my work demanded sufficient attention to keep me from moping, had I been inclined to so unmanly a weakness.

On the 23d December, 1884, I felt a little feverish. There was a full moon at the time, and, in consequence, every dog near my tent was baying it. The brutes assembled in twos and threes and drove me frantic. A few days previously I had shot one loud-mouthed singer and suspended his carcass in terrorem about fifty yards from my tent-door. But his friends fell upon, fought for, and ultimately devoured the body; and, as it seemed to me, sang their hymns of thanksgiving afterward with renewed energy.

The light-heartedness which accompanies fever acts differently on different men. My irritation gave way, after a short time, to a fixed determination to slaughter one huge black and white beast who had been foremost in song and first in flight throughout the evening. Thanks to a shaking hand and a giddy head I had already missed him twice with both barrels of my shot-gun, when it struck me that my best plan would be to ride him down in the open and finish him off with a hog-spear. This, of course, was merely the semi-delirious notion of a fever patient; but I remember that it struck me at the time as being eminently practical and feasible.

I therefore ordered my groom to saddle Pornic and bring him round quietly to the rear of my tent. When the pony was ready, I stood at his head prepared to mount and dash out as soon as the dog should again lift up his voice. Pornic, by the way, had not been out of his pickets for a couple of days; the night air was crisp and chilly; and I was armed with a specially long and sharp pair of persuaders with which I had been rousing a sluggish cob that afternoon. You will easily believe, then, that when he was let go he went quickly. In one moment, for the brute bolted as straight as a die, the tent was left far behind, and we were flying over the smooth sandy soil at racing speed.

In another we had passed the wretched dog, and I had almost forgotten why it was that I had taken the horse and hogspear.

The delirium of fever and the excitement of rapid motion through the air must have taken away the remnant of my senses. I have a faint recollection of standing upright in my stirrups, and of brandishing my hog-spear at the great white Moon that looked down so calmly on my mad gallop; and of shouting challenges to the camel-thorn bushes as they whizzed past. Once or twice I believe, I swayed forward on Pornic's neck, and literally hung on by my spurs—as the marks next morning showed.

The wretched beast went forward like a thing possessed, over what seemed to be a limitless expanse of moonlit sand. Next, I remember, the ground rose suddenly in front of us, and as we topped the ascent I saw the waters of the Sutlej shining like a silver bar below. Then Pornic blundered heavily on his nose, and we rolled together down some unseen slope.

I must have lost consciousness, for when I recovered I was lying on my stomach in a heap of soft white sand, and the dawn was beginning to break dimly over the edge of the slope down which I had fallen. As the light grew stronger I saw that I was at the bottom of a horse-shoe shaped crater of sand, opening on one side directly on to the shoals of the Sutlej. My fever had altogether left me, and, with the exception of a slight dizziness in the head, I felt no had effects from the fall over night.

Pornic, who was standing a few yards away, was naturally a good deal exhausted, but had not hurt himself in the least. His saddle, a favorite polo one, was much knocked about, and had been twisted under his belly. It took me some time to put him to rights, and in the meantime I had ample opportunities of observing the spot into which I had so foolishly dropped.

At the risk of being considered tedious, I must describe it at length: inasmuch as an accurate mental picture of its peculiarities will be of material assistance in enabling the reader to understand what follows.

Imagine then, as I have said before, a horseshoe-shaped crater of sand with steeply graded sand walls about thirty-five feet high. (The slope, I fancy, must have been about 65 degrees.) This crater enclosed a level piece of ground about fifty yards long by thirty at its broadest part, with a crude well in the centre. Round the bottom of the crater, about three feet from the level of the ground proper, ran a series of eighty-three semi-circular ovoid, square, and multilateral holes, all about three feet at the mouth. Each hole on inspection showed that it was carefully shored internally with drift-wood and bamboos, and over the mouth a wooden drip-board projected, like the peak of a jockey's cap, for two feet. No sign of life was visible in these tunnels, but a most sickening stench pervaded the entire amphitheatre—a stench fouler than any which my wanderings in Indian villages have introduced me to.

Having remounted Pornic, who was as anxious as I to get back to camp, I rode round the base of the horseshoe to find some place whence an exit would be practicable. The inhabitants, whoever they might be, had not thought fit to put in an appearance, so I was left to my own devices. My first attempt to "rush" Pornic up the steep sand-banks showed me that I had fallen into a trap exactly on the same model as that which the ant-lion sets for its prey. At each step the shifting sand poured down from above in tons, and rattled on the drip-boards of the holes like small shot. A couple of ineffectual charges sent us both rolling down to the bottom, half choked with the torrents of sand; and I was constrained to turn my attention to the river-bank.

Here everything seemed easy enough. The sand hills ran down to the river edge, it is true, but there were plenty of shoals and shallows across which I could gallop Pornic, and find my way back to terra firma by turning sharply to the right or left. As I led Pornic over the sands I was

startled by the faint pop of a rifle across the river; and at the same moment a bullet dropped with a sharp "whit" close to Pornic's head.

There was no mistaking the nature of the missile-a regulation Martini-Henry "picket." About five hundred yards away a country-boat was anchored in midstream; and a jet of smoke drifting away from its bows in the still morning air showed me whence the delicate attention had come. Was ever a respectable gentleman in such an impasse? The treacherous sand slope allowed no escape from a spot which I had visited most involuntarily, and a promenade on the river frontage was the signal for a bombardment from some insane native in a boat. I'm afraid that I lost my temper very much indeed.

Another bullet reminded me that I had better save my breath to cool my porridge; and I retreated hastily up the sands and back to the horseshoe, where I saw that the noise of the rifle had drawn sixty-five human beings from the badger-holes which I had up till that point supposed to be untenanted. I found myself in the midst of a crowd of spectators—about forty men, twenty women, and one child who could not have been more than five years old. They were all scantily clothed in that salmon-colored cloth which one associates with Hindu mendicants, and, at first sight, gave me the impression of a band of loathsome fakirs. The filth and repulsiveness of the assembly were beyond all description, and I shuddered to think what their life in the badger-holes must be.

Even in these days, when local self government has destroyed the greater part of a native's respect for a Sahib, I have been accustomed to a certain amount of civility from my inferiors, and on approaching the crowd naturally expected that there would be some recognition of my presence. As a matter of fact there was; but it was by no means what I had looked for.

The ragged crew actually laughed at me—such laughter I hope I may never hear again. They cackled, yelled, whistled, and howled as I walked into their midst; some of them literally throwing themselves down on the ground in convulsions of unholy mirth. In a moment I had let go Pornic's head, and irritated beyond expression at the morning's adventure, commenced cuffing those nearest to me with all the force I could. The wretches dropped under my blows like nine-pins, and the laughter gave place to wails for mercy; while those yet untouched clasped me round the knees, imploring me in all sorts of uncouth tongues to spare them.

In the tumult, and just when I was feeling very much ashamed of myself for having thus easily given way to my temper, a thin, high voice murmured in English from behind my shoulder: "—Sahib! Sahib! Do you not know me? Sahib, it is Gunga Dass, the telegraph-master."

I spun round quickly and faced the speaker.

Gunga Dass, (I have, of course, no hesitation in mentioning the man's real name) I had known four years before as a Deccanee Brahmin loaned by the Punjab Government to one of the Khalsia States. He was in charge of a branch telegraph-office there, and when I had last met him was a jovial, full-stomached, portly Government servant with a marvelous capacity for making had puns in English—a peculiarity which made me remember him long after I had forgotten his services to me in his official capacity. It is seldom that a Hindu makes English puns.

Now, however, the man was changed beyond all recognition. Caste-mark, stomach, slate-colored continuations, and unctuous speech were all gone. I looked at a withered skeleton, turban-less and almost naked, with long matted hair and deep-set codfish-eyes.

But for a crescent-shaped scar on the left cheek—the result of an accident for which I was responsible I should never have known him. But it was indubitably Gunga Dass, and—for this I was thankful—an English-speaking native who might at least tell me the meaning of all that I had gone through that day.

The crowd retreated to some distance as I turned toward the miserable figure, and ordered him to show me some method of escaping from the crate. He held a freshly plucked crow in his hand, and in reply to my question climbed slowly on a platform of sand which ran in front of the holes, and commenced lighting a fire there in silence. Dried bents, sand-poppies, and driftwood burn quickly; and I derived much consolation from the fact that he lit them with an ordinary sulphur-match. When they were in a bright glow, and the crow was neatly spitted in front thereof, Gunga Dass began without a word of preamble:

"There are only two kinds of men, Sar. The alive and the dead. When you are dead you are dead, but when you are alive you live." (Here the crow demanded his attention for an instant as it twirled before the fire in danger of being burned to a cinder.) "If you die at home and do not die when you come to the ghat to be burned you come here."

The nature of the reeking village was made plain now, and all that I had known or read of the grotesque and the horrible paled before the fact just communicated by the ex-Brahmin. Sixteen years ago, when I first landed in Bombay, I had been told by a wandering Armenian of the existence, somewhere in India, of a place to which such Hindus as had the misfortune to recover from trance or catalepsy were conveyed and kept, and I recollect laughing heartily at what I was then pleased to consider a traveler's tale.

Sitting at the bottom of the sand-trap, the memory of Watson's Hotel, with its swinging punkahs, white-robed attendants, and the sallow-faced Armenian, rose up in my mind as vividly as a photograph, and I burst into a loud fit of laughter. The contrast was too absurd!

Gunga Dass, as he bent over the unclean bird, watched me curiously. Hindus seldom laugh, and his surroundings were not such as to move Gunga Dass to any undue excess of hilarity. He removed the crow solemnly from the wooden spit and as solemnly devoured it. Then he continued his story, which I give in his own words:

"In epidemics of the cholera you are carried to be burned almost before you are dead. When you come to the riverside the cold air, perhaps, makes you alive, and then, if you are only little alive, mud is put on your nose and mouth and you die conclusively. If you are rather more alive, more mud is put; but if you are too lively they let you go and take you away. I was too lively, and made protestation with anger against the indignities that they endeavored to press upon me. In those days I was Brahmin and proud man.

"Now I am dead man and eat"—here he eyed the well-gnawed breast bone with the first sign of emotion that I had seen in him since we met—"crows, and other things. They took me from my sheets when they saw that I was too lively and gave me medicines for one week, and I survived successfully. Then they sent me by rail from my place to Okara Station, with a man to take care of me; and at Okara Station we met two other men, and they conducted we three on camels, in the night, from Okara Station to this place, and they propelled me from the top to the bottom, and the other two succeeded, and I have been here ever since two and a half years. Once I was Brahmin and proud man, and now I eat crows."

"There is no way of getting out?"

"None of what kind at all. When I first came I made experiments frequently and all the others also, but we have always succumbed to the sand which is precipitated upon our heads."

"But surely," I broke in at this point, "the river-front is open, and it is worth while dodging the bullets; while at night"—I had already matured a rough plan of escape which a natural instinct of selfishness forbade me sharing with Gunga Dass. He, however, divined my unspoken thought almost as soon as it was formed; and, to my intense astonishment, gave vent to a long low

chuckle of derision—the laughter, be it understood, of a superior or at least of an equal.

"You will not"—he had dropped the Sir completely after his opening sentence—"make any escape that way. But you can try. I have tried. Once only."

The sensation of nameless terror and abject fear which I had in vain attempted to strive against overmastered me completely. My long fast—it was now close upon ten o'clock, and I had eaten nothing since tiffin on the previous day—combined with the violent and unnatural agitation of the ride had exhausted me, and I verily believe that, for a few minutes, I acted as one mad. I hurled myself against the pitiless sand-slope. I ran round the base of the crater, blaspheming and praying by turns. I crawled out among the sedges of the river-front, only to be driven back each time in an agony of nervous dread by the rifle-bullets which cut up the sand round me—for I dared not face the death of a mad dog among that hideous crowd—and finally fell, spent and raving, at the curb of the well. No one had taken the slightest notion of an exhibition which makes me blush hotly even when I think of it now.

Two or three men trod on my panting body as they drew water, but they were evidently used to this sort of thing, and had no time to waste upon me. The situation was humiliating. Gunga Dass, indeed, when he had banked the embers of his fire with sand, was at some pains to throw half a cupful of fetid water over my head, an attention for which I could have fallen on my knees and thanked him, but he was laughing all the while in the same mirthless, wheezy key that greeted me on my first attempt to force the shoals. And so, in a semi-comatose condition, I lay till noon.

Then, being only a man after all, I felt hungry, and intimated as much to Gunga Dass, whom I had begun to regard as my natural protector. Following the impulse of the outer world when dealing with natives, I put my hand into my pocket and drew out four annas. The absurdity of the gift struck me at once, and I was about to replace the money.

Gunga Dass, however, was of a different opinion. "Give me the money," said he; "all you have, or I will get help, and we will kill you!" All this as if it were the most natural thing in the world!

A Briton's first impulse, I believe, is to guard the contents of his pockets; but a moment's reflection convinced me of the futility of differing with the one man who had it in his power to make me comfortable; and with whose help it was possible that I might eventually escape from the crater. I gave him all the money in my possession, Rs. 9-8-5—nine rupees eight annas and five pie—for I always keep small change as bakshish when I am in camp. Gunga Dass clutched the coins, and hid them at once in his ragged loin cloth, his expression changing to something diabolical as he looked round to assure himself that no one had observed us.

"Now I will give you something to eat," said he.

What pleasure the possession of my money could have afforded him I am unable to say; but inasmuch as it did give him evident delight I was not sorry that I had parted with it so readily, for I had no doubt that he would have had me killed if I had refused. One does not protest against the vagaries of a den of wild beasts; and my companions were lower than any beasts. While I devoured what Gunga Dass had provided, a coarse chapatti and a cupful of the foul well-water, the people showed not the faintest sign of curiosity—that curiosity which is so rampant, as a rule, in an Indian village.

I could even fancy that they despised me. At all events they treated me with the most chilling indifference, and Gunga Dass was nearly as bad. I plied him with questions about the terrible village, and received extremely unsatisfactory answers. So far as I could gather, it had been in existence from time immemorial—whence I concluded that it was at least a century old—

and during that time no one had ever been known to escape from it. [I had to control myself here with both hands, lest the blind terror should lay hold of me a second time and drive me raving round the crater.] Gunga Dass took a malicious pleasure in emphasizing this point and in watching me wince. Nothing that I could do would induce him to tell me who the mysterious "They" were.

"It is so ordered," he would reply, "and I do not yet know any one who has disobeyed the orders."

"Only wait till my servants find that I am missing," I retorted, "and I promise you that this place shall be cleared off the face of the earth, and I'll give you a lesson in civility, too, my friend."

"Your servants would be torn in pieces before they came near this place; and, besides, you are dead, my dear friend. It is not your fault, of course, but none the less you are dead and buried."

At irregular intervals supplies of food, I was told, were dropped down from the land side into the amphitheatre, and the inhabitants fought for them like wild beasts. When a man felt his death coming on he retreated to his lair and died there. The body was sometimes dragged out of the hole and thrown on to the sand, or allowed to rot where it lay.

The phrase "thrown on to the sand" caught my attention, and I asked Gunga Dass whether this sort of thing was not likely to breed a pestilence.

"That," said he, with another of his wheezy chuckles, "you may see for yourself subsequently. You will have much time to make observations."

Whereat, to his great delight, I winced once more and hastily continued the conversation:— "And how do you live here from day to day? What do you do?" The question elicited exactly the same answer as before coupled with the information that "this place is like your European heaven; there is neither marrying nor giving in marriage."

Gunga Dass had been educated at a Mission School, and, as he himself admitted, had he only changed his religion "like a wise man," might have avoided the living grave which was now his portion. But as long as I was with him I fancy he was happy.

Here was a Sahib, a representative of the dominant race, helpless as a child and completely at the mercy of his native neighbors. In a deliberate lazy way he set himself to torture me as a schoolboy would devote a rapturous half-hour to watching the agonies of an impaled beetle, or as a ferret in a blind burrow might glue himself comfortably to the neck of a rabbit. The burden of his conversation was that there was no escape "of no kind whatever," and that I should stay here till I died and was "thrown on to the sand." If it were possible to forejudge the conversation of the Damned on the advent of a new soul in their abode, I should say that they would speak as Gunga Dass did to me throughout that long afternoon. I was powerless to protest or answer; all my energies being devoted to a struggle against the inexplicable terror that threatened to overwhelm me again and again. I can compare the feeling to nothing except the struggles of a man against the overpowering nausea of the Channel passage—only my agony was of the spirit and infinitely more terrible.

As the day wore on, the inhabitants began to appear in full strength to catch the rays of the afternoon sun, which were now sloping in at the mouth of the crater. They assembled in little knots, and talked among themselves without even throwing a glance in my direction. About four o'clock, as far as I could judge Gunga Dass rose and dived into his lair for a moment, emerging with a live crow in his hands. The wretched bird was in a most draggled and deplorable condition, but seemed to be in no way afraid of its master, Advancing cautiously to the river

front, Gunga Dass stepped from tussock to tussock until he had reached a smooth patch of sand directly in the line of the boat's fire. The occupants of the boat took no notice. Here he stopped, and, with a couple of dexterous turns of the wrist, pegged the bird on its back with outstretched wings. As was only natural, the crow began to shriek at once and beat the air with its claws. In a few seconds the clamor had attracted the attention of a bevy of wild crows on a shoal a few hundred yards away, where they were discussing something that looked like a corpse. Half a dozen crows flew over at once to see what was going on, and also, as it proved, to attack the pinioned bird. Gunga Dass, who had lain down on a tussock, motioned to me to be quiet, though I fancy this was a needless precaution. In a moment, and before I could see how it happened, a wild crow, who had grappled with the shrieking and helpless bird, was entangled in the latter's claws, swiftly disengaged by Gunga Dass, and pegged down beside its companion in adversity. Curiosity, it seemed, overpowered the rest of the flock, and almost before Gunga Dass and I had time to withdraw to the tussock, two more captives were struggling in the upturned claws of the decoys. So the chase—if I can give it so dignified a name—continued until Gunga Dass had captured seven crows. Five of them he throttled at once, reserving two for further operations another day. I was a good deal impressed by this, to me, novel method of securing food, and complimented Gunga Dass on his skill.

"It is nothing to do," said he. "Tomorrow you must do it for me. You are stronger than I am."

This calm assumption of superiority Upset me not a little, and I answered peremptorily;—"Indeed, you old ruffian! What do you think I have given you money for?"

"Very well," was the unmoved reply. "Perhaps not tomorrow, nor the day after, nor subsequently; but in the end, and for many years, you will catch crows and eat crows, and you will thank your European God that you have crows to catch and eat."

I could have cheerfully strangled him for this; but judged it best under the circumstances to smother my resentment. An hour later I was eating one of the crows; and, as Gunga Dass had said, thanking my God that I had a crow to eat. Never as long as I live shall I forget that evening meal. The whole population were squatting on the hard sand platform opposite their dens, huddled over tiny fires of refuse and dried rushes. Death, having once laid his hand upon these men and forborne to strike, seemed to stand aloof from them now; for most of our company were old men, bent and worn and twisted with years, and women aged to all appearance as the Fates themselves. They sat together in knots and talked—God only knows what they found to discuss—in low equable tones, curiously in contrast to the strident babble with which natives are accustomed to make day hideous. Now and then an access of that sudden fury which had possessed me in the morning would lay hold on a man or woman; and with yells and imprecations the sufferer would attack the steep slope until, baffled and bleeding, he fell back on the platform incapable of moving a limb. The others would never even raise their eyes when this happened, as men too well aware of the futility of their fellows' attempts and wearied with their useless repetition. I saw four such outbursts in the course of the evening.

Gunga Dass took an eminently business-like view of my situation, and while we were dining—I can afford to laugh at the recollection now, but it was painful enough at the time-propounded the terms on which he would consent to "do" for me. My nine rupees eight annas, he argued, at the rate of three annas a day, would provide me with food for fifty-one days, or about seven weeks; that is to say, he would be willing to cater for me for that length of time. At the end of it I was to look after myself. For a further consideration—videlicet my boots—he would be willing to allow me to occupy the den next to his own, and would supply me with as much dried grass for bedding as he could spare.

"Very well, Gunga Dass," I replied; "to the first terms I cheerfully agree, but, as there is nothing

on earth to prevent my killing you as you sit here and taking everything that you have" (I thought of the two invaluable crows at the time), "I flatly refuse to give you my boots and shall take whichever den I please."

The stroke was a bold one, and I was glad when I saw that it had succeeded. Gunga Dass changed his tone immediately, and disavowed all intention of asking for my boots. At the time it did not strike me as at all strange that I, a Civil Engineer, a man of thirteen years' standing in the Service, and, I trust, an average Englishman, should thus calmly threaten murder and violence against the man who had, for a consideration it is true, taken me under his wing. I had left the world, it seemed, for centuries. I was as certain then as I am now of my own existence, that in the accursed settlement there was no law save that of the strongest; that the living dead men had thrown behind them every canon of the world which had cast them out; and that I had to depend for my own life on my strength and vigilance alone. The crew of the ill-fated Mignonette are the only men who would understand my frame of mind. "At present," I argued to myself, "I am strong and a match for six of these wretches. It is imperatively necessary that I should, for my own sake, keep both health and strength until the hour of my release comes—if it ever does."

Fortified with these resolutions, I ate and drank as much as I could, and made Gunga Dass understand that I intended to be his master, and that the least sign of insubordination on his part would be visited with the only punishment I had it in my power to inflict—sudden and violent death. Shortly after this I went to bed.

That is to say, Gunga Dass gave me a double armful of dried bents which I thrust down the mouth of the lair to the right of his, and followed myself, feet foremost; the hole running about nine feet into the sand with a slight downward inclination, and being neatly shored with timbers. From my den, which faced the river-front, I was able to watch the waters of the Sutlej flowing past under the light of a young moon and compose myself to sleep as best I might.

The horrors of that night I shall never forget. My den was nearly as narrow as a coffin, and the sides had been worn smooth and greasy by the contact of innumerable naked bodies, added to which it smelled abominably. Sleep was altogether out of question to one in my excited frame of mind. As the night wore on, it seemed that the entire amphitheatre was filled with legions of unclean devils that, trooping up from the shoals below, mocked the unfortunates in their lairs.

Personally I am not of an imaginative temperament,—very few Engineers are,—but on that occasion I was as completely prostrated with nervous terror as any woman. After half an hour or so, however, I was able once more to calmly review my chances of escape. Any exit by the steep sand walls was, of course, impracticable. I had been thoroughly convinced of this some time before. It was possible, just possible, that I might, in the uncertain moonlight, safely run the gauntlet of the rifle shots. The place was so full of terror for me that I was prepared to undergo any risk in leaving it. Imagine my delight, then, when after creeping stealthily to the river-front I found that the infernal boat was not there. My freedom lay before me in the next few steps!

By walking out to the first shallow pool that lay at the foot of the projecting left horn of the horseshoe, I could wade across, turn the flank of the crater, and make my way inland. Without a moment's hesitation I marched briskly past the tussocks where Gunga Dass had snared the crows, and out in the direction of the smooth white sand beyond. My first step from the tufts of dried grass showed me how utterly futile was any hope of escape; for, as I put my foot down, I felt an indescribable drawing, sucking motion of the sand below. Another moment and my leg was swallowed up nearly to the knee. In the moonlight the whole surface of the sand seemed to be shaken with devilish delight at my disappointment. I struggled clear, sweating with terror and exertion, back to the tussocks behind me and fell on my face.

My only means of escape from the semicircle was protected with a quicksand!

How long I lay I have not the faintest idea; but I was roused at last by the malevolent chuckle of Gunga Dass at my ear. "I would advise you, Protector of the Poor" (the ruffian was speaking English) "to return to your house. It is unhealthy to lie down here. Moreover, when the boat returns, you will most certainly be rifled at." He stood over me in the dim light of the dawn, chuckling and laughing to himself. Suppressing my first impulse to catch the man by the neck and throw him on to the quicksand, I rose sullenly and followed him to the platform below the burrows.

Suddenly, and futilely as I thought while I spoke, I asked—"Gunga Dass, what is the good of the boat if I can't get out anyhow?" I recollect that even in my deepest trouble I had been speculating vaguely on the waste of ammunition in guarding an already well protected foreshore.

Gunga Dass laughed again and made answer:—"They have the boat only in daytime. It is for the reason that there is a way. I hope we shall have the pleasure of your company for much longer time. It is a pleasant spot when you have been here some years and eaten roast crow long enough."

I staggered, numbed and helpless, toward the fetid burrow allotted to me, and fell asleep. An hour or so later I was awakened by a piercing scream—the shrill, high-pitched scream of a horse in pain. Those who have once heard that will never forget the sound. I found some little difficulty in scrambling out of the burrow. When I was in the open, I saw Pornic, my poor old Pornic, lying dead on the sandy soil. How they had killed him I cannot guess. Gunga Dass explained that horse was better than crow, and "greatest good of greatest number is political maxim. We are now Republic, Mister Jukes, and you are entitled to a fair share of the beast. If you like, we will pass a vote of thanks. Shall I propose?"

Yes, we were a Republic indeed! A Republic of wild beasts penned at the bottom of a pit, to eat and fight and sleep till we died. I attempted no protest of any kind, but sat down and stared at the hideous sight in front of me. In less time almost than it takes me to write this, Pornic's body was divided, in some unclear way or other; the men and women had dragged the fragments on to the platform and were preparing their normal meal. Gunga Dass cooked mine. The almost irresistible impulse to fly at the sand walls until I was wearied laid hold of me afresh, and I had to struggle against it with all my might. Gunga Dass was offensively jocular till I told him that if he addressed another remark of any kind whatever to me I should strangle him where he sat. This silenced him till silence became insupportable, and I bade him say something.

"You will live here till you die like the other Feringhi," he said, coolly, watching me over the fragment of gristle that he was gnawing.

"What other Sahib, you swine? Speak at once, and don't stop to tell me a lie."

"He is over there," answered Gunga Dass, pointing to a burrow-mouth about four doors ta the left of my own. "You can see for yourself. He died in the burrow as you will die, and I will die, and as all these men and women and the one child will also die."

"For pity's sake tell me all you know about him. Who was he? When did he come, and when did he die?"

This appeal was a weak step on my part. Gunga Dass only leered and replied:—"I will not—unless you give me something first."

Then I recollected where I was, and struck the man between the eyes, partially stunning him. He stepped down from the platform at once, and, cringing and fawning and weeping and attempting to embrace my feet, led me round to the burrow which he had indicated.

"I know nothing whatever about the gentleman. Your God be my witness that I do not. He was as anxious to escape as you were, and he was shot from the boat, though we all did all things to prevent him from attempting. He was shot here." Gunga Dass laid his hand on his lean stomach and bowed to the earth.

"Well, and what then? Go on!"

"And then—and then, Your Honor, we carried him in to his house and gave him water, and put wet cloths on the wound, and he laid down in his house and gave up the ghost."

"In how long? In how long?"

"About half an hour, after he received his wound. I call Vishnu to witness," yelled the wretched man, "that I did everything for him. Everything which was possible, that I did!"

He threw himself down on the ground and clasped my ankles. But I had my doubts about Gunga Dass's benevolence, and kicked him off as he lay protesting.

"I believe you robbed him of everything he had. But I can find out in a minute or two. How long was the Sahib here?"

"Nearly a year and a half. I think he must have gone mad. But hear me swear, Protector of the Poor! Won't Your Honor hear me swear that I never touched an article that belonged to him? What is Your Worship going to do?"

I had taken Gunga Dass by the waist and had hauled him on to the platform opposite the deserted burrow. As I did so I thought of my wretched fellow-prisoner's unspeakable misery among all these horrors for eighteen months, and the final agony of dying like a rat in a hole, with a bullet-wound in the stomach. Gunga Dass fancied I was going to kill him and howled pitifully. The rest of the population, in the plethora that follows a full flesh meal, watched us without stirring.

"Go inside, Gunga Dass," said I, "and fetch it out."

I was feeling sick and faint with horror now. Gunga Dass nearly rolled off the platform and howled aloud.

"But I am Brahmin, Sahib—a high-caste Brahmin. By your soul, by your father's soul, do not make me do this thing!"

"Brahmin or no Brahmin, by my soul and my father's soul, in you go!" I said, and, seizing him by the shoulders, I crammed his head into the mouth of the burrow, kicked the rest of him in, and, sitting down, covered my face with my hands.

At the end of a few minutes I heard a rustle and a creak; then Gunga Dass in a sobbing, choking whisper speaking to himself; then a soft thud—and I uncovered my eyes.

The dry sand had turned the corpse entrusted to its keeping into a yellow-brown mummy. I told Gunga Dass to stand off while I examined it.

The body—clad in an olive-green hunting-suit much stained and worn, with leather pads on the shoulders—was that of a man between thirty and forty, above middle height, with light, sandy hair, long mustache, and a rough unkempt beard. The left canine of the upper jaw was missing, and a portion of the lobe of the right ear was gone. On the second finger of the left hand was a ring—a shield-shaped bloodstone set in gold, with a monogram that might have been either "B.K." or "B.L." On the third finger of the right hand was a silver ring in the shape

of a coiled cobra, much worn and tarnished. Gunga Dass deposited a handful of trifles he had picked out of the burrow at my feet, and, covering the face of the body with my handkerchief, I turned to examine these. I give the full list in the hope that it may lead to the identification of the unfortunate man:

1. Bowl of a briarwood pipe, serrated at the edge; much worn and blackened; bound with string at the crew.

2. Two patent-lever keys; wards of both broken.

3. Tortoise-shell-handled penknife, silver or nickel name-plate, marked with monogram "B.K."

4. Envelope, postmark Undecipherable, bearing a Victorian stamp, addressed to "Miss Mon-" (rest illegible) -"ham-'nt."

5. Imitation crocodile-skin notebook with pencil. First forty-five pages blank; four and a half illegible; fifteen others filled with private memoranda relating chiefly to three persons—a Mrs. L. Singleton, abbreviated several times to "Lot Single," "Mrs. S. May," and "Garmison," referred to in places as "Jerry" or "Jack."

6. Handle of small-sized hunting-knife. Blade snapped short. Buck's horn, diamond cut, with swivel and ring on the butt; fragment of cotton cord attached.

It must not be supposed that I inventoried all these things on the spot as fully as I have here written them down. The notebook first attracted my attention, and I put it in my pocket with a view of studying it later on.

The rest of the articles I conveyed to my burrow for safety's sake, and there being a methodical man, I inventoried them. I then returned to the corpse and ordered Gunga Dass to help me to carry it out to the river-front. While we were engaged in this, the exploded shell of an old brown cartridge dropped out of one of the pockets and rolled at my feet. Gunga Dass had not seen it; and I fell to thinking that a man does not carry exploded cartridge-cases, especially "browns," which will not bear loading twice, about with him when shooting. In other words, that cartridge-case had been fired inside the crater. Consequently there must be a gun somewhere. I was on the verge of asking Gunga Dass, but checked myself, knowing that he would lie. We laid the body down on the edge of the quicksand by the tussocks. It was my intention to push it out and let it be swallowed up—the only possible mode of burial that I could think of. I ordered Gunga Dass to go away.

Then I gingerly put the corpse out on the quicksand. In doing so—it was lying face downward—I tore the frail and rotten khaki shooting-coat open, disclosing a hideous cavity in the back. I have already told you that the dry sand had, as it were, mummified the body. A moment's glance showed that the gaping hole had been caused by a gun-shot wound; the gun must have been fired with the muzzle almost touching the back. The shooting-coat, being intact, had been drawn over the body after death, which must have been instantaneous. The secret of the poor wretch's death was plain to me in a flash. Some one of the crater, presumably Gunga Dass, must have shot him with his own gun—the gun that fitted the brown cartridges. He had never attempted to escape in the face of the rifle-fire from the boat.

I pushed the corpse out hastily, and saw it sink from sight literally in a few seconds. I shuddered as I watched. In a dazed, half-conscious way I turned to peruse the notebook. A stained and discolored slip of paper bad been inserted between the binding and the back, and dropped out as I opened the pages. This is what it contained:—"Four out from crow-clump: three left; nine out; two right; three back; two left; fourteen out; two left; seven out; one left; nine back; two right;

six back; four right; seven back." The paper had been burned and charred at the edges. What it meant I could not understand. I sat down on the dried bents turning it over and over between my fingers, until I was aware of Gunga Dass standing immediately behind me with glowing eyes and outstretched hands.

"Have you got it?" he panted. "Will you not let me look at it also? I swear that I will return it."

"Got what? Return what?" asked.

"That which you have in your hands. It will help us both." He stretched out his long, bird-like talons, trembling with eagerness.

"I could never find it," he continued. "He had secreted it about his person. Therefore I shot him, but nevertheless I was unable to obtain it."

Gunga Dass had quite forgotten his little fiction about the rifle-bullet. I received the information perfectly calmly. Morality is blunted by consorting with the Dead who are alive.

"What on earth are you raving about? What is it you want me to give you?"

"The piece of paper in the notebook. It will help us both. Oh, you fool! You fool! Can you not see what it will do for us? We shall escape!"

His voice rose almost to a scream, and he danced with excitement before me. I own I was moved at the chance of my getting away.

"Don't skip! Explain yourself. Do you mean to say that this slip of paper will help us? What does it mean?"

"Read it aloud! Read it aloud! I beg and I pray you to read it aloud."

I did so. Gunga Dass listened delightedly, and drew an irregular line in the sand with his fingers.

"See now! It was the length of his gun-barrels without the stock. I have those barrels. Four gun-barrels out from the place where I caught crows straight out; do you follow me? Then three left—Ah! how well I remember when that man worked it out night after night Then nine out, and so on. Out is always straight before you across the quicksand. He told me so before I killed him."

"But if you knew all this why didn't you get out before?"

"I did not know it. He told me that he was working it out a year and a half ago, and how he was working it out night after night when the boat had gone away, and he could get out near the quicksand safely. Then he said that we would get away together. But I was afraid that he would leave me behind one night when he had worked it all out, and so I shot him. Besides, it is not advisable that the men who once get in here should escape. Only I, and I am a Brahmin."

The prospect of escape had brought Gunga Dass's caste back to him. He stood up, walked about and gesticulated violently. Eventually I managed to make him talk soberly, and he told me how this Englishman had spent six months night after night in exploring, inch by inch, the passage across the quicksand; how he had declared it to be simplicity itself up to within about twenty yards of the river bank after turning the flank of the left horn of the horseshoe. This much he had evidently not completed when Gunga Dass shot him with his own gun.

In my frenzy of delight at the possibilities of escape I recollect shaking hands effusively with

Gunga Dass, after we had decided that we were to make an attempt to get away that very night. It was weary work waiting throughout the afternoon.

About ten o'clock, as far as I could judge, when the Moon had just risen above the lip of the crater, Gunga Dass made a move for his burrow to bring out the gun-barrels whereby to measure our path. All the other wretched inhabitants had retired to their lairs long ago. The guardian boat drifted downstream some hours before, and we were utterly alone by the crow-clump. Gunga Dass, while carrying the gun-barrels, let slip the piece of paper which was to be our guide. I stooped down hastily to recover it, and, as I did so, I was aware that the diabolical Brahmin was aiming a violent blow at the back of my head with the gun-barrels. It was too late to turn round. I must have received the blow somewhere on the nape of my neck. A hundred thousand fiery stars danced before my eyes, and I fell forwards senseless at the edge of, the quicksand.

When I recovered consciousness, the Moon was going down, and I was sensible of intolerable pain in the back of my head. Gunga Dass had disappeared and my mouth was full of blood. I lay down again and prayed that I might die without more ado. Then the unreasoning fury which I had before mentioned, laid hold upon me, and I staggered inland toward the walls of the crater. It seemed that some one was calling to me in a whisper—"Sahib! Sahib! Sahib!" exactly as my bearer used to call me in the morning I fancied that I was delirious until a handful of sand fell at my feet. Then I looked up and saw a head peering down into the amphitheatre—the head of Dunnoo, my dog-boy, who attended to my collies. As soon as he had attracted my attention, he held up his hand and showed a rope. I motioned, staggering to and fro for the while, that he should throw it down. It was a couple of leather punkah-ropes knotted together, with a loop at one end. I slipped the loop over my head and under my arms; heard Dunnoo urge something forward; was conscious that I was being dragged, face downward, up the steep sand slope, and the next instant found myself choked and half fainting on the sand hills overlooking the crater. Dunnoo, with his face ashy grey in the moonlight, implored me not to stay but to get back to my tent at once.

It seems that he had tracked Pornic's footprints fourteen miles across the sands to the crater; had returned and told my servants, who flatly refused to meddle with any one, white or black, once fallen into the hideous Village of the Dead; whereupon Dunnoo had taken one of my ponies and a couple of punkah-ropes, returned to the crater, and hauled me out as I have described.

To cut a long story short, Dunnoo is now my personal servant on a gold mohur a month—a sum which I still think far too little for the services he has rendered. Nothing on earth will induce me to go near that devilish spot again, or to reveal its whereabouts more clearly than I have done. Of Gunga Dass I have never found a trace, nor do I wish to do. My sole motive in giving this to be published is the hope that some one may possibly identify, from the details and the inventory which I have given above, the corpse of the man in the olive-green hunting-suit.

THE MAN WHO WOULD BE KING

Brother to a Prince and fellow to a beggar if he be found worthy.

The Law, as quoted, lays down a fair conduct of life, and one not easy to follow. I have been fellow to a beggar again and again under circumstances which prevented either of us finding out whether the other was worthy. I have still to be brother to a Prince, though I once came near to kinship with what might have been a veritable King, and was promised the reversion of a Kingdom—army, law-courts, revenue, and policy all complete. But, today, I greatly fear that my King is dead, and if I want a crown I must go hunt it for myself.

The beginning of everything was in a railway-train upon the road to Mhow from Ajmir. There had been a Deficit in the Budget, which necessitated travelling, not Second-class, which is only half as dear as First-Class, but by Intermediate, which is very awful indeed. There are no cushions in the Intermediate class, and the population are either Intermediate, which is Eurasian, or native, which for a long night journey is nasty, or Loafer, which is amusing though intoxicated. Intermediates do not buy from refreshment-rooms. They carry their food in bundles and pots, and buy sweets from the native sweetmeat-sellers, and drink the roadside water. This is why in hot weather Intermediates are taken out of the carriages dead, and in all weathers are most properly looked down upon.

My particular Intermediate happened to be empty till I reached Nasirabad, when the big black-browed gentleman in shirt-sleeves entered, and, following the custom of Intermediates, passed the time of day. He was a wanderer and a vagabond like myself, but with an educated taste for whisky. He told tales of things he had seen and done, of out-of-the-way corners of the Empire into which he had penetrated, and of adventures in which he risked his life for a few days' food.

"If India was filled with men like you and me, not knowing more than the crows where they'd get their next day's rations, it isn't seventy millions of revenue the land would be paying—it's seven hundred millions," said he; and as I looked at his mouth and chin I was disposed to agree with him.

We talked politics,—the politics of Loaferdom that sees things from the under side where the lath and plaster is not smoothed off,—and we talked postal arrangements because my friend wanted to send a telegram back from the next station to Ajmir, the turning-off place from the Bombay to the Mhow line as you travel westward. My friend had no money beyond eight annas which he wanted for dinner, and I had no money at all, owing to the hitch in the Budget before mentioned. Further, I was going into a wilderness where, though I should resume touch with the Treasury, there were no telegraph offices. I was, therefore, unable to help him in any way.

"We might threaten a Station-master, and make him send a wire on tick," said my friend, "but that'd mean inquiries for you and for me, and I've got my hands full these days. Did you say you were travelling back along this line within any days?"

"Within ten," I said.

"Can't you make it eight?" said he. "Mine is rather urgent business."

"I can send your telegrams within ten days if that will serve you," I said.

"I couldn't trust the wire to fetch him, now I think of it. It's this way. He leaves Delhi on the 23rd for Bombay. That means he'll be running through Ajmir about the night of the 23rd."

"But I'm going into the Indian Desert," I explained.

"Well and good," said he. "You'll be changing at Marwar Junction to get into Jodhpore territory,—you must do that,—and he'll be coming through Marwar Junction in the early morning of the 24th by the Bombay Mail. Can you be at Marwar Junction on that time? 'T won't be inconveniencing you, because I know that there's precious few pickings to be got out of these Central India States—even though you pretend to be correspondent of the 'Backwoodsman.'"

"Have you ever tried that trick?" I asked.

"Again and again, but the Residents find you out, and then you get escorted to the Border before you've time to get your knife into them. But about my friend here. I must give him a word o' mouth to tell him what's come to me, or else he won't know where to go. I would take it more than kind of you if you was to come out of Central India in time to catch him at Marwar Junction, and say to him, 'He has gone South for the week.' He'll know what that means. He's a big man with a red beard, and a great swell he is.

"You'll find him sleeping like a gentleman with all his luggage round him in a Second-class apartment. But don't you be afraid.

"Slip down the window and say, 'He has gone South for the week,' and he'll tumble. It's only cutting your time of stay in those parts by two days. I ask you as a stranger—going to the West," he said, with emphasis.

"Where have you come from?" said I.

"From the East," said he, "and I am hoping that you will give him the message on the square— for the sake of my Mother as well as your own."

Englishmen are not usually softened by appeals to the memory of their mothers; but for certain reasons, which will be fully apparent, I saw fit to agree.

"It's more than a little matter," said he, "and that's why I asked you to do it—and now I know that I can depend on you doing it. A Second-class carriage at Marwar Junction, and a red-haired man asleep in it. You'll be sure to remember. I get out at the next station, and I must hold on there till he comes or sends me what I want."

"I'll give the message if I catch him," I said, "and for the sake of your Mother as well as mine I'll give you a word of advice. Don't try to run the Central India States just now as the correspondent of the 'Backwoodsman.' There's a real one knocking about here, and it might lead to trouble."

"Thank you," said he, simply; "and when will the swine be gone? I can't starve because he's ruining my work. I wanted to get hold of the Degumber Rajah down here about his father's widow, and give him a jump."

"What did he do to his father's widow, then?"

"Filled her up with red pepper and slippered her to death as she hung from a beam. I found that out myself, and I'm the only man that would dare going into the State to get hush-money for it. They'll try to poison me, same as they did in Chortumna when I went on the loot there. But you'll give the man at Marwar Junction my message?"

He got out at a little roadside station, and I reflected. I had heard, more than once, of men personating correspondents of newspapers and bleeding small Native States with threats of

exposure, but I had never met any of the caste before. They lead a hard life, and generally die with great suddenness. The Native States have a wholesome horror of English newspapers, which may throw light on their peculiar methods of government, and do their best to choke correspondents with champagne, or drive them out of their mind with four-in-hand barouches. They do not understand that nobody cares a straw for the internal administration of Native States so long as oppression and crime are kept within decent limits, and the ruler is not drugged, drunk, or diseased from one end of the year to the other. They are the dark places of the earth, full of unimaginable cruelty, touching the Railway and the Telegraph on one side, and, on the other, the days of Harun-al-Raschid. When I left the train I did business with divers Kings, and in eight days passed through many changes of life. Sometimes I wore dress-clothes and consorted with Princes and Politicals, drinking from crystal and eating from silver. Sometimes I lay out upon the ground and devoured what I could get, from a plate made of leaves, and drank the running water, and slept under the same rug as my servant. It was all in the day's work.

Then I headed for the Great Indian Desert upon the proper date, as I had promised, and the night Mail set me down at Marwar Junction, where a funny little, happy-go-lucky, native managed railway runs to Jodhpore. The Bombay Mail from Delhi makes a short halt at Marwar. She arrived just as I got in, and I had just time to hurry to her platform and go down the carriages. There was only one Second-class on the train. I slipped the window and looked down upon a flaming-red beard, half covered by a railway-rug. That was my man, fast asleep, and I dug him gently in the ribs.

He woke with a grunt, and I saw his face in the light of the lamps.

It was a great and shining face.

"Tickets again?" said he.

"No," said I. "I am to tell you that he is gone South for the week. He has gone South for the week!"

The train had begun to move out. The red man rubbed his eyes.

"He has gone South for the week," he repeated. "Now that's just like his impidence. Did he say that I was to give you anything? 'Cause I won't."

"He didn't," I said, and dropped away, and watched the red lights die out in the dark. It was horribly cold because the wind was blowing off the sands. I climbed into my own train—not an Intermediate carriage this time—and went to sleep.

If the man with the beard had given me a rupee I should have kept it as a memento of a rather curious affair. But the consciousness of having done my duty was my only reward.

Later on I reflected that two gentlemen like my friends could not do any good if they foregathered and personated correspondents of newspapers, and might, if they blackmailed one of the little rat-trap States of Central India or Southern Rajputana, get themselves into serious difficulties. I therefore took some trouble to describe them as accurately as I could remember to people who would be interested in deporting them; and succeeded, so I was later informed, in having them headed back from the Degumber borders.

Then I became respectable, and returned to an office where there were no Kings and no incidents outside the daily manufacture of a newspaper. A newspaper office seems to attract every conceivable sort of person, to the prejudice of discipline. Zenana-mission ladies arrive, and beg that the Editor will instantly abandon all his duties to describe a Christian prize-giving in a back

slum of a perfectly inaccessible village; Colonels who have been overpassed for command sit down and sketch the outline of a series of ten, twelve, or twenty-four leading articles on Seniority versus Selection; missionaries wish to know why they have not been permitted to escape from their regular vehicles of abuse, and swear at a brother missionary under special patronage of the editorial We. Stranded theatrical companies troop up to explain that they cannot pay for their advertisements, but on their return from New Zealand or Tahiti will do so with interest; inventors of patent punka-pulling machines, carriage couplings, and unbreakable swords and axletrees call with specifications in their pockets and hours at their disposal; tea companies enter and elaborate their prospectuses with the office pens; secretaries of ball committees clamour to have the glories of their last dance more fully described; strange ladies rustle in and say, "I want a hundred lady's cards printed at once, please," which is manifestly part of an Editor's duty; and every dissolute ruffian that ever tramped the Grand Trunk Road makes it his business to ask for employment as a proof-reader. And, all the time, the telephone-bell is ringing madly, and Kings are being killed on the Continent, and Empires are saying, "You're another," and Mister Gladstone is calling down brimstone upon the British Dominions, and the little black copyboys are whining, "kaa-pi chay-ha-yeh" ("Copy wanted"), like tired bees, and most of the paper is as blank as Modred's shield.

But that is the amusing part of the year. There are six other months when none ever come to call, and the thermometer walks inch by inch up to the top of the glass, and the office is darkened to just above reading-light, and the press-machines are red-hot to touch, and nobody writes anything but accounts of amusements in the Hill-stations or obituary notices. Then the telephone becomes a tinkling terror, because it tells you of the sudden deaths of men and women that you knew intimately, and the prickly heat covers you with a garment, and you sit down and write: "A slight increase of sickness is reported from the Khuda Janta Khan District. The outbreak is purely sporadic in its nature, and, thanks to the energetic efforts of the District authorities, is now almost at an end. It is, however, with deep regret we record the death," etc.

Then the sickness really breaks out, and the less recording and reporting the better for the peace of the subscribers. But the Empires and the Kings continue to divert themselves as selfishly as before, and the Foreman thinks that a daily paper really ought to come out once in twenty-four hours, and all the people at the Hill-stations in the middle of their amusements say, "Good gracious! why can't the paper be sparkling? I'm sure there's plenty going on up here."

That is the dark half of the moon, and, as the advertisements say, "must be experienced to be appreciated."

It was in that season, and a remarkably evil season, that the paper began running the last issue of the week on Saturday night, which is to say Sunday morning, after the custom of a London paper. This was a great convenience, for immediately after the paper was put to bed the dawn would lower the thermometer from 96 degrees to almost 84 degrees for half an hour, and in that chill—you have no idea how cold is 84 degrees on the grass until you begin to pray for it—a very tired man could get off to sleep ere the heat roused him.

One Saturday night it was my pleasant duty to put the paper to bed alone. A King or courtier or a courtesan or a Community was going to die or get a new Constitution, or do something that was important on the other side of the world, and the paper was to be held open till the latest possible minute in order to catch the telegram.

It was a pitchy-black night, as stifling as a June night can be, and the loo, the red-hot wind from the westward, was booming among the tinder-dry trees and pretending that the rain was on its heels.

Now and again a spot of almost boiling water would fall on the dust with the flop of a frog,

but all our weary world knew that was only pretence. It was a shade cooler in the press-room than the office, so I sat there, while the type ticked and clicked, and the night-jars hooted at the windows, and the all but naked compositors wiped the sweat from their foreheads and called for water. The thing that was keeping us back, whatever it was, would not come off, though the loo dropped and the last type was set, and the whole round earth stood still in the choking heat, with its finger on its lip, to wait the event. I drowsed, and wondered whether the telegraph was a blessing, and whether this dying man, or struggling people, might be aware of the inconvenience the delay was causing. There was no special reason beyond the heat and worry to make tension, but, as the clock-hands crept up to three o'clock and the machines spun their fly-wheels two and three times to see that all was in order, before I said the word that would set them off, I could have shrieked aloud.

Then the roar and rattle of the wheels shivered the quiet into little bits. I rose to go away, but two men in white clothes stood in front of me. The first one said, "It's him!" The second said, "So it is!" And they both laughed almost as loudly as the machinery roared, and mopped their foreheads. We seed there was a light burning across the road, and we were sleeping in that ditch there for coolness, and I said to my friend here, "The office is open. Let's come along and speak to him as turned us back from Degumber State," said the smaller of the two. He was the man I had met in the Mhow train, and his fellow was the red-bearded man of Marwar Junction. There was no mistaking the eyebrows of the one or the beard of the other.

I was not pleased, because I wished to go to sleep, not to squabble with loafers. "What do you want?" I asked.

"Half an hour's talk with you, cool and comfortable, in the office," said the red-bearded man. "We'd like some drink,—the Contrack doesn't begin yet, Peachey, so you needn't look,—but what we really want is advice. We don't want money. We ask you as a favour, because we found out you did us a bad turn about Degumber State."

I led from the press-room to the stifling office with the maps on the walls, and the red-haired man rubbed his hands. "That's something like," said he. "This was the proper shop to come to."

"Now, Sir, let me introduce you to Brother Peachey Carnehan, that's him, and Brother Daniel Dravot, that is me, and the less said about our professions the better, for we have been most things in our time—soldier, sailor, compositor, photographer, proof-reader, street-preacher, and correspondents of the 'Backwoodsman' when we thought the paper wanted one. Carnehan is sober, and so am I. Look at us first, and see that's sure. It will save you cutting into my talk. We'll take one of your cigars apiece, and you shall see us light up."

I watched the test. The men were absolutely sober, so I gave them each a tepid whisky-and-soda.

"Well and good," said Carnehan of the eyebrows, wiping the froth from his moustache. "Let me talk now, Dan. We have been all over India, mostly on foot. We have been boiler-fitters, engine-drivers, petty contractors, and all that, and we have decided that India isn't big enough for such as us."

They certainly were too big for the office. Dravot's beard seemed to fill half the room and Carnehan's shoulders the other half, as they sat on the big table. Carnehan continued: "The country isn't half worked out because they that governs it won't let you touch it. They spend all their blessed time in governing it, and you can't lift a spade, nor chip a rock, nor look for oil, nor anything like that, without all the Government saying, 'Leave it alone, and let us govern.' Therefore, such as it is, we will let it alone, and go away to some other place where a man isn't crowded and can come to his own. We are not little men, and there is nothing that we are afraid of except Drink, and we have signed a Contrack on that.

"Therefore we are going away to be Kings."

"Kings in our own right," muttered Dravot.

"Yes, of course," I said. "You've been tramping in the sun, and it's a very warm night, and hadn't you better sleep over the notion? Come tomorrow."

"Neither drunk nor sunstruck," said Dravot. "We have slept over the notion half a year, and require to see Books and Atlases, and we have decided that there is only one place now in the world that two strong men can Sar-a-whack. They call it Kafiristan. By my reckoning it's the top right-hand corner of Afghanistan, not more than three hundred miles from Peshawar. They have two and thirty heathen idols there, and we'll be the thirty-third and fourth. It's a mountaineous country, the women of those parts are very beautiful."

"But that is provided against in the Contrack," said Carnehan. "Neither Women nor Liquor, Daniel."

"And that's all we know, except that no one has gone there, and they fight, and in any place where they fight a man who knows how to drill men can always be a King. We shall go to those parts and say to any King we find, 'D' you want to vanquish your foes?' and we will show him how to drill men; for that we know better than anything else. Then we will subvert that King and seize his Throne and establish a Dy-nasty."

"You'll be cut to pieces before you're fifty miles across the Border," I said. "You have to travel through Afghanistan to get to that country. It's one mass of mountains and peaks and glaciers, and no Englishman has been through it. The people are utter brutes, and even if you reached them you couldn't do anything."

"That's more like," said Carnehan. "If you could think us a little more mad we would be more pleased. We have come to you to know about this country, to read a book about it, and to be shown maps. We want you to tell us that we are fools and to show us your books." He turned to the bookcases.

"Are you at all in earnest?" I said.

"A little," said Dravot, sweetly. "As big a map as you have got, even if it's all blank where Kafiristan is, and any books you've got. We can read, though we aren't very educated."

I uncased the big thirty-two-miles-to-the-inch map of India and two smaller Frontier maps, hauled down volume INF-KAN of the "Encyclopaedia Britannica," and the men consulted them.

"See here!" said Dravot, his thumb on the map. "Up to Jagdallak, Peachey and me know the road. We was there with Robert's Army. We'll have to turn off to the right at Jagdallak through Laghmann territory. Then we get among the hills—fourteen thousand feet—fifteen thousand— it will be cold work there, but it don't look very far on the map."

I handed him Wood on the "Sources of the Oxus." Carnehan was deep in the "Encyclopaedia."

"They're a mixed lot," said Dravot, reflectively; "and it won't help us to know the names of their tribes. The more tribes the more they'll fight, and the better for us. From Jagdallak to Ashang. H'mm!"

"But all the information about the country is as sketchy and inaccurate as can be," I protested. "No one knows anything about it really. Here's the file of the 'United Services' Institute.' Read what Bellew says."

"Blow Bellew!" said Carnehan. "Dan, they're a stinkin' lot of heathens, but this book here says they think they're related to us English."

I smoked while the men poured over Raverty, Wood, the maps, and the "Encyclopaedia."

"There is no use your waiting," said Dravot, politely. "It's about four o'clock now. We'll go before six o'clock if you want to sleep, and we won't steal any of the papers. Don't you sit up. We're two harmless lunatics, and if you come tomorrow evening down to the Serai we'll say goodbye to you."

"You are two fools," I answered. "You'll be turned back at the Frontier or cut up the minute you set foot in Afghanistan. Do you want any money or a recommendation down-country? I can help you to the chance of work next week."

"Next week we shall be hard at work ourselves, thank you," said Dravot. "It isn't so easy being a King as it looks. When we've got our Kingdom in going order we'll let you know, and you can come up and help us govern it."

"Would two lunatics make a Contrack like that?" said Carnehan, with subdued pride, showing me a greasy half-sheet of notepaper on which was written the following. I copied it, then and there, as a curiosity.

This Contrack between me and you persuing witnesseth in the name of God—Amen and so forth.

(One) That me and you will settle this matter together; i.e., to be Kings of Kafiristan.

(Two) That you and me will not, while this matter is being settled, look at any Liquor, nor any Woman, black, white, or brown, so as to get mixed up with one or the other harmful.

(Three) That we conduct ourselves with Dignity and Discretion, and if one of us gets into trouble the other will stay by him.

Signed by you and me this day.

Peachey Taliaferro Carnehan.

Daniel Dravot.

Both Gentlemen at Large.

"There was no need for the last article," said Carnehan, blushing modestly; "but it looks regular. Now you know the sort of men that loafers are,—we are loafers, Dan, until we get out of India,—and do you think that we would sign a Contrack like that unless we was in earnest? We have kept away from the two things that make life worth having."

"You won't enjoy your lives much longer if you are going to try this idiotic adventure. Don't set the office on fire," I said, "and go away before nine o'clock."

I left them still poring over the maps and making notes on the back of the "Contrack." "Be sure to come down to the Serai tomorrow," were their parting words.

The Kumharsen Serai is the great foursquare sink of humanity where the strings of camels and horses from the North load and unload. All the nationalities of Central Asia may be found there, and most of the folk of India proper. Balkh and Bokhara there meet Bengal and Bombay,

and try to draw eye-teeth. You can buy ponies, turquoises, Persian pussy-cats, saddle-bags, fat-tailed sheep, and musk in the Kumharsen Serai, and get many strange things for nothing. In the afternoon I went down to see whether my friends intended to keep their word or were lying there drunk.

A priest attired in fragments of ribbons and rags stalked up to me, gravely twisting a child's paper whirligig. Behind him was his servant bending under the load of a crate of mud toys. The two were loading up two camels, and the inhabitants of the Serai watched them with shrieks of laughter.

"The priest is mad," said a horse-dealer to me. "He is going up to Kabul to sell toys to the Amir. He will either be raised to honour or have his head cut off. He came in here this morning and has been behaving madly ever since."

"The witless are under the protection of God," stammered a flat-cheeked Usbeg in broken Hindi. "They foretell future events."

"Would they could have foretold that my caravan would have been cut up by the Shinwaris almost within shadow of the Pass!" grunted the Eusufzai agent of a Rajputana trading-house whose goods had been diverted into the hands of other robbers just across the Border, and whose misfortunes were the laughing-stock of the bazaar. "Ohe', priest, whence come you and whither do you go?"

"From Roum have I come," shouted the priest, waving his whirligig; "from Roum, blown by the breath of a hundred devils across the sea! O thieves, robbers, liars, the blessing of Pir Khan on pigs, dogs, and perjurers! Who will take the Protected of God to the North to sell charms that are never still to the Amir? The camels shall not gall, the sons shall not fall sick, and the wives shall remain faithful while they are away, of the men who give me place in their caravan. Who will assist me to slipper the King of the Roos with a golden slipper with a silver heel? The protection of Pir Khan be upon his labours!" He spread out the skirts of his gabardine and pirouetted between the lines of tethered horses.

"There starts a caravan from Peshawar to Kabul in twenty days, Huzrut," said the Eusufzai trader. "My camels go therewith. Do thou also go and bring us good luck."

"I will go even now!" shouted the priest. "I will depart upon my winged camels, and be at Peshawar in a day! Ho! Hazar Mir Khan," he yelled to his servant, "drive out the camels, but let me first mount my own."

He leaped on the back of his beast as it knelt, and, turning round to me, cried, "Come thou also, Sahib, a little along the road, and I will sell thee a charm—an amulet that shall make thee King of Kafiristan."

Then the light broke upon me, and I followed the two camels out of the Serai till we reached open road and the priest halted.

"What d' you think o' that?" said he in English. "Carnehan can't talk their patter, so I've made him my servant. He makes a handsome servant. 'T isn't for nothing that I've been knocking about the country for fourteen years. Didn't I do that talk neat? We'll hitch on to a caravan at Peshawar till we get to Jagdallak, and then we'll see if we can get donkeys for our camels, and strike into Kafiristan. Whirligigs for the Amir, O Lor'! Put your hand under the camelbags and tell me what you feel."

I felt the butt of a Martini, and another and another.

"Twenty of 'em," said Dravot, placidly. "Twenty of 'em and ammunition to correspond, under the whirligigs and the mud dolls."

"Heaven help you if you are caught with those things!" I said. "A Martini is worth her weight in silver among the Pathans."

"Fifteen hundred rupees of capital—every rupee we could beg, borrow, or steal—are invested on these two camels," said Dravot.

"We won't get caught. We're going through the Khaiber with a regular caravan. Who'd touch a poor mad priest?"

"Have you got everything you want?" I asked, overcome with astonishment.

"Not yet, but we shall soon. Give us a memento of your kindness, Brother. You did me a service yesterday, and that time in Marwar. Half my Kingdom shall you have, as the saying is." I slipped a small charm compass from my watch-chain and handed it up to the priest.

"Goodbye," said Dravot, giving me hand cautiously. "It's the last time we'll shake hands with an Englishman these many days. Shake hands with him, Carnehan," he cried, as the second camel passed me.

Carnehan leaned down and shook hands. Then the camels passed away along the dusty road, and I was left alone to wonder. My eye could detect no failure in the disguises. The scene in the Serai proved that they were complete to the native mind. There was just the chance, therefore, that Carnehan and Dravot would be able to wander through Afghanistan without detection. But, beyond, they would find death—certain and awful death.

Ten days later a native correspondent, giving me the news of the day from Peshawar, wound up his letter with: "There has been much laughter here on account of a certain mad priest who is going in his estimation to sell petty gauds and insignificant trinkets which he ascribes as great charms to H. H. the Amir of Bokhara. He passed through Peshawar and associated himself to the Second Summer caravan that goes to Kabul. The merchants are pleased because through superstition they imagine that such mad fellows bring good fortune."

The two, then, were beyond the Border. I would have prayed for them, but that night a real King died in Europe, and demanded an obituary notice.

The wheel of the world swings through the same phases again and again. Summer passed and winter thereafter, and came and passed again. The daily paper continued and I with it, and upon the third summer there fell a hot night, a night issue, and a strained waiting for something to be telegraphed from the other side of the world, exactly as had happened before. A few great men had died in the past two years, the machines worked with more clatter, and some of the trees in the office garden were a few feet taller. But that was all the difference.

I passed over to the press-room, and went through just such a scene as I have already described. The nervous tension was stronger than it had been two years before, and I felt the heat more acutely. At three o'clock I cried, "Print off," and turned to go, when there crept to my chair what was left of a man. He was bent into a circle, his head was sunk between his shoulders, and he moved his feet one over the other like a bear. I could hardly see whether he walked or crawled—this rag-wrapped, whining cripple who addressed me by name, crying that he was come back. "Can you give me a drink?" he whimpered. "For the Lord's sake, give me a drink!"

I went back to the office, the man following with groans of pain, and I turned up the lamp.

"Don't you know me?" he gasped, dropping into a chair, and he turned his drawn face, surmounted by a shock of gray hair, to the light.

I looked at him intently. Once before had I seen eyebrows that met over the nose in an inch-broad black band, but for the life of me I could not tell where.

"I don't know you," I said, handing him the whisky. "What can I do for you?"

He took a gulp of the spirit raw, and shivered in spite of the suffocating heat.

"I've come back," he repeated; "and I was the King of Kafiristan—me and Dravot—crowned Kings we was! In this office we settled it—you setting there and giving us the books. I am Peachey,—Peachey Taliaferro Carnehan,—and you've been setting here ever since—O Lord!"

I was more than a little astonished, and expressed my feelings accordingly.

"It's true," said Carnehan, with a dry cackle, nursing his feet, which were wrapped in rags— "true as gospel. Kings we were, with crowns upon our heads—me and Dravot—poor Dan—oh, poor, poor Dan, that would never take advice, not though I begged of him!"

"Take the whisky," I said, "and take your own time. Tell me all you can recollect of everything from beginning to end. You got across the Border on your camels, Dravot dressed as a mad priest and you his servant. Do you remember that?"

"I ain't mad—yet, but I shall be that way soon. Of course I remember. Keep looking at me, or maybe my words will go all to pieces. Keep looking at me in my eyes and don't say anything."

I leaned forward and looked into his face as steadily as I could. He dropped one hand upon the table and I grasped it by the wrist. It was twisted like a bird's claw, and upon the back was a ragged, red, diamond-shaped scar.

"No, don't look there. Look at me," said Carnehan. "That comes afterward, but for the Lord's sake don't distrack me. We left with that caravan, me and Dravot playing all sorts of antics to amuse the people we were with. Dravot used to make us laugh in the evenings when all the people was cooking their dinners—cooking their dinners, and... what did they do then? They lit little fires with sparks that went into Dravot's beard, and we all laughed—fit to die. Little red fires they was, going into Dravot's big red beard—so funny." His eyes left mine and he smiled foolishly.

"You went as far as Jagdallak with that caravan," I said, at a venture, "after you had lit those fires. To Jagdallak, where you turned off to try to get into Kafiristan."

"No, we didn't, neither. What are you talking about? We turned off before Jagdallak, because we heard the roads was good. But they wasn't good enough for our two camels—mine and Dravot's. When we left the caravan, Dravot took off all his clothes and mine too, and said we would be heathen, because the Kafirs didn't allow Mohammedans to talk to them. So we dressed betwixt and between, and such a sight as Daniel Dravot I never saw yet nor expect to see again. He burned half his beard, and slung a sheepskin over his shoulder, and shaved his head into patterns. He shaved mine too, and made me wear outrageous things to look like a heathen. That was in a most mountaineous country, and our camels couldn't go along any more because of the mountains. They were tall and black, and coming home I saw them fight like wild goats—there are lots of goats in Kafiristan. And these mountains, they never keep still, no more than the goats. Always fighting they are, and don't let you sleep at night."

"Take some more whisky," I said, very slowly. "What did you and Daniel Dravot do when the

camels could go no farther because of the rough roads that led into Kafiristan?"

"What did which do? There was a party called Peachey Taliaferro Carnehan that was with Dravot. Shall I tell you about him? He died out there in the cold. Slap from the bridge fell old Peachey, turning and twisting in the air like a penny whirligig that you can sell to the Amir. No; they was two for three ha'pence, those whirligigs, or I am much mistaken and woful sore... And then these camels were no use, and Peachey said to Dravot, 'For the Lord's sake let's get out of this before our heads are chopped off,' and with that they killed the camels all among the mountains, not having anything in particular to eat, but first they took off the boxes with the guns and the ammunition, till two men came along driving four mules. Dravot up and dances in front of them, singing, 'Sell me four mules.' Says the first man, 'If you are rich enough to buy, you are rich enough to rob;' but before ever he could put his hand to his knife, Dravot breaks his neck over his knee, and the other party runs away. So Carnehan loaded the mules with the rifles that was taken off the camels, and together we starts forward into those bitter-cold mountaineous parts, and never a road broader than the back of your hand."

He paused for a moment, while I asked him if he could remember the nature of the country through which he had journeyed.

"I am telling you as straight as I can, but my head isn't as good as it might be. They drove nails through it to make me hear better how Dravot died. The country was mountaineous and the mules were most contrary, and the inhabitants was dispersed and solitary. They went up and up, and down and down, and that other party, Carnehan, was imploring of Dravot not to sing and whistle so loud, for fear of bringing down the tremenjus avalanches. But Dravot says that if a King couldn't sing it wasn't worth being King, and whacked the mules over the rump, and never took no heed for ten cold days. We came to a big level valley all among the mountains, and the mules were near dead, so we killed them, not having anything in special for them or us to eat. We sat upon the boxes, and played odd and even with the cartridges that was jolted out.

"Then ten men with bows and arrows ran down that valley, chasing twenty men with bows and arrows, and the row was tremenjus.

"They was fair men—fairer than you or me—with yellow hair and remarkable well built. Says Dravot, unpacking the guns, 'This is the beginning of the business. We'll fight for the ten men,' and with that he fires two rifles at the twenty men, and drops one of them at two hundred yards from the rock where he was sitting. The other men began to run, but Carnehan and Dravot sits on the boxes picking them off at all ranges, up and down the valley. Then we goes up to the ten men that had run across the snow too, and they fires a footy little arrow at us. Dravot he shoots above their heads, and they all falls down flat. Then he walks over them and kicks them, and then he lifts them up and shakes hands all round to make them friendly like. He calls them and gives them the boxes to carry, and waves his hand for all the world as though he was King already. They takes the boxes and him across the valley and up the hill into a pine wood on the top, where there was half a dozen big stone idols. Dravot he goes to the biggest—a fellow they call Imbra—and lays a rifle and a cartridge at his feet, rubbing his nose respectfully with his own nose, patting him on the head, and nods his head, and says, 'That's all right. I'm in the know too, and these old jimjams are my friends.' Then he opens his mouth and points down it, and when the first man brings him food, he says, 'No;' and when the second man brings him food, he says 'no;' but when one of the old priests and the boss of the village brings him food, he says, 'Yes;' very haughty, and eats it slow. That was how he came to our first village without any trouble, just as though we had tumbled from the skies. But we tumbled from one of those damned rope-bridges, you see, and—you couldn't expect a man to laugh much after that?"

"Take some more whisky and go on," I said. "That was the first village you came into. How did you get to be King?"

"I wasn't King," said Carnehan. "Dravot he was the King, and a handsome man he looked with the gold crown on his head and all. Him and the other party stayed in that village, and every morning Dravot sat by the side of old Imbra, and the people came and worshipped. That was Dravot's order. Then a lot of men came into the valley, and Carnehan Dravot picks them off with the rifles before they knew where they was, and runs down into the valley and up again the other side, and finds another village, same as the first one, and the people all falls down flat on their faces, and Dravot says, 'Now what is the trouble between you two villages?' and the people points to a woman, as fair as you or me, that was carried off, and Dravot takes her back to the first village and counts up the dead—eight there was. For each dead man Dravot pours a little milk on the ground and waves his arms like a whirligig, and 'That's all right,' says he. Then he and Carnehan takes the big boss of each village by the arm, and walks them down the valley, and shows them how to scratch a line with a spear right down the valley, and gives each a sod of turf from both sides of the line. Then all the people comes down and shouts like the devil and all, and Dravot says, 'Go and dig the land, and be fruitful and multiply,' which they did, though they didn't understand. Then we asks the names of things in their lingo—bread and water and fire and idols and such; and Dravot leads the priest of each village up to the idol, and says he must sit there and judge the people, and if anything goes wrong he is to be shot.

"Next week they was all turning up the land in the valley as quiet as bees and much prettier, and the priests heard all the complaints and told Dravot in dumb-show what it was about. 'That's just the beginning,' says Dravot. 'They think we're Gods.' He and Carnehan picks out twenty good men and shows them how to click off a rifle and form fours and advance in line; and they was very pleased to do so, and clever to see the hang of it. Then he takes out his pipe and his baccy-pouch, and leaves one at one village and one at the other, and off we two goes to see what was to be done in the next valley. That was all rock, and there was a little village there, and Carnehan says, 'Send 'em to the old valley to plant,' and takes 'em there and gives 'em some land that wasn't took before. They were a poor lot, and we blooded 'em with a kid before letting 'em into the new Kingdom. That was to impress the people, and then they settled down quiet, and Carnehan went back to Dravot, who had got into another valley, all snow and ice and most mountaineous.

"There was no people there, and the Army got afraid; so Dravot shoots one of them, and goes on till he finds some people in a village, and the Army explains that unless the people wants to be killed they had better not shoot their little matchlocks, for they had matchlocks. We makes friends with the priest, and I stays there alone with two of the Army, teaching the men how to drill; and a thundering big Chief comes across the snow with kettledrums and horns twanging, because he heard there was a new God kicking about. Carnehan sights for the brown of the men half a mile across the snow and wings one of them. Then he sends a message to the Chief that, unless he wished to be killed, he must come and shake hands with me and leave his arms behind. The Chief comes alone first, and Carnehan shakes hands with him and whirls his arms about, same as Dravot used, and very much surprised that Chief was, and strokes my eyebrows. Then Carnehan goes alone to the Chief, and asks him in dumb-show if he had an enemy he hated. 'I have,' says the chief. So Carnehan weeds out the pick of his men, and sets the two of the Army to show them drill, and at the end of two weeks the men can manoeuvre about as well as Volunteers. So he marches with the Chief to a great big plain on the top of a mountain, and the Chief's men rushes into a village and takes it, we three Martinis firing into the brown of the enemy. So we took that village too, and I gives the Chief a rag from my coat, and says, 'Occupy till I come;' which was scriptural. By way of a reminder, when me and the Army was eighteen hundred yards away, I drops a bullet near him standing on the snow, and all the people falls flat on their faces. Then I sends a letter to Dravot wherever he be by land or by sea."

At the risk of throwing the creature out of train I interrupted: "How could you write a letter up yonder?"

"The letter?—oh!—the letter! Keep looking at me between the eyes, please. It was a string-talk letter, that we'd learned the way of it from a blind beggar in the Punjab."

I remember that there had once come to the office a blind man with a knotted twig, and a piece of string which he wound round the twig according to some cipher of his own. He could, after the lapse of days or hours, repeat the sentence which he had reeled up.

He had reduced the alphabet to eleven primitive sounds, and tried to teach me his method, but I could not understand.

"I sent that letter to Dravot," said Carnehan, "and told him to come back because this Kingdom was growing too big for me to handle; and then I struck for the first valley, to see how the priests were working. They called the village we took along with the Chief, Bashkai, and the first village we took, Er-Heb. The priests at Er-Heb was doing all right, but they had a lot of pending cases about land to show me, and some men from another village had been firing arrows at night. I went out and looked for that village, and fired four rounds at it from a thousand yards. That used all the cartridges I cared to spend, and I waited for Dravot, who had been away two or three months, and I kept my people quiet.

"One morning I heard the devil's own noise of drums and horns, and Dan Dravot marches down the hill with his Army and a tail of hundreds of men, and, which was the most amazing, a great gold crown on his head. 'My Gord, Carnehan,' says Daniel, 'this is a tremenjus business, and we've got the whole country as far as it's worth having. I am the son of Alexander by Queen Semiramis, and you're my younger brother and a God too! It's the biggest thing we've ever seen. I've been marching and fighting for six weeks with the Army, and every footy little village for fifty miles has come in rejoiceful; and more than that, I've got the key of the whole show, as you'll see, and I've got a crown for you! I told 'em to make two of 'em at a place called Shu, where the gold lies in the rock like suet in mutton. Gold I've seen, and turquoise I've kicked out of the cliffs, and there's garnets in the sands of the river, and here's a chunk of amber that a man brought me. Call up all the priests and, here, take your crown.'

"One of the men opens a black hair bag, and I slips the crown on. It was too small and too heavy, but I wore it for the glory. Hammered gold it was—five pounds weight, like a hoop of a barrel.

"'Peachey,' says Dravot, 'we don't want to fight no more. The Craft's the trick, so help me!' and he brings forward that same Chief that I left at Bashkai—Billy Fish we called him afterward, because he was so like Billy Fish that drove the big tank-engine at Mach on the Bolan in the old days. 'Shake hands with him,' says Dravot; and I shook hands and nearly dropped, for Billy Fish gave me the Grip. I said nothing, but tried him with the Fellow-craft Grip. He answers all right, and I tried the Master's Grip, but that was a slip. 'A Fellow-craft he is!' I says to Dan. 'Does he know the word?' 'He does,' says Dan, 'and all the priests know. It's a miracle! The Chiefs and the priests can work a Fellow-craft Lodge in a way that's very like ours, and they've cut the marks on the rocks, but they don't know the Third Degree, and they've come to find out. It's Gord's Truth. I've known these long years that the Afghans knew up to the Fellow-craft Degree, but this is a miracle. A God and a Grand Master of the Craft am I, and a Lodge in the Third Degree I will open, and we'll raise the head priests and the Chiefs of the villages.'

"'It's against all the law,' I says, 'holding a Lodge without warrant from any one; and you know we never held office in any Lodge.'

"'It's a master stroke o' policy,' says Dravot. 'It means running the country as easy as a four-wheeled bogie on a down grade. We can't stop to inquire now, or they'll turn against us. I've forty Chiefs at my heel, and passed and raised according to their merit they shall be. Billet these men on the villages, and see that we run up a Lodge of some kind. The temple of Imbra will do

for a Lodge-room. The women must make aprons as you show them. I'll hold a levee of Chiefs tonight and Lodge tomorrow.'

"I was fair run off my legs, but I wasn't such a fool as not to see what a pull this Craft business gave us. I showed the priests' families how to make aprons of the degrees, but for Dravot's apron the blue border and marks was made of turquoise lumps on white hide, not cloth. We took a great square stone in the temple for the Master's chair, and little stones for the officer's chairs, and painted the black pavement with white squares, and did what we could to make things regular.

"At the levee which was held that night on the hillside with big bonfires, Dravot gives out that him and me were Gods and sons of Alexander, and Passed Grand Masters in the Craft, and was come to make Kafiristan a country where every man should eat in peace and drink in quiet, and specially obey us. Then the Chiefs come round to shake hands, and they were so hairy and white and fair it was just shaking hands with old friends. We gave them names according as they was like men we had known in India—Billy Fish, Holly Dilworth, Pikky Kergan, that was Bazaar-master when I was at Mhow, and so on, and so on.

"The most amazing miracles was at Lodge next night. One of the old priests was watching us continuous, and I felt uneasy, for I knew we'd have to fudge the Ritual, and I didn't know what the men knew. The old priest was a stranger come in from beyond the village of Bashkai. The minute Dravot puts on the Master's apron that the girls had made for him, the priest fetches a whoop and a howl, and tries to overturn the stone that Dravot was sitting on. 'It's all up now,' I says. 'That comes of meddling with the Craft without warrant!' Dravot never winked an eye, not when ten priests took and tilted over the Grand Master's chair—which was to say, the stone of Imbra. The priest begins rubbing the bottom end of it to clear away the black dirt, and presently he shows all the other priests the Master's Mark, same as was on Dravot's apron, cut into the stone. Not even the priests of the temple of Imbra knew it was there. The old chap falls flat on his face at Dravot's feet and kisses 'em. 'Luck again,' says Dravot, across the Lodge, to me; 'they say it's the missing Mark that no one could understand the why of.'

"'We're more than safe now.' Then he bangs the butt of his gun for a gavel and says, 'By virtue of the authority vested in me by my own right hand and the help of Peachey, I declare myself Grand Master of all Freemasonry in Kafiristan in this the Mother Lodge o' the country, and King of Kafiristan equally with Peachey!' At that he puts on his crown and I puts on mine,—I was doing Senior Warden,—and we opens the Lodge in most ample form. It was an amazing miracle! The priests moved in Lodge through the first two degrees almost without telling, as if the memory was coming back to them. After that Peachey and Dravot raised such as was worthy—high priests and Chiefs of far-off villages. Billy Fish was the first, and I can tell you we scared the soul out of him. It was not in any way according to Ritual, but it served our turn. We didn't raise more than ten of the biggest men, because we didn't want to make the Degree common. And they was clamouring to be raised.

"'In another six months,' says Dravot, 'we'll hold another Communication and see how you are working.' Then he asks them about their villages, and learns that they was fighting one against the other, and were sick and tired of it. And when they wasn't doing that they was fighting with the Mohammedans. 'You can fight those when they come into our country,' says Dravot. 'Tell off every tenth man of your tribes for a Frontier guard, and send two hundred at a time to this valley to be drilled. Nobody is going to be shot or speared any more so long as he does well, and I know that you won't cheat me, because you're white people—sons of Alexander—and not like common black Mohammedans. You are my people, and, by God,' says he, running off into English at the end, 'I'll make a damned fine Nation of you, or I'll die in the making!'

"I can't tell all we did for the next six months, because Dravot did a lot I couldn't see the hang of, and he learned their lingo in a way I never could. My work was to help the people plough, and now and again go out with some of the Army and see what the other villages were doing, and make 'em throw rope bridges across the ravines which cut up the country horrid. Dravot was very kind to me, but when he walked up and down in the pine wood pulling that bloody red beard of his with both fists I knew he was thinking plans I could not advise about, and I just waited for orders.

"But Dravot never showed me disrespect before the people. They were afraid of me and the Army, but they loved Dan. He was the best of friends with the priests and the Chiefs; but any one could come across the hills with a complaint, and Dravot would hear him out fair, and call four priests together and say what was to be done.

"He used to call in Billy Fish from Bashkai, and Pikky Kergan from Shu, and an old Chief we called Kafuzelum,—it was like enough to his real name,—and hold councils with 'em when there was any fighting to be done in small villages. That was his Council of War, and the four priests of Bashkai, Shu, Khawak, and Madora was his Privy Council. Between the lot of 'em they sent me, with forty men and twenty rifles, and sixty men carrying turquoises, into the Ghorband country to buy those hand-made Martini rifles, that come out of the Amir's workshops at Kabul, from one of the Amir's Herati regiments that would have sold the very teeth out of their mouths for turquoises.

"I stayed in Ghorband a month, and gave the Governor there the pick of my baskets for hush-money, and bribed the Colonel of the regiment some more, and, between the two and the tribes-people, we got more than a hundred hand-made Martinis, a hundred good Kohat Jezails that'll throw to six hundred yards, and forty man—loads of very bad ammunition for the rifles. I came back with what I had, and distributed 'em among the men that the Chiefs sent in to me to drill. Dravot was too busy to attend to those things, but the old Army that we first made helped me, and we turned out five hundred men that could drill, and two hundred that knew how to hold arms pretty straight. Even those cork-screwed, hand-made guns was a miracle to them. Dravot talked big about powder-shops and factories, walking up and down in the pine wood when the winter was coming on.

"'I won't make a Nation,' says he. 'I'll make an Empire! These men aren't niggers; they're English! Look at their eyes—look at their mouths. Look at the way they stand up. They sit on chairs in their own houses. They're the Lost Tribes, or something like it, and they've grown to be English. I'll take a census in the spring if the priests don't get frightened. There must be a fair two million of 'em in these hills. The villages are full o' little children. Two million people—two hundred and fifty thousand fighting men—and all English! They only want the rifles and a little drilling. Two hundred and fifty thousand men, ready to cut in on Russia's right flank when she tries for India! Peachey, man,' he says, chewing his beard in great hunks, 'we shall be Emperors—Emperors of the Earth! Rajah Brooke will be a suckling to us. I'll treat with the Viceroy on equal terms. I'll ask him to send me twelve picked English—twelve that I know of—to help us govern a bit. There's Mackray, Serjeant Pensioner at Segowli—many's the good dinner he's given me, and his wife a pair of trousers. There's Donkin, the Warder of Tounghoo Jail; there's hundreds that I could lay my hand on if I was in India. The Viceroy shall do it for me; I'll send a man through in the spring for those men, and I'll write for a dispensation from the Grand Lodge for what I've done as Grand Master. That—and all the Sniders that'll be thrown out when the native troops in India take up the Martini. They'll be worn smooth, but they'll do for fighting in these hills. Twelve English, a hundred thousand Sniders run through the Amir's country in driblets,—I'd be content with twenty thousand in one year,—and we'd be an Empire.

"When everything was shipshape I'd hand over the crown—this crown I'm wearing now—to

Queen Victoria on my knees, and she'd say, 'Rise up, Sir Daniel Dravot.' Oh, it's big! It's big, I tell you! But there's so much to be done in every place—Bashkai, Khawak, Shu, and everywhere else.

"'What is it?' I says. 'There are no more men coming in to be drilled this autumn. Look at those fat black clouds. They're bringing the snow.'

"'It isn't that,' says Daniel, putting his hand very hard on my shoulder; 'and I don't wish to say anything that's against you, for no other living man would have followed me and made me what I am as you have done. You're a first-class Commander-in-Chief, and the people know you; but—it's a big country, and somehow you can't help me, Peachey, in the way I want to be helped.'

"'Go to your blasted priests, then!' I said, and I was sorry when I made that remark, but it did hurt me sore to find Daniel talking so superior, when I'd drilled all the men and done all he told me.

"'Don't let's quarrel, Peachey,' says Daniel, without cursing. 'You're a King too, and the half of this Kingdom is yours; but can't you see, Peachey, we want cleverer men than us now—three or four of 'em, that we can scatter about for our Deputies. It's a hugeous great State, and I can't always tell the right thing to do, and I haven't time for all I want to do, and here's the winter coming on and all.'

"He put half his beard into his mouth, all red like the gold of his crown.

"'I'm sorry, Daniel,' says I. 'I've done all I could. I've drilled the men and shown the people how to stack their oats better; and I've brought in those tinware rifles from Ghorband—but I know what you're driving at. I take it Kings always feel oppressed that way.'

"'There's another thing too,' says Dravot, walking up and down. 'The winter's coming, and these people won't be giving much trouble, and if they do we can't move about. I want a wife.'

"'For Gord's sake leave the women alone!' I says. 'We've both got all the work we can, though I am a fool. Remember the Contrack, and keep clear o' women.'"

"'The Contrack only lasted till such time as we was Kings; and Kings we have been these months past,' says Dravot, weighing his crown in his hand. 'You go get a wife too, Peachey—a nice, strappin', plump girl that'll keep you warm in the winter. They're prettier than English girls, and we can take the pick of 'em. Boil 'em once or twice in hot water, and they'll come out like chicken and ham.'

"'Don't tempt me!' I says. 'I will not have any dealings with a woman, not till we are a dam' side more settled than we are now. I've been doing the work o' two men, and you've been doing the work of three. Let's lie off a bit, and see if we can get some better tobacco from Afghan country and run in some good liquor; and no women.'"

"'Who's talking o' women?' says Dravot. 'I said wife—a Queen to breed a King's son for the King. A Queen out of the strongest tribe, that'll make them your blood-brothers, and that'll lie by your side and tell you all the people thinks about you and their own affairs. That's what I want.'

"'Do you remember that Bengali woman I kept at Mogul Serai when I was a plate-layer?' says I. 'A fat lot o' good she was to me. She taught me the lingo and one or two other things; but what happened? She ran away with the Station-master's servant and half my month's pay. Then

she turned up at Dadur Junction in tow of a half-caste, and had the impidence to say I was her husband—all among the drivers in the running-shed too!'

"'We've done with that,' says Dravot; 'these women are whiter than you or me, and a Queen I will have for the winter months.'

"'For the last time o' asking, Dan, do not,' I says. 'It'll only bring us harm. The Bible says that Kings ain't to waste their strength on women, 'specially when they've got a new raw Kingdom to work over.'

"'For the last time of answering, I will,' said Dravot, and he went away through the pine trees looking like a big red devil, the sun being on his crown and beard and all.

"But getting a wife was not as easy as Dan thought. He put it before the Council, and there was no answer till Billy Fish said that he'd better ask the girls. Dravot damned them all round.

"'What's wrong with me?' he shouts, standing by the idol Imbra. 'Am I a dog, or am I not enough of a man for your wenches? Haven't I put the shadow of my hand over this country? Who stopped the last Afghan raid?' It was me really, but Dravot was too angry to remember. 'Who bought your guns? Who repaired the bridges? Who's the Grand Master of the sign cut in the stone?' says he, and he thumped his hand on the block that he used to sit on in Lodge, and at Council, which opened like Lodge always. Billy Fish said nothing, and no more did the others. 'Keep your hair on, Dan,' said I, 'and ask the girls. That's how it's done at Home, and these people are quite English.'

"'The marriage of the King is a matter of State,' says Dan, in a white-hot rage, for he could feel, I hope, that he was going against his better mind. He walked out of the Council-room, and the others sat still, looking at the ground.

"'Billy Fish,' says I to the Chief of Bashkai, 'what's the difficulty here? A straight answer to a true friend.'

"'You know,' says Billy Fish. 'How should a man tell you who knows everything? How can daughters of men marry Gods or Devils? It's not proper.'

"I remembered something like that in the Bible; but, if after seeing us as long as they had, they still believed we were Gods, it wasn't for me to undeceive them.

"'A God can do anything,' says I. 'If the King is fond of a girl he'll not let her die.' 'She'll have to,' said Billy Fish. 'There are all sorts of Gods and Devils in these mountains, and now and again a girl marries one of them and isn't seen any more. Besides, you two know the Mark cut in the stone. Only the Gods know that. We thought you were men till you showed the sign of the Master.'

"I wished then that we had explained about the loss of the genuine secrets of a Master Mason at the first go-off; but I said nothing. All that night there was a blowing of horns in a little dark temple half-way down the hill, and I heard the girl crying fit to die. One of the priests told us that she was being prepared to marry the King.

"'I'll have no nonsense of that kind,' says Dan. 'I don't want to interfere with your customs, but I'll take my own wife.' 'The girl's a little bit afraid,' says the priest. 'She thinks she's going to die, and they are a-heartening of her up down in the temple.'

"'Hearten her very tender, then,' says Dravot, 'or I'll hearten you with the butt of a gun so you'll never want to be heartened again.'

"He licked his lips, did Dan, and stayed up walking about more than half the night, thinking of the wife that he was going to get in the morning. I wasn't any means comfortable, for I knew that dealings with a woman in foreign parts, though you was a crowned King twenty times over, could not but be risky. I got up very early in the morning while Dravot was asleep, and I saw the priests talking together in whispers, and the Chiefs talking together too, and they looked at me out of the corners of their eyes.

"'What is up, Fish?' I say to the Bashkai man, who was wrapped up in his furs and looking splendid to behold.

"'I can't rightly say,' says he; 'but if you can make the King drop all this nonsense about marriage, you'll be doing him and me and yourself a great service.'

"'That I do believe,' says I. 'But sure, you know, Billy, as well as me, having fought against and for us, that the King and me are nothing more than two of the finest men that God Almighty ever made. Nothing more, I do assure you.'

"'That may be,' says Billy Fish, 'and yet I should be sorry if it was.' He sinks his head upon his great fur cloak for a minute and thinks. 'King,' says he, 'be you man or God or Devil, I'll stick by you today. I have twenty of my men with me, and they will follow me. We'll go to Bashkai until the storm blows over.'

"A little snow had fallen in the night, and everything was white except the greasy fat clouds that blew down and down from the north. Dravot came out with his crown on his head, swinging his arms and stamping his feet, and looking more pleased than Punch.

"'For the last time, drop it, Dan,' says I, in a whisper; 'Billy Fish here says that there will be a row.'

"'A row among my people!' says Dravot. 'Not much. Peachey, you're a fool not to get a wife too. Where's the girl?' says he, with a voice as loud as the braying of a jackass. 'Call up all the Chiefs and priests, and let the Emperor see if his wife suits him.'

"There was no need to call any one. They were all there leaning on their guns and spears round the clearing in the centre of the pine wood. A lot of priests went down to the little temple to bring up the girl, and the horns blew fit to wake the dead. Billy Fish saunters round and gets as close to Daniel as he could, and behind him stood his twenty men with matchlocks—not a man of them under six feet. I was next to Dravot, and behind me was twenty men of the regular Army. Up comes the girl, and a strapping wench she was, covered with silver and turquoises, but white as death, and looking back every minute at the priests.

"'She'll do,' said Dan, looking her over. 'What's to be afraid of, lass? Come and kiss me.' He puts his arm round her. She shuts her eyes, gives a bit of a squeak, and down goes her face in the side of Dan's flaming-red beard.

"'The slut's bitten me!' says he, clapping his hand to his neck, and, sure enough, his hand was red with blood. Billy Fish and two of his matchlock men catches hold of Dan by the shoulders and drags him into the Bashkai lot, while the priests howls in their lingo, 'Neither God nor Devil, but a man!' I was all taken aback, for a priest cut at me in front, and the Army behind began firing into the Bashkai men.

"'God A'mighty!' says Dan, 'what is the meaning o' this?'

"'Come back! Come away!' says Billy Fish. 'Ruin and Mutiny is the matter. We'll break for Bashkai if we can.'

"I tried to give some sort of orders to my men,—the men o' the regular Army,—but it was no use, so I fired into the brown of 'em with an English Martini and drilled three beggars in a line. The valley was full of shouting, howling creatures, and every soul was shrieking, 'Not a God nor a Devil, but only a man!' The Bashkai troops stuck to Billy Fish all they were worth, but their matchlocks wasn't half as good as the Kabul breech-loaders, and four of them dropped. Dan was bellowing like a bull, for he was very wrathy; and Billy Fish had a hard job to prevent him running out at the crowd.

"'We can't stand,' says Billy Fish. 'Make a run for it down the valley! The whole place is against us.' The matchlock-men ran, and we went down the valley in spite of Dravot. He was swearing horrible and crying out that he was a King. The priests rolled great stones on us, and the regular Army fired hard, and there wasn't more than six men, not counting Dan, Billy Fish, and Me, that came down to the bottom of the valley alive.

"Then they stopped firing, and the horns in the temple blew again.

"'Come away—for Gord's sake come away!' says Billy Fish. 'They'll send runners out to all the villages before ever we get to Bashkai. I can protect you there, but I can't do anything now.'"

"My own notion is that Dan began to go mad in his head from that hour. He stared up and down like a stuck pig. Then he was all for walking back alone and killing the priests with his bare hands; which he could have done. 'An Emperor am I,' says Daniel, 'and next year I shall be a Knight of the Queen.'

"'All right, Dan,' says I; 'but come along now while there's time.'

"'It's your fault,' says he, 'for not looking after your Army better. There was mutiny in the midst, and you didn't know—you damned engine-driving, plate-laying, missionary's-pass-hunting hound!' He sat upon a rock and called me every foul name he could lay tongue to. I was too heart-sick to care, though it was all his foolishness that brought the smash.

"'I'm sorry, Dan,' says I, 'but there's no accounting for natives. This business is our Fifty-seven. Maybe we'll make something out of it yet, when we've got to Bashkai.'

"'Let's get to Bashkai, then,' says Dan, 'and, by God, when I come back here again I'll sweep the valley so there isn't a bug in a blanket left!'

"We walked all that day, and all that night Dan was stumping up and down on the snow, chewing his beard and muttering to himself.

"'There's no hope o' getting clear,' said Billy Fish. 'The priests have sent runners to the villages to say that you are only men. Why didn't you stick on as Gods till things was more settled? I'm a dead man,' says Billy Fish, and he throws himself down on the snow and begins to pray to his Gods.

"Next morning we was in a cruel bad country—all up and down, no level ground at all, and no food, either. The six Bashkai men looked at Billy Fish hungry-way as if they wanted to ask something, but they never said a word. At noon we came to the top of a flat mountain all covered with snow, and when we climbed up into it, behold, there was an Army in position waiting in the middle!

"'The runners have been very quick,' says Billy Fish, with a little bit of a laugh. 'They are waiting for us.'

"Three or four men began to fire from the enemy's side, and a chance shot took Daniel in the

calf of the leg. That brought him to his senses. He looks across the snow at the Army, and sees the rifles that we had brought into the country.

"'We're done for,' says he. 'They are Englishmen, these people,—and it's my blasted nonsense that has brought you to this. Get back, Billy Fish, and take your men away; you've done what you could, and now cut for it. Carnehan,' says he, 'shake hands with me and go along with Billy, Maybe they won't kill you. I'll go and meet 'em alone. It's me that did it! Me, the King!'

"'Go!' says I. 'Go to Hell, Dan! I'm with you here. Billy Fish, you clear out, and we two will meet those folk.'

"'I'm a Chief,' says Billy Fish, quite quiet. 'I stay with you. My men can go.'

"The Bashkai fellows didn't wait for a second word, but ran off, and Dan and Me and Billy Fish walked across to where the drums were drumming and the horns were horning. It was cold—awful cold. I've got that cold in the back of my head now. There's a lump of it there."

The punka-coolies had gone to sleep. Two kerosene lamps were blazing in the office, and the perspiration poured down my face and splashed on the blotter as I leaned forward. Carnehan was shivering, and I feared that his mind might go. I wiped my face, took a fresh grip of the piteously mangled hands, and said, "What happened after that?"

The momentary shift of my eyes had broken the clear current.

"What was you pleased to say?" whined Carnehan. "They took them without any sound. Not a little whisper all along the snow, not though the King knocked down the first man that set hand on him—not though old Peachey fired his last cartridge into the brown of 'em. Not a single solitary sound did those swines make. They just closed up tight, and I tell you their furs stunk. There was a man called Billy Fish, a good friend of us all, and they cut his throat, Sir, then and there, like a pig; and the King kicks up the bloody snow and says, 'We've had a dashed fine run for our money. What's coming next?' But Peachey, Peachey Taliaferro, I tell you, Sir, in confidence as betwixt two friends, he lost his head, Sir. No, he didn't, neither. The King lost his head, so he did, all along o' one of those cunning rope bridges. Kindly let me have the paper-cutter, Sir. It tilted this way. They marched him a mile across that snow to a rope bridge over a ravine with a river at the bottom. You may have seen such. They prodded him behind like an ox. 'Damn your eyes!' says the King. 'D' you suppose I can't die like a gentleman?'

"He turns to Peachey—Peachey that was crying like a child. 'I've brought you to this, Peachey,' says he. 'Brought you out of your happy life to be killed in Kafiristan, where you was late Commander-in-Chief of the Emperor's forces. Say you forgive me, Peachey.' 'I do,' says Peachey. 'Fully and freely do I forgive you, Dan.' 'Shake hands, Peachey,' says he. 'I'm going now.' Out he goes, looking neither right nor left, and when he was plumb in the middle of those dizzy dancing ropes, 'Cut you beggars,' he shouts; and they cut, and old Dan fell, turning round and round and round, twenty thousand miles, for he took half an hour to fall till he struck the water, and I could see his body caught on a rock with the gold crown close beside.

"But do you know what they did to Peachey between two pine trees? They crucified him, Sir, as Peachey's hand will show. They used wooden pegs for his hands and feet; but he didn't die. He hung there and screamed, and they took him down next day, and said it was a miracle that he wasn't dead. They took him down—poor old Peachey that hadn't done them any harm—that hadn't done them any—"

He rocked to and fro and wept bitterly, wiping his eyes with the back of his scarred hands and moaning like a child for some ten minutes.

"They was cruel enough to feed him up in the temple, because they said he was more of a God than old Daniel that was a man. Then they turned him out on the snow, and told him to go home, and Peachey came home in about a year, begging along the roads quite safe; for Daniel Dravot he walked before and said, 'Come along, Peachey. It's a big thing we're doing.' The mountains they danced at night, and the mountains they tried to fall on Peachey's head, but Dan he held up his hand, and Peachey came along bent double. He never let go of Dan's hand, and he never let go of Dan's head. They gave it to him as a present in the temple, to remind him not to come again; and though the crown was pure gold and Peachey was starving, never would Peachey sell the same. You know Dravot, Sir! You knew Right Worshipful Brother Dravot! Look at him now!"

He fumbled in the mass of rags round his bent waist; brought out a black horsehair bag embroidered with silver thread; and shook therefrom on to my table—the dried, withered head of Daniel Dravot! The morning sun, that had long been paling the lamps, struck the red beard and blind sunken eyes; struck, too, a heavy circlet of gold studded with raw turquoises, that Carnehan placed tenderly on the battered temples.

"You be'old now," said Carnehan, "the Emperor in his 'abit as he lived—the King of Kafiristan with his crown upon his head. Poor old Daniel that was a monarch once!"

I shuddered, for, in spite of defacements manifold, I recognised the head of the man of Marwar Junction. Carnehan rose to go. I attempted to stop him. He was not fit to walk abroad. "Let me take away the whisky, and give me a little money," he gasped. "I was a King once. I'll go to the Deputy Commissioner and ask to set in the Poorhouse till I get my health. No, thank you, I can't wait till you get a carriage for me. I've urgent private affairs—in the south—at Marwar."

He shambled out of the office and departed in the direction of the Deputy Commissioner's house. That day at noon I had occasion to go down the blinding-hot Mall, and I saw a crooked man crawling along the white dust of the roadside, his hat in his hand, quavering dolorously after the fashion of street-singers at Home. There was not a soul in sight, and he was out of all possible earshot of the houses. And he sang through his nose, turning his head from right to left:

"The Son of Man goes forth to war,

A golden crown to gain;

His blood-red banner streams afar—

Who follows in His train?"

I waited to hear no more, but put the poor wretch into my carriage and drove him off to the nearest missionary for eventual transfer to the Asylum. He repeated the hymn twice while he was with me, whom he did not in the least recognise, and I left him singing it to the missionary.

Two days later I inquired after his welfare of the Superintendent of the Asylum.

"He was admitted suffering from sunstroke. He died early yesterday morning," said the Superintendent. "Is it true that he was half an hour bareheaded in the sun at midday?"

"Yes," said I; "but do you happen to know if he had anything upon him by any chance when he died?"

"Not to my knowledge," said the Superintendent.

And there the matter rests.

"THE FINEST STORY IN THE WORLD"

"O' ever the knightly years were gone

With the old world to the grave,

I was a king in Babylon

And you were a Christian slave."

—W. E. Henley.

His name was Charlie Mears; he was the only son of his mother who was a widow, and he lived in the north of London, coming into the City every day to work in a bank. He was twenty years old and suffered from aspirations. I met him in a public billiard-saloon where the marker called him by his given name, and he called the marker "Bulls-eyes." Charley explained, a little nervously, that he had only come to the place to look on, and since looking on at games of skill is not a cheap amusement for the young, I suggested that Charlie should go back to his mother.

That was our first step toward better acquaintance. He would call on me sometimes in the evenings instead of running about London with his fellow-clerks; and before long, speaking of himself as a young man must, he told me of his aspirations, which were all literary. He desired to make himself an undying name chiefly through verse, though he was not above sending stories of love and death to the drop-a-penny-in-the-slot journals. It was my fate to sit still while Charlie read me poems of many hundred lines, and bulky fragments of plays that would surely shake the world. My reward was his unreserved confidence, and the self-revelations and troubles of a young man are almost as holy as those of a maiden.

Charlie had never fallen in love, but was anxious to do so on the first opportunity; he believed in all things good and all things honorable, but, at the same time, was curiously careful to let me see that he knew his way about the world as befitted a bank clerk on twenty-five shillings a week. He rhymed "dove" with "love" and "moon" with "June," and devoutly believed that they had never so been rhymed before. The long lame gaps in his plays he filled up with hasty words of apology and description and swept on, seeing all that he intended to do so clearly that he esteemed it already done, and turned to me for applause.

I fancy that his mother did not encourage his aspirations, and I know that his writing-table at home was the edge of his washstand. This he told me almost at the outset of our acquaintance; when he was ravaging my bookshelves, and a little before I was implored to speak the truth as to his chances of "writing something really great, you know." Maybe I encouraged him too much, for, one night, he called on me, his eyes flaming with excitement, and said breathlessly:

"Do you mind—can you let me stay here and write all this evening? I won't interrupt you, I won't really. There's no place for me to write in at my mother's."

"What's the trouble?" I said, knowing well what that trouble was.

"I've a notion in my head that would make the most splendid story that was ever written. Do let me write it out here. It's such a notion!"

There was no resisting the appeal. I set him a table; he hardly thanked me, but plunged into the work at once. For half an hour the pen scratched without stopping. Then Charlie sighed and tugged his hair. The scratching grew slower, there were more erasures, and at last ceased. The

finest story in the world would not come forth.

"It looks such awful rot now" he said, mournfully. "And yet it seemed so good when I was thinking about it. What's wrong?"

I could not dishearten him by saying the truth. So I answered: "Perhaps you don't feel in the mood for writing."

"Yes I do—except when I look at this stuff. Ugh!"

"Read me what you've done," I said. He read, and it was wondrous bad and he paused at all the specially turgid sentences, expecting a little approval; for he was proud of those sentences, as I knew he would be.

"It needs compression," I suggested, cautiously.

"I hate cutting my things down. I don't think you could alter a word here without spoiling the sense. It reads better aloud than when I was writing it."

"Charlie, you're suffering from an alarming disease afflicting a numerous class. Put the thing by, and tackle it again in a week."

"I want to do it at once. What do you think of it?"

"How can I judge from a half-written tale? Tell me the story as it lies in your head."

Charlie told, and in the telling there was everything that his ignorance had so carefully prevented from escaping into the written word. I looked at him, and wondering whether it were possible, that he did not know the originality, the power of the notion that had come in his way? It was distinctly a Notion among notions. Men had been puffed up with pride by notions not a tithe as excellent and practicable. But Charlie babbled on serenely, interrupting the current of pure fancy with samples of horrible sentences that he purposed to use. I heard him out to the end. It would be folly to allow his idea to remain in his own inept hands, when I could do so much with it. Not all that could be done indeed; but, oh so much!

"What do you think?" he said, at last. "I fancy I shall call it 'The Story of a Ship.'"

"I think the idea's pretty good; but you won't Be able to handle it for ever so long. Now I—"

"Would it be of any use to you? Would you care to take it? I should be proud," said Charlie, promptly.

There are few things sweeter in this world than the guileless, hot-headed, intemperate, open admiration of a junior. Even a woman in her blindest devotion does not fall into the gait of the man she adores, tilt her bonnet to the angle at which he wears his hat, or interlard her speech with his pet oaths. And Charlie did all these things. Still it was necessary to salve my conscience before I possessed myself of Charlie's thoughts.

"Let's make a bargain. I'll give you a fiver for the notion," I said.

Charlie became a bank-clerk at once.

"Oh, that's impossible. Between two pals, you know, if I may call you so, and speaking as a man of the world, I couldn't. Take the notion if it's any use to you. I've heaps more."

He had—none knew this better than I—but they were the notions of other men.

"Look at it as a matter of business—between men of the world," I returned. "Five pounds will buy you any number of poetry-books. Business is business, and you may be sure I shouldn't give that price unless—"

"Oh, if you put it that way," said Charlie, visibly moved by the thought of the books. The bargain was clinched with an agreement that he should at unstated intervals come to me with all the notions that he possessed, should have a table of his own to write at, and unquestioned right to inflict upon me all his poems and fragments of poems. Then I said, "Now tell me how you came by this idea."

"It came by itself." Charlie's eyes opened a little.

"Yes, but you told me a great deal about the hero that you must have read before somewhere."

"I haven't any time for reading, except when you let me sit here, and on Sundays I'm on my bicycle or down the river all day. There's nothing wrong about the hero, is there?"

"Tell me again and I shall understand clearly. You say that your hero went pirating. How did he live?"

"He was on the lower deck of this ship-thing that I was telling you about."

"What sort of ship?"

"It was the kind rowed with oars, and the sea spurts through the oar-holes and the men row sitting up to their knees in water. Then there's a bench running down between the two lines of oars and an overseer with a whip walks up and down the bench to make the men work."

"How do you know that?"

"It's in the table. There's a rope running overhead, looped to the upper deck, for the overseer to catch hold of when the ship rolls. When the overseer misses the rope once and falls among the rowers, remember the hero laughs at him and gets licked for it. He's chained to his oar of course—the hero."

"How is he chained?"

"With an iron band round his waist fixed to the bench he sits on, and a sort of handcuff on his left wrist chaining him to the oar. He's on the lower deck where the worst men are sent, and the only light comes from the hatchways and through the oar-holes. Can't you imagine the sunlight just squeezing through between the handle and the hole and wobbling about as the ship moves?"

"I can, but I can't imagine your imagining it."

"How could it be any other way? Now you listen to me. The long oars on the upper deck are managed by four men to each bench, the lower ones by three, and the lowest of all by two. Remember it's quite dark on the lowest deck and all the men there go mad. When a man dies at his oar on that deck he isn't thrown overboard, but cut up in his chains and stuffed through the oar-hole in little pieces."

"Why?" I demanded, amazed, not so much at the information as the tone of command in which it was flung out.

"To save trouble and to frighten the others. It needs two overseers to drag a man's body up to the top deck; and if the men at the lower deck oars were left alone, of course they'd stop rowing

and try to pull up the benches by all standing up together in their chains."

"You've a most provident imagination. Where have you been reading about galleys and galley-slaves?"

"Nowhere that I remember. I row a little when I get the chance. But, perhaps, if you say so, I may have read something."

He went away shortly afterward to deal with booksellers, and I wondered how a bank clerk aged twenty could put into my hands with a profligate abundance of detail, all given with absolute assurance, the story of extravagant and bloodthirsty adventure, riot, piracy, and death in unnamed seas. He had led his hero a desperate dance through revolt against the overseas, to command of a ship of his own, and ultimate establishment of a kingdom on an island "somewhere in the sea, you know"; and, delighted with my paltry five pounds, had gone out to buy the notions of other men, that these might teach him how to write. I had the consolation of knowing that this notion was mine by right of purchase, and I thought that I could make something of it.

When next he came to me he was drunk—royally drunk on many poets for the first time revealed to him. His pupils were dilated, his words tumbled over each other, and he wrapped himself in quotations. Most of all was he drunk with Longfellow.

"Isn't it splendid? Isn't it superb?" he cried, after hasty greetings.

"Listen to this—

"'Wouldst thou,' so the helmsman answered, 'Know the secret of the sea? Only those who brave its dangers Comprehend its mystery.'

"By gum!

"'Only those who brave its dangers Comprehend its mystery.'" he repeated twenty times, walking up and down the room and forgetting me. "But I can understand it too," he said to himself. "I don't know how to thank you for that fiver. And this; listen—

"'I remember the black wharves and the ships And the sea-tides tossing free, And the Spanish sailors with bearded lips, And the beauty and mystery of the ships, And the magic of the sea.'

"I haven't braved any dangers, but I feel as if I knew all about it."

"You certainly seem to have a grip of the sea. Have you ever seen it?"

"When I was a little chap I went to Brighton once; we used to live in Coventry, though, before we came to London. I never saw it.

"'When descends on the Atlantic The gigantic Storm-wind of the Equinox.'"

He shook me by the shoulder to make me understand the passion that was shaking himself.

"When that storm comes," he continued, "I think that all the oars in the ship that I was talking about get broken, and the rowers have their chests smashed in by the bucking oar-heads. By the way, have you done anything with that notion of mine yet?"

"No. I was waiting to hear more of it from you. Tell me how in the world you're so certain about the fittings of the ship. You know nothing of ships."

"I don't know. It's as real as anything to me until I try to write it down. I was thinking about it

only last night in bed, after you had loaned me 'Treasure Island'; and I made up a whole lot of new things to go into the story."

"What sort of things?"

"About the food the men ate; rotten figs and black beans and wine in a skin bag, passed from bench to bench."

"Was the ship built so long ago as that?"

"As what? I don't know whether it was long ago or not. It's only a notion, but sometimes it seems just as real as if it was true. Do I bother you with talking about it?"

"Not in the least. Did you make up anything else?"

"Yes, but it's nonsense." Charlie flushed a little.

"Never mind; let's hear about it."

"Well, I was thinking over the story, and after awhile I got out of bed and wrote down on a piece of paper the sort of stuff the men might be supposed to scratch on their oars with the edges of their handcuffs. It seemed to make the thing more lifelike. It is so real to me, y'know."

"Have you the paper on you?"

"Ye-es, but what's the use of showing it? It's only a lot of scratches. All the same, we might have 'em reproduced in the book on the front page."

"I'll attend to those details. Show me what your men wrote."

He pulled out of his pocket a sheet of note-paper, with a single line of scratches upon it, and I put this carefully away.

"What is it supposed to mean in English?" I said.

"Oh, I don't know. Perhaps it means 'I'm beastly tired.' It's great nonsense," he repeated, "but all those men in the ship seem as real people to me. Do do something to the notion soon; I should like to see it written and printed."

"But all you've told me would make a long book."

"Make it then. You've only to sit down and write it out."

"Give me a little time. Have you any more notions?"

"Not just now. I'm reading all the books I've bought. They're splendid."

When he had left I looked at the sheet of note-paper with the inscription upon it. Then I took my head tenderly between both hands, to make certain that it was not coming off or turning round.

Then—but there seemed to be no interval between quitting my rooms and finding myself arguing with a policeman outside a door marked Private in a corridor of the British Museum. All I demanded, as politely as possible, was "the Greek antiquity man." The policeman knew nothing except the rules of the Museum, and it became necessary to forage through all the houses and offices inside the gates. An elderly gentleman called away from his lunch put an end to my search by holding the note-paper between finger and thumb and sniffing at it scornfully.

"What does this mean? H'mm," said he. "So far as I can ascertain it is an attempt to write extremely corrupt Greek on the part"—here he glared at me with intention—"of an extremely illiterate—ah—person." He read slowly from the paper, "Pollock, Erckman, Tauchnitz, Henniker"—four names familiar to me.

"Can you tell me what the corruption is supposed to mean—the gist of the thing?" I asked.

"'I have been—many times—overcome with weariness in this particular employment. That is the meaning.'" He returned me the paper, and I fled without a word of thanks, explanation, or apology.

I might have been excused for forgetting much. To me of all men had been given the chance to write the most marvelous tale in the world, nothing less than the story of a Greek galley-slave, as told by himself. Small wonder that his dreaming had seemed real to Charlie. The Fates that are so careful to shut the doors of each successive life behind us had, in this case, been neglectful, and Charlie was looking, though that he did not know, where never man had been permitted to look with full knowledge since Time began. Above all he was absolutely ignorant of the knowledge sold to me for five pounds; and he would retain that ignorance, for bank-clerks do not understand metempsychosis, and a sound commercial education does not include Greek. He would supply me—here I capered among the dumb gods of Egypt and laughed in their battered faces—with material to make my tale sure—so sure that the world would hail it as an impudent and vamped fiction. And I—I alone would know that it was absolutely and literally true. I alone held this jewel to my hand for the cutting and polishing.

Therefore I danced again among the gods till a policeman saw me and took steps in my direction.

It remained now only to encourage Charlie to talk, and here there was no difficulty. But I had forgotten those accursed books of poetry. He came to me time after time, as useless as a surcharged phonograph—drunk on Byron, Shelley, or Keats. Knowing now what the boy had been in his past lives, and desperately anxious not to lose one word of his babble, I could not hide from him my respect and interest. He misconstrued both into respect for the present soul of Charlie Mears, to whom life was as new as it was to Adam, and interest in his readings; and stretched my patience to breaking point by reciting poetry—not his own now, but that of others. I wished every English poet blotted out of the memory of mankind. I blasphemed the mightiest names of song because they had drawn Charlie from the path of direct narrative, and would, later, spur him to imitate them; but I choked down my impatience until the first flood of enthusiasm should have spent itself and the boy returned to his dreams.

"What's the use of my telling you what I think, when these chaps wrote things for the angels to read?" he growled, one evening. "Why don't you write something like theirs?"

"I don't think you're treating me quite fairly," I said, speaking under strong restraint.

"I've given you the story," he said, shortly replunging into "Lara."

"But I want the details."

"The things I make up about that damned ship that you call a galley? They're quite easy. You can just make 'em up yourself. Turn up the gas a little, I want to go on reading."

I could have broken the gas globe over his head for his amazing stupidity. I could indeed make up things for myself did I only know what Charlie did not know that he knew. But since the doors were shut behind me I could only wait his youthful pleasure and strive to keep him in good temper. One minute's want of guard might spoil a priceless revelation: now and again

he would toss his books aside—he kept them in my rooms, for his mother would have been shocked at the waste of good money had she seen them—and launched into his sea dreams. Again I cursed all the poets of England. The plastic mind of the bank-clerk had been overlaid, colored and distorted by that which he had read, and the result as delivered was a confused tangle of other voices most like the muttered song through a City telephone in the busiest part of the day.

He talked of the galley—his own galley had he but known it—with illustrations borrowed from the "Bride of Abydos." He pointed the experiences of his hero with quotations from "The Corsair," and threw in deep and desperate moral reflections from "Cain" and "Manfred," expecting me to use them all. Only when the talk turned on Longfellow were the jarring cross-currents dumb, and I knew that Charlie was speaking the truth as he remembered it.

"What do you think of this?" I said one evening, as soon as I understood the medium in which his memory worked best, and, before he could expostulate read him the whole of "The Saga of King Olaf!"

He listened open-mouthed, flushed his hands drumming on the back of the sofa where he lay, till I came to the Songs of Emar Tamberskelver and the verse:

"Emar then, the arrow taking From the loosened string, Answered: 'That was Norway breaking 'Neath thy hand, O King.'"

He gasped with pure delight of sound.

"That's better than Byron, a little," I ventured.

"Better? Why it's true! How could he have known?"

I went back and repeated:

"'What was that?' said Olaf, standing

On the quarter-deck,

'Something heard I like the stranding

Of a shattered wreck.'"

"How could he have known how the ships crash and the oars rip out and go z-zzp all along the line? Why only the other night—But go back please and read 'The Skerry of Shrieks' again."

"No, I'm tired. Let's talk. What happened the other night?"

"I had an awful nightmare about that galley of ours. I dreamed I was drowned in a fight. You see we ran alongside another ship in harbor. The water was dead still except where our oars whipped it up. You know where I always sit in the galley?" He spoke haltingly at first, under a fine English fear of being laughed at.

"No. That's news to me," I answered, meekly, my heart beginning to beat.

"On the fourth oar from the bow on the right side on the upper deck. There were four of us at the oar, all chained. I remember watching the water and trying to get my handcuffs off before the row began. Then we closed up on the other ship, and all their fighting men jumped over our

bulwarks, and my bench broke and I was pinned down with the three other fellows on top of me, and the big oar jammed across our backs."

"Well?" Charlie's eyes were alive and alight. He was looking at the wall behind my chair.

"I don't know how we fought. The men were trampling all over my back, and I lay low. Then our rowers on the left side—tied to their oars, you know—began to yell and back water. I could hear the water sizzle, and we spun round like a cockchafer and I knew, lying where I was, that there was a galley coming up bow-on, to ram us on the left side. I could just lift up my head and see her sail over the bulwarks. We wanted to meet her bow to bow, but it was too late. We could only turn a little bit because the galley on our right had hooked herself on to us and stopped our moving. Then, by gum! there was a crash! Our left oars began to break as the other galley, the moving one y'know, stuck her nose into them. Then the lower-deck oars shot up through the deck-planking, butt first, and one of them jumped clean up into the air and came down again close to my head."

"How was that managed?"

"The moving galley's bow was plunking them back through their own oarholes, and I could hear the devil of a shindy in the decks below. Then her nose caught us nearly in the middle, and we tilted sideways, and the fellows in the right-hand galley unhitched their hooks and ropes, and threw things on to our upper deck—arrows, and hot pitch or something that stung, and we went up and up and up on the left side, and the right side dipped, and I twisted my head round and saw the water stand still as it topped the right bulwarks, and then it curled over and crashed down on the whole lot of us on the right side, and I felt it hit my back, and I woke."

"One minute, Charlie. When the sea topped the bulwarks, what did it look like?" I had my reasons for asking. A man of my acquaintance had once gone down with a leaking ship in a still sea, and had seen the water-level pause for an instant ere it fell on the deck.

"It looked just like a banjo-string drawn tight, and it seemed to stay there for years," said Charlie.

Exactly! The other man had said: "It looked like a silver wire laid down along the bulwarks, and I thought it was never going to break." He had paid everything except the bare life for this little valueless piece of knowledge, and I had traveled ten thousand weary miles to meet him and take his knowledge at second hand. But Charlie, the bank-clerk, on twenty-five shillings a week, he who had never been out of sight of a London omnibus, knew it all. It was no consolation to me that once in his lives he had been forced to die for his gains. I also must have died scores of times, but behind me, because I could have used my knowledge, the doors were shut.

"And then?" I said, trying to put away the devil of envy.

"The funny thing was, though, in all the mess I didn't feel a bit astonished or frightened. It seemed as if I'd been in a good many fights, because I told my next man so when the row began. But that cad of an overseer on my deck wouldn't unloose our chains and give us a chance. He always said that we'd all Be set free after a battle, but we never were; We never were." Charlie shook his head mournfully.

"What a scoundrel!"

"I should say he was. He never gave us enough to eat, and sometimes we were so thirsty that we used to drink salt-water. I can taste that salt-water still.''

"Now tell me something about the harbor where the fight was fought."

"I didn't dream about that. I know it was a harbor, though; because we were tied up to a ring on a white wall and all the face of the stone under water was covered with wood to prevent our ram getting chipped when the tide made us rock."

"That's curious. Our hero commanded the galley? Didn't he?"

"Didn't he just! He stood by the bows and shouted like a good 'un. He was the man who killed the overseer."

"But you were all drowned together, Charlie, weren't you?"

"I can't make that fit quite," he said with a puzzled look. "The galley must have gone down with all hands and yet I fancy that the hero went on living afterward. Perhaps he climbed into the attacking ship. I wouldn't see that, of course. I was dead, you know."

He shivered slightly and protested that he could remember no more.

I did not press him further, but to satisfy myself that he lay in ignorance of the workings of his own mind, deliberately introduced him to Mortimer Collins's "Transmigration," and gave him a sketch of the plot before he opened the pages.

"What rot it all is!" he said, frankly, at the end of an hour. "I don't understand his nonsense about the Red Planet Mars and the King, and the rest of it. Chuck me the Longfellow again."

I handed him the book and wrote out as much as I could remember of his description of the sea-fight, appealing to him from time to time for confirmation of fact or detail. He would answer without raising his eyes from the book, as assuredly as though all his knowledge lay before flint on the printed page. I spoke under the normal key of my voice that the current might not be broken, and I know that he was not aware of what he was saying, for his thoughts were out on the sea with Longfellow.

"Charlie," I asked, "when the rowers on the galleys mutinied how did they kill their overseers?"

"Tore up the benches and brained 'em. That happened when a heavy sea was running. An overseer on the lower deck slipped from the centre plank and fell among the rowers. They choked him to death against the side of the ship with their chained hands quite quietly, and it was too dark for the other overseer to see what had happened. When he asked, he was pulled down too and choked, and the lower deck fought their way up deck by deck, with the pieces of the broken benches banging behind 'em. How they howled!"

"And what happened after that?"

"I don't know. The hero went away—red hair and red beard and all. That was after he had captured our galley, I think."

The sound of my voice irritated him, and he motioned slightly with his left hand as a man does when interruption jars.

"You never told me he was redheaded before, or that he captured your galley," I said, after a discreet interval.

Charlie did not raise his eyes.

"He was as red as a red bear," said he, abstractedly. "He came from the north; they said so in the galley when he looked for rowers—not slaves, but free men. Afterward—years and years afterward—news came from another ship, or else he came back"—His lips moved in silence. He was rapturously retasting some poem before him.

"Where had he been, then?" I was almost whispering that the sentence might come gentle to whichever section of Charlie's brain was working on my behalf.

"To the Beaches—the Long and Wonderful Beaches!" was the reply, after a minute of silence.

"To Furdurstrandi?" I asked, tingling from head to foot.

"Yes, to Furdurstrandi," he pronounced the word in a new fashion "And I too saw"—The voice failed.

"Do you know what you have said?" I shouted, incautiously.

He lifted his eyes, fully roused now. "No!" he snapped. "I wish you'd let a chap go on reading. Hark to this:

"'But Othere, the old sea captain, He neither paused nor stirred Till the king listened, and then

Once more took up his pen

And wrote down every word.

"'And to the King of the Saxons

In witness of the truth,

Raising his noble head,

He stretched his brown hand and said,

"Behold this walrus tooth.""

"By Jove, what chaps those must have been, to go sailing all over the shop never knowing where they'd fetch the land! Hah!"

"Charlie," I pleaded, "if you'll only be sensible for a minute or two I'll make our hero in our tale every inch as good as Othere."

"Umph! Longfellow wrote that poem. I don't care about writing things any more. I want to read." He was thoroughly out of tune now, and raging over my own ill-luck, I left him.

Conceive yourself at the door of the world's treasure-house guarded by a child—an idle irresponsible child playing knuckle-bones—on whose favor depends the gift of the key, and you will imagine one-half my torment. Till that evening Charlie had spoken nothing that might not lie within the experiences of a Greek galley-slave. But now, or there was no virtue in books, he had talked of some desperate adventure of the Vikings, of Thorfin Karlsefne's sailing to Wineland, which is America, in the ninth or tenth century. The battle in the harbor he had seen; and his own death he had described. But this was a much more startling plunge into the past.

Was it possible that he had skipped half a dozen lives and was then dimly remembering some episode of a thousand years later? It was a maddening jumble, and the worst of it was that Charlie Mears in his normal condition was the last person in the world to clear it up. I could only wait and watch, but I went to bed that night full of the wildest imaginings. There was nothing that was not possible if Charlie's detestable memory only held good.

I might rewrite the Saga of Thorfin Karlsefne as it had never been written before, might tell the story of the first discovery of America, myself the discoverer. But I was entirely at Charlie's mercy, and so long as there was a three-and-six-penny Bohn volume within his reach Charlie would not tell. I dared not curse him openly; I hardly dared jog his memory, for I was dealing with the experiences of a thousand years ago, told through the mouth of a boy of today; and a boy of today is affected by every change of tone and gust of opinion, so that he lies even when he desires to speak the truth.

I saw no more of him for nearly a week. When next I met him it was in Gracechurch Street with a billbook chained to his waist.

Business took him over London Bridge and I accompanied him. He was very full of the importance of that book and magnified it.

As we passed over the Thames we paused to look at a steamer unloading great slabs of white and brown marble. A barge drifted under the steamer's stern and a lonely cow in that barge bellowed.

Charlie's face changed from the face of the bank-clerk to that of an unknown and—though he would not have believed this—a much shrewder man. He flung out his arm across the parapet of the bridge, and laughing very loudly, said: "When they heard our bulls bellow the Skroelings ran away!"

I waited only for an instant, but the barge and the cow had disappeared under the bows of the steamer before I answered.

"Charlie, what do you suppose are Skroelings?"

"Never heard of 'em before. They sound like a new kind of seagull. What a chap you are for asking questions!" he replied. "I have to go to the cashier of the Omnibus Company yonder. Will you wait for me and we can lunch somewhere together? I've a notion for a poem."

"No, thanks. I'm off. You're sure you know nothing about Skroelings?"

"Not unless he's been entered for the Liverpool Handicap." He nodded and disappeared in the crowd.

Now it is written in the Saga of Eric the Red or that of Thorfin Karlsefne, that nine hundred years ago when Karlsefne's galleys came to Leif's booths, which Leif had erected in the unknown land called Markland, which may or may not have been Rhode Island, the Skroelings—and the Lord He knows who these may or may not have been—came to trade with the Vikings, and ran away because they were frightened at the bellowing of the cattle which Thorfin had brought with him in the ships. But what in the world could a Greek slave know of that affair? I wandered up and down among the streets trying to unravel the mystery, and the more I considered it, the more baffling it grew. One thing only seemed certain and that certainty took away my breath for the moment. If I came to full knowledge of anything at all, it would not be one life of the soul in Charlie Mears's body, but half a dozen—half a dozen several and separate existences spent on blue water in the morning of the world!

Then I walked round the situation.

Obviously if I used my knowledge I should stand alone and unapproachable until all men were as wise as myself. That would be something, but manlike I was ungrateful. It seemed bitterly unfair that Charlie's memory should fail me when I needed it most.

Great Powers above—I looked up at them through the fog smoke—did the Lords of Life and Death know what this meant to me? Nothing less than eternal fame of the best kind; that comes from One, and is shared by one alone. I would be content—remembering Clive, I stood astounded at my own moderation,—with the mere right to tell one story, to work out one little contribution to the light literature of the day. If Charlie were permitted full recollection for one hour—for sixty short minutes—of existences that had extended over a thousand years—I would forego all profit and honor from all that I should make of his speech. I would take no share in the commotion that would follow throughout the particular corner of the earth that calls itself "the world." The thing should be put forth anonymously. Nay, I would make other men believe that they had written it. They would hire bull-hided self-advertising Englishmen to bellow it abroad. Preachers would found a fresh conduct of life upon it, swearing that it was new and that they had lifted the fear of death from all mankind. Every Orientalist in Europe would patronize it discursively with Sanskrit and Pali texts. Terrible women would invent unclean variants of the men's belief for the elevation of their sisters. Churches and religions would war over it. Between the hailing and re-starting of an omnibus I foresaw the scuffles that would arise among half a dozen denominations all professing "the doctrine of the True Metempsychosis as applied to the world and the New Era"; and saw, too, the respectable English newspapers shying, like frightened kine, over the beautiful simplicity of the tale. The mind leaped forward a hundred—two hundred—a thousand years. I saw with sorrow that men would mutilate and garble the story; that rival creeds would turn it upside down till, at last, the western world which clings to the dread of death more closely than the hope of life, would set it aside as an interesting superstition and stampede after some faith so long forgotten that it seemed altogether new. Upon this I changed the terms of the bargain that I would make with the Lords of Life and Death. Only let me know, let me write, the story with sure knowledge that I wrote the truth, and I would burn the manuscript as a solemn sacrifice. Five minutes after the last line was written I would destroy it all. But I must be allowed to write it with absolute certainty.

There was no answer. The flaming colors of an Aquarium poster caught my eye and I wondered whether it would be wise or prudent to lure Charlie into the hands of the professional mesmerist, and whether, if he were under his power, he would speak of his past lives. If he did, and if people believed him—but Charlie would be frightened and flustered, or made conceited by the interviews. In either case he would begin to lie, through fear or vanity. He was safest in my own hands.

"They are very funny fools, your English," said a voice at my elbow, and turning round I recognized a casual acquaintance, a young Bengali law student, called Grish Chunder, whose father had sent him to England to become civilized. The old man was a retired native official, and on an income of five pounds a month contrived to allow his son two hundred pounds a year, and the run of his teeth in a city where he could pretend to be the cadet of a royal house, and tell stories of the brutal Indian bureaucrats who ground the faces of the poor.

Grish Chunder was a young, fat, full-bodied Bengali dressed with scrupulous care in frock coat, tall hat, light trousers and tan gloves. But I had known him in the days when the brutal Indian Government paid for his university education, and he contributed cheap sedition to Sachi Durpan, and intrigued with the wives of his schoolmates.

"That is very funny and very foolish," he said, nodding at the poster. "I am going down to the

Northbrook Club. Will you come too?"

I walked with him for some time. "You are not well," he said. "What is there in your mind? You do not talk."

"Grish Chunder, you've been too well educated to believe in a God, haven't you?"

"Oah, yes, here! But when I go home I must conciliate popular superstition, and make ceremonies of purification, and my women will anoint idols."

"And bang up tulsi and feast the purohit, and take you back into caste again and make a good khuttri of you again, you advanced social Free-thinker. And you'll eat desi food, and like it all, from the smell in the courtyard to the mustard oil over you."

"I shall very much like it," said Grish Chunder, unguardedly. "Once a Hindu—always a Hindu. But I like to know what the English think they know."

"I'll tell you something that one Englishman knows. It's an old tale to you."

I began to tell the story of Charlie in English, but Grish Chunder put a question in the vernacular, and the history went forward naturally in the tongue best suited for its telling. After all it could never have been told in English. Grish Chunder heard me, nodding from time to time, and then came up to my rooms where I finished the tale.

"Beshak," he said, philosophically. "Lekin darwaza band hai. (Without doubt, but the door is shut.) I have heard of this remembering of previous existences among my people. It is of course an old tale with us, but, to happen to an Englishman—a cow-fed Malechk—an outcast. By Jove, that is most peculiar!"

"Outcast yourself, Grish Chunder! You eat cow-beef every day. Let's think the thing over. The boy remembers his incarnations."

"Does he know that?" said Grish Chunder, quietly, swinging his legs as he sat on my table. He was speaking in English now.

"He does not know anything. Would I speak to you if he did? Go on!"

"There is no going on at all. If you tell that to your friends they will say you are mad and put it in the papers. Suppose, now, you prosecute for libel."

"Let's leave that out of the question entirely. Is there any chance of his being made to speak?"

"There is a chance. Oah, yess! But if he spoke it would mean that all this world would end now—instanto—fall down on your head. These things are not allowed, you know. As I said, the door is shut."

"Not a ghost of a chance?"

"How can there be? You are a Christian, and it is forbidden to eat, in your books, of the Tree of Life, or else you would never die. How shall you all fear death if you all know what your friend does not know that he knows? I am afraid to be kicked, but I am not afraid to die, because I know what I know. You are not afraid to be kicked, but you are afraid to die. If you were not, by God! you English would be all over the shop in an hour, upsetting the balances of power, and making commotions. It would not be good. But no fear. He will remember a little and a little less, and he will call it dreams. Then he will forget altogether. When I passed my First

Arts Examination in Calcutta that was all in the cram-book on Wordsworth. Trailing clouds of glory, you know."

"This seems to be an exception to the rule."

"There are no exceptions to rules. Some are not so hard-looking as others, but they are all the same when you touch. If this friend of yours said so-and-so and so-and-so, indicating that he remembered all his lost lives, or one piece of a lost life, he would not be in the bank another hour. He would be what you called sack because he was mad, and they would send him to an asylum for lunatics. You can see that, my friend."

"Of course I can, but I wasn't thinking of him. His name need never appear in the story."

"Ah! I see. That story will never be written. You can try."

"I am going to."

"For your own credit and for the sake of money, of course?"

"No. For the sake of writing the story. On my honor that will be all."

"Even then there is no chance. You cannot play with the Gods. It is a very pretty story now. As they say, Let it go on that—I mean at that. Be quick; he will not last long."

"How do you mean?"

"What I say. He has never, so far, thought about a woman."

"Hasn't he though!" I remembered some of Charlie's confidences.

"I mean no woman has thought about him. When that comes; bushogya—all up' I know. There are millions of women here. Housemaids, for instance."

I winced at the thought of my story being ruined by a housemaid.

And yet nothing was more probable.

Grish Chunder grinned.

"Yes—also pretty girls—cousins of his house, and perhaps not of his house. One kiss that he gives back again and remembers will cure all this nonsense or else"—

"Or else what? Remember he does not know that he knows."

"I know that. Or else, if nothing happens he will become immersed in the trade and the financial speculations like the rest. It must be so. You can see that it must be so. But the woman will come first, I think."

There was a rap at the door, and Charlie charged in impetuously. He had been released from office, and by the look in his eyes I could see that he had come over for a long talk; most probably with poems in his pockets. Charlie's poems were very wearying, but sometimes they led him to talk about the galley.

Grish Chunder looked at him keenly for a minute.

"I beg your pardon," Charlie said, uneasily; "I didn't know you had any one with you."

"I am going," said Grish Chunder.

He drew me into the lobby as he departed.

"That is your man," he said, quickly. "I tell you he will never speak all you wish. That is rot—bosh. But he would be most good to make to see things. Suppose now we pretend that it was only play"—I had never seen Grish Chunder so excited—"and pour the ink-pool into his hand. Eh, what do you think? I tell you that he could see anything that a man could see. Let me get the ink and the camphor. He is a seer and he will tell us very many things."

"He may be all you say, but I'm not going to trust him to your Gods and devils."

"It will not hurt him. He will only feel a little stupid and dull when he wakes up. You have seen boys look into the ink-pool before."

"That is the reason why I am not going to see it any more. You'd better go, Grish Chunder."

He went, declaring far down the staircase that it was throwing away my only chance of looking into the future.

This left me unmoved, for I was concerned for the past, and no peering of hypnotized boys into mirrors and ink-pools would help me do that. But I recognized Grish Chunder's point of view and sympathized with it.

"What a big black brute that was!" said Charlie, when I returned to him. "Well, look here, I've just done a poem; dil it instead of playing dominoes after lunch. May I read it?"

"Let me read it to myself."

"Then you miss the proper expression. Besides, you always make my things sound as if the rhymes were all wrong."

"Read it aloud, then. You're like the rest of 'em."

Charlie mouthed me his poem, and it was not much worse than the average of his verses. He had been reading his book faithfully, but he was not pleased when I told him that I preferred my Longfellow undiluted with Charlie.

Then we began to go through the MS. line by line; Charlie parrying every objection and correction with: "Yes, that may be better, but you don't catch what I'm driving at."

Charlie was, in one way at least, very like one kind of poet.

There was a pencil scrawl at the back of the paper and "What's that?" I said.

"Oh that's not poetry 't all. It's some rot I wrote last night before I went to bed and it was too much bother to hunt for rhymes; so I made it a sort of a blank verse instead."

Here is Charlie's "blank verse":

"We pulled for you when the wind was against us and the sails were low.

"Will you never let us go?

"We ate bread and onions when you took towns or ran aboard quickly when you were beaten back by the foe,

"The captains walked up and down the deck in fair weather singing songs, but we were below,

"We fainted with our chins on the oars and you did not see that we were idle for we still swung to and fro.

"Will you never let us go?

"The salt made the oar handles like sharkskin; our knees were cut to the bone with salt cracks; our hair was stuck to our foreheads; and our lips were cut to our gums and you whipped us because we could not row.

"Will you never let us go?

"But in a little time we shall run out of the portholes as the water runs along the oarblade, and though you tell the others to row after us you will never catch us till you catch the oar-thresh and tie up the winds in the belly of the sail. Aho! "Will you never let us go?"

"H'm. What's oar-thresh, Charlie?"

"The water washed up by the oars. That's the sort of song they might sing in the galley, y'know. Aren't you ever going to finish that story and give me some of the profits?"

"It depends on yourself. If you had only told me more about your hero in the first instance it might have been finished by now. You're so hazy in your notions."

"I only want to give you the general notion of it—the knocking about from place to place and the fighting and all that. Can't you fill in the rest yourself? Make the hero save a girl on a pirate-galley and marry her or do something."

"You're a really helpful collaborator. I suppose the hero went through some few adventures before he married."

"Well then, make him a very artful card—a low sort of man—a sort of political man who went about making treaties and breaking them—a black-haired chap who hid behind the mast when the fighting began."

"But you said the other day that he was red-haired."

"I couldn't have. Make him black-haired of course. You've no imagination."

Seeing that I had just discovered the entire principles upon which the half-memory falsely called imagination is based, I felt entitled to laugh, but forbore, for the sake of the tale.

"You're right. You're the man with imagination. A black-haired chap in a decked ship," I said.

"No, an open ship—like a big boat."

This was maddening.

"Your ship has been built and designed, closed and decked in; you said so yourself," I protested.

"No, no, not that ship. That was open, or half decked because—By Jove you're right. You made me think of the hero as a red-haired chap. Of course if he were red, the ship would be an open one with painted sails."

Surely, I thought he would remember now that he had served in two galleys at least—in a

three-decked Greek one under the black-haired "political man," and again in a Viking's open sea-serpent under the man "red as a red bear" who went to Markland. The devil prompted me to speak.

"Why, 'of course,' Charlie?" said I. "I don't know. Are you making fun of me?"

The current was broken for the time being. I took up a notebook and pretended to make many entries in it.

"It's a pleasure to work with an imaginative chap like yourself," I said after a pause. "The way that you've brought out the character of the hero is simply wonderful."

"Do you think so?" he answered, with a pleased flush. "I often tell myself that there's more in me than my—than people think."

"There's an enormous amount in you."

"Then, won't you let me send an essay on The Ways of Bank Clerks to Tit-Bits, and get the guinea prize?"

"That wasn't exactly what I meant, old fellow: perhaps it would be better to wait a little and go ahead with the galley-story."

"Ah, but I sha'n't get the credit of that. Tit-Bits would publish my name and address if I win. What are you grinning at? They would."

"I know it. Suppose you go for a walk. I want to look through my notes about our story."

Now this reprehensible youth who left me, a little hurt and put back, might for aught he or I knew have been one of the crew of the Argo—had been certainly slave or comrade to Thorfin Karlsefne. Therefore he was deeply interested in guinea competitions. Remembering what Grish Chunder had said I laughed aloud. The Lords of Life and Death would never allow Charlie Mears to speak with full knowledge of his pasts, and I must even piece out what he had told me with my own poor inventions while Charlie wrote of the ways of bank-clerks.

I got together and placed on one file all my notes; and the net result was not cheering. I read them a second time. There was nothing that might not have been compiled at second-hand from other people's books—except, perhaps, the story of the fight in the harbor. The adventures of a Viking bad been written many times before; the history of a Greek galley-slave was no new thing, and though I wrote both, who could challenge or confirm the accuracy of my details? I might as well tell a tale of two thousand years hence. The Lords of Life and Death were as cunning as Grish Chunder had hinted. They would allow nothing to escape that might trouble or make easy the minds of men. Though I was convinced of this, yet I could not leave the tale alone. Exaltation followed reaction, not once, but twenty times in the next few weeks. My moods varied with the March sunlight and flying clouds. By night or in the beauty of a spring morning I perceived that I could write that tale and shift continents thereby. In the wet, windy afternoons, I saw that the tale might indeed be written, but would be nothing more than a faked, false-varnished, sham-rusted piece of Wardour Street work at the end. Then I blessed Charlie in many ways—though it was no fault of his. He seemed to be busy with prize competitions, and I saw less and less of him as the weeks went by and the earth cracked and grew ripe to spring, and the buds swelled in their sheaths. He did not care to read or talk of what he had read, and there was a new ring of self-assertion in his voice. I hardly cared to remind him of the galley when we met; but Charlie alluded to it on every occasion, always as a story from which money was to be made.

"I think I deserve twenty-five per cent., don't I, at least," he said, with beautiful frankness. "I supplied all the ideas, didn't I?"

This greediness for silver was a new side in his nature. I assumed that it had been developed in the City, where Charlie was picking up the curious nasal drawl of the underbred City man.

"When the thing's done we'll talk about it. I can't make anything of it at present. Red-haired or black-haired hero are equally difficult."

He was sitting by the fire staring at the red coals. "I can't understand what you find so difficult. It's all as clean as mud to me," he replied. A jet of gas puffed out between the bars, took light and whistled softly. "Suppose we take the red-haired hero's adventures first, from the time that he came south to my galley and captured it and sailed to the Beaches."

I knew better now than to interrupt Charlie. I was out of reach of pen and paper, and dared not move to get them lest I should break the current. The gas-jet puffed and whinnied, Charlie's voice dropped almost to a whisper, and he told a tale of the sailing of an open galley to Furdurstrandi, of sunsets on the open sea, seen under the curve of the one sail evening after evening when the galley's beak was notched into the centre of the sinking disc, and "we sailed by that for we had no other guide," quoth Charlie. He spoke of a landing on an island and explorations in its woods, where the crew killed three men whom they found asleep under the pines. Their ghosts, Charlie said, followed the galley, swimming and choking in the water, and the crew cast lots and threw one of their number overboard as a sacrifice to the strange gods whom they had offended. Then they ate sea-weed when their provisions failed, and their legs swelled, and their leader, the red-haired man, killed two rowers who mutinied, and after a year spent among the woods they set sail for their own country, and a wind that never failed carried them back so safely that they all slept at night. This and much more Charlie told. Sometimes the voice fell so low that I could not catch the words, though every nerve was on the strain. He spoke of their leader, the red-haired man, as a pagan speaks of his God; for it was he who cheered them and slew them impartially as he thought best for their needs; and it was he who steered them for three days among floating ice, each floe crowded with strange beasts that "tried to sail with us," said Charlie, "and we beat them back with the handles of the oars."

The gas-jet went out, a burned coal gave way, and the fire settled down with a tiny crash to the bottom of the grate. Charlie ceased speaking, and I said no word.

"By Jove!" he said, at last, shaking his head. "I've been staring at the fire till I'm dizzy. What was I going to say?"

"Something about the galley."

"I remember now. It's 25 per cent. of the profits, isn't it?"

"It's anything you like when I've done the tale."

"I wanted to be sure of that. I must go now. I've, I've an appointment." And he left me.

Had my eyes not been held I might have known that that broken muttering over the fire was the swan-song of Charlie Mears. But I thought it the prelude to fuller revelation. At last and at last I should cheat the Lords of Life and Death!

When next Charlie came to me I received him with rapture. He was nervous and embarrassed, but his eyes were very full of light, and his lips a little parted.

"I've done a poem," he said; and then quickly: "it's the best I've ever done. Read it." He thrust

it into my hand and retreated to the window.

I groaned inwardly. It would be the work of half an hour to criticise—that is to say praise—the poem sufficiently to please Charlie. Then I had good reason to groan, for Charlie, discarding his favorite centipede metres, had launched into shorter and choppier verse, and verse with a motive at the back of it. This is what I read:

"The day is most fair, the cheery wind

Halloos behind the hill,

Where bends the wood as seemeth good,

And the sapling to his will!

Riot O wind; there is that in my blood

That would not have thee still!

"She gave me herself, O Earth, O Sky:

Grey sea, she is mine alone—I

Let the sullen boulders hear my cry,

And rejoice tho' they be but stone!

'Mine! I have won her O good brown earth,

Make merry! 'Tis bard on Spring;

Make merry; my love is doubly worth

All worship your fields can bring!

Let the hind that tills you feel my mirth

At the early harrowing."

"Yes, it's the early harrowing, past a doubt," I said, with a dread at my heart. Charlie smiled, but did not answer.

"Red cloud of the sunset, tell it abroad; I am victor.

Greet me O Sun, Dominant master and absolute lord

Over the soul of one!"

"Well?" said Charlie, looking over my shoulder.

I thought it far from well, and very evil indeed, when he silently laid a photograph on the paper—the photograph of a girl with a curly head, and a foolish slack mouth.

"Isn't it—isn't it wonderful?" he whispered, pink to the tips of his ears, wrapped in the rosy mystery of first love. "I didn't know; I didn't think—it came like a thunderclap."

"Yes. It comes like a thunderclap. Are you very happy, Charlie?"

"My God—she—she loves me!" He sat down repeating the last words to himself. I looked at the hairless face, the narrow shoulders already bowed by desk-work, and wondered when, where, and bow he had loved in his past lives.

"What will your mother say?" I asked, cheerfully.

"I don't care a damn what she says."

At twenty the things for which one does not care a damn should, properly, be many, but one must not include mothers in the list. I told him this gently; and he described Her, even as Adam must have described to the newly named beasts the glory and tenderness and beauty of Eve. Incidentally I learned that She was a tobacconist's assistant with a weakness for pretty dress, and had told him four or five times already that She had never been kissed by a man before.

Charlie spoke on, and on, and on; while I, separated from him by thousands of years, was considering the beginnings of things. Now I understood why the Lords of Life and Death shut the doors so carefully behind us. It is that we may not remember our first wooings. Were it not so, our world would be without inhabitants in a hundred years.

"Now, about that galley-story," I said, still more cheerfully, in a pause in the rush of the speech.

Charlie looked up as though he had been hit. "The galley—what galley? Good heavens, don't joke, man! This is serious! You don't know how serious it is!"

Grish Chunder was right. Charlie had tasted the love of woman that kills remembrance, and the "finest story" in the world would never be written.

VOLUME IV UNDER THE DEODARS
THE EDUCATION OF OTIS YEERE
I

In the pleasant orchard-closes

"God bless all our gains," say we;

But "May God bless all our losses,"

Better suits with our degree.

 —The Lost Bower.

This is the history of a failure; but the woman who failed said that it might be an instructive tale to put into print for the benefit of the younger generation. The younger generation does not want instruction, being perfectly willing to instruct if any one will listen to it. None the less, here begins the story where every right-minded story should begin, that is to say at Simla, where all things begin and many come to an evil end.

The mistake was due to a very clever woman making a blunder and not retrieving it. Men are licensed to stumble, but a clever woman's mistake is outside the regular course of Nature and Providence; since all good people know that a woman is the only infallible thing in this world, except Government Paper of the '70 issue, bearing interest at four and a half per cent. Yet, we have to remember that six consecutive days of rehearsing the leading part of The Fallen Age, at the New Gaiety Theatre where the plaster is not yet properly dry, might have brought about an unhingement of spirits which, again, might have led to eccentricities.

Mrs. Hauksbee came to "The Foundry" to tiffin with Mrs. Mallowe, her one bosom friend, for she was in no sense "a woman's woman." And it was a woman's tiffin, the door shut to all the world; and they both talked chiffons, which is French for Mysteries.

"I've enjoyed an interval of sanity," Mrs. Hauksbee announced, after tiffin was over and the two were comfortably settled in the little writing-room that opened out of Mrs. Mallowe's bedroom.

"My dear girl, what has he done?" said Mrs. Mallowe, sweetly. It is noticeable that ladies of a certain age call each other "dear girl," just as commissioners of twenty-eight years' standing address their equals in the Civil List as "my boy."

"There's no he in the case. Who am I that an imaginary man should be always credited to me? Am I an Apache?"

"No, dear, but somebody's scalp is generally drying at your wigwam-door. Soaking, rather."

This was an allusion to the Hawley Boy, who was in the habit of riding all across Simla in the Rains, to call on Mrs. Hauksbee. That lady laughed.

"For my sins, the Aide at Tyrconnel last night told me off to The Mussuck. Hsh! Don't laugh. One of my most devoted admirers. When the duff came—some one really ought to teach them to make pudding at Tyrconnel—The Mussuck was at liberty to attend to me."

"Sweet soul! I know his appetite," said Mrs. Mallowe. "Did he, oh did he, begin his wooing?"

"By a special mercy of Providence, no. He explained his importance as a Pillar of the Empire. I didn't laugh."

"Lucy, I don't believe you."

"Ask Captain Sangar; he was on the other side. Well, as I was saying, The Mussuck dilated."

"I think I can see him doing it," said Mrs. Mallowe, pensively, scratching her fox-terrier's ears.

"I was properly impressed. Most properly. I yawned openly. 'Strict supervision, and play them off one against the other,' said The Mussuck, shoveling down his ice by tureenfuls, I assure you. 'That, Mrs. Hauksbee, is the secret of our Government.'"

Mrs. Mallowe laughed long and merrily. "And what did you say?"

"Did you ever know me at loss for an answer yet? I said: 'So I have observed in my dealings with you.' The Mussuck swelled with pride. He is coming to call on me tomorrow. The Hawley Boy is coming too."

"'Strict supervision and play them off one against the other. That, Mrs. Hauksbee, is the secret of our Government.' And I dare say if we could get to The Mussuck's heart, we should find that he considers himself a man of the world."

"As he is of the other two things. I like The Mussuck, and I won't have you call him names. He amuses me."

"He has reformed you, too, by what appears. Explain the interval of sanity, and hit Tim on the nose with the paper-cutter, please. That dog is too fond of sugar. Do you take milk in yours?"

"No, thanks. Polly, I'm wearied of this life. It's hollow."

"Turn religious, then. I always said that Rome would be your fate."

"Only exchanging half a dozen attaches in red for one and in black, and if I fasted, the wrinkles would come, and never, never go. Has it ever struck you, dear, that I'm getting old?"

"Thanks for your courtesy. I'll return it. Ye-es we are both not exactly—how shall I put it?"

"What we have been. 'I feel it in my bones,' as Mrs. Crossley says. Polly, I've wasted my life."

"As how?"

"Never mind how. I feel it. I want to be a Power before I die."

"Be a Power then. You've wits enough for anything—and beauty?"

Mrs. Hauksbee pointed a teaspoon straight at her hostess. "Polly, if you heap compliments on me like this, I shall cease to believe that you're a woman. Tell me how I am to be a Power."

"Inform The Mussuck that he is the most fascinating and slimmest man in Asia, and he'll tell you anything and everything you please."

"Bother The Mussuck! I mean an intellectual Power—not a gas-power. Polly, I'm going to start a salon."

Mrs. Mallowe turned lazily on the sofa and rested her head on her hand. "Hear the words of the

Preacher, the son of Baruch," she said.

"Will you talk sensibly?"

"I will, dear, for I see that you are going to make a mistake."

"I never made a mistake in my life at least, never one that I couldn't explain away afterward."

"Going to make a mistake," went on Mrs. Mallowe, composedly. "It is impossible to start a salon in Simla. A bar would be much more to the point."

"Perhaps, but why? It seems so easy."

"Just what makes it so difficult. How many clever women are there in Simla?"

"Myself and yourself," said Mrs. Hauksbee, without a moment's hesitation.

"Modest woman! Mrs. Feardon would thank you for that. And how many clever men?"

"Oh—er—hundreds," said Mrs. Hauksbee, vaguely.

"What a fatal blunder! Not one. They are all bespoke of the Government. Take my husband, for instance. Jack was a clever man, though I say so who shouldn't. Government has eaten him up. All his ideas and powers of conversation—he really used to be a good talker, even to his wife, in the old days—are taken from him by this—this kitchen-sink of a Government. That's the case with every man up here who is at work. I don't suppose a Russian convict under the knout is able to amuse the rest of his gang; and all our men-folk here are gilded convicts."

"But there are scores—"

"I know what you're going to say. Scores of idle men up on leave. I admit it, but they are all of two objectionable sets, The Civilian who'd be delightful if he had the military man's knowledge of the world and style, and the military man who'd be adorable if lie had the Civilian's culture."

"Detestable word! Have Civilians Culchaw? I never studied the breed deeply."

"Don't make fun of Jack's service. Yes. They're like the teapots in the Lakka Bazar—good material but not polished. They can't help themselves, poor dears. A Civilian only begins to be tolerable after he has knocked about the world for fifteen years."

"And a military man?"

"When he has had the same amount of service. The young of both species are horrible. You would have scores of them in your salon."

"I would not!" said Mrs. Hauksbee, fiercely. "I would tell the bearer to darwaza band them. I'd put their own colonels and commissioners at the door to turn them away. I'd give them to the Topsham girl to play with."

"The Topsham girl would be grateful for the gift. But to go back to the salon. Allowing that you had gathered all your men and women together, what would you do with them? Make them talk? They would all with one accord begin to flirt. Your salon would become a glorified Peliti's—a 'Scandal Point' by lamplight."

"There's a certain amount of wisdom in that view."

"There's all the wisdom in the world in it. Surely, twelve Simla seasons ought to have taught you that you can't focus anything in India; and a salon, to be any good at all, must be permanent. In two seasons your roomful would be scattered all over Asia. We are only little bits of dirt on the hillsides—here one day and blown down the khud the next. We have lost the art of talking— at least our men have. We have no cohesion"—

"George Eliot in the flesh," interpolated Mrs. Hauksbee, wickedly.

"And collectively, my dear scoffer, we, men and women alike, have no influence.

"Come into the veranda and look at the Mall!"

The two looked down on the now rapidly filling road, for all Simla was abroad to steal a stroll between a shower and a fog.

"How do you propose to fix that river? Look! There's The Mussuck—head of goodness knows what. He is a power in the land, though he does eat like a costermonger. There's Colonel Blone, and General Grucher, and Sir Dugald Delane, and Sir Henry Haughton, and Mr. Jellalatty. All Heads of Departments, and all powerful."

"And all my fervent admirers," said Mrs. Hauksbee, piously. "Sir Henry Haughton raves about me. But go on."

"One by one, these men are worth something. Collectively, they're just a mob of Anglo-Indians. Who cares for what Anglo-Indians say? Your salon won't weld the Departments together and make you mistress of India, dear. And these creatures won't talk administrative 'shop' in a crowd—your salon—because they are so afraid of the men in the lower ranks overhearing it. They have forgotten what of Literature and Art they ever knew, and the women"—

"Can't talk about anything except the last Gymkhana, or the sins of their last nurse. I was calling on Mrs. Derwills this morning."

"You admit that? They can talk to the subalterns though, and the subalterns can talk to them. Your salon would suit their views admirably, if you respected the religious prejudices of the country and provided plenty of kala juggahs."

"Plenty of kala juggahs. Oh my poor little idea! Kala juggahs in a salon! But who made you so awfully clever?"

"Perhaps I've tried myself; or perhaps I know a woman who has. I have preached and expounded the whole matter and the conclusion thereof"—

"You needn't go on. 'Is Vanity.' Polly, I thank you. These vermin—" Mrs. Hauksbee waved her hand from the veranda to two men in the crowd below who had raised their hats to her—"these vermin shall not rejoice in a new Scandal Point or an extra Peliti's. I will abandon the notion of a salon. It did seem so tempting, though. But what shall I do? I must do something."

"Why? Are not Abana and Pharphar"—

"Jack has made you nearly as bad as himself! I want to, of course. I'm tired of everything and everybody, from a moonlight picnic at Seepee to the blandishments of The Mussuck."

"Yes—that comes, too, sooner or later, Have you nerve enough to make your bow yet?"

Mrs. Hauksbee's mouth shut grimly. Then she laughed. "I think I see myself doing it. Big pink

placards on the Mall: 'Mrs. Hauksbee! Positively her last appearance on any stage! This is to give notice!' No more dances; no more rides; no more luncheons; no more theatricals with supper to follow; no more sparring with one's dearest, dearest friend; no more fencing with an inconvenient man who hasn't wit enough to clothe what he's pleased to call his sentiments in passable speech; no more parading of The Mussuck while Mrs. Tarkass calls all round Simla, spreading horrible stories about me? No more of anything that is thoroughly wearying, abominable and detestable, but, all the same, makes life worth the having. Yes! I see it all! Don't interrupt, Polly, I'm inspired. A mauve and white striped 'cloud' round my excellent shoulders, a seat in the fifth row of the Gaiety, and both horses sold. Delightful vision! A comfortable armchair, situated in three different draughts, at every ballroom; and nice, large, sensible shoes for all the couples to stumble over as they go into the veranda! Then at supper. Can't you imagine the scene? The greedy mob gone away. Reluctant subaltern, pink all over like a newly-powdered baby—they really ought to tan subalterns before they are exported—Polly—sent back by the hostess to do his duty. Slouches up to me across the room, tugging at a glove two sizes too large for him—I hate a man who wears gloves like overcoats—and trying to look as if he'd thought of it from the first. 'May I ah—have the pleasure 'f takin' you 'nt' supper?' Then I get up with a hungry smile. Just like this."

"Lucy, how can you be so absurd?"

"And sweep out on his arm. So! After supper I shall go away early, you know, because I shall be afraid of catching cold. No one will look for my 'rickshaw. Mine, so please you! I shall stand, always with that mauve and white 'cloud' over my head, while the wet soaks into my dear, old, venerable feet and Tom swears and shouts for the mem-sahib's gharri. Then home to bed at half-past eleven! Truly excellent life helped out by the visits of the Padri, just fresh from burying somebody down below there." She pointed through the pines, toward the Cemetery, and continued with vigorous dramatic gesture—"Listen! I see it all down, down even to the stays! Such stays! Six-eight a pair, Polly, with red flannel—or list is it?—that they put into the tops of those fearful things. I can draw you a picture of them."

"Lucy, for Heaven's sake, don't go waving your arms about in that idiotic manner! Recollect, every one can see you from the Mall."

"Let them see! They'll think I am rehearsing for The Fallen Angel. Look! There's The Mussuck. How badly he rides. There!"

She blew a kiss to the venerable Indian administrator with infinite grace.

"Now," she continued, "he'll be chaffed about that at the Club in the delicate manner those brutes of men affect, and the Hawley Boy will tell me all about it—softening the details for fear of shocking me. That boy is too good to live, Polly. I've serious thoughts of recommending him to throw up his Commission and go into the Church. In his present frame of mind he would obey me. Happy, happy child."

"Never again," said Mrs. Mallowe, with an affectation of indignation, "shall you tiffin here! 'Lucindy, your behavior is scand'lus.'"

"All your fault," retorted Mrs. Hauksbee, "for suggesting such a thing as my abdication. No! Jamais—nevaire! I will act, dance, ride, frivol, talk scandal, dine out, and appropriate the legitimate captives of any woman I choose until I d-r-r-rop or a better woman than I puts me to shame before all Simla—and it's dust and ashes in my mouth while I'm doing it!"

She swept into the drawing-room, Mrs. Mallowe followed and put an arm round her waist.

"I'm not!" said Mrs. Hauksbee, defiantly, rummaging for her handkerchief. "I've been dining out the last ten nights, and rehearsing in the afternoon. You'd be tired yourself. It's only because I'm tired."

Mrs. Mallowe did not offer Mrs. Hauksbee any pity or ask her to lie down, but gave her another cup of tea, and went on with the talk.

"I've been through that too, dear," she said.

"I remember," said Mrs. Hauksbee, a gleam of fun on her face. "In '84 wasn't it? You went out a great deal less next season."

Mrs. Mallowe smiled in a superior and Sphinxlike fashion.

"I became an Influence," said she.

"Good gracious, child, you didn't join the Theosophists and kiss Buddha's big toe, did you? I tried to get into their set once, but they cast me out for a skeptic—without a chance of improving my poor little mind, too."

"No, I didn't Theosophilander. Jack says"—

"Never mind Jack. What a husband says is known before. What did you do?"

"I made a lasting impression."

"So have I—for four months. But that didn't console me in the least. I hated the man. Will you stop smiling in that inscrutable way and tell me what you mean?"

Mrs. Mallowe told.

* * * * * *

"And—you—mean—to—say that it is absolutely Platonic on both sides?"

"Absolutely, or I should never have taken it up."

"And his last promotion was due to you?"

Mrs. Mallowe nodded.

"And you warned him against the Topsham girl?"

Another nod.

"And told him of Sir Dugald Delane's private memo about him?"

A third nod.

"Why?"

"What a question to ask a woman! Because it amused me at first. I am proud of my property now. If I live he shall continue to be successful. Yes, I will put him upon the straight road to Knighthood, and everything else that a man values. The rest depends upon himself."

"Polly, you are a most extraordinary woman."

"Not in the least. I'm concentrated, that's all. You diffuse yourself, dear; and though all Simla knows your skill in managing a team"—

"Can't you choose a prettier word?"

"Team, of half a dozen, from The Mussuck to the Hawley Boy, you gain nothing by it. Not even amusement."

"And you?"

"Try my recipe. Take a man, not a boy, mind, but an almost mature, unattached man, and be this guide, philosopher, and friend. You'll find it the most interesting occupation that you ever embarked on. It can be done—you needn't look like that—because I've done it."

"There's an element of risk about it that makes the notion attractive. I'll get such a man and say to him, 'Now, understand that there must be no flirtation. Do exactly what I tell you, profit by my instruction and counsels, and all will yet be well,' as Toole says. Is that the idea?"

"More or less," said Mrs. Mallowe with an unfathomable smile. "But be sure he understands that there must be no flirtation."

II

Dribble-dribble-trickle-trickle

What a lot of raw dust!

My dollie's had an accident

And out came all the sawdust! —Nursery Rhyme.

So Mrs. Hauksbee, in "The Foundry" which overlooks Simla Mall, sat at the feet of Mrs. Mallowe and gathered wisdom. The end of the Conference was the Great Idea upon which Mrs. Hauksbee so plumed herself.

"I warn you," said Mrs. Mallowe, beginning to repent of her suggestion, "that the matter is not half so easy as it looks. Any woman—even the Topsham girl—can catch a man, but very, very few know how to manage him when caught."

"My child," was the answer, "I've been a female St. Simon Stylites looking down upon men for these—these years past. Ask The Mussuck whether I can manage them."

Mrs. Hauksbee departed humming, "I'll go to him and say to him in manner most ironical." Mrs. Mallowe laughed to herself. Then she grew suddenly sober. "I wonder whether I've done well in advising that amusement? Lucy's a clever woman, but a thought too careless."

A week later, the two met at a Monday Pop. "Well?" said Mrs. Mallowe.

"I've caught him!" said Mrs. Hauksbee; her eyes were dancing with merriment.

"Who is it, mad woman? I'm sorry I ever spoke to you about it."

"Look between the pillars. In the third row; fourth from the end. You can see his face now. Look!"

"Otis Yeere! Of all the improbable and impossible people! I don't believe you."

"Hsh! Wait till Mrs. Tarkass begins murdering Milton Wellings; and I'll tell you all about it. S-s-ss! That woman's voice always reminds me of an Underground train coming into Earl's Court with the brakes on. Now listen. It is really Otis Yeere."

"So I see, but does it follow that he is your property?"

"He is! By right of trove. I found him, lonely and unbefriended, the very next night after our talk, at the Dugald Delane's burra-khana. I liked his eyes, and I talked to him. Next day he called. Next day we went for a ride together, and today he's tied to my 'rickshaw-wheels hand and foot. You'll see when the concert's over. He doesn't know I'm here yet."

"Thank goodness you haven't chosen a boy. What are you going to do with him, assuming that you've got him?"

"Assuming, indeed! Does a woman—do I—ever make a mistake in that sort of thing? First"— Mrs. Hauksbee ticked off the items ostentatiously on her little gloved fingers—"First, my dear, I shall dress him properly. At present his raiment is a disgrace, and he wears a dress shirt like a crumpled sheet of the 'Pioneer'. Secondly, after I have made him presentable, I shall form his

manners—his morals are above reproach."

"You seem to have discovered a great deal about him considering the shortness of your acquaintance."

"Surely you ought to know that the first proof a man gives of his interest in a woman is by talking to her about his own sweet self. If the woman listens without yawning, he begins to like her. If she flatters the animal's vanity, he ends by adoring her."

"In some cases."

"Never mind the exceptions. I know which one you are thinking of. Thirdly, and lastly, after he is polished and made pretty, I shall, as you said, be his guide, philosopher and friend, and he shall become a success—as great a success as your friend. I always wondered how that man got on. Did The Mussuck come to you with the Civil List and, dropping on one knee—no, two knees, a' la Gibbon—hand it to you and say, 'Adorable angel, choose your friend's appointment'?"

"Lucy, your long experiences of the Military Department have demoralized you. One doesn't do that sort of thing on the Civil Side."

"No disrespect meant to Jack's Service, my dear. I only asked for information. Give me three months, and see what changes I shall work in my prey."

"Go your own way since you must. But I'm sorry that I was weak enough to suggest the amusement."

"'I am all discretion, and may be trusted to an in-finite extent,'" quoted Mrs. Hauksbee from The Fallen Angel; and the conversation ceased with Mrs. Tarkass's last, long-drawn war-whoop.

Her bitterest enemies—and she had many—could hardly accuse Mrs. Hauksbee of wasting her time. Otis Yeere was one of those wandering "dumb" characters, foredoomed through life to be nobody's property. Ten years in Her Majesty's Bengal Civil Service, spent, for the most part, in undesirable Districts, had given him little to be proud of, and nothing to bring confidence. Old enough to have lost the first fine careless rapture that showers on the immature 'Stunt imaginary Commissionerships and Stars, and sends him into the collar with coltish earnestness and abandon; too young to be yet able to look back upon the progress he had made, and thank Providence that under the conditions of the day he had come even so far, he stood upon the "dead-centre" of his career. And when a man stands still, he feels the slightest impulse from without. Fortune had ruled that Otis Yeere should be, for the first part of his service, one of the rank and file who are ground up in the wheels of the Administration; losing heart and soul, and mind and strength, in the process. Until steam replaces manual power in the working of the Empire, there must always be this percentage—must always be the men who are used up, expended, in the mere mechanical routine. For these promotion is far off and the mill-grind of every day very near and instant. The Secretariats know them only by name; they are not the picked men of the Districts with the Divisions and Collectorates awaiting them. They are simply the rank and file—the food for fever—sharing with the ryot and the plough-bullock the honor of being the plinth on which the State rests. The older ones have lost their aspirations; the younger are putting theirs aside with a sigh. Both learn to endure patiently until the end of the day. Twelve years in the rank and file, men say, will sap the hearts of the bravest and dull the wits of the most keen.

Out of this life Otis Yeere had fled for a few months, drifting, for the sake of a little masculine society, into Simla. When his leave was over he would return to his swampy, sour-green,

undermanned district, the native Assistant, the native Doctor, the native Magistrate, the steaming, sweltering Station, the ill-kempt City, and the undisguised insolence of the Municipality that babbled away the lives of men. Life was cheap, however. The soil spawned humanity, as it bred frogs in the Rains, and the gap of the sickness of one season was filled to overflowing by the fecundity of the next. Otis was unfeignedly thankful to lay down his work for a little while and escape from the seething, whining, weakly hive, impotent to help itself, but strong in its power to cripple, thwart, and annoy the weary-eyed man who, by official irony, was said to be "in charge" of it.

"I knew there were women-dowdies in Bengal. They come up here sometimes. But I didn't know that there were men-dowdies, too."

Then, for the first time, it occurred to Otis Yeere that his clothes were rather ancestral in appearance. It will be seen from the above that his friendship with Mrs Hauksbee had made great strides.

As that lady truthfully says, a man is never so happy as when he is talking about himself. From Otis Yeere's lips Mrs Hauksbee, before long, learned everything that she wished to know about the subject of her experiment; learned what manner of life he had led in what she vaguely called "those awful cholera districts"; learned too, but this knowledge came later, what manner of life he had purposed to lead and what dreams he had dreamed in the year of grace '77, before the reality had knocked the heart out of him. Very pleasant are the shady bridle-paths round Prospect Hill for the telling of such confidences.

"Not yet," said Mrs. Hauksbee to Mrs. Mallowe. "Not yet. I must wait until the man is properly dressed, at least. Great Heavens, is it possible that he doesn't know what an honor it is to be taken up by Me!"

Mrs. Hauksbee did not reckon false modesty as one of her failings.

"Always with Mrs. Hauksbee!" murmured Mrs. Mallowe, with her sweetest smile, to Otis. "Oh you men, you men! Here are our Punjabis growling because you've monopolized the nicest woman in Simla. They'll tear you to pieces on the Mall, some day, Mr. Yeere."

Mrs. Mallowe rattled down-hill, having satisfied herself, by a glance through the fringe of her sunshade, of the effect of her words.

The shot went home. Of a surety Otis Yeere was somebody in this bewildering whirl of Simla— had monopolized the nicest woman in it and the Punjabis were growling. The notion justified a mild glow of vanity. He had never looked upon his acquaintance with Mrs. Hauksbee as a matter for general interest.

The knowledge of envy was a pleasant feeling to the man of no account. It was intensified later in the day when a luncher at the Club said, spitefully, "Well, for a debilitated Ditcher, Yeere, you are going it. Hasn't any kind friend told you that she's the most dangerous woman in Simla?"

Yeere chuckled and passed out. When, oh when, would his new clothes be ready? He descended into the Mall to inquire; and Mrs. Hauksbee, coming over the Church Ridge in her 'rickshaw, looked down upon him approvingly. "He's learning to carry himself as if he were a man, instead of a piece of furniture, and"—she screwed up her eyes to see the better through the sunlight— "he is a man when he holds himself like that. Oh blessed Conceit, what should we be without you?"

With the new clothes came a new stock of self-confidence. Otis Yeere discovered that he could enter a room without breaking into a gentle perspiration—could cross one, even to talk to Mrs. Hauksbee, as though rooms were meant to be crossed. He was for the first time in nine years proud of himself, and contented with his life, satisfied with his new clothes, and rejoicing in the friendship of Mrs. Hauksbee.

"Conceit is what the poor fellow wants," she said in confidence to Mrs. Mallowe. "I believe they must use Civilians to plough the fields with in Lower Bengal. You see I have to begin from the very beginning—haven't I? But you'll admit, won't you, dear, that he is immensely improved since I took him in hand. Only give me a little more time and he won't know himself."

Indeed, Yeere was rapidly beginning to forget what he had been. One of his own rank and file put the matter brutally when he asked Yeere, in reference to nothing, "And who has been making you a Member of Council, lately? You carry the side of half a dozen of 'em."

"I—I'm awf'ly sorry. I didn't mean it, you know," said Yeere, apologetically.

"There'll be no holding you," continued the old stager, grimly. "Climb down, Otis—climb down, and get all that beastly affectation knocked out of you with fever! Three thousand a month wouldn't support it."

Yeere repeated the incident to Mrs. Hauksbee. He had come to look upon her as his Mother Confessor.

"And you apologized!" she said. "Oh, shame! I hate a man who apologizes. Never apologize for what your friend called 'side.' Never! It's a man's business to be insolent and overbearing until he meets with a stronger. Now, you bad boy, listen to me."

Simply and straightforwardly, as the 'rickshaw loitered round Jakko, Mrs. Hauksbee preached to Otis Yeere the Great Gospel of Conceit, illustrating it with living pictures encountered during their Sunday afternoon stroll.

"Good gracious!" she ended, with the personal argument, "you'll apologize next for being my attache?"

"Never!" said Otis Yeere. "That's another thing altogether. I shall always be"—

"What's coming?" thought Mrs. Hauksbee.

"Proud of that," said Otis.

"Safe for the present," she said to herself.

"But I'm afraid I have grown conceited. Like Jeshurun, you know. When he waxed fat, then he kicked. It's the having no worry on one's mind and the Hill air, I suppose."

"Hill air, indeed!" said Mrs. Hauksbee to herself. "He'd have been hiding in the Club till the last day of his leave, if I hadn't discovered him." And aloud—"Why shouldn't you be? You have every right to."

"I! Why?"

"Oh, hundreds of things. I'm not going to waste this lovely afternoon by explaining; but I know you have. What was that heap of manuscript you showed me about the grammar of the aboriginal—what's their names?"

"Gullals. A piece of nonsense. I've far too much work to do to bother over Gullals now. You should see my District. Come down with your husband some day and I'll show you round. Such a lovely place in the Rains! A sheet of water with the railway-embankment and the snakes sticking out, and, in the summer, green flies and green squash. The people would die of fear if you shook a dogwhip at 'em. But they know you're forbidden to do that, so they conspire to make your life a burden to you. My District's worked by some man at Darjiling, on the strength of u native pleader's false reports. Oh, it's a heavenly place!"

Otis Yeere laughed bitterly.

"There's not the least necessity that you should stay in it. Why do you?"

"Because I must. How'm I to get out of it?"

"How! In a hundred and fifty ways. If there weren't so many people on the road, I'd like to box your ears. Ask, my dear boy, ask! Look, There is young Hexarly with six years' service and half your talents. He asked for what he wanted, and he got it. See, down by the Convent! There's McArthurson who has come to his present position by asking—sheer, downright asking—after he had pushed himself out of the rank and file. One man is as good as another in your service—believe me. I've seen Simla for more seasons than I care to think about. Do you suppose men are chosen for appointments because of their special fitness beforehand? You have all passed a high test—what do you call it?—in the beginning, and, except for the few who have gone altogether to the bad, you can all work hard. Asking does the rest. Call it cheek, call it insolence, call it anything you like, but ask! Men argue—yes, I know what men say—that a man, by the mere audacity of his request, must have some good in him. A weak man doesn't say: 'Give me this and that.' He whines 'Why haven't I been given this and that?' If you were in the Army, I should say learn to spin plates or play a tambourine with your toes. As it is—ask! You belong to a Service that ought to be able to command the Channel Fleet, or set a leg at twenty minutes' notice, and yet you hesitate over asking to escape from a squashy green district where you admit you are not master. Drop the Bengal Government altogether. Even Darjiling is a little out-of-the-way hole. I was there once, and the rents were extortionate. Assert yourself. Get the Government of India to take you over. Try to get on the Frontier, where every man has a grand chance if he can trust himself. Go somewhere! Do something! You have twice the wits and three times the presence of the men up here, and, and"—

Mrs. Hauksbee paused for breath; then continued—"and in any way you look at it, you ought to. You who could go so far!"

"I don't know," said Yeere, rather taken aback by the unexpected eloquence. "1 haven't such a good opinion of myself."

It was not strictly Platonic, but it was Policy. Mrs. Hauksbee laid her hand lightly upon the ungloved paw that rested on the turned-back 'rickshaw hood, and, looking the man full in the face, said tenderly, almost too tenderly, "I believe in you if you mistrust yourself. Is that enough, my friend?"

"It is enough," answered Otis, very solemnly.

He was silent for a long time, redreaming the dreams that he had dreamed eight years ago, but through them all ran, as sheet-lightning through golden cloud, the light of Mrs. Hauksbee's violet eyes.

Curious and impenetrable are the mazes of Simla life—the only existence in this desolate land worth the living. Gradually it went abroad among men and women, in the pauses between

dance, play and Gymkhana, that Otis Yeere, the man with the newly-lit light of self-confidence in his eyes, had "done something decent" in the wilds whence he came. He had brought an erring Municipality to reason, appropriated the funds on his own responsibility, and saved the lives of hundreds, He knew more about the Gullals than any living man. Had a vast knowledge of the aboriginal tribes; was, in spite of his juniority, the greatest authority on the aboriginal Gullals. No one quite knew who or what the Gullals were till The Mussuck, who had been calling on Mrs. Hauksbee, and prided himself upon picking people's brains, explained they were a tribe of ferocious hillmen, somewhere near Sikkim, whose friendship even the Great Indian Empire would find it worth her while to secure. Now we know that Otis Yeere had showed Mrs. Hauksbee his MS notes of six years' standing on the same Gullals. He had told her, too, how, sick and shaken with the fever their negligence had bred, crippled by the loss of his pet clerk, and savagely angry at the desolation in his charge, he had once damned the collective eyes of his "intelligent local board" for a set of haramzadas. Which act of "brutal and tyrannous oppression" won him a Reprimand Royal from the Bengal Government; but in the anecdote as amended for Northern consumption we find no record of this. Hence we are forced to conclude that Mrs. Hauksbee "edited" his reminiscences before sowing them in idle ears, ready, as she well knew, to exaggerate good or evil. And Otis Yeere bore himself as befitted the hero of many tales.

"You can talk to me when you don't fall into a brown study. Talk now, and talk your brightest and best," said Mrs. Hauksbee.

Otis needed no spur. Look to a man who has the counsel of a woman of or above the world to back him. So long as he keeps his head, he can meet both sexes on equal ground—an advantage never intended by Providence, who fashioned Man on one day and Woman on another, in sign that neither should know more than a very little of the other's life. Such a man goes far, or, the counsel being withdrawn, collapses suddenly while his world seeks the reason.

Generalled by Mrs. Hauksbee who, again, had all Mrs. Mallowe's wisdom at her disposal, proud of himself and, in the end, believing in himself because he was believed in, Otis Yeere stood ready for any fortune that might befall, certain that it would be good. He would fight for his own hand, and intended that this second struggle should lead to better issue than the first helpless surrender of the bewildered 'Stunt.

What might have happened, it is impossible to say. This lamentable thing befell, bred directly by a statement of Mrs. Hauksbee that she would spend the next season in Darjiling.

"Are you certain of that?" said Otis Yeere.

"Quite. We're writing about a house now."

Otis Yeere "stopped dead," as Mrs. Hauksbee put it in discussing the relapse with Mrs. Mallowe.

"He has behaved," she said, angrily, "just like Captain Kerrington's pony—only Otis is a donkey—at the last Gymkhana. Planted his forefeet and refused to go on another step. Polly, my man's going to disappoint me. What shall I do?"

As a rule, Mrs. Mallowe does not approve of staring, but on this occasion she opened her eyes to the utmost.

"You have managed cleverly so far," she said. "Speak to him, and ask him what he means."

"I will—at tonight's dance."

"No-o, not at a dance," said Mrs. Mallowe, cautiously. "Men are never themselves quite at dances. Better wait till tomorrow morning."

"Nonsense. If he's going to revert in this insane way, there isn't a day to lose. Are you going? No? Then sit up for me, there's a dear. I shan't stay longer than supper under any circumstances."

Mrs. Mallowe waited through the evening, looking long and earnestly into the fire, and sometimes smiling to herself.

"Oh! oh! oh! The man's an idiot! A raving, positive idiot! I'm sorry I ever saw him!"

Mrs. Hauksbee burst into Mrs. Mallowe's house, at midnight, almost in tears.

"What in the world has happened?" said Mrs. Mallowe, but her eyes showed that she had guessed an answer.

"Happened! Everything has happened! He was there. I went to him and said, 'Now, what does this nonsense mean?' Don't laugh, dear, I can't bear it. But you know what I mean I said. Then it was a square, and I sat it out with him and wanted an explanation, and he said—Oh! I haven't patience with such idiots! You know what I said about going to Darjiling next year? It doesn't matter to me where I go. I'd have changed the Station and lost the rent to have saved this. He said, in so many words, that he wasn't going to try to work up any more, because—because he would be shifted into a province away from Darjiling, and his own District, where these creatures are, is within a day's journey"—

"Ah-hh!" said Mrs. Mallowe, in a tone of one who has successfully tracked an obscure word through a large dictionary.

"Did you ever hear of anything so mad—so absurd? And he had the ball at his feet. He had only to kick it! I would have made him anything! Anything in the wide world. He could have gone to the world's end. I would have helped him. I made him, didn't I, Polly? Didn't I create that man? Doesn't he owe everything to me? And to reward me, just when everything was nicely arranged, by this lunacy that spoiled everything!"

"Very few men understand your devotion thoroughly."

"Oh, Polly, don't laugh at me! I give men up from this hour. I could have killed him then and there. What right had this man—this Thing I had picked out of his filthy paddy-fields—to make love to me?"

"He did that, did he?"

"He did. I don't remember half he said, I was so angry. Oh, but such a funny thing happened! I can't help laughing at it now, though I felt nearly ready to cry with rage. He raved and I stormed—I'm afraid we must have made an awful noise in our kala juggah. Protect my character, dear, if it's all over Simla by tomorrow—and then he bobbed forward in the middle of this insanity—I firmly believe the man's demented—and kissed me!"

"Morals above reproach," purred Mrs. Mallowe.

"So they were—so they are! It was the most absurd kiss. I don't believe he'd ever kissed a woman in his life before. I threw my head back, and it was a sort of slidy, pecking dab, just on the end of the chin—here." Mrs. Hauksbee tapped her masculine little chin with her fan. "Then, of course, I was furiously angry, and told him that he was no gentleman, and I was sorry I'd ever met him, and so on. He was crushed so easily that I couldn't be very angry. Then I came

away straight to you."

"Was this before or after supper?"

"Oh! before—oceans before. Isn't it perfectly disgusting?"

"Let me think. I withhold judgment till tomorrow. Morning brings counsel."

But morning brought only a servant with a dainty bouquet of Annandale roses for Mrs. Hauksbee to wear at the dance at Viceregal Lodge that night.

"He doesn't seem to be very penitent," said Mrs. Mallowe. "What's the billet-doux in the centre?"

Mrs. Hauksbee opened the neatly folded note,—another accomplishment that she had taught Otis,—read it, and groaned tragically.

"Last wreck of a feeble intellect! Poetry! Is it his own, do you think? Oh, that I ever built my hopes on such a maudlin idiot!"

"No. It's a quotation from Mrs. Browning, and, in view of the facts of the case, as Jack says, uncommonly well chosen. Listen:

"'Sweet thou has trod on a heart—

Pass! There's a world full of men

And women as fair as thou art,

Must do such things now and then.

"'Thou only hast stepped unaware—

Malice not one can impute;

And why should a heart have been there,

In the way of a fair woman's foot?'

"I didn't—I didn't—I didn't!" said Mrs. Hauksbee, angrily, her eyes filling with tears; "there was no malice at all. Oh, it's too vexatious!"

"You've misunderstood the compliment," said Mrs. Mallowe. "He clears you completely and— ahem—I should think by this, that he has cleared completely too. My experience of men is that when they begin to quote poetry, they are going to flit. Like swans singing before they die, you know."

"Polly, you take my sorrows in a most unfeeling way."

"Do I? Is it so terrible? If he's hurt your vanity, I should say that you've done a certain amount of damage to his heart."

"Oh, you never can tell about a man!" said Mrs. Hauksbee, with deep scorn.

Reviewing the matter as an impartial outsider, it strikes me that I'm about the only person who has profited by the education of Otis Yeere. It comes to twenty-seven pages and bittock.

AT THE PIT'S MOUTH

Men say it was a stolen tide—

The Lord that sent it he knows all,

But in mine ear will aye abide

The message that the bells let fall,

And awesome bells they were to me,

That in the dark rang, "Enderby."

—Jean Ingelow.

Once upon a time there was a man and his Wife and a Tertium Quid.

All three were unwise, but the Wife was the unwisest. The Man should have looked after his Wife, who should have avoided the Tertium Quid, who, again, should have married a wife of his own, after clean and open flirtations, to which nobody can possibly object, round Jakko or Observatory Hill. When you see a young man with his pony in a white lather, and his hat on the back of his head flying down-hill at fifteen miles an hour to meet a girl who will be properly surprised to meet him, you naturally approve of that young man, and wish him Staff Appointments, and take an interest in his welfare, and, as the proper time comes, give them sugar-tongs or side-saddles, according to your means and generosity.

The Tertium Quid flew down-hill on horseback, but it was to meet the Man's Wife; and when he flew up-hill it was for the same end. The Man was in the Plains, earning money for his Wife to spend on dresses and four-hundred-rupee bracelets, and inexpensive luxuries of that kind. He worked very hard, and sent her a letter or a post-card daily. She also wrote to him daily, and said that she was longing for him to come up to Simla. The Tertium Quid used to lean over her shoulder and laugh as she wrote the notes. Then the two would ride to the Post Office together.

Now, Simla is a strange place and its customs are peculiar; nor is any man who has not spent at least ten seasons there qualified to pass judgment on circumstantial evidence, which is the most untrustworthy in the Courts. For these reasons, and for others which need not appear, I decline to state positively whether there was anything irretrievably wrong in the relations between the Man's Wife and the Tertium Quid. If there was, and hereon you must form your own opinion, it was the Man's Wife's fault. She was kittenish in her manners, wearing generally an air of soft and fluffy innocence. But she was deadly learned and evil-instructed; and, now and again, when the mask dropped, men saw this, shuddered and almost drew back. Men are occasionally particular, and the least particular men are always the most exacting.

Simla is eccentric in its fashion of tearing friendships. Certain attachments which have set and crystallized through half a dozen seasons acquire almost the sanctity of the marriage bond, and are revered as such. Again, certain attachments equally old, and, to all appearance, equally venerable, never seem to win any recognized official status; while a chance-sprung acquaintance now two months born, steps into the place which by right belongs to the senior. There is no law reducible to print which regulates these affairs.

Some people have a gift which secures them infinite toleration, and others have not. The Man's Wife had not. If she looked over the garden wall, for instance, women taxed her with stealing

their husbands. She complained pathetically that she was not allowed to choose her own friends. When she put up her big white muff to her lips, and gazed over it and under her eyebrows at you as she said this thing, you felt that she had been infamously misjudged, and that all the other women's instincts were all wrong; which was absurd. She was not allowed to own the Tertium Quid in peace; and was so strangely constructed that she would not have enjoyed peace had she been so permitted. She preferred some semblance of intrigue to cloak even her most commonplace actions.

After two months of riding, first round Jakko, then Elysium, then Summer Hill, then Observatory Hill, then under Jutogh, and lastly up and down the Cart Road as far as the Tara Devi gap in the dusk, she said to the Tertium Quid, "Frank, people say we are too much together, and people are so horrid."

The Tertium Quid pulled his moustache, and replied that horrid people were unworthy of the consideration of nice people.

"But they have done more than talk—they have written—written to my hubby—I'm sure of it," said the Man's Wife, and she pulled a letter from her husband out of her saddle-pocket and gave it to the Tertium Quid.

It was an honest letter, written by an honest man, then stewing in the Plains on two hundred rupees a month (for he allowed his wife eight hundred and fifty), and in a silk banian and cotton trousers. It is said that, perhaps, she had no thought of the unwisdom of allowing her name to be so generally coupled with the Tertium Quid's; that she was too much of a child to understand the dangers of that sort of thing; that he, her husband, was the last man in the world to interfere jealously with her little amusements and interests, but that it would be better were she to drop the Tertium Quid quietly and for her husband's sake. The letter was sweetened with many pretty little pet names, and it amused the Tertium Quid considerably. He and She laughed over it, so that you, fifty yards away, could see their shoulders shaking while the horses slouched along side by side.

Their conversation was not worth reporting. The upshot of it was that, next day, no one saw the Man's Wife and the Tertium Quid together. They had both gone down to the Cemetery, which, as a rule, is only visited officially by the inhabitants of Simla.

A Simla funeral with the clergyman riding, the mourners riding, and the coffin creaking as it swings between the bearers, is one of the most depressing things on this earth, particularly when the procession passes under the wet, dank dip beneath the Rockcliffe Hotel, where the sun is shut out and all the hill streams are wailing and weeping together as they go down the valleys.

Occasionally folk tend the graves, but we in India shift and are transferred so often that, at the end of the second year, the Dead have no friends—only acquaintances who are far too busy amusing themselves up the hill to attend to old partners. The idea of using a Cemetery as a rendezvous is distinctly a feminine one. A man would have said simply "Let people talk. We'll go down the Mall." A woman is made differently, especially if she be such a woman as the Man's Wife. She and the Tertium Quid enjoyed each other's society among the graves of men and women whom they had known and danced with aforetime.

They used to take a big horse-blanket and sit on the grass a little to the left of the lower end, where there is a dip in the ground and where the occupied graves stop short and the ready-made ones are not ready. Each well-regulated India Cemetery keeps half a dozen graves permanently open for contingencies and incidental wear and tear. In the Hills these are more usually baby's size, because children who come up weakened and sick from the Plains often succumb to the effects of the Rains in the Hills or get pneumonia from their ayahs taking them through damp

pine-woods after the sun has set. In Cantonments, of course, the man's size is more in request; these arrangements varying with the climate and population.

One day when the Man's Wife and the Tertium Quid had just arrived in the Cemetery, they saw some coolies breaking ground. They had marked out a full-size grave, and the Tertium Quid asked them whether any Sahib was sick. They said that they did not know; but it was an order that they should dig a Sahib's grave.

"Work away," said the Tertium Quid, "and let's see how it's done."

The coolies worked away, and the Man's Wife and the Tertium Quid watched and talked for a couple of hours while the grave was being deepened Then a coolie, taking the earth in blankets as it was thrown up, jumped over the grave.

"That's queer," said the Tertium Quid. "Where's my ulster?"

"What's queer?" said the Man's Wife.

"I have got a chill down my back just as if a goose had walked over my grave."

"Why do you look at the thing, then?" said the Man's Wife. "Let us go."

The Tertium Quid stood at the head of the grave, and stared without answering for a space. Then he said, dropping a pebble down, "It is nasty and cold; horribly cold. I don't think I shall come to the Cemetery any more. I don't think grave-digging is cheerful."

The two talked and agreed that the Cemetery was depressing. They also arranged for a ride next day out from the Cemetery through the Mashobra Tunnel up to Fagoo and back, because all the world was going to a garden-party at Viceregal Lodge, and all the people of Mashobra would go too.

Coming up the Cemetery road, the Tertium Quid's horse tried to bolt up hill, being tired with standing so long, and managed to strain a back sinew.

"I shall have to take the mare tomorrow," said the Tertium Quid, "and she will stand nothing heavier than a snaffle."

They made their arrangements to meet in the Cemetery, after allowing all the Mashobra people time to pass into Simla. That night it rained heavily, and next day, when the Tertium Quid came to the trysting-place, he saw that the new grave had a foot of water in it, the ground being a tough and sour clay.

"'Jove! That looks beastly," said the Tertium Quid. "Fancy being boarded up and dropped into that well!"

They then started off to Fagoo, the mare playing with the snaffle and picking her way as though she were shod with satin, and the sun shining divinely. The road below Mashobra to Fagoo is officially styled the Himalayan-Thibet Road; but in spite of its name it is not much more than six feet wide in most places, and the drop into the valley below must be anything between one and two thousand feet.

"Now we're going to Thibet," said the Man's Wife merrily, as the horses drew near to Fagoo. She was riding on the cliff-side.

"Into Thibet," said the Tertium Quid, "ever so far from people who say horrid things, and

hubbies who write stupid letters. With you—to the end of the world!"

A coolie carrying a log of wood came round a corner, and the mare went wide to avoid him—forefeet in and haunches out, as a sensible mare should go.

"To the world's end," said the Man's Wife, and looked unspeakable things over her near shoulder at the Tertium Quid.

He was smiling, but, while she looked, the smile froze stiff as it were on his face, and changed to a nervous grin—the sort of grin men wear when they are not quite easy in their saddles. The mare seemed to be sinking by the stem, and her nostrils cracked while she was trying to realize what was happening. The rain of the night before had rotted the drop-side of the Himalayan-Thibet Road, and it was giving way under her. "What are you doing?" said the Man's Wife. The Tertium Quid gave no answer. He grinned nervously and set his spurs into the mare, who rapped with her forefeet on the road, and the struggle began. The Man's Wife screamed, "Oh, Frank, get off!"

But the Tertium Quid was glued to the saddle—his face blue and white—and he looked into the Man's Wife's eyes. Then the Man's Wife clutched at the mare's head and caught her by the nose instead of the bridle. The brute threw up her head and went down with a scream, the Tertium Quid upon her, and the nervous grin still set on his face.

The Man's Wife heard the tinkle-tinkle of little stones and loose earth falling off the roadway, and the sliding roar of the man and horse going down. Then everything was quiet, and she called on Frank to leave his mare and walk up. But Frank did not answer. He was underneath the mare, nine hundred feet below, spoiling a patch of Indian corn.

As the revellers came back from Viceregal Lodge in the mists of the evening, they met a temporarily insane woman, on a temporarily mad horse, swinging round the corners, with her eyes and her mouth open, and her head like the head of the Medusa. She was stopped by a man at the risk of his life, and taken out of the saddle, a limp heap, and put on the bank to explain herself. This wasted twenty minutes, and then she was sent home in a lady's 'rickshaw, still with her mouth open and her hands picking at her riding-gloves.

She was in bed through the following three days, which were rainy; so she missed attending the funeral of the Tertium Quid, who was lowered into eighteen inches of water, instead of the twelve to which he had first objected.

A WAYSIDE COMEDY

Because to every purpose there is time and judgment, therefore

the misery of man is great upon him.

—Eccles. viii. 6.

Fate and the Government of India have turned the Station of Kashima into a prison; and, because there is no help for the poor souls who are now lying there in torment, I write this story, praying that the Government of India may be moved to scatter the European population to the four winds.

Kashima is bound on all sides by the rock-tipped circle of the Dosehri hills. In Spring, it is ablaze with roses; in Summer, the roses die and the hot winds blow from the hills; in Autumn, the white mists from the hills cover the place as with water; and in Winter the frosts nip everything young and tender to earth-level. There is but one view in Kashima—a stretch of perfectly flat pasture and plough-land, running up to the grey-blue scrub of the Dosehri hills.

There are no amusements, except snipe and tiger shooting; but the tigers have been long since hunted from their lairs in the rock-caves, and the snipe only come once a year. Narkarra—one hundred and forty-three miles by road—is the nearest station to Kashima. But Kashima never goes to Narkarra, where there are at least twelve English people. It stays within the circle of the Dosehri hills.

All Kashima acquits Mrs. Vansuythen of any intention to do harm; but all Kashima knows that she, and she alone, brought about their pain.

Boulte, the Engineer, Mrs. Boulte, and Captain Kurrell know this. They are the English population of Kashima, if we except Major Vansuythen, who is of no importance whatever, and Mrs. Vansuythen, who is the most important of all.

You must remember, though you will not understand, that all laws weaken in a small and hidden community where there is no public opinion. When a man is absolutely alone in a Station he runs a certain risk of falling into evil ways. The risk is multiplied by every addition to the population up to twelve—the Jury-number. After that, fear and consequent restraint begin, and human action becomes less grotesquely jerky.

There was deep peace in Kashima till Mrs. Vansuythen arrived. She was a charming woman, every one said so everywhere; and she charmed every one. In spite of this, or, perhaps, because of this, since Fate is so perverse, she cared only for one man, and he was Major Vansuythen. Had she been plain or stupid, this matter would have been intelligible to Kashima. But she was a fair woman, with very still grey eyes, the color of a lake just before the light of the sun touches it. No man who had seen those eyes, could, later on, explain what fashion of woman she was to look upon. The eyes dazzled him. Her own sex said that she was "not bad looking, but spoiled by pretending to be so grave." And yet her gravity was natural It was not her habit to smile. She merely went through life, looking at those who passed; and the women objected while the men fell down and worshipped.

She knows and is deeply sorry for the evil she has done to Kashima; but Major Vansuythen cannot understand why Mrs. Boulte does not drop in to afternoon tea at least three times a week. "When there are only two women in one Station, they ought to see a great deal of each other," says Major Vansuythen.

Long and long before ever Mrs. Vansuythen came out of those far-away places where there is society and amusement, Kurrell had discovered that Mrs. Boulte was the one woman in the world for him and—you dare not blame them. Kashima was as out of the world as Heaven or the Other Place, and the Dosehri hills kept their secret well. Boulte had no concern in the matter. He was in camp for a fortnight at a time. He was a hard, heavy man, and neither Mrs. Boulte nor Kurrell pitied him. They had all Kashima and each other for their very, very own; and Kashima was the Garden of Eden in those days. When Boulte returned from his wanderings he would slap Kurrell between the shoulders and call him "old fellow," and the three would dine together. Kashima was happy then when the judgment of God seemed almost as distant as Narkarra or the railway that ran down to the sea. But the Government sent Major Vansuythen to Kashima, and with him came his wife.

The etiquette of Kashima is much the same as that of a desert island. When a stranger is cast away there, all hands go down to the shore to make him welcome. Kashima assembled at the masonry platform close to the Narkarra Road, and spread tea for the Vansuythens. That ceremony was reckoned a formal call, and made them free of the Station, its rights and privileges. When the Vansuythens were settled down, they gave a tiny housewarming to all Kashima; and that made Kashima free of their house, according to the immemorial usage of the Station.

Then the Rains came, when no one could go into camp, and the Narkarra Road was washed away by the Kasun River, and in the cup-like pastures of Kashima the cattle waded knee-deep. The clouds dropped down from the Dosehri hills and covered everything.

At the end of the Rains, Boulte's manner toward his wife changed and became demonstratively affectionate. They had been married twelve years, and the change startled Mrs. Boulte, who hated her husband with the hate of a woman who has met with nothing but kindness from her mate, and, in the teeth of this kindness, had done him a great wrong. Moreover, she had her own trouble to fight with—her watch to keep over her own property, Kurrell. For two months the Rains had hidden the Dosehri hills and many other things besides; but when they lifted, they showed Mrs. Boulte that her man among men, her Ted—for she called him Ted in the old days when Boulte was out of earshot—was slipping the links of the allegiance.

"The Vansuythen Woman has taken him," Mrs. Boulte said to herself; and when Boulte was away, wept over her belief, in the face of the over-vehement blandishments of Ted. Sorrow in Kashima is as fortunate as Love, because there is nothing to weaken it save the flight of Time. Mrs. Boulte had never breathed her suspicion to Kurrell because she was not certain; and her nature led her to be very certain before she took steps in any direction. That is why she behaved as she did.

Boulte came into the house one evening, and leaned against the door-posts of the drawing-room, chewing his moustache. Mrs. Boulte was putting some flowers into a vase. There is a pretence of civilization even in Kashima.

"Little woman," said Boulte, quietly, "do you care for me?"

"Immensely," said she, with a laugh. "Can you ask it?"

"But I'm serious," said Boulte. "Do you care for me?"

Mrs. Boulte dropped the flowers, and turned round quickly. "Do you want an honest answer?"

"Ye-es, I've asked for it."

Mrs. Boulte spoke in a low, even voice for five minutes, very distinctly, that there might be no

misunderstanding her meaning. When Samson broke the pillars of Gaza, he did a little thing, and one not to be compared to the deliberate pulling down of a woman's homestead about her own ears. There was no wise female friend to advise Mrs. Boulte, the singularly cautious wife, to hold her hand. She struck at Boulte's heart, because her own was sick with suspicion of Kurrell, and worn out with the long strain of watching alone through the Rains. There was no plan or purpose in her speaking. The sentences made themselves; and Boulte listened leaning against the door-post with his hands in his pockets. When all was over, and Mrs. Boulte began to breathe through her nose before breaking out into tears, he laughed and stared straight in front of him at the Dosehri hills.

"Is that all?" he said. "Thanks, I only wanted to know, you know."

"What are you going to do?" said the woman, between her sobs.

"Do! Nothing. What should I do? Kill Kurrell or send you Home, or apply for leave to get a divorce? It's two days' dak into Narkarra." He laughed again and went on: "I'll tell you what you can do. You can ask Kurrell to dinner tomorrow—no, on Thursday, that will allow you time to pack—and you can bolt with him. I give you my word I won't follow."

He took up his helmet and went out of the room, and Mrs. Boulte sat till the moonlight streaked the floor, thinking and thinking and thinking. She had done her best upon the spur of the moment to pull the house down; but it would not fall. Moreover, she could not understand her husband, and she was afraid. Then the folly of her useless truthfulness struck her, and she was ashamed to write to Kurrell, saying: "I have gone mad and told everything. My husband says that I am free to elope with you. Get a dak for Thursday, and we will fly after dinner." There was a cold-bloodedness about that procedure which did not appeal to her. So she sat still in her own house and thought.

At dinner-time Boulte came back from his walk, white and worn and haggard, and the woman was touched at his distress. As the evening wore on, she muttered some expression of sorrow, something approaching to contrition. Boulte came out of a brown study and said, "Oh, that! I wasn't thinking about that. By the way, what does Kurrell say to the elopement?"

"I haven't seen him," said Mrs. Boulte. "Good God! is that all?"

But Boulte was not listening, and her sentence ended in a gulp.

The next day brought no comfort to Mrs. Boulte, for Kurrell did not appear, and the new life that she, in the five minutes' madness of the previous evening, had hoped to build out of the ruins of the old, seemed to be no nearer.

Boulte ate his breakfast, advised her to see her Arab pony fed in the veranda, and went out. The morning wore through, and at midday the tension became unendurable. Mrs. Boulte could not cry. She had finished her crying in the night, and now she did not want to be left alone. Perhaps the Vansuythen woman would talk to her; and, since talking opens the heart, perhaps there might be some comfort to be found in her company. She was the only other woman in the Station.

In Kashima there are no regular calling-hours. Every one can drop in upon every one else at pleasure. Mrs. Boulte put on a big terai hat, and walked across to the Vansuythens's house to borrow last week's Queen. The two compounds touched, and instead of going up the drive, she crossed through the gap in the cactus-hedge, entering the house from the back. As she passed through the dining-room, she heard, behind the purdah that cloaked the drawing-room door, her husband's voice, saying—"But on my Honor! On my Soul and Honor, I tell you she doesn't

care for me. She told me so last night. I would have told you then if Vansuythen hadn't been with you. If it is for her sake that you'll have nothing to say to me, you can make your mind easy. It's Kurrell."

"What?" said Mrs. Vansuythen, with an hysterical little laugh. "Kurrell! Oh, it can't be. You two must have made some horrible mistake. Perhaps you—you lost your temper, or misunderstood, or something. Things can't be as wrong as you say."

Mrs. Vansuythen had shifted her defence to avoid the man's pleading, and was desperately trying to keep him to a side-issue.

"There must be some mistake," she insisted, "and it can be all put right again."

Boulte laughed grimly.

"It can't be Captain Kurrell! He told me that he had never taken the least—the least interest in your wife, Mr. Boulte. Oh, do listen! He said he had not. He swore he had not," said Mrs. Vansuythen.

The purdah rustled, and the speech was cut short by the entry of a little, thin woman with big rings round her eyes. Mrs. Vansuythen stood up with a gasp.

"What was that you said?" asked Mrs. Boulte. "Never mind that man. What did Ted say to you? What did he say to you? What did he say to you?"

Mrs. Vansuythen sat down helplessly on the sofa, overborne by the trouble of her questioner.

"He said—I can't remember exactly what he said—but I understood him to say—that is—But, really, Mrs. Boulte, isn't it rather a strange question?"

"Will you tell me what he said?" repeated Mrs. Boulte.

Even a tiger will fly before a bear robbed of her whelps, and Mrs. Vansuythen was only an ordinarily good woman. She began in a sort of desperation: "Well, he said that he never cared for you at all, and, of course, there was not the least reason why he should have, and—and—that was all."

"You said he swore he had not cared for me. Was that true?"

"Yes," said Mrs. Vansuythen, very softly.

Mrs. Boulte wavered for an instant where she stood, and then fell forward fainting.

"What did I tell you?" said Boulte, as though the conversation had been unbroken. "You can see for yourself she cares for him." The light began to break into his dull mind, and he went on—"And he—what was he saying to you?"

But Mrs. Vansuythen, with no heart for explanations or impassioned protestations, was kneeling over Mrs. Boulte.

"Oh, you brute!" she cried. "Are all men like this? Help me to get her into my room—and her face is cut against the table. Oh, will you be quiet, and help me to carry her? I hate you, and I hate Captain Kurrell. Lift her up carefully and now—go! Go away!"

Boulte carried his wife into Mrs. Vansuythen's bedroom and departed before the storm of that lady's wrath and disgust, impenitent and burning with jealousy. Kurrell had been making love

to Mrs. Vansuythen—would do Vansuythen as great a wrong as he had done Boulte, who caught himself considering whether Mrs. Vansuythen would faint if she discovered that the man she loved had foresworn her.

In the middle of these meditations, Kurrell came cantering along the road and pulled up with a cheery, "Good mornin'. 'Been mashing Mrs. Vansuythen as usual, eh? Bad thing for a sober, married man, that. What will Mrs Boulte say?"

Boulte raised his head and said, slowly, "Oh, you liar!"

Kurrell's face changed. "What's that?" he asked, quickly.

"Nothing much," said Boulte. "Has my wife told you that you two are free to go off whenever you please? She has been good enough to explain the situation to me. You've been a true friend to me, Kurrell—old man—haven't you?"

Kurrell groaned, and tried to frame some sort of idiotic sentence about being willing to give "satisfaction." But his interest in the woman was dead, had died out in the Rains, and, mentally, he was abusing her for her amazing indiscretion. It would have been so easy to have broken off the thing gently and by degrees, and now he was saddled with—Boulte's voice recalled him.

"I don't think I should get any satisfaction from killing you, and I'm pretty sure you'd get none from killing me."

Then in a querulous tone, ludicrously disproportioned to his wrongs, Boulte added—"'Seems rather a pity that you haven't the decency to keep to the woman, now you've got her. You've been a true friend to her too, haven't you?"

Kurrell stared long and gravely. The situation was getting beyond him.

"What do you mean?" he said.

Boulte answered, more to himself than the questioner: "My wife came over to Mrs. Vansuythen's just now; and it seems you'd been telling Mrs. Vansuythen that you'd never cared for Emma. I suppose you lied, as usual. What had Mrs. Vansuythen to do with you, or you with her? Try to speak the truth for once in a way."

Kurrell took the double insult without wincing, and replied by another question: "Go on. What happened?"

"Emma fainted," said Boulte, simply. "But, look here, what had you been saying to Mrs. Vansuythen?"

Kurrell laughed. Mrs. Boulte had, with unbridled tongue, made havoc of his plans; and he could at least retaliate by hurting the man in whose eyes he was humiliated and shown dishonorable.

"Said to her? What does a man tell a lie like that for? I suppose I said pretty much what you've said, unless I'm a good deal mistaken."

"I spoke the truth," said Boulte, again more to himself than Kurrell. "Emma told me she hated me. She has no right in me."

"No! I suppose not. You're only her husband, y'know. And what did Mrs. Vansuythen say after you had laid your disengaged heart at her feet?"

Kurrell felt almost virtuous as he put the question.

"I don't think that matters," Boulte replied; "and it doesn't concern you."

"But it does! I tell you it does" began Kurrell, shamelessly.

The sentence was cut by a roar of laughter from Boulte's lips. Kurrell was silent for an instant, and then he, too, laughed—laughed long and loudly, rocking in his saddle. It was an unpleasant sound—the mirthless mirth of these men on the long, white line of the Narkarra Road. There were no strangers in Kashima, or they might have thought that captivity within the Dosehri hills had driven half the European population mad. The laughter ended abruptly, and Kurrell was the first to speak.

"Well, what are you going to do?"

Boulte looked up the road, and at the hills. "Nothing," said he, quietly; "what's the use? It's too ghastly for anything. We must let the old life go on. I can only call you a hound and a liar, and I can't go on calling you names forever. Besides which, I don't feel that I'm much better. We can't get out of this place. What is there to do?"

Kurrell looked round the rat-pit of Kashima and made no reply. The injured husband took up the wondrous tale.

"Ride on, and speak to Emma if you want to. God knows I don't care what you do."

He walked forward and left Kurrell gazing blankly after him. Kurrell did not ride on either to see Mrs. Boulte or Mrs. Vansuythen. He sat in his saddle and thought, while his pony grazed by the roadside.

The whir of approaching wheels roused him. Mrs. Vansuythen was driving home Mrs. Boulte, white and wan, with a cut on her forehead.

"Stop, please," said Mrs. Boulte "I want to speak to Ted."

Mrs. Vansuythen obeyed, but as Mrs. Boulte leaned forward, putting her hand upon the splash-board of the dog-cart, Kurrell spoke.

"I've seen your husband, Mrs. Boulte."

There was no necessity for any further explanation. The man's eyes were fixed, not upon Mrs. Boulte, but her companion. Mrs. Boulte saw the look.

"Speak to him!" she pleaded, turning to the woman at her side. "Oh, speak to him! Tell him what you told me just now. Tell him you hate him. Tell him you hate him!"

She bent forward and wept bitterly, while the sais, impassive, went forward to hold the horse. Mrs. Vansuythen turned scarlet and dropped the reins. She wished to be no party to such unholy explanations.

"I've nothing to do with it," she began, coldly; but Mrs. Boulte's sobs overcame her, and she addressed herself to the man. "I don't know what I am to say, Captain Kurrell. I don't know what I can call you. I think you've—you've behaved abominably, and she has cut her forehead terribly against the table."

"It doesn't hurt. It isn't anything," said Mrs. Boulte feebly. "That doesn't matter. Tell him what

you told me. Say you don't care for him. Oh, Ted, won't you believe her?"

"Mrs. Boulte has made me understand that you were—that you were fond of her once upon a time," went on Mrs. Vansuythen.

"Well!" said Kurrell brutally. "It seems to me that Mrs. Boulte had better be fond of her own husband first."

"Stop!" said Mrs. Vansuythen. "Hear me first. I don't care—I don't want to know anything about you and Mrs. Boulte; but I want you to know that I hate you, that I think you are a cur, and that I'll never, never speak to you again. Oh, I don't dare to say what I think of you, you— man! Sais, gorah ko jane do."

"I want to speak to Ted," moaned Mrs. Boulte, but the dog-cart rattled on, and Kurrell was left on the road, shamed, and boiling with wrath against Mrs. Boulte.

He waited till Mrs. Vansuythen was driving back to her own house, and, she being freed from the embarrassment of Mrs. Boulte's presence, learned for the second time her opinion of himself and his actions.

In the evenings, it was the wont of all Kashima to meet at the platform on the Narkarra Road, to drink tea, and discuss the trivialities of the day. Major Vansuythen and his wife found themselves alone at the gathering-place for almost the first time in their remembrance; and the cheery Major, in the teeth of his wife's remarkably reasonable suggestion that the rest of the Station might be sick, insisted upon driving round to the two bungalows and unearthing the population.

"Sitting in the twilight!" said he, with great indignation to the Boultes. "That'll never do! Hang it all, we're one family here! You must come out, and so must Kurrell. I'll make him bring his banjo." So great is the power of honest simplicity and a good digestion over guilty consciences that all Kashima did turn out, even down to the banjo; and the Major embraced the company in one expansive grin. As he grinned, Mrs. Vansuythen raised her eyes for an instant and looked at all Kashima. Her meaning was clear. Major Vansuythen would never know anything. He was to be the outsider in that happy family whose cage was the Dosehri hills.

"You're singing villainously out of tune, Kurrell," said the Major, truthfully. "Pass me that banjo."

And he sang in excruciating-wise till the stars came out and all Kashima went to dinner.

That was the beginning of the New Life of Kashima—the life that Mrs. Boulte made when her tongue was loosened in the twilight.

Mrs. Vansuythen has never told the Major; and since be insists upon keeping up a burdensome geniality, she has been compelled to break her vow of not speaking to Kurrell. This speech, which must of necessity preserve the semblance of politeness and interest, serves admirably to keep alive the flame of jealousy and dull hatred in Boulte's bosom, as it awakens the same passions in his wife's heart. Mrs. Boulte hates Mrs. Vansuythen because she has taken Ted from her, and, in some curious fashion, hates her because Mrs. Vansuythen—and here the wife's eyes see far more clearly than the husband's—detests Ted. And Ted—that gallant captain and honorable man—knows now that it is possible to hate a woman once loved, to the verge of wishing to silence her forever with blows. Above all, is he shocked that Mrs. Boulte cannot see the error of her ways.

Boulte and he go out tiger-shooting together in all friendship. Boulte has put their relationship on a most satisfactory footing.

"You're a blackguard," he says to Kurrell, "and I've lost any self-respect I may ever have had; but when you're with me, I can feel certain that you are not with Mrs. Vansuythen, or making Emma miserable."

Kurrell endures anything that Boulte may say to him. Sometimes they are away for three days together, and then the Major insists upon his wife going over to sit with Mrs. Boulte; although Mrs. Vansuythen has repeatedly declared that she prefers her husband's company to any in the world. From the way in which she clings to him, she would certainly seem to be speaking the truth.

But of course, as the Major says, "in a little Station we must all be friendly."

THE HILL OF ILLUSION

What rendered vain their deep desire?

A God, a God their severance ruled,

And bade between their shores to be

The unplumbed, salt, estranging sea.

 —Matthew Arnold.

HE. Tell your jhampanis not to hurry so, dear. They forget I'm fresh from the Plains.

SHE. Sure proof that I have not been going out with any one. Yes, they are an untrained crew. Where do we go?

HE. As usual—to the world's end. No, Jakko.

SHE. Have your pony led after you, then. It's a long round.

HE. And for the last time, thank Heaven!

SHE. Do you mean that still? I didn't dare to write to you about it... all these months.

HE. Mean it! I've been shaping my affairs to that end since Autumn. What makes you speak as though it had occurred to you for the first time?

SHE. I! Oh! I don't know. I've had long enough to think, too.

HE. And you've changed your mind?

SHE. No. You ought to know that I am a miracle of constancy. What are your—arrangements?

HE. Ours, Sweetheart, please.

SHE. Ours, be it then. My poor boy, how the prickly heat has marked your forehead! Have you ever tried sulphate of copper in water?

HE. It'll go away in a day or two up here. The arrangements are simple enough. Tonga in the early morning—reach Kalka at twelve—Umballa at seven—down, straight by night train, to Bombay, and then the steamer of the 21st for Rome. That's my idea. The Continent and Sweden—a ten-week honeymoon.

SHE. Ssh! Don't talk of it in that way. It makes me afraid. Guy, how long have we two been insane?

HE. Seven months and fourteen days; I forget the odd hours exactly, but I'll think.

SHE. I only wanted to see if you remembered. Who are those two on the Blessington Road?

HE. Eabrey and the Penner woman. What do they matter to us? Tell me everything that you've been doing and saying and thinking.

SHE. Doing little, saying less, and thinking a great deal. I've hardly been out at all.

Ha. That was wrong of you. You haven't been moping?

SHE. Not very much. Can you wonder that I'm disinclined for amusement?

HE. Frankly, I do. Where was the difficulty?

SHE. In this only. The more people I know and the more I'm known here, the wider spread will be the news of the crash when it comes. I don't like that.

HE. Nonsense. We shall be out of it.

SHE. You think so?

HE. I'm sure of it, if there is any power in steam or horse-flesh to carry us away. Ha! ha!

SHE. And the fun of the situation comes in—where, my Lancelot?

HE. Nowhere, Guinevere. I was only thinking of something.

SHE. They say men have a keener sense of humor than women. Now I was thinking of the scandal.

HE. Don't think of anything so ugly. We shall be beyond it.

SHE. It will be there all the same in the mouths of Simla—telegraphed over India, and talked of at the dinners—and when He goes out they will stare at Him to see how He takes it. And we shall be dead, Guy dear—dead and cast into the outer darkness where there is—

HE. Love at least. Isn't that enough?

SHE. I have said so.

HE. And you think so still?

SHE. What do you think?

Ha. What have I done? It means equal ruin to me, as the world reckons it—outcasting, the loss of my appointment, the breaking of my life's work. I pay my price.

SHE. And are you so much above the world that you can afford to pay it? Am I?

Ha. My Divinity—what else?

SHE. A very ordinary woman I'm afraid, but, so far, respectable. How'd you do, Mrs. Middleditch? Your husband? I think he's riding down to Annandale with Colonel Statters. Yes, isn't it divine after the rain?—Guy, how long am I to be allowed to bow to Mrs. Middleditch? Till the 17th?

HE. Frowsy Scotchwoman? What is the use of bringing her into the discussion? You were saying?

SHE. Nothing. Have you ever seen a man hanged?

HE. Yes. Once.

SHE. What was it for?

HE. Murder, of course.

SHE. Murder. Is that so great a sin after all? I wonder how he felt before the drop fell.

HE. I don't think he felt much. What a gruesome little woman it is this evening! You're shivering. Put on your cape, dear.

SHE. I think I will. Oh! Look at the mist coming over Sanjaoli; and I thought we should have sunshine on the Ladies' Mile! Let's turn back.

HE. What's the good? There's a cloud on Elysium Hill, and that means it's foggy all down the Mall. We'll go on. It'll blow away before we get to the Convent, perhaps. 'Jove! It is chilly.

SHE. You feel it, fresh from below. Put on your ulster. What do you think of my cape?

HE. Never ask a man his opinion of a woman's dress when he is desperately and abjectly in love with the wearer. Let me look. Like everything else of yours it's perfect. Where did you get it from?

SHE. He gave it me, on Wednesday... our wedding-day, you know.

HE. The deuce He did! He's growing generous in his old age. D'you like all that frilly, bunchy stuff at the throat? I don't.

SHE. Don't you?

"Kind Sir, O' your courtesy,

As you go by the town, Sir,

Pray you O' your love for me,

Buy me a russet gown, Sir."

HE. I won't say: "Keek into the draw-well, Janet, Janet." Only wait a little, darling, and you shall be stocked with russet gowns and everything else.

SHE. And when the frocks wear out, you'll get me new ones—and everything else?

HE. Assuredly.

SHE. I wonder!

HE. Look here, Sweetheart, I didn't spend two days and two nights in the train to hear you wonder. I thought we'd settled all that at Shaifazehat.

SHE (dreamily). At Shaifazehat? Does the Station go on still? That was ages and ages ago. It must be crumbling to pieces. All except the Amirtollah kutcha road. I don't believe that could crumble till the Day of Judgment.

Ha. You think so? What is the mood now?

SHE. I can't tell. How cold it is! Let us get on quickly.

Ha. Better walk a little. Stop your jhampanis and get out. What's the matter with you this evening, dear?

SHE. Nothing. You must grow accustomed to my ways. If I'm boring you I can go home. Here's Captain Congleton coming; I dare say he'll be willing to escort me.

Ha. Goose! Between us, too! Damn Captain Congleton. There!

SHE. Chivalrous Knight! Is it your habit to swear much in talking? It jars a little, and you might swear at me.

HE. My angel! I didn't know what I was saying; and you changed so quickly that I couldn't follow. I'll apologize in dust and ashes.

SHE. There'll be enough of those later on. Good night, Captain Congleton. Going to the singing-quadrilles already? What dances am I giving you next week? No! You must have written them down wrong. Five and Seven, I said. If you've made a mistake, I certainly don't intend to suffer for it. You must alter your programme.

HE. I thought you told me that you had not been going out much this season?

SHE. Quite true, but when I do I dance with Captain Congleton. He dances very nicely.

HE. And sit out with him, I suppose?

SHE. Yes. Have you any objection? Shall I stand under the chandelier in future?

HE. What does he talk to you about?

SHE. What do men talk about when they sit out?

Ha. Ugh! Don't! Well now I'm up, you must dispense with the fascinating Congleton for a while. I don't like him.

SHE. (after a pause). Do you know what you have said?

HE. 'Can't say that I do exactly. I'm not in the best of tempers.

SHE. So I see... and feel. My true and faithful lover, where is your "eternal constancy," "unalterable trust," and "reverent devotion"? I remember those phrases; you seem to have forgotten them. I mention a man's name—

HE. A good deal more than that.

SHE. Well, speak to him about a dance—perhaps the last dance that I shall ever dance in my life before I... before I go away; and you at once distrust and insult me.

HE. I never said a word.

SHE. How much did you imply? Guy, is this amount of confidence to be our stock to start the new life on?

HE. No, of course not. I didn't mean that. On my word of honor, I didn't. Let it pass, dear. Please let it pass.

SHE. This once—yes—and a second time, and again and again, all through the years when I shall be unable to resent it. You want too much, my Lancelot, and... you know too much.

HE. How do you mean?

SHE. That is a part of the punishment. There cannot be perfect trust between us.

HE. In Heaven's name, why not?

SHE. Hush! The Other Place is quite enough. Ask yourself.

HE. I don't follow.

SHE. You trust me so implicitly that when I look at another man—Never mind, Guy. Have you ever made love to a girl—a good girl?

HE. Something of the sort. Centuries ago—in the Dark Ages, before I ever met you, dear.

SHE. Tell me what you said to her.

HE. What does a man say to a girl? I've forgotten.

SHE. I remember. He tells her that he trusts her and worships the ground she walks on, and that he'll love and honor and protect her till her dying day; and so she marries in that belief. At least, I speak of one girl who was not protected.

HE. Well, and then?

SHE. And then, Guy, and then, that girl needs ten times the love and trust and honor—yes, honor—that was enough when she was only a mere wife if—if—the other life she chooses to lead is to be made even bearable. Do you understand?

HE. Even bearable! It'll he Paradise.

SHE. Ah! Can you give me all I've asked for—not now, nor a few months later, but when you begin to think of what you might have done if you had kept your own appointment and your caste here—when you begin to look upon me as a drag and a burden? I shall want it most, then, Guy, for there will be no one in the wide world but you.

HE. You're a little over-tired tonight, Sweetheart, and you're taking a stage view of the situation. After the necessary business in the Courts, the road is clear to—

SHE. "The holy state of matrimony!" Ha! ha! ha!

HE. Ssh! Don't laugh in that horrible way!

SHE. I-I c-c-c-can't help it! Isn't it too absurd! Ah! Ha! ha! ha! Guy, stop me quick or I shall—l-l-laugh till we get to the Church.

HE. For goodness' sake, stop! Don't make an exhibition of yourself. What is the matter with you?

SHE. N-nothing. I'm better now.

HE. That's all right. One moment, dear. There's a little wisp of hair got loose from behind your right ear and it's straggling over your cheek. So!

SHE. Thank'oo. I'm 'fraid my hat's on one side, too.

HE. What do you wear these huge dagger bonnet-skewers for? They're big enough to kill a man with.

SHE. Oh! Don't kill me, though. You're sticking it into my head! Let me do it. You men are so clumsy.

HE. Have you had many opportunities of comparing us—in this sort of work?

SHE. Guy, what is my name?

HE. Eh! I don't follow.

SHE. Here's my cardcase. Can you read?

HE. Yes. Well?

SHE. Well, that answers your question. You know the other man's name. Am I sufficiently humbled, or would you like to ask me if there is any one else?

HE. I see now. My darling, I never meant that for an instant. I was only joking. There! Lucky there's no one on the road. They'd be scandalized.

SHE. They'll be more scandalized before the end.

HE. Do-on't! I don't like you to talk in that way.

SHE. Unreasonable man! Who asked me to face the situation and accept it? Tell me, do I look like Mrs. Penner? Do I look like a naughty woman? Swear I don't! Give me your word of honor, my honorable friend, that I'm not like Mrs. Buzgago. That's the way she stands, with her hands clasped at the back of her head. D'you like that?

HE. Don't be affected.

SHE. I'm not. I'm Mrs. Buzgago. Listen!

Pendant une anne' toute entiere

Le regiment n'a pas r'paru.

Au Ministere de la Guerre

On le r'porta comme perdu.

On se r'noncait a r'trouver sa trace,

Quand un matin subitement,

On le vit r'paraitre sur la place

L'Colonel toujours en avant.

That's the way she rolls her r's. Am I like her?

HE. No, but I object when you go on like an actress and sing stuff of that kind. Where in the world did you pick up the Chanson du Colonel? It isn't a drawing-room song. It isn't proper.

SHE. Mrs. Buzgago taught it me. She is both drawing-room and proper, and in another month she'll shut her drawing-room to me, and thank God she isn't as improper as I am. Oh, Guy, Guy! I wish I was like some women and had no scruples about—what is it Keene says?—"Wearing

a corpse's hair and being false to the bread they eat."

HE. I am only a man of limited intelligence, and just now, very bewildered. When you have quite finished flashing through all your moods tell me, and I'll try to understand the last one.

SHE. Moods, Guy! I haven't any. I'm sixteen years old and you're just twenty, and you've been waiting for two hours outside the school in the cold. And now I've met you, and now we're walking home together. Does that suit you, My Imperial Majesty?

HE. No. We aren't children. Why can't you be rational?

SHE. He asks me that when I'm going to commit suicide for his sake, and, and—I don't want to be French and rave about my mother, but have I ever told you that I have a mother, and a brother who was my pet before I married? He's married now. Can't you imagine the pleasure that the news of the elopement will give him? Have you any people at Home, Guy, to be pleased with your performances?

HE. One or two. One can't make omelets without breaking eggs.

SHE (slowly). I don't see the necessity—

HE. Hah! What do you mean?

SHE. Shall I speak the truth?

HE. Under the circumstances, perhaps it would be as well.

SHE. Guy, I'm afraid.

HE. I thought we'd settled all that. What of?

SHE. Of you.

HE. Oh, damn it all! The old business! This is too had!

SHE. Of you.

HE. And what now?

SHE. What do you think of me?

HE. Beside the question altogether. What do you intend to do?

SHE. I daren't risk it. I'm afraid. If I could only cheat—

HE. A la Buzgago? No, thanks. That's the one point on which I have any notion of Honor. I won't eat his salt and steal too. I'll loot openly or not at all.

SHE. I never meant anything else.

HE. Then, why in the world do you pretend not to be willing to come?

SHE. It's not pretence, Guy. I am afraid.

HE. Please explain.

SHE. It can't last, Guy. It can't last. You'll get angry, and then you'll swear, and then you'll get

jealous, and then you'll mistrust me—you do now—and you yourself will be the best reason for doubting. And I—what shall I do? I shall be no better than Mrs. Buzgago found out—no better than any one. And you'll know that. Oh, Guy, can't you see?

HE. I see that you are desperately unreasonable, little woman.

SHE. There! The moment I begin to object, you get angry. What will you do when I am only your property—stolen property? It can't be, Guy. It can't be! I thought it could, but it can't. You'll get tired of me.

HE. I tell you I shall not. Won't anything make you understand that?

SHE. There, can't you see? If you speak to me like that now, you'll call me horrible names later, if I don't do everything as you like. And if you were cruel to me, Guy, where should I go—where should I go? I can't trust you. Oh! I can't trust you!

HE. I suppose I ought to say that I can trust you. I've ample reason.

SHE. Please don't, dear. It hurts as much as if you hit me.

HE. It isn't exactly pleasant for me.

SHE. I can't help it. I wish I were dead! I can't trust you, and I don't trust myself. Oh, Guy, let it die away and be forgotten!

HE. Too late now. I don't understand you—I won't—and I can't trust myself to talk this evening. May I call tomorrow?

SHE. Yes. No! Oh, give me time! The day after. I get into my 'rickshaw here and meet Him at Peliti's. You ride.

HE. I'll go on to Peliti's too. I think I want a drink. My world's knocked about my ears and the stars are falling. Who are those brutes howling in the Old Library?

SHE. They're rehearsing the singing-quadrilles for the Fancy Ball. Can't you hear Mrs. Buzgago's voice? She has a solo. It's quite a new idea. Listen.

MRS. BUZGAGO (in the Old Library, con. molt. exp.).

See-saw! Margery Daw! Sold her bed to lie upon straw. Wasn't she a silly slut To sell her bed and lie upon dirt?

Captain Congleton, I'm going to alter that to "flirt." It sound better.

HE. No, I've changed my mind about the drink. Good night, little lady. I shall see you tomorrow?

SHE. Yes. Good night, Guy. Don't be angry with me.

HE. Angry! You know I trust you absolutely. Good night and—God bless you!

(Three seconds later. Alone.) Hmm! I'd give something to discover whether there's another man at the back of all this.

A SECOND-RATE WOMAN

Est fuga, volvitur rota,

On we drift; where looms the dim port?

One Two Three Four Five contribute their quota:

Something is gained if one caught but the import,

Show it us, Hugues of Saxe-Gotha.

—Master Hugues of Saxe-Gotha.

"DRESSED! Don't tell me that woman ever dressed in her life. She stood in the middle of her room while her ayah—no, her husband—it must have been a man—threw her clothes at her. She then did her hair with her fingers, and rubbed her bonnet in the flue under the bed. I know she did, as well as if I had assisted at the orgy. Who is she?" said Mrs. Hauksbee.

"Don't!" said Mrs. Mallowe, feebly. "You make my head ache. I'm miserable today. Stay me with fondants, comfort me with chocolates, for I am—Did you bring anything from Peliti's?"

"Questions to begin with. You shall have the sweets when you have answered them. Who and what is the creature? There were at least half a dozen men round her, and she appeared to be going to sleep in their midst."

"Delville," said Mrs. Mallowe, "'Shady' Delville, to distinguish her from Mrs. Jim of that ilk. She dances as untidily as she dresses, I believe, and her husband is somewhere in Madras. Go and call, if you are so interested."

"What have I to do with Shigramitish women? She merely caught my attention for a minute, and I wondered at the attraction that a dowd has for a certain type of man. I expected to see her walk out of her clothes—until I looked at her eyes."

"Hooks and eyes, surely," drawled Mrs. Mallowe.

"Don't be clever, Polly. You make my head ache. And round this hayrick stood a crowd of men—a positive crowd!"

"Perhaps they also expected"—

"Polly, don't be Rabelaisian!"

Mrs. Mallowe curled herself up comfortably on the sofa, and turned her attention to the sweets. She and Mrs. Hauksbee shared the same house at Simla; and these things befell two seasons after the matter of Otis Yeere, which has been already recorded.

Mrs. Hauksbee stepped into the veranda and looked down upon the Mall, her forehead puckered with thought.

"Hah!" said Mrs. Hauksbee, shortly. "Indeed!"

"What is it?" said Mrs. Mallowe, sleepily.

"That dowd and The Dancing Master—to whom I object."

"Why to The Dancing Master? He is a middle-aged gentleman, of reprobate and romantic tendencies, and tries to be a friend of mine."

"Then make up your mind to lose him. Dowds cling by nature, and I should imagine that this animal—how terrible her bonnet looks from above!—is specially clingsome."

"She is welcome to The Dancing Master so far as I am concerned. I never could take an interest in a monotonous liar. The frustrated aim of his life is to persuade people that he is a bachelor."

"0—oh! I think I've met that sort of man before. And isn't he?"

"No. He confided that to me a few days ago. Ugh! Some men ought to Be killed."

"What happened then?"

"He posed as the horror of horrors—a misunderstood man. Heaven knows the femme incomprise is sad enough and had enough—but the other thing!"

"And so fat too! I should have laughed in his face. Men seldom confide in me. How is it they come to you?"

"For the sake of impressing me with their careers in the past. Protect me from men with confidences!"

"And yet you encourage them?"

"What can I do? They talk. I listen, and they vow that I am sympathetic. I know I always profess astonishment even when the plot is—of the most old possible."

"Yes. Men are so unblushingly explicit if they are once allowed to talk, whereas women's confidences are full of reservations and fibs, except"—

"When they go mad and babble of the Unutterabilities after a week's acquaintance. Really, if you come to consider, we know a great deal more of men than of our own sex."

"And the extraordinary thing is that men will never believe it. They say we are trying to hide something."

"They are generally doing that on their own account. Alas! These chocolates pall upon me, and I haven't eaten more than a dozen. I think I shall go to sleep."

"Then you'll get fat dear. If you took more exercise and a more intelligent interest in your neighbors you would—"

"Be as much loved as Mrs. Hauksbee. You're a darling in many ways and I like you—you are not a woman's woman—but why do you trouble yourself about mere human beings?"

"Because in the absence of angels, who I am sure would be horribly dull, men and women are the most fascinating things in the whole wide world, lazy one. I am interested in The Dowd—I am interested in The Dancing Master—I am interested in the Hawley Boy—and I am interested in you."

"Why couple me with the Hawley Boy? He is your property."

"Yes, and in his own guileless speech, I'm making a good thing out of him. When he is slightly more reformed, and has passed his Higher Standard, or whatever the authorities think fit to exact from him, I shall select a pretty little girl, the Holt girl, I think, and"—here she waved her hands airily—"'whom Mrs. Hauksbee hath joined together let no man put asunder.' That's all."

"And when you have yoked May Holt with the most notorious detrimental in Simla, and earned the undying hatred of Mamma Holt, what will you do with me, Dispenser of the Destinies of the Universe?"

Mrs. Hauksbee dropped into a low chair in front of the fire, and, chin in band, gazed long and steadfastly at Mrs. Mallowe.

"I do not know," she said, shaking her head, "what I shall do with you, dear. It's obviously impossible to marry you to some one else—your husband would object and the experiment might not be successful after all. I think I shall begin by preventing you from—what is it?— 'sleeping on ale-house benches and snoring in the sun.'"

"Don't! I don't like your quotations. They are so rude. Go to the Library and bring me new books."

"While you sleep? No! If you don't come with me, I shall spread your newest frock on my 'rickshaw-bow, and when any one asks me what I am doing, I shall say that I am going to Phelps's to get it let out. I shall take care that Mrs. MacNamara sees me. Put your things on, there's a good girl."

Mrs. Mallowe groaned and obeyed, and the two went off to the Library, where they found Mrs. Delville and the man who went by the nickname of The Dancing Master. By that time Mrs Mallowe was awake and eloquent.

"That is the Creature!" said Mrs Hauksbee, with the air of one pointing out a slug in the road.

"No," said Mrs. Mallowe. "The man is the Creature. Ugh! Good-evening, Mr. Bent. I thought you were coming to tea this evening."

"Surely it was for tomorrow, was it not?" answered The Dancing Master. "I understood... I fancied... I'm so sorry... How very unfortunate!..."

But Mrs. Mallowe had passed on.

"For the practiced equivocator you said he was," murmured Mrs. Hauksbee, "he strikes me as a failure. Now wherefore should he have preferred a walk with The Dowd to tea with us? Elective affinities, I suppose—both grubby. Polly, I'd never forgive that woman as long as the world rolls."

"I forgive every woman everything," said Mrs. Mallowe. "He will be a sufficient punishment for her. What a common voice she has!"

Mrs. Delville's voice was not pretty, her carriage was even less lovely, and her raiment was strikingly neglected. All these things Mrs. Mallowe noticed over the top of a magazine.

"Now what is there in her?" said Mrs. Hauksbee. "Do you see what I meant about the clothes falling off? If I were a man I would perish sooner than be seen with that rag-bag. And yet, she has good eyes, but—oh!"

"What is it?"

"She doesn't know how to use them! On my Honor, she does not. Look! Oh look! Untidiness I can endure, but ignorance never! The woman's a fool."

"H'sh! She'll hear you."

"All the women in Simla are fools. She'll think I mean some one else. Now she's going out. What a thoroughly objectionable couple she and The Dancing Master make! Which reminds me. Do you suppose they'll ever dance together?"

"Wait and see. I don't envy her the conversation of The Dancing Master—loathly man. His wife ought to be up here before long."

"Do you know anything about him?"

"Only what he told me. It may be all a fiction. He married a girl bred in the country, I think, and, being an honorable, chivalrous soul, told me that he repented his bargain and sent her to her mother as often as possible—a person who has lived in the Doon since the memory of man and goes to Mussoorie when other people go Home. The wife is with her at present. So he says."

'Babies?'

"One only, but he talks of his wife in a revolting way. I hated him for it. He thought he was being epigrammatic and brilliant."

"That is a vice peculiar to men. I dislike him because he is generally in the wake of some girl, disappointing the Eligibles. He will persecute May Holt no more, unless I am much mistaken."

"No. I think Mrs. Delville may occupy his attention for a while."

"Do you suppose she knows that he is the head of a family?"

"Not from his lips. He swore me to eternal secrecy. Wherefore I tell you. Don't you know that type of man?"

"Not intimately, thank goodness! As a general rule, when a man begins to abuse his wife to me, I find that the Lord gives me wherewith to answer him according to his folly; and we part with a coolness between us. I laugh."

"I'm different. I've no sense of humor."

"Cultivate it, then. It has been my mainstay for more years than I care to think about. A well-educated sense of Humor will save a woman when Religion, Training, and Home influences fail; and we may all need salvation sometimes."

"Do you suppose that the Delville woman has humor?"

"Her dress betrays her. How can a Thing who wears her supple'ment under her left arm have any notion of the fitness of things—much less their folly? If she discards The Dancing Master after having once seen him dance, I may respect her, Otherwise—

"But are we not both assuming a great deal too much, dear? You saw the woman at Peliti's— half an hour later you saw her walking with The Dancing Master—an hour later you met her here at the Library."

"Still with The Dancing Master, remember."

"Still with The Dancing Master, I admit, but why on the strength of that should you imagine"—

"I imagine nothing. I have no imagination. I am only convinced that The Dancing Master is attracted to The Dowd because he is objectionable in every way and she in every other. If I know the man as you have described him, he holds his wife in slavery at present."

"She is twenty years younger than he."

"Poor wretch! And, in the end, after he has posed and swaggered and lied—he has a mouth under that ragged moustache simply made for lies—he will be rewarded according to his merits."

"I wonder what those really are," said Mrs. Mallowe.

But Mrs. Hauksbee, her face close to the shelf of the new books, was humming softly: "What shall he have who killed the Deer!" She was a lady of unfettered speech.

One month later, she announced her intention of calling upon Mrs. Delville. Both Mrs. Hauksbee and Mrs. Mallowe were in morning wrappers, and there was a great peace in the land.

"I should go as I was," said Mrs. Mallowe. "It would be a delicate compliment to her style."

Mrs. Hauksbee studied herself in the glass.

"Assuming for a moment that she ever darkened these doors, I should put on this robe, after all the others, to show her what a morning wrapper ought to be. It might enliven her. As it is, I shall go in the dove-colored—sweet emblem of youth and innocence—and shall put on my new gloves."

"If you really are going, dirty tan would be too good; and you know that dove—color spots with the rain."

"I care not. I may make her envious. At least I shall try, though one cannot expect very much from a woman who puts a lace tucker into her habit."

"Just Heavens! When did she do that?"

"Yesterday—riding with The Dancing Master. I met them at the back of Jakko, and the rain had made the lace lie down. To complete the effect, she was wearing an unclean terai with the elastic under her chin. I felt almost too well content to take the trouble to despise her."

"The Hawley Boy was riding with you. What did he think?"

"Does a boy ever notice these things? Should I like him if he did? He stared in the rudest way, and just when I thought he had seen the elastic, he said, 'There's something very taking about that face.' I rebuked him on the spot. I don't approve of boys being taken by faces."

"Other than your own. I shouldn't be in the least surprised if the Hawley Boy immediately went to call."

"I forbade him. Let her be satisfied with The Dancing Master, and his wife when she comes up. I'm rather curious to see Mrs. Bent and the Delville woman together."

Mrs. Hauksbee departed and, at the end of an hour, returned slightly flushed.

"There is no limit to the treachery of youth! I ordered the Hawley Boy, as he valued my patronage, not to call. The first person I stumble over—literally stumble over—in her poky, dark, little drawing-room is, of course, the Hawley Boy. She kept us waiting ten minutes, and then emerged as though he had been tipped out of the dirty-clothes basket. You know my way, dear, when I am all put out. I was Superior, crrrushingly Superior! 'Lifted my eyes to Heaven, and had heard of nothing—'dropped my eyes on the carpet and 'really didn't know'—'played with my cardcase and 'supposed so.' The Hawley Boy giggled like a girl, and I had to freeze him with scowls between the sentences."

"And she?"

"She sat in a heap on the edge of a couch, and managed to convey the impression that she was suffering from stomach-ache, at the very least. It was all I could do not to ask after her symptoms. When I rose she grunted just like a buffalo in the water—too lazy to move."

"Are you certain?"—

"Am I blind, Polly? Laziness, sheer laziness, nothing else—or her garments were only constructed for sitting down in. I stayed for a quarter of an hour trying to penetrate the gloom, to guess what her surroundings were like, while she stuck out her tongue."

"Lu—cy!"

"Well—I'll withdraw the tongue, though I'm sure if she didn't do it when I was in the room, she did the minute I was outside. At any rate, she lay in a lump and grunted. Ask the Hawley Boy, dear. I believe the grunts were meant for sentences, but she spoke so indistinctly that I can't swear to it."

"You are incorrigible, simply."

"I am not! Treat me civilly, give me peace with honor, don't put the only available seat facing the window, and a child may eat jam in my lap before Church. But I resent being grunted at. Wouldn't you? Do you suppose that she communicates her views on life and love to The Dancing Master in a set of modulated 'Grmphs'?"

"You attach too much importance to The Dancing Master."

"He came as we went, and The Dowd grew almost cordial at the sight of him. He smiled greasily, and moved about that darkened dog-kennel in a suspiciously familiar way."

"Don't be uncharitable. Any sin but that I'll forgive."

"Listen to the voice of History. I am only describing what I saw. He entered, the heap on the sofa revived slightly, and the Hawley Boy and I came away together. He is disillusioned, but I felt it my duty to lecture him severely for going there. And that's all."

"Now for Pity's sake leave the wretched creature and The Dancing Master alone. They never did you any harm."

"No harm? To dress as an example and a stumbling-block for half Simla, and then to find this Person who is dressed by the hand of God—not that I wish to disparage Him for a moment, but you know the tikka-dhurzie way He attires those lilies of the field—this Person draws the eyes of men—and some of them nice men? It's almost enough to make one discard clothing. I told the Hawley Boy so."

"And what did that sweet youth do?"

"Turned shell-pink and looked across the far blue hills like a distressed cherub. Am I talking wildly, Polly? Let me say my say, and I shall be calm. Otherwise I may go abroad and disturb Simla with a few original reflections. Excepting always your own sweet self, there isn't a single woman in the land who understands me when I am—what's the word?"

"Tete-Fele'e," suggested Mrs. Mallowe.

"Exactly! And now let us have tiffin. The demands of Society are exhausting, and as Mrs. Delville says"—Here Mrs. Hauksbee, to the horror of the khitmatgars, lapsed into a series of grunts, while Mrs. Mallowe stared in lazy surprise.

"'God gie us a gude conceit of oorselves,'" said Mrs. Hauksbee, piously, returning to her natural speech. "Now, in any other woman that would have been vulgar. I am consumed with curiosity to see Mrs. Bent. I expect complications."

"Woman of one idea," said Mrs. Mallowe, shortly; "all complications are as old as the hills! I have lived through or near all—all—ALL!"

"And yet do not understand that men and women never behave twice alike. I am old who was young—if ever I put my head in your lap, you dear, big sceptic, you will learn that my parting is gauze—but never, no never have I lost my interest in men and women. Polly, I shall see this business Out to the bitter end."

"I am going to sleep," said Mrs. Mallowe, calmly. "I never interfere with men or women unless I am compelled," and she retired with dignity to her own room.

Mrs. Hauksbee's curiosity was not long left ungratified, for Mrs. Bent came up to Simla a few days after the conversation faithfully reported above, and pervaded the Mall by her husband's side.

"Behold!" said Mrs. Hauksbee, thoughtfully rubbing her nose. "That is the last link of the chain, if we omit the husband of the Delville, whoever he may be. Let me consider. The Bents and the Delvilles inhabit the same hotel; and the Delville is detested by the Waddy—do you know the Waddy?—who is almost as big a dowd. The Waddy also abominates the male Bent, for which, if her other sins do not weigh too heavily, she will eventually be caught up to Heaven."

"Don't be irreverent," said Mrs. Mallowe. "I like Mrs. Bent's face."

"I am discussing the Waddy," returned Mrs. Hauksbee, loftily. "The Waddy will take the female Bent apart, after having borrowed—yes!—everything that she can, from hairpins to babies' bottles. Such, my dear, is life in a hotel. The Waddy will tell the female Bent facts and fictions about The Dancing Master and The Dowd."

"Lucy, I should like you better if you were not always looking into people's back bedrooms."

"Anybody can look into their front drawing-rooms; and remember whatever I do, and whatever I look, I never talk—as the Waddy will. Let us hope that The Dancing Master's greasy smile and manner of the pedagogue will soften the heart of that cow, his wife. If mouths speak truth, I should think that little Mrs. Bent could get very angry on occasion."

"But what reason has she for being angry?"

"What reason! The Dancing Master in himself is a reason. How does it go? 'If in his life some

trivial errors fall, Look in his face and you'll believe them all.' I am prepared to credit any evil of The Dancing Master, because I hate him so. And The Dowd is so disgustingly badly dressed"—

"That she, too, is capable of every iniquity? I always prefer to believe the best of everybody. It saves so much trouble."

"Very good. I prefer to believe the worst. It saves useless expenditure of sympathy. And you may be quite certain that the Waddy believes with me."

Mrs. Mallowe sighed and made no answer.

The conversation was holden after dinner while Mrs. Hauksbee was dressing for a dance.

"I am too tired to go," pleaded Mrs. Mallowe, and Mrs. Hauksbee left her in peace till two in the morning, when she was aware of emphatic knocking at her door.

"Don't be very angry, dear," said Mrs. Hauksbee. "My idiot of an ayah has gone home, and, as I hope to sleep tonight, there isn't a soul in the place to unlace me."

"Oh, this is too bad!" said Mrs. Mallowe sulkily.

"'Can't help it. I'm a lone, lorn grass-widow, dear, but I will not sleep in my stays. And such news, too! Oh, do unlace me, there's a darling! The Dowd—The Dancing Master—I and the Hawley Boy—You know the North veranda?"

"How can I do anything if you spin round like this?" protested Mrs. Mallowe, fumbling with the knot of the laces.

"Oh, I forget. I must tell my tale without the aid of your eyes. Do you know you've lovely eyes, dear? Well to begin with, I took the Hawley Boy to a kala juggah."

"Did he want much taking?"

"Lots! There was an arrangement of loose-boxes in kanats, and she was in the next one talking to him."

"Which? How? Explain."

"You know what I mean—The Dowd and The Dancing Master. We could hear every word and we listened shamelessly—'specially the Hawley Boy. Polly, I quite love that woman!"

"This is interesting. There! Now turn round. What happened?"

"One moment. Ah-h! Blessed relief. I've been looking forward to taking them off for the last half-hour—which is ominous at my time of life. But, as I was saying, we listened and heard The Dowd drawl worse than ever. She drops her final g's like a barmaid or a blue-blooded Aide-de-Camp. 'Look he-ere, you're gettin' too fond o' me,' she said, and The Dancing Master owned it was so in language that nearly made me ill. The Dowd reflected for a while. Then we heard her say, 'Look he-ere, Mister Bent, why are you such an awful liar?' I nearly exploded while The Dancing Master denied the charge. It seems that he never told her he was a married man."

"I said he wouldn't."

"And she had taken this to heart, on personal grounds, I suppose. She drawled along for five minutes, reproaching him with his perfidy and grew quite motherly. 'Now you've got a nice

little wife of your own—you have,' she said. 'She's ten times too good for a fat old man like you, and, look he-ere, you never told me a word about her, and I've been thinkin' about it a good deal, and I think you're a liar.' Wasn't that delicious? The Dancing Master maundered and raved till the Hawley Boy suggested that he should burst in and beat him. His voice runs up into an impassioned squeak when he is afraid. The Dowd must be an extraordinary woman. She explained that had he been a bachelor she might not have objected to his devotion; but since he was a married man and the father of a very nice baby, she considered him a hypocrite, and this she repeated twice. She wound up her drawl with: 'An I'm tellin' you this because your wife is angry with me, an' I hate quarrellin' with any other woman, an' I like your wife. You know how you have behaved for the last six weeks. You shouldn't have done it, indeed you shouldn't. You're too old an' fat.' Can't you imagine how The Dancing Master would wince at that! 'Now go away,' she said. 'I don't want to tell you what I think of you, because I think you are not nice. I'll stay he-ere till the next dance begins.' Did you think that the creature had so much in her?"

"I never studied her as closely as you did. It sounds unnatural. What happened?"

"The Dancing Master attempted blandishment, reproof, jocularity, and the style of the Lord High Warden, and I had almost to pinch the Hawley Boy to make him keep quiet. She grunted at the end of each sentence and, in the end he went away swearing to himself, quite like a man in a novel. He looked more objectionable than ever. I laughed. I love that woman—in spite of her clothes. And now I'm going to bed. What do you think of it?"

"I sha'n't begin to think till the morning," said Mrs. Mallowe, yawning "Perhaps she spoke the truth. They do fly into it by accident sometimes."

Mrs. Hauksbee's account of her eavesdropping was an ornate one but truthful in the main. For reasons best known to herself, Mrs. "Shady" Delville had turned upon Mr Bent and rent him limb from limb, casting him away limp and disconcerted ere she withdrew the light of her eyes from him permanently. Being a man of resource, and anything but pleased in that he had been called both old and fat, he gave Mrs. Bent to understand that he had, during her absence in the Doon, been the victim of unceasing persecution at the hands of Mrs. Delville, and he told the tale so often and with such eloquence that he ended in believing it, while his wife marvelled at the manners and customs of "some women." When the situation showed signs of languishing, Mrs. Waddy was always on hand to wake the smouldering fires of suspicion in Mrs. Bent's bosom and to contribute generally to the peace and comfort of the hotel. Mr. Bent's life was not a happy one, for if Mrs. Waddy's story were true, he was, argued his wife, untrustworthy to the last degree. If his own statement was true, his charms of manner and conversation were so great that he needed constant surveillance. And he received it, till he repented genuinely of his marriage and neglected his personal appearance. Mrs. Delville alone in the hotel was unchanged. She removed her chair some six paces toward the head of the table, and occasionally in the twilight ventured on timid overtures of friendship to Mrs. Bent, which were repulsed.

"She does it for my sake," hinted the Virtuous Bent.

"A dangerous and designing woman," purred Mrs. Waddy.

Worst of all, every other hotel in Simla was full!

"Polly, are you afraid of diphtheria?"

"Of nothing in the world except smallpox. Diphtheria kills, but it doesn't disfigure. Why do you ask?"

"Because the Bent baby has got it, and the whole hotel is upside down in consequence. The

Waddy has 'set her five young on the rail' and fled. The Dancing Master fears for his precious throat, and that miserable little woman, his wife, has no notion of what ought to be done. She wanted to put it into a mustard bath—for croup!"

"Where did you learn all this?"

"Just now, on the Mall. Dr. Howlen told me. The Manager of the hotel is abusing the Bents, and the Bents are abusing the manager. They are a feckless couple."

"Well. What's on your mind?"

"This; and I know it's a grave thing to ask. Would you seriously object to my bringing the child over here, with its mother?"

"On the most strict understanding that we see nothing of The Dancing Master."

"He will be only too glad to stay away. Polly, you're an angel. The woman really is at her wits' end."

"And you know nothing about her, careless, and would hold her up to public scorn if it gave you a minute's amusement. Therefore you risk your life for the sake of her brat. No, Loo, I'm not the angel. I shall keep to my rooms and avoid her. But do as you please—only tell me why you do it."

Mrs. Hauksbee's eyes softened; she looked out of the window and back into Mrs. Mallowe's face.

"I don't know," said Mrs. Hauksbee, simply.

"You dear!"

"Polly!—and for aught you knew you might have taken my fringe off. Never do that again without warning. Now we'll get the rooms ready. I don't suppose I shall be allowed to circulate in society for a month."

"And I also. Thank goodness I shall at last get all the sleep I want."

Much to Mrs. Bent's surprise she and the baby were brought over to the house almost before she knew where she was. Bent was devoutly and undisguisedly thankful, for he was afraid of the infection, and also hoped that a few weeks in the hotel alone with Mrs. Delville might lead to explanations. Mrs. Bent had thrown her jealousy to the winds in her fear for her child's life.

"We can give you good milk," said Mrs. Hauksbee to her, "and our house is much nearer to the Doctor's than the hotel, and you won't feel as though you were living in a hostile camp Where is the dear Mrs. Waddy? She seemed to be a particular friend of yours."

"They've all left me," said Mrs. Bent, bitterly. "Mrs. Waddy went first. She said I ought to be ashamed of myself for introducing diseases there, and I am sure it wasn't my fault that little Dora"—

"How nice!" cooed Mrs. Hauksbee. "The Waddy is an infectious disease herself—'more quickly caught than the plague and the taker runs presently mad.' I lived next door to her at the Elysium, three years ago. Now see, you won't give us the least trouble, and I've ornamented all the house with sheets soaked in carbolic. It smells comforting, doesn't it? Remember I'm always in call, and my ayah's at your service when yours goes to her meals and—and... if you cry I'll never forgive you."

Dora Bent occupied her mother's unprofitable attention through the day and the night. The Doctor called thrice in the twenty-four hours, and the house reeked with the smell of the Condy's Fluid, chlorine-water, and carbolic acid washes. Mrs. Mallowe kept to her own rooms—she considered that she had made sufficient concessions in the cause of humanity—and Mrs. Hauksbee was more esteemed by the Doctor as a help in the sick-room than the half-distraught mother.

"I know nothing of illness," said Mrs. Hauksbee to the Doctor. "Only tell me what to do, and I'll do it."

"Keep that crazy woman from kissing the child, and let her have as little to do with the nursing as you possibly can," said the Doctor; "I'd turn her out of the sick-room, but that I honestly believe she'd die of anxiety. She is less than no good, and I depend on you and the ayahs, remember."

Mrs. Hauksbee accepted the responsibility, though it painted olive hollows under her eyes and forced her to her oldest dresses. Mrs. Bent clung to her with more than childlike faith.

"I know you'll, make Dora well, won't you?" she said at least twenty times a day; and twenty times a day Mrs. Hauksbee answered valiantly, "Of course I will."

But Dora did not improve, and the Doctor seemed to be always in the house.

"There's some danger of the thing taking a bad turn," he said; "I'll come over between three and four in the morning tomorrow."

"Good gracious!" said Mrs. Hauksbee. "He never told me what the turn would be! My education has been horribly neglected; and I have only this foolish mother-woman to fall back upon."

The night wore through slowly, and Mrs. Hauksbee dozed in a chair by the fire. There was a dance at the Viceregal Lodge, and she dreamed of it till she was aware of Mrs. Bent's anxious eyes staring into her own.

"Wake up! Wake up! Do something!" cried Mrs. Bent, piteously. "Dora's choking to death! Do you mean to let her die?"

Mrs. Hauksbee jumped to her feet and bent over the bed. The child was fighting for breath, while the mother wrung her hands despairing.

"Oh, what can I do? What can you do? She won't stay still! I can't hold her. Why didn't the Doctor say this was coming?" screamed Mrs. Bent. "Won't you help me? She's dying!"

"I-I've never seen a child die before!" stammered Mrs. Hauksbee, feebly, and then—let none blame her weakness after the strain of long watching—she broke down, and covered her face with her hands. The ayahs on the threshold snored peacefully.

There was a rattle of 'rickshaw wheels below, the clash of an opening door, a heavy step on the stairs, and Mrs. Delville entered to find Mrs. Bent screaming for the Doctor as she ran round the room. Mrs. Hauksbee, her hands to her ears, and her face buried in the chintz of a chair, was quivering with pain at each cry from the bed, and murmuring, "Thank God, I never bore a child! Oh! thank God, I never bore a child!"

Mrs. Delville looked at the bed for an instant, took Mrs. Bent by the shoulders, and said, quietly, "Get me some caustic. Be quick."

The mother obeyed mechanically. Mrs. Delville had thrown herself down by the side of the child and was opening its mouth.

"Oh, you're killing her!" cried Mrs. Bent. "Where's the Doctor! Leave her alone!"

Mrs. Delville made no reply for a minute, but busied herself with the child.

"Now the caustic, and hold a lamp behind my shoulder. Will you do as you are told? The acid-bottle, if you don't know what I mean," she said.

A second time Mrs. Delville bent over the child. Mrs. Hauksbee, her face still hidden, sobbed and shivered. One of the ayahs staggered sleepily into the room, yawning: "Doctor Sahib come."

Mrs. Delville turned her head.

"You're only just in time," she said. "It was chokin' her when I came in, an' I've burned it."

"There was no sign of the membrane getting to the air-passages after the last steaming. It was the general weakness, I feared," said the Doctor half to himself, and he whispered as he looked. "You've done what I should have been afraid to do without consultation."

"She was dyin'," said Mrs. Delville, under her breath. "Can you do anythin'? What a mercy it was I went to the dance!"

Mrs. Hauksbee raised her head.

"Is it all over?" she gasped. "I'm useless—I'm worse than useless! What are you doing here?"

She stared at Mrs. Delville, and Mrs. Bent, realizing for the first time who was the Goddess from the Machine, stared also.

Then Mrs. Delville made explanation, putting on a dirty long glove and smoothing a crumpled and ill-fitting ball-dress.

"I was at the dance, an' the Doctor was tellin' me about your baby bein' so ill. So I came away early, an' your door was open, an' I-I lost my boy this way six months ago, an' I've been tryin' to forget it ever since, an' I-I-I-am very sorry for intrudin' an' anythin' that has happened."

Mrs. Bent was putting out the Doctor's eye with a lamp as he stooped over Dora.

"Take it away," said the Doctor. "I think the child will do, thanks to you, Mrs. Delville. I should have come too late, but, I assure you"—he was addressing himself to Mrs. Delville—"I had not the faintest reason to expect this. The membrane must have grown like a mushroom. Will one of you help me, please?"

He had reason for the last sentence. Mrs. Hauksbee had thrown herself into Mrs. Delville's arms, where she was weeping bitterly, and Mrs. Bent was unpicturesquely mixed up with both, while from the tangle came the sound of many sobs and much promiscuous kissing.

"Good gracious! I've spoilt all your beautiful roses!" said Mrs. Hauksbee, lifting her head from the lump of crushed gum and calico atrocities on Mrs. Delville's shoulder and hurrying to the Doctor.

Mrs. Delville picked up her shawl, and slouched out of the room, mopping her eyes with the glove that she had not put on.

"I always said she was more than a woman," sobbed Mrs. Hauksbee, hysterically, "and that proves it!"

Six weeks later, Mrs. Bent and Dora had returned to the hotel. Mrs. Hauksbee had come out of the Valley of Humiliation, had ceased to reproach herself for her collapse in an hour of need, and was even beginning to direct the affairs of the world as before.

"So nobody died, and everything went off as it should, and I kissed The Dowd, Polly. I feel so old. Does it show in my face?"

"Kisses don't as a rule, do they? Of course you know what the result of The Dowd's providential arrival has been."

"They ought to build her a statue—only no sculptor dare copy those skirts."

"Ah!" said Mrs. Mallowe, quietly. "She has found another reward. The Dancing Master has been smirking through Simla giving every one to understand that she came because of her undying love for him—for him—to save his child, and all Simla naturally believes this."

"But Mrs. Bent"—

"Mrs. Bent believes it more than any one else. She won't speak to The Dowd now. Isn't The Dancing Master an angel?"

Mrs. Hauksbee lifted up her voice and raged till bedtime. The doors of the two rooms stood open.

"Polly," said a voice from the darkness, "what did that American-heiress-globe-trotter-girl say last season when she was tipped out of her 'rickshaw turning a corner? Some absurd adjective that made the man who picked her up explode."

"'Paltry,'" said Mrs. Mallowe. "Through her nose—like this—'Ha-ow pahltry!'"

"Exactly," said the voice. "Ha-ow pahltry it all is!"

"Which?"

"Everything. Babies, Diphtheria, Mrs. Bent and The Dancing Master, I whooping in a chair, and The Dowd dropping in from the clouds. I wonder what the motive was—all the motives."

"Um!"

"What do you think?"

"Don't ask me. She was a woman. Go to sleep."

ONLY A SUBALTERN

... Not only to enforce by command but to encourage by

example the energetic discharge of duty and the steady

endurance of the difficulties and privations inseparable

from Military Service. —Bengal Army Regulations.

THEY made Bobby Wick pass an examination at Sandhurst. He was a gentleman before he was gazetted, so, when the Empress announced that "Gentleman-Cadet Robert Hanna Wick" was posted as Second Lieutenant to the Tyneside Tail Twisters at Kram Bokhar, he became an officer and a gentleman, which is an enviable thing; and there was joy in the house of Wick where Mamma Wick and all the little Wicks fell upon their knees and offered incense to Bobby by virtue of his achievements.

Papa Wick had been a Commissioner in his day, holding authority over three millions of men in the Chota-Buldana Division, building great works for the good of the land, and doing his best to make two blades of grass grow where there was but one before. Of course, nobody knew anything about this in the little English village where he was just "old Mr. Wick" and had forgotten that he was a Companion of the Order of the Star of India.

He patted Bobby on the shoulder and said: "Well done, my boy!"

There followed, while the uniform was being prepared, an interval of pure delight, during which Bobby took brevet-rank as a "man" at the women-swamped tennis-parties and tea-fights of the village, and, I dare say, had his joining-time been extended, would have fallen in love with several girls at once. Little country villages at Home are very full of nice girls, because all the young men come out to India to make their fortunes.

"India," said Papa Wick, "is the place. I've had thirty years of it and, begad, I'd like to go back again. When you join the Tail Twisters you'll be among friends, if every one hasn't forgotten Wick of Chota-Buldana, and a lot of people will be kind to you for our sakes. The mother will tell you more about outfit than I can, but remember this. Stick to your Regiment, Bobby—stick to your Regiment. You'll see men all round you going into the Staff Corps, and doing every possible sort of duty but regimental, and you may be tempted to follow suit. Now so long as you keep within your allowance, and I haven't stinted you there, stick to the Line, the whole Line and nothing but the Line. Be careful how you back another young fool's bill, and if you fall in love with a woman twenty years older than yourself, don't tell me about it, that's all."

With these counsels, and many others equally valuable, did Papa Wick fortify Bobby ere that last awful night at Portsmouth when the Officers' Quarters held more inmates than were provided for by the Regulations, and the liberty-men of the ships fell foul of the drafts for India, and the battle raged from the Dockyard Gates even to the slums of Longport, while the drabs of Fratton came down and scratched the faces of the Queen's Officers.

Bobby Wick, with an ugly bruise on his freckled nose, a sick and shaky detachment to manoeuvre inship and the comfort of fifty scornful females to attend to, had no time to feel homesick till the Malabar reached mid-Channel, when he doubled his emotions with a little guard-visiting and a great many other matters.

The Tail Twisters were a most particular Regiment. Those who knew them least said that they

were eaten up with "side." But their reserve and their internal arrangements generally were merely protective diplomacy. Some five years before, the Colonel commanding had looked into the fourteen fearless eyes of seven plump and juicy subalterns who had all applied to enter the Staff Corps, and had asked them why the three stars should he, a colonel of the Line, command a dashed nursery for double-dashed bottle-suckers who put on condemned tin spurs and rode qualified mokes at the hiatused heads of forsaken Black Regiments. He was a rude man and a terrible. Wherefore the remnant took measures [with the half-butt as an engine of public opinion] till the rumor went abroad that young men who used the Tail Twisters as a crutch to the Staff Corps, had many and varied trials to endure. However a regiment had just as much right to its own secrets as a woman.

When Bobby came up from Deolali and took his place among the Tail Twisters, it was gently But firmly borne in upon him that the Regiment was his father and his mother and his indissolubly wedded wife, and that there was no crime under the canopy of heaven blacker than that of bringing shame on the Regiment, which was the best-shooting, best-drilled, best-set-up, bravest, most illustrious, and in all respects most desirable Regiment within the compass of the Seven Seas. He was taught the legends of the Mess Plate from the great grinning Golden Gods that had come out of the Summer Palace in Pekin to the silver-mounted markhor-horn snuff-mull presented by the last C. 0. [he who spake to the seven subalterns]. And every one of those legends told him of battles fought at long odds, without fear as without support; of hospitality catholic as an Arab's; of friendships deep as the sea and steady as the fighting-line; of honor won by hard roads for honor's sake; and of instant and unquestioning devotion to the Regiment—the Regiment that claims the lives of all and lives forever.

More than once, too, he came officially into contact with the Regimental colors, which looked like the lining of a bricklayer's hat on the end of a chewed stick. Bobby did not kneel and worship them, because British subalterns are not constructed in that manner. Indeed, he condemned them for their weight at the very moment that they were filling with awe and other more noble sentiments.

But best of all was the occasion when he moved with the Tail Twisters, in review order at the breaking of a November day. Allowing for duty-men and sick, the Regiment was one thousand and eighty strong, and Bobby belonged to them; for was he not a Subaltern of the Line the whole Line and nothing but the Line—as the tramp of two thousand one hundred and sixty sturdy ammunition boots attested. He would not have changed places with Deighton of the Horse Battery, whirling by in a pillar of cloud to a chorus of "Strong right! Strong left!" or Hogan-Yale of the White Hussars, leading his squadron for all it was worth, with the price of horseshoes thrown in; or "Tick" Boileau, trying to live up to his fierce blue and gold turban while the wasps of the Bengal Cavalry stretched to a gallop in the wake of the long, lollopping Walers of the White Hussars.

They fought through the clear cool day, and Bobby felt a little thrill run down his spine when he heard the tinkle-tinkle-tinkle of the empty cartridge-cases hopping from the breech-blocks after the roar of the volleys; for he knew that he should live to hear that sound in action. The review ended in a glorious chase across the plain—batteries thundering after cavalry to the huge disgust of the White Hussars, and the Tyneside Tail Twisters hunting a Sikh Regiment, till the lean lathy Singhs panted with exhaustion. Bobby was dusty and dripping long before noon, but his enthusiasm was merely focused—not diminished.

He returned to sit at the feet of Revere, his "skipper," that is to say, the Captain of his Company, and to be instructed in the dark art and mystery of managing men, which is a very large part of the Profession of Arms.

"If you haven't a taste that way," said Revere, between his puffs of his cheroot, "you'll never be able to get the hang of it, but remember Bobby, 'tisn't the best drill, though drill is nearly everything, that hauls a Regiment through Hell and out on the other side. It's the man who knows how to handle men—goat-men, swine-men, dog-men, and so on."

"Dormer, for instance," said Bobby. "I think he comes under the head of fool-men. He mopes like a sick owl."

"That's where you make your mistake, my son. Dormer isn't a fool yet, but he's a dashed dirty soldier, and his room corporal makes fun of his socks before kit-inspection. Dormer, being two-thirds pure brute, goes into a corner and growls."

"How do you know?" said Bobby, admiringly.

"Because a Company commander has to know these things—because, if he does not know, he may have crime—ay, murder—brewing under his very nose and yet not see that it's there. Dormer is being badgered out of his mind—big as he is—and he hasn't intellect enough to resent it. He's taken to quiet boozing and, Bobby, when the butt of a room goes on the drink, or takes to moping by himself, measures are necessary to pull him out of himself."

"What measures? 'Man can't run round coddling his men forever."

"No. The men would precious soon show him that he was not wanted. You've got to"—Here the Color-sergeant entered with some papers; Bobby reflected for a while as Revere looked through the Company forms.

"Does Dormer do anything, Sergeant?" Bobby asked, with the air of one continuing an interrupted conversation.

"No, sir. Does 'is dooty like a hortomato," said the Sergeant, who delighted in long words. "A dirty soldier, and 'e's under full stoppages for new kit. It's covered with scales, sir."

"Scales? What scales?"

"Fish-scales, sir. 'E's always pokin' in the mud by the river an' a-cleanin' them muchly-fish with 'is thumbs." Revere was still absorbed in the Company papers, and the Sergeant, who was sternly fond of Bobby, continued,—"'E generally goes down there when 'e's got 'is skinful, beggin' your pardon, sir, an' they do say that the more lush in-he-briated 'e is, the more fish 'e catches. They call 'im the Looney Fish-monger in the Comp'ny, sir."

Revere signed the last paper and the Sergeant retreated.

"It's a filthy amusement," sighed Bobby to himself. Then aloud to Revere: "Are you really worried about Dormer?"

"A little. You see he's never mad enough to send to a hospital, or drunk enough to run in, but at any minute he may flare up, brooding and sulking as he does. He resents any interest being shown in him, and the only time I took him out shooting he all but shot me by accident."

"I fish," said Bobby, with a wry face. "I hire a country-boat and go down the river from Thursday to Sunday, and the amiable Dormer goes with me—if you can spare us both."

"You blazing young fool!" said Revere, but his heart was full of much more pleasant words.

Bobby, the Captain of a dhoni, with Private Dormer for mate, dropped down the river on

Thursday morning—the Private at the bow, the Subaltern at the helm. The Private glared uneasily at the Subaltern, who respected the reserve of the Private.

After six hours, Dormer paced to the stern, saluted, and said—"Beg y'pardon, sir, but was you ever on the Durh'm Canal?"

"No," said Bobby Wick. "Come and have some tiffin."

They ate in silence. As the evening fell, Private Dormer broke forth, speaking to himself—"Hi was on the Durh'm Canal, jes' such a night, come next week twelve month, a-trailin' of my toes in the water." He smoked and said no more till bedtime.

The witchery of the dawn turned the grey river-reaches to purple, gold, and opal; and it was as though the lumbering dhoni crept across the splendors of a new heaven.

Private Dormer popped his head out of his blanket and gazed at the glory below and around.

"Well—damn-my-eyes!" said Private Dormer, in an awed whisper. "This 'ere is like a bloomin' gallantry-show!" For the rest of the day he was dumb, but achieved an ensanguined filthiness through the cleaning of big fish.

The boat returned on Saturday evening. Dormer had been struggling with speech since noon. As the lines and luggage were being disembarked, he found tongue.

"Beg y'pardon—sir," he said, "but would you—would you min' shakin' 'ands with me, sir?"

"Of course not," said Bobby, and he shook accordingly. Dormer returned to barracks and Bobby to mess.

"He wanted a little quiet and some fishing, I think," said Bobby. "My aunt, but he's a filthy sort of animal! Have you ever seen him clean 'them, muchly-fish with 'is thumbs'?"

"Anyhow," said Revere, three weeks later, "he's doing his best to keep his things clean."

When the spring died, Bobby joined in the general scramble for Hill leave, and to his surprise and delight secured three months.

"As good a boy as I want," said Revere, the admiring skipper.

"The best of the batch," said the Adjutant to the Colonel. "Keep back that young skrim-shanker Porkiss, sir, and let Revere make him sit up."

So Bobby departed joyously to Simla Pahar with a tin box of gorgeous raiment.

"Son of Wick—old Wick of Chota-Buldana? Ask him to dinner, dear," said the aged men.

"What a nice boy!" said the matrons and the maids.

"First-class place, Simla. Oh, ri-ipping!" said Bobby Wick, and ordered new white cord breeches on the strength of it.

"We're in a bad way," wrote Revere to Bobby at the end of two months. "Since you left, the Regiment has taken to fever and is fairly rotten with it—two hundred in hospital, about a hundred in cells—drinking to keep off fever—and the Companies on parade fifteen file strong at the outside. There's rather more sickness in the out-villages than I care for, but then I'm so blistered with prickly-heat that I'm ready to hang myself. What's the yarn about your mashing a

Miss Haverley up there? Not serious, I hope? You're over-young to hang millstones round your neck, and the Colonel will turf you out of that in double-quick time if you attempt it."

It was not the Colonel that brought Bobby out of Simla, but a much more to be respected Commandant. The sick ness in the out-villages spread, the Bazar was put out of bounds, and then came the news that the Tail Twisters must go into camp. The message flashed to the Hill stations.—"Cholera—Leave stopped—Officers recalled." Alas, for the white gloves in the neatly soldered boxes, the rides and the dances and picnics that were to he, the loves half spoken, and the debts unpaid! Without demur and without question, fast as tongue could fly or pony gallop, back to their Regiments and their Batteries, as though they were hastening to their weddings, fled the subalterns.

Bobby received his orders on returning from a dance at Viceregal Lodge where he had—but only the Haverley girl knows what Bobby had said or how many waltzes he had claimed for the next ball. Six in the morning saw Bobby at the Tonga Office in the drenching rain, the whirl of the last waltz still in his ears, and an intoxication due neither to wine nor waltzing in his brain.

"Good man!" shouted Deighton of the Horse Battery, through the mists. "Whar you raise dat tonga? I'm coming with you. Ow! But I've had a head and a half. I didn't sit out all night. They say the Battery's awful bad," and he hummed dolorously—Leave the what at the what's-its-name, Leave the flock without shelter, Leave the corpse uninterred, Leave the bride at the altar!

"My faith! It'll be more bally corpse than bride, though, this journey. Jump in, Bobby. Get on, Coachman!"

On the Umballa platform waited a detachment of officers discussing the latest news from the stricken cantonment, and it was here that Bobby learned the real condition of the Tail Twisters.

"They went into camp," said an elderly Major recalled from the whist-tables at Mussoorie to a sickly Native Regiment, "they went into camp with two hundred and ten sick in carts. Two hundred and ten fever cases only, and the balance looking like so many ghosts with sore eyes. A Madras Regiment could have walked through 'em."

"But they were as fit as be-damned when I left them!" said Bobby.

"Then you'd better make them as fit as be-damned when you rejoin," said the Major, brutally.

Bobby pressed his forehead against the rain-splashed windowpane as the train lumbered across the sodden Doab, and prayed for the health of the Tyneside Tail Twisters. Naini Tal had sent down her contingent with all speed; the lathering ponies of the Dalhousie Road staggered into Pathankot, taxed to the full stretch of their strength; while from cloudy Darjiling the Calcutta Mail whirled up the last straggler of the little army that was to fight a fight, in which was neither medal nor honor for the winning, against an enemy none other than "the sickness that destroyeth in the noonday."

And as each man reported himself, he said: "This is a bad business," and went about his own forthwith, for every Regiment and Battery in the cantonment was under canvas, the sickness bearing them company.

Bobby fought his way through the rain to the Tail Twisters' temporary mess, and Revere could have fallen on the boy's neck for the joy of seeing that ugly, wholesome phiz once more.

"Keep 'em amused and interested," said Revere. "They went on the drink, poor fools, after the first two cases, and there was no improvement. Oh, it's good to have you back, Bobby! Porkiss is a—never mind."

Deighton came over from the Artillery camp to attend a dreary mess dinner, and contributed to the general gloom by nearly weeping over the condition of his beloved Battery. Porkiss so far forgot himself as to insinuate that the presence of the officers could do no earthly good, and that the best thing would be to send the entire Regiment into hospital and "let the doctors look after them." Porkiss was demoralized with fear, nor was his peace of mind restored when Revere said coldly: "Oh! The sooner you go out the better, if that's your way of thinking. Any public school could send us fifty good men in your place, but it takes time, time, Porkiss, and money, and a certain amount of trouble, to make a Regiment. 'S'pose you're the person we go into camp for, eh?'"

Whereupon Porkiss was overtaken with a great and chilly fear which a drenching in the rain did not allay, and, two days later, quitted this world for another where, men do fondly hope, allowances are made for the weaknesses of the flesh. The Regimental Sergeant-Major looked wearily across the Sergeants' Mess tent when the news was announced.

"There goes the worst of them," he said. "It'll take the best, and then, please God, it'll stop." The Sergeants were silent till one said: "It couldn't be him!" and all knew of whom Travis was thinking.

Bobby Wick stormed through the tents of his Company, rallying, rebuking mildly, as is consistent with the Regulations, chaffing the faint-hearted: haling the sound into the watery sunlight when there was a break in the weather, and bidding them be of good cheer for their trouble was nearly at an end; scuttling on his dun pony round the outskirts of the camp and heading back men who, with the innate perversity of British soldier's, were always wandering into infected villages, or drinking deeply from rain-flooded marshes; comforting the panic-stricken with rude speech, and more than once tending the dying who had no friends—the men without "townies"; organizing, with banjos and burned cork, Sing-songs which should allow the talent of the Regiment full play; and generally, as he explained, "playing the giddy garden-goat all round."

"You're worth half a dozen of us, Bobby," said Revere in a moment of enthusiasm. "How the devil do you keep it up?"

Bobby made no answer, but had Revere looked into the breast-pocket of his coat he might have seen there a sheaf of badly-written letters which perhaps accounted for the power that possessed the boy. A letter came to Bobby every other day. The spelling was not above reproach, but the sentiments must have been most satisfactory, for on receipt Bobby's eyes softened marvelously, and he was wont to fall into a tender abstraction for a while ere, shaking his cropped head, he charged into his work.

By what power he drew after him the hearts of the roughest, and the Tail Twisters counted in their ranks some rough diamonds indeed, was a mystery to both skipper and C. O., who learned from the regimental chaplain that Bobby was considerably more in request in the hospital tents than the Reverend John Emery.

"The men seem fond of you. Are you in the hospitals much?" said the Colonel, who did his daily round and ordered the men to get well with a hardness that did not cover his bitter grief.

"A little, sir," said Bobby.

"Shouldn't go there too often if I were you. They say it's not contagious, but there's no use in running unnecessary risks. We can't afford to have you down, y'know."

Six days later, it was with the utmost difficulty that the post-runner plashed his way out to the

camp with mailbags, for the rain was falling in torrents. Bobby received a letter, bore it off to his tent, and, the programme for the next week's Sing-song being satisfactorily disposed of, sat down to answer it. For an hour the unhandy pen toiled over the paper, and where sentiment rose to more than normal tide-level Bobby Wick stuck out his tongue and breathed heavily. He was not used to letter-writing.

"Beg y'pardon, sir," said a voice at the tent door; "but Dormer's 'orrid bad, sir, an' they've taken him orf, sir.

"Damn Private Dormer and you too!" said Bobby Wick running the blotter over the half-finished letter. "Tell him I'll come in the morning."

"'E's awful bad, sir," said the voice, hesitatingly. There was an undecided squelching of heavy boots.

"Well?" said Bobby, impatiently.

"Excusin' 'imself before an' for takin' the liberty, 'e says it would be a comfort for to assist 'im, sir, if"—

"Tattoo lao! Get my pony! Here, come in out of the rain till I'm ready. What blasted nuisances you are! That's brandy. Drink some; you want it. Hang on to my stirrup and tell me if I go mo fast."

Strengthened by a four-finger "nip" which he swallowed without a wink, the Hospital Orderly kept up with the slipping, mud-stained, and very disgusted pony as it shambled to the hospital tent.

Private Dormer was certainly "'orrid bad." He had all but reached the stage of collapse and was not pleasant to look upon.

"What's this, Dormer?" said Bobby, bending over the man. "You're not going out this time. You've got to come fishin' with me once or twice more yet."

The blue lips parted and in the ghost of a whisper said,—"Beg y'pardon, sir, disturbin' of you now, but would you min' 'oldin' my 'and, sir?"

Bobby sat on the side of the bed, and the icy cold hand closed on his own like a vice, forcing a lady's ring which was on the little finger deep into the flesh. Bobby set his lips and waited, the water dripping from the hem of his trousers. An hour passed and the grasp of the hand did not relax, nor did the expression on the drawn face change. Bobby with infinite craft lit himself a cheroot with the left hand—his right arm was numbed to the elbow—and resigned himself to a night of pain.

Dawn showed a very white-faced Subaltern sitting on the side of a sick man's cot, and a Doctor in the doorway using language unfit for publication.

"Have you been here all night, you young ass?" said the Doctor.

"There or thereabouts," said Bobby, ruefully. "He's frozen on to me."

Dormer's mouth shut with a click. He turned his head and sighed. The clinging band opened, and Bobby's arm fell useless at his side.

"He'll do," said the Doctor, quietly. "It must have been a toss-up all through the night. 'Think

you're to be congratulated on this case."

"Oh, bosh!" said Bobby. "I thought the man had gone out long ago—only—only I didn't care to take my hand away. Rub my arm down, there's a good chap. What a grip the brute has! I'm chilled to the marrow!" He passed out of the tent shivering.

Private Dormer was allowed to celebrate his repulse of Death by strong waters. Four days later, he sat on the side of his cot and said to the patients mildly: "I'd 'a' liken to 'a' spoken to 'im—so I should."

But at that time Bobby was reading yet another letter—he had the most persistent correspondent of any man in camp—and was even then about to write that the sickness had abated, and in another week at the outside would be gone. He did not intend to say that the chill of a sick man's hand seemed to have struck into the heart whose capacities for affection he dwelt on at such length. He did intend to enclose the illustrated programme of the forthcoming Sing-song whereof he was not a little proud. He also intended to write on many other matters which do not concern us, and doubtless would have done so but for the slight feverish headache which made him dull and unresponsive at mess.

"You are overdoing it, Bobby," said his skipper. "'Might give the rest of us credit of doing a little work. You go on as if you were the whole Mess rolled into one. Take it easy."

"I will," said Bobby. "I'm feeling done up, somehow." Revere looked at him anxiously and said nothing.

There was a flickering of lanterns about the camp that night, and a rumor that brought men out of their cots to the tent doors, a paddling of the naked feet of doolie-bearers and the rush of a galloping horse.

"Wot's up?" asked twenty tents; and through twenty tents ran the answer—"Wick, 'e's down."

They brought the news to Revere and he groaned. "Any one but Bobby and I shouldn't have cared! The Sergeant-Major was right."

"Not going out this journey," gasped Bobby, as he was lifted from the doolie. "Not going out this journey." Then with an air of supreme conviction—"I can't, you see."

"Not if I can do anything!" said the Surgeon-Major, who had hastened over from the mess where he had been dining.

He and the Regimental Surgeon fought together with Death for the life of Bobby Wick. Their work was interrupted by a hairy apparition in a blue-grey dressing-gown who stared in horror at the bed and cried—"Oh, my Gawd. It can't be 'im!" until an indignant Hospital Orderly whisked him away.

If care of man and desire to live could have done aught, Bobby would have been saved. As it was, he made a fight of three days, and the Surgeon-Major's brow uncreased. "We'll save him yet," he said; and the Surgeon, who, though he ranked with the Captain, had a very youthful heart, went out upon the word and pranced joyously in the mud.

"Not going out this journey," whispered Bobby Wick, gallantly, at the end of the third day.

"Bravo!" said the Surgeon-Major. "That's the way to look at it, Bobby."

As evening fell a grey shade gathered round Bobby's mouth, and he turned his face to the tent

wall wearily. The Surgeon-Major frowned.

"I'm awfully tired," said Bobby, very faintly. "What's the use of bothering me with medicine? I-don't-want-it. Let me alone."

The desire for life had departed, and Bobby was content to drift away on the easy tide of Death.

"It's no good," said the Surgeon-Major. "He doesn't want to live. He's meeting it, poor child." And he blew his nose.

Half a mile away, the regimental band was playing the overture to the Sing-song, for the men had been told that Bobby was out of danger. The clash of the brass and the wail of the horns reached Bobby's ears.

Is there a single joy or pain,

That I should never kno-ow?

You do not love me, 'tis in vain,

Bid me goodbye and go!

An expression of hopeless irritation crossed the boy's face, and he tried to shake his head.

The Surgeon-Major bent down—"What is it? Bobby?"—

"Not that waltz," muttered Bobby. "That's our own—our very ownest own. Mummy dear."

With this he sank into the stupor that gave place to death early next morning.

Revere, his eyes red at the rims and his nose very white, went into Bobby's tent to write a letter to Papa Wick which should bow the white head of the ex-Commissioner of Chota-Buldana in the keenest sorrow of his life. Bobby's little store of papers lay in confusion on the table, and among them a half-finished letter. The last sentence ran: "So you see, darling, there is really no fear, because as long as I know you care for me and I care for you, nothing can touch me."

Revere stayed in the tent for an hour. When he came out, his eyes were redder than ever.

Private Conklin sat on a turned-down bucket, and listened to a not unfamiliar tune. Private Conklin was a convalescent and should have been tenderly treated.

"Ho!" said Private Conklin. "There's another bloomin' orf'cer dead."

The bucket shot from under him, and his eyes filled with a smithyful of sparks. A tall man in a blue-grey bedgown was regarding him with deep disfavor.

"You ought to take shame for yourself, Conky! Orf'cer?—bloomin' orf'cer? I'll learn you to misname the likes of 'im. Hangel! Bloomin' Hangel! That's wot 'e is!"

And the Hospital Orderly was so satisfied with the justice of the punishment that he did not even order Private Dormer back to his cot.

IN THE MATTER OF A PRIVATE

Hurrah! hurrah! a soldier's life for me!

Shout, boys, shout! for it makes you jolly and free.

—The Ramrod Corps.

People who have seen, say that one of the quaintest spectacles of human frailty is an outbreak of hysterics in a girls' school. It starts without warning, generally on a hot afternoon among the elder pupils. A girl giggles till the giggle gets beyond control. Then she throws up her head, and cries, "Honk, honk, honk," like a wild goose, and tears mix with the laughter. If the mistress be wise she will rap out something severe at this point to check matters. If she be tender-hearted, and send for a drink of water, the chances are largely in favor of another girl laughing at the afflicted one and herself collapsing. Thus the trouble spreads, and may end in half of what answers to the Lower Sixth of a boys' school rocking and whooping together. Given a week of warm weather, two stately promenades per diem, a heavy mutton and rice meal in the middle of the day, a certain amount of nagging from the teachers, and a few other things, some amazing effects develop. At least this is what folk say who have had experience.

Now, the Mother Superior of a Convent and the Colonel of a British Infantry Regiment would be justly shocked at any comparison being made between their respective charges. But it is a fact that, under certain circumstances, Thomas in bulk can be worked up into dithering, rippling hysteria. He does not weep, but he shows his trouble unmistakably, and the consequences get into the newspapers, and all the good people who hardly know a Martini from a Snider say: "Take away the brute's ammunition!"

Thomas isn't a brute, and his business, which is to look after the virtuous people, demands that he shall have his ammunition to his hand. He doesn't wear silk stockings, and he really ought to be supplied with a new Adjective to help him to express his opinions; but, for all that, he is a great man. If you call him "the heroic defender of the national honor" one day, and "a brutal and licentious soldiery" the next, you naturally bewilder him, and he looks upon you with suspicion. There is nobody to speak for Thomas except people who have theories to work off on him; and nobody understands Thomas except Thomas, and he does not always know what is the matter with himself.

That is the prologue. This is the story:

Corporal Slane was engaged to be married to Miss Jhansi M'Kenna, whose history is well known in the regiment and elsewhere. He had his Colonel's permission, and, being popular with the men, every arrangement had been made to give the wedding what Private Ortheris called "eeklar." It fell in the heart of the hot weather, and, after the wedding, Slane was going up to the Hills with the Bride. None the less, Slane's grievance was that the affair would Be only a hired-carriage wedding, and he felt that the "eeklar" of that was meagre. Miss M'Kenna did not care so much. The Sergeant's wife was helping her to make her wedding-dress, and she was very busy. Slane was, just then, the only moderately contented man in barracks. All the rest were more or less miserable.

And they had so much to make them happy, too. All their work was over at eight in the morning, and for the rest of the day they could lie on their backs and smoke Canteen-plug and swear at the punkah-coolies. They enjoyed a fine, full flesh meal in the middle of the day, and then threw themselves down on their cots and sweated and slept till it was cool enough to go out with their

"towny," whose vocabulary contained less than six hundred words, and the Adjective, and whose views on every conceivable question they had heard many times before.

There was the Canteen, of course, and there was the Temperance Room with the second-hand papers in it; but a man of any profession cannot read for eight hours a day in a temperature of 96 degrees or 98 degrees in the shade, running up sometimes to 103 degrees at midnight. Very few men, even though they get a pannikin of flat, stale, muddy beer and hide it under their cots, can continue drinking for six hours a day. One man tried, but he died, and nearly the whole regiment went to his funeral because it gave them something to do. It was too early for the excitement of fever or cholera. The men could only wait and wait and wait, and watch the shadow of the barrack creeping across the blinding white dust. That was a gay life.

They lounged about cantonments—it was too hot for any sort of game, and almost too hot for vice—and fuddled themselves in the evening, and filled themselves to distension with the healthy nitrogenous food provided for them, and the more they stoked the less exercise they took and more explosive they grew. Then tempers began to wear away, and men fell a-brooding over insults real or imaginary, for they had nothing else to think of. The tone of the repartees changed, and instead of saying light-heartedly: "I'll knock your silly face in," men grew laboriously polite and hinted that the cantonments were not big enough for themselves and their enemy, and that there would be more space for one of the two in another place.

It may have been the Devil who arranged the thing, but the fact of the case is that Losson had for a long time been worrying Simmons in an aimless way. It gave him occupation. The two had their cots side by side, and would sometimes spend a long afternoon swearing at each other; but Simmons was afraid of Losson and dared not challenge him to a fight. He thought over the words in the hot still nights, and half the hate he felt toward Losson be vented on the wretched punkah-coolie.

Losson bought a parrot in the bazar, and put it into a little cage, and lowered the cage into the cool darkness of a well, and sat on the well-curb, shouting bad language down to the parrot. He taught it to say: "Simmons, ye so-oor," which means swine, and several other things entirely unfit for publication. He was a big gross man, and he shook like a jelly when the parrot had the sentence correctly. Simmons, however, shook with rage, for all the room were laughing at him—the parrot was such a disreputable puff of green feathers and it looked so human when it chattered. Losson used to sit, swinging his fat legs, on the side of the cot, and ask the parrot what it thought of Simmons. The parrot would answer: "Simmons, ye so-oor." "Good boy," Losson used to say, scratching the parrot's head; "ye 'ear that, Sim?"

And Simmons used to turn over on his stomach and make answer: "I 'ear. Take 'eed you don't 'ear something one of these days."

In the restless nights, after he had been asleep all day, fits of blind rage came upon Simmons and held him till he trembled all over, while he thought in how many different ways he would slay Losson. Sometimes he would picture himself trampling the life out of the man, with heavy ammunition-boots, and at others smashing in his face with the butt, and at others jumping on his shoulders and dragging the head back till the neckbone cracked. Then his mouth would feel hot and fevered, and he would reach out for another sup of the beer in the pannikin.

But the fancy that came to him most frequently and stayed with him longest was one connected with the great roll of fat under Losson's right ear. He noticed it first on a moonlight night, and thereafter it was always before his eyes. It was a fascinating roll of fat. A man could get his hand upon it and tear away one side of the neck; or he could place the muzzle of a rifle on it and blow away all the head in a flash. Losson had no right to be sleek and contented and well-to-do, when he, Simmons, was the butt of the room, Some day, perhaps, he would show those who

laughed at the "Simmons, ye so-oor" joke, that he was as good as the rest, and held a man's life in the crook of his forefinger. When Losson snored, Simmons hated him more bitterly than ever. Why should Losson be able to sleep when Simmons had to stay awake hour after hour, tossing and turning on the tapes, with the dull liver pain gnawing into his right side and his head throbbing and aching after Canteen? He thought over this for many nights, and the world became unprofitable to him. He even blunted his naturally fine appetite with beer and tobacco; and all the while the parrot talked at and made a mock of him.

The heat continued and the tempers wore away more quickly than before. A Sergeant's wife died of heat-apoplexy in the night, and the rumor ran abroad that it was cholera. Men rejoiced openly, hoping that it would spread and send them into camp. But that was a false alarm.

It was late on a Tuesday evening, and the men were waiting in the deep double verandas for "Last Posts," when Simmons went to the box at the foot of his bed, took out his pipe, and slammed the lid down with a bang that echoed through the deserted barrack like the crack of a rifle. Ordinarily speaking, the men would have taken no notice; but their nerves were fretted to fiddle-strings. They jumped up, and three or four clattered into the barrack-room only to find Simmons kneeling by his box.

"Owl It's you, is it?" they said and laughed foolishly. "We t h o u g h t 'twas"—Simmons rose slowly. If the accident had so shaken his fellows, what would not the reality do?

"You thought it was—did you? And what makes you think?" he said, lashing himself into madness as he went on; "to Hell with your thinking, ye dirty spies."

"Simmons, ye so-oor," chuckled the parrot in the veranda, sleepily, recognizing a well-known voice. Now that was absolutely all.

The tension snapped. Simmons fell back on the arm-rack deliberately,—the men were at the far end of the room,—and took out his rifle and packet of ammunition. "Don't go playing the goat, Sim!" said Losson. "Put it down," but there was a quaver in his voice. Another man stooped, slipped his boot and hurled it at Simmons's head. The prompt answer was a shot which, fired at random, found its billet in Losson's throat. Losson fell forward without a word, and the others scattered.

"You thought it was!" yelled Simmons. "You're drivin' me to it! I tell you you're drivin' me to it! Get up, Losson, an' don't lie shammin' there—you an' your blasted parrit that druv me to it!"

But there was an unaffected reality about Losson's pose that showed Simmons what he had done. The men were still clamoring on the veranda. Simmons appropriated two more packets of ammunition and ran into the moonlight, muttering: "I'll make a night of it. Thirty roun's, an' the last for myself. Take you that, you dogs!"

He dropped on one knee and fired into the brown of the men on the veranda, but the bullet flew high, and landed in the brickwork with a vicious phat that made some of the younger ones turn pale. It is, as musketry theorists observe, one thing to fire and another to be fired at.

Then the instinct of the chase flared up. The news spread from barrack to barrack, and the men doubled out intent on the capture of Simmons, the wild beast, who was heading for the Cavalry parade-ground, stopping now and again to send back a shot and a curse in the direction of his pursuers.

"I'll learn you to spy on me!" he shouted; "I'll learn you to give me dorg's names! Come on the 'ole lot o' you! Colonel John Anthony Deever, C.B.!"—he turned toward the Infantry Mess and

shook his rifle—"you think yourself the devil of a man—but I tell you that if you put your ugly old carcass outside o' that door, I'll make you the poorest-lookin' man in the army. Come out, Colonel John Anthony Deever, C.B.! Come out and see me practiss on the rainge. I'm the crack shot of the 'ole bloomin' battalion." In proof of which statement Simmons fired at the lighted windows of the mess-house.

"Private Simmons, E Comp'ny, on the Cavalry p'rade-ground, Sir, with thirty rounds," said a Sergeant breathlessly to the Colonel. "Shootin' right and lef', Sir. Shot Private Losson. What's to be done, Sir?"

Colonel John Anthony Deever, C.B., sallied out, only to be saluted by s spurt of dust at his feet.

"Pull up!" said the Second in Command; "I don't want my step in that way, Colonel. He's as dangerous as a mad dog."

"Shoot him like one, then," said the Colonel, bitterly, "if he won't take his chance, My regiment, too! If it had been the Towheads I could have under stood."

Private Simmons had occupied a strong position near a well on the edge of the parade-ground, and was defying the regiment to come on. The regiment was not anxious to comply, for there is small honor in being shot by a fellow-private. Only Corporal Slane, rifle in band, threw himself down on the ground, and wormed his way toward the well.

"Don't shoot," said he to the men round him; "like as not you'll hit me. I'll catch the beggar, livin'."

Simmons ceased shouting for a while, and the noise of trap-wheels could be heard across the plain. Major Oldyn, commanding the Horse Battery, was coming back from a dinner in the Civil Lines; was driving after his usual custom—that is to say, as fast as the horse could go.

"A orf'cer! A blooming spangled orf'cer," shrieked Simmons; "I'll make a scarecrow of that orf'cer!" The trap stopped.

"What's this?" demanded the Major of Gunners. "You there, drop your rifle."

"Why, it's Jerry Blazes! I ain't got no quarrel with you, Jerry Blazes. Pass frien', an' all's well!"

But Jerry Blazes had not the faintest intention of passing a dangerous murderer. He was, as his adoring Battery swore long and fervently, without knowledge of fear, and they were surely the best judges, for Jerry Blazes, it was notorious, had done his possible to kill a man each time the Battery went out.

He walked toward Simmons, with the intention of rushing him, and knocking him down.

"Don't make me do it, Sir," said Simmons; "I ain't got nothing agin you. Ah! you would?"—the Major broke into a run—"Take that then!"

The Major dropped with a bullet through his shoulder, and Simmons stood over him. He had lost the satisfaction of killing Losson in the desired way: hut here was a helpless body to his hand. Should be slip in another cartridge, and blow off the head, or with the butt smash in the white face? He stopped to consider, and a cry went up from the far side of the parade-ground: "He's killed Jerry Blazes!" But in the shelter of the well-pillars Simmons was safe except when he stepped out to fire. "I'll blow yer 'andsome 'ead off, Jerry Blazes," said Simmons, reflectively. "Six an' three is nine an one is ten, an' that leaves me another nineteen, an' one for myself." He tugged at the string of the second packet of ammunition. Corporal Slane crawled

out of the shadow of a bank into the moonlight.

"I see you!" said Simmons. "Come a bit furder on an' I'll do for you."

"I'm comm'," said Corporal Slane, briefly; "you've done a bad day's work, Sim. Come out 'ere an' come back with me."

"Come to,"—laughed Simmons, sending a cartridge home with his thumb. "Not before I've settled you an' Jerry Blazes."

The Corporal was lying at full length in the dust of the parade-ground, a rifle under him. Some of the less-cautious men in the distance shouted: "Shoot 'im! Shoot 'im, Slane!"

"You move 'and or foot, Slane," said Simmons, "an' I'll kick Jerry Blazes' 'ead in, and shoot you after."

"I ain't movin'," said the Corporal, raising his head; "you daren't 'it a man on 'is legs. Let go o' Jerry Blazes an' come out o' that with your fistes. Come an' 'it me. You daren't, you bloomin' dog-shooter!"

"I dare."

"You lie, you man-sticker. You sneakin', Sheeny butcher, you lie. See there!" Slane kicked the rifle away, and stood up in the peril of his life. "Come on, now!"

The temptation was more than Simmons could resist, for the Corporal in his white clothes offered a perfect mark.

"Don't misname me," shouted Simmons, firing as he spoke. The shot missed, and the shooter, blind with rage, threw his rifle down and rushed at Slane from the protection of the well. Within striking distance, he kicked savagely at Slane's stomach, but the weedy Corporal knew something of Simmons's weakness, and knew, too, the deadly guard for that kick. Bowing forward and drawing up his right leg till the heel of the right foot was set some three inches above the inside of the left knee-cap, he met the blow standing on one leg—exactly as Gonds stand when they meditate—and ready for the fall that would follow. There was an oath, the Corporal fell over his own left as shinbone met shinbone, and the Private collapsed, his right leg broken an inch above the ankle.

"'Pity you don't know that guard, Sim," said Slane, spitting out the dust as he rose. Then raising his voice, "Come an' take him orf. I've bruk 'is leg." This was not strictly true, for the Private had accomplished his own downfall, since it is the special merit of that leg-guard that the harder the kick the greater the kicker's discomfiture.

Slane walked to Jerry Blazes and hung over him with ostentatious anxiety, while Simmons, weeping with pain, was carried away. "'Ope you ain't 'urt badly, Sir," said Slane. The Major had fainted, and there was an ugly, ragged hole through the top of his arm. Slane knelt down and murmured. "S'elp me, I believe 'e's dead. Well, if that ain't my blooming luck all over!"

But the Major was destined to lead his Battery afield for many a long day with unshaken nerve. He was removed, and nursed and petted into convalescence, while the Battery discussed the wisdom of capturing Simmons, and blowing him from a gun. They idolized their Major, and his reappearance on parade brought about a scene nowhere provided for in the Army Regulations.

Great, too, was the glory that fell to Slane's share. The Gunners would have made him drunk thrice a day for at least a fortnight. Even the Colonel of his own regiment complimented him

upon his coolness, and the local paper called him a hero. These things did not puff him up. When the Major offered him money and thanks, the virtuous Corporal took the one and put aside the other. But he had a request to make and prefaced it with many a "Beg y'pardon, Sir." Could the Major see his way to letting the Slane-M'Kenna wedding be adorned by the presence of four Battery horses to pull a hired barouche? The Major could, and so could the Battery. Excessively so. It was a gorgeous wedding.

"Wot did I do it for?" said Corporal Slane. "For the 'orses O' course. Jhansi ain't a beauty to look at, but I wasn't goin' to 'ave a hired turn-out. Jerry Blazes? If I 'adn't 'a' wanted something, Sim might ha' blowed Jerry Blazes' blooming 'ead into Hirish stew for aught I'd 'a' cared."

And they hanged Private Simmons—hanged him as high as Haman in hollow square of the regiment; and the Colonel said it was Drink; and the Chaplain was sure it was the Devil; and Simmons fancied it was both, but he didn't know, and only hoped his fate would be a warning to his companions; and half a dozen "intelligent publicists" wrote six beautiful leading articles on "'The Prevalence of Crime in the Army."

But not a soul thought of comparing the "bloody-minded Simmons" to the squawking, gaping schoolgirl with which this story opens.

THE ENLIGHTENMENTS OF PAGETT, M.P.

"Because half a dozen grasshoppers under a fern make the field ring

with their importunate chink while thousands of great cattle,

reposed beneath the shadow of the British oak, chew the cud and are

silent, pray do not imagine that those who make the noise are the

only inhabitants of the field—that, of course, they are many in

number or that, after all, they are other than the little,

shrivelled, meagre, hopping, though loud and troublesome insects of

the hour."

—Burke: "Reflections on the Revolution in France."

They were sitting in the veranda of "the splendid palace of an Indian Pro-Consul"; surrounded by all the glory and mystery of the immemorial East. In plain English it was a one-storied, ten-roomed, whitewashed, mud-roofed bungalow, set in a dry garden of dusty tamarisk trees and divided from the road by a low mud wall. The green parrots screamed overhead as they flew in battalions to the river for their morning drink. Beyond the wall, clouds of fine dust showed where the cattle and goats of the city were passing afield to graze. The remorseless white light of the winter sunshine of Northern India lay upon everything and improved nothing, from the whining Persian-wheel by the lawn-tennis court to the long perspective of level road and the blue, domed tombs of Mohammedan saints just visible above the trees.

"A Happy New Year," said Orde to his guest. "It's the first you've ever spent out of England, isn't it?"

"Yes. 'Happy New Year," said Pagett, smiling at the sunshine. "What a divine climate you have here! Just think of the brown cold fog hanging over London now!" And he rubbed his hands.

It was more than twenty years since he had last seen Orde, his schoolmate, and their paths in the world had divided early. The one had quitted college to become a cog-wheel in the machinery of the great Indian Government; the other more blessed with goods, had been whirled into a similar position in the English scheme. Three successive elections had not affected Pagett's position with a loyal constituency, and he had grown insensibly to regard himself in some sort as a pillar of the Empire, whose real worth would be known later on. After a few years of conscientious attendance at many divisions, after newspaper battles innumerable and the publication of interminable correspondence, and more hasty oratory than in his calmer moments he cared to think upon, it occurred to him, as it had occurred to many of his fellows in Parliament, that a tour to India would enable him to sweep a larger lyre and address himself to the problems of Imperial administration with a firmer hand. Accepting, therefore, a general invitation extended to him by Orde some years before, Pagett bad taken ship to Karachi, and only overnight had been received with joy by the Deputy-Commissioner of Amara. They had sat late, discussing the changes and chances of twenty years, recalling the names of the dead, and weighing the futures of the living, as is the custom of men meeting after intervals of action.

Next morning they smoked the after-breakfast pipe in the veranda, still regarding each other curiously, Pagett, in a light grey frock-coat and garments much too thin for the time of the year, and a puggried sun-hat carefully and wonderfully made, Orde in a shooting coat, riding breeches, brown cowhide boots with spurs, and a battered flax helmet. He had ridden some miles in the early morning to inspect a doubtful river dam. The men's faces differed as much as their attire. Orde's worn and wrinkled around the eyes, and grizzled at the temples, was the harder and more square of the two, and it was with something like envy that the owner looked at the comfortable outlines of Pagett's blandly receptive countenance, the clear skin, the untroubled eye, and the mobile, clean-shaved lips.

"And this is India!" said Pagett for the twentieth time staring long and intently at the grey feathering of the tamarisks.

"One portion of India only. It's very much like this for 300 miles in every direction. By the way, now that you have rested a little—I wouldn't ask the old question before—what d'you think of the country?"

"'Tis the most pervasive country that ever yet was seen. I acquired several pounds of your country coming up from Karachi. The air is heavy with it, and for miles and miles along that distressful eternity of rail there's no horizon to show where air and earth separate."

"Yes. It isn't easy to see truly or far in India. But you had a decent passage out, hadn't you?"

"Very good on the whole. Your Anglo-Indian may be unsympathetic about one's political views; but he has reduced ship life to a science."

"The Anglo-Indian is a political orphan, and if he's wise he won't be in a hurry to be adopted by your party grandmothers. But how were your companions, unsympathetic?"

"Well, there was a man called Dawlishe, a judge somewhere in this country it seems, and a capital partner at whist by the way, and when I wanted to talk to him about the progress of India in a political sense (Orde hid a grin, which might or might not have been sympathetic), the National Congress movement, and other things in which, as a Member of Parliament, I'm of course interested, he shifted the subject, and when I once cornered him, he looked me calmly in the eye, and said: 'That's all Tommy rot. Come and have a game at Bull.' You may laugh; but that isn't the way to treat a great and important question; and, knowing who I was, well, I thought it rather rude, don't you know; and yet Dawlishe is a thoroughly good fellow."

"Yes; he's a friend of mine, and one of the straightest men I know. I suppose, like many Anglo-Indians, he felt it was hopeless to give you any just idea of any Indian question without the documents before you, and in this case the documents you want are the country and the people."

"Precisely. That was why I came straight to you, bringing an open mind to bear on things. I'm anxious to know what popular feeling in India is really like y'know, now that it has wakened into political life. The National Congress, in spite of Dawlishe, must have caused great excitement among the masses?"

"On the contrary, nothing could be more tranquil than the state of popular feeling; and as to excitement, the people would as soon be excited over the 'Rule of Three' as over the Congress."

"Excuse me, Orde, but do you think you are a fair judge? Isn't the official Anglo-Indian naturally jealous of any external influences that might move the masses, and so much opposed to liberal ideas, truly liberal ideas, that he can scarcely be expected to regard a popular movement with fairness?"

"What did Dawlishe say about Tommy Rot? Think a moment, old man. You and I were brought up together; taught by the same tutors, read the same books, lived the same life, and new languages, and work among new races; while you, more fortunate, remain at home. Why should I change my mind—our mind—because I change my sky? Why should I and the few hundred Englishmen in my service become unreasonable, prejudiced fossils, while you and your newer friends alone remain bright and open-minded? You surely don't fancy civilians are members of a Primrose League?"

"Of course not, but the mere position of an English official gives him a point of view which cannot but bias his mind on this question." Pagett moved his knee up and down a little uneasily as he spoke.

"That sounds plausible enough, but, like more plausible notions on Indian matters, I believe it's a mistake. You'll find when you come to consult the unofficial Briton that our fault, as a class—I speak of the civilian now—is rather to magnify the progress that has been made toward liberal institutions. It is of English origin, such as it is, and the stress of our work since the Mutiny—only thirty years ago—has been in that direction. No, I think you will get no fairer or more dispassionate view of the Congress business than such men as I can give you. But I may as well say at once that those who know most of India, from the inside, are inclined to wonder at the noise our scarcely begun experiment makes in England."

"But surely the gathering together of Congress delegates is of itself a new thing."

"There's nothing new under the sun When Europe was a jungle half Asia flocked to the canonical conferences of Buddhism; and for centuries the people have gathered at Pun, Hurdwar, Trimbak, and Benares in immense numbers. A great meeting, what you call a mass meeting, is really one of the oldest and most popular of Indian institutions in this topsy-turvy land, and though they have been employed in clerical work for generations they have no practical knowledge of affairs. A ship's clerk is a useful person, but he is scarcely the captain; and an orderly room writer, however smart he may be, is not the colonel. You see, the writer class in India has never till now aspired to anything like command. It wasn't allowed to. The Indian gentleman, for thousands of years past, has resembled Victor Hugo's noble:

"'Un vrai sire Chatelain Laisse ecrire Le vilain. Sa main digne Quand il signe Egratigne Le velin.'

"And the little egratignures he most likes to make have been scored pretty deeply by the sword."

"But this is childish and mediaeval nonsense!"

"Precisely; and from your, or rather our, point of view the pen is mightier than the sword. In this country it's otherwise. The fault lies in our Indian balances, not yet adjusted to civilized weights and measures."

"Well, at all events, this literary class represent the natural aspirations and wishes of the people at large, though it may not exactly lead them, and, in spite of all you say, Orde, I defy you to find a really sound English Radical who would not sympathize with those aspirations."

Pagett spoke with some warmth, and he had scarcely ceased when a well-appointed dog-cart turned into the compound gates, and Orde rose saying: "Here is Edwards, the Master of the Lodge I neglect so diligently, come to talk about accounts, I suppose."

As the vehicle drove up under the porch Pagett also rose, saying with the trained effusion born of much practice: "But this is also my friend, my old and valued friend Edwards. I'm delighted

to see you. I knew you were in India, but not exactly where."

"Then it isn't accounts, Mr. Edwards," said Orde, cheerily.

"Why, no, sir; I heard Mr. Pagett was coming, and as our works were closed for the New Year I thought I would drive over and see him."

"A very happy thought. Mr. Edwards, you may not know, Orde, was a leading member of our Radical Club at Switchton when I was beginning political life, and I owe much to his exertions. There's no pleasure like meeting an old friend, except, perhaps, making a new one. I suppose, Mr. Edwards, you stick to the good old cause?"

"Well, you see, sir, things are different out here. There's precious little one can find to say against the Government, which was the main of our talk at home, and them that do say things are not the sort o' people a man who respects himself would like to be mixed up with. There are no politics, in a manner of speaking, in India. It's all work."

"Surely you are mistaken, my good friend. Why I have come all the way from England just to see the working of this great National movement."

"I don't know where you're going to find the nation as moves to begin with, and then you'll be hard put to it to find what they are moving about. It's like this, sir," said Edwards, who had not quite relished being called "my good friend." "They haven't got any grievance—nothing to hit with, don't you see, sir; and then there's not much to hit against, because the Government is more like a kind of general Providence, directing an old-established state of things, than that at home, where there's something new thrown down for us to fight about every three months."

"You are probably, in your workshops, full of English mechanics, out of the way of learning what the masses think."

"I don't know so much about that. There are four of us English foremen, and between seven and eight hundred native fitters, smiths, carpenters, painters, and such like."

"And they are full of the Congress, of course?"

"Never hear a word of it from year's end to year's end, and I speak the talk too. But I wanted to ask how things are going on at home—old Tyler and Brown and the rest?"

"We will speak of them presently, but your account of the indifference of your men surprises me almost as much as your own. I fear you are a backslider from the good old doctrine, Edwards." Pagett spoke as one who mourned the death of a near relative.

"Not a bit, Sir, but I should be if I took up with a parcel of baboos, pleaders, and schoolboys, as never did a day's work in their lives, and couldn't if they tried. And if you was to poll us English railway men, mechanics, tradespeople, and the like of that all up and down the country from Peshawur to Calcutta, you would find us mostly in a tale together. And yet you'd know we're the same English you pay some respect to at home at 'lection time, and we have the pull o' knowing something about it."

"This is very curious, but you will let me come and see you, and perhaps you will kindly show me the railway works, and we will talk things over at leisure. And about all old friends and old times," added Pagett, detecting with quick insight a look of disappointment in the mechanic's face.

Nodding briefly to Orde, Edwards mounted his dog-cart and drove off.

"It's very disappointing," said the Member to Orde, who, while his friend discoursed with Edwards, had been looking over a bundle of sketches drawn on grey paper in purple ink, brought to him by a Chuprassee.

"Don't let it trouble you, old chap," 'said Orde, sympathetically. "Look here a moment, here are some sketches by the man who made the carved wood screen you admired so much in the dining-room, and wanted a copy of, and the artist himself is here too."

"A native?" said Pagett.

"Of course," was the reply, "Bishen Singh is his name, and he has two brothers to help him. When there is an important job to do, the three go into partnership, but they spend most of their time and all their money in litigation over an inheritance, and I'm afraid they are getting involved, Thoroughbred Sikhs of the old rock, obstinate, touchy, bigoted, and cunning, but good men for all that. Here is Bishen Singh—shall we ask him about the Congress?"

But Bishen Singh, who approached with a respectful salaam, had never heard of it, and he listened with a puzzled face and obviously feigned interest to Orde's account of its aims and objects, finally shaking his vast white turban with great significance when he learned that it was promoted by certain pleaders named by Orde, and by educated natives. He began with labored respect to explain how he was a poor man with no concern in such matters, which were all under the control of God, but presently broke out of Urdu into familiar Punjabi, the mere sound of which had a rustic smack of village smoke-reek and plough-tail, as he denounced the wearers of white coats, the jugglers with words who filched his field from him, the men whose backs were never bowed in honest work; and poured ironical scorn on the Bengali. He and one of his brothers had seen Calcutta, and being at work there had Bengali carpenters given to them as assistants.

"Those carpenters!" said Bishen Singh. "Black apes were more efficient workmates, and as for the Bengali babu—tchick!" The guttural click needed no interpretation, but Orde translated the rest, while Pagett gazed with interest at the wood-carver.

"He seems to have a most illiberal prejudice against the Bengali," said the M.P.

"Yes, it's very sad that for ages outside Bengal there should be so bitter a prejudice. Pride of race, which also means race-hatred, is the plague and curse of India and it spreads far," Orde pointed with his riding-whip to the large map of India on the veranda wall.

"See! I begin with the North," said he. "There's the Afghan, and, as a highlander, he despises all the dwellers in Hindoostan—with the exception of the Sikh, whom he hates as cordially as the Sikh hates him. The Hindu loathes Sikh and Afghan, and the Rajput—that's a little lower down across this yellow blot of desert—has a strong objection, to put it mildly, to the Maratha who, by the way, poisonously hates the Afghan. Let's go North a minute. The Sindhi hates everybody I've mentioned. Very good, we'll take less warlike races. The cultivator of Northern India domineers over the man in the next province, and the Behari of the Northwest ridicules the Bengali. They are all at one on that point. I'm giving you merely the roughest possible outlines of the facts, of course."

Bishen Singh, his clean cut nostrils still quivering, watched the large sweep of the whip as it traveled from the frontier, through Sindh, the Punjab and Rajputana, till it rested by the valley of the Jumna.

"Hate—eternal and inextinguishable hate," concluded Orde, flicking the lash of the whip across the large map from East to West as he sat down. "Remember Canning's advice to Lord

Granville, 'Never write or speak of Indian things without looking at a map.'"

Pagett opened his eyes, Orde resumed. "And the race-hatred is only a part of it. What's really the matter with Bishen Singh is class-hatred, which, unfortunately, is even more intense and more widely spread. That's one of the little drawbacks of caste, which some of your recent English writers find an impeccable system."

The wood-carver was glad to be recalled to the business of his craft, and his eyes shone as he received instructions for a carved wooden doorway for Pagett, which he promised should be splendidly executed and despatched to England in six months. It is an irrelevant detail, but in spite of Orde's reminders, fourteen months elapsed before the work was finished. Business over, Bishen Singh hung about, reluctant to take his leave, and at last joining his hands and approaching Orde with bated breath and whispering humbleness, said he had a petition to make. Orde's face suddenly lost all trace of expression. "Speak on, Bishen Singh," said he, and the carver in a whining tone explained that his case against his brothers was fixed for hearing before a native judge and—here he dropped his voice still lower till he was summarily stopped by Orde, who sternly pointed to the gate with an emphatic Begone!

Bishen Singh, showing but little sign of discomposure, salaamed respectfully to the friends and departed.

Pagett looked inquiry; Orde, with complete recovery of his usual urbanity, replied: "It's nothing, only the old story, he wants his case to be tried by an English judge—they all do that—but when he began to hint that the other side were in improper relations with the native judge I had to shut him up. Gunga Ram, the man he wanted to make insinuations about, may not be very bright; but he's as honest as daylight on the bench. But that's just what one can't get a native to believe."

"Do you really mean to say these people prefer to have their cases tried by English judges?"

"Why, certainly."

Pagett drew a long breath. "I didn't know that before." At this point a phaeton entered the compound, and Orde rose with "Confound it, there's old Rasul Ali Khan come to pay one of his tiresome duty calls. I'm afraid we shall never get through our little Congress discussion."

Pagett was an almost silent spectator of the grave formalities of a visit paid by a punctilious old Mahommedan gentleman to an Indian official; and was much impressed by the distinction of manner and fine appearance of the Mohammedan landholder. When the exchange of polite banalities came to a pause, he expressed a wish to learn the courtly visitor's opinion of the National Congress.

Orde reluctantly interpreted, and with a smile which even Mohammedan politeness could not save from bitter scorn, Rasul Ali Khan intimated that he knew nothing about it and cared still less. It was a kind of talk encouraged by the Government for some mysterious purpose of its own, and for his own part he wondered and held his peace.

Pagett was far from satisfied with this, and wished to have the old gentleman's opinion on the propriety of managing all Indian affairs on the basis of an elective system.

Orde did his best to explain, but it was plain the visitor was bored and bewildered. Frankly, he didn't think much of committees; they had a Municipal Committee at Lahore and had elected a menial servant, an orderly, as a member. He had been informed of this on good authority, and after that, committees had ceased to interest him. But all was according to the rule of Government, and, please God, it was all for the best.

"What an old fossil it is!" cried Pagett, as Orde returned from seeing his guest to the door; "just like some old blue-blooded hidalgo of Spain. What does he really think of the Congress after all, and of the elective system?"

"Hates it all like poison. When you are sure of a majority, election is a fine system; but you can scarcely expect the Mahommedans, the most masterful and powerful minority in the country, to contemplate their own extinction with joy. The worst of it is that he and his co-religionists, who are many, and the landed proprietors, also, of Hindu race, are frightened and put out by this election business and by the importance we have bestowed on lawyers, pleaders, writers, and the like, who have, up to now, been in abject submission to them. They say little, but after all they are the most important fagots in the great bundle of communities, and all the glib bunkum in the world would not pay for their estrangement. They have controlled the land."

"But I am assured that experience of local self-government in your municipalities has been most satisfactory, and when once the principle is accepted in your centres, don't you know, it is bound to spread, and these important—ah—people of yours would learn it like the rest. I see no difficulty at all," and the smooth lips closed with the complacent snap habitual to Pagett, M.P., the "man of cheerful yesterdays and confident tomorrows."

Orde looked at him with a dreary smile.

"The privilege of election has been most reluctantly withdrawn from scores of municipalities, others have had to be summarily suppressed, and, outside the Presidency towns, the actual work done has been badly performed. This is of less moment, perhaps—it only sends up the local death-rates—than the fact that the public interest in municipal elections, never very strong, has waned, and is waning, in spite of careful nursing on the part of Government servants."

"Can you explain this lack of interest?" said Pagett, putting aside the rest of Orde's remarks.

"You may find a ward of the key in the fact that only one in every thousand of our population can spell. Then they are infinitely more interested in religion and caste questions than in any sort of politics. When the business of mere existence is over, their minds are occupied by a series of interests, pleasures, rituals, superstitions, and the like, based on centuries of tradition and usage. You, perhaps, find it hard to conceive of people absolutely devoid of curiosity, to whom the book, the daily paper, and the printed speech are unknown, and you would describe their life as blank. That's a profound mistake. You are in another land, another century, down on the bed-rock of society, where the family merely, and not the community, is all-important. The average Oriental cannot be brought to look beyond his clan. His life, too, is more complete and self-sufficing, and less sordid and low-thoughted than you might imagine. It is bovine and slow in some respects, but it is never empty. You and I are inclined to put the cart before the horse, and to forget that it is the man that is elemental, not the book. 'The corn and the cattle are all my care, And the rest is the will of God.' Why should such folk look up from their immemorially appointed round of duty and interests to meddle with the unknown and fuss with voting-papers. How would you, atop of all your interests care to conduct even one-tenth of your life according to the manners and customs of the Papuans, let's say? That's what it comes to."

"But if they won't take the trouble to vote, why do you anticipate that Mohammedans, proprietors, and the rest would be crushed by majorities of them?"

Again Pagett disregarded the closing sentence.

"Because, though the landholders would not move a finger on any purely political question, they could be raised in dangerous excitement by religious hatreds. Already the first note of this has been sounded by the people who are trying to get up an agitation on the cow-killing

question, and every year there is trouble over the Mohammedan Muharrum processions.

"But who looks after the popular rights, being thus unrepresented?"

"The Government of Her Majesty the Queen, Empress of India, in which, if the Congress promoters are to be believed, the people have an implicit trust; for the Congress circular, specially prepared for rustic comprehension, says the movement is 'for the remission of tax, the advancement of Hindustan, and the strengthening of the British Government.' This paper is headed in large letters-'MAY THE PROSPERITY OF THE EMPIRE OF INDIA ENDURE.'"

"Really!" said Pagett, "that shows some cleverness. But there are things better worth imitation in our English methods of—er—political statement than this sort of amiable fraud."

"Anyhow," resumed Orde, "you perceive that not a word is said about elections and the elective principle, and the reticence of the Congress promoters here shows they are wise in their generation."

"But the elective principle must triumph in the end, and the little difficulties you seem to anticipate would give way on the introduction of a well-balanced scheme, capable of indefinite extension."

"But is it possible to devise a scheme which, always assuming that the people took any interest in it, without enormous expense, ruinous dislocation of the administration and danger to the public peace, can satisfy the aspirations of Mr. Hume and his following, and yet safeguard the interests of the Mahommedans, the landed and wealthy classes, the Conservative Hindus, the Eurasians, Parsees, Sikhs, Rajputs, native Christians, domiciled Europeans and others, who are each important and powerful in their way?"

Pagett's attention, however, was diverted to the gate, where a group of cultivators stood in apparent hesitation.

"Here are the twelve Apostles, by Jove—come straight out of Raffaele's cartoons," said the M.P., with the fresh appreciation of a newcomer.

Orde, loth to be interrupted, turned impatiently toward the villagers, and their leader, handing his long staff to one of his companions, advanced to the house.

"It is old Jelbo, the Lumherdar, or head-man of Pind Sharkot, and a very intelligent man for a villager."

The Jat farmer had removed his shoes and stood smiling on the edge of the veranda. His strongly marked features glowed with russet bronze, and his bright eyes gleamed under deeply set brows, contracted by lifelong exposure to sunshine. His beard and moustache streaked with grey swept from bold cliffs of brow and cheek in the large sweeps one sees drawn by Michael Angelo, and strands of long black hair mingled with the irregularly piled wreaths and folds of his turban. The drapery of stout blue cotton cloth thrown over his broad shoulders and girt round his narrow loins, hung from his tall form in broadly sculptured folds, and he would have made a superb model for an artist in search of a patriarch.

Orde greeted him cordially, and after a polite pause the countryman started off with a long story told with impressive earnestness. Orde listened and smiled, interrupting the speaker at times to argue and reason with him in a tone which Pagett could hear was kindly, and finally checking the flux of words was about to dismiss him, when Pagett suggested that he should be asked about the National Congress.

But Jelbo had never heard of it. He was a poor man and such things, by the favor of his Honor, did not concern him.

"What's the matter with your big friend that he was so terribly in earnest?" asked Pagett, when he had left.

"Nothing much. He wants the blood of the people in the next village, who have had smallpox and cattle plague pretty badly, and by the help of a wizard, a currier, and several pigs have passed it on to his own village. 'Wants to know if they can't be run in for this awful crime. It seems they made a dreadful charivari at the village boundary, threw a quantity of spell-bearing objects over the border, a buffalo's skull and other things; then branded a chamur—what you would call a currier—on his hinder parts and drove him and a number of pigs over into Jelbo's village. Jelbo says he can bring evidence to prove that the wizard directing these proceedings, who is a Sansi, has been guilty of theft, arson, cattle-killing, perjury and murder, but would prefer to have him punished for bewitching them and inflicting smallpox."

"And how on earth did you answer such a lunatic?"

"Lunatic!—the old fellow is as sane as you or I; and he has some ground of complaint against those Sansis. I asked if he would like a native superintendent of police with some men to make inquiries, but he objected on the grounds the police were rather worse than smallpox and criminal tribes put together."

"Criminal tribes—er—I don't quite understand," said Pagett.

"We have in India many tribes of people who in the slack anti-British days became robbers, in various kind, and preyed on the people. They are being restrained and reclaimed little by little, and in time will become useful citizens, but they still cherish hereditary traditions of crime, and are a difficult lot to deal with. By the way what about the political rights of these folk under your schemes? The country people call them vermin, but I suppose they would be electors with the rest."

"Nonsense—special provision would be made for them in a well-considered electoral scheme, and they would doubtless be treated with fitting severity," said Pagett, with a magisterial air.

"Severity, yes—but whether it would be fitting is doubtful. Even those poor devils have rights, and, after all, they only practice what they have been taught."

"But criminals, Orde!"

"Yes, criminals with codes and rituals of crime, gods and godlings of crime, and a hundred songs and sayings in praise of it. Puzzling, isn't it?"

"It's simply dreadful. They ought to be put down at once. Are there many of them?"

"Not more than about sixty thousand in this province, for many of the tribes broadly described as criminal are really vagabond and criminal only on occasion, while others are being settled and reclaimed. They are of great antiquity, a legacy from the past, the golden, glorious Aryan past of Max Muller, Birdwood and the rest of your spindrift philosophers."

An orderly brought a card to Orde, who took it with a movement of irritation at the interruption, and banded it to Pagett; a large card with a ruled border in red ink, and in the centre in schoolboy copper plate, Mr. Dma Nath. "Give salaam," said the civilian, and there entered in haste a slender youth, clad in a closely fitting coat of grey homespun, tight trousers, patent-leather shoes, and a small black velvet cap. His thin cheek twitched, and his eyes wandered restlessly,

for the young man was evidently nervous and uncomfortable, though striving to assume a free and easy air.

"Your honor may perhaps remember me," he said in English, and Orde scanned him keenly.

"I know your face somehow. You belonged to the Shershah district I think, when I was in charge there?"

"Yes, Sir, my father is writer at Shershah, and your honor gave me a prize when I was first in the Middle School examination five years ago. Since then I have prosecuted my studies, and I am now second year's student in the Mission College—"

"Of course: you are Kedar Nath's son—the boy who said he liked geography better than play or sugar cakes, and I didn't believe you. How is your father getting on?"

"He is well, and he sends his salaam, but his circumstances are depressed, and he also is down on his luck."

"You learn English idioms at the Mission College, it seems."

"Yes, sir, they are the best idioms, and my father ordered me to ask your honor to say a word for him to the present incumbent of your honor's shoes, the latchet of which he is not worthy to open, and who knows not Joseph; for things are different at Shershah now, and my father wants promotion."

"Your father is a good man, and I will do what I can for him."

At this point a telegram was handed to Orde, who, after glancing at it, said he must leave his young friend whom he introduced to Pagett, "a member of the English House of Commons who wishes to learn about India."

Orde had scarcely retired with his telegram when Pagett began:

"Perhaps you can tell me something of the National Congress movement?"

"Sir, it is the greatest movement of modern times, and one in which all educated men like us must join. All our students are for the Congress."

"Excepting, I suppose, Mahommedans, and the Christians?" said Pagett, quick to use his recent instruction.

"These are some mere exceptions to the universal rule."

"But the people outside the College, the working classes, the agriculturists; your father and mother, for instance."

"My mother," said the young man, with a visible effort to bring himself to pronounce the word, "has no ideas, and my father is not agriculturist, nor working class; he is of the Kayeth caste; but he had not the advantage of a collegiate education, and he does not know much of the Congress. It is a movement for the educated young-man"—connecting adjective and noun in a sort of vocal hyphen.

"Ah, yes," said Pagett, feeling he was a little off the rails, "and what are the benefits you expect to gain by it?"

"Oh, sir, everything. England owes its greatness to Parliamentary institutions, and we should

at once gain the same high position in scale of nations. Sir, we wish to have the sciences, the arts, the manufactures, the industrial factories, with steam engines, and other motive powers and public meetings, and debates. Already we have a debating club in connection with the college, and elect a Mr. Speaker. Sir, the progress must come. You also are a Member of Parliament and worship the great Lord Ripon," said the youth, breathlessly, and his black eyes flashed as he finished his commaless sentences.

"Well," said Pagett, drily, "it has not yet occurred to me to worship his Lordship, although I believe he is a very worthy man, and I am not sure that England owes quite all the things you name to the House of Commons. You see, my young friend, the growth of a nation like ours is slow, subject to many influences, and if you have read your history aright"—

"Sir. I know it all—all! Norman Conquest, Magna Charta, Runnymede, Reformation, Tudors, Stuarts, Mr. Milton and Mr. Burke, and I have read something of Mr. Herbert Spencer and Gibbon's 'Decline and Fall,' Reynolds' 'Mysteries of the Court,' and"—

Pagett felt like one who had pulled the string of a shower-bath unawares, and hastened to stop the torrent with a question as to what particular grievances of the people of India the attention of an elected assembly should be first directed. But young Mr. Dma Nath was slow to particularize. There were many, very many demanding consideration. Mr. Pagett would like to hear of one or two typical examples. The Repeal of the Arms Act was at last named, and the student learned for the first time that a license was necessary before an Englishman could carry a gun in England. Then natives of India ought to be allowed to become Volunteer Riflemen if they chose, and the absolute equality of the Oriental with his European fellow-subject in civil status should be proclaimed on principle, and the Indian Army should be considerably reduced. The student was not, however, prepared with answers to Mr. Pagett's mildest questions on these points, and he returned to vague generalities, leaving the M.P. so much impressed with the crudity of his views that he was glad on Orde's return to say goodbye to his "very interesting" young friend.

"What do you think of young India?" asked Orde.

"Curious, very curious—and callow."

"And yet," the civilian replied, "one can scarcely help sympathizing with him for his mere youth's sake. The young orators of the Oxford Union arrived at the same conclusions and showed doubtless just the same enthusiasm. If there were any political analogy between India and England, if the thousand races of this Empire were one, if there were any chance even of their learning to speak one language, if, in short, India were a Utopia of the debating-room, and not a real land, this kind of talk might be worth listening to, but it is all based on false analogy and ignorance of the facts."

"But he is a native and knows the facts."

"He is a sort of English schoolboy, but married three years, and the father of two weaklings, and knows less than most English schoolboys. You saw all he is and knows, and such ideas as he has acquired are directly hostile to the most cherished convictions of the vast majority of the people."

"But what does he mean by saying he is a student of a mission college? Is he a Christian?"

"He meant just what he said, and he is not a Christian, nor ever will he be. Good people in America, Scotland and England, most of whom would never dream of collegiate education for their own sons, are pinching themselves to bestow it in pure waste on Indian youths. Their

scheme is an oblique, subterranean attack on heathenism; the theory being that with the jam of secular education, leading to a University degree, the pill of moral or religious instruction may be coaxed down the heathen gullet."

"But does it succeed; do they make converts?"

"They make no converts, for the subtle Oriental swallows the jam and rejects the pill; but the mere example of the sober, righteous, and godly lives of the principals and professors who are most excellent and devoted men, must have a certain moral value. Yet, as Lord Lansdowne pointed out the other day, the market is dangerously overstocked with graduates of our Universities who look for employment in the administration. An immense number are employed, but year by year the college mills grind out increasing lists of youths foredoomed to failure and disappointment, and meanwhile, trades, manufactures, and the industrial arts are neglected, and in fact regarded with contempt by our new literary mandarins in posse."

"But our young friend said he wanted steam-engines and factories," said Pagett.

"Yes, he would like to direct such concerns. He wants to begin at the top, for manual labor is held to be discreditable, and he would never defile his hands by the apprenticeship which the architects, engineers, and manufacturers of England cheerfully undergo; and he would be aghast to learn that the leading names of industrial enterprise in England belonged a generation or two since, or now belong, to men who wrought with their own hands. And, though he talks glibly of manufacturers, he refuses to see that the Indian manufacturer of the future will be the despised workman of the present. It was proposed, for example, a few weeks ago, that a certain municipality in this province should establish an elementary technical school for the sons of workmen. The stress of the opposition to the plan came from a pleader who owed all he had to a college education bestowed on him gratis by Government and missions. You would have fancied some fine old crusted Tory squire of the last generation was speaking. 'These people,' he said, 'want no education, for they learn their trades from their fathers, and to teach a workman's son the elements of mathematics and physical science would give him ideas above his business. They must be kept in their place, and it was idle to imagine that there was any science in wood or iron work.' And he carried his point. But the Indian workman will rise in the social scale in spite of the new literary caste."

"In England we have scarcely begun to realize that there is an industrial class in this country, yet, I suppose, the example of men, like Edwards for instance, must tell," said Pagett, thoughtfully.

"That you shouldn't know much about it is natural enough, for there are but few sources of information. India in this, as in other respects, is like a badly kept ledger—not written up to date. And men like Edwards are, in reality, missionaries, who by precept and example are teaching more lessons than they know. Only a few, however, of their crowds of subordinates seem to care to try to emulate them, and aim at individual advancement; the rest drop into the ancient Indian caste groove."

"How do you mean?" asked Pagett.

"Well, it is found that the new railway and factory workmen, the fitter, the smith, the engine-driver, and the rest are already forming separate hereditary castes. You may notice this down at Jamalpur in Bengal, one of the oldest railway centres; and at other places, and in other industries, they are following the same inexorable Indian law."

"Which means?" queried Pagett.

"It means that the rooted habit of the people is to gather in small self-contained, self-sufficing

family groups with no thought or care for any interests but their own—a habit which is scarcely compatible with the right acceptation of the elective principle."

"Yet you must admit, Orde, that though our young friend was not able to expound the faith that is in him, your Indian army is too big."

"Not nearly big enough for its main purpose. And, as a side issue, there are certain powerful minorities of fighting folk whose interests an Asiatic Government is bound to consider. Arms is as much a means of livelihood as civil employ under Government and law. And it would be a heavy strain on British bayonets to hold down Sikhs, Jats, Bilochis, Rohillas, Rajputs, Bhils, Dogras, Pathans, and Gurkhas to abide by the decisions of a numerical majority opposed to their interests. Leave the 'numerical majority' to itself without the British bayonets—a flock of sheep might as reasonably hope to manage a troop of collies."

"This complaint about excessive growth of the army is akin to another contention of the Congress party. They protest against the malversation of the whole of the moneys raised by additional taxes as a Famine Insurance Fund to other purposes. You must be aware that this special Famine Fund has all been spent on frontier roads and defences and strategic railway schemes as a protection against Russia."

"But there was never a special famine fund raised by special taxation and put by as in a box. No sane administrator would dream of such a thing. In a time of prosperity a finance minister, rejoicing in a margin, proposed to annually apply a million and a half to the construction of railways and canals for the protection of districts liable to scarcity, and to the reduction of the annual loans for public works. But times were not always prosperous, and the finance minister had to choose whether he would bang up the insurance scheme for a year or impose fresh taxation. When a farmer hasn't got the little surplus he hoped to have for buying a new wagon and draining a low-lying field corner, you don't accuse him of malversation, if he spends what he has on the necessary work of the rest of his farm."

A clatter of hoofs was heard, and Orde looked up with vexation, but his brow cleared as a horseman halted under the porch.

"Hello, Orde! just looked in to ask if you are coming to polo on Tuesday: we want you badly to help to crumple up the Krab Bokhar team."

Orde explained that he had to go out into the District, and while the visitor complained that though good men wouldn't play, duffers were always keen, and that his side would probably be beaten, Pagett rose to look at his mount, a red, lathered Biloch mare, with a curious lyrelike incurving of the ears. "Quite a little thoroughbred in all other respects," said the M.P., and Orde presented Mr. Reginald Burke, Manager of the Siad and Sialkote Bank to his friend.

"Yes, she's as good as they make 'em, and she's all the female I possess and spoiled in consequence, aren't you, old girl?" said Burke, patting the mare's glossy neck as she backed and plunged.

"Mr. Pagett," said Orde, "has been asking me about the Congress. What is your opinion?" Burke turned to the M. P. with a frank smile.

"Well, if it's all the same to you, sir, I should say, Damn the Congress, but then I'm no politician, but only a business man."

"You find it a tiresome subject?"

"Yes, it's all that, and worse than that, for this kind of agitation is anything but wholesome for the country."

"How do you mean?"

"It would be a long job to explain, and Sara here won't stand, but you know how sensitive capital is, and how timid investors are. All this sort of rot is likely to frighten them, and we can't afford to frighten them. The passengers aboard an Ocean steamer don't feel reassured when the ship's way is stopped, and they hear the workmen's hammers tinkering at the engines down below. The old Ark's going on all right as she is, and only wants quiet and room to move. Them's my sentiments, and those of some other people who have to do with money and business."

"Then you are a thick-and-thin supporter of the Government as it is."

"Why, no! The Indian Government is much too timid with its money—like an old maiden aunt of mine—always in a funk about her investments. They don't spend half enough on railways for instance, and they are slow in a general way, and ought to be made to sit up in all that concerns the encouragement of private enterprise, and coaxing out into use the millions of capital that lie dormant in the country."

The mare was dancing with impatience, and Burke was evidently anxious to be off, so the men wished him goodbye.

"Who is your genial friend who condemns both Congress and Government in a breath?" asked Pagett, with an amused smile.

"Just now he is Reggie Burke, keener on polo than on anything else, but if you go to the Sind and Sialkote Bank tomorrow you would find Mr. Reginald Burke a very capable man of business, known and liked by an immense constituency North and South of this."

"Do you think he is right about the Government's want of enterprise?"

"I should hesitate to say. Better consult the merchants and chambers of commerce in Cawnpore, Madras, Bombay, and Calcutta. But though these bodies would like, as Reggie puts it, to make Government sit up, it is an elementary consideration in governing a country like India, which must be administered for the benefit of the people at large, that the counsels of those who resort to it for the sake of making money should be judiciously weighed and not allowed to overpower the rest. They are welcome guests here, as a matter of course, but it has been found best to restrain their influence. Thus the rights of plantation laborers, factory operatives, and the like, have been protected, and the capitalist, eager to get on, has not always regarded Government action with favor. It is quite conceivable that under an elective system the commercial communities of the great towns might find means to secure majorities on labor questions and on financial matters."

"They would act at least with intelligence and consideration."

"Intelligence, yes; but as to consideration, who at the present moment most bitterly resents the tender solicitude of Lancashire for the welfare and protection of the Indian factory operative? English and native capitalists running cotton mills and factories."

"But is the solicitude of Lancashire in this matter entirely disinterested?"

"It is no business of mine to say. I merely indicate an example of how a powerful commercial interest might hamper a Government intent in the first place on the larger interests of humanity."

Orde broke off to listen a moment. "There's Dr. Lathrop talking to my wife in the drawing-room," said he.

"Surely not; that's a lady's voice, and if my ears don't deceive me, an American."

"Exactly, Dr. Eva McCreery Lathrop, chief of the new Women's Hospital here, and a very good fellow forbye. Good morning, Doctor," he said, as a graceful figure came out on the veranda, "you seem to be in trouble. I hope Mrs. Orde was able to help you."

"Your wife is real kind and good, I always come to her when I'm in a fix but I fear it's more than comforting I want."

"You work too hard and wear yourself out," said Orde, kindly. "Let me introduce my friend, Mr. Pagett, just fresh from home, and anxious to learn his India. You could tell him something of that more important half of which a mere man knows so little."

"Perhaps I could if I'd any heart to do it, but I'm in trouble, I've lost a case, a case that was doing well, through nothing in the world but inattention on the part of a nurse I had begun to trust. And when I spoke only a small piece of my mind she collapsed in a whining heap on the floor. It is hopeless."

The men were silent, for the blue eyes of the lady doctor were dim. Recovering herself she looked up with a smile, half sad, half humorous, "And I am in a whining heap, too; but what phase of Indian life are you particularly interested in, sir?"

"Mr. Pagett intends to study the political aspect of things and the possibility of bestowing electoral institutions on the people."

"Wouldn't it be as much to the purpose to bestow point-lace collars on them? They need many things more urgently than votes. Why it's like giving a bread-pill for a broken leg."

"Er—I don't quite follow," said Pagett, uneasily.

"Well, what's the matter with this country is not in the least political, but an all round entanglement of physical, social, and moral evils and corruptions, all more or less due to the unnatural treatment of women. You can't gather figs from thistles, and so long as the system of infant marriage, the prohibition of the remarriage of widows, the lifelong imprisonment of wives and mothers in a worse than penal confinement, and the withholding from them of any kind of education or treatment as rational beings continues, the country can't advance a step. Half of it is morally dead, and worse than dead, and that's just the half from which we have a right to look for the best impulses. It's right here where the trouble is, and not in any political considerations whatsoever."

"But do they marry so early?" said Pagett, vaguely.

"The average age is seven, but thousands are married still earlier. One result is that girls of twelve and thirteen have to bear the burden of wifehood and motherhood, and, as might be expected, the rate of mortality both for mothers and children is terrible. Pauperism, domestic unhappiness, and a low state of health are only a few of the consequences of this. Then, when, as frequently happens, the boy-husband dies prematurely, his widow is condemned to worse than death. She may not remarry, must live a secluded and despised life, a life so unnatural that she sometimes prefers suicide; more often she goes astray. You don't know in England what such words as 'infant-marriage,' 'baby-wife,' 'girl-mother,' and 'virgin-widow' mean; but they mean unspeakable horrors here."

"Well, but the advanced political party here will surely make it their business to advocate social reforms as well as political ones," said Pagett.

"Very surely they will do no such thing," said the lady doctor, emphatically. "I wish I could make you understand. Why, even of the funds devoted to the Marchioness of Dufferin's organization for medical aid to the women of India, it was said in print and in speech, that they would be better spent on more college scholarships for men. And in all the advanced parties' talk—God forgive them—and in all their programmes, they carefully avoid all such subjects. They will talk about the protection of the cow, for that's an ancient superstition—they can all understand that; but the protection of the women is a new and dangerous idea." She turned to Pagett impulsively:

"You are a member of the English Parliament. Can you do nothing? The foundations of their life are rotten—utterly and bestially rotten. I could tell your wife things that I couldn't tell you. I know the inner life that belongs to the native, and I know nothing else; and believe me you might as well try to grow golden-rod in a mushroom-pit as to make anything of a people that are born and reared as these—these things 're. The men talk of their rights and privileges. I have seen the women that bear these very men, and again—may God forgive the men!"

Pagett's eyes opened with a large wonder. Dr. Lathrop rose tempestuously.

"I must be off to lecture," said she, "and I'm sorry that I can't show you my hospitals; but you had better believe, sir, that it's more necessary for India than all the elections in creation."

"That's a woman with a mission, and no mistake," said Pagett, after a pause.

"Yes; she believes in her work, and so do I," said Orde. "I've a notion that in the end it will be found that the most helpful work done for India in this generation was wrought by Lady Dufferin in drawing attention—what work that was, by the way, even with her husband's great name to back it to the needs of women here. In effect, native habits and beliefs are an organized conspiracy against the laws of health and happy life—but there is some dawning of hope now."

"How d'you account for the general indifference, then?"

"I suppose it's due in part to their fatalism and their utter indifference to all human suffering. How much do you imagine the great province of the Punjab with over twenty million people and half a score rich towns has contributed to the maintenance of civil dispensaries last year? About seven thousand rupees."

"That's seven hundred pounds," said Pagett, quickly.

"I wish it was," replied Orde; "but anyway, it's an absurdly inadequate sum, and shows one of the blank sides of Oriental character."

Pagett was silent for a long time. The question of direct and personal pain did not lie within his researches. He preferred to discuss the weightier matters of the law, and contented himself with murmuring: "They'll do better later on." Then, with a rush, returning to his first thought:

"But, my dear Orde, if it's merely a class movement of a local and temporary character, how d' you account for Bradlaugh, who is at least a man of sense, taking it up?"

"I know nothing of the champion of the New Brahmins but what I see in the papers. I suppose there is something tempting in being hailed by a large assemblage as the representative of the aspirations of two hundred and fifty millions of people. Such a man looks 'through all the roaring and the wreaths,' and does not reflect that it is a false perspective, which, as a matter of fact, hides the real complex and manifold India from his gaze. He can scarcely be expected to distinguish between the ambitions of a new oligarchy and the real wants of the people of

whom he knows nothing. But it's strange that a professed Radical should come to be the chosen advocate of a movement which has for its aim the revival of an ancient tyranny. Shows how even Radicalism can fall into academic grooves and miss the essential truths of its own creed. Believe me, Pagett, to deal with India you want first-hand knowledge and experience. I wish he would come and live here for a couple of years or so."

"Is not this rather an ad hominem style of argument?"

"Can't help it in a case like this. Indeed, I am not sure you ought not to go further and weigh the whole character and quality and upbringing of the man. You must admit that the monumental complacency with which he trotted out his ingenious little Constitution for India showed a strange want of imagination and the sense of humor."

"No, I don't quite admit it," said Pagett.

"Well, you know him and I don't, but that's how it strikes a stranger." He turned on his heel and paced the veranda thoughtfully. "And, after all, the burden of the actual, daily unromantic toil falls on the shoulders of the men out here, and not on his own. He enjoys all the privileges of recommendation without responsibility, and we—well, perhaps, when you've seen a little more of India you'll understand. To begin with, our death rate's five times higher than yours—I speak now for the brutal bureaucrat—and we work on the refuse of worked-out cities and exhausted civilizations, among the bones of the dead. In the case of the Congress meetings, the only notable fact is that the priests of the altar are British, not Buddhist, Jain or Brahminical, and that the whole thing is a British contrivance kept alive by the efforts of Messrs. Hume, Eardley, Norton, and Digby."

"You mean to say, then, it's not a spontaneous movement?"

"What movement was ever spontaneous in any true sense of the word? This seems to be more factitious than usual. You seem to know a great deal about it; try it by the touchstone of subscriptions, a coarse but fairly trustworthy criterion, and there is scarcely the color of money in it. The delegates write from England that they are out of pocket for working expenses, railway fares, and stationery—the mere pasteboard and scaffolding of their show. It is, in fact, collapsing from mere financial inanition."

"But you cannot deny that the people of India, who are, perhaps, too poor to subscribe, are mentally and morally moved by the agitation," Pagett insisted.

"That is precisely what I do deny. The native side of the movement is the work of a limited class, a microscopic minority, as Lord Dufferin described it, when compared with the people proper, but still a very interesting class, seeing that it is of our own creation. It is composed almost entirely of those of the literary or clerkly castes who have received an English education."

"Surely that's a very important class. Its members must be the ordained leaders of popular thought."

"Anywhere else they might be leaders, but they have no social weight here."

Pagett laughed. "That's an epigrammatic way of putting it, Orde."

"Is it? Let's see," said the Deputy Commissioner of Amara, striding into the sunshine toward a half-naked gardener potting roses. He took the man's hoe, and went to a rain-scarped bank at the bottom of the garden.

"Come here, Pagett," he said, and cut at the sun-baked soil. After three strokes there rolled

from under the blade of the hoe the half of a clanking skeleton that settled at Pagett's feet in an unseemly jumble of bones. The M.P. drew back.

"Our houses are built on cemeteries," said Orde. "There are scores of thousands of graves within ten miles."

Pagett was contemplating the skull with the awed fascination of a man who has but little to do with the dead. "India's a very curious place," said he, after a pause.

"Ah? You'll know all about it in three months. Come in to lunch," said Orde.

VOLUME V PLAIN TALES FROM THE HILLS
LISPETH

Look, you have cast out Love! What Gods are these

 You bid me please?

The Three in One, the One in Three? Not so!

 To my own Gods I go.

It may be they shall give me greater ease

Than your cold Christ and tangled Trinities.

 —The Convert.

She was the daughter of Sonoo, a Hill-man, and Jadeh his wife. One year their maize failed, and two bears spent the night in their only poppy-field just above the Sutlej Valley on the Kotgarh side; so, next season, they turned Christian, and brought their baby to the Mission to be baptized. The Kotgarh Chaplain christened her Elizabeth, and "Lispeth" is the Hill or pahari pronunciation.

Later, cholera came into the Kotgarh Valley and carried off Sonoo and Jadeh, and Lispeth became half-servant, half-companion to the wife of the then Chaplain of Kotgarh. This was after the reign of the Moravian missionaries, but before Kotgarh had quite forgotten her title of "Mistress of the Northern Hills."

Whether Christianity improved Lispeth, or whether the gods of her own people would have done as much for her under any circumstances, I do not know; but she grew very lovely. When a Hill girl grows lovely, she is worth traveling fifty miles over bad ground to look upon. Lispeth had a Greek face—one of those faces people paint so often, and see so seldom. She was of a pale, ivory color and, for her race, extremely tall. Also, she possessed eyes that were wonderful; and, had she not been dressed in the abominable print-cloths affected by Missions, you would, meeting her on the hill-side unexpectedly, have thought her the original Diana of the Romans going out to slay.

Lispeth took to Christianity readily, and did not abandon it when she reached womanhood, as do some Hill girls. Her own people hated her because she had, they said, become a memsahib and washed herself daily; and the Chaplain's wife did not know what to do with her. Somehow, one cannot ask a stately goddess, five foot ten in her shoes, to clean plates and dishes. So she played with the Chaplain's children and took classes in the Sunday School, and read all the books in the house, and grew more and more beautiful, like the Princesses in fairy tales. The Chaplain's wife said that the girl ought to take service in Simla as a nurse or something "genteel." But Lispeth did not want to take service. She was very happy where she was.

When travellers—there were not many in those years—came to Kotgarh, Lispeth used to lock herself into her own room for fear they might take her away to Simla, or somewhere out into the unknown world.

One day, a few months after she was seventeen years old, Lispeth went out for a walk. She did not walk in the manner of English ladies—a mile and a half out, and a ride back again.

She covered between twenty and thirty miles in her little constitutionals, all about and about, between Kotgarh and Narkunda. This time she came back at full dusk, stepping down the breakneck descent into Kotgarh with something heavy in her arms. The Chaplain's wife was dozing in the drawing-room when Lispeth came in breathing hard and very exhausted with her burden. Lispeth put it down on the sofa, and said simply:

"This is my husband. I found him on the Bagi Road. He has hurt himself. We will nurse him, and when he is well, your husband shall marry him to me."

This was the first mention Lispeth had ever made of her matrimonial views, and the Chaplain's wife shrieked with horror. However, the man on the sofa needed attention first. He was a young Englishman, and his head had been cut to the bone by something jagged. Lispeth said she had found him down the khud, so she had brought him in.

He was breathing queerly and was unconscious.

He was put to bed and tended by the Chaplain, who knew something of medicine; and Lispeth waited outside the door in case she could be useful. She explained to the Chaplain that this was the man she meant to marry; and the Chaplain and his wife lectured her severely on the impropriety of her conduct. Lispeth listened quietly, and repeated her first proposition. It takes a great deal of Christianity to wipe out uncivilized Eastern instincts, such as falling in love at first sight. Lispeth, having found the man she worshipped, did not see why she should keep silent as to her choice. She had no intention of being sent away, either. She was going to nurse that Englishman until he was well enough to marry her. This was her little programme.

After a fortnight of slight fever and inflammation, the Englishman recovered coherence and thanked the Chaplain and his wife, and Lispeth—especially Lispeth—for their kindness. He was a traveller in the East, he said—they never talked about "globe-trotters" in those days, when the P. & O. fleet was young and small—and had come from Dehra Dun to hunt for plants and butterflies among the Simla hills. No one at Simla, therefore, knew anything about him. He fancied he must have fallen over the cliff while stalking a fern on a rotten tree-trunk, and that his coolies must have stolen his baggage and fled. He thought he would go back to Simla when he was a little stronger. He desired no more mountaineering.

He made small haste to go away, and recovered his strength slowly.

Lispeth objected to being advised either by the Chaplain or his wife; so the latter spoke to the Englishman, and told him how matters stood in Lispeth's heart. He laughed a good deal, and said it was very pretty and romantic, a perfect idyl of the Himalayas; but, as he was engaged to a girl at Home, he fancied that nothing would happen. Certainly he would behave with discretion. He did that. Still he found it very pleasant to talk to Lispeth, and walk with Lispeth, and say nice things to her, and call her pet names while he was getting strong enough to go away. It meant nothing at all to him, and everything in the world to Lispeth. She was very happy while the fortnight lasted, because she had found a man to love.

Being a savage by birth, she took no trouble to hide her feelings, and the Englishman was amused. When he went away, Lispeth walked with him, up the Hill as far as Narkunda, very troubled and very miserable. The Chaplain's wife, being a good Christian and disliking anything in the shape of fuss or scandal—Lispeth was beyond her management entirely—had told the Englishman to tell Lispeth that he was coming back to marry her. "She is but a child, you know, and, I fear, at heart a heathen," said the Chaplain's wife. So all the twelve miles up the hill the Englishman, with his arm around Lispeth's waist, was assuring the girl that he would come back and marry her; and Lispeth made him promise over and over again. She wept on the Narkunda Ridge till he had passed out of sight along the Muttiani path.

Then she dried her tears and went in to Kotgarh again, and said to the Chaplain's wife: "He will come back and marry me. He has gone to his own people to tell them so." And the Chaplain's wife soothed Lispeth and said: "He will come back." At the end of two months, Lispeth grew impatient, and was told that the Englishman had gone over the seas to England. She knew where England was, because she had read little geography primers; but, of course, she had no conception of the nature of the sea, being a Hill girl.

There was an old puzzle-map of the World in the House. Lispeth had played with it when she was a child. She unearthed it again, and put it together of evenings, and cried to herself, and tried to imagine where her Englishman was. As she had no ideas of distance or steamboats, her notions were somewhat erroneous. It would not have made the least difference had she been perfectly correct; for the Englishman had no intention of coming back to marry a Hill girl. He forgot all about her by the time he was butterfly-hunting in Assam. He wrote a book on the East afterwards. Lispeth's name did not appear.

At the end of three months, Lispeth made daily pilgrimage to Narkunda to see if her Englishman was coming along the road. It gave her comfort, and the Chaplain's wife, finding her happier, thought that she was getting over her "barbarous and most indelicate folly." A little later the walks ceased to help Lispeth and her temper grew very bad. The Chaplain's wife thought this a profitable time to let her know the real state of affairs—that the Englishman had only promised his love to keep her quiet—that he had never meant anything, and that it was "wrong and improper" of Lispeth to think of marriage with an Englishman, who was of a superior clay, besides being promised in marriage to a girl of his own people. Lispeth said that all this was clearly impossible, because he had said he loved her, and the Chaplain's wife had, with her own lips, asserted that the Englishman was coming back.

"How can what he and you said be untrue?" asked Lispeth.

"We said it as an excuse to keep you quiet, child," said the Chaplain's wife.

"Then you have lied to me," said Lispeth, "you and he?"

The Chaplain's wife bowed her head, and said nothing. Lispeth was silent, too for a little time; then she went out down the valley, and returned in the dress of a Hill girl—infamously dirty, but without the nose and ear rings. She had her hair braided into the long pig-tail, helped out with black thread, that Hill women wear.

"I am going back to my own people," said she. "You have killed Lispeth. There is only left old Jadeh's daughter—the daughter of a pahari and the servant of Tarka Devi. You are all liars, you English."

By the time that the Chaplain's wife had recovered from the shock of the announcement that Lispeth had 'verted to her mother's gods, the girl had gone; and she never came back.

She took to her own unclean people savagely, as if to make up the arrears of the life she had stepped out of; and, in a little time, she married a wood-cutter who beat her, after the manner of paharis, and her beauty faded soon.

"There is no law whereby you can account for the vagaries of the heathen," said the Chaplain's wife, "and I believe that Lispeth was always at heart an infidel." Seeing she had been taken into the Church of England at the mature age of five weeks, this statement does not do credit to the Chaplain's wife.

Lispeth was a very old woman when she died. She always had a perfect command of English,

and when she was sufficiently drunk, could sometimes be induced to tell the story of her first love-affair.

It was hard then to realize that the bleared, wrinkled creature, so like a wisp of charred rag, could ever have been "Lispeth of the Kotgarh Mission."

THREE AND—AN EXTRA.

"When halter and heel ropes are slipped, do not give chase with

sticks but with gram." —Punjabi Proverb.

After marriage arrives a reaction, sometimes a big, sometimes a little one; but it comes sooner or later, and must be tided over by both parties if they desire the rest of their lives to go with the current.

In the case of the Cusack-Bremmils this reaction did not set in till the third year after the wedding. Bremmil was hard to hold at the best of times; but he was a beautiful husband until the baby died and Mrs. Bremmil wore black, and grew thin, and mourned as if the bottom of the universe had fallen out. Perhaps Bremmil ought to have comforted her. He tried to do so, I think; but the more he comforted the more Mrs. Bremmil grieved, and, consequently, the more uncomfortable Bremmil grew. The fact was that they both needed a tonic. And they got it. Mrs. Bremmil can afford to laugh now, but it was no laughing matter to her at the time.

You see, Mrs. Hauksbee appeared on the horizon; and where she existed was fair chance of trouble. At Simla her bye-name was the "Stormy Petrel." She had won that title five times to my own certain knowledge. She was a little, brown, thin, almost skinny, woman, with big, rolling, violet-blue eyes, and the sweetest manners in the world. You had only to mention her name at afternoon teas for every woman in the room to rise up, and call her—well—NOT blessed. She was clever, witty, brilliant, and sparkling beyond most of her kind; but possessed of many devils of malice and mischievousness. She could be nice, though, even to her own sex. But that is another story.

Bremmil went off at score after the baby's death and the general discomfort that followed, and Mrs. Hauksbee annexed him. She took no pleasure in hiding her captives. She annexed him publicly, and saw that the public saw it. He rode with her, and walked with her, and talked with her, and picnicked with her, and tiffined at Peliti's with her, till people put up their eyebrows and said: "Shocking!" Mrs. Bremmil stayed at home turning over the dead baby's frocks and crying into the empty cradle. She did not care to do anything else. But some eight dear, affectionate lady-friends explained the situation at length to her in case she should miss the cream of it. Mrs. Bremmil listened quietly, and thanked them for their good offices. She was not as clever as Mrs. Hauksbee, but she was no fool. She kept her own counsel, and did not speak to Bremmil of what she had heard. This is worth remembering. Speaking to, or crying over, a husband never did any good yet.

When Bremmil was at home, which was not often, he was more affectionate than usual; and that showed his hand. The affection was forced partly to soothe his own conscience and partly to soothe Mrs. Bremmil. It failed in both regards.

Then "the A.-D.-C. in Waiting was commanded by Their Excellencies, Lord and Lady Lytton, to invite Mr. and Mrs. Cusack-Bremmil to Peterhoff on July 26th at 9.30 P. M."—"Dancing" in the bottom-left-hand corner.

"I can't go," said Mrs. Bremmil, "it is too soon after poor little Florrie—but it need not stop you, Tom."

She meant what she said then, and Bremmil said that he would go just to put in an appearance. Here he spoke the thing which was not; and Mrs. Bremmil knew it. She guessed—a woman's

guess is much more accurate than a man's certainty—that he had meant to go from the first, and with Mrs. Hauksbee. She sat down to think, and the outcome of her thoughts was that the memory of a dead child was worth considerably less than the affections of a living husband.

She made her plan and staked her all upon it. In that hour she discovered that she knew Tom Bremmil thoroughly, and this knowledge she acted on.

"Tom," said she, "I shall be dining out at the Longmores' on the evening of the 26th. You'd better dine at the club."

This saved Bremmil from making an excuse to get away and dine with Mrs. Hauksbee, so he was grateful, and felt small and mean at the same time—which was wholesome. Bremmil left the house at five for a ride. About half-past five in the evening a large leather-covered basket came in from Phelps' for Mrs. Bremmil. She was a woman who knew how to dress; and she had not spent a week on designing that dress and having it gored, and hemmed, and herring-boned, and tucked and rucked (or whatever the terms are) for nothing. It was a gorgeous dress—slight mourning. I can't describe it, but it was what The Queen calls "a creation"—a thing that hit you straight between the eyes and made you gasp. She had not much heart for what she was going to do; but as she glanced at the long mirror she had the satisfaction of knowing that she had never looked so well in her life. She was a large blonde and, when she chose, carried herself superbly.

After the dinner at the Longmores, she went on to the dance—a little late—and encountered Bremmil with Mrs. Hauksbee on his arm.

That made her flush, and as the men crowded round her for dances she looked magnificent. She filled up all her dances except three, and those she left blank. Mrs. Hauksbee caught her eye once; and she knew it was war—real war—between them. She started handicapped in the struggle, for she had ordered Bremmil about just the least little bit in the world too much; and he was beginning to resent it. Moreover, he had never seen his wife look so lovely.

He stared at her from doorways, and glared at her from passages as she went about with her partners; and the more he stared, the more taken was he. He could scarcely believe that this was the woman with the red eyes and the black stuff gown who used to weep over the eggs at breakfast.

Mrs. Hauksbee did her best to hold him in play, but, after two dances, he crossed over to his wife and asked for a dance.

"I'm afraid you've come too late, MISTER Bremmil," she said, with her eyes twinkling.

Then he begged her to give him a dance, and, as a great favor, she allowed him the fifth waltz. Luckily it stood vacant on his programme. They danced it together, and there was a little flutter round the room. Bremmil had a sort of notion that his wife could dance, but he never knew she danced so divinely. At the end of that waltz he asked for another—as a favor, not as a right; and Mrs. Bremmil said: "Show me your programme, dear!" He showed it as a naughty little schoolboy hands up contraband sweets to a master.

There was a fair sprinkling of "H" on it besides "H" at supper.

Mrs. Bremmil said nothing, but she smiled contemptuously, ran her pencil through 7 and 9—two "H's"—and returned the card with her own name written above—a pet name that only she and her husband used. Then she shook her finger at him, and said, laughing: "Oh, you silly, SILLY boy!"

Mrs. Hauksbee heard that, and—she owned as much—felt that she had the worst of it. Bremmil accepted 7 and 9 gratefully. They danced 7, and sat out 9 in one of the little tents. What Bremmil said and what Mrs. Bremmil said is no concern of any one's.

When the band struck up "The Roast Beef of Old England," the two went out into the verandah, and Bremmil began looking for his wife's dandy (this was before 'rickshaw days) while she went into the cloak-room. Mrs. Hauksbee came up and said: "You take me in to supper, I think, Mr. Bremmil." Bremmil turned red and looked foolish. "Ah—h'm! I'm going home with my wife, Mrs. Hauksbee. I think there has been a little mistake." Being a man, he spoke as though Mrs. Hauksbee were entirely responsible.

Mrs. Bremmil came out of the cloak-room in a swansdown cloak with a white "cloud" round her head. She looked radiant; and she had a right to.

The couple went off in the darkness together, Bremmil riding very close to the dandy.

Then says Mrs. Hauksbee to me—she looked a trifle faded and jaded in the lamplight: "Take my word for it, the silliest woman can manage a clever man; but it needs a very clever woman to manage a fool."

Then we went in to supper.

THROWN AWAY.

"And some are sulky, while some will plunge

 [So ho! Steady! Stand still, you!]

Some you must gentle, and some you must lunge.

 [There! There! Who wants to kill you?]

Some—there are losses in every trade—

 Will break their hearts ere bitted and made,

 Will fight like fiends as the rope cuts hard,

And die dumb-mad in the breaking-yard."

 —Toolungala Stockyard Chorus.

To rear a boy under what parents call the "sheltered life system" is, if the boy must go into the world and fend for himself, not wise. Unless he be one in a thousand he has certainly to pass through many unnecessary troubles; and may, possibly, come to extreme grief simply from ignorance of the proper proportions of things.

Let a puppy eat the soap in the bath-room or chew a newly-blacked boot. He chews and chuckles until, by and by, he finds out that blacking and Old Brown Windsor make him very sick; so he argues that soap and boots are not wholesome. Any old dog about the house will soon show him the unwisdom of biting big dogs' ears. Being young, he remembers and goes abroad, at six months, a well-mannered little beast with a chastened appetite. If he had been kept away from boots, and soap, and big dogs till he came to the trinity full-grown and with developed teeth, just consider how fearfully sick and thrashed he would be! Apply that motion to the "sheltered life," and see how it works. It does not sound pretty, but it is the better of two evils.

There was a Boy once who had been brought up under the "sheltered life" theory; and the theory killed him dead. He stayed with his people all his days, from the hour he was born till the hour he went into Sandhurst nearly at the top of the list. He was beautifully taught in all that wins marks by a private tutor, and carried the extra weight of "never having given his parents an hour's anxiety in his life." What he learnt at Sandhurst beyond the regular routine is of no great consequence. He looked about him, and he found soap and blacking, so to speak, very good. He ate a little, and came out of Sandhurst not so high as he went in.

Them there was an interval and a scene with his people, who expected much from him. Next a year of living "unspotted from the world" in a third-rate depot battalion where all the juniors were children, and all the seniors old women; and lastly he came out to India, where he was cut off from the support of his parents, and had no one to fall back on in time of trouble except himself.

Now India is a place beyond all others where one must not take things too seriously—the midday sun always excepted. Too much work and too much energy kill a man just as effectively as too much assorted vice or too much drink. Flirtation does not matter because every one is being transferred and either you or she leave the Station, and never return. Good work does not matter, because a man is judged by his worst output and another man takes all the credit of his

best as a rule. Bad work does not matter, because other men do worse, and incompetents hang on longer in India than anywhere else. Amusements do not matter, because you must repeat them as soon as you have accomplished them once, and most amusements only mean trying to win another person's money.

Sickness does not matter, because it's all in the day's work, and if you die another man takes over your place and your office in the eight hours between death and burial. Nothing matters except Home furlough and acting allowances, and these only because they are scarce. This is a slack, kutcha country where all men work with imperfect instruments; and the wisest thing is to take no one and nothing in earnest, but to escape as soon as ever you can to some place where amusement is amusement and a reputation worth the having.

But this Boy—the tale is as old as the Hills—came out, and took all things seriously. He was pretty and was petted. He took the pettings seriously, and fretted over women not worth saddling a pony to call upon. He found his new free life in India very good.

It DOES look attractive in the beginning, from a Subaltern's point of view—all ponies, partners, dancing, and so on. He tasted it as the puppy tastes the soap. Only he came late to the eating, with a growing set of teeth. He had no sense of balance—just like the puppy—and could not understand why he was not treated with the consideration he received under his father's roof. This hurt his feelings.

He quarrelled with other boys, and, being sensitive to the marrow, remembered these quarrels, and they excited him. He found whist, and gymkhanas, and things of that kind (meant to amuse one after office) good; but he took them seriously too, just as he took the "head" that followed after drink. He lost his money over whist and gymkhanas because they were new to him.

He took his losses seriously, and wasted as much energy and interest over a two-gold-mohur race for maiden ekka-ponies with their manes hogged, as if it had been the Derby. One-half of this came from inexperience—much as the puppy squabbles with the corner of the hearth-rug—and the other half from the dizziness bred by stumbling out of his quiet life into the glare and excitement of a livelier one. No one told him about the soap and the blacking because an average man takes it for granted that an average man is ordinarily careful in regard to them. It was pitiful to watch The Boy knocking himself to pieces, as an over-handled colt falls down and cuts himself when he gets away from the groom.

This unbridled license in amusements not worth the trouble of breaking line for, much less rioting over, endured for six months—all through one cold weather—and then we thought that the heat and the knowledge of having lost his money and health and lamed his horses would sober The Boy down, and he would stand steady. In ninety-nine cases out of a hundred this would have happened. You can see the principle working in any Indian Station. But this particular case fell through because The Boy was sensitive and took things seriously—as I may have said some seven times before. Of course, we couldn't tell how his excesses struck him personally.

They were nothing very heart-breaking or above the average. He might be crippled for life financially, and want a little nursing.

Still the memory of his performances would wither away in one hot weather, and the shroff would help him to tide over the money troubles. But he must have taken another view altogether and have believed himself ruined beyond redemption. His Colonel talked to him severely when the cold weather ended. That made him more wretched than ever; and it was only an ordinary "Colonel's wigging!"

What follows is a curious instance of the fashion in which we are all linked together and made responsible for one another. THE thing that kicked the beam in The Boy's mind was a remark that a woman made when he was talking to her. There is no use in repeating it, for it was only a cruel little sentence, rapped out before thinking, that made him flush to the roots of his hair. He kept himself to himself for three days, and then put in for two days' leave to go shooting near a Canal Engineer's Rest House about thirty miles out. He got his leave, and that night at Mess was noisier and more offensive than ever. He said that he was "going to shoot big game," and left at half-past ten o'clock in an ekka.

Partridge—which was the only thing a man could get near the Rest House—is not big game; so every one laughed.

Next morning one of the Majors came in from short leave, and heard that The Boy had gone out to shoot "big game." The Major had taken an interest in The Boy, and had, more than once, tried to check him in the cold weather. The Major put up his eyebrows when he heard of the expedition and went to The Boy's room, where he rummaged.

Presently he came out and found me leaving cards on the Mess.

There was no one else in the ante-room.

He said: "The Boy has gone out shooting. DOES a man shoot [missing] with a revolver and a writing-case?"

I said: "Nonsense, Major!" for I saw what was in his mind.

He said: "Nonsense or nonsense, I'm going to the Canal now—at once. I don't feel easy."

Then he thought for a minute, and said: "Can you lie?"

"You know best," I answered. "It's my profession."

"Very well," said the Major; "you must come out with me now—at once—in an ekka to the Canal to shoot black-buck. Go and put on shikar-kit—quick—and drive here with a gun."

The Major was a masterful man; and I knew that he would not give orders for nothing. So I obeyed, and on return found the Major packed up in an ekka—gun-cases and food slung below—all ready for a shooting-trip.

He dismissed the driver and drove himself. We jogged along quietly while in the station; but as soon as we got to the dusty road across the plains, he made that pony fly. A country-bred can do nearly anything at a pinch. We covered the thirty miles in under three hours, but the poor brute was nearly dead.

Once I said: "What's the blazing hurry, Major?"

He said, quietly: "The Boy has been alone, by himself, for—one, two, five—fourteen hours now! I tell you, I don't feel easy."

This uneasiness spread itself to me, and I helped to beat the pony.

When we came to the Canal Engineer's Rest House the Major called for The Boy's servant; but there was no answer. Then we went up to the house, calling for The Boy by name; but there was no answer.

"Oh, he's out shooting," said I.

Just then I saw through one of the windows a little hurricane-lamp burning. This was at four in the afternoon. We both stopped dead in the verandah, holding our breath to catch every sound; and we heard, inside the room, the "brr—brr—brr" of a multitude of flies. The Major said nothing, but he took off his helmet and we entered very softly.

The Boy was dead on the charpoy in the centre of the bare, lime-washed room. He had shot his head nearly to pieces with his revolver. The gun-cases were still strapped, so was the bedding, and on the table lay The Boy's writing-case with photographs. He had gone away to die like a poisoned rat!

The Major said to himself softly: "Poor Boy! Poor, POOR devil!" Then he turned away from the bed and said: "I want your help in this business."

Knowing The Boy was dead by his own hand, I saw exactly what that help would be, so I passed over to the table, took a chair, lit a cheroot, and began to go through the writing-case; the Major looking over my shoulder and repeating to himself: "We came too late!—Like a rat in a hole!—Poor, POOR devil!"

The Boy must have spent half the night in writing to his people, and to his Colonel, and to a girl at Home; and as soon as he had finished, must have shot himself, for he had been dead a long time when we came in.

I read all that he had written, and passed over each sheet to the Major as I finished it.

We saw from his accounts how very seriously he had taken everything. He wrote about "disgrace which he was unable to bear"—"indelible shame"—"criminal folly"—"wasted life," and so on; besides a lot of private things to his Father and Mother too much too sacred to put into print. The letter to the girl at Home was the most pitiful of all; and I choked as I read it. The Major made no attempt to keep dry-eyed. I respected him for that. He read and rocked himself to and fro, and simply cried like a woman without caring to hide it. The letters were so dreary and hopeless and touching. We forgot all about The Boy's follies, and only thought of the poor Thing on the charpoy and the scrawled sheets in our hands. It was utterly impossible to let the letters go Home.

They would have broken his Father's heart and killed his Mother after killing her belief in her son.

At last the Major dried his eyes openly, and said: "Nice sort of thing to spring on an English family! What shall we do?"

I said, knowing what the Major had brought me but for: "The Boy died of cholera. We were with him at the time. We can't commit ourselves to half-measures. Come along."

Then began one of the most grimy comic scenes I have ever taken part in—the concoction of a big, written lie, bolstered with evidence, to soothe The Boy's people at Home. I began the rough draft of a letter, the Major throwing in hints here and there while he gathered up all the stuff that The Boy had written and burnt it in the fireplace. It was a hot, still evening when we began, and the lamp burned very badly. In due course I got the draft to my satisfaction, setting forth how The Boy was the pattern of all virtues, beloved by his regiment, with every promise of a great career before him, and so on; how we had helped him through the sickness—it was no time for little lies, you will understand—and how he had died without pain. I choked while I was putting down these things and thinking of the poor people who would read them.

Then I laughed at the grotesqueness of the affair, and the laughter mixed itself up with the choke—and the Major said that we both wanted drinks.

I am afraid to say how much whiskey we drank before the letter was finished. It had not the least effect on us. Then we took off The Boy's watch, locket, and rings.

Lastly, the Major said: "We must send a lock of hair too. A woman values that."

But there were reasons why we could not find a lock fit to send.

The Boy was black-haired, and so was the Major, luckily. I cut off a piece of the Major's hair above the temple with a knife, and put it into the packet we were making. The laughing-fit and the chokes got hold of me again, and I had to stop. The Major was nearly as bad; and we both knew that the worst part of the work was to come.

We sealed up the packet, photographs, locket, seals, ring, letter, and lock of hair with The Boy's sealing-wax and The Boy's seal.

Then the Major said: "For God's sake let's get outside—away from the room—and think!"

We went outside, and walked on the banks of the Canal for an hour, eating and drinking what we had with us, until the moon rose. I know now exactly how a murderer feels. Finally, we forced ourselves back to the room with the lamp and the Other Thing in it, and began to take up the next piece of work. I am not going to write about this. It was too horrible. We burned the bedstead and dropped the ashes into the Canal; we took up the matting of the room and treated that in the same way. I went off to a village and borrowed two big hoes—I did not want the villagers to help—while the Major arranged—the other matters. It took us four hours' hard work to make the grave. As we worked, we argued out whether it was right to say as much as we remembered of the Burial of the Dead.

We compromised things by saying the Lord's Prayer with a private unofficial prayer for the peace of the soul of The Boy. Then we filled in the grave and went into the verandah—not the house—to lie down to sleep. We were dead-tired.

When we woke the Major said, wearily: "We can't go back till tomorrow. We must give him a decent time to die in. He died early THIS morning, remember. That seems more natural." So the Major must have been lying awake all the time, thinking.

I said: "Then why didn't we bring the body back to the cantonments?"

The Major thought for a minute:—"Because the people bolted when they heard of the cholera. And the ekka has gone!"

That was strictly true. We had forgotten all about the ekka-pony, and he had gone home.

So, we were left there alone, all that stifling day, in the Canal Rest House, testing and re-testing our story of The Boy's death to see if it was weak at any point. A native turned up in the afternoon, but we said that a Sahib was dead of cholera, and he ran away. As the dusk gathered, the Major told me all his fears about The Boy, and awful stories of suicide or nearly-carried-out suicide—tales that made one's hair crisp. He said that he himself had once gone into the same Valley of the Shadow as the Boy, when he was young and new to the country; so he understood how things fought together in The Boy's poor jumbled head. He also said that youngsters, in their repentant moments, consider their sins much more serious and ineffaceable than they really are. We talked together all through the evening, and rehearsed the story of the death of The Boy. As soon as the moon was up, and The Boy, theoretically, just buried, we struck across

country for the Station. We walked from eight till six o'clock in the morning; but though we were dead-tired, we did not forget to go to The Boy's room and put away his revolver with the proper amount of cartridges in the pouch. Also to set his writing-case on the table. We found the Colonel and reported the death, feeling more like murderers than ever. Then we went to bed and slept the clock round; for there was no more in us.

The tale had credence as long as was necessary, for every one forgot about The Boy before a fortnight was over. Many people, however, found time to say that the Major had behaved scandalously in not bringing in the body for a regimental funeral. The saddest thing of all was a letter from The Boy's mother to the Major and me—with big inky blisters all over the sheet. She wrote the sweetest possible things about our great kindness, and the obligation she would be under to us as long as she lived.

All things considered, she WAS under an obligation; but not exactly as she meant.

MISS YOUGHAL'S SAIS.

When Man and Woman are agreed, what can the Kazi do? —Mahomedan

Proverb.

Some people say that there is no romance in India. Those people are wrong. Our lives hold quite as much romance as is good for us.

Sometimes more.

Strickland was in the Police, and people did not understand him; so they said he was a doubtful sort of man and passed by on the other side. Strickland had himself to thank for this. He held the extraordinary theory that a Policeman in India should try to know as much about the natives as the natives themselves. Now, in the whole of Upper India, there is only ONE man who can pass for Hindu or Mohammedan, chamar or faquir, as he pleases. He is feared and respected by the natives from the Ghor Kathri to the Jamma Musjid; and he is supposed to have the gift of invisibility and executive control over many Devils. But what good has this done him with the Government? None in the world. He has never got Simla for his charge; and his name is almost unknown to Englishmen.

Strickland was foolish enough to take that man for his model; and, following out his absurd theory, dabbled in unsavory places no respectable man would think of exploring—all among the native riff-raff. He educated himself in this peculiar way for seven years, and people could not appreciate it. He was perpetually "going Fantee" among the natives, which, of course, no man with any sense believes in. He was initiated into the Sat Bhai at Allahabad once, when he was on leave; he knew the Lizard-Song of the Sansis, and the Halli-Hukk dance, which is a religious can-can of a startling kind. When a man knows who dances the Halli-Hukk, and how, and when, and where, he knows something to be proud of. He has gone deeper than the skin. But Strickland was not proud, though he had helped once, at Jagadhri, at the Painting of the Death Bull, which no Englishman must even look upon; had mastered the thieves'-patter of the changars; had taken a Eusufzai horse-thief alone near Attock; and had stood under the mimbar-board of a Border mosque and conducted service in the manner of a Sunni Mollah.

His crowning achievement was spending eleven days as a faquir in the gardens of Baba Atal at Amritsar, and there picking up the threads of the great Nasiban Murder Case. But people said, justly enough: "Why on earth can't Strickland sit in his office and write up his diary, and recruit, and keep quiet, instead of showing up the incapacity of his seniors?" So the Nasiban Murder Case did him no good departmentally; but, after his first feeling of wrath, he returned to his outlandish custom of prying into native life. By the way, when a man once acquires a taste for this particular amusement, it abides with him all his days. It is the most fascinating thing in the world; Love not excepted. Where other men took ten days to the Hills, Strickland took leave for what he called shikar, put on the disguise that appealed to him at the time, stepped down into the brown crowd, and was swallowed up for a while. He was a quiet, dark young fellow—spare, black-eyes—and, when he was not thinking of something else, a very interesting companion. Strickland on Native Progress as he had seen it was worth hearing. Natives hated Strickland; but they were afraid of him. He knew too much.

When the Youghals came into the station, Strickland—very gravely, as he did everything—fell in love with Miss Youghal; and she, after a while, fell in love with him because she could not understand him. Then Strickland told the parents; but Mrs. Youghal said she was not going to throw her daughter into the worst paid Department in the Empire, and old Youghal said, in so

many words, that he mistrusted Strickland's ways and works, and would thank him not to speak or write to his daughter any more. "Very well," said Strickland, for he did not wish to make his lady-love's life a burden. After one long talk with Miss Youghal he dropped the business entirely.

The Youghals went up to Simla in April.

In July, Strickland secured three months' leave on "urgent private affairs." He locked up his house—though not a native in the Providence would wittingly have touched "Estreekin Sahib's" gear for the world—and went down to see a friend of his, an old dyer, at Tarn Taran.

Here all trace of him was lost, until a sais met me on the Simla Mall with this extraordinary note:

"Dear old man,

"Please give bearer a box of cheroots—Supers, No. I, for preference. They are freshest at the Club. I'll repay when I reappear; but at present I'm out of Society.

"Yours,

"E. STRICKLAND."

I ordered two boxes, and handed them over to the sais with my love.

That sais was Strickland, and he was in old Youghal's employ, attached to Miss Youghal's Arab. The poor fellow was suffering for an English smoke, and knew that whatever happened I should hold my tongue till the business was over.

Later on, Mrs. Youghal, who was wrapped up in her servants, began talking at houses where she called of her paragon among saises—the man who was never too busy to get up in the morning and pick flowers for the breakfast-table, and who blacked—actually BLACKED—the hoofs of his horse like a London coachman! The turnout of Miss Youghal's Arab was a wonder and a delight. Strickland—Dulloo, I mean—found his reward in the pretty things that Miss Youghal said to him when she went out riding. Her parents were pleased to find she had forgotten all her foolishness for young Strickland and said she was a good girl.

Strickland vows that the two months of his service were the most rigid mental discipline he has ever gone through. Quite apart from the little fact that the wife of one of his fellow-saises fell in love with him and then tried to poison him with arsenic because he would have nothing to do with her, he had to school himself into keeping quiet when Miss Youghal went out riding with some man who tried to flirt with her, and he was forced to trot behind carrying the blanket and hearing every word! Also, he had to keep his temper when he was slanged in "Benmore" porch by a policeman—especially once when he was abused by a Naik he had himself recruited from Isser Jang village—or, worse still, when a young subaltern called him a pig for not making way quickly enough.

But the life had its compensations. He obtained great insight into the ways and thefts of saises—enough, he says, to have summarily convicted half the chamar population of the Punjab if he had been on business. He became one of the leading players at knuckle-bones, which all jhampanis and many saises play while they are waiting outside the Government House or the Gaiety Theatre of nights; he learned to smoke tobacco that was three-fourths cowdung; and he heard the wisdom of the grizzled Jemadar of the Government House saises, whose words are valuable. He saw many things which amused him; and he states, on honor, that no man can appreciate Simla properly, till he has seen it from the sais's point of view.

He also says that, if he chose to write all he saw, his head would be broken in several places.

Strickland's account of the agony he endured on wet nights, hearing the music and seeing the lights in "Benmore," with his toes tingling for a waltz and his head in a horse-blanket, is rather amusing. One of these days, Strickland is going to write a little book on his experiences. That book will be worth buying; and even more, worth suppressing.

Thus, he served faithfully as Jacob served for Rachel; and his leave was nearly at an end when the explosion came. He had really done his best to keep his temper in the hearing of the flirtations I have mentioned; but he broke down at last. An old and very distinguished General took Miss Youghal for a ride, and began that specially offensive "you're-only-a-little-girl" sort of flirtation—most difficult for a woman to turn aside deftly, and most maddening to listen to. Miss Youghal was shaking with fear at the things he said in the hearing of her sais. Dulloo—Strickland—stood it as long as he could. Then he caught hold of the General's bridle, and, in most fluent English, invited him to step off and be heaved over the cliff. Next minute Miss Youghal began crying; and Strickland saw that he had hopelessly given himself away, and everything was over.

The General nearly had a fit, while Miss Youghal was sobbing out the story of the disguise and the engagement that wasn't recognized by the parents. Strickland was furiously angry with himself and more angry with the General for forcing his hand; so he said nothing, but held the horse's head and prepared to thrash the General as some sort of satisfaction, but when the General had thoroughly grasped the story, and knew who Strickland was, he began to puff and blow in the saddle, and nearly rolled off with laughing. He said Strickland deserved a V. C., if it were only for putting on a sais's blanket. Then he called himself names, and vowed that he deserved a thrashing, but he was too old to take it from Strickland. Then he complimented Miss Youghal on her lover.

The scandal of the business never struck him; for he was a nice old man, with a weakness for flirtations. Then he laughed again, and said that old Youghal was a fool. Strickland let go of the cob's head, and suggested that the General had better help them, if that was his opinion. Strickland knew Youghal's weakness for men with titles and letters after their names and high official position.

"It's rather like a forty-minute farce," said the General, "but begad, I WILL help, if it's only to escape that tremendous thrashing I deserved. Go along to your home, my sais-Policeman, and change into decent kit, and I'll attack Mr. Youghal. Miss Youghal, may I ask you to canter home and wait?".........

About seven minutes later, there was a wild hurroosh at the Club.

A sais, with a blanket and head-rope, was asking all the men he knew: "For Heaven's sake lend me decent clothes!" As the men did not recognize him, there were some peculiar scenes before Strickland could get a hot bath, with soda in it, in one room, a shirt here, a collar there, a pair of trousers elsewhere, and so on. He galloped off, with half the Club wardrobe on his back, and an utter stranger's pony under him, to the house of old Youghal.

The General, arrayed in purple and fine linen, was before him.

What the General had said Strickland never knew, but Youghal received Strickland with moderate civility; and Mrs. Youghal, touched by the devotion of the transformed Dulloo, was almost kind.

The General beamed, and chuckled, and Miss Youghal came in, and almost before old Youghal knew where he was, the parental consent had been wrenched out and Strickland had departed with Miss Youghal to the Telegraph Office to wire for his kit. The final embarrassment was when an utter stranger attacked him on the Mall and asked for the stolen pony.

So, in the end, Strickland and Miss Youghal were married, on the strict understanding that Strickland should drop his old ways, and stick to Departmental routine, which pays best and leads to Simla.

Strickland was far too fond of his wife, just then, to break his word, but it was a sore trial to him; for the streets and the bazars, and the sounds in them, were full of meaning to Strickland, and these called to him to come back and take up his wanderings and his discoveries. Some day, I will tell you how he broke his promise to help a friend. That was long since, and he has, by this time, been nearly spoilt for what he would call shikar. He is forgetting the slang, and the beggar's cant, and the marks, and the signs, and the drift of the undercurrents, which, if a man would master, he must always continue to learn.

But he fills in his Departmental returns beautifully.

YOKED WITH AN UNBELIEVER.

I am dying for you, and you are dying for another. —Punjabi

Proverb.

When the Gravesend tender left the P. & 0. steamer for Bombay and went back to catch the train to Town, there were many people in it crying. But the one who wept most, and most openly was Miss Agnes Laiter. She had reason to cry, because the only man she ever loved—or ever could love, so she said—was going out to India; and India, as every one knows, is divided equally between jungle, tigers, cobras, cholera, and sepoys.

Phil Garron, leaning over the side of the steamer in the rain, felt very unhappy too; but he did not cry. He was sent out to "tea." What "tea" meant he had not the vaguest idea, but fancied that he would have to ride on a prancing horse over hills covered with tea-vines, and draw a sumptuous salary for doing so; and he was very grateful to his uncle for getting him the berth. He was really going to reform all his slack, shiftless ways, save a large proportion of his magnificent salary yearly, and, in a very short time, return to marry Agnes Laiter. Phil Garron had been lying loose on his friends' hands for three years, and, as he had nothing to do, he naturally fell in love. He was very nice; but he was not strong in his views and opinions and principles, and though he never came to actual grief his friends were thankful when he said good-bye, and went out to this mysterious "tea" business near Darjiling. They said:—"God bless you, dear boy! Let us never see your face again,"—or at least that was what Phil was given to understand.

When he sailed, he was very full of a great plan to prove himself several hundred times better than any one had given him credit for—to work like a horse, and triumphantly marry Agnes Laiter. He had many good points besides his good looks; his only fault being that he was weak, the least little bit in the world weak. He had as much notion of economy as the Morning Sun; and yet you could not lay your hand on any one item, and say: "Herein Phil Garron is extravagant or reckless." Nor could you point out any particular vice in his character; but he was "unsatisfactory" and as workable as putty.

Agnes Laiter went about her duties at home—her family objected to the engagement—with red eyes, while Phil was sailing to Darjiling—"a port on the Bengal Ocean," as his mother used to tell her friends. He was popular enough on board ship, made many acquaintances and a moderately large liquor bill, and sent off huge letters to Agnes Laiter at each port. Then he fell to work on this plantation, somewhere between Darjiling and Kangra, and, though the salary and the horse and the work were not quite all he had fancied, he succeeded fairly well, and gave himself much unnecessary credit for his perseverance.

In the course of time, as he settled more into collar, and his work grew fixed before him, the face of Agnes Laiter went out of his mind and only came when he was at leisure, which was not often. He would forget all about her for a fortnight, and remember her with a start, like a school-boy who has forgotten to learn his lesson.

She did not forget Phil, because she was of the kind that never forgets. Only, another man—a really desirable young man—presented himself before Mrs. Laiter; and the chance of a marriage with Phil was as far off as ever; and his letters were so unsatisfactory; and there was a certain amount of domestic pressure brought to bear on the girl; and the young man really was an eligible person as incomes go; and the end of all things was that Agnes married him, and wrote a tempestuous whirlwind of a letter to Phil in the wilds of Darjiling, and said she should never know a happy moment all the rest of her life. Which was a true prophecy.

Phil got that letter, and held himself ill-treated. This was two years after he had come out; but by dint of thinking fixedly of Agnes Laiter, and looking at her photograph, and patting himself on the back for being one of the most constant lovers in history, and warming to the work as he went on, he really fancied that he had been very hardly used. He sat down and wrote one final letter—a really pathetic "world without end, amen," epistle; explaining how he would be true to Eternity, and that all women were very much alike, and he would hide his broken heart, etc., etc.; but if, at any future time, etc., etc., he could afford to wait, etc., etc., unchanged affections, etc., etc., return to her old love, etc., etc., for eight closely-written pages. From an artistic point of view, it was very neat work, but an ordinary Philistine, who knew the state of Phil's real feelings—not the ones he rose to as he went on writing—would have called it the thoroughly mean and selfish work of a thoroughly mean and selfish, weak man. But this verdict would have been incorrect. Phil paid for the postage, and felt every word he had written for at least two days and a half.

It was the last flicker before the light went out.

That letter made Agnes Laiter very unhappy, and she cried and put it away in her desk, and became Mrs. Somebody Else for the good of her family. Which is the first duty of every Christian maid.

Phil went his ways, and thought no more of his letter, except as an artist thinks of a neatly touched-in sketch. His ways were not bad, but they were not altogether good until they brought him across Dunmaya, the daughter of a Rajput ex-Subadar-Major of our Native Army. The girl had a strain of Hill blood in her, and, like the Hill women, was not a purdah nashin. Where Phil met her, or how he heard of her, does not matter. She was a good girl and handsome, and, in her way, very clever and shrewd; though, of course, a little hard. It is to be remembered that Phil was living very comfortably, denying himself no small luxury, never putting by an anna, very satisfied with himself and his good intentions, was dropping all his English correspondents one by one, and beginning more and more to look upon this land as his home. Some men fall this way; and they are of no use afterwards. The climate where he was stationed was good, and it really did not seem to him that there was anything to go Home for.

He did what many planters have done before him—that is to say, he made up his mind to marry a Hill girl and settle down. He was seven and twenty then, with a long life before him, but no spirit to go through with it. So he married Dunmaya by the forms of the English Church, and some fellow-planters said he was a fool, and some said he was a wise man. Dunmaya was a thoroughly honest girl, and, in spite of her reverence for an Englishman, had a reasonable estimate of her husband's weaknesses. She managed him tenderly, and became, in less than a year, a very passable imitation of an English lady in dress and carriage. [It is curious to think that a Hill man, after a lifetime's education, is a Hill man still; but a Hill woman can in six months master most of the ways of her English sisters. There was a coolie woman once. But that is another story.] Dunmaya dressed by preference in black and yellow, and looked well.

Meantime the letter lay in Agnes's desk, and now and again she would think of poor resolute hard-working Phil among the cobras and tigers of Darjiling, toiling in the vain hope that she might come back to him. Her husband was worth ten Phils, except that he had rheumatism of the heart. Three years after he was married—and after he had tried Nice and Algeria for his complaint—he went to Bombay, where he died, and set Agnes free. Being a devout woman, she looked on his death and the place of it, as a direct interposition of Providence, and when she had recovered from the shock, she took out and reread Phil's letter with the "etc., etc.," and the big dashes, and the little dashes, and kissed it several times. No one knew her in Bombay; she had her husband's income, which was a large one, and Phil was close at hand. It was wrong and improper, of course, but she decided, as heroines do in novels, to find her old lover,

to offer him her hand and her gold, and with him spend the rest of her life in some spot far from unsympathetic souls. She sat for two months, alone in Watson's Hotel, elaborating this decision, and the picture was a pretty one. Then she set out in search of Phil Garron, Assistant on a tea plantation with a more than usually unpronounceable name..........

She found him. She spent a month over it, for his plantation was not in the Darjiling district at all, but nearer Kangra. Phil was very little altered, and Dunmaya was very nice to her.

Now the particular sin and shame of the whole business is that Phil, who really is not worth thinking of twice, was and is loved by Dunmaya, and more than loved by Agnes, the whole of whose life he seems to have spoilt.

Worst of all, Dunmaya is making a decent man of him; and he will be ultimately saved from perdition through her training.

Which is manifestly unfair.

FALSE DAWN.

Tonight God knows what thing shall tide,

 The Earth is racked and faint—

Expectant, sleepless, open-eyed;

And we, who from the Earth were made,

 Thrill with our Mother's pain.

 —In Durance.

No man will ever know the exact truth of this story; though women may sometimes whisper it to one another after a dance, when they are putting up their hair for the night and comparing lists of victims. A man, of course, cannot assist at these functions. So the tale must be told from the outside—in the dark—all wrong.

Never praise a sister to a sister, in the hope of your compliments reaching the proper ears, and so preparing the way for you later on. Sisters are women first, and sisters afterwards; and you will find that you do yourself harm.

Saumarez knew this when he made up his mind to propose to the elder Miss Copleigh. Saumarez was a strange man, with few merits, so far as men could see, though he was popular with women, and carried enough conceit to stock a Viceroy's Council and leave a little over for the Commander-in-Chief's Staff. He was a Civilian. Very many women took an interest in Saumarez, perhaps, because his manner to them was offensive. If you hit a pony over the nose at the outset of your acquaintance, he may not love you, but he will take a deep interest in your movements ever afterwards. The elder Miss Copleigh was nice, plump, winning and pretty. The younger was not so pretty, and, from men disregarding the hint set forth above, her style was repellant and unattractive. Both girls had, practically, the same figure, and there was a strong likeness between them in look and voice; though no one could doubt for an instant which was the nicer of the two.

Saumarez made up his mind, as soon as they came into the station from Behar, to marry the elder one. At least, we all made sure that he would, which comes to the same thing. She was two and twenty, and he was thirty-three, with pay and allowances of nearly fourteen hundred rupees a month. So the match, as we arranged it, was in every way a good one. Saumarez was his name, and summary was his nature, as a man once said. Having drafted his Resolution, he formed a Select Committee of One to sit upon it, and resolved to take his time. In our unpleasant slang, the Copleigh girls "hunted in couples." That is to say, you could do nothing with one without the other. They were very loving sisters; but their mutual affection was sometimes inconvenient. Saumarez held the balance-hair true between them, and none but himself could have said to which side his heart inclined; though every one guessed. He rode with them a good deal and danced with them, but he never succeeded in detaching them from each other for any length of time.

Women said that the two girls kept together through deep mistrust, each fearing that the other would steal a march on her. But that has nothing to do with a man. Saumarez was silent for good or bad, and as business—likely attentive as he could be, having due regard to his work and his polo. Beyond doubt both girls were fond of him.

As the hot weather drew nearer, and Saumarez made no sign, women said that you could see their trouble in the eyes of the girls—that they were looking strained, anxious, and irritable. Men are quite blind in these matters unless they have more of the woman than the man in their composition, in which case it does not matter what they say or think. I maintain it was the hot April days that took the color out of the Copleigh girls' cheeks. They should have been sent to the Hills early. No one—man or woman—feels an angel when the hot weather is approaching. The younger sister grew more cynical—not to say acid—in her ways; and the winningness of the elder wore thin. There was more effort in it.

Now the Station wherein all these things happened was, though not a little one, off the line of rail, and suffered through want of attention. There were no gardens or bands or amusements worth speaking of, and it was nearly a day's journey to come into Lahore for a dance. People were grateful for small things to interest them.

About the beginning of May, and just before the final exodus of Hill-goers, when the weather was very hot and there were not more than twenty people in the Station, Saumarez gave a moonlight riding-picnic at an old tomb, six miles away, near the bed of the river. It was a "Noah's Ark" picnic; and there was to be the usual arrangement of quarter-mile intervals between each couple, on account of the dust. Six couples came altogether, including chaperons. Moonlight picnics are useful just at the very end of the season, before all the girls go away to the Hills. They lead to understandings, and should be encouraged by chaperones; especially those whose girls look sweetish in riding habits. I knew a case once. But that is another story. That picnic was called the "Great Pop Picnic," because every one knew Saumarez would propose then to the eldest Miss Copleigh; and, beside his affair, there was another which might possibly come to happiness.

The social atmosphere was heavily charged and wanted clearing.

We met at the parade-ground at ten: the night was fearfully hot.

The horses sweated even at walking-pace, but anything was better than sitting still in our own dark houses. When we moved off under the full moon we were four couples, one triplet, and Mr. Saumarez rode with the Copleigh girls, and I loitered at the tail of the procession, wondering with whom Saumarez would ride home. Every one was happy and contented; but we all felt that things were going to happen. We rode slowly: and it was nearly midnight before we reached the old tomb, facing the ruined tank, in the decayed gardens where we were going to eat and drink. I was late in coming up; and before I went into the garden, I saw that the horizon to the north carried a faint, dun-colored feather. But no one would have thanked me for spoiling so well-managed an entertainment as this picnic—and a dust-storm, more or less, does no great harm.

We gathered by the tank. Some one had brought out a banjo—which is a most sentimental instrument—and three or four of us sang.

You must not laugh at this. Our amusements in out-of-the-way Stations are very few indeed. Then we talked in groups or together, lying under the trees, with the sun-baked roses dropping their petals on our feet, until supper was ready. It was a beautiful supper, as cold and as iced as you could wish; and we stayed long over it.

I had felt that the air was growing hotter and hotter; but nobody seemed to notice it until the moon went out and a burning hot wind began lashing the orange-trees with a sound like the noise of the sea. Before we knew where we were, the dust-storm was on us, and everything was roaring, whirling darkness. The supper-table was blown bodily into the tank. We were afraid of staying anywhere near the old tomb for fear it might be blown down. So we felt our way to the orange-trees where the horses were picketed and waited for the storm to blow over. Then

the little light that was left vanished, and you could not see your hand before your face. The air was heavy with dust and sand from the bed of the river, that filled boots and pockets and drifted down necks and coated eyebrows and moustaches. It was one of the worst dust-storms of the year.

We were all huddled together close to the trembling horses, with the thunder clattering overhead, and the lightning spurting like water from a sluice, all ways at once. There was no danger, of course, unless the horses broke loose. I was standing with my head downward and my hands over my mouth, hearing the trees thrashing each other. I could not see who was next me till the flashes came.

Then I found that I was packed near Saumarez and the eldest Miss Copleigh, with my own horse just in front of me. I recognized the eldest Miss Copleigh, because she had a pagri round her helmet, and the younger had not. All the electricity in the air had gone into my body and I was quivering and tingling from head to foot—exactly as a corn shoots and tingles before rain. It was a grand storm.

The wind seemed to be picking up the earth and pitching it to leeward in great heaps; and the heat beat up from the ground like the heat of the Day of Judgment.

The storm lulled slightly after the first half-hour, and I heard a despairing little voice close to my ear, saying to itself, quietly and softly, as if some lost soul were flying about with the wind: "O my God!" Then the younger Miss Copleigh stumbled into my arms, saying: "Where is my horse? Get my horse. I want to go home. I WANT to go home. Take me home."

I thought that the lightning and the black darkness had frightened her; so I said there was no danger, but she must wait till the storm blew over. She answered: "It is not THAT! It is not THAT! I want to go home! O take me away from here!"

I said that she could not go till the light came; but I felt her brush past me and go away. It was too dark to see where. Then the whole sky was split open with one tremendous flash, as if the end of the world were coming, and all the women shrieked.

Almost directly after this, I felt a man's hand on my shoulder and heard Saumarez bellowing in my ear. Through the rattling of the trees and howling of the wind, I did not catch his words at once, but at last I heard him say: "I've proposed to the wrong one! What shall I do?" Saumarez had no occasion to make this confidence to me. I was never a friend of his, nor am I now; but I fancy neither of us were ourselves just then. He was shaking as he stood with excitement, and I was feeling queer all over with the electricity.

I could not think of anything to say except:—"More fool you for proposing in a dust-storm." But I did not see how that would improve the mistake.

Then he shouted: "Where's Edith—Edith Copleigh?" Edith was the youngest sister. I answered out of my astonishment:—"What do you want with HER?" Would you believe it, for the next two minutes, he and I were shouting at each other like maniacs—he vowing that it was the youngest sister he had meant to propose to all along, and I telling him till my throat was hoarse that he must have made a mistake! I can't account for this except, again, by the fact that we were neither of us ourselves. Everything seemed to me like a bad dream—from the stamping of the horses in the darkness to Saumarez telling me the story of his loving Edith Copleigh since the first. He was still clawing my shoulder and begging me to tell him where Edith Copleigh was, when another lull came and brought light with it, and we saw the dust-cloud forming on the plain in front of us. So we knew the worst was over. The moon was low down, and there was just the glimmer of the false dawn that comes about an hour before the real one. But the

light was very faint, and the dun cloud roared like a bull. I wondered where Edith Copleigh had gone; and as I was wondering I saw three things together: First Maud Copleigh's face come smiling out of the darkness and move towards Saumarez, who was standing by me. I heard the girl whisper, "George," and slide her arm through the arm that was not clawing my shoulder, and I saw that look on her face which only comes once or twice in a lifetime—when a woman is perfectly happy and the air is full of trumpets and gorgeous-colored fire and the Earth turns into cloud because she loves and is loved. At the same time, I saw Saumarez's face as he heard Maud Copleigh's voice, and fifty yards away from the clump of orange-trees I saw a brown holland habit getting upon a horse.

It must have been my state of over-excitement that made me so quick to meddle with what did not concern me. Saumarez was moving off to the habit; but I pushed him back and said:—"Stop here and explain. I'll fetch her back!" and I ran out to get at my own horse. I had a perfectly unnecessary notion that everything must be done decently and in order, and that Saumarez's first care was to wipe the happy look out of Maud Copleigh's face. All the time I was linking up the curb-chain I wondered how he would do it.

I cantered after Edith Copleigh, thinking to bring her back slowly on some pretence or another. But she galloped away as soon as she saw me, and I was forced to ride after her in earnest. She called back over her shoulder—"Go away! I'm going home. Oh, go away!" two or three times; but my business was to catch her first, and argue later. The ride just fitted in with the rest of the evil dream. The ground was very bad, and now and again we rushed through the whirling, choking "dust-devils" in the skirts of the flying storm. There was a burning hot wind blowing that brought up a stench of stale brick-kilns with it; and through the half light and through the dust-devils, across that desolate plain, flickered the brown holland habit on the gray horse. She headed for the Station at first. Then she wheeled round and set off for the river through beds of burnt down jungle-grass, bad even to ride a pig over. In cold blood I should never have dreamed of going over such a country at night, but it seemed quite right and natural with the lightning crackling overhead, and a reek like the smell of the Pit in my nostrils. I rode and shouted, and she bent forward and lashed her horse, and the aftermath of the dust-storm came up and caught us both, and drove us downwind like pieces of paper.

I don't know how far we rode; but the drumming of the horse-hoofs and the roar of the wind and the race of the faint blood-red moon through the yellow mist seemed to have gone on for years and years, and I was literally drenched with sweat from my helmet to my gaiters when the gray stumbled, recovered himself, and pulled up dead lame. My brute was used up altogether. Edith Copleigh was in a sad state, plastered with dust, her helmet off, and crying bitterly. "Why can't you let me alone?" she said. "I only wanted to get away and go home. Oh, PLEASE let me go!"

"You have got to come back with me, Miss Copleigh. Saumarez has something to say to you."

It was a foolish way of putting it; but I hardly knew Miss Copleigh; and, though I was playing Providence at the cost of my horse, I could not tell her in as many words what Saumarez had told me. I thought he could do that better himself. All her pretence about being tired and wanting to go home broke down, and she rocked herself to and fro in the saddle as she sobbed, and the hot wind blew her black hair to leeward. I am not going to repeat what she said, because she was utterly unstrung.

This, if you please, was the cynical Miss Copleigh. Here was I, almost an utter stranger to her, trying to tell her that Saumarez loved her and she was to come back to hear him say so! I believe I made myself understood, for she gathered the gray together and made him hobble somehow, and we set off for the tomb, while the storm went thundering down to Umballa and a few big drops of warm rain fell. I found out that she had been standing close to Saumarez when he

proposed to her sister and had wanted to go home and cry in peace, as an English girl should. She dabbled her eyes with her pocket-handkerchief as we went along, and babbled to me out of sheer lightness of heart and hysteria. That was perfectly unnatural; and yet, it seemed all right at the time and in the place. All the world was only the two Copleigh girls, Saumarez and I, ringed in with the lightning and the dark; and the guidance of this misguided world seemed to lie in my hands.

When we returned to the tomb in the deep, dead stillness that followed the storm, the dawn was just breaking and nobody had gone away. They were waiting for our return. Saumarez most of all.

His face was white and drawn. As Miss Copleigh and I limped up, he came forward to meet us, and, when he helped her down from her saddle, he kissed her before all the picnic. It was like a scene in a theatre, and the likeness was heightened by all the dust-white, ghostly-looking men and women under the orange-trees, clapping their hands, as if they were watching a play—at Saumarez's choice. I never knew anything so un-English in my life.

Lastly, Saumarez said we must all go home or the Station would come out to look for us, and WOULD I be good enough to ride home with Maud Copleigh? Nothing would give me greater pleasure, I said.

So, we formed up, six couples in all, and went back two by two; Saumarez walking at the side of Edith Copleigh, who was riding his horse.

The air was cleared; and little by little, as the sun rose, I felt we were all dropping back again into ordinary men and women and that the "Great Pop Picnic" was a thing altogether apart and out of the world—never to happen again. It had gone with the dust-storm and the tingle in the hot air.

I felt tired and limp, and a good deal ashamed of myself as I went in for a bath and some sleep.

There is a woman's version of this story, but it will never be written. ... unless Maud Copleigh cares to try.

THE RESCUE OF PLUFFLES.

Thus, for a season, they fought it fair—

 She and his cousin May—

Tactful, talented, debonnaire,

 Decorous foes were they;

But never can battle of man compare

 With merciless feminine fray.

 —Two and One.

Mrs. Hauksbee was sometimes nice to her own sex. Here is a story to prove this; and you can believe just as much as ever you please.

Pluffles was a subaltern in the "Unmentionables." He was callow, even for a subaltern. He was callow all over—like a canary that had not finished fledging itself. The worst of it was he had three times as much money as was good for him; Pluffles' Papa being a rich man and Pluffles being the only son. Pluffles' Mamma adored him. She was only a little less callow than Pluffles and she believed everything he said.

Pluffles' weakness was not believing what people said. He preferred what he called "trusting to his own judgment." He had as much judgment as he had seat or hands; and this preference tumbled him into trouble once or twice. But the biggest trouble Pluffles ever manufactured came about at Simla—some years ago, when he was four-and-twenty.

He began by trusting to his own judgment, as usual, and the result was that, after a time, he was bound hand and foot to Mrs. Reiver's 'rickshaw wheels.

There was nothing good about Mrs. Reiver, unless it was her dress.

She was bad from her hair—which started life on a Brittany's girl's head—to her boot-heels, which were two and three-eighth inches high. She was not honestly mischievous like Mrs. Hauksbee; she was wicked in a business-like way.

There was never any scandal—she had not generous impulses enough for that. She was the exception which proved the rule that Anglo-Indian ladies are in every way as nice as their sisters at Home.

She spent her life in proving that rule.

Mrs. Hauksbee and she hated each other fervently. They heard far too much to clash; but the things they said of each other were startling—not to say original. Mrs. Hauksbee was honest—honest as her own front teeth—and, but for her love of mischief, would have been a woman's woman. There was no honesty about Mrs. Reiver; nothing but selfishness. And at the beginning of the season, poor little Pluffles fell a prey to her. She laid herself out to that end, and who was Pluffles, to resist? He went on trusting to his judgment, and he got judged.

I have seen Hayes argue with a tough horse—I have seen a tonga-driver coerce a stubborn pony—I have seen a riotous setter broken to gun by a hard keeper—but the breaking-in of

Pluffles of the "Unmentionables" was beyond all these. He learned to fetch and carry like a dog, and to wait like one, too, for a word from Mrs. Reiver. He learned to keep appointments which Mrs. Reiver had no intention of keeping. He learned to take thankfully dances which Mrs. Reiver had no intention of giving him. He learned to shiver for an hour and a quarter on the windward side of Elysium while Mrs. Reiver was making up her mind to come for a ride. He learned to hunt for a 'rickshaw, in a light dress-suit under a pelting rain, and to walk by the side of that 'rickshaw when he had found it. He learned what it was to be spoken to like a coolie and ordered about like a cook. He learned all this and many other things besides. And he paid for his schooling.

Perhaps, in some hazy way, he fancied that it was fine and impressive, that it gave him a status among men, and was altogether the thing to do. It was nobody's business to warn Pluffles that he was unwise. The pace that season was too good to inquire; and meddling with another man's folly is always thankless work.

Pluffles' Colonel should have ordered him back to his regiment when he heard how things were going. But Pluffles had got himself engaged to a girl in England the last time he went home; and if there was one thing more than another which the Colonel detested, it was a married subaltern. He chuckled when he heard of the education of Pluffles, and said it was "good training for the boy." But it was not good training in the least. It led him into spending money beyond his means, which were good: above that, the education spoilt an average boy and made it a tenth-rate man of an objectionable kind. He wandered into a bad set, and his little bill at Hamilton's was a thing to wonder at.

Then Mrs. Hauksbee rose to the occasion. She played her game alone, knowing what people would say of her; and she played it for the sake of a girl she had never seen. Pluffles' fiancée was to come out, under the chaperonage of an aunt, in October, to be married to Pluffles.

At the beginning of August, Mrs. Hauksbee discovered that it was time to interfere. A man who rides much knows exactly what a horse is going to do next before he does it. In the same way, a woman of Mrs. Hauksbee's experience knows accurately how a boy will behave under certain circumstances—notably when he is infatuated with one of Mrs. Reiver's stamp. She said that, sooner or later, little Pluffles would break off that engagement for nothing at all—simply to gratify Mrs. Reiver, who, in return, would keep him at her feet and in her service just so long as she found it worth her while.

She said she knew the signs of these things. If she did not, no one else could.

Then she went forth to capture Pluffles under the guns of the enemy; just as Mrs. Cusack-Bremmil carried away Bremmil under Mrs. Hauksbee's eyes.

This particular engagement lasted seven weeks—we called it the Seven Weeks' War—and was fought out inch by inch on both sides. A detailed account would fill a book, and would be incomplete then.

Any one who knows about these things can fit in the details for himself. It was a superb fight—there will never be another like it as long as Jakko stands—and Pluffles was the prize of victory.

People said shameful things about Mrs. Hauksbee. They did not know what she was playing for. Mrs. Reiver fought, partly because Pluffles was useful to her, but mainly because she hated Mrs. Hauksbee, and the matter was a trial of strength between them. No one knows what Pluffles thought. He had not many ideas at the best of times, and the few he possessed made him conceited. Mrs. Hauksbee said:—"The boy must be caught; and the only way of catching him is by treating him well."

So she treated him as a man of the world and of experience so long as the issue was doubtful. Little by little, Pluffles fell away from his old allegiance and came over to the enemy, by whom he was made much of. He was never sent on out-post duty after 'rickshaws any more, nor was he given dances which never came off, nor were the drains on his purse continued. Mrs. Hauksbee held him on the snaffle; and after his treatment at Mrs. Reiver's hands, he appreciated the change.

Mrs. Reiver had broken him of talking about himself, and made him talk about her own merits. Mrs. Hauksbee acted otherwise, and won his confidence, till he mentioned his engagement to the girl at Home, speaking of it in a high and mighty way as a "piece of boyish folly." This was when he was taking tea with her one afternoon, and discoursing in what he considered a gay and fascinating style.

Mrs. Hauksbee had seen an earlier generation of his stamp bud and blossom, and decay into fat Captains and tubby Majors.

At a moderate estimate there were about three and twenty sides to that lady's character. Some men say more. She began to talk to Pluffles after the manner of a mother, and as if there had been three hundred years, instead of fifteen, between them. She spoke with a sort of throaty quaver in her voice which had a soothing effect, though what she said was anything but soothing. She pointed out the exceeding folly, not to say meanness, of Pluffles' conduct, and the smallness of his views. Then he stammered something about "trusting to his own judgment as a man of the world;" and this paved the way for what she wanted to say next. It would have withered up Pluffles had it come from any other woman; but in the soft cooing style in which Mrs. Hauksbee put it, it only made him feel limp and repentant—as if he had been in some superior kind of church. Little by little, very softly and pleasantly, she began taking the conceit out of Pluffles, as you take the ribs out of an umbrella before re-covering it. She told him what she thought of him and his judgment and his knowledge of the world; and how his performances had made him ridiculous to other people; and how it was his intention to make love to herself if she gave him the chance. Then she said that marriage would be the making of him; and drew a pretty little picture—all rose and opal—of the Mrs. Pluffles of the future going through life relying on the "judgment" and "knowledge of the world" of a husband who had nothing to reproach himself with. How she reconciled these two statements she alone knew. But they did not strike Pluffles as conflicting.

Hers was a perfect little homily—much better than any clergyman could have given—and it ended with touching allusions to Pluffles' Mamma and Papa, and the wisdom of taking his bride Home.

Then she sent Pluffles out for a walk, to think over what she had said. Pluffles left, blowing his nose very hard and holding himself very straight. Mrs. Hauksbee laughed.

What Pluffles had intended to do in the matter of the engagement only Mrs. Reiver knew, and she kept her own counsel to her death. She would have liked it spoiled as a compliment, I fancy.

Pluffles enjoyed many talks with Mrs. Hauksbee during the next few days. They were all to the same end, and they helped Pluffles in the path of Virtue.

Mrs. Hauksbee wanted to keep him under her wing to the last.

Therefore she discountenanced his going down to Bombay to get married. "Goodness only knows what might happen by the way!" she said. "Pluffles is cursed with the curse of Reuben, and India is no fit place for him!"

In the end, the fiancee arrived with her aunt; and Pluffles, having reduced his affairs to some sort of order—here again Mrs. Hauksbee helped him—was married.

Mrs. Hauksbee gave a sigh of relief when both the "I wills" had been said, and went her way.

Pluffles took her advice about going Home. He left the Service, and is now raising speckled cattle inside green painted fences somewhere at Home. I believe he does this very judiciously. He would have come to extreme grief out here.

For these reasons if any one says anything more than usually nasty about Mrs. Hauksbee, tell him the story of the Rescue of Pluffles.

CUPID'S ARROWS.

Pit where the buffalo cooled his hide,

By the hot sun emptied, and blistered and dried;

Log in the reh-grass, hidden and alone;

Bund where the earth-rat's mounds are strown;

Cave in the bank where the sly stream steals;

Aloe that stabs at the belly and heels,

Jump if you dare on a steed untried—Safer it is to go wide—

go wide!

Hark, from in front where the best men ride:—

"Pull to the off, boys! Wide! Go wide!"

—The Peora Hunt.

Once upon a time there lived at Simla a very pretty girl, the daughter of a poor but honest District and Sessions Judge. She was a good girl, but could not help knowing her power and using it.

Her Mamma was very anxious about her daughter's future, as all good Mammas should be.

When a man is a Commissioner and a bachelor and has the right of wearing open-work jam-tart jewels in gold and enamel on his clothes, and of going through a door before every one except a Member of Council, a Lieutenant-Governor, or a Viceroy, he is worth marrying. At least, that is what ladies say. There was a Commissioner in Simla, in those days, who was, and wore, and did, all I have said. He was a plain man—an ugly man—the ugliest man in Asia, with two exceptions. His was a face to dream about and try to carve on a pipe-head afterwards. His name was Saggott—Barr-Saggott—Anthony Barr-Saggott and six letters to follow.

Departmentally, he was one of the best men the Government of India owned. Socially, he was like a blandishing gorilla.

When he turned his attentions to Miss Beighton, I believe that Mrs.

Beighton wept with delight at the reward Providence had sent her in her old age.

Mr. Beighton held his tongue. He was an easy-going man.

Now a Commissioner is very rich. His pay is beyond the dreams of avarice—is so enormous that he can afford to save and scrape in a way that would almost discredit a Member of Council. Most Commissioners are mean; but Barr-Saggott was an exception. He entertained royally; he horsed himself well; he gave dances; he was a power in the land; and he behaved as such.

Consider that everything I am writing of took place in an almost pre-historic era in the history of British India. Some folk may remember the years before lawn-tennis was born when we all

played croquet. There were seasons before that, if you will believe me, when even croquet had not been invented, and archery—which was revived in England in 1844—was as great a pest as lawn-tennis is now. People talked learnedly about "holding" and "loosing," "steles," "reflexed bows," "56-pound bows," "backed" or "self-yew bows," as we talk about "rallies," "volleys," "smashes," "returns," and "16-ounce rackets."

Miss Beighton shot divinely over ladies' distance—60 yards, that is—and was acknowledged the best lady archer in Simla. Men called her "Diana of Tara-Devi."

Barr-Saggott paid her great attention; and, as I have said, the heart of her mother was uplifted in consequence. Kitty Beighton took matters more calmly. It was pleasant to be singled out by a Commissioner with letters after his name, and to fill the hearts of other girls with bad feelings. But there was no denying the fact that Barr-Saggott was phenomenally ugly; and all his attempts to adorn himself only made him more grotesque. He was not christened "The Langur"—which means gray ape—for nothing. It was pleasant, Kitty thought, to have him at her feet, but it was better to escape from him and ride with the graceless Cubbon—the man in a Dragoon Regiment at Umballa—the boy with a handsome face, and no prospects. Kitty liked Cubbon more than a little. He never pretended for a moment the he was anything less than head over heels in love with her; for he was an honest boy. So Kitty fled, now and again, from the stately wooings of Barr-Saggott to the company of young Cubbon, and was scolded by her Mamma in consequence. "But, Mother," she said, "Mr. Saggott is such—such a—is so FEARFULLY ugly, you know!"

"My dear," said Mrs. Beighton, piously, "we cannot be other than an all-ruling Providence has made us. Besides, you will take precedence of your own Mother, you know! Think of that and be reasonable."

Then Kitty put up her little chin and said irreverent things about precedence, and Commissioners, and matrimony. Mr. Beighton rubbed the top of his head; for he was an easy-going man.

Late in the season, when he judged that the time was ripe, Barr-Saggott developed a plan which did great credit to his administrative powers. He arranged an archery tournament for ladies, with a most sumptuous diamond-studded bracelet as prize.

He drew up his terms skilfully, and every one saw that the bracelet was a gift to Miss Beighton; the acceptance carrying with it the hand and the heart of Commissioner Barr-Saggott. The terms were a St. Leonard's Round—thirty-six shots at sixty yards—under the rules of the Simla Toxophilite Society.

All Simla was invited. There were beautifully arranged tea-tables under the deodars at Annandale, where the Grand Stand is now; and, alone in its glory, winking in the sun, sat the diamond bracelet in a blue velvet case. Miss Beighton was anxious—almost too anxious to compete. On the appointed afternoon, all Simla rode down to Annandale to witness the Judgment of Paris turned upside down.

Kitty rode with young Cubbon, and it was easy to see that the boy was troubled in his mind. He must be held innocent of everything that followed. Kitty was pale and nervous, and looked long at the bracelet. Barr-Saggott was gorgeously dressed, even more nervous than Kitty, and more hideous than ever.

Mrs. Beighton smiled condescendingly, as befitted the mother of a potential Commissioneress, and the shooting began; all the world standing in a semicircle as the ladies came out one after the other.

Nothing is so tedious as an archery competition. They shot, and they shot, and they kept on shooting, till the sun left the valley, and little breezes got up in the deodars, and people waited for Miss Beighton to shoot and win. Cubbon was at one horn of the semicircle round the shooters, and Barr-Saggott at the other. Miss Beighton was last on the list. The scoring had been weak, and the bracelet, PLUS Commissioner Barr-Saggott, was hers to a certainty.

The Commissioner strung her bow with his own sacred hands. She stepped forward, looked at the bracelet, and her first arrow went true to a hair—full into the heart of the "gold"—counting nine points.

Young Cubbon on the left turned white, and his Devil prompted Barr-Saggott to smile. Now horses used to shy when Barr-Saggott smiled.

Kitty saw that smile. She looked to her left-front, gave an almost imperceptible nod to Cubbon, and went on shooting.

I wish I could describe the scene that followed. It was out of the ordinary and most improper. Miss Kitty fitted her arrows with immense deliberation, so that every one might see what she was doing. She was a perfect shot; and her 46-pound bow suited her to a nicety. She pinned the wooden legs of the target with great care four successive times. She pinned the wooden top of the target once, and all the ladies looked at each other. Then she began some fancy shooting at the white, which, if you hit it, counts exactly one point. She put five arrows into the white. It was wonderful archery; but, seeing that her business was to make "golds" and win the bracelet, Barr-Saggott turned a delicate green like young water-grass. Next, she shot over the target twice, then wide to the left twice—always with the same deliberation—while a chilly hush fell over the company, and Mrs. Beighton took out her handkerchief. Then Kitty shot at the ground in front of the target, and split several arrows. Then she made a red—or seven points—just to show what she could do if she liked, and finished up her amazing performance with some more fancy shooting at the target-supports. Here is her score as it was picked off:—

Gold.	Red.	Blue.	Black.	White.	Total Hits.	Total Score Miss Beighton
1	1	0	0	5	7	21

Barr-Saggott looked as if the last few arrowheads had been driven into his legs instead of the target's, and the deep stillness was broken by a little snubby, mottled, half-grown girl saying in a shrill voice of triumph: "Then I'VE won!"

Mrs. Beighton did her best to bear up; but she wept in the presence of the people. No training could help her through such a disappointment. Kitty unstrung her bow with a vicious jerk, and went back to her place, while Barr-Saggott was trying to pretend that he enjoyed snapping the bracelet on the snubby girl's raw, red wrist. It was an awkward scene—most awkward. Every one tried to depart in a body and leave Kitty to the mercy of her Mamma.

But Cubbon took her away instead, and—the rest isn't worth printing.

HIS CHANCE IN LIFE.

Then a pile of heads be laid—

Thirty thousand heaped on high—

All to please the Kafir maid,

Where the Oxus ripples by.

Grimly spake Atulla Khan:—

"Love hath made this thing a Man."

 —Oatta's Story.

If you go straight away from Levees and Government House Lists, past Trades' Balls—far beyond everything and everybody you ever knew in your respectable life—you cross, in time, the Border line where the last drop of White blood ends and the full tide of Black sets in. It would be easier to talk to a new-made Duchess on the spur of the moment than to the Borderline folk without violating some of their conventions or hurting their feelings. The Black and the White mix very quaintly in their ways. Sometimes the White shows in spurts of fierce, childish pride—which is Pride of Race run crooked—and sometimes the Black in still fiercer abasement and humility, half heathenish customs and strange, unaccountable impulses to crime. One of these days, this people—understand they are far lower than the class whence Derozio, the man who imitated Byron, sprung—will turn out a writer or a poet; and then we shall know how they live and what they feel. In the meantime, any stories about them cannot be absolutely correct in fact or inference.

Miss Vezzis came from across the Borderline to look after some children who belonged to a lady until a regularly ordained nurse could come out. The lady said Miss Vezzis was a bad, dirty nurse and inattentive. It never struck her that Miss Vezzis had her own life to lead and her own affairs to worry over, and that these affairs were the most important things in the world to Miss Vezzis.

Very few mistresses admit this sort of reasoning. Miss Vezzis was as black as a boot, and to our standard of taste, hideously ugly.

She wore cotton-print gowns and bulged shoes; and when she lost her temper with the children, she abused them in the language of the Borderline—which is part English, part Portuguese, and part Native. She was not attractive; but she had her pride, and she preferred being called "Miss Vezzis."

Every Sunday she dressed herself wonderfully and went to see her Mamma, who lived, for the most part, on an old cane chair in a greasy tussur-silk dressing-gown and a big rabbit-warren of a house full of Vezzises, Pereiras, Ribieras, Lisboas and Gansalveses, and a floating population of loafers; besides fragments of the day's bazar, garlic, stale incense, clothes thrown on the floor, petticoats hung on strings for screens, old bottles, pewter crucifixes, dried immortelles, pariah puppies, plaster images of the Virgin, and hats without crowns. Miss Vezzis drew twenty rupees a month for acting as nurse, and she squabbled weekly with her Mamma as to the percentage to be given towards housekeeping.

When the quarrel was over, Michele D'Cruze used to shamble across the low mud wall of the compound and make love to Miss Vezzis after the fashion of the Borderline, which is hedged about with much ceremony. Michele was a poor, sickly weed and very black; but he had his pride. He would not be seen smoking a huqa for anything; and he looked down on natives as only a man with seven-eighths native blood in his veins can. The Vezzis Family had their pride too. They traced their descent from a mythical plate-layer who had worked on the Sone Bridge when railways were new in India, and they valued their English origin. Michele was a Telegraph Signaller on Rs. 35 a month. The fact that he was in Government employ made Mrs. Vezzis lenient to the shortcomings of his ancestors.

There was a compromising legend—Dom Anna the tailor brought it from Poonani—that a black Jew of Cochin had once married into the D'Cruze family; while it was an open secret that an uncle of Mrs. D'Cruze was at that very time doing menial work, connected with cooking, for a Club in Southern India! He sent Mrs D'Cruze seven rupees eight annas a month; but she felt the disgrace to the family very keenly all the same.

However, in the course of a few Sundays, Mrs. Vezzis brought herself to overlook these blemishes and gave her consent to the marriage of her daughter with Michele, on condition that Michele should have at least fifty rupees a month to start married life upon. This wonderful prudence must have been a lingering touch of the mythical plate-layer's Yorkshire blood; for across the Borderline people take a pride in marrying when they please—not when they can.

Having regard to his departmental prospects, Miss Vezzis might as well have asked Michele to go away and come back with the Moon in his pocket. But Michele was deeply in love with Miss Vezzis, and that helped him to endure. He accompanied Miss Vezzis to Mass one Sunday, and after Mass, walking home through the hot stale dust with her hand in his, he swore by several Saints, whose names would not interest you, never to forget Miss Vezzis; and she swore by her Honor and the Saints—the oath runs rather curiously; "In nomine Sanctissimae—" (whatever the name of the she-Saint is) and so forth, ending with a kiss on the forehead, a kiss on the left cheek, and a kiss on the mouth—never to forget Michele.

Next week Michele was transferred, and Miss Vezzis dropped tears upon the window-sash of the "Intermediate" compartment as he left the Station.

If you look at the telegraph-map of India you will see a long line skirting the coast from Backergunge to Madras. Michele was ordered to Tibasu, a little Sub-office one-third down this line, to send messages on from Berhampur to Chicacola, and to think of Miss Vezzis and his chances of getting fifty rupees a month out of office hours. He had the noise of the Bay of Bengal and a Bengali Babu for company; nothing more. He sent foolish letters, with crosses tucked inside the flaps of the envelopes, to Miss Vezzis.

When he had been at Tibasu for nearly three weeks his chance came.

Never forget that unless the outward and visible signs of Our Authority are always before a native he is as incapable as a child of understanding what authority means, or where is the danger of disobeying it. Tibasu was a forgotten little place with a few Orissa Mohamedans in it. These, hearing nothing of the Collector-Sahib for some time, and heartily despising the Hindu Sub-Judge, arranged to start a little Mohurrum riot of their own. But the Hindus turned out and broke their heads; when, finding lawlessness pleasant, Hindus and Mahomedans together raised an aimless sort of Donnybrook just to see how far they could go. They looted each other's shops, and paid off private grudges in the regular way. It was a nasty little riot, but not worth putting in the newspapers.

Michele was working in his office when he heard the sound that a man never forgets all his

life—the "ah-yah" of an angry crowd.

[When that sound drops about three tones, and changes to a thick, droning ut, the man who hears it had better go away if he is alone.] The Native Police Inspector ran in and told Michele that the town was in an uproar and coming to wreck the Telegraph Office.

The Babu put on his cap and quietly dropped out of the window; while the Police Inspector, afraid, but obeying the old race-instinct which recognizes a drop of White blood as far as it can be diluted, said:—"What orders does the Sahib give?"

The "Sahib" decided Michele. Though horribly frightened, he felt that, for the hour, he, the man with the Cochin Jew and the menial uncle in his pedigree, was the only representative of English authority in the place. Then he thought of Miss Vezzis and the fifty rupees, and took the situation on himself. There were seven native policemen in Tibasu, and four crazy smooth-bore muskets among them. All the men were gray with fear, but not beyond leading. Michele dropped the key of the telegraph instrument, and went out, at the head of his army, to meet the mob. As the shouting crew came round a corner of the road, he dropped and fired; the men behind him loosing instinctively at the same time.

The whole crowd—curs to the backbone—yelled and ran; leaving one man dead, and another dying in the road. Michele was sweating with fear, but he kept his weakness under, and went down into the town, past the house where the Sub-Judge had barricaded himself. The streets were empty. Tibasu was more frightened than Michele, for the mob had been taken at the right time.

Michele returned to the Telegraph-Office, and sent a message to Chicacola asking for help. Before an answer came, he received a deputation of the elders of Tibasu, telling him that the Sub-Judge said his actions generally were "unconstitional," and trying to bully him. But the heart of Michele D'Cruze was big and white in his breast, because of his love for Miss Vezzis, the nurse-girl, and because he had tasted for the first time Responsibility and Success. Those two make an intoxicating drink, and have ruined more men than ever has Whiskey. Michele answered that the Sub-Judge might say what he pleased, but, until the Assistant Collector came, the Telegraph Signaller was the Government of India in Tibasu, and the elders of the town would be held accountable for further rioting. Then they bowed their heads and said: "Show mercy!" or words to that effect, and went back in great fear; each accusing the other of having begun the rioting.

Early in the dawn, after a night's patrol with his seven policemen, Michele went down the road, musket in hand, to meet the Assistant Collector, who had ridden in to quell Tibasu. But, in the presence of this young Englishman, Michele felt himself slipping back more and more into the native, and the tale of the Tibasu Riots ended, with the strain on the teller, in an hysterical outburst of tears, bred by sorrow that he had killed a man, shame that he could not feel as uplifted as he had felt through the night, and childish anger that his tongue could not do justice to his great deeds. It was the White drop in Michele's veins dying out, though he did not know it.

But the Englishman understood; and, after he had schooled those men of Tibasu, and had conferred with the Sub-Judge till that excellent official turned green, he found time to draught an official letter describing the conduct of Michele. Which letter filtered through the Proper Channels, and ended in the transfer of Michele up-country once more, on the Imperial salary of sixty-six rupees a month.

So he and Miss Vezzis were married with great state and ancientry; and now there are several little D'Cruzes sprawling about the verandahs of the Central Telegraph Office.

But, if the whole revenue of the Department he serves were to be his reward Michele could never, never repeat what he did at Tibasu for the sake of Miss Vezzis the nurse-girl.

Which proves that, when a man does good work out of all proportion to his pay, in seven cases out of nine there is a woman at the back of the virtue.

The two exceptions must have suffered from sunstroke.

WATCHES OF THE NIGHT.

What is in the Brahmin's books that is in the Brahmin's heart.

Neither you nor I knew there was so much evil in the world.

 —Hindu Proverb.

This began in a practical joke; but it has gone far enough now, and is getting serious.

Platte, the Subaltern, being poor, had a Waterbury watch and a plain leather guard.

The Colonel had a Waterbury watch also, and for guard, the lip-strap of a curb-chain. Lip-straps make the best watch guards.

They are strong and short. Between a lip-strap and an ordinary leather guard there is no great difference; between one Waterbury watch and another there is none at all. Every one in the station knew the Colonel's lip-strap. He was not a horsey man, but he liked people to believe he had been one once; and he wove fantastic stories of the hunting-bridle to which this particular lip-strap had belonged. Otherwise he was painfully religious.

Platte and the Colonel were dressing at the Club—both late for their engagements, and both in a hurry. That was Kismet. The two watches were on a shelf below the looking-glass—guards hanging down. That was carelessness. Platte changed first, snatched a watch, looked in the glass, settled his tie, and ran. Forty seconds later, the Colonel did exactly the same thing; each man taking the other's watch.

You may have noticed that many religious people are deeply suspicious. They seem—for purely religious purposes, of course—to know more about iniquity than the Unregenerate. Perhaps they were specially bad before they became converted! At any rate, in the imputation of things evil, and in putting the worst construction on things innocent, a certain type of good people may be trusted to surpass all others. The Colonel and his Wife were of that type. But the Colonel's Wife was the worst. She manufactured the Station scandal, and—TALKED TO HER AYAH! Nothing more need be said. The Colonel's Wife broke up the Laplaces's home. The Colonel's Wife stopped the Ferris-Haughtrey engagement. The Colonel's Wife induced young Buxton to keep his wife down in the Plains through the first year of the marriage. Whereby little Mrs.

Buxton died, and the baby with her. These things will be remembered against the Colonel's Wife so long as there is a regiment in the country.

But to come back to the Colonel and Platte. They went their several ways from the dressing-room. The Colonel dined with two Chaplains, while Platte went to a bachelor-party, and whist to follow.

Mark how things happen! If Platte's sais had put the new saddle-pad on the mare, the butts of the terrets would not have worked through the worn leather, and the old pad into the mare's withers, when she was coming home at two o'clock in the morning. She would not have reared, bolted, fallen into a ditch, upset the cart, and sent Platte flying over an aloe-hedge on to Mrs. Larkyn's well-kept lawn; and this tale would never have been written. But the mare did all these things, and while Platte was rolling over and over on the turf, like a shot rabbit, the watch and guard flew from his waistcoat—as an Infantry Major's sword hops out of the scabbard when they are firing a feu de joie—and rolled and rolled in the moonlight, till it stopped under a window.

Platte stuffed his handkerchief under the pad, put the cart straight, and went home.

Mark again how Kismet works! This would not happen once in a hundred years. Towards the end of his dinner with the two Chaplains, the Colonel let out his waistcoat and leaned over the table to look at some Mission Reports. The bar of the watch-guard worked through the buttonhole, and the watch—Platte's watch—slid quietly on to the carpet. Where the bearer found it next morning and kept it.

Then the Colonel went home to the wife of his bosom; but the driver of the carriage was drunk and lost his way. So the Colonel returned at an unseemly hour and his excuses were not accepted. If the Colonel's Wife had been an ordinary "vessel of wrath appointed for destruction," she would have known that when a man stays away on purpose, his excuse is always sound and original. The very baldness of the Colonel's explanation proved its truth.

See once more the workings of Kismet! The Colonel's watch which came with Platte hurriedly on to Mrs. Larkyn's lawn, chose to stop just under Mrs. Larkyn's window, where she saw it early in the morning, recognized it, and picked it up. She had heard the crash of Platte's cart at two o'clock that morning, and his voice calling the mare names. She knew Platte and liked him. That day she showed him the watch and heard his story. He put his head on one side, winked and said:—"How disgusting! Shocking old man! with his religious training, too! I should send the watch to the Colonel's Wife and ask for explanations."

Mrs. Larkyn thought for a minute of the Laplaces—whom she had known when Laplace and his wife believed in each other—and answered:—"I will send it. I think it will do her good. But remember, we must NEVER tell her the truth."

Platte guessed that his own watch was in the Colonel's possession, and thought that the return of the lip-strapped Waterbury with a soothing note from Mrs. Larkyn, would merely create a small trouble for a few minutes. Mrs. Larkyn knew better. She knew that any poison dropped would find good holding-ground in the heart of the Colonel's Wife.

The packet, and a note containing a few remarks on the Colonel's calling-hours, were sent over to the Colonel's Wife, who wept in her own room and took counsel with herself.

If there was one woman under Heaven whom the Colonel's Wife hated with holy fervor, it was Mrs. Larkyn. Mrs. Larkyn was a frivolous lady, and called the Colonel's Wife "old cat." The Colonel's Wife said that somebody in Revelations was remarkably like Mrs. Larkyn.

She mentioned other Scripture people as well. From the Old Testament. [But the Colonel's Wife was the only person who cared or dared to say anything against Mrs. Larkyn. Every one else accepted her as an amusing, honest little body.] Wherefore, to believe that her husband had been shedding watches under that "Thing's" window at ungodly hours, coupled with the fact of his late arrival on the previous night, was.....

At this point she rose up and sought her husband. He denied everything except the ownership of the watch. She besought him, for his Soul's sake, to speak the truth. He denied afresh, with two bad words. Then a stony silence held the Colonel's Wife, while a man could draw his breath five times.

The speech that followed is no affair of mine or yours. It was made up of wifely and womanly jealousy; knowledge of old age and sunken cheeks; deep mistrust born of the text that says even little babies' hearts are as bad as they make them; rancorous hatred of Mrs. Larkyn, and the tenets of the creed of the Colonel's Wife's upbringing.

Over and above all, was the damning lip-strapped Waterbury, ticking away in the palm of her shaking, withered hand. At that hour, I think, the Colonel's Wife realized a little of the restless suspicions she had injected into old Laplace's mind, a little of poor Miss Haughtrey's misery, and some of the canker that ate into Buxton's heart as he watched his wife dying before his eyes. The Colonel stammered and tried to explain. Then he remembered that his watch had disappeared; and the mystery grew greater. The Colonel's Wife talked and prayed by turns till she was tired, and went away to devise means for "chastening the stubborn heart of her husband." Which translated, means, in our slang, "tail-twisting."

You see, being deeply impressed with the doctrine of Original Sin, she could not believe in the face of appearances. She knew too much, and jumped to the wildest conclusions.

But it was good for her. It spoilt her life, as she had spoilt the life of the Laplaces. She had lost her faith in the Colonel, and—here the creed suspicion came in—he might, she argued, have erred many times, before a merciful Providence, at the hands of so unworthy an instrument as Mrs. Larkyn, had established his guilt.

He was a bad, wicked, gray-haired profligate. This may sound too sudden a revulsion for a long-wedded wife; but it is a venerable fact that, if a man or woman makes a practice of, and takes a delight in, believing and spreading evil of people indifferent to him or her, he or she will end in believing evil of folk very near and dear. You may think, also, that the mere incident of the watch was too small and trivial to raise this misunderstanding. It is another aged fact that, in life as well as racing, all the worst accidents happen at little ditches and cut-down fences. In the same way, you sometimes see a woman who would have made a Joan of Arc in another century and climate, threshing herself to pieces over all the mean worry of housekeeping. But that is another story.

Her belief only made the Colonel's Wife more wretched, because it insisted so strongly on the villainy of men. Remembering what she had done, it was pleasant to watch her unhappiness, and the penny-farthing attempts she made to hide it from the Station. But the Station knew and laughed heartlessly; for they had heard the story of the watch, with much dramatic gesture, from Mrs. Larkyn's lips.

Once or twice Platte said to Mrs. Larkyn, seeing that the Colonel had not cleared himself:— "This thing has gone far enough. I move we tell the Colonel's Wife how it happened." Mrs. Larkyn shut her lips and shook her head, and vowed that the Colonel's Wife must bear her punishment as best she could. Now Mrs. Larkyn was a frivolous woman, in whom none would have suspected deep hate. So Platte took no action, and came to believe gradually, from the Colonel's silence, that the Colonel must have "run off the line" somewhere that night, and, therefore, preferred to stand sentence on the lesser count of rambling into other people's compounds out of calling hours. Platte forgot about the watch business after a while, and moved down-country with his regiment. Mrs. Larkyn went home when her husband's tour of Indian service expired. She never forgot.

But Platte was quite right when he said that the joke had gone too far. The mistrust and the tragedy of it—which we outsiders cannot see and do not believe in—are killing the Colonel's Wife, and are making the Colonel wretched. If either of them read this story, they can depend upon its being a fairly true account of the case, and can "kiss and make friends."

Shakespeare alludes to the pleasure of watching an Engineer being shelled by his own Battery. Now this shows that poets should not write about what they do not understand. Any one could have told him that Sappers and Gunners are perfectly different branches of the Service. But, if you correct the sentence, and substitute Gunner for Sapper, the moral comes just the same.

THE OTHER MAN.

When the earth was sick and the skies were gray,

And the woods were rotted with rain,

The Dead Man rode through the autumn day

To visit his love again.

—Old Ballad.

Far back in the "seventies," before they had built any Public Offices at Simla, and the broad road round Jakko lived in a pigeon-hole in the P. W. D. hovels, her parents made Miss Gaurey marry Colonel Schreiderling. He could not have been MUCH more than thirty-five years her senior; and, as he lived on two hundred rupees a month and had money of his own, he was well off. He belonged to good people, and suffered in the cold weather from lung complaints. In the hot weather he dangled on the brink of heat-apoplexy; but it never quite killed him.

Understand, I do not blame Schreiderling. He was a good husband according to his lights, and his temper only failed him when he was being nursed. Which was some seventeen days in each month. He was almost generous to his wife about money matters, and that, for him, was a concession. Still Mrs. Schreiderling was not happy. They married her when she was this side of twenty and had given all her poor little heart to another man. I have forgotten his name, but we will call him the Other Man. He had no money and no prospects.

He was not even good-looking; and I think he was in the Commissariat or Transport. But, in spite of all these things, she loved him very madly; and there was some sort of an engagement between the two when Schreiderling appeared and told Mrs. Gaurey that he wished to marry her daughter. Then the other engagement was broken off—washed away by Mrs. Gaurey's tears, for that lady governed her house by weeping over disobedience to her authority and the lack of reverence she received in her old age. The daughter did not take after her mother. She never cried. Not even at the wedding.

The Other Man bore his loss quietly, and was transferred to as bad a station as he could find. Perhaps the climate consoled him. He suffered from intermittent fever, and that may have distracted him from his other trouble. He was weak about the heart also. Both ways. One of the valves was affected, and the fever made it worse.

This showed itself later on.

Then many months passed, and Mrs. Schreiderling took to being ill.

She did not pine away like people in story books, but she seemed to pick up every form of illness that went about a station, from simple fever upwards. She was never more than ordinarily pretty at the best of times; and the illness made her ugly. Schreiderling said so. He prided himself on speaking his mind.

When she ceased being pretty, he left her to her own devices, and went back to the lairs of his bachelordom. She used to trot up and down Simla Mall in a forlorn sort of way, with a gray Terai hat well on the back of her head, and a shocking bad saddle under her.

Schreiderling's generosity stopped at the horse. He said that any saddle would do for a woman

as nervous as Mrs. Schreiderling. She never was asked to dance, because she did not dance well; and she was so dull and uninteresting, that her box very seldom had any cards in it. Schreiderling said that if he had known that she was going to be such a scare-crow after her marriage, he would never have married her. He always prided himself on speaking his mind, did Schreiderling!

He left her at Simla one August, and went down to his regiment.

Then she revived a little, but she never recovered her looks. I found out at the Club that the Other Man is coming up sick—very sick—on an off chance of recovery. The fever and the heart-valves had nearly killed him. She knew that, too, and she knew—what I had no interest in knowing—when he was coming up. I suppose he wrote to tell her. They had not seen each other since a month before the wedding. And here comes the unpleasant part of the story.

A late call kept me down at the Dovedell Hotel till dusk one evening. Mrs. Schreidlerling had been flitting up and down the Mall all the afternoon in the rain. Coming up along the Cart-road, a tonga passed me, and my pony, tired with standing so long, set off at a canter. Just by the road down to the Tonga Office Mrs. Schreiderling, dripping from head to foot, was waiting for the tonga. I turned up-hill, as the tonga was no affair of mine; and just then she began to shriek. I went back at once and saw, under the Tonga Office lamps, Mrs. Schreiderling kneeling in the wet road by the back seat of the newly-arrived tonga, screaming hideously.

Then she fell face down in the dirt as I came up.

Sitting in the back seat, very square and firm, with one hand on the awning-stanchion and the wet pouring off his hat and moustache, was the Other Man—dead. The sixty-mile up-hill jolt had been too much for his valve, I suppose. The tonga-driver said:—"The Sahib died two stages out of Solon. Therefore, I tied him with a rope, lest he should fall out by the way, and so came to Simla. Will the Sahib give me bukshish? IT," pointing to the Other Man, "should have given one rupee."

The Other Man sat with a grin on his face, as if he enjoyed the joke of his arrival; and Mrs. Schreiderling, in the mud, began to groan. There was no one except us four in the office and it was raining heavily. The first thing was to take Mrs. Schreiderling home, and the second was to prevent her name from being mixed up with the affair. The tonga-driver received five rupees to find a bazar 'rickshaw for Mrs. Schreiderling. He was to tell the tonga Babu afterwards of the Other Man, and the Babu was to make such arrangements as seemed best.

Mrs. Schreiderling was carried into the shed out of the rain, and for three-quarters of an hour we two waited for the 'rickshaw. The Other Man was left exactly as he had arrived. Mrs. Schreiderling would do everything but cry, which might have helped her. She tried to scream as soon as her senses came back, and then she began praying for the Other Man's soul. Had she not been as honest as the day, she would have prayed for her own soul too. I waited to hear her do this, but she did not. Then I tried to get some of the mud off her habit. Lastly, the 'rickshaw came, and I got her away—partly by force. It was a terrible business from beginning to end; but most of all when the 'rickshaw had to squeeze between the wall and the tonga, and she saw by the lamp-light that thin, yellow hand grasping the awning-stanchion.

She was taken home just as every one was going to a dance at Viceregal Lodge—"Peterhoff" it was then—and the doctor found that she had fallen from her horse, that I had picked her up at the back of Jakko, and really deserved great credit for the prompt manner in which I had secured medical aid. She did not die—men of Schreiderling's stamp marry women who don't die easily. They live and grow ugly.

She never told of her one meeting, since her marriage, with the Other Man; and, when the chill and cough following the exposure of that evening, allowed her abroad, she never by word or sign alluded to having met me by the Tonga Office. Perhaps she never knew.

She used to trot up and down the Mall, on that shocking bad saddle, looking as if she expected to meet some one round the corner every minute. Two years afterward, she went Home, and died—at Bournemouth, I think.

Schreiderling, when he grew maudlin at Mess, used to talk about "my poor dear wife." He always set great store on speaking his mind, did Schreiderling!

CONSEQUENCES.

Rosicrucian subtleties

In the Orient had rise;

Ye may find their teachers still

Under Jacatala's Hill.

Seek ye Bombast Paracelsus,

Read what Flood the Seeker tells us

Of the Dominant that runs

Through the cycles of the Suns—

Read my story last and see

Luna at her apogee.

There are yearly appointments, and two-yearly appointments, and five-yearly appointments at Simla, and there are, or used to be, permanent appointments, whereon you stayed up for the term of your natural life and secured red cheeks and a nice income. Of course, you could descend in the cold weather; for Simla is rather dull then.

Tarrion came from goodness knows where—all away and away in some forsaken part of Central India, where they call Pachmari a "Sanitarium," and drive behind trotting bullocks, I believe. He belonged to a regiment; but what he really wanted to do was to escape from his regiment and live in Simla forever and ever. He had no preference for anything in particular, beyond a good horse and a nice partner. He thought he could do everything well; which is a beautiful belief when you hold it with all your heart. He was clever in many ways, and good to look at, and always made people round him comfortable—even in Central India.

So he went up to Simla, and, because he was clever and amusing, he gravitated naturally to Mrs. Hauksbee, who could forgive everything but stupidity. Once he did her great service by changing the date on an invitation-card for a big dance which Mrs. Hauksbee wished to attend, but couldn't because she had quarrelled with the A.-D.-C., who took care, being a mean man, to invite her to a small dance on the 6th instead of the big Ball of the 26th. It was a very clever piece of forgery; and when Mrs. Hauksbee showed the A.-D.-C. her invitation-card, and chaffed him mildly for not better managing his vendettas, he really thought he had made a mistake; and—which was wise—realized that it was no use to fight with Mrs. Hauksbee. She was grateful to Tarrion and asked what she could do for him. He said simply: "I'm a Freelance up here on leave, and on the lookout for what I can loot. I haven't a square inch of interest in all Simla. My name isn't known to any man with an appointment in his gift, and I want an appointment—a good, sound, pukka one. I believe you can do anything you turn yourself to do. Will you help me?" Mrs. Hauksbee thought for a minute, and passed the last of her riding-whip through her lips, as was her custom when thinking.

Then her eyes sparkled, and she said:—"I will;" and she shook hands on it. Tarrion, having perfect confidence in this great woman, took no further thought of the business at all. Except to wonder what sort of an appointment he would win.

Mrs. Hauksbee began calculating the prices of all the Heads of Departments and Members of Council she knew, and the more she thought the more she laughed, because her heart was in the game and it amused her. Then she took a Civil List and ran over a few of the appointments. There are some beautiful appointments in the Civil List. Eventually, she decided that, though Tarrion was too good for the Political Department, she had better begin by trying to get him in there. What were her own plans to this end, does not matter in the least, for Luck or Fate played into her hands, and she had nothing to do but to watch the course of events and take the credit of them.

All Viceroys, when they first come out, pass through the "Diplomatic Secrecy" craze. It wears off in time; but they all catch it in the beginning, because they are new to the country.

The particular Viceroy who was suffering from the complaint just then—this was a long time ago, before Lord Dufferin ever came from Canada, or Lord Ripon from the bosom of the English Church—had it very badly; and the result was that men who were new to keeping official secrets went about looking unhappy; and the Viceroy plumed himself on the way in which he had instilled notions of reticence into his Staff.

Now, the Supreme Government have a careless custom of committing what they do to printed papers. These papers deal with all sorts of things—from the payment of Rs. 200 to a "secret service" native, up to rebukes administered to Vakils and Motamids of Native States, and rather brusque letters to Native Princes, telling them to put their houses in order, to refrain from kidnapping women, or filling offenders with pounded red pepper, and eccentricities of that kind. Of course, these things could never be made public, because Native Princes never err officially, and their States are, officially, as well administered as Our territories. Also, the private allowances to various queer people are not exactly matters to put into newspapers, though they give quaint reading sometimes.

When the Supreme Government is at Simla, these papers are prepared there, and go round to the people who ought to see them in office-boxes or by post. The principle of secrecy was to that Viceroy quite as important as the practice, and he held that a benevolent despotism like Ours should never allow even little things, such as appointments of subordinate clerks, to leak out till the proper time. He was always remarkable for his principles.

There was a very important batch of papers in preparation at that time. It had to travel from one end of Simla to the other by hand.

It was not put into an official envelope, but a large, square, pale-pink one; the matter being in MS. on soft crinkly paper. It was addressed to "The Head Clerk, etc., etc." Now, between "The Head Clerk, etc., etc.," and "Mrs. Hauksbee" and a flourish, is no very great difference if the address be written in a very bad hand, as this was. The chaprassi who took the envelope was not more of an idiot than most chaprassis. He merely forgot where this most unofficial cover was to be delivered, and so asked the first Englishman he met, who happened to be a man riding down to Annandale in a great hurry. The Englishman hardly looked, said: "Hauksbee Sahib ki Mem," and went on. So did the chaprassi, because that letter was the last in stock and he wanted to get his work over. There was no book to sign; he thrust the letter into Mrs. Hauksbee's bearer's hands and went off to smoke with a friend.

Mrs. Hauksbee was expecting some cut-out pattern things in flimsy paper from a friend. As soon as she got the big square packet, therefore, she said, "Oh, the DEAR creature!" and tore it open with a paper-knife, and all the MS. enclosures tumbled out on the floor.

Mrs. Hauksbee began reading. I have said the batch was rather important. That is quite enough for you to know. It referred to some correspondence, two measures, a peremptory order to a

native chief and two dozen other things. Mrs. Hauksbee gasped as she read, for the first glimpse of the naked machinery of the Great Indian Government, stripped of its casings, and lacquer, and paint, and guard-rails, impresses even the most stupid man. And Mrs. Hauksbee was a clever woman. She was a little afraid at first, and felt as if she had laid hold of a lightning-flash by the tail, and did not quite know what to do with it. There were remarks and initials at the side of the papers; and some of the remarks were rather more severe than the papers. The initials belonged to men who are all dead or gone now; but they were great in their day.

Mrs. Hauksbee read on and thought calmly as she read. Then the value of her trove struck her, and she cast about for the best method of using it. Then Tarrion dropped in, and they read through all the papers together, and Tarrion, not knowing how she had come by them, vowed that Mrs. Hauksbee was the greatest woman on earth.

Which I believe was true, or nearly so.

"The honest course is always the best," said Tarrion after an hour and a half of study and conversation. "All things considered, the Intelligence Branch is about my form. Either that or the Foreign Office. I go to lay siege to the High Gods in their Temples."

He did not seek a little man, or a little big man, or a weak Head of a strong Department, but he called on the biggest and strongest man that the Government owned, and explained that he wanted an appointment at Simla on a good salary. The compound insolence of this amused the Strong Man, and, as he had nothing to do for the moment, he listened to the proposals of the audacious Tarrion.

"You have, I presume, some special qualifications, besides the gift of self-assertion, for the claims you put forwards?" said the Strong Man. "That, Sir," said Tarrion, "is for you to judge." Then he began, for he had a good memory, quoting a few of the more important notes in the papers—slowly and one by one as a man drops chlorodyne into a glass. When he had reached the peremptory order—and it WAS a peremptory order—the Strong Man was troubled.

Tarrion wound up:—"And I fancy that special knowledge of this kind is at least as valuable for, let us say, a berth in the Foreign Office, as the fact of being the nephew of a distinguished officer's wife." That hit the Strong Man hard, for the last appointment to the Foreign Office had been by black favor, and he knew it. "I'll see what I can do for you," said the Strong Man. "Many thanks," said Tarrion. Then he left, and the Strong Man departed to see how the appointment was to be blocked..........

Followed a pause of eleven days; with thunders and lightnings and much telegraphing. The appointment was not a very important one, carrying only between Rs. 500 and Rs. 700 a month; but, as the Viceroy said, it was the principle of diplomatic secrecy that had to be maintained, and it was more than likely that a boy so well supplied with special information would be worth translating. So they translated him. They must have suspected him, though he protested that his information was due to singular talents of his own. Now, much of this story, including the after-history of the missing envelope, you must fill in for yourself, because there are reasons why it cannot be written. If you do not know about things Up Above, you won't understand how to fill it in, and you will say it is impossible.

What the Viceroy said when Tarrion was introduced to him was:—"So, this is the boy who 'rusked' the Government of India, is it? Recollect, Sir, that is not done TWICE." So he must have known something.

What Tarrion said when he saw his appointment gazetted was:—"If Mrs. Hauksbee were twenty years younger, and I her husband, I should be Viceroy of India in twenty years."

What Mrs. Hauksbee said, when Tarrion thanked her, almost with tears in his eyes, was first:— "I told you so!" and next, to herself:—"What fools men are!"

THE CONVERSION OF AURELIAN McGOGGIN.

Ride with an idle whip, ride with an unused heel.

But, once in a way, there will come a day

When the colt must be taught to feel

The lash that falls, and the curb that galls,

And the sting of the rowelled steel.

—Life's Handicap.

This is not a tale exactly. It is a Tract; and I am immensely proud of it. Making a Tract is a Feat.

Every man is entitled to his own religious opinions; but no man—least of all a junior—has a right to thrust these down other men's throats. The Government sends out weird Civilians now and again; but McGoggin was the queerest exported for a long time. He was clever—brilliantly clever—but his cleverness worked the wrong way. Instead of keeping to the study of the vernaculars, he had read some books written by a man called Comte, I think, and a man called Spencer, and a Professor Clifford. [You will find these books in the Library.] They deal with people's insides from the point of view of men who have no stomachs. There was no order against his reading them; but his Mamma should have smacked him.

They fermented in his head, and he came out to India with a rarefied religion over and above his work. It was not much of a creed. It only proved that men had no souls, and there was no God and no hereafter, and that you must worry along somehow for the good of Humanity.

One of its minor tenets seemed to be that the one thing more sinful than giving an order was obeying it. At least, that was what McGoggin said; but I suspect he had misread his primers.

I do not say a word against this creed. It was made up in Town, where there is nothing but machinery and asphalt and building—all shut in by the fog. Naturally, a man grows to think that there is no one higher than himself, and that the Metropolitan Board of Works made everything. But in this country, where you really see humanity—raw, brown, naked humanity—with nothing between it and the blazing sky, and only the used-up, over-handled earth underfoot, the notion somehow dies away, and most folk come back to simpler theories. Life, in India, is not long enough to waste in proving that there is no one in particular at the head of affairs.

For this reason. The Deputy is above the Assistant, the Commissioner above the Deputy, the Lieutenant-Governor above the Commissioner, and the Viceroy above all four, under the orders of the Secretary of State, who is responsible to the Empress. If the Empress be not responsible to her Maker—if there is no Maker for her to be responsible to—the entire system of Our administration must be wrong. Which is manifestly impossible. At Home men are to be excused. They are stalled up a good deal and get intellectually "beany." When you take a gross, "beany" horse to exercise, he slavers and slobbers over the bit till you can't see the horns.

But the bit is there just the same. Men do not get "beany" in India. The climate and the work are against playing bricks with words.

If McGoggin had kept his creed, with the capital letters and the endings in "isms," to himself, no one would have cared; but his grandfathers on both sides had been Wesleyan preachers, and

the preaching strain came out in his mind. He wanted every one at the Club to see that they had no souls too, and to help him to eliminate his Creator. As a good many men told him, HE undoubtedly had no soul, because he was so young, but it did not follow that his seniors were equally undeveloped; and, whether there was another world or not, a man still wanted to read his papers in this. "But that is not the point—that is not the point!" Aurelian used to say. Then men threw sofa-cushions at him and told him to go to any particular place he might believe in. They christened him the "Blastoderm"—he said he came from a family of that name somewhere, in the pre-historic ages—and, by insult and laughter, strove to choke him dumb, for he was an unmitigated nuisance at the Club; besides being an offence to the older men. His Deputy Commissioner, who was working on the Frontier when Aurelian was rolling on a bed-quilt, told him that, for a clever boy, Aurelian was a very big idiot. And, you know, if he had gone on with his work, he would have been caught up to the Secretariat in a few years. He was just the type that goes there—all head, no physique and a hundred theories. Not a soul was interested in McGoggin's soul. He might have had two, or none, or somebody's else's. His business was to obey orders and keep abreast of his files instead of devastating the Club with "isms."

He worked brilliantly; but he could not accept any order without trying to better it. That was the fault of his creed. It made men too responsible and left too much to their honor. You can sometimes ride an old horse in a halter; but never a colt.

McGoggin took more trouble over his cases than any of the men of his year. He may have fancied that thirty-page judgments on fifty-rupee cases—both sides perjured to the gullet— advanced the cause of Humanity. At any rate, he worked too much, and worried and fretted over the rebukes he received, and lectured away on his ridiculous creed out of office, till the Doctor had to warn him that he was overdoing it. No man can toil eighteen annas in the rupee in June without suffering. But McGoggin was still intellectually "beany" and proud of himself and his powers, and he would take no hint. He worked nine hours a day steadily.

"Very well," said the doctor, "you'll break down because you are over-engined for your beam." McGoggin was a little chap.

One day, the collapse came—as dramatically as if it had been meant to embellish a Tract.

It was just before the Rains. We were sitting in the verandah in the dead, hot, close air, gasping and praying that the black-blue clouds would let down and bring the cool. Very, very far away, there was a faint whisper, which was the roar of the Rains breaking over the river. One of the men heard it, got out of his chair, listened, and said, naturally enough:—"Thank God!"

Then the Blastoderm turned in his place and said:—"Why? I assure you it's only the result of perfectly natural causes—atmospheric phenomena of the simplest kind. Why you should, therefore, return thanks to a Being who never did exist—who is only a figment—"

"Blastoderm," grunted the man in the next chair, "dry up, and throw me over the Pioneer. We know all about your figments." The Blastoderm reached out to the table, took up one paper, and jumped as if something had stung him. Then he handed the paper over.

"As I was saying," he went on slowly and with an effort—"due to perfectly natural causes— perfectly natural causes. I mean—"

"Hi! Blastoderm, you've given me the Calcutta Mercantile Advertiser."

The dust got up in little whorls, while the treetops rocked and the kites whistled. But no one was looking at the coming of the Rains.

We were all staring at the Blastoderm, who had risen from his chair and was fighting with his

speech. Then he said, still more slowly:—

"Perfectly conceivable—dictionary—red oak—amenable—cause—retaining—shuttlecock—alone."

"Blastoderm's drunk," said one man. But the Blastoderm was not drunk. He looked at us in a dazed sort of way, and began motioning with his hands in the half light as the clouds closed overhead.

Then—with a scream:—

"What is it?—Can't—reserve—attainable—market—obscure—"

But his speech seemed to freeze in him, and—just as the lightning shot two tongues that cut the whole sky into three pieces and the rain fell in quivering sheets—the Blastoderm was struck dumb. He stood pawing and champing like a hard-held horse, and his eyes were full of terror.

The Doctor came over in three minutes, and heard the story. "It's aphasia," he said. "Take him to his room. I KNEW the smash would come." We carried the Blastoderm across, in the pouring rain, to his quarters, and the Doctor gave him bromide of potassium to make him sleep.

Then the Doctor came back to us and told us that aphasia was like all the arrears of "Punjab Head" falling in a lump; and that only once before—in the case of a sepoy—had he met with so complete a case. I myself have seen mild aphasia in an overworked man, but this sudden dumbness was uncanny—though, as the Blastoderm himself might have said, due to "perfectly natural causes."

"He'll have to take leave after this," said the Doctor. "He won't be fit for work for another three months. No; it isn't insanity or anything like it. It's only complete loss of control over the speech and memory. I fancy it will keep the Blastoderm quiet, though."

Two days later, the Blastoderm found his tongue again. The first question he asked was: "What was it?" The Doctor enlightened him.

"But I can't understand it!" said the Blastoderm; "I'm quite sane; but I can't be sure of my mind, it seems—my OWN memory—can I?"

"Go up into the Hills for three months, and don't think about it," said the Doctor.

"But I can't understand it," repeated the Blastoderm. "It was my OWN mind and memory."

"I can't help it," said the Doctor; "there are a good many things you can't understand; and, by the time you have put in my length of service, you'll know exactly how much a man dare call his own in this world."

The stroke cowed the Blastoderm. He could not understand it. He went into the Hills in fear and trembling, wondering whether he would be permitted to reach the end of any sentence he began.

This gave him a wholesome feeling of mistrust. The legitimate explanation, that he had been overworking himself, failed to satisfy him. Something had wiped his lips of speech, as a mother wipes the milky lips of her child, and he was afraid—horribly afraid.

So the Club had rest when he returned; and if ever you come across Aurelian McGoggin laying down the law on things Human—he doesn't seem to know as much as he used to about things Divine—put your forefinger on your lip for a moment, and see what happens.

Don't blame me if he throws a glass at your head!

A GERM DESTROYER.

Pleasant it is for the Little Tin Gods,

 When great Jove nods;

But Little Tin Gods make their little mistakes

 In missing the hour when great Jove wakes.

As a general rule, it is inexpedient to meddle with questions of State in a land where men are highly paid to work them out for you.

This tale is a justifiable exception.

Once in every five years, as you know, we indent for a new Viceroy; and each Viceroy imports, with the rest of his baggage, a Private Secretary, who may or may not be the real Viceroy, just as Fate ordains. Fate looks after the Indian Empire because it is so big and so helpless.

There was a Viceroy once, who brought out with him a turbulent Private Secretary—a hard man with a soft manner and a morbid passion for work. This Secretary was called Wonder— John Fennil Wonder. The Viceroy possessed no name—nothing but a string of counties and two-thirds of the alphabet after them. He said, in confidence, that he was the electro-plated figurehead of a golden administration, and he watched in a dreamy, amused way Wonder's attempts to draw matters which were entirely outside his province into his own hands. "When we are all cherubims together," said His Excellency once, "my dear, good friend Wonder will head the conspiracy for plucking out Gabriel's tail-feathers or stealing Peter's keys. THEN I shall report him."

But, though the Viceroy did nothing to check Wonder's officiousness, other people said unpleasant things. Maybe the Members of Council began it; but, finally, all Simla agreed that there was "too much Wonder, and too little Viceroy," in that regime. Wonder was always quoting "His Excellency." It was "His Excellency this," "His Excellency that," "In the opinion of His Excellency," and so on. The Viceroy smiled; but he did not heed.

He said that, so long as his old men squabbled with his "dear, good Wonder," they might be induced to leave the "Immemorial East" in peace.

"No wise man has a policy," said the Viceroy. "A Policy is the blackmail levied on the Fool by the Unforeseen. I am not the former, and I do not believe in the latter."

I do not quite see what this means, unless it refers to an Insurance Policy. Perhaps it was the Viceroy's way of saying:—"Lie low."

That season, came up to Simla one of these crazy people with only a single idea. These are the men who make things move; but they are not nice to talk to. This man's name was Mellish, and he had lived for fifteen years on land of his own, in Lower Bengal, studying cholera. He held that cholera was a germ that propagated itself as it flew through a muggy atmosphere; and stuck in the branches of trees like a wool-flake. The germ could be rendered sterile, he said, by "Mellish's Own Invincible Fumigatory"—a heavy violet-black powder—"the result of fifteen years' scientific investigation, Sir!"

Inventors seem very much alike as a caste. They talk loudly, especially about "conspiracies

of monopolists;" they beat upon the table with their fists; and they secrete fragments of their inventions about their persons.

Mellish said that there was a Medical "Ring" at Simla, headed by the Surgeon-General, who was in league, apparently, with all the Hospital Assistants in the Empire. I forget exactly how he proved it, but it had something to do with "skulking up to the Hills;" and what Mellish wanted was the independent evidence of the Viceroy—"Steward of our Most Gracious Majesty the Queen, Sir." So Mellish went up to Simla, with eighty-four pounds of Fumigatory in his trunk, to speak to the Viceroy and to show him the merits of the invention.

But it is easier to see a Viceroy than to talk to him, unless you chance to be as important as Mellishe of Madras. He was a six-thousand-rupee man, so great that his daughters never "married." They "contracted alliances." He himself was not paid. He "received emoluments," and his journeys about the country were "tours of observation." His business was to stir up the people in Madras with a long pole—as you stir up stench in a pond—and the people had to come up out of their comfortable old ways and gasp:—"This is Enlightenment and progress. Isn't it fine!" Then they gave Mellishe statues and jasmine garlands, in the hope of getting rid of him.

Mellishe came up to Simla "to confer with the Viceroy." That was one of his perquisites. The Viceroy knew nothing of Mellishe except that he was "one of those middle-class deities who seem necessary to the spiritual comfort of this Paradise of the Middle-classes," and that, in all probability, he had "suggested, designed, founded, and endowed all the public institutions in Madras." Which proves that His Excellency, though dreamy, had experience of the ways of six-thousand-rupee men.

Mellishe's name was E. Mellishe and Mellish's was E. S. Mellish, and they were both staying at the same hotel, and the Fate that looks after the Indian Empire ordained that Wonder should blunder and drop the final "e;" that the Chaprassi should help him, and that the note which ran: "Dear Mr. Mellish.—Can you set aside your other engagements and lunch with us at two tomorrow? His Excellency has an hour at your disposal then," should be given to Mellish with the Fumigatory. He nearly wept with pride and delight, and at the appointed hour cantered off to Peterhoff, a big paper-bag full of the Fumigatory in his coat-tail pockets. He had his chance, and he meant to make the most of it. Mellishe of Madras had been so portentously solemn about his "conference," that Wonder had arranged for a private tiffin—no A.-D.-C.'s, no Wonder, no one but the Viceroy, who said plaintively that he feared being left alone with unmuzzled autocrats like the great Mellishe of Madras.

But his guest did not bore the Viceroy. On the contrary, he amused him. Mellish was nervously anxious to go straight to his Fumigatory, and talked at random until tiffin was over and His Excellency asked him to smoke. The Viceroy was pleased with Mellish because he did not talk "shop."

As soon as the cheroots were lit, Mellish spoke like a man; beginning with his cholera-theory, reviewing his fifteen years' "scientific labors," the machinations of the "Simla Ring," and the excellence of his Fumigatory, while the Viceroy watched him between half-shut eyes and thought: "Evidently, this is the wrong tiger; but it is an original animal." Mellish's hair was standing on end with excitement, and he stammered. He began groping in his coat-tails and, before the Viceroy knew what was about to happen, he had tipped a bagful of his powder into the big silver ash-tray.

"J-j-judge for yourself, Sir," said Mellish. "Y' Excellency shall judge for yourself! Absolutely infallible, on my honor."

He plunged the lighted end of his cigar into the powder, which began to smoke like a volcano,

and send up fat, greasy wreaths of copper-colored smoke. In five seconds the room was filled with a most pungent and sickening stench—a reek that took fierce hold of the trap of your windpipe and shut it. The powder then hissed and fizzed, and sent out blue and green sparks, and the smoke rose till you could neither see, nor breathe, nor gasp. Mellish, however, was used to it.

"Nitrate of strontia," he shouted; "baryta, bone-meal, etcetera! Thousand cubic feet smoke per cubic inch. Not a germ could live—not a germ, Y' Excellency!"

But His Excellency had fled, and was coughing at the foot of the stairs, while all Peterhoff hummed like a hive. Red Lancers came in, and the Head Chaprassi, who speaks English, came in, and mace-bearers came in, and ladies ran downstairs screaming "fire;" for the smoke was drifting through the house and oozing out of the windows, and bellying along the verandahs, and wreathing and writhing across the gardens. No one could enter the room where Mellish was lecturing on his Fumigatory, till that unspeakable powder had burned itself out.

Then an Aide-de-Camp, who desired the V. C., rushed through the rolling clouds and hauled Mellish into the hall. The Viceroy was prostrate with laughter, and could only waggle his hands feebly at Mellish, who was shaking a fresh bagful of powder at him.

"Glorious! Glorious!" sobbed his Excellency. "Not a germ, as you justly observe, could exist! I can swear it. A magnificent success!"

Then he laughed till the tears came, and Wonder, who had caught the real Mellishe snorting on the Mall, entered and was deeply shocked at the scene. But the Viceroy was delighted, because he saw that Wonder would presently depart. Mellish with the Fumigatory was also pleased, for he felt that he had smashed the Simla Medical "Ring.".........

Few men could tell a story like His Excellency when he took the trouble, and the account of "my dear, good Wonder's friend with the powder" went the round of Simla, and flippant folk made Wonder unhappy by their remarks.

But His Excellency told the tale once too often—for Wonder. As he meant to do. It was at a Seepee Picnic. Wonder was sitting just behind the Viceroy.

"And I really thought for a moment," wound up His Excellency, "that my dear, good Wonder had hired an assassin to clear his way to the throne!"

Every one laughed; but there was a delicate subtinkle in the Viceroy's tone which Wonder understood. He found that his health was giving way; and the Viceroy allowed him to go, and presented him with a flaming "character" for use at Home among big people.

"My fault entirely," said His Excellency, in after seasons, with a twinkling in his eye. "My inconsistency must always have been distasteful to such a masterly man."

KIDNAPPED.

There is a tide in the affairs of men,

Which, taken any way you please, is bad,

And strands them in forsaken guts and creeks

No decent soul would think of visiting.

You cannot stop the tide; but now and then,

You may arrest some rash adventurer

Who—h'm—will hardly thank you for your pains.

　　　—Vibart's Moralities.

We are a high-caste and enlightened race, and infant-marriage is very shocking and the consequences are sometimes peculiar; but, nevertheless, the Hindu notion—which is the Continental notion—which is the aboriginal notion—of arranging marriages irrespective of the personal inclinations of the married, is sound. Think for a minute, and you will see that it must be so; unless, of course, you believe in "affinities." In which case you had better not read this tale. How can a man who has never married; who cannot be trusted to pick up at sight a moderately sound horse; whose head is hot and upset with visions of domestic felicity, go about the choosing of a wife? He cannot see straight or think straight if he tries; and the same disadvantages exist in the case of a girl's fancies. But when mature, married and discreet people arrange a match between a boy and a girl, they do it sensibly, with a view to the future, and the young couple live happily ever afterwards. As everybody knows.

Properly speaking, Government should establish a Matrimonial Department, efficiently officered, with a Jury of Matrons, a Judge of the Chief Court, a Senior Chaplain, and an Awful Warning, in the shape of a love-match that has gone wrong, chained to the trees in the courtyard. All marriages should be made through the Department, which might be subordinate to the Educational Department, under the same penalty as that attaching to the transfer of land without a stamped document. But Government won't take suggestions. It pretends that it is too busy. However, I will put my notion on record, and explain the example that illustrates the theory.

Once upon a time there was a good young man—a first-class officer in his own Department—a man with a career before him and, possibly, a K. C. G. E. at the end of it. All his superiors spoke well of him, because he knew how to hold his tongue and his pen at the proper times. There are today only eleven men in India who possess this secret; and they have all, with one exception, attained great honor and enormous incomes.

This good young man was quiet and self-contained—too old for his years by far. Which always carries its own punishment. Had a Subaltern, or a Tea-Planter's Assistant, or anybody who enjoys life and has no care for tomorrow, done what he tried to do not a soul would have cared. But when Peythroppe—the estimable, virtuous, economical, quiet, hard-working, young Peythroppe—fell, there was a flutter through five Departments.

The manner of his fall was in this way. He met a Miss Castries—d'Castries it was originally,

but the family dropped the d' for administrative reasons—and he fell in love with her even more energetically than he worked. Understand clearly that there was not a breath of a word to be said against Miss Castries—not a shadow of a breath. She was good and very lovely—possessed what innocent people at home call a "Spanish" complexion, with thick blue-black hair growing low down on her forehead, into a "widow's peak," and big violet eyes under eyebrows as black and as straight as the borders of a Gazette Extraordinary when a big man dies. But—but—but—. Well, she was a VERY sweet girl and very pious, but for many reasons she was "impossible." Quite so. All good Mammas know what "impossible" means. It was obviously absurd that Peythroppe should marry her. The little opal-tinted onyx at the base of her finger-nails said this as plainly as print. Further, marriage with Miss Castries meant marriage with several other Castries—Honorary Lieutenant Castries, her Papa, Mrs. Eulalie Castries, her Mamma, and all the ramifications of the Castries family, on incomes ranging from Rs. 175 to Rs. 470 a month, and THEIR wives and connections again.

It would have been cheaper for Peythroppe to have assaulted a Commissioner with a dog-whip, or to have burned the records of a Deputy Commissioner's Office, than to have contracted an alliance with the Castries. It would have weighted his after-career less—even under a Government which never forgets and NEVER forgives.

Everybody saw this but Peythroppe. He was going to marry Miss Castries, he was—being of age and drawing a good income—and woe betide the house that would not afterwards receive Mrs. Virginie Saulez Peythroppe with the deference due to her husband's rank.

That was Peythroppe's ultimatum, and any remonstrance drove him frantic.

These sudden madnesses most afflict the sanest men. There was a case once—but I will tell you of that later on. You cannot account for the mania, except under a theory directly contradicting the one about the Place wherein marriages are made. Peythroppe was burningly anxious to put a millstone round his neck at the outset of his career and argument had not the least effect on him. He was going to marry Miss Castries, and the business was his own business.

He would thank you to keep your advice to yourself. With a man in this condition, mere words only fix him in his purpose. Of course he cannot see that marriage out here does not concern the individual but the Government he serves.

Do you remember Mrs. Hauksbee—the most wonderful woman in India? She saved Pluffles from Mrs. Reiver, won Tarrion his appointment in the Foreign Office, and was defeated in open field by Mrs. Cusack-Bremmil. She heard of the lamentable condition of Peythroppe, and her brain struck out the plan that saved him. She had the wisdom of the Serpent, the logical coherence of the Man, the fearlessness of the Child, and the triple intuition of the Woman. Never—no, never—as long as a tonga buckets down the Solon dip, or the couples go a-riding at the back of Summer Hill, will there be such a genius as Mrs. Hauksbee. She attended the consultation of Three Men on Peythroppe's case; and she stood up with the lash of her riding-whip between her lips and spake....... ...

Three weeks later, Peythroppe dined with the Three Men, and the Gazette of India came in. Peythroppe found to his surprise that he had been gazetted a month's leave. Don't ask me how this was managed. I believe firmly that if Mrs. Hauksbee gave the order, the whole Great Indian Administration would stand on its head.

The Three Men had also a month's leave each. Peythroppe put the Gazette down and said bad words. Then there came from the compound the soft "pad-pad" of camels—"thieves' camels," the bikaneer breed that don't bubble and howl when they sit down and get up.

After that I don't know what happened. This much is certain.

Peythroppe disappeared—vanished like smoke—and the long foot-rest chair in the house of the Three Men was broken to splinters. Also a bedstead departed from one of the bedrooms.

Mrs. Hauksbee said that Mr. Peythroppe was shooting in Rajputana with the Three Men; so we were compelled to believe her.

At the end of the month, Peythroppe was gazetted twenty days' extension of leave; but there was wrath and lamentation in the house of Castries. The marriage-day had been fixed, but the bridegroom never came; and the D'Silvas, Pereiras, and Ducketts lifted their voices and mocked Honorary Lieutenant Castries as one who had been basely imposed upon. Mrs. Hauksbee went to the wedding, and was much astonished when Peythroppe did not appear. After seven weeks, Peythroppe and the Three Men returned from Rajputana. Peythroppe was in hard, tough condition, rather white, and more self-contained than ever.

One of the Three Men had a cut on his nose, cause by the kick of a gun. Twelve-bores kick rather curiously.

Then came Honorary Lieutenant Castries, seeking for the blood of his perfidious son-in-law to be. He said things—vulgar and "impossible" things which showed the raw rough "ranker" below the "Honorary," and I fancy Peythroppe's eyes were opened. Anyhow, he held his peace till the end; when he spoke briefly. Honorary Lieutenant Castries asked for a "peg" before he went away to die or bring a suit for breach of promise.

Miss Castries was a very good girl. She said that she would have no breach of promise suits. She said that, if she was not a lady, she was refined enough to know that ladies kept their broken hearts to themselves; and, as she ruled her parents, nothing happened. Later on, she married a most respectable and gentlemanly person. He travelled for an enterprising firm in Calcutta, and was all that a good husband should be.

So Peythroppe came to his right mind again, and did much good work, and was honored by all who knew him. One of these days he will marry; but he will marry a sweet pink-and-white maiden, on the Government House List, with a little money and some influential connections, as every wise man should. And he will never, all his life, tell her what happened during the seven weeks of his shooting-tour in Rajputana.

But just think how much trouble and expense—for camel hire is not cheap, and those Bikaneer brutes had to be fed like humans—might have been saved by a properly conducted Matrimonial Department, under the control of the Director General of Education, but corresponding direct with the Viceroy.

THE ARREST OF LIEUTENANT GOLIGHTLY.

"'I've forgotten the countersign,' sez 'e.

'Oh! You 'ave, 'ave you?' sez I.

'But I'm the Colonel,' sez 'e.

'Oh! You are, are you?' sez I. 'Colonel nor no Colonel, you

waits 'ere till I'm relieved, an' the Sarjint reports on

your ugly old mug. Coop!' sez I.

.........

An' s'help me soul, 'twas the Colonel after all! But I was

a recruity then."

> The Unedited Autobiography of Private Ortheris.

IF there was one thing on which Golightly prided himself more than another, it was looking like "an Officer and a gentleman." He said it was for the honor of the Service that he attired himself so elaborately; but those who knew him best said that it was just personal vanity. There was no harm about Golightly—not an ounce.

He recognized a horse when he saw one, and could do more than fill a cantle. He played a very fair game at billiards, and was a sound man at the whist-table. Everyone liked him; and nobody ever dreamed of seeing him handcuffed on a station platform as a deserter. But this sad thing happened.

He was going down from Dalhousie, at the end of his leave—riding down. He had cut his leave as fine as he dared, and wanted to come down in a hurry.

It was fairly warm at Dalhousie, and knowing what to expect below, he descended in a new khaki suit—tight fitting—of a delicate olive-green; a peacock-blue tie, white collar, and a snowy white solah helmet. He prided himself on looking neat even when he was riding post. He did look neat, and he was so deeply concerned about his appearance before he started that he quite forgot to take anything but some small change with him. He left all his notes at the hotel. His servants had gone down the road before him, to be ready in waiting at Pathankote with a change of gear. That was what he called travelling in "light marching-order." He was proud of his faculty of organization—what we call bundobust.

Twenty-two miles out of Dalhousie it began to rain—not a mere hill-shower, but a good, tepid monsoonish downpour. Golightly bustled on, wishing that he had brought an umbrella. The dust on the roads turned into mud, and the pony mired a good deal. So did Golightly's khaki gaiters. But he kept on steadily and tried to think how pleasant the coolth was.

His next pony was rather a brute at starting, and Golightly's hands being slippery with the rain, contrived to get rid of Golightly at a corner. He chased the animal, caught it, and went ahead briskly.

The spill had not improved his clothes or his temper, and he had lost one spur. He kept the

other one employed. By the time that stage was ended, the pony had had as much exercise as he wanted, and, in spite of the rain, Golightly was sweating freely. At the end of another miserable half-hour, Golightly found the world disappear before his eyes in clammy pulp. The rain had turned the pith of his huge and snowy solah-topee into an evil-smelling dough, and it had closed on his head like a half-opened mushroom. Also the green lining was beginning to run.

Golightly did not say anything worth recording here. He tore off and squeezed up as much of the brim as was in his eyes and ploughed on. The back of the helmet was flapping on his neck and the sides stuck to his ears, but the leather band and green lining kept things roughly together, so that the hat did not actually melt away where it flapped.

Presently, the pulp and the green stuff made a sort of slimy mildew which ran over Golightly in several directions—down his back and bosom for choice. The khaki color ran too—it was really shockingly bad dye—and sections of Golightly were brown, and patches were violet, and contours were ochre, and streaks were ruddy red, and blotches were nearly white, according to the nature and peculiarities of the dye. When he took out his handkerchief to wipe his face and the green of the hat-lining and the purple stuff that had soaked through on to his neck from the tie became thoroughly mixed, the effect was amazing.

Near Dhar the rain stopped and the evening sun came out and dried him up slightly. It fixed the colors, too. Three miles from Pathankote the last pony fell dead lame, and Golightly was forced to walk. He pushed on into Pathankote to find his servants. He did not know then that his khitmatgar had stopped by the roadside to get drunk, and would come on the next day saying that he had sprained his ankle. When he got into Pathankote, he couldn't find his servants, his boots were stiff and ropy with mud, and there were large quantities of dirt about his body. The blue tie had run as much as the khaki. So he took it off with the collar and threw it away. Then he said something about servants generally and tried to get a peg. He paid eight annas for the drink, and this revealed to him that he had only six annas more in his pocket—or in the world as he stood at that hour.

He went to the Station-Master to negotiate for a first-class ticket to Khasa, where he was stationed. The booking-clerk said something to the Station-Master, the Station-Master said something to the Telegraph Clerk, and the three looked at him with curiosity. They asked him to wait for half-an-hour, while they telegraphed to Umritsar for authority. So he waited, and four constables came and grouped themselves picturesquely round him. Just as he was preparing to ask them to go away, the Station-Master said that he would give the Sahib a ticket to Umritsar, if the Sahib would kindly come inside the booking-office. Golightly stepped inside, and the next thing he knew was that a constable was attached to each of his legs and arms, while the Station-Master was trying to cram a mailbag over his head.

There was a very fair scuffle all round the booking-office, and Golightly received a nasty cut over his eye through falling against a table. But the constables were too much for him, and they and the Station-Master handcuffed him securely. As soon as the mail-bag was slipped, he began expressing his opinions, and the head-constable said:—"Without doubt this is the soldier-Englishman we required. Listen to the abuse!" Then Golightly asked the Station-Master what the this and the that the proceedings meant. The Station-Master told him he was "Private John Binkle of the——Regiment, 5 ft. 9 in., fair hair, gray eyes, and a dissipated appearance, no marks on the body," who had deserted a fortnight ago. Golightly began explaining at great length; and the more he explained the less the Station-Master believed him. He said that no Lieutenant could look such a ruffian as did Golightly, and that his instructions were to send his capture under proper escort to Umritsar. Golightly was feeling very damp and uncomfortable, and the language he used was not fit for publication, even in an expurgated form. The four constables saw him safe to Umritsar in an "intermediate" compartment, and he spent the four-

hour journey in abusing them as fluently as his knowledge of the vernaculars allowed.

At Umritsar he was bundled out on the platform into the arms of a Corporal and two men of the——Regiment. Golightly drew himself up and tried to carry off matters jauntily. He did not feel too jaunty in handcuffs, with four constables behind him, and the blood from the cut on his forehead stiffening on his left cheek. The Corporal was not jocular either. Golightly got as far as—"This is a very absurd mistake, my men," when the Corporal told him to "stow his lip" and come along. Golightly did not want to come along. He desired to stop and explain. He explained very well indeed, until the Corporal cut in with:—"YOU a orficer! It's the like o' YOU as brings disgrace on the likes of US. Bloom-in' fine orficer you are! I know your regiment. The Rogue's March is the quickstep where you come from. You're a black shame to the Service."

Golightly kept his temper, and began explaining all over again from the beginning. Then he was marched out of the rain into the refreshment-room and told not to make a qualified fool of himself.

The men were going to run him up to Fort Govindghar. And "running up" is a performance almost as undignified as the Frog March.

Golightly was nearly hysterical with rage and the chill and the mistake and the handcuffs and the headache that the cut on his forehead had given him. He really laid himself out to express what was in his mind. When he had quite finished and his throat was feeling dry, one of the men said:—"I've 'eard a few beggars in the click blind, stiff and crack on a bit; but I've never 'eard any one to touch this 'ere 'orficer.'" They were not angry with him. They rather admired him. They had some beer at the refreshment-room, and offered Golightly some too, because he had "swore won'erful." They asked him to tell them all about the adventures of Private John Binkle while he was loose on the countryside; and that made Golightly wilder than ever. If he had kept his wits about him he would have kept quiet until an officer came; but he attempted to run.

Now the butt of a Martini in the small of your back hurts a great deal, and rotten, rain-soaked khaki tears easily when two men are jerking at your collar.

Golightly rose from the floor feeling very sick and giddy, with his shirt ripped open all down his breast and nearly all down his back.

He yielded to his luck, and at that point the down-train from Lahore came in carrying one of Golightly's Majors.

This is the Major's evidence in full:—

"There was the sound of a scuffle in the second-class refreshment-room, so I went in and saw the most villainous loafer that I ever set eyes on. His boots and breeches were plastered with mud and beer-stains. He wore a muddy-white dunghill sort of thing on his head, and it hung down in slips on his shoulders, which were a good deal scratched. He was half in and half out of a shirt as nearly in two pieces as it could be, and he was begging the guard to look at the name on the tail of it. As he had rucked the shirt all over his head, I couldn't at first see who he was, but I fancied that he was a man in the first stage of D. T. from the way he swore while he wrestled with his rags. When he turned round, and I had made allowance for a lump as big as a pork-pie over one eye, and some green war-paint on the face, and some violet stripes round the neck, I saw that it was Golightly. He was very glad to see me," said the Major, "and he hoped I would not tell the Mess about it. I didn't, but you can if you like, now that Golightly has gone Home."

Golightly spent the greater part of that summer in trying to get the Corporal and the two soldiers tried by Court-Martial for arresting an "officer and a gentleman." They were, of course, very sorry for their error. But the tale leaked into the regimental canteen, and thence ran about the Province.

THE HOUSE OF SUDDHOO

A stone's throw out on either hand

From that well-ordered road we tread,

 And all the world is wild and strange;

Churel and ghoul and Djinn and sprite

Shall bear us company tonight,

For we have reached the Oldest Land

 Wherein the Powers of Darkness range.

 —From the Dusk to the Dawn.

The house of Suddhoo, near the Taksali Gate, is two-storied, with four carved windows of old brown wood, and a flat roof. You may recognize it by five red hand-prints arranged like the Five of Diamonds on the whitewash between the upper windows. Bhagwan Dass, the bunnia, and a man who says he gets his living by seal-cutting, live in the lower story with a troop of wives, servants, friends, and retainers. The two upper rooms used to be occupied by Janoo and Azizun and a little black-and-tan terrier that was stolen from an Englishman's house and given to Janoo by a soldier. Today, only Janoo lives in the upper rooms. Suddhoo sleeps on the roof generally, except when he sleeps in the street. He used to go to Peshawar in the cold weather to visit his son, who sells curiosities near the Edwardes' Gate, and then he slept under a real mud roof.

Suddhoo is a great friend of mine, because his cousin had a son who secured, thanks to my recommendation, the post of head-messenger to a big firm in the Station. Suddhoo says that God will make me a Lieutenant-Governor one of these days. I daresay his prophecy will come true. He is very, very old, with white hair and no teeth worth showing, and he has outlived his wits—outlived nearly everything except his fondness for his son at Peshawar. Janoo and Azizun are Kashmiris, Ladies of the City, and theirs was an ancient and more or less honorable profession; but Azizun has since married a medical student from the North-West and has settled down to a most respectable life somewhere near Bareilly. Bhagwan Dass is an extortionate and an adulterator. He is very rich. The man who is supposed to get his living by seal-cutting pretends to be very poor.

This lets you know as much as is necessary of the four principal tenants in the house of Suddhoo. Then there is Me, of course; but I am only the chorus that comes in at the end to explain things. So I do not count.

Suddhoo was not clever. The man who pretended to cut seals was the cleverest of them all—Bhagwan Dass only knew how to lie—except Janoo. She was also beautiful, but that was her own affair.

Suddhoo's son at Peshawar was attacked by pleurisy, and old Suddhoo was troubled. The seal-cutter man heard of Suddhoo's anxiety and made capital out of it. He was abreast of the times. He got a friend in Peshawar to telegraph daily accounts of the son's health.

And here the story begins.

Suddhoo's cousin's son told me, one evening, that Suddhoo wanted to see me; that he was too old and feeble to come personally, and that I should be conferring an everlasting honor on the House of Suddhoo if I went to him. I went; but I think, seeing how well-off Suddhoo was then, that he might have sent something better than an ekka, which jolted fearfully, to haul out a future Lieutenant-Governor to the City on a muggy April evening. The ekka did not run quickly.

It was full dark when we pulled up opposite the door of Ranjit Singh's Tomb near the main gate of the Fort. Here was Suddhoo and he said that, by reason of my condescension, it was absolutely certain that I should become a Lieutenant-Governor while my hair was yet black. Then we talked about the weather and the state of my health, and the wheat crops, for fifteen minutes, in the Huzuri Bagh, under the stars.

Suddhoo came to the point at last. He said that Janoo had told him that there was an order of the Sirkar against magic, because it was feared that magic might one day kill the Empress of India. I didn't know anything about the state of the law; but I fancied that something interesting was going to happen. I said that so far from magic being discouraged by the Government it was highly commended.

The greatest officials of the State practiced it themselves. (If the Financial Statement isn't magic, I don't know what is.) Then, to encourage him further, I said that, if there was any jadoo afoot, I had not the least objection to giving it my countenance and sanction, and to seeing that it was clean jadoo—white magic, as distinguished from the unclean jadoo which kills folk. It took a long time before Suddhoo admitted that this was just what he had asked me to come for. Then he told me, in jerks and quavers, that the man who said he cut seals was a sorcerer of the cleanest kind; that every day he gave Suddhoo news of the sick son in Peshawar more quickly than the lightning could fly, and that this news was always corroborated by the letters. Further, that he had told Suddhoo how a great danger was threatening his son, which could be removed by clean jadoo; and, of course, heavy payment. I began to see how the land lay, and told Suddhoo that I also understood a little jadoo in the Western line, and would go to his house to see that everything was done decently and in order. We set off together; and on the way Suddhoo told me he had paid the seal-cutter between one hundred and two hundred rupees already; and the jadoo of that night would cost two hundred more. Which was cheap, he said, considering the greatness of his son's danger; but I do not think he meant it.

The lights were all cloaked in the front of the house when we arrived. I could hear awful noises from behind the seal-cutter's shop-front, as if some one were groaning his soul out. Suddhoo shook all over, and while we groped our way upstairs told me that the jadoo had begun. Janoo and Azizun met us at the stair-head, and told us that the jadoo-work was coming off in their rooms, because there was more space there. Janoo is a lady of a freethinking turn of mind. She whispered that the jadoo was an invention to get money out of Suddhoo, and that the seal-cutter would go to a hot place when he died. Suddhoo was nearly crying with fear and old age. He kept walking up and down the room in the half light, repeating his son's name over and over again, and asking Azizun if the seal-cutter ought not to make a reduction in the case of his own landlord.

Janoo pulled me over to the shadow in the recess of the carved bow-windows. The boards were up, and the rooms were only lit by one tiny lamp. There was no chance of my being seen if I stayed still.

Presently, the groans below ceased, and we heard steps on the staircase. That was the seal-cutter. He stopped outside the door as the terrier barked and Azizun fumbled at the chain, and he told Suddhoo to blow out the lamp. This left the place in jet darkness, except for the red glow from the two huqas that belonged to Janoo and Azizun. The seal-cutter came in, and I heard Suddhoo

throw himself down on the floor and groan. Azizun caught her breath, and Janoo backed to one of the beds with a shudder. There was a clink of something metallic, and then shot up a pale blue-green flame near the ground. The light was just enough to show Azizun, pressed against one corner of the room with the terrier between her knees; Janoo, with her hands clasped, leaning forward as she sat on the bed; Suddhoo, face down, quivering, and the seal-cutter.

I hope I may never see another man like that seal-cutter. He was stripped to the waist, with a wreath of white jasmine as thick as my wrist round his forehead, a salmon-colored loin-cloth round his middle, and a steel bangle on each ankle. This was not awe-inspiring. It was the face of the man that turned me cold. It was blue-gray in the first place. In the second, the eyes were rolled back till you could only see the whites of them; and, in the third, the face was the face of a demon—a ghoul—anything you please except of the sleek, oily old ruffian who sat in the day-time over his turning-lathe downstairs. He was lying on his stomach, with his arms turned and crossed behind him, as if he had been thrown down pinioned. His head and neck were the only parts of him off the floor. They were nearly at right angles to the body, like the head of a cobra at spring. It was ghastly. In the centre of the room, on the bare earth floor, stood a big, deep, brass basin, with a pale blue-green light floating in the centre like a night-light. Round that basin the man on the floor wriggled himself three times. How he did it I do not know. I could see the muscles ripple along his spine and fall smooth again; but I could not see any other motion.

The head seemed the only thing alive about him, except that slow curl and uncurl of the laboring back-muscles. Janoo from the bed was breathing seventy to the minute; Azizun held her hands before her eyes; and old Suddhoo, fingering at the dirt that had got into his white beard, was crying to himself. The horror of it was that the creeping, crawly thing made no sound—only crawled! And, remember, this lasted for ten minutes, while the terrier whined, and Azizun shuddered, and Janoo gasped, and Suddhoo cried.

I felt the hair lift at the back of my head, and my heart thump like a thermantidote paddle. Luckily, the seal-cutter betrayed himself by his most impressive trick and made me calm again. After he had finished that unspeakable triple crawl, he stretched his head away from the floor as high as he could, and sent out a jet of fire from his nostrils. Now, I knew how fire-spouting is done—I can do it myself—so I felt at ease. The business was a fraud. If he had only kept to that crawl without trying to raise the effect, goodness knows what I might not have thought. Both the girls shrieked at the jet of fire and the head dropped, chin down, on the floor with a thud; the whole body lying then like a corpse with its arms trussed.

There was a pause of five full minutes after this, and the blue-green flame died down. Janoo stooped to settle one of her anklets, while Azizun turned her face to the wall and took the terrier in her arms. Suddhoo put out an arm mechanically to Janoo's huqa, and she slid it across the floor with her foot. Directly above the body and on the wall, were a couple of flaming portraits, in stamped paper frames, of the Queen and the Prince of Wales. They looked down on the performance, and, to my thinking, seemed to heighten the grotesqueness of it all.

Just when the silence was getting unendurable, the body turned over and rolled away from the basin to the side of the room, where it lay stomach up. There was a faint "plop" from the basin—exactly like the noise a fish makes when it takes a fly—and the green light in the centre revived.

I looked at the basin, and saw, bobbing in the water, the dried, shrivelled, black head of a native baby—open eyes, open mouth and shaved scalp. It was worse, being so very sudden, than the crawling exhibition. We had no time to say anything before it began to speak.

Read Poe's account of the voice that came from the mesmerized dying man, and you will realize less than one-half of the horror of that head's voice.

There was an interval of a second or two between each word, and a sort of "ring, ring, ring," in the note of the voice, like the timbre of a bell. It pealed slowly, as if talking to itself, for several minutes before I got rid of my cold sweat. Then the blessed solution struck me. I looked at the body lying near the doorway, and saw, just where the hollow of the throat joins on the shoulders, a muscle that had nothing to do with any man's regular breathing, twitching away steadily. The whole thing was a careful reproduction of the Egyptian teraphin that one read about sometimes and the voice was as clever and as appalling a piece of ventriloquism as one could wish to hear. All this time the head was "lip-lip-lapping" against the side of the basin, and speaking. It told Suddhoo, on his face again whining, of his son's illness and of the state of the illness up to the evening of that very night. I always shall respect the seal-cutter for keeping so faithfully to the time of the Peshawar telegrams. It went on to say that skilled doctors were night and day watching over the man's life; and that he would eventually recover if the fee to the potent sorcerer, whose servant was the head in the basin, were doubled.

Here the mistake from the artistic point of view came in. To ask for twice your stipulated fee in a voice that Lazarus might have used when he rose from the dead, is absurd. Janoo, who is really a woman of masculine intellect, saw this as quickly as I did. I heard her say "Asli nahin! Fareib!" scornfully under her breath; and just as she said so, the light in the basin died out, the head stopped talking, and we heard the room door creak on its hinges. Then Janoo struck a match, lit the lamp, and we saw that head, basin, and seal-cutter were gone. Suddhoo was wringing his hands and explaining to any one who cared to listen, that, if his chances of eternal salvation depended on it, he could not raise another two hundred rupees. Azizun was nearly in hysterics in the corner; while Janoo sat down composedly on one of the beds to discuss the probabilities of the whole thing being a bunao, or "make-up."

I explained as much as I knew of the seal-cutter's way of jadoo; but her argument was much more simple:—"The magic that is always demanding gifts is no true magic," said she. "My mother told me that the only potent love-spells are those which are told you for love. This seal-cutter man is a liar and a devil. I dare not tell, do anything, or get anything done, because I am in debt to Bhagwan Dass the bunnia for two gold rings and a heavy anklet. I must get my food from his shop. The seal-cutter is the friend of Bhagwan Dass, and he would poison my food. A fool's jadoo has been going on for ten days, and has cost Suddhoo many rupees each night. The seal-cutter used black hens and lemons and mantras before. He never showed us anything like this till tonight. Azizun is a fool, and will be a purdah nashin soon. Suddhoo has lost his strength and his wits. See now! I had hoped to get from Suddhoo many rupees while he lived, and many more after his death; and behold, he is spending everything on that offspring of a devil and a she-ass, the seal-cutter!"

Here I said:—"But what induced Suddhoo to drag me into the business? Of course I can speak to the seal-cutter, and he shall refund. The whole thing is child's talk—shame—and senseless."

"Suddhoo IS an old child," said Janoo. "He has lived on the roofs these seventy years and is as senseless as a milch-goat. He brought you here to assure himself that he was not breaking any law of the Sirkar, whose salt he ate many years ago. He worships the dust off the feet of the seal-cutter, and that cow-devourer has forbidden him to go and see his son. What does Suddhoo know of your laws or the lightning-post? I have to watch his money going day by day to that lying beast below."

Janoo stamped her foot on the floor and nearly cried with vexation; while Suddhoo was whimpering under a blanket in the corner, and Azizun was trying to guide the pipe-stem to his foolish old mouth....... ...

Now the case stands thus. Unthinkingly, I have laid myself open to the charge of aiding and

abetting the seal-cutter in obtaining money under false pretences, which is forbidden by Section 420 of the Indian Penal Code. I am helpless in the matter for these reasons, I cannot inform the Police. What witnesses would support my statements? Janoo refuses flatly, Azizun is a veiled woman somewhere near Bareilly—lost in this big India of ours. I cannot again take the law into my own hands, and speak to the seal-cutter; for certain am I that, not only would Suddhoo disbelieve me, but this step would end in the poisoning of Janoo, who is bound hand and foot by her debt to the bunnia. Suddhoo is an old dotard; and whenever we meet mumbles my idiotic joke that the Sirkar rather patronizes the Black Art than otherwise. His son is well now; but Suddhoo is completely under the influence of the seal-cutter, by whose advice he regulates the affairs of his life. Janoo watches daily the money that she hoped to wheedle out of Suddhoo taken by the seal-cutter, and becomes daily more furious and sullen.

She will never tell, because she dare not; but, unless something happens to prevent her, I am afraid that the seal-cutter will die of cholera—the white arsenic kind—about the middle of May. And thus I shall have to be privy to a murder in the House of Suddhoo.

HIS WEDDED WIFE.

Cry "Murder!" in the market-place, and each

Will turn upon his neighbor anxious eyes

That ask:—"Art thou the man?"

 We hunted Cain,

Some centuries ago, across the world,

That bred the fear our own misdeeds maintain

Today.

 —Vibart's Moralities.

Shakespeare says something about worms, or it may be giants or beetles, turning if you tread on them too severely. The safest plan is never to tread on a worm—not even on the last new subaltern from Home, with his buttons hardly out of their tissue paper, and the red of sappy English beef in his cheeks. This is the story of the worm that turned. For the sake of brevity, we will call Henry Augustus Ramsay Faizanne, "The Worm," although he really was an exceedingly pretty boy, without a hair on his face, and with a waist like a girl's when he came out to the Second "Shikarris" and was made unhappy in several ways. The "Shikarris" are a high-caste regiment, and you must be able to do things well—play a banjo or ride more than a little, or sing, or act—to get on with them.

The Worm did nothing except fall off his pony, and knock chips out of gate-posts with his trap. Even that became monotonous after a time. He objected to whist, cut the cloth at billiards, sang out of tune, kept very much to himself, and wrote to his Mamma and sisters at Home. Four of these five things were vices which the "Shikarris" objected to and set themselves to eradicate. Every one knows how subalterns are, by brother subalterns, softened and not permitted to be ferocious. It is good and wholesome, and does no one any harm, unless tempers are lost; and then there is trouble. There was a man once—but that is another story.

The "Shikarris" shikarred The Worm very much, and he bore everything without winking. He was so good and so anxious to learn, and flushed so pink, that his education was cut short, and he was left to his own devices by every one except the Senior Subaltern, who continued to make life a burden to The Worm. The Senior Subaltern meant no harm; but his chaff was coarse, and he didn't quite understand where to stop. He had been waiting too long for his company; and that always sours a man. Also he was in love, which made him worse.

One day, after he had borrowed The Worm's trap for a lady who never existed, had used it himself all the afternoon, had sent a note to The Worm purporting to come from the lady, and was telling the Mess all about it, The Worm rose in his place and said, in his quiet, ladylike voice: "That was a very pretty sell; but I'll lay you a month's pay to a month's pay when you get your step, that I work a sell on you that you'll remember for the rest of your days, and the Regiment after you when you're dead or broke." The Worm wasn't angry in the least, and the rest of the Mess shouted. Then the Senior Subaltern looked at The Worm from the boots upwards, and down again, and said, "Done, Baby." The Worm took the rest of the Mess to witness that the bet had been taken, and retired into a book with a sweet smile.

Two months passed, and the Senior Subaltern still educated The Worm, who began to move about a little more as the hot weather came on. I have said that the Senior Subaltern was in love. The curious thing is that a girl was in love with the Senior Subaltern. Though the Colonel said awful things, and the Majors snorted, and married Captains looked unutterable wisdom, and the juniors scoffed, those two were engaged.

The Senior Subaltern was so pleased with getting his Company and his acceptance at the same time that he forgot to bother The Worm. The girl was a pretty girl, and had money of her own. She does not come into this story at all.

One night, at the beginning of the hot weather, all the Mess, except The Worm, who had gone to his own room to write Home letters, were sitting on the platform outside the Mess House. The Band had finished playing, but no one wanted to go in. And the Captains' wives were there also. The folly of a man in love is unlimited.

The Senior Subaltern had been holding forth on the merits of the girl he was engaged to, and the ladies were purring approval, while the men yawned, when there was a rustle of skirts in the dark, and a tired, faint voice lifted itself:

"Where's my husband?"

I do not wish in the least to reflect on the morality of the "Shikarris;" but it is on record that four men jumped up as if they had been shot. Three of them were married men. Perhaps they were afraid that their wives had come from Home unbeknownst. The fourth said that he had acted on the impulse of the moment. He explained this afterwards.

Then the voice cried:—"Oh, Lionel!" Lionel was the Senior Subaltern's name. A woman came into the little circle of light by the candles on the peg-tables, stretching out her hands to the dark where the Senior Subaltern was, and sobbing. We rose to our feet, feeling that things were going to happen and ready to believe the worst. In this bad, small world of ours, one knows so little of the life of the next man—which, after all, is entirely his own concern—that one is not surprised when a crash comes. Anything might turn up any day for any one. Perhaps the Senior Subaltern had been trapped in his youth. Men are crippled that way occasionally. We didn't know; we wanted to hear; and the Captains' wives were as anxious as we. If he HAD been trapped, he was to be excused; for the woman from nowhere, in the dusty shoes, and gray travelling dress, was very lovely, with black hair and great eyes full of tears. She was tall, with a fine figure, and her voice had a running sob in it pitiful to hear. As soon as the Senior Subaltern stood up, she threw her arms round his neck, and called him "my darling," and said she could not bear waiting alone in England, and his letters were so short and cold, and she was his to the end of the world, and would he forgive her. This did not sound quite like a lady's way of speaking. It was too demonstrative.

Things seemed black indeed, and the Captains' wives peered under their eyebrows at the Senior Subaltern, and the Colonel's face set like the Day of Judgment framed in gray bristles, and no one spoke for a while.

Next the Colonel said, very shortly:—"Well, Sir?" and the woman sobbed afresh. The Senior Subaltern was half choked with the arms round his neck, but he gasped out:—"It's a d——d lie! I never had a wife in my life!" "Don't swear," said the Colonel. "Come into the Mess. We must sift this clear somehow," and he sighed to himself, for he believed in his "Shikarris," did the Colonel.

We trooped into the ante-room, under the full lights, and there we saw how beautiful the woman was. She stood up in the middle of us all, sometimes choking with crying, then hard and proud,

and then holding out her arms to the Senior Subaltern. It was like the fourth act of a tragedy. She told us how the Senior Subaltern had married her when he was Home on leave eighteen months before; and she seemed to know all that we knew, and more too, of his people and his past life. He was white and ashy gray, trying now and again to break into the torrent of her words; and we, noting how lovely she was and what a criminal he looked, esteemed him a beast of the worst kind. We felt sorry for him, though.

I shall never forget the indictment of the Senior Subaltern by his wife. Nor will he. It was so sudden, rushing out of the dark, unannounced, into our dull lives. The Captains' wives stood back; but their eyes were alight, and you could see that they had already convicted and sentenced the Senior Subaltern. The Colonel seemed five years older. One Major was shading his eyes with his hand and watching the woman from underneath it. Another was chewing his moustache and smiling quietly as if he were witnessing a play. Full in the open space in the centre, by the whist-tables, the Senior Subaltern's terrier was hunting for fleas. I remember all this as clearly as though a photograph were in my hand. I remember the look of horror on the Senior Subaltern's face. It was rather like seeing a man hanged; but much more interesting. Finally, the woman wound up by saying that the Senior Subaltern carried a double F. M. in tattoo on his left shoulder. We all knew that, and to our innocent minds it seemed to clinch the matter. But one of the Bachelor Majors said very politely:—"I presume that your marriage certificate would be more to the purpose?"

That roused the woman. She stood up and sneered at the Senior Subaltern for a cur, and abused the Major and the Colonel and all the rest. Then she wept, and then she pulled a paper from her breast, saying imperially:—"Take that! And let my husband—my lawfully wedded husband— read it aloud—if he dare!"

There was a hush, and the men looked into each other's eyes as the Senior Subaltern came forward in a dazed and dizzy way, and took the paper. We were wondering as we stared, whether there was anything against any one of us that might turn up later on. The Senior Subaltern's throat was dry; but, as he ran his eye over the paper, he broke out into a hoarse cackle of relief, and said to the woman:—"You young blackguard!"

But the woman had fled through a door, and on the paper was written:—"This is to certify that I, The Worm, have paid in full my debts to the Senior Subaltern, and, further, that the Senior Subaltern is my debtor, by agreement on the 23d of February, as by the Mess attested, to the extent of one month's Captain's pay, in the lawful currency of the India Empire."

Then a deputation set off for The Worm's quarters and found him, betwixt and between, unlacing his stays, with the hat, wig, serge dress, etc., on the bed. He came over as he was, and the "Shikarris" shouted till the Gunners' Mess sent over to know if they might have a share of the fun. I think we were all, except the Colonel and the Senior Subaltern, a little disappointed that the scandal had come to nothing. But that is human nature. There could be no two words about The Worm's acting. It leaned as near to a nasty tragedy as anything this side of a joke can. When most of the Subalterns sat upon him with sofa-cushions to find out why he had not said that acting was his strong point, he answered very quietly:—"I don't think you ever asked me. I used to act at Home with my sisters." But no acting with girls could account for The Worm's display that night. Personally, I think it was in bad taste.

Besides being dangerous. There is no sort of use in playing with fire, even for fun.

The "Shikarris" made him President of the Regimental Dramatic Club; and, when the Senior Subaltern paid up his debt, which he did at once, The Worm sank the money in scenery and dresses. He was a good Worm; and the "Shikarris" are proud of him. The only drawback is that he has been christened "Mrs. Senior Subaltern;" and as there are now two Mrs. Senior Subalterns in the Station, this is sometimes confusing to strangers.

Later on, I will tell you of a case something like, this, but with all the jest left out and nothing in it but real trouble.

THE BROKEN LINK HANDICAPPED.

While the snaffle holds, or the "long-neck" stings,

While the big beam tilts, or the last bell rings,

While horses are horses to train and to race,

Then women and wine take a second place

For me—for me—

While a short "ten-three"

Has a field to squander or fence to face!

————Song of the G. R.

There are more ways of running a horse to suit your book than pulling his head off in the straight. Some men forget this.

Understand clearly that all racing is rotten—as everything connected with losing money must be. Out here, in addition to its inherent rottenness, it has the merit of being two-thirds sham; looking pretty on paper only. Every one knows every one else far too well for business purposes. How on earth can you rack and harry and post a man for his losings, when you are fond of his wife, and live in the same Station with him? He says, "on the Monday following," "I can't settle just yet." "You say, 'All right, old man,'" and think your self lucky if you pull off nine hundred out of a two-thousand rupee debt. Any way you look at it, Indian racing is immoral, and expensively immoral. Which is much worse. If a man wants your money, he ought to ask for it, or send round a subscription-list, instead of juggling about the country, with an Australian larrikin; a "brumby," with as much breed as the boy; a brace of chumars in gold-laced caps; three or four ekka-ponies with hogged manes, and a switch-tailed demirep of a mare called Arab because she has a kink in her flag. Racing leads to the shroff quicker than anything else. But if you have no conscience and no sentiments, and good hands, and some knowledge of pace, and ten years' experience of horses, and several thousand rupees a month, I believe that you can occasionally contrive to pay your shoeing-bills.

Did you ever know Shackles—b. w. g., 15.13.8—coarse, loose, mule-like ears—barrel as long as a gate-post—tough as a telegraph-wire—and the queerest brute that ever looked through a bridle? He was of no brand, being one of an ear-nicked mob taken into the Bucephalus at 4l.-10s. a head to make up freight, and sold raw and out of condition at Calcutta for Rs. 275. People who lost money on him called him a "brumby;" but if ever any horse had Harpoon's shoulders and The Gin's temper, Shackles was that horse. Two miles was his own particular distance. He trained himself, ran himself, and rode himself; and, if his jockey insulted him by giving him hints, he shut up at once and bucked the boy off. He objected to dictation. Two or three of his owners did not understand this, and lost money in consequence. At last he was bought by a man who discovered that, if a race was to be won, Shackles, and Shackles only, would win it in his own way, so long as his jockey sat still.

This man had a riding-boy called Brunt—a lad from Perth, West Australia—and he taught Brunt, with a trainer's whip, the hardest thing a jock can learn—to sit still, to sit still, and to keep on sitting still. When Brunt fairly grasped this truth, Shackles devastated the country. No weight could stop him at his own distance; and The fame of Shackles spread from Ajmir in the

South, to Chedputter in the North. There was no horse like Shackles, so long as he was allowed to do his work in his own way. But he was beaten in the end; and the story of his fall is enough to make angels weep.

At the lower end of the Chedputter racecourse, just before the turn into the straight, the track passes close to a couple of old brick-mounds enclosing a funnel-shaped hollow. The big end of the funnel is not six feet from the railings on the off-side. The astounding peculiarity of the course is that, if you stand at one particular place, about half a mile away, inside the course, and speak at an ordinary pitch, your voice just hits the funnel of the brick-mounds and makes a curious whining echo there. A man discovered this one morning by accident while out training with a friend. He marked the place to stand and speak from with a couple of bricks, and he kept his knowledge to himself. EVERY peculiarity of a course is worth remembering in a country where rats play the mischief with the elephant-litter, and Stewards build jumps to suit their own stables.

This man ran a very fairish country-bred, a long, racking high mare with the temper of a fiend, and the paces of an airy wandering seraph—a drifty, glidy stretch. The mare was, as a delicate tribute to Mrs. Reiver, called "The Lady Regula Baddun"—or for short, Regula Baddun.

Shackles' jockey, Brunt, was a quiet, well-behaved boy, but his nerves had been shaken. He began his career by riding jump-races in Melbourne, where a few Stewards want lynching, and was one of the jockeys who came through the awful butchery—perhaps you will recollect it—of the Maribyrnong Plate. The walls were colonial ramparts—logs of jarrak spiked into masonry—with wings as strong as Church buttresses. Once in his stride, a horse had to jump or fall. He couldn't run out. In the Maribyrnong Plate, twelve horses were jammed at the second wall. Red Hat, leading, fell this side, and threw out The Glen, and the ruck came up behind and the space between wing and wing was one struggling, screaming, kicking shambles. Four jockeys were taken out dead; three were very badly hurt, and Brunt was among the three. He told the story of the Maribyrnong Plate sometimes; and when he described how Whalley on Red Hat, said, as the mare fell under him:—"God ha' mercy, I'm done for!" and how, next instant, Sithee There and White Otter had crushed the life out of poor Whalley, and the dust hid a small hell of men and horses, no one marvelled that Brunt had dropped jump-races and Australia together. Regula Baddun's owner knew that story by heart. Brunt never varied it in the telling. He had no education.

Shackles came to the Chedputter Autumn races one year, and his owner walked about insulting the sportsmen of Chedputter generally, till they went to the Honorary Secretary in a body and said:—"Appoint Handicappers, and arrange a race which shall break Shackles and humble the pride of his owner." The Districts rose against Shackles and sent up of their best; Ousel, who was supposed to be able to do his mile in 1-53; Petard, the stud-bred, trained by a cavalry regiment who knew how to train; Gringalet, the ewe-lamb of the 75th; Bobolink, the pride of Peshawar; and many others.

They called that race The Broken-Link Handicap, because it was to smash Shackles; and the Handicappers piled on the weights, and the Fund gave eight hundred rupees, and the distance was "round the course for all horses." Shackles' owner said:—"You can arrange the race with regard to Shackles only. So long as you don't bury him under weight-cloths, I don't mind." Regula Baddun's owner said:—"I throw in my mare to fret Ousel. Six furlongs is Regula's distance, and she will then lie down and die. So also will Ousel, for his jockey doesn't understand a waiting race." Now, this was a lie, for Regula had been in work for two months at Dehra, and her chances were good, always supposing that Shackles broke a blood-vessel—OR BRUNT MOVED ON HIM.

The plunging in the lotteries was fine. They filled eight thousand rupee lotteries on the Broken Link Handicap, and the account in the Pioneer said that "favoritism was divided." In plain English, the various contingents were wild on their respective horses; for the Handicappers had done their work well. The Honorary Secretary shouted himself hoarse through the din; and the smoke of the cheroots was like the smoke, and the rattling of the dice-boxes like the rattle of small-arm fire.

Ten horses started—very level—and Regula Baddun's owner cantered out on his back to a place inside the circle of the course, where two bricks had been thrown. He faced towards the brick-mounds at the lower end of the course and waited.

he story of the running is in the Pioneer. At the end of the first mile, Shackles crept out of the ruck, well on the outside, ready to get round the turn, lay hold of the bit and spin up the straight before the others knew he had got away. Brunt was sitting still, perfectly happy, listening to the "drum, drum, drum" of the hoofs behind, and knowing that, in about twenty strides, Shackles would draw one deep breath and go up the last half-mile like the "Flying Dutchman." As Shackles went short to take the turn and came abreast of the brick-mound, Brunt heard, above the noise of the wind in his ears, a whining, wailing voice on the offside, saying:—"God ha' mercy, I'm done for!" In one stride, Brunt saw the whole seething smash of the Maribyrnong Plate before him, started in his saddle and gave a yell of terror. The start brought the heels into Shackles' side, and the scream hurt Shackles' feelings. He couldn't stop dead; but he put out his feet and slid along for fifty yards, and then, very gravely and judicially, bucked off Brunt—a shaking, terror-stricken lump, while Regula Baddun made a neck-and-neck race with Bobolink up the straight, and won by a short head—Petard a bad third. Shackles' owner, in the Stand, tried to think that his field-glasses had gone wrong. Regula Baddun's owner, waiting by the two bricks, gave one deep sigh of relief, and cantered back to the stand. He had won, in lotteries and bets, about fifteen thousand.

It was a broken-link Handicap with a vengeance. It broke nearly all the men concerned, and nearly broke the heart of Shackles' owner.

He went down to interview Brunt. The boy lay, livid and gasping with fright, where he had tumbled off. The sin of losing the race never seemed to strike him. All he knew was that Whalley had "called" him, that the "call" was a warning; and, were he cut in two for it, he would never get up again. His nerve had gone altogether, and he only asked his master to give him a good thrashing, and let him go. He was fit for nothing, he said. He got his dismissal, and crept up to the paddock, white as chalk, with blue lips, his knees giving way under him. People said nasty things in the paddock; but Brunt never heeded. He changed into tweeds, took his stick and went down the road, still shaking with fright, and muttering over and over again:—"God ha' mercy, I'm done for!" To the best of my knowledge and belief he spoke the truth.

So now you know how the Broken-Link Handicap was run and won. Of course you don't believe it. You would credit anything about Russia's designs on India, or the recommendations of the Currency Commission; but a little bit of sober fact is more than you can stand!

BEYOND THE PALE.

"Love heeds not caste nor sleep a broken bed. I went in search of

love and lost myself." Hindu Proverb.

A man should, whatever happens, keep to his own caste, race and breed. Let the White go to the White and the Black to the Black.

Then, whatever trouble falls is in the ordinary course of things—neither sudden, alien, nor unexpected.

This is the story of a man who wilfully stepped beyond the safe limits of decent every-day society, and paid for it heavily.

He knew too much in the first instance; and he saw too much in the second. He took too deep an interest in native life; but he will never do so again.

Deep away in the heart of the City, behind Jitha Megji's bustee, lies Amir Nath's Gully, which ends in a dead-wall pierced by one grated window. At the head of the Gully is a big cow-byre, and the walls on either side of the Gully are without windows. Neither Suchet Singh nor Gaur Chand approved of their women-folk looking into the world. If Durga Charan had been of their opinion, he would have been a happier man today, and little Bisesa would have been able to knead her own bread. Her room looked out through the grated window into the narrow dark Gully where the sun never came and where the buffaloes wallowed in the blue slime. She was a widow, about fifteen years old, and she prayed the Gods, day and night, to send her a lover; for she did not approve of living alone.

One day the man—Trejago his name was—came into Amir Nath's Gully on an aimless wandering; and, after he had passed the buffaloes, stumbled over a big heap of cattle food.

Then he saw that the Gully ended in a trap, and heard a little laugh from behind the grated window. It was a pretty little laugh, and Trejago, knowing that, for all practical purposes, the old Arabian Nights are good guides, went forward to the window, and whispered that verse of "The Love Song of Har Dyal" which begins:

Can a man stand upright in the face of the naked Sun;

or a Lover in the Presence of his Beloved?

If my feet fail me, O Heart of my Heart, am I to blame,

being blinded by the glimpse of your beauty?

There came the faint tchinks of a woman's bracelets from behind the grating, and a little voice went on with the song at the fifth verse:

Alas! alas! Can the Moon tell the Lotus of her love when the

Gate of Heaven is shut and the clouds gather for the rains?

They have taken my Beloved, and driven her with the pack-horses

to the North.

There are iron chains on the feet that were set on my heart.

Call to the bowman to make ready—

The voice stopped suddenly, and Trejago walked out of Amir Nath's Gully, wondering who in the world could have capped "The Love Song of Har Dyal" so neatly.

Next morning, as he was driving to the office, an old woman threw a packet into his dog-cart. In the packet was the half of a broken glass bangle, one flower of the blood red dhak, a pinch of bhusa or cattle-food, and eleven cardamoms. That packet was a letter—not a clumsy compromising letter, but an innocent, unintelligible lover's epistle.

Trejago knew far too much about these things, as I have said. No Englishman should be able to translate object-letters. But Trejago spread all the trifles on the lid of his office-box and began to puzzle them out.

A broken glass-bangle stands for a Hindu widow all India over; because, when her husband dies a woman's bracelets are broken on her wrists. Trejago saw the meaning of the little bit of the glass.

The flower of the dhak means diversely "desire," "come," "write," or "danger," according to the other things with it. One cardamom means "jealousy;" but when any article is duplicated in an object-letter, it loses its symbolic meaning and stands merely for one of a number indicating time, or, if incense, curds, or saffron be sent also, place. The message ran then:—"A widow dhak flower and bhusa—at eleven o'clock." The pinch of bhusa enlightened Trejago. He saw—this kind of letter leaves much to instinctive knowledge—that the bhusa referred to the big heap of cattle-food over which he had fallen in Amir Nath's Gully, and that the message must come from the person behind the grating; she being a widow. So the message ran then:—"A widow, in the Gully in which is the heap of bhusa, desires you to come at eleven o'clock."

Trejago threw all the rubbish into the fireplace and laughed. He knew that men in the East do not make love under windows at eleven in the forenoon, nor do women fix appointments a week in advance.

So he went, that very night at eleven, into Amir Nath's Gully, clad in a boorka, which cloaks a man as well as a woman. Directly the gongs in the City made the hour, the little voice behind the grating took up "The Love Song of Har Dyal" at the verse where the Panthan girl calls upon Har Dyal to return. The song is really pretty in the Vernacular. In English you miss the wail of it. It runs something like this:—

Alone upon the housetops, to the North

I turn and watch the lightning in the sky,—

The glamour of thy footsteps in the North,

Come back to me, Beloved, or I die!

Below my feet the still bazar is laid

Far, far below the weary camels lie,—

The camels and the captives of thy raid,

Come back to me, Beloved, or I die!

My father's wife is old and harsh with years,

 And drudge of all my father's house am I.—

My bread is sorrow and my drink is tears,

 Come back to me, Beloved, or I die!

As the song stopped, Trejago stepped up under the grating and whispered:—"I am here."

Bisesa was good to look upon.

That night was the beginning of many strange things, and of a double life so wild that Trejago today sometimes wonders if it were not all a dream. Bisesa or her old handmaiden who had thrown the object-letter had detached the heavy grating from the brick-work of the wall; so that the window slid inside, leaving only a square of raw masonry, into which an active man might climb.

In the day-time, Trejago drove through his routine of office-work, or put on his calling-clothes and called on the ladies of the Station; wondering how long they would know him if they knew of poor little Bisesa. At night, when all the City was still, came the walk under the evil-smelling boorka, the patrol through Jitha Megji's bustee, the quick turn into Amir Nath's Gully between the sleeping cattle and the dead walls, and then, last of all, Bisesa, and the deep, even breathing of the old woman who slept outside the door of the bare little room that Durga Charan allotted to his sister's daughter. Who or what Durga Charan was, Trejago never inquired; and why in the world he was not discovered and knifed never occurred to him till his madness was over, and Bisesa... But this comes later.

Bisesa was an endless delight to Trejago. She was as ignorant as a bird; and her distorted versions of the rumors from the outside world that had reached her in her room, amused Trejago almost as much as her lisping attempts to pronounce his name—"Christopher." The first syllable was always more than she could manage, and she made funny little gestures with her rose-leaf hands, as one throwing the name away, and then, kneeling before Trejago, asked him, exactly as an Englishwoman would do, if he were sure he loved her. Trejago swore that he loved her more than any one else in the world. Which was true.

After a month of this folly, the exigencies of his other life compelled Trejago to be especially attentive to a lady of his acquaintance. You may take it for a fact that anything of this kind is not only noticed and discussed by a man's own race, but by some hundred and fifty natives as well. Trejago had to walk with this lady and talk to her at the Band-stand, and once or twice to drive with her; never for an instant dreaming that this would affect his dearer out-of-the-way life. But the news flew, in the usual mysterious fashion, from mouth to mouth, till Bisesa's duenna heard of it and told Bisesa. The child was so troubled that she did the household work evilly, and was beaten by Durga Charan's wife in consequence.

A week later, Bisesa taxed Trejago with the flirtation. She understood no gradations and spoke openly. Trejago laughed and Bisesa stamped her little feet—little feet, light as marigold flowers, that could lie in the palm of a man's one hand.

Much that is written about "Oriental passion and impulsiveness" is exaggerated and compiled at second-hand, but a little of it is true; and when an Englishman finds that little, it is quite as startling as any passion in his own proper life. Bisesa raged and stormed, and finally threatened to kill herself if Trejago did not at once drop the alien Memsahib who had come between them. Trejago tried to explain, and to show her that she did not understand these things from a

Western standpoint. Bisesa drew herself up, and said simply:

"I do not. I know only this—it is not good that I should have made you dearer than my own heart to me, Sahib. You are an Englishman. I am only a black girl"—she was fairer than bar-gold in the Mint—and the widow of a black man.

Then she sobbed and said: "But on my soul and my Mother's soul, I love you. There shall no harm come to you, whatever happens to me."

Trejago argued with the child, and tried to soothe her, but she seemed quite unreasonably disturbed. Nothing would satisfy her save that all relations between them should end. He was to go away at once. And he went. As he dropped out at the window, she kissed his forehead twice, and he walked away wondering.

A week, and then three weeks, passed without a sign from Bisesa.

Trejago, thinking that the rupture had lasted quite long enough, went down to Amir Nath's Gully for the fifth time in the three weeks, hoping that his rap at the sill of the shifting grating would be answered. He was not disappointed.

There was a young moon, and one stream of light fell down into Amir Nath's Gully, and struck the grating, which was drawn away as he knocked. From the black dark, Bisesa held out her arms into the moonlight. Both hands had been cut off at the wrists, and the stumps were nearly healed.

Then, as Bisesa bowed her head between her arms and sobbed, some one in the room grunted like a wild beast, and something sharp—knife, sword or spear—thrust at Trejago in his boorka. The stroke missed his body, but cut into one of the muscles of the groin, and he limped slightly from the wound for the rest of his days.

The grating went into its place. There was no sign whatever from inside the house—nothing but the moonlight strip on the high wall, and the blackness of Amir Nath's Gully behind.

The next thing Trejago remembers, after raging and shouting like a madman between those pitiless walls, is that he found himself near the river as the dawn was breaking, threw away his boorka and went home bareheaded.

What the tragedy was—whether Bisesa had, in a fit of causeless despair, told everything, or the intrigue had been discovered and she tortured to tell, whether Durga Charan knew his name, and what became of Bisesa—Trejago does not know to this day. Something horrible had happened, and the thought of what it must have been comes upon Trejago in the night now and again, and keeps him company till the morning. One special feature of the case is that he does not know where lies the front of Durga Charan's house. It may open on to a courtyard common to two or more houses, or it may lie behind any one of the gates of Jitha Megji's bustee. Trejago cannot tell.

He cannot get Bisesa—poor little Bisesa—back again. He has lost her in the City, where each man's house is as guarded and as unknowable as the grave; and the grating that opens into Amir Nath's Gully has been walled up.

But Trejago pays his calls regularly, and is reckoned a very decent sort of man.

There is nothing peculiar about him, except a slight stiffness, caused by a riding-strain, in the right leg.

IN ERROR.

They burnt a corpse upon the sand—

 The light shone out afar;

It guided home the plunging boats

 That beat from Zanzibar.

Spirit of Fire, where'er Thy altars rise.

Thou art Light of Guidance to our eyes!

 ——Salsette Boat-Song.

There is hope for a man who gets publicly and riotously drunk more often that he ought to do; but there is no hope for the man who drinks secretly and alone in his own house—the man who is never seen to drink.

This is a rule; so there must be an exception to prove it.

Moriarty's case was that exception.

He was a Civil Engineer, and the Government, very kindly, put him quite by himself in an out-district, with nobody but natives to talk to and a great deal of work to do. He did his work well in the four years he was utterly alone; but he picked up the vice of secret and solitary drinking, and came up out of the wilderness more old and worn and haggard than the dead-alive life had any right to make him.

You know the saying that a man who has been alone in the jungle for more than a year is never quite sane all his life after. People credited Moriarty's queerness of manner and moody ways to the solitude, and said it showed how Government spoilt the futures of its best men. Moriarty had built himself the plinth of a very god reputation in the bridge-dam-girder line. But he knew, every night of the week, that he was taking steps to undermine that reputation with L. L. L. and "Christopher" and little nips of liqueurs, and filth of that kind. He had a sound constitution and a great brain, or else he would have broken down and died like a sick camel in the district, as better men have done before him.

Government ordered him to Simla after he had come out of the desert; and he went up meaning to try for a post then vacant. That season, Mrs. Reiver—perhaps you will remember her—was in the height of her power, and many men lay under her yoke. Everything bad that could be said has already been said about Mrs. Reiver, in another tale.

Moriarty was heavily-built and handsome, very quiet and nervously anxious to please his neighbors when he wasn't sunk in a brown study. He started a good deal at sudden noises or if spoken to without warning; and, when you watched him drinking his glass of water at dinner, you could see the hand shake a little. But all this was put down to nervousness, and the quiet, steady, "sip-sip-sip, fill and sip-sip-sip, again," that went on in his own room when he was by himself, was never known. Which was miraculous, seeing how everything in a man's private life is public property out here.

Moriarty was drawn, not into Mrs. Reiver's set, because they were not his sort, but into the power of Mrs. Reiver, and he fell down in front of her and made a goddess of her. This was due to his coming fresh out of the jungle to a big town. He could not scale things properly or see who was what.

Because Mrs. Reiver was cold and hard, he said she was stately and dignified. Because she had no brains, and could not talk cleverly, he said she was reserved and shy. Mrs. Reiver shy! Because she was unworthy of honor or reverence from any one, he reverenced her from a distance and dowered her with all the virtues in the Bible and most of those in Shakespeare.

This big, dark, abstracted man who was so nervous when a pony cantered behind him, used to moon in the train of Mrs. Reiver, blushing with pleasure when she threw a word or two his way. His admiration was strictly platonic: even other women saw and admitted this. He did not move out in Simla, so he heard nothing against his idol: which was satisfactory. Mrs. Reiver took no special notice of him, beyond seeing that he was added to her list of admirers, and going for a walk with him now and then, just to show that he was her property, claimable as such. Moriarty must have done most of the talking, for Mrs. Reiver couldn't talk much to a man of his stamp; and the little she said could not have been profitable. What Moriarty believed in, as he had good reason to, was Mrs. Reiver's influence over him, and, in that belief, set himself seriously to try to do away with the vice that only he himself knew of.

His experiences while he was fighting with it must have been peculiar, but he never described them. Sometimes he would hold off from everything except water for a week. Then, on a rainy night, when no one had asked him out to dinner, and there was a big fire in his room, and everything comfortable, he would sit down and make a big night of it by adding little nip to little nip, planning big schemes of reformation meanwhile, until he threw himself on his bed hopelessly drunk. He suffered next morning.

One night, the big crash came. He was troubled in his own mind over his attempts to make himself "worthy of the friendship" of Mrs. Reiver. The past ten days had been very bad ones, and the end of it all was that he received the arrears of two and three-quarter years of sipping in one attack of delirium tremens of the subdued kind; beginning with suicidal depression, going on to fits and starts and hysteria, and ending with downright raving. As he sat in a chair in front of the fire, or walked up and down the room picking a handkerchief to pieces, you heard what poor Moriarty really thought of Mrs. Reiver, for he raved about her and his own fall for the most part; though he ravelled some P. W. D. accounts into the same skein of thought. He talked, and talked, and talked in a low dry whisper to himself, and there was no stopping him. He seemed to know that there was something wrong, and twice tried to pull himself together and confer rationally with the Doctor; but his mind ran out of control at once, and he fell back to a whisper and the story of his troubles. It is terrible to hear a big man babbling like a child of all that a man usually locks up, and puts away in the deep of his heart. Moriarty read out his very soul for the benefit of any one who was in the room between ten-thirty that night and two-forty-five next morning.

From what he said, one gathered how immense an influence Mrs. Reiver held over him, and how thoroughly he felt for his own lapse. His whisperings cannot, of course, be put down here; but they were very instructive as showing the errors of his estimates..........

When the trouble was over, and his few acquaintances were pitying him for the bad attack of jungle-fever that had so pulled him down, Moriarty swore a big oath to himself and went abroad again with Mrs. Reiver till the end of the season, adoring her in a quiet and deferential way as an angel from heaven. Later on he took to riding—not hacking, but honest riding—which was good proof that he was improving, and you could slam doors behind him without his jumping to his feet with a gasp. That, again, was hopeful.

How he kept his oath, and what it cost him in the beginning, nobody knows. He certainly managed to compass the hardest thing that a man who has drank heavily can do. He took his peg and wine at dinner, but he never drank alone, and never let what he drank have the least hold on him.

Once he told a bosom-friend the story of his great trouble, and how the "influence of a pure honest woman, and an angel as well" had saved him. When the man—startled at anything good being laid to Mrs. Reiver's door—laughed, it cost him Moriarty's friendship.

Moriarty, who is married now to a woman ten thousand times better than Mrs. Reiver—a woman who believes that there is no man on earth as good and clever as her husband—will go down to his grave vowing and protesting that Mrs. Reiver saved him from ruin in both worlds.

That she knew anything of Moriarty's weakness nobody believed for a moment. That she would have cut him dead, thrown him over, and acquainted all her friends with her discovery, if she had known of it, nobody who knew her doubted for an instant.

oriarty thought her something she never was, and in that belief saved himself. Which was just as good as though she had been everything that he had imagined.

But the question is, what claim will Mrs. Reiver have to the credit of Moriarty's salvation, when her day of reckoning comes?

A BANK FRAUD.

He drank strong waters and his speech was coarse;

He purchased raiment and forebore to pay;

He struck a trusting junior with a horse,

And won Gymkhanas in a doubtful way.

Then, 'twixt a vice and folly, turned aside

To do good deeds and straight to cloak them, lied.

—THE MESS ROOM.

If Reggie Burke were in India now, he would resent this tale being told; but as he is in Hong-Kong and won't see it, the telling is safe. He was the man who worked the big fraud on the Sind and Sialkote Bank. He was manager of an up-country Branch, and a sound practical man with a large experience of native loan and insurance work. He could combine the frivolities of ordinary life with his work, and yet do well. Reggie Burke rode anything that would let him get up, danced as neatly as he rode, and was wanted for every sort of amusement in the Station.

As he said himself, and as many men found out rather to their surprise, there were two Burkes, both very much at your service.

"Reggie Burke," between four and ten, ready for anything from a hot-weather gymkhana to a riding-picnic; and, between ten and four, "Mr. Reginald Burke, Manager of the Sind and Sialkote Branch Bank." You might play polo with him one afternoon and hear him express his opinions when a man crossed; and you might call on him next morning to raise a two-thousand rupee loan on a five hundred pound insurance-policy, eighty pounds paid in premiums. He would recognize you, but you would have some trouble in recognizing him.

The Directors of the Bank—it had its headquarters in Calcutta and its General Manager's word carried weight with the Government—picked their men well. They had tested Reggie up to a fairly severe breaking-strain. They trusted him just as much as Directors ever trust Managers. You must see for yourself whether their trust was misplaced.

Reggie's Branch was in a big Station, and worked with the usual staff—one Manager, one Accountant, both English, a Cashier, and a horde of native clerks; besides the Police patrol at nights outside.

The bulk of its work, for it was in a thriving district, was hoondi and accommodation of all kinds. A fool has no grip of this sort of business; and a clever man who does not go about among his clients, and know more than a little of their affairs, is worse than a fool.

Reggie was young-looking, clean-shaved, with a twinkle in his eye, and a head that nothing short of a gallon of the Gunners' Madeira could make any impression on.

One day, at a big dinner, he announced casually that the Directors had shifted on to him a Natural Curiosity, from England, in the Accountant line. He was perfectly correct. Mr. Silas Riley, Accountant, was a MOST curious animal—a long, gawky, rawboned Yorkshireman, full

of the savage self-conceit that blossoms only in the best county in England. Arrogance was a mild word for the mental attitude of Mr. S. Riley. He had worked himself up, after seven years, to a Cashier's position in a Huddersfield Bank; and all his experience lay among the factories of the North. Perhaps he would have done better on the Bombay side, where they are happy with one-half per cent. profits, and money is cheap. He was useless for Upper India and a wheat Province, where a man wants a large head and a touch of imagination if he is to turn out a satisfactory balance-sheet.

He was wonderfully narrow-minded in business, and, being new to the country, had no notion that Indian banking is totally distinct from Home work. Like most clever self-made men, he had much simplicity in his nature; and, somehow or other, had construed the ordinarily polite terms of his letter of engagement into a belief that the Directors had chosen him on account of his special and brilliant talents, and that they set great store by him. This notion grew and crystallized; thus adding to his natural North-country conceit.

Further, he was delicate, suffered from some trouble in his chest, and was short in his temper.

You will admit that Reggie had reason to call his new Accountant a Natural Curiosity. The two men failed to hit it off at all. Riley considered Reggie a wild, feather-headed idiot, given to Heaven only knew what dissipation in low places called "Messes," and totally unfit for the serious and solemn vocation of banking. He could never get over Reggie's look of youth and "you-be-damned" air; and he couldn't understand Reggie's friends—clean-built, careless men in the Army—who rode over to big Sunday breakfasts at the Bank, and told sultry stories till Riley got up and left the room. Riley was always showing Reggie how the business ought to be conducted, and Reggie had more than once to remind him that seven years' limited experience between Huddersfield and Beverly did not qualify a man to steer a big up-country business. Then Riley sulked and referred to himself as a pillar of the Bank and a cherished friend of the Directors, and Reggie tore his hair. If a man's English subordinates fail him in this country, he comes to a hard time indeed, for native help has strict limitations. In the winter Riley went sick for weeks at a time with his lung complaint, and this threw more work on Reggie. But he preferred it to the everlasting friction when Riley was well.

One of the Travelling Inspectors of the Bank discovered these collapses and reported them to the Directors. Now Riley had been foisted on the Bank by an M. P., who wanted the support of Riley's father, who, again, was anxious to get his son out to a warmer climate because of those lungs. The M. P. had an interest in the Bank; but one of the Directors wanted to advance a nominee of his own; and, after Riley's father had died, he made the rest of the Board see that an Accountant who was sick for half the year, had better give place to a healthy man. If Riley had known the real story of his appointment, he might have behaved better; but knowing nothing, his stretches of sickness alternated with restless, persistent, meddling irritation of Reggie, and all the hundred ways in which conceit in a subordinate situation can find play. Reggie used to call him striking and hair-curling names behind his back as a relief to his own feelings; but he never abused him to his face, because he said: "Riley is such a frail beast that half of his loathsome conceit is due to pains in the chest."

Late one April, Riley went very sick indeed. The doctor punched him and thumped him, and told him he would be better before long. Then the doctor went to Reggie and said:—"Do you know how sick your Accountant is?" "No!" said Reggie—"The worse the better, confound him! He's a clacking nuisance when he's well. I'll let you take away the Bank Safe if you can drug him silent for this hot-weather."

But the doctor did not laugh—"Man, I'm not joking," he said. "I'll give him another three months in his bed and a week or so more to die in. On my honor and reputation that's all the

grace he has in this world. Consumption has hold of him to the marrow."

Reggie's face changed at once into the face of "Mr. Reginald Burke," and he answered:— "What can I do?"

"Nothing," said the doctor. "For all practical purposes the man is dead already. Keep him quiet and cheerful and tell him he's going to recover. That's all. I'll look after him to the end, of course."

The doctor went away, and Reggie sat down to open the evening mail.

His first letter was one from the Directors, intimating for his information that Mr. Riley was to resign, under a month's notice, by the terms of his agreement, telling Reggie that their letter to Riley would follow and advising Reggie of the coming of a new Accountant, a man whom Reggie knew and liked.

Reggie lit a cheroot, and, before he had finished smoking, he had sketched the outline of a fraud. He put away—"burked"—the Directors letter, and went in to talk to Riley, who was as ungracious as usual, and fretting himself over the way the bank would run during his illness. He never thought of the extra work on Reggie's shoulders, but solely of the damage to his own prospects of advancement. Then Reggie assured him that everything would be well, and that he, Reggie, would confer with Riley daily on the management of the Bank. Riley was a little soothed, but he hinted in as many words that he did not think much of Reggie's business capacity.

Reggie was humble. And he had letters in his desk from the Directors that a Gilbarte or a Hardie might have been proud of!

The days passed in the big darkened house, and the Directors' letter of dismissal to Riley came and was put away by Reggie, who, every evening, brought the books to Riley's room, and showed him what had been going forward, while Riley snarled. Reggie did his best to make statements pleasing to Riley, but the Accountant was sure that the Bank was going to rack and ruin without him. In June, as the lying in bed told on his spirit, he asked whether his absence had been noted by the Directors, and Reggie said that they had written most sympathetic letters, hoping that he would be able to resume his valuable services before long. He showed Riley the letters: and Riley said that the Directors ought to have written to him direct.

A few days later, Reggie opened Riley's mail in the half-light of the room, and gave him the sheet—not the envelope—of a letter to Riley from the Directors. Riley said he would thank Reggie not to interfere with his private papers, specially as Reggie knew he was too weak to open his own letters. Reggie apologized.

Then Riley's mood changed, and he lectured Reggie on his evil ways: his horses and his bad friends. "Of course, lying here on my back, Mr. Burke, I can't keep you straight; but when I'm well, I DO hope you'll pay some heed to my words." Reggie, who had dropped polo, and dinners, and tennis, and all to attend to Riley, said that he was penitent and settled Riley's head on the pillow and heard him fret and contradict in hard, dry, hacking whispers, without a sign of impatience. This at the end of a heavy day's office work, doing double duty, in the latter half of June.

When the new Accountant came, Reggie told him the facts of the case, and announced to Riley that he had a guest staying with him. Riley said that he might have had more consideration than to entertain his "doubtful friends" at such a time. Reggie made Carron, the new Accountant, sleep at the Club in consequence. Carron's arrival took some of the heavy work off his shoulders,

and he had time to attend to Riley's exactions—to explain, soothe, invent, and settle and resettle the poor wretch in bed, and to forge complimentary letters from Calcutta. At the end of the first month, Riley wished to send some money home to his mother. Reggie sent the draft. At the end of the second month, Riley's salary came in just the same. Reggie paid it out of his own pocket; and, with it, wrote Riley a beautiful letter from the Directors.

Riley was very ill indeed, but the flame of his life burnt unsteadily. Now and then he would be cheerful and confident about the future, sketching plans for going Home and seeing his mother.

Reggie listened patiently when the office work was over, and encouraged him.

At other times Riley insisted on Reggie's reading the Bible and grim "Methody" tracts to him. Out of these tracts he pointed morals directed at his Manager. But he always found time to worry Reggie about the working of the Bank, and to show him where the weak points lay.

This in-door, sick-room life and constant strains wore Reggie down a good deal, and shook his nerves, and lowered his billiard-play by forty points. But the business of the Bank, and the business of the sick-room, had to go on, though the glass was 116 degrees in the shade.

At the end of the third month, Riley was sinking fast, and had begun to realize that he was very sick. But the conceit that made him worry Reggie, kept him from believing the worst. "He wants some sort of mental stimulant if he is to drag on," said the doctor.

"Keep him interested in life if you care about his living." So Riley, contrary to all the laws of business and the finance, received a 25-per-cent, rise of salary from the Directors. The "mental stimulant" succeeded beautifully. Riley was happy and cheerful, and, as is often the case in consumption, healthiest in mind when the body was weakest. He lingered for a full month, snarling and fretting about the Bank, talking of the future, hearing the Bible read, lecturing Reggie on sin, and wondering when he would be able to move abroad.

But at the end of September, one mercilessly hot evening, he rose up in his bed with a little gasp, and said quickly to Reggie:—"Mr. Burke, I am going to die. I know it in myself. My chest is all hollow inside, and there's nothing to breathe with. To the best of my knowledge I have done nowt"—he was returning to the talk of his boyhood—"to lie heavy on my conscience. God be thanked, I have been preserved from the grosser forms of sin; and I counsel YOU, Mr. Burke...."

Here his voice died down, and Reggie stooped over him.

"Send my salary for September to my mother.... done great things with the Bank if I had been spared.... mistaken policy.... no fault of mine."

Then he turned his face to the wall and died.

Reggie drew the sheet over Its face, and went out into the verandah, with his last "mental stimulant"—a letter of condolence and sympathy from the Directors—unused in his pocket.

"If I'd been only ten minutes earlier," thought Reggie, "I might have heartened him up to pull through another day."

TODS' AMENDMENT.

The World hath set its heavy yoke

Upon the old white-bearded folk

Who strive to please the King.

God's mercy is upon the young,

God's wisdom in the baby tongue

That fears not anything.

—The Parable of Chajju Bhagat.

Now Tods' Mamma was a singularly charming woman, and every one in Simla knew Tods. Most men had saved him from death on occasions.

He was beyond his ayah's control altogether, and perilled his life daily to find out what would happen if you pulled a Mountain Battery mule's tail. He was an utterly fearless young Pagan, about six years old, and the only baby who ever broke the holy calm of the supreme Legislative Council.

It happened this way: Tods' pet kid got loose, and fled up the hill, off the Boileaugunge Road, Tods after it, until it burst into the Viceregal Lodge lawn, then attached to "Peterhoff." The Council were sitting at the time, and the windows were open because it was warm. The Red Lancer in the porch told Tods to go away; but Tods knew the Red Lancer and most of the Members of Council personally.

Moreover, he had firm hold of the kid's collar, and was being dragged all across the flower-beds. "Give my salaam to the long Councillor Sahib, and ask him to help me take Moti back!" gasped Tods. The Council heard the noise through the open windows; and, after an interval, was seen the shocking spectacle of a Legal Member and a Lieutenant-Governor helping, under the direct patronage of a Commander-in-Chief and a Viceroy, one small and very dirty boy in a sailor's suit and a tangle of brown hair, to coerce a lively and rebellious kid. They headed it off down the path to the Mall, and Tods went home in triumph and told his Mamma that ALL the Councillor Sahibs had been helping him to catch Moti. Whereat his Mamma smacked Tods for interfering with the administration of the Empire; but Tods met the Legal Member the next day, and told him in confidence that if the Legal Member ever wanted to catch a goat, he, Tods, would give him all the help in his power. "Thank you, Tods," said the Legal Member.

Tods was the idol of some eighty jhampanis, and half as many saises.

He saluted them all as "O Brother." It never entered his head that any living human being could disobey his orders; and he was the buffer between the servants and his Mamma's wrath. The working of that household turned on Tods, who was adored by every one from the dhoby to the dog-boy. Even Futteh Khan, the villainous loafer khit from Mussoorie, shirked risking Tods' displeasure for fear his co-mates should look down on him.

So Tods had honor in the land from Boileaugunge to Chota Simla, and ruled justly according to

his lights. Of course, he spoke Urdu, but he had also mastered many queer side-speeches like the chotee bolee of the women, and held grave converse with shopkeepers and Hill-coolies alike. He was precocious for his age, and his mixing with natives had taught him some of the more bitter truths of life; the meanness and the sordidness of it. He used, over his bread and milk, to deliver solemn and serious aphorisms, translated from the vernacular into the English, that made his Mamma jump and vow that Tods MUST go home next hot weather.

Just when Tods was in the bloom of his power, the Supreme Legislature were hacking out a Bill, for the Sub-Montane Tracts, a revision of the then Act, smaller than the Punjab Land Bill, but affecting a few hundred thousand people none the less. The Legal Member had built, and bolstered, and embroidered, and amended that Bill, till it looked beautiful on paper. Then the Council began to settle what they called the "minor details." As if any Englishman legislating for natives knows enough to know which are the minor and which are the major points, from the native point of view, of any measure! That Bill was a triumph of "safe-guarding the interests of the tenant." One clause provided that land should not be leased on longer terms than five years at a stretch; because, if the landlord had a tenant bound down for, say, twenty years, he would squeeze the very life out of him. The notion was to keep up a stream of independent cultivators in the Sub-Montane Tracts; and ethnologically and politically the notion was correct. The only drawback was that it was altogether wrong. A native's life in India implies the life of his son. Wherefore, you cannot legislate for one generation at a time. You must consider the next from the native point of view. Curiously enough, the native now and then, and in Northern India more particularly, hates being over-protected against himself. There was a Naga village once, where they lived on dead AND buried Commissariat mules.... But that is another story.

For many reasons, to be explained later, the people concerned objected to the Bill. The Native Member in Council knew as much about Punjabis as he knew about Charing Cross. He had said in Calcutta that "the Bill was entirely in accord with the desires of that large and important class, the cultivators;" and so on, and so on. The Legal Member's knowledge of natives was limited to English-speaking Durbaris, and his own red chaprassis, the Sub-Montane Tracts concerned no one in particular, the Deputy Commissioners were a good deal too driven to make representations, and the measure was one which dealt with small landholders only. Nevertheless, the Legal Member prayed that it might be correct, for he was a nervously conscientious man. He did not know that no man can tell what natives think unless he mixes with them with the varnish off. And not always then. But he did the best he knew. And the measure came up to the Supreme Council for the final touches, while Tods patrolled the Burra Simla Bazar in his morning rides, and played with the monkey belonging to Ditta Mull, the bunnia, and listened, as a child listens to all the stray talk about this new freak of the Lat Sahib's.

One day there was a dinner-party, at the house of Tods' Mamma, and the Legal Member came. Tods was in bed, but he kept awake till he heard the bursts of laughter from the men over the coffee. Then he paddled out in his little red flannel dressing-gown and his night-suit, and took refuge by the side of his father, knowing that he would not be sent back. "See the miseries of having a family!" said Tods' father, giving Tods three prunes, some water in a glass that had been used for claret, and telling him to sit still. Tods sucked the prunes slowly, knowing that he would have to go when they were finished, and sipped the pink water like a man of the world, as he listened to the conversation. Presently, the Legal Member, talking "shop," to the Head of a Department, mentioned his Bill by its full name—"The Sub-Montane Tracts Ryotwari Revised Enactment." Tods caught the one native word, and lifting up his small voice said:—"Oh, I know ALL about that! Has it been murramutted yet, Councillor Sahib?"

"How much?" said the Legal Member.

"Murramutted—mended.—Put theek, you know—made nice to please Ditta Mull!"

The Legal Member left his place and moved up next to Tods.

"What do you know about Ryotwari, little man?" he said.

"I'm not a little man, I'm Tods, and I know ALL about it. Ditta Mull, and Choga Lall, and Amir Nath, and—oh, lakhs of my friends tell me about it in the bazars when I talk to them."

"Oh, they do—do they? What do they say, Tods?"

Tods tucked his feet under his red flannel dressing-gown and said:—"I must fink."

The Legal Member waited patiently. Then Tods, with infinite compassion:

"You don't speak my talk, do you, Councillor Sahib?"

"No; I am sorry to say I do not," said the Legal' Member.

"Very well," said Tods. "I must fink in English."

He spent a minute putting his ideas in order, and began very slowly, translating in his mind from the vernacular to English, as many Anglo-Indian children do. You must remember that the Legal Member helped him on by questions when he halted, for Tods was not equal to the sustained flight of oratory that follows.

"Ditta Mull says:—'This thing is the talk of a child, and was made up by fools.' But I don't think you are a fool, Councillor Sahib," said Tods, hastily. "You caught my goat. This is what Ditta Mull says:—'I am not a fool, and why should the Sirkar say I am a child? I can see if the land is good and if the landlord is good. If I am a fool, the sin is upon my own head. For five years I take my ground for which I have saved money, and a wife I take too, and a little son is born.' Ditta Mull has one daughter now, but he SAYS he will have a son, soon. And he says: 'At the end of five years, by this new bundobust, I must go. If I do not go, I must get fresh seals and takkus-stamps on the papers, perhaps in the middle of the harvest, and to go to the law-courts once is wisdom, but to go twice is Jehannum.' That is QUITE true," explained Tods, gravely. "All my friends say so. And Ditta Mull says:—'Always fresh takkus and paying money to vakils and chaprassis and law-courts every five years or else the landlord makes me go. Why do I want to go? Am I fool? If I am a fool and do not know, after forty years, good land when I see it, let me die! But if the new bundobust says for FIFTEEN years, then it is good and wise. My little son is a man, and I am burnt, and he takes the ground or another ground, paying only once for the takkus-stamps on the papers, and his little son is born, and at the end of fifteen years is a man too. But what profit is there in five years and fresh papers? Nothing but dikh, trouble, dikh. We are not young men who take these lands, but old ones—not jais, but tradesmen with a little money—and for fifteen years we shall have peace. Nor are we children that the Sirkar should treat us so.'"

Here Tods stopped short, for the whole table were listening. The Legal Member said to Tods: "Is that all?"

"All I can remember," said Tods. "But you should see Ditta Mull's big monkey. It's just like a Councillor Sahib."

"Tods! Go to bed," said his father.

Tods gathered up his dressing-gown tail and departed.

The Legal Member brought his hand down on the table with a crash—"By Jove!" said the Legal

Member, "I believe the boy is right. The short tenure IS the weak point."

He left early, thinking over what Tods had said. Now, it was obviously impossible for the Legal Member to play with a bunnia's monkey, by way of getting understanding; but he did better. He made inquiries, always bearing in mind the fact that the real native—not the hybrid, University-trained mule—is as timid as a colt, and, little by little, he coaxed some of the men whom the measure concerned most intimately to give in their views, which squared very closely with Tods' evidence.

So the Bill was amended in that clause; and the Legal Member was filled with an uneasy suspicion that Native Members represent very little except the Orders they carry on their bosoms. But he put the thought from him as illiberal. He was a most Liberal Man.

After a time the news spread through the bazars that Tods had got the Bill recast in the tenure clause, and if Tods' Mamma had not interfered, Tods would have made himself sick on the baskets of fruit and pistachio nuts and Cabuli grapes and almonds that crowded the verandah. Till he went Home, Tods ranked some few degrees before the Viceroy in popular estimation. But for the little life of him Tods could not understand why.

In the Legal Member's private-paper-box still lies the rough draft of the Sub-Montane Tracts Ryotwari Revised Enactment; and, opposite the twenty-second clause, pencilled in blue chalk, and signed by the Legal Member, are the words "Tods' Amendment."

IN THE PRIDE OF HIS YOUTH.

"Stopped in the straight when the race was his own!

Look at him cutting it—cur to the bone!"

"Ask ere the youngster be rated and chidden,

What did he carry and how was he ridden?

Maybe they used him too much at the start;

Maybe Fate's weight-cloths are breaking his heart."

—Life's Handicap.

When I was telling you of the joke that The Worm played off on the Senior Subaltern, I promised a somewhat similar tale, but with all the jest left out. This is that tale:

Dicky Hatt was kidnapped in his early, early youth—neither by landlady's daughter, housemaid, barmaid, nor cook, but by a girl so nearly of his own caste that only a woman could have said she was just the least little bit in the world below it. This happened a month before he came out to India, and five days after his one-and-twentieth birthday. The girl was nineteen—six years older than Dicky in the things of this world, that is to say—and, for the time, twice as foolish as he.

Excepting, always, falling off a horse there is nothing more fatally easy than marriage before the Registrar. The ceremony costs less than fifty shillings, and is remarkably like walking into a pawn-shop. After the declarations of residence have been put in, four minutes will cover the rest of the proceedings—fees, attestation, and all. Then the Registrar slides the blotting-pad over the names, and says grimly, with his pen between his teeth:—"Now you're man and wife;" and the couple walk out into the street, feeling as if something were horribly illegal somewhere.

But that ceremony holds and can drag a man to his undoing just as thoroughly as the "long as ye both shall live" curse from the altar-rails, with the bridesmaids giggling behind, and "The Voice that breathed o'er Eden" lifting the roof off. In this manner was Dicky Hatt kidnapped, and he considered it vastly fine, for he had received an appointment in India which carried a magnificent salary from the Home point of view. The marriage was to be kept secret for a year. Then Mrs. Dicky Hatt was to come out and the rest of life was to be a glorious golden mist. That was how they sketched it under the Addison Road Station lamps; and, after one short month, came Gravesend and Dicky steaming out to his new life, and the girl crying in a thirty-shillings a week bed-and-living room, in a back street off Montpelier Square near the Knightsbridge Barracks.

But the country that Dicky came to was a hard land, where "men" of twenty-one were reckoned very small boys indeed, and life was expensive. The salary that loomed so large six thousand miles away did not go far. Particularly when Dicky divided it by two, and remitted more than the fair half, at 1-6, to Montpelier Square. One hundred and thirty-five rupees out of three hundred and thirty is not much to live on; but it was absurd to suppose that Mrs. Hatt could exist forever on the 20 pounds held back by Dicky, from his outfit allowance. Dicky saw this, and remitted at once; always remembering that Rs. 700 were to be paid, twelve months later, for a first-class passage out for a lady. When you add to these trifling details the natural instincts of a boy beginning a new life in a new country and longing to go about and enjoy himself, and

the necessity for grappling with strange work—which, properly speaking, should take up a boy's undivided attention—you will see that Dicky started handicapped. He saw it himself for a breath or two; but he did not guess the full beauty of his future.

As the hot weather began, the shackles settled on him and ate into his flesh. First would come letters—big, crossed, seven sheet letters—from his wife, telling him how she longed to see him, and what a Heaven upon earth would be their property when they met.

Then some boy of the chummery wherein Dicky lodged would pound on the door of his bare little room, and tell him to come out and look at a pony—the very thing to suit him. Dicky could not afford ponies. He had to explain this. Dicky could not afford living in the chummery, modest as it was. He had to explain this before he moved to a single room next the office where he worked all day. He kept house on a green oil-cloth table-cover, one chair, one charpoy, one photograph, one tooth-glass, very strong and thick, a seven-rupee eight-anna filter, and messing by contract at thirty-seven rupees a month. Which last item was extortion. He had no punkah, for a punkah costs fifteen rupees a month; but he slept on the roof of the office with all his wife's letters under his pillow. Now and again he was asked out to dinner where he got both a punkah and an iced drink. But this was seldom, for people objected to recognizing a boy who had evidently the instincts of a Scotch tallow-chandler, and who lived in such a nasty fashion. Dicky could not subscribe to any amusement, so he found no amusement except the pleasure of turning over his Bank-book and reading what it said about "loans on approved security." That cost nothing. He remitted through a Bombay Bank, by the way, and the Station knew nothing of his private affairs.

Every month he sent Home all he could possibly spare for his wife—and for another reason which was expected to explain itself shortly and would require more money.

About this time, Dicky was overtaken with the nervous, haunting fear that besets married men when they are out of sorts. He had no pension to look to. What if he should die suddenly, and leave his wife unprovided for? The thought used to lay hold of him in the still, hot nights on the roof, till the shaking of his heart made him think that he was going to die then and there of heart-disease.

Now this is a frame of mind which no boy has a right to know. It is a strong man's trouble; but, coming when it did, it nearly drove poor punkah-less, perspiring Dicky Hatt mad. He could tell no one about it.

A certain amount of "screw" is as necessary for a man as for a billiard-ball. It makes them both do wonderful things. Dicky needed money badly, and he worked for it like a horse. But, naturally, the men who owned him knew that a boy can live very comfortably on a certain income—pay in India is a matter of age, not merit, you see—and if their particular boy wished to work like two boys, Business forbid that they should stop him! But Business forbid that they should give him an increase of pay at his present ridiculously immature age! So Dicky won certain rises of salary—ample for a boy—not enough for a wife and child—certainly too little for the seven-hundred-rupee passage that he and Mrs. Hatt had discussed so lightly once upon a time. And with this he was forced to be content.

Somehow, all his money seemed to fade away in Home drafts and the crushing Exchange, and the tone of the Home letters changed and grew querulous. "Why wouldn't Dicky have his wife and the baby out? Surely he had a salary—a fine salary—and it was too bad of him to enjoy himself in India. But would he—could he—make the next draft a little more elastic?" Here followed a list of baby's kit, as long as a Parsee's bill. Then Dicky, whose heart yearned to his wife and the little son he had never seen—which, again, is a feeling no boy is entitled to—enlarged the draft and wrote queer half-boy, half-man letters, saying that life was not so

enjoyable after all and would the little wife wait yet a little longer? But the little wife, however much she approved of money, objected to waiting, and there was a strange, hard sort of ring in her letters that Dicky didn't understand. How could he, poor boy?

Later on still—just as Dicky had been told—apropos of another youngster who had "made a fool of himself," as the saying is—that matrimony would not only ruin his further chances of advancement, but would lose him his present appointment—came the news that the baby, his own little, little son, had died, and, behind this, forty lines of an angry woman's scrawl, saying that death might have been averted if certain things, all costing money, had been done, or if the mother and the baby had been with Dicky. The letter struck at Dicky's naked heart; but, not being officially entitled to a baby, he could show no sign of trouble.

How Dicky won through the next four months, and what hope he kept alight to force him into his work, no one dare say. He pounded on, the seven-hundred-rupee passage as far away as ever, and his style of living unchanged, except when he launched into a new filter.

There was the strain of his office-work, and the strain of his remittances, and the knowledge of his boy's death, which touched the boy more, perhaps, than it would have touched a man; and, beyond all, the enduring strain of his daily life. Gray-headed seniors, who approved of his thrift and his fashion of denying himself everything pleasant, reminded him of the old saw that says:

"If a youth would be distinguished in his art, art, art,

He must keep the girls away from his heart, heart, heart."

And Dicky, who fancied he had been through every trouble that a man is permitted to know, had to laugh and agree; with the last line of his balanced Bank-book jingling in his head day and night.

But he had one more sorrow to digest before the end. There arrived a letter from the little wife— the natural sequence of the others if Dicky had only known it—and the burden of that letter was "gone with a handsomer man than you." It was a rather curious production, without stops, something like this:—"She was not going to wait forever and the baby was dead and Dicky was only a boy and he would never set eyes on her again and why hadn't he waved his handkerchief to her when he left Gravesend and God was her judge she was a wicked woman but Dicky was worse enjoying himself in India and this other man loved the ground she trod on and would Dicky ever forgive her for she would never forgive Dicky; and there was no address to write to."

Instead of thanking his lucky stars that he was free, Dicky discovered exactly how an injured husband feels—again, not at all the knowledge to which a boy is entitled—for his mind went back to his wife as he remembered her in the thirty-shilling "suite" in Montpelier Square, when the dawn of his last morning in England was breaking, and she was crying in the bed. Whereat he rolled about on his bed and bit his fingers. He never stopped to think whether, if he had met Mrs. Hatt after those two years, he would have discovered that he and she had grown quite different and new persons. This, theoretically, he ought to have done. He spent the night after the English Mail came in rather severe pain.

Next morning, Dicky Hatt felt disinclined to work. He argued that he had missed the pleasure of youth. He was tired, and he had tasted all the sorrow in life before three-and-twenty. His Honor was gone—that was the man; and now he, too, would go to the Devil—that was the boy in him. So he put his head down on the green oil-cloth table-cover, and wept before resigning his post, and all it offered.

But the reward of his services came. He was given three days to reconsider himself, and the

Head of the establishment, after some telegraphings, said that it was a most unusual step, but, in view of the ability that Mr. Hatt had displayed at such and such a time, at such and such junctures, he was in a position to offer him an infinitely superior post—first on probation, and later, in the natural course of things, on confirmation. "And how much does the post carry?" said Dicky. "Six hundred and fifty rupees," said the Head slowly, expecting to see the young man sink with gratitude and joy.

And it came then! The seven hundred rupee passage, and enough to have saved the wife, and the little son, and to have allowed of assured and open marriage, came then. Dicky burst into a roar of laughter—laughter he could not check—nasty, jangling merriment that seemed as if it would go on forever. When he had recovered himself he said, quite seriously:—"I'm tired of work. I'm an old man now. It's about time I retired. And I will."

"The boy's mad!" said the Head.

I think he was right; but Dicky Hatt never reappeared to settle the question.

PIG.

Go, stalk the red deer o'er the heather

 Ride, follow the fox if you can!

But, for pleasure and profit together,

 Allow me the hunting of Man,—

The chase of the Human, the search for the Soul

 To its ruin,—the hunting of Man.

 —The Old Shikarri.

I believe the difference began in the matter of a horse, with a twist in his temper, whom Pinecoffin sold to Nafferton and by whom Nafferton was nearly slain. There may have been other causes of offence; the horse was the official stalking-horse. Nafferton was very angry; but Pinecoffin laughed and said that he had never guaranteed the beast's manners. Nafferton laughed, too, though he vowed that he would write off his fall against Pinecoffin if he waited five years. Now, a Dalesman from beyond Skipton will forgive an injury when the Strid lets a man live; but a South Devon man is as soft as a Dartmoor bog. You can see from their names that Nafferton had the race-advantage of Pinecoffin. He was a peculiar man, and his notions of humor were cruel. He taught me a new and fascinating form of shikar. He hounded Pinecoffin from Mithankot to Jagadri, and from Gurgaon to Abbottabad up and across the Punjab, a large province and in places remarkably dry. He said that he had no intention of allowing Assistant Commissioners to "sell him pups," in the shape of ramping, screaming countrybreds, without making their lives a burden to them.

Most Assistant Commissioners develop a bent for some special work after their first hot weather in the country. The boys with digestions hope to write their names large on the Frontier and struggle for dreary places like Bannu and Kohat. The bilious ones climb into the Secretariat. Which is very bad for the liver.

Others are bitten with a mania for District work, Ghuznivide coins or Persian poetry; while some, who come of farmers' stock, find that the smell of the Earth after the Rains gets into their blood, and calls them to "develop the resources of the Province." These men are enthusiasts. Pinecoffin belonged to their class. He knew a great many facts bearing on the cost of bullocks and temporary wells, and opium-scrapers, and what happens if you burn too much rubbish on a field, in the hope of enriching used-up soil. All the Pinecoffins come of a landholding breed, and so the land only took back her own again. Unfortunately—most unfortunately for Pinecoffin— he was a Civilian, as well as a farmer. Nafferton watched him, and thought about the horse. Nafferton said:—"See me chase that boy till he drops!" I said:—"You can't get your knife into an Assistant Commissioner." Nafferton told me that I did not understand the administration of the Province.

Our Government is rather peculiar. It gushes on the agricultural and general information side, and will supply a moderately respectable man with all sorts of "economic statistics," if he speaks to it prettily. For instance, you are interested in gold-washing in the sands of the Sutlej. You pull the string, and find that it wakes up half a dozen Departments, and finally communicates, say, with a friend of yours in the Telegraph, who once wrote some notes on the customs of the gold-washers when he was on construction-work in their part of the Empire. He may or may

not be pleased at being ordered to write out everything he knows for your benefit. This depends on his temperament. The bigger man you are, the more information and the greater trouble can you raise.

Nafferton was not a big man; but he had the reputation of being very "earnest." An "earnest" man can do much with a Government. There was an earnest man who once nearly wrecked... but all India knows THAT story. I am not sure what real "earnestness" is. A very fair imitation can be manufactured by neglecting to dress decently, by mooning about in a dreamy, misty sort of way, by taking office-work home after staying in office till seven, and by receiving crowds of native gentlemen on Sundays. That is one sort of "earnestness."

Nafferton cast about for a peg whereon to hang his earnestness, and for a string that would communicate with Pinecoffin. He found both.

They were Pig. Nafferton became an earnest inquirer after Pig. He informed the Government that he had a scheme whereby a very large percentage of the British Army in India could be fed, at a very large saving, on Pig. Then he hinted that Pinecoffin might supply him with the "varied information necessary to the proper inception of the scheme." So the Government wrote on the back of the letter:—"Instruct Mr. Pinecoffin to furnish Mr. Nafferton with any information in his power." Government is very prone to writing things on the backs of letters which, later, lead to trouble and confusion.

Nafferton had not the faintest interest in Pig, but he knew that Pinecoffin would flounce into the trap. Pinecoffin was delighted at being consulted about Pig. The Indian Pig is not exactly an important factor in agricultural life; but Nafferton explained to Pinecoffin that there was room for improvement, and corresponded direct with that young man.

You may think that there is not much to be evolved from Pig. It all depends how you set to work. Pinecoffin being a Civilian and wishing to do things thoroughly, began with an essay on the Primitive Pig, the Mythology of the Pig, and the Dravidian Pig.

Nafferton filed that information—twenty-seven foolscap sheets—and wanted to know about the distribution of the Pig in the Punjab, and how it stood the Plains in the hot weather. From this point onwards, remember that I am giving you only the barest outlines of the affair—the guy-ropes, as it were, of the web that Nafferton spun round Pinecoffin.

Pinecoffin made a colored Pig-population map, and collected observations on the comparative longevity of the Pig (a) in the sub-montane tracts of the Himalayas, and (b) in the Rechna Doab.

Nafferton filed that, and asked what sort of people looked after Pig. This started an ethnological excursus on swineherds, and drew from Pinecoffin long tables showing the proportion per thousand of the caste in the Derajat. Nafferton filed that bundle, and explained that the figures which he wanted referred to the Cis-Sutlej states, where he understood that Pigs were very fine and large, and where he proposed to start a Piggery. By this time, Government had quite forgotten their instructions to Mr. Pinecoffin.

They were like the gentlemen, in Keats' poem, who turned well-oiled wheels to skin other people. But Pinecoffin was just entering into the spirit of the Pig-hunt, as Nafferton well knew he would do. He had a fair amount of work of his own to clear away; but he sat up of nights reducing Pig to five places of decimals for the honor of his Service. He was not going to appear ignorant of so easy a subject as Pig.

Then Government sent him on special duty to Kohat, to "inquire into" the big-seven-foot, iron-shod spades of that District. People had been killing each other with those peaceful tools;

and Government wished to know "whether a modified form of agricultural implement could not, tentatively and as a temporary measure, be introduced among the agricultural population without needlessly or unduly exasperating the existing religious sentiments of the peasantry."

Between those spades and Nafferton's Pig, Pinecoffin was rather heavily burdened.

Nafferton now began to take up "(a) The food-supply of the indigenous Pig,

with a view to the improvement of its capacities as a flesh-former.

(b) The acclimatization of the exotic Pig, maintaining its distinctive

peculiarities." Pinecoffin replied exhaustively that the exotic Pig

would become merged in the indigenous type; and quoted horse-breeding

statistics to prove this.

The side-issue was debated, at great length on Pinecoffin's side, till Nafferton owned that he had been in the wrong, and moved the previous question. When Pinecoffin had quite written himself out about flesh-formers, and fibrins, and glucose and the nitrogenous constituents of maize and lucerne, Nafferton raised the question of expense. By this time Pinecoffin, who had been transferred from Kohat, had developed a Pig theory of his own, which he stated in thirty-three folio pages—all carefully filed by Nafferton. Who asked for more.

These things took ten months, and Pinecoffin's interest in the potential Piggery seemed to die down after he had stated his own views. But Nafferton bombarded him with letters on "the Imperial aspect of the scheme, as tending to officialize the sale of pork, and thereby calculated to give offence to the Mahomedan population of Upper India." He guessed that Pinecoffin would want some broad, free-hand work after his niggling, stippling, decimal details.

Pinecoffin handled the latest development of the case in masterly style, and proved that no "popular ebullition of excitement was to be apprehended." Nafferton said that there was nothing like Civilian insight in matters of this kind, and lured him up a bye-path—"the possible profits to accrue to the Government from the sale of hog-bristles." There is an extensive literature of hog-bristles, and the shoe, brush, and colorman's trades recognize more varieties of bristles than you would think possible. After Pinecoffin had wondered a little at Nafferton's rage for information, he sent back a monograph, fifty-one pages, on "Products of the Pig." This led him, under Nafferton's tender handling, straight to the Cawnpore factories, the trade in hog-skin for saddles—and thence to the tanners. Pinecoffin wrote that pomegranate-seed was the best cure for hog-skin, and suggested—for the past fourteen months had wearied him—that Nafferton should "raise his pigs before he tanned them."

Nafferton went back to the second section of his fifth question.

How could the exotic Pig be brought to give as much pork as it did in the West and yet "assume the essentially hirsute characteristics of its oriental congener?" Pinecoffin felt dazed, for he had forgotten what he had written sixteen month's before, and fancied that he was about to reopen the entire question. He was too far involved in the hideous tangle to retreat, and, in a weak moment, he wrote:—"Consult my first letter." Which related to the Dravidian Pig. As a matter of fact, Pinecoffin had still to reach the acclimatization stage; having gone off on a side-issue on the merging of types.

THEN Nafferton really unmasked his batteries! He complained to the Government, in stately language, of "the paucity of help accorded to me in my earnest attempts to start a potentially

remunerative industry, and the flippancy with which my requests for information are treated by a gentleman whose pseudo-scholarly attainments should at lest have taught him the primary differences between the Dravidian and the Berkshire variety of the genus Sus. If I am to understand that the letter to which he refers me contains his serious views on the acclimatization of a valuable, though possibly uncleanly, animal, I am reluctantly compelled to believe," etc., etc.

There was a new man at the head of the Department of Castigation.

The wretched Pinecoffin was told that the Service was made for the Country, and not the Country for the Service, and that he had better begin to supply information about Pigs.

Pinecoffin answered insanely that he had written everything that could be written about Pig, and that some furlough was due to him.

Nafferton got a copy of that letter, and sent it, with the essay on the Dravidian Pig, to a down-country paper, which printed both in full. The essay was rather highflown; but if the Editor had seen the stacks of paper, in Pinecoffin's handwriting, on Nafferton's table, he would not have been so sarcastic about the "nebulous discursiveness and blatant self-sufficiency of the modern Competition-wallah, and his utter inability to grasp the practical issues of a practical question." Many friends cut out these remarks and sent them to Pinecoffin.

I have already stated that Pinecoffin came of a soft stock. This last stroke frightened and shook him. He could not understand it; but he felt he had been, somehow, shamelessly betrayed by Nafferton.

He realized that he had wrapped himself up in the Pigskin without need, and that he could not well set himself right with his Government. All his acquaintances asked after his "nebulous discursiveness" or his "blatant self-sufficiency," and this made him miserable.

He took a train and went to Nafferton, whom he had not seen since the Pig business began. He also took the cutting from the paper, and blustered feebly and called Nafferton names, and then died down to a watery, weak protest of the "I-say-it's-too-bad-you-know" order.

Nafferton was very sympathetic.

"I'm afraid I've given you a good deal of trouble, haven't I?" said he.

"Trouble!" whimpered Pinecoffin; "I don't mind the trouble so much, though that was bad enough; but what I resent is this showing up in print. It will stick to me like a burr all through my service. And I DID do my best for your interminable swine. It's too bad of you, on my soul it is!"

"I don't know," said Nafferton; "have you ever been stuck with a horse? It isn't the money I mind, though that is bad enough; but what I resent is the chaff that follows, especially from the boy who stuck me. But I think we'll cry quite now."

Pinecoffin found nothing to say save bad words; and Nafferton smiled ever so sweetly, and asked him to dinner.

THE ROUT OF THE WHITE HUSSARS.

It was not in the open fight

 We threw away the sword,

But in the lonely watching

 In the darkness by the ford.

The waters lapped, the night-wind blew,

Full-armed the Fear was born and grew,

And we were flying ere we knew

 From panic in the night.

 —Beoni Bar.

Some people hold that an English Cavalry regiment cannot run. This is a mistake. I have seen four hundred and thirty-seven sabres flying over the face of the country in abject terror—have seen the best Regiment that ever drew bridle, wiped off the Army List for the space of two hours. If you repeat this tale to the White Hussars they will, in all probability, treat you severely. They are not proud of the incident.

You may know the White Hussars by their "side," which is greater than that of all the Cavalry Regiments on the roster. If this is not a sufficient mark, you may know them by their old brandy. It has been sixty years in the Mess and is worth going far to taste.

Ask for the "McGaire" old brandy, and see that you get it. If the Mess Sergeant thinks that you are uneducated, and that the genuine article will be lost on you, he will treat you accordingly. He is a good man. But, when you are at Mess, you must never talk to your hosts about forced marches or long-distance rides. The Mess are very sensitive; and, if they think that you are laughing at them, will tell you so.

As the White Hussars say, it was all the Colonel's fault. He was a new man, and he ought never to have taken the Command. He said that the Regiment was not smart enough. This to the White Hussars, who knew they could walk round any Horse and through any Guns, and over any Foot on the face of the earth! That insult was the first cause of offence.

Then the Colonel cast the Drum-Horse—the Drum-Horse of the White Hussars! Perhaps you do not see what an unspeakable crime he had committed. I will try to make it clear. The soul of the Regiment lives in the Drum-Horse, who carries the silver kettle-drums. He is nearly always a big piebald Waler. That is a point of honor; and a Regiment will spend anything you please on a piebald. He is beyond the ordinary laws of casting. His work is very light, and he only manoeuvres at a foot-pace. Wherefore, so long as he can step out and look handsome, his well-being is assured. He knows more about the Regiment than the Adjutant, and could not make a mistake if he tried.

The Drum-Horse of the White Hussars was only eighteen years old, and perfectly equal to his duties. He had at least six years' more work in him, and carried himself with all the pomp and

dignity of a Drum-Major of the Guards. The Regiment had paid Rs. 1,200 for him.

But the Colonel said that he must go, and he was cast in due form and replaced by a washy, bay beast as ugly as a mule, with a ewe-neck, rat-tail, and cow-hocks. The Drummer detested that animal, and the best of the Band-horses put back their ears and showed the whites of their eyes at the very sight of him. They knew him for an upstart and no gentleman. I fancy that the Colonel's ideas of smartness extended to the Band, and that he wanted to make it take part in the regular parade movements. A Cavalry Band is a sacred thing. It only turns out for Commanding Officers' parades, and the Band Master is one degree more important than the Colonel. He is a High Priest and the "Keel Row" is his holy song. The "Keel Row" is the Cavalry Trot; and the man who has never heard that tune rising, high and shrill, above the rattle of the Regiment going past the saluting-base, has something yet to hear and understand.

When the Colonel cast the Drum-horse of the White Hussars, there was nearly a mutiny.

The officers were angry, the Regiment were furious, and the Bandsman swore—like troopers. The Drum-Horse was going to be put up to auction—public auction—to be bought, perhaps, by a Parsee and put into a cart! It was worse than exposing the inner life of the Regiment to the whole world, or selling the Mess Plate to a Jew—a black Jew.

The Colonel was a mean man and a bully. He knew what the Regiment thought about his action; and, when the troopers offered to buy the Drum-Horse, he said that their offer was mutinous and forbidden by the Regulations.

But one of the Subalterns—Hogan-Yale, an Irishman—bought the Drum-Horse for Rs. 160 at the sale; and the Colonel was wroth. Yale professed repentance—he was unnaturally submissive—and said that, as he had only made the purchase to save the horse from possible ill-treatment and starvation, he would now shoot him and end the business. This appeared to soothe the Colonel, for he wanted the Drum-Horse disposed of. He felt that he had made a mistake, and could not of course acknowledge it. Meantime, the presence of the Drum-Horse was an annoyance to him.

Yale took to himself a glass of the old brandy, three cheroots, and his friend, Martyn; and they all left the Mess together. Yale and Martyn conferred for two hours in Yale's quarters; but only the bull-terrier who keeps watch over Yale's boot-trees knows what they said. A horse, hooded and sheeted to his ears, left Yale's stables and was taken, very unwillingly, into the Civil Lines. Yale's groom went with him. Two men broke into the Regimental Theatre and took several paint-pots and some large scenery brushes. Then night fell over the Cantonments, and there was a noise as of a horse kicking his loose-box to pieces in Yale's stables. Yale had a big, old, white Waler trap-horse.

The next day was a Thursday, and the men, hearing that Yale was going to shoot the Drum-Horse in the evening, determined to give the beast a regular regimental funeral—a finer one than they would have given the Colonel had he died just then. They got a bullock-cart and some sacking, and mounds and mounds of roses, and the body, under sacking, was carried out to the place where the anthrax cases were cremated; two-thirds of the Regiment followed. There was no Band, but they all sang "The Place where the old Horse died" as something respectful and appropriate to the occasion. When the corpse was dumped into the grave and the men began throwing down armfuls of roses to cover it, the Farrier-Sergeant ripped out an oath and said aloud:—"Why, it ain't the Drum-Horse any more than it's me!" The Troop-Sergeant-Majors asked him whether he had left his head in the Canteen. The Farrier-Sergeant said that he knew the Drum-Horse's feet as well as he knew his own; but he was silenced when he saw the regimental number burnt in on the poor stiff, upturned near-fore.

Thus was the Drum-Horse of the White Hussars buried; the Farrier-Sergeant grumbling. The

sacking that covered the corpse was smeared in places with black paint; and the Farrier-Sergeant drew attention to this fact. But the Troop-Sergeant-Major of E Troop kicked him severely on the shin, and told him that he was undoubtedly drunk.

On the Monday following the burial, the Colonel sought revenge on the White Hussars. Unfortunately, being at that time temporarily in Command of the Station, he ordered a Brigade field-day. He said that he wished to make the regiment "sweat for their damned insolence," and he carried out his notion thoroughly. That Monday was one of the hardest days in the memory of the White Hussars.

They were thrown against a skeleton-enemy, and pushed forward, and withdrawn, and dismounted, and "scientifically handled" in every possible fashion over dusty country, till they sweated profusely.

Their only amusement came late in the day, when they fell upon the battery of Horse Artillery and chased it for two mile's. This was a personal question, and most of the troopers had money on the event; the Gunners saying openly that they had the legs of the White Hussars. They were wrong. A march-past concluded the campaign, and when the Regiment got back to their Lines, the men were coated with dirt from spur to chin-strap.

The White Hussars have one great and peculiar privilege. They won it at Fontenoy, I think.

Many Regiments possess special rights, such as wearing collars with undress uniform, or a bow of ribbon between the shoulders, or red and white roses in their helmets on certain days of the year. Some rights are connected with regimental saints, and some with regimental successes. All are valued highly; but none so highly as the right of the White Hussars to have the Band playing when their horses are being watered in the Lines. Only one tune is played, and that tune never varies. I don't know its real name, but the White Hussars call it:—"Take me to London again." It sounds very pretty. The Regiment would sooner be struck off the roster than forego their distinction.

After the "dismiss" was sounded, the officers rode off home to prepare for stables; and the men filed into the lines, riding easy.

That is to say, they opened their tight buttons, shifted their helmets, and began to joke or to swear as the humor took them; the more careful slipping off and easing girths and curbs. A good trooper values his mount exactly as much as he values himself, and believes, or should believe, that the two together are irresistible where women or men, girls or guns, are concerned.

Then the Orderly-Officer gave the order:—"Water horses," and the Regiment loafed off to the squadron-troughs, which were in rear of the stables and between these and the barracks. There were four huge troughs, one for each squadron, arranged en echelon, so that the whole Regiment could water in ten minutes if it liked. But it lingered for seventeen, as a rule, while the Band played.

The band struck up as the squadrons filed off the troughs and the men slipped their feet out of the stirrups and chaffed each other.

The sun was just setting in a big, hot bed of red cloud, and the road to the Civil Lines seemed to run straight into the sun's eye.

There was a little dot on the road. It grew and grew till it showed as a horse, with a sort of gridiron thing on his back. The red cloud glared through the bars of the gridiron. Some of the troopers shaded their eyes with their hands and said:—"What the mischief as that there 'orse got on 'im!"

In another minute they heard a neigh that every soul—horse and man—in the Regiment knew, and saw, heading straight towards the Band, the dead Drum-Horse of the White Hussars!

On his withers banged and bumped the kettle-drums draped in crape, and on his back, very stiff and soldierly, sat a bare-headed skeleton.

The band stopped playing, and, for a moment, there was a hush.

Then some one in E troop—men said it was the Troop-Sergeant-Major—swung his horse round and yelled. No one can account exactly for what happened afterwards; but it seems that, at least, one man in each troop set an example of panic, and the rest followed like sheep. The horses that had barely put their muzzles into the trough's reared and capered; but, as soon as the Band broke, which it did when the ghost of the Drum-Horse was about a furlong distant, all hooves followed suit, and the clatter of the stampede—quite different from the orderly throb and roar of a movement on parade, or the rough horse-play of watering in camp—made them only more terrified. They felt that the men on their backs were afraid of something. When horses once know THAT, all is over except the butchery.

Troop after troop turned from the troughs and ran—anywhere, and everywhere—like spilt quicksilver. It was a most extraordinary spectacle, for men and horses were in all stages of easiness, and the carbine-buckets flopping against their sides urged the horses on. Men were shouting and cursing, and trying to pull clear of the Band which was being chased by the Drum-Horse whose rider had fallen forward and seemed to be spurring for a wager.

The Colonel had gone over to the Mess for a drink. Most of the officers were with him, and the Subaltern of the Day was preparing to go down to the lines, and receive the watering reports from the Troop-Sergeant Majors. When "Take me to London again" stopped, after twenty bars, every one in the Mess said:—"What on earth has happened?" A minute later, they heard unmilitary noises, and saw, far across the plain, the White Hussars scattered, and broken, and flying.

The Colonel was speechless with rage, for he thought that the Regiment had risen against him or was unanimously drunk. The Band, a disorganized mob, tore past, and at its heels labored the Drum-Horse—the dead and buried Drum-Horse—with the jolting, clattering skeleton. Hogan-Yale whispered softly to Martyn:—"No wire will stand that treatment," and the Band, which had doubled like a hare, came back again. But the rest of the Regiment was gone, was rioting all over the Province, for the dusk had shut in and each man was howling to his neighbor that the Drum-Horse was on his flank.

Troop-Horses are far too tenderly treated as a rule. They can, on emergencies, do a great deal, even with seventeen stone on their backs. As the troopers found out.

How long this panic lasted I cannot say. I believe that when the moon rose the men saw they had nothing to fear, and, by twos and threes and half-troops, crept back into Cantonments very much ashamed of themselves. Meantime, the Drum-Horse, disgusted at his treatment by old friends, pulled up, wheeled round, and trotted up to the Mess verandah-steps for bread. No one liked to run; but no one cared to go forward till the Colonel made a movement and laid hold of the skeleton's foot. The Band had halted some distance away, and now came back slowly. The Colonel called it, individually and collectively, every evil name that occurred to him at the time; for he had set his hand on the bosom of the Drum-Horse and found flesh and blood. Then he beat the kettle-drums with his clenched fist, and discovered that they were but made of silvered paper and bamboo. Next, still swearing, he tried to drag the skeleton out of the saddle, but found that it had been wired into the cantle. The sight of the Colonel, with his arms round the skeleton's pelvis and his knee in the old Drum-Horse's stomach, was striking. Not to say

amusing. He worried the thing off in a minute or two, and threw it down on the ground, saying to the Band:—"Here, you curs, that's what you're afraid of." The skeleton did not look pretty in the twilight. The Band-Sergeant seemed to recognize it, for he began to chuckle and choke. "Shall I take it away, sir?" said the Band-Sergeant. "Yes," said the Colonel, "take it to Hell, and ride there yourselves!"

The Band-Sergeant saluted, hoisted the skeleton across his saddle-bow, and led off to the stables. Then the Colonel began to make inquiries for the rest of the Regiment, and the language he used was wonderful. He would disband the Regiment—he would court-martial every soul in it—he would not command such a set of rabble, and so on, and so on. As the men dropped in, his language grew wilder, until at last it exceeded the utmost limits of free speech allowed even to a Colonel of Horse.

Martyn took Hogan-Yale aside and suggested compulsory retirement from the service as a necessity when all was discovered. Martyn was the weaker man of the two, Hogan-Yale put up his eyebrows and remarked, firstly, that he was the son of a Lord, and secondly, that he was as innocent as the babe unborn of the theatrical resurrection of the Drum-Horse.

"My instructions," said Yale, with a singularly sweet smile, "were that the Drum-Horse should be sent back as impressively as possible. I ask you, AM I responsible if a mule-headed friend sends him back in such a manner as to disturb the peace of mind of a regiment of Her Majesty's Cavalry?"

Martyn said:—"you are a great man and will in time become a General; but I'd give my chance of a troop to be safe out of this affair."

Providence saved Martyn and Hogan-Yale. The Second-in-Command led the Colonel away to the little curtained alcove wherein the subalterns of the white Hussars were accustomed to play poker of nights; and there, after many oaths on the Colonel's part, they talked together in low tones. I fancy that the Second-in-Command must have represented the scare as the work of some trooper whom it would be hopeless to detect; and I know that he dwelt upon the sin and the shame of making a public laughingstock of the scare.

"They will call us," said the Second-in-Command, who had really a fine imagination, "they will call us the 'Fly-by-Nights'; they will call us the 'Ghost Hunters'; they will nickname us from one end of the Army list to the other. All the explanations in the world won't make outsiders understand that the officers were away when the panic began. For the honor of the Regiment and for your own sake keep this thing quiet."

The Colonel was so exhausted with anger that soothing him down was not so difficult as might be imagined. He was made to see, gently and by degrees, that it was obviously impossible to court-martial the whole Regiment, and equally impossible to proceed against any subaltern who, in his belief, had any concern in the hoax.

"But the beast's alive! He's never been shot at all!" shouted the Colonel. "It's flat, flagrant disobedience! I've known a man broke for less, d——d sight less. They're mocking me, I tell you, Mutman! They're mocking me!"

Once more, the Second-in-Command set himself to sooth the Colonel, and wrestled with him for half-an-hour. At the end of that time, the Regimental Sergeant-Major reported himself. The situation was rather novel tell to him; but he was not a man to be put out by circumstances. He saluted and said: "Regiment all come back, Sir." Then, to propitiate the Colonel:—"An' none of the horses any the worse, Sir."

The Colonel only snorted and answered:—"You'd better tuck the men into their cots, then, and see that they don't wake up and cry in the night." The Sergeant withdrew.

His little stroke of humor pleased the Colonel, and, further, he felt slightly ashamed of the language he had been using. The Second-in-Command worried him again, and the two sat talking far into the night.

Next day but one, there was a Commanding Officer's parade, and the Colonel harangued the White Hussars vigorously. The pith of his speech was that, since the Drum-Horse in his old age had proved himself capable of cutting up the Whole Regiment, he should return to his post of pride at the head of the band, BUT the Regiment were a set of ruffians with bad consciences.

The White Hussars shouted, and threw everything movable about them into the air, and when the parade was over, they cheered the Colonel till they couldn't speak. No cheers were put up for Lieutenant Hogan-Yale, who smiled very sweetly in the background.

Said the Second-in-Command to the Colonel, unofficially:—"These little things ensure popularity, and do not the least affect discipline."

"But I went back on my word," said the Colonel.

"Never mind," said the Second-in-Command. "The White Hussars will follow you anywhere from today. Regiments are just like women. They will do anything for trinketry."

A week later, Hogan-Yale received an extraordinary letter from some one who signed himself "Secretary Charity and Zeal, 3709, E. C.," and asked for "the return of our skeleton which we have reason to believe is in your possession."

"Who the deuce is this lunatic who trades in bones?" said Hogan-Yale.

"Beg your pardon, Sir," said the Band-Sergeant, "but the skeleton is with me, an' I'll return it if you'll pay the carriage into the Civil Lines. There's a coffin with it, Sir."

Hogan-Yale smiled and handed two rupees to the Band-Sergeant, saying:—"Write the date on the skull, will you?"

If you doubt this story, and know where to go, you can see the date on the skeleton. But don't mention the matter to the White Hussars.

I happen to know something about it, because I prepared the Drum-Horse for his resurrection. He did not take kindly to the skeleton at all.

THE BRONCKHORST DIVORCE-CASE.

In the daytime, when she moved about me,

In the night, when she was sleeping at my side,—

I was wearied, I was wearied of her presence.

Day by day and night by night I grew to hate her—

Would to God that she or I had died!

 —Confessions.

There was a man called Bronckhorst—a three-cornered, middle-aged man in the Army—gray as a badger, and, some people said, with a touch of country-blood in him. That, however, cannot be proved.

Mrs. Bronckhorst was not exactly young, though fifteen years younger than her husband. She was a large, pale, quiet woman, with heavy eyelids, over weak eyes, and hair that turned red or yellow as the lights fell on it.

Bronckhorst was not nice in any way. He had no respect for the pretty public and private lies that make life a little less nasty than it is. His manner towards his wife was coarse. There are many things—including actual assault with the clenched fist—that a wife will endure; but seldom a wife can bear—as Mrs. Bronckhorst bore—with a long course of brutal, hard chaff, making light of her weaknesses, her headaches, her small fits of gaiety, her dresses, her queer little attempts to make herself attractive to her husband when she knows that she is not what she has been, and—worst of all—the love that she spends on her children. That particular sort of heavy-handed jest was specially dear to Bronckhorst. I suppose that he had first slipped into it, meaning no harm, in the honeymoon, when folk find their ordinary stock of endearments run short, and so go to the other extreme to express their feelings. A similar impulse makes a man say:—"Hutt, you old beast!" when a favorite horse nuzzles his coat-front. Unluckily, when the reaction of marriage sets in, the form of speech remains, and, the tenderness having died out, hurts the wife more than she cares to say. But Mrs. Bronckhorst was devoted to her "Teddy," as she called him.

Perhaps that was why he objected to her. Perhaps—this is only a theory to account for his infamous behavior later on—he gave way to the queer savage feeling that sometimes takes by the throat a husband twenty years' married, when he sees, across the table, the same face of his wedded wife, and knows that, as he has sat facing it, so must he continue to sit until day of its death or his own.

Most men and all women know the spasm. It only lasts for three breaths as a rule, must be a "throw-back" to times when men and women were rather worse than they are now, and is too unpleasant to be discussed.

Dinner at the Bronckhorst's was an infliction few men cared to undergo. Bronckhorst took a pleasure in saying things that made his wife wince. When their little boy came in at dessert, Bronckhorst used to give him half a glass of wine, and naturally enough, the poor little mite got first riotous, next miserable, and was removed screaming. Bronckhorst asked if that was the

way Teddy usually behaved, and whether Mrs. Bronckhorst could not spare some of her time to teach the "little beggar decency." Mrs. Bronckhorst, who loved the boy more than her own life, tried not to cry—her spirit seemed to have been broken by her marriage. Lastly, Bronckhorst used to say:—"There! That'll do, that'll do. For God's sake try to behave like a rational woman. Go into the drawing-room." Mrs. Bronckhorst would go, trying to carry it all off with a smile; and the guest of the evening would feel angry and uncomfortable.

After three years of this cheerful life—for Mrs. Bronckhorst had no woman-friends to talk to—the Station was startled by the news that Bronckhorst had instituted proceedings ON THE CRIMINAL COUNT, against a man called Biel, who certainly had been rather attentive to Mrs. Bronckhorst whenever she had appeared in public. The utter want of reserve with which Bronckhorst treated his own dishonor helped us to know that the evidence against Biel would be entirely circumstantial and native. There were no letters; but Bronckhorst said openly that he would rack Heaven and Earth until he saw Biel superintending the manufacture of carpets in the Central Jail. Mrs. Bronckhorst kept entirely to her house, and let charitable folks say what they pleased. Opinions were divided. Some two-thirds of the Station jumped at once to the conclusion that Biel was guilty; but a dozen men who knew and liked him held by him. Biel was furious and surprised. He denied the whole thing, and vowed that he would thrash Bronckhorst within an inch of his life. No jury, we knew, could convict a man on the criminal count on native evidence in a land where you can buy a murder-charge, including the corpse, all complete for fifty-four rupees; but Biel did not care to scrape through by the benefit of a doubt. He wanted the whole thing cleared: but as he said one night:—"He can prove anything with servants' evidence, and I've only my bare word." This was about a month before the case came on; and beyond agreeing with Biel, we could do little. All that we could be sure of was that the native evidence would be bad enough to blast Biel's character for the rest of his service; for when a native begins perjury he perjures himself thoroughly. He does not boggle over details.

Some genius at the end of the table whereat the affair was being talked over, said:—"Look here! I don't believe lawyers are any good. Get a man to wire to Strickland, and beg him to come down and pull us through."

Strickland was about a hundred and eighty miles up the line. He had not long been married to Miss Youghal, but he scented in the telegram a chance of return to the old detective work that his soul lusted after, and next night he came in and heard our story. He finished his pipe and said oracularly:—"We must get at the evidence. Oorya bearer, Mussalman khit and methraniayah, I suppose, are the pillars of the charge. I am on in this piece; but I'm afraid I'm getting rusty in my talk."

He rose and went into Biel's bedroom where his trunk had been put, and shut the door. An hour later, we heard him say:—"I hadn't the heart to part with my old makeups when I married. Will this do?" There was a lothely faquir salaaming in the doorway.

"Now lend me fifty rupees," said Strickland, "and give me your Words of Honor that you won't tell my Wife."

He got all that he asked for, and left the house while the table drank his health. What he did only he himself knows. A faquir hung about Bronckhorst's compound for twelve days. Then a mehter appeared, and when Biel heard of HIM, he said that Strickland was an angel full-fledged. Whether the mehter made love to Janki, Mrs. Bronckhorst's ayah, is a question which concerns Strickland exclusively.

He came back at the end of three weeks, and said quietly:—"You spoke the truth, Biel. The whole business is put up from beginning to end. Jove! It almost astonishes ME! That Bronckhorst-beast isn't fit to live."

There was uproar and shouting, and Biel said:—"How are you going to prove it? You can't say that you've been trespassing on Bronckhorst's compound in disguise!"

"No," said Strickland. "Tell your lawyer-fool, whoever he is, to get up something strong about 'inherent improbabilities' and 'discrepancies of evidence.' He won't have to speak, but it will make him happy. I'M going to run this business."

Biel held his tongue, and the other men waited to see what would happen. They trusted Strickland as men trust quiet men. When the case came off the Court was crowded. Strickland hung about in the verandah of the Court, till he met the Mohammedan khitmatgar. Then he murmured a faquir's blessing in his ear, and asked him how his second wife did. The man spun round, and, as he looked into the eyes of "Estreeken Sahib," his jaw dropped. You must remember that before Strickland was married, he was, as I have told you already, a power among natives. Strickland whispered a rather coarse vernacular proverb to the effect that he was abreast of all that was going on, and went into the Court armed with a gut trainer's-whip.

The Mohammedan was the first witness and Strickland beamed upon him from the back of the Court. The man moistened his lips with his tongue and, in his abject fear of "Estreeken Sahib" the faquir, went back on every detail of his evidence—said he was a poor man and God was his witness that he had forgotten every thing that Bronckhorst Sahib had told him to say. Between his terror of Strickland, the Judge, and Bronckhorst he collapsed, weeping.

Then began the panic among the witnesses. Janki, the ayah, leering chastely behind her veil, turned gray, and the bearer left the Court. He said that his Mamma was dying and that it was not wholesome for any man to lie unthriftily in the presence of "Estreeken Sahib."

Biel said politely to Bronckhorst:—"Your witnesses don't seem to work. Haven't you any forged letters to produce?" But Bronckhorst was swaying to and fro in his chair, and there was a dead pause after Biel had been called to order.

Bronckhorst's Counsel saw the look on his client's face, and without more ado, pitched his papers on the little green baize table, and mumbled something about having been misinformed. The whole Court applauded wildly, like soldiers at a theatre, and the Judge began to say what he thought..........

Biel came out of the place, and Strickland dropped a gut trainer's-whip in the verandah. Ten minutes later, Biel was cutting Bronckhorst into ribbons behind the old Court cells, quietly and without scandal. What was left of Bronckhorst was sent home in a carriage; and his wife wept over it and nursed it into a man again.

Later on, after Biel had managed to hush up the counter-charge against Bronckhorst of fabricating false evidence, Mrs. Bronckhorst, with her faint watery smile, said that there had been a mistake, but it wasn't her Teddy's fault altogether. She would wait till her Teddy came back to her. Perhaps he had grown tired of her, or she had tried his patience, and perhaps we wouldn't cut her any more, and perhaps the mothers would let their children play with "little Teddy" again. He was so lonely. Then the Station invited Mrs. Bronckhorst everywhere, until Bronckhorst was fit to appear in public, when he went Home and took his wife with him. According to the latest advices, her Teddy did "come back to her," and they are moderately happy. Though, of course, he can never forgive her the thrashing that she was the indirect means of getting for him..

What Biel wants to know is:—"Why didn't I press home the charge against the Bronckhorst-brute, and have him run in?"

What Mrs. Strickland wants to know is:—"How DID my husband bring such a lovely, lovely Waler from your Station? I know ALL his money-affairs; and I'm CERTAIN he didn't BUY it."

"What I want to know is:—How do women like Mrs. Bronckhorst come to marry men like Bronckhorst?"

And my conundrum is the most unanswerable of the three.

VENUS ANNODOMINI.

And the years went on as the years must do;

But our great Diana was always new—

Fresh, and blooming, and blonde, and fair,

With azure eyes and with aureate hair;

And all the folk, as they came or went,

Offered her praise to her heart's content.

—Diana of Ephesus.

She had nothing to do with Number Eighteen in the Braccio Nuovo of the Vatican, between Visconti's Ceres and the God of the Nile. She was purely an Indian deity—an Anglo-Indian deity, that is to say—and we called her THE Venus Annodomini, to distinguish her from other Annodominis of the same everlasting order. There was a legend among the Hills that she had once been young; but no living man was prepared to come forward and say boldly that the legend was true.

Men rode up to Simla, and stayed, and went away and made their name and did their life's work, and returned again to find the Venus Annodomini exactly as they had left her. She was as immutable as the Hills. But not quite so green. All that a girl of eighteen could do in the way of riding, walking, dancing, picnicking and over-exertion generally, the Venus Annodomini did, and showed no sign of fatigue or trace of weariness. Besides perpetual youth, she had discovered, men said, the secret of perpetual health; and her fame spread about the land. From a mere woman, she grew to be an Institution, insomuch that no young man could be said to be properly formed, who had not, at some time or another, worshipped at the shrine of the Venus Annodomini. There was no one like her, though there were many imitations. Six years in her eyes were no more than six months to ordinary women; and ten made less visible impression on her than does a week's fever on an ordinary woman. Every one adored her, and in return she was pleasant and courteous to nearly every one. Youth had been a habit of hers for so long, that she could not part with it—never realized, in fact, the necessity of parting with it—and took for her more chosen associates young people.

Among the worshippers of the Venus Annodomini was young Gayerson.

"Very Young" Gayerson, he was called to distinguish him from his father "Young" Gayerson, a Bengal Civilian, who affected the customs—as he had the heart—of youth. "Very Young" Gayerson was not content to worship placidly and for form's sake, as the other young men did, or to accept a ride or a dance, or a talk from the Venus Annodomini in a properly humble and thankful spirit. He was exacting, and, therefore, the Venus Annodomini repressed him. He worried himself nearly sick in a futile sort of way over her; and his devotion and earnestness made him appear either shy or boisterous or rude, as his mood might vary, by the side of the older men who, with him, bowed before the Venus Annodomini. She was sorry for him. He reminded her of a lad who, three-and-twenty years ago, had professed a boundless devotion for her, and for whom in return she had felt something more than a week's weakness. But that lad had fallen away and married another woman less than a year after he had worshipped her; and the Venus Annodomini had almost—not quite—forgotten his name. "Very Young" Gayerson had the same big blue eyes and the same way of pouting his underlip when he was excited or

troubled. But the Venus Annodomini checked him sternly none the less. Too much zeal was a thing that she did not approve of; preferring instead, a tempered and sober tenderness.

"Very Young" Gayerson was miserable, and took no trouble to conceal his wretchedness. He was in the Army—a Line regiment I think, but am not certain—and, since his face was a looking-glass and his forehead an open book, by reason of his innocence, his brothers in arms made his life a burden to him and embittered his naturally sweet disposition. No one except "Very Young" Gayerson, and he never told his views, knew how old "Very Young" Gayerson believed the Venus Annodomini to be. Perhaps he thought her five and twenty, or perhaps she told him that she was this age. "Very Young" Gayerson would have forded the Gugger in flood to carry her lightest word, and had implicit faith in her. Every one liked him, and every one was sorry when they saw him so bound a slave of the Venus Annodomini. Every one, too, admitted that it was not her fault; for the Venus Annodomini differed from Mrs. Hauksbee and Mrs. Reiver in this particular—she never moved a finger to attract any one; but, like Ninon de l'Enclos, all men were attracted to her. One could admire and respect Mrs. Hauksbee, despise and avoid Mrs. Reiver, but one was forced to adore the Venus Annodomini.

"Very Young" Gayerson's papa held a Division or a Collectorate or something administrative in a particularly unpleasant part of Bengal—full of Babus who edited newspapers proving that "Young" Gayerson was a "Nero" and a "Scylla" and a "Charybdis"; and, in addition to the Babus, there was a good deal of dysentery and cholera abroad for nine months of the year. "Young" Gayerson—he was about five and forty—rather liked Babus, they amused him, but he objects to dysentery, and when he could get away, went to Darjiling for the most part. This particular season he fancied that he would come up to Simla, and see his boy. The boy was not altogether pleased. He told the Venus Annodomini that his father was coming up, and she flushed a little and said that she should be delighted to make his acquaintance. Then she looked long and thoughtfully at "Very Young" Gayerson; because she was very, very sorry for him, and he was a very, very big idiot.

"My daughter is coming out in a fortnight, Mr. Gayerson," she said.

"Your WHAT?" said he.

"Daughter," said the Venus Annodomini. "She's been out for a year at Home already, and I want her to see a little of India. She is nineteen and a very sensible, nice girl I believe."

"Very Young" Gayerson, who was a short twenty-two years old, nearly fell

out of his chair with astonishment; for he had persisted in believing,

against all belief, in the youth of the Venus Annodomini.

She, with her back to the curtained window, watched the effect of her

sentences and smiled.

"Very Young" Gayerson's papa came up twelve days later, and had not been in Simla four and twenty hours, before two men, old acquaintances of his, had told him how "Very Young" Gayerson had been conducting himself.

"Young" Gayerson laughed a good deal, and inquired who the Venus Annodomini might be. Which proves that he had been living in Bengal where nobody knows anything except the rate of Exchange. Then he said "boys will be boys," and spoke to his son about the matter.

"Very Young" Gayerson said that he felt wretched and unhappy; and "Young" Gayerson said that he repented of having helped to bring a fool into the world. He suggested that his son had better cut his leave short and go down to his duties. This led to an unfilial answer, and relations were strained, until "Young" Gayerson demanded that they should call on the Venus Annodomini. "Very Young" Gayerson went with his papa, feeling, somehow, uncomfortable and small.

The Venus Annodomini received them graciously and "Young" Gayerson said:—"By Jove! It's Kitty!" "Very Young" Gayerson would have listened for an explanation, if his time had not been taken up with trying to talk to a large, handsome, quiet, well-dressed girl—introduced to him by the Venus Annodomini as her daughter. She was far older in manners, style and repose than "Very Young" Gayerson; and, as he realized this thing, he felt sick.

Presently, he heard the Venus Annodomini saying:—"Do you know that your son is one of my most devoted admirers?"

"I don't wonder," said "Young" Gayerson. Here he raised his voice:—"He follows his father's footsteps. Didn't I worship the ground you trod on, ever so long ago, Kitty—and you haven't changed since then. How strange it all seems!"

"Very Young" Gayerson said nothing. His conversation with the daughter of the Venus Annodomini was, through the rest of the call, fragmentary and disjointed..........

"At five, tomorrow then," said the Venus Annodomini. "And mind you are punctual."

"At five punctual," said "Young" Gayerson. "You can lend your old father a horse I dare say, youngster, can't you? I'm going for a ride tomorrow afternoon."

"Certainly," said "Very Young" Gayerson. "I am going down tomorrow morning. My ponies are at your service, Sir."

The Venus Annodomini looked at him across the half-light of the room, and her big gray eyes filled with moisture. She rose and shook hands with him.

"Goodbye, Tom," whispered the Venus Annodomini.

THE BISARA OF POOREE.

Little Blind Fish, thou art marvellous wise,

Little Blind Fish, who put out thy eyes?

Open thine ears while I whisper my wish—

Bring me a lover, thou little Blind Fish.

—The Charm of the Bisara.

Some natives say that it came from the other side of Kulu, where the eleven-inch Temple Sapphire is. Others that it was made at the Devil-Shrine of Ao-Chung in Thibet, was stolen by a Kafir, from him by a Gurkha, from him again by a Lahouli, from him by a khitmatgar, and by this latter sold to an Englishman, so all its virtue was lost: because, to work properly, the Bisara of Pooree must be stolen—with bloodshed if possible, but, at any rate, stolen.

These stories of the coming into India are all false. It was made at Pooree ages since—the manner of its making would fill a small book—was stolen by one of the Temple dancing-girls there, for her own purposes, and then passed on from hand to hand, steadily northward, till it reached Hanla: always bearing the same name—the Bisara of Pooree. In shape it is a tiny, square box of silver, studded outside with eight small balas-rubies. Inside the box, which opens with a spring, is a little eyeless fish, carved from some sort of dark, shiny nut and wrapped in a shred of faded gold-cloth. That is the Bisara of Pooree, and it were better for a man to take a king cobra in his hand than to touch the Bisara of Pooree.

All kinds of magic are out of date and done away with except in India where nothing changes in spite of the shiny, toy-scum stuff that people call "civilization." Any man who knows about the Bisara of Pooree will tell you what its powers are—always supposing that it has been honestly stolen. It is the only regularly working, trustworthy love-charm in the country, with one exception.

[The other charm is in the hands of a trooper of the Nizam's Horse, at a place called Tuprani, due north of Hyderabad.] This can be depended upon for a fact. Some one else may explain it.

If the Bisara be not stolen, but given or bought or found, it turns against its owner in three years, and leads to ruin or death. This is another fact which you may explain when you have time.

Meanwhile, you can laugh at it. At present, the Bisara is safe on an ekka-pony's neck, inside the blue bead-necklace that keeps off the Evil-eye. If the ekka-driver ever finds it, and wears it, or gives it to his wife, I am sorry for him.

A very dirty hill-cooly woman, with goitre, owned it at Theog in 1884. It came into Simla from the north before Churton's khitmatgar bought it, and sold it, for three times its silver-value, to Churton, who collected curiosities. The servant knew no more what he had bought than the master; but a man looking over Churton's collection of curiosities—Churton was an Assistant Commissioner by the way—saw and held his tongue. He was an Englishman; but knew how to believe. Which shows that he was different from most Englishmen. He knew that it was dangerous to have any share in the little box when working or dormant; for unsought Love is a terrible gift.

Pack—"Grubby" Pack, as we used to call him—was, in every way, a nasty little man who

must have crawled into the Army by mistake. He was three inches taller than his sword, but not half so strong. And the sword was a fifty-shilling, tailor-made one. Nobody liked him, and, I suppose, it was his wizenedness and worthlessness that made him fall so hopelessly in love with Miss Hollis, who was good and sweet, and five foot seven in her tennis shoes. He was not content with falling in love quietly, but brought all the strength of his miserable little nature into the business. If he had not been so objectionable, one might have pitied him. He vapored, and fretted, and fumed, and trotted up and down, and tried to make himself pleasing in Miss Hollis's big, quiet, gray eyes, and failed. It was one of the cases that you sometimes meet, even in this country where we marry by Code, of a really blind attachment all on one side, without the faintest possibility of return. Miss Hollis looked on Pack as some sort of vermin running about the road. He had no prospects beyond Captain's pay, and no wits to help that out by one anna. In a large-sized man, love like his would have been touching.

In a good man it would have been grand. He being what he was, it was only a nuisance.

You will believe this much. What you will not believe, is what follows: Churton, and The Man who Knew that the Bisara was, were lunching at the Simla Club together. Churton was complaining of life in general. His best mare had rolled out of stable down the hill and had broken her back; his decisions were being reversed by the upper Courts, more than an Assistant Commissioner of eight years' standing has a right to expect; he knew liver and fever, and, for weeks past, had felt out of sorts. Altogether, he was disgusted and disheartened.

Simla Club dining-room is built, as all the world knows, in two sections, with an arch-arrangement dividing them. Come in, turn to your own left, take the table under the window, and you cannot see any one who has come in, turning to the right, and taken a table on the right side of the arch. Curiously enough, every word that you say can be heard, not only by the other diner, but by the servants beyond the screen through which they bring dinner. This is worth knowing: an echoing-room is a trap to be forewarned against.

Half in fun, and half hoping to be believed, The Man who Knew told Churton the story of the Bisara of Pooree at rather greater length than I have told it to you in this place; winding up with the suggestion that Churton might as well throw the little box down the hill and see whether all his troubles would go with it. In ordinary ears, English ears, the tale was only an interesting bit of folk-lore. Churton laughed, said that he felt better for his tiffin, and went out. Pack had been tiffining by himself to the right of the arch, and had heard everything. He was nearly mad with his absurd infatuation for Miss Hollis that all Simla had been laughing about.

It is a curious thing that, when a man hates or loves beyond reason, he is ready to go beyond reason to gratify his feelings. Which he would not do for money or power merely. Depend upon it, Solomon would never have built altars to Ashtaroth and all those ladies with queer names, if there had not been trouble of some kind in his zenana, and nowhere else. But this is beside the story. The facts of the case are these: Pack called on Churton next day when Churton was out, left his card, and STOLE the Bisara of Pooree from its place under the clock on the mantelpiece! Stole it like the thief he was by nature. Three days later, all Simla was electrified by the news that Miss Hollis had accepted Pack—the shrivelled rat, Pack! Do you desire clearer evidence than this? The Bisara of Pooree had been stolen, and it worked as it had always done when won by foul means.

There are three or four times in a man's life when he is justified in meddling with other people's affairs to play Providence.

The Man who Knew felt that he WAS justified; but believing and acting on a belief are quite different things. The insolent satisfaction of Pack as he ambled by the side of Miss Hollis, and Churton's striking release from liver, as soon as the Bisara of Pooree had gone, decided

the Man. He explained to Churton and Churton laughed, because he was not brought up to believe that men on the Government House List steal—at least little things. But the miraculous acceptance by Miss Hollis of that tailor, Pack, decided him to take steps on suspicion. He vowed that he only wanted to find out where his ruby-studded silver box had vanished to. You cannot accuse a man on the Government House List of stealing. And if you rifle his room you are a thief yourself. Churton, prompted by The Man who Knew, decided on burglary. If he found nothing in Pack's room.... but it is not nice to think of what would have happened in that case.

Pack went to a dance at Benmore—Benmore WAS Benmore in those days, and not an office— and danced fifteen waltzes out of twenty-two with Miss Hollis. Churton and The Man took all the keys that they could lay hands on, and went to Pack's room in the hotel, certain that his servants would be away. Pack was a cheap soul. He had not purchased a decent cash-box to keep his papers in, but one of those native imitations that you buy for ten rupees. It opened to any sort of key, and there at the bottom, under Pack's Insurance Policy, lay the Bisara of Pooree!

Churton called Pack names, put the Bisara of Pooree in his pocket, and went to the dance with The Man. At least, he came in time for supper, and saw the beginning of the end in Miss Hollis's eyes. She was hysterical after supper, and was taken away by her Mamma.

At the dance, with the abominable Bisara in his pocket, Churton twisted his foot on one of the steps leading down to the old Rink, and had to be sent home in a rickshaw, grumbling. He did not believe in the Bisara of Pooree any the more for this manifestation, but he sought out Pack and called him some ugly names; and "thief" was the mildest of them. Pack took the names with the nervous smile of a little man who wants both soul and body to resent an insult, and went his way. There was no public scandal.

A week later, Pack got his definite dismissal from Miss Hollis.

There had been a mistake in the placing of her affections, she said.

So he went away to Madras, where he can do no great harm even if he lives to be a Colonel.

Churton insisted upon The Man who Knew taking the Bisara of Pooree as a gift. The Man took it, went down to the Cart Road at once, found an ekka pony with a blue head-necklace, fastened the Bisara of Pooree inside the necklace with a piece of shoe-string and thanked Heaven that he was rid of a danger. Remember, in case you ever find it, that you must not destroy the Bisara of Pooree. I have not time to explain why just now, but the power lies in the little wooden fish. Mister Gubernatis or Max Muller could tell you more about it than I.

You will say that all this story is made up. Very well. If ever you come across a little silver, ruby-studded box, seven-eighths of an inch long by three-quarters wide, with a dark-brown wooden fish, wrapped in gold cloth, inside it, keep it. Keep it for three years, and then you will discover for yourself whether my story is true or false.

Better still, steal it as Pack did, and you will be sorry that you had not killed yourself in the beginning.

THE GATE OF A HUNDRED SORROWS.

"If I can attain Heaven for a pice, why should you be envious?"

—Opium Smoker's Proverb.

This is no work of mine. My friend, Gabral Misquitta, the half-caste, spoke it all, between moonset and morning, six weeks before he died; and I took it down from his mouth as he answered my questions so:—

It lies between the Copper-smith's Gully and the pipe-stem sellers' quarter, within a hundred yards, too, as the crow flies, of the Mosque of Wazir Khan. I don't mind telling any one this much, but I defy him to find the Gate, however well he may think he knows the City. You might even go through the very gully it stands in a hundred times, and be none the wiser. We used to call the gully, "the Gully of the Black Smoke," but its native name is altogether different of course. A loaded donkey couldn't pass between the walls; and, at one point, just before you reach the Gate, a bulged house-front makes people go along all sideways.

It isn't really a gate though. It's a house. Old Fung-Tching had it first five years ago. He was a boot-maker in Calcutta. They say that he murdered his wife there when he was drunk. That was why he dropped bazar-rum and took to the Black Smoke instead. Later on, he came up north and opened the Gate as a house where you could get your smoke in peace and quiet. Mind you, it was a pukka, respectable opium-house, and not one of those stifling, sweltering chandoo-khanas, that you can find all over the City. No; the old man knew his business thoroughly, and he was most clean for a Chinaman. He was a one-eyed little chap, not much more than five feet high, and both his middle fingers were gone. All the same, he was the handiest man at rolling black pills I have ever seen. Never seemed to be touched by the Smoke, either; and what he took day and night, night and day, was a caution. I've been at it five years, and I can do my fair share of the Smoke with any one; but I was a child to Fung-Tching that way. All the same, the old man was keen on his money, very keen; and that's what I can't understand. I heard he saved a good deal before he died, but his nephew has got all that now; and the old man's gone back to China to be buried.

He kept the big upper room, where his best customers gathered, as neat as a new pin. In one corner used to stand Fung-Tching's Joss—almost as ugly as Fung-Tching—and there were always sticks burning under his nose; but you never smelt 'em when the pipes were going thick. Opposite the Joss was Fung-Tching's coffin. He had spent a good deal of his savings on that, and whenever a new man came to the Gate he was always introduced to it. It was lacquered black, with red and gold writings on it, and I've heard that Fung-Tching brought it out all the way from China. I don't know whether that's true or not, but I know that, if I came first in the evening, I used to spread my mat just at the foot of it. It was a quiet corner you see, and a sort of breeze from the gully came in at the window now and then. Besides the mats, there was no other furniture in the room—only the coffin, and the old Joss all green and blue and purple with age and polish.

Fung-Tching never told us why he called the place "The Gate of a Hundred Sorrows." (He was the only Chinaman I know who used bad-sounding fancy names. Most of them are flowery. As you'll see in Calcutta.) We used to find that out for ourselves. Nothing grows on you so much, if you're white, as the Black Smoke. A yellow man is made different. Opium doesn't tell on him scarcely at all; but white and black suffer a good deal. Of course, there are some people that the Smoke doesn't touch any more than tobacco would at first. They just doze a bit, as one would fall asleep naturally, and next morning they are almost fit for work. Now, I was one of that sort

when I began, but I've been at it for five years pretty steadily, and its different now. There was an old aunt of mine, down Agra way, and she left me a little at her death. About sixty rupees a month secured. Sixty isn't much. I can recollect a time, seems hundreds and hundreds of years ago, that I was getting my three hundred a month, and pickings, when I was working on a big timber contract in Calcutta.

I didn't stick to that work for long. The Black Smoke does not allow of much other business; and even though I am very little affected by it, as men go, I couldn't do a day's work now to save my life. After all, sixty rupees is what I want. When old Fung-Tching was alive he used to draw the money for me, give me about half of it to live on (I eat very little), and the rest he kept himself. I was free of the Gate at any time of the day and night, and could smoke and sleep there when I liked, so I didn't care. I know the old man made a good thing out of it; but that's no matter. Nothing matters, much to me; and, besides, the money always came fresh and fresh each month.

There was ten of us met at the Gate when the place was first opened. Me, and two Baboos from a Government Office somewhere in Anarkulli, but they got the sack and couldn't pay (no man who has to work in the daylight can do the Black Smoke for any length of time straight on); a Chinaman that was Fung-Tching's nephew; a bazar-woman that had got a lot of money somehow; an English loafer—Mac-Somebody I think, but I have forgotten—that smoked heaps, but never seemed to pay anything (they said he had saved Fung-Tching's life at some trial in Calcutta when he was a barrister): another Eurasian, like myself, from Madras; a half-caste woman, and a couple of men who said they had come from the North. I think they must have been Persians or Afghans or something. There are not more than five of us living now, but we come regular. I don't know what happened to the Baboos; but the bazar-woman she died after six months of the Gate, and I think Fung-Tching took her bangles and nose-ring for himself. But I'm not certain. The Englishman, he drank as well as smoked, and he dropped off. One of the Persians got killed in a row at night by the big well near the mosque a long time ago, and the Police shut up the well, because they said it was full of foul air.

They found him dead at the bottom of it. So, you see, there is only me, the Chinaman, the half-caste woman that we call the Memsahib (she used to live with Fung-Tching), the other Eurasian, and one of the Persians. The Memsahib looks very old now. I think she was a young woman when the Gate was opened; but we are all old for the matter of that. Hundreds and hundreds of years old. It is very hard to keep count of time in the Gate, and besides, time doesn't matter to me. I draw my sixty rupees fresh and fresh every month.

A very, very long while ago, when I used to be getting three hundred and fifty rupees a month, and pickings, on a big timber-contract at Calcutta, I had a wife of sorts. But she's dead now. People said that I killed her by taking to the Black Smoke. Perhaps I did, but it's so long since it doesn't matter. Sometimes when I first came to the Gate, I used to feel sorry for it; but that's all over and done with long ago, and I draw my sixty rupees fresh and fresh every month, and am quite happy. Not DRUNK happy, you know, but always quiet and soothed and contented.

How did I take to it? It began at Calcutta. I used to try it in my own house, just to see what it was like. I never went very far, but I think my wife must have died then. Anyhow, I found myself here, and got to know Fung-Tching. I don't remember rightly how that came about; but he told me of the Gate and I used to go there, and, somehow, I have never got away from it since. Mind you, though, the Gate was a respectable place in Fung-Tching's time where you could be comfortable, and not at all like the chandoo-khanas where the niggers go. No; it was clean and quiet, and not crowded. Of course, there were others beside us ten and the man; but we always had a mat apiece with a wadded woollen head-piece, all covered with black and red dragons and things; just like a coffin in the corner.

At the end of one's third pipe the dragons used to move about and fight. I've watched 'em, many and many a night through. I used to regulate my Smoke that way, and now it takes a dozen pipes to make 'em stir. Besides, they are all torn and dirty, like the mats, and old Fung-Tching is dead. He died a couple of years ago, and gave me the pipe I always use now—a silver one, with queer beasts crawling up and down the receiver-bottle below the cup. Before that, I think, I used a big bamboo stem with a copper cup, a very small one, and a green jade mouthpiece. It was a little thicker than a walking-stick stem, and smoked sweet, very sweet. The bamboo seemed to suck up the smoke. Silver doesn't, and I've got to clean it out now and then, that's a great deal of trouble, but I smoke it for the old man's sake. He must have made a good thing out of me, but he always gave me clean mats and pillows, and the best stuff you could get anywhere.

When he died, his nephew Tsin-ling took up the Gate, and he called it the "Temple of the Three Possessions;" but we old ones speak of it as the "Hundred Sorrows," all the same. The nephew does things very shabbily, and I think the Memsahib must help him. She lives with him; same as she used to do with the old man. The two let in all sorts of low people, niggers and all, and the Black Smoke isn't as good as it used to be. I've found burnt bran in my pipe over and over again. The old man would have died if that had happened in his time. Besides, the room is never cleaned, and all the mats are torn and cut at the edges. The coffin has gone—gone to China again—with the old man and two ounces of smoke inside it, in case he should want 'em on the way.

The Joss doesn't get so many sticks burnt under his nose as he used to; that's a sign of ill-luck, as sure as Death. He's all brown, too, and no one ever attends to him. That's the Memsahib's work, I know; because, when Tsin-ling tried to burn gilt paper before him, she said it was a waste of money, and, if he kept a stick burning very slowly, the Joss wouldn't know the difference. So now we've got the sticks mixed with a lot of glue, and they take half-an-hour longer to burn, and smell stinky. Let alone the smell of the room by itself. No business can get on if they try that sort of thing.

The Joss doesn't like it. I can see that. Late at night, sometimes, he turns all sorts of queer colors—blue and green and red—just as he used to do when old Fung-Tching was alive; and he rolls his eyes and stamps his feet like a devil.

I don't know why I don't leave the place and smoke quietly in a little room of my own in the bazar. Most like, Tsin-ling would kill me if I went away—he draws my sixty rupees now—and besides, it's so much trouble, and I've grown to be very fond of the Gate. It's not much to look at. Not what it was in the old man's time, but I couldn't leave it. I've seen so many come in and out. And I've seen so many die here on the mats that I should be afraid of dying in the open now. I've seen some things that people would call strange enough; but nothing is strange when you're on the Black Smoke, except the Black Smoke. And if it was, it wouldn't matter.

Fung-Tching used to be very particular about his people, and never got in any one who'd give trouble by dying messy and such. But the nephew isn't half so careful. He tells everywhere that he keeps a "first-chop" house. Never tries to get men in quietly, and make them comfortable like Fung-Tching did. That's why the Gate is getting a little bit more known than it used to be. Among the niggers of course. The nephew daren't get a white, or, for matter of that, a mixed skin into the place. He has to keep us three of course—me and the Memsahib and the other Eurasian. We're fixtures.

But he wouldn't give us credit for a pipeful—not for anything.

One of these days, I hope, I shall die in the Gate. The Persian and the Madras man are terrible shaky now. They've got a boy to light their pipes for them. I always do that myself. Most like, I shall see them carried out before me. I don't think I shall ever outlive the Memsahib or Tsin-

ling. Women last longer than men at the Black-Smoke, and Tsin-ling has a deal of the old man's blood in him, though he DOES smoke cheap stuff. The bazar-woman knew when she was going two days before her time; and SHE died on a clean mat with a nicely wadded pillow, and the old man hung up her pipe just above the Joss. He was always fond of her, I fancy. But he took her bangles just the same.

I should like to die like the bazar-woman—on a clean, cool mat with a pipe of good stuff between my lips. When I feel I'm going, I shall ask Tsin-ling for them, and he can draw my sixty rupees a month, fresh and fresh, as long as he pleases, and watch the black and red dragons have their last big fight together; and then....

Well, it doesn't matter. Nothing matters much to me—only I wished Tsin-ling wouldn't put bran into the Black Smoke.

THE STORY OF MUHAMMAD DIN.

"Who is the happy man? He that sees in his own house at home little

children crowned with dust, leaping and falling and crying."

—Munichandra, translated by Professor Peterson.

The polo-ball was an old one, scarred, chipped, and dinted. It stood on the mantelpiece among the pipe-stems which Imam Din, khitmatgar, was cleaning for me.

"Does the Heaven-born want this ball?" said Imam Din, deferentially.

The Heaven-born set no particular store by it; but of what use was a polo-ball to a khitmatgar?

"By Your Honor's favor, I have a little son. He has seen this ball, and desires it to play with. I do not want it for myself."

No one would for an instant accuse portly old Imam Din of wanting to play with polo-balls. He carried out the battered thing into the verandah; and there followed a hurricane of joyful squeaks, a patter of small feet, and the thud-thud-thud of the ball rolling along the ground. Evidently the little son had been waiting outside the door to secure his treasure. But how had he managed to see that polo-ball?

Next day, coming back from office half an hour earlier than usual, I was aware of a small figure in the dining-room—a tiny, plump figure in a ridiculously inadequate shirt which came, perhaps, half-way down the tubby stomach. It wandered round the room, thumb in mouth, crooning to itself as it took stock of the pictures. Undoubtedly this was the "little son."

He had no business in my room, of course; but was so deeply absorbed in his discoveries that he never noticed me in the doorway. I stepped into the room and startled him nearly into a fit. He sat down on the ground with a gasp. His eyes opened, and his mouth followed suit. I knew what was coming, and fled, followed by a long, dry howl which reached the servants' quarters far more quickly than any command of mine had ever done. In ten seconds Imam Din was in the dining-room. Then despairing sobs arose, and I returned to find Imam Din admonishing the small sinner who was using most of his shirt as a handkerchief.

"This boy," said Imam Din, judicially, "is a budmash, a big budmash. He will, without doubt, go to the jail-khana for his behavior." Renewed yells from the penitent, and an elaborate apology to myself from Imam Din.

"Tell the baby," said I, "that the Sahib is not angry, and take him away." Imam Din conveyed my forgiveness to the offender, who had now gathered all his shirt round his neck, string-wise, and the yell subsided into a sob. The two set off for the door. "His name," said Imam Din, as though the name were part of the crime, "is Muhammad Din, and he is a budmash." Freed from present danger, Muhammad Din turned round, in his father's arms, and said gravely:—"It is true that my name is Muhammad Din, Tahib, but I am not a budmash. I am a MAN!"

From that day dated my acquaintance with Muhammad Din. Never again did he come into my dining-room, but on the neutral ground of the compound, we greeted each other with much state, though our conversation was confined to "Talaam, Tahib" from his side and "Salaam Muhammad Din" from mine. Daily on my return from office, the little white shirt, and the fat little body used to rise from the shade of the creeper-covered trellis where they had been

hid; and daily I checked my horse here, that my salutation might not be slurred over or given unseemly.

Muhammad Din never had any companions. He used to trot about the compound, in and out of the castor-oil bushes, on mysterious errands of his own. One day I stumbled upon some of his handiwork far down the ground. He had half buried the polo-ball in dust, and stuck six shrivelled old marigold flowers in a circle round it. Outside that circle again, was a rude square, traced out in bits of red brick alternating with fragments of broken china; the whole bounded by a little bank of dust. The bhistie from the well-curb put in a plea for the small architect, saying that it was only the play of a baby and did not much disfigure my garden.

Heaven knows that I had no intention of touching the child's work then or later; but, that evening, a stroll through the garden brought me unawares full on it; so that I trampled, before I knew, marigold-heads, dust-bank, and fragments of broken soap-dish into confusion past all hope of mending. Next morning I came upon Muhammad Din crying softly to himself over the ruin I had wrought.

Some one had cruelly told him that the Sahib was very angry with him for spoiling the garden, and had scattered his rubbish using bad language the while. Muhammad Din labored for an hour at effacing every trace of the dust-bank and pottery fragments, and it was with a tearful apologetic face that he said, "Talaam Tahib," when I came home from the office. A hasty inquiry resulted in Imam Din informing Muhammad Din that by my singular favor he was permitted to disport himself as he pleased. Whereat the child took heart and fell to tracing the ground-plan of an edifice which was to eclipse the marigold-polo-ball creation.

For some months, the chubby little eccentricity revolved in his humble orbit among the castor-oil bushes and in the dust; always fashioning magnificent palaces from stale flowers thrown away by the bearer, smooth water-worn pebbles, bits of broken glass, and feathers pulled, I fancy, from my fowls—always alone and always crooning to himself.

A gayly-spotted sea-shell was dropped one day close to the last of his little buildings; and I looked that Muhammad Din should build something more than ordinarily splendid on the strength of it. Nor was I disappointed. He meditated for the better part of an hour, and his crooning rose to a jubilant song. Then he began tracing in dust. It would certainly be a wondrous palace, this one, for it was two yards long and a yard broad in ground-plan. But the palace was never completed.

Next day there was no Muhammad Din at the head of the carriage-drive, and no "Talaam Tahib" to welcome my return. I had grown accustomed to the greeting, and its omission troubled me. Next day, Imam Din told me that the child was suffering slightly from fever and needed quinine. He got the medicine, and an English Doctor.

"They have no stamina, these brats," said the Doctor, as he left Imam Din's quarters.

A week later, though I would have given much to have avoided it, I met on the road to the Mussulman burying-ground Imam Din, accompanied by one other friend, carrying in his arms, wrapped in a white cloth, all that was left of little Muhammad Din.

ON THE STRENGTH OF A LIKENESS.

If your mirror be broken, look into still water; but have a care

that you do not fall in.

—Hindu Proverb.

Next to a requited attachment, one of the most convenient things that a young man can carry about with him at the beginning of his career, is an unrequited attachment. It makes him feel important and business-like, and blasé, and cynical; and whenever he has a touch of liver, or suffers from want of exercise, he can mourn over his lost love, and be very happy in a tender, twilight fashion.

Hannasyde's affair of the heart had been a Godsend to him. It was four years old, and the girl had long since given up thinking of it.

She had married and had many cares of her own. In the beginning, she had told Hannasyde that, "while she could never be anything more than a sister to him, she would always take the deepest interest in his welfare." This startlingly new and original remark gave Hannasyde something to think over for two years; and his own vanity filled in the other twenty-four months. Hannasyde was quite different from Phil Garron, but, none the less, had several points in common with that far too lucky man.

He kept his unrequited attachment by him as men keep a well-smoked pipe—for comfort's sake, and because it had grown dear in the using. It brought him happily through the Simla season. Hannasyde was not lovely. There was a crudity in his manners, and a roughness in the way in which he helped a lady on to her horse, that did not attract the other sex to him. Even if he had cast about for their favor, which he did not. He kept his wounded heart all to himself for a while.

Then trouble came to him. All who go to Simla, know the slope from the Telegraph to the Public Works Office. Hannasyde was loafing up the hill, one September morning between calling hours, when a 'rickshaw came down in a hurry, and in the 'rickshaw sat the living, breathing image of the girl who had made him so happily unhappy.

Hannasyde leaned against the railing and gasped. He wanted to run downhill after the 'rickshaw, but that was impossible; so he went forward with most of his blood in his temples. It was impossible, for many reasons, that the woman in the 'rickshaw could be the girl he had known. She was, he discovered later, the wife of a man from Dindigul, or Coimbatore, or some out-of-the-way place, and she had come up to Simla early in the season for the good of her health.

She was going back to Dindigul, or wherever it was, at the end of the season; and in all likelihood would never return to Simla again, her proper Hill-station being Ootacamund. That night, Hannasyde, raw and savage from the raking up of all old feelings, took counsel with himself for one measured hour. What he decided upon was this; and you must decide for yourself how much genuine affection for the old love, and how much a very natural inclination to go abroad and enjoy himself, affected the decision. Mrs. Landys-Haggert would never in all human likelihood cross his path again. So whatever he did didn't much matter. She was marvellously like the girl who "took a deep interest" and the rest of the formula. All things considered, it would be pleasant to make the acquaintance of Mrs. Landys-Haggert, and for a little time—only a very little time—to make believe that he was with Alice Chisane again. Every one is more

or less mad on one point. Hannasyde's particular monomania was his old love, Alice Chisane.

He made it his business to get introduced to Mrs. Haggert, and the introduction prospered. He also made it his business to see as much as he could of that lady. When a man is in earnest as to interviews, the facilities which Simla offers are startling. There are garden-parties, and tennis-parties, and picnics, and luncheons at Annandale, and rifle-matches, and dinners and balls; besides rides and walks, which are matters of private arrangement.

Hannasyde had started with the intention of seeing a likeness, and he ended by doing much more. He wanted to be deceived, he meant to be deceived, and he deceived himself very thoroughly. Not only were the face and figure, the face and figure of Alice Chisane, but the voice and lower tones were exactly the same, and so were the turns of speech; and the little mannerisms, that every woman has, of gait and gesticulation, were absolutely and identically the same. The turn of the head was the same; the tired look in the eyes at the end of a long walk was the same; the sloop and wrench over the saddle to hold in a pulling horse was the same; and once, most marvellous of all, Mrs. Landys-Haggert singing to herself in the next room, while Hannasyde was waiting to take her for a ride, hummed, note for note, with a throaty quiver of the voice in the second line:—"Poor Wandering One!" exactly as Alice Chisane had hummed it for Hannasyde in the dusk of an English drawing-room. In the actual woman herself—in the soul of her—there was not the least likeness; she and Alice Chisane being cast in different moulds. But all that Hannasyde wanted to know and see and think about, was this maddening and perplexing likeness of face and voice and manner. He was bent on making a fool of himself that way; and he was in no sort disappointed.

Open and obvious devotion from any sort of man is always pleasant to any sort of woman; but Mrs. Landys-Haggert, being a woman of the world, could make nothing of Hannasyde's admiration.

He would take any amount of trouble—he was a selfish man habitually—to meet and forestall, if possible, her wishes.

Anything she told him to do was law; and he was, there could be no doubting it, fond of her company so long as she talked to him, and kept on talking about trivialities. But when she launched into expression of her personal views and her wrongs, those small social differences that make the spice of Simla life, Hannasyde was neither pleased nor interested. He didn't want to know anything about Mrs. Landys-Haggert, or her experiences in the past—she had travelled nearly all over the world, and could talk cleverly—he wanted the likeness of Alice Chisane before his eyes and her voice in his ears.

Anything outside that, reminding him of another personality jarred, and he showed that it did.

Under the new Post Office, one evening, Mrs. Landys-Haggert turned on him, and spoke her mind shortly and without warning. "Mr. Hannasyde," said she, "will you be good enough to explain why you have appointed yourself my special cavalier servente? I don't understand it. But I am perfectly certain, somehow or other, that you don't care the least little bit in the world for ME." This seems to support, by the way, the theory that no man can act or tell lies to a woman without being found out. Hannasyde was taken off his guard. His defence never was a strong one, because he was always thinking of himself, and he blurted out, before he knew what he was saying, this inexpedient answer:—"No more I do."

The queerness of the situation and the reply, made Mrs. Haggert laugh. Then it all came out; and at the end of Hannasyde's lucid explanation, Mrs. Haggert said, with the least little touch of scorn in her voice:—"So I'm to act as the lay-figure for you to hang the rags of your tattered affections on, am I?"

Hannasyde didn't see what answer was required, and he devoted himself generally and vaguely to the praise of Alice Chisane, which was unsatisfactory. Now it is to be thoroughly made clear that Mrs. Haggert had not the shadow of a ghost of an interest in Hannasyde.

Only—only no woman likes being made love through instead of to—specially on behalf of a musty divinity of four years' standing.

Hannasyde did not see that he had made any very particular exhibition of himself. He was glad to find a sympathetic soul in the arid wastes of Simla.

When the season ended, Hannasyde went down to his own place and Mrs. Haggert to hers. "It was like making love to a ghost," said Hannasyde to himself, "and it doesn't matter; and now I'll get to my work." But he found himself thinking steadily of the Haggert-Chisane ghost; and he could not be certain whether it was Haggert or Chisane that made up the greater part of the pretty phantom..........

He got understanding a month later.

A peculiar point of this peculiar country is the way in which a heartless Government transfers men from one end of the Empire to the other. You can never be sure of getting rid of a friend or an enemy till he or she dies. There was a case once—but that's another story.

Haggert's Department ordered him up from Dindigul to the Frontier at two days' notice, and he went through, losing money at every step, from Dindigul to his station. He dropped Mrs. Haggert at Lucknow, to stay with some friends there, to take part in a big ball at the Chutter Munzil, and to come on when he had made the new home a little comfortable. Lucknow was Hannasyde's station, and Mrs. Haggert stayed a week there. Hannasyde went to meet her. And the train came in, he discovered which he had been thinking of for the past month. The unwisdom of his conduct also struck him. The Lucknow week, with two dances, and an unlimited quantity of rides together, clinched matters; and Hannasyde found himself pacing this circle of thought:—He adored Alice Chisane—at least he HAD adored her. AND he admired Mrs. Landys-Haggert because she was like Alice Chisane. BUT Mrs. Landys-Haggert was not in the least like Alice Chisane, being a thousand times more adorable. NOW Alice Chisane was "the bride of another," and so was Mrs. Landys-Haggert, and a good and honest wife too. THEREFORE, he, Hannasyde, was.... here he called himself several hard names, and wished that he had been wise in the beginning.

Whether Mrs. Landys-Haggert saw what was going on in his mind, she alone knows. He seemed to take an unqualified interest in everything connected with herself, as distinguished from the Alice-Chisane likeness, and he said one or two things which, if Alice Chisane had been still betrothed to him, could scarcely have been excused, even on the grounds of the likeness. But Mrs. Haggert turned the remarks aside, and spent a long time in making Hannasyde see what a comfort and a pleasure she had been to him because of her strange resemblance to his old love. Hannasyde groaned in his saddle and said, "Yes, indeed," and busied himself with preparations for her departure to the Frontier, feeling very small and miserable.

The last day of her stay at Lucknow came, and Hannasyde saw her off at the Railway Station. She was very grateful for his kindness and the trouble he had taken, and smiled pleasantly and sympathetically as one who knew the Alice-Chisane reason of that kindness. And Hannasyde abused the coolies with the luggage, and hustled the people on the platform, and prayed that the roof might fall in and slay him.

As the train went out slowly, Mrs. Landys-Haggert leaned out of the window to say goodbye:— "On second thoughts au revoir, Mr. Hannasyde. I go Home in the Spring, and perhaps I may meet you in Town."

Hannasyde shook hands, and said very earnestly and adoringly:—"I hope to Heaven I shall never see your face again!"

And Mrs. Haggert understood.

WRESSLEY OF THE FOREIGN OFFICE.

I closed and drew for my love's sake,

That now is false to me,

And I slew the Riever of Tarrant Moss,

And set Dumeny free.

And ever they give me praise and gold,

And ever I moan my loss,

For I struck the blow for my false love's sake,

And not for the men at the Moss.

—Tarrant Moss.

One of the many curses of our life out here is the want of atmosphere in the painter's sense. There are no half-tints worth noticing. Men stand out all crude and raw, with nothing to tone them down, and nothing to scale them against. They do their work, and grow to think that there is nothing but their work, and nothing like their work, and that they are the real pivots on which the administration turns. Here is an instance of this feeling. A half-caste clerk was ruling forms in a Pay Office. He said to me:—"Do you know what would happen if I added or took away one single line on this sheet?" Then, with the air of a conspirator:—"It would disorganize the whole of the Treasury payments throughout the whole of the Presidency Circle! Think of that?"

If men had not this delusion as to the ultra-importance of their own particular employments, I suppose that they would sit down and kill themselves. But their weakness is wearisome, particularly when the listener knows that he himself commits exactly the same sin.

Even the Secretariat believes that it does good when it asks an over-driven Executive Officer to take census of wheat-weevils through a district of five thousand square miles.

There was a man once in the Foreign Office—a man who had grown middle-aged in the department, and was commonly said, by irreverent juniors, to be able to repeat Aitchison's "Treaties and Sunnuds" backwards, in his sleep. What he did with his stored knowledge only the Secretary knew; and he, naturally, would not publish the news abroad. This man's name was Wressley, and it was the Shibboleth, in those days, to say:—"Wressley knows more about the Central Indian States than any living man." If you did not say this, you were considered one of mean understanding.

Now-a-days, the man who says that he knows the ravel of the inter-tribal complications across the Border is of more use; but in Wressley's time, much attention was paid to the Central Indian States. They were called "foci" and "factors," and all manner of imposing names.

And here the curse of Anglo-Indian life fell heavily. When Wressley lifted up his voice, and spoke about such-and-such a succession to such-and-such a throne, the Foreign Office were silent, and Heads of Departments repeated the last two or three words of Wressley's sentences, and tacked "yes, yes," on them, and knew that they were "assisting the Empire to grapple with

seriouspolitical contingencies." In most big undertakings, one or two men do the work while the rest sit near and talk till the ripe decorations begin to fall.

Wressley was the working-member of the Foreign Office firm, and, to keep him up to his duties when he showed signs of flagging, he was made much of by his superiors and told what a fine fellow he was.

He did not require coaxing, because he was of tough build, but what he received confirmed him in the belief that there was no one quite so absolutely and imperatively necessary to the stability of India as Wressley of the Foreign Office. There might be other good men, but the known, honored and trusted man among men was Wressley of the Foreign Office. We had a Viceroy in those days who knew exactly when to "gentle" a fractious big man and to hearten up a collar-galled little one, and so keep all his team level. He conveyed to Wressley the impression which I have just set down; and even tough men are apt to be disorganized by a Viceroy's praise. There was a case once—but that is another story.

All India knew Wressley's name and office—it was in Thacker and Spink's Directory—but who he was personally, or what he did, or what his special merits were, not fifty men knew or cared. His work filled all his time, and he found no leisure to cultivate acquaintances beyond those of dead Rajput chiefs with Ahir blots in their 'scutcheons. Wressley would have made a very good Clerk in the Herald's College had he not been a Bengal Civilian.

Upon a day, between office and office, great trouble came to Wressley—overwhelmed him, knocked him down, and left him gasping as though he had been a little school-boy. Without reason, against prudence, and at a moment's notice, he fell in love with a frivolous, golden-haired girl who used to tear about Simla Mall on a high, rough waler, with a blue velvet jockey-cap crammed over her eyes. Her name was Venner—Tillie Venner—and she was delightful.

She took Wressley's heart at a hand-gallop, and Wressley found that it was not good for man to live alone; even with half the Foreign Office Records in his presses.

Then Simla laughed, for Wressley in love was slightly ridiculous.

He did his best to interest the girl in himself—that is to say, his work—and she, after the manner of women, did her best to appear interested in what, behind his back, she called "Mr. Wressley's Wajahs"; for she lisped very prettily. She did not understand one little thing about them, but she acted as if she did. Men have married on that sort of error before now.

Providence, however, had care of Wressley. He was immensely struck with Miss Venner's intelligence. He would have been more impressed had he heard her private and confidential accounts of his calls. He held peculiar notions as to the wooing of girls. He said that the best work of a man's career should be laid reverently at their feet.

Ruskin writes something like this somewhere, I think; but in ordinary life a few kisses are better and save time.

About a month after he had lost his heart to Miss Venner, and had been doing his work vilely in consequence, the first idea of his "Native Rule in Central India" struck Wressley and filled him with joy. It was, as he sketched it, a great thing—the work of his life—a really comprehensive survey of a most fascinating subject—to be written with all the special and laboriously acquired knowledge of Wressley of the Foreign Office—a gift fit for an Empress.

He told Miss Venner that he was going to take leave, and hoped, on his return, to bring her a present worthy of her acceptance. Would she wait? Certainly she would. Wressley drew

seventeen hundred rupees a month. She would wait a year for that. Her mamma would help her to wait.

So Wressley took one year's leave and all the available documents, about a truck-load, that he could lay hands on, and went down to Central India with his notion hot in his head. He began his book in the land he was writing of. Too much official correspondence had made him a frigid workman, and he must have guessed that he needed the white light of local color on his palette. This is a dangerous paint for amateurs to play with.

Heavens, how that man worked! He caught his Rajahs, analyzed his Rajahs, and traced them up into the mists of Time and beyond, with their queens and their concubines. He dated and cross-dated, pedigreed and triple-pedigreed, compared, noted, connoted, wove, strung, sorted, selected, inferred, calendared and counter-calendared for ten hours a day. And, because this sudden and new light of Love was upon him, he turned those dry bones of history and dirty records of misdeeds into things to weep or to laugh over as he pleased. His heart and soul were at the end of his pen, and they got into the ink. He was dowered with sympathy, insight, humor and style for two hundred and thirty days and nights; and his book was a Book. He had his vast special knowledge with him, so to speak; but the spirit, the woven-in human Touch, the poetry and the power of the output, were beyond all special knowledge. But I doubt whether he knew the gift that was in him then, and thus he may have lost some happiness. He was toiling for Tillie Venner, not for himself.

Men often do their best work blind, for some one else's sake.

Also, though this has nothing to do with the story, in India where every one knows every one else, you can watch men being driven, by the women who govern them, out of the rank-and-file and sent to take up points alone. A good man once started, goes forward; but an average man, so soon as the woman loses interest in his success as a tribute to her power, comes back to the battalion and is no more heard of.

Wressley bore the first copy of his book to Simla and, blushing and stammering, presented it to Miss Venner. She read a little of it.

I give her review verbatim:—"Oh, your book? It's all about those how-wid Wajahs. I didn't understand it.".........

Wressley of the Foreign Office was broken, smashed,—I am not exaggerating—by this one frivolous little girl. All that he could say feebly was:—"But, but it's my magnum opus! The work of my life." Miss Venner did not know what magnum opus meant; but she knew that Captain Kerrington had won three races at the last Gymkhana. Wressley didn't press her to wait for him any longer. He had sense enough for that.

Then came the reaction after the year's strain, and Wressley went back to the Foreign Office and his "Wajahs," a compiling, gazetteering, report-writing hack, who would have been dear at three hundred rupees a month. He abided by Miss Venner's review. Which proves that the inspiration in the book was purely temporary and unconnected with himself. Nevertheless, he had no right to sink, in a hill-tarn, five packing-cases, brought up at enormous expense from Bombay, of the best book of Indian history ever written.

When he sold off before retiring, some years later, I was turning over his shelves, and came across the only existing copy of "Native Rule in Central India"—the copy that Miss Venner could not understand. I read it, sitting on his mule-trucks, as long as the light lasted, and offered him his own price for it. He looked over my shoulder for a few pages and said to himself drearily:—"Now, how in the world did I come to write such damned good stuff as that?" Then

to me:—"Take it and keep it. Write one of your penny-farthing yarns about its birth. Perhaps—perhaps—the whole business may have been ordained to that end."

Which, knowing what Wressley of the Foreign Office was once, struck me as about the bitterest thing that I had ever heard a man say of his own work.

BY WORD OF MOUTH.

Not though you die tonight, O Sweet, and wail,

 A spectre at my door,

Shall mortal Fear make Love immortal fail—

 I shall but love you more,

Who from Death's house returning, give me still

One moment's comfort in my matchless ill.

 —Shadow Houses.

This tale may be explained by those who know how souls are made, and where the bounds of the Possible are put down. I have lived long enough in this country to know that it is best to know nothing, and can only write the story as it happened.

Dumoise was our Civil Surgeon at Meridki, and we called him "Dormouse," because he was a round little, sleepy little man. He was a good Doctor and never quarrelled with any one, not even with our Deputy Commissioner, who had the manners of a bargee and the tact of a horse. He married a girl as round and as sleepy-looking as himself. She was a Miss Hillardyce, daughter of "Squash" Hillardyce of the Berars, who married his Chief's daughter by mistake. But that is another story.

A honeymoon in India is seldom more than a week long; but there is nothing to hinder a couple from extending it over two or three years. This is a delightful country for married folk who are wrapped up in one another. They can live absolutely alone and without interruption—just as the Dormice did. These two little people retired from the world after their marriage, and were very happy. They were forced, of course, to give occasional dinners, but they made no friends hereby, and the Station went its own way and forgot them; only saying, occasionally, that Dormouse was the best of good fellows, though dull. A Civil Surgeon who never quarrels is a rarity, appreciated as such.

Few people can afford to play Robinson Crusoe anywhere—least of all in India, where we are few in the land, and very much dependent on each other's kind offices. Dumoise was wrong in shutting himself from the world for a year, and he discovered his mistake when an epidemic of typhoid broke out in the Station in the heart of the cold weather, and his wife went down. He was a shy little man, and five days were wasted before he realized that Mrs. Dumoise was burning with something worse than simple fever, and three days more passed before he ventured to call on Mrs. Shute, the Engineer's wife, and timidly speak about his trouble. Nearly every household in India knows that Doctors are very helpless in typhoid. The battle must be fought out between Death and the Nurses, minute by minute and degree by degree. Mrs. Shute almost boxed Dumoise's ears for what she called his "criminal delay," and went off at once to look after the poor girl. We had seven cases of typhoid in the Station that winter and, as the average of death is about one in every five cases, we felt certain that we should have to lose somebody. But all did their best. The women sat up nursing the women, and the men turned to and tended the bachelors who were down, and we wrestled with those typhoid cases for fifty-six days, and brought them through the Valley of the Shadow in triumph. But, just when we thought all was over, and were going to give a dance to celebrate the victory, little Mrs. Dumoise got a relapse and died in a week and the Station went to the funeral. Dumoise broke down utterly at the brink of the grave, and had to be taken away.

After the death, Dumoise crept into his own house and refused to be comforted. He did his duties perfectly, but we all felt that he should go on leave, and the other men of his own Service told him so. Dumoise was very thankful for the suggestion—he was thankful for anything in those days—and went to Chini on a walking-tour.

Chini is some twenty marches from Simla, in the heart of the Hills, and the scenery is good if you are in trouble. You pass through big, still deodar-forests, and under big, still cliffs, and over big, still grass-downs swelling like a woman's breasts; and the wind across the grass, and the rain among the deodars says:—"Hush—hush—hush." So little Dumoise was packed off to Chini, to wear down his grief with a full-plate camera, and a rifle. He took also a useless bearer, because the man had been his wife's favorite servant. He was idle and a thief, but Dumoise trusted everything to him.

On his way back from Chini, Dumoise turned aside to Bagi, through the Forest Reserve which is on the spur of Mount Huttoo. Some men who have travelled more than a little say that the march from Kotegarh to Bagi is one of the finest in creation. It runs through dark wet forest, and ends suddenly in bleak, nipped hill-side and black rocks. Bagi dak-bungalow is open to all the winds and is bitterly cold. Few people go to Bagi. Perhaps that was the reason why Dumoise went there. He halted at seven in the evening, and his bearer went down the hill-side to the village to engage coolies for the next day's march. The sun had set, and the night-winds were beginning to croon among the rocks. Dumoise leaned on the railing of the verandah, waiting for his bearer to return. The man came back almost immediately after he had disappeared, and at such a rate that Dumoise fancied he must have crossed a bear. He was running as hard as he could up the face of the hill.

But there was no bear to account for his terror. He raced to the verandah and fell down, the blood spurting from his nose and his face iron-gray. Then he gurgled:—"I have seen the Memsahib! I have seen the Memsahib!"

"Where?" said Dumoise.

"Down there, walking on the road to the village. She was in a blue dress, and she lifted the veil of her bonnet and said:—'Ram Dass, give my salaams to the Sahib, and tell him that I shall meet him next month at Nuddea.' Then I ran away, because I was afraid."

What Dumoise said or did I do not know. Ram Dass declares that he said nothing, but walked up and down the verandah all the cold night, waiting for the Memsahib to come up the hill and stretching out his arms into the dark like a madman. But no Memsahib came, and, next day, he went on to Simla cross-questioning the bearer every hour.

Ram Dass could only say that he had met Mrs. Dumoise and that she had lifted up her veil and given him the message which he had faithfully repeated to Dumoise. To this statement Ram Dass adhered.

He did not know where Nuddea was, had no friends at Nuddea, and would most certainly never go to Nuddea; even though his pay were doubled.

Nuddea is in Bengal, and has nothing whatever to do with a doctor serving in the Punjab. It must be more than twelve hundred miles from Meridki.

Dumoise went through Simla without halting, and returned to Meridki there to take over charge from the man who had been officiating for him during his tour. There were some Dispensary accounts to be explained, and some recent orders of the Surgeon-General to be noted, and, altogether, the taking-over was a full day's work. In the evening, Dumoise told his locum

tenens, who was an old friend of his bachelor days, what had happened at Bagi; and the man said that Ram Dass might as well have chosen Tuticorin while he was about it.

At that moment a telegraph-peon came in with a telegram from Simla, ordering Dumoise not to take over charge at Meridki, but to go at once to Nuddea on special duty. There was a nasty outbreak of cholera at Nuddea, and the Bengal Government, being shorthanded, as usual, had borrowed a Surgeon from the Punjab.

Dumoise threw the telegram across the table and said:—"Well?"

The other Doctor said nothing. It was all that he could say.

Then he remembered that Dumoise had passed through Simla on his way from Bagi; and thus might, possibly, have heard the first news of the impending transfer.

He tried to put the question, and the implied suspicion into words, but Dumoise stopped him with:—"If I had desired THAT, I should never have come back from Chini. I was shooting there. I wish to live, for I have things to do.... but I shall not be sorry."

The other man bowed his head, and helped, in the twilight, to pack up Dumoise's just opened trunks. Ram Dass entered with the lamps.

"Where is the Sahib going?" he asked.

"To Nuddea," said Dumoise, softly.

Ram Dass clawed Dumoise's knees and boots and begged him not to go.

Ram Dass wept and howled till he was turned out of the room. Then he wrapped up all his belongings and came back to ask for a character. He was not going to Nuddea to see his Sahib die, and, perhaps to die himself.

So Dumoise gave the man his wages and went down to Nuddea alone; the other Doctor bidding him goodbye as one under sentence of death.

Eleven days later, he had joined his Memsahib; and the Bengal Government had to borrow a fresh Doctor to cope with that epidemic at Nuddea. The first importation lay dead in Chooadanga Dak-Bungalow.

TO BE HELD FOR REFERENCE.

By the hoof of the Wild Goat up-tossed

From the Cliff where She lay in the Sun,

 Fell the Stone To the Tarn where the daylight is lost;

So She fell from the light of the Sun,

 And alone.

Now the fall was ordained from the first,

With the Goat and the Cliff and the Tarn,

 But the Stone Knows only Her life is accursed,

As She sinks in the depths of the Tarn,

 And alone.

Oh, Thou who has builded the world,

Oh, Thou who hast lighted the Sun!

Oh, Thou who hast darkened the Tarn!

 Judge Thou The Sin of the Stone that was hurled

By the Goat from the light of the Sun,

As She sinks in the mire of the Tarn,

 Even now—even now—even now!

 —From the Unpublished Papers of McIntosh Jellaludin.

"Say, is it dawn, is it dusk in thy Bower,

Thou whom I long for, who longest for me?

Oh be it night—be it—"

Here he fell over a little camel-colt that was sleeping in the Serai where the horse-traders and the best of the blackguards from Central Asia live; and, because he was very drunk indeed and the night was dark, he could not rise again till I helped him. That was the beginning of my

[780] RUDYARD KIPLING

acquaintance with McIntosh Jellaludin. When a loafer, and drunk, sings The Song of the Bower, he must be worth cultivating. He got off the camel's back and said, rather thickly:—"I—I—I'm a bit screwed, but a dip in Loggerhead will put me right again; and I say, have you spoken to Symonds about the mare's knees?"

Now Loggerhead was six thousand weary miles away from us, close to Mesopotamia, where you mustn't fish and poaching is impossible, and Charley Symonds' stable a half mile further across the paddocks. It was strange to hear all the old names, on a May night, among the horses and camels of the Sultan Caravanserai. Then the man seemed to remember himself and sober down at the same time. He leaned against the camel and pointed to a corner of the Serai where a lamp was burning:—

"I live there," said he, "and I should be extremely obliged if you would be good enough to help my mutinous feet thither; for I am more than usually drunk—most—most phenomenally tight. But not in respect to my head. 'My brain cries out against'—how does it go? But my head rides on the—rolls on the dung-hill I should have said, and controls the qualm."

I helped him through the gangs of tethered horses and he collapsed on the edge of the verandah in front of the line of native quarters.

"Thanks—a thousand thanks! O Moon and little, little Stars! To think that a man should so shamelessly.... Infamous liquor, too. Ovid in exile drank no worse. Better. It was frozen. Alas! I had no ice. Good night. I would introduce you to my wife were I sober—or she civilized."

A native woman came out of the darkness of the room, and began calling the man names; so I went away. He was the most interesting loafer that I had the pleasure of knowing for a long time; and later on, he became a friend of mine. He was a tall, well-built, fair man fearfully shaken with drink, and he looked nearer fifty than the thirty-five which, he said, was his real age. When a man begins to sink in India, and is not sent Home by his friends as soon as may be, he falls very low from a respectable point of view. By the time that he changes his creed, as did McIntosh, he is past redemption.

In most big cities, natives will tell you of two or three Sahibs, generally low-caste, who have turned Hindu or Mussulman, and who live more or less as such. But it is not often that you can get to know them. As McIntosh himself used to say:—"If I change my religion for my stomach's sake, I do not seek to become a martyr to missionaries, nor am I anxious for notoriety."

At the outset of acquaintance McIntosh warned me. "Remember this. I am not an object for charity. I require neither your money, your food, nor your cast-off raiment. I am that rare animal, a self-supporting drunkard. If you choose, I will smoke with you, for the tobacco of the bazars does not, I admit, suit my palate; and I will borrow any books which you may not specially value. It is more than likely that I shall sell them for bottles of excessively filthy country-liquors. In return, you shall share such hospitality as my house affords. Here is a charpoy on which two can sit, and it is possible that there may, from time to time, be food in that platter. Drink, unfortunately, you will find on the premises at any hour: and thus I make you welcome to all my poor establishments."

I was admitted to the McIntosh household—I and my good tobacco.

But nothing else. Unluckily, one cannot visit a loafer in the Serai by day. Friends buying horses would not understand it.

Consequently, I was obliged to see McIntosh after dark. He laughed at this, and said simply:—"You are perfectly right. When I enjoyed a position in society, rather higher than yours, I should

have done exactly the same thing, Good Heavens! I was once"—he spoke as though he had fallen from the Command of a Regiment—"an Oxford Man!" This accounted for the reference to Charley Symonds' stable.

"You," said McIntosh, slowly, "have not had that advantage; but, to outward appearance, you do not seem possessed of a craving for strong drinks. On the whole, I fancy that you are the luckier of the two. Yet I am not certain. You are—forgive my saying so even while I am smoking your excellent tobacco—painfully ignorant of many things."

We were sitting together on the edge of his bedstead, for he owned no chairs, watching the horses being watered for the night, while the native woman was preparing dinner. I did not like being patronized by a loafer, but I was his guest for the time being, though he owned only one very torn alpaca-coat and a pair of trousers made out of gunny-bags. He took the pipe out of his mouth, and went on judicially:—"All things considered, I doubt whether you are the luckier. I do not refer to your extremely limited classical attainments, or your excruciating quantities, but to your gross ignorance of matters more immediately under your notice. That for instance."— He pointed to a woman cleaning a samovar near the well in the centre of the Serai. She was flicking the water out of the spout in regular cadenced jerks.

"There are ways and ways of cleaning samovars. If you knew why she was doing her work in that particular fashion, you would know what the Spanish Monk meant when he said—

'I the Trinity illustrate,

 Drinking watered orange-pulp—

In three sips the Aryan frustrate,

 While he drains his at one gulp.—'

and many other things which now are hidden from your eyes. However, Mrs. McIntosh has prepared dinner. Let us come and eat after the fashion of the people of the country—of whom, by the way, you know nothing."

The native woman dipped her hand in the dish with us. This was wrong. The wife should always wait until the husband has eaten.

McIntosh Jellaludin apologized, saying:—

"It is an English prejudice which I have not been able to overcome; and she loves me. Why, I have never been able to understand. I fore-gathered with her at Jullundur, three years ago, and she has remained with me ever since. I believe her to be moral, and know her to be skilled in cookery."

He patted the woman's head as he spoke, and she cooed softly. She was not pretty to look at.

McIntosh never told me what position he had held before his fall.

He was, when sober, a scholar and a gentleman. When drunk, he was rather more of the first than the second. He used to get drunk about once a week for two days. On those occasions the native woman tended him while he raved in all tongues except his own. One day, indeed, he began reciting Atalanta in Calydon, and went through it to the end, beating time to the swing of the verse with a bedstead-leg. But he did most of his ravings in Greek or German. The man's mind was a perfect rag-bag of useless things. Once, when he was beginning to get sober, he told me that I was the only rational being in the Inferno into which he had descended—a Virgil in

the Shades, he said—and that, in return for my tobacco, he would, before he died, give me the materials of a new Inferno that should make me greater than Dante. Then he fell asleep on a horse-blanket and woke up quite calm.

"Man," said he, "when you have reached the uttermost depths of degradation, little incidents which would vex a higher life, are to you of no consequence. Last night, my soul was among the gods; but I make no doubt that my bestial body was writhing down here in the garbage."

"You were abominably drunk if that's what you mean," I said.

"I WAS drunk—filthy drunk. I who am the son of a man with whom you have no concern—I who was once Fellow of a College whose buttery-hatch you have not seen. I was loathsomely drunk. But consider how lightly I am touched. It is nothing to me. Less than nothing; for I do not even feel the headache which should be my portion. Now, in a higher life, how ghastly would have been my punishment, how bitter my repentance! Believe me, my friend with the neglected education, the highest is as the lowest—always supposing each degree extreme."

He turned round on the blanket, put his head between his fists and continued:—

"On the Soul which I have lost and on the Conscience which I have killed, I tell you that I CANNOT feel! I am as the gods, knowing good and evil, but untouched by either. Is this enviable or is it not?"

When a man has lost the warning of "next morning's head," he must be in a bad state, I answered, looking at McIntosh on the blanket, with his hair over his eyes and his lips blue-white, that I did not think the insensibility good enough.

"For pity's sake, don't say that! I tell you, it IS good and most enviable. Think of my consolations!"

"Have you so many, then, McIntosh?"

"Certainly; your attempts at sarcasm which is essentially the weapon of a cultured man, are crude. First, my attainments, my classical and literary knowledge, blurred, perhaps, by immoderate drinking—which reminds me that before my soul went to the Gods last night, I sold the Pickering Horace you so kindly lent me. Ditta Mull the Clothesman has it. It fetched ten annas, and may be redeemed for a rupee—but still infinitely superior to yours. Secondly, the abiding affection of Mrs. McIntosh, best of wives. Thirdly, a monument, more enduring than brass, which I have built up in the seven years of my degradation."

He stopped here, and crawled across the room for a drink of water.

He was very shaky and sick.

He referred several times to his "treasure"—some great possession that he owned—but I held this to be the raving of drink. He was as poor and as proud as he could be. His manner was not pleasant, but he knew enough about the natives, among whom seven years of his life had been spent, to make his acquaintance worth having. He used actually to laugh at Strickland as an ignorant man—"ignorant West and East"—he said. His boast was, first, that he was an Oxford Man of rare and shining parts, which may or may not have been true—I did not know enough to check his statements—and, secondly, that he "had his hand on the pulse of native life"—which was a fact. As an Oxford man, he struck me as a prig: he was always throwing his education about. As a Mahommedan faquir—as McIntosh Jellaludin—he was all that I wanted for my own ends. He smoked several pounds of my tobacco, and taught me several ounces of things

worth knowing; but he would never accept any gifts, not even when the cold weather came, and gripped the poor thin chest under the poor thin alpaca-coat. He grew very angry, and said that I had insulted him, and that he was not going into hospital. He had lived like a beast and he would die rationally, like a man.

As a matter of fact, he died of pneumonia; and on the night of his death sent over a grubby note asking me to come and help him to die.

The native woman was weeping by the side of the bed. McIntosh, wrapped in a cotton cloth, was too weak to resent a fur coat being thrown over him. He was very active as far as his mind was concerned, and his eyes were blazing. When he had abused the Doctor who came with me so foully that the indignant old fellow left, he cursed me for a few minutes and calmed down.

Then he told his wife to fetch out "The Book" from a hole in the wall. She brought out a big bundle, wrapped in the tail of a petticoat, of old sheets of miscellaneous note-paper, all numbered and covered with fine cramped writing. McIntosh ploughed his hand through the rubbish and stirred it up lovingly.

"This," he said, "is my work—the Book of McIntosh Jellaludin, showing what he saw and how he lived, and what befell him and others; being also an account of the life and sins and death of Mother Maturin. What Mirza Murad Ali Beg's book is to all other books on native life, will my work be to Mirza Murad Ali Beg's!"

This, as will be conceded by any one who knows Mirza Ali Beg's book, was a sweeping statement. The papers did not look specially valuable; but McIntosh handled them as if they were currency-notes.

Then he said slowly:—"In despite the many weaknesses of your education, you have been good to me. I will speak of your tobacco when I reach the Gods. I owe you much thanks for many kindnesses.

"But I abominate indebtedness. For this reason I bequeath to you now the monument more enduring than brass—my one book—rude and imperfect in parts, but oh, how rare in others! I wonder if you will understand it. It is a gift more honorable than... Bah! where is my brain rambling to? You will mutilate it horribly. You will knock out the gems you call 'Latin quotations,' you Philistine, and you will butcher the style to carve into your own jerky jargon; but you cannot destroy the whole of it. I bequeath it to you.

"Ethel... My brain again!.. Mrs. McIntosh, bear witness that I give the sahib all these papers. They would be of no use to you, Heart of my heart; and I lay it upon you," he turned to me here, "that you do not let my book die in its present form. It is yours unconditionally—the story of McIntosh Jellaludin, which is NOT the story of McIntosh Jellaludin, but of a greater man than he, and of a far greater woman. Listen now! I am neither mad nor drunk! That book will make you famous."

I said, "thank you," as the native woman put the bundle into my arms.

"My only baby!" said McIntosh with a smile. He was sinking fast, but he continued to talk as long as breath remained. I waited for the end: knowing that, in six cases out of ten the dying man calls for his mother. He turned on his side and said:—

"Say how it came into your possession. No one will believe you, but my name, at least, will live. You will treat it brutally, I know you will. Some of it must go; the public are fools and prudish fools. I was their servant once. But do your mangling gently—very gently. It is a great work,

and I have paid for it in seven years' damnation."

His voice stopped for ten or twelve breaths, and then he began mumbling a prayer of some kind in Greek. The native woman cried very bitterly. Lastly, he rose in bed and said, as loudly as slowly:—"Not guilty, my Lord!"

Then he fell back, and the stupor held him till he died. The native woman ran into the Serai among the horses and screamed and beat her breasts; for she had loved him.

Perhaps his last sentence in life told what McIntosh had once gone through; but, saving the big bundle of old sheets in the cloth, there was nothing in his room to say who or what he had been.

The papers were in a hopeless muddle.

Strickland helped me to sort them, and he said that the writer was either an extreme liar or a most wonderful person. He thought the former. One of these days, you may be able to judge for yourself.

The bundle needed much expurgation and was full of Greek nonsense, at the head of the chapters, which has all been cut out.

If the things are ever published some one may perhaps remember this story, now printed as a safeguard to prove that McIntosh Jellaludin and not I myself wrote the Book of Mother Maturin.

I don't want the Giant's Robe to come true in my case.

VOLUME VI THE LIGHT THAT FAILED
THE LIGHT THAT FAILED
CHAPTER I

So we settled it all when the storm was done

As comf'y as comf'y could be;

And I was to wait in the barn, my dears,

Because I was only three;

And Teddy would run to the rainbow's foot,

Because he was five and a man;

And that's how it all began, my dears,

And that's how it all began.

> —Big Barn Stories.

"WHAT do you think she'd do if she caught us? We oughtn't to have it, you know," said Maisie.

"Beat me, and lock you up in your bedroom," Dick answered, without hesitation. "Have you got the cartridges?"

"Yes; they're in my pocket, but they are joggling horribly. Do pin-fire cartridges go off of their own accord?"

"Don't know. Take the revolver, if you are afraid, and let me carry them."

"I'm not afraid." Maisie strode forward swiftly, a hand in her pocket and her chin in the air. Dick followed with a small pin-fire revolver.

The children had discovered that their lives would be unendurable without pistol-practice. After much forethought and self-denial, Dick had saved seven shillings and sixpence, the price of a badly constructed Belgian revolver. Maisie could only contribute half a crown to the syndicate for the purchase of a hundred cartridges. "You can save better than I can, Dick," she explained; "I like nice things to eat, and it doesn't matter to you. Besides, boys ought to do these things."

Dick grumbled a little at the arrangement, but went out and made the purchase, which the children were then on their way to test. Revolvers did not lie in the scheme of their daily life as decreed for them by the guardian who was incorrectly supposed to stand in the place of a mother to these two orphans. Dick had been under her care for six years, during which time she had made her profit of the allowances supposed to be expended on his clothes, and, partly through thoughtlessness, partly through a natural desire to pain,—she was a widow of some years anxious to marry again,—had made his days burdensome on his young shoulders.

Where he had looked for love, she gave him first aversion and then hate.

Where he growing older had sought a little sympathy, she gave him ridicule. The many hours

that she could spare from the ordering of her small house she devoted to what she called the home-training of Dick Heldar. Her religion, manufactured in the main by her own intelligence and a keen study of the Scriptures, was an aid to her in this matter. At such times as she herself was not personally displeased with Dick, she left him to understand that he had a heavy account to settle with his Creator; wherefore Dick learned to loathe his God as intensely as he loathed Mrs. Jennett; and this is not a wholesome frame of mind for the young. Since she chose to regard him as a hopeless liar, when dread of pain drove him to his first untruth he naturally developed into a liar, but an economical and self-contained one, never throwing away the least unnecessary fib, and never hesitating at the blackest, were it only plausible, that might make his life a little easier. The treatment taught him at least the power of living alone,—a power that was of service to him when he went to a public school and the boys laughed at his clothes, which were poor in quality and much mended. In the holidays he returned to the teachings of Mrs. Jennett, and, that the chain of discipline might not be weakened by association with the world, was generally beaten, on one account or another, before he had been twelve hours under her roof.

The autumn of one year brought him a companion in bondage, a long-haired, gray-eyed little atom, as self-contained as himself, who moved about the house silently and for the first few weeks spoke only to the goat that was her chiefest friend on earth and lived in the back-garden. Mrs. Jennett objected to the goat on the grounds that he was un-Christian,—which he certainly was. "Then," said the atom, choosing her words very deliberately, "I shall write to my lawyer-peoples and tell them that you are a very bad woman. Amomma is mine, mine, mine!" Mrs. Jennett made a movement to the hall, where certain umbrellas and canes stood in a rack. The atom understood as clearly as Dick what this meant. "I have been beaten before," she said, still in the same passionless voice; "I have been beaten worse than you can ever beat me. If you beat me I shall write to my lawyer-peoples and tell them that you do not give me enough to eat. I am not afraid of you." Mrs. Jennett did not go into the hall, and the atom, after a pause to assure herself that all danger of war was past, went out, to weep bitterly on Amomma's neck.

Dick learned to know her as Maisie, and at first mistrusted her profoundly, for he feared that she might interfere with the small liberty of action left to him. She did not, however; and she volunteered no friendliness until Dick had taken the first steps. Long before the holidays were over, the stress of punishment shared in common drove the children together, if it were only to play into each other's hands as they prepared lies for Mrs. Jennett's use. When Dick returned to school, Maisie whispered, "Now I shall be all alone to take care of myself; but," and she nodded her head bravely, "I can do it. You promised to send Amomma a grass collar. Send it soon." A week later she asked for that collar by return of post, and was not pleased when she learned that it took time to make. When at last Dick forwarded the gift, she forgot to thank him for it.

Many holidays had come and gone since that day, and Dick had grown into a lanky hobbledehoy more than ever conscious of his bad clothes. Not for a moment had Mrs. Jennett relaxed her tender care of him, but the average canings of a public school—Dick fell under punishment about three times a month—filled him with contempt for her powers. "She doesn't hurt," he explained to Maisie, who urged him to rebellion, "and she is kinder to you after she has whacked me." Dick shambled through the days unkempt in body and savage in soul, as the smaller boys of the school learned to know, for when the spirit moved him he would hit them, cunningly and with science. The same spirit made him more than once try to tease Maisie, but the girl refused to be made unhappy. "We are both miserable as it is," said she. "What is the use of trying to make things worse? Let's find things to do, and forget things."

The pistol was the outcome of that search. It could only be used on the muddiest foreshore of the beach, far away from the bathing-machines and pierheads, below the grassy slopes of Fort Keeling. The tide ran out nearly two miles on that coast, and the many-coloured mud-banks,

touched by the sun, sent up a lamentable smell of dead weed. It was late in the afternoon when Dick and Maisie arrived on their ground, Amomma trotting patiently behind them.

"Mf!" said Maisie, sniffing the air. "I wonder what makes the sea so smelly? I don'tlike it!"

"You never like anything that isn't made just for you," said Dick bluntly. "Give me the cartridges, and I'll try first shot. How far does one of these little revolvers carry?"

"Oh, half a mile," said Maisie, promptly. "At least it makes an awful noise. Be careful with the cartridges; I don't like those jagged stick-up things on the rim. Dick, do be careful."

"All right. I know how to load. I'll fire at the breakwater out there."

He fired, and Amomma ran away bleating. The bullet threw up a spurt of mud to the right of the wood-wreathed piles.

"Throws high and to the right. You try, Maisie. Mind, it's loaded all round."

Maisie took the pistol and stepped delicately to the verge of the mud, her hand firmly closed on the butt, her mouth and left eye screwed up.

Dick sat down on a tuft of bank and laughed. Amomma returned very cautiously. He was accustomed to strange experiences in his afternoon walks, and, finding the cartridge-box unguarded, made investigations with his nose. Maisie fired, but could not see where the bullet went.

"I think it hit the post," she said, shading her eyes and looking out across the sailless sea.

"I know it has gone out to the Marazion Bell-buoy," said Dick, with a chuckle. "Fire low and to the left; then perhaps you'll get it. Oh, look at Amomma!—he's eating the cartridges!"

Maisie turned, the revolver in her hand, just in time to see Amomma scampering away from the pebbles Dick threw after him. Nothing is sacred to a billy-goat. Being well fed and the adored of his mistress, Amomma had naturally swallowed two loaded pin-fire cartridges. Maisie hurried up to assure herself that Dick had not miscounted the tale.

"Yes, he's eaten two."

"Horrid little beast! Then they'll joggle about inside him and blow up, and serve him right.... Oh, Dick! have I killed you?"

Revolvers are tricky things for young hands to deal with. Maisie could not explain how it had happened, but a veil of reeking smoke separated her from Dick, and she was quite certain that the pistol had gone off in his face. Then she heard him sputter, and dropped on her knees beside him, crying, "Dick, you aren't hurt, are you? I didn't mean it."

"Of course you didn't," said Dick, coming out of the smoke and wiping his cheek. "But you nearly blinded me. That powder stuff stings awfully." A neat little splash of gray led on a stone showed where the bullet had gone. Maisie began to whimper.

"Don't," said Dick, jumping to his feet and shaking himself. "I'm not a bit hurt."

"No, but I might have killed you," protested Maisie, the corners of her mouth drooping. "What should I have done then?"

"Gone home and told Mrs. Jennett." Dick grinned at the thought; then, softening, "Please don't

worry about it. Besides, we are wasting time. We've got to get back to tea. I'll take the revolver for a bit."

Maisie would have wept on the least encouragement, but Dick's indifference, albeit his hand was shaking as he picked up the pistol, restrained her. She lay panting on the beach while Dick methodically bombarded the breakwater. "Got it at last!" he exclaimed, as a lock of weed flew from the wood.

"Let me try," said Maisie, imperiously. "I'm all right now."

They fired in turns till the rickety little revolver nearly shook itself to pieces, and Amomma the outcast—because he might blow up at any moment—browsed in the background and wondered why stones were thrown at him. Then they found a balk of timber floating in a pool which was commanded by the seaward slope of Fort Keeling, and they sat down together before this new target.

"Next holidays," said Dick, as the now thoroughly fouled revolver kicked wildly in his hand, "we'll get another pistol,—central fire,—that will carry farther."

"There won't be any next holidays for me," said Maisie. "I'm going away."

"Where to?"

"I don't know. My lawyers have written to Mrs. Jennett, and I've got to be educated somewhere,—in France, perhaps,—I don'tknow where; but I shall be glad to go away."

"I shan't like it a bit. I suppose I shall be left. Look here, Maisie, is it really true you're going? Then these holidays will be the last I shall see anything of you; and I go back to school next week. I wish——"

The young blood turned his cheeks scarlet. Maisie was picking grass-tufts and throwing them down the slope at a yellow sea-poppy nodding all by itself to the illimitable levels of the mud-flats and the milk-white sea beyond.

"I wish," she said, after a pause, "that I could see you again sometime. You wish that, too?"

"Yes, but it would have been better if—if—you had—shot straight over there—down by the breakwater."

Maisie looked with large eyes for a moment. And this was the boy who only ten days before had decorated Amomma's horns with cut-paper ham-frills and turned him out, a bearded derision, among the public ways! Then she dropped her eyes: this was not the boy.

"Don't be stupid," she said reprovingly, and with swift instinct attacked the side-issue. "How selfish you are! Just think what I should have felt if that horrid thing had killed you! I'm quite miserable enough already."

"Why? Because you're going away from Mrs. Jennett?"

"No."

"From me, then?"

No answer for a long time. Dick dared not look at her. He felt, though he did not know, all that the past four years had been to him, and this the more acutely since he had no knowledge to put his feelings in words.

"I don't know," she said. "I suppose it is."

"Maisie, you must know. I'm not supposing."

"Let's go home," said Maisie, weakly.

But Dick was not minded to retreat.

"I can't say things," he pleaded, "and I'm awfully sorry for teasing you about Amomma the other day. It's all different now, Maisie, can't you see? And you might have told me that you were going, instead of leaving me to find out."

"You didn't. I did tell. Oh, Dick, what's the use of worrying?"

"There isn't any; but we've been together years and years, and I didn't know how much I cared."

"I don't believe you ever did care."

"No, I didn't; but I do,—I care awfully now, Maisie," he gulped,—"Maisie, darling, say you care too, please."

"I do, indeed I do; but it won't be any use."

"Why?"

"Because I am going away."

"Yes, but if you promise before you go. Only say—will you?" A second "darling" came to his lips more easily than the first. There were few endearments in Dick's home or school life; he had to find them by instinct. Dick caught the little hand blackened with the escaped gas of the revolver.

"I promise," she said solemnly; "but if I care there is no need for promising."

"And do you care?" For the first time in the past few minutes their eyes met and spoke for them who had no skill in speech....

"Oh, Dick, don't! Please don't! It was all right when we said good-morning; but now it's all different!" Amomma looked on from afar.

He had seen his property quarrel frequently, but he had never seen kisses exchanged before. The yellow sea-poppy was wiser, and nodded its head approvingly. Considered as a kiss, that was a failure, but since it was the first, other than those demanded by duty, in all the world that either had ever given or taken, it opened to them new worlds, and every one of them glorious, so that they were lifted above the consideration of any worlds at all, especially those in which tea is necessary, and sat still, holding each other's hands and saying not a word.

"You can't forget now," said Dick, at last. There was that on his cheek that stung more than gunpowder.

"I shouldn't have forgotten anyhow," said Maisie, and they looked at each other and saw that each was changed from the companion of an hour ago to a wonder and a mystery they could not understand. The sun began to set, and a night-wind thrashed along the bents of the foreshore.

"We shall be awfully late for tea," said Maisie. "Let's go home."

"Let's use the rest of the cartridges first," said Dick; and he helped Maisie down the slope of the fort to the sea,—a descent that she was quite capable of covering at full speed. Equally gravely Maisie took the grimy hand. Dick bent forward clumsily; Maisie drew the hand away, and Dick blushed.

"It's very pretty," he said.

"Pooh!" said Maisie, with a little laugh of gratified vanity. She stood close to Dick as he loaded the revolver for the last time and fired over the sea with a vague notion at the back of his head that he was protecting Maisie from all the evils in the world. A puddle far across the mud caught the last rays of the sun and turned into a wrathful red disc. The light held Dick's attention for a moment, and as he raised his revolver there fell upon him a renewed sense of the miraculous, in that he was standing by Maisie who had promised to care for him for an indefinite length of time till such date as——A gust of the growing wind drove the girl's long black hair across his face as she stood with her hand on his shoulder calling Amomma "a little beast," and for a moment he was in the dark,—a darkness that stung. The bullet went singing out to the empty sea.

"Spoilt my aim," said he, shaking his head. "There aren't any more cartridges; we shall have to run home." But they did not run. They walked very slowly, arm in arm. And it was a matter of indifference to them whether the neglected Amomma with two pin-fire cartridges in his inside blew up or trotted beside them; for they had come into a golden heritage and were disposing of it with all the wisdom of all their years.

"And I shall be——" quoth Dick, valiantly. Then he checked himself: "I don't know what I shall be. I don't seem to be able to pass any exams, but I can make awful caricatures of the masters. Ho! Ho!"

"Be an artist, then," said Maisie. "You're always laughing at my trying to draw; and it will do you good."

"I'll never laugh at anything you do," he answered. "I'll be an artist, and I'll do things."

"Artists always want money, don'tthey?"

"I've got a hundred and twenty pounds a year of my own. My guardians tell me I'm to have it when I come of age. That will be enough to begin with."

"Ah, I'm rich," said Maisie. "I've got three hundred a year all my own when I'm twenty-one. That's why Mrs. Jennett is kinder to me than she is to you. I wish, though, that I had somebody that belonged to me,—just a father or a mother."

"You belong to me," said Dick, "for ever and ever."

"Yes, we belong—for ever. It's very nice." She squeezed his arm. The kindly darkness hid them both, and, emboldened because he could only just see the profile of Maisie's cheek with the long lashes veiling the gray eyes, Dick at the front door delivered himself of the words he had been boggling over for the last two hours.

"And I—love you, Maisie," he said, in a whisper that seemed to him to ring across the world,—the world that he would tomorrow or the next day set out to conquer.

There was a scene, not, for the sake of discipline, to be reported, when Mrs. Jennett would have fallen upon him, first for disgraceful unpunctuality, and secondly for nearly killing himself with a forbidden weapon.

"I was playing with it, and it went off by itself," said Dick, when the powder-pocked cheek could no longer be hidden, "but if you think you're going to lick me you're wrong. You are never going to touch me again. Sit down and give me my tea. You can't cheat us out of that, anyhow."

Mrs. Jennett gasped and became livid. Maisie said nothing, but encouraged Dick with her eyes, and he behaved abominably all that evening. Mrs. Jennett prophesied an immediate judgment of Providence and a descent into Tophet later, but Dick walked in Paradise and would not hear. Only when he was going to bed Mrs. Jennett recovered and asserted herself. He had bidden Maisie good night with down-dropped eyes and from a distance.

"If you aren't a gentleman you might try to behave like one," said Mrs. Jennett, spitefully. "You've been quarrelling with Maisie again."

This meant that the usual good-night kiss had been omitted. Maisie, white to the lips, thrust her cheek forward with a fine air of indifference, and was duly pecked by Dick, who tramped out of the room red as fire. That night he dreamed a wild dream. He had won all the world and brought it to Maisie in a cartridge-box, but she turned it over with her foot, and, instead of saying "Thank you," cried—"Where is the grass collar you promised for Amomma? Oh, how selfish you are!"

CHAPTER II

Then we brought the lances down, then the bugles blew,

When we went to Kandahar, ridin' two an'' two,

Ridin', ridin', ridin', two an'' two,

Ta-ra-ra-ra-ra-ra-ra,

All the way to Kandahar, ridin' two an'' two.

—Barrack-Room Ballad.

"I'M NOT angry with the British public, but I wish we had a few thousand of them scattered among these rooks. They wouldn't be in such a hurry to get at their morning papers then. Can't you imagine the regulation householder—Lover of Justice, Constant Reader, Paterfamilias, and all that lot—frizzling on hot gravel?"

"With a blue veil over his head, and his clothes in strips. Has any man here a needle? I've got a piece of sugar-sack."

"I'll lend you a packing-needle for six square inches of it then. Both my knees are worn through."

"Why not six square acres, while you're about it? But lend me the needle, and I'll see what I can do with the selvage. I don't think there's enough to protect my royal body from the cold blast as it is. What are you doing with that everlasting sketch-book of yours, Dick?"

"Study of our Special Correspondent repairing his wardrobe," said Dick, gravely, as the other man kicked off a pair of sorely worn riding-breeches and began to fit a square of coarse canvas over the most obvious open space. He grunted disconsolately as the vastness of the void developed itself.

"Sugar-bags, indeed! Hi! you pilot man there! lend me all the sails for that whale-boat."

A fez-crowned head bobbed up in the stern-sheets, divided itself into exact halves with one flashing grin, and bobbed down again. The man of the tattered breeches, clad only in a Norfolk jacket and a gray flannel shirt, went on with his clumsy sewing, while Dick chuckled over the sketch.

Some twenty whale-boats were nuzzling a sand-bank which was dotted with English soldiery of half a dozen corps, bathing or washing their clothes. A heap of boat-rollers, commissariat-boxes, sugar-bags, and flour—and small-arm-ammunition-cases showed where one of the whale-boats had been compelled to unload hastily; and a regimental carpenter was swearing aloud as he tried, on a wholly insufficient allowance of white lead, to plaster up the sun-parched gaping seams of the boat herself.

"First the bloomin' rudder snaps," said he to the world in general; "then the mast goes; an' then, s' help me, when she can't do nothin' else, she opens 'erself out like a cock-eyed Chinese lotus."

"Exactly the case with my breeches, whoever you are," said the tailor, without looking up. "Dick, I wonder when I shall see a decent shop again."

There was no answer, save the incessant angry murmur of the Nile as it raced round a basalt-walled bend and foamed across a rock-ridge half a mile upstream. It was as though the brown weight of the river would drive the white men back to their own country. The indescribable scent of Nile mud in the air told that the stream was falling and the next few miles would be no light thing for the whale-boats to overpass. The desert ran down almost to the banks, where, among gray, red, and black hillocks, a camel-corps was encamped. No man dared even for a day lose touch of the slow-moving boats; there had been no fighting for weeks past, and throughout all that time the Nile had never spared them. Rapid had followed rapid, rock rock, and island-group island-group, till the rank and file had long since lost all count of direction and very nearly of time. They were moving somewhere, they did not know why, to do something, they did not know what. Before them lay the Nile, and at the other end of it was one Gordon, fighting for the dear life, in a town called Khartoum. There were columns of British troops in the desert, or in one of the many deserts; there were yet more columns waiting to embark on the river; there were fresh drafts waiting at Assioot and Assuan; there were lies and rumours running over the face of the hopeless land from Suakin to the Sixth Cataract, and men supposed generally that there must be some one in authority to direct the general scheme of the many movements. The duty of that particular river-column was to keep the whale-boats afloat in the water, to avoid trampling on the villagers' crops when the gangs "tracked" the boats with lines thrown from midstream, to get as much sleep and food as was possible, and, above all, to press on without delay in the teeth of the churning Nile.

With the soldiers sweated and toiled the correspondents of the newspapers, and they were almost as ignorant as their companions. But it was above all things necessary that England at breakfast should be amused and thrilled and interested, whether Gordon lived or died, or half the British army went to pieces in the sands. The Soudan campaign was a picturesque one, and lent itself to vivid word-painting. Now and again a "Special" managed to get slain,—which was not altogether a disadvantage to the paper that employed him,—and more often the hand-to-hand nature of the fighting allowed of miraculous escapes which were worth telegraphing home at eighteenpence the word. There were many correspondents with many corps and columns,—from the veterans who had followed on the heels of the cavalry that occupied Cairo in '82, what time Arabi Pasha called himself king, who had seen the first miserable work round Suakin when the sentries were cut up nightly and the scrub swarmed with spears, to youngsters jerked into the business at the end of a telegraph-wire to take the places of their betters killed or invalided.

Among the seniors—those who knew every shift and change in the perplexing postal arrangements, the value of the seediest, weediest Egyptian garron offered for sale in Cairo or Alexandria, who could talk a telegraph-clerk into amiability and soothe the ruffled vanity of a newly appointed staff-officer when press regulations became burdensome—was the man in the flannel shirt, the black-browed Torpenhow. He represented the Central Southern Syndicate in the campaign, as he had represented it in the Egyptian war, and elsewhere. The syndicate did not concern itself greatly with criticisms of attack and the like. It supplied the masses, and all it demanded was picturesqueness and abundance of detail; for there is more joy in England over a soldier who insubordinately steps out of square to rescue a comrade than over twenty generals slaving even to baldness at the gross details of transport and commissariat.

He had met at Suakin a young man, sitting on the edge of a recently abandoned redoubt about the size of a hat-box, sketching a clump of shell-torn bodies on the gravel plain.

"What are you for?" said Torpenhow. The greeting of the correspondent is that of the commercial traveller on the road.

"My own hand," said the young man, without looking up. "Have you any tobacco?"

Torpenhow waited till the sketch was finished, and when he had looked at it said, "What's your business here?"

"Nothing; there was a row, so I came. I'm supposed to be doing something down at the painting-slips among the boats, or else I'm in charge of the condenser on one of the water-ships. I've forgotten which."

"You've cheek enough to build a redoubt with," said Torpenhow, and took stock of the new acquaintance. "Do you always draw like that?"

The young man produced more sketches. "Row on a Chinese pig-boat," said he, sententiously, showing them one after another.—"Chief mate dirked by a comprador.—Junk ashore off Hakodate.—Somali muleteer being flogged.—Star-shell bursting over camp at Berbera.—Slave-dhow being chased round Tajurrah Bah.—Soldier lying dead in the moonlight outside Suakin.—throat cut by Fuzzies."

"H'm!" said Torpenhow, "can't say I care for Verestchagin-and-water myself, but there's no accounting for tastes. Doing anything now, are you?"

"No. I'm amusing myself here."

Torpenhow looked at the sketches again, and nodded. "Yes, you're right to take your first chance when you can get it."

He rode away swiftly through the Gate of the Two War-Ships, rattled across the causeway into the town, and wired to his syndicate, "Got man here, picture-work. Good and cheap. Shall I arrange? Will do letterpress with sketches."

The man on the redoubt sat swinging his legs and murmuring, "I knew the chance would come, sooner or later. By Gad, they'll have to sweat for it if I come through this business alive!"

In the evening Torpenhow was able to announce to his friend that the Central Southern Agency was willing to take him on trial, paying expenses for three months. "And, by the way, what's your name?" said Torpenhow.

"Heldar. Do they give me a free hand?"

"They've taken you on chance. You must justify the choice. You'd better stick to me. I'm going up-country with a column, and I'll do what I can for you. Give me some of your sketches taken here, and I'll send 'em along." To himself he said, "That's the best bargain the Central Southern has ever made; and they got me cheaply enough."

So it came to pass that, after some purchase of horse-flesh and arrangements financial and political, Dick was made free of the New and Honourable Fraternity of war correspondents, who all possess the inalienable right of doing as much work as they can and getting as much for it as Providence and their owners shall please. To these things are added in time, if the brother be worthy, the power of glib speech that neither man nor woman can resist when a meal or a bed is in question, the eye of a horse-cope, the skill of a cook, the constitution of a bullock, the digestion of an ostrich, and an infinite adaptability to all circumstances. But many die before they attain to this degree, and the past-masters in the craft appear for the most part in dress-clothes when they are in England, and thus their glory is hidden from the multitude.

Dick followed Torpenhow wherever the latter's fancy chose to lead him, and between the two they managed to accomplish some work that almost satisfied themselves. It was not an easy life in any way, and under its influence the two were drawn very closely together, for they ate from

the same dish, they shared the same water-bottle, and, most binding tie of all, their mails went off together. It was Dick who managed to make gloriously drunk a telegraph-clerk in a palm hut far beyond the Second Cataract, and, while the man lay in bliss on the floor, possessed himself of some laboriously acquired exclusive information, forwarded by a confiding correspondent of an opposition syndicate, made a careful duplicate of the matter, and brought the result to Torpenhow, who said that all was fair in love or war correspondence, and built an excellent descriptive article from his rival's riotous waste of words. It was Torpenhow who—but the tale of their adventures, together and apart, from Philae to the waste wilderness of Herawi and Muella, would fill many books. They had been penned into a square side by side, in deadly fear of being shot by over-excited soldiers; they had fought with baggage-camels in the chill dawn; they had jogged along in silence under blinding sun on indefatigable little Egyptian horses; and they had floundered on the shallows of the Nile when the whale-boat in which they had found a berth chose to hit a hidden rock and rip out half her bottom-planks.

Now they were sitting on the sand-bank, and the whale-boats were bringing up the remainder of the column.

"Yes," said Torpenhow, as he put the last rude stitches into his over-long-neglected gear, "it has been a beautiful business."

"The patch or the campaign?" said Dick. "Don't think much of either, myself."

"You want the Euryalus brought up above the Third Cataract, don't you? and eighty-one-ton guns at Jakdul? Now, I'm quite satisfied with my breeches." He turned round gravely to exhibit himself, after the manner of a clown.

"It's very pretty. Specially the lettering on the sack. G.B.T. Government Bullock Train. That's a sack from India."

"It's my initials,—Gilbert Belling Torpenhow. I stole the cloth on purpose. What the mischief are the camel-corps doing yonder?" Torpenhow shaded his eyes and looked across the scrub-strewn gravel.

A bugle blew furiously, and the men on the bank hurried to their arms and accoutrements.

"'Pisan soldiery surprised while bathing,'" remarked Dick, calmly.

"D'you remember the picture? It's by Michael Angelo; all beginners copy it. That scrub's alive with enemy."

The camel-corps on the bank yelled to the infantry to come to them, and a hoarse shouting down the river showed that the remainder of the column had wind of the trouble and was hastening to take share in it. As swiftly as a reach of still water is crisped by the wind, the rock-strewn ridges and scrub-topped hills were troubled and alive with armed men.

Mercifully, it occurred to these to stand far off for a time, to shout and gesticulate joyously. One man even delivered himself of a long story. The camel-corps did not fire. They were only too glad of a little breathing-space, until some sort of square could be formed. The men on the sand-bank ran to their side; and the whale-boats, as they toiled up within shouting distance, were thrust into the nearest bank and emptied of all save the sick and a few men to guard them. The Arab orator ceased his outcries, and his friends howled.

"They look like the Mahdi's men," said Torpenhow, elbowing himself into the crush of the square; "but what thousands of 'em there are! The tribes hereabout aren't against us, I know."

"Then the Mahdi's taken another town," said Dick, "and set all these yelping devils free to show us up. Lend us your glass."

"Our scouts should have told us of this. We've been trapped," said a subaltern. "Aren't the camel guns ever going to begin? Hurry up, you men!"

There was no need of any order. The men flung themselves panting against the sides of the square, for they had good reason to know that whoso was left outside when the fighting began would very probably die in an extremely unpleasant fashion. The little hundred-and-fifty-pound camel-guns posted at one corner of the square opened the ball as the square moved forward by its right to get possession of a knoll of rising ground. All had fought in this manner many times before, and there was no novelty in the entertainment; always the same hot and stifling formation, the smell of dust and leather, the same boltlike rush of the enemy, the same pressure on the weakest side, the few minutes of hand-to-hand scuffle, and then the silence of the desert, broken only by the yells of those whom their handful of cavalry attempted to purse. They had become careless. The camel-guns spoke at intervals, and the square slouched forward amid the protesting of the camels. Then came the attack of three thousand men who had not learned from books that it is impossible for troops in close order to attack against breech-loading fire.

A few dropping shots heralded their approach, and a few horsemen led, but the bulk of the force was naked humanity, mad with rage, and armed with the spear and the sword. The instinct of the desert, where there is always much war, told them that the right flank of the square was the weakest, for they swung clear of the front. The camel-guns shelled them as they passed and opened for an instant lanes through their midst, most like those quick-closing vistas in a Kentish hop-garden seen when the train races by at full speed; and the infantry fire, held till the opportune moment, dropped them in close-packing hundreds. No civilised troops in the world could have endured the hell through which they came, the living leaping high to avoid the dying who clutched at their heels, the wounded cursing and staggering forward, till they fell—a torrent black as the sliding water above a mill-dam—full on the right flank of the square.

Then the line of the dusty troops and the faint blue desert sky overhead went out in rolling smoke, and the little stones on the heated ground and the tinder-dry clumps of scrub became matters of surpassing interest, for men measured their agonised retreat and recovery by these things, counting mechanically and hewing their way back to chosen pebble and branch. There was no semblance of any concerted fighting. For aught the men knew, the enemy might be attempting all four sides of the square at once. Their business was to destroy what lay in front of them, to bayonet in the back those who passed over them, and, dying, to drag down the slayer till he could be knocked on the head by some avenging gun-butt.

Dick waited with Torpenhow and a young doctor till the stress grew unendurable. It was hopeless to attend to the wounded till the attack was repulsed, so the three moved forward gingerly towards the weakest side of the square. There was a rush from without, the short hough-hough of the stabbing spears, and a man on a horse, followed by thirty or forty others, dashed through, yelling and hacking. The right flank of the square sucked in after them, and the other sides sent help. The wounded, who knew that they had but a few hours more to live, caught at the enemy's feet and brought them down, or, staggering into a discarded rifle, fired blindly into the scuffle that raged in the centre of the square.

Dick was conscious that somebody had cut him violently across his helmet, that he had fired his revolver into a black, foam-flecked face which forthwith ceased to bear any resemblance to a face, and that Torpenhow had gone down under an Arab whom he had tried to "collar low," and was turning over and over with his captive, feeling for the man's eyes. The doctor jabbed at a venture with a bayonet, and a helmetless soldier fired over Dick's shoulder: the flying grains of

powder stung his cheek. It was to Torpenhow that Dick turned by instinct. The representative of the Central Southern Syndicate had shaken himself clear of his enemy, and rose, wiping his thumb on his trousers. The Arab, both hands to his forehead, screamed aloud, then snatched up his spear and rushed at Torpenhow, who was panting under shelter of Dick's revolver. Dick fired twice, and the man dropped limply. His upturned face lacked one eye. The musketry-fire redoubled, but cheers mingled with it. The rush had failed and the enemy were flying. If the heart of the square were shambles, the ground beyond was a butcher's shop. Dick thrust his way forward between the maddened men. The remnant of the enemy were retiring, as the few—the very few—English cavalry rode down the laggards.

Beyond the lines of the dead, a broad blood-stained Arab spear cast aside in the retreat lay across a stump of scrub, and beyond this again the illimitable dark levels of the desert. The sun caught the steel and turned it into a red disc. Some one behind him was saying, "Ah, get away, you brute!" Dick raised his revolver and pointed towards the desert. His eye was held by the red splash in the distance, and the clamour about him seemed to die down to a very far-away whisper, like the whisper of a level sea. There was the revolver and the red light. ... and the voice of some one scaring something away, exactly as had fallen somewhere before,—a darkness that stung. He fired at random, and the bullet went out across the desert as he muttered, "Spoilt my aim. There aren't any more cartridges. We shall have to run home." He put his hand to his head and brought it away covered with blood.

"Old man, you're cut rather badly," said Torpenhow. "I owe you something for this business. Thanks. Stand up! I say, you can't be ill here."

Throughout the night, when the troops were encamped by the whale-boats, a black figure danced in the strong moonlight on the sand-bar and shouted that Khartoum the accursed one was dead,—was dead,—was dead,—that two steamers were rock-staked on the Nile outside the city, and that of all their crews there remained not one; and Khartoum was dead,—was dead,— was dead! But Torpenhow took no heed. He was watching Dick, who called aloud to the restless Nile for Maisie,—and again Maisie! "Behold a phenomenon," said Torpenhow, rearranging the blanket. "Here is a man, presumably human, who mentions the name of one woman only. And I've seen a good deal of delirium, too.—Dick, here's some fizzy drink."

"Thank you, Maisie," said Dick.

CHAPTER III

So he thinks he shall take to the sea again

For one more cruise with his buccaneers,

To singe the beard of the King of Spain,

And capture another Dean of Jaen

And sell him in Algiers.

—Dutch Picture. Longfellow

THE SOUDAN campaign and Dick's broken head had been some months ended and mended, and the Central Southern Syndicate had paid Dick a certain sum on account for work done, which work they were careful to assure him was not altogether up to their standard. Dick heaved the letter into the Nile at Cairo, cashed the draft in the same town, and bade a warm farewell to Torpenhow at the station.

"I am going to lie up for a while and rest," said Torpenhow. "I don't know where I shall live in London, but if God brings us to meet, we shall meet. Are you staying here on the off-chance of another row? There will be none till the Southern Soudan is reoccupied by our troops. Mark that. Goodbye; bless you; come back when your money's spent; and give me your address."

Dick loitered in Cairo, Alexandria, Ismailia, and Port Said,—especially Port Said. There is iniquity in many parts of the world, and vice in all, but the concentrated essence of all the iniquities and all the vices in all the continents finds itself at Port Said. And through the heart of that sand-bordered hell, where the mirage flickers day long above the Bitter Lake, move, if you will only wait, most of the men and women you have known in this life. Dick established himself in quarters more riotous than respectable. He spent his evenings on the quay, and boarded many ships, and saw very many friends,—gracious Englishwomen with whom he had talked not too wisely in the veranda of Shepherd's Hotel, hurrying war correspondents, skippers of the contract troop-ships employed in the campaign, army officers by the score, and others of less reputable trades.

He had choice of all the races of the East and West for studies, and the advantage of seeing his subjects under the influence of strong excitement, at the gaming-tables, saloons, dancing-hells, and elsewhere. For recreation there was the straight vista of the Canal, the blazing sands, the procession of shipping, and the white hospitals where the English soldiers lay. He strove to set down in black and white and colour all that Providence sent him, and when that supply was ended sought about for fresh material. It was a fascinating employment, but it ran away with his money, and he had drawn in advance the hundred and twenty pounds to which he was entitled yearly. "Now I shall have to work and starve!" thought he, and was addressing himself to this new fate when a mysterious telegram arrived from Torpenhow in England, which said, "Come back, quick; you have caught on. Come."

A large smile overspread his face. "So soon! that's a good hearing," said he to himself. "There will be an orgy tonight. I'll stand or fall by my luck. Faith, it's time it came!" He deposited half of his funds in the hands of his well-known friends Monsieur and Madame Binat, and ordered himself a Zanzibar dance of the finest. Monsieur Binat was shaking with drink, but Madame smiles sympathetically—"Monsieur needs a chair, of course, and of course Monsieur will sketch; Monsieur amuses himself strangely."

Binat raised a blue-white face from a cot in the inner room. "I understand," he quavered. "We all know Monsieur. Monsieur is an artist, as I have been." Dick nodded. "In the end," said Binat, with gravity, "Monsieur will descend alive into hell, as I have descended." And he laughed.

"You must come to the dance, too," said Dick; "I shall want you."

"For my face? I knew it would be so. For my face? My God! and for my degradation so tremendous! I will not. Take him away. He is a devil. Or at least do thou, Celeste, demand of him more." The excellent Binat began to kick and scream.

"All things are for sale in Port Said," said Madame. "If my husband comes it will be so much more. Eh, how you call 'alf a sovereign."

The money was paid, and the mad dance was held at night in a walled courtyard at the back of Madame Binat's house. The lady herself, in faded mauve silk always about to slide from her yellow shoulders, played the piano, and to the tin-pot music of a Western waltz the naked Zanzibari girls danced furiously by the light of kerosene lamps. Binat sat upon a chair and stared with eyes that saw nothing, till the whirl of the dance and the clang of the rattling piano stole into the drink that took the place of blood in his veins, and his face glistened. Dick took him by the chin brutally and turned that face to the light. Madame Binat looked over her shoulder and smiled with many teeth. Dick leaned against the wall and sketched for an hour, till the kerosene lamps began to smell, and the girls threw themselves panting on the hard-beaten ground. Then he shut his book with a snap and moved away, Binat plucking feebly at his elbow. "Show me," he whimpered. "I too was once an artist, even I!" Dick showed him the rough sketch. "Am I that?" he screamed. "Will you take that away with you and show all the world that it is I,—Binat?" He moaned and wept.

"Monsieur has paid for all," said Madame. "To the pleasure of seeing Monsieur again."

The courtyard gate shut, and Dick hurried up the sandy street to the nearest gambling-hell, where he was well known. "If the luck holds, it's an omen; if I lose, I must stay here." He placed his money picturesquely about the board, hardly daring to look at what he did. The luck held.

Three turns of the wheel left him richer by twenty pounds, and he went down to the shipping to make friends with the captain of a decayed cargo-steamer, who landed him in London with fewer pounds in his pocket than he cared to think about.

A thin gray fog hung over the city, and the streets were very cold; for summer was in England.

"It's a cheerful wilderness, and it hasn't the knack of altering much," Dick thought, as he tramped from the Docks westward. "Now, what must I do?"

The packed houses gave no answer. Dick looked down the long lightless streets and at the appalling rush of traffic. "Oh, you rabbit-hutches!" said he, addressing a row of highly respectable semi-detached residences. "Do you know what you've got to do later on? You have to supply me with men-servants and maid-servants,"—here he smacked his lips,—"and the peculiar treasure of kings. Meantime I'll clothes and boots, and presently I will return and trample on you." He stepped forward energetically; he saw that one of his shoes was burst at the side. As he stooped to make investigations, a man jostled him into the gutter. "All right," he said. "That's another nick in the score. I'll jostle you later on."

Good clothes and boots are not cheap, and Dick left his last shop with the certainty that he would be respectably arrayed for a time, but with only fifty shillings in his pocket. He returned to streets by the Docks, and lodged himself in one room, where the sheets on the bed were

almost audibly marked in case of theft, and where nobody seemed to go to bed at all. When his clothes arrived he sought the Central Southern Syndicate for Torpenhow's address, and got it, with the intimation that there was still some money waiting for him.

"How much?" said Dick, as one who habitually dealt in millions.

"Between thirty and forty pounds. If it would be any convenience to you, of course we could let you have it at once; but we usually settle accounts monthly."

"If I show that I want anything now, I'm lost," he said to himself. "All I need I'll take later on." Then, aloud, "It's hardly worth while; and I'm going to the country for a month, too. Wait till I come back, and I'll see about it."

"But we trust, Mr. Heldar, that you do not intend to sever your connection with us?"

Dick's business in life was the study of faces, and he watched the speaker keenly. "That man means something," he said. "I'll do no business till I've seen Torpenhow. There's a big deal coming." So he departed, making no promises, to his one little room by the Docks. And that day was the seventh of the month, and that month, he reckoned with awful distinctness, had thirty-one days in it! It is not easy for a man of catholic tastes and healthy appetites to exist for twenty-four days on fifty shillings. Nor is it cheering to begin the experiment alone in all the loneliness of London. Dick paid seven shillings a week for his lodging, which left him rather less than a shilling a day for food and drink. Naturally, his first purchase was of the materials of his craft; he had been without them too long. Half a day's investigations and comparison brought him to the conclusion that sausages and mashed potatoes, twopence a plate, were the best food. Now, sausages once or twice a week for breakfast are not unpleasant. As lunch, even, with mashed potatoes, they become monotonous. At dinner they are impertinent.

At the end of three days Dick loathed sausages, and, going, forth, pawned his watch to revel on sheep's head, which is not as cheap as it looks, owing to the bones and the gravy. Then he returned to sausages and mashed potatoes. Then he confined himself entirely to mashed potatoes for a day, and was unhappy because of pain in his inside. Then he pawned his waistcoat and his tie, and thought regretfully of money thrown away in times past. There are few things more edifying unto Art than the actual belly-pinch of hunger, and Dick in his few walks abroad,—he did not care for exercise; it raised desires that could not be satisfied—found himself dividing mankind into two classes,—those who looked as if they might give him something to eat, and those who looked otherwise. "I never knew what I had to learn about the human face before," he thought; and, as a reward for his humility, Providence caused a cab-driver at a sausage-shop where Dick fed that night to leave half eaten a great chunk of bread. Dick took it,—would have fought all the world for its possession,—and it cheered him.

The month dragged through at last, and, nearly prancing with impatience, he went to draw his money. Then he hastened to Torpenhow's address and smelt the smell of cooking meats all along the corridors of the chambers. Torpenhow was on the top floor, and Dick burst into his room, to be received with a hug which nearly cracked his ribs, as Torpenhow dragged him to the light and spoke of twenty different things in the same breath.

"But you're looking tucked up," he concluded.

"Got anything to eat?" said Dick, his eye roaming round the room.

"I shall be having breakfast in a minute. What do you say to sausages?"

"No, anything but sausages! Torp, I've been starving on that accursed horse-flesh for thirty days and thirty nights."

"Now, what lunacy has been your latest?"

Dick spoke of the last few weeks with unbridled speech. Then he opened his coat; there was no waistcoat below. "I ran it fine, awfully fine, but I've just scraped through."

"You haven't much sense, but you've got a backbone, anyhow. Eat, and talk afterwards." Dick fell upon eggs and bacon and gorged till he could gorge no more. Torpenhow handed him a filled pipe, and he smoked as men smoke who for three weeks have been deprived of good tobacco.

"Ouf!" said he. "That's heavenly! Well?"

"Why in the world didn't you come to me?"

"Couldn't; I owe you too much already, old man. Besides I had a sort of superstition that this temporary starvation—that's what it was, and it hurt—would bring me luck later. It's over and done with now, and none of the syndicate know how hard up I was. Fire away. What's the exact state of affairs as regards myself?"

"You had my wire? You've caught on here. People like your work immensely. I don't know why, but they do. They say you have a fresh touch and a new way of drawing things. And, because they're chiefly home-bred English, they say you have insight. You're wanted by half a dozen papers; you're wanted to illustrate books."

Dick grunted scornfully.

"You're wanted to work up your smaller sketches and sell them to the dealers. They seem to think the money sunk in you is a good investment. Good Lord! who can account for the fathomless folly of the public?"

"They're a remarkably sensible people."

"They are subject to fits, if that's what you mean; and you happen to be the object of the latest fit among those who are interested in what they call Art. Just now you're a fashion, a phenomenon, or whatever you please. I appeared to be the only person who knew anything about you here, and I have been showing the most useful men a few of the sketches you gave me from time to time. Those coming after your work on the Central Southern Syndicate appear to have done your business. You're in luck."

"Huh! call it luck! Do call it luck, when a man has been kicking about the world like a dog, waiting for it to come! I'll luck 'em later on. I want a place to work first."

"Come here," said Torpenhow, crossing the landing. "This place is a big box room really, but it will do for you. There's your skylight, or your north light, or whatever window you call it, and plenty of room to thrash about in, and a bedroom beyond. What more do you need?"

"Good enough," said Dick, looking round the large room that took up a third of a top story in the rickety chambers overlooking the Thames. A pale yellow sun shone through the skylight and showed the much dirt of the place. Three steps led from the door to the landing, and three more to Torpenhow's room. The well of the staircase disappeared into darkness, pricked by tiny gas-jets, and there were sounds of men talking and doors slamming seven flights below, in the warm gloom.

"Do they give you a free hand here?" said Dick, cautiously. He was Ishmael enough to know the value of liberty.

"Anything you like; latch-keys and license unlimited. We are permanent tenants for the most part here. 'Tisn't a place I would recommend for a Young Men's Christian Association, but it will serve. I took these rooms for you when I wired."

"You're a great deal too kind, old man."

"You didn't suppose you were going away from me, did you?" Torpenhow put his hand on Dick's shoulder, and the two walked up and down the room, henceforward to be called the studio, in sweet and silent communion. They heard rapping at Torpenhow's door. "That's some ruffian come up for a drink," said Torpenhow; and he raised his voice cheerily. There entered no one more ruffianly than a portly middle-aged gentleman in a satin-faced frockcoat. His lips were parted and pale, and there were deep pouches under the eyes.

"Weak heart," said Dick to himself, and, as he shook hands, "very weak heart. His pulse is shaking his fingers."

The man introduced himself as the head of the Central Southern Syndicate and "one of the most ardent admirers of your work, Mr. Heldar. I assure you, in the name of the syndicate, that we are immensely indebted to you; and I trust, Mr. Heldar, you won't forget that we were largely instrumental in bringing you before the public." He panted because of the seven flights of stairs.

Dick glanced at Torpenhow, whose left eyelid lay for a moment dead on his cheek.

"I shan't forget," said Dick, every instinct of defence roused in him.

"You've paid me so well that I couldn't, you know. By the way, when I am settled in this place I should like to send and get my sketches. There must be nearly a hundred and fifty of them with you."

"That is er—is what I came to speak about. I fear we can't allow it exactly, Mr. Heldar. In the absence of any specified agreement, the sketches are our property, of course."

"Do you mean to say that you are going to keep them?"

"Yes; and we hope to have your help, on your own terms, Mr. Heldar, to assist us in arranging a little exhibition, which, backed by our name and the influence we naturally command among the press, should be of material service to you. Sketches such as yours——"

"Belong to me. You engaged me by wire, you paid me the lowest rates you dared. You can't mean to keep them! Good God alive, man, they're all I've got in the world!"

Torpenhow watched Dick's face and whistled.

Dick walked up and down, thinking. He saw the whole of his little stock in trade, the first weapon of his equipment, annexed at the outset of his campaign by an elderly gentleman whose name Dick had not caught aright, who said that he represented a syndicate, which was a thing for which Dick had not the least reverence. The injustice of the proceedings did not much move him; he had seen the strong hand prevail too often in other places to be squeamish over the moral aspects of right and wrong.

But he ardently desired the blood of the gentleman in the frockcoat, and when he spoke again, it was with a strained sweetness that Torpenhow knew well for the beginning of strife.

"Forgive me, sir, but you have no—no younger man who can arrange this business with me?"

"I speak for the syndicate. I see no reason for a third party to——"

"You will in a minute. Be good enough to give back my sketches."

The man stared blankly at Dick, and then at Torpenhow, who was leaning against the wall. He was not used to ex-employees who ordered him to be good enough to do things.

"Yes, it is rather a cold-blooded steal," said Torpenhow, critically; "but I'm afraid, I am very much afraid, you've struck the wrong man. Be careful, Dick; remember, this isn't the Soudan."

"Considering what services the syndicate have done you in putting your name before the world——"

This was not a fortunate remark; it reminded Dick of certain vagrant years lived out in loneliness and strife and unsatisfied desires. The memory did not contrast well with the prosperous gentleman who proposed to enjoy the fruit of those years.

"I don't know quite what to do with you," began Dick, meditatively. "Of course you're a thief, and you ought to be half killed, but in your case you'd probably die. I don't want you dead on this floor, and, besides, it's unlucky just as one's moving in. Don't hit, sir; you'll only excite yourself."

He put one hand on the man's forearm and ran the other down the plump body beneath the coat. "My goodness!" said he to Torpenhow, "and this gray oaf dares to be a thief! I have seen an Esneh camel-driver have the black hide taken off his body in strips for stealing half a pound of wet dates, and he was as tough as whipcord. This thing's soft all over—like a woman."

There are few things more poignantly humiliating than being handled by a man who does not intend to strike. The head of the syndicate began to breathe heavily. Dick walked round him, pawing him, as a cat paws a soft hearth-rug. Then he traced with his forefinger the leaden pouches underneath the eyes, and shook his head. "You were going to steal my things,—mine, mine, mine!—you, who don't know when you may die. Write a note to your office,—you say you're the head of it,—and order them to give Torpenhow my sketches,—every one of them. Wait a minute: your hand's shaking. Now!" He thrust a pocket-book before him. The note was written. Torpenhow took it and departed without a word, while Dick walked round and round the spellbound captive, giving him such advice as he conceived best for the welfare of his soul. When Torpenhow returned with a gigantic portfolio, he heard Dick say, almost soothingly, "Now, I hope this will be a lesson to you; and if you worry me when I have settled down to work with any nonsense about actions for assault, believe me, I'll catch you and manhandle you, and you'll die. You haven't very long to live, anyhow. Go! Imshi, Vootsak,—get out!" The man departed, staggering and dazed. Dick drew a long breath: "Phew! what a lawless lot these people are! The first thing a poor orphan meets is gang robbery, organised burglary! Think of the hideous blackness of that man's mind! Are my sketches all right, Torp?"

"Yes; one hundred and forty-seven of them. Well, I must say, Dick, you've begun well."

"He was interfering with me. It only meant a few pounds to him, but it was everything to me. I don't think he'll bring an action. I gave him some medical advice gratis about the state of his body. It was cheap at the little flurry it cost him. Now, let's look at my things."

Two minutes later Dick had thrown himself down on the floor and was deep in the portfolio, chuckling lovingly as he turned the drawings over and thought of the price at which they had been bought.

The afternoon was well advanced when Torpenhow came to the door and saw Dick dancing a wild saraband under the skylight.

"I builded better than I knew, Torp," he said, without stopping the dance. "They're good! They're damned good! They'll go like flame! I shall have an exhibition of them on my own brazen hook. And that man would have cheated me out of it! Do you know that I'm sorry now that I didn't actually hit him?"

"Go out," said Torpenhow,—"go out and pray to be delivered from the sin of arrogance, which you never will be. Bring your things up from whatever place you're staying in, and we'll try to make this barn a little more shipshape."

"And then—oh, then," said Dick, still capering, "we will spoil the Egyptians!"

CHAPTER IV

The wolf-cub at even lay hid in the corn,

When the smoke of the cooking hung gray:

He knew where the doe made a couch for her fawn,

And he looked to his strength for his prey.

But the moon swept the smoke-wreaths away.

And he turned from his meal in the villager's close,

And he bayed to the moon as she rose.

 —In Seonee.

"WELL, and how does success taste?" said Torpenhow, some three months later. He had just returned to chambers after a holiday in the country.

"Good," said Dick, as he sat licking his lips before the easel in the studio.

"I want more,—heaps more. The lean years have passed, and I approve of these fat ones."

"Be careful, old man. That way lies bad work."

Torpenhow was sprawling in a long chair with a small fox-terrier asleep on his chest, while Dick was preparing a canvas. A dais, a background, and a lay-figure were the only fixed objects in the place. They rose from a wreck of oddments that began with felt-covered water-bottles, belts, and regimental badges, and ended with a small bale of second-hand uniforms and a stand of mixed arms. The mark of muddy feet on the dais showed that a military model had just gone away. The watery autumn sunlight was falling, and shadows sat in the corners of the studio.

"Yes," said Dick, deliberately, "I like the power; I like the fun; I like the fuss; and above all I like the money. I almost like the people who make the fuss and pay the money. Almost. But they're a queer gang,—an amazingly queer gang!"

"They have been good enough to you, at any rate. That tin-pot exhibition of your sketches must have paid. Did you see that the papers called it the 'Wild Work Show'?"

"Never mind. I sold every shred of canvas I wanted to; and, on my word, I believe it was because they believed I was a self-taught flagstone artist. I should have got better prices if I worked my things on wool or scratched them on camel-bone instead of using mere black and white and colour. Verily, they are a queer gang, these people. Limited isn't the word to describe 'em. I met a fellow the other day who told me that it was impossible that shadows on white sand should be blue,—ultramarine,—as they are. I found out, later, that the man had been as far as Brighton beach; but he knew all about Art, confound him. He gave me a lecture on it, and recommended me to go to school to learn technique. I wonder what old Kami would have said to that."

"When were you under Kami, man of extraordinary beginnings?"

"I studied with him for two years in Paris. He taught by personal magnetism. All he ever said was, 'Continuez, mes enfants,' and you had to make the best you could of that. He had a divine touch, and he knew something about colour. Kami used to dream colour; I swear he could never have seen the genuine article; but he evolved it; and it was good."

"Recollect some of those views in the Soudan?" said Torpenhow, with a provoking drawl.

Dick squirmed in his place. "Don't! It makes me want to get out there again. What colour that was! Opal and umber and amber and claret and brick-red and sulphur—cockatoo-crest-sulphur—against brown, with a nigger-black rock sticking up in the middle of it all, and a decorative frieze of camels festooning in front of a pure pale turquoise sky." He began to walk up and down. "And yet, you know, if you try to give these people the thing as God gave it, keyed down to their comprehension and according to the powers He has given you——"

"Modest man! Go on."

"Half a dozen epicene young pagans who haven't even been to Algiers will tell you, first, that your notion is borrowed, and, secondly, that it isn't Art."

"This comes of my leaving town for a month. Dickie, you've been promenading among the toy-shops and hearing people talk."

"I couldn't help it," said Dick, penitently. "You weren't here, and it was lonely these long evenings. A man can't work for ever."

"A man might have gone to a pub, and got decently drunk."

"I wish I had; but I forgathered with some men of sorts. They said they were artists, and I knew some of them could draw,—but they wouldn't draw. They gave me tea,—tea at five in the afternoon!—and talked about Art and the state of their souls. As if their souls mattered. I've heard more about Art and seen less of her in the last six months than in the whole of my life. Do you remember Cassavetti, who worked for some continental syndicate, out with the desert column? He was a regular Christmas-tree of contraptions when he took the field in full fig, with his water-bottle, lanyard, revolver, writing-case, housewife, gig-lamps, and the Lord knows what all. He used to fiddle about with 'em and show us how they worked; but he never seemed to do much except fudge his reports from the Nilghai. See?"

"Dear old Nilghai! He's in town, fatter than ever. He ought to be up here this evening. I see the comparison perfectly. You should have kept clear of all that man-millinery. Serves you right; and I hope it will unsettle your mind."

"It won't. It has taught me what Art—holy sacred Art—means."

"You've learnt something while I've been away. What is Art?"

"Give 'em what they know, and when you've done it once do it again."

Dick dragged forward a canvas laid face to the wall. "Here's a sample of real Art. It's going to be a facsimile reproduction for a weekly. I called it 'His Last Shot.' It's worked up from the little water-colour I made outside El Maghrib. Well, I lured my model, a beautiful rifleman, up here with drink; I drored him, and I redrored him, and I redrored him, and I made him a flushed, dishevelled, bedevilled scallawag, with his helmet at the back of his head, and the living fear of death in his eye, and the blood oozing out of a cut over his ankle-bone. He wasn't pretty, but he was all soldier and very much man."

"Once more, modest child!"

Dick laughed. "Well, it's only to you I'm talking. I did him just as well as I knew how, making allowance for the slickness of oils. Then the art-manager of that abandoned paper said that his subscribers wouldn't like it. It was brutal and coarse and violent,—man being naturally gentle when he's fighting for his life. They wanted something more restful, with a little more colour. I could have said a good deal, but you might as well talk to a sheep as an art-manager. I took my 'Last Shot' back. Behold the result! I put him into a lovely red coat without a speck on it. That is Art. I polished his boots,—observe the high light on the toe. That is Art. I cleaned his rifle,— rifles are always clean on service,—because that is Art. I pipeclayed his helmet,—pipeclay is always used on active service, and is indispensable to Art. I shaved his chin, I washed his hands, and gave him an air of fatted peace. Result, military tailor's pattern-plate. Price, thank Heaven, twice as much as for the first sketch, which was moderately decent."

"And do you suppose you're going to give that thing out as your work?"

"Why not? I did it. Alone I did it, in the interests of sacred, home-bred Art and Dickenson's Weekly."

Torpenhow smoked in silence for a while. Then came the verdict, delivered from rolling clouds: "If you were only a mass of blathering vanity, Dick, I wouldn't mind,—I'd let you go to the deuce on your own mahl-stick; but when I consider what you are to me, and when I find that to vanity you add the twopenny-halfpenny pique of a twelve-year-old girl, then I bestir myself in your behalf. Thus!"

The canvas ripped as Torpenhow's booted foot shot through it, and the terrier jumped down, thinking rats were about.

"If you have any bad language to use, use it. You have not. I continue. You are an idiot, because no man born of woman is strong enough to take liberties with his public, even though they be— which they ain't—all you say they are."

"But they don't know any better. What can you expect from creatures born and bred in this light?" Dick pointed to the yellow fog. "If they want furniture-polish, let them have furniture-polish, so long as they pay for it. They are only men and women. You talk as if they were gods."

"That sounds very fine, but it has nothing to do with the case. They are they people you have to do work for, whether you like it or not. They are your masters. Don't be deceived, Dickie, you aren't strong enough to trifle with them,—or with yourself, which is more important.

"Moreover,—Come back, Binkie: that red daub isn't going anywhere,—unless you take precious good care, you will fall under the damnation of the check-book, and that's worse than death. You will get drunk—you're half drunk already—on easily acquired money. For that money and you own infernal vanity you are willing to deliberately turn out bad work. You'll do quite enough bad work without knowing it. And, Dickie, as I love you and as I know you love me, I am not going to let you cut off your nose to spite your face for all the gold in England. That's settled. Now swear."

"Don't know," said Dick. "I've been trying to make myself angry, but I can't, you're so abominably reasonable. There will be a row on Dickenson's Weekly, I fancy."

"Why the Dickenson do you want to work on a weekly paper? It's slow bleeding of power."

"It brings in the very desirable dollars," said Dick, his hands in his pockets.

Torpenhow watched him with large contempt. "Why, I thought it was a man!" said he. "It's a child."

"No, it isn't," said Dick, wheeling quickly. "You've no notion what the certainty of cash means to a man who has always wanted it badly. Nothing will pay me for some of my life's joys; on that Chinese pig-boat, for instance, when we ate bread and jam for every meal, because Ho-Wang wouldn't allow us anything better, and it all tasted of pig,—Chinese pig. I've worked for this, I've sweated and I've starved for this, line on line and month after month. And now I've got it I am going to make the most of it while it lasts. Let them pay—they've no knowledge."

"What does Your Majesty please to want? You can't smoke more than you do; you won't drink; you're a gross feeder; and you dress in the dark, by the look of you. You wouldn't keep a horse the other day when I suggested, because, you said, it might fall lame, and whenever you cross the street you take a hansom. Even you are not foolish enough to suppose that theatres and all the live things you can by thereabouts mean Life. What earthly need have you for money?"

"It's there, bless its golden heart," said Dick. "It's there all the time. Providence has sent me nuts while I have teeth to crack 'em with. I haven't yet found the nut I wish to crack, but I'm keeping my teeth filed. Perhaps some day you and I will go for a walk round the wide earth."

"With no work to do, nobody to worry us, and nobody to compete with? You would be unfit to speak to in a week. Besides, I shouldn't go. I don't care to profit by the price of a man's soul,—for that's what it would mean. Dick, it's no use arguing. You're a fool."

"Don't see it. When I was on that Chinese pig-boat, our captain got credit for saving about twenty-five thousand very seasick little pigs, when our old tramp of a steamer fell foul of a timber-junk. Now, taking those pigs as a parallel——"

"Oh, confound your parallels! Whenever I try to improve your soul, you always drag in some anecdote from your very shady past. Pigs aren't the British public; and self-respect is self-respect the world over. Go out for a walk and try to catch some self-respect. And, I say, if the Nilghai comes up this evening can I show him your diggings?"

"Surely." And Dick departed, to take counsel with himself in the rapidly gathering London fog.

Half an hour after he had left, the Nilghai laboured up the staircase. He was the chiefest, as he was the youngest, of the war correspondents, and his experiences dated from the birth of the needle-gun. Saving only his ally, Keneu the Great War Eagle, there was no man higher in the craft than he, and he always opened his conversation with the news that there would be trouble in the Balkans in the spring. Torpenhow laughed as he entered.

"Never mind the trouble in the Balkans. Those little states are always screeching. You've heard about Dick's luck?"

"Yes; he has been called up to notoriety, hasn't he? I hope you keep him properly humble. He wants suppressing from time to time."

"He does. He's beginning to take liberties with what he thinks is his reputation."

"Already! By Jove, he has cheek! I don't know about his reputation, but he'll come a cropper if he tries that sort of thing."

"So I told him. I don't think he believes it."

"They never do when they first start off. What's that wreck on the ground there?"

"Specimen of his latest impertinence." Torpenhow thrust the torn edges of the canvas together and showed the well-groomed picture to the Nilghai, who looked at it for a moment and whistled.

"It's a chromo," said he,—"a chromo-litholeomargarine fake! What possessed him to do it? And yet how thoroughly he has caught the note that catches a public who think with their boots and read with their elbows! The cold-blooded insolence of the work almost saves it; but he mustn't go on with this. Hasn't he been praised and cockered up too much? You know these people here have no sense of proportion. They'll call him a second Detaille and a third-hand Meissonier while his fashion lasts. It's windy diet for a colt."

"I don't think it affects Dick much. You might as well call a young wolf a lion and expect him to take the compliment in exchange for a shin-bone. Dick's soul is in the bank. He's working for cash."

"Now he has thrown up war work, I suppose he doesn't see that the obligations of the service are just the same, only the proprietors are changed."

"How should he know? He thinks he is his own master."

"Does he? I could undeceive him for his good, if there's any virtue in print. He wants the whiplash."

"Lay it on with science, then. I'd flay him myself, but I like him too much."

"I've no scruples. He had the audacity to try to cut me out with a woman at Cairo once. I forgot that, but I remember now."

"Did he cut you out?"

"You'll see when I have dealt with him. But, after all, what's the good? Leave him alone and he'll come home, if he has any stuff in him, dragging or wagging his tail behind him. There's more in a week of life than in a lively weekly. None the less I'll slate him. I'll slate him ponderously in the Cataclysm."

"Good luck to you; but I fancy nothing short of a crowbar would make Dick wince. His soul seems to have been fired before we came across him. He's intensely suspicious and utterly lawless."

"Matter of temper," said the Nilghai. "It's the same with horses. Some you wallop and they work, some you wallop and they jib, and some you wallop and they go out for a walk with their hands in their pockets."

"That's exactly what Dick has done," said Torpenhow. "Wait till he comes back. In the meantime, you can begin your slating here. I'll show you some of his last and worst work in his studio."

Dick had instinctively sought running water for a comfort to his mood of mind. He was leaning over the Embankment wall, watching the rush of the Thames through the arches of Westminster Bridge. He began by thinking of Torpenhow's advice, but, as of custom, lost himself in the study of the faces flocking past. Some had death written on their features, and Dick marvelled that they could laugh. Others, clumsy and coarse-built for the most part, were alight with love; others were merely drawn and lined with work; but there was something, Dick knew, to be made out of them all. The poor at least should suffer that he might learn, and the rich should pay for the output of his learning. Thus his credit in the world and his cash balance at the bank would be increased. So much the better for him. He had suffered. Now he would take toll of the ills of others.

The fog was driven apart for a moment, and the sun shone, a blood-red wafer, on the water. Dick watched the spot till he heard the voice of the tide between the piers die down like the wash of the sea at low tide. A girl hard pressed by her lover shouted shamelessly, "Ah, get away, you beast!" and a shift of the same wind that had opened the fog drove across Dick's face the black smoke of a river-steamer at her berth below the wall. He was blinded for the moment, then spun round and found himself face to face with—Maisie.

There was no mistaking. The years had turned the child to a woman, but they had not altered the dark-gray eyes, the thin scarlet lips, or the firmly modelled mouth and chin; and, that all should be as it was of old, she wore a closely fitting gray dress.

Since the human soul is finite and not in the least under its own command, Dick, advancing, said "Halloo!" after the manner of schoolboys, and Maisie answered, "Oh, Dick, is that you?" Then, against his will, and before the brain newly released from considerations of the cash balance had time to dictate to the nerves, every pulse of Dick's body throbbed furiously and his palate dried in his mouth. The fog shut down again, and Maisie's face was pearl-white through it. No word was spoken, but Dick fell into step at her side, and the two paced the Embankment together, keeping the step as perfectly as in their afternoon excursions to the mud-flats. Then Dick, a little hoarsely—"What has happened to Amomma?"

"He died, Dick. Not cartridges; over-eating. He was always greedy. Isn't it funny?"

"Yes. No. Do you mean Amomma?"

"Ye—es. No. This. Where have you come from?"

"Over there," He pointed eastward through the fog. "And you?"

"Oh, I'm in the north,—the black north, across all the Park. I am very busy."

"What do you do?"

"I paint a great deal. That's all I have to do."

"Why, what's happened? You had three hundred a year."

"I have that still. I am painting; that's all."

"Are you alone, then?"

"There's a girl living with me. Don't walk so fast, Dick; you're out of step."

"Then you noticed it too?"

"Of course I did. You're always out of step."

"So I am. I'm sorry. You went on with the painting?"

"Of course. I said I should. I was at the Slade, then at Merton's in St. John's Wood, the big studio, then I pepper-potted,—I mean I went to the National,—and now I'm working under Kami."

"But Kami is in Paris surely?"

"No; he has his teaching studio in Vitry-sur-Marne. I work with him in the summer, and I live in London in the winter. I'm a householder."

"Do you sell much?"

"Now and again, but not often. There is my 'bus. I must take it or lose half an hour. Goodbye, Dick."

"Goodbye, Maisie. Won't you tell me where you live? I must see you again; and perhaps I could help you. I—I paint a little myself."

"I may be in the Park tomorrow, if there is no working light. I walk from the Marble Arch down and back again; that is my little excursion. But of course I shall see you again." She stepped into the omnibus and was swallowed up by the fog.

"Well—I—am—damned!" exclaimed Dick, and returned to the chambers.

Torpenhow and the Nilghai found him sitting on the steps to the studio door, repeating the phrase with an awful gravity.

"You'll be more damned when I'm done with you," said the Nilghai, upheaving his bulk from behind Torpenhow's shoulder and waving a sheaf of half-dry manuscript. "Dick, it is of common report that you are suffering from swelled head."

"Halloo, Nilghai. Back again? How are the Balkans and all the little Balkans? One side of your face is out of drawing, as usual."

"Never mind that. I am commissioned to smite you in print. Torpenhow refuses from false delicacy. I've been overhauling the pot-boilers in your studio. They are simply disgraceful."

"Oho! that's it, is it? If you think you can slate me, you're wrong. You can only describe, and you need as much room to turn in, on paper, as a P. and O. cargo-boat. But continue, and be swift. I'm going to bed."

"H'm! h'm! h'm! The first part only deals with your pictures. Here's the peroration: 'For work done without conviction, for power wasted on trivialities, for labour expended with levity for the deliberate purpose of winning the easy applause of a fashion-driven public——"

"That's 'His Last Shot,' second edition. Go on."

"——'public, there remains but one end,—the oblivion that is preceded by toleration and cenotaphed with contempt. From that fate Mr. Heldar has yet to prove himself out of danger."

"Wow—wow—wow—wow—wow!" said Dick, profanely. "It's a clumsy ending and vile journalese, but it's quite true. And yet,"—he sprang to his feet and snatched at the manuscript,— "you scarred, deboshed, battered old gladiator! you're sent out when a war begins, to minister to the blind, brutal, British public's bestial thirst for blood. They have no arenas now, but they must have special correspondents. You're a fat gladiator who comes up through a trap-door and talks of what he's seen. You stand on precisely the same level as an energetic bishop, an affable actress, a devastating cyclone, or—mine own sweet self. And you presume to lecture me about my work! Nilghai, if it were worth while I'd caricature you in four papers!"

The Nilghai winced. He had not thought of this.

"As it is, I shall take this stuff and tear it small—so!" The manuscript fluttered in slips down the dark well of the staircase. "Go home, Nilghai," said Dick; "go home to your lonely little bed, and leave me in peace. I am about to turn in till to-morrow."

"Why, it isn't seven yet!" said Torpenhow, with amazement.

"It shall be two in the morning, if I choose," said Dick, backing to the studio door. "I go to grapple with a serious crisis, and I shan't want any dinner."

The door shut and was locked.

"What can you do with a man like that?" said the Nilghai.

"Leave him alone. He's as mad as a hatter."

At eleven there was a kicking on the studio door. "Is the Nilghai with you still?" said a voice from within. "Then tell him he might have condensed the whole of his lumbering nonsense into an epigram: 'Only the free are bond, and only the bond are free.' Tell him he's an idiot, Torp, and tell him I'm another."

"All right. Come out and have supper. You're smoking on an empty stomach."

There was no answer.

CHAPTER V

"I have a thousand men," said he,

"To wait upon my will,

And towers nine upon the Tyne,

And three upon the Till."

"And what care I for you men," said she,

"Or towers from Tyne to Till,

"Sith you must go with me," she said,

"To wait upon my will?"

—Sir Hoggie and the Fairies

Next morning Torpenhow found Dick sunk in deepest repose of tobacco.

"Well, madman, how d'you feel?"

"I don't know. I'm trying to find out."

"You had much better do some work."

"Maybe; but I'm in no hurry. I've made a discovery. Torp, there's too much Ego in my Cosmos."

"Not really! Is this revelation due to my lectures, or the Nilghai's?"

"It came to me suddenly, all on my own account. Much too much Ego; and now I'm going to work."

He turned over a few half-finished sketches, drummed on a new canvas, cleaned three brushes, set Binkie to bite the toes of the lay figure, rattled through his collection of arms and accoutrements, and then went out abruptly, declaring that he had done enough for the day.

"This is positively indecent," said Torpenhow, "and the first time that Dick has ever broken up a light morning. Perhaps he has found out that he has a soul, or an artistic temperament, or something equally valuable. That comes of leaving him alone for a month. Perhaps he has been going out of evenings. I must look to this." He rang for the bald-headed old housekeeper, whom nothing could astonish or annoy.

"Beeton, did Mr. Heldar dine out at all while I was out of town?"

"Never laid 'is dress-clothes out once, sir, all the time. Mostly 'e dined in; but 'e brought some most remarkable young gentlemen up 'ere after theatres once or twice. Remarkable fancy they was. You gentlemen on the top floor does very much as you likes, but it do seem to me, sir, droppin' a walkin'-stick down five flights o' stairs an' then goin' down four abreast to pick it up again at half-past two in the mornin', singin' 'Bring back the whiskey, Willie darlin','—not

once or twice, but scores o' times,—isn't charity to the other tenants. What I say is, 'Do as you would be done by.' That's my motto."

"Of course! of course! I'm afraid the top floor isn't the quietest in the house."

"I make no complaints, sir. I have spoke to Mr. Heldar friendly, an' he laughed, an' did me a picture of the missis that is as good as a coloured print. It 'asn't the high shine of a photograph, but what I say is, 'Never look a gift-horse in the mouth.' Mr. Heldar's dress-clothes 'aven't been on him for weeks."

"Then it's all right," said Torpenhow to himself. "Orgies are healthy, and Dick has a head of his own, but when it comes to women making eyes I'm not so certain,—Binkie, never you be a man, little dorglums. They're contrary brutes, and they do things without any reason."

Dick had turned northward across the Park, but he was walking in the spirit on the mud-flats with Maisie. He laughed aloud as he remembered the day when he had decked Amomma's horns with the ham-frills, and Maisie, white with rage, had cuffed him. How long those four years seemed in review, and how closely Maisie was connected with every hour of them! Storm across the sea, and Maisie in a gray dress on the beach, sweeping her drenched hair out of her eyes and laughing at the homeward race of the fishing-smacks; hot sunshine on the mud-flats, and Maisie sniffing scornfully, with her chin in the air; Maisie flying before the wind that threshed the foreshore and drove the sand like small shot about her ears; Maisie, very composed and independent, telling lies to Mrs. Jennett while Dick supported her with coarser perjuries; Maisie picking her way delicately from stone to stone, a pistol in her hand and her teeth firm-set; and Maisie in a gray dress sitting on the grass between the mouth of a cannon and a nodding yellow sea-poppy. The pictures passed before him one by one, and the last stayed the longest.

Dick was perfectly happy with a quiet peace that was as new to his mind as it was foreign to his experiences. It never occurred to him that there might be other calls upon his time than loafing across the Park in the forenoon.

"There's a good working light now," he said, watching his shadow placidly. "Some poor devil ought to be grateful for this. And there's Maisie."

She was walking towards him from the Marble Arch, and he saw that no mannerism of her gait had been changed. It was good to find her still Maisie, and, so to speak, his next-door neighbour. No greeting passed between them, because there had been none in the old days.

"What are you doing out of your studio at this hour?" said Dick, as one who was entitled to ask.

"Idling. Just idling. I got angry with a chin and scraped it out. Then I left it in a little heap of paint-chips and came away."

"I know what palette-knifing means. What was the piccy?"

"A fancy head that wouldn't come right,—horrid thing!"

"I don't like working over scraped paint when I'm doing flesh. The grain comes up woolly as the paint dries."

"Not if you scrape properly." Maisie waved her hand to illustrate her methods. There was a dab of paint on the white cuff. Dick laughed.

"You're as untidy as ever."

"That comes well from you. Look at your own cuff."

"By Jove, yes! It's worse than yours. I don't think we've much altered in anything. Let's see, though." He looked at Maisie critically. The pale blue haze of an autumn day crept between the tree-trunks of the Park and made a background for the gray dress, the black velvet toque above the black hair, and the resolute profile.

"No, there's nothing changed. How good it is! D'you remember when I fastened your hair into the snap of a hand-bag?"

Maisie nodded, with a twinkle in her eyes, and turned her full face to Dick.

"Wait a minute," said he. "That mouth is down at the corners a little. Who's been worrying you, Maisie?"

"No one but myself. I never seem to get on with my work, and yet I try hard enough, and Kami says——"

"'Continuez, mesdemoiselles. Continuez toujours, mes enfants.' Kami is depressing. I beg your pardon."

"Yes, that's what he says. He told me last summer that I was doing better and he'd let me exhibit this year."

"Not in this place, surely?"

"Of course not. The Salon."

"You fly high."

"I've been beating my wings long enough. Where do you exhibit, Dick?"

"I don't exhibit. I sell."

"What is your line, then?"

"Haven't you heard?" Dick's eyes opened. Was this thing possible? He cast about for some means of conviction. They were not far from the Marble Arch. "Come up Oxford Street a little and I'll show you."

A small knot of people stood round a print-shop that Dick knew well.

"Some reproduction of my work inside," he said, with suppressed triumph. Never before had success tasted so sweet upon the tongue. "You see the sort of things I paint. D'you like it?"

Maisie looked at the wild whirling rush of a field-battery going into action under fire. Two artillery-men stood behind her in the crowd.

"They've chucked the off lead-'orse" said one to the other. "'E's tore up awful, but they're makin' good time with the others. That lead-driver drives better nor you, Tom. See 'ow cunnin' 'e's nursin' 'is 'orse."

"Number Three'll be off the limber, next jolt," was the answer.

"No, 'e won't. See 'ow 'is foot's braced against the iron? 'E's all right."

Dick watched Maisie's face and swelled with joy—fine, rank, vulgar triumph. She was more interested in the little crowd than in the picture.

That was something that she could understand.

"And I wanted it so! Oh, I did want it so!" she said at last, under her breath.

"Me,—all me!" said Dick, placidly. "Look at their faces. It hits 'em. They don't know what makes their eyes and mouths open; but I know. And I know my work's right."

"Yes. I see. Oh, what a thing to have come to one!"

"Come to one, indeed! I had to go out and look for it. What do you think?"

"I call it success. Tell me how you got it."

They returned to the Park, and Dick delivered himself of the saga of his own doings, with all the arrogance of a young man speaking to a woman.

From the beginning he told the tale, the I—I—I's flashing through the records as telegraph-poles fly past the traveller. Maisie listened and nodded her head. The histories of strife and privation did not move her a hair's-breadth. At the end of each canto he would conclude, "And that gave me some notion of handling colour," or light, or whatever it might be that he had set out to pursue and understand. He led her breathless across half the world, speaking as he had never spoken in his life before.

And in the flood-tide of his exaltation there came upon him a great desire to pick up this maiden who nodded her head and said, "I understand. Go on,"—to pick her up and carry her away with him, because she was Maisie, and because she understood, and because she was his right, and a woman to be desired above all women.

Then he checked himself abruptly. "And so I took all I wanted," he said, "and I had to fight for it. Now you tell."

Maisie's tale was almost as gray as her dress. It covered years of patient toil backed by savage pride that would not be broken though dealers laughed, and fogs delayed work, and Kami was unkind and even sarcastic, and girls in other studios were painfully polite. It had a few bright spots, in pictures accepted at provincial exhibitions, but it wound up with the oft repeated wail, "And so you see, Dick, I had no success, though I worked so hard."

Then pity filled Dick. Even thus had Maisie spoken when she could not hit the breakwater, half an hour before she had kissed him. And that had happened yesterday.

"Never mind," he said. "I'll tell you something, if you'll believe it." The words were shaping themselves of their own accord. "The whole thing, lock, stock, and barrel, isn't worth one big yellow sea-poppy below Fort Keeling."

Maisie flushed a little. "It's all very well for you to talk, but you've had the success and I haven't."

"Let me talk, then. I know you'll understand. Maisie, dear, it sounds a bit absurd, but those ten years never existed, and I've come back again. It really is just the same. Can't you see? You're alone now and I'm alone. What's the use of worrying? Come to me instead, darling."

Maisie poked the gravel with her parasol. They were sitting on a bench.

"I understand," she said slowly. "But I've got my work to do, and I must do it."

"Do it with me, then, dear. I won't interrupt."

"No, I couldn't. It's my work,—mine,—mine,—mine! I've been alone all my life in myself, and I'm not going to belong to anybody except myself. I remember things as well as you do, but that doesn't count. We were babies then, and we didn't know what was before us. Dick, don't be selfish. I think I see my way to a little success next year. Don't take it away from me."

"I beg your pardon, darling. It's my fault for speaking stupidly. I can't expect you to throw up all your life just because I'm back. I'll go to my own place and wait a little."

"But, Dick, I don't want you to—go—out of—my life, now you've just come back."

"I'm at your orders; forgive me." Dick devoured the troubled little face with his eyes. There was triumph in them, because he could not conceive that Maisie should refuse sooner or later to love him, since he loved her.

"It's wrong of me," said Maisie, more slowly than before; "it's wrong and selfish; but, oh, I've been so lonely! No, you misunderstand. Now I've seen you again,—it's absurd, but I want to keep you in my life."

"Naturally. We belong."

"We don't; but you always understood me, and there is so much in my work that you could help me in. You know things and the ways of doing things. You must."

"I do, I fancy, or else I don't know myself. Then you won't care to lose sight of me altogether, and—you want me to help you in your work?"

"Yes; but remember, Dick, nothing will ever come of it. That's why I feel so selfish. Can't things stay as they are? I do want your help."

"You shall have it. But let's consider. I must see your pics first, and overhaul your sketches, and find out about your tendencies. You should see what the papers say about my tendencies! Then I'll give you good advice, and you shall paint according. Isn't that it, Maisie?"

Again there was triumph in Dick's eye.

"It's too good of you,—much too good. Because you are consoling yourself with what will never happen, and I know that, and yet I want to keep you. Don't blame me later, please."

"I'm going into the matter with my eyes open. Moreover the Queen can do no wrong. It isn't your selfishness that impresses me. It's your audacity in proposing to make use of me."

"Pooh! You're only Dick,—and a print-shop."

"Very good: that's all I am. But, Maisie, you believe, don't you, that I love you? I don't want you to have any false notions about brothers and sisters."

Maisie looked up for a moment and dropped her eyes.

"It's absurd, but—I believe. I wish I could send you away before you get angry with me. But—but the girl that lives with me is red-haired, and an impressionist, and all our notions clash."

"So do ours, I think. Never mind. Three months from today we shall be laughing at this together."

Maisie shook her head mournfully. "I knew you wouldn't understand, and it will only hurt you more when you find out. Look at my face, Dick, and tell me what you see."

They stood up and faced each other for a moment. The fog was gathering, and it stifled the roar of the traffic of London beyond the railings. Dick brought all his painfully acquired knowledge of faces to bear on the eyes, mouth, and chin underneath the black velvet toque.

"It's the same Maisie, and it's the same me," he said. "We've both nice little wills of our own, and one or other of us has to be broken. Now about the future. I must come and see your pictures some day,—I suppose when the red-haired girl is on the premises."

"Sundays are my best times. You must come on Sundays. There are such heaps of things I want to talk about and ask your advice about. Now I must get back to work."

"Try to find out before next Sunday what I am," said Dick. "Don't take my word for anything I've told you. Good-bye, darling, and bless you."

Maisie stole away like a little gray mouse. Dick watched her till she was out of sight, but he did not hear her say to herself, very soberly, "I'm a wretch,—a horrid, selfish wretch. But it's Dick, and Dick will understand."

No one has yet explained what actually happens when an irresistible force meets the immovable post, though many have thought deeply, even as Dick thought. He tried to assure himself that Maisie would be led in a few weeks by his mere presence and discourse to a better way of thinking. Then he remembered much too distinctly her face and all that was written on it.

"If I know anything of heads," he said, "there's everything in that face but love. I shall have to put that in myself; and that chin and mouth won't be won for nothing. But she's right. She knows what she wants, and she's going to get it. What insolence! Me! Of all the people in the wide world, to use me! But then she's Maisie. There's no getting over that fact; and it's good to see her again. This business must have been simmering at the back of my head for years.... She'll use me as I used Binat at Port Said. She's quite right. It will hurt a little. I shall have to see her every Sunday,—like a young man courting a housemaid. She's sure to come around; and yet—that mouth isn't a yielding mouth. I shall be wanting to kiss her all the time, and I shall have to look at her pictures,—I don't even know what sort of work she does yet,—and I shall have to talk about Art,—Woman's Art! Therefore, particularly and perpetually, damn all varieties of Art. It did me a good turn once, and now it's in my way. I'll go home and do some Art."

Half-way to the studio, Dick was smitten with a terrible thought. The figure of a solitary woman in the fog suggested it.

"She's all alone in London, with a red-haired impressionist girl, who probably has the digestion of an ostrich. Most red-haired people have. Maisie's a bilious little body. They'll eat like lone women,—meals at all hours, and tea with all meals. I remember how the students in Paris used to pig along. She may fall ill at any minute, and I shan't be able to help. Whew! this is ten times worse than owning a wife."

Torpenhow entered the studio at dusk, and looked at Dick with eyes full of the austere love that springs up between men who have tugged at the same oar together and are yoked by custom and use and the intimacies of toil. This is a good love, and, since it allows, and even encourages, strife, recrimination, and brutal sincerity, does not die, but grows, and is proof against any absence and evil conduct.

Dick was silent after he handed Torpenhow the filled pipe of council. He thought of Maisie and her possible needs. It was a new thing to think of anybody but Torpenhow, who could think for himself. Here at last was an outlet for that cash balance. He could adorn Maisie barbarically with jewelry,—a thick gold necklace round that little neck, bracelets upon the rounded arms, and rings of price upon her hands,—the cool, temperate, ringless hands that he had taken between his own. It was an absurd thought, for Maisie would not even allow him to put one ring on one finger, and she would laugh at golden trappings. It would be better to sit with her quietly in the dusk, his arm around her neck and her face on his shoulder, as befitted husband and wife. Torpenhow's boots creaked that night, and his strong voice jarred. Dick's brows contracted and he murmured an evil word because he had taken all his success as a right and part payment for past discomfort, and now he was checked in his stride by a woman who admitted all the success and did not instantly care for him.

"I say, old man," said Torpenhow, who had made one or two vain attempts at conversation, "I haven't put your back up by anything I've said lately, have I?"

"You! No. How could you?"

"Liver out of order?"

"The truly healthy man doesn't know he has a liver. I'm only a bit worried about things in general. I suppose it's my soul."

"The truly healthy man doesn't know he has a soul. What business have you with luxuries of that kind?"

"It came of itself. Who's the man that says that we're all islands shouting lies to each other across seas of misunderstanding?"

"He's right, whoever he is,—except about the misunderstanding. I don't think we could misunderstand each other."

The blue smoke curled back from the ceiling in clouds. Then Torpenhow, insinuatingly—"Dick, is it a woman?"

"Be hanged if it's anything remotely resembling a woman; and if you begin to talk like that, I'll hire a red-brick studio with white paint trimmings, and begonias and petunias and blue Hungarias to play among three-and-sixpenny pot-palms, and I'll mount all my pics in aniline-dye plush plasters, and I'll invite every woman who maunders over what her guide-books tell her is Art, and you shall receive 'em, Torp,—in a snuff-brown velvet coat with yellow trousers and an orange tie. You'll like that?"

"Too thin, Dick. A better man than you once denied with cursing and swearing. You've overdone it, just as he did. It's no business of mine, of course, but it's comforting to think that somewhere under the stars there's saving up for you a tremendous thrashing. Whether it'll come from heaven or earth, I don't know, but it's bound to come and break you up a little. You want hammering."

Dick shivered. "All right," said he. "When this island is disintegrated, it will call for you."

"I shall come round the corner and help to disintegrate it some more. We're talking nonsense. Come along to a theatre."

CHAPTER VI

"And you may lead a thousand men,

Nor ever draw the rein,

But ere ye lead the Faery Queen

'Twill burst your heart in twain."

He has slipped his foot from the stirrup-bar,

The bridle from his hand,

And he is bound by hand and foot

To the Queen 'o Faery-land.

———Sir Hoggie and the Fairies.

Some weeks later, on a very foggy Sunday, Dick was returning across the Park to his studio. "This," he said, "is evidently the thrashing that Torp meant. It hurts more than I expected; but the Queen can do no wrong; and she certainly has some notion of drawing."

He had just finished a Sunday visit to Maisie,—always under the green eyes of the red-haired impressionist girl, whom he learned to hate at sight,—and was tingling with a keen sense of shame. Sunday after Sunday, putting on his best clothes, he had walked over to the untidy house north of the Park, first to see Maisie's pictures, and then to criticise and advise upon them as he realised that they were productions on which advice would not be wasted. Sunday after Sunday, and his love grew with each visit, he had been compelled to cram his heart back from between his lips when it prompted him to kiss Maisie several times and very much indeed. Sunday after Sunday, the head above the heart had warned him that Maisie was not yet attainable, and that it would be better to talk as connectedly as possible upon the mysteries of the craft that was all in all to her. Therefore it was his fate to endure weekly torture in the studio built out over the clammy back garden of a frail stuffy little villa where nothing was ever in its right place and nobody every called,—to endure and to watch Maisie moving to and fro with the teacups. He abhorred tea, but, since it gave him a little longer time in her presence, he drank it devoutly, and the red-haired girl sat in an untidy heap and eyed him without speaking. She was always watching him.

Once, and only once, when she had left the studio, Maisie showed him an album that held a few poor cuttings from provincial papers,—the briefest of hurried notes on some of her pictures sent to outlying exhibitions. Dick stooped and kissed the paint-smudged thumb on the open page. "Oh, my love, my love," he muttered, "do you value these things? Chuck 'em into the waste-paper basket!"

"Not till I get something better," said Maisie, shutting the book.

Then Dick, moved by no respect for his public and a very deep regard for the maiden, did deliberately propose, in order to secure more of these coveted cuttings, that he should paint a picture which Maisie should sign.

"That's childish," said Maisie, "and I didn't think it of you. It must be my work. Mine,—mine,—mine!"

"Go and design decorative medallions for rich brewers' houses. You are thoroughly good at that." Dick was sick and savage.

"Better things than medallions, Dick," was the answer, in tones that recalled a gray-eyed atom's fearless speech to Mrs. Jennett. Dick would have abased himself utterly, but that other girl trailed in.

Next Sunday he laid at Maisie's feet small gifts of pencils that could almost draw of themselves and colours in whose permanence he believed, and he was ostentatiously attentive to the work in hand. It demanded, among other things, an exposition of the faith that was in him.

Torpenhow's hair would have stood on end had he heard the fluency with which Dick preached his own gospel of Art.

A month before, Dick would have been equally astonished; but it was Maisie's will and pleasure, and he dragged his words together to make plain to her comprehension all that had been hidden to himself of the whys and wherefores of work. There is not the least difficulty in doing a thing if you only know how to do it; the trouble is to explain your method.

"I could put this right if I had a brush in my hand," said Dick, despairingly, over the modelling of a chin that Maisie complained would not "look flesh,"—it was the same chin that she had scraped out with the palette knife,—"but I find it almost impossible to teach you. There's a queer grim Dutch touch about your painting that I like; but I've a notion that you're weak in drawing. You foreshorten as though you never used the model, and you've caught Kami's pasty way of dealing with flesh in shadow. Then, again, though you don't know it yourself, you shirk hard work. Suppose you spend some of your time on line lone. Line doesn't allow of shirking. Oils do, and three square inches of flashy, tricky stuff in the corner of a pic sometimes carry a bad thing off,—as I know. That's immoral. Do line-work for a little while, and then I can tell more about your powers, as old Kami used to say."

Maisie protested; she did not care for the pure line.

"I know," said Dick. "You want to do your fancy heads with a bunch of flowers at the base of the neck to hide bad modelling." The red-haired girl laughed a little. "You want to do landscapes with cattle knee-deep in grass to hide bad drawing. You want to do a great deal more than you can do. You have sense of colour, but you want form. Colour's a gift,—put it aside and think no more about it,—but form you can be drilled into. Now, all your fancy heads—and some of them are very good—will keep you exactly where you are. With line you must go forward or backward, and it will show up all your weaknesses."

"But other people——" began Maisie.

"You mustn't mind what other people do. If their souls were your soul, it would be different. You stand and fall by your own work, remember, and it's waste of time to think of any one else in this battle."

Dick paused, and the longing that had been so resolutely put away came back into his eyes. He looked at Maisie, and the look asked as plainly as words, Was it not time to leave all this barren wilderness of canvas and counsel and join hands with Life and Love? Maisie assented to the new programme of schooling so adorably that Dick could hardly restrain himself from picking her up then and there and carrying her off to the nearest registrar's office. It was the implicit

obedience to the spoken word and the blank indifference to the unspoken desire that baffled and buffeted his soul. He held authority in that house,—authority limited, indeed, to one-half of one afternoon in seven, but very real while it lasted. Maisie had learned to appeal to him on many subjects, from the proper packing of pictures to the condition of a smoky chimney. The red-haired girl never consulted him about anything.

On the other hand, she accepted his appearances without protest, and watched him always. He discovered that the meals of the establishment were irregular and fragmentary. They depended chiefly on tea, pickles, and biscuit, as he had suspected from the beginning. The girls were supposed to market week and week about, but they lived, with the help of a charwoman, as casually as the young ravens. Maisie spent most of her income on models, and the other girl revelled in apparatus as refined as her work was rough. Armed with knowledge, dear-bought from the Docks, Dick warned Maisie that the end of semi-starvation meant the crippling of power to work, which was considerably worse than death.

Maisie took the warning, and gave more thought to what she ate and drank. When his trouble returned upon him, as it generally did in the long winter twilights, the remembrance of that little act of domestic authority and his coercion with a hearth-brush of the smoky drawing-room chimney stung Dick like a whip-lash.

He conceived that this memory would be the extreme of his sufferings, till one Sunday, the red-haired girl announced that she would make a study of Dick's head, and that he would be good enough to sit still, and—quite as an afterthought—look at Maisie. He sat, because he could not well refuse, and for the space of half an hour he reflected on all the people in the past whom he had laid open for the purposes of his own craft. He remembered Binat most distinctly,—that Binat who had once been an artist and talked about degradation.

It was the merest monochrome roughing in of a head, but it presented the dumb waiting, the longing, and, above all, the hopeless enslavement of the man, in a spirit of bitter mockery.

"I'll buy it," said Dick, promptly, "at your own price."

"My price is too high, but I dare say you'll be as grateful if——" The wet sketch, fluttered from the girl's hand and fell into the ashes of the studio stove. When she picked it up it was hopelessly smudged.

"Oh, it's all spoiled!" said Maisie. "And I never saw it. Was it like?"

"Thank you," said Dick under his breath to the red-haired girl, and he removed himself swiftly.

"How that man hates me!" said the girl. "And how he loves you, Maisie!"

"What nonsense? I knew Dick's very fond of me, but he had his work to do, and I have mine."

"Yes, he is fond of you, and I think he knows there is something in impressionism, after all. Maisie, can't you see?"

"See? See what?"

"Nothing; only, I know that if I could get any man to look at me as that man looks at you, I'd—I don't know what I'd do. But he hates me. Oh, how he hates me!"

She was not altogether correct. Dick's hatred was tempered with gratitude for a few moments, and then he forgot the girl entirely. Only the sense of shame remained, and he was nursing it across the Park in the fog. "There'll be an explosion one of these days," he said wrathfully. "But

it isn't Maisie's fault; she's right, quite right, as far as she knows, and I can't blame her. This business has been going on for three months nearly. Three months!—and it cost me ten years" knocking about to get at the notion, the merest raw notion, of my work. That's true; but then I didn't have pins, drawing-pins, and palette-knives, stuck into me every Sunday.

"Oh, my little darling, if ever I break you, somebody will have a very bad time of it. No, she won't. I'd be as big a fool about her as I am now. I'll poison that red-haired girl on my wedding-day,—she's unwholesome,—and now I'll pass on these present bad times to Torp."

Torpenhow had been moved to lecture Dick more than once lately on the sin of levity, and Dick and listened and replied not a word. In the weeks between the first few Sundays of his discipline he had flung himself savagely into his work, resolved that Maisie should at least know the full stretch of his powers. Then he had taught Maisie that she must not pay the least attention to any work outside her own, and Maisie had obeyed him all too well. She took his counsels, but was not interested in his pictures.

"Your things smell of tobacco and blood," she said once. "Can't you do anything except soldiers?"

"I could do a head of you that would startle you," thought Dick,—this was before the red-haired girl had brought him under the guillotine,—but he only said, "I am very sorry," and harrowed Torpenhow's soul that evening with blasphemies against Art. Later, insensibly and to a large extent against his own will, he ceased to interest himself in his own work.

For Maisie's sake, and to soothe the self-respect that it seemed to him he lost each Sunday, he would not consciously turn out bad stuff, but, since Maisie did not care even for his best, it were better not to do anything at all save wait and mark time between Sunday and Sunday. Torpenhow was disgusted as the weeks went by fruitless, and then attacked him one Sunday evening when Dick felt utterly exhausted after three hours' biting self-restraint in Maisie's presence. There was Language, and Torpenhow withdrew to consult the Nilghai, who had come it to talk continental politics.

"Bone-idle, is he? Careless, and touched in the temper?" said the Nilghai. "It isn't worth worrying over. Dick is probably playing the fool with a woman."

"Isn't that bad enough?"

"No. She may throw him out of gear and knock his work to pieces for a while. She may even turn up here some day and make a scene on the staircase: one never knows. But until Dick speaks of his own accord you had better not touch him. He is no easy-tempered man to handle."

"No; I wish he were. He is such an aggressive, cocksure, you-be-damned fellow."

"He'll get that knocked out of him in time. He must learn that he can't storm up and down the world with a box of moist tubes and a slick brush. You're fond of him?"

"I'd take any punishment that's in store for him if I could; but the worst of it is, no man can save his brother."

"No, and the worser of it is, there is no discharge in this war. Dick must learn his lesson like the rest of us. Talking of war, there'll be trouble in the Balkans in the spring."

"That trouble is long coming. I wonder if we could drag Dick out there when it comes off?"

Dick entered the room soon afterwards, and the question was put to him.

"Not good enough," he said shortly. "I'm too comf'y where I am."

"Surely you aren't taking all the stuff in the papers seriously?" said the Nilghai. "Your vogue will be ended in less than six months,—the public will know your touch and go on to something new,—and where will you be then?"

"Here, in England."

"When you might be doing decent work among us out there? Nonsense! I shall go, the Keneu will be there, Torp will be there, Cassavetti will be there, and the whole lot of us will be there, and we shall have as much as ever we can do, with unlimited fighting and the chance for you of seeing things that would make the reputation of three Verestchagins."

"Um!" said Dick, pulling at his pipe.

"You prefer to stay here and imagine that all the world is gaping at your pictures? Just think how full an average man's life is of his own pursuits and pleasures. When twenty thousand of him find time to look up between mouthfuls and grunt something about something they aren't the least interested in, the net result is called fame, reputation, or notoriety, according to the taste and fancy of the speller my lord."

"I know that as well as you do. Give me credit for a little gumption."

"Be hanged if I do!"

"Be hanged, then; you probably will be,—for a spy, by excited Turks. Heigh-ho! I'm weary, dead weary, and virtue has gone out of me." Dick dropped into a chair, and was fast asleep in a minute.

"That's a bad sign," said the Nilghai, in an undertone.

Torpenhow picked the pipe from the waistcoat where it was beginning to burn, and put a pillow behind the head. "We can't help; we can't help," he said. "It's a good ugly sort of old cocoanut, and I'm fond of it. There's the scar of the wipe he got when he was cut over in the square."

"Shouldn't wonder if that has made him a trifle mad."

"I should. He's a most businesslike madman."

Then Dick began to snore furiously.

"Oh, here, no affection can stand this sort of thing. Wake up, Dick, and go and sleep somewhere else, if you intend to make a noise about it."

"When a cat has been out on the tiles all night," said the Nilghai, in his beard, "I notice that she usually sleeps all day. This is natural history."

Dick staggered away rubbing his eyes and yawning. In the night-watches he was overtaken with an idea, so simple and so luminous that he wondered he had never conceived it before. It was full of craft. He would seek Maisie on a week-day,—would suggest an excursion, and would take her by train to Fort Keeling, over the very ground that they two had trodden together ten years ago.

"As a general rule," he explained to his chin-lathered reflection in the morning, "it isn't safe to cross an old trail twice. Things remind one of things, and a cold wind gets up, and you feel sad;

but this is an exception to every rule that ever was. I'll go to Maisie at once."

Fortunately, the red-haired girl was out shopping when he arrived, and Maisie in a paint-spattered blouse was warring with her canvas. She was not pleased to see him; for week-day visits were a stretch of the bond; and it needed all his courage to explain his errand.

"I know you've been working too hard," he concluded, with an air of authority. "If you do that, you'll break down. You had much better come."

"Where?" said Maisie, wearily. She had been standing before her easel too long, and was very tired.

"Anywhere you please. We'll take a train tomorrow and see where it stops. We'll have lunch somewhere, and I'll bring you back in the evening."

"If there's a good working light tomorrow, I lose a day." Maisie balanced the heavy white chestnut palette irresolutely.

Dick bit back an oath that was hurrying to his lips. He had not yet learned patience with the maiden to whom her work was all in all.

"You'll lose ever so many more, dear, if you use every hour of working light. Overwork's only murderous idleness. Don't be unreasonable. I'll call for you tomorrow after breakfast early."

"But surely you are going to ask——"

"No, I am not. I want you and nobody else. Besides, she hates me as much as I hate her. She won't care to come. Tomorrow, then; and pray that we get sunshine."

Dick went away delighted, and by consequence did no work whatever.

He strangled a wild desire to order a special train, but bought a great gray kangaroo cloak lined with glossy black marten, and then retired into himself to consider things.

"I'm going out for the day tomorrow with Dick," said Maisie to the red-haired girl when the latter returned, tired, from marketing in the Edgware road.

"He deserves it. I shall have the studio floor thoroughly scrubbed while you're away. It's very dirty."

Maisie had enjoyed no sort of holiday for months and looked forward to the little excitement, but not without misgivings.

"There's nobody nicer than Dick when he talks sensibly," she thought, "but I'm sure he'll be silly and worry me, and I'm sure I can't tell him anything he'd like to hear. If he'd only be sensible, I should like him so much better."

Dick's eyes were full of joy when he made his appearance next morning and saw Maisie, gray-ulstered and black-velvet-hatted, standing in the hallway. Palaces of marble, and not sordid imitation of grained wood, were surely the fittest background for such a divinity. The red-haired girl drew her into the studio for a moment and kissed her hurriedly.

Maisie's eyebrows climbed to the top of her forehead; she was altogether unused to these demonstrations. "Mind my hat," she said, hurrying away, and ran down the steps to Dick waiting by the hansom.

"Are you quite warm enough! Are you sure you wouldn't like some more breakfast? Put the cloak over your knees."

"I'm quite comf'y, thanks. Where are we going, Dick? Oh, do stop singing like that. People will think we're mad."

"Let 'em think,—if the exertion doesn't kill them. They don't know who we are, and I'm sure I don't care who they are. My faith, Maisie, you're looking lovely!"

Maisie stared directly in front of her and did not reply. The wind of a keen clear winter morning had put colour into her cheeks. Overhead, the creamy-yellow smoke-clouds were thinning away one by one against a pale-blue sky, and the improvident sparrows broke off from water-spout committees and cab-rank cabals to clamour of the coming of spring.

"It will be lovely weather in the country," said Dick.

"But where are we going?"

"Wait and see."

The stopped at Victoria, and Dick sought tickets. For less than half the fraction of an instant it occurred to Maisie, comfortably settled by the waiting-room fire, that it was much more pleasant to send a man to the booking-office than to elbow one's own way through the crowd. Dick put her into a Pullman,—solely on account of the warmth there; and she regarded the extravagance with grave scandalised eyes as the train moved out into the country.

"I wish I knew where we are going," she repeated for the twentieth time.

The name of a well-remembered station flashed by, towards the end of the run, and Maisie was delighted.

"Oh, Dick, you villain!"

"Well, I thought you might like to see the place again. You haven't been here since the old times, have you?"

"No. I never cared to see Mrs. Jennett again; and she was all that was ever there."

"Not quite. Look out a minute. There's the windmill above the potato-fields; they haven't built villas there yet; d'you remember when I shut you up in it?"

"Yes. How she beat you for it! I never told it was you."

"She guessed. I jammed a stick under the door and told you that I was burying Amomma alive in the potatoes, and you believed me. You had a trusting nature in those days."

They laughed and leaned to look out, identifying ancient landmarks with many reminiscences. Dick fixed his weather eye on the curve of Maisie's cheek, very near his own, and watched the blood rise under the clear skin. He congratulated himself upon his cunning, and looked that the evening would bring him a great reward.

When the train stopped they went out to look at an old town with new eyes. First, but from a distance, they regarded the house of Mrs. Jennett.

"Suppose she should come out now, what would you do?" said Dick, with mock terror.

"I should make a face."

"Show, then," said Dick, dropping into the speech of childhood.

Maisie made that face in the direction of the mean little villa, and Dick laughed.

"'This is disgraceful,'" said Maisie, mimicking Mrs. Jennett's tone. "'Maisie, you run in at once, and learn the collect, gospel, and epistle for the next three Sundays. After all I've taught you, too, and three helps every Sunday at dinner! Dick's always leading you into mischief. If you aren't a gentleman, Dick, you might at least...'"

The sentence ended abruptly. Maisie remembered when it had last been used.

"'Try to behave like one,'" said Dick, promptly. "Quite right. Now we'll get some lunch and go on to Fort Keeling,—unless you'd rather drive there?"

"We must walk, out of respect to the place. How little changed it all is!"

They turned in the direction of the sea through unaltered streets, and the influence of old things lay upon them. Presently they passed a confectioner's shop much considered in the days when their joint pocket-money amounted to a shilling a week.

"Dick, have you any pennies?" said Maisie, half to herself.

"Only three; and if you think you're going to have two of 'em to buy peppermints with, you're wrong. She says peppermints aren't ladylike."

Again they laughed, and again the colour came into Maisie's cheeks as the blood boiled through Dick's heart. After a large lunch they went down to the beach and to Fort Keeling across the waste, wind-bitten land that no builder had thought it worth his while to defile. The winter breeze came in from the sea and sang about their ears.

"Maisie," said Dick, "your nose is getting a crude Prussian blue at the tip. I'll race you as far as you please for as much as you please."

She looked round cautiously, and with a laugh set off, swiftly as the ulster allowed, till she was out of breath.

"We used to run miles," she panted. "It's absurd that we can't run now."

"Old age, dear. This it is to get fat and sleek in town. When I wished to pull your hair you generally ran for three miles, shrieking at the top of your voice. I ought to know, because those shrieks of yours were meant to call up Mrs. Jennett with a cane and——"

"Dick, I never got you a beating on purpose in my life."

"No, of course you never did. Good heavens! look at the sea."

"Why, it's the same as ever!" said Maisie.

Torpenhow had gathered from Mr. Beeton that Dick, properly dressed and shaved, had left the house at half-past eight in the morning with a travelling-rug over his arm. The Nilghai rolled in at mid-day for chess and polite conversation.

"It's worse than anything I imagined," said Torpenhow.

"Oh, the everlasting Dick, I suppose! You fuss over him like a hen with one chick. Let him run riot if he thinks it'll amuse him. You can whip a young pup off feather, but you can't whip a young man."

"It isn't a woman. It's one woman; and it's a girl."

"Where's your proof?"

"He got up and went out at eight this morning,—got up in the middle of the night, by Jove! a thing he never does except when he's on service. Even then, remember, we had to kick him out of his blankets before the fight began at El-Maghrib. It's disgusting."

"It looks odd; but maybe he's decided to buy a horse at last. He might get up for that, mightn't he?"

"Buy a blazing wheelbarrow! He'd have told us if there was a horse in the wind. It's a girl."

"Don't be certain. Perhaps it's only a married woman."

"Dick has some sense of humour, if you haven't. Who gets up in the gray dawn to call on another man's wife? It's a girl."

"Let it be a girl, then. She may teach him that there's somebody else in the world besides himself."

"She'll spoil his hand. She'll waste his time, and she'll marry him, and ruin his work for ever. He'll be a respectable married man before we can stop him, and—he'll ever go on the long trail again."

"All quite possible, but the earth won't spin the other way when that happens.... No! ho! I'd give something to see Dick 'go wooing with the boys.' Don't worry about it. These things be with Allah, and we can only look on. Get the chessmen."

The red-haired girl was lying down in her own room, staring at the ceiling. The footsteps of people on the pavement sounded, as they grew indistinct in the distance, like a many-times-repeated kiss that was all one long kiss. Her hands were by her side, and they opened and shut savagely from time to time.

The charwoman in charge of the scrubbing of the studio knocked at her door: "Beg y' pardon, miss, but in cleanin' of a floor there's two, not to say three, kind of soap, which is yaller, an' mottled, an' disinfectink. Now, jist before I took my pail into the passage I though it would be pre'aps jest as well if I was to come up 'ere an' ask you what sort of soap you was wishful that I should use on them boards. The yaller soap, miss——"

There was nothing in the speech to have caused the paroxysm of fury that drove the red-haired girl into the middle of the room, almost shouting—"Do you suppose I care what you use? Any kind will do!—any kind!"

The woman fled, and the red-haired girl looked at her own reflection in the glass for an instant and covered her face with her hands. It was as though she had shouted some shameless secret aloud.

CHAPTER VII

Roses red and roses white

Plucked I for my love's delight.

She would none of all my posies,—

Bade me gather her blue roses.

Half the world I wandered through,

Seeking where such flowers grew;

Half the world unto my quest

Answered but with laugh and jest.

It may be beyond the grave

She shall find what she would have.

Mine was but an idle quest,—

Roses white and red are best!

——Blue Roses

Indeed the sea had not changed. Its waters were low on the mud-banks, and the Marazion Bell-buoy clanked and swung in the tide-way. On the white beach-sand dried stumps of sea-poppy shivered and chattered.

"I don't see the old breakwater," said Maisie, under her breath.

"Let's be thankful that we have as much as we have. I don't believe they've mounted a single new gun on the fort since we were here. Come and look."

They came to the glacis of Fort Keeling, and sat down in a nook sheltered from the wind under the tarred throat of a forty-pounder cannon.

"Now, if Ammoma were only here!" said Maisie.

For a long time both were silent. Then Dick took Maisie's hand and called her by her name.

She shook her head and looked out to sea.

"Maisie, darling, doesn't it make any difference?"

"No!" between clenched teeth. "I'd—I'd tell you if it did; but it doesn't. Oh, Dick, please be sensible."

"Don't you think that it ever will?"

"No, I'm sure it won't."

"Why?"

Maisie rested her chin on her hand, and, still regarding the sea, spoke hurriedly—"I know what you want perfectly well, but I can't give it to you, Dick. It isn't my fault; indeed, it isn't. If I felt that I could care for any one——But I don't feel that I care. I simply don't understand what the feeling means."

"Is that true, dear?"

"You've been very good to me, Dickie; and the only way I can pay you back is by speaking the truth. I daren't tell a fib. I despise myself quite enough as it is."

"What in the world for?"

"Because—because I take everything that you give me and I give you nothing in return. It's mean and selfish of me, and whenever I think of it it worries me."

"Understand once for all, then, that I can manage my own affairs, and if I choose to do anything you aren't to blame. You haven't a single thing to reproach yourself with, darling."

"Yes, I have, and talking only makes it worse."

"Then don't talk about it."

"How can I help myself? If you find me alone for a minute you are always talking about it; and when you aren't you look it. You don't know how I despise myself sometimes."

"Great goodness!" said Dick, nearly jumping to his feet. "Speak the truth now, Maisie, if you never speak it again! Do I—does this worrying bore you?"

"No. It does not."

"You'd tell me if it did?"

"I should let you know, I think."

"Thank you. The other thing is fatal. But you must learn to forgive a man when he's in love. He's always a nuisance. You must have known that?"

Maisie did not consider the last question worth answering, and Dick was forced to repeat it.

"There were other men, of course. They always worried just when I was in the middle of my work, and wanted me to listen to them."

"Did you listen?"

"At first; and they couldn't understand why I didn't care. And they used to praise my pictures; and I thought they meant it. I used to be proud of the praise, and tell Kami, and—I shall never forget—once Kami laughed at me."

"You don't like being laughed at, Maisie, do you?"

"I hate it. I never laugh at other people unless—unless they do bad work. Dick, tell me honestly what you think of my pictures generally,—of everything of mine that you've seen."

"'Honest, honest, and honest over!'" quoted Dick from a catchword of long ago. "Tell me what Kami always says."

Maisie hesitated. "He—he says that there is feeling in them."

"How dare you tell me a fib like that? Remember, I was under Kami for two years. I know exactly what he says."

"It isn't a fib."

"It's worse; it's a half-truth. Kami says, when he puts his head on one side,—so, 'Il y a du sentiment, mais il n'y a pas de parti pris.'" He rolled the r threateningly, as Kami used to do.

"Yes, that is what he says; and I'm beginning to think that he is right."

"Certainly he is." Dick admitted that two people in the world could do and say no wrong. Kami was the man.

"And now you say the same thing. It's so disheartening."

"I'm sorry, but you asked me to speak the truth. Besides, I love you too much to pretend about your work. It's strong, it's patient sometimes,—not always,—and sometimes there's power in it, but there's no special reason why it should be done at all. At least, that's how it strikes me."

"There's no special reason why anything in the world should ever be done. You know that as well as I do. I only want success."

"You're going the wrong way to get it, then. Hasn't Kami ever told you so?"

"Don't quote Kami to me. I want to know what you think. My work's bad, to begin with."

"I didn't say that, and I don't think it."

"It's amateurish, then."

"That it most certainly is not. You're a work-woman, darling, to your boot-heels, and I respect you for that."

"You don't laugh at me behind my back?"

"No, dear. You see, you are more to me than any one else. Put this cloak thing round you, or you'll get chilled."

Maisie wrapped herself in the soft marten skins, turning the gray kangaroo fur to the outside. "This is delicious," she said, rubbing her chin thoughtfully along the fur.

"Well? Why am I wrong in trying to get a little success?"

"Just because you try. Don't you understand, darling? Good work has nothing to do with—doesn't belong to—the person who does it. It's put into him or her from outside."

"But how does that affect———"

"Wait a minute. All we can do is to learn how to do our work, to be masters of our materials instead of servants, and never to be afraid of anything."

"I understand that."

"Everything else comes from outside ourselves. Very good. If we sit down quietly to work out notions that are sent to us, we may or we may not do something that isn't bad. A great deal depends on being master of the bricks and mortar of the trade. But the instant we begin to think about success and the effect of our work—to play with one eye on the gallery—we lose power and touch and everything else. At least that's how I have found it. Instead of being quiet and giving every power you possess to your work, you're fretting over something which you can neither help no hinder by a minute. See?"

"It's so easy for you to talk in that way. People like what you do. Don't you ever think about the gallery?"

"Much too often; but I'm always punished for it by loss of power. It's as simple as the Rule of Three. If we make light of our work by using it for our own ends, our work will make light of us, and, as we're the weaker, we shall suffer."

"I don't treat my work lightly. You know that it's everything to me."

"Of course; but, whether you realise it or not, you give two strokes for yourself to one for your work. It isn't your fault, darling. I do exactly the same thing, and know that I'm doing it. Most of the French schools, and all the schools here, drive the students to work for their own credit, and for the sake of their pride. I was told that all the world was interested in my work, and everybody at Kami's talked turpentine, and I honestly believed that the world needed elevating and influencing, and all manner of impertinences, by my brushes. By Jove, I actually believed that! When my little head was bursting with a notion that I couldn't handle because I hadn't sufficient knowledge of my craft, I used to run about wondering at my own magnificence and getting ready to astonish the world."

"But surely one can do that sometimes?"

"Very seldom with malice aforethought, darling. And when it's done it's such a tiny thing, and the world's so big, and all but a millionth part of it doesn't care. Maisie, come with me and I'll show you something of the size of the world. One can no more avoid working than eating,—that goes on by itself,—but try to see what you are working for. I know such little heavens that I could take you to,—islands tucked away under the Line. You sight them after weeks of crashing through water as black as black marble because it's so deep, and you sit in the fore-chains day after day and see the sun rise almost afraid because the sea's so lonely."

"Who is afraid?—you, or the sun?"

"The sun, of course. And there are noises under the sea, and sounds overhead in a clear sky. Then you find your island alive with hot moist orchids that make mouths at you and can do everything except talk. There's a waterfall in it three hundred feet high, just like a sliver of green jade laced with silver; and millions of wild bees live up in the rocks; and you can hear the fat cocoanuts falling from the palms; and you order an ivory-white servant to sling you a long yellow hammock with tassels on it like ripe maize, and you put up your feet and hear the bees hum and the water fall till you go to sleep."

"Can one work there?"

"Certainly. One must do something always. You hang your canvas up in a palm tree and let the parrots criticise. When the scuffle you heave a ripe custard-apple at them, and it bursts in a lather of cream. There are hundreds of places. Come and see them."

"I don't quite like that place. It sounds lazy. Tell me another."

"What do you think of a big, red, dead city built of red sandstone, with raw green aloes growing between the stones, lying out neglected on honey-coloured sands? There are forty dead kings there, Maisie, each in a gorgeous tomb finer than all the others. You look at the palaces and streets and shops and tanks, and think that men must live there, till you find a wee gray squirrel rubbing its nose all alone in the market-place, and a jewelled peacock struts out of a carved doorway and spreads its tail against a marble screen as fine pierced as point-lace. Then a monkey—a little black monkey—walks through the main square to get a drink from a tank forty feet deep. He slides down the creepers to the water's edge, and a friend holds him by the tail, in case he should fall in."

"Is that all true?"

"I have been there and seen. Then evening comes, and the lights change till it's just as though you stood in the heart of a king-opal. A little before sundown, as punctually as clockwork, a big bristly wild boar, with all his family following, trots through the city gate, churning the foam on his tusks. You climb on the shoulder of a blind black stone god and watch that pig choose himself a palace for the night and stump in wagging his tail. Then the night-wind gets up, and the sands move, and you hear the desert outside the city singing, 'Now I lay me down to sleep,' and everything is dark till the moon rises. Maisie, darling, come with me and see what the world is really like. It's very lovely, and it's very horrible,—but I won't let you see anything horrid,—and it doesn't care your life or mine for pictures or anything else except doing its own work and making love. Come, and I'll show you how to brew sangaree, and sling a hammock, and—oh, thousands of things, and you'll see for yourself what colour means, and we'll find out together what love means, and then, maybe, we shall be allowed to do some good work. Come away!"

"Why?" said Maisie.

"How can you do anything until you have seen everything, or as much as you can? And besides, darling, I love you. Come along with me. You have no business here; you don't belong to this place; you're half a gipsy,—your face tells that; and I—even the smell of open water makes me restless. Come across the sea and be happy!"

He had risen to his feet, and stood in the shadow of the gun, looking down at the girl. The very short winter afternoon had worn away, and, before they knew, the winter moon was walking the untroubled sea. Long ruled lines of silver showed where a ripple of the rising tide was turning over the mud-banks. The wind had dropped, and in the intense stillness they could hear a donkey cropping the frosty grass many yards away. A faint beating, like that of a muffled drum, came out of the moon-haze.

"What's that?" said Maisie, quickly. "It sounds like a heart beating. Where is it?"

Dick was so angry at this sudden wrench to his pleadings that he could not trust himself to speak, and in this silence caught the sound. Maisie from her seat under the gun watched him with a certain amount of fear.

She wished so much that he would be sensible and cease to worry her with over-sea emotion

that she both could and could not understand. She was not prepared, however, for the change in his face as he listened.

"It's a steamer," he said,—"a twin-screw steamer, by the beat. I can't make her out, but she must be standing very close inshore. Ah!" as the red of a rocket streaked the haze, "she's standing in to signal before she clears the Channel."

"Is it a wreck?" said Maisie, to whom these words were as Greek.

Dick's eyes were turned to the sea. "Wreck! What nonsense! She's only reporting herself. Red rocket forward—there's a green light aft now, and two red rockets from the bridge."

"What does that mean?"

"It's the signal of the Cross Keys Line running to Australia. I wonder which steamer it is." The note of his voice had changed; he seemed to be talking to himself, and Maisie did not approve of it. The moonlight broke the haze for a moment, touching the black sides of a long steamer working down Channel. "Four masts and three funnels—she's in deep draught, too. That must be the Barralong, or the Bhutia. No, the Bhutia has a clipper bow. It's the Barralong, to Australia. She'll lift the Southern Cross in a week,—lucky old tub!—oh, lucky old tub!"

He stared intently, and moved up the slope of the fort to get a better view, but the mist on the sea thickened again, and the beating of the screws grew fainter. Maisie called to him a little angrily, and he returned, still keeping his eyes to seaward. "Have you ever seen the Southern Cross blazing right over your head?" he asked. "It's superb!"

"No," she said shortly, "and I don't want to. If you think it's so lovely, why don't you go and see it yourself?"

She raised her face from the soft blackness of the marten skins about her throat, and her eyes shone like diamonds. The moonlight on the gray kangaroo fur turned it to frosted silver of the coldest.

"By Jove, Maisie, you look like a little heathen idol tucked up there." The eyes showed that they did not appreciate the compliment. "I'm sorry," he continued. "The Southern Cross isn't worth looking at unless someone helps you to see. That steamer's out of hearing."

"Dick," she said quietly, "suppose I were to come to you now,—be quiet a minute,—just as I am, and caring for you just as much as I do."

"Not as a brother, though. You said you didn't—in the Park."

"I never had a brother. Suppose I said, 'Take me to those places, and in time, perhaps, I might really care for you,' what would you do?"

"Send you straight back to where you came from, in a cab. No, I wouldn't; I'd let you walk. But you couldn't do it, dear. And I wouldn't run the risk. You're worth waiting for till you can come without reservation."

"Do you honestly believe that?"

"I have a hazy sort of idea that I do. Has it never struck you in that light?"

"Ye—es. I feel so wicked about it."

"Wickeder than usual?"

"You don't know all I think. It's almost too awful to tell."

"Never mind. You promised to tell me the truth—at least."

"It's so ungrateful of me, but—but, though I know you care for me, and I like to have you with me, I'd—I'd even sacrifice you, if that would bring me what I want."

"My poor little darling! I know that state of mind. It doesn't lead to good work."

"You aren't angry? Remember, I do despise myself."

"I'm not exactly flattered,—I had guessed as much before,—but I'm not angry. I'm sorry for you. Surely you ought to have left a littleness like that behind you, years ago."

"You've no right to patronise me! I only want what I have worked for so long. It came to you without any trouble, and—and I don't think it's fair."

"What can I do? I'd give ten years of my life to get you what you want. But I can't help you; even I can't help."

A murmur of dissent from Maisie. He went on—"And I know by what you have just said that you're on the wrong road to success. It isn't got at by sacrificing other people,—I've had that much knocked into me; you must sacrifice yourself, and live under orders, and never think for yourself, and never have real satisfaction in your work except just at the beginning, when you're reaching out after a notion."

"How can you believe all that?"

"There's no question of belief or disbelief. That's the law, and you take it or refuse it as you please. I try to obey, but I can't, and then my work turns bad on my hands. Under any circumstances, remember, four-fifths of everybody's work must be bad. But the remnant is worth the trouble for its own sake."

"Isn't it nice to get credit even for bad work?"

"It's much too nice. But——May I tell you something? It isn't a pretty tale, but you're so like a man that I forget when I'm talking to you."

"Tell me."

"Once when I was out in the Soudan I went over some ground that we had been fighting on for three days. There were twelve hundred dead; and we hadn't time to bury them."

"How ghastly!"

"I had been at work on a big double-sheet sketch, and I was wondering what people would think of it at home. The sight of that field taught me a good deal. It looked just like a bed of horrible toadstools in all colours, and—I'd never seen men in bulk go back to their beginnings before. So I began to understand that men and women were only material to work with, and that what they said or did was of no consequence. See? Strictly speaking, you might just as well put your ear down to the palette to catch what your colours are saying."

"Dick, that's disgraceful!"

"Wait a minute. I said, strictly speaking. Unfortunately, everybody must be either a man or a woman."

"I'm glad you allow that much."

"In your case I don't. You aren't a woman. But ordinary people, Maisie, must behave and work ·as such. That's what makes me so savage." He hurled a pebble towards the sea as he spoke. "I know that it is outside my business to care what people say; I can see that it spoils my output if I listen to 'em; and yet, confound it all,"—another pebble flew seaward,—"I can't help purring when I'm rubbed the right way. Even when I can see on a man's forehead that he is lying his way through a clump of pretty speeches, those lies make me happy and play the mischief with my hand."

"And when he doesn't say pretty things?"

"Then, belovedest,"—Dick grinned,—"I forget that I am the steward of these gifts, and I want to make that man love and appreciate my work with a thick stick. It's too humiliating altogether; but I suppose even if one were an angel and painted humans altogether from outside, one would lose in touch what one gained in grip."

Maisie laughed at the idea of Dick as an angel.

"But you seem to think," she said, "that everything nice spoils your hand."

"I don't think. It's the law,—just the same as it was at Mrs. Jennett's. Everything that is nice does spoil your hand. I'm glad you see so clearly."

"I don't like the view."

"Nor I. But—have got orders: what can do? Are you strong enough to face it alone?"

"I suppose I must."

"Let me help, darling. We can hold each other very tight and try to walk straight. We shall blunder horribly, but it will be better than stumbling apart. Maisie, can't you see reason?"

"I don't think we should get on together. We should be two of a trade, so we should never agree."

"How I should like to meet the man who made that proverb! He lived in a cave and ate raw bear, I fancy. I'd make him chew his own arrow-heads. Well?"

"I should be only half married to you. I should worry and fuss about my work, as I do now. Four days out of the seven I'm not fit to speak to."

"You talk as if no one else in the world had ever used a brush. D'you suppose that I don't know the feeling of worry and bother and can't-get-at-ness? You're lucky if you only have it four days out of the seven. What difference would that make?"

"A great deal—if you had it too."

"Yes, but I could respect it. Another man might not. He might laugh at you. But there's no use talking about it. If you can think in that way you can't care for me—yet."

The tide had nearly covered the mud-banks and twenty little ripples broke on the beach before Maisie chose to speak.

"Dick," she said slowly, "I believe very much that you are better than I am."

"This doesn't seem to bear on the argument—but in what way?"

"I don't quite know, but in what you said about work and things; and then you're so patient. Yes, you're better than I am."

Dick considered rapidly the murkiness of an average man's life. There was nothing in the review to fill him with a sense of virtue. He lifted the hem of the cloak to his lips.

"Why," said Maisie, making as though she had not noticed, "can you see things that I can't? I don't believe what you believe; but you're right, I believe."

"If I've seen anything, God knows I couldn't have seen it but for you, and I know that I couldn't have said it except to you. You seemed to make everything clear for a minute; but I don't practice what I preach. You would help me... There are only us two in the world for all purposes, and—and you like to have me with you?"

"Of course I do. I wonder if you can realise how utterly lonely I am!"

"Darling, I think I can."

"Two years ago, when I first took the little house, I used to walk up and down the back-garden trying to cry. I never can cry. Can you?"

"It's some time since I tried. What was the trouble? Overwork?"

"I don't know; but I used to dream that I had broken down, and had no money, and was starving in London. I thought about it all day, and it frightened me—oh, how it frightened me!"

"I know that fear. It's the most terrible of all. It wakes me up in the night sometimes. You oughtn't to know anything about it."

"How do you know?"

"Never mind. Is your three hundred a year safe?"

"It's in Consols."

"Very well. If any one comes to you and recommends a better investment,—even if I should come to you,—don't you listen. Never shift the money for a minute, and never lend a penny of it,—even to the red-haired girl."

"Don't scold me so! I'm not likely to be foolish."

"The earth is full of men who'd sell their souls for three hundred a year; and women come and talk, and borrow a five-pound note here and a ten-pound note there; and a woman has no conscience in a money debt. Stick to your money, Maisie, for there's nothing more ghastly in the world than poverty in London. It's scared me. By Jove, it put the fear into me! And one oughtn't to be afraid of anything."

To each man is appointed his particular dread,—the terror that, if he does not fight against it, must cow him even to the loss of his manhood. Dick's experience of the sordid misery of want had entered into the deeps of him, and, lest he might find virtue too easy, that memory stood behind him, tempting to shame, when dealers came to buy his wares. As the Nilghai quaked against his will at the still green water of a lake or a mill-dam, as Torpenhow flinched before

any white arm that could cut or stab and loathed himself for flinching, Dick feared the poverty he had once tasted half in jest. His burden was heavier than the burdens of his companions.

Maisie watched the face working in the moonlight.

"You've plenty of pennies now," she said soothingly.

"I shall never have enough," he began, with vicious emphasis. Then, laughing, "I shall always be three-pence short in my accounts."

"Why threepence?"

"I carried a man's bag once from Liverpool Street Station to Blackfriar's Bridge. It was a sixpenny job,—you needn't laugh; indeed it was,—and I wanted the money desperately. He only gave me threepence; and he hadn't even the decency to pay in silver. Whatever money I make, I shall never get that odd threepence out of the world."

This was not language befitting the man who had preached of the sanctity of work. It jarred on Maisie, who preferred her payment in applause, which, since all men desire it, must be of the right. She hunted for her little purse and gravely took out a threepenny bit.

"There it is," she said. "I'll pay you, Dickie; and don't worry any more; it isn't worth while. Are you paid?"

"I am," said the very human apostle of fair craft, taking the coin. "I'm paid a thousand times, and we'll close that account. It shall live on my watch-chain; and you're an angel, Maisie."

"I'm very cramped, and I'm feeling a little cold. Good gracious! the cloak is all white, and so is your moustache! I never knew it was so chilly."

A light frost lay white on the shoulder of Dick's ulster. He, too, had forgotten the state of the weather. They laughed together, and with that laugh ended all serious discourse.

They ran inland across the waste to warm themselves, then turned to look at the glory of the full tide under the moonlight and the intense black shadows of the furze bushes. It was an additional joy to Dick that Maisie could see colour even as he saw it,—could see the blue in the white of the mist, the violet that is in gray palings, and all things else as they are,—not of one hue, but a thousand. And the moonlight came into Maisie's soul, so that she, usually reserved, chattered of herself and of the things she took interest in,—of Kami, wisest of teachers, and of the girls in the studio,—of the Poles, who will kill themselves with overwork if they are not checked; of the French, who talk at great length of much more than they will ever accomplish; of the slovenly English, who toil hopelessly and cannot understand that inclination does not imply power; of the Americans, whose rasping voices in the hush of a hot afternoon strain tense-drawn nerves to breaking-point, and whose suppers lead to indigestion; of tempestuous Russians, neither to hold nor to bind, who tell the girls ghost-stories till the girls shriek; of stolid Germans, who come to learn one thing, and, having mastered that much, stolidly go away and copy pictures for evermore. Dick listened enraptured because it was Maisie who spoke. He knew the old life.

"It hasn't changed much," he said. "Do they still steal colours at lunch-time?"

"Not steal. Attract is the word. Of course they do. I'm good—I only attract ultramarine; but there are students who'd attract flake-white."

"I've done it myself. You can't help it when the palettes are hung up. Every colour is common property once it runs down,—even though you do start it with a drop of oil. It teaches people

not to waste their tubes."

"I should like to attract some of your colours, Dick. Perhaps I might catch your success with them."

"I mustn't say a bad word, but I should like to. What in the world, which you've just missed a lovely chance of seeing, does success or want of success, or a three-storied success, matter compared with——No, I won't open that question again. It's time to go back to town."

"I'm sorry, Dick, but——"

"You're much more interested in that than you are in me."

"I don't know, I don't think I am."

"What will you give me if I tell you a sure short-cut to everything you want,—the trouble and the fuss and the tangle and all the rest? Will you promise to obey me?"

"Of course."

"In the first place, you must never forget a meal because you happen to be at work. You forgot your lunch twice last week," said Dick, at a venture, for he knew with whom he was dealing.

"No, no,—only once, really."

"That's bad enough. And you mustn't take a cup of tea and a biscuit in place of a regular dinner, because dinner happens to be a trouble."

"You're making fun of me!"

"I never was more in earnest in my life. Oh, my love, my love, hasn't it dawned on you yet what you are to me? Here's the whole earth in a conspiracy to give you a chill, or run over you, or drench you to the skin, or cheat you out of your money, or let you die of overwork and underfeeding, and I haven't the mere right to look after you. Why, I don't even know if you have sense enough to put on warm things when the weather's cold."

"Dick, you're the most awful boy to talk to—really! How do you suppose I managed when you were away?"

"I wasn't here, and I didn't know. But now I'm back I'd give everything I have for the right of telling you to come in out of the rain."

"Your success too?"

This time it cost Dick a severe struggle to refrain from bad words.

"As Mrs. Jennett used to say, you're a trial, Maisie! You've been cooped up in the schools too long, and you think every one is looking at you. There aren't twelve hundred people in the world who understand pictures. The others pretend and don't care. Remember, I've seen twelve hundred men dead in toadstool-beds. It's only the voice of the tiniest little fraction of people that makes success. The real world doesn't care a tinker's—doesn't care a bit. For aught you or I know, every man in the world may be arguing with a Maisie of his own."

"Poor Maisie!"

"Poor Dick, I think. Do you believe while he's fighting for what's dearer than his life he wants to

look at a picture? And even if he did, and if all the world did, and a thousand million people rose up and shouted hymns to my honour and glory, would that make up to me for the knowledge that you were out shopping in the Edgware Road on a rainy day without an umbrella? Now we'll go to the station."

"But you said on the beach——" persisted Maisie, with a certain fear.

Dick groaned aloud: "Yes, I know what I said. My work is everything I have, or am, or hope to be, to me, and I believe I've learnt the law that governs it; but I've some lingering sense of fun left,—though you've nearly knocked it out of me. I can just see that it isn't everything to all the world. Do what I say, and not what I do."

Maisie was careful not to reopen debatable matters, and they returned to London joyously. The terminus stopped Dick in the midst of an eloquent harangue on the beauties of exercise. He would buy Maisie a horse,—such a horse as never yet bowed head to bit,—would stable it, with a companion, some twenty miles from London, and Maisie, solely for her health's sake should ride with him twice or thrice a week.

"That's absurd," said she. "It wouldn't be proper."

"Now, who in all London tonight would have sufficient interest or audacity to call us two to account for anything we chose to do?"

Maisie looked at the lamps, the fog, and the hideous turmoil. Dick was right; but horseflesh did not make for Art as she understood it.

"You're very nice sometimes, but you're very foolish more times. I'm not going to let you give me horses, or take you out of your way tonight. I'll go home by myself. Only I want you to promise me something. You won't think any more about that extra threepence, will you? Remember, you've been paid; and I won't allow you to be spiteful and do bad work for a little thing like that. You can be so big that you mustn't be tiny."

This was turning the tables with a vengeance. There remained only to put Maisie into her hansom.

"Goodbye," she said simply. "You'll come on Sunday. It has been a beautiful day, Dick. Why can't it be like this always?"

"Because love's like line-work: you must go forward or backward; you can't stand still. By the way, go on with your line-work. Good night, and, for my—for my sake, take care of yourself."

He turned to walk home, meditating. The day had brought him nothing that he hoped for, but—surely this was worth many days—it had brought him nearer to Maisie. The end was only a question of time now, and the prize well worth the waiting. By instinct, once more, he turned to the river.

"And she understood at once," he said, looking at the water. "She found out my pet besetting sin on the spot, and paid it off. My God, how she understood! And she said I was better than she was! Better than she was!" He laughed at the absurdity of the notion. "I wonder if girls guess at one-half a man's life. They can't, or—they wouldn't marry us." He took her gift out of his pocket, and considered it in the light of a miracle and a pledge of the comprehension that, one day, would lead to perfect happiness. Meantime, Maisie was alone in London, with none to save her from danger. And the packed wilderness was very full of danger.

Dick made his prayer to Fate disjointedly after the manner of the heathen as he threw the piece

of silver into the river. If any evil were to befal, let him bear the burden and let Maisie go unscathed, since the threepenny piece was dearest to him of all his possessions. It was a small coin in itself, but Maisie had given it, and the Thames held it, and surely the Fates would be bribed for this once.

The drowning of the coin seemed to cut him free from thought of Maisie for the moment. He took himself off the bridge and went whistling to his chambers with a strong yearning for some man-talk and tobacco after his first experience of an entire day spent in the society of a woman. There was a stronger desire at his heart when there rose before him an unsolicited vision of the Barralong dipping deep and sailing free for the Southern Cross.

CHAPTER VIII

And these two, as I have told you,

Were the friends of Hiawatha,

Chibiabos, the musician,

And the very strong man, Kwasind.

—Hiawatha

Torpenhow was paging the last sheets of some manuscript, while the Nilghai, who had come for chess and remained to talk tactics, was reading through the first part, commenting scornfully the while.

"It's picturesque enough and it's sketchy," said he; "but as a serious consideration of affairs in Eastern Europe, it's not worth much."

"It's off my hands at any rate.... Thirty-seven, thirty-eight, thirty-nine slips altogether, aren't there? That should make between eleven and twelve pages of valuable misinformation. Heigh-ho!" Torpenhow shuffled the writing together and hummed—

'Young lambs to sell, young lambs to sell,

If I'd as much money as I could tell,

I never would cry, Young lambs to sell!'"

Dick entered, self-conscious and a little defiant, but in the best of tempers with all the world.

"Back at last?" said Torpenhow.

"More or less. What have you been doing?"

"Work. Dickie, you behave as though the Bank of England were behind you. Here's Sunday, Monday, and Tuesday gone and you haven't done a line. It's scandalous."

"The notions come and go, my children—they come and go like our 'baccy," he answered, filling his pipe. "Moreover," he stooped to thrust a spill into the grate, "Apollo does not always stretch his——Oh, confound your clumsy jests, Nilghai!"

"This is not the place to preach the theory of direct inspiration," said the Nilghai, returning Torpenhow's large and workmanlike bellows to their nail on the wall. "We believe in cobblers' wax. La!—where you sit down."

"If you weren't so big and fat," said Dick, looking round for a weapon, "I'd——"

"No skylarking in my rooms. You two smashed half my furniture last time you threw the cushions about. You might have the decency to say How d'you do? to Binkie. Look at him."

Binkie had jumped down from the sofa and was fawning round Dick's knee, and scratching at his boots.

"Dear man!" said Dick, snatching him up, and kissing him on the black patch above his right eye. "Did ums was, Binks? Did that ugly Nilghai turn you off the sofa? Bite him, Mr. Binkie." He pitched him on the Nilghai's stomach, as the big man lay at ease, and Binkie pretended to destroy the Nilghai inch by inch, till a sofa cushion extinguished him, and panting he stuck out his tongue at the company.

"The Binkie-boy went for a walk this morning before you were up, Torp. I saw him making love to the butcher at the corner when the shutters were being taken down—just as if he hadn't enough to eat in his own proper house," said Dick.

"Binks, is that a true bill?" said Torpenhow, severely. The little dog retreated under the sofa cushion, and showed by the fat white back of him that he really had no further interest in the discussion.

"Strikes me that another disreputable dog went for a walk, too," said the Nilghai. "What made you get up so early? Torp said you might be buying a horse."

"He knows it would need three of us for a serious business like that. No, I felt lonesome and unhappy, so I went out to look at the sea, and watch the pretty ships go by."

"Where did you go?"

"Somewhere on the Channel. Progly or Snigly, or some watering-place was its name; I've forgotten; but it was only two hours' run from London and the ships went by."

"Did you see anything you knew?"

"Only the Barralong outwards to Australia, and an Odessa grain-boat loaded down by the head. It was a thick day, but the sea smelt good."

"Wherefore put on one's best trousers to see the Barralong?" said Torpenhow, pointing.

"Because I've nothing except these things and my painting duds. Besides, I wanted to do honour to the sea."

"Did She make you feel restless?" asked the Nilghai, keenly.

"Crazy. Don't speak of it. I'm sorry I went."

Torpenhow and the Nilghai exchanged a look as Dick, stooping, busied himself among the former's boots and trees.

"These will do," he said at last; "I can't say I think much of your taste in slippers, but the fit's the thing." He slipped his feet into a pair of sock-like sambhur-skin foot coverings, found a long chair, and lay at length.

"They're my own pet pair," Torpenhow said. "I was just going to put them on myself."

"All your reprehensible selfishness. Just because you see me happy for a minute, you want to worry me and stir me up. Find another pair."

"Good for you that Dick can't wear your clothes, Torp. You two live communistically," said the Nilghai.

"Dick never has anything that I can wear. He's only useful to sponge upon."

"Confound you, have you been rummaging round among my clothes, then?" said Dick. "I put a sovereign in the tobacco-jar yesterday. How do you expect a man to keep his accounts properly if you——"

Here the Nilghai began to laugh, and Torpenhow joined him.

"Hid a sovereign yesterday! You're no sort of financier. You lent me a fiver about a month back. Do you remember?" Torpenhow said.

"Yes, of course."

"Do you remember that I paid it you ten days later, and you put it at the bottom of the tobacco?"

"By Jove, did I? I thought it was in one of my colour-boxes."

"You thought! About a week ago I went into your studio to get some 'baccy and found it."

"What did you do with it?"

"Took the Nilghai to a theatre and fed him."

"You couldn't feed the Nilghai under twice the money—not though you gave him Army beef. Well, I suppose I should have found it out sooner or later. What is there to laugh at?"

"You're a most amazing cuckoo in many directions," said the Nilghai, still chuckling over the thought of the dinner. "Never mind. We had both been working very hard, and it was your unearned increment we spent, and as you're only a loafer it didn't matter."

"That's pleasant—from the man who is bursting with my meat, too. I'll get that dinner back one of these days. Suppose we go to a theatre now."

"Put our boots on,—and dress,—and wash?" The Nilghai spoke very lazily.

"I withdraw the motion."

"Suppose, just for a change—as a startling variety, you know—we, that is to say we, get our charcoal and our canvas and go on with our work."

Torpenhow spoke pointedly, but Dick only wriggled his toes inside the soft leather moccasins.

"What a one-ideaed clucker that is! If I had any unfinished figures on hand, I haven't any model; if I had my model, I haven't any spray, and I never leave charcoal unfixed overnight; and if I had my spray and twenty photographs of backgrounds, I couldn't do anything tonight. I don't feel that way."

"Binkie-dog, he's a lazy hog, isn't he?" said the Nilghai.

"Very good, I will do some work," said Dick, rising swiftly. "I'll fetch the Nungapunga Book, and we'll add another picture to the Nilghai Saga."

"Aren't you worrying him a little too much?" asked the Nilghai, when Dick had left the room.

"Perhaps, but I know what he can turn out if he likes. It makes me savage to hear him praised for past work when I know what he ought to do. You and I are arranged for——"

"By Kismet and our own powers, more's the pity. I have dreamed of a good deal."

"So have I, but we know our limitations now. I'm dashed if I know what Dick's may be when he gives himself to his work. That's what makes me so keen about him."

"And when all's said and done, you will be put aside—quite rightly—for a female girl."

"I wonder... Where do you think he has been today?"

"To the sea. Didn't you see the look in his eyes when he talked about her? He's as restless as a swallow in autumn."

"Yes; but did he go alone?"

"I don't know, and I don't care, but he has the beginnings of the go-fever upon him. He wants to up-stakes and move out. There's no mistaking the signs. Whatever he may have said before, he has the call upon him now."

"It might be his salvation," Torpenhow said.

"Perhaps—if you care to take the responsibility of being a saviour."

Dick returned with the big clasped sketch-book that the Nilghai knew well and did not love too much. In it Dick had drawn all manner of moving incidents, experienced by himself or related to him by the others, of all the four corners of the earth. But the wider range of the Nilghai's body and life attracted him most. When truth failed he fell back on fiction of the wildest, and represented incidents in the Nilghai's career that were unseemly,—his marriages with many African princesses, his shameless betrayal, for Arab wives, of an army corps to the Mahdi, his tattooment by skilled operators in Burmah, his interview (and his fears) with the yellow headsman in the blood-stained execution-ground of Canton, and finally, the passings of his spirit into the bodies of whales, elephants, and toucans. Torpenhow from time to time had added rhymed descriptions, and the whole was a curious piece of art, because Dick decided, having regard to the name of the book which being interpreted means "naked," that it would be wrong to draw the Nilghai with any clothes on, under any circumstances. Consequently the last sketch, representing that much-enduring man calling on the War Office to press his claims to the Egyptian medal, was hardly delicate. He settled himself comfortably on Torpenhow's table and turned over the pages.

"What a fortune you would have been to Blake, Nilghai!" he said. "There's a succulent pinkness about some of these sketches that's more than life-like. 'The Nilghai surrounded while bathing by the Mahdieh'—that was founded on fact, eh?"

"It was very nearly my last bath, you irreverent dauber. Has Binkie come into the Saga yet?"

"No; the Binkie-boy hasn't done anything except eat and kill cats. Let's see. Here you are as a stained-glass saint in a church. Deuced decorative lines about your anatomy; you ought to be grateful for being handed down to posterity in this way. Fifty years hence you'll exist in rare and curious facsimiles at ten guineas each. What shall I try this time? The domestic life of the Nilghai?"

"Hasn't got any."

"The undomestic life of the Nilghai, then. Of course. Mass-meeting of his wives in Trafalgar Square. That's it. They came from the ends of the earth to attend Nilghai's wedding to an English bride. This shall be an epic. It's a sweet material to work with."

"It's a scandalous waste of time," said Torpenhow.

"Don't worry; it keeps one's hand in—specially when you begin without the pencil." He set to work rapidly. "That's Nelson's Column. Presently the Nilghai will appear shinning up it."

"Give him some clothes this time."

"Certainly—a veil and an orange-wreath, because he's been married."

"Gad, that's clever enough!" said Torpenhow over his shoulder, as Dick brought out of the paper with three twirls of the brush a very fat back and labouring shoulder pressed against stone.

"Just imagine," Dick continued, "if we could publish a few of these dear little things every time the Nilghai subsidises a man who can write, to give the public an honest opinion of my pictures."

"Well, you'll admit I always tell you when I have done anything of that kind. I know I can't hammer you as you ought to be hammered, so I give the job to another. Young Maclagan, for instance——"

"No-o—one half-minute, old man; stick your hand out against the dark of the wall-paper—you only burble and call me names. That left shoulder's out of drawing. I must literally throw a veil over that. Where's my pen-knife? Well, what about Maclagan?"

"I only gave him his riding-orders to—to lambast you on general principles for not producing work that will last."

"Whereupon that young fool,"—Dick threw back his head and shut one eye as he shifted the page under his hand,—"being left alone with an ink-pot and what he conceived were his own notions, went and spilt them both over me in the papers. You might have engaged a grown man for the business, Nilghai. How do you think the bridal veil looks now, Torp?"

"How the deuce do three dabs and two scratches make the stuff stand away from the body as it does?" said Torpenhow, to whom Dick's methods were always new.

"It just depends on where you put 'em. If Maclagan had know that much about his business he might have done better."

"Why don't you put the damned dabs into something that will stay, then?" insisted the Nilghai, who had really taken considerable trouble in hiring for Dick's benefit the pen of a young gentleman who devoted most of his waking hours to an anxious consideration of the aims and ends of Art, which, he wrote, was one and indivisible.

"Wait a minute till I see how I am going to manage my procession of wives. You seem to have married extensively, and I must rough 'em in with the pencil—Medes, Parthians, Edomites.... Now, setting aside the weakness and the wickedness and—and the fat-headedness of deliberately trying to do work that will live, as they call it, I'm content with the knowledge that I've done my best up to date, and I shan't do anything like it again for some hours at least—probably years. Most probably never."

"What! any stuff you have in stock your best work?" said Torpenhow.

"Anything you've sold?" said the Nilghai.

"Oh no. It isn't here and it isn't sold. Better than that, it can't be sold, and I don't think any one knows where it is. I'm sure I don't.... And yet more and more wives, on the north side of the square. Observe the virtuous horror of the lions!"

"You may as well explain," said Torpenhow, and Dick lifted his head from the paper.

"The sea reminded me of it," he said slowly. "I wish it hadn't. It weighs some few thousand tons—unless you cut it out with a cold chisel."

"Don't be an idiot. You can't pose with us here," said the Nilghai.

"There's no pose in the matter at all. It's a fact. I was loafing from Lima to Auckland in a big, old, condemned passenger-ship turned into a cargo-boat and owned by a second-hand Italian firm. She was a crazy basket. We were cut down to fifteen ton of coal a day, and we thought ourselves lucky when we kicked seven knots an hour out of her. Then we used to stop and let the bearings cool down, and wonder whether the crack in the shaft was spreading."

"Were you a steward or a stoker in those days?"

"I was flush for the time being, so I was a passenger, or else I should have been a steward, I think," said Dick, with perfect gravity, returning to the procession of angry wives. "I was the only other passenger from Lima, and the ship was half empty, and full of rats and cockroaches and scorpions."

"But what has this to do with the picture?"

"Wait a minute. She had been in the China passenger trade and her lower decks had bunks for two thousand pigtails. Those were all taken down, and she was empty up to her nose, and the lights came through the port holes—most annoying lights to work in till you got used to them. I hadn't anything to do for weeks. The ship's charts were in pieces and our skipper daren't run south for fear of catching a storm. So he did his best to knock all the Society Islands out of the water one by one, and I went into the lower deck, and did my picture on the port side as far forward in her as I could go. There was some brown paint and some green paint that they used for the boats, and some black paint for ironwork, and that was all I had."

"The passengers must have thought you mad."

"There was only one, and it was a woman; but it gave me the notion of my picture."

"What was she like?" said Torpenhow.

"She was a sort of Negroid-Jewess-Cuban; with morals to match. She couldn't read or write, and she didn't want to, but she used to come down and watch me paint, and the skipper didn't like it, because he was paying her passage and had to be on the bridge occasionally."

"I see. That must have been cheerful."

"It was the best time I ever had. To begin with, we didn't know whether we should go up or go down any minute when there was a sea on; and when it was calm it was paradise; and the woman used to mix the paints and talk broken English, and the skipper used to steal down every few minutes to the lower deck, because he said he was afraid of fire. So, you see, we could never tell when we might be caught, and I had a splendid notion to work out in only three keys of colour."

"What was the notion?"

"Two lines in Poe—

 'Neither the angels in Heaven above nor the demons down under the sea,

Can ever dissever my soul from the soul of the beautiful Annabel Lee.'

It came out of the sea—all by itself. I drew that fight, fought out in green water over the naked, choking soul, and the woman served as the model for the devils and the angels both—sea-devils and sea-angels, and the soul half drowned between them. It doesn't sound much, but when there was a good light on the lower deck it looked very fine and creepy. It was seven by fourteen feet, all done in shifting light for shifting light."

"Did the woman inspire you much?" said Torpenhow.

"She and the sea between them—immensely. There was a heap of bad drawing in that picture. I remember I went out of my way to foreshorten for sheer delight of doing it, and I foreshortened damnably, but for all that it's the best thing I've ever done; and now I suppose the ship's broken up or gone down. Whew! What a time that was!"

"What happened after all?"

"It all ended. They were loading her with wool when I left the ship, but even the stevedores kept the picture clear to the last. The eyes of the demons scared them, I honestly believe."

"And the woman?"

"She was scared too when it was finished. She used to cross herself before she went down to look at it. Just three colours and no chance of getting any more, and the sea outside and unlimited love-making inside, and the fear of death atop of everything else, O Lord!" He had ceased to look at the sketch, but was staring straight in front of him across the room.

"Why don't you try something of the same kind now?" said the Nilghai.

"Because those things come not by fasting and prayer. When I find a cargo-boat and a Jewess-Cuban and another notion and the same old life, I may."

"You won't find them here," said the Nilghai.

"No, I shall not." Dick shut the sketch-book with a bang. "This room's as hot as an oven. Open the window, some one."

He leaned into the darkness, watching the greater darkness of London below him. The chambers stood much higher than the other houses, commanding a hundred chimneys—crooked cowls that looked like sitting cats as they swung round, and other uncouth brick and zinc mysteries supported by iron stanchions and clamped by 8-pieces. Northward the lights of Piccadilly Circus and Leicester Square threw a copper-coloured glare above the black roofs, and southward by all the orderly lights of the Thames. A train rolled out across one of the railway bridges, and its thunder drowned for a minute the dull roar of the streets. The Nilghai looked at his watch and said shortly, "That's the Paris night-mail. You can book from here to St. Petersburg if you choose."

Dick crammed head and shoulders out of the window and looked across the river. Torpenhow came to his side, while the Nilghai passed over quietly to the piano and opened it. Binkie, making himself as large as possible, spread out upon the sofa with the air of one who is not to be lightly disturbed.

"Well," said the Nilghai to the two pairs of shoulders, "have you never seen this place before?"

A steam-tug on the river hooted as she towed her barges to wharf. Then the boom of the traffic

came into the room. Torpenhow nudged Dick.

"Good place to bank in—bad place to bunk in, Dickie, isn't it?"

Dick's chin was in his hand as he answered, in the words of a general not without fame, still looking out on the darkness—"'My God, what a city to loot!'"

Binkie found the night air tickling his whiskers and sneezed plaintively.

"We shall give the Binkie-dog a cold," said Torpenhow. "Come in," and they withdrew their heads. "You'll be buried in Kensal Green, Dick, one of these days, if it isn't closed by the time you want to go there—buried within two feet of some one else, his wife and his family."

"Allah forbid! I shall get away before that time comes. Give a man room to stretch his legs, Mr. Binkie." Dick flung himself down on the sofa and tweaked Binkie's velvet ears, yawning heavily the while.

"You'll find that wardrobe-case very much out of tune," Torpenhow said to the Nilghai. "It's never touched except by you."

"A piece of gross extravagance," Dick grunted. "The Nilghai only comes when I'm out."

"That's because you're always out. Howl, Nilghai, and let him hear."

"The life of the Nilghai is fraud and slaughter, His writings are watered Dickens and water; But the voice of the Nilghai raised on high Makes even the Mahdieh glad to die!"

Dick quoted from Torpenhow's letterpress in the Nungapunga Book.

"How do they call moose in Canada, Nilghai?"

The man laughed. Singing was his one polite accomplishment, as many Press-tents in far-off lands had known.

"What shall I sing?" said he, turning in the chair.

"'Moll Roe in the Morning,'" said Torpenhow, at a venture.

"No," said Dick, sharply, and the Nilghai opened his eyes. The old chanty whereof he, among a very few, possessed all the words was not a pretty one, but Dick had heard it many times before without wincing. Without prelude he launched into that stately tune that calls together and troubles the hearts of the gipsies of the sea—

"Farewell and adieu to you, Spanish ladies, Farewell and adieu to you, ladies of Spain."

Dick turned uneasily on the sofa, for he could hear the bows of the Barralong crashing into the green seas on her way to the Southern Cross.

Then came the chorus—

"We'll rant and we'll roar like true British sailors, We'll rant and we'll roar across the salt seas, Until we take soundings in the Channel of Old England From Ushant to Scilly 'tis forty-five leagues."

"Thirty-five-thirty-five," said Dick, petulantly. "Don't tamper with Holy Writ. Go on, Nilghai."

"The first land we made it was called the Deadman," and they sang to the end very vigourously.

"That would be a better song if her head were turned the other way—to the Ushant light, for instance," said the Nilghai.

"Flinging his arms about like a mad windmill," said Torpenhow. "Give us something else, Nilghai. You're in fine fog-horn form tonight."

"Give us the 'Ganges Pilot'; you sang that in the square the night before El-Maghrib. By the way, I wonder how many of the chorus are alive tonight," said Dick.

Torpenhow considered for a minute. "By Jove! I believe only you and I. Raynor, Vicery, and Deenes—all dead; Vincent caught smallpox in Cairo, carried it here and died of it. Yes, only you and I and the Nilghai."

"Umph! And yet the men here who've done their work in a well-warmed studio all their lives, with a policeman at each corner, say that I charge too much for my pictures."

"They are buying your work, not your insurance policies, dear child," said the Nilghai.

"I gambled with one to get at the other. Don't preach. Go on with the 'Pilot.' Where in the world did you get that song?"

"On a tombstone," said the Nilghai. "On a tombstone in a distant land. I made it an accompaniment with heaps of base chords."

"Oh, Vanity! Begin." And the Nilghai began—

"I have slipped my cable, messmates, I'm drifting down with the tide, I have my sailing orders, while yet at anchor ride. And never on fair June morning have I put out to sea With clearer conscience or better hope, or a heart more light and free.

"Shoulder to shoulder, Joe, my boy, into the crowd like a wedge. Strike with the hangers, messmates, but do not cut with the edge." Cries Charnock, "Scatter the faggots, double that Brahmin in two, The tall pale widow for me, Joe, the little brown girl for you!"

"Young Joe (you're nearing sixty), why is your hide so dark? Katie has soft fair blue eyes, who blackened yours?—Why, hark!"

They were all singing now, Dick with the roar of the wind of the open sea about his ears as the deep bass voice let itself go.

"The morning gun—Ho, steady! the arquebuses to me! I ha' sounded the Dutch High Admiral's heart as my lead doth sound the sea.

"Sounding, sounding the Ganges, floating down with the tide, Moore me close to Charnock, next to my nut-brown bride. My blessing to Kate at Fairlight—Holwell, my thanks to you; Steady! We steer for heaven, through sand-drifts cold and blue."

"Now what is there in that nonsense to make a man restless?" said Dick, hauling Binkie from his feet to his chest.

"It depends on the man," said Torpenhow.

"The man who has been down to look at the sea," said the Nilghai.

"I didn't know she was going to upset me in this fashion."

"That's what men say when they go to say good-bye to a woman. It's more easy though to get rid of three women than a piece of one's life and surroundings."

"But a woman can be——" began Dick, unguardedly.

"A piece of one's life," continued Torpenhow. "No, she can't." His face darkened for a moment. "She says she wants to sympathise with you and help you in your work, and everything else that clearly a man must do for himself. Then she sends round five notes a day to ask why the dickens you haven't been wasting your time with her."

"Don't generalise," said the Nilghai. "By the time you arrive at five notes a day you must have gone through a good deal and behaved accordingly. Shouldn't begin these things, my son."

"I shouldn't have gone down to the sea," said Dick, just a little anxious to change the conversation. "And you shouldn't have sung."

"The sea isn't sending you five notes a day," said the Nilghai.

"No, but I'm fatally compromised. She's an enduring old hag, and I'm sorry I ever met her. Why wasn't I born and bred and dead in a three-pair back?"

"Hear him blaspheming his first love! Why in the world shouldn't you listen to her?" said Torpenhow.

Before Dick could reply the Nilghai lifted up his voice with a shout that shook the windows, in "The Men of the Sea," that begins, as all know, "The sea is a wicked old woman," and after wading through eight lines whose imagery is truthful, ends in a refrain, slow as the clacking of a capstan when the boat comes unwillingly up to the bars where the men sweat and tramp in the shingle.

"'Ye that bore us, O restore us! She is kinder than ye; For the call is on our heart-strings!' Said The Men of the Sea."

The Nilghai sang that verse twice, with simple cunning, intending that Dick should hear. But Dick was waiting for the farewell of the men to their wives.

"'Ye that love us, can ye move us? She is dearer than ye; And your sleep will be the sweeter,' Said The Men of the Sea."

The rough words beat like the blows of the waves on the bows of the rickety boat from Lima in the days when Dick was mixing paints, making love, drawing devils and angels in the half dark, and wondering whether the next minute would put the Italian captain's knife between his shoulder-blades. And the go-fever which is more real than many doctors' diseases, waked and raged, urging him who loved Maisie beyond anything in the world, to go away and taste the old hot, unregenerate life again,—to scuffle, swear, gamble, and love light loves with his fellows; to take ship and know the sea once more, and by her beget pictures; to talk to Binat among the sands of Port Said while Yellow Tina mixed the drinks; to hear the crackle of musketry, and see the smoke roll outward, thin and thicken again till the shining black faces came through, and in that hell every man was strictly responsible for his own head, and his own alone, and struck with an unfettered arm. It was impossible, utterly impossible, but—

"'Oh, our fathers in the churchyard, She is older than ye, And our graves will be the greener,' Said The Men of the Sea."

"What is there to hinder?" said Torpenhow, in the long hush that followed the song.

"You said a little time since that you wouldn't come for a walk round the world, Torp."

"That was months ago, and I only objected to your making money for travelling expenses. You've shot your bolt here and it has gone home. Go away and do some work, and see some things."

"Get some of the fat off you; you're disgracefully out of condition," said the Nilghai, making a plunge from the chair and grasping a handful of Dick generally over the right ribs. "Soft as putty—pure tallow born of over-feeding. Train it off, Dickie."

"We're all equally gross, Nilghai. Next time you have to take the field you'll sit down, wink your eyes, gasp, and die in a fit."

"Never mind. You go away on a ship. Go to Lima again, or to Brazil. There's always trouble in South America."

"Do you suppose I want to be told where to go? Great Heavens, the only difficulty is to know where I'm to stop. But I shall stay here, as I told you before."

"Then you'll be buried in Kensal Green and turn into adipocere with the others," said Torpenhow. "Are you thinking of commissions in hand? Pay forfeit and go. You've money enough to travel as a king if you please."

"You've the grisliest notions of amusement, Torp. I think I see myself shipping first class on a six-thousand-ton hotel, and asking the third engineer what makes the engines go round, and whether it isn't very warm in the stokehold. Ho! ho! I should ship as a loafer if ever I shipped at all, which I'm not going to do. I shall compromise, and go for a small trip to begin with."

"That's something at any rate. Where will you go?" said Torpenhow. "It would do you all the good in the world, old man."

The Nilghai saw the twinkle in Dick's eye, and refrained from speech.

"I shall go in the first place to Rathray's stable, where I shall hire one horse, and take him very carefully as far as Richmond Hill. Then I shall walk him back again, in case he should accidentally burst into a lather and make Rathray angry. I shall do that tomorrow, for the sake of air and exercise."

"Bah!" Dick had barely time to throw up his arm and ward off the cushion that the disgusted Torpenhow heaved at his head.

"Air and exercise indeed," said the Nilghai, sitting down heavily on Dick.

"Let's give him a little of both. Get the bellows, Torp."

At this point the conference broke up in disorder, because Dick would not open his mouth till the Nilghai held his nose fast, and there was some trouble in forcing the nozzle of the bellows between his teeth; and even when it was there he weakly tried to puff against the force of the blast, and his cheeks blew up with a great explosion; and the enemy becoming helpless with laughter he so beat them over the head with a soft sofa cushion that became unsewn and distributed its feathers, and Binkie, interfering in Torpenhow's interests, was bundled into the half-empty bag and advised to scratch his way out, which he did after a while, travelling rapidly up and down the floor in the shape of an agitated green haggis, and when he came out looking

for satisfaction, the three pillars of his world were picking feathers out of their hair.

"A prophet has no honour in his own country," said Dick, ruefully, dusting his knees. "This filthy fluff will never brush off my legs."

"It was all for your own good," said the Nilghai. "Nothing like air and exercise."

"All for your good," said Torpenhow, not in the least with reference to past clowning. "It would let you focus things at their proper worth and prevent your becoming slack in this hothouse of a town. Indeed it would, old man. I shouldn't have spoken if I hadn't thought so. Only, you make a joke of everything."

"Before God I do no such thing," said Dick, quickly and earnestly. "You don't know me if you think that."

"I don't think it," said the Nilghai.

"How can fellows like ourselves, who know what life and death really mean, dare to make a joke of anything? I know we pretend it, to save ourselves from breaking down or going to the other extreme. Can't I see, old man, how you're always anxious about me, and try to advise me to make my work better? Do you suppose I don't think about that myself? But you can't help me—you can't help me—not even you. I must play my own hand alone in my own way."

"Hear, hear," from the Nilghai.

"What's the one thing in the Nilghai Saga that I've never drawn in the Nungapunga Book?" Dick continued to Torpenhow, who was a little astonished at the outburst.

Now there was one blank page in the book given over to the sketch that Dick had not drawn of the crowning exploit in the Nilghai's life; when that man, being young and forgetting that his body and bones belonged to the paper that employed him, had ridden over sunburned slippery grass in the rear of Bredow's brigade on the day that the troopers flung themselves at Caurobert's artillery, and for aught they knew twenty battalions in front, to save the battered 24th German Infantry, to give time to decide the fate of Vionville, and to learn ere their remnant came back to Flavigay that cavalry can attack and crumple and break unshaken infantry. Whenever he was inclined to think over a life that might have been better, an income that might have been larger, and a soul that might have been considerably cleaner, the Nilghai would comfort himself with the thought, "I rode with Bredow's brigade at Vionville," and take heart for any lesser battle the next day might bring.

"I know," he said very gravely. "I was always glad that you left it out."

"I left it out because Nilghai taught me what the Germany army learned then, and what Schmidt taught their cavalry. I don't know German. What is it? 'Take care of the time and the dressing will take care of itself.' I must ride my own line to my own beat, old man."

"Tempe ist richtung. You've learned your lesson well," said the Nilghai.

"He must go alone. He speaks truth, Torp."

"Maybe I'm as wrong as I can be—hideously wrong. I must find that out for myself, as I have to think things out for myself, but I daren't turn my head to dress by the next man. It hurts me a great deal more than you know not to be able to go, but I cannot, that's all. I must do my own work and live my own life in my own way, because I'm responsible for both. Only don't think I frivol about it, Torp. I have my own matches and sulphur, and I'll make my own hell, thanks."

There was an uncomfortable pause. Then Torpenhow said blandly, "What did the Governor of North Carolina say to the Governor of South Carolina?"

"Excellent notion. It is a long time between drinks. There are the makings of a very fine prig in you, Dick," said the Nilghai.

"I've liberated my mind, estimable Binkie, with the feathers in his mouth." Dick picked up the still indignant one and shook him tenderly. "You're tied up in a sack and made to run about blind, Binkie-wee, without any reason, and it has hurt your little feelings. Never mind. Sic volo, sic jubeo, stet pro ratione voluntas, and don't sneeze in my eye because I talk Latin. Good night."

He went out of the room.

"That's distinctly one for you," said the Nilghai. "I told you it was hopeless to meddle with him. He's not pleased."

"He'd swear at me if he weren't. I can't make it out. He has the go-fever upon him and he won't go. I only hope that he mayn't have to go some day when he doesn't want to," said Torpenhow.

In his own room Dick was settling a question with himself—and the question was whether all the world, and all that was therein, and a burning desire to exploit both, was worth one threepenny piece thrown into the Thames.

"It came of seeing the sea, and I'm a cur to think about it," he decided. "After all, the honeymoon will be that tour—with reservations; only... only I didn't realise that the sea was so strong. I didn't feel it so much when I was with Maisie. These damnable songs did it. He's beginning again."

But it was only Herrick's Nightpiece to Julia that the Nilghai sang, and before it was ended Dick reappeared on the threshold, not altogether clothed indeed, but in his right mind, thirsty and at peace.

The mood had come and gone with the rising and the falling of the tide by Fort Keeling.

CHAPTER IX

"If I have taken the common clay

And wrought it cunningly

In the shape of a god that was digged a clod,

The greater honour to me."

"If thou hast taken the common clay,

And thy hands be not free

From the taint of the soil,

thou hast made thy spoil

The greater shame to thee."

—The Two Potters

HE DID no work of any kind for the rest of the week. Then came another Sunday. He dreaded and longed for the day always, but since the red-haired girl had sketched him there was rather more dread than desire in his mind.

He found that Maisie had entirely neglected his suggestions about line-work. She had gone off at score filed with some absurd notion for a "fancy head." It cost Dick something to command his temper.

"What's the good of suggesting anything?" he said pointedly.

"Ah, but this will be a picture,—a real picture; and I know that Kami will let me send it to the Salon. You don't mind, do you?"

"I suppose not. But you won't have time for the Salon."

Maisie hesitated a little. She even felt uncomfortable.

"We're going over to France a month sooner because of it. I shall get the idea sketched out here and work it up at Kami's."

Dick's heart stood still, and he came very near to being disgusted with his queen who could do no wrong. "Just when I thought I had made some headway, she goes off chasing butterflies. It's too maddening!"

There was no possibility of arguing, for the red-haired girl was in the studio. Dick could only look unutterable reproach.

"I'm sorry," he said, "and I think you make a mistake. But what's the idea of your new picture?"

"I took it from a book."

"That's bad, to begin with. Books aren't the places for pictures. And——"

"It's this," said the red-haired girl behind him. "I was reading it to Maisie the other day from The City of Dreadful Night. D'you know the book?"

"A little. I am sorry I spoke. There are pictures in it. What has taken her fancy?"

"The description of the Melancolia—

'Her folded wings as of a mighty eagle,

But all too impotent to lift the regal

Robustness of her earth-born strength and pride.

And here again. (Maisie, get the tea, dear.)

'The forehead charged with baleful thoughts and dreams,

The household bunch of keys, the housewife's gown,

Voluminous indented, and yet rigid

As though a shell of burnished metal frigid,

Her feet thick-shod to tread all weakness down."

There was no attempt to conceal the scorn of the lazy voice. Dick winced.

"But that has been done already by an obscure artist by the name of Durer," said he. "How does the poem run?—

'Three centuries and threescore years ago,

With phantasies of his peculiar thought.'

You might as well try to rewrite Hamlet. It will be a waste of time."

"No, it won't," said Maisie, putting down the teacups with a clatter to reassure herself. "And I mean to do it. Can't you see what a beautiful thing it would make?"

"How in perdition can one do work when one hasn't had the proper training? Any fool can get a notion. It needs training to drive the thing through,—training and conviction; not rushing after the first fancy." Dick spoke between his teeth.

"You don't understand," said Maisie. "I think I can do it."

Again the voice of the girl behind him—

"Baffled and beaten back, she works on still;

Weary and sick of soul, she works the more.

 Sustained by her indomitable will,

 The hands shall fashion, and the brain shall pore,

 And all her sorrow shall be turned to labour——

I fancy Maisie means to embody herself in the picture."

"Sitting on a throne of rejected pictures? No, I shan't, dear. The notion in itself has fascinated me.—Of course you don't care for fancy heads, Dick. I don't think you could do them. You like blood and bones."

"That's a direct challenge. If you can do a Melancolia that isn't merely a sorrowful female head, I can do a better one; and I will, too. What d'you know about Melacolias?" Dick firmly believed that he was even then tasting three-quarters of all the sorrow in the world.

"She was a woman," said Maisie, "and she suffered a great deal,—till she could suffer no more. Then she began to laugh at it all, and then I painted her and sent her to the Salon."

The red-haired girl rose up and left the room, laughing.

Dick looked at Maisie humbly and hopelessly.

"Never mind about the picture," he said. "Are you really going back to Kami's for a month before your time?"

"I must, if I want to get the picture done."

"And that's all you want?"

"Of course. Don't be stupid, Dick."

"You haven't the power. You have only the ideas—the ideas and the little cheap impulses. How you could have kept at your work for ten years steadily is a mystery to me. So you are really going,—a month before you need?"

"I must do my work."

"Your work—bah!... No, I didn't mean that. It's all right, dear. Of course you must do your work, and—I think I'll say goodbye for this week."

"Won't you even stay for tea?"

"No, thank you. Have I your leave to go, dear? There's nothing more you particularly want me to do, and the line-work doesn't matter."

"I wish you could stay, and then we could talk over my picture. If only one single picture's a success, it draws attention to all the others. I know some of my work is good, if only people could see. And you needn't have been so rude about it."

"I'm sorry. We'll talk the Melancolia over some one of the other Sundays. There are four more—yes, one, two, three, four—before you go. Goodbye, Maisie."

Maisie stood by the studio window, thinking, till the red-haired girl returned, a little white at the corners of her lips.

"Dick's gone off," said Maisie. "Just when I wanted to talk about the picture. Isn't it selfish of him?"

Her companion opened her lips as if to speak, shut them again, and went on reading The City of Dreadful Night.

Dick was in the Park, walking round and round a tree that he had chosen as his confidante for many Sundays past. He was swearing audibly, and when he found that the infirmities of the English tongue hemmed in his rage, he sought consolation in Arabic, which is expressly designed for the use of the afflicted. He was not pleased with the reward of his patient service; nor was he pleased with himself; and it was long before he arrived at the proposition that the queen could do no wrong.

"It's a losing game," he said. "I'm worth nothing when a whim of hers is in question. But in a losing game at Port Said we used to double the stakes and go on. She do a Melancolia! She hasn't the power, or the insight, or the training. Only the desire. She's cursed with the curse of Reuben. She won't do line-work, because it means real work; and yet she's stronger than I am. I'll make her understand that I can beat her on her own Melancolia. Even then she wouldn't care. She says I can only do blood and bones. I don't believe she has blood in her veins. All the same I lover her; and I must go on loving her; and if I can humble her inordinate vanity I will. I'll do a Melancolia that shall be something like a Melancolia 'the Melancolia that transcends all wit.' I'll do it at once, con—bless her."

He discovered that the notion would not come to order, and that he could not free his mind for an hour from the thought of Maisie's departure. He took very small interest in her rough studies for the Melancolia when she showed them next week. The Sundays were racing past, and the time was at hand when all the church bells in London could not ring Maisie back to him. Once or twice he said something to Binkie about 'hermaphroditic futilities,' but the little dog received so many confidences both from Torpenhow and Dick that he did not trouble his tulip-ears to listen.

Dick was permitted to see the girls off. They were going by the Dover night-boat; and they hoped to return in August. It was then February, and Dick felt that he was being hardly used. Maisie was so busy stripping the small house across the Park, and packing her canvases, that she had not time for thought. Dick went down to Dover and wasted a day there fretting over a wonderful possibility. Would Maisie at the very last allow him one small kiss? He reflected that he might capture her by the strong arm, as he had seem women captured in the Southern Soudan, and lead her away; but Maisie would never be led. She would turn her gray eyes upon him and say, "Dick, how selfish you are!" Then his courage would fail him. It would be better, after all, to beg for that kiss.

Maisie looked more than usually kissable as she stepped from the night-mail on to the windy pier, in a gray waterproof and a little gray cloth travelling-cap. The red-haired girl was not so lovely. Her green eyes were hollow and her lips were dry. Dick saw the trunks aboard, and went to Maisie's side in the darkness under the bridge. The mail-bags were thundering into the forehold, and the red-haired girl was watching them.

"You'll have a rough passage tonight," said Dick. "It's blowing outside. I suppose I may come over and see you if I'm good?"

"You mustn't. I shall be busy. At least, if I want you I'll send for you. But I shall write from Vitry-sur-Marne. I shall have heaps of things to consult you about. Oh, Dick, you have been so good to me!—so good to me!"

"Thank you for that, dear. It hasn't made any difference, has it?"

"I can't tell a fib. It hasn't—in that way. But don't think I'm not grateful."

"Damn the gratitude!" said Dick, huskily, to the paddle-box.

"What's the use of worrying? You know I should ruin your life, and you'd ruin mine, as things are now. You remember what you said when you were so angry that day in the Park? One of us has to be broken. Can't you wait till that day comes?"

"No, love. I want you unbroken—all to myself."

Maisie shook her head. "My poor Dick, what can I say!"

"Don't say anything. Give me a kiss. Only one kiss, Maisie. I'll swear I won't take any more. You might as well, and then I can be sure you're grateful."

Maisie put her cheek forward, and Dick took his reward in the darkness.

It was only one kiss, but, since there was no time-limit specified, it was a long one. Maisie wrenched herself free angrily, and Dick stood abashed and tingling from head to toe.

"Goodbye, darling. I didn't mean to scare you. I'm sorry. Only—keep well and do good work,—specially the Melancolia. I'm going to do one, too. Remember me to Kami, and be careful what you drink. Country drinking-water is bad everywhere, but it's worse in France. Write to me if you want anything, and good-bye. Say good-bye to the whatever-you-call-um girl, and—can't I have another kiss? No. You're quite right. Goodbye."

A shout told him that it was not seemly to charge of the mail-bag incline. He reached the pier as the steamer began to move off, and he followed her with his heart.

"And there's nothing—nothing in the wide world—to keep us apart except her obstinacy. These Calais night-boats are much too small. I'll get Torp to write to the papers about it. She's beginning to pitch already."

Maisie stood where Dick had left her till she heard a little gasping cough at her elbow. The red-haired girl's eyes were alight with cold flame.

"He kissed you!" she said. "How could you let him, when he wasn't anything to you? How dared you to take a kiss from him? Oh, Maisie, let's go to the ladies' cabin. I'm sick,—deadly sick."

"We aren't into open water yet. Go down, dear, and I'll stay here. I don't like the smell of the engines.... Poor Dick! He deserved one,—only one. But I didn't think he'd frighten me so."

Dick returned to town next day just in time for lunch, for which he had telegraphed. To his disgust, there were only empty plates in the studio.

He lifted up his voice like the bears in the fairy-tale, and Torpenhow entered, looking guilty.

"H'sh!" said he. "Don't make such a noise. I took it. Come into my rooms, and I'll show you why."

Dick paused amazed at the threshold, for on Torpenhow's sofa lay a girl asleep and breathing heavily. The little cheap sailor-hat, the blue-and-white dress, fitter for June than for February, dabbled with mud at the skirts, the jacket trimmed with imitation Astrakhan and ripped at the

shoulder-seams, the one-and-elevenpenny umbrella, and, above all, the disgraceful condition of the kid-topped boots, declared all things.

"Oh, I say, old man, this is too bad! You mustn't bring this sort up here. They steal things from the rooms."

"It looks bad, I admit, but I was coming in after lunch, and she staggered into the hall. I thought she was drunk at first, but it was collapse. I couldn't leave her as she was, so I brought her up here and gave her your lunch. She was fainting from want of food. She went fast asleep the minute she had finished."

"I know something of that complaint. She's been living on sausages, I suppose. Torp, you should have handed her over to a policeman for presuming to faint in a respectable house. Poor little wretch! Look at the face! There isn't an ounce of immorality in it. Only folly,—slack, fatuous, feeble, futile folly. It's a typical head. D'you notice how the skull begins to show through the flesh padding on the face and cheek-bone?"

"What a cold-blooded barbarian it is! Don't hit a woman when she's down. Can't we do anything? She was simply dropping with starvation. She almost fell into my arms, and when she got to the food she ate like a wild beast. It was horrible."

"I can give her money, which she would probably spend in drinks. Is she going to sleep for ever?"

The girl opened her eyes and glared at the men between terror and effrontery.

"Feeling better?" said Torpenhow.

"Yes. Thank you. There aren't many gentlemen that are as kind as you are. Thank you."

"When did you leave service?" said Dick, who had been watching the scarred and chapped hands.

"How did you know I was in service? I was. General servant. I didn't like it."

"And how do you like being your own mistress?"

"Do I look as if I liked it?"

"I suppose not. One moment. Would you be good enough to turn your face to the window?"

The girl obeyed, and Dick watched her face keenly,—so keenly that she made as if to hide behind Torpenhow.

"The eyes have it," said Dick, walking up and down. "They are superb eyes for my business. And, after all, every head depends on the eyes. This has been sent from heaven to make up for— what was taken away. Now the weekly strain's off my shoulders, I can get to work in earnest. Evidently sent from heaven. Yes. Raise your chin a little, please."

"Gently, old man, gently. You're scaring somebody out of her wits," said Torpenhow, who could see the girl trembling.

"Don't let him hit me! Oh, please don't let him hit me! I've been hit cruel today because I spoke to a man. Don't let him look at me like that! He's reg'lar wicked, that one. Don't let him look at me like that, neither! Oh, I feel as if I hadn't nothing on when he looks at me like that!"

The overstrained nerves in the frail body gave way, and the girl wept like a little child and began to scream. Dick threw open the window, and Torpenhow flung the door back.

"There you are," said Dick, soothingly. "My friend here can call for a policeman, and you can run through that door. Nobody is going to hurt you."

The girl sobbed convulsively for a few minutes, and then tried to laugh.

"Nothing in the world to hurt you. Now listen to me for a minute. I'm what they call an artist by profession. You know what artists do?"

"They draw the things in red and black ink on the pop-shop labels."

"I dare say. I haven't risen to pop-shop labels yet. Those are done by the Academicians. I want to draw your head."

"What for?"

"Because it's pretty. That is why you will come to the room across the landing three times a week at eleven in the morning, and I'll give you three quid a week just for sitting still and being drawn. And there's a quid on account."

"For nothing? Oh, my!" The girl turned the sovereign in her hand, and with more foolish tears, "Ain't neither 'o you two gentlemen afraid of my bilking you?"

"No. Only ugly girls do that. Try and remember this place. And, by the way, what's your name?"

"I'm Bessie,—Bessie——It's no use giving the rest. Bessie Broke,—Stone-broke, if you like. What's your names? But there,—no one ever gives the real ones."

Dick consulted Torpenhow with his eyes.

"My name's Heldar, and my friend's called Torpenhow; and you must be sure to come here. Where do you live?"

"South-the-water,—one room,—five and sixpence a week. Aren't you making fun of me about that three quid?"

"You'll see later on. And, Bessie, next time you come, remember, you needn't wear that paint. It's bad for the skin, and I have all the colours you'll be likely to need."

Bessie withdrew, scrubbing her cheek with a ragged pocket-handkerchief. The two men looked at each other.

"You're a man," said Torpenhow.

"I'm afraid I've been a fool. It isn't our business to run about the earth reforming Bessie Brokes. And a woman of any kind has no right on this landing."

"Perhaps she won't come back."

"She will if she thinks she can get food and warmth here. I know she will, worse luck. But remember, old man, she isn't a woman; she's my model; and be careful."

"The idea! She's a dissolute little scarecrow,—a gutter-snippet and nothing more."

"So you think. Wait till she has been fed a little and freed from fear. That fair type recovers itself very quickly. You won't know her in a week or two, when that abject fear has died out of her eyes. She'll be too happy and smiling for my purposes."

"But surely you're not taking her out of charity?—to please me?"

"I am not in the habit of playing with hot coals to please anybody. She has been sent from heaven, as I may have remarked before, to help me with my Melancolia."

"Never heard a word about the lady before."

"What's the use of having a friend, if you must sling your notions at him in words? You ought to know what I'm thinking about. You've heard me grunt lately?"

"Even so; but grunts mean anything in your language, from bad 'baccy to wicked dealers. And I don't think I've been much in your confidence for some time."

"It was a high and soulful grunt. You ought to have understood that it meant the Melancolia." Dick walked Torpenhow up and down the room, keeping silence. Then he smote him in the ribs, "Now don't you see it? Bessie's abject futility, and the terror in her eyes, welded on to one or two details in the way of sorrow that have come under my experience lately. Likewise some orange and black,—two keys of each. But I can't explain on an empty stomach."

"It sounds mad enough. You'd better stick to your soldiers, Dick, instead of maundering about heads and eyes and experiences."

"Think so?" Dick began to dance on his heels, singing—

"They're as proud as a turkey when they hold the ready cash, You ought to 'ear the way they laugh an' joke; They are tricky an' they're funny when they've got the ready money,—Ow! but see 'em when they're all stone-broke."

Then he sat down to pour out his heart to Maisie in a four-sheet letter of counsel and encouragement, and registered an oath that he would get to work with an undivided heart as soon as Bessie should reappear.

The girl kept her appointment unpainted and unadorned, afraid and overbold by turns. When she found that she was merely expected to sit still, she grew calmer, and criticised the appointments of the studio with freedom and some point. She liked the warmth and the comfort and the release from fear of physical pain. Dick made two or three studies of her head in monochrome, but the actual notion of the Melancolia would not arrive.

"What a mess you keep your things in!" said Bessie, some days later, when she felt herself thoroughly at home. "I s'pose your clothes are just as bad. Gentlemen never think what buttons and tape are made for."

"I buy things to wear, and wear 'em till they go to pieces. I don't know what Torpenhow does."

Bessie made diligent inquiry in the latter's room, and unearthed a bale of disreputable socks. "Some of these I'll mend now," she said, "and some I'll take home. D'you know, I sit all day long at home doing nothing, just like a lady, and no more noticing them other girls in the house than if they was so many flies. I don't have any unnecessary words, but I put 'em down quick, I can tell you, when they talk to me. No; it's quite nice these days. I lock my door, and they can only call me names through the keyhole, and I sit inside, just like a lady, mending socks. Mr. Torpenhow wears his socks out both ends at once."

"Three quid a week from me, and the delights of my society. No socks mended. Nothing from Torp except a nod on the landing now and again, and all his socks mended. Bessie is very much a woman," thought Dick; and he looked at her between half-shut eyes. Food and rest had transformed the girl, as Dick knew they would.

"What are you looking at me like that for?" she said quickly. "Don't. You look reg'lar bad when you look that way. You don't think much o' me, do you?"

"That depends on how you behave."

Bessie behaved beautifully. Only it was difficult at the end of a sitting to bid her go out into the gray streets. She very much preferred the studio and a big chair by the stove, with some socks in her lap as an excuse for delay. Then Torpenhow would come in, and Bessie would be moved to tell strange and wonderful stories of her past, and still stranger ones of her present improved circumstances. She would make them tea as though she had a right to make it; and once or twice on these occasions Dick caught Torpenhow's eyes fixed on the trim little figure, and because Bessie's flittings about the room made Dick ardently long for Maisie, he realised whither Torpenhow's thoughts were tending. And Bessie was exceedingly careful of the condition of Torpenhow's linen. She spoke very little to him, but sometimes they talked together on the landing.

"I was a great fool," Dick said to himself. "I know what red firelight looks like when a man's tramping through a strange town; and ours is a lonely, selfish sort of life at the best. I wonder Maisie doesn't feel that sometimes. But I can't order Bessie away. That's the worst of beginning things. One never knows where they stop."

One evening, after a sitting prolonged to the last limit of the light, Dick was roused from a nap by a broken voice in Torpenhow's room. He jumped to his feet. "Now what ought I to do? It looks foolish to go in.—Oh, bless you, Binkie!" The little terrier thrust Torpenhow's door open with his nose and came out to take possession of Dick's chair. The door swung wide unheeded, and Dick across the landing could see Bessie in the half-light making her little supplication to Torpenhow. She was kneeling by his side, and her hands were clasped across his knee.

"I know,—I know," she said thickly. "'Tisn't right 'o me to do this, but I can't help it; and you were so kind,—so kind; and you never took any notice 'o me. And I've mended all your things so carefully,—I did. Oh, please, 'tisn't as if I was asking you to marry me. I wouldn't think of it. But you—couldn't you take and live with me till Miss Right comes along? I'm only Miss Wrong, I know, but I'd work my hands to the bare bone for you. And I'm not ugly to look at. Say you will!"

Dick hardly recognised Torpenhow's voice in reply—"But look here. It's no use. I'm liable to be ordered off anywhere at a minute's notice if a war breaks out. At a minute's notice—dear."

"What does that matter? Until you go, then. Until you go. 'Tisn't much I'm asking, and—you don't know how good I can cook." She had put an arm round his neck and was drawing his head down.

"Until—I—go, then."

"Torp," said Dick, across the landing. He could hardly steady his voice.

"Come here a minute, old man. I'm in trouble"—

"Heaven send he'll listen to me!" There was something very like an oath from Bessie's lips. She

was afraid of Dick, and disappeared down the staircase in panic, but it seemed an age before Torpenhow entered the studio. He went to the mantelpiece, buried his head on his arms, and groaned like a wounded bull.

"What the devil right have you to interfere?" he said, at last.

"Who's interfering with which? Your own sense told you long ago you couldn't be such a fool. It was a tough rack, St. Anthony, but you're all right now."

"I oughtn't to have seen her moving about these rooms as if they belonged to her. That's what upset me. It gives a lonely man a sort of hankering, doesn't it?" said Torpenhow, piteously.

"Now you talk sense. It does. But, since you aren't in a condition to discuss the disadvantages of double housekeeping, do you know what you're going to do?"

"I don't. I wish I did."

"You're going away for a season on a brilliant tour to regain tone. You're going to Brighton, or Scarborough, or Prawle Point, to see the ships go by. And you're going at once. Isn't it odd? I'll take care of Binkie, but out you go immediately. Never resist the devil. He holds the bank. Fly from him. Pack your things and go."

"I believe you're right. Where shall I go?"

"And you call yourself a special correspondent! Pack first and inquire afterwards."

An hour later Torpenhow was despatched into the night for a hansom.

"You'll probably think of some place to go to while you're moving," said Dick. "On to Euston, to begin with, and—oh yes—get drunk tonight."

He returned to the studio, and lighted more candles, for he found the room very dark.

"Oh, you Jezebel! you futile little Jezebel! Won't you hate me tomorrow!—Binkie, come here."

Binkie turned over on his back on the hearth-rug, and Dick stirred him with a meditative foot.

"I said she was not immoral. I was wrong. She said she could cook. That showed premeditated sin. Oh, Binkie, if you are a man you will go to perdition; but if you are a woman, and say that you can cook, you will go to a much worse place."

CHAPTER X

What's you that follows at my side?—

The foe that ye must fight, my lord.—

That hirples swift as I can ride?—

The shadow of the night, my lord.—

Then wheel my horse against the foe!—

He's down and overpast, my lord.

Ye war against the sunset glow;

The darkness gathers fast, my lord.

——The Fight of Heriot's Ford

"This is a cheerful life," said Dick, some days later. "Torp's away; Bessie hates me; I can't get at the notion of the Melancolia; Maisie's letters are scrappy; and I believe I have indigestion. What give a man pains across the head and spots before his eyes, Binkie? Shall us take some liver pills?"

Dick had just gone through a lively scene with Bessie. She had for the fiftieth time reproached him for sending Torpenhow away. She explained her enduring hatred for Dick, and made it clear to him that she only sat for the sake of his money. "And Mr. Torpenhow's ten times a better man than you," she concluded.

"He is. That's why he went away. I should have stayed and made love to you."

The girl sat with her chin on her hand, scowling. "To me! I'd like to catch you! If I wasn't afraid 'o being hung I'd kill you. That's what I'd do. D'you believe me?"

Dick smiled wearily. It is not pleasant to live in the company of a notion that will not work out, a fox-terrier that cannot talk, and a woman who talks too much. He would have answered, but at that moment there unrolled itself from one corner of the studio a veil, as it were, of the flimsiest gauze. He rubbed his eyes, but the gray haze would not go.

"This is disgraceful indigestion. Binkie, we will go to a medicine-man. We can't have our eyes interfered with, for by these we get our bread; also mutton-chop bones for little dogs."

The doctor was an affable local practitioner with white hair, and he said nothing till Dick began to describe the gray film in the studio.

"We all want a little patching and repairing from time to time," he chirped. "Like a ship, my dear sir,—exactly like a ship. Sometimes the hull is out of order, and we consult the surgeon; sometimes the rigging, and then I advise; sometimes the engines, and we go to the brain-specialist; sometimes the look-out on the bridge is tired, and then we see an oculist. I should recommend you to see an oculist. A little patching and repairing from time to time is all we want. An oculist, by all means."

Dick sought an oculist,—the best in London. He was certain that the local practitioner did not know anything about his trade, and more certain that Maisie would laugh at him if he were forced to wear spectacles.

"I've neglected the warnings of my lord the stomach too long. Hence these spots before the eyes, Binkie. I can see as well as I ever could."

As he entered the dark hall that led to the consulting-room a man cannoned against him. Dick saw the face as it hurried out into the street.

"That's the writer-type. He has the same modelling of the forehead as Torp. He looks very sick. Probably heard something he didn't like."

Even as he thought, a great fear came upon Dick, a fear that made him hold his breath as he walked into the oculist's waiting room, with the heavy carved furniture, the dark-green paper, and the sober-hued prints on the wall. He recognised a reproduction of one of his own sketches.

Many people were waiting their turn before him. His eye was caught by a flaming red-and-gold Christmas-carol book. Little children came to that eye-doctor, and they needed large-type amusement.

"That's idolatrous bad Art," he said, drawing the book towards himself.

"From the anatomy of the angels, it has been made in Germany." He opened in mechanically, and there leaped to his eyes a verse printed in red ink—

The next good joy that Mary had,

It was the joy of three,

To see her good Son Jesus Christ

Making the blind to see;

Making the blind to see, good Lord,

And happy we may be.

Praise Father, Son, and Holy Ghost

To all eternity!

Dick read and re-read the verse till his turn came, and the doctor was bending above him seated in an arm-chair. The blaze of the gas-microscope in his eyes made him wince. The doctor's hand touched the scar of the sword-cut on Dick's head, and Dick explained briefly how he had come by it. When the flame was removed, Dick saw the doctor's face, and the fear came upon him again. The doctor wrapped himself in a mist of words. Dick caught allusions to "scar," "frontal bone," "optic nerve," "extreme caution," and the "avoidance of mental anxiety."

"Verdict?" he said faintly. "My business is painting, and I daren't waste time. What do you make of it?"

Again the whirl of words, but this time they conveyed a meaning.

"Can you give me anything to drink?"

Many sentences were pronounced in that darkened room, and the prisoners often needed cheering. Dick found a glass of liqueur brandy in his hand.

"As far as I can gather," he said, coughing above the spirit, "you call it decay of the optic nerve, or something, and therefore hopeless. What is my time-limit, avoiding all strain and worry?"

"Perhaps one year."

"My God! And if I don't take care of myself?"

"I really could not say. One cannot ascertain the exact amount of injury inflicted by the sword-cut. The scar is an old one, and—exposure to the strong light of the desert, did you say?—with excessive application to fine work? I really could not say?"

"I beg your pardon, but it has come without any warning. If you will let me, I'll sit here for a minute, and then I'll go. You have been very good in telling me the truth. Without any warning; without any warning. Thanks."

Dick went into the street, and was rapturously received by Binkie.

"We've got it very badly, little dog! Just as badly as we can get it. We'll go to the Park to think it out."

They headed for a certain tree that Dick knew well, and they sat down to think, because his legs were trembling under him and there was cold fear at the pit of his stomach.

"How could it have come without any warning? It's as sudden as being shot. It's the living death, Binkie. We're to be shut up in the dark in one year if we're careful, and we shan't see anybody, and we shall never have anything we want, not though we live to be a hundred!" Binkie wagged his tail joyously. "Binkie, we must think. Let's see how it feels to be blind." Dick shut his eyes, and flaming commas and Catherine-wheels floated inside the lids. Yet when he looked across the Park the scope of his vision was not contracted. He could see perfectly, until a procession of slow-wheeling fireworks defiled across his eyeballs.

"Little dorglums, we aren't at all well. Let's go home. If only Torp were back, now!"

But Torpenhow was in the south of England, inspecting dockyards in the company of the Nilghai. His letters were brief and full of mystery.

Dick had never asked anybody to help him in his joys or his sorrows. He argued, in the loneliness of his studio, henceforward to be decorated with a film of gray gauze in one corner, that, if his fate were blindness, all the Torpenhows in the world could not save him. "I can't call him off his trip to sit down and sympathise with me. I must pull through this business alone," he said. He was lying on the sofa, eating his moustache and wondering what the darkness of the night would be like. Then came to his mind the memory of a quaint scene in the Soudan. A soldier had been nearly hacked in two by a broad-bladed Arab spear. For one instant the man felt no pain. Looking down, he saw that his life-blood was going from him. The stupid bewilderment on his face was so intensely comic that both Dick and Torpenhow, still panting and unstrung from a fight for life, had roared with laughter, in which the man seemed as if he would join, but, as his lips parted in a sheepish grin, the agony of death came upon him, and he pitched grunting at their feet. Dick laughed again, remembering the horror. It seemed so exactly like his own case.

"But I have a little more time allowed me," he said. He paced up and down the room, quietly at first, but afterwards with the hurried feet of fear. It was as though a black shadow stood at his elbow and urged him to go forward; and there were only weaving circles and floating pin-dots before his eyes.

"We need to be calm, Binkie; we must be calm." He talked aloud for the sake of distraction. "This isn't nice at all. What shall we do? We must do something. Our time is short. I shouldn't have believed that this morning; but now things are different. Binkie, where was Moses when the light went out?"

Binkie smiled from ear to ear, as a well-bred terrier should, but made no suggestion.

"'Were there but world enough and time, This coyness, Binkie, were not crime.... But at my back I always hear——'" He wiped his forehead, which was unpleasantly damp. "What can I do? What can I do? I haven't any notions left, and I can't think connectedly, but I must do something, or I shall go off my head."

The hurried walk recommenced, Dick stopping every now and again to drag forth long-neglected canvases and old note-books; for he turned to his work by instinct, as a thing that could not fail. "You won't do, and you won't do," he said, at each inspection. "No more soldiers. I couldn't paint 'em. Sudden death comes home too nearly, and this is battle and murder for me."

The day was failing, and Dick thought for a moment that the twilight of the blind had come upon him unaware. "Allah Almighty!" he cried despairingly, "help me through the time of waiting, and I won't whine when my punishment comes. What can I do now, before the light goes?"

There was no answer. Dick waited till he could regain some sort of control over himself. His hands were shaking, and he prided himself on their steadiness; he could feel that his lips were quivering, and the sweat was running down his face. He was lashed by fear, driven forward by the desire to get to work at once and accomplish something, and maddened by the refusal of his brain to do more than repeat the news that he was about to go blind. "It's a humiliating exhibition," he thought, "and I'm glad Torp isn't here to see. The doctor said I was to avoid mental worry. Come here and let me pet you, Binkie."

The little dog yelped because Dick nearly squeezed the bark out of him.

Then he heard the man speaking in the twilight, and, doglike, understood that his trouble stood off from him—"Allah is good, Binkie. Not quite so gentle as we could wish, but we'll discuss that later. I think I see my way to it now. All those studies of Bessie's head were nonsense, and they nearly brought your master into a scrape. I hold the notion now as clear as crystal, 'the Melancolia that transcends all wit.' There shall be Maisie in that head, because I shall never get Maisie; and Bess, of course, because she knows all about Melancolia, though she doesn't know she knows; and there shall be some drawing in it, and it shall all end up with a laugh. That's for myself. Shall she giggle or grin? No, she shall laugh right out of the canvas, and every man and woman that ever had a sorrow of their own shall—what is it the poem says?— 'Understand the speech and feel a stir Of fellowship in all disastrous fight.'

"'In all disastrous fight'? That's better than painting the thing merely to pique Maisie. I can do it now because I have it inside me. Binkie, I'm going to hold you up by your tail. You're an omen. Come here."

Binkie swung head downward for a moment without speaking.

"Rather like holding a guinea-pig; but you're a brave little dog, and you don't yelp when you're hung up. It is an omen."

Binkie went to his own chair, and as often as he looked saw Dick walking up and down, rubbing his hands and chuckling. That night Dick wrote a letter to Maisie full of the tenderest regard for her health, but saying very little about his own, and dreamed of the Melancolia to be born. Not

till morning did he remember that something might happen to him in the future.

He fell to work, whistling softly, and was swallowed up in the clean, clear joy of creation, which does not come to man too often, lest he should consider himself the equal of his God, and so refuse to die at the appointed time. He forgot Maisie, Torpenhow, and Binkie at his feet, but remembered to stir Bessie, who needed very little stirring, into a tremendous rage, that he might watch the smouldering lights in her eyes.

He threw himself without reservation into his work, and did not think of the doom that was to overtake him, for he was possessed with his notion, and the things of this world had no power upon him.

"You're pleased today," said Bessie.

Dick waved his mahl-stick in mystic circles and went to the sideboard for a drink. In the evening, when the exaltation of the day had died down, he went to the sideboard again, and after some visits became convinced that the eye-doctor was a liar, since he could still see everything very clearly.

He was of opinion that he would even make a home for Maisie, and that whether she liked it or not she should be his wife. The mood passed next morning, but the sideboard and all upon it remained for his comfort.

Again he set to work, and his eyes troubled him with spots and dashes and blurs till he had taken counsel with the sideboard, and the Melancolia both on the canvas and in his own mind appeared lovelier than ever. There was a delightful sense of irresponsibility upon him, such as they feel who walking among their fellow-men know that the death-sentence of disease is upon them, and, seeing that fear is but waste of the little time left, are riotously happy. The days passed without event.

Bessie arrived punctually always, and, though her voice seemed to Dick to come from a distance, her face was always very near. The Melancolia began to flame on the canvas, in the likeness of a woman who had known all the sorrow in the world and was laughing at it. It was true that the corners of the studio draped themselves in gray film and retired into the darkness, that the spots in his eyes and the pains across his head were very troublesome, and that Maisie's letters were hard to read and harder still to answer. He could not tell her of his trouble, and he could not laugh at her accounts of her own Melancolia which was always going to be finished. But the furious days of toil and the nights of wild dreams made amends for all, and the sideboard was his best friend on earth.

Bessie was singularly dull. She used to shriek with rage when Dick stared at her between half-closed eyes. Now she sulked, or watched him with disgust, saying very little.

Torpenhow had been absent for six weeks. An incoherent note heralded his return. "News! great news!" he wrote. "The Nilghai knows, and so does the Keneu. We're all back on Thursday. Get lunch and clean your accoutrements."

Dick showed Bessie the letter, and she abused him for that he had ever sent Torpenhow away and ruined her life.

"Well," said Dick, brutally, "you're better as you are, instead of making love to some drunken beast in the street." He felt that he had rescued Torpenhow from great temptation.

"I don't know if that's any worse than sitting to a drunken beast in a studio. You haven't been

sober for three weeks. You've been soaking the whole time; and yet you pretend you're better than me!"

"What d'you mean?" said Dick.

"Mean! You'll see when Mr. Torpenhow comes back."

It was not long to wait. Torpenhow met Bessie on the staircase without a sign of feeling. He had news that was more to him than many Bessies, and the Keneu and the Nilghai were trampling behind him, calling for Dick.

"Drinking like a fish," Bessie whispered. "He's been at it for nearly a month." She followed the men stealthily to hear judgment done.

They came into the studio, rejoicing, to be welcomed over effusively by a drawn, lined, shrunken, haggard wreck,—unshaven, blue-white about the nostrils, stooping in the shoulders, and peering under his eyebrows nervously. The drink had been at work as steadily as Dick.

"Is this you?" said Torpenhow.

"All that's left of me. Sit down. Binkie's quite well, and I've been doing some good work." He reeled where he stood.

"You've done some of the worst work you've ever done in your life. Man alive, you're——"

Torpenhow turned to his companions appealingly, and they left the room to find lunch elsewhere. Then he spoke; but, since the reproof of a friend is much too sacred and intimate a thing to be printed, and since Torpenhow used figures and metaphors which were unseemly, and contempt untranslatable, it will never be known what was actually said to Dick, who blinked and winked and picked at his hands. After a time the culprit began to feel the need of a little self-respect. He was quite sure that he had not in any way departed from virtue, and there were reasons, too, of which Torpenhow knew nothing. He would explain.

He rose, tried to straighten his shoulders, and spoke to the face he could hardly see.

"You are right," he said. "But I am right, too. After you went away I had some trouble with my eyes. So I went to an oculist, and he turned a gasogene—I mean a gas-engine—into my eye. That was very long ago. He said, 'Scar on the head,—sword-cut and optic nerve.' Make a note of that. So I am going blind. I have some work to do before I go blind, and I suppose that I must do it. I cannot see much now, but I can see best when I am drunk. I did not know I was drunk till I was told, but I must go on with my work. If you want to see it, there it is." He pointed to the all but finished Melancolia and looked for applause.

Torpenhow said nothing, and Dick began to whimper feebly, for joy at seeing Torpenhow again, for grief at misdeeds—if indeed they were misdeeds—that made Torpenhow remote and unsympathetic, and for childish vanity hurt, since Torpenhow had not given a word of praise to his wonderful picture.

Bessie looked through the keyhole after a long pause, and saw the two walking up and down as usual, Torpenhow's hand on Dick's shoulder.

Hereat she said something so improper that it shocked even Binkie, who was dribbling patiently on the landing with the hope of seeing his master again.

CHAPTER XI

The lark will make her hymn to God,

The partridge call her brood,

While I forget the heath I trod,

The fields wherein I stood.

'Tis dule to know not night from morn,

But deeper dule to know

I can but hear the hunter's horn

That once I used to blow.

—The Only Son

IT WAS the third day after Torpenhow's return, and his heart was heavy.

"Do you mean to tell me that you can't see to work without whiskey? It's generally the other way about."

"Can a drunkard swear on his honour?" said Dick.

"Yes, if he has been as good a man as you."

"Then I give you my word of honour," said Dick, speaking hurriedly through parched lips. "Old man, I can hardly see your face now. You've kept me sober for two days,—if I ever was drunk,—and I've done no work. Don't keep me back any more. I don't know when my eyes may give out. The spots and dots and the pains and things are crowding worse than ever. I swear I can see all right when I'm—when I'm moderately screwed, as you say. Give me three more sittings from Bessie and all—the stuff I want, and the picture will be done. I can't kill myself in three days. It only means a touch of D. T. at the worst."

"If I give you three days more will you promise me to stop work and—the other thing, whether the picture's finished or not?"

"I can't. You don't know what that picture means to me. But surely you could get the Nilghai to help you, and knock me down and tie me up. I shouldn't fight for the whiskey, but I should for the work."

"Go on, then. I give you three days; but you're nearly breaking my heart."

Dick returned to his work, toiling as one possessed; and the yellow devil of whiskey stood by him and chased away the spots in his eyes. The Melancolia was nearly finished, and was all or nearly all that he had hoped she would be. Dick jested with Bessie, who reminded him that he was "a drunken beast"; but the reproof did not move him.

"You can't understand, Bess. We are in sight of land now, and soon we shall lie back and think

about what we've done. I'll give you three months' pay when the picture's finished, and next time I have any more work in hand—but that doesn't matter. Won't three months' pay make you hate me less?"

"No, it won't! I hate you, and I'll go on hating you. Mr. Torpenhow won't speak to me any more. He's always looking at maps."

Bessie did not say that she had again laid siege to Torpenhow, or that at the end of our passionate pleading he had picked her up, given her a kiss, and put her outside the door with the recommendation not to be a little fool. He spent most of his time in the company of the Nilghai, and their talk was of war in the near future, the hiring of transports, and secret preparations among the dockyards. He did not wish to see Dick till the picture was finished.

"He's doing first-class work," he said to the Nilghai, "and it's quite out of his regular line. But, for the matter of that, so's his infernal soaking."

"Never mind. Leave him alone. When he has come to his senses again we'll carry him off from this place and let him breathe clean air. Poor Dick! I don't envy you, Torp, when his eyes fail."

"Yes, it will be a case of 'God help the man who's chained to our Davie.' The worst is that we don't know when it will happen, and I believe the uncertainty and the waiting have sent Dick to the whiskey more than anything else."

"How the Arab who cut his head open would grin if he knew!"

"He's at perfect liberty to grin if he can. He's dead. That's poor consolation now."

In the afternoon of the third day Torpenhow heard Dick calling for him.

"All finished!" he shouted. "I've done it! Come in! Isn't she a beauty? Isn't she a darling? I've been down to hell to get her; but isn't she worth it?"

Torpenhow looked at the head of a woman who laughed,—a full-lipped, hollow-eyed woman who laughed from out of the canvas as Dick had intended she would.

"Who taught you how to do it?" said Torpenhow. "The touch and notion have nothing to do with your regular work. What a face it is! What eyes, and what insolence!" Unconsciously he threw back his head and laughed with her. "She's seen the game played out,—I don't think she had a good time of it,—and now she doesn't care. Isn't that the idea?"

"Exactly."

"Where did you get the mouth and chin from? They don't belong to Bess."

"They're—some one else's. But isn't it good? Isn't it thundering good? Wasn't it worth the whiskey? I did it. Alone I did it, and it's the best I can do." He drew his breath sharply, and whispered, "Just God! what could I not do ten years hence, if I can do this now!—By the way, what do you think of it, Bess?"

The girl was biting her lips. She loathed Torpenhow because he had taken no notice of her.

"I think it's just the horridest, beastliest thing I ever saw," she answered, and turned away.

"More than you will be of that way of thinking, young woman.—Dick, there's a sort of murderous, viperine suggestion in the poise of the head that I don't understand," said Torpenhow.

"That's trick-work," said Dick, chuckling with delight at being completely understood. "I couldn't resist one little bit of sheer swagger. It's a French trick, and you wouldn't understand; but it's got at by slewing round the head a trifle, and a tiny, tiny foreshortening of one side of the face from the angle of the chin to the top of the left ear. That, and deepening the shadow under the lobe of the ear. It was flagrant trick-work; but, having the notion fixed, I felt entitled to play with it,—Oh, you beauty!"

"Amen! She is a beauty. I can feel it."

"So will every man who has any sorrow of his own," said Dick, slapping his thigh. "He shall see his trouble there, and, by the Lord Harry, just when he's feeling properly sorry for himself he shall throw back his head and laugh,—as she is laughing. I've put the life of my heart and the light of my eyes into her, and I don't care what comes.... I'm tired,—awfully tired. I think I'll get to sleep. Take away the whiskey, it has served its turn, and give Bessie thirty-six quid, and three over for luck. Cover the picture."

He dropped asleep in the long chair, his face white and haggard, almost before he had finished the sentence. Bessie tried to take Torpenhow's hand. "Aren't you never going to speak to me any more?" she said; but Torpenhow was looking at Dick.

"What a stock of vanity the man has! I'll take him in hand tomorrow and make much of him. He deserves it.—Eh! what was that, Bess?"

"Nothing. I'll put things tidy here a little, and then I'll go. You couldn't give Me that three months' pay now, could you? He said you were to."

Torpenhow gave her a check and went to his own rooms. Bessie faithfully tidied up the studio, set the door ajar for flight, emptied half a bottle of turpentine on a duster, and began to scrub the face of the Melancolia viciously. The paint did not smudge quickly enough. She took a palette-knife and scraped, following each stroke with the wet duster. In five minutes the picture was a formless, scarred muddle of colours. She threw the paint-stained duster into the studio stove, stuck out her tongue at the sleeper, and whispered, "Bilked!" as she turned to run down the staircase. She would never see Torpenhow any more, but she had at least done harm to the man who had come between her and her desire and who used to make fun of her. Cashing the check was the very cream of the jest to Bessie. Then the little privateer sailed across the Thames, to be swallowed up in the gray wilderness of South-the-Water.

Dick slept till late in the evening, when Torpenhow dragged him off to bed. His eyes were as bright as his voice was hoarse. "Let's have another look at the picture," he said, insistently as a child.

"You—go—to—bed," said Torpenhow. "You aren't at all well, though you mayn't know it. You're as jumpy as a cat."

"I reform tomorrow. Good night."

As he repassed through the studio, Torpenhow lifted the cloth above the picture, and almost betrayed himself by outcries: "Wiped out!—scraped out and turped out! He's on the verge of jumps as it is. That's Bess,—the little fiend! Only a woman could have done that!—with the ink not dry on the check, too! Dick will be raving mad tomorrow. It was all my fault for trying to help gutter-devils. Oh, my poor Dick, the Lord is hitting you very hard!"

Dick could not sleep that night, partly for pure joy, and partly because the well-known Catherine-wheels inside his eyes had given place to crackling volcanoes of many-coloured fire. "Spout away," he said aloud.

"I've done my work, and now you can do what you please." He lay still, staring at the ceiling, the long-pent-up delirium of drink in his veins, his brain on fire with racing thoughts that would not stay to be considered, and his hands crisped and dry. He had just discovered that he was painting the face of the Melancolia on a revolving dome ribbed with millions of lights, and that all his wondrous thoughts stood embodied hundreds of feet below his tiny swinging plank, shouting together in his honour, when something cracked inside his temples like an overstrained bowstring, the glittering dome broke inward, and he was alone in the thick night.

"I'll go to sleep. The room's very dark. Let's light a lamp and see how the Melancolia looks. There ought to have been a moon."

It was then that Torpenhow heard his name called by a voice that he did not know,—in the rattling accents of deadly fear.

"He's looked at the picture," was his first thought, as he hurried into the bedroom and found Dick sitting up and beating the air with his hands.

"Torp! Torp! where are you? For pity's sake, come to me!"

"What's the matter?"

Dick clutched at his shoulder. "Matter! I've been lying here for hours in the dark, and you never heard me. Torp, old man, don't go away. I'm all in the dark. In the dark, I tell you!"

Torpenhow held the candle within a foot of Dick's eyes, but there was no light in those eyes. He lit the gas, and Dick heard the flame catch. The grip of his fingers on Torpenhow's shoulder made Torpenhow wince.

"Don't leave me. You wouldn't leave me alone now, would you? I can't see. D'you understand? It's black,—quite black,—and I feel as if I was falling through it all."

"Steady does it." Torpenhow put his arm round Dick and began to rock him gently to and fro.

"That's good. Now don't talk. If I keep very quiet for a while, this darkness will lift. It seems just on the point of breaking. H'sh!" Dick knit his brows and stared desperately in front of him. The night air was chilling Torpenhow's toes.

"Can you stay like that a minute?" he said. "I'll get my dressing-gown and some slippers."

Dick clutched the bed-head with both hands and waited for the darkness to clear away. "What a time you've been!" he cried, when Torpenhow returned. "It's as black as ever. What are you banging about in the door-way?"

"Long chair,—horse-blanket,—pillow. Going to sleep by you. Lie down now; you'll be better in the morning."

"I shan't!" The voice rose to a wail. "My God! I'm blind! I'm blind, and the darkness will never go away." He made as if to leap from the bed, but Torpenhow's arms were round him, and Torpenhow's chin was on his shoulder, and his breath was squeezed out of him. He could only gasp, "Blind!" and wriggle feebly.

"Steady, Dickie, steady!" said the deep voice in his ear, and the grip tightened. "Bite on the bullet, old man, and don't let them think you're afraid." The grip could draw no closer. Both men were breathing heavily.

Dick threw his head from side to side and groaned.

"Let me go," he panted. "You're cracking my ribs. We—we mustn't let them think we're afraid, must we,—all the powers of darkness and that lot?"

"Lie down. It's all over now."

"Yes," said Dick, obediently. "But would you mind letting me hold your hand? I feel as if I wanted something to hold on to. One drops through the dark so."

Torpenhow thrust out a large and hairy paw from the long chair. Dick clutched it tightly, and in half an hour had fallen asleep. Torpenhow withdrew his hand, and, stooping over Dick, kissed him lightly on the forehead, as men do sometimes kiss a wounded comrade in the hour of death, to ease his departure.

In the gray dawn Torpenhow heard Dick talking to himself. He was adrift on the shoreless tides of delirium, speaking very quickly—"It's a pity,—a great pity; but it's helped, and it must be eaten, Master George. Sufficient unto the day is the blindness thereof, and, further, putting aside all Melancolias and false humours, it is of obvious notoriety—such as mine was—that the queen can do no wrong. Torp doesn't know that. I'll tell him when we're a little farther into the desert.

"What a bungle those boatmen are making of the steamer-ropes! They'll have that four-inch hawser chafed through in a minute. I told you so—there she goes! White foam on green water, and the steamer slewing round. How good that looks! I'll sketch it. No, I can't. I'm afflicted with ophthalmia. That was one of the ten plagues of Egypt, and it extends up the Nile in the shape of cataract. Ha! that's a joke, Torp. Laugh, you graven image, and stand clear of the hawser.... It'll knock you into the water and make your dress all dirty, Maisie dear."

"Oh!" said Torpenhow. "This happened before. That night on the river."

"She'll be sure to say it's my fault if you get muddy, and you're quite near enough to the breakwater. Maisie, that's not fair. Ah! I knew you'd miss. Low and to the left, dear. But you've no conviction. Don't be angry, darling. I'd cut my hand off if it would give you anything more than obstinacy. My right hand, if it would serve."

"Now we mustn't listen. Here's an island shouting across seas of misunderstanding with a vengeance. But it's shouting truth, I fancy," said Torpenhow.

The babble continued. It all bore upon Maisie. Sometimes Dick lectured at length on his craft, then he cursed himself for his folly in being enslaved. He pleaded to Maisie for a kiss—only one kiss—before she went away, and called to her to come back from Vitry-sur-Marne, if she would; but through all his ravings he bade heaven and earth witness that the queen could do no wrong.

Torpenhow listened attentively, and learned every detail of Dick's life that had been hidden from him. For three days Dick raved through the past, and then a natural sleep. "What a strain he has been running under, poor chap!" said Torpenhow. "Dick, of all men, handing himself over like a dog! And I was lecturing him on arrogance! I ought to have known that it was no use to judge a man. But I did it. What a demon that girl must be! Dick's given her his life,—confound him!—and she's given him one kiss apparently."

"Torp," said Dick, from the bed, "go out for a walk. You've been here too long. I'll get up. Hi! This is annoying. I can't dress myself. Oh, it's too absurd!"

Torpenhow helped him into his clothes and led him to the big chair in the studio. He sat quietly waiting under strained nerves for the darkness to lift. It did not lift that day, nor the next. Dick adventured on a voyage round the walls. He hit his shins against the stove, and this suggested to him that it would be better to crawl on all fours, one hand in front of him. Torpenhow found him on the floor.

"I'm trying to get the geography of my new possessions," said he. "D'you remember that nigger you gouged in the square? Pity you didn't keep the odd eye. It would have been useful. Any letters for me? Give me all the ones in fat gray envelopes with a sort of crown thing outside. They're of no importance."

Torpenhow gave him a letter with a black M. on the envelope flap. Dick put it into his pocket. There was nothing in it that Torpenhow might not have read, but it belonged to himself and to Maisie, who would never belong to him.

"When she finds that I don't write, she'll stop writing. It's better so. I couldn't be any use to her now," Dick argued, and the tempter suggested that he should make known his condition. Every nerve in him revolted. "I have fallen low enough already. I'm not going to beg for pity. Besides, it would be cruel to her." He strove to put Maisie out of his thoughts; but the blind have many opportunities for thinking, and as the tides of his strength came back to him in the long employless days of dead darkness, Dick's soul was troubled to the core. Another letter, and another, came from Maisie. Then there was silence, and Dick sat by the window, the pulse of summer in the air, and pictured her being won by another man, stronger than himself. His imagination, the keener for the dark background it worked against, spared him no single detail that might send him raging up and down the studio, to stumble over the stove that seemed to be in four places at once. Worst of all, tobacco would not taste in the darkness. The arrogance of the man had disappeared, and in its place were settled despair that Torpenhow knew, and blind passion that Dick confided to his pillow at night. The intervals between the paroxysms were filled with intolerable waiting and the weight of intolerable darkness.

"Come out into the Park," said Torpenhow. "You haven't stirred out since the beginning of things."

"What's the use? There's no movement in the dark; and, besides,"—he paused irresolutely at the head of the stairs,—"something will run over me."

"Not if I'm with you. Proceed gingerly."

The roar of the streets filled Dick with nervous terror, and he clung to Torpenhow's arm. "Fancy having to feel for a gutter with your foot!" he said petulantly, as he turned into the Park. "Let's curse God and die."

"Sentries are forbidden to pay unauthorised compliments. By Jove, there are the Guards!"

Dick's figure straightened. "Let's get near 'em. Let's go in and look. Let's get on the grass and run. I can smell the trees."

"Mind the low railing. That's all right!" Torpenhow kicked out a tuft of grass with his heel. "Smell that," he said. "Isn't it good?" Dick sniffed luxuriously. "Now pick up your feet and run." They approached as near to the regiment as was possible. The clank of bayonets being unfixed made Dick's nostrils quiver.

"Let's get nearer. They're in column, aren't they?"

"Yes. How did you know?"

"Felt it. Oh, my men!—my beautiful men!" He edged forward as though he could see. "I could draw those chaps once. Who'll draw 'em now?"

"They'll move off in a minute. Don't jump when the band begins."

"Huh! I'm not a new charger. It's the silences that hurt. Nearer, Torp!—nearer! Oh, my God, what wouldn't I give to see 'em for a minute!—one half-minute!"

He could hear the armed life almost within reach of him, could hear the slings tighten across the bandsman's chest as he heaved the big drum from the ground.

"Sticks crossed above his head," whispered Torpenhow.

"I know. I know! Who should know if I don't? H'sh!"

The drum-sticks fell with a boom, and the men swung forward to the crash of the band. Dick felt the wind of the massed movement in his face, heard the maddening tramp of feet and the friction of the pouches on the belts. The big drum pounded out the tune. It was a music-hall refrain that made a perfect quickstep—

"He must be a man of decent height,

He must be a man of weight,

He must come home on a Saturday night

In a thoroughly sober state;

He must know how to love me,

And he must know how to kiss;

And if he's enough to keep us both

I can't refuse him bliss."

"What's the matter?" said Torpenhow, as he saw Dick's head fall when the last of the regiment had departed.

"Nothing. I feel a little bit out of the running,—that's all. Torp, take me back. Why did you bring me out?"

CHAPTER XII

There were three friends that buried the fourth,

The mould in his mouth and the dust in his eyes

And they went south and east, and north,—

The strong man fights, but the sick man dies.

There were three friends that spoke of the dead,—

The strong man fights, but the sick man dies.—

"And would he were with us now," they said,

"The sun in our face and the wind in our eyes."

　　　　　—Ballad.

The Nilghai was angry with Torpenhow. Dick had been sent to bed,—blind men are ever under the orders of those who can see,—and since he had returned from the Park had fluently sworn at Torpenhow because he was alive, and all the world because it was alive and could see, while he, Dick, was dead in the death of the blind, who, at the best, are only burdens upon their associates. Torpenhow had said something about a Mrs. Gummidge, and Dick had retired in a black fury to handle and re-handle three unopened letters from Maisie.

The Nilghai, fat, burly, and aggressive, was in Torpenhow's rooms.

Behind him sat the Keneu, the Great War Eagle, and between them lay a large map embellished with black-and-white-headed pins.

"I was wrong about the Balkans," said the Nilghai. "But I'm not wrong about this business. The whole of our work in the Southern Soudan must be done over again. The public doesn't care, of course, but the government does, and they are making their arrangements quietly. You know that as well as I do."

"I remember how the people cursed us when our troops withdrew from Omdurman. It was bound to crop up sooner or later. But I can't go," said Torpenhow. He pointed through the open door; it was a hot night. "Can you blame me?"

The Keneu purred above his pipe like a large and very happy cat—"Don't blame you in the least. It's uncommonly good of you, and all the rest of it, but every man—even you, Torp—must consider his work. I know it sounds brutal, but Dick's out of the race,—down,—gastados expended, finished, done for. He has a little money of his own. He won't starve, and you can't pull out of your slide for his sake. Think of your own reputation."

"Dick's was five times bigger than mine and yours put together."

"That was because he signed his name to everything he did. It's all ended now. You must hold yourself in readiness to move out. You can command your own prices, and you do better work than any three of us."

"Don't tell me how tempting it is. I'll stay here to look after Dick for a while. He's as cheerful as a bear with a sore head, but I think he likes to have me near him."

The Nilghai said something uncomplimentary about soft-headed fools who throw away their careers for other fools. Torpenhow flushed angrily. The constant strain of attendance on Dick had worn his nerves thin.

"There remains a third fate," said the Keneu, thoughtfully. "Consider this, and be not larger fools than necessary. Dick is—or rather was—an able-bodied man of moderate attractions and a certain amount of audacity."

"Oho!" said the Nilghai, who remembered an affair at Cairo. "I begin to see,—Torp, I'm sorry."

Torpenhow nodded forgiveness: "You were more sorry when he cut you out, though.—Go on, Keneu."

"I've often thought, when I've seen men die out in the desert, that if the news could be sent through the world, and the means of transport were quick enough, there would be one woman at least at each man's bedside."

"There would be some mighty quaint revelations. Let us be grateful things are as they are," said the Nilghai.

"Let us rather reverently consider whether Torp's three-cornered ministrations are exactly what Dick needs just now.—What do you think yourself, Torp?"

"I know they aren't. But what can I do?"

"Lay the matter before the board. We are all Dick's friends here. You've been most in his life."

"But I picked it up when he was off his head."

"The greater chance of its being true. I thought we should arrive. Who is she?"

Then Torpenhow told a tale in plain words, as a special correspondent who knows how to make a verbal precis should tell it. The men listened without interruption.

"Is it possible that a man can come back across the years to his calf-love?"

said the Keneu. "Is it possible?"

"I give the facts. He says nothing about it now, but he sits fumbling three letters from her when he thinks I'm not looking. What am I to do?"

"Speak to him," said the Nilghai.

"Oh yes! Write to her,—I don't know her full name, remember,—and ask her to accept him out of pity. I believe you once told Dick you were sorry for him, Nilghai. You remember what happened, eh? Go into the bedroom and suggest full confession and an appeal to this Maisie girl, whoever she is. I honestly believe he'd try to kill you; and the blindness has made him rather muscular."

"Torpenhow's course is perfectly clear," said the Keneu. "He will go to Vitry-sur-Marne, which is on the Bezieres-Landes Railway,—single track from Tourgas. The Prussians shelled it out in '70 because there was a poplar on the top of a hill eighteen hundred yards from the church spire. There's a squadron of cavalry quartered there,—or ought to be. Where this studio Torp

spoke about may be I cannot tell. That is Torp's business. I have given him his route. He will dispassionately explain the situation to the girl, and she will come back to Dick,—the more especially because, to use Dick's words, 'there is nothing but her damned obstinacy to keep them apart.'"

"And they have four hundred and twenty pounds a year between 'em."

Dick never lost his head for figures, even in his delirium. "You haven't the shadow of an excuse for not going," said the Nilghai.

Torpenhow looked very uncomfortable. "But it's absurd and impossible. I can't drag her back by the hair."

"Our business—the business for which we draw our money—is to do absurd and impossible things,—generally with no reason whatever except to amuse the public. Here we have a reason. The rest doesn't matter. I shall share these rooms with the Nilghai till Torpenhow returns. There will be a batch of unbridled 'specials' coming to town in a little while, and these will serve as their headquarters. Another reason for sending Torpenhow away. Thus Providence helps those who help others, and"—here the Keneu dropped his measured speech—"we can't have you tied by the leg to Dick when the trouble begins. It's your only chance of getting away; and Dick will be grateful."

"He will,—worse luck! I can but go and try. I can't conceive a woman in her senses refusing Dick."

"Talk that out with the girl. I have seen you wheedle an angry Mahdieh woman into giving you dates. This won't be a tithe as difficult. You had better not be here tomorrow afternoon, because the Nilghai and I will be in possession. It is an order. Obey."

"Dick," said Torpenhow, next morning, "can I do anything for you?"

"No! Leave me alone. How often must I remind you that I'm blind?"

"Nothing I could go for to fetch for to carry for to bring?"

"No. Take those infernal creaking boots of yours away."

"Poor chap!" said Torpenhow to himself. "I must have been sitting on his nerves lately. He wants a lighter step." Then, aloud, "Very well. Since you're so independent, I'm going off for four or five days. Say goodbye at least. The housekeeper will look after you, and Keneu has my rooms."

Dick's face fell. "You won't be longer than a week at the outside? I know I'm touched in the temper, but I can't get on without you."

"Can't you? You'll have to do without me in a little time, and you'll be glad I'm gone."

Dick felt his way back to the big chair, and wondered what these things might mean. He did not wish to be tended by the housekeeper, and yet Torpenhow's constant tenderness jarred on him. He did not exactly know what he wanted. The darkness would not lift, and Maisie's unopened letters felt worn and old from much handling. He could never read them for himself as long as life endured; but Maisie might have sent him some fresh ones to play with. The Nilghai entered with a gift,—a piece of red modelling-wax. He fancied that Dick might find interest in using his hands. Dick poked and patted the stuff for a few minutes, and, "Is it like anything in the world?" he said drearily. "Take it away. I may get the touch of the blind in fifty years. Do you know where Torpenhow has gone?"

The Nilghai knew nothing. "We're staying in his rooms till he comes back. Can we do anything for you?"

"I'd like to be left alone, please. Don't think I'm ungrateful; but I'm best alone."

The Nilghai chuckled, and Dick resumed his drowsy brooding and sullen rebellion against fate. He had long since ceased to think about the work he had done in the old days, and the desire to do more work had departed from him. He was exceedingly sorry for himself, and the completeness of his tender grief soothed him. But his soul and his body cried for Maisie— Maisie who would understand. His mind pointed out that Maisie, having her own work to do, would not care. His experience had taught him that when money was exhausted women went away, and that when a man was knocked out of the race the others trampled on him. "Then at the least," said Dick, in reply, "she could use me as I used Binat,—for some sort of a study. I wouldn't ask more than to be near her again, even though I knew that another man was making love to her. Ugh! what a dog I am!"

A voice on the staircase began to sing joyfully—

"When we go—go—go away from here, Our creditors will weep and they will wail, Our absence much regretting when they find that we've been getting Out of England by next Tuesday's Indian mail."

Following the trampling of feet, slamming of Torpenhow's door, and the sound of voices in strenuous debate, some one squeaked, "And see, you good fellows, I have found a new water-bottle—firs'-class patent—eh, how you say? Open himself inside out."

Dick sprang to his feet. He knew the voice well. "That's Cassavetti, come back from the Continent. Now I know why Torp went away. There's a row somewhere, and—I'm out of it!"

The Nilghai commanded silence in vain. "That's for my sake," Dick said bitterly. "The birds are getting ready to fly, and they wouldn't tell me. I can hear Morten-Sutherland and Mackaye. Half the War Correspondents in London are there;—and I'm out of it."

He stumbled across the landing and plunged into Torpenhow's room. He could feel that it was full of men. "Where's the trouble?" said he. "In the Balkans at last? Why didn't some one tell me?"

"We thought you wouldn't be interested," said the Nilghai, shamefacedly.

"It's in the Soudan, as usual."

"You lucky dogs! Let me sit here while you talk. I shan't be a skeleton at the feast.—Cassavetti, where are you? Your English is as bad as ever."

Dick was led into a chair. He heard the rustle of the maps, and the talk swept forward, carrying him with it. Everybody spoke at once, discussing press censorships, railway-routes, transport, water-supply, the capacities of generals,—these in language that would have horrified a trusting public,—ranting, asserting, denouncing, and laughing at the top of their voices. There was the glorious certainty of war in the Soudan at any moment. The Nilghai said so, and it was well to be in readiness. The Keneu had telegraphed to Cairo for horses; Cassavetti had stolen a perfectly inaccurate list of troops that would be ordered forward, and was reading it out amid profane interruptions, and the Keneu introduced to Dick some man unknown who would be employed as war artist by the Central Southern Syndicate. "It's his first outing," said the Keneu. "Give him some tips—about riding camels."

"Oh, those camels!" groaned Cassavetti. "I shall learn to ride him again, and now I am so much all soft! Listen, you good fellows. I know your military arrangement very well. There will go the Royal Argalshire Sutherlanders. So it was read to me upon best authority."

A roar of laughter interrupted him.

"Sit down," said the Nilghai. "The lists aren't even made out in the War Office."

"Will there be any force at Suakin?" said a voice.

Then the outcries redoubled, and grew mixed, thus: "How many Egyptian troops will they use?—God help the Fellaheen!—There's a railway in Plumstead marshes doing duty as a fives-court.—We shall have the Suakin-Berber line built at last.—Canadian voyageurs are too careful. Give me a half-drunk Krooman in a whale-boat.—Who commands the Desert column?—No, they never blew up the big rock in the Ghineh bend. We shall have to be hauled up, as usual.—Somebody tell me if there's an Indian contingent, or I'll break everybody's head.—Don't tear the map in two.—It's a war of occupation, I tell you, to connect with the African companies in the South.—There's Guinea-worm in most of the wells on that route." Then the Nilghai, despairing of peace, bellowed like a fog-horn and beat upon the table with both hands.

"But what becomes of Torpenhow?" said Dick, in the silence that followed.

"Torp's in abeyance just now. He's off love-making somewhere, I suppose," said the Nilghai.

"He said he was going to stay at home," said the Keneu.

"Is he?" said Dick, with an oath. "He won't. I'm not much good now, but if you and the Nilghai hold him down I'll engage to trample on him till he sees reason. He'll stay behind, indeed! He's the best of you all. There'll be some tough work by Omdurman. We shall come there to stay, this time.

"But I forgot. I wish I were going with you."

"So do we all, Dickie," said the Keneu.

"And I most of all," said the new artist of the Central Southern Syndicate.

"Could you tell me——"

"I'll give you one piece of advice," Dick answered, moving towards the door. "If you happen to be cut over the head in a scrimmage, don't guard. Tell the man to go on cutting. You'll find it cheapest in the end. Thanks for letting me look in."

"There's grit in Dick," said the Nilghai, an hour later, when the room was emptied of all save the Keneu.

"It was the sacred call of the war-trumpet. Did you notice how he answered to it? Poor fellow! Let's look at him," said the Keneu.

The excitement of the talk had died away. Dick was sitting by the studio table, with his head on his arms, when the men came in. He did not change his position.

"It hurts," he moaned. "God forgive me, but it hurts cruelly; and yet, y'know, the world has a knack of spinning round all by itself. Shall I see Torp before he goes?"

"Oh, yes. You'll see him," said the Nilghai.

CHAPTER XIII

The sun went down an hour ago,

I wonder if I face towards home;

If I lost my way in the light of day

How shall I find it now night is come?

 —Old Song

"Maisie, come to bed."

"It's so hot I can't sleep. Don't worry."

Maisie put her elbows on the window-sill and looked at the moonlight on the straight, poplar-flanked road. Summer had come upon Vitry-sur-Marne and parched it to the bone. The grass was dry-burnt in the meadows, the clay by the bank of the river was caked to brick, the roadside flowers were long since dead, and the roses in the garden hung withered on their stalks. The heat in the little low bedroom under the eaves was almost intolerable. The very moonlight on the wall of Kami's studio across the road seemed to make the night hotter, and the shadow of the big bell-handle by the closed gate cast a bar of inky black that caught Maisie's eye and annoyed her.

"Horrid thing! It should be all white," she murmured. "And the gate isn't in the middle of the wall, either. I never noticed that before."

Maisie was hard to please at that hour. First, the heat of the past few weeks had worn her down; secondly, her work, and particularly the study of a female head intended to represent the Melancolia and not finished in time for the Salon, was unsatisfactory; thirdly, Kami had said as much two days before; fourthly,—but so completely fourthly that it was hardly worth thinking about,—Dick, her property, had not written to her for more than six weeks. She was angry with the heat, with Kami, and with her work, but she was exceedingly angry with Dick.

She had written to him three times,—each time proposing a fresh treatment of her Melancolia. Dick had taken no notice of these communications. She had resolved to write no more. When she returned to England in the autumn—for her pride's sake she could not return earlier—she would speak to him. She missed the Sunday afternoon conferences more than she cared to admit. All that Kami said was, "Continuez, mademoiselle, continuez toujours," and he had been repeating the wearisome counsel through the hot summer, exactly like a cicada,—an old gray cicada in a black alpaca coat, white trousers, and a huge felt hat.

But Dick had tramped masterfully up and down her little studio north of the cool green London park, and had said things ten times worse than continuez, before he snatched the brush out of her hand and showed her where the error lay. His last letter, Maisie remembered, contained some trivial advice about not sketching in the sun or drinking water at wayside farmhouses; and he had said that not once, but three times,—as if he did not know that Maisie could take care of herself.

But what was he doing, that he could not trouble to write? A murmur of voices in the road made her lean from the window. A cavalryman of the little garrison in the town was talking to Kami's cook. The moonlight glittered on the scabbard of his sabre, which he was holding in his hand

lest it should clank inopportunely. The cook's cap cast deep shadows on her face, which was close to the conscript's. He slid his arm round her waist, and there followed the sound of a kiss.

"Faugh!" said Maisie, stepping back.

"What's that?" said the red-haired girl, who was tossing uneasily outside her bed.

"Only a conscript kissing the cook," said Maisie.

"They've gone away now." She leaned out of the window again, and put a shawl over her nightgown to guard against chills. There was a very small night-breeze abroad, and a sun-baked rose below nodded its head as one who knew unutterable secrets. Was it possible that Dick should turn his thoughts from her work and his own and descend to the degradation of Suzanne and the conscript? He could not! The rose nodded its head and one leaf therewith. It looked like a naughty little devil scratching its ear.

Dick could not, "because," thought Maisie, "he is mine,—mine,—mine. He said he was. I'm sure I don't care what he does. It will only spoil his work if he does; and it will spoil mine too."

The rose continued to nod in the futile way peculiar to flowers. There was no earthly reason why Dick should not disport himself as he chose, except that he was called by Providence, which was Maisie, to assist Maisie in her work. And her work was the preparation of pictures that went sometimes to English provincial exhibitions, as the notices in the scrap-book proved, and that were invariably rejected by the Salon when Kami was plagued into allowing her to send them up. Her work in the future, it seemed, would be the preparation of pictures on exactly similar lines which would be rejected in exactly the same way——The red-haired girl threshed distressfully across the sheets. "It's too hot to sleep," she moaned; and the interruption jarred.

Exactly the same way. Then she would divide her years between the little studio in England and Kami's big studio at Vitry-sur-Marne. No, she would go to another master, who should force her into the success that was her right, if patient toil and desperate endeavour gave one a right to anything. Dick had told her that he had worked ten years to understand his craft. She had worked ten years, and ten years were nothing. Dick had said that ten years were nothing,— but that was in regard to herself only. He had said—this very man who could not find time to write—that he would wait ten years for her, and that she was bound to come back to him sooner or later. He had said this in the absurd letter about sunstroke and diphtheria; and then he had stopped writing. He was wandering up and down moonlit streets, kissing cooks. She would like to lecture him now,—not in her nightgown, of course, but properly dressed, severely and from a height. Yet if he was kissing other girls he certainly would not care whether she lecture him or not. He would laugh at her. Very good.

She would go back to her studio and prepare pictures that went, etc., etc.

The mill-wheel of thought swung round slowly, that no section of it might be slurred over, and the red-haired girl tossed and turned behind her.

Maisie put her chin in her hands and decided that there could be no doubt whatever of the villainy of Dick. To justify herself, she began, unwomanly, to weigh the evidence. There was a boy, and he had said he loved her. And he kissed her,—kissed her on the cheek,—by a yellow sea-poppy that nodded its head exactly like the maddening dry rose in the garden. Then there was an interval, and men had told her that they loved her—just when she was busiest with her work. Then the boy came back, and at their very second meeting had told her that he loved her. Then he had——But there was no end to the things he had done. He had given her his time and his powers. He had spoken to her of Art, housekeeping, technique, teacups, the abuse of pickles

as a stimulant,—that was rude,—sable hair-brushes,—he had given her the best in her stock,—she used them daily; he had given her advice that she profited by, and now and again—a look. Such a look! The look of a beaten hound waiting for the word to crawl to his mistress's feet. In return she had given him nothing whatever, except—here she brushed her mouth against the open-work sleeve of her nightgown—the privilege of kissing her once. And on the mouth, too. Disgraceful! Was that not enough, and more than enough? and if it was not, had he not cancelled the debt by not writing and—probably kissing other girls? "Maisie, you'll catch a chill. Do go and lie down," said the wearied voice of her companion. "I can't sleep a wink with you at the window."

Maisie shrugged her shoulders and did not answer. She was reflecting on the meannesses of Dick, and on other meannesses with which he had nothing to do. The moonlight would not let her sleep. It lay on the skylight of the studio across the road in cold silver; she stared at it intently and her thoughts began to slide one into the other. The shadow of the big bell-handle in the wall grew short, lengthened again, and faded out as the moon went down behind the pasture and a hare came limping home across the road. Then the dawn-wind washed through the upland grasses, and brought coolness with it, and the cattle lowed by the drought-shrunk river. Maisie's head fell forward on the window-sill, and the tangle of black hair covered her arms.

"Maisie, wake up. You'll catch a chill."

"Yes, dear; yes, dear." She staggered to her bed like a wearied child, and as she buried her face in the pillows she muttered, "I think—I think—But he ought to have written."

Day brought the routine of the studio, the smell of paint and turpentine, and the monotone wisdom of Kami, who was a leaden artist, but a golden teacher if the pupil were only in sympathy with him. Maisie was not in sympathy that day, and she waited impatiently for the end of the work.

She knew when it was coming; for Kami would gather his black alpaca coat into a bunch behind him, and, with faded flue eyes that saw neither pupils nor canvas, look back into the past to recall the history of one Binat. "You have all done not so badly," he would say. "But you shall remember that it is not enough to have the method, and the art, and the power, nor even that which is touch, but you shall have also the conviction that nails the work to the wall. Of the so many I taught,"—here the students would begin to unfix drawing-pins or get their tubes together,—"the very so many that I have taught, the best was Binat. All that comes of the study and the work and the knowledge was to him even when he came. After he left me he should have done all that could be done with the colour, the form, and the knowledge. Only, he had not the conviction. So today I hear no more of Binat,—the best of my pupils,—and that is long ago. So today, too, you will be glad to hear no more of me. Continuez, mesdemoiselles, and, above all, with conviction."

He went into the garden to smoke and mourn over the lost Binat as the pupils dispersed to their several cottages or loitered in the studio to make plans for the cool of the afternoon.

Maisie looked at her very unhappy Melancolia, restrained a desire to grimace before it, and was hurrying across the road to write a letter to Dick, when she was aware of a large man on a white troop-horse. How Torpenhow had managed in the course of twenty hours to find his way to the hearts of the cavalry officers in quarters at Vitry-sur-Marne, to discuss with them the certainty of a glorious revenge for France, to reduce the colonel to tears of pure affability, and to borrow the best horse in the squadron for the journey to Kami's studio, is a mystery that only special correspondents can unravel.

"I beg your pardon," said he. "It seems an absurd question to ask, but the fact is that I don't

know her by any other name: Is there any young lady here that is called Maisie?"

"I am Maisie," was the answer from the depths of a great sun-hat.

"I ought to introduce myself," he said, as the horse capered in the blinding white dust. "My name is Torpenhow. Dick Heldar is my best friend, and—and—the fact is that he has gone blind."

"Blind!" said Maisie, stupidly. "He can't be blind."

"He has been stone-blind for nearly two months."

Maisie lifted up her face, and it was pearly white. "No! No! Not blind! I won't have him blind!"

"Would you care to see for yourself?" said Torpenhow.

"Now,—at once?"

"Oh, no! The Paris train doesn't go through this place till tonight. There will be ample time."

"Did Mr. Heldar send you to me?"

"Certainly not. Dick wouldn't do that sort of thing. He's sitting in his studio, turning over some letters that he can't read because he's blind."

There was a sound of choking from the sun-hat. Maisie bowed her head and went into the cottage, where the red-haired girl was on a sofa, complaining of a headache.

"Dick's blind!" said Maisie, taking her breath quickly as she steadied herself against a chair-back. "My Dick's blind!"

"What?" The girl was on the sofa no longer.

"A man has come from England to tell me. He hasn't written to me for six weeks."

"Are you going to him?"

"I must think."

"Think! I should go back to London and see him and I should kiss his eyes and kiss them and kiss them until they got well again! If you don't go I shall. Oh, what am I talking about? You wicked little idiot! Go to him at once. Go!"

Torpenhow's neck was blistering, but he preserved a smile of infinite patience as Maisie's appeared bareheaded in the sunshine.

"I am coming," said she, her eyes on the ground.

"You will be at Vitry Station, then, at seven this evening." This was an order delivered by one who was used to being obeyed. Maisie said nothing, but she felt grateful that there was no chance of disputing with this big man who took everything for granted and managed a squealing horse with one hand. She returned to the red-haired girl, who was weeping bitterly, and between tears, kisses,—very few of those,—menthol, packing, and an interview with Kami, the sultry afternoon wore away.

Thought might come afterwards. Her present duty was to go to Dick,—Dick who owned the

wondrous friend and sat in the dark playing with her unopened letters.

"But what will you do," she said to her companion.

"I? Oh, I shall stay here and—finish your Melancolia," she said, smiling pitifully. "Write to me afterwards."

That night there ran a legend through Vitry-sur-Marne of a mad Englishman, doubtless suffering from sunstroke, who had drunk all the officers of the garrison under the table, had borrowed a horse from the lines, and had then and there eloped, after the English custom, with one of those more mad English girls who drew pictures down there under the care of that good Monsieur Kami.

"They are very droll," said Suzanne to the conscript in the moonlight by the studio wall. "She walked always with those big eyes that saw nothing, and yet she kisses me on both cheeks as though she were my sister, and gives me—see—ten francs!"

The conscript levied a contribution on both gifts; for he prided himself on being a good soldier.

Torpenhow spoke very little to Maisie during the journey to Calais; but he was careful to attend to all her wants, to get her a compartment entirely to herself, and to leave her alone. He was amazed of the ease with which the matter had been accomplished.

"The safest thing would be to let her think things out. By Dick's showing,—when he was off his head,—she must have ordered him about very thoroughly. Wonder how she likes being under orders."

Maisie never told. She sat in the empty compartment often with her eyes shut, that she might realise the sensation of blindness. It was an order that she should return to London swiftly, and she found herself at last almost beginning to enjoy the situation. This was better than looking after luggage and a red-haired friend who never took any interest in her surroundings. But there appeared to be a feeling in the air that she, Maisie,—of all people,—was in disgrace. Therefore she justified her conduct to herself with great success, till Torpenhow came up to her on the steamer and without preface began to tell the story of Dick's blindness, suppressing a few details, but dwelling at length on the miseries of delirium. He stopped before he reached the end, as though he had lost interest in the subject, and went forward to smoke. Maisie was furious with him and with herself.

She was hurried on from Dover to London almost before she could ask for breakfast, and—she was past any feeling of indignation now—was bidden curtly to wait in a hall at the foot of some lead-covered stairs while Torpenhow went up to make inquiries. Again the knowledge that she was being treated like a naughty little girl made her pale cheeks flame. It was all Dick's fault for being so stupid as to go blind.

Torpenhow led her up to a shut door, which he opened very softly. Dick was sitting by the window, with his chin on his chest. There were three envelopes in his hand, and he turned them over and over. The big man who gave orders was no longer by her side, and the studio door snapped behind her.

Dick thrust the letters into his pocket as he heard the sound. "Hullo, Torp! Is that you? I've been so lonely."

His voice had taken the peculiar flatness of the blind. Maisie pressed herself up into a corner of the room. Her heart was beating furiously, and she put one hand on her breast to keep it quiet.

Dick was staring directly at her, and she realised for the first time that he was blind.

Shutting her eyes in a rail-way carriage to open them when she pleased was child's play. This man was blind though his eyes were wide open.

"Torp, is that you? They said you were coming." Dick looked puzzled and a little irritated at the silence.

"No; it's only me," was the answer, in a strained little whisper. Maisie could hardly move her lips.

"H'm!" said Dick, composedly, without moving. "This is a new phenomenon. Darkness I'm getting used to; but I object to hearing voices."

Was he mad, then, as well as blind, that he talked to himself? Maisie's heart beat more wildly, and she breathed in gasps. Dick rose and began to feel his way across the room, touching each table and chair as he passed. Once he caught his foot on a rug, and swore, dropping on his knees to feel what the obstruction might be. Maisie remembered him walking in the Park as though all the earth belonged to him, tramping up and down her studio two months ago, and flying up the gangway of the Channel steamer. The beating of her heart was making her sick, and Dick was coming nearer, guided by the sound of her breathing. She put out a hand mechanically to ward him off or to draw him to herself, she did not know which. It touched his chest, and he stepped back as though he had been shot.

"It's Maisie!" said he, with a dry sob. "What are you doing here?"

"I came—I came—to see you, please."

Dick's lips closed firmly.

"Won't you sit down, then? You see, I've had some bother with my eyes, and——"

"I know. I know. Why didn't you tell me?"

"I couldn't write."

"You might have told Mr. Torpenhow."

"What has he to do with my affairs?"

"He—he brought me from Vitry-sur-Marne. He thought I ought to see you."

"Why, what has happened? Can I do anything for you? No, I can't. I forgot."

"Oh, Dick, I'm so sorry! I've come to tell you, and——Let me take you back to your chair."

"Don't! I'm not a child. You only do that out of pity. I never meant to tell you anything about it. I'm no good now. I'm down and done for. Let me alone!"

He groped back to his chair, his chest labouring as he sat down.

Maisie watched him, and the fear went out of her heart, to be followed by a very bitter shame. He had spoken a truth that had been hidden from the girl through every step of the impetuous flight to London; for he was, indeed, down and done for—masterful no longer but rather a little abject; neither an artist stronger than she, nor a man to be looked up to—only some blind one that sat in a chair and seemed on the point of crying. She was immensely and unfeignedly sorry

for him—more sorry than she had ever been for any one in her life, but not sorry enough to deny his words.

So she stood still and felt ashamed and a little hurt, because she had honestly intended that her journey should end triumphantly; and now she was only filled with pity most startlingly distinct from love.

"Well?" said Dick, his face steadily turned away. "I never meant to worry you any more. What's the matter?"

He was conscious that Maisie was catching her breath, but was as unprepared as herself for the torrent of emotion that followed. She had dropped into a chair and was sobbing with her face hidden in her hands.

"I can't—I can't!" she cried desperately. "Indeed, I can't. It isn't my fault. I'm so sorry. Oh, Dickie, I'm so sorry."

Dick's shoulders straightened again, for the words lashed like a whip.

Still the sobbing continued. It is not good to realise that you have failed in the hour of trial or flinched before the mere possibility of making sacrifices.

"I do despise myself—indeed I do. But I can't. Oh, Dickie, you wouldn't ask me—would you?" wailed Maisie.

She looked up for a minute, and by chance it happened that Dick's eyes fell on hers. The unshaven face was very white and set, and the lips were trying to force themselves into a smile. But it was the worn-out eyes that Maisie feared. Her Dick had gone blind and left in his place some one that she could hardly recognise till he spoke.

"Who is asking you to do anything, Maisie? I told you how it would be. What's the use of worrying? For pity's sake don't cry like that; it isn't worth it."

"You don't know how I hate myself. Oh, Dick, help me—help me!" The passion of tears had grown beyond her control and was beginning to alarm the man. He stumbled forward and put his arm round her, and her head fell on his shoulder.

"Hush, dear, hush! Don't cry. You're quite right, and you've nothing to reproach yourself with—you never had. You're only a little upset by the journey, and I don't suppose you've had any breakfast. What a brute Torp was to bring you over."

"I wanted to come. I did indeed," she protested.

"Very well. And now you've come and seen, and I'm—immensely grateful. When you're better you shall go away and get something to eat. What sort of a passage did you have coming over?"

Maisie was crying more subduedly, for the first time in her life glad that she had something to lean against. Dick patted her on the shoulder tenderly but clumsily, for he was not quite sure where her shoulder might be.

She drew herself out of his arms at last and waited, trembling and most unhappy. He had felt his way to the window to put the width of the room between them, and to quiet a little the tumult in his heart.

"Are you better now?" he said.

"Yes, but—don't you hate me?"

"I hate you? My God! I?"

"Isn't—isn't there anything I could do for you, then? I'll stay here in England to do it, if you like. Perhaps I could come and see you sometimes."

"I think not, dear. It would be kindest not to see me any more, please. I don't want to seem rude, but—don't you think—perhaps you had almost better go now."

He was conscious that he could not bear himself as a man if the strain continued much longer.

"I don't deserve anything else. I'll go, Dick. Oh, I'm so miserable."

"Nonsense. You've nothing to worry about; I'd tell you if you had. Wait a moment, dear. I've got something to give you first. I meant it for you ever since this little trouble began. It's my Melancolia; she was a beauty when I last saw her. You can keep her for me, and if ever you're poor you can sell her. She's worth a few hundreds at any state of the market." He groped among his canvases. "She's framed in black. Is this a black frame that I have my hand on? There she is. What do you think of her?"

He turned a scarred formless muddle of paint towards Maisie, and the eyes strained as though they would catch her wonder and surprise. One thing and one thing only could she do for him.

"Well?"

The voice was fuller and more rounded, because the man knew he was speaking of his best work. Maisie looked at the blur, and a lunatic desire to laugh caught her by the throat. But for Dick's sake—whatever this mad blankness might mean—she must make no sign. Her voice choked with hard-held tears as she answered, still gazing at the wreck—"Oh, Dick, it is good!"

He heard the little hysterical gulp and took it for tribute. "Won't you have it, then? I'll send it over to your house if you will."

"I? Oh yes—thank you. Ha! ha!" If she did not fly at once the laughter that was worse than tears would kill her. She turned and ran, choking and blinded, down the staircases that were empty of life to take refuge in a cab and go to her house across the Parks. There she sat down in the dismantled drawing-room and thought of Dick in his blindness, useless till the end of life, and of herself in her own eyes. Behind the sorrow, the shame, and the humiliation, lay fear of the cold wrath of the red-haired girl when Maisie should return. Maisie had never feared her companion before. Not until she found herself saying, "Well, he never asked me," did she realise her scorn of herself. And that is the end of Maisie.

For Dick was reserved more searching torment. He could not realise at first that Maisie, whom he had ordered to go had left him without a word of farewell. He was savagely angry against Torpenhow, who had brought upon him this humiliation and troubled his miserable peace. Then his dark hour came and he was alone with himself and his desires to get what help he could from the darkness. The queen could do no wrong, but in following the right, so far as it served her work, she had wounded her one subject more than his own brain would let him know.

"It's all I had and I've lost it," he said, as soon as the misery permitted clear thinking. "And Torp will think that he has been so infernally clever that I shan't have the heart to tell him. I must think this out quietly."

"Hullo!" said Torpenhow, entering the studio after Dick had enjoyed two hours of thought. "I'm back. Are you feeling any better?"

"Torp, I don't know what to say. Come here." Dick coughed huskily, wondering, indeed, what he should say, and how to say it temperately.

"What's the need for saying anything? Get up and tramp." Torpenhow was perfectly satisfied.

They walked up and down as of custom, Torpenhow's hand on Dick's shoulder, and Dick buried in his own thoughts.

"How in the world did you find it all out?" said Dick, at last.

"You shouldn't go off your head if you want to keep secrets, Dickie. It was absolutely impertinent on my part; but if you'd seen me rocketing about on a half-trained French troop-horse under a blazing sun you'd have laughed. There will be a charivari in my rooms tonight. Seven other devils——"

"I know—the row in the Southern Soudan. I surprised their councils the other day, and it made me unhappy. Have you fixed your flint to go? Who d'you work for?"

"Haven't signed any contracts yet. I wanted to see how your business would turn out."

"Would you have stayed with me, then, if—things had gone wrong?" He put his question cautiously.

"Don't ask me too much. I'm only a man."

"You've tried to be an angel very successfully."

"Oh ye—es!... Well, do you attend the function tonight? We shall be half screwed before the morning. All the men believe the war's a certainty."

"I don't think I will, old man, if it's all the same to you. I'll stay quiet here."

"And meditate? I don't blame you. You observe a good time if ever a man did."

That night there was a tumult on the stairs. The correspondents poured in from theatre, dinner, and music-hall to Torpenhow's room that they might discuss their plan of campaign in the event of military operations becoming a certainty. Torpenhow, the Keneu, and the Nilghai had bidden all the men they had worked with to the orgy; and Mr. Beeton, the housekeeper, declared that never before in his checkered experience had he seen quite such a fancy lot of gentlemen. They waked the chambers with shoutings and song; and the elder men were quite as bad as the younger. For the chances of war were in front of them, and all knew what those meant.

Sitting in his own room a little perplexed by the noise across the landing, Dick suddenly began to laugh to himself.

"When one comes to think of it the situation is intensely comic. Maisie's quite right—poor little thing. I didn't know she could cry like that before; but now I know what Torp thinks, I'm sure he'd be quite fool enough to stay at home and try to console me—if he knew. Besides, it isn't nice to own that you've been thrown over like a broken chair. I must carry this business through alone—as usual. If there isn't a war, and Torp finds out, I shall look foolish, that's all. If there is a way I mustn't interfere with another man's chances. Business is business, and I want to be alone—I want to be alone. What a row they're making!"

Somebody hammered at the studio door.

"Come out and frolic, Dickie," said the Nilghai.

"I should like to, but I can't. I'm not feeling frolicsome."

"Then, I'll tell the boys and they'll drag you like a badger."

"Please not, old man. On my word, I'd sooner be left alone just now."

"Very good. Can we send anything in to you? Fizz, for instance. Cassavetti is beginning to sing songs of the Sunny South already."

For one minute Dick considered the proposition seriously.

"No, thanks, I've a headache already."

"Virtuous child. That's the effect of emotion on the young. All my congratulations, Dick. I also was concerned in the conspiracy for your welfare."

"Go to the devil—oh, send Binkie in here."

The little dog entered on elastic feet, riotous from having been made much of all the evening. He had helped to sing the choruses; but scarcely inside the studio he realised that this was no place for tail-wagging, and settled himself on Dick's lap till it was bedtime. Then he went to bed with Dick, who counted every hour as it struck, and rose in the morning with a painfully clear head to receive Torpenhow's more formal congratulations and a particular account of the last night's revels.

"You aren't looking very happy for a newly accepted man," said Torpenhow.

"Never mind that—it's my own affair, and I'm all right. Do you really go?"

"Yes. With the old Central Southern as usual. They wired, and I accepted on better terms than before."

"When do you start?"

"The day after tomorrow—for Brindisi."

"Thank God." Dick spoke from the bottom of his heart.

"Well, that's not a pretty way of saying you're glad to get rid of me. But men in your condition are allowed to be selfish."

"I didn't mean that. Will you get a hundred pounds cashed for me before you leave?"

"That's a slender amount for housekeeping, isn't it?"

"Oh, it's only for—marriage expenses."

Torpenhow brought him the money, counted it out in fives and tens, and carefully put it away in the writing table.

"Now I suppose I shall have to listen to his ravings about his girl until I go. Heaven send us patience with a man in love!" he said to himself.

But never a word did Dick say of Maisie or marriage. He hung in the doorway of Torpenhow's room when the latter was packing and asked innumerable questions about the coming campaign, till Torpenhow began to feel annoyed.

"You're a secretive animal, Dickie, and you consume your own smoke, don't you?" he said on the last evening.

"I—I suppose so. By the way, how long do you think this war will last?"

"Days, weeks, or months. One can never tell. It may go on for years."

"I wish I were going."

"Good Heavens! You're the most unaccountable creature! Hasn't it occurred to you that you're going to be married—thanks to me?"

"Of course, yes. I'm going to be married—so I am. Going to be married. I'm awfully grateful to you. Haven't I told you that?"

"You might be going to be hanged by the look of you," said Torpenhow.

And the next day Torpenhow bade him good-bye and left him to the loneliness he had so much desired.

CHAPTER XIV

Yet at the last, ere our spearmen had found him,

Yet at the last, ere a sword-thrust could save,

Yet at the last, with his masters around him,

He of the Faith spoke as master to slave;

Yet at the last, tho' the Kafirs had maimed him,

Broken by bondage and wrecked by the reiver,—

Yet at the last, tho' the darkness had claimed him,

He called upon Allah and died a believer.—Kizzilbashi.

"Beg your pardon, Mr. Heldar, but—but isn't nothin' going to happen?" said Mr. Beeton.

"No!" Dick had just waked to another morning of blank despair and his temper was of the shortest.

"'Tain't my regular business, 'o course, sir; and what I say is, 'Mind your own business and let other people mind theirs;' but just before Mr. Torpenhow went away he give me to understand, like, that you might be moving into a house of your own, so to speak—a sort of house with rooms upstairs and downstairs where you'd be better attended to, though I try to act just by all our tenants. Don't I?"

"Ah! That must have been a mad-house. I shan't trouble you to take me there yet. Get me my breakfast, please, and leave me alone."

"I hope I haven't done anything wrong, sir, but you know I hope that as far as a man can I tries to do the proper thing by all the gentlemen in chambers—and more particular those whose lot is hard—such as you, for instance, Mr. Heldar. You likes soft-roe bloater, don't you? Soft-roe bloaters is scarcer than hard-roe, but what I says is, 'Never mind a little extra trouble so long as you give satisfaction to the tenants.'"

Mr. Beeton withdrew and left Dick to himself. Torpenhow had been long away; there was no more rioting in the chambers, and Dick had settled down to his new life, which he was weak enough to consider nothing better than death.

It is hard to live alone in the dark, confusing the day and night; dropping to sleep through sheer weariness at mid-day, and rising restless in the chill of the dawn. At first Dick, on his awakenings, would grope along the corridors of the chambers till he heard some one snore. Then he would know that the day had not yet come, and return wearily to his bedroom.

Later he learned not to stir till there was a noise and movement in the house and Mr. Beeton advised him to get up. Once dressed—and dressing, now that Torpenhow was away, was a lengthy business, because collars, ties, and the like hid themselves in far corners of the room, and search meant head-beating against chairs and trunks—once dressed, there was nothing whatever to do except to sit still and brood till the three daily meals came. Centuries separated breakfast from lunch and lunch from dinner, and though a man prayed for hundreds of years that his mind might be taken from him, God would never hear. Rather the mind was quickened

and the revolving thoughts ground against each other as millstones grind when there is no corn between; and yet the brain would not wear out and give him rest. It continued to think, at length, with imagery and all manner of reminiscences. It recalled Maisie and past success, reckless travels by land and sea, the glory of doing work and feeling that it was good, and suggested all that might have happened had the eyes only been faithful to their duty. When thinking ceased through sheer weariness, there poured into Dick's soul tide on tide of overwhelming, purposeless fear—dread of starvation always, terror lest the unseen ceiling should crush down upon him, fear of fire in the chambers and a louse's death in red flame, and agonies of fiercer horror that had nothing to do with any fear of death. Then Dick bowed his head, and clutching the arms of his chair fought with his sweating self till the tinkle of plates told him that something to eat was being set before him.

Mr. Beeton would bring the meal when he had time to spare, and Dick learned to hang upon his speech, which dealt with badly fitted gas-plugs, waste-pipes out of repair, little tricks for driving picture-nails into walls, and the sins of the charwoman or the housemaids. In the lack of better things the small gossip of a servants' hall becomes immensely interesting, and the screwing of a washer on a tap an event to be talked over for days.

Once or twice a week, too, Mr. Beeton would take Dick out with him when he went marketing in the morning to haggle with tradesmen over fish, lamp-wicks, mustard, tapioca, and so forth, while Dick rested his weight first on one foot and then on the other and played aimlessly with the tins and string-ball on the counter. Then they would perhaps meet one of Mr. Beeton's friends, and Dick, standing aside a little, would hold his peace till Mr. Beeton was willing to go on again.

The life did not increase his self-respect. He abandoned shaving as a dangerous exercise, and being shaved in a barber's shop meant exposure of his infirmity. He could not see that his clothes were properly brushed, and since he had never taken any care of his personal appearance he became every known variety of sloven. A blind man cannot deal with cleanliness till he has been some months used to the darkness. If he demand attendance and grow angry at the want of it, he must assert himself and stand upright. Then the meanest menial can see that he is blind and, therefore, of no consequence. A wise man will keep his eyes on the floor and sit still. For amusement he may pick coal lump by lump out of the scuttle with the tongs and pile it in a little heap in the fender, keeping count of the lumps, which must all be put back again, one by one and very carefully. He may set himself sums if he cares to work them out; he may talk to himself or to the cat if she chooses to visit him; and if his trade has been that of an artist, he may sketch in the air with his forefinger; but that is too much like drawing a pig with the eyes shut. He may go to his bookshelves and count his books, ranging them in order of their size; or to his wardrobe and count his shirts, laying them in piles of two or three on the bed, as they suffer from frayed cuffs or lost buttons.

Even this entertainment wearies after a time; and all the times are very, very long.

Dick was allowed to sort a tool-chest where Mr. Beeton kept hammers, taps and nuts, lengths of gas-pipes, oil-bottles, and string.

"If I don't have everything just where I know where to look for it, why, then, I can't find anything when I do want it. You've no idea, sir, the amount of little things that these chambers uses up," said Mr. Beeton.

Fumbling at the handle of the door as he went out: "It's hard on you, sir, I do think it's hard on you. Ain't you going to do anything, sir?"

"I'll pay my rent and messing. Isn't that enough?"

"I wasn't doubting for a moment that you couldn't pay your way, sir; but I 'ave often said to my wife, 'It's 'ard on 'im because it isn't as if he was an old man, nor yet a middle-aged one, but quite a young gentleman. That's where it comes so 'ard.'"

"I suppose so," said Dick, absently. This particular nerve through long battering had ceased to feel—much.

"I was thinking," continued Mr. Beeton, still making as if to go, "that you might like to hear my boy Alf read you the papers sometimes of an evening. He do read beautiful, seeing he's only nine."

"I should be very grateful," said Dick. "Only let me make it worth his while."

"We wasn't thinking of that, sir, but of course it's in your own 'ands; but only to 'ear Alf sing 'A Boy's best Friend is 'is Mother!' Ah!"

"I'll hear him sing that too. Let him come this evening with the newspapers."

Alf was not a nice child, being puffed up with many school-board certificates for good conduct, and inordinately proud of his singing. Mr. Beeton remained, beaming, while the child wailed his way through a song of some eight eight-line verses in the usual whine of a young Cockney, and, after compliments, left him to read Dick the foreign telegrams. Ten minutes later Alf returned to his parents rather pale and scared.

"'E said 'e couldn't stand it no more," he explained.

"He never said you read badly, Alf?" Mrs. Beeton spoke.

"No. 'E said I read beautiful. Said 'e never 'eard any one read like that, but 'e said 'e couldn't abide the stuff in the papers."

"P'raps he's lost some money in the Stocks. Were you readin' him about Stocks, Alf?"

"No; it was all about fightin' out there where the soldiers is gone—a great long piece with all the lines close together and very hard words in it. 'E give me 'arf a crown because I read so well. And 'e says the next time there's anything 'e wants read 'e'll send for me."

"That's good hearing, but I do think for all the half-crown—put it into the kicking-donkey money-box, Alf, and let me see you do it—he might have kept you longer. Why, he couldn't have begun to understand how beautiful you read."

"He's best left to hisself—gentlemen always are when they're downhearted," said Mr. Beeton.

Alf's rigorously limited powers of comprehending Torpenhow's special correspondence had waked the devil of unrest in Dick. He could hear, through the boy's nasal chant, the camels grunting in the squares behind the soldiers outside Suakin; could hear the men swearing and chaffing across the cooking pots, and could smell the acrid wood-smoke as it drifted over camp before the wind of the desert.

That night he prayed to God that his mind might be taken from him, offering for proof that he was worthy of this favour the fact that he had not shot himself long ago. That prayer was not answered, and indeed Dick knew in his heart of hearts that only a lingering sense of humour and no special virtue had kept him alive. Suicide, he had persuaded himself, would be a ludicrous insult to the gravity of the situation as well as a weak-kneed confession of fear.

"Just for the fun of the thing," he said to the cat, who had taken Binkie's place in his establishment, "I should like to know how long this is going to last. I can live for a year on the hundred pounds Torp cashed for me. I must have two or three thousand at least in the Bank—twenty or thirty years more provided for, that is to say. Then I fall back on my hundred and twenty a year, which will be more by that time. Let's consider.

"Twenty-five—thirty-five—a man's in his prime then, they say—forty-five—a middle-aged man just entering politics—fifty-five 'died at the comparatively early age of fifty-five,' according to the newspapers. Bah! How these Christians funk death! Sixty-five—we're only getting on in years. Seventy-five is just possible, though. Great hell, cat O! fifty years more of solitary confinement in the dark! You'll die, and Beeton will die, and Torp will die, and Mai—everybody else will die, but I shall be alive and kicking with nothing to do. I'm very sorry for myself. I should like some one else to be sorry for me. Evidently I'm not going mad before I die, but the pain's just as bad as ever. Some day when you're vivisected, cat O! they'll tie you down on a little table and cut you open—but don't be afraid; they'll take precious good care that you don't die. You'll live, and you'll be very sorry then that you weren't sorry for me. Perhaps Torp will come back or... I wish I could go to Torp and the Nilghai, even though I were in their way."

Pussy left the room before the speech was ended, and Alf, as he entered, found Dick addressing the empty hearth-rug.

"There's a letter for you, sir," he said. "Perhaps you'd like me to read it."

"Lend it to me for a minute and I'll tell you."

The outstretched hand shook just a little and the voice was not over-steady. It was within the limits of human possibility that—that was no letter from Maisie. He knew the heft of three closed envelopes only too well. It was a foolish hope that the girl should write to him, for he did not realise that there is a wrong which admits of no reparation though the evildoer may with tears and the heart's best love strive to mend all. It is best to forget that wrong whether it be caused or endured, since it is as remediless as bad work once put forward.

"Read it, then," said Dick, and Alf began intoning according to the rules of the Board School—"'I could have given you love, I could have given you loyalty, such as you never dreamed of. Do you suppose I cared what you were? But you chose to whistle everything down the wind for nothing. My only excuse for you is that you are so young.' That's all," he said, returning the paper to be dropped into the fire.

"What was in the letter?" asked Mrs. Beeton, when Alf returned.

"I don't know. I think it was a circular or a tract about not whistlin' at everything when you're young."

"I must have stepped on something when I was alive and walking about and it has bounced up and hit me. God help it, whatever it is—unless it was all a joke. But I don't know any one who'd take the trouble to play a joke on me—Love and loyalty for nothing. It sounds tempting enough. I wonder whether I have lost anything really?"

Dick considered for a long time but could not remember when or how he had put himself in the way of winning these trifles at a woman's hands.

Still, the letter as touching on matters that he preferred not to think about stung him into a fit of frenzy that lasted for a day and night. When his heart was so full of despair that it would hold no more, body and soul together seemed to be dropping without check through the darkness.

Then came fear of darkness and desperate attempts to reach the light again. But there was no light to be reached. When that agony had left him sweating and breathless, the downward flight would recommence till the gathering torture of it spurred him into another fight as hopeless as the first. Followed some few minutes of sleep in which he dreamed that he saw. Then the procession of events would repeat itself till he was utterly worn out and the brain took up its everlasting consideration of Maisie and might-have-beens.

At the end of everything Mr. Beeton came to his room and volunteered to take him out. "Not marketing this time, but we'll go into the Parks if you like."

"Be damned if I do," quoth Dick. "Keep to the streets and walk up and down. I like to hear the people round me."

This was not altogether true. The blind in the first stages of their infirmity dislike those who can move with a free stride and unlifted arms—but Dick had no earthly desire to go to the Parks. Once and only once since Maisie had shut her door he had gone there under Alf's charge. Alf forgot him and fished for minnows in the Serpentine with some companions. After half an hour's waiting Dick, almost weeping with rage and wrath, caught a passer-by, who introduced him to a friendly policeman, who led him to a four-wheeler opposite the Albert Hall. He never told Mr. Beeton of Alf's forgetfulness, but... this was not the manner in which he was used to walk the Parks aforetime.

"What streets would you like to walk down, then?" said Mr. Beeton, sympathetically. His own ideas of a riotous holiday meant picnicking on the grass of Green Park with his family, and half a dozen paper bags full of food.

"Keep to the river," said Dick, and they kept to the river, and the rush of it was in his ears till they came to Blackfriars Bridge and struck thence on to the Waterloo Road, Mr. Beeton explaining the beauties of the scenery as he went on.

"And walking on the other side of the pavement," said he, "unless I'm much mistaken, is the young woman that used to come to your rooms to be drawed. I never forgets a face and I never remembers a name, except paying tenants, 'o course!"

"Stop her," said Dick. "It's Bessie Broke. Tell her I'd like to speak to her again. Quick, man!"

Mr. Beeton crossed the road under the noses of the omnibuses and arrested Bessie then on her way northward. She recognised him as the man in authority who used to glare at her when she passed up Dick's staircase, and her first impulse was to run.

"Wasn't you Mr. Heldar's model?" said Mr. Beeton, planting himself in front of her. "You was. He's on the other side of the road and he'd like to see you."

"Why?" said Bessie, faintly. She remembered—indeed had never for long forgotten—an affair connected with a newly finished picture.

"Because he has asked me to do so, and because he's most particular blind."

"Drunk?"

"No. 'Orspital blind. He can't see. That's him over there."

Dick was leaning against the parapet of the bridge as Mr. Beeton pointed him out—a stub-bearded, bowed creature wearing a dirty magenta-coloured neckcloth outside an unbrushed coat. There was nothing to fear from such an one. Even if he chased her, Bessie thought, he

could not follow far. She crossed over, and Dick's face lighted up. It was long since a woman of any kind had taken the trouble to speak to him.

"I hope you're well, Mr. Heldar?" said Bessie, a little puzzled. Mr. Beeton stood by with the air of an ambassador and breathed responsibly.

"I'm very well indeed, and, by Jove! I'm glad to see—hear you, I mean, Bess. You never thought it worth while to turn up and see us again after you got your money. I don't know why you should. Are you going anywhere in particular just now?"

"I was going for a walk," said Bessie.

"Not the old business?" Dick spoke under his breath.

"Lor, no! I paid my premium"—Bessie was very proud of that word—"for a barmaid, sleeping in, and I'm at the bar now quite respectable. Indeed I am."

Mr. Beeton had no special reason to believe in the loftiness of human nature. Therefore he dissolved himself like a mist and returned to his gas-plugs without a word of apology. Bessie watched the flight with a certain uneasiness; but so long as Dick appeared to be ignorant of the harm that had been done to him...

"It's hard work pulling the beer-handles," she went on, "and they've got one of them penny-in-the-slot cash-machines, so if you get wrong by a penny at the end of the day—but then I don't believe the machinery is right. Do you?"

"I've only seen it work. Mr. Beeton."

"He's gone.

"I'm afraid I must ask you to help me home, then. I'll make it worth your while. You see." The sightless eyes turned towards her and Bessie saw.

"It isn't taking you out of your way?" he said hesitatingly. "I can ask a policeman if it is."

"Not at all. I come on at seven and I'm off at four. That's easy hours."

"Good God!—but I'm on all the time. I wish I had some work to do too. Let's go home, Bess."

He turned and cannoned into a man on the sidewalk, recoiling with an oath. Bessie took his arm and said nothing—as she had said nothing when he had ordered her to turn her face a little more to the light. They walked for some time in silence, the girl steering him deftly through the crowd.

"And where's—where's Mr. Torpenhow?" she inquired at last.

"He has gone away to the desert."

"Where's that?"

Dick pointed to the right. "East—out of the mouth of the river," said he.

"Then west, then south, and then east again, all along the under-side of Europe. Then south again, God knows how far." The explanation did not enlighten Bessie in the least, but she held her tongue and looked to Dick's patch till they came to the chambers.

"We'll have tea and muffins," he said joyously. "I can't tell you, Bessie, how glad I am to find you again. What made you go away so suddenly?"

"I didn't think you'd want me any more," she said, emboldened by his ignorance.

"I didn't, as a matter of fact—but afterwards—At any rate I'm glad you've come. You know the stairs."

So Bessie led him home to his own place—there was no one to hinder—and shut the door of the studio.

"What a mess!" was her first word. "All these things haven't been looked after for months and months."

"No, only weeks, Bess. You can't expect them to care."

"I don't know what you expect them to do. They ought to know what you've paid them for. The dust's just awful. It's all over the easel."

"I don't use it much now."

"All over the pictures and the floor, and all over your coat. I'd like to speak to them housemaids."

"Ring for tea, then." Dick felt his way to the one chair he used by custom.

Bessie saw the action and, as far as in her lay, was touched. But there remained always a keen sense of new-found superiority, and it was in her voice when she spoke.

"How long have you been like this?" she said wrathfully, as though the blindness were some fault of the housemaids.

"How?"

"As you are."

"The day after you went away with the check, almost as soon as my picture was finished; I hardly saw her alive."

"Then they've been cheating you ever since, that's all. I know their nice little ways."

A woman may love one man and despise another, but on general feminine principles she will do her best to save the man she despises from being defrauded. Her loved one can look to himself, but the other man, being obviously an idiot, needs protection.

"I don't think Mr. Beeton cheats much," said Dick. Bessie was flouncing up and down the room, and he was conscious of a keen sense of enjoyment as he heard the swish of her skirts and the light step between.

"Tea and muffins," she said shortly, when the ring at the bell was answered; "two teaspoonfuls and one over for the pot. I don't want the old teapot that was here when I used to come. It don't draw. Get another."

The housemaid went away scandalised, and Dick chuckled. Then he began to cough as Bessie banged up and down the studio disturbing the dust.

"What are you trying to do?"

"Put things straight. This is like unfurnished lodgings. How could you let it go so?"

"How could I help it? Dust away."

She dusted furiously, and in the midst of all the pother entered Mrs. Beeton. Her husband on his return had explained the situation, winding up with the peculiarly felicitous proverb, "Do unto others as you would be done by." She had descended to put into her place the person who demanded muffins and an uncracked teapot as though she had a right to both.

"Muffins ready yet?" said Bess, still dusting. She was no longer a drab of the streets but a young lady who, thanks to Dick's check, had paid her premium and was entitled to pull beer-handles with the best. Being neatly dressed in black she did not hesitate to face Mrs. Beeton, and there passed between the two women certain regards that Dick would have appreciated. The situation adjusted itself by eye. Bessie had won, and Mrs. Beeton returned to cook muffins and make scathing remarks about models, hussies, trollops, and the like, to her husband.

"There's nothing to be got of interfering with him, Liza," he said. "Alf, you go along into the street to play. When he isn't crossed he's as kindly as kind, but when he's crossed he's the devil and all. We took too many little things out of his rooms since he was blind to be that particular about what he does. They ain't no objects to a blind man, of course, but if it was to come into court we'd get the sack. Yes, I did introduce him to that girl because I'm a feelin' man myself."

"Much too feelin'!" Mrs. Beeton slapped the muffins into the dish, and thought of comely housemaids long since dismissed on suspicion.

"I ain't ashamed of it, and it isn't for us to judge him hard so long as he pays quiet and regular as he do. I know how to manage young gentlemen, you know how to cook for them, and what I says is, let each stick to his own business and then there won't be any trouble. Take them muffins down, Liza, and be sure you have no words with that young woman. His lot is cruel hard, and if he's crossed he do swear worse than any one I've ever served."

"That's a little better," said Bessie, sitting down to the tea. "You needn't wait, thank you, Mrs. Beeton."

"I had no intention of doing such, I do assure you."

Bessie made no answer whatever. This, she knew, was the way in which real ladies routed their foes, and when one is a barmaid at a first-class public-house one may become a real lady at ten minutes' notice.

Her eyes fell on Dick opposite her and she was both shocked and displeased. There were droppings of food all down the front of his coat; the mouth under the ragged ill-grown beard drooped sullenly; the forehead was lined and contracted; and on the lean temples the hair was a dusty indeterminate colour that might or might not have been called gray. The utter misery and self-abandonment of the man appealed to her, and at the bottom of her heart lay the wicked feeling that he was humbled and brought low who had once humbled her.

"Oh! it is good to hear you moving about," said Dick, rubbing his hands. "Tell us all about your bar successes, Bessie, and the way you live now."

"Never mind that. I'm quite respectable, as you'd see by looking at me. You don't seem to live too well. What made you go blind that sudden? Why isn't there any one to look after you?"

Dick was too thankful for the sound of her voice to resent the tone of it.

"I was cut across the head a long time ago, and that ruined my eyes. I don't suppose anybody thinks it worth while to look after me any more. Why should they?—and Mr. Beeton really does everything I want."

"Don't you know any gentlemen and ladies, then, while you was—well?"

"A few, but I don't care to have them looking at me."

"I suppose that's why you've growed a beard. Take it off, it don't become you."

"Good gracious, child, do you imagine that I think of what becomes of me these days?"

"You ought. Get that taken off before I come here again. I suppose I can come, can't I?"

"I'd be only too grateful if you did. I don't think I treated you very well in the old days. I used to make you angry."

"Very angry, you did."

"I'm sorry for it, then. Come and see me when you can and as often as you can. God knows, there isn't a soul in the world to take that trouble except you and Mr. Beeton."

"A lot of trouble he's taking and she too." This with a toss of the head.

"They've let you do anyhow and they haven't done anything for you. I've only to look and see that much. I'll come, and I'll be glad to come, but you must go and be shaved, and you must get some other clothes—those ones aren't fit to be seen."

"I have heaps somewhere," he said helplessly.

"I know you have. Tell Mr. Beeton to give you a new suit and I'll brush it and keep it clean. You may be as blind as a barn-door, Mr. Heldar, but it doesn't excuse you looking like a sweep."

"Do I look like a sweep, then?"

"Oh, I'm sorry for you. I'm that sorry for you!" she cried impulsively, and took Dick's hands. Mechanically, he lowered his head as if to kiss—she was the only woman who had taken pity on him, and he was not too proud for a little pity now. She stood up to go.

"Nothing 'o that kind till you look more like a gentleman. It's quite easy when you get shaved, and some clothes."

He could hear her drawing on her gloves and rose to say good-bye. She passed behind him, kissed him audaciously on the back of the neck, and ran away as swiftly as on the day when she had destroyed the Melancolia.

"To think of me kissing Mr. Heldar," she said to herself, "after all he's done to me and all! Well, I'm sorry for him, and if he was shaved he wouldn't be so bad to look at, but... Oh them Beetons, how shameful they've treated him! I know Beeton's wearing his shirt on his back today just as well as if I'd aired it. Tomorrow, I'll see... I wonder if he has much of his own. It might be worth more than the bar—I wouldn't have to do any work—and just as respectable as if no one knew."

Dick was not grateful to Bessie for her parting gift. He was acutely conscious of it in the nape of his neck throughout the night, but it seemed, among very many other things, to enforce the wisdom of getting shaved.

He was shaved accordingly in the morning, and felt the better for it. A fresh suit of clothes, white linen, and the knowledge that some one in the world said that she took an interest in his personal appearance made him carry himself almost upright; for the brain was relieved for a while from thinking of Maisie, who, under other circumstances, might have given that kiss and a million others.

"Let us consider," said he, after lunch. "The girl can't care, and it's a toss-up whether she comes again or not, but if money can buy her to look after me she shall be bought. Nobody else in the world would take the trouble, and I can make it worth her while. She's a child of the gutter holding brevet rank as a barmaid; so she shall have everything she wants if she'll only come and talk and look after me." He rubbed his newly shorn chin and began to perplex himself with the thought of her not coming. "I suppose I did look rather a sweep," he went on. "I had no reason to look otherwise. I knew things dropped on my clothes, but it didn't matter. It would be cruel if she didn't come. She must. Maisie came once, and that was enough for her. She was quite right. She had something to work for. This creature has only beer-handles to pull, unless she has deluded some young man into keeping company with her. Fancy being cheated for the sake of a counter-jumper! We're falling pretty low."

Something cried aloud within him:—This will hurt more than anything that has gone before. It will recall and remind and suggest and tantalise, and in the end drive you mad.

"I know it, I know it!" Dick cried, clenching his hands despairingly; "but, good heavens! is a poor blind beggar never to get anything out of his life except three meals a day and a greasy waistcoat? I wish she'd come."

Early in the afternoon time she came, because there was no young man in her life just then, and she thought of material advantages which would allow her to be idle for the rest of her days.

"I shouldn't have known you," she said approvingly. "You look as you used to look—a gentleman that was proud of himself."

"Don't you think I deserve another kiss, then?" said Dick, flushing a little.

"Maybe—but you won't get it yet. Sit down and let's see what I can do for you. I'm certain sure Mr. Beeton cheats you, now that you can't go through the housekeeping books every month. Isn't that true?"

"You'd better come and housekeep for me then, Bessie."

"Couldn't do it in these chambers—you know that as well as I do."

"I know, but we might go somewhere else, if you thought it worth your while."

"I'd try to look after you, anyhow; but I shouldn't care to have to work for both of us." This was tentative.

Dick laughed.

"Do you remember where I used to keep my bank-book?" said he. "Torp took it to be balanced just before he went away. Look and see."

"It was generally under the tobacco-jar. Ah!"

"Well?"

"Oh! Four thousand two hundred and ten pounds nine shillings and a penny! Oh my!"

"You can have the penny. That's not bad for one year's work. Is that and a hundred and twenty pounds a year good enough?"

The idleness and the pretty clothes were almost within her reach now, but she must, by being housewifely, show that she deserved them.

"Yes; but you'd have to move, and if we took an inventory, I think we'd find that Mr. Beeton has been prigging little things out of the rooms here and there. They don't look as full as they used."

"Never mind, we'll let him have them. The only thing I'm particularly anxious to take away is that picture I used you for—when you used to swear at me. We'll pull out of this place, Bess, and get away as far as ever we can."

"Oh yes," she said uneasily.

"I don't know where I can go to get away from myself, but I'll try, and you shall have all the pretty frocks that you care for. You'll like that. Give me that kiss now, Bess. Ye gods! it's good to put one's arm round a woman's waist again."

Then came the fulfilment of the prophecy within the brain. If his arm were thus round Maisie's waist and a kiss had just been given and taken between them,—why then... He pressed the girl more closely to himself because the pain whipped him. She was wondering how to explain a little accident to the Melancolia. At any rate, if this man really desired the solace of her company—and certainly he would relapse into his original slough if she withdrew it—he would not be more than just a little vexed.

It would be delightful at least to see what would happen, and by her teachings it was good for a man to stand in certain awe of his companion.

She laughed nervously, and slipped out of his reach.

"I shouldn't worrit about that picture if I was you," she began, in the hope of turning his attention.

"It's at the back of all my canvases somewhere. Find it, Bess; you know it as well as I do."

"I know—but—"

"But what? You've wit enough to manage the sale of it to a dealer. Women haggle much better than men. It might be a matter of eight or nine hundred pounds to—to us. I simply didn't like to think about it for a long time. It was mixed up with my life so.—But we'll cover up our tracks and get rid of everything, eh? Make a fresh start from the beginning, Bess."

Then she began to repent very much indeed, because she knew the value of money. Still, it was probable that the blind man was overestimating the value of his work. Gentlemen, she knew, were absurdly particular about their things. She giggled as a nervous housemaid giggles when she tries to explain the breakage of a pipe.

"I'm very sorry, but you remember I was—I was angry with you before Mr. Torpenhow went away?"

"You were very angry, child; and on my word I think you had some right to be."

"Then I—but aren't you sure Mr. Torpenhow didn't tell you?"

"Tell me what? Good gracious, what are you making such a fuss about when you might just as well be giving me another kiss?"

He was beginning to learn, not for the first time in his experience, that kissing is a cumulative poison. The more you get of it, the more you want.

Bessie gave the kiss promptly, whispering, as she did so, "I was so angry I rubbed out that picture with the turpentine. You aren't angry, are you?"

"What? Say that again." The man's hand had closed on her wrist.

"I rubbed it out with turps and the knife," faltered Bessie. "I thought you'd only have to do it over again. You did do it over again, didn't you? Oh, let go of my wrist; you're hurting me."

"Isn't there anything left of the thing?"

"N'nothing that looks like anything. I'm sorry—I didn't know you'd take on about it; I only meant to do it in fun. You aren't going to hit me?"

"Hit you! No! Let's think."

He did not relax his hold upon her wrist but stood staring at the carpet.

Then he shook his head as a young steer shakes it when the lash of the stock-whip cross his nose warns him back to the path on to the shambles that he would escape. For weeks he had forced himself not to think of the Melancolia, because she was a part of his dead life. With Bessie's return and certain new prospects that had developed themselves, the Melancolia—lovelier in his imagination than she had ever been on canvas—reappeared. By her aid he might have procured more money wherewith to amuse Bess and to forget Maisie, as well as another taste of an almost forgotten success. Now, thanks to a vicious little housemaid's folly, there was nothing to look for—not even the hope that he might some day take an abiding interest in the housemaid. Worst of all, he had been made to appear ridiculous in Maisie's eyes. A woman will forgive the man who has ruined her life's work so long as he gives her love; a man may forgive those who ruin the love of his life, but he will never forgive the destruction of his work.

"Tck—tck—tck," said Dick between his teeth, and then laughed softly. "It's an omen, Bessie, and—a good many things considered, it serves me right for doing what I have done. By Jove! that accounts for Maisie's running away. She must have thought me perfectly mad—small blame to her! The whole picture ruined, isn't it so? What made you do it?"

"Because I was that angry. I'm not angry now—I'm awful sorry."

"I wonder.—It doesn't matter, anyhow. I'm to blame for making the mistake."

"What mistake?"

"Something you wouldn't understand, dear. Great heavens! to think that a little piece of dirt like you could throw me out of stride!" Dick was talking to himself as Bessie tried to shake off his grip on her wrist.

"I ain't a piece of dirt, and you shouldn't call me so! I did it 'cause I hated you, and I'm only sorry now 'cause you're 'cause you're——"

"Exactly—because I'm blind. There's noting like tact in little things."

Bessie began to sob. She did not like being shackled against her will; she was afraid of the blind face and the look upon it, and was sorry too that her great revenge had only made Dick laugh.

"Don't cry," he said, and took her into his arms. "You only did what you thought right."

"I—I ain't a little piece of dirt, and if you say that I'll never come to you again."

"You don't know what you've done to me. I'm not angry—indeed, I'm not. Be quiet for a minute."

Bessie remained in his arms shrinking. Dick's first thought was connected with Maisie, and it hurt him as white-hot iron hurts an open sore.

Not for nothing is a man permitted to ally himself to the wrong woman.

The first pang—the first sense of things lost is but the prelude to the play, for the very just Providence who delights in causing pain has decreed that the agony shall return, and that in the midst of keenest pleasure.

They know this pain equally who have forsaken or been forsaken by the love of their life, and in their new wives' arms are compelled to realise it.

It is better to remain alone and suffer only the misery of being alone, so long as it is possible to find distraction in daily work. When that resource goes the man is to be pitied and left alone.

These things and some others Dick considered while he was holding Bessie to his heart.

"Though you mayn't know it," he said, raising his head, "the Lord is a just and a terrible God, Bess; with a very strong sense of humour. It serves me right—how it serves me right! Torp could understand it if he were here; he must have suffered something at your hands, child, but only for a minute or so. I saved him. Set that to my credit, some one."

"Let me go," said Bess, her face darkening. "Let me go."

"All in good time. Did you ever attend Sunday school?"

"Never. Let me go, I tell you; you're making fun of me."

"Indeed, I'm not. I'm making fun of myself.... Thus. 'He saved others, himself he cannot save.' It isn't exactly a school-board text." He released her wrist, but since he was between her and the door, she could not escape. "What an enormous amount of mischief one little woman can do!"

"I'm sorry; I'm awful sorry about the picture."

"I'm not. I'm grateful to you for spoiling it.... What were we talking about before you mentioned the thing?"

"About getting away—and money. Me and you going away."

"Of course. We will get away—that is to say, I will."

"And me?"

"You shall have fifty whole pounds for spoiling a picture."

"Then you won't——?"

"I'm afraid not, dear. Think of fifty pounds for pretty things all to yourself."

"You said you couldn't do anything without me."

"That was true a little while ago. I'm better now, thank you. Get me my hat."

"S'pose I don't?"

"Beeton will, and you'll lose fifty pounds. That's all. Get it."

Bessie cursed under her breath. She had pitied the man sincerely, had kissed him with almost equal sincerity, for he was not unhandsome; it pleased her to be in a way and for a time his protector, and above all there were four thousand pounds to be handled by some one. Now through a slip of the tongue and a little feminine desire to give a little, not too much, pain she had lost the money, the blessed idleness and the pretty things, the companionship, and the chance of looking outwardly as respectable as a real lady.

"Now fill me a pipe. Tobacco doesn't taste, but it doesn't matter, and I'll think things out. What's the day of the week, Bess?"

"Tuesday."

"Then Thursday's mail-day. What a fool—what a blind fool I have been! Twenty-two pounds covers my passage home again. Allow ten for additional expenses. We must put up at Madam Binat's for old time's sake. Thirty-two pounds altogether. Add a hundred for the cost of the last trip—Gad, won't Torp stare to see me!—a hundred and thirty-two leaves seventy-eight for baksheesh—I shall need it—and to play with. What are you crying for, Bess? It wasn't your fault, child; it was mine altogether. Oh, you funny little opossum, mop your eyes and take me out! I want the pass-book and the check-book. Stop a minute. Four thousand pounds at four per cent—that's safe interest—means a hundred and sixty pounds a year; one hundred and twenty pounds a year—also safe—is two eighty, and two hundred and eighty pounds added to three hundred a year means gilded luxury for a single woman. Bess, we'll go to the bank."

Richer by two hundred and ten pounds stored in his money-belt, Dick caused Bessie, now thoroughly bewildered, to hurry from the bank to the P. and O. offices, where he explained things tersely.

"Port Said, single first; cabin as close to the baggage-hatch as possible. What ship's going?"

"The Colgong," said the clerk.

"She's a wet little hooker. Is it Tilbury and a tender, or Galleons and the docks?"

"Galleons. Twelve-forty, Thursday."

"Thanks. Change, please. I can't see very well—will you count it into my hand?"

"If they all took their passages like that instead of talking about their trunks, life would be worth something," said the clerk to his neighbour, who was trying to explain to a harassed mother of many that condensed milk is just as good for babes at sea as daily dairy. Being nineteen and unmarried, he spoke with conviction.

"We are now," quoth Dick, as they returned to the studio, patting the place where his money-

belt covered ticket and money, "beyond the reach of man, or devil, or woman—which is much more important. I've had three little affairs to carry through before Thursday, but I needn't ask you to help, Bess. Come here on Thursday morning at nine. We'll breakfast, and you shall take me down to Galleons Station."

"What are you going to do?"

"Going away, of course. What should I stay for?"

"But you can't look after yourself?"

"I can do anything. I didn't realise it before, but I can. I've done a great deal already. Resolution shall be treated to one kiss if Bessie doesn't object." Strangely enough, Bessie objected and Dick laughed. "I suppose you're right. Well, come at nine the day after tomorrow and you'll get your money."

"Shall I sure?"

"I don't bilk, and you won't know whether I do or not unless you come. Oh, but it's long and long to wait! Good-bye, Bessie,—send Beeton here as you go out."

The housekeeper came.

"What are all the fittings of my rooms worth?" said Dick, imperiously.

"'Tisn't for me to say, sir. Some things is very pretty and some is wore out dreadful."

"I'm insured for two hundred and seventy."

"Insurance policies is no criterion, though I don't say——"

"Oh, damn your longwindedness! You've made your pickings out of me and the other tenants. Why, you talked of retiring and buying a public-house the other day. Give a straight answer to a straight question."

"Fifty," said Mr. Beeton, without a moment's hesitation.

"Double it; or I'll break up half my sticks and burn the rest."

He felt his way to a bookstand that supported a pile of sketch-books, and wrenched out one of the mahogany pillars.

"That's sinful, sir," said the housekeeper, alarmed.

"It's my own. One hundred or——"

"One hundred it is. It'll cost me three and six to get that there pilaster mended."

"I thought so. What an out and out swindler you must have been to spring that price at once!"

"I hope I've done nothing to dissatisfy any of the tenants, least of all you, sir."

"Never mind that. Get me the money tomorrow, and see that all my clothes are packed in the little brown bullock-trunk. I'm going."

"But the quarter's notice?"

"I'll pay forfeit. Look after the packing and leave me alone."

Mr. Beeton discussed this new departure with his wife, who decided that Bessie was at the bottom of it all. Her husband took a more charitable view.

"It's very sudden—but then he was always sudden in his ways. Listen to him now!"

There was a sound of chanting from Dick's room.

"We'll never come back any more, boys, We'll never come back no more; We'll go to the deuce on any excuse, And never come back no more! Oh say we're afloat or ashore, boys, Oh say we're afloat or ashore; But we'll never come back any more, boys, We'll never come back no more!"

"Mr. Beeton! Mr. Beeton! Where the deuce is my pistol?"

"Quick, he's going to shoot himself 'avin' gone mad!" said Mrs. Beeton.

Mr. Beeton addressed Dick soothingly, but it was some time before the latter, threshing up and down his bedroom, could realise the intention of the promises to 'find everything tomorrow, sir.'

"Oh, you copper-nosed old fool—you impotent Academician!" he shouted at last. "Do you suppose I want to shoot myself? Take the pistol in your silly shaking hand then. If you touch it, it will go off, because it's loaded. It's among my campaign-kit somewhere—in the parcel at the bottom of the trunk."

Long ago Dick had carefully possessed himself of a forty-pound weight field-equipment constructed by the knowledge of his own experience. It was this put-away treasure that he was trying to find and rehandle. Mr. Beeton whipped the revolver out of its place on the top of the package, and Dick drove his hand among the khaki coat and breeches, the blue cloth leg-bands, and the heavy flannel shirts doubled over a pair of swan-neck spurs. Under these and the water-bottle lay a sketch-book and a pigskin case of stationery.

"These we don't want; you can have them, Mr. Beeton. Everything else I'll keep. Pack 'em on the top right-hand side of my trunk. When you've done that come into the studio with your wife. I want you both. Wait a minute; get me a pen and a sheet of notepaper."

It is not an easy thing to write when you cannot see, and Dick had particular reasons for wishing that his work should be clear. So he began, following his right hand with his left: "The badness of this writing is because I am blind and cannot see my pen." H'mph!—even a lawyer can't mistake that. It must be signed, I suppose, but it needn't be witnessed. Now an inch lower—why did I never learn to use a type-writer?—"This is the last will and testament of me, Richard Heldar. I am in sound bodily and mental health, and there is no previous will to revoke."—That's all right. Damn the pen! Whereabouts on the paper was I?—" "I leave everything that I possess in the world, including four thousand pounds, and two thousand seven hundred and twenty eight pounds held for me—oh, I can't get this straight." He tore off half the sheet and began again with the caution about the handwriting. Then: "I leave all the money I possess in the world to"—here followed Maisie's name, and the names of the two banks that held the money.

"It mayn't be quite regular, but no one has a shadow of a right to dispute it, and I've given Maisie's address. Come in, Mr. Beeton. This is my signature; I want you and your wife to witness it. Thanks. Tomorrow you must take me to the landlord and I'll pay forfeit for leaving

without notice, and I'll lodge this paper with him in case anything happens while I'm away. Now we're going to light up the studio stove. Stay with me, and give me my papers as I want 'em."

No one knows until he has tried how fine a blaze a year's accumulation of bills, letters, and dockets can make. Dick stuffed into the stove every document in the studio—saving only three unopened letters; destroyed sketch-books, rough note-books, new and half-finished canvases alike.

"What a lot of rubbish a tenant gets about him if he stays long enough in one place, to be sure," said Mr. Beeton, at last.

"He does. Is there anything more left?" Dick felt round the walls.

"Not a thing, and the stove's nigh red-hot."

"Excellent, and you've lost about a thousand pounds' worth of sketches. Ho! ho! Quite a thousand pounds' worth, if I can remember what I used to be."

"Yes, sir," politely. Mr. Beeton was quite sure that Dick had gone mad, otherwise he would have never parted with his excellent furniture for a song. The canvas things took up storage room and were much better out of the way.

There remained only to leave the little will in safe hands: that could not be accomplished til tomorrow. Dick groped about the floor picking up the last pieces of paper, assured himself again and again that there remained no written word or sign of his past life in drawer or desk, and sat down before the stove till the fire died out and the contracting iron cracked in the silence of the night.

CHAPTER XV

With a heart of furious fancies,

Whereof I am commander;

With a burning spear and a horse of air,

To the wilderness I wander.

With a knight of ghosts and shadows

I summoned am to tourney—

Ten leagues beyond the wide world's end,

Methinks it is no journey.

　　—Tom o' Bedlam's Song

"Goodbye, Bess; I promised you fifty. Here's a hundred—all that I got for my furniture from Beeton. That will keep you in pretty frocks for some time. You've been a good little girl, all things considered, but you've given me and Torpenhow a fair amount of trouble."

"Give Mr. Torpenhow my love if you see him, won't you?"

"Of course I will, dear. Now take me up the gang-plank and into the cabin. Once aboard the lugger and the maid is—and I am free, I mean."

"Who'll look after you on this ship?"

"The head-steward, if there's any use in money. The doctor when we come to Port Said, if I know anything of P. and O. doctors. After that, the Lord will provide, as He used to do."

Bess found Dick his cabin in the wild turmoil of a ship full of leavetakers and weeping relatives. Then he kissed her, and laid himself down in his bunk until the decks should be clear. He who had taken so long to move about his own darkened rooms well understood the geography of a ship, and the necessity of seeing to his own comforts was as wine to him.

Before the screw began to thrash the ship along the Docks he had been introduced to the head-steward, had royally tipped him, secured a good place at table, opened out his baggage, and settled himself down with joy in the cabin. It was scarcely necessary to feel his way as he moved about, for he knew everything so well. Then God was very kind: a deep sleep of weariness came upon him just as he would have thought of Maisie, and he slept till the steamer had cleared the mouth of the Thames and was lifting to the pulse of the Channel.

The rattle of the engines, the reek of oil and paint, and a very familiar sound in the next cabin roused him to his new inheritance.

"Oh, it's good to be alive again!" He yawned, stretched himself vigorously, and went on deck to be told that they were almost abreast of the lights of Brighton. This is no more open water than Trafalgar Square is a common; the free levels begin at Ushant; but none the less Dick could

feel the healing of the sea at work upon him already. A boisterous little cross-swell swung the steamer disrespectfully by the nose; and one wave breaking far aft spattered the quarterdeck and the pile of new deck-chairs. He heard the foam fall with the clash of broken glass, was stung in the face by a cupful, and sniffing luxuriously, felt his way to the smoking-room by the wheel. There a strong breeze found him, blew his cap off and left him bareheaded in the doorway, and the smoking-room steward, understanding that he was a voyager of experience, said that the weather would be stiff in the chops off the Channel and more than half a gale in the Bay. These things fell as they were foretold, and Dick enjoyed himself to the utmost. It is allowable and even necessary at sea to lay firm hold upon tables, stanchions, and ropes in moving from place to place. On land the man who feels with his hands is patently blind. At sea even a blind man who is not sea-sick can jest with the doctor over the weakness of his fellows. Dick told the doctor many tales—and these are coin of more value than silver if properly handled—smoked with him till unholy hours of the night, and so won his short-lived regard that he promised Dick a few hours of his time when they came to Port Said.

And the sea roared or was still as the winds blew, and the engines sang their song day and night, and the sun grew stronger day by day, and Tom the Lascar barber shaved Dick of a morning under the opened hatch-grating where the cool winds blew, and the awnings were spread and the passengers made merry, and at last they came to Port Said.

"Take me," said Dick, to the doctor, "to Madame Binat's—if you know where that is."

"Whew!" said the doctor, "I do. There's not much to choose between 'em; but I suppose you're aware that that's one of the worst houses in the place. They'll rob you to begin with, and knife you later."

"Not they. Take me there, and I can look after myself."

So he was brought to Madame Binat's and filled his nostrils with the well-remembered smell of the East, that runs without a change from the Canal head to Hong-Kong, and his mouth with the villainous Lingua Franca of the Levant. The heat smote him between the shoulder-blades with the buffet of an old friend, his feet slipped on the sand, and his coat-sleeve was warm as new-baked bread when he lifted it to his nose.

Madame Binat smiled with the smile that knows no astonishment when Dick entered the drinking-shop which was one source of her gains. But for a little accident of complete darkness he could hardly realise that he had ever quitted the old life that hummed in his ears. Somebody opened a bottle of peculiarly strong Schiedam. The smell reminded Dick of Monsieur Binat, who, by the way, had spoken of art and degradation.

Binat was dead; Madame said as much when the doctor departed, scandalised, so far as a ship's doctor can be, at the warmth of Dick's reception. Dick was delighted at it. "They remember me here after a year. They have forgotten me across the water by this time. Madame, I want a long talk with you when you're at liberty. It is good to be back again."

In the evening she set an iron-topped cafe-table out on the sands, and Dick and she sat by it, while the house behind them filled with riot, merriment, oaths, and threats. The stars came out and the lights of the shipping in the harbour twinkled by the head of the Canal.

"Yes. The war is good for trade, my friend; but what dost thou do here? We have not forgotten thee."

"I was over there in England and I went blind."

"But there was the glory first. We heard of it here, even here—I and Binat; and thou hast used the head of Yellow 'Tina—she is still alive—so often and so well that 'Tina laughed when the papers arrived by the mail-boats. It was always something that we here could recognise in the paintings. And then there was always the glory and the money for thee."

"I am not poor—I shall pay you well."

"Not to me. Thou hast paid for everything." Under her breath, "Mon Dieu, to be blind and so young! What horror!"

Dick could not see her face with the pity on it, or his own with the discoloured hair at the temples. He did not feel the need of pity; he was too anxious to get to the front once more, and explained his desire.

"And where? The Canal is full of the English ships. Sometimes they fire as they used to do when the war was here—ten years ago. Beyond Cairo there is fighting, but how canst thou go there without a correspondent's passport? And in the desert there is always fighting, but that is impossible also," said she.

"I must go to Suakin." He knew, thanks to Alf's readings, that Torpenhow was at work with the column that was protecting the construction of the Suakin-Berber line. P. and O. steamers do not touch at that port, and, besides, Madame Binat knew everybody whose help or advice was worth anything. They were not respectable folk, but they could cause things to be accomplished, which is much more important when there is work toward.

"But at Suakin they are always fighting. That desert breeds men always—and always more men. And they are so bold! Why to Suakin?"

"My friend is there.

"Thy friend! Chtt! Thy friend is death, then."

Madame Binat dropped a fat arm on the table-top, filled Dick's glass anew, and looked at him closely under the stars. There was no need that he should bow his head in assent and say—"No. He is a man, but—if it should arrive... blamest thou?"

"I blame?" she laughed shrilly. "Who am I that I should blame any one—except those who try to cheat me over their consommations. But it is very terrible."

"I must go to Suakin. Think for me. A great deal has changed within the year, and the men I knew are not here. The Egyptian lighthouse steamer goes down the Canal to Suakin—and the post-boats—But even then——"

"Do not think any longer. I know, and it is for me to think. Thou shalt go—thou shalt go and see thy friend. Be wise. Sit here until the house is a little quiet—I must attend to my guests—and afterwards go to bed. Thou shalt go, in truth, thou shalt go."

"Tomorrow?"

"As soon as may be." She was talking as though he were a child.

He sat at the table listening to the voices in the harbour and the streets, and wondering how soon the end would come, till Madame Binat carried him off to bed and ordered him to sleep. The house shouted and sang and danced and revelled, Madame Binat moving through it with one eye on the liquor payments and the girls and the other on Dick's interests. To this latter end she

smiled upon scowling and furtive Turkish officers of fellaheen regiments, and was more than kind to camel agents of no nationality whatever.

In the early morning, being then appropriately dressed in a flaming red silk ball-dress, with a front of tarnished gold embroidery and a necklace of plate-glass diamonds, she made chocolate and carried it in to Dick.

"It is only I, and I am of discreet age, eh? Drink and eat the roll too. Thus in France mothers bring their sons, when those behave wisely, the morning chocolate." She sat down on the side of the bed whispering:—"It is all arranged. Thou wilt go by the lighthouse boat. That is a bribe of ten pounds English. The captain is never paid by the Government. The boat comes to Suakin in four days. There will go with thee George, a Greek muleteer. Another bribe of ten pounds. I will pay; they must not know of thy money. George will go with thee as far as he goes with his mules. Then he comes back to me, for his well-beloved is here, and if I do not receive a telegram from Suakin saying that thou art well, the girl answers for George."

"Thank you." He reached out sleepily for the cup. "You are much too kind, Madame."

"If there were anything that I might do I would say, stay here and be wise; but I do not think that would be best for thee." She looked at her liquor-stained dress with a sad smile. "Nay, thou shalt go, in truth, thou shalt go. It is best so. My boy, it is best so."

She stooped and kissed Dick between the eyes. "That is for good-morning," she said, going away. "When thou art dressed we will speak to George and make everything ready. But first we must open the little trunk. Give me the keys."

"The amount of kissing lately has been simply scandalous. I shall expect Torp to kiss me next. He is more likely to swear at me for getting in his way, though. Well, it won't last long.—Ohe, Madame, help me to my toilette of the guillotine! There will be no chance of dressing properly out yonder."

He was rummaging among his new campaign-kit, and rowelling his hands with the spurs. There are two ways of wearing well-oiled ankle-jacks, spotless blue bands, khaki coat and breeches, and a perfectly pipeclayed helmet. The right way is the way of the untired man, master of himself, setting out upon an expedition, well pleased.

"Everything must be very correct," Dick explained. "It will become dirty afterwards, but now it is good to feel well dressed. Is everything as it should be?"

He patted the revolver neatly hidden under the fulness of the blouse on the right hip and fingered his collar.

"I can do no more," Madame said, between laughing and crying. "Look at thyself—but I forgot."

"I am very content." He stroked the creaseless spirals of his leggings.

"Now let us go and see the captain and George and the lighthouse boat. Be quick, Madame."

"But thou canst not be seen by the harbour walking with me in the daylight. Figure to yourself if some English ladies——"

"There are no English ladies; and if there are, I have forgotten them. Take me there."

In spite of this burning impatience it was nearly evening ere the lighthouse boat began to move. Madame had said a great deal both to George and the captain touching the arrangements that

were to be made for Dick's benefit. Very few men who had the honour of her acquaintance cared to disregard Madame's advice. That sort of contempt might end in being knifed by a stranger in a gambling hell upon surprisingly short provocation.

For six days—two of them were wasted in the crowded Canal—the little steamer worked her way to Suakin, where she was to pick up the superintendent of the lighthouse; and Dick made it his business to propitiate George, who was distracted with fears for the safety of his light-of-love and half inclined to make Dick responsible for his own discomfort. When they arrived George took him under his wing, and together they entered the red-hot seaport, encumbered with the material and wastage of the Suakin-Berger line, from locomotives in disconsolate fragments to mounds of chairs and pot-sleepers.

"If you keep with me," said George, "nobody will ask for passports or what you do. They are all very busy."

"Yes; but I should like to hear some of the Englishmen talk. They might remember me. I was known here a long time ago—when I was some one indeed."

"A long time ago is a very long time ago here. The graveyards are full. Now listen. This new railway runs out so far as Tanai-el-Hassan—that is seven miles. Then there is a camp. They say that beyond Tanai-el-Hassan the English troops go forward, and everything that they require will be brought to them by this line."

"Ah! Base camp. I see. That's a better business than fighting Fuzzies in the open."

"For this reason even the mules go up in the iron-train."

"Iron what?"

"It is all covered with iron, because it is still being shot at."

"An armoured train. Better and better! Go on, faithful George."

"And I go up with my mules tonight. Only those who particularly require to go to the camp go out with the train. They begin to shoot not far from the city."

"The dears—they always used to!" Dick snuffed the smell of parched dust, heated iron, and flaking paint with delight. Certainly the old life was welcoming him back most generously.

"When I have got my mules together I go up tonight, but you must first send a telegram of Port Said, declaring that I have done you no harm."

"Madame has you well in hand. Would you stick a knife into me if you had the chance?"

"I have no chance," said the Greek. "She is there with that woman."

"I see. It's a bad thing to be divided between love of woman and the chance of loot. I sympathise with you, George."

They went to the telegraph-office unquestioned, for all the world was desperately busy and had scarcely time to turn its head, and Suakin was the last place under sky that would be chosen for holiday-ground. On their return the voice of an English subaltern asked Dick what he was doing. The blue goggles were over his eyes and he walked with his hand on George's elbow as he replied—"Egyptian Government—mules. My orders are to give them over to the A. C. G. at Tanai-el-Hassan. Any occasion to show my papers?"

"Oh, certainly not. I beg your pardon. I'd no right to ask, but not seeing your face before I——"

"I go out in the train tonight, I suppose," said Dick, boldly. "There will be no difficulty in loading up the mules, will there?"

"You can see the horse-platforms from here. You must have them loaded up early." The young man went away wondering what sort of broken-down waif this might be who talked like a gentleman and consorted with Greek muleteers. Dick felt unhappy. To outface an English officer is no small thing, but the bluff loses relish when one plays it from the utter dark, and stumbles up and down rough ways, thinking and eternally thinking of what might have been if things had fallen out otherwise, and all had been as it was not.

George shared his meal with Dick and went off to the mule-lines. His charge sat alone in a shed with his face in his hands. Before his tight-shut eyes danced the face of Maisie, laughing, with parted lips. There was a great bustle and clamour about him. He grew afraid and almost called for George.

"I say, have you got your mules ready?" It was the voice of the subaltern over his shoulder.

"My man's looking after them. The—the fact is I've a touch of ophthalmia and can't see very well.

"By Jove! that's bad. You ought to lie up in hospital for a while. I've had a turn of it myself. It's as bad as being blind."

"So I find it. When does this armoured train go?"

"At six o'clock. It takes an hour to cover the seven miles."

"Are the Fuzzies on the rampage—eh?"

"About three nights a week. Fact is I'm in acting command of the night-train. It generally runs back empty to Tanai for the night."

"Big camp at Tanai, I suppose?"

"Pretty big. It has to feed our desert-column somehow."

"Is that far off?"

"Between thirty and forty miles—in an infernal thirsty country."

"Is the country quiet between Tanai and our men?"

"More or less. I shouldn't care to cross it alone, or with a subaltern's command for the matter of that, but the scouts get through it in some extraordinary fashion."

"They always did."

"Have you been here before, then?"

"I was through most of the trouble when it first broke out."

"In the service and cashiered," was the subaltern's first thought, so he refrained from putting any questions.

"There's your man coming up with the mules. It seems rather queer——"

"That I should be mule-leading?" said Dick.

"I didn't mean to say so, but it is. Forgive me—it's beastly impertinence I know, but you speak like a man who has been at a public school. There's no mistaking the tone."

"I am a public school man."

"I thought so. I say, I don't want to hurt your feelings, but you're a little down on your luck, aren't you? I saw you sitting with your head in your hands, and that's why I spoke."

"Thanks. I am about as thoroughly and completely broke as a man need be."

"Suppose—I mean I'm a public school man myself. Couldn't I perhaps—take it as a loan y'know and——"

"You're much too good, but on my honour I've as much money as I want. ... I tell you what you could do for me, though, and put me under an everlasting obligation. Let me come into the bogie truck of the train. There is a fore-truck, isn't there?"

"Yes. How d'you know?"

"I've been in an armoured train before. Only let me see—hear some of the fun I mean, and I'll be grateful. I go at my own risk as a non-combatant."

The young man thought for a minute. "All right," he said. "We're supposed to be an empty train, and there's no one to blow me up at the other end."

George and a horde of yelling amateur assistants had loaded up the mules, and the narrow-gauge armoured train, plated with three-eighths inch boiler-plate till it looked like one long coffin, stood ready to start.

Two bogie trucks running before the locomotive were completely covered in with plating, except that the leading one was pierced in front for the muzzle of a machine-gun, and the second at either side for lateral fire.

The trucks together made one long iron-vaulted chamber in which a score of artillerymen were rioting.

"Whitechapel—last train! Ah, I see yer kissin' in the first class there!" somebody shouted, just as Dick was clamouring into the forward truck.

"Lordy! 'Ere's a real live passenger for the Kew, Tanai, Acton, and Ealin' train. Echo, sir. Speshul edition! Star, sir."—"Shall I get you a foot-warmer?" said another.

"Thanks. I'll pay my footing," said Dick, and relations of the most amiable were established ere silence came with the arrival of the subaltern, and the train jolted out over the rough track.

"This is an immense improvement on shooting the unimpressionable Fuzzy in the open," said Dick, from his place in the corner.

"Oh, but he's still unimpressed. There he goes!" said the subaltern, as a bullet struck the outside of the truck. "We always have at least one demonstration against the night-train. Generally they attack the rear-truck, where my junior commands. He gets all the fun of the fair."

"Not tonight though! Listen!" said Dick. A flight of heavy-handed bullets was succeeded by yelling and shouts. The children of the desert valued their nightly amusement, and the train was an excellent mark.

"Is it worth giving them half a hopper full?" the subaltern asked of the engine, which was driven by a Lieutenant of Sappers.

"I should think so! This is my section of the line. They'll be playing old Harry with my permanent way if we don't stop 'em."

"Right O!"

"Hrrmph!" said the machine gun through all its five noses as the subaltern drew the lever home. The empty cartridges clashed on the floor and the smoke blew back through the truck. There was indiscriminate firing at the rear of the train, and return fire from the darkness without and unlimited howling. Dick stretched himself on the floor, wild with delight at the sounds and the smells.

"God is very good—I never thought I'd hear this again. Give 'em hell, men. Oh, give 'em hell!" he cried.

The train stopped for some obstruction on the line ahead and a party went out to reconnoitre, but came back, cursing, for spades. The children of the desert had piled sand and gravel on the rails, and twenty minutes were lost in clearing it away. Then the slow progress recommenced, to be varied with more shots, more shoutings, the steady clack and kick of the machine guns, and a final difficulty with a half-lifted rail ere the train came under the protection of the roaring camp at Tanai-el-Hassan.

"Now, you see why it takes an hour and a half to fetch her through," said the subaltern, unshipping the cartridge-hopper above his pet gun.

"It was a lark, though. I only wish it had lasted twice as long. How superb it must have looked from outside!" said Dick, sighing regretfully.

"It palls after the first few nights. By the way, when you've settled about your mules, come and see what we can find to eat in my tent. I'm Bennil of the Gunners—in the artillery lines—and mind you don't fall over my tent-ropes in the dark."

But it was all dark to Dick. He could only smell the camels, the hay-bales, the cooking, the smoky fires, and the tanned canvas of the tents as he stood, where he had dropped from the train, shouting for George. There was a sound of light-hearted kicking on the iron skin of the rear trucks, with squealing and grunting. George was unloading the mules.

The engine was blowing off steam nearly in Dick's ear; a cold wind of the desert danced between his legs; he was hungry, and felt tired and dirty—so dirty that he tried to brush his coat with his hands. That was a hopeless job; he thrust his hands into his pockets and began to count over the many times that he had waited in strange or remote places for trains or camels, mules or horses, to carry him to his business. In those days he could see—few men more clearly—and the spectacle of an armed camp at dinner under the stare was an ever fresh pleasure to the eye. There was colour, light, and motion, without which no man has much pleasure in living. This night there remained for him only one more journey through the darkness that never lifts to tell a man how far he has travelled. Then he would grip Torpenhow's hand again—Torpenhow, who was alive and strong, and lived in the midst of the action that had once made the reputation of a man called Dick Heldar: not in the least to be confused with the blind, bewildered vagabond

who seemed to answer to the same name. Yes, he would find Torpenhow, and come as near to the old life as might be. Afterwards he would forget everything: Bessie, who had wrecked the Melancolia and so nearly wrecked his life; Beeton, who lived in a strange unreal city full of tin-tacks and gas-plugs and matters that no men needed; that irrational being who had offered him love and loyalty for nothing, but had not signed her name; and most of all Maisie, who, from her own point of view, was undeniably right in all she did, but oh, at this distance, so tantalisingly fair.

George's hand on his arm pulled him back to the situation.

"And what now?" said George.

"Oh yes of course. What now? Take me to the camel-men. Take me to where the scouts sit when they come in from the desert. They sit by their camels, and the camels eat grain out of a black blanket held up at the corners, and the men eat by their side just like camels. Take me there!"

The camp was rough and rutty, and Dick stumbled many times over the stumps of scrub. The scouts were sitting by their beasts, as Dick knew they would. The light of the dung-fires flickered on their bearded faces, and the camels bubbled and mumbled beside them at rest. It was no part of Dick's policy to go into the desert with a convoy of supplies. That would lead to impertinent questions, and since a blind non-combatant is not needed at the front, he would probably be forced to return to Suakin.

He must go up alone, and go immediately.

"Now for one last bluff—the biggest of all," he said. "Peace be with you, brethren!" The watchful George steered him to the circle of the nearest fire. The heads of the camel-sheiks bowed gravely, and the camels, scenting a European, looked sideways curiously like brooding hens, half ready to get to their feet.

"A beast and a driver to go to the fighting line tonight," said Dick.

"A Mulaid?" said a voice, scornfully naming the best baggage-breed that he knew.

"A Bisharin," returned Dick, with perfect gravity. "A Bisharin without saddle-galls. Therefore no charge of thine, shock-head."

Two or three minutes passed. Then—"We be knee-haltered for the night. There is no going out from the camp."

"Not for money?"

"H'm! Ah! English money?"

Another depressing interval of silence.

"How much?"

"Twenty-five pounds English paid into the hand of the driver at my journey's end, and as much more into the hand of the camel-sheik here, to be paid when the driver returns."

This was royal payment, and the sheik, who knew that he would get his commission on this deposit, stirred in Dick's behalf.

"For scarcely one night's journey—fifty pounds. Land and wells and good trees and wives to make a man content for the rest of his days. Who speaks?" said Dick.

"I," said a voice. "I will go—but there is no going from the camp."

"Fool! I know that a camel can break his knee-halter, and the sentries do not fire if one goes in chase. Twenty-five pounds and another twenty-five pounds. But the beast must be a good Bisharin; I will take no baggage-camel."

Then the bargaining began, and at the end of half an hour the first deposit was paid over to the sheik, who talked in low tones to the driver.

Dick heard the latter say: "A little way out only. Any baggage-beast will serve. Am I a fool to waste my cattle for a blind man?"

"And though I cannot see"—Dick lifted his voice a little—"yet I carry that which has six eyes, and the driver will sit before me. If we do not reach the English troops in the dawn he will be dead."

"But where, in God's name, are the troops?"

"Unless thou knowest let another man ride. Dost thou know? Remember it will be life or death to thee."

"I know," said the driver, sullenly. "Stand back from my beast. I am going to slip him."

"Not so swiftly. George, hold the camel's head a moment. I want to feel his cheek." The hands wandered over the hide till they found the branded half-circle that is the mark of the Biharin, the light-built riding-camel.

"That is well. Cut this one loose. Remember no blessing of God comes on those who try to cheat the blind."

The men chuckled by the fires at the camel-driver's discomfiture. He had intended to substitute a slow, saddle-galled baggage-colt.

"Stand back!" one shouted, lashing the Biharin under the belly with a quirt. Dick obeyed as soon as he felt the nose-string tighten in his hand,—and a cry went up, "Illaha! Aho! He is loose."

With a roar and a grunt the Biharin rose to his feet and plunged forward toward the desert, his driver following with shouts and lamentation.

George caught Dick's arm and hurried him stumbling and tripping past a disgusted sentry who was used to stampeding camels.

"What's the row now?" he cried.

"Every stitch of my kit on that blasted dromedary," Dick answered, after the manner of a common soldier.

"Go on, and take care your throat's not cut outside—you and your dromedary's."

The outcries ceased when the camel had disappeared behind a hillock, and his driver had called him back and made him kneel down.

"Mount first," said Dick. Then climbing into the second seat and gently screwing the pistol muzzle into the small of his companion's back, "Go on in God's name, and swiftly. Goodbye, George. Remember me to Madame, and have a good time with your girl. Get forward, child of the Pit!"

A few minutes later he was shut up in a great silence, hardly broken by the creaking of the saddle and the soft pad of the tireless feet. Dick adjusted himself comfortably to the rock and pitch of the pace, girthed his belt tighter, and felt the darkness slide past. For an hour he was conscious only of the sense of rapid progress.

"A good camel," he said at last.

"He was never underfed. He is my own and clean bred," the driver replied.

"Go on."

His head dropped on his chest and he tried to think, but the tenor of his thoughts was broken because he was very sleepy. In the half doze in seemed that he was learning a punishment hymn at Mrs. Jennett's. He had committed some crime as bad as Sabbath-breaking, and she had locked him up in his bedroom. But he could never repeat more than the first two lines of the hymn—

When Israel of the Lord believed Out of the land of bondage came.

He said them over and over thousands of times. The driver turned in the saddle to see if there were any chance of capturing the revolver and ending the ride. Dick roused, struck him over the head with the butt, and stormed himself wide awake. Somebody hidden in a clump of camel-thorn shouted as the camel toiled up rising ground. A shot was fired, and the silence shut down again, bringing the desire to sleep. Dick could think no longer. He was too tired and stiff and cramped to do more than nod uneasily from time to time, waking with a start and punching the driver with the pistol.

"Is there a moon?" he asked drowsily.

"She is near her setting."

"I wish that I could see her. Halt the camel. At least let me hear the desert talk."

The man obeyed. Out of the utter stillness came one breath of wind. It rattled the dead leaves of a shrub some distance away and ceased. A handful of dry earth detached itself from the edge of a rail trench and crumbled softly to the bottom.

"Go on. The night is very cold."

Those who have watched till the morning know how the last hour before the light lengthens itself into many eternities. It seemed to Dick that he had never since the beginning of original darkness done anything at all save jolt through the air. Once in a thousand years he would finger the nailheads on the saddle-front and count them all carefully. Centuries later he would shift his revolver from his right hand to his left and allow the eased arm to drop down at his side. From the safe distance of London he was watching himself thus employed,—watching critically. Yet whenever he put out his hand to the canvas that he might paint the tawny yellow desert under the glare of the sinking moon, the black shadow of a camel and the two bowed figures atop, that hand held a revolver and the arm was numbed from wrist to collar-bone. Moreover, he was in the dark, and could see no canvas of any kind whatever.

The driver grunted, and Dick was conscious of a change in the air.

"I smell the dawn," he whispered.

"It is here, and yonder are the troops. Have I done well?"

The camel stretched out its neck and roared as there came down wind the pungent reek of camels in the square.

"Go on. We must get there swiftly. Go on."

"They are moving in their camp. There is so much dust that I cannot see what they do."

"Am I in better case? Go forward."

They could hear the hum of voices ahead, the howling and the bubbling of the beasts and the hoarse cries of the soldiers girthing up for the day.

Two or three shots were fired.

"Is that at us? Surely they can see that I am English," Dick spoke angrily.

"Nay, it is from the desert," the driver answered, cowering in his saddle.

"Go forward, my child! Well it is that the dawn did not uncover us an hour ago."

The camel headed straight for the column and the shots behind multiplied. The children of the desert had arranged that most uncomfortable of surprises, a dawn attack for the English troops, and were getting their distance by snap-shots at the only moving object without the square.

"What luck! What stupendous and imperial luck!" said Dick. "It's 'just before the battle, mother.' Oh, God has been most good to me! Only"—the agony of the thought made him screw up his eyes for an instant—"Maisie..."

"Allahu! We are in," said the man, as he drove into the rearguard and the camel knelt.

"Who the deuce are you? Despatches or what? What's the strength of the enemy behind that ridge? How did you get through?" asked a dozen voices. For all answer Dick took a long breath, unbuckled his belt, and shouted from the saddle at the top of a wearied and dusty voice, "Torpenhow! Ohe, Torp! Coo-ee, Tor-pen-how."

A bearded man raking in the ashes of a fire for a light to his pipe moved very swiftly towards that cry, as the rearguard, facing about, began to fire at the puffs of smoke from the hillocks around. Gradually the scattered white cloudlets drew out into the long lines of banked white that hung heavily in the stillness of the dawn before they turned over wave-like and glided into the valleys. The soldiers in the square were coughing and swearing as their own smoke obstructed their view, and they edged forward to get beyond it. A wounded camel leaped to its feet and roared aloud, the cry ending in a bubbling grunt. Some one had cut its throat to prevent confusion. Then came the thick sob of a man receiving his death-wound from a bullet; then a yell of agony and redoubled firing.

There was no time to ask any questions.

"Get down, man! Get down behind the camel!"

"No. Put me, I pray, in the forefront of the battle." Dick turned his face to Torpenhow and raised his hand to set his helmet straight, but, miscalculating the distance, knocked it off. Torpenhow saw that his hair was gray on the temples, and that his face was the face of an old man.

"Come down, you damned fool! Dickie, come off!"

And Dick came obediently, but as a tree falls, pitching sideways from the Bisharin's saddle at

Torpenhow's feet. His luck had held to the last, even to the crowning mercy of a kindly bullet through his head.

Torpenhow knelt under the lee of the camel, with Dick's body in his arms.

THE END

VOLUME VII THE STORY OF THE GADSBYS
RUDYARD KIPLING.

P. S.—On second thoughts I should recommend you to keep the book away from Mrs. Mafflin.

POOR DEAR MAMMA

The wild hawk to the wind-swept sky,

The deer to the wholesome wold,

And the heart of a man to the heart of a maid,

As it was in the days of old.

—Gypsy Song.

SCENE. Interior of Miss MINNIE THREEGAN'S Bedroom at Simla. Miss THREEGAN, in window-seat, turning over a drawerful of things. Miss EMMA DEERCOURT, bosom—friend, who has come to spend the day, sitting on the bed, manipulating the bodice of a ballroom frock, and a bunch of artificial lilies of the valley. Time, 5:30 P. M. on a hot May afternoon.

Miss DEERCOURT. And he said: "I shall never forget this dance," and, of course, I said: "Oh, how can you be so silly!" Do you think he meant anything, dear?

Miss THREEGAN. (Extracting long lavender silk stocking from the rubbish.) You know him better than I do.

Miss D. Oh, do be sympathetic, Minnie! I'm sure he does. At least I would be sure if he wasn't always riding with that odious Mrs. Hagan.

Miss T. I suppose so. How does one manage to dance through one's heels first? Look at this—isn't it shameful? (Spreads stocking-heel on open hand for inspection.)

Miss D. Never mind that! You can't mend it. Help me with this hateful bodice. I've run the string so, and I've run the string so, and I can't make the fulness come right. Where would you put this? (Waves lilies of the valley.)

Miss T. As high up on the shoulder as possible.

Miss D. Am I quite tall enough? I know it makes May Older look lopsided.

Miss T. Yes, but May hasn't your shoulders. Hers are like a hock-bottle.

BEARER. (Rapping at door.) Captain Sahib aya.

Miss D. (Jumping up wildly, and hunting for bodice, which she has discarded owing to the heat of the day.) Captain Sahib! What Captain Sahib? Oh, good gracious, and I'm only half dressed! Well, I sha'n't bother.

Miss T. (Calmly.) You needn't. It isn't for us. That's Captain Gadsby. He is going for a ride

with Mamma. He generally comes five days out of the seven.

AGONIZED VOICE. (Prom an inner apartment.) Minnie, run out and give Captain Gadsby some tea, and tell him I shall be ready in ten minutes; and, O Minnie, come to me an instant, there's a dear girl!

Miss T. Oh, bother! (Aloud.) Very well, Mamma.

Exit, and reappears, after five minutes, flushed, and rubbing her fingers.

Miss D. You look pink. What has happened?

Miss T. (In a stage whisper.) A twenty-four-inch waist, and she won't let it out. Where are my bangles? (Rummages on the toilet-table, and dabs at her hair with a brush in the interval.)

Miss D. Who is this Captain Gadsby? I don't think I've met him.

Miss T. You must have. He belongs to the Harrar set. I've danced with him, but I've never talked to him. He's a big yellow man, just like a newly-hatched chicken, with an enormous moustache. He walks like this (imitates Cavalry swagger), and he goes "Ha-Hmmm!" deep down in his throat when he can't think of anything to say. Mamma likes him. I don't.

Miss D. (Abstractedly.) Does he wax that moustache?

Miss T. (Busy with Powder-puff.) Yes, I think so. Why?

Miss D. (Bending over the bodice and sewing furiously.) Oh, nothing—only—

Miss T. (Sternly.) Only what? Out with it, Emma.

Miss D. Well, May Olger—she's engaged to Mr. Charteris, you know—said—Promise you won't repeat this?

Miss T. Yes, I promise. What did she say?

Miss D. That—that being kissed (with a rush) with a man who didn't wax his moustache was—like eating an egg without salt.

Miss T. (At her full height, with crushing scorn.) May Olger is a horrid, nasty Thing, and you can tell her I said so. I'm glad she doesn't belong to my set—I must go and feed this man! Do I look presentable?

Miss D. Yes, perfectly. Be quick and hand him over to your Mother, and then we can talk. I shall listen at the door to hear what you say to him.

Miss T. 'Sure I don't care. I'm not afraid of Captain Gadsby.

In proof of this swings into the drawing-room with a mannish stride followed by two short steps, which produces the effect of a restive horse entering. Misses CAPTAIN GADSBY, who is sitting in the shadow of the window-curtain, and gazes round helplessly.

CAPTAIN GADSBY. (Aside.) The filly, by Jove! 'Must ha' picked up that action from the sire. (Aloud, rising.) Good evening, Miss Threegan.

Miss T. (Conscious that she is flushing.) Good evening, Captain Gadsby. Mamma told me to say that she will be ready in a few minutes. Won't you have some tea? (Aside.) I hope Mamma will

be quick. What am I to say to the creature? (Aloud and abruptly.) Milk and sugar?

Capt. G. No sugar, tha-anks, and very little milk. Ha-Hmmm.

Miss T. (Aside.) If he's going to do that, I'm lost. I shall laugh. I know I shall!

Capt. G. (Pulling at his moustache and watching it sideways down his nose.) Ha-Hmmm. (Aside.) 'Wonder what the little beast can talk about. 'Must make a shot at it.

Miss T. (Aside.) Oh, this is agonizing. I must say something.

Both Together. Have you Been—

Capt. G. I beg your pardon. You were going to say—

Miss T. (Who has been watching the moustache with awed fascination.) Won't you have some eggs?

Capt. G. (Looking bewilderedly at the tea-table.) Eggs! (Aside.) O Hades! She must have a nursery-tea at this hour. S'pose they've wiped her mouth and sent her to me while the Mother is getting on her duds. (Aloud.) No, thanks.

Miss T. (Crimson with confusion.) Oh! I didn't mean that. I wasn't thinking of mou—eggs for an instant. I mean salt. Won't you have some sa—sweets? (Aside.) He'll think me a raving lunatic. I wish Mamma would come.

Capt. G. (Aside.) It was a nursery-tea and she's ashamed of it. By Jove! She doesn't look half bad when she colors up like that. (Aloud, helping himself from the dish.) Have you seen those new chocolates at Peliti's?

Miss T. No, I made these myself. What are they like?

Capt. G. These! De-licious. (Aside.) And that's a fact.

Miss T. (Aside.) Oh, bother! he'll think I'm fishing for compliments. (Aloud.) No, Peliti's of course.

Capt. G. (Enthusiastically.) Not to compare with these. How d'you make them? I can't get my khansamah to understand the simplest thing beyond mutton and fowl.

Miss T. Yes? I'm not a khansamah, you know. Perhaps you frighten him. You should never frighten a servant. He loses his head. It's very bad policy.

Capt. G. He's so awf'ly stupid.

Miss T. (Folding her hands in her lap.) You should call him quietly and say: 'O khansamah jee!'

Capt. G. (Getting interested.) Yes? (Aside.) Fancy that little featherweight saying, 'O khansamah jee' to my bloodthirsty Mir Khan!

Miss T Then you should explain the dinner, dish by dish.

Capt. G. But I can't speak the vernacular.

Miss T. (Patronizingly.) You should pass the Higher Standard and try.

Capt. G. I have, but I don't seem to be any the wiser. Are you?

Miss T. I never passed the Higher Standard. But the khansamah is very patient with me. He doesn't get angry when I talk about sheep's topees, or order maunds of grain when I mean seers.

Capt. G. (Aside with intense indignation.) I'd like to see Mir Khan being rude to that girl! Hullo! Steady the Buffs! (Aloud.) And do you understand about horses, too?

Miss T. A little—not very much. I can't doctor them, but I know what they ought to eat, and I am in charge of our stable.

Capt. G. Indeed! You might help me then. What ought a man to give his sais in the Hills? My ruffian says eight rupees, because everything is so dear.

Miss T. Six rupees a month, and one rupee Simla allowance—neither more nor less. And a grass-cut gets six rupees. That's better than buying grass in the bazar.

Capt. G. (Admiringly.) How do you know?

Miss T. I have tried both ways.

Capt. G. Do you ride much, then? I've never seen you on the Mall.

Miss T. (Aside.) I haven't passed him more than fifty times. (Aloud.) Nearly every day.

Capt. G. By Jove! I didn't know that. Ha-Hmmm (Pulls at his moustache and is silent for forty seconds.)

Miss T. (Desperately, and wondering what will happen next.) It looks beautiful. I shouldn't touch it if I were you. (Aside.) It's all Mamma's fault for not coming before. I will be rude!

Capt. G. (Bronzing under the tan and bringing down his hand very quickly.) Eh! Wha-at! Oh, yes! Ha! Ha! (Laughs uneasily.) (Aside.) Well, of all the dashed cheek! I never had a woman say that to me yet. She must be a cool hand or else—Ah! that nursery-tea!

VOICE PROM THE UNKNOWN. Tchk! Tchk! Tchk!

Capt. G. Good gracious! What's that?

Miss T. The dog, I think. (Aside.) Emma has been listening, and I'll never forgive her!

Capt. G. (Aside.) They don't keep dogs here. (Aloud.) Didn't sound like a dog, did it?

Miss T. Then it must have been the cat. Let's go into the veranda. What a lovely evening it is!

Steps into veranda and looks out across the hills into sunset. The CAPTAIN follows.

Capt. G. (Aside.) Superb eyes! I wonder that I never noticed them before! (Aloud.) There's going to be a dance at Viceregal Lodge on Wednesday. Can you spare me one?

Miss T. (Shortly.) No! I don't want any of your charity-dances. You only ask me because Mamma told you to. I hop and I bump. You know I do!

Capt. G. (Aside.) That's true, but little girls shouldn't understand these things. (Aloud.) No, on my word, I don't. You dance beautifully.

Miss T. Then why do you always stand out after half a dozen turns? I thought officers in the Army didn't tell fibs.

Capt. G. It wasn't a fib, believe me. I really do want the pleasure of a dance with you.

Miss T. (Wickedly.) Why? Won't Mamma dance with you any more?

Capt. G. (More earnestly than the necessity demands.) I wasn't thinking of your Mother. (Aside.) You little vixen!

Miss T. (Still looking out of the window.) Eh? Oh, I beg your pardon. I was thinking of something else.

Capt. G. (Aside.) Well! I wonder what she'll say next. I've never known a woman treat me like this before. I might b—Dash it, I might be an Infantry subaltern! (Aloud.) Oh, please don't trouble. I'm not worth thinking about. Isn't your Mother ready yet?

Miss T. I should think so; but promise me, Captain Gamsby, you won't take poor dear Mamma twice round Jakko any more. It tires her so.

Capt. G. She says that no exercise tires her.

Miss T. Yes, but she suffers afterward. You don't know what rheumatism is, and you oughtn't to keep her out so late, when it gets chill in the evenings.

Capt. G. (Aside.) Rheumatism. I thought she came off her horse rather in a bunch. Whew! One lives and learns. (Aloud.) I'm sorry to hear that. She hasn't mentioned it to me.

Miss T. (Flurried.) Of course not! Poor dear Mamma never would. And you mustn't say that I told you either. Promise me that you won't. Oh, Captain Gamsby, promise me you won't!

Capt. G. I am dumb, or—I shall be as soon as you've given me that dance, and another—if you can trouble yourself to think about me for a minute.

Miss T. But you won't like it one little bit. You'll be awfully sorry afterward.

Capt. G. I shall like it above all things, and I shall only be sorry that I didn't get more. (Aside.) Now what in the world am I saying?

Miss T. Very well. You will have only yourself to thank if your toes are trodden on. Shall we say Seven?

Capt. G. And Eleven. (Aside.) She can't be more than eight stone, but, even then, it's an absurdly small foot. (Looks at his own riding boots.)

Miss T. They're beautifully shiny. I can almost see my face in them.

Capt. G. I was thinking whether I should have to go on crutches for the rest of my life if you trod on my toes.

Miss T. Very likely. Why not change Eleven for a square?

Capt. G. No, please! I want them both waltzes. Won't you write them down?

Miss T. I don't get so many dances that I shall confuse them. You will be the offender.

Capt. G. Wait and see! (Aside.) She doesn't dance perfectly, perhaps, but—

Miss T. Your tea must have got cold by this time. Won't you have another cup?

Capt. G. No, thanks. Don't you think it's pleasanter out in the veranda? (Aside.) I never saw hair take that color in the sunshine before. (Aloud.) It's like one of Dicksee's pictures.

Miss T. Yes I It's a wonderful sunset, isn't it? (Bluntly.) But what do you know about Dicksee's pictures?

Capt. G. I go Home occasionally. And I used to know the Galleries. (Nervously.) You mustn't think me only a Philistine with a moustache.

Miss T. Don't! Please don't. I'm so sorry for what I said then. I was horribly rude. It slipped out before j thought. Don't you know the temptation to say frightful and shocking things just for the mere sake of saying them? I'm afraid I gave way to it.

Capt. G. (Watching the girl as she flushes.) I think I know the feeling. It would be terrible if we all yielded to it, wouldn't it? For instance, I might say—

POOR DEAR MAMMA. (Entering, habited, hatted, and booted.) Ah, Captain Gamsby? 'Sorry to keep you waiting. 'Hope you haven't been bored. 'My little girl been talking to you?

Miss T. (Aside.) I'm not sorry I spoke about the rheumatism. I'm not! I'm NOT! I only wished I'd mentioned the corns too.

Capt. G. (Aside.) What a shame! I wonder how old she is. It never occurred to me before. (Aloud.) We've been discussing 'Shakespeare and the musical glasses' in the veranda.

Miss T. (Aside.) Nice man! He knows that quotation. He isn't a Philistine with a moustache. (Aloud.) Goodbye, Captain Gadsby. (Aside.) What a huge hand and what a squeeze! I don't suppose he meant it, but he has driven the rings into my fingers.

Poor Dear Mamma. Has Vermillion come round yet? Oh, yes! Captain Gadsby, don't you think that the saddle is too far forward? (They pass into the front veranda.)

Capt. G. (Aside.) How the dickens should I know what she prefers? She told me that she doted on horses. (Aloud.) I think it is.

Miss T. (Coming out into front veranda.) Oh! Bad Buldoo! I must speak to him for this. He has taken up the curb two links, and Vermillion bates that. (Passes out and to horse's head.)

Capt. G. Let me do it!

Miss. T. No, Vermillion understands me. Don't you, old man? (Loosens curb-chain skilfully, and pats horse on nose and throttle.) Poor Vermillion! Did they want to cut his chin off? There!

Captain Gadsby watches the interlude with undisguised admiration.

Poor Dear Mamma. (Tartly to Miss T.) You've forgotten your guest, I think, dear.

Miss T. Good gracious! So I have! Goodbye. (Retreats indoors hastily.)

Poor Dear Mamma. (Bunching reins in fingers hampered by too tight gauntlets.) CAPTAIN Gadsby!

CAPTAIN GADSBY stoops and makes the foot-rest. Poor Dear Mamma blunders, halts too long, and breaks through it.

Capt. G. (Aside.) Can't hold up seven stone forever. It's all your rheumatism. (Aloud.) Can't imagine why I was so clumsy. (Aside.) Now Little Featherweight would have gone up like a bird.

They ride out of the garden. The Captain falls back.

Capt. G. (Aside.) How that habit catches her under the arms! Ugh!

Poor Dear Mamma. (With the worn smile of sixteen seasons, the worse for exchange.) You're dull this afternoon, Captain Gadsby.

Capt. G. (Spurring up wearily.) Why did you keep me waiting so long?

Et cetera, et cetera, et cetera.

(AN INTERVAL OF THREE WEEKS.)

GILDED YOUTH. (Sitting on railings opposite Town Hall.) Hullo, Gadsby! 'Been trotting out the Gorgonzola! We all thought it was the Gorgon you're mashing.

Capt. G. (With withering emphasis.) You young cub! What the—does it matter to you?

Proceeds to read GILDED YOUTH a lecture on discretion and deportment, which crumbles latter like a Chinese Lantern. Departs fuming.

(FURTHER INTERVAL OF FIVE WEEKS.) SCENE. Exterior of New Simla Library on a foggy evening. Miss THREEGAN and Miss DEERCOURT meet among the 'rickshaws. Miss T. is carrying a bundle of books under her left arm.

Miss D. (Level intonation.) Well?

Miss T. (Ascending intonation.) Well?

Miss D. (Capturing her friend's left arm, taking away all the books, placing books in 'rickshaw, returning to arm, securing hand by third finger and investigating.) Well! You bad girl! And you never told me.

Miss T. (Demurely.) He—he—he only spoke yesterday afternoon.

Miss D. Bless you, dear! And I'm to be bridesmaid, aren't I? You know you promised ever so long ago.

Miss T. Of course. I'll tell you all about it tomorrow. (Gets into 'rickshaw.) O Emma!

Miss D. (With intense interest.) Yes, dear?

Miss T. (Piano.) It's quite true—about-the-egg.

Miss D. What egg?

Miss T. (Pianissimo prestissimo.) The egg without the salt. (Forte.) Chalo ghar ko jaldi, jhampani! (Go home, jhampani.)

THE WORLD WITHOUT

Certain people of importance.

SCENE. Smoking-room of the Degchi Club. Time, 10.30 P. M. of a stuffy night in the Rains. Four men dispersed in picturesque attitudes and easy-chairs. To these enter BLAYNE of the Irregular Moguls, in evening dress.

BLAYNE. Phew! The Judge ought to be hanged in his own store-godown. Hi, khitmatgar! Pour a whiskey-peg, to take the taste out of my mouth.

CURTISS. (Royal Artillery.) That's it, is it? What the deuce made you dine at the Judge's? You know his bandobust.

Blayne. 'Thought it couldn't be worse than the Club, but I'll swear he buys ullaged liquor and doctors it with gin and ink (looking round the room.) Is this all of you tonight?

DOONE. (P.W.D.) Anthony was called out at dinner. Mingle had a pain in his tummy.

Curtiss. Miggy dies of cholera once a week in the Rains, and gets drunk on chlorodyne in between. Good little chap, though. Any one at the Judge's, Blayne?

Blayne. Cockley and his memsahib looking awfully white and fagged. Female girl—couldn'tcatch the name—on her way to the Hills, under the Cockleys' charge—the Judge, and Markyn fresh from Simla—disgustingly fit.

Curtiss. Good Lord, how truly magnificent! Was there enough ice? When I mangled garbage there I got one whole lump—nearly as big as a walnut. What had Markyn to say for himself?

Blayne. Seems that every one is having a fairly good time up there in spite of the rain. By Jove, that reminds me! I know I hadn'tcome across just for the pleasure of your society. News! Great news! Markyn told me.

DOONE. Who's dead now?

Blayne. No one that I know of; but Gadsby's hooked at last!

DROPPING CHORUS. How much? The Devil! Markyn was pulling your leg. Not GADSBY!

Blayne. (Humming.) "Yea, verily, verily, verily! Verily, verily, I say unto thee." Theodore, the gift 'o God! Our Phillup! It's been given out up above.

MACKESY. (Barrister-at-Law.) Huh! Women will give out anything. What does accused say?

Blayne. Markyn told me that he congratulated him warily—one hand held out, t'other ready to guard. Gadsby turned pink and said it was so.

Curtiss. Poor old Caddy! They all do it. Who's she? Let's hear the details.

Blayne. She's a girl—daughter of a Colonel Somebody.

Doone. Simla's stiff with Colonels' daughters. Be more explicit.

Blayne. Wait a shake. What was her name? Thresomething. Three—

Curtiss. Stars, perhaps. Caddy knows that brand.

Blayne. Threegan—Minnie Threegan.

Mackesy. Threegan Isn't she a little bit of a girl with red hair?

Blayne. 'Bout that—from what from what Markyn said.

Mackesy. Then I've met her. She was at Lucknow last season. 'Owned a permanently juvenile Mamma, and danced damnably. I say, Jervoise, you knew the Threegans, didn't you?

JERVOISE. (Civilian of twenty-five years' service, waking up from his doze.) Eh? What's that? Knew who? How? I thought I was at Home, confound you!

Mackesy. The Threegan girl's engaged, so Blayne says.

Jervoise. (Slowly.) Engaged—en-gaged! Bless my soul! I'm getting an old man! Little Minnie Threegan engaged. It was only the other day I went home with them in the Surat—no, the Massilia—and she was crawling about on her hands and knees among the ayahs. 'Used to call me the "Tick Tack Sahib" because I showed her my watch. And that was in Sixty-Seven—no, Seventy. Good God, how time flies! I'm an old man. I remember when Threegan married Miss Derwent—daughter of old Hooky Derwent—but that was before your time. And so the little baby's engaged to have a little baby of her own! Who's the other fool?

Mackesy. Gadsby of the Pink Hussars.

Jervoise. 'Never met him. Threegan lived in debt, married in debt, and'll die in debt. 'Must be glad to get the girl off his hands.

Blayne. Caddy has money—lucky devil. Place at Home, too.

Doone. He comes of first-class stock. 'Can't quite understand his being caught by a Colonel's daughter, and (looking cautiously round room.) Black Infantry at that! No offence to you, Blayne.

Blayne. (Stiffly.) Not much, thaanks.

Curtiss. (Quoting motto of Irregular Moguls.) "We are what we are," eh, old man? But Gadsby was such a superior animal as a rule. Why didn't he go Home and pick his wife there?

Mackesy. They are all alike when they come to the turn into the straight. About thirty a man begins to get sick of living alone.

Curtiss. And of the eternal mutton—chop in the morning.

Doone. It's a dead goat as a rule, but go on, Mackesy.

Mackesy. If a man's once taken that way nothing will hold him, Do you remember Benoit of your service, Doone? They transferred him to Tharanda when his time came, and he married a platelayer's daughter, or something of that kind. She was the only female about the place.

Doone. Yes, poor brute. That smashed Benoit's chances of promotion altogether. Mrs. Benoit used to ask "Was you goin' to the dance this evenin'?"

Curtiss. Hang it all! Gadsby hasn't married beneath him. There's no tar-brush in the family, I suppose.

Jervoise. Tar-brush! Not an anna. You young fellows talk as though the man was doing the girl an honor in marrying her. You're all too conceited—nothing's good enough for you.

Blayne. Not even an empty Club, a dam' bad dinner at the Judge's, and a Station as sickly as a hospital. You're quite right. We're a set of Sybarites.

Doone. Luxurious dogs, wallowing in—

Curtiss. Prickly heat between the shoulders. I'm covered with it. Let's hope Beora will be cooler.

Blayne. Whew! Are you ordered into camp, too? I thought the Gunners had a clean sheet.

Curtiss. No, worse luck. Two cases yesterday—one died—and if we have a third, out we go. Is there any shooting at Beora, Doone?

Doone. The country's under water, except the patch by the Grand Trunk Road. I was there yesterday, looking at a bund, and came across four poor devils in their last stage. It's rather bad from here to Kuchara.

Curtiss. Then we're pretty certain to have a heavy go of it. Heigho! I shouldn't mind changing places with Gaddy for a while. 'Sport with Amaryllis in the shade of the Town Hall, and all that. Oh, why doesn't somebody come and marry me, instead of letting me go into cholera-camp?

Mackesy. Ask the Committee.

Curtiss. You ruffian! You'll stand me another peg for that. Blayne, what will you take? Mackesy is fine on moral grounds. Doone, have you any preference?

Doone. Small glass Kummel, please. Excellent carminative, these days. Anthony told me so.

Mackesy. (Signing voucher for four drinks.) Most unfair punishment. I only thought of Curtiss as Actaeon being chivied round the billiard tables by the nymphs of Diana.

Blayne. Curtiss would have to import his nymphs by train. Mrs. Cockley's the only woman in the Station. She won't leave Cockley, and he's doing his best to get her to go.

Curtiss. Good, indeed! Here's Mrs. Cockley's health. To the only wife in the Station and a damned brave woman!

OMNES. (Drinking.) A damned brave woman

Blayne. I suppose Gadsby will bring his wife here at the end of the cold weather. They are going to be married almost immediately, I believe.

Curtiss. Gadsby may thank his luck that the Pink Hussars are all detachment and no headquarters this hot weather, or he'd be torn from the arms of his love as sure as death. Have you ever noticed the thorough-minded way British Cavalry take to cholera? It's because they are so expensive. If the Pinks had stood fast here, they would have been out in camp a month ago. Yes, I should decidedly like to be Gadsby.

Mackesy. He'll go Home after he's married, and send in his papers—see if he doesn't.

Blayne. Why shouldn't he? Hasn't he money? Would any one of us be here if we weren't paupers?

Doone. Poor old pauper! What has become of the six hundred you rooked from our table last month?

Blayne. It took unto itself wings. I think an enterprising tradesman got some of it, and a shroff gobbled the rest—or else I spent it.

Curtiss. Gadsby never had dealings with a shroff in his life.

Doone. Virtuous Gadsby! If I had three thousand a month, paid from England, I don't think I'd deal with a shroff either.

Mackesy. (Yawning.) Oh, it's a sweet life! I wonder whether matrimony would make it sweeter.

Curtiss. Ask Cockley—with his wife dying by inches!

Blayne. Go home and get a fool of a girl to come out to—what is it Thackeray says?—"the splendid palace of an Indian pro-consul."

Doone. Which reminds me. My quarters leak like a sieve. I had fever last night from sleeping in a swamp. And the worst of it is, one can't do anything to a roof till the Rains are over.

Curtiss. What's wrong with you? You haven't eighty rotting Tommies to take into a running stream.

Doone. No: but I'm mixed boils and bad language. I'm a regular Job all over my body. It's sheer poverty of blood, and I don't see any chance of getting richer—either way.

Blayne. Can't you take leave?

Doone. That's the pull you Army men have over us. Ten days are nothing in your sight. I'm so important that Government can't find a substitute if I go away. Ye-es, I'd like to be Gadsby, whoever his wife may be.

Curtiss. You've passed the turn of life that Mackesy was speaking of.

Doone. Indeed I have, but I never yet had the brutality to ask a woman to share my life out here.

Blayne. On my soul I believe you're right. I'm thinking of Mrs. Cockley. The woman's an absolute wreck.

Doone. Exactly. Because she stays down here. The only way to keep her fit would be to send her to the Hills for eight months—and the same with any woman. I fancy I see myself taking a wife on those terms.

Mackesy. With the rupee at one and sixpence. The little Doones would be little Debra Doones, with a fine Mussoorie @chi-chi anent to bring home for the holidays.

Curtiss. And a pair of be-ewtiful sambhur—horns for Doone to wear, free of expense, presented by—Doone. Yes, it's an enchanting prospect. By the way, the rupee hasn't done falling yet. The time will come when we shall think ourselves lucky if we only lose half our pay.

Curtiss. Surely a third's loss enough. Who gains by the arrangement? That's what I want to know.

Blayne. The Silver Question! I'm going to bed if you begin squabbling Thank Goodness, here's Anthony—looking like a ghost.

Enter ANTHONY, Indian Medical Staff, very white and tired.

Anthony. 'Evening, Blayne. It's raining in sheets. Whiskey peg lao, khitmatgar. The roads are something ghastly.

Curtiss. How's Mingle?

Anthony. Very bad, and more frightened. I handed him over to Fewton. Mingle might just as well have called him in the first place, instead of bothering me.

Blayne. He's a nervous little chap. What has he got, this time?

Anthony. 'Can't quite say. A very bad tummy and a blue funk so far. He asked me at once if it was cholera, and I told him not to be a fool. That soothed him.

Curtiss. Poor devil! The funk does half the business in a man of that build.

Anthony. (Lighting a cheroot.) I firmly believe the funk will kill him if he stays down. You know the amount of trouble he's been giving Fewton for the last three weeks. He's doing his very best to frighten himself into the grave.

GENERAL CHORUS. Poor little devil! Why doesn't he get away?

Anthony. 'Can't. He has his leave all right, but he's so dipped he can't take it, and I don't think his name on paper would raise four annas. That's in confidence, though.

Mackesy. All the Station knows it.

Anthony. "I suppose I shall have to die here," he said, squirming all across the bed. He's quite made up his mind to Kingdom Come. And I know he has nothing more than a wet-weather tummy if he could only keep a hand on himself.

Blayne. That's bad. That's very bad. Poor little Miggy. Good little chap, too. I say—

Anthony. What do you say?

Blayne. Well, look here—anyhow. If it's like that—as you say—I say fifty.

Curtiss. I say fifty.

Mackesy. I go twenty better.

Doone. Bloated Croesus of the Bar! I say fifty. Jervoise, what do you say? Hi! Wake up!

Jervoise. Eh? What's that? What's that?

Curtiss. We want a hundred rupees from you. You're a bachelor drawing a gigantic income, and there's a man in a hole.

Jervoise. What man? Any one dead?

Blayne. No, but he'll die if you don't—give the hundred. Here! Here's a peg-voucher. You can see what we've signed for, and Anthony's man will come round tomorrow to collect it. So there will be no trouble.

Jervoise. (Signing.) One hundred, E. M. J. There you are (feebly). It isn't one of your jokes, is it?

Blayne. No, it really is wanted. Anthony, you were the biggest poker-winner last week, and you've defrauded the tax-collector too long. Sign!

Anthony. Let's see. Three fifties and a seventy-two twenty-three twenty—say four hundred and twenty. That'll give him a month clear at the Hills. Many thanks, you men. I'll send round the chaprassi tomorrow.

Curtiss. You must engineer his taking the stuff, and of course you mustn't—

Anthony. Of course. It would never do. He'd weep with gratitude over his evening drink.

Blayne. That's just what he would do, damn him. Oh! I say, Anthony, you pretend to know everything. Have you heard about Gadsby?

Anthony. No. Divorce Court at last?

Blayne. Worse. He's engaged!

Anthony. How much? He can't be!

Blayne. He is. He's going to be married in a few weeks. Markyn told me at the Judge's this evening. It's pukka.

Anthony. You don't say so? Holy Moses! There'll be a shine in the tents of Kedar.

Curtiss. 'Regiment cut up rough, think you?

Anthony. 'Don't know anything about the Regiment.

Mackesy. It is bigamy, then?

Anthony. Maybe. Do you mean to say that you men have forgotten, or is there more charity in the world than I thought?

Doone. You don't look pretty when you are trying to keep a secret. You bloat. Explain.

Anthony. Mrs. Herriott!

Blayne. (After a long pause, to the room generally.) It's my notion that we are a set of fools.

Mackesy. Nonsense. That business was knocked on the head last season. Why, young Mallard—

Anthony. Mallard was a candlestick, paraded as such. Think awhile. Recollect last season and the talk then. Mallard or no Mallard, did Gadsby ever talk to any other woman?

Curtiss. There's something in that. It was slightly noticeable now you come to mention it. But she's at Naini Tal and he's at Simla.

Anthony. He had to go to Simla to look after a globe-trotter relative of his—a person with a title. Uncle or aunt.

Blayne And there he got engaged. No law prevents a man growing tired of a woman.

Anthony. Except that he mustn't do it till the woman is tired of him. And the Herriott woman was not that.

Curtiss. She may be now. Two months of Naini Tal works wonders.

Doone. Curious thing how some women carry a Fate with them. There was a Mrs. Deegie in the Central Provinces whose men invariably fell away and got married. It became a regular proverb with us when I was down there. I remember three men desperately devoted to her, and they all, one after another, took wives.

Curtiss. That's odd. Now I should have thought that Mrs. Deegie's influence would have led them to take other men's wives. It ought to have made them afraid of the judgment of Providence.

Anthony. Mrs. Herriott will make Gadsby afraid of something more than the judgment of Providence, I fancy.

Blayne. Supposing things are as you say, he'll be a fool to face her. He'll sit tight at Simla.

Anthony. Shouldn't be a bit surprised if he went off to Naini to explain. He's an unaccountable sort of man, and she's likely to be a more than unaccountable woman.

Doone. What makes you take her character away so confidently?

Anthony. Primum tempus. Caddy was her first and a woman doesn't allow her first man to drop away without expostulation. She justifies the first transfer of affection to herself by swearing that it is forever and ever. Consequently—

Blayne. Consequently, we are sitting here till past one o'clock, talking scandal like a set of Station cats. Anthony, it's all your fault. We were perfectly respectable till you came in. Go to bed. I'm off, Good night all.

Curtiss. Past one! It's past two by Jove, and here's the khit coming for the late charge. Just Heavens! One, two, three, four, five rupees to pay for the pleasure of saying that a poor little beast of a woman is no better than she should be. I'm ashamed of myself. Go to bed, you slanderous villains, and if I'm sent to Beora tomorrow, be prepared to hear I'm dead before paying my card account!

THE TENTS OF KEDAR

Only why should it be with pain at all?

Why must I 'twixt the leaves of coronal

Put any kiss of pardon on thy brow?

Why should the other women know so much,

And talk together—

Such the look and such

The smile he used to love with, then as now.

—Any Wife to any Husband.

SCENE. A Naini Tal dinner for thirty-four. Plate, wines, crockery, and khitmatgars carefully calculated to scale of Rs. 6000 per mensem, less Exchange. Table split lengthways by bank of flowers.

MRS. HERRIOTT. (After conversation has risen to proper pitch.) Ah! 'Didn't see you in the crush in the drawing-room. (Sotto voce.) Where have you been all this while, Pip?

CAPTAIN GADSBY. (Turning from regularly ordained dinner partner and settling hock glasses.) Good evening. (Sotto voce.) Not quite so loud another time. You've no notion how your voice carries. (Aside.) So much for shirking the written explanation. It'll have to be a verbal one now. Sweet prospect! How on earth am I to tell her that I am a respectable, engaged member of society and it's all over between us?

MRS. H. I've a heavy score against you. Where were you at the Monday Pop? Where were you on Tuesday? Where were you at the Lamonts' tennis? I was looking everywhere.

Capt. G. For me! Oh, I was alive somewhere, I suppose. (Aside.) It's for Minnie's sake, but it's going to be dashed unpleasant.

Mrs. H. Have I done anything to offend you? I never meant it if I have. I couldn't help going for a ride with the Vaynor man. It was promised a week before you came up.

Capt. G. I didn't know—

Mrs. H. It really was.

Capt. G. Anything about it, I mean.

Mrs. H. What has upset you today? All these days? You haven't been near me for four whole days—nearly one hundred hours. Was it kind of you, Pip? And I've been looking forward so much to your coming.

Capt. G. Have you?

Mrs. H. You know I have! I've been as foolish as a schoolgirl about it. I made a little calendar and put it in my card-case, and every time the twelve o'clock gun went off I scratched out a square and said: "That brings me nearer to Pip. My Pip!"

Capt. G. (With an uneasy laugh). What will Mackler think if you neglect him so?

Mrs. H. And it hasn't brought you nearer. You seem farther away than ever. Are you sulking about something? I know your temper.

Capt. G. No.

Mrs. H. Have I grown old in the last few months, then? (Reaches forward to bank of flowers for menu-card.)

PARTNER ON LEFT. Allow me. (Hands menu-card. Mrs. H. keeps her arm at full stretch for three seconds.)

Mrs. H. (To partner.) Oh, thanks. I didn't see. (Turns right again.) Is anything in me changed at all?

Capt. G. For Goodness's sake go on with your dinner! You must eat something. Try one of those cutlet arrangements. (Aside.) And I fancied she had good shoulders, once upon a time! What an ass a man can make of himself!

Mrs. H. (Helping herself to a paper frill, seven peas, some stamped carrots and a spoonful of gravy.) That isn't an answer. Tell me whether I have done anything.

Capt. G. (Aside.) If it isn't ended here there will be a ghastly scene some-where else. If only I'd written to her and stood the racket at long range! (To Khitmatgar.) Han! Simpkin do. (Aloud.) I'll tell you later on.

Mrs. H. Tell me now. It must be some foolish misunderstanding, and you know that there was to be nothing of that sort between us. We, of all people in the world, can't afford it. Is it the Vaynor man, and don't you like to say so? On my honor—

Capt. G. I haven't given the Vaynor man a thought.

Mrs. H. But how d'you know that I haven't?

Capt. G. (Aside.) Here's my chance and may the Devil help me through with it. (Aloud and measuredly.) Believe me, I do not care how often or how tenderly you think of the Vaynor man.

Mrs. H. I wonder if you mean that! Oh, what is the good of squabbling and pretending to misunderstand when you are only up for so short a time? Pip, don't be a stupid!

Follows a pause, during which he crosses his left leg over his right and continues his dinner.

Capt. G. (In answer to the thunderstorm in her eyes.) Corns—my worst.

Mrs. H. Upon my word, you are the very rudest man in the world! I'll never do it again.

Capt. G. (Aside.) No, I don't think you will; but I wonder what you will do before it's all over. (To Khitmatgar.) Thorah ur Simpkin do.

Mrs. H. Well! Haven't you the grace to apologize, bad man?

Capt. G. (Aside.) I mustn't let it drift back now. Trust a woman for being as blind as a bat when she won't see.

Mrs. H. I'm waiting; or would you like me to dictate a form of apology?

Capt. G. (Desperately.) By all means dictate.

Mrs. H. (Lightly.) Very well. Rehearse your several Christian names after me and go on: "Profess my sincere repentance."

Capt. G. "Sincere repentance."

Mrs. H. "For having behaved"—

Capt. G. (Aside.) At last! I wish to Goodness she'd look away. "For having behaved"—as I have behaved, and declare that I am thoroughly and heartily sick of the whole business, and take this opportunity of making clear my intention of ending it, now, henceforward, and forever. (Aside.) If any one had told me I should be such a blackguard!—

Mrs. H. (Shaking a spoonful of potato chips into her plate.) That's not a pretty joke.

Capt. G. No. It's a reality. (Aside.) I wonder if smashes of this kind are always so raw.

Mrs. H. Really, Pip, you're getting more absurd every day.

Capt. G. I don't think you quite understand me. Shall I repeat it?

Mrs. H. No! For pity's sake don't do that. It's too terrible, even in fur.

Capt. G. I'll let her think it over for a while. But I ought to be horsewhipped.

Mrs. H. I want to know what you meant by what you said just now.

Capt. G. Exactly what I said. No less.

Mrs. H. But what have I done to deserve it? What have I done?

Capt. G. (Aside.) If she only wouldn't look at me. (Aloud and very slowly, his eyes on his plate.) D'you remember that evening in July, before the Rains broke, when you said that the end would have to come sooner or later—and you wondered for which of US it would come first?

Mrs. H. Yes! I was only joking. And you swore that, as long as there was breath in your body, it should never come. And I believed you.

Capt. G. (Fingering menu-card.) Well, it has. That's all.

A long pause, during which Mrs. H. bows her head and rolls the bread-twist into little pellets; G. stares at the oleanders.

Mrs. H. (Throwing back her head and laughing naturally.) They train us women well, don't they, Pip?

Capt. G. (Brutally, touching shirt-stud.) So far as the expression goes. (Aside.) It isn't in her nature to take things quietly. There'll be an explosion yet.

Mrs. H. (With a shudder.) Thank you. B-but even Red Indians allow people to wriggle when

they're being tortured, I believe. (Slips fan from girdle and fans slowly: rim of fan level with chin.)

PARTNER ON LEFT. Very close tonight, isn't it? 'You find it too much for you?

Mrs. H. Oh, no, not in the least. But they really ought to have punkahs, even in your cool Naini Tal, oughtn't they? (Turns, dropping fan and raising eyebrows.)

Capt. G. It's all right. (Aside.) Here comes the storm!

Mrs. H. (Her eyes on the tablecloth: fan ready in right hand.) It was very cleverly managed, Pip, and I congratulate you. You swore—you never contented yourself with merely Saying a thing—you swore that, as far as lay in your power, you'd make my wretched life pleasant for me. And you've denied me the consolation of breaking down. I should have done it—indeed I should. A woman would hardly have thought of this refinement, my kind, considerate friend. (Fan-guard as before.) You have explained things so tenderly and truthfully, too! You haven't spoken or written a word of warning, and you have let me believe in you till the last minute. You haven't condescended to give me your reason yet. No! A woman could not have managed it half so well. Are there many men like you in the world?

Capt. G. I'm sure I don't know. (To Khitmatgar.) Ohe! Simpkin do.

Mrs. H. You call yourself a man of the world, don't you? Do men of the world behave like Devils when they do a woman the honor to get tired of her?

Capt. G. I'm sure I don't know. Don't speak so loud!

Mrs. H. Keep us respectable, O Lord, whatever happens. Don't be afraid of my compromising you. You've chosen your ground far too well, and I've been properly brought up. (Lowering fan.) Haven't you any pity, Pip, except for yourself?

Capt. G. Wouldn't it be rather impertinent of me to say that I'm sorry for you?

Mrs. H. I think you have said it once or twice before. You're growing very careful of my feelings. My God, Pip, I was a good woman once! You said I was. You've made me what I am. What are you going to do with me? What are you going to do with me? Won't you say that you are sorry? (Helps herself to iced asparagus.)

Capt. G. I am sorry for you, if you WANT the pity of such a brute as I am. I'm awf'ly sorry for you.

Mrs. H. Rather tame for a man of the world. Do you think that that admission clears you?

Capt. G. What can I do? I can only tell you what I think of myself. You can't think worse than that?

Mrs. H. Oh, yes, I can! And now, will you tell me the reason of all this? Remorse? Has Bayard been suddenly conscience-stricken?

Capt. G. (Angrily, his eyes still lowered.) No! The thing has come to an end on my side. That's all. Mafisch!

Mrs. H. "That's all. Mafisch!" As though I were a Cairene Dragoman. You used to make prettier speeches. D'you remember when you said?—

Capt. G. For Heaven's sake don't bring that back! Call me anything you like and I'll admit it—

Mrs. H. But you don't care to be reminded of old lies? If I could hope to hurt you one-tenth as much as you have hurt me tonight—No, I wouldn't—I couldn't do it—liar though you are.

Capt. G. I've spoken the truth.

Mrs. H. My dear Sir, you flatter yourself. You have lied over the reason. Pip, remember that I know you as you don't know yourself. You have been everything to me, though you are—(Fanguard.) Oh, what a contemptible Thing it is! And so you are merely tired of me?

Capt. G. Since you insist upon my repeating it—Yes.

Mrs. H. Lie the first. I wish I knew a coarser word. Lie seems so ineffectual in your case. The fire has just died out and there is no fresh one? Think for a minute, Pip, if you care whether I despise you more than I do. Simply Mafisch, is it?

Capt. G. Yes. (Aside.) I think I deserve this.

Mrs. H. Lie number two. Before the next glass chokes you, tell me her name.

Capt. G. (Aside.) I'll make her pay for dragging Minnie into the business! (Aloud.) Is it likely?

Mrs. H. Very likely if you thought that it would flatter your vanity. You'd cry my name on the house-tops to make people turn round.

Capt. G. I wish I had. There would have been an end to this business.

Mrs. H. Oh, no, there would not—And so you were going to be virtuous and blase', were you? To come to me and say: "I've done with you. The incident is clo-osed." I ought to be proud of having kept such a man so long.

Capt. G. (Aside.) It only remains to pray for the end of the dinner. (Aloud.) You know what I think of myself.

Mrs. H. As it's the only person in he world you ever do think of, and as I know your mind thoroughly, I do. You want to get it all over and—Oh, I can't keep you back! And you're going—think of it, Pip—to throw me over for another woman. And you swore that all other women were—Pip, my Pip! She can't care for you as I do. Believe me, she can't. Is it any one that I know?

Capt. G. Thank Goodness it isn't. (Aside.) I expected a cyclone, but not an earthquake.

Mrs. H. She can't! Is there anything that I wouldn't do for you—or haven't done? And to think that I should take this trouble over you, knowing what you are! Do you despise me for it?

Capt. G. (Wiping his mouth to hide a smile.) Again? It's entirely a work of charity on your part.

Mrs. H. Ahhh! But I have no right to resent it.—Is she better-looking than I? Who was it said?—

Capt. G. No—not that!

Mrs. H. I'll be more merciful than you were. Don't you know that all women are alike?

Capt. G. (Aside.) Then this is the exception that proves the rule.

Mrs. H. All of them! I'll tell you anything you like. I will, upon my word! They only want the admiration—from anybody—no matter who—anybody! But there is always one man that they care for more than any one else in the world, and would sacrifice all the others to. Oh, do listen! I've kept the Vaynor man trotting after me like a poodle, and he believes that he is the only man I am interested in. I'll tell you what he said to me.

Capt. G. Spare him. (Aside.) I wonder what his version is.

Mrs. H. He's been waiting for me to look at him all through dinner. Shall I do it, and you can see what an idiot he looks?

Capt. G. "But what imports the nomination of this gentleman?"

Mrs. H. Watch! (Sends a glance to the Vaynor man, who tries vainly to combine a mouthful of ice pudding, a smirk of self-satisfaction, a glare of intense devotion, and the stolidity of a British dining countenance.)

Capt. G. (Critically.) He doesn't look pretty. Why didn't you wait till the spoon was out of his mouth?

Mrs. H. To amuse you. She'll make an exhibition of you as I've made of him; and people will laugh at you. Oh, Pip, can't you see that? It's as plain as the noonday Sun. You'll be trotted about and told lies, and made a fool of like the others. I never made a fool of you, did I?

Capt. G. (Aside.) What a clever little woman it is!

Mrs. H. Well, what have you to say?

Capt. G. I feel better.

Mrs. H. Yes, I suppose so, after I have come down to your level. I couldn't have done it if I hadn't cared for you so much. I have spoken the truth.

Capt. G. It doesn't alter the situation.

Mrs. H. (Passionately.) Then she has said that she cares for you! Don't believe her, Pip. It's a lie—as bad as yours to me!

Capt. G. Ssssteady! I've a notion that a friend of yours is looking at you.

Mrs. H. He! I hate him. He introduced you to me.

Capt. G. (Aside.) And some people would like women to assist in making the laws. Introduction to imply condonement. (Aloud.) Well, you see, if you can remember so far back as that, I couldn't, in common politeness, refuse the offer.

Mrs. H. In common politeness I—We have got beyond that!

Capt. G. (Aside.) Old ground means fresh trouble. (Aloud.) On my honor—

Mrs. H. Your what? Ha, ha!

Capt. G. Dishonor, then. She's not what you imagine. I meant to—

Mrs. H. Don't tell me anything about her! She won't care for you, and when you come back, after having made an exhibition of yourself, you'll find me occupied with—

Capt. G. (Insolently.) You couldn't while I am alive. (Aside.) If that doesn't bring her pride to her rescue, nothing will.

Mrs. H. (Drawing herself up.) Couldn't do it? I—(Softening.) You're right. I don't believe I could—though you are what you are—a coward and a liar in grain.

Capt. G. It doesn't hurt so much after your little lecture—with demonstrations.

Mrs. H. One mass of vanity! Will nothing ever touch you in this life? There must be a Hereafter if it's only for the benefit of—But you will have it all to yourself.

Capt. G. (Under his eyebrows.) Are you certain of that?

Mrs. H. I shall have had mine in this life; and it will serve me right,

Capt. G. But the admiration that you insisted on so strongly a moment ago? (Aside.) Oh, I am a brute!

Mrs. H. (Fiercely.) Will that console me for knowing that you will go to her with the same words, the same arguments, and the—the same pet names you used to me? And if she cares for you, you two will laugh over my story. Won't that be punishment heavy enough even for me—even for me?—And it's all useless. That's another punishment.

Capt. G. (Feebly.) Oh, come! I'm not so low as you think.

Mrs. H. Not now, perhaps, but you will be. Oh, Pip, if a woman flatters your vanity, there's nothing on earth that you would not tell her; and no meanness that you would not do. Have I known you so long without knowing that?

Capt. G. If you can trust me in nothing else—and I don't see why I should be trusted—you can count upon my holding my tongue.

Mrs. H. If you denied everything you've said this evening and declared it was all in fun (a long pause), I'd trust you. Not otherwise. All I ask is, don't tell her my name. Please don't. A man might forget: a woman never would. (Looks up table and sees hostess beginning to collect eyes.) So it's all ended, through no fault of mine—Haven't I behaved beautifully? I've accepted your dismissal, and you managed it as cruelly as you could, and I have made you respect my sex, haven't I? (Arranging gloves and fan.) I only pray that she'll know you some day as I know you now. I wouldn't be you then, for I think even your conceit will be hurt. I hope she'll pay you back the humiliation you've brought on me. I hope—No. I don't! I can't give you up! I must have something to look forward to or I shall go crazy. When it's all over, come back to me, come back to me, and you'll find that you're my Pip still!

Capt. G. (Very clearly.) False move, and you pay for it. It's a girl!

Mrs. H. (Rising.) Then it was true! They said—but I wouldn't insult you by asking. A girl! I was a girl not very long ago. Be good to her, Pip. I daresay she believes in you.

Goes out with an uncertain smile. He watches her through the door, and settles into a chair as the men redistribute themselves.

Capt. G. Now, if there is any Power who looks after this world, will He kindly tell me what I have done? (Reaching out for the claret, and half aloud.) What have I done?

WITH ANY AMAZEMENT

And are not afraid with any amazement. —Marriage Service.

SCENE. bachelor's bedroom-toilet-table arranged with unnatural neatness.

CAPTAIN GADSBY asleep and snoring heavily. Time, 10:30 A. M.—a glorious autumn day at Simla. Enter delicately Captain MAFFLIN of GADSBY's regiment. Looks at sleeper, and shakes his head murmuring "Poor Gaddy." Performs violent fantasia with hair-brushes on chairback.

Capt. M. Wake up, my sleeping beauty! (Roars.)

"Uprouse ye, then, my merry merry men!

It is our opening day!

It is our opening da-ay!"

Gaddy, the little dicky-birds have been billing and cooing for ever so long; and I'm here!

Capt. G. (Sitting up and yawning.) Mornin'. This is awf'ly good of you, old fellow. Most awf'ly good of you. Don't know what I should do without you. 'Pon my soul, I don't. 'Haven't slept a wink all night.

Capt. M. I didn't get in till half-past eleven. 'Had a look at you then, and you seemed to be sleeping as soundly as a condemned criminal.

Capt. G. Jack, if you want to make those disgustingly worn-out jokes, you'd better go away. (With portentous gravity.) It's the happiest day in my life.

Capt. M. (Chuckling grimly.) Not by a very long chalk, my son. You're going through some of the most refined torture you've ever known. But be calm. I am with you. 'Shun! Dress!

Capt. G. Eh! Wha-at?

Capt. M. Do you suppose that you are your own master for the next twelve hours? If you do, of course—(Makes for the door.)

Capt. G. No! For Goodness' sake, old man, don't do that! You'll see me through, won't you? I've been mugging up that beastly drill, and can't remember a line of it.

Capt. M. (Overturning G.'s uniform.) Go and tub. Don't bother me. I'll give you ten minutes to dress in.

INTERVAL, filled by the noise as of one splashing in the bath-room..

Capt. G. (Emerging from dressing-room.) What time is it?

Capt. M. Nearly eleven.

Capt. G. Five hours more. O Lord!

Capt. M. (Aside.) 'First sign of funk, that. 'Wonder if it's going to spread. (Aloud.) Come along to breakfast.

Capt. G. I can't eat anything. I don't want any breakfast.

Capt. M. (Aside.) So early! (Aloud) CAPTAIN Gadsby, I order you to eat breakfast, and a dashed good breakfast, too. None of your bridal airs and graces with me!

Leads G. downstairs and stands over him while he eats two chops.

Capt. G. (Who has looked at his watch thrice in the last five minutes.) What time is it?

Capt. M. Time to come for a walk. Light up.

Capt. G. I haven't smoked for ten days, and I won't now. (Takes cheroot which M. has cut for him, and blows smoke through his nose luxuriously.) We aren't going down the Mall, are we?

Capt. M. (Aside.) They're all alike in these stages. (Aloud.) No, my Vestal. We're going along the quietest road we can find.

Capt. G. Any chance of seeing Her?

Capt. M. Innocent! No! Come along, and, if you want me for the final obsequies, don't cut my eye out with your stick.

Capt. G. (Spinning round.) I say, isn't She the dearest creature that ever walked? What's the time? What comes after "wilt thou take this woman"?

Capt. M. You go for the ring. R'c'lect it'll be on the top of my right-hand little finger, and just be careful how you draw it off, because I shall have the Verger's fees somewhere in my glove.

Capt. G. (Walking forward hastily.) D—the Verger! Come along! It's past twelve and I haven't seen Her since yesterday evening. (Spinning round again.) She's an absolute angel, Jack, and She's a dashed deal too good for me. Look here, does She come up the aisle on my arm, or how?

Capt. M. If I thought that there was the least chance of your remembering anything for two consecutive minutes, I'd tell you. Stop passaging about like that!

Capt. G. (Halting in the middle of the road.) I say, Jack.

Capt. M. Keep quiet for another ten minutes if you can, you lunatic; and walk!

The two tramp at five miles an hour for fifteen minutes.

Capt. G. What's the time? How about the cursed wedding-cake and the slippers? They don't throw 'em about in church, do they?

Capt. M. Invariably. The Padre leads off with his boots.

Capt. G. Confound your silly soul! Don't make fun of me. I can't stand it, and I won't!

Capt. M. (Untroubled.) So-ooo, old horse You'll have to sleep for a couple of hours this afternoon.

Capt. G. (Spinning round.) I'm not going to be treated like a dashed child, understand that.

Capt. M. (Aside.) Nerves gone to fiddle-strings. What a day we're having! (Tenderly putting his hand on G.'s shoulder.) My David, how long have you known this Jonathan? Would I come up here to make a fool of you—after all these years?

Capt. G. (Penitently.) I know, I know, Jack—but I'm as upset as I can be. Don't mind what I say. Just hear me run through the drill and see if I've got it all right:—"To have and to hold for better or worse, as it was in the beginning, is now, and ever shall be, world without end, so help me God. Amen."

Capt. M. (Suffocating with suppressed laughter.) Yes. That's about the gist of it. I'll prompt if you get into a hat.

Capt. G. (Earnestly.) Yes, you'll stick by me, Jack, won't you? I'm awfully happy, but I don't mind telling you that I'm in a blue funk!

Capt. M. (Gravely.) Are you? I should never have noticed it. You don't look like it.

Capt. G. Don't I? That's all right. (Spinning round.) On my soul and honor, Jack, She's the sweetest little angel that ever came down from the sky. There isn't a woman on earth fit to speak to Her.

Capt. M. (Aside.) And this is old Gadsby! (Aloud.) Go on if it relieves you.

Capt. G. You can laugh! That's all you wild asses of bachelors are fit for.

Capt. M. (Drawling.) You never would wait for the troop to come up. You aren't quite married yet, y'know.

Capt. G. Ugh! That reminds me. I don't believe I shall be able to get into any boots Let's go home and try 'em on (Hurries forward.)

Capt. M. 'Wouldn't be in your shoes for anything that Asia has to offer.

Capt. G. (Spinning round.) That just shows your hideous blackness of soul—your dense stupidity—your brutal narrow-mindedness. There's only one fault about you. You're the best of good fellows, and I don't know what I should have done without you, but—you aren't married. (Wags his head gravely.) Take a wife, Jack.

Capt. M. (With a face like a wall.) Ya-as. Whose for choice?

Capt. G. If you're going to be a blackguard, I'm going on—What's the time?

Capt. M. (Hums.) An' since 'twas very clear we drank only ginger-beer, Faith, there must ha' been some stingo in the ginger. Come back, you maniac. I'm going to take you home, and you're going to lie down.

Capt. G. What on earth do I want to lie down for?

Capt. M. Give me a light from your cheroot and see.

Capt. G. (Watching cheroot-butt quiver like a tuning-fork.) Sweet state I'm in!

Capt. M. You are. I'll get you a peg and you'll go to sleep.

They return and M. compounds a four-finger peg.

Capt. G. O bus! bus! It'll make me as drunk as an owl.

Capt. M. 'Curious thing, 'twon't have the slightest effect on you. Drink it off, chuck yourself down there, and go to bye-bye.

Capt. G. It's absurd. I sha'n't sleep, I know I sha'n't!

Falls into heavy doze at end of seven minutes. Capt. M. watches him tenderly.

Capt. M. Poor old Gadsby! I've seen a few turned off before, but never one who went to the gallows in this condition. 'Can't tell how it affects 'em, though. It's the thoroughbreds that sweat when they're backed into double-harness.—And that's the man who went through the guns at Amdheran like a devil possessed of devils. (Leans over G.) But this is worse than the guns, old pal—worse than the guns, isn't it? (G. turns in his sleep, and M. touches him clumsily on the forehead.) Poor, dear old Gaddy! Going like the rest of 'em—going like the rest of 'em—Friend that sticketh closer than a brother—eight years. Dashed bit of a slip of a girl—eight weeks! And—where's your friend? (Smokes disconsolately till church clock strikes three.)

Capt. M. Up with you! Get into your kit.

Capt. C. Already? Isn't it too soon? Hadn't I better have a shave?

Capt. M. No! You're all right. (Aside.) He'd chip his chin to pieces.

Capt. C. What's the hurry?

Capt. M. You've got to be there first.

Capt. C. To be stared at?

Capt. M. Exactly. You're part of the show. Where's the burnisher? Your spurs are in a shameful state.

Capt. G. (Gruffly.) Jack, I be damned if you shall do that for me.

Capt. M. (More gruffly.) Dry up and get dressed! If I choose to clean your spurs, you're under my orders.

Capt. G. dresses. M. follows suit.

Capt. M. (Critically, walking round.) M'—yes, you'll do. Only don't look so like a criminal. Ring, gloves, fees—that's all right for me. Let your moustache alone. Now, if the ponies are ready, we'll go.

Capt. G. (Nervously.) It's much too soon. Let's light up! Let's have a peg! Let's—

Capt. M. Let's make bally asses of ourselves!

BELLS. (Without.)—"Good-peo-ple-all To prayers-we call."

Capt. M. There go the bells! Come on—unless you'd rather not. (They ride off.)

BELLS.—"We honor the King And Brides joy do bring—Good tidings we tell, And ring the Dead's knell."

Capt. G. (Dismounting at the door of the Church.) I say, aren't we much too soon? There are no

end of people inside. I say, aren't we much too late? Stick by me, Jack! What the devil do I do?

Capt. M. Strike an attitude at the head of the aisle and wait for Her. (G. groans as M. wheels him into position before three hundred eyes.)

Capt. M. (Imploringly.) Gaddy, if you love me, for pity's sake, for the Honor of the Regiment, stand up! Chuck yourself into your uniform! Look like a man! I've got to speak to the Padre a minute. (G. breaks into a gentle Perspiration.) If you wipe your face I'll never be your best man again. Stand up! (G. trembles visibly.)

Capt. M. (Returning.) She's coming now. Look out when the music starts. There's the organ beginning to clack.

Bride steps out of 'rickshaw at Church door. G. catches a glimpse of her and takes heart.

ORGAN.—"The Voice that breathed o'er Eden, That earliest marriage day, The primal marriage-blessing, It hath not passed away."

Capt. M. (Watching G.) By Jove! He is looking well. 'Didn't think he had it in him.

Capt. G. How long does this hymn go on for?

Capt. M. It will be over directly. (Anxiously.) (Beginning to bleach and gulp.) Hold on, Gabby, and think 'o the Regiment.

Capt. G. (Measuredly.) I say, there's a big brown lizard crawling up that wall.

Capt. M. My Sainted Mother! The last stage of collapse!

Bride comes up to left of altar, lifts her eyes once to G., who is suddenly smitten mad.

Capt. G. (To himself again and again.) Little Featherweight's a woman—a woman! And I thought she was a little girl.

Capt. M. (In a whisper.) Form the halt—inward wheel.

Capt. G. obeys mechanically and the ceremony proceeds.

PADRE.... only unto her as ye both shall live?

Capt. G. (His throat useless.) Ha-hmmm!

Capt. M. Say you will or you won't. There's no second deal here.

Bride gives response with perfect coolness, and is given away by the father.

Capt. G. (Thinking to show his learning.) Jack give me away now, quick!

Capt. M. You've given yourself away quite enough. Her right hand, man! Repeat! Repeat! "Theodore Philip." Have you forgotten your own name?

Capt. G. stumbles through Affirmation, which Bride repeats without a tremor.

Capt. M. Now the ring! Follow the Padre! Don't pull off my glove! Here it is! Great Cupid, he's found his voice.

Capt. G. repeats Troth in a voice to be heard to the end of the Church and turns on his heel.

Capt. M. (Desperately.) Rein back! Back to your troop! 'Tisn't half legal yet.

PADRE.... joined together let no man put asunder.

Capt. G. paralyzed with fear jibs after Blessing.

Capt. M. (Quickly.) On your own front—one length. Take her with you. I don't come. You've nothing to say. (Capt. G. jingles up to altar.)

Capt. M. (In a piercing rattle meant to be a whisper.) Kneel, you stiff-necked ruffian! Kneel!

PADRE... whose daughters are ye so long as ye do well and are not afraid with any amazement.

Capt. M. Dismiss! Break off! Left wheel!

All troop to vestry. They sign.

Capt. M. Kiss Her, Gaddy.

Capt. G. (Rubbing the ink into his glove.) Eh! Wha-at?

Capt. M. (Taking one pace to Bride.) If you don't, I shall.

Capt. G. (Interposing an arm.) Not this journey!

General kissing, in which Capt. G. is pursued by unknown female.

Capt. G. (Faintly to M.) This is Hades! Can I wipe my face now?

Capt. M. My responsibility has ended. Better ask Misses GADSBY.

Capt. G. winces as though shot and procession is Mendelssohned out of Church to house, where usual tortures take place over the wedding-cake.

Capt. M. (At table.) Up with you, Gaddy. They expect a speech.

Capt. G. (After three minutes' agony.) Ha-hmmm. (Thunders Of applause.)

Capt. M. Doocid good, for a first attempt. Now go and change your kit while Mamma is weeping over "the Missus." (Capt. G. disappears. Capt. M. starts up tearing his hair.) It's not half legal. Where are the shoes? Get an ayah.

AYAH. Missie Captain Sahib done gone band karo all the jutis.

Capt. M. (Brandishing scab larded sword.) Woman, produce those shoes! Some one lend me a bread-knife. We mustn't crack Gaddy's head more than it is. (Slices heel off white satin slipper and puts slipper up his sleeve.)

Where is the Bride? (To the company at large.) Be tender with that rice. It's a heathen custom. Give me the big bag.

Bride slips out quietly into 'rickshaw and departs toward the sunset.

Capt. M. (In the open.) Stole away, by Jove! So much the worse for Gaddy! Here he is. Now Gaddy, this'll be livelier than Amdberan! Where's your horse?

Capt. G. (Furiously, seeing that the women are out of an earshot.) Where the d——'s my Wife?

Capt. M. Half-way to Mahasu by this time. You'll have to ride like Young Lochinvar.

Horse comes round on his hind legs; refuses to let G. handle him.

Capt. G. Oh you will, will you? Get 'round, you brute—you hog—you beast! Get round!

Wrenches horse's head over, nearly breaking lower jaw: swings himself into saddle, and sends home both spurs in the midst of a spattering gale of Best Patna.

Capt. M. For your life and your love—ride, Gaddy—And God bless you!

Throws half a pound of rice at G. who disappears, bowed forward on the saddle, in a cloud of sunlit dust.

Capt. M. I've lost old Gaddy. (Lights cigarette and strolls off, singing absently):—"You may carve it on his tombstone, you may cut it on his card, That a young man married is a young man marred!"

Miss DEERCOURT. (From her horse.) Really, Captain Mafflin! You are more plain spoken than polite!

Capt. M. (Aside.) They say marriage is like cholera. 'Wonder who'll be the next victim.

White satin slipper slides from his sleeve and falls at his feet. Left wondering.

THE GARDEN OF EDEN

And ye shall be as—Gods!

SCENE. Thymy grass-plot at back of the Mahasu dak-bungalow, overlooking little wooded valley. On the left, glimpse of the Dead Forest of Fagoo; on the right, Simla Hills. In background, line of the Snows. CAPTAIN GADSBY, now three weeks a husband, is smoking the pipe of peace on a rug in the sunshine. Banjo and tobacco-pouch on rug. Overhead the Fagoo eagles. Mrs. G. comes out of bungalow.

Mrs. G. My husband!

Capt. G. (Lazily, with intense enjoyment.) Eh, wha-at? Say that again.

Mrs. G. I've written to Mamma and told her that we shall be back on the 17th.

Capt. G. Did you give her my love?

Mrs. G. No, I kept all that for myself. (Sitting down by his side.) I thought you wouldn't mind.

Capt. G. (With mock sternness.) I object awf'ly. How did you know that it was yours to keep?

Mrs. G. I guessed, Phil.

Capt. G. (Rapturously.) Lit-tle Featherweight!

Mrs. G. I won' t be called those sporting pet names, bad boy.

Capt. G. You'll be called anything I choose. Has it ever occurred to you, Madam, that you are my Wife?

Mrs. G. It has. I haven't ceased wondering at it yet.

Capt. G. Nor I. It seems so strange; and yet, somehow, it doesn't. (Confidently.) You see, it could have been no one else.

Mrs. G. (Softly.) No. No one else—for me or for you. It must have been all arranged from the beginning. Phil, tell me again what made you care for me.

Capt. G. How could I help it? You were you, you know.

Mrs. G. Did you ever want to help it? Speak the truth!

Capt. G. (A twinkle in his eye.) I did, darling, just at the first. Rut only at the very first. (Chuckles.) I called you—stoop low and I'll whisper—"a little beast." Ho! Ho! Ho!

Mrs. G. (Taking him by the moustache and making him sit up.) "A-little-beast!" Stop laughing over your crime! And yet you had the—the—awful cheek to propose to me!

Capt. C. I'd changed my mind then. And you weren't a little beast any more.

Mrs. G. Thank you, sir! And when was I ever?

Capt. G. Never! But that first day, when you gave me tea in that peach-colored muslin gown thing, you looked—you did indeed, dear—such an absurd little mite. And I didn't know what to say to you.

Mrs. G. (Twisting moustache.) So you said "little beast." Upon my word, Sir! I called you a "Crrrreature," but I wish now I had called you something worse.

Capt. G. (Very meekly.) I apologize, but you're hurting me awf'ly. (Interlude.) You're welcome to torture me again on those terms.

Mrs. G. Oh, why did you let me do it?

Capt. G. (Looking across valley.) No reason in particular, but—if it amused you or did you any good—you might—wipe those dear little boots of yours on me.

Mrs. G. (Stretching out her hands.) Don't! Oh, don't! Philip, my King, please don't talk like that. It's how I feel. You're so much too good for me. So much too good!

Capt. G. Me! I'm not fit to put my arm around you. (Puts it round.)

Mrs. C. Yes, you are. But I—what have I ever done?

Capt. G. Given me a wee bit of your heart, haven't you, my Queen!

Mrs. G. That's nothing. Any one would do that. They cou—couldn't help it.

Capt. G. Pussy, you'll make me horribly conceited. Just when I was beginning to feel so humble, too.

Mrs. G. Humble! I don't believe it's in your character.

Capt. G. What do you know of my character, Impertinence?

Mrs. G. Ah, but I shall, shan't I, Phil? I shall have time in all the years and years to come, to know everything about you; and there will be no secrets between us.

Capt. G. Little witch! I believe you know me thoroughly already.

Mrs. G. I think I can guess. You're selfish?

Capt. G. Yes.

Mrs. G. Foolish?

Capt. G. Very.

Mrs. G. And a dear?

Capt. G. That is as my lady pleases.

Mrs. G. Then your lady is pleased. (A pause.) D'you know that we're two solemn, serious, grown-up people—

Capt. G. (Tilting her straw hat over her eyes.) You grown-up! Pooh! You're a baby.

Mrs. G. And we're talking nonsense.

Capt. G. Then let's go on talking nonsense. I rather like it. Pussy, I'll tell you a secret. Promise not to repeat?

Mrs. G. Ye-es. Only to you.

Capt. G. I love you.

Mrs. G. Re-ally! For how long?

Capt. G. Forever and ever.

Mrs. G. That's a long time.

Capt. G. 'Think so? It's the shortest I can do with.

Mrs. G. You're getting quite clever.

Capt. G. I'm talking to you.

Mrs. G. Prettily turned. Hold up your stupid old head and I'll pay you for it.

Capt. G. (Affecting supreme contempt.) Take it yourself if you want it.

Mrs. G. I've a great mind to—and I will! (Takes it and is repaid with interest.)

Capt. G, Little Featherweight, it's my opinion that we are a couple of idiots.

Mrs. G. We're the only two sensible people in the world. Ask the eagle. He's coming by.

Capt. G. Ah! I dare say he's seen a good many sensible people at Mahasu. They say that those birds live for ever so long.

Mrs. G. How long?

Capt. G. A hundred and twenty years.

Mrs. G. A hundred and twenty years! O-oh! And in a hundred and twenty years where will these two sensible people be?

Capt. G. What does it matter so long as we are together now?

Mrs. G. (Looking round the horizon.) Yes. Only you and I—I and you—in the whole wide, wide world until the end. (Sees the line of the Snows.) How big and quiet the hills look! D'you think they care for us?

Capt. G. 'Can't say I've consulted 'em particularly. I care, and that's enough for me.

Mrs. G. (Drawing nearer to him.) Yes, now—but afterward. What's that little black blur on the Snows?

Capt. G. A snowstorm, forty miles away. You'll see it move, as the wind carries it across the face of that spur and then it will be all gone.

Mrs. G. And then it will be all gone. (Shivers.)

Capt. G. (Anxiously.) 'Not chilled, pet, are you? 'Better let me get your cloak.

Mrs. G. No. Don't leave me, Phil. Stay here. I believe I am afraid. Oh, why are the hills so horrid! Phil, promise me that you'll always love me.

Capt. G. What's the trouble, darling? I can't promise any more than I have; but I'll promise that again and again if you like.

Mrs. G. (Her head on his shoulder.) Say it, then—say it! N-no—don't! The—the—eagles would laugh. (Recovering.) My husband, you've married a little goose.

Capt. G. (Very tenderly.) Have I? I am content whatever she is, so long as she is mine.

Mrs. G. (Quickly.) Because she is yours or because she is me mineself?

Capt. G. Because she is both. (Piteously.) I'm not clever, dear, and I don't think I can make myself understood properly.

Mrs. G. I understand. Pip, will you tell me something?

Capt. G. Anything you like. (Aside.) I wonder what's coming now.

Mrs. G. (Haltingly, her eyes lowered.) You told me once in the old days—centuries and centuries ago—that you had been engaged before. I didn't say anything—then.

Capt. G. (Innocently.) Why not?

Mrs. G. (Raising her eyes to his.) Because—because I was afraid of losing you, my heart. But now—tell about it—please.

Capt. G. There's nothing to tell. I was awf'ly old then—nearly two and twenty—and she was quite that.

Mrs. G. That means she was older than you. I shouldn't like her to have been younger. Well?

Capt. G. Well, I fancied myself in love and raved about a bit, and—oh, yes, by Jove! I made up poetry. Ha! Ha!

Mrs. G. You never wrote any for me! What happened?

Capt. G. I came out here, and the whole thing went phut. She wrote to say that there had been a mistake, and then she married.

Mrs. G. Did she care for you much?

Capt. G. No. At least she didn't show it as far as I remember.

Mrs. G. As far as you remember! Do you remember her name? (Hears it and bows her head.) Thank you, my husband.

Capt. G. Who but you had the right? Now, Little Featherweight, have you ever been mixed up in any dark and dismal tragedy?

Mrs. G. If you call me Mrs. Gadsby, p'raps I'll tell.

Capt. G. (Throwing Parade rasp into his voice.) Mrs. Gadsby, confess!

Mrs. G. Good Heavens, Phil! I never knew that you could speak in that terrible voice.

Capt. G. You don't know half my accomplishments yet. Wait till we are settled in the Plains, and I'll show you how I bark at my troop. You were going to say, darling?

Mrs. G. I—I don't like to, after that voice. (Tremulously.) Phil, never you dare to speak to me in that tone, whatever I may do!

Capt. G. My poor little love! Why, you're shaking all over. I am so sorry. Of course I never meant to upset you Don't tell me anything, I'm a brute.

Mrs. G. No, you aren't, and I will tell—There was a man.

Capt. G. (Lightly.) Was there? Lucky man!

Mrs. G. (In a whisper.) And I thought I cared for him.

Capt. G. Still luckier man! Well?

Mrs. G. And I thought I cared for him—and I didn't—and then you came—and I cared for you very, very much indeed. That's all. (Face hidden.) You aren't angry, are you?

Capt. G. Angry? Not in the least. (Aside.) Good Lord, what have I done to deserve this angel?

Mrs. G. (Aside.) And he never asked for the name! How funny men are! But perhaps it's as well.

Capt. G. That man will go to heaven because you once thought you cared for him. 'Wonder if you'll ever drag me up there?

Mrs. G. (Firmly.) 'Sha'n't go if you don't.

Capt. G. Thanks. I say, Pussy, I don't know much about your religious beliefs. You were brought up to believe in a heaven and all that, weren't you?

Mrs. G. Yes. But it was a pincushion heaven, with hymn-books in all the pews.

Capt. G. (Wagging his head with intense conviction.) Never mind. There is a pukka heaven.

Mrs. G. Where do you bring that message from, my prophet?

Capt. G. Here! Because we care for each other. So it's all right.

Mrs. G. (As a troop of langurs crash through the branches.) So it's all right. But Darwin says that we came from those!

Capt. G. (Placidly.) Ah! Darwin was never in love with an angel. That settles it. Sstt, you brutes! Monkeys, indeed! You shouldn't read those books.

Mrs. G. (Folding her hands.) If it pleases my Lord the King to issue proclamation.

Capt. G. Don't, dear one. There are no orders between us. Only I'd rather you didn't. They lead to nothing, and bother people's heads.

Mrs. G. Like your first engagement.

Capt. G. (With an immense calm.) That was a necessary evil and led to you. Are you nothing?

Mrs. G. Not so very much, am I?

Capt. G. All this world and the next to me.

Mrs. G. (Very softly.) My boy of boys! Shall I tell you something?

Capt. G. Yes, if it's not dreadful—about other men.

Mrs. G. It's about my own bad little self.

Capt. G. Then it must be good. Go on, dear.

Mrs. G. (Slowly.) I don't know why I'm telling you, Pip; but if ever you marry again—(Interlude.) Take your hand from my mouth or I'll bite! In the future, then remember—I don't know quite how to put it!

Capt. G. (Snorting indignantly.) Don't try. "Marry again," indeed!

Mrs. G. I must. Listen, my husband. Never, never, never tell your wife anything that you do not wish her to remember and think over all her life. Because a woman—yes, I am a woman—can't forget.

Capt. G. By Jove, how do you know that?

Mrs. G. (Confusedly.) I don't. I'm only guessing. I am—I was—a silly little girl; but I feel that I know so much, oh, so very much more than you, dearest. To begin with, I'm your wife.

Capt. G. So I have been led to believe.

Mrs. G. And I shall want to know every one of your secrets—to share everything you know with you. (Stares round desperately.)

Capt. G. So you shall, dear, so you shall—but don't look like that.

Mrs. G. For your own sake don't stop me, Phil. I shall never talk to you in this way again. You must not tell me! At least, not now. Later on, when I'm an old matron it won't matter, but if you love me, be very good to me now; for this part of my life I shall never forget! Have I made you understand?

Capt. G. I think so, child. Have I said anything yet that you disapprove of?

Mrs. G. Will you be very angry? That—that voice, and what you said about the engagement—

Capt. G. But you asked to be told that, darling.

Mrs. G. And that's why you shouldn't have told me! You must be the Judge, and, oh, Pip, dearly as I love you, I shan't be able to help you! I shall hinder you, and you must judge in spite of me!

Capt. G. (Meditatively.) We have a great many things to find out together, God help us both—say so, Pussy—but we shall understand each other better every day; and I think I'm beginning to see now. How in the world did you come to know just the importance of giving me just that lead?

Mrs. G. I've told you that I don't know. Only somehow it seemed that, in all this new life, I was being guided for your sake as well as my own.

Capt. G. (Aside.) Then Mafflin was right! They know, and we—we're blind all of us. (Lightly.) 'Getting a little beyond our depth, dear, aren't we? I'll remember, and, if I fail, let me be punished as I deserve.

Mrs. G. There shall be no punishment. We'll start into life together from here—you and I—and no one else.

Capt. G. And no one else. (A pause.) Your eyelashes are all wet, Sweet? Was there ever such a quaint little Absurdity?

Mrs. G. Was there ever such nonsense talked before?

Capt. G. (Knocking the ashes out of his pipe.) 'Tisn't what we say, it's what we don't say, that helps. And it's all the profoundest philosophy. But no one would understand—even if it were put into a book.

Mrs. G. The idea! No—only we ourselves, or people like ourselves—if there are any people like us.

Capt. G. (Magisterially.) All people, not like ourselves, are blind idiots.

Mrs. G. (Wiping her eyes.) Do you think, then, that there are any people as happy as we are?

Capt. G. 'Must be—unless we've appropriated all the happiness in the world.

Mrs. G. (Looking toward Simla.) Poor dears! Just fancy if we have!

Capt. G. Then we'll hang on to the whole show, for it's a great deal too jolly to lose—eh, wife 'o mine?

Mrs. G. O Pip! Pip! How much of you is a solemn, married man and how much a horrid slangy schoolboy?

Capt. G. When you tell me how much of you was eighteen last birthday and how much is as old as the Sphinx and twice as mysterious, perhaps I'll attend to you. Lend me that banjo. The spirit moveth me to yowl at the sunset.

Mrs. G. Mind! It's not tuned. Ah! How that jars!

Capt. G. (Turning pegs.) It's amazingly different to keep a banjo to proper pitch.

Mrs. G. It's the same with all musical instruments, What shall it be?

Capt. G. "Vanity," and let the hills hear. (Sings through the first and half of the second verse. Turning to Mrs. G.) Now, chorus! Sing, Pussy!

BOTH TOGETHER. (Con brio, to the horror of the monkeys who are settling for the night.)—

"Vanity, all is Vanity," said Wisdom, scorning me—I clasped my true Love's tender hand and answered frank and free-ee "If this be Vanity who'd be wise? If this be Vanity who'd be wise? If this be Vanity who'd be wi-ise (Crescendo.) Vanity let it be!"

Mrs. G. (Defiantly to the grey of the evening sky.) "Vanity let it be!"

ECHO. (Prom the Fagoo spur.) Let it be!

FATIMA

And you may go in every room of the house and see everything that is there, but into the Blue Room you must not go. —The Story of Blue Beard.

SCENE. The GADSBYS' bungalow in the Plains. Time, 11 A. M. on a Sunday morning. Captain GADSBY, in his shirt-sleeves, is bending over a complete set of Hussar's equipment, from saddle to picketing-rope, which is neatly spread over the floor of his study. He is smoking an unclean briar, and his forehead is puckered with thought.

Capt. G. (To himself, fingering a headstall.) Jack's an ass. There's enough brass on this to load a mule—and, if the Americans know anything about anything, it can be cut down to a bit only. 'Don't want the watering-bridle, either. Humbug!—Half a dozen sets of chains and pulleys for one horse! Rot! (Scratching his head.) Now, let's consider it all over from the beginning. By Jove, I've forgotten the scale of weights! Never mind. 'Keep the bit only, and eliminate every boss from the crupper to breastplate. No breastplate at all. Simple leather strap across the breast—like the Russians. Hi! Jack never thought of that!

Mrs. G. (Entering hastily, her hand bound in a cloth.) Oh, Pip, I've scalded my hand over that horrid, horrid Tiparee jam!

Capt. G. (Absently.) Eh! Wha-at?

Mrs. G. (With round-eyed reproach.) I've scalded it aw-fully! Aren't you sorry? And I did so want that jam to jam properly.

Capt. G. Poor little woman! Let me kiss the place and make it well. (Unrolling bandage.) You small sinner! Where's that scald? I can't see it.

Mrs. G. On the top of the little finger. There!—It's a most 'normous big burn!

Capt. G. (Kissing little finger.) Baby! Let Hyder look after the jam. You know I don't care for sweets.

Mrs. G. Indeed?—Pip!

Capt. G. Not of that kind, anyhow. And now run along, Minnie, and leave me to my own base devices. I'm busy.

Mrs. G. (Calmly settling herself in long chair.) So I see. What a mess you're making! Why have you brought all that smelly leather stuff into the house?

Capt. G. To play with. Do you mind, dear?

Mrs. G. Let me play too. I'd like it.

Capt. G. I'm afraid you wouldn't. Pussy—Don't you think that jam will burn, or whatever it is that jam does when it's not looked after by a clever little housekeeper?

Mrs. G. I thought you said Hyder could attend to it. I left him in the veranda, stirring—when I hurt myself so.

Capt. G. (His eye returning to the equipment.) Po-oor little woman!—Three pounds four and seven is three eleven, and that can be cut down to two eight, with just a lee-tle care, without

weakening anything. Farriery is all rot in incompetent hands. What's the use of a shoe-case when a man's scouting? He can't stick it on with a lick—like a stamp—the shoe! Skittles—

Mrs. G. What's skittles? Pah! What is this leather cleaned with?

Capt. G. Cream and champagne and—Look here, dear, do you really want to talk to me about anything important?

Mrs. G. No. I've done my accounts, and I thought I'd like to see what you're doing.

Capt. G. Well, love, now you've seen and—Would you mind?—That is to say—Minnie, I really am busy.

Mrs. G. You want me to go?

Capt. G, Yes, dear, for a little while. This tobacco will hang in your dress, and saddlery doesn't interest you.

Mrs. G. Everything you do interests me, Pip.

Capt. G. Yes, I know, I know, dear. I'll tell you all about it some day when I've put a head on this thing. In the meantime—

Mrs. G. I'm to be turned out of the room like a troublesome child?

Capt. G. No-o. I don't mean that exactly. But, you see, I shall be tramping up and down, shifting these things to and fro, and I shall be in your way. Don't you think so?

Mrs. G. Can't I lift them about? Let me try. (Reaches forward to trooper's saddle.)

Capt. G. Good gracious, child, don't touch it. You'll hurt yourself. (Picking up saddle.) Little girls aren't expected to handle numdahs. Now, where would you like it put? (Holds saddle above his head.)

Mrs. G. (A break in her voice.) Nowhere. Pip, how good you are—and how strong! Oh, what's that ugly red streak inside your arm?

Capt. G. (Lowering saddle quickly.) Nothing. It's a mark of sorts. (Aside.) And Jack's coming to tiffin with his notions all cut and dried!

Mrs. G. I know it's a mark, but I've never seen it before. It runs all up the arm. What is it?

Capt. G. A cut—if you want to know.

Mrs. G. Want to know! Of course I do! I can't have my husband cut to pieces in this way. How did it come? Was it an accident? Tell me, Pip.

Capt. G. (Grimly.) No. 'Twasn't an accident. I got it—from a man—in Afghanistan.

Mrs. G. In action? Oh, Pip, and you never told me!

Capt. G. I'd forgotten all about it.

Mrs. G. Hold up your arm! What a horrid, ugly scar! Are you sure it doesn't hurt now! How did the man give it you?

Capt. G. (Desperately looking at his watch.) With a knife. I came down—old Van Loo did, that's to say—and fell on my leg, so I couldn't run. And then this man came up and began chopping at me as I sprawled.

Mrs. G. Oh, don't, don't! That's enough!—Well, what happened?

Capt. G. I couldn't get to my holster, and Mafflin came round the corner and stopped the performance.

Mrs. G. How? He's such a lazy man, I don't believe he did.

Capt. G. Don't you? I don't think the man had much doubt about it. Jack cut his head off.

Mrs. G. Cut-his-head-off! "With one blow," as they say in the books?

Capt. G. I'm not sure. I was too interested in myself to know much about it. Anyhow, the head was off, and Jack was punching old Van Loo in the ribs to make him get up. Now you know all about it, dear, and now—

Mrs. G. You want me to go, of course. You never told me about this, though I've been married to you for ever so long; and you never would have told me if I hadn't found out; and you never do tell me anything about yourself, or what you do, or what you take an interest in.

Capt. G. Darling, I'm always with you, aren't I?

Mrs. G. Always in my pocket, you were going to say. I know you are; but you are always thinking away from me.

Capt. G. (Trying to hide a smile.) Am I? I wasn't aware of it. I'm awf'ly sorry.

Mrs. G. (Piteously.) Oh, don't make fun of me! Pip, you know what I mean. When you are reading one of those things about Cavalry, by that idiotic Prince—why doesn't he be a Prince instead of a stable-boy?

Capt. G. Prince Kraft a stable-boy—Oh, my Aunt! Never mind, dear. You were going to say?

Mrs. G. It doesn't matter; you don't care for what I say. Only—only you get up and walk about the room, staring in front of you, and then Mafflin comes in to dinner, and after I'm in the drawing-room I can hear you and him talking, and talking, and talking, about things I can't understand, and—oh, I get so tired and feel so lonely!—I don't want to complain and be a trouble, Pip; but I do indeed I do!

Capt. G. My poor darling! I never thought of that. Why don't you ask some nice people in to dinner?

Mrs. G. Nice people! Where am I to find them? Horrid frumps! And if I did, I shouldn't be amused. You know I only want you.

Capt. G. And you have me surely, Sweetheart?

Mrs. G. I have not! Pip why don't you take me into your life?

Capt. G. More than I do? That would be difficult, dear.

Mrs. G. Yes, I suppose it would—to you. I'm no help to you—no companion to you; and you like to have it so.

Capt. G. Aren't you a little unreasonable, Pussy?

Mrs. G. (Stamping her foot.) I'm the most reasonable woman in the world—when I'm treated properly.

Capt. G. And since when have I been treating you improperly?

Mrs. G. Always—and since the beginning. You know you have.

Capt. G. I don't; but I'm willing to be convinced.

Mrs. G. (Pointing to saddlery.) There!

Capt. G. How do you mean?

Mrs. G. What does all that mean? Why am I not to be told? Is it so precious?

Capt. G. I forget its exact Government value just at present. It means that it is a great deal too heavy.

Mrs. G. Then why do you touch it?

Capt. G. To make it lighter. See here, little love, I've one notion and Jack has another, but we are both agreed that all this equipment is about thirty pounds too heavy. The thing is how to cut it down without weakening any part of it, and, at the same time, allowing the trooper to carry everything he wants for his own comfort—socks and shirts and things of that kind.

Mrs. G. Why doesn't he pack them in a little trunk?

Capt. G. (Kissing her.) Oh, you darling! Pack them in a little trunk, indeed! Hussars don't carry trunks, and it's a most important thing to make the horse do all the carrying.

Mrs. G. But why need you bother about it? You're not a trooper.

Capt. G. No; but I command a few score of him; and equipment is nearly everything in these days.

Mrs. G. More than me?

Capt. G. Stupid! Of course not; but it's a matter that I'm tremendously interested in, because if I or Jack, or I and Jack, work out some sort of lighter saddlery and all that, it's possible that we may get it adopted.

Mrs. G. How?

Capt. G. Sanctioned at Home, where they will make a sealed pattern—a pattern that all the saddlers must copy—and so it will be used by all the regiments.

Mrs. G. And that interests you?

Capt. G. It's part of my profession, y'know, and my profession is a good deal to me. Everything in a soldier's equipment is important, and if we can improve that equipment, so much the better for the soldiers and for us.

Mrs. G. Who's "us"?

Capt. G. Jack and I; only Jack's notions are too radical. What's that big sigh for, Minnie?

Mrs. G. Oh, nothing—and you've kept all this a secret from me! Why?

Capt. G. Not a secret, exactly, dear. I didn't say anything about it to you because I didn't think it would amuse you.

Mrs. G. And am I only made to be amused?

Capt. G. No, of course. I merely mean that it couldn't interest you.

Mrs. G. It's your work and—and if you'd let me, I'd count all these things up. If they are too heavy, you know by how much they are too heavy, and you must have a list of things made out to your scale of lightness, and—

Capt. G. I have got both scales somewhere in my head; but it's hard to tell how light you can make a head-stall, for instance, until you've actually had a model made.

Mrs. G. But if you read out the list, I could copy it down, and pin it up there just above your table. Wouldn't that do?

Capt. G. It would be awf'ly nice, dear, but it would be giving you trouble for nothing. I can't work that way. I go by rule of thumb. I know the present scale of weights, and the other one—the one that I'm trying to work to—will shift and vary so much that I couldn't be certain, even if I wrote it down.

Mrs. G. I'm so sorry. I thought I might help. Is there anything else that I could be of use in?

Capt. G. (Looking round the room.) I can't think of anything. You're always helping me you know.

Mrs. G. Am I? How?

Capt. G. You are of course, and as long as you're near me—I can't explain exactly, but it's in the air.

Mrs. G. And that's why you wanted to send me away?

Capt. G. That's only when I'm trying to do work—grubby work like this.

Mrs. G. Mafflin's better, then, isn't he?

Capt. G. (Rashly.) Of course he is. Jack and I have been thinking along the same groove for two or three years about this equipment. It's our hobby, and it may really be useful some day.

Mrs. G. (After a pause.) And that's all that you have away from me?

Capt. G. It isn't very far away from you now. Take care the oil on that bit doesn't come off on your dress.

Mrs. G. I wish—I wish so much that I could really help you. I believe I could—if I left the room. But that's not what I mean.

Capt. G. (Aside.) Give me patience! I wish she would go. (Aloud.) I assure you you can't do anything for me, Minnie, and I must really settle down to this. Where's my pouch?

Mrs. G. (Crossing to writing-table.) Here you are, Bear. What a mess you keep your table in!

Capt. G. Don' ttouch it. There's a method in my madness, though you mightn't think of it.

Mrs. G. (At table.) I want to look—Do you keep accounts, Pip?

Capt. G. (Bending over saddlery.) Of a sort. Are you rummaging among the Troop papers? Be careful.

Mrs. G. Why? I sha'n't disturb anything. Good gracious! I had no idea that you had anything to do with so many sick horses.

Capt. G. 'Wish I hadn't, but they insist on falling sick. Minnie, if I were you I really should not investigate those papers. You may come across something that you won't like.

Mrs. G. Why will you always treat me like a child? I know I'm not displacing the horrid things.

Capt. G. (Resignedly.) Very well, then. Don't blame me if anything happens. Play with the table and let me go on with the saddlery. (Slipping hand into trousers-pocket.) Oh, the deuce!

Mrs. G. (Her back to G.) What's that for?

Capt. G. Nothing. (Aside.) There's not much in it, but I wish I'd torn it up.

Mrs. G. (Turning over contents of table.) I know you'll hate me for this; but I do want to see what your work is like. (A pause.) Pip, what are "farcybuds"?

Capt. G. Hah! Would you really like to know? They aren't pretty things.

Mrs. G. This Journal of Veterinary Science says they are of "absorbing interest." Tell me.

Capt. G. (Aside.) It may turn her attention.

Gives a long and designedly loathsome account of glanders and farcy.

Mrs. G. Oh, that's enough. Don't go on!

Capt. G. But you wanted to know—Then these things suppurate and matterate and spread—

Mrs. G. Pin, you're making me sick! You're a horrid, disgusting schoolboy.

Capt. G. (On his knees among the bridles.) You asked to be told. It's not my fault if you worry me into talking about horrors.

Mrs. G. Why didn't you say No?

Capt. G. Good Heavens, child! Have you come in here simply to bully me?

Mrs. G. I bully you? How could I! You're so strong. (Hysterically.) Strong enough to pick me up and put me outside the door and leave me there to cry. Aren't you?

Capt. G. It seems to me that you're an irrational little baby. Are you quite well?

Mrs. G. Do I look ill? (Returning to table). Who is your lady friend with the big grey envelope and the fat monogram outside?

Capt. G. (Aside.) Then it wasn't locked up, confound it. (Aloud.) "God made her, therefore let

her pass for a woman." You remember what farcybuds are like?

Mrs. G. (Showing envelope.) This has nothing to do with them. I'm going to open it. May I?

Capt. G. Certainly, if you want to. I'd sooner you didn't though. I don't ask to look at your letters to the Deercourt girl.

Mrs. G. You'd better not, Sir! (Takes letter from envelope.) Now, may I look? If you say no, I shall cry.

Capt. G. You've never cried in my knowledge of you, and I don't believe you could.

Mrs. G. I feel very like it today, Pip. Don't be hard on me. (Reads letter.) It begins in the middle, without any "Dear Captain Gadsby," or anything. How funny!

Capt. G. (Aside.) No, it's not Dear Captain Gadsby, or anything, now. How funny!

Mrs. G. What a strange letter! (Reads.) "And so the moth has come too near the candle at last, and has been singed into—shall I say Respectability? I congratulate him, and hope he will be as happy as he deserves to be." What does that mean? Is she congratulating you about our marriage?

Capt. G. Yes, I suppose so.

Mrs. G. (Still reading letter.) She seems to be a particular friend of yours.

Capt. G. Yes. She was an excellent matron of sorts—a Mrs. Herriott—wife of a Colonel Herriott. I used to know some of her people at Home long ago—before I came out.

Mrs. G. Some Colonel's wives are young—as young as me. I knew one who was younger.

Capt. G. Then it couldn't have been Mrs. Herriott. She was old enough to have been your mother, dear.

Mrs. G. I remember now. Mrs. Scargill was talking about her at the Dutfins' tennis, before you came for me, on Tuesday. Captain Mafflin said she was a "dear old woman." Do you know, I think Mafflin is a very clumsy man with his feet.

Capt. G. (Aside.) Good old Jack! (Aloud.) Why, dear?

Mrs. G. He had put his cup down on the ground then, and he literally stepped into it. Some of the tea spirted over my dress—the grey one. I meant to tell you about it before.

Capt. G. (Aside.) There are the makings of a strategist about Jack though his methods are coarse. (Aloud.) You'd better get a new dress, then. (Aside.) Let us pray that that will turn her.

Mrs. G. Oh, it isn't stained in the least. I only thought that I'd tell you. (Returning to letter.) What an extraordinary person! (Reads.) "But need I remind you that you have taken upon yourself a charge of wardship"—what in the world is a charge of wardship?—"which as you yourself know, may end in Consequences"—

Capt. G. (Aside.) It's safest to let em see everything as they come across it; but 'seems to me that there are exceptions to the rule. (Aloud.) I told you that there was nothing to be gained from rearranging my table.

Mrs. G. (Absently.) What does the woman mean? She goes on talking about Consequences—

"almost inevitable Consequences" with a capital C—for half a page. (Flushing scarlet.) Oh, good gracious! How abominable!

Capt. G. (Promptly.) Do you think so? Doesn't it show a sort of motherly interest in us? (Aside.) Thank Heaven. Harry always wrapped her meaning up safely! (Aloud.) Is it absolutely necessary to go on with the letter, darling?

Mrs. G. It's impertinent—it's simply horrid. What right has this woman to write in this way to you? She oughtn't to.

Capt. G. When you write to the Deercourt girl, I notice that you generally fill three or four sheets. Can't you let an old woman babble on paper once in a way? She means well.

Mrs. G. I don't care. She shouldn't write, and if she did, you ought to have shown me her letter.

Capt. G. Can't you understand why I kept it to myself, or must I explain at length—as I explained the farcybuds?

Mrs. G. (Furiously.) Pip I hate you! This is as bad as those idiotic saddle-bags on the floor. Never mind whether it would please me or not, you ought to have given it to me to read.

Capt. G. It comes to the same thing. You took it yourself.

Mrs. G. Yes, but if I hadn't taken it, you wouldn't have said a word. I think this Harriet Herriott—it's like a name in a book—is an interfering old Thing.

Capt. G. (Aside.) So long as you thoroughly understand that she is old, I don't much care what you think. (Aloud.) Very good, dear. Would you like to write and tell her so? She's seven thousand miles away.

Mrs. G. I don't want to have anything to do with her, but you ought to have told me. (Turning to last page of letter.) And she patronizes me, too. I've never seen her! (Reads.) "I do not know how the world stands with you; in all human probability I shall never know; but whatever I may have said before, I pray for her sake more than for yours that all may be well. I have learned what misery means, and I dare not wish that any one dear to you should share my knowledge."

Capt. G. Good God! Can't you leave that letter alone, or, at least, can't you refrain from reading it aloud? I've been through it once. Put it back on the desk. Do you hear me?

Mrs. G. (Irresolutely.) I sh-sha'n't! (Looks at G.'s eyes.) Oh, Pip, please! I didn't mean to make you angry—'Deed, I didn't. Pip, I'm so sorry. I know I've wasted your time—

Capt. G. (Grimly.) You have. Now, will you be good enough to go—if there is nothing more in my room that you are anxious to pry into?

Mrs. G. (Putting out her hands.) Oh, Pip, don't look at me like that! I've never seen you look like that before and it hu-urts me! I'm sorry. I oughtn't to have been here at all, and—and—and—(sobbing.) Oh, be good to me! Be good to me! There's only you—anywhere! Breaks down in long chair, hiding face in cushions.

Capt. G. (Aside.) She doesn't know how she flicked me on the raw. (Aloud, bending over chair.) I didn't mean to be harsh, dear—I didn't really. You can stay here as long as you please, and do what you please. Don't cry like that. You'll make yourself sick. (Aside.) What on earth has come over her? (Aloud.) Darling, what's the matter with you?

Mrs. G. (Her face still hidden.) Let me go—let me go to my own room. Only—only say you aren't angry with me.

Capt. G. Angry with you, love! Of course not. I was angry with myself. I'd lost my temper over the saddlery—Don't hide your face, Pussy. I want to kiss it.

Bends lower, Mrs. G. slides right arm round his neck. Several interludes and much sobbing.

Mrs. G. (In a whisper.) I didn't mean about the jam when I came in to tell you— CAPT. G. Bother the jam and the equipment! (Interlude.)

Mrs. G. (Still more faintly.) My finger wasn't scalded at all. I—wanted to speak to you about— about—something else, and—I didn't know how.

Capt. G. Speak away, then. (Looking into her eyes.) Eh! Wha-at? Minnie! Here, don't go away! You don't mean?

Mrs. G. (Hysterically, backing to portiere and hiding her face in its folds.) The—the Almost Inevitable Consequences! (Flits through portiere as G. attempts to catch her, and bolts her self in her own room.)

Capt. G. (His arms full of portiere.) Oh! (Sitting down heavily in chair.) I'm a brute, a pig—a bully, and a blackguard. My poor, poor little darling! "Made to be amused only?"—

THE VALLEY OF THE SHADOW,
KNOWING GOOD AND EVIL.

SCENE. The GADSBYS' bungalow in the Plains, in June. Punkah-coolies asleep in veranda where Captain GADSBY is walking up and down. DOCTOR'S trap in porch. JUNIOR CHAPLAIN drifting generally and uneasily through the house. Time, 3:40 A. M. Heat 94 degrees in veranda.

DOCTOR. (Coming into veranda and touching G. on the shoulder.) You had better go in and see her now.

Capt. G. (The color of good cigar-ash.) Eh, wha-at? Oh, yes, of course. What did you say?

DOCTOR. (Syllable by syllable.) Go-in-to-the-room-and-see-her. She wants to speak to you. (Aside, testily.) I shall have him on my hands next.

JUNIOR CHAPLAIN. (In half-lighted dining room.) Isn't there any?—

DOCTOR. (Savagely.) Ha, you little fool!

JUNIOR CHAPLAIN. Let me do my work. Gadsby, stop a minute—I (Edges after G.)

DOCTOR. Wait till she sends for you at least—at least. Man alive, he'll kill you if you go in there! What are you bothering him for?

JUNIOR CHAPLAIN. (Coming into veranda.) I've given him a stiff brandy-peg. He wants it. You've forgotten him for the last ten hours and—forgotten yourself too.

G. enters bedroom, which is lit by one night-lamp. Ayah on the floor pretending to be asleep.

VOICE. (From the bed.) All down the street—such bonfires! Ayah, go and put them out! (Appealingly.) How can I sleep with an installation of the C.I.E. in my room? No—not C.I.E. Something else. What was it?

Capt. G. (Trying to control his voice.) Minnie, I'm here. (Bending over bed.) Don't you know me, Minnie? It's me—it's Phil—it's your husband.

VOICE. (Mechanically.) It's me—it's Phil—it's your husband.

Capt. G. She doesn't know me!—It's your own husband, darling.

VOICE. Your own husband, darling.

Ayah. (With an inspiration.) Memsahib understanding all I saying.

Capt. G. Make her understand me then—quick!

Ayah. (Hand on Mrs. G.'s fore-head.) Memsahib! Captain Sahib here.

VOICE. Salaem do. (Fretfully.) I know I'm not fit to be seen.

Ayah. (Aside to G.) Say "marneen" same as breakfash.

Capt. G. Good morning, little woman. How are we today?

VOICE. That's Phil. Poor old Phil. (Viciously.) Phil, you fool, I can't see you. Come nearer.

Capt. G. Minnie! Minnie! It's me—you know me?

VOICE. (Mockingly.) Of course I do. Who does not know the man who was so cruel to his wife—almost the only one he ever had?

Capt. G. Yes, dear. Yes—of course, of course. But won't you speak to him? He wants to speak to you so much.

VOICE. They'd never let him in. The Doctor would give darwaza band even if he were in the house. He'll never come. (Despairingly.) O Judas! Judas! Judas!

Capt. G. (Putting out his arms.) They have let him in, and he always was in the house Oh, my love—don't you know me?

VOICE. (In a half chant.) "And it came to pass at the eleventh hour that this poor soul repented." It knocked at the gates, but they were shut—tight as a plaster—a great, burning plaster. They had pasted our marriage certificate all across the door, and it was made of red-hot iron—people really ought to be more careful, you know.

Capt. G. What am I to do? (Taking her in his arms.) Minnie! speak to me—to Phil.

VOICE. What shall I say? Oh, tell me what to say before it's too late! They are all going away and I can't say anything.

Capt. G. Say you know me! Only say you know me!

DOCTOR. (Who has entered quietly.) For pity's sake don't take it too much to heart, Gadsby. It's this way sometimes. They won't recognize. They say all sorts of queer things—don't you see?

Capt. G. All right! All right! Go away now; she'll recognize me; you're bothering her. She must—mustn't she?

DOCTOR. She will before—Have I your leave to try?—

Capt. G. Anything you please, so long as she'll know me. It's only a question of hours, isn't it?

DOCTOR. (Professionally.) While there's life there's hope y'know. But don't build on it.

Capt. G. I don't. Pull her together if it's possible. (Aside.) What have I done to deserve this?

DOCTOR. (Bending over bed.) Now, Mrs. Gadsby! We shall be all right tomorrow. You must take it, or I sha'n't let Phil see you. It isn't nasty, is it?

Voice. Medicines! Always more medicines! Can't you leave me alone?

Capt. G. Oh, leave her in peace, Doc!

DOCTOR. (Stepping back,—aside.) May I be forgiven if I've done wrong. (Aloud.) In a few minutes she ought to be sensible; but I daren't tell you to look for anything. It's only—

Capt. G. What? Go on, man.

DOCTOR. (In a whisper.) Forcing the last rally.

Capt. G. Then leave us alone.

DOCTOR. Don't mind what she says at first, if you can. They—they—they turn against those they love most sometimes in this.—It's hard, but—

Capt. G. Am I her husband or are you? Leave us alone for what time we have together.

VOICE. (Confidentially.) And we were engaged quite suddenly, Emma. I assure you that I never thought of it for a moment; but, oh, my little Me!—I don't know what I should have done if he hadn't proposed.

Capt. G. She thinks of that Deercourt girl before she thinks of me. (Aloud.) Minnie!

VOICE. Not from the shops, Mummy dear. You can get the real leaves from Kaintu, and (laughing weakly) never mind about the blossoms—Dead white silk is only fit for widows, and I won't wear it. It's as bad as a winding sheet. (A long pause.)

Capt. G. I never asked a favor yet. If there is anybody to listen to me, let her know me—even if I die too!

VOICE. (Very faintly.) Pip, Pip dear.

Capt. G. I'm here, darling.

VOICE. What has happened? They've been bothering me so with medicines and things, and they wouldn't let you come and see me. I was never ill before. Am I ill now?

Capt. G. You—you aren't quite well.

VOICE. How funny! Have I been ill long?

Capt. G. Some days; but you'll be all right in a little time.

VOICE. Do you think so, Pip? I don't feel well and—Oh! what have they done to my hair?

Capt. G. I d-d-on't know.

VOICE. They've cut it off. What a shame!

Capt. G. It must have been to make your head cooler.

VOICE. Just like a boy's wig. Don't I look horrid?

Capt. G. Never looked prettier in your life, dear. (Aside.) How am I to ask her to say goodbye?

VOICE. I don't feel pretty. I feel very ill. My heart won't work. It's nearly dead inside me, and there's a funny feeling in my eyes. Everything seems the same distance—you and the almirah and the table inside my eyes or miles away. What does it mean, Pip?

Capt. G. You're a little feverish, Sweetheart—very feverish. (Breaking down.) My love! my love! How can I let you go?

VOICE. I thought so. Why didn't you tell me that at first?

Capt. G. What?

VOICE. That I am going to—die.

Capt. G. But you aren't! You sha'n't.

Ayah to punkah-coolie. (Stepping into veranda after a glance at the bed.). Punkah chor do! (Stop pulling the punkah.)

VOICE. It's hard, Pip. So very, very hard after one year—just one year. (Wailing.) And I'm only twenty. Most girls aren't even married at twenty. Can't they do anything to help me? I don't want to die.

Capt. G. Hush, dear. You won't.

VOICE. What's the use of talking? Help me! You've never failed me yet. Oh, Phil, help me to keep alive. (Feverishly.) I don't believe you wish me to live. You weren't a bit sorry when that horrid Baby thing died. I wish I'd killed it!

Capt. G. (Drawing his hand across his forehead.) It's more than a man's meant to bear—it's not right. (Aloud.) Minnie, love, I'd die for you if it would help.

VOICE. No more death. There's enough already. Pip, don't you die too.

Capt. G. I wish I dared.

VOICE. It says: "Till Death do us part." Nothing after that—and so it would be no use. It stops at the dying. Why does it stop there? Only such a very short life, too. Pip, I'm sorry we married.

Capt. G. No! Anything but that, Min!

VOICE. Because you'll forget and I'll forget. Oh, Pip, don't forget! I always loved you, though I was cross sometimes. If I ever did anything that you didn't like, say you forgive me now.

Capt. G. You never did, darling. On my soul and honor you never did. I haven't a thing to forgive you.

VOICE. I sulked for a whole week about those petunias. (With a laugh.) What a little wretch I was, and how grieved you were! Forgive me that, Pp.

Capt. G. There's nothing to forgive. It was my fault. They were too near the drive. For God's sake don't talk so, Minnie! There's such a lot to say and so little time to say it in.

VOICE. Say that you'll always love me—until the end.

Capt. G. Until the end. (Carried away.) It's a lie. It must be, because we've loved each other. This isn't the end.

VOICE. (Relapsing into semi-delirium.) My Church-service has an ivory cross on the back, and it says so, so it must be true. "Till Death do us part."—but that's a lie. (With a parody of G.'s manner.) A damned lie! (Recklessly.) Yes, I can swear as well as a Trooper, Pip. I can't make my head think, though. That's because they cut off my hair. How can one think with one's head all fuzzy? (Pleadingly.) Hold me, Pip! Keep me with you always and always. (Relapsing.) But if you marry the Thorniss girl when I'm dead, I'll come back and howl under our bedroom window all night. Oh, bother! You'll think I'm a jackal. Pip, what time is it?

Capt. G. A little before the dawn, dear.

VOICE. I wonder where I shall be this time tomorrow?

Capt. G. Would you like to see the Padre?

VOICE. Why should I? He'd tell me that I am going to heaven; and that wouldn't be true, because you are here. Do you recollect when he upset the cream-ice all over his trousers at the Gassers' tennis?

Capt. G. Yes, dear.

VOICE. I often wondered whether he got another pair of trousers; but then his are so shiny all over that you really couldn't tell unless you were told. Let's call him in and ask.

Capt. G. (Gravely.) No. I don't think he'd like that. Your head comfy, Sweetheart?

VOICE. (Faintly with a sigh of contentment.) Yeth! Gracious, Pip, when did you shave last? Your chin's worse than the barrel of a musical box.—No, don't lift it up. I like it. (A pause.) You said you've never cried at all. You're crying all over my cheek.

Capt. G. I-I-I can't help it, dear.

VOICE. How funny! I couldn't cry now to save my life. (G. shivers.) I want to sing.

Capt. G. Won't it tire you? 'Better not, perhaps.

VOICE. Why? I won't be bothered about. (Begins in a hoarse quaver)

"Minnie bakes oaten cake, Minnie brews ale,

All because her Johnnie's coming home from the sea." (That's parade, Pip.)

"And she grows red as a rose, who was so pale;

And 'Are you sure the church-clock goes?' says she."

(Pettishly.) I knew I couldn't take the last note. How do the bass chords run? (Puts out her hands and begins playing piano on the sheet.)

Capt. G. (Catching up hands.) Ahh! Don't do that, Pussy, if you love me.

VOICE. Love you? Of course I do. Who else should it be? (A pause.)

VOICE. (Very clearly.) Pip, I'm going now. Something's choking me cruelly. (Indistinctly.) Into the dark—without you, my heart—But it's a lie, dear—we mustn't believe it.—Forever and ever, living or dead. Don't let me go, my husband—hold me tight.—They can't—whatever happens. (A cough.) Pip—my Pip! Not for always—and—so—soon! (Voice ceases.)

Pause of ten minutes. G. buries his face in the side of the bed while AYAH bends over bed from opposite side and feels Mrs. G.'s breast and forehead.

Capt. G. (Rising.) Doctor Sahib ko salaam do.

Ayah. (Still by bedside, with a shriek.) Ail Ail Tuta-phuta! My Memsahib! Not getting—not have got!—Pusseena agyal (The sweat has come.) (Fiercely to G.) TUM jao Doctor Sahib ko jaldi! (You go to the doctor.) Oh, my Memsahib!

DOCTOR. (Entering hastily.) Come away, Gadsby. (Bends over bed.) Eh! The Dev—What inspired you to stop the punkah? Get out, man—go away—wait outside! Go! Here, Ayah! (Over his shoulder to G.) Mind I promise nothing.

The dawn breaks as G. stumbles into the garden.

Capt. M. (Rehung up at the gate on his way to parade and very soberly.) Old man, how goes?

Capt. G. (Dazed.) I don't quite know. Stay a bit. Have a drink or something. Don't run away. You're just getting amusing. Ha! ha!

Capt. M. (Aside.) What am I let in for? Gaddy has aged ten years in the night.

Capt. G. (Slowly, fingering charger's headstall.) Your curb's too loose.

Capt. M. So it is. Put it straight, will you? (Aside.) I shall be late for parade. Poor Gaddy.

Capt. G. links and unlinks curb-chain aimlessly, and finally stands staring toward the veranda. The day brightens.

DOCTOR. (Knocked out of professional gravity, tramping across flower-beds and shaking G's hands.) It'-it's-it's!—Gadsby, there's a fair chance—a dashed fair chance. The flicker, y'know. The sweat, y'know I saw how it would be. The punkah, y'know. Deuced clever woman that Ayah of yours. Stopped the punkah just at the right time. A dashed good chance! No—you don't go in. We'll pull her through yet I promise on my reputation—under Providence. Send a man with this note to Bingle. Two heads better than one. 'Specially the Ayah! We'll pull her round. (Retreats hastily to house.)

Capt. G. (His head on neck of M.'s charger.) Jack! I bub-bu-believe, I'm going to make a bu-bub-bloody exhibitiod of byself.

Capt. M. (Sniffing openly and feeling in his left cuff.) I b-b-believe, I'b doing it already. Old bad, what cad I say? I'b as pleased as—Cod dab you, Gaddy! You're one big idiot and I'b adother. (Pulling himself together.) Sit tight! Here comes the Devil-dodger.

JUNIOR CHAPLAIN. (Who is not in the Doctor's confidence.) We—we are only men in these things, Gadsby. I know that I can say nothing now to help.

Capt. M. (jealously.) Then don't say it Leave him alone. It's not bad enough to croak over. Here, Gaddy, take the chit to Bingle and ride hell-for-leather. It'll do you good. I can't go.

JUNIOR CHAPLAIN. Do him good! (Smiling.) Give me the chit and I'll drive. Let him lie down. Your horse is blocking my cart—please!

Capt. M. (Slowly without reining back.) I beg your pardon—I'll apologize. On paper if you like.

JUNIOR CHAPLAIN. (Flicking M.'s charger.) That'll do, thanks. Turn in, Gadsby, and I'll bring Bingle back—ahem—"hell-for-leather."

Capt. M. (Solus.) It would have served me right if he'd cut me across the face. He can drive too. I shouldn't care to go that pace in a bamboo cart. What a faith he must have in his Maker—of harness! Come hup, you brute! (Gallops off to parade, blowing his nose, as the sun rises.)

(INTERVAL OF FIVE WEEKS.)

Mrs. G. (Very white and pinched, in morning wrapper at breakfast table.) How big and strange

the room looks, and how glad I am to see it again! What dust, though! I must talk to the servants. Sugar, Pip? I've almost forgotten. (Seriously.) Wasn't I very ill?

Capt. G. Iller than I liked. (Tenderly.) Oh, you bad little Pussy, what a start you gave me!

Mrs. G. I'll never do it again.

Capt. G. You'd better not. And now get those poor pale cheeks pink again, or I shall be angry. Don't try to lift the urn. You'll upset it. Wait. (Comes round to head of table and lifts urn.)

Mrs. G. (Quickly.) Khitmatgar, howarchikhana see kettly lao. Butler, get a kettle from the cookhouse. (Drawing down G.'s face to her own.) Pip dear, I remember.

Capt. G. What?

Mrs. G. That last terrible night.

CAPT. G. Then just you forget all about it.

Mrs. G. (Softly, her eyes filling.) Never. It has brought us very close together, my husband. There! (Interlude.) I'm going to give Junda a saree.

Capt. G. I gave her fifty dibs.

Mrs. G. So she told me. It was a 'normous reward. Was I worth it? (Several interludes.) Don't! Here's the khitmatgar.—Two lumps or one Sir?

THE SWELLING OF JORDAN

If thou hast run with the footmen and they have wearied thee, then how canst thou contend with horses? And if in the land of peace wherein thou trustedst they wearied thee, then how wilt thou do in the swelling of Jordan?

SCENE. The GADSBYS' bungalow in the Plains, on a January morning. Mrs. G. arguing with bearer in back veranda.

Capt. M. rides up.

Capt. M. 'Mornin', Mrs. Gadsby. How's the Infant Phenomenon and the Proud Proprietor?

Mrs. G. You'll find them in the front veranda; go through the house. I'm Martha just now.

Capt. M, 'Cumbered about with cares of Khitmatgars? I fly.

Passes into front veranda, where GADSBV is watching GADSBY JUNIOR, aged ten months, crawling about the matting.

Capt. M. What's the trouble, Gaddy-spoiling an honest man's Europe morning this way? (Seeing G. JUNIOR.) By Jove, that yearling's comin' on amazingly! Any amount of bone below the knee there.

Capt. G. Yes, he's a healthy little scoundrel. Don't you think his hair's growing?

Capt. M. Let's have a look. Hi! Hst Come here, General Luck, and we'll report on you.

Mrs. G. (Within.) What absurd name will you give him next? Why do you call him that?

Capt. M. Isn't he our Inspector-General of Cavalry? Doesn't he come down in his seventeen-two perambulator every morning the Pink Hussars parade? Don't wriggle, Brigadier. Give us your private opinion on the way the third squadron went past. 'Trifle ragged, weren't they?

Capt. G. A bigger set of tailors than the new draft I don't wish to see. They've given me more than my fair share—knocking the squadron out of shape. It's sickening!

Capt. M. When you're in command, you'll do better, young 'un. Can'tyou walk yet? Grip my finger and try. (To G.) 'Twon't hurt his hocks, will it?

Capt. G. Oh, no. Don't let him flop, though, or he'll lick all the blacking off your boots.

Mrs. G. (Within.) Who's destroying my son's character?

Capt. M. And my Godson's. I'm ashamed of you, Gaddy. Punch your father in the eye, Jack! Don't you stand it! Hit him again!

Capt. G. (Sotto voce.) Put The Butcha down and come to the end of the veranda. I'd rather the Wife didn't hear—just now.

Capt. M. You look awf'ly serious. Anything wrong?

Capt. G. 'Depends on your view entirely. I say, Jack, you won't think more hardly of me than you can help, will you? Come further this way.—The fact of the matter is, that I've made up my mind—at least I'm thinking seriously of—cutting the Service.

Capt. M. Hwhatt?

Capt. G. Don't shout. I'm going to send in my papers.

Capt. M. You! Are you mad?

Capt. G. No—only married.

Capt. M. Look here! What's the meaning of it all? You never intend to leave us. You can't. Isn't the best squadron of the best regiment of the best cavalry in all the world good enough for you?

Capt. G. (Jerking his head over his shoulder.) She doesn't seem to thrive in this God-forsaken country, and there's The Butcha to be considered and all that, you know.

Capt. M. Does she say that she doesn't like India?

Capt. G. That's the worst of it. She won't for fear of leaving me.

Capt. M. What are the Hills made for?

Capt. G. Not for my wife, at any rate.

Capt. M. You know too much, Gaddy, and—I don't like you any the better for it!

Capt. G. Never mind that. She wants England, and The Butcha would be all the better for it. I'm going to chuck. You don't understand.

Capt. M. (Hotly.) I understand this!—One hundred and thirty-seven new horse to be licked into shape somehow before Luck comes round again; a hairy-heeled draft who'll give more trouble than the horses; a camp next cold weather for a certainty; ourselves the first on the roster; the Russian shindy ready to come to a head at five minutes' notice, and you, the best of us all, backing out of it all! Think a little, Gaddy. You won't do it.

Capt. G. Hang it, a man has some duties toward his family, I suppose.

Capt. M. I remember a man, though, who told me, the night after Amdheran, when we were picketed under Jagai, and he'd left his sword—by the way, did you ever pay Ranken for that sword?—in an Utmanzai's head—that man told me that he'd stick by me and the Pinks as long as he lived. I don't blame him for not sticking by me—I'm not much of a man—but I do blame him for not sticking by the Pink Hussars.

Capt. G. (Uneasily.) We were little more than boys then. Can't you see, Jack, how things stand? 'Tisn't as if we were serving for our bread. We've all of us, more or less, got the filthy lucre. I'm luckier than some, perhaps. There's no call for me to serve on.

Capt. M. None in the world for you or for us, except the Regimental. If you don't choose to answer to that, of course—

Capt. G. Don't be too hard on a man. You know that a lot of us only take up the thing for a few years and then go back to Town and catch on with the rest.

Capt. M. Not lots, and they aren't some of Us.

Capt. G. And then there are one's affairs at Home to be considered—my place and the rents, and all that. I don't suppose my father can last much longer, and that means the title, and so on.

Capt. M. 'Fraid you won't be entered in the Stud Book correctly unless you go Home? Take six months, then, and come out in October. If I could slay off a brother or two, I s'pose I should be a Marquis of sorts. Any fool can be that; but it needs men, Gaddy—men like you—to lead flanking squadrons properly. Don't you delude yourself into the belief that you're going Home to take your place and prance about among pink-nosed Kabuli dowagers. You aren't built that way. I know better.

Capt. G. A man has a right to live his life as happily as he can. You aren't married.

Capt. M. No—praise be to Providence and the one or two women who have had the good sense to jawab me.

Capt. G. Then you don't know what it is to go into your own room and see your wife's head on the pillow, and when everything else is safe and the house shut up for the night, to wonder whether the roof-beams won't give and kill her.

Capt. M. (Aside.) Revelations first and second! (Aloud.) So-o! I knew a man who got squiffy at our Mess once and confided to me that he never helped his wife on to her horse without praying that she'd break her neck before she came back. All husbands aren't alike, you see.

Capt. G. What on earth has that to do with my case? The man must ha' been mad, or his wife as bad as they make 'em.

Capt. M. (Aside.) 'No fault of yours if either weren't all you say. You've forgotten the time when you were insane about the Herriott woman. You always were a good hand at forgetting. (Aloud.) Not more mad than men who go to the other extreme. Be reasonable, Gaddy. Your roof-beams are sound enough.

Capt. G. That was only a way of speaking. I've been uneasy and worried about the Wife ever since that awful business three years ago—when—I nearly lost her. Can you wonder?

Capt. M. Oh, a shell never falls twice in the same place. You've paid your toll to misfortune— why should your Wife be picked out more than anybody else's?

Capt. G. I can talk just as reasonably as you can, but you don't understand—you don't understand. And then there's The Butcha. Deuce knows where the Ayah takes him to sit in the evening! He has a bit of a cough. Haven't you noticed it?

Capt. M. Bosh! The Brigadier's jumping out of his skin with pure condition. He's got a muzzle like a rose-leaf and the chest of a two-year-old. What's demoralized you?

Capt. G. Funk. That's the long and the short of it. Funk!

Capt. M. But what is there to funk?

Capt. G. Everything. It's ghastly.

Capt. M. Ah! I see. You don't want to fight, And by Jingo when we do,

You've got the kid, you've got the Wife,

You've got the money, too.

That's about the case, eh?

Capt. G. I suppose that's it. But it's not for myself. It's because of them. At least I think it is.

Capt. M. Are you sure? Looking at the matter in a cold-blooded light, the Wife is provided for even if you were wiped out tonight. She has an ancestral home to go to, money and the Brigadier to carry on the illustrious name.

Capt. G. Then it is for myself or because they are part of me. You don't see it. My life's so good, so pleasant, as it is, that I want to make it quite safe. Can't you understand?

Capt. M. Perfectly. "Shelter-pit for the Off'cer's charger," as they say in the Line.

Capt. G. And I have everything to my hand to make it so. I'm sick of the strain and the worry for their sakes out here; and there isn't a single real difficulty to prevent my dropping it altogether. It'll only cost me—Jack, I hope you'll never know the shame that I've been going through for the past six months.

Capt. M. Hold on there! I don't wish to be told. Every man has his moods and tenses sometimes.

Capt. G. (Laughing bitterly.) Has he? What do you call craning over to see where your near-fore lands?

Capt. M. In my case it means that I have been on the Considerable Bend, and have come to parade with a Head and a Hand. It passes in three strides.

Capt. G. (Lowering voice.) It never passes with me, Jack. I'm always thinking about it. Phil Gadsby funking a fall on parade! Sweet picture, isn't it! Draw it for me.

Capt. M. (Gravely.) Heaven forbid! A man like you can't be as bad as that. A fall is no nice thing, but one never gives it a thought.

Capt. G. Doesn't one? Wait till you've got a wife and a youngster of your own, and then you'll know how the roar of the squadron behind you turns you cold all up the back.

Capt. M. (Aside.) And this man led at Amdheran after Bagal Deasin went under, and we were all mixed up together, and he came out of the snow dripping like a butcher. (Aloud.) Skittles! The men can always open out, and you can always pick your way more or less. We haven't the dust to bother us, as the men have, and whoever heard of a horse stepping on a man?

Capt. G. Never—as long as he can see. But did they open out for poor Errington?

Capt. M. Oh, this is childish!

Capt. G. I know it is, worse than that. I don't care. You've ridden Van Loo. Is he the sort of brute to pick his way—'specially when we're coming up in column of troop with any pace on?

Capt. M. Once in a Blue Moon do we gallop in column of troop, and then only to save time. Aren't three lengths enough for you?

Capt. G. Yes—quite enough. They just allow for the full development of the smash. I'm talking like a cur, I know: but I tell you that, for the past three months, I've felt every hoof of the squadron in the small of my back every time that I've led.

Capt. M. But, Gaddy, this is awful!

Capt. G. Isn't it lovely? Isn't it royal? A Captain of the Pink Hussars watering up his charger before parade like the blasted boozing Colonel of a Black Regiment!

Capt. M. You never did!

Capt. G. Once only. He squelched like a mussuck, and the Troop-Sergeant-Major cocked his eye at me. You know old Haffy's eye. I was afraid to do it again.

Capt. M. I should think so. That was the best way to rupture old Van Loo's tummy, and make him crumple you up. You knew that.

Capt. G. I didn't care. It took the edge off him.

Capt. M. "Took the edge off him"? Gaddy, you—you—you mustn't, you know! Think of the men.

Capt. G. That's another thing I am afraid of. D'you s'pose they know?

Capt. M. Let's hope not; but they're deadly quick to spot skirm—little things of that kind. See here, old man, send the Wife Home for the hot weather and come to Kashmir with me. We'll start a boat on the Dal or cross the Rhotang—shoot ibex or loaf—which you please. Only come! You're a bit off your oats and you're talking nonsense. Look at the Colonel—swag-bellied rascal that he is. He has a wife and no end of a bow-window of his own. Can any one of us ride round him—chalkstones and all? I can't, and I think I can shove a crock along a bit.

Capt. G. Some men are different. I haven't any nerve. Lord help me, I haven't the nerve! I've taken up a hole and a half to get my knees well under the wallets. I can't help it. I'm so afraid of anything happening to me. On my soul, I ought to be broke in front of the squadron, for cowardice.

Capt. M. Ugly word, that. I should never have the courage to own up.

Capt. G. I meant to lie about my reasons when I began, but—I've got out of the habit of lying to you, old man. Jack, you won't?—But I know you won't.

Capt. M. Of course not. (Half aloud.) The Pinks are paying dearly for their Pride.

Capt. G. Eh! Wha-at?

Capt. M. Don't you know? The men have called Mrs. Gadsby the Pride of the Pink Hussars ever since she came to us.

Capt. G. 'Tisn't her fault. Don't think that. It's all mine.

Capt. M. What does she say?

Capt. G. I haven't exactly put it before her. She's the best little woman in the world, Jack, and all that—but she wouldn't counsel a man to stick to his calling if it came between him and her. At least, I think—

Capt. M. Never mind. Don't tell her what you told me. Go on the Peerage and Landed-Gentry tack.

Capt. G. She'd see through it. She's five times cleverer than I am.

Capt. M. (Aside.) Then she'll accept the sacrifice and think a little bit worse of him for the rest of her days.

Capt. G. (Absently.) I say, do you despise me?

Capt. M. 'Queer way of putting it. Have you ever been asked that question? Think a minute.

What answer used you to give?

Capt. G. So bad as that? I'm not entitled to expect anything more, but it's a bit hard when one's best friend turns round and—

Capt. M. So I have found. But you will have consolations—Bailiffs and Drains and Liquid Manure and the Primrose League, and, perhaps, if you're lucky, the Colonelcy of a Yeomanry Cav-al-ry Regiment—all uniform and no riding, I believe. How old are you?

Capt. G. Thirty-three. I know it's—

Capt. M. At forty you'll be a fool of a J. P. landlord. At fifty you'll own a bath-chair, and The Brigadier, if he takes after you, will be fluttering the dovecotes of—what's the particular dunghill you're going to? Also, Mrs. Gadsby will be fat.

Capt. G. (Limply.) This is rather more than a joke.

Capt. M. D'you think so? Isn't cutting the Service a joke? It generally takes a man fifty years to arrive at it. You're quite right, though. It is more than a joke. You've managed it in thirty-three.

Capt. G. Don't make me feel worse than I do. Will it satisfy you if I own that I am a shirker, a skrim-shanker, and a coward?

Capt. M. It will not, because I'm the only man in the world who can talk to you like this without being knocked down. You mustn't take all that I've said to heart in this way. I only spoke—a lot of it at least—out of pure selfishness, because, because—Oh, damn it all, old man,—I don't know what I shall do without you. Of course, you've got the money and the place and all that—and there are two very good reasons why you should take care of yourself.

Capt. G. 'Doesn't make it any sweeter. I'm backing out—I know I am. I always had a soft drop in me somewhere—and I daren't risk any danger to them.

Capt. M. Why in the world should you? You're bound to think of your family—bound to think. Er—hmm. If I wasn't a younger son I'd go too—be shot if I wouldn't!

Capt. G. Thank you, Jack. It's a kind lie, but it's the blackest you've told for some time. I know what I'm doing, and I'm going into it with my eyes open. Old man, I can't help it. What would you do if you were in my place?

Capt. M. (Aside.) 'Couldn't conceive any woman getting permanently between me and the Regiment. (Aloud.) 'Can't say. 'Very likely I should do no better. I'm sorry for you—awf'ly sorry—but "if them's your sentiments," I believe, I really do, that you are acting wisely.

Capt. G. Do you? I hope you do. (In a whisper.) Jack, be very sure of yourself before you marry. I'm an ungrateful ruffian to say this, but marriage—even as good a marriage as mine has been—hampers a man's work, it cripples his sword-arm, and oh, it plays Hell with his notions of duty. Sometimes—good and sweet as she is—sometimes I could wish that I had kept my freedom—No, I don't mean that exactly.

Mrs. G. (Coming down veranda.) What are you wagging your head over, Pip?

Capt. M. (Turning quickly.) Me, as usual. The old sermon. Your husband is recommending me to get married. 'Never saw such a one-ideaed man.

Mrs. G. Well, why don't you? I dare say you would make some woman very happy.

Capt. G. There's the Law and the Prophets, Jack. Never mind the Regiment. Make a woman happy. (Aside.) O Lord!

Capt. M. We'll see. I must be off to make a Troop Cook desperately unhappy. I won't have the wily Hussar fed on Government Bullock Train shinbones—(Hastily.) Surely black ants can't be good for The Brigadier. He's picking em off the matting and eating 'em. Here, Senor Comandante Don Grubbynose, come and talk to me. (Lifts G. JUNIOR in his arms.) 'Want my watch? You won't be able to put it into your mouth, but you can try. (G. JUNIOR drops watch, breaking dial and hands.)

Mrs. G. Oh, Captain Mafflin, I am so sorry! Jack, you bad, bad little villain. Ahhh!

Capt. M. It's not the least consequence, I assure you. He'd treat the world in the same way if he could get it into his hands. Everything's made to be played, with and broken, isn't it, young 'un?

Mrs. G. Mafflin didn't at all like his watch being broken, though he was too polite to say so. It was entirely his fault for giving it to the child. Dem little puds are werry, werry feeble, aren't dey, by Jack-in-de-box? (To G.) What did he want to see you for?

Capt. G. Regimental shop as usual.

Mrs. G. The Regiment! Always the Regiment. On my word, I sometimes feel jealous of Mafflin.

Capt. G. (Wearily.) Poor old Jack? I don't think you need. Isn't it time for The Butcha to have his nap? Bring a chair out here, dear. I've got some thing to talk over with you.

THIS IS THE END OF THE STORY OF THE GADSBYS
VOLUME VIII from MINE OWN PEOPLE

BIMI

THE orangoutang in the big iron cage lashed to the sheep-pen began the discussion. The night was stiflingly hot, and as Hans Breitmann and I passed him, dragging our bedding to the fore-peak of the steamer, he roused himself and chattered obscenely. He had been caught somewhere in the Malayan Archipelago, and was going to England to be exhibited at a shilling a head. For four days he had struggled, yelled, and wrenched at the heavy iron bars of his prison without ceasing, and had nearly slain a Lascar incautious enough to come within reach of the great hairy paw.

"It would be well for you, mine friend, if you was a liddle seasick," said Hans Breitmann, pausing by the cage. "You haf too much Ego in your Cosmos."

The orangoutang's arm slid out negligently from between the bars. No one would have believed that it would make a sudden snake-like rush at the German's breast. The thin silk of the sleeping-suit tore out: Hans stepped back unconcernedly, to pluck a banana from a bunch hanging close to one of the boats.

"Too much Ego," said he, peeling the fruit and offering it to the caged devil, who was rending the silk to tatters.

Then we laid out our bedding in the bows, among the sleeping Lascars, to catch any breeze that the pace of the ship might give us. The sea was like smoky oil, except where it turned to fire under our forefoot and whirled back into the dark in smears of dull flame. There was a thunderstorm some miles away: we could see the glimmer of the lightning. The ship's cow, distressed by the heat and the smell of the ape-beast in the cage, lowed unhappily from time to time in exactly the same key as the lookout man at the bows answered the hourly call from the bridge. The trampling tune of the engines was very distinct, and the jarring of the ash-lift, as it was tipped into the sea, hurt the procession of hushed noise. Hans lay down by my side and lighted a good-night cigar. This was naturally the beginning of conversation. He owned a voice as soothing as the wash of the sea, and stores of experiences as vast as the sea itself; for his business in life was to wander up and down the world, collecting orchids and wild beasts and ethnological specimens for German and American dealers. I watched the glowing end of his cigar wax and wane in the gloom, as the sentences rose and fell, till I was nearly asleep. The orangoutang, troubled by some dream of the forests of his freedom, began to yell like a soul in purgatory, and to wrench madly at the bars of the cage.

"If he was out now dere would not be much of us left hereabouts," said Hans, lazily. "He screams good. See, now, how I shall tame him when he stops himself."

There was a pause in the outcry, and from Hans' mouth came an imitation of a snake's hiss, so

perfect that I almost sprung to my feet. The sustained murderous sound ran along the deck, and the wrenching at the bars ceased. The orangoutang was quaking in an ecstasy of pure terror.

"Dot stop him," said Hans. "I learned dot trick in Mogoung Tanjong when I was collecting liddle monkeys for some peoples in Berlin. Efery one in der world is afraid of der monkeys except der snake. So I blay snake against monkey, and he keep quite still. Dere was too much Ego in his Cosmos. Dot is der soul-custom of monkeys. Are you asleep, or will you listen, and I will tell a dale dot you shall not pelief?"

"There's no tale in the wide world that I can't believe," I said.

"If you have learned pelief you haf learned somedings. Now I shall try your pelief. Good! When I was collecting dose liddle monkeys—it was in '79 or '80, und I was in der islands of der Archipelago—over dere in der dark"—he pointed southward to New Guinea generally—"Mein Gott! I would sooner collect life red devils than liddle monkeys. When dey do not bite off your thumbs dey are always dying from nostalgia—homesick—for dey haf der imperfect soul, which is midway arrested in defelopment—und too much Ego. I was dere for nearly a year, und dere I found a man dot was called Bertran. He was a Frenchman, und he was a goot man—naturalist to the bone. Dey said he was an escaped convict, but he was a naturalist, und dot was enough for me. He would call all her life beasts from der forests, und dey would come. I said he was St. Francis of Assisi in a new dransmigration produced, und he laughed und said he had never preach to der fishes. He sold dem for trepang—beche-de-mer.

"Und dot man, who was king of beasts-tamer men, he had in der house shush such anoder as dot devil-animal in der cage—a great orangoutang dot thought he was a man. He haf found him when he was a child—der orangoutang—und he was child and brother and opera comique all round to Bertran. He had his room in dot house—not a cage, but a room—mit a bed and sheets, and he would go to bed and get up in der morning and smoke his cigar und eat his dinner mit Bertran, und walk mit him hand-in-hand, which was most horrible. Herr Gott! I haf seen dot beast throw himself back in his chair and laugh when Bertran haf made fun of me. He was not a beast; he was a man, and he talked to Bertran, und Bertran comprehended, for I have seen dem. Und he was always politeful to me except when I talk too long to Bertran und say nodings at all to him. Den he would pull me away—dis great, dark devil, mit his enormous paws shush as if I was a child. He was not a beast, he was a man. Dis I saw pefore I know him three months, und Bertran he haf saw the same; and Bimi, der orangoutang, haf understood us both, mit his cigar between his big-dog teeth und der blue gum.

"I was dere a year, dere und at dere oder islands—somedimes for monkeys and somedimes for butterflies und orchits. One time Bertran says to me dot he will be married, because he hass found a girl dot was goot, and he inquire if this marrying idea was right. I would not say, pecause it was not me dot was going to be married. Den he go off courting der girl—she was a half-caste French girl—very pretty. Haf you got a new light for my cigar? Oof! Very pretty. Only I say 'Haf you thought of Bimi? If he pulls me away when I talk to you, what will he do to your wife? He will pull her in pieces. If I was you, Bertran, I would gif my wife for wedding present der stuff figure of Bimi.' By dot time I bad learned somedings about der monkey peoples. 'Shoot him?' says Bertran. 'He is your beast,' I said; 'if he was mine he would be shot now.'

"Den I felt at der back of my neck der fingers of Bimi. Mein Gott! I tell you dot he talked through dose fingers. It was der deaf-and-dumb alphabet all gomplete. He slide his hairy arm round my neck, and he tilt up my chin and look into my face, shust to see if I understood his talk so well as he understood mine.

"'See now dere!' says Bertran, 'und you would shoot him while he is cuddling you? Dot is der Teuton ingrate!'

"But I knew dot I had made Bimi a life's enemy, pecause his fingers haf talk murder through the back of my neck. Next dime I see Bimi dere was a pistol in my belt, und he touch it once, and I open de breech to show him it was loaded. He haf seen der liddle monkeys killed in der woods, and he understood.

"So Bertran he was married, and he forgot clean about Bimi dot was skippin' alone on the beach mit der haf of a human soul in his belly. I was see him skip, und he took a big bough und thrash der sand till he haf made a great hole like a grave. So I says to Bertran 'For any sakes, kill Bimi. He is mad mit der jealousy.'

"Bertran haf said: 'He is not mad at all. He haf obey and love my wife, und if she speaks he will get her slippers,' und he looked at his wife across der room. She was a very pretty girl.

"Den I said to him: 'Dost thou pretend to know monkeys und dis beast dot is lashing himself mad upon der sands, pecause you do not talk to him? Shoot him when he comes to der house, for he haf der light in his eyes dot means killing—und killing.' Bimi come to der house, but dere was no light in his eyes. It was all put away, cunning—so cunning—und he fetch der girl her slippers, and Bertran turn to me und say: 'Dost thou know him in nine months more dan I haf known him in twelve years? Shall a child stab his fader? I have fed him, und he was my child. Do not speak this nonsense to my wife or to me any more.'

"Dot next day Bertran came to my house to help me make some wood cases for der specimens, und he tell me dot he haf left his wife a liddle while mit Bimi in der garden. Den I finish my cases quick, und I say: 'Let us go to your house und get a trink.' He laugh und say: 'Come along, dry mans.'

"His wife was not in der garden, und Bimi did not come when Bertran called. Und his wife did not come when he called, und he knocked at her bedroom door und dot was shut tight-locked. Den he looked at me, und his face was white. I broke down der door mit my shoulder, und der thatch of der roof was torn into a great hole, und der sun came in upon der floor. Haf you ever seen paper in der waste-basket, or cards at whist on der table scattered? Dere was no wife dot could be seen. I tell you dere was noddings in dot room dot might be a woman. Dere was stuff on der floor, und dot was all. I looked at dese things und I was very sick; but Bertran looked a little longer at what was upon the floor und der walls, und der hole in der thatch. Den he pegan to laugh, soft and low, und I know und thank God dot he was mad. He nefer cried, he nefer prayed. He stood still in der doorway und laugh to himself. Den he said: 'She haf locked herself in dis room, and he haf torn up der thatch. Fi donc. Dot is so. We will mend der thatch und wait for Bimi. He will surely come.'

"I tell you we waited ten days in dot house, after der room was made into a room again, and once or twice we saw Bimi comin' a liddle way from der woods. He was afraid pecause he haf done wrong. Bertran called him when he was come to look on the tenth day, und Bimi come skipping along der beach und making noises, mit a long piece of Nack hair in his hands. Den Bertran laugh and say, 'Fi donc' shust as if it was a glass broken upon der table; und Bimi come nearer, und Bertran was honey-sweet in his voice and laughed to himself. For three days he made love to Bimi, pecause Bimi would not let himself be touched Den Bimi come to dinner at der same table mit us, und der hair on his hands was all black und thick mit—mit what had dried on his hands. Bertran gave him sangaree till Bimi was drunk and stupid, und den—"

Hans paused to puff at his cigar.

"And then?" said I.

"Und den Bertran kill him with his hands, und I go for a walk upon der heach. It was Bertran's

own piziness. When I come back der ape he was dead, und Bertran he was dying abofe him; but still he laughed a liddle und low, and he was quite content. Now you know der formula uf der strength of der orangoutang—it is more as seven to one in relation to man. But Bertran, he haf killed Bimi mit sooch dings as Gott gif him. Dot was der mericle."

The infernal clamor in the cage recommenced. "Aha! Dot friend of ours haf still too much Ego in his Cosmos, Be quiet, thou!"

Hans hissed long and venomously. We could hear the great beast quaking in his cage.

"But why in the world didn't you help Bertran instead of letting him be killed?" I asked.

"My friend," said Hans, composedly stretching himself to slumber, "it was not nice even to mineself dot I should lif after I had seen dot room wit der hole in der thatch. Und Bertran, he was her husband. Good-night, und sleep well."

NAMGAY DOOLA

ONCE upon a time there was a king who lived on the road to Thibet, very many miles in the Himalaya Mountains. His kingdom was 11,000 feet above the sea, and exactly four miles square, but most of the miles stood on end, owing to the nature of the country. His revenues were rather less than 400 pounds yearly, and they were expended on the maintenance of one elephant and a standing army of five men. He was tributary to the Indian government, who allowed him certain sums for keeping a section of the Himalaya-Thibet road in repair. He further increased his revenues by selling timber to the railway companies, for he would cut the great deodar trees in his own forest and they fell thundering into the Sutlej River and were swept down to the Plains, 300 miles away, and became railway ties. Now and again this king, whose name does not matter, would mount a ring-streaked horse and ride scores of miles to Simlatown to confer with the lieutenant-governor on matters of state, or assure the viceroy that his sword was at the service of the queen-empress. Then the viceroy would cause a ruffle of drums to be sounded and the ring-streaked horse and the cavalry of the state—two men in tatters—and the herald who bore the Silver Stick before the king would trot back to their own place, which was between the tail of a heaven-climbing glacier and a dark birch forest.

Now, from such a king, always remembering that he possessed one veritable elephant and could count his descent for 1,200 years, I expected, when it was my fate to wander through his dominions, no more than mere license to live.

The night had closed in rain, and rolling clouds blotted out the lights of the villages in the valley. Forty miles away, untouched by cloud or storm, the white shoulder of Dongo Pa—the Mountain of the Council of the Gods—upheld the evening star. The monkeys sung sorrowfully to each other as they hunted for dry roots in the fern-draped trees, and the last puff of the day-wind brought from the unseen villages the scent of damp wood smoke, hot cakes, dripping undergrowth, and rotting pine-cones. That smell is the true smell of the Himalayas, and if it once gets into the blood of a man he will, at the last, forgetting everything else, return to the Hills to die. The clouds closed and the smell went away, and there remained nothing in all the world except chilling white mists and the boom of the Sutlej River.

A fat-tailed sheep, who did not want to die, bleated lamentably at my tent-door. He was scuffling with the prime minister and the director-general of public education, and he was a royal gift to me and my camp servants. I expressed my thanks suitably and inquired if I might have audience of the king. The prime minister readjusted his turban—it had fallen off in the struggle—and assured me that the king would be very pleased to see me. Therefore I dispatched two bottles as a foretaste, and when the sheep had entered upon another incarnation, climbed up to the king's palace through the wet. He had sent his army to escort me, but it stayed to talk with my cook. Soldiers are very much alike all the world over.

The palace was a four-roomed, white-washed mud-and-timber house, the finest in all the Hills for a day's journey. The king was dressed in a purple velvet jacket, white muslin trousers, and a saffron-yellow turban of price. He gave me audience in a little carpeted room opening off the palace courtyard, which was occupied by the elephant of state. The great beast was sheeted and anchored from trunk to tail, and the curve of his back stood out against the sky line.

The prime minister and the director-general of public instruction were present to introduce me; but all the court had been dismissed lest the two bottles aforesaid should corrupt their morals. The king cast a wreath of heavy, scented flowers round my neck as I bowed, and inquired how my honored presence had the felicity to be. I said that through seeing his auspicious countenance the mists of the night had turned into sunshine, and that by reason of his beneficent sheep his

good deeds would be remembered by the gods. He said that since I had set my magnificent foot in his kingdom the crops would probably yield seventy per cent more than the average. I said that the fame of the king had reached to the four corners of the earth, and that the nations gnashed their teeth when they heard daily of the glory of his realm and the wisdom of his moon-like prime minister and lotus-eyed director-general of public education.

Then we sat down on clean white cushions, and I was at the king's right hand. Three minutes later he was telling me that the condition of the maize crop was something disgraceful, and that the railway companies would not pay him enough for his timber. The talk shifted to and fro with the bottles. We discussed very many quaint things, and the king became confidential on the subject of government generally. Most of all he dwelt on the shortcomings of one of his subjects, who, from what I could gather, had been paralyzing the executive.

"In the old days," said the king, "I could have ordered the elephant yonder to trample him to death. Now I must e'en send him seventy miles across the hills to be tried, and his keep for that time would be upon the state. And the elephant eats everything."

"What be the man's crimes, Rajah Sahib?" said I.

"Firstly, he is an 'outlander,' and no man of mine own people. Secondly, since of my favor I gave him land upon his coming, he refuses to pay revenue. Am I not the lord of the earth, above and below—entitled by right and custom to one-eighth of the crop? Yet this devil, establishing himself, refuses to pay a single tax... and he brings a poisonous spawn of babes."

"Cast him into jail," I said.

"Sahib," the king answered, shifting a little on the cushions, "once and only once in these forty years sickness came upon me so that I was not able to go abroad. In that hour I made a vow to my God that I would never again cut man or woman from the light of the sun and the air of God, for I perceived the nature of the punishment. How can I break my vow? Were it only the lopping off of a hand or a foot, I should not delay. But even that is impossible now that the English have rule. One or another of my people"—he looked obliquely at the director-general of public education—"would at once write a letter to the viceroy, and perhaps I should be deprived of that ruffle of drums."

He unscrewed the mouthpiece of his silver water-pipe, fitted a plain amber one, and passed the pipe to me. "Not content with refusing revenue," he continued, "this outlander refuses also to beegar" (this is the corvee or forced labor on the roads), "and stirs my people up to the like treason. Yet he is, if so he wills, an expert log-snatcher. There is none better or bolder among my people to clear a block of the river when the logs stick fast."

"But he worships strange gods," said the prime minister, deferentially.

"For that I have no concern," said the king, who was as tolerant as Akbar in matters of belief. "To each man his own god, and the fire or Mother Earth for us all at the last. It is the rebellion that offends me."

"The king has an army," I suggested. "Has not the king burned the man's house, and left him naked to the night dews?"

"Nay. A hut is a hut, and it holds the life of a man. But once I sent my army against him when his excuses became wearisome. Of their heads he brake three across the top with a stick. The other two men ran away. Also the guns would not shoot."

I had seen the equipment of the infantry. One-third of it was an old muzzle-loading fowling-piece with ragged rust holes where the nipples should have been; one-third a wirebound matchlock with a worm-eaten stock, and one-third a four-bore flint duck-gun, without a flint.

"But it is to be remembered," said the king, reaching out for the bottle, "that he is a very expert log-snatcher and a man of a merry face. What shall I do to him, sahib?"

This was interesting. The timid hill-folk would as soon have refused taxes to their king as offerings to their gods. The rebel must be a man of character.

"If it be the king's permission," I said, "I will not strike my tents till the third day, and I will see this man. The mercy of the king is godlike, and rebellion is like unto the sin of witchcraft. Moreover, both the bottles, and another, be empty."

"You have my leave to go," said the king.

Next morning the crier went through the stare proclaiming that there was a log-jam on the river and that it behooved all loyal subjects to clear it. The people poured down from their villages to the moist, warm valley of poppy fields, and the king and I went with them.

Hundreds of dressed deodar logs had caught on a snag of rock, and the river was bringing down more logs every minute to complete the blockade. The water snarled and wrenched and worried at the timber, while the population of the state prodded at the nearest logs with poles, in the hope of easing the pressure. Then there went up a shout of "Namgay Doola! Namgay Doola!" and a large, red-haired villager hurried up, stripping off his clothes as he ran.

"That he is. That is the rebel!" said the king. "Now will the dam be cleared."

"But why has he red hair?" I asked, since red hair among hill-folk is as uncommon as blue or green.

"He is an outlander," said the king. "Well done! Oh, well done!"

Namgay Doola had scrambled on the jam and was clawing out the butt of a log with a rude sort of a boat-hook. It slid forward slowly, as an alligator moves, and three or four others followed it. The green water spouted through the gaps. Then the villagers howled and shouted and leaped among the logs, pulling and pushing the obstinate timber, and the red head of Namgay Doola was chief among them all. The logs swayed and chafed and groaned as fresh consignments from up-stream battered the now weakening dam. It gave way at last in a smother of foam, racing butts, bobbing black heads, and a confusion indescribable, as the river tossed everything before it. I saw the red head go down with the last remnants of the jam and disappear between the great grinding tree trunks. It rose close to the hank, and blowing like a grampus, Namgay Doola wiped the water out of his eyes and made obeisance to the king.

I had time to observe the man closely. The virulent redness of his shock head and beard was most startling, and in the thicket of hair twinkled above high cheek-bones two very merry blue eyes. He was indeed an outlander, but yet a Thibetan in language, habit and attire. He spoke the Lepcha dialect with an indescribable softening of the gutturals. It was not so much a lisp as an accent.

"Whence comest thou?" I asked, wondering.

"From Thibet." He pointed across the hills and grinned. That grin went straight to my heart. Mechanically I held out my hand and Namgay Doola took it. No pure Thibetan would have understood the meaning of the gesture. He went away to look for his clothes, and as he climbed

back to his village, I heard a joyous yell that seemed unaccountably familiar. It was the whooping of Namgay Doola.

"You see now," said the king, "why I would not kill him. He is a bold man among my logs, but," and he shook his head like a schoolmaster, "I know that before long there will be complaints of him in the court. Let us return to the palace and do justice."

It was that king's custom to judge his subjects every day between eleven and three o'clock. I heard him do justice equitably on weighty matters of trespass, slander, and a little wife-stealing. Then his brow clouded and he summoned me.

"Again it is Namgay Doola," he said, despairingly. "Not content with refusing revenue on his own part, he has bound half his village by an oath to the like treason. Never before has such a thing befallen me! Nor are my taxes heavy."

A rabbit-faced villager, with a blush-rose stuck behind his ear, advanced trembling. He had been in Namgay Doola's conspiracy, but had told everything and hoped for the king's favor.

"Oh, king!" said I, "if it be the king's will, let this matter stand over till the morning. Only the gods can do right in a hurry, and it may be that yonder villager has lied."

"Nay, for I know the nature of Namgay Doola; but since a guest asks, let the matter remain. Wilt thou, for my sake, speak harshly to this red-headed outlander? He may listen to thee."

I made an attempt that very evening, but for the life of me I could not keep my countenance. Namgay Doola grinned so persuasively and began to tell me about a big brown bear in a poppy field by the river. Would I care to shoot that bear? I spoke austerely on the sin of detected conspiracy and the certainty of punishment. Namgay Doola's face clouded for a moment. Shortly afterward he withdrew from my tent, and I heard him singing softly among the pines. The words were unintelligible to me, but the tune, like his liquid, insinuating speech, seemed the ghost of something strangely familiar.

"Dir hane mard-i-yemen dir To weeree ala gee," crooned Namgay Doola again and again, and I racked my brain for that lost tune. It was not till after dinner that I discovered some one had cut a square foot of velvet from the centre of my best camera-cloth. This made me so angry that I wandered down the valley in the hope of meeting the big brown bear. I could hear him grunting like a discontented pig in the poppy field as I waited shoulder deep in the dew-dripping Indian corn to catch him after his meal. The moon was at full and drew out the scent of the tasseled crop. Then I heard the anguished bellow of a Himalayan cow—one of the little black crummies no bigger than Newfoundland dogs. Two shadows that looked like a bear and her cub hurried past me. I was in the act of firing when I saw that each bore a brilliant red head. The lesser animal was trailing something rope-like that left a dark track on the path. They were within six feet of me, and the shadow of the moonlight lay velvet-black on their faces. Velvet-black was exactly the word, for by all the powers of moonlight they were masked in the velvet of my camera-cloth. I marveled, and went to bed.

Next morning the kingdom was in an uproar. Namgay Doola, men said, had gone forth in the night and with a sharp knife had cut off the tail of a cow belonging to the rabbit-faced villager who had betrayed him. It was sacrilege unspeakable against the holy cow. The state desired his blood, but he had retreated into his hut, barricaded the doors and windows with big stones, and defied the world.

The king and I and the populace approached the hut cautiously. There was no hope of capturing our man without loss of life, for from a hole in the wall projected the muzzle of an extremely

well-cared-for gun—the only gun in the state that could shoot. Namgay Doola had narrowly missed a villager just before we came up.

The standing army stood.

It could do no more, for when it advanced pieces of sharp shale flew from the windows. To these were added from time to time showers of scalding water. We saw red beads bobbing up and down within. The family of Namgay Doola were aiding their sire. Blood-curdling yells of defiance were the only answer to our prayers.

"Never," said the king, puffing, "has such a thing befallen my state. Next year I will certainly buy a little cannon." He looked at me imploringly.

"Is there any priest in the kingdom to whom he will listen?" said I, for a light was beginning to break upon me.

"He worships his own god," said the prime minister. "We can but starve him out."

"Let the white man approach," said Namgay Doola from within. "All others I will kill. Send me the white man."

The door was thrown open and I entered the smoky interior of a Thibetan hut crammed with children. And every child had flaming red hair. A freshgathered cow's tail lay on the floor, and by its side two pieces of black velvet—my black velvet—rudely hacked into the semblance of masks.

"And what is this shame, Namgay Doola?" I asked.

He grinned more charmingly than ever. "There is no shame," said he. "I did but cut off the tail of that man's cow. He betrayed me. I was minded to shoot him, sahib, but not to death. Indeed, not to death; only in the legs."

"And why at all, since it is the custom to pay revenue to the king? Why at all?"

"By the god of my father, I cannot tell," said Namgay Doola.

"And who was thy father?"

"The same that had this gun." He showed me his weapon, a Tower musket, bearing date 1832 and the stamp of the Honorable East India Company.

"And thy father's name?" said I.

He obeyed, and I understood whence the puzzling accent in his speech came. "Thimla Dhula!" said he, excitedly. "To this hour I worship his god."

"May I see that god?"

"In a little while—at twilight time."

"Rememberest thou aught of thy father's speech?"

"It is long ago. But there was one word which he said often. Thus, ''Shun!' Then I and my brethren stood upon our feet, our hands to our sides, thus."

"Even so. And what was thy mother?"

"A woman of the Hills. We be Lepchas of Darjiling, but me they call an outlander because my hair is as thou seest."

The Thibetan woman, his wife, touched him on the arm gently. The long parley outside the fort had lasted far into the day. It was now close upon twilight—the hour of the Angelus. Very solemnly the red-headed brats rose from the floor and formed a semicircle. Namgay Doola laid his gun aside, lighted a little oil-lamp, and set it before a recess in the wall. Pulling back a wisp of dirty cloth, he revealed a worn brass crucifix leaning against the helmet badge of a long-forgotten East India Company's regiment. "Thus did my father," he said, crossing himself clumsily. The wife and children followed suit. Then, all together, they struck up the wailing cham that I heard on the hillside:

"Dir bane mard-i-yemen dir To weeree ala gee."

I was puzzled no longer. Again and again they sung, as if their hearts would break, their version of the chorus of "The Wearing of the Green":

"They're hanging men and women, too,

For the wearing of the green,"

A diabolical inspiration came to me. One of the brats, a boy about eight years old—could he have been in the fields last night?—was watching me as he sung. I pulled out a rupee, held the coin between finger and thumb, and looked—only looked—at the gun leaning against the wall. A grin of brilliant and perfect comprehension overspread his porringer-like face. Never for an instant stopping the song, he held out his hand for the money, and then slid the gun to my hand. I might have shot Namgay Doola dead as he chanted, but I was satisfied. The inevitable blood-instinct held true. Namgay Doola drew the curtain across the recess. Angelus was over.

"Thus my father sung. There was much more, but I have forgotten, and I do not know the purport of even these words, but it may be that the god will understand. I am not of this people, and I will not pay revenue."

"And why?"

Again that soul-compelling grin. "What occupation would be to me between crop and crop? It is better than scaring bears. But these people do not understand."

He picked the masks off the floor and looked in my face as simply as a child.

"By what road didst thou attain knowledge to make those deviltries?" I said, pointing.

"I cannot tell. I am but a Lepcha of Darjiling, and yet the stuff"—

"Which thou hast stolen," said I.

"Nay, surely. Did I steal? I desired it so. The stuff—the stuff. What else should I have done with the stuff?" He twisted the velvet between his fingers.

"But the sin of maiming the cow—consider that."

"Oh, sahib, the man betrayed me; the heifer's tail waved in the moonlight, and I had my knife. What else should I have done? The tail came off ere I was aware. Sahib, thou knowest more than I."

"That is true," said I. "Stay within the door. I go to speak to the king." The population of the state were ranged on the hillside. I went forth and spoke.

"O king," said I, "touching this man, there be two courses open to thy wisdom. Thou canst either hang him from a tree—him and his brood—till there remains no hair that is red within thy land."

"Nay," said the king. "Why should I hurt the little children?"

They had poured out of the hut and were making plump obeisances to everybody. Namgay Doola waited at the door with his gun across his arm.

"Or thou canst, discarding their impiety of the cow-maiming, raise him to honor in thy army. He comes of a race that will not pay revenue. A red flame is in his blood which comes out at the top of his head in that glowing hair. Make him chief of thy army. Give him honor as may befall and full allowance of work, but look to it, oh, king, that neither he nor his hold a foot of earth from thee henceforward. Feed him with words and favor, and also liquor from certain bottles that thou knowest of, and he will be a bulwark of defense. But deny him even a tuftlet of grass for his own. This is the nature that God has given him. Moreover, he has brethren"—

The state groaned unanimously.

"But if his brethren come they will surely fight with each other till they die; or else the one will always give information concerning the other. Shall he be of thy army, oh, king? Choose!"

The king bowed his head, and I said:

"Come forth, Namgay Doola, and command the king's army. Thy name shall no more be Namgay in the mouths of men, but Patsay Doola, for, as thou hast truly said, I know."

Then Namgay Doola, never christened Patsay Doola, son of Timlay Doola—which is Tim Doolan—clasped the king's feet, cuffed the standing army, and hurried in an agony of contrition from temple to temple making offerings for the sin of the cattle—maiming.

And the king was so pleased with my perspicacity that he offered to sell me a village for 20 pounds sterling. But I buy no village in the Himalayas so long as one red head flares between the tail of the heaven-climbing glacier and the dark birch forest.

I know that breed.

THE RECRUDESCENCE OF IMRAY

Imray had achieved the impossible. Without warning, for no conceivable motive, in his youth and at the threshold of his career he had chosen to disappear from the world—which is to say, the little Indian station where he lived. Upon a day he was alive, well, happy, and in great evidence at his club, among the billiard-tables. Upon a morning he was not, and no manner of search could make sure where he might be. He had stepped out of his place; he had not appeared at his office at the proper time, and his dog-cart was not upon the public roads. For these reasons and because he was hampering in a microscopical degree the administration of the Indian Empire, the Indian Empire paused for one microscopical moment to make inquiry into the fate of Imray. Ponds were dragged, wells were plumbed, telegrams were dispatched down the lines of railways and to the nearest seaport town—1,200 miles away—but Imray was not at the end of the drag-ropes nor the telegrams. He was gone, and his place knew him no more. Then the work of the great Indian Empire swept forward, because it could not be delayed, and Imray, from being a man, became a mystery—such a thing as men talk over at their tables in the club for a month and then forget utterly. His guns, horses, and carts were sold to the highest bidder. His superior officer wrote an absurd letter to his mother, saying that Imray had unaccountably disappeared and his bungalow stood empty on the road.

After three or four months of the scorching hot weather had gone by, my friend Strickland, of the police force, saw fit to rent the bungalow from the native landlord. This was before he was engaged to Miss Youghal—an affair which has been described in another place—and while he was pursuing his investigations into native life. His own life was sufficiently peculiar, and men complained of his manners and customs. There was always food in his house, but there were no regular times for meals. He ate, standing up and walking about, whatever he might find on the sideboard, and this is not good for the insides of human beings. His domestic equipment was limited to six rifles, three shotguns, five saddles, and a collection of stiff-jointed masheer rods, bigger and stronger than the largest salmon rods. These things occupied one half of his bungalow, and the other half was given up to Strickland and his dog Tietjens—an enormous Rampur slut, who sung when she was ordered, and devoured daily the rations of two men. She spoke to Strickland in a language of her own, and whenever, in her walks abroad she saw things calculated to destroy the peace of Her Majesty the Queen Empress, she returned to her master and gave him information. Strickland would take steps at once, and the end of his labors was trouble and fine and imprisonment for other people. The natives believed that Tietjens was a familiar spirit, and treated her with the great reverence that is born of hate and fear One room in the bungalow was set apart for her special use. She owned a bedstead, a blanket, and a drinking-trough, and if any one came into Strickland's room at night, her custom was to knock down the invader and give tongue till some one came with a light. Strickland owes his life to her. When he was on the frontier in search of the local murderer who came in the grey dawn to send Strickland much further than the Andaman Islands, Tietjens caught him as he was crawling into Strickland's tent with a dagger between his teeth, and after his record of iniquity was established in the eyes of the law, he was hanged. From that date Tietjens wore a collar of rough silver and employed a monogram on her night blanket, and the blanket was double-woven Kashmir cloth, for she was a delicate dog.

Under no circumstances would she be separated from Strickland, and when he was ill with fever she made great trouble for the doctors because she did not know how to help her master and would not allow another creature to attempt aid. Macarnaght, of the Indian Medical Service, beat her over the head with a gun, before she could understand that she must give room for those who could give quinine.

A short time after Strickland had taken Imray's bungalow, my business took me through that station, and naturally, the club quarters being full, I quartered myself upon Strickland. It was a desirable bungalow, eight-roomed, and heavily thatched against any chance of leakage from rain. Under the pitch of the roof ran a ceiling cloth, which looked just as nice as a whitewashed ceiling. The landlord had repainted it when Strickland took the bungalow, and unless you knew how Indian bungalows were built you would never have suspected that above the cloth lay the dark, three-cornered cavern of the roof, where the beams and the under side of the thatch harbored all manner of rats, hats, ants, and other things.

Tietjens met me in the veranda with a bay like the boom of the bells of St. Paul's, and put her paws on my shoulders and said she was glad to see me. Strickland had contrived to put together that sort of meal which he called lunch, and immediately after it was finished went out about his business. I was left alone with Tietjens and my own affairs. The heat of the summer had broken up and given place to the warm damp of the rains. There was no motion in the heated air, but the rain fell like bayonet rods on the earth, and flung up a blue mist where it splashed back again. The bamboos and the custard apples, the poinsettias and the mango-trees in the garden stood still while the warm water lashed through them, and the frogs began to sing among the aloe hedges. A little before the light failed, and when the rain was at its worst, I sat in the back veranda and heard the water roar from the eaves, and scratched myself because I was covered with the thing they called prickly heat. Tietjens came out with me and put her head in my lap, and was very sorrowful, so I gave her biscuits when tea was ready, and I took tea in the back veranda on account of the little coolness I found there. The rooms of the house were dark behind me. I could smell Strickland's saddlery and the oil on his guns, and I did not the least desire to sit among these things. My own servant came to me in the twilight, the muslin of his clothes clinging tightly to his drenched body, and told me that a gentleman had called and wished to see some one. Very much against my will, and because of the darkness of the rooms, I went into the naked drawing-room, telling my man to bring the lights. There might or might not have been a caller in the room—it seems to me that I saw a figure by one of the windows, but when the lights came there was nothing save the spikes of the rain without and the smell of the drinking earth in my nostrils. I explained to my man that he was no wiser than he ought to be, and went back to the veranda to talk to Tietjens. She had gone out into the wet and I could hardly coax her back to me—even with biscuits with sugar on top. Strickland rode back, dripping wet, just before dinner, and the first thing he said was:

"Has any one called?"

I explained, with apologies, that my servant had called me into the drawing-room on a false alarm; or that some loafer had tried to call on Strickland, and, thinking better of it, fled after giving his name. Strickland ordered dinner without comment, and since it was a real dinner, with white tablecloth attached, we sat down.

At nine o'clock Strickland wanted to go to bed, and I was tired too. Tietjens, who had been lying underneath the table, rose up and went into the least exposed veranda as soon as her master moved to his own room, which was next to the stately chamber set apart for Tietjens. If a mere wife had wished to sleep out-of-doors in that pelting rain, it would not have mattered, but Tietjens was a dog, and therefore the better animal. I looked at Strickland, expecting to see him flog her with a whip. He smiled queerly, as a man would smile after telling some hideous domestic tragedy. "She has done this ever since I moved in here."

The dog was Strickland's dog, so I said nothing, but I felt all that Strickland felt in being made light of. Tietjens encamped outside my bedroom window, and storm after storm came up, thundered on the thatch, and died away. The lightning spattered the sky as a thrown egg spattered a barn door, but the light was pale blue, not yellow; and looking through my slit

bamboo blinds, I could see the great dog standing, not sleeping, in the veranda, the hackles alift on her back, and her feet planted as tensely as the drawn wire rope of a suspension bridge. In the very short pauses of the thunder I tried to sleep, but it seemed that some one wanted me very badly. He, whoever he was, was trying to call me by name, but his voice was no more than a husky whisper. Then the thunder ceased and Tietjens went into the garden and howled at the low moon. Somebody tried to open my door, and walked about and through the house, and stood breathing heavily in the verandas, and just when I was falling asleep I fancied that I heard a wild hammering and clamoring above my head or on the door.

I ran into Strickland's room and asked him whether he was ill and had been calling for me. He was lying on the bed half-dressed, with a pipe in his mouth. "I thought you'd come," he said. "Have I been walking around the house at all?"

I explained that he had been in the dining-room and the smoking-room and two or three other places; and he laughed and told me to go back to bed. I went back to bed and slept till the morning, but in all my dreams I was sure I was doing some one an injustice in not attending to his wants. What those wants were I could not tell, but a fluttering, whispering, bolt-fumbling, luring, loitering some one was reproaching me for my slackness, and through all the dreams I heard the howling of Tietjens in the garden and the thrashing of the rain.

I was in that house for two days, and Strickland went to his office daily, leaving me alone for eight or ten hours a day, with Tietjens for my only companion. As long as the full light lasted I was comfortable, and so was Tietjens; but in the twilight she and I moved into the back veranda and cuddled each other for company. We were alone in the house, but for all that it was fully occupied by a tenant with whom I had no desire to interfere. I never saw him, but I could see the curtains between the rooms quivering where he had just passed through; I could hear the chairs creaking as the bamboos sprung under a weight that had just quitted them; and I could feel when I went to get a book from the dining-room that somebody was waiting in the shadows of the front veranda till I should have gone away. Tietjens made the twilight more interesting by glaring into the darkened rooms, with every hair erect, and following the motions of something that I could not see. She never entered the rooms, but her eyes moved, and that was quite sufficient. Only when my servant came to trim the lamps and make all light and habitable, she would come in with me and spend her time sitting on her haunches watching an invisible extra man as he moved about behind my shoulder. Dogs are cheerful companions.

I explained to Strickland, gently as might be, that I would go over to the club and find for myself quarters there. I admired his hospitality, was pleased with his guns and rods, but I did not much care for his house and its atmosphere. He heard me out to the end, and then smiled very wearily, but without contempt, for he is a man who understands things. "Stay on," he said, "and see what this thing means. All you have talked about I have known since I took the bungalow. Stay on and wait. Tietjens has left me. Are you going too?"

I had seen him through one little affair connected with an idol that had brought me to the doors of a lunatic asylum, and I had no desire to help him through further experiences. He was a man to whom unpleasantnesses arrived as do dinners to ordinary people.

Therefore I explained more clearly than ever that I liked him immensely, and would be happy to see him in the daytime, but that I didn't care to sleep under his roof. This was after dinner, when Tietjens had gone out to lie in the veranda.

"'Pon my soul, I don't wonder," said Strickland, with his eyes on the ceiling-cloth. "Look at that."

The tails of two snakes were hanging between the cloth and the cornice of the wall. They threw

long shadows in the lamp-light. "If you are afraid of snakes, of course"—said Strickland. "I hate and fear snakes, because if you look into the eyes of any snake you will see that it knows all and more of man's fall, and that it feels all the contempt that the devil felt when Adam was evicted from Eden. Besides which its bite is generally fatal, and it bursts up trouser legs."

"You ought to get your thatch over-hauled," I said. "Give me a masheer rod, and we'll poke 'em down."

"They'll hide among the roof beams," said Strickland. "I can't stand snakes overhead. I'm going up. If I shake 'em down, stand by with a cleaning-rod and break their backs."

I was not anxious to assist Strickland in his work, but I took the loading-rod and waited in the dining-room, while Strickland brought a gardener's ladder from the veranda and set it against the side of the room. The snake tails drew themselves up and disappeared. We could hear the dry rushing scuttle of long bodies running over the baggy cloth. Strickland took a lamp with him, while I tried to make clear the danger of hunting roof snakes between a ceiling cloth and a thatch, apart from the deterioration of property caused by ripping out ceiling-cloths.

"N o n s en s e," said Strickland. "They're sure to hide near the walls by the cloth. The bricks are too cold for 'em, and the heat of the room is just what they like." He put his hands to the corner of the cloth and ripped the rotten stuff from the cornice. It gave great sound of tearing, and Strickland put his head through the opening into the dark of the angle of the roof beams. I set my teeth and lifted the loading-rod, for I had not the least knowledge of what might descend.

"H'm," said Strickland; and his voice rolled and rumbled in the roof. "There's room for another set of rooms up here, and, by Jove! some one is occupying em."

"Snakes?" I said down below.

"No. It's a buffalo. Hand me up the two first joints of a masheer rod, and I'll prod it. It's lying on the main beam."

I handed up the rod.

"What a nest for owls and serpents! No wonder the snakes live here," said Strickland, climbing further into the roof. I could see his elbow thrusting with the rod. "Come out of that, whoever you are! Look out! Heads below there! It's tottering."

I saw the ceiling-cloth nearly in the centre of the room bag with a shape that was pressing it downward and downward toward the lighted lamps on the table. I snatched a lamp out of danger and stood back. Then the cloth ripped out from the walls, tore, split, swayed, and shot down upon the table something that I dared not look at till Strickland had slid down the ladder and was standing by my side.

He did not say much, being a man of few words, but he picked up the loose end of the table-cloth and threw it over the thing on the table.

"It strikes me," said he, pulling down the lamp, "our friend Imray has come back. Oh! you would, would you?"

There was a movement under the cloth, and a little snake wriggled out, to be back-broken by the butt of the masheer rod. I was sufficiently sick to make no remarks worth recording.

Strickland meditated and helped himself to drinks liberally. The thing under the cloth made no more signs of life.

"Is it Imray?" I said.

Strickland turned back the cloth for a moment and looked. "It is Imray," he said, "and his throat is cut from ear to ear."

Then we spoke both together and to ourselves:

"That's why he whispered about the house."

Tietjens, in the garden, began to bay furiously. A little later her great nose heaved upon the dining-room door.

She sniffed and was still. The broken and tattered ceiling-cloth hung down almost to the level of the table, and there was hardly room to move away from the discovery.

Then Tietjens came in and sat down, her teeth bared and her forepaws planted. She looked at Strickland.

"It's bad business, old lady," said he. "Men don't go up into the roofs of their bungalows to die, and they don't fasten up the ceiling-cloth behind 'em. Let's think it out."

"Let's think it out somewhere else," I said.

"Excellent idea! Turn the lamps out. We'll get into my room."

I did not turn the lamps out. I went into Strickland's room first and allowed him to make the darkness. Then he followed me, and we lighted tobacco and thought. Strickland did the thinking. I smoked furiously because I was afraid.

"Imray is back," said Strickland. "The question is, who killed Imray? Don't talk—I have a notion of my own. When I took this bungalow I took most of Imray's servants. Imray was guileless and inoffensive, wasn't he?"

I agreed, though the heap under the cloth looked neither one thing nor the other.

"If I call the servants they will stand fast in a crowd and lie like Aryans. What do you suggest?"

"Call 'em in one by one," I said.

"They'll run away and give the news to all their fellows," said Strickland.

"We must segregate 'em. Do you suppose your servant knows anything about it?"

"He may, for aught I know, but I don't think it's likely. He has only been here two or three days."

"What's your notion?" I asked.

"I can't quite tell. How the dickens did the man get the wrong side of the ceiling-cloth?"

There was a heavy coughing outside Strickland's bedroom door. This showed that Bahadur Khan, his body-servant, had waked from sleep and wished to put Strickland to bed.

"Come in," said Strickland. "It is a very warm night, isn't it?"

Bahadur Khan, a great, green-turbaned, six-foot Mohammedan, said that it was a very warm

night, but that there was more rain pending, which, by his honor's favor, would bring relief to the country.

"It will be so, if God pleases," said Strickland, tugging off his boots. "It is in my mind, Bahadur Khan, that I have worked thee remorselessly for many days—ever since that time when thou first came into my service. What time was that?"

"Has the heaven-born forgotten? It was when Imray Sahib went secretly to Europe without warning given, and I—even I—came into the honored service of the protector of the poor."

"And Imray Sahib went to Europe?"

"It is so said among the servants."

"And thou wilt take service with him when he returns?"

"Assuredly, sahib. He was a good master and cherished his dependents."

"That is true. I am very tired, but I can go buck-shooting tomorrow. Give me the little rifle that I use for black buck; it is in the case yonder."

The man stooped over the case, banded barrels, stock, and fore-end to Strickland, who fitted them together. Yawning dolefully, then he reached down to the gun-case, took a solid drawn cartridge, and slipped it into the breech of the .360 express.

"And Imray Sahib has gone to Europe secretly? That is very strange, Bahadur Khan, is it not?"

"What do I know of the ways of the white man, heaven-born?"

"Very little, truly. But thou shalt know more. It has reached me that Imray Sahib has returned from his so long journeyings, and that even now he lies in the next room, waiting his servant."

"Sahib!"

The lamp-light slid along the barrels of the rifle as they leveled themselves against Bahadur Khan's broad breast.

"Go, then, and look!" said Strickland. "Take a lamp. Thy master is tired, and he waits. Go!"

The man picked up a lamp and went into the dining-room, Strickland following, and almost pushing him with the muzzle of the rifle. He looked for a moment at the black depths behind the ceiling-cloth, at the carcass of the mangled snake under foot, and last, a grey glaze setting on his face, at the thing under the table-cloth.

"Hast thou seen?" said Strickland, after a pause.

"I have seen. I am clay in the white man's hands. What does the presence do?"

"Hang thee within a month! What else?"

"For killing him? Nay, sahib, consider. Walking among us, his servants, he cast his eyes upon my child, who was four years old. Him he bewitched, and in ten days he died of the fever. My child!"

"What said Imray Sahib?"

"He said he was a handsome child, and patted him on the head; wherefore my child died. Wherefore I killed Imray Sahib in the twilight, when he came back from office and was sleeping. The heaven-born knows all things. I am the servant of the heaven-born."

Strickland looked at me above the rifle, and said, in the vernacular: "Thou art witness to this saying. He has killed."

Bahadur Khan stood ashen grey in the light of the one lamp. The need for justification came upon him very swiftly.

"I am trapped," he said, "but the offence was that man's. He cast an evil eye upon my child, and I killed and hid him. Only such as are served by devils," he glared at Tietjens, crouched stolidly before him, "only such could know what I did."

"It was clever. But thou shouldst have lashed him to the beam with a rope. Now, thou thyself wilt hang by a rope. Orderly!"

A drowsy policeman answered Strickland's call. He was followed by another, and Tietjens sat still.

"Take him to the station," said Strickland. "There is a case toward."

"Do I hang, then?" said Bahadur Khan, making no attempt to escape and keeping his eyes on the ground.

"If the sun shines, or the water runs, thou wilt hang," said Strickland. Bahadur Khan stepped back one pace, quivered, and stood still. The two policemen waited further orders.

"Go!" said Strickland.

"Nay; but I go very swiftly," said Bahadur Khan. "Look! I am even now a dead man."

He lifted his foot, and to the little toe there clung the head of the half-killed snake, firm fixed in the agony of death.

"I come of land-holding stock," said Bahadur Khan, rocking where he stood. "It were a disgrace for me to go to the public scaffold, therefore I take this way. Be it remembered that the sahib's shirts are correctly enumerated, and that there is an extra piece of soap in his washbasin. My child was bewitched, and I slew the wizard. Why should you seek to slay me? My honor is saved, and—and—I die."

At the end of an hour he died as they die who are bitten by the little kariat, and the policeman bore him and the thing under the table-cloth to their appointed places. They were needed to make clear the disappearance of Imray.

"This," said Strickland, very calmly, as he climbed into bed, "is called the nineteenth century. Did you hear what that man said?"

"I heard," I answered. "Imray made a mistake."

"Simply and solely through not knowing the nature and coincidence of a little seasonal fever. Bahadur Khan has been with him for four years."

I shuddered. My own servant had been with me for exactly that length of time. When I went over to my own room I found him waiting, impassive as the copper head on a penny, to pull off my boots.

"What has befallen Bahadur Khan?" said I.

"He was bitten by a snake and died; the rest the sahib knows," was the answer.

"And how much of the matter hast thou known?"

"As much as might be gathered from one coming in the twilight to seek satisfaction. Gently, sahib. Let me pull off those boots."

I had just settled to the sleep of exhaustion when I heard Strickland shouting from his side of the house:

"Tietjens has come back to her room!"

And so she had. The great deer-hound was couched on her own bedstead, on her own blanket, and in the next room the idle, empty ceiling-cloth wagged light-heartedly as it flailed on the table.

MOTI GUJ—MUTINEER

ONCE upon a time there was a coffee-planter in India who wished to clear some forest land for coffee-planting. When he had cut down all the trees and burned the underwood, the stumps still remained. Dynamite is expensive and slow fire slow. The happy medium for stump-clearing is the lord of all beasts, who is the elephant. He will either push the stump out of the ground with his tusks, if he has any, or drag it out with ropes. The planter, therefore, hired elephants by ones and twos and threes, and fell to work. The very best of all the elephants belonged to the very worst of all the drivers or mahouts; and this superior beast's name was Moti Guj. He was the absolute property of his mahout, which would never have been the case under native rule; for Moti Guj was a creature to be desired by kings, and his name, being translated, meant the Pearl Elephant. Because the British government was in the land, Deesa, the mahout, enjoyed his property undisturbed. He was dissipated. When he had made much money through the strength of his elephant, he would get extremely drunk and give Moti Guj a beating with a tent-peg over the tender nails of the forefeet. Moti Guj never trampled the life out of Deesa on these occasions, for he knew that after the beating was over, Deesa would embrace his trunk and weep and call him his love and his life and the liver of his soul, and give him some liquor. Moti Guj was very fond of liquor—arrack for choice, though he would drink palm-tree toddy if nothing better offered. Then Deesa would go to sleep between Moti Guj's forefeet, and as Deesa generally chose the middle of the public road, and as Moti Guj mounted guard over him, and would not permit horse, foot, or cart to pass by, traffic was congested till Deesa saw fit to wake up.

There was no sleeping in the daytime on the planter's clearing: the wages were too high to risk. Deesa sat on Moti Guj's neck and gave him orders, while Moti Guj rooted up the stumps—for he owned a magnificent pair of tusks; or pulled at the end of a rope—for he had a magnificent pair of shoulders—while Deesa kicked him behind the ears and said he was the king of elephants. At evening time Moti Guj would wash down his three hundred pounds' weight of green food with a quart of arrack, and Deesa would take a share, and sing songs between Moti Guj's legs till it was time to go to bed. Once a week Deesa led Moti Guj down to the river, and Moti Gui lay on his side luxuriously in the shallows, while Deesa went over him with a coir swab and a brick. Moti Guj never mistook the pounding blow of the latter for the smack of the former that warned him to get up and turn over on the other side. Then Deesa would look at his feet and examine his eyes, and turn up the fringes of his mighty ears in case of sores or budding ophthalmia. After inspection the two would come up with a song from the sea, Moti Guj, all black and shining, waving a torn tree branch twelve feet long in his trunk, and Deesa knotting up his own long wet hair.

It was a peaceful, well-paid life till Deesa felt the return of the desire to drink deep. He wished for an orgy. The little draughts that led nowhere were taking the manhood out of him.

He went to the planter, and "My mother's dead," said he, weeping.

"She died on the last plantation two months ago, and she died once before that when you were working for me last year," said the planter, who knew something of the ways of nativedom.

"Then it's my aunt, and she was just the same as a mother to me," said Deesa, weeping more than ever. "She has left eighteen small children entirely without bread, and it is I who must fill their little stomachs," said Deesa, beating his head on the floor.

"Who brought the news?" said the planter.

"The post," said Deesa.

"There hasn't been a post here for the past week. Get back to your lines!",

"A devastating sickness has fallen on my village, and all my wives are dying," yelled Deesa, really in tears this time.

"Call Chihun, who comes from Deesa's village," said the planter. "Chihun, has this man got a wife?"

"He?" said Chihun. "No. Not a woman of our village would look at him. They'd sooner marry the elephant!"

Chihun snorted. Deesa wept and bellowed.

"You will get into a difficulty in a minute," said the planter. "Go back to your work!"

"Now I will speak Heaven's truth," gulped Deesa, with an inspiration. "I haven't been drunk for two months. I desire to depart in order to get properly drunk afar off and distant from this heavenly plantation. Thus I shall cause no trouble."

A flickering smile crossed the planter's face. "Deesa," said he, "you've spoken the truth, and I'd give you leave on the spot if anything could be done with Moti Guj while you're away. You know that he will only obey your orders."

"May the light of the heavens live forty thousand years. I shall be absent but ten little days. After that, upon my faith and honor and soul, I return. As to the inconsiderable interval, have I the gracious permission of the heaven-born to call up Moti Guj?"

Permission was granted, and in answer of Deesa's shrill yell, the mighty tusker swung out of the shade of a clump of trees where he had been squirting dust over himself till his master should return.

"Light of my heart, protector of the drunken, mountain of might, give ear!" said Deesa, standing in front of him.

Moti Guj gave ear, and saluted with his trunk. "I am going away," said Deesa.

Moti Guj's eyes twinkled. He liked jaunts as well as his master. One could snatch all manner of nice things from the roadside then.

"But you, you fussy old pig, must stay behind and work."

The twinkle died out as Moti Guj tried to look delighted. He hated stump-hauling on the plantation. It hurt his teeth.

"I shall be gone for ten days, oh, delectable one! Hold up your near forefoot and I'll impress the fact upon it, warty toad of a dried mud-puddle." Deesa took a tent-peg and banged Moti Guj ten times on the nails. Moti Guj grunted and shuffled from foot to foot.

"Ten days," said Deesa, "you will work and haul and root the trees as Chihun here shall order you. Take up Chihun and set him on your neck!" Moti Guj curled the tip of his trunk, Chihun put his foot there, and was swung on to the neck. Deesa handed Chihun the heavy ankus—the iron elephant goad.

Chihun thumped Moti Guj's bald head as a paver thumps a curbstone.

Moti Guj trumpeted.

"Be still, hog of the backwoods! Chihun's your mahout for ten days. And now bid me goodbye, beast after mine own heart. Oh, my lord, my king! Jewel of all created elephants, lily of the herd, preserve your honored health; be virtuous. Adieu!"

Moti Guj lapped his trunk round Deesa and swung him into the air twice. That was his way of bidding him goodbye.

"He'll work now," said Deesa to the planter. "Have I leave to go?"

The planter nodded, and Deesa dived into the woods. Moti Guj went back to haul stumps.

Chihun was very kind to him, but he felt unhappy and forlorn for all that. Chihun gave him a ball of spices, and tickled him under the chin, and Chihun's little baby cooed to him after work was over, and Chihun's wife called him a darling; but Moti Guj was a bachelor by instinct, as Deesa was. He did not understand the domestic emotions. He wanted the light of his universe back again—the drink and the drunken slumber, the savage beatings and the savage caresses.

None the less he worked well, and the planter wondered. Deesa had wandered along the roads till he met a marriage procession of his own caste, and, drinking, dancing, and tippling, had drifted with it past all knowledge of the lapse of time.

The morning of the eleventh day dawned, and there returned no Deesa, Moti Guj was loosed from his ropes for the daily stint. He swung clear, looked round, shrugged his shoulders, and began to walk away, as one having business elsewhere.

"Hi! ho! Come back you!" shouted Chihun. "Come back and put me on your neck, misborn mountain! Return, splendor of the hillsides! Adornment of all India, heave to, or I'll bang every toe off your forefoot!"

Moti Guj gurgled gently, but did not obey. Chihun ran after him with a rope and caught him up. Moti Guj put his ears forward, and Chihun knew what that meant, though he tried to carry it off with high words.

"None of your nonsense with me," said he. "To your pickets, devil-son!"

"Hrrump!" said Moti Guj, and that was all—that and the forebent ears.

Moti Guj put his hands in his pockets, chewed a branch for a toothpick, and strolled about the clearing, making fun of the other elephants who had just set to work.

Chihun reported the state of affairs to the planter, who came out with a dog-whip and cracked it furiously. Moti Guj paid the white man the compliment of charging him nearly a quarter of a mile across the clearing and "Hrrumphing" him into his veranda. Then he stood outside the house, chuckling to himself and shaking all over with the fun of it, as an elephant will.

"We'll thrash him," said the planter. "He shall have the finest thrashing ever elephant received. Give Kala Nag and Nazim twelve foot of chain apiece, and tell them to lay on twenty."

Kala Nag—which means Black Snake—and Nazim were two of the biggest elephants in the lines, and one of their duties was to administer the graver punishment, since no man can beat an elephant properly.

They took the whipping-chains and rattled them in their trunks as they sidled up to Moti Guj, meaning to hustle him between them. Moti Guj had never, in all his life of thirty-nine years, been whipped, and he did not intend to begin a new experience. So he waited, waving his head

from right to left, and measuring the precise spot in Kala Nag's fat side where a blunt tusk could sink deepest. Kala Nag had no tusks; the chain was the badge of his authority; but for all that, he swung wide of Moti Guj at the last minute, and tried to appear as if he had brought the chain out for amusement. Nazim turned round and went home early. He did not feel fighting fit that morning, and so Moti Guj was left standing alone with his ears cocked.

That decided the planter to argue no more, and Moti Guj rolled back to his amateur inspection of the clearing. An elephant who will not work and is not tied up is about as manageable as an eighty-one-ton gun loose in a heavy seaway. He slapped old friends on the back and asked them if the stumps were coming away easily; he talked nonsense concerning labor and the inalienable rights of elephants to a long 'nooning'; and, wandering to and fro, he thoroughly demoralized the garden till sundown, when he returned to his picket for food.

"If you won't work, you sha'n't eat," said Chihun, angrily. "You're a wild elephant, and no educated animal at all. Go back to your jungle."

Chihun's little brown baby was rolling on the floor of the hut, and stretching out its fat arms to the huge shadow in the doorway. Moti Guj knew well that it was the dearest thing on earth to Chihun. He swung out his trunk with a fascinating crook at the end, and the brown baby threw itself, shouting, upon it. Moti Guj made fast and pulled up till the brown baby was crowing in the air twelve feet above his father's head.

"Great Lord!" said Chihun. "Flour cakes of the best, twelve in number, two feet across and soaked in rum, shall be yours on the instant, and two hundred pounds weight of fresh-cut young sugar-cane therewith. Deign only to put down safely that insignificant brat who is my heart and my life to me!"

Moti Guj tucked the brown baby comfortably between his forefeet, that could have knocked into toothpicks all Chihun's hut, and waited for his food. He ate it, and the brown baby crawled away. Moti Guj dozed and thought of Deesa. One of many mysteries connected with the elephant is that his huge body needs less sleep than anything else that lives. Four or five hours in the night suffice—two just before midnight, lying down on one side; two just after one o'clock, lying down on the other. The rest of the silent hours are filled with eating and fidgeting, and long grumbling soliloquies.

At midnight, therefore, Moti Guj strode out of his pickets, for a thought had come to him that Deesa might be lying drunk somewhere in the dark forest with none to look after him. So all that night he chased through the undergrowth, blowing and trumpeting and shaking his ears. He went down to the river and blared across the shallows where Deesa used to wash him, but there was no answer. He could not find Deesa, but he disturbed all the other elephants in the lines, and nearly frightened to death some gypsies in the woods.

At dawn Deesa returned to the plantation. He had been very drunk in deed, and he expected to get into trouble for outstaying his leave. He drew a long breath when he saw that the bungalow and the plantation were still uninjured, for he knew something of Moti Guj's temper, and reported himself with many lies and salaams. Moti Guj had gone to his pickets for breakfast. The night exercise had made him hungry.

"Call up your beast," said the planter; and Deesa shouted in the mysterious elephant language that some mahouts believe came from China at the birth of the world, when elephants and not men were masters. Moti Guj heard and came. Elephants do not gallop They move from places at varying rates of speed. If an elephant wished to catch an express train he could not gallop, but he could catch the train. So Moti Guj was at the planter's door almost before Chihun noticed that he had left his pickets. He fell into Deesa's arms trumpeting with joy, and the man and

beast wept and slobbered over each other, and handled each other from head to heel to see that no harm had befallen.

"Now we will get to work," said Deesa. "Lift me up, my son and my joy!"

Moti Guj swung him up, and the two went to the coffee-clearing to look for difficult stumps.

The planter was too astonished to be very angry.

Printed in the USA
CPSIA information can be obtained
at www.ICGtesting.com
LVHW092316081123
763464LV00006B/112

9 789358 370898